Dan Simmons, a former teacher and director of programmes for gifted children, now writes full time. He lives with his wife and daughter in Colorado, USA. He has always been interested in writing, composing his first short stories at the age of nine. Since then he has been co-winner of the first *Twilight Zone Magazine* short story contest, winner of the Rod Serling Memorial Award and the winner of the World Fantasy Award for Best Novel with *Song of Kali*.

Dan Simmons is also the author of the internationally acclaimed *Hyperion*, winner of the 1990 Hugo Award and Locus Award for Best Science Fiction Novel, *Phases of Gravity* and *Carrion Comfort*, winner of the 1990 Bram Stoker Award, British Fantasy Society Award and Locus Award for Best Horror Novel.

THE
HYPERION
OMNIBUS

◆

Hyperion

AND

The Fall of Hyperion

◆

DAN SIMMONS

GOLLANCZ

LONDON

First published in Great Britain in 2004 by

Gollancz
An imprint of the Orion Publishing Group
Orion House, 5 Upper St Martin's Lane,
London WC2H 9EA

The authorised representative in the EEA is Hachette Ireland,
8 Castlecourt Centre, Dublin 15, D15 XTP3, Ireland (email: info@hbgi.ie)

15

A CIP catalogue record for this book
is available from the British Library

ISBN-13 978 0 575 07626 6

Typeset at The Spartan Press Ltd,
Lymington, Hants

Printed in Great Britain by
Clays Ltd, Elcograf S.p.A.

The Orion Publishing Group's policy is to use papers that
are natural, renewable and recyclable products and
made from wood grown in sustainable forests. The logging
and manufacturing processes are expected to conform to
the environmental regulations of the country of origin.

www.orionbooks.co.uk

HYPERION

This is for Ted

PROLOGUE

The Hegemony Consul sat on the balcony of his ebony spaceship and played Rachmaninov's Prelude in C-sharp Minor on an ancient but well-maintained Steinway while great, green, saurian things surged and bellowed in the swamps below. A thunderstorm was brewing to the north. Bruise-black clouds silhouetted a forest of giant gymnosperms while stratocumulus towered nine kilometers high in a violent sky. Lightning rippled along the horizon. Closer to the ship, occasional vague, reptilian shapes would blunder into the interdiction field, cry out, and then crash away through indigo mists. The Consul concentrated on a difficult section of the Prelude and ignored the approach of storm and nightfall.

The fatline receiver chimed.

The Consul stopped, fingers hovering above the keyboard, and listened. Thunder rumbled through the heavy air. From the direction of the gymnosperm forest there came the mournful ululation of a carrion-breed pack. Somewhere in the darkness below, a small-brained beast trumpeted its answering challenge and fell quiet. The interdiction field added its sonic undertones to the sudden silence. The fatline chimed again.

'Damn,' said the Consul and went in to answer it.

While the computer took a few seconds to convert and decode the burst of decaying tachyons, the Consul poured himself a glass of Scotch. He settled into the cushions of the projection pit just as the diskey blinked green. 'Play,' he said.

'You have been chosen to return to Hyperion,' came a woman's husky voice. Full visuals had not yet formed; the air remained empty except for the pulse of transmission codes which told the Consul that this fatline squirt had originated on the Hegemony administrative world of Tau Ceti Center. The Consul did not need the transmission coordinates to know this. The aged but still beautiful voice of Meina Gladstone was unmistakable. 'You have been chosen to return to Hyperion as a member of the Shrike Pilgrimage,' continued the voice.

The hell you say, thought the Consul and rose to leave the pit.

'You and six others have been selected by the Church of the Shrike and confirmed by the All Thing,' said Meina Gladstone. 'It is in the interest of the Hegemony that you accept.'

The Consul stood motionless in the pit, his back to the flickering transmission codes. Without turning, he raised his glass and drained the last of the Scotch.

'The situation is very confused,' said Meina Gladstone. Her voice was weary. 'The consulate and Home Rule Council fatlined us three standard weeks ago with the news that the Time Tombs showed signs of opening. The anti-entropic fields around them were expanding rapidly and the Shrike has begun ranging as far south as the Bridle Range.'

The Consul turned and dropped into the cushions. A holo had formed of Meina Gladstone's ancient face. Her eyes looked as tired as her voice sounded.

'A FORCE:space task force was immediately dispatched from Parvati to evacuate the Hegemony citizens on Hyperion before the Time Tombs open. Their time-debt will be a little more than three Hyperion years.' Meina Gladstone paused. The Consul thought he had never seen the Senate CEO look so grim. 'We do not know if the evacuation fleet will arrive in time,' she said, 'but the situation is even more complicated. An Ouster migration cluster of at least four thousand . . . units . . . has been detected approaching the Hyperion system. Our evacuation task force should arrive only a short while before the Ousters.'

The Consul understood Gladstone's hesitation. An Ouster migration cluster might consist of ships ranging in size from single-person ramscouts to can cities and comet forts holding tens of thousands of the interstellar barbarians.

'The FORCE joint chiefs believe that this is the Ousters' big push,' said Meina Gladstone. The ship's computer had positioned the holo so that the woman's sad brown eyes seemed to be staring directly at the Consul. 'Whether they seek to control just Hyperion for the Time Tombs or whether this is an all-out attack on the Worldweb remains to be seen. In the meantime, a full FORCE:space battle fleet complete with a farcaster construction battalion has spun up from the Camn System to join the evacuation task force, but this fleet may be recalled depending upon circumstances.'

The Consul nodded and absently raised the Scotch to his lips. He frowned at the empty glass and dropped it onto the thick carpeting of the holopit. Even with no military training he understood the difficult tactical decision Gladstone and the joint chiefs were faced with. Unless a military farcaster were hurriedly constructed in the Hyperion system – at staggering expense – there would be no way to resist the Ouster invasion. Whatever secrets the Time Tombs might hold would go to the Hegemony's enemy. If the fleet *did* construct a farcaster in time and the Hegemony committed the total resources of FORCE to defending the single, distant, colonial world of Hyperion, the Worldweb ran the terrible risk of suffering an Ouster attack elsewhere on the perimeter, or – in a worst-case scenario – having the barbarians actually seizing the farcaster and penetrating the Web itself. The Consul tried to imagine the reality of armored Ouster troops stepping through farcaster portals into the undefended home cities on a hundred worlds.

The Consul walked through the holo of Meina Gladstone, retrieved his glass, and went to pour another Scotch.

4

'You have been chosen to join the pilgrimage to the Shrike,' said the image of the old CEO whom the press loved to compare to Lincoln or Churchill or Alvarez-Temp or whatever other pre-Hegira legend was in historical vogue at the time. 'The Templars are sending their treeship *Yggdrasill*,' said Gladstone, 'and the evacuation task force commander has instructions to let it pass. With a three-week time-debt, you can rendezvous with the *Yggdrasill* before it goes quantum from the Parvati system. The six other pilgrims chosen by the Shrike Church will be aboard the treeship. Our intelligence reports suggest that at least one of the seven pilgrims is an agent of the Ousters. We do not . . . at this time . . . have any way of knowing which one it is.'

The Consul had to smile. Among all the other risks Gladstone was taking, the old woman had to consider the possibility that *he* was the spy and that she was fatlining crucial information to an Ouster agent. Or *had* she given him any crucial information? The fleet movements were detectable as soon as the ships used their Hawking drives, and if the Consul *were* the spy, the CEO's revelation might be a way to scare him off. The Consul's smile faded and he drank his Scotch.

'Sol Weintraub and Fedmahn Kassad are among the seven pilgrims chosen,' said Gladstone.

The Consul's frown deepened. He stared at the cloud of digits flickering like dust motes around the old woman's image. Fifteen seconds of fatline transmission time remained.

'We need your help,' said Meina Gladstone. 'It is essential that the secrets of the Time Tombs and Shrike be uncovered. This pilgrimage may be our last chance. If the Ousters conquer Hyperion, their agent must be eliminated and the Time Tombs sealed at all cost. The fate of the Hegemony may depend upon it.'

The transmission ended except for the pulse of rendezvous coordinates. 'Response?' asked the ship's computer. Despite the tremendous energies involved, the spacecraft was capable of placing a brief, coded squirt into the incessant babble of FTL bursts which tied the human portions of the galaxy together.

'No,' said the Consul and went outside to lean on the balcony railing. Night had fallen and the clouds were low. No stars were visible. The darkness would have been absolute except for the intermittent flash of lightning to the north and a soft phosphorescence rising from the marshes. The Consul was suddenly very aware that he was, at that second, the only sentient being on an unnamed world. He listened to the antediluvian night sounds rising from the swamps and he thought about morning, about setting out in the Vikken EMV at first light, about spending the day in sunshine, about hunting big game in the fern forests to the south and then returning to the ship in the evening for a good steak and a cold beer. The Consul thought about the sharp pleasure of the hunt and the equally sharp solace of solitude: solitude he had earned through the pain and nightmare he had already suffered on Hyperion.

Hyperion.

The Consul went inside, brought the balcony in, and sealed the ship just as the first heavy raindrops began to fall. He climbed the spiral staircase to his sleeping cabin at the apex of the ship. The circular room was dark except for silent explosions of lightning which outlined rivulets of rain coursing the skylight. The Consul stripped, lay back on the firm mattress, and switched on the sound system and external audio pickups. He listened as the fury of the storm blended with the violence of Wagner's 'Flight of the Valkyries'. Hurricane winds buffeted the ship. The sound of thunderclaps filled the room as the skylight flashed white, leaving afterimages burning in the Consul's retinas.

Wagner is good only for thunderstorms, he thought. He closed his eyes but the lightning was visible through closed eyelids. He remembered the glint of ice crystals blowing through the tumbled ruins on the low hills near the Time Tombs and the colder gleam of steel on the Shrike's impossible tree of metal thorns. He remembered screams in the night and the hundred-facet, ruby-and-blood gaze of the Shrike itself.

Hyperion.

The Consul silently commanded the computer to shut off all speakers and raised his wrist to cover his eyes. In the sudden silence he lay thinking about how insane it would be to return to Hyperion. During his eleven years as Consul on that distant and enigmatic world, the mysterious Church of the Shrike had allowed a dozen barges of offworld pilgrims to depart for the windswept barrens around the Time Tombs, north of the mountains. No one had returned. And that had been in normal times, when the Shrike had been prisoner to the tides of time and forces no one understood, and the anti-entropic fields had been contained to a few dozen meters around the Time Tombs. And there had been no threat of an Ouster invasion.

The Consul thought of the Shrike, free to wander everywhere on Hyperion, of the millions of indigenies and thousands of Hegemony citizens helpless before a creature which defied physical laws and which communicated only through death, and he shivered despite the warmth of the cabin.

Hyperion.

The night and storm passed. Another stormfront raced ahead of the approaching dawn. Gymnosperms two hundred meters tall bent and whipped before the coming torrent. Just before first light, the Consul's ebony spaceship rose on a tail of blue plasma and punched through thickening clouds as it climbed toward space and rendezvous.

ONE

The Consul awoke with the peculiar headache, dry throat, and sense of having forgotten a thousand dreams which only periods in cryogenic fugue could bring. He blinked, sat upright on a low couch, and groggily pushed away the last sensor tapes clinging to his skin. There were two very short crew clones and one very tall, hooded Templar with him in the windowless ovoid of a room. One of the clones offered the Consul the traditional post-thaw glass of orange juice. He accepted it and drank greedily.

'The Tree is two light-minutes and five hours of travel from Hyperion,' said the Templar, and the Consul realized that he was being addressed by Het Masteen, captain of the Templar treeship and True Voice of the Tree. The Consul vaguely realized that it was a great honor to be awakened by the Captain, but he was too groggy and disoriented from fugue to appreciate it.

'The others have been awake for some hours,' said Het Masteen and gestured for the clones to leave them. 'They have assembled on the foremost dining platform.'

'Hhrghn,' said the Consul and took a drink. He cleared his throat and tried again. 'Thank you, Het Masteen,' he managed. Looking around at the egg-shaped room with its carpet of dark grass, translucent walls, and support ribs of continuous, curved weirwood, the Consul realized that he must be in one of the smaller environment pods. Closing his eyes, he tried to recall his memories of rendezvous just before the Templar ship went quantum.

The Consul remembered his first glimpse of the kilometer-long treeship as he closed for rendezvous, the treeship's details blurred by the redundant machine and erg-generated containment fields which surrounded it like a spherical mist, but its leafy bulk clearly ablaze with thousands of lights which shone softly through leaves and thin-walled environment pods, or along countless platforms, bridges, command decks, stairways, and bowers. Around the base of the treeship, engineering and cargo spheres clustered like oversized galls while blue and violet drive streamers trailed behind like ten-kilometer-long roots.

'The others await,' Het Masteen said softly and nodded toward low cushions where the Consul's luggage lay ready to open upon his command. The Templar gazed thoughtfully at the weirwood rafters while the Consul dressed in semiformal evening wear of loose black trousers, polished ship boots, a white silk blouse which ballooned at waist and elbows, topaz collar cinch, black demi-coat complete with slashes of Hegemony crimson on the epaulets, and a soft gold tricorne. A section of curved wall became a mirror and the Consul stared at the image there: a more than middle-aged man in semiformal evening wear, sunburned skin but oddly pale under the sad eyes. The Consul frowned, nodded, and turned away.

Het Masteen gestured and the Consul followed the tall, robed figure through a dilation in the pod onto an ascending walkway which curved up and out of sight around the massive bark wall of the treeship's trunk. The Consul paused, moved to the edge of the walkway, and took a quick step back. It was at least six hundred meters down – down being created by the one-sixth standard gravity being generated by the singularities imprisoned at the base of the tree – and there were no railings.

They resumed their silent ascent, turning off from the main trunk walkway thirty meters and half a trunk-spiral later to cross a flimsy suspension bridge to a five-meter-wide branch. They followed this outward to where the riot of leaves caught the glare of Hyperion's sun.

'Has my ship been brought out of storage?' asked the Consul.

'It is fueled and ready in sphere eleven,' said Het Masteen. They passed into the shadow of the trunk and stars became visible in the black patches between the dark latticework of leaves. 'The other pilgrims have agreed to ferry down in your ship if the FORCE authorities give permission,' added the Templar.

The Consul rubbed his eyes and wished that he had been allowed more time to retrieve his wits from the cold grip of cryonic fugue. 'You've been in touch with the task force?'

'Oh, yes, we were challenged the moment we tunneled down from quantum leap. A Hegemony warship is . . . escorting us . . . this very moment.' Het Masteen gestured toward a patch of sky above them.

The Consul squinted upward but at that second segments of the upper tiers of branches revolved out of the treeship's shadow and acres of leaves ignited in sunset hues. Even in the still shadowed places, glowbirds nestled like Japanese lanterns above lighted walkways, glowing swingvines, and illuminated hanging bridges, while fireflies from Old Earth and radiant gossamers from Maui-Covenant blinked and coded their way through labyrinths of leaves, mixing with constellations sufficiently to fool even the most starwise traveler.

Het Masteen stepped into a basket lift hanging from a whiskered-carbon cable which disappeared into the three hundred meters of tree above them. The Consul followed and they were borne silently upward. He noted that the walkways, pods, and platforms were conspicuously empty except for a few Templars and their diminutive crew clone counterparts. The Consul could recall seeing no other passengers during his rushed hour between rendezvous and fugue, but he had put that down to the imminence of the treeship going quantum, assuming then that the passengers were safe in their fugue couches. Now, however, the treeship was traveling far below relativistic velocities and its branches should be crowded with gawking passengers. He mentioned his observation to the Templar.

'The six of you are our only passengers,' said Het Masteen. The basket stopped in a maze of foliage and the treeship captain led the way up a wooden escalator worn with age.

The Consul blinked in surprise. A Templar treeship normally carried between two and five thousand passengers; it was easily the most desirable way to travel between the stars. Treeships rarely accrued more than a four- or five-month time-debt, making short, scenic crossings where star systems were a very few light-years apart, thus allowing their affluent passengers to spend as little time as necessary in fugue. For the treeship to make the trip to Hyperion and back, accumulating six years of Web time *with no paying passengers* would mean a staggering financial loss to the Templars.

Then the Consul realized, belatedly, that the treeship would be ideal for the upcoming evacuation, its expenses ultimately to be reimbursed by the Hegemony. Still, the Consul knew, to bring a ship as beautiful and vulnerable as the *Yggdrasill* – one of only five of its kind – into a war zone was a terrible risk for the Templar Brotherhood.

'Your fellow pilgrims,' announced Het Masteen as he and the Consul emerged onto a broad platform where a small group waited at one end of a long wooden table. Above them the stars burned, rotating occasionally as the treeship changed its pitch or yaw, while to either side a solid sphere of foliage curved away like the green skin of some great fruit. The Consul immediately recognized the setting as the Captain's dining platform, even before the five other passengers rose to let Het Masteen take his place at the head of the table. The Consul found an empty chair waiting for him to the left of the Captain.

When everyone was seated and quiet, Het Masteen made formal introductions. Although the Consul knew none of the others from personal experience, several of the names were familiar and he used his diplomat's long training to file away identities and impressions.

To the Consul's left sat Father Lenar Hoyt, a priest of the old-style Christian sect known as Catholic. For a second the Consul had forgotten the significance of the black clothing and Roman collar, but then he remembered St Francis Hospital on Hebron where he had received alcohol trauma therapy after his disastrous first diplomatic assignment there almost four standard decades earlier. And at the mention of Hoyt's name he remembered another priest, one who had disappeared on Hyperion half-way through his own tenure there.

Lenar Hoyt was a young man by the Consul's reckoning – no more than his early thirties – but it appeared that something had aged the man terribly in the not too distant past. The Consul looked at the thin face, cheekbones pressing against sallow flesh, eyes large but hooded in deep hollows, thin lips set in a permanent twitch of muscle too downturned to be called even a cynical smile, the hairline not so much receding as ravaged by radiation, and he felt he was looking at a man who had been ill for years. Still, the Consul was surprised that behind that mask of concealed pain there remained the physical echo of the boy in the man – the faintest

9

remnants of the round face, fair skin, and soft mouth which had belonged to a younger, healthier, less cynical Lenar Hoyt.

Next to the priest sat a man whose image had been familiar to most citizens of the Hegemony some years before. The Consul wondered if the collective attention span in the Worldweb was as short now as it had been when he had lived there. Shorter, probably. If so, then Colonel Fedmahn Kassad, the so-called Butcher of South Bressia, was probably no longer either infamous or famous. To the Consul's generation and to all those who lived in the slow, expatriate fringe of things, Kassad was not someone one was likely to forget.

Colonel Fedmahn Kassad was tall – almost tall enough to look the two-meter Het Masteen in the eye – and dressed in FORCE black with no rank insignia or citations showing. The black uniform was oddly similar to Father Hoyt's garb, but there was no real resemblance between the two men. In lieu of Hoyt's wasted appearance, Kassad was brown, obviously fit, and whip-handle lean, with strands of muscle showing in shoulder, wrist, and throat. The Colonel's eyes were small, dark, and as all-encompassing as the lenses of some primitive video camera. His face was all angles: shadows, planes, and facets. Not gaunt like Father Hoyt's, merely carved from cold stone. A thin line of beard along his jawline served to accent the sharpness of his countenance as surely as blood on a knife blade.

The Colonel's intense, slow movements reminded the Consul of an Earth-bred jaguar he had seen in a private seedship zoo on Lusus many years before. Kassad's voice was soft but the Consul did not fail to notice that even the Colonel's silences commanded attention.

Most of the long table was empty, the group clustered at one end. Across from Fedmahn Kassad sat a man introduced as the poet Martin Silenus.

Silenus appeared to be quite the opposite of the military man across from him. Where Kassad was lean and tall, Martin Silenus was short and visibly out of shape. Countering Kassad's stone-cut features, the poet's face was as mobile and expressive as an Earth primate's. His voice was a loud, profane rasp. There was something, thought the Consul, almost pleasantly de-monic about Martin Silenus, with his ruddy cheeks, broad mouth, pitched eyebrows, sharp ears, and constantly moving hands sporting fingers long enough to serve a concert pianist. Or a strangler. The poet's silver hair had been cropped into rough-hewn bangs.

Martin Silenus seemed to be in his late fifties, but the Consul noticed the telltale blue tinge to throat and palms and suspected that the man had been through more than a few Poulsen treatments. Silenus's true age might be anywhere from ninety to a hundred and fifty standard years. If he were close to the latter age, the Consul knew, the odds were that the poet was quite mad.

As boisterous and animated as Martin Silenus seemed upon first encoun-ter, so the next guest at the table exuded an immediate and equally impressive sense of intelligent reticence. Sol Weintraub looked up upon introduction and the Consul noted the short gray beard, lined forehead, and sad, luminous eyes of the well-known scholar. The Consul had heard tales of the Wandering Jew and his hopeless quest, but he was shocked to realize that the old man now held the infant in his arms – his daughter Rachel, no more than a few weeks old. The Consul looked away.

The sixth pilgrim and only woman at the table was Brawne Lamia. When introduced, the detective stared at the Consul with such intensity that he could feel the pressure of her gaze even after she looked away.

A former citizen of the 1.3-g world of Lusus, Brawne Lamia was no taller than the poet two chairs to her right, but even her loose corduroy shipsuit did not conceal the heavy layers of muscle on her compact form. Black curls reached to her shoulders, her eyebrows were two dark lines dabbed horizontally across a wide brow, and her nose was solid and sharp, intensifying the aquiline quality of her stare. Lamia's mouth was wide and expressive to the point of being sensuous, curled slightly at the corners in a slight smile which might be cruel or merely playful. The woman's dark eyes seemed to dare the observer to discover which was the case.

It occurred to the Consul that Brawne Lamia might well be considered beautiful.

Introductions completed, the Consul cleared his throat and turned toward the Templar. 'Het Masteen, you said that there were seven pilgrims. Is M. Weintraub's child the seventh?'

Het Masteen's hood moved slowly from side to side. 'No. Only those who make a conscious decision to seek the Shrike may be counted among the pilgrims.'

The group at the table stirred slightly. Each must know what the Consul knew; only a group comprising a prime number of pilgrims might make the Shrike Church-sponsored trip north.

'I am the seventh,' said Het Masteen, captain of the Templar treeship *Yggdrasill* and the True Voice of the Tree. In the silence which followed the announcement, Het Masteen gestured and a group of crew clones began serving the pilgrims their last meal before planet fall.

'So the Ousters are not in-system yet?' asked Brawne Lamia. Her voice had a husky, throaty quality which strangely stirred the Consul.

'No,' said Het Masteen. 'But we cannot be more than a few standard days ahead of them. Our instruments have detected fusion skirmishes within the system's Oört cloud.'

'Will there be war?' asked Father Hoyt. His voice seemed as fatigued as his expression. When no one volunteered a response, the priest turned to his right as if retroactively directing the question to the Consul.

The Consul sighed. The crew clones had served wine; he wished it had been whiskey. 'Who knows what the Ousters will do?' he said. 'They no longer appear to be motivated by human logic.'

Martin Silenus laughed loudly, spilling his wine as he gestured. 'As if we fucking *humans* were ever motivated by human logic!' He took a deep drink, wiped his mouth, and laughed again.

Brawne Lamia frowned. 'If the serious fighting starts too soon,' she said, 'perhaps the authorities will not allow us to land.'

'We will be allowed to pass,' said Het Masteen. Sunlight found its way past folds in his cowl to fall on yellowish skin.

'Saved from certain death in war to be delivered to certain death at the hands of the Shrike,' murmured Father Hoyt.

'There is no death in all the Universe!' intoned Martin Silenus in a voice which the Consul felt sure could have awakened someone deep in cryogenic fugue. The poet drained the last of his wine and raised the empty goblet in an apparent toast to the stars:

'No smell of death – there shall be no death, moan, moan;
Moan, Cybele, moan; for thy pernicious Babes
Have changed a god into a shaking palsy.
Moan, brethren, moan, for I have no strength left;
Weak as the reed – weak – feeble as my voice—
Oh, oh, the pain, the pain of feebleness.
Moan, moan, for still I thaw . . .'

Silenus abruptly broke off and poured more wine, belching once into the silence which had followed his recitation. The other six looked at one another. The Consul noticed that Sol Weintraub was smiling slightly until the baby in his arms stirred and distracted him.

'Well,' said Father Hoyt hesitantly, as if trying to retrieve an earlier strand of thought, 'if the Hegemony convoy leaves and the Ousters take Hyperion, perhaps the occupation will be bloodless and they'll let us go about our business.'

Colonel Fedmahn Kassad laughed softly. 'The Ousters don't want to *occupy* Hyperion,' he said. 'If they take the planet they'll loot what they want and then do what they do best. They'll burn the cities into charred rubble, break the rubble into smaller pieces, and then bake the pieces until they glow. They'll melt the poles, boil the oceans, and then use the residue to salt what's left of the continents so nothing will ever grow there again.'

'Well . . .' began Father Hoyt and then trailed off.

There was no conversation as the clones cleared the soup and salad dishes and brought on the main course.

'You said that there was a Hegemony warship escorting us,' the Consul said to Het Masteen as they finished their roast beef and boiled sky squid.

The Templar nodded and pointed. The Consul squinted but could make out nothing moving against the rotating starfield.

'Here,' said Fedmahn Kassad and leaned across Father Hoyt to hand the Consul a collapsible pair of military binoculars.

The Consul nodded his thanks, thumbed on the power, and scanned the patch of sky Het Masteen had indicated. Gyroscopic crystals in the binoculars hummed slightly as they stabilized the optics and swept the area in a programmed search pattern. Suddenly the image froze, blurred, expanded, and steadied.

The Consul could not avoid an involuntary intake of breath as the Hegemony ship filled the viewer. Neither the expected field-blurred seed of a solo ramscout nor the bulb of a torchship, the electronically outlined image was of a matte-black attack carrier. The thing was impressive in the way only warships through the centuries had succeeded in being. The Hegemony spinship was incongruously streamlined with its four sets of boom arms retracted in battle readiness, its sixty-meter command probe sharp as a Clovis point, and its Hawking drive and fusion blisters set far back along the launch shaft like feathers on an arrow.

The Consul handed the binoculars back to Kassad without comment. If the task force was using a full attack carrier to escort the *Yggdrasill*, what kind of firepower were they setting in place to meet the Ouster invasion?

'How long until we land?' asked Brawne Lamia. She had been using her comlog to access the treeship's datasphere and obviously was frustrated with what she had found. Or had not found.

'Four hours until orbit,' murmured Het Masteen. 'A few minutes more by dropship. Our consular friend has offered his private craft to ferry you down.'

'To Keats?' said Sol Weintraub. It was the first time the scholar had spoken since dinner had been served.

The Consul nodded. 'It's still the only spaceport on Hyperion set to handle passenger vehicles,' he said.

'Spaceport?' Father Hoyt sounded angry. 'I thought that we were going straight to the north. To the Shrike's realm.'

Het Masteen patiently shook his head. 'The pilgrimage always begins from the capital,' he said. 'It will take several days to reach the Time Tombs.'

'Several *days*,' snapped Brawne Lamia. 'That's absurd.'

'Perhaps,' agreed Het Masteen, 'but it is the case, nonetheless.'

Father Hoyt looked as if something in the meal had caused him indigestion even though he had eaten almost nothing. 'Look,' he said, 'couldn't we change the rules this once – I mean, given the war scare and all? And just land near the Time Tombs or wherever and get it over with?'

The Consul shook his head. 'Spacecraft and aircraft have been trying to take the short route to the northern moors for almost four hundred years,' he said. 'I know of none who made it.'

'May one inquire,' said Martin Silenus, happily raising his hand like a schoolboy, 'just what the gibbering fuck *happens* to these legions of ships?'

Father Hoyt frowned at the poet. Fedmahn Kassad smiled slightly. Sol Weintraub said, 'The Consul did not mean to suggest that the area is inaccessible. One may travel by ship or various land routes. Nor do spacecraft and aircraft disappear. They easily land near the ruins or the Time Tombs and just as easily return to whatever point their computers command. It is merely the pilots and passengers who are never seen again.'

13

Weintraub lifted the sleeping baby from his lap and set her in an infant carrier slung around his neck.

'So the tired old legend goes,' said Brawne Lamia. 'What do the ship logs show?'

'Nothing,' said the Consul. 'No violence. No forced entry. No deviation from course. No unexplained time lapses. No unusual energy emissions or depletions. No physical phenomena of any sort.'

'No passengers,' said Het Masteen.

The Consul did a slow double take. If Het Masteen had, indeed, just attempted a joke, it was the first sign in all of the Consul's decades of dealing with the Templars that one of them had shown even a nascent sense of humour. What the Consul could see of the Captain's vaguely oriental features beneath the cowl gave no hint that a joke had been attempted.

'Marvelous melodrama,' laughed Silenus. 'A real-life, Christ-weeping Sargasso of Souls and we're for it. Who orchestrates this shitpot of a plot, anyway?'

'Shut up,' said Brawne Lamia. 'You're drunk, old man.'

The Consul sighed. The group had been together for less than a standard hour.

Crew clones swept away the dishes and brought dessert trays showcasing sherbets, coffees, treeship fruit, draums, tortes, and concoctions made of Renaissance chocolate. Martin Silenus waved away the desserts and told the clones to bring him another bottle of wine. The Consul reflected a few seconds and then asked for a whiskey.

'It occurs to me,' Sol Weintraub said as the group was finishing dessert, 'that our survival may depend upon our talking to one another.'

'What do you mean?' asked Brawne Lamia.

Weintraub unconsciously rocked the child sleeping against his chest. 'For instance, does anyone here know why he or she was chosen by the Shrike Church and the All Thing to go on this voyage?'

No one spoke.

'I thought not,' said Weintraub. 'Even more fascinating, is anyone here a member or follower of the Church of the Shrike? I, for one, am a Jew, and however confused my religious notions have become these days, they do not include the worship of an organic killing machine.' Weintraub raised eyebrows and looked around the table.

'I am the True Voice of the Tree,' said Het Masteen. 'While many Templars believe that the Shrike is the Avatar of punishment for those who do not feed from the root, I must consider this a heresy not founded in the Covenant or the writings of the Muir.'

To the Captain's left, the Consul shrugged. 'I am an atheist,' he said, holding the glass of whiskey to the light. 'I have never been in contact with the Shrike cult.'

Father Hoyt smiled without humor. 'The Catholic Church ordained me,' he said. 'Shrike-worship contradicts everything the Church defends.'

14

Colonel Kassad shook his head, whether in refusal to respond or to indicate that he was not a member of the Shrike Church, it was not clear.

Martin Silenus made an expansive gesture. 'I was baptized a Lutheran,' he said. 'A subset which no longer exists. I helped create Zen Gnosticism before any of your parents were born. I have been a Catholic, a revelationist, a neo-Marxist, an interface zealot, a Bound Shaker, a satanist, a bishop in the Church of Jake's Nada, and a dues-paying subscriber to the Assured Reincarnation Institute. Now, I am happy to say, I am a simple pagan.' He smiled at everyone. 'To a pagan,' he concluded, 'the Shrike is a most acceptable deity.'

'I ignore religions,' said Brawne Lamia. 'I do not succumb to them.'

'My point has been made, I believe,' said Sol Weintraub. 'None of us admits to subscribing to the Shrike cult dogma, yet the elders of that perceptive group have chosen us over many millions of the petitioning faithful to visit the Time Tombs . . . and their fierce god . . . in what may be the last such pilgrimage.'

The Consul shook his head. 'Your point may be made, M. Weintraub,' he said, 'but I fail to see it.'

The scholar absently stroked his beard. 'It would seem that our reasons for returning to Hyperion are so compelling that even the Shrike Church and the Hegemony probability intelligences agree that we deserve to return,' he said. 'Some of these reasons – mine, for instance – may appear to be public knowledge, but I am certain that none are known in their entirety except to the individuals at this table. I suggest that we share our stories in the few days remaining to us.'

'Why?' said Colonel Kassad. 'It would seem to serve no purpose.'

Weintraub smiled. 'On the contrary, it would – at the very least – amuse us and give at least a glimpse of our fellow travelers' souls before the Shrike or some other calamity distracts us. Beyond that, it might just give us enough insight to save all of our lives if we are intelligent enough to find the common thread of experience which binds all our fates to the whim of the Shrike.'

Martin Silenus laughed and closed his eyes. He said:

'Straddling each a dolphin's back
And steadied by a fin,
Those Innocents re-live their death,
Their wounds open again.'

'That's Lenista, isn't it?' said Father Hoyt. 'I studied her in seminary.'

'Close,' said Silenus, opening his eyes and pouring more wine. 'It's Yeats. Bugger lived five hundred years before Lenista tugged at her mother's metal teat.'

'Look,' said Lamia, 'what good would telling each other stories do? When we meet the Shrike, we tell *it* what we want, one of us is granted the wish, and the others die. Correct?'

'So goes the myth,' said Weintraub.

'The Shrike is no myth,' said Kassad. 'Nor its steel tree.'

'So why bore each other with stories?' asked Brawne Lamia, spearing the last of her chocolate cheesecake.

Weintraub gently touched the back of his sleeping infant's head. 'We live in strange times,' he said. 'Because we are part of that one tenth of one tenth of one percent of the Hegemony's citizens who travel *between* the stars rather than along the Web, we represent odd epochs of our own recent past. I, for example, am sixty-eight standard years old, but because of the time-debts my travels could have incurred, I might have spread these threescore and eight years across well more than a century of Hegemony history.'

'So?' said the woman next to him.

Weintraub opened his hand in a gesture which included everyone at the table. 'Among us we represent islands of time as well as separate oceans of perspective. Or perhaps more aptly put, each of us may hold a piece to a puzzle no one else has been able to solve since humankind first landed on Hyperion.' Weintraub scratched his nose. 'It is a mystery,' he said, 'and to tell the truth, I am intrigued by mysteries even if this is to be my last week of enjoying them. I would welcome some glimmer of understanding but, failing that, working on the puzzle will suffice.'

'I agree,' said Het Masteen with no emotion. 'It had not occurred to me, but I see the wisdom of telling our tales before we confront the Shrike.'

'But what's to keep us from lying?' asked Brawne Lamia.

'Nothing.' Martin Silenus grinned. 'That's the beauty of it.'

'We should put it to a vote,' said the Consul. He was thinking about Meina Gladstone's contention that one of the group was an Ouster agent. Would hearing the stories be a way of revealing the spy? The Consul smiled at the thought of an agent so stupid.

'Who decided that we are a happy little democracy?' Colonel Kassad asked dryly.

'We had better be,' said the Consul. 'To reach our individual goals, this group needs to reach the Shrike regions together. We require some means of making decisions.'

'We could appoint a leader,' said Kassad.

'Piss on that,' the poet said in a pleasant tone. Others at the table also shook their heads.

'All right,' said the Consul, 'we vote. Our first decision relates to M. Weintraub's suggestion that we tell the stories of our past involvement with Hyperion.'

'All or nothing,' said Het Masteen. 'We each share our story or none does. We will abide by the will of the majority.'

'Agreed,' said the Consul, suddenly curious to hear the others tell their stories and equally sure that he would never tell his own. 'Those in favor of telling our tales?'

'Yes,' said Sol Weintraub.

'Yes,' said Het Masteen.

'Absolutely,' said Martin Silenus. 'I wouldn't miss this little comic farce for a month in the orgasm baths on Shote.'

'I vote yes also,' said the Consul, surprising himself. 'Those opposed?'

'Nay,' said Father Hoyt but there was no energy in his voice.

'I think it's stupid,' said Brawne Lamia.

The Consul turned to Kassad. 'Colonel?'

Fedmahn Kassad shrugged.

'I register four yes votes, two negatives, and one abstention,' said the Consul. 'The ayes have it. Who wants to start?'

The table was silent. Finally Martin Silenus looked up from where he had been writing on a small pad of paper. He tore a sheet into several smaller strips. 'I've recorded numbers from one to seven,' he said. 'Why don't we draw lots and go in the order we draw?'

'That seems rather childish, doesn't it?' said M. Lamia.

'I'm a childish fellow,' responded Silenus with his satyr's smile. 'Ambassador' – he nodded toward the Consul – 'could I borrow that gilded pillow you're wearing for a hat?'

The Consul handed over his tricorne, the folded slips were dropped in, and the hat passed around. Sol Weintraub was the first to draw, Martin Silenus the last.

The Consul unfolded his slip, making sure that no one else could see it. He was number seven. Tension ebbed out of him like air out of an over-inflated balloon. It was quite possible, he reasoned, that events would intercede before he had to tell his story. Or the war would make everything academic. Or the group could lose interest in stories. Or the king could die. Or the horse could die. Or he could teach the horse how to talk.

No more whiskey, thought the Consul.

'Who's first?' asked Martin Silenus.

In the brief silence, the Consul could hear leaves stirring to unfelt breezes.

'I am,' said Father Hoyt. The priest's expression showed the same barely submerged acceptance of pain which the Consul had seen on the faces of terminally ill friends. Hoyt held up his slip of paper with a large 1 clearly scrawled on it.

'All right,' said Silenus. 'Start.'

'Now?' asked the priest.

'Why not?' said the poet. The only sign that Silenus had finished at least two bottles of wine was a slight darkening of the already ruddy cheeks and a somewhat more demonic tilt to the pitched eyebrows. 'We have a few hours before planetfall,' he said, 'and I for one plan to sleep off the freezer fugue when we're safely down and settled among the simple natives.'

'Our friend has a point,' Sol Weintraub said softly. 'If the tales are to be told, the hour after dinner each day is a civilized time to tell them.'

Father Hoyt sighed and stood. 'Just a minute,' he said and left the dining platform.

After some minutes had passed, Brawne Lamia said, 'Do you think he's lost his nerve?'

'No,' said Lenar Hoyt, emerging from the darkness at the head of the wooden escalator which served as the main staircase. 'I needed these.' He dropped two small, stained notebooks on the table as he took his seat.

'No fair reading stories from a primer,' said Silenus. 'These are to be our own tall tales, Magus!'

'Shut up, damn it!' cried Hoyt. He ran a hand across his face, touched his chest. For the second time that night, the Consul knew that he was looking at a seriously ill man.

'I'm sorry,' said Father Hoyt. 'But if I'm to tell my . . . my tale, I have to tell someone else's story as well. These journals belong to the man who was the reason for my coming to Hyperion . . . and why I am returning today.' Hoyt took a deep breath.

The Consul touched the journals. They were begrimed and charred, as if they had survived a fire. 'Your friend has old-fashioned tastes,' he said, 'if he still keeps a written journal.'

'Yes,' said Hoyt. 'If you're all ready, I will begin.'

The group at the table nodded. Beneath the dining platform, a kilometer of treeship drove through the cold night with the strong pulse of a living thing. Sol Weintraub lifted his sleeping child from the infant carrier and carefully set her on a cushioned mat on the floor near his chair. He removed his comlog, set it near the mat, and programmed the diskey for white noise. The week-old infant lay on her stomach and slept.

The Consul leaned far back and found the blue and green star which was Hyperion. It seemed to grow larger even as he watched. Het Masteen drew his cowl forward until only shadows showed for his face. Sol Weintraub lighted a pipe. Others accepted refills of coffee and settled back in their chairs.

Martin Silenus seemed the most avid and expectant of the listeners as he leaned forward and whispered:

'He seyde, "Syn I shal bigynne the game,
What, welcome be the cut, a Goddes name!
Now lat us ryde, and herkneth what I seye."
And with that word we ryden forth oure weye;
And he bigan with right a myrie cheere
His tale anon, and seyde as ye may heere.'

THE PRIEST'S TALE:
'THE MAN WHO CRIED GOD'

'Sometimes there is a thin line separating orthodox zeal from apostasy,' said Father Lenar Hoyt.

So began the priest's story. Later, dictating the tale into his comlog, the Consul remembered it as a seamless whole, minus the pauses, hoarse voice, false starts, and small redundancies which were the timeless failings of human speech.

Lenar Hoyt had been a young priest, born, raised, and only recently ordained on the Catholic world of Pacem, when he was given his first offworld assignment: he was ordered to escort the respected Jesuit Father Paul Duré into quiet exile on the colony world of Hyperion.

In another time, Father Paul Duré certainly would have become a bishop and perhaps a pope. Tall, thin, ascetic, with white hair receding from a noble brow and eyes too filled with the sharp edge of experience to hide their pain, Paul Duré was a follower of St Teilhard as well as an archae-ologist, ethnologist, and eminent Jesuit theologian. Despite the decline of the Catholic Church into what amounted to a half-forgotten cult tolerated because of its quaintness and isolation from the mainstream of Hegemony life, Jesuit logic had not lost its bite. Nor had Father Duré lost his con-viction that the Holy Catholic Apostolic Church continued to be human-kind's last, best hope for immortality.

To Lenar Hoyt as a boy, Father Duré had been a somewhat godlike figure when glimpsed during his rare visits to the preseminary schools, or on the would-be seminarian's even rarer visits to the New Vatican. Then, during the years of Hoyt's study in seminary, Duré had been on an important Church-sponsored archaeological dig on the nearby world of Armaghast. When the Jesuit returned, a few weeks after Hoyt's ordination, it had been under a cloud. No one outside the highest circles of the New Vatican knew precisely what had happened, but there were whispers of excommunica-tion and even of a hearing before the Holy Office of the Inquisition, dormant the four centuries since the confusion following the death of Earth.

Instead, Father Duré had asked for a posting to Hyperion, a world most people knew of only because of the bizarre Shrike cult which had origin-ated there, and Father Hoyt had been chosen to accompany him. It would be a thankless job, traveling in a role which combined the worst aspects of apprentice, escort, and spy without even the satisfaction of seeing a new world; Hoyt was under orders to see Father Duré down to the Hyperion spaceport and then reboard the same spinship for its return voyage to the Worldweb. What the bishopric was offering Lenar Hoyt was twenty months in cryogenic fugue, a few weeks of in-system travel at either end of the voyage, and a time-debt which would return him to Pacem eight years behind his former classmates in the quest for Vatican careers and mis-sionary postings.

Bound by obedience and schooled in discipline, Lenar Hoyt accepted without question.

Their transport, the aging spinship *HS Nadia Oleg*, was a pockmarked metal tub with no artificial gravity of any sort when it was not under drive, no viewports for the passengers, and no on-board recreation except for the stimsims piped into the datalink to keep passengers in their hammocks and fugue couches. After awakening from fugue, the passengers – mostly offworld workers and economy-rate tourists with a few cult mystics and would-be Shrike suicides thrown in for good measure – slept in those same hammocks and fugue couches, ate recycled food in featureless mess decks, and generally tried to cope with spacesickness and boredom during their twelve-day, zero-g glide from their spinout point to Hyperion.

Father Hoyt learned little from Father Duré during those days of forced intimacy, nothing at all about the events on Armaghast which had sent the senior priest into exile. The younger man had keyed his comlog implant to seek out as much data as it could on Hyperion and, by the time they were three days out from planetfall, Father Hoyt considered himself somewhat of an expert on the world.

'There are records of Catholics coming to Hyperion but no mention of a diocese there,' said Hoyt one evening as they hung talking in their zero-g hammocks while most of their fellow passengers lay tuned into erotic stimsims. 'I presume you're going down to do some mission work?'

'Not at all,' replied Father Duré. 'The good people of Hyperion have done nothing to foist their religious opinions on me, so I see no reason to offend them with my proselytizing. Actually, I hope to travel to the southern continent – Aquila – and then find a way inland from the city of Port Romance. But not in the guise of a missionary. I plan to set up an ethnological research station along the Cleft.'

'Research?' Father Hoyt had echoed in surprise. He closed his eyes to key his implant. Looking again at Father Duré, he said, 'That section of the Pinion Plateau isn't inhabited, Father. The flame forests make it totally inaccessible most of the year.'

Father Duré smiled and nodded. He carried no implant and his ancient comlog had been in his luggage for the duration of the trip. 'Not quite inaccessible,' he said softly. 'And not quite uninhabited. The Bikura live there.'

'Bikura,' Father Hoyt said and closed his eyes. 'But they're just a legend,' he said at last.

'Hmmm,' said Father Duré. 'Try cross-indexing through Mamet Spedling.'

Father Hoyt closed his eyes again. General Index told him that Mamet Spedling had been a minor explorer affiliated with the Shackleton Institute on Renaissance Minor who, almost a standard century and a half earlier, had filed a short report with the Institute in which he told of hacking his way inland from the then newly settled Port Romance, through swamplands which had since been reclaimed for fiberplastic plantations, passing through the flame forests during a period of rare quietude, and climbing high enough on the Pinion Plateau to encounter the Cleft and a small tribe of humans who fit the profile of the legendary Bikura.

Spedling's brief notes hypothesized that the humans were survivors of a missing seedship colony from three centuries earlier and clearly described a group suffering all of the classic retrograde cultural effects of extreme isolation, inbreeding, and overadaptaflon. In Spedling's blunt words,

'. . . even after less than two days here it is obvious that the Bikura are too stupid, lethargic, and dull to waste time describing.' As it turned out, the flame forests then began to show some signs of becoming active and Spedling had *not* wasted any more time observing his discovery but had rushed to reach the coast, losing four indigenie bearers, all of his equipment and records, and his left arm to the 'quiet' forest in the three months it took him to escape.

'My God,' Father Hoyt had said as he lay in his hammock on the *Nadia Oleg*, 'why the Bikura?'

'Why not?' had been Father Duré's mild reply. 'Very little is known about them.'

'Very little is known about *most* of Hyperion,' said the younger priest, becoming somewhat agitated. 'What about the Time Tombs and the legendary Shrike north of the Bridle Range on Equus?' he said. 'They're *famous*!'

'Precisely,' said Father Duré. 'Lenar, how many learned papers have been written on the Tombs and the Shrike creature? Hundreds? Thousands?' The aging priest had tamped in tobacco and now lighted his pipe: no small feat in zero-g, Hoyt observed. 'Besides,' said Paul Duré, 'even if the Shrike-thing is real, it is not human. I am partial to human beings.'

'Yes,' said Hoyt, ransacking his mental arsenal for potent arguments, 'but the Bikura are such a *small* mystery. At the most you're going to find a few dozen indigenies living in a region so cloudy and smoky and . . . *unimportant* that even the colony's own mapsats haven't noticed them. Why choose them when there are *big* mysteries to study on Hyperion . . . like the labyrinths!' Hoyt had brightened. 'Did you know that Hyperion is one of the nine labyrinthine worlds, Father?'

'Of course,' said Duré. A rough hemisphere of smoke expanded from him until air currents broke it into tendrils and tributaries. 'But the labyrinths have their researchers and admirers throughout the Web, Lenar, and the tunnels have been there – on all nine worlds – for how long? Half a million standard years? Closer to three quarters of a million, I believe. Their secret will last. But how long will the Bikura culture last before they're absorbed into modern colonial society or, more likely, are simply wiped out by circumstances?'

Hoyt shrugged. 'Perhaps they're already gone. It's been a long time since Spedling's encounter with them and there haven't been any other confirmed reports. If they *are* extinct as a group, then all of your time-debt and labor and pain of getting there will be for nothing.'

'Precisely,' was all that Father Paul Duré had said and puffed calmly on his pipe.

It was in their last hour together, during the dropship ride down, that Father Hoyt had gained the slightest glimpse into his companion's thoughts. The limb of Hyperion had been glowing white and green and lapis above them for hours when suddenly the old dropship had cut into the upper layers of atmosphere, flame had briefly filled the window, and then they were flying silently some sixty kilometers above dark cloud masses and starlit seas with the hurtling terminator of Hyperion's sunrise rushing toward them like a spectral tidal wave of light.

'Marvelous,' Paul Duré had whispered, more to himself than to his young companion. 'Marvelous. It is at times like this that I have the sense . . . the slightest sense . . . of what a sacrifice it must have been for the Son of God to condescend to become the Son of Man.'

Hoyt had wanted to talk then, but Father Duré had continued to stare out the window, lost in thought. Ten minutes later they had landed at Keats Interstellar, Father Duré was soon swept into the whirlpool of customs and luggage rituals, and twenty minutes after that a thoroughly disappointed Lenar Hoyt was rising toward space and the *Nadia Oleg* once again.

'Five weeks later of my time, I returned to Pacem,' said Father Hoyt. 'I had mislaid eight years but for some reason my sense of loss ran deeper than that simple fact. Immediately upon my return, the bishop informed me that there had been no word from Paul Duré during the four years of his stay on Hyperion. The New Vatican had spent a fortune on fatline inquiries, but neither the colonial authorities nor the consulate in Keats had been able to locate the missing priest.'

Hoyt paused to sip from his water glass and the Consul said, 'I remember the search. I never met Duré of course, but we did our best to trace him. Theo, my aide, spent a lot of energy over the years trying to solve the case of the missing cleric. Other than a few contradictory reports of sightings in Port Romance, there was no trace of him. And those sightings went back to the weeks right after his arrival, years before. There were hundreds of plantations out there with no radios or comlines, primarily because they were harvesting bootleg drugs as well as fiberplastic. I guess we never talked to the people at the right plantation. At least I know Father Duré's file was still open when I left.'

Father Hoyt nodded. 'I landed in Keats a month after your replacement had taken over at the consulate. The bishop had been astonished when I volunteered to return. His Holiness himself granted me an audience. I was on Hyperion less than seven of its local months. By the time I left to return to the Web, I had discovered the fate of Father Duré.' Hoyt tapped the two stained leather books on the table. 'If I am to complete this,' he said, his voice thick, 'I must read excerpts from these.'

The treeship *Yggdrasill* had turned so the bulk of the tree had blocked the sun. The effect was to plunge the dining platform and the curved canopy of leaves beneath it into night, but instead of a few thousand stars dotting the sky, as would have been the case from a planet's surface, literally a million suns blazed above, beside, and beneath the group at the table. Hyperion was a distinct sphere now, hurtling directly at them like some deadly missile.

'Read,' said Martin Silenus.

22

FROM THE JOURNAL OF FATHER PAUL DURÉ:

Day 1:

So begins my exile.

I am somewhat at a loss as to how to date my new journal. By the monastic calendar on Pacem, it is the seventeenth day of Thomasmonth in the Year of Our Lord 2732. By Hegemony Standard, it is October 12, 589 P.C. By Hyperion reckoning, or so I am told by the wizened little clerk in the old hotel where I am staying, it is the twenty-third day of Lycius (the last of their seven forty-day months), either 426 A.D.C. (after dropship crash!) or the hundred and twenty-eighth year of the reign of Sad King Billy, who has not reigned for at least a hundred of those years.

To hell with it. I'll call it Day 1 of my exile.

Exhausting day. (Strange to be tired after months of sleep, but that is said to be a common reaction after awakening from fugue. My cells feel the fatigue of these past months of travel even if I do not remember them. I don't remember feeling this tired from travel when I was younger.)

I felt bad about not getting to know young Hoyt better. He seems a decent sort, all proper catechism and bright eyes. It's no fault of youngsters like him that the Church is in its final days. It's just that his brand of happy naiveté can do nothing to arrest that slide into oblivion which the Church seems destined for.

Well, my contributions have not helped either.

Brilliant view of my new world as the dropship brought us down. I was able to make out two of the three continents – Equus and Aquila. The third one, Ursa, was not visible.

Planetfall at Keats and hours of effort getting through customs and taking ground transit into the city. Confused images: the mountain range to the north with its shifting, blue haze, foothills forested with orange and yellow trees, pale sky with its green-blue undercoating, the sun too small but more brilliant than Pacem's. Colors seem more vivid from a distance, dissolving and scattering as one approaches, like a pointillist's palette. The great sculpture of Sad King Billy which I had heard so much about was oddly disappointing. Seen from the highway, it looked raw and rough, a hasty sketch chiseled from the dark mountain, rather than the regal figure I had expected. It does brood over this ramshackle city of half a million people in a way that the neurotic poet-king probably would have appreciated.

The town itself seems to be separated into the sprawling maze of slums and saloons which the locals call Jacktown and Keats itself, the so-called Old City although it dates back only four centuries, all polished stone and studied sterility. I will take the tour soon.

I had scheduled a month in Keats but already I am eager to press on. Oh, Monsignor Edouard, if you could see me now. Punished but still unrepentant. More alone than ever but strangely satisfied with my new exile. If my punishment for past excesses brought about by my zeal is to be banishment

23

to the seventh circle of desolation, then Hyperion was well chosen. I could forget my self-appointed mission to the distant Bikura (are they real? I think not this night) and content myself with living out the remainder of my years in this provincial capital on this godforsaken backwater world. My exile would be no less complete.

Ah, Edouard, boys together, classmates together (although I was not so brilliant nor so orthodox as you), now old men together. But now you are four years wiser and I am still the mischievous, unrepentant boy you remember. I pray that you are alive and well and praying for me.

Tired. Will sleep. Tomorrow, take the tour of Keats, eat well, and arrange transport to Aquila and points south.

Day 5:

There is a cathedral in Keats. Or, rather, there was one. It has been abandoned for at least two standard centuries. It lies in ruins with its transept open to the green-blue skies, one of its western towers unfinished, and the other tower a skeletal framework of tumbled stone and rusted reinforcement rods.

I stumbled upon it while wandering, lost, along the banks of the Hoolie River in the sparsely populated section of town where the Old City decays into Jacktown amid a jumble of tall warehouses which prevent even a glimpse of the ruined towers of the cathedral until one turns a corner onto a narrow cul-de-sac and there is the shell of the cathedral; its chapter house has half fallen away into the river, its facade is pocked with remnants of the mournful, apocalyptic statuary of the post-Hegira expansionist period.

I wandered through the latticework of shadows and fallen blocks into the nave. The bishopric on Pacem had not mentioned any history of Catholicism on Hyperion, much less the presence of a cathedral. It is almost inconceivable that the scattered seedship colony of four centuries ago could have supported a large enough congregation to warrant the presence of a bishop, much less a cathedral. Yet there it was.

I poked through the shadows of the sacristy. Dust and powdered plaster hung in the air like incense, outlining two shafts of sunlight streaming down from narrow windows high above. I stepped out into a broader patch of sunlight and approached an altar stripped of all decoration except for chips and cracks caused by falling masonry. The great cross which had hung on the east wall behind the altar had also fallen and now lay in ceramic splinters among the heap of stones there. Without conscious thought I stepped behind the altar, raised my arms, and began the celebration of the Eucharist. There was no sense of parody or melodrama in this act, no symbolism or hidden intention; it was merely the automatic reaction of a priest who had said Mass almost daily for more than forty-six years of his life and who now faced the prospect of never again participating in the reassuring ritual of that celebration.

It was with some shock that I realized I had a congregation. The old woman was kneeling in the fourth row of pews. The black of her dress and scarf blended so perfectly with the shadows there that only the pale oval of her face was visible, lined and ancient, floating disembodied in the darkness. Startled, I stopped speaking the litany of consecration. She was looking at me but something about her eyes, even at a distance, instantly convinced me that she was blind. For a moment I could not speak and stood there mute, squinting in the dusty light bathing the altar, trying to explain this spectral image to myself while at the same time attempting to frame an explanation of my own presence and actions.

When I did find my voice and called to her – the words echoing in the great hall – I realized that she had moved. I could hear her feet scraping on the stone floor. There was a rasping sound and then a brief flare of light illuminated her profile far to the right of the altar. I shielded my eyes from the shafts of sunlight and began picking my way over the detritus where the altar railing had once stood. I called to her again, offered reassurances, and told her not to be afraid, even though it was I who had chills coursing up my back. I moved quickly but when I reached the sheltered corner of the nave she was gone. A small door led to the crumbling chapter house and the riverbank. There was no sign of her. I returned to the dark interior and would have gladly attributed her appearance to my imagination, a waking dream after so many months of enforced cryogenic dreamlessness, but for a single, tangible proof of her presence. There in the cool darkness burned a lone red votive candle, its tiny flame flickering to unseen drafts and currents.

I am tired of this city. I am tired of its pagan pretensions and false histories. Hyperion is a poet's world devoid of poetry. Keats itself is a mixture of tawdry, false classicism and mindless, boomtown energy. There are three Zen Gnostic assemblies and four High Muslim mosques in the town, but the real houses of worship are the countless saloons and brothels, the huge marketplaces handling the fiberplastic shipments from the south, and the Shrike Cult temples where lost souls hide their suicidal hopelessness behind a shield of shallow mysticism. The whole planet reeks of mysticism without revelation.

To hell with it.

Tomorrow I head south. There are skimmers and other aircraft on this absurd world but, for the Common Folk, travel between these accursed island continents seems restricted to boat – which takes forever, I am told – or one of the huge passenger dirigibles which depart from Keats only once a week.

I leave early tomorrow by dirigible.

Day 10:
Animals.

The firstdown team for this planet must have had a fixation on animals. Horse, Bear, Eagle. For three days we were creeping down the east coast of Equus over an irregular coastline called the Mane. We've spent the last day making the crossing of a short span of the Middle Sea to a large island called Cat Key. Today we are offloading passengers and freight at Felix, the 'major city' of the island. From what I can see from the observation promenade and the mooring tower, there can't be more than five thousand people living in that random collection of hovels and barracks.

Next the ship will make its eight-hundred-kilometer crawl down a series of smaller islands called the Nine Tails and then take a bold leap across seven hundred kilometers of open sea and the equator. The next land we see then is the northwest coast of Aquila, the so-called Beak.

Animals.

To call this conveyance a 'passenger dirigible' is an exercise in creative semantics. It is a huge lifting device with cargo holds large enough to carry the town of Felix out to sea and still have room for thousands of bales of fiberplastic. Meanwhile, the less important cargo – we passengers – make do where we can. I have set up a cot near the aft loading portal and made a rather comfortable niche for myself with my personal luggage and three large trunks of expedition gear. Near me is a family of eight – indigenie plantation workers returning from a biannual shopping expedition of their own to Keats – and although I do not mind the sound or scent of their caged pigs or the squeal of their food hamsters, the incessant, confused crowing of their poor befuddled rooster is more than I can stand some nights.

Animals!

Day 11:
Dinner tonight in the salon above the promenade deck with Citizen Heremis Denzel, a retired professor from a small planters' college near Endymion. He informed me that the Hyperion firstdown team had no animal fetish after all; the official names of the three continents are not Equus, Ursa, and Aquila, but Creighton, Allensen, and Lopez. He went on to say that this was in honor of three middle-level bureaucrats in the old Survey Service. Better the animal fetish!

It is after dinner. I am alone on the outside promenade to watch the sunset. The walkway here is sheltered by the forward cargo modules so the wind is little more than a salt-tinged breeze. Above me curves the orange and green skin of the dirigible. We are between islands; the sea is a rich lapis shot through with verdant undertones, a reversal of sky tones. A scattering of high cirrus catches the last light of Hyperion's too-small sun and ignites like burning coral. There is no sound except for the faintest hum of the electric turbines. Three hundred meters below, the shadow of a huge, mantalike undersea creature keeps pace with the dirigible. A second ago an insect or bird the size and color of a hummingbird but with gossamer wings a meter across paused five meters out to inspect me before diving toward the sea with folded wings.

Edouard, I feel very alone tonight. It would help if I knew you were alive, still working in the garden, writing evenings in your study. I thought my travels would stir my old beliefs in St Teilhard's concept of the God in

Whom the Christ of Evolution, the Personal, and the Universal, the *En Haut* and the *En Avant* are joined, but no such renewal is forthcoming.

It is growing dark. I am growing old. I feel something . . . not yet remorse . . . at my sin of falsifying the evidence on the Armaghast dig. But, Edouard, Your Excellency, if the artifacts *had* indicated the presence of a Christ-oriented culture there, six hundred light-years from Old Earth, almost three thousand years *before* man left the surface of the home-world . . .

Was it so dark a sin to interpret such ambiguous data in a way which would have meant the resurgence of Christianity in our life-time?

Yes, it was. But not, I think, because of the sin of tampering with the data, but the deeper sin of thinking that Christianity could be saved. The Church is dying, Edouard. And not merely our beloved branch of the Holy Tree, but all of its offshoots, vestiges and cankers. The entire Body of Christ is dying as surely as this poorly used body of mine, Edouard. You and I knew this in Armaghast, where the blood-sun illuminated only dust and death. We knew it that cool, green summer at the College when we took our first vows. We knew it as boys in the quiet playfields of Villefranche-sur-Saône. We know it now.

The light is gone now; I must write by the slight glow from the salon windows a deck above. The stars lie in strange constellations. The Middle Sea glows at night with a greenish, unhealthy phosphorescence. There is a dark mass on the horizon to the southeast. It may be a storm or it may be the next island in the chain, the third of the nine 'tails'. (What mythology deals with a cat with nine tails? I know of none.)

For the sake of the bird I saw earlier – if it was a bird – I pray that it is an island ahead and not a storm.

Day 28:

I have been in Port Romance eight days and I have seen three dead men.

The first was a beached corpse, a bloated, white parody of a man, that had washed up on the mud flats beyond the mooring tower my first evening in town. Children threw stones at it.

The second man I watched being pulled from the burned wreckage of a methane-unit shop in the poor section of town near my hotel. His body was charred beyond recognition and shrunken by the heat, his arms and legs pulled tight in the prizefighter posture burning victims have been reduced to since time immemorial. I had been fasting all day and I confess with shame that I began to salivate when the air filled with the rich, frying-fat odor of burned flesh.

The third man was murdered not three meters from me. I had just emerged from the hotel onto the maze of mud-splattered planks that serve as sidewalks in this miserable town when shots rang out and a man several paces ahead of me lurched as if his foot had slipped, spun toward me with a quizzical look on his face, and fell sideways into the mud and sewage.

He had been shot three times with some sort of projectile weapon. Two of the bullets had struck his chest, the third entered just below the left eye. Incredibly, he was still breathing when I reached him. Without thinking about it, I removed my stole from my carrying bag, fumbled for the vial of holy water I had carried for so long, and proceeded to perform the sacrament of Extreme Unction. No one in the gathering crowd objected. The fallen man stirred once, cleared his throat as if he were about to speak, and died. The crowd dispersed even before the body was removed.

The man was middle-aged, sandy-haired, and slightly overweight. He carried no identification, not even a universal card or comlog. There were six silver coins in his pocket.

For some reason, I elected to stay with the body the rest of that day. The doctor was a short and cynical man who allowed me to stay during the required autopsy. I suspect that he was starved for conversation.

'This is what the whole thing's worth,' he said as he opened the poor man's belly like a pink satchel, pulling the folds of skin and muscle back and pinning them down like tent flaps.

'What thing?' I asked.

'His life,' said the doctor and pulled the skin of the corpse's face up and back like a greasy mask. 'Your life. My life.' The red and white stripes of overlapping muscle turned to blue bruise around the ragged hole just above the cheekbone.

'There has to be more than this,' I said.

The doctor looked up from his grim work with a bemused smile. 'Is there?' he said. 'Please show me.' He lifted the man's heart and seemed to weigh it in one hand. 'In the Web worlds, this'd be worth some money on the open market. There're those too poor to keep vat-grown, cloned parts in store, but too well off to die just for want of a heart. But out here it's just offal.'

'There has to be more,' I said, although I felt little conviction. I remembered the funeral of His Holiness Pope Urban XV shortly before I left Pacem. As has been the custom since pre-Hegira days, the corpse was not embalmed. It waited in the anteroom off the main basilica to be fitted for the plain wooden coffin. As I helped Edouard and Monsignor Frey place the vestments on the stiffened corpse I noticed the browning skin and slackening mouth.

The doctor shrugged and finished the perfunctory autopsy. There was the briefest of formal inquiries. No suspect was found, no motive put forward. A description of the murdered man was sent to Keats but the man himself was buried the next day in a pauper's field between the mud flats and the yellow jungle.

Port Romance is a jumble of yellow, weirwood structures set on a maze of scaffolds and planks stretching far out onto the tidal mud flats at the mouth of the Kans. The river is almost two kilometers wide here where it spills out into Toschahai Bay, but only a few channels are navigable and the dredging goes on day and night. I lie awake each night in my cheap room with the window open to the pounding of the dredge-hammer sounding like the booming of this vile city's heart, the distant susurration of the surf its wet breathing. Tonight I listen to the city breathe and cannot help but give it the flayed face of the murdered man.

The companies keep a skimmerport on the edge of town to ferry men and matériel inland to the larger plantations, but I do not have enough money to bribe my way aboard. Rather, I could get *myself* aboard but cannot afford to transport my three trunks of medical and scientific gear. I am still tempted. My service among the Bikura seems more absurd and irrational now than ever before. Only my strange need for a destination and a certain masochistic determination to complete the terms of my self-imposed exile keep me moving upriver.

There is a riverboat departing up the Kans in two days. I have booked passage and will move my trunks onto it tomorrow. It will not be hard to leave Port Romance behind.

Day 41:

The *Emporotic Girandole* continues its slow progress upriver. No sight of human habitation since we left Melton's Landing two days ago. The jungle presses down to the riverbank like a solid wall now; more, it almost completely overhangs us in places where the river narrows to thirty or forty meters. The light itself is yellow, rich as liquid butter, filtered as it is through foliage and fronds eighty meters above the brown surface of the Kans. I sit on the rusted tin roof of the center passenger barge and strain to make out my first glimpse of a tesla tree. Old Kady sitting nearby pauses in his whittling, spits over the side through a gap in his teeth, and laughs at me. 'Ain't going to be no flame trees this far down,' he says. 'If they was the forest sure all hell wouldn't look like this. You got to get up in the Pinions before you see a tesla. We ain't out of the rain forest yet, Padre.'

It rains every afternoon. Actually, rain is too gentle a term for the deluge that strikes us each day, obscuring the shore, pounding the tin roofs of the barges with a deafening roar, and slowing our upstream crawl until it seems we are standing still. It is as if the river becomes a vertical torrent each afternoon, a waterfall which the ship must climb if we are to go on.

The *Girandole* is an ancient, flat-bottomed tow with five barges lashed around it like ragged children clinging to their tired mother's skirts. Three of the two-level barges carry bales of goods to be traded or sold at the few plantations and settlements along the river. The other two offer a simulacrum of lodging for the indigenies traveling upriver, although I suspect that some of the barge's residents are permanent. My own berth boasts a stained mattress on the floor and lizard-like insects on the walls.

After the rains everyone gathers on the decks to watch the evening mists rise from the cooling river. The air is very hot and supersaturated with moisture most of the day now. Old Kady tells me that I have come too late to make the climb through the rain and flame forests before the tesla trees become active. We shall see.

Tonight the mists rise like the spirits of all the dead who sleep beneath the river's dark surface. The last tattered remnants of the afternoon's cloud cover dissipate through the treetops and color returns to the world. I watch as the dense forest shifts from chrome yellow to a translucent saffron and then slowly fades through ocher to umber to gloom. Aboard the *Girandole*, Old Kady lights the lanterns and candle-globes hanging from the sagging second tier and, as if not to be outdone, the darkened jungle begins to glow with the faint phosphorescence of decay while glowbirds and multihued gossamers can be seen floating from branch to branch in the darker upper regions.

Hyperion's small moon is not visible tonight but this world moves through more debris than is common for a planet so close to its sun and the night skies are illuminated by frequent meteor showers. Tonight the heavens are especially fertile and when we move onto wide sections of the river we can see a tracery of brilliant meteor trails weaving the stars together. Their images burn the retina after a while and I look down at the river only to see the same optic echo there in the dark waters.

There is a bright glow on the eastern horizon and Old Kady tells me that this is from the orbital mirrors which give light to a few of the larger plantations.

It is too warm to return to my cabin. I spread my thin mat on the rooftop of my barge and watch the celestial light show while clusters of indigenie families sing haunting songs in an argot I have not even tried to learn. I wonder about the Bikura, still far away from here, and a strange anxiety rises in me.

Somewhere in the forest an animal screams with the voice of a frightened woman.

Day 60:
Arrived Perecebo Plantation. Sick.

Day 62:
Very ill. Fever, fits of shaking. All yesterday I was vomiting black bile. The rain is deafening. At night the clouds are lit from above by orbital mirrors. The sky seems to be on fire. My fever is very high.

A woman takes care of me. Bathes me. Too sick to be ashamed. Her hair is darker than most indigenies'. She says little. Dark, gentle eyes.

Oh, God, to be sick so far from home.

Day
sheis waiting spying comesin from the rain the thin shirt

on purpose to tempt me, knows what iam my skin burning on fire thin cotton nipples dark against it i knowwho they are they are watching, here hear their voices at night they bathe me in poison burns me they think I don't know but i hear their voices above the rain when the screaming stops stop stop

My skin is almost gone. red underneath can feel the hole in my cheek.

when I find the bullet iwill spit it out it out. agnusdeiquitolispecattamundi miserer nobis misere nobis miserere

Day 65:
Thank you, dear Lord, for deliverance from illness.

Day 66:
Shaved today. Was able to make it to the shower.

Semfa helped me prepare for the administrator's visit. I expected him to be one of the large, gruff types I've seen out the window working in the sorting compound, but he was a quiet black man with a slight lisp. He was most helpful. I had been concerned about paying for my medical care but he reassured me that there would be no charge. Even better – he will assign a man to lead me into the high country! He says it is late in the season but if I can travel in ten days we should be able to make it through the flame forest to the Cleft before the tesla trees are fully active.

After he left I sat and talked to Semfa a bit. Her husband died here three local months ago in a harvesting accident. Semfa herself had come from Port Romance; her marriage to Mikel had been a salvation for her and she has chosen to stay on here doing odd jobs rather than go back downriver. I do not blame her.

After a massage, I will sleep. Many dreams about my mother recently.

Ten days. I will be ready in ten days.

Day 75:
Before leaving with Tuk, I went down to the matrix paddies to say goodbye to Semfa. She said little but I could see in her eyes that she was sad to see me go. Without premeditation, I blessed her and then kissed her on the forehead. Tuk stood nearby, smiling and bobbing. Then we were off, leading the two packbrids. Supervisor Orlandi came to the end of the road and waved as we entered the narrow lane hacked into the aureate foliage.

Domine, dirige nos.

Day 82:
After a week on the trail – what trail? – after a week in the trackless, yellow rain forest, after a week of exhausting climb up the ever steeper shoulder of the Pinion Plateau, we emerged this morning onto a rocky outcropping that allowed us a view back across an expanse of jungle toward the Beak and the Middle Sea. The plateau here is almost three thousand meters above sea level and the view was impressive. Heavy rain clouds spread out below us to the foot of the Pinion Hills, but through gaps in the white and gray carpet of cloud we caught glimpses of the Kans in its leisurely uncoiling toward Port R. and the sea, chrome-yellow swatches of the forest we had struggled through, and a hint of magenta far to the east that Tuk swore was the lower matrix of fiberplastic fields near Perecebo.

31

We continued onward and upward late into the evening. Tuk is obviously worried that we will be caught in the flame forests when the tesla trees become active. I struggle to keep up, tugging at the heavily laden 'brid and saying silent prayers to keep my mind off my aches, pains, and general misgivings.

Day 83:
Loaded and moving before dawn today. The air smells of smoke and ashes.

The change in vegetation here on the Plateau is startling. No longer evident are the ubiquitous weirwood and leafy chalma. After passing through an intermediate zone of short evergreens and everblues, then after climbing again through dense strands of mutated lodgepole pines and triaspen, we came into the flame forest proper with its groves of tall prometheus, trailers of ever present phoenix, and round stands of amber lambents. Occasionally we encountered impenetrable breaks of the white-fibrous, bifurcated bestos plants that Tuk picturesquely referred to as '. . . looking like de rotting cocks o' some dead giants what be buried shallow here, dat be sure.' My guide has a way with words.

It was late afternoon before we saw our first tesla tree. For half an hour we had been trudging over an ash-covered forest floor, trying not to tread on the tender shoots of phoenix and firewhip gamely pushing up through the sooty soil, when suddenly Tuk stopped and pointed.

The tesla tree, still half a kilometer away, stood at least a hundred meters tall, half again as high as the tallest prometheus. Near its crown it bulged with the distinctive onion-shaped dome of its accumulator gall. The radial branches above the gall trailed dozens of nimbus vines, each looking silver and metallic against the clear green and lapis sky. The whole thing made me think of some elegant High Muslim mosque on New Mecca irreverently garlanded with tinsel.

'We got to get de 'brids and our asses de hell out o' here,' grunted Tuk. He insisted that we change into flame forest gear right then and there. We spent the rest of the afternoon and evening trudging on in our osmosis masks and thick, rubber-soled boots, sweating under layers of leathery gamma-cloth. Both of the 'brids acted nervous, their long ears pricking at the slightest sound. Even through my mask I could smell the ozone; it reminded me of electric trains I had played with as a child on lazy Christmas Day afternoons in Villefranche-sur-Saône.

We are camping as close as we can to a bestos break this night. Tuk showed me how to set out the ring of arrestor rods, all the time clucking dire warnings to himself and searching the evening sky for clouds.

I plan to sleep well in spite of everything.

Day 84:
0400 hours—
    Sweet Mother of Christ.

For three hours we have been caught up in the middle of the end of the world.

The explosions started shortly after midnight, mere lightning crashes at first, and against our better judgment Tuk and I slid our heads through the tent flap to watch the pyrotechnics. I am used to the Matthewmonth monsoon storms on Pacem, so the first hour of lightning displays did not seem too unusual. Only the sight of distant tesla trees as the unerring focus of the aerial discharge was a bit unnerving. But soon the forest behemoths were glowing and spitting with their own accumulated energy and then – just as I was drifting off to sleep despite the continued noise – true Armageddon was unleashed.

At least a hundred arcs of electricity must have been released in the first ten seconds of the tesla trees' opening spasms of violent energy. A prometheus less than thirty meters from us exploded, dropping flaming brands fifty meters to the forest floor. The arrestor rods glowed, hissed, and deflected arc after arc of blue-white death over and around our small campsite. Tuk screamed something but no mere human sound was audible over the onslaught of light and noise. A patch of trailing phoenix burst into flame near the tethered 'brids and one of the terrified animals – hobbled and blindfolded as it was – broke free and lunged through the circle of glowing arrestor rods. Instantly half a dozen bolts of lightning from the nearest tesla arced to the hapless animal. For a mad second I could have sworn I saw the beast's skeleton glowing through boiling flesh and then it spasmed high into the air and simply ceased to be.

For three hours we have watched the end of the world. Two of the arrestor rods have fallen but the other eight continue to function. Tuk and I huddle in the hot cave of our tent, osmosis masks filtering enough cool oxygen out of the superheated, smoky air to allow us to breathe. Only the lack of undergrowth and Tuk's skill in placing our tent away from other targets and near the sheltering bestos plants have allowed us to survive. That and the eight whiskered-alloy rods that stand between us and eternity.

'They seem to be holding up well!' I shout to Tuk over the hiss and crackle, crash and split of the storm.

'Dey be made to stand de hour, mebbe two,' grunts my guide. 'Any time, mebbe sooner, dey fuse, we die.'

I nod and sip at lukewarm water through the slipstrip of my osmosis mask. If I survive this night, I shall always thank God for His generosity in allowing me to see this sight.

Day 87:

Tuk and I emerged from the smoldering northeastern edge of the flame forest at noon yesterday, promptly set up camp by the edge of a small stream, and slept for eighteen hours straight; making up for three nights of no sleep and two grueling days moving without rest through a nightmare of flame and ash. Everywhere we looked as we approached the hogback ridge that marked the terminus of the forest, we could see seedpods and cones burst open with new life for the various fire species that had died in the conflagration of the previous two nights. Five of our arrestor rods still functioned, although neither Tuk nor I was eager to test them another night. Our surviving packbrid collapsed and died the instant the heavy load was lifted off its back.

I awoke this morning at dawn to the sound of running water. I followed the small stream a kilometer to the northeast, following a deepening in its sound, until suddenly it dropped from sight.

The Cleft! I had almost forgotten our destination. This morning, stumbling through the fog, leaping from one wet rock to another alongside the widening stream, I took a leap to a final boulder, teetered there, regained my balance, and looked straight down above a waterfall that dropped almost three thousand meters to mist, rock, and river far below.

The Cleft was not carved out of the rising plateau as was the legendary Grand Canyon on Old Earth or World Crack on Hebron. In spite of its active oceans and seemingly earthlike continents, Hyperion is tectonically quite dead; more like Mars, Lusus, or Armaghast in its total lack of continental drift. And like Mars and Lusus, Hyperion is afflicted with its Deep Ice Ages, although here the periodicity is spread to thirty-seven million years by the long ellipse of the currently absent binary dwarf. The comlog compares the Cleft to the pre-terraformed Mariner Valley on Mars, both being caused by the weakening of crust through periodic freeze and thaw over the aeons, followed by the flow of subterranean rivers such as the Kans. Then the massive collapse, running like a long scar through the mountainous wing of the continent Aquila.

Tuk joined me as I stood on the edge of the Cleft. I was naked, rinsing the ash smell from my traveling clothes and cassock. I splashed cold water over my pale flesh and laughed out loud as the echoes of Tuk's shouts came back from the North Wall two thirds of a kilometer away. Because of the nature of the crust collapse, Tuk and I stood far out on an overhang that hid the South Wall below us. Although perilously exposed, we assumed that the rocky cornice which had defied gravity for millions of years would last a few more hours as we bathed, relaxed, shouted echoing hallos until we were hoarse, and generally acted like children liberated from school. Tuk confessed that he had never penetrated the full width of the flame forest – nor known anyone who had in this season – and announced that, now that the tesla trees were becoming fully active, he would have at least a three-month wait until he could return. He did not seem too sorry and I was glad to have him with me.

In the afternoon we transported my gear in relays, setting up camp near the stream a hundred meters back from the cornice and stacking my flowfoam boxes of scientific gear for further sorting in the morning.

It was cold this evening. After dinner, just before sunset, I pulled on my thermal jacket and walked alone to a rocky ledge southwest of where I had first encountered the Cleft. From my vantage point far out over the river, the view was memorable. Mists rose from unseen waterfalls tumbling to the river far below, spray rising in shifting curtains of mist to multiply the setting sun into a dozen violet spheres and twice that many rainbows. I watched as each spectrum was born, rose toward the darkening dome of sky, and died. As the cooling air settled into the cracks and caverns of the plateau and the warm air rushed skyward, pulling leaves, twigs, and mist upward in a vertical gale, a sound ebbed up out of the Cleft as if the continent itself was calling with the voices of stone giants, gigantic bamboo flutes, church organs the size of palaces, the clear, perfect notes ranging from the shrillest soprano to the deepest bass. I speculated on wind vectors against the fluted rock walls, on caverns far below venting deep cracks in the motionless crust, and on the illusion of human voices that random harmonics can generate. But in the end I set aside speculation and simply listened as the Cleft sang its farewell hymn to the sun.

I walked back to our tent and its circle of bioluminescent lantern light as the first fusillade of meteor showers burned the skies overhead and distant explosions from the flame forests rippled along the southern and western horizons like cannon fire from some ancient war on pre-Hegira Old Earth.

Once in the tent I try the long-range comlog bands but there is nothing but static. I suspect that even if the primitive comsats that serve the fiberplastic plantations were ever to broadcast this far east, anything but the tightest laser or fatline beams would be masked by the mountains and tesla activity. On Pacem, few of us at the monastery wore or carried personal comlogs, but the datasphere was always there if we needed to tap into it. Here there is no choice.

I sit and listen to the last notes from the canyon wind die, watch the skies simultaneously darken and blaze, smile at the sound of Tuk's snoring from his bedroll outside the tent, and I think to myself, *If this is exile, so be it.*

Day 88:
Tuk is dead. Murdered.

I found his body when I left the tent at sunrise. He had been sleeping outside, not more than four meters from me. He had said that he wished to sleep under the stars.

The murderers cut his throat while he slept. I heard no cry. I did dream, however: dreams of Semfa ministering to me during my fever. Dreams of cool hands touching my neck and chest, touching the crucifix I have worn since childhood. I stood over Tuk's body, staring at the wide, dark circle where his blood had soaked into Hyperion's uncaring soil, and I shivered at the thought that the dream had been more than a dream – that hands *had* touched me in the night.

I confess that I reacted more like a frightened old fool than as a priest. I did administer Extreme Unction, but then the panic struck me and I left my poor guide's body, desperately searched through the supplies for a weapon, and took away the machete I had used in the rain forest and the low-voltage maser with which I had planned to hunt small game. Whether

I would have used a weapon on a human being, even to save my own life, I do not know. But, in my panic, I carried the machete, the maser, and the powered binoculars to a high boulder near the Cleft and searched the region for any signs of the murderers. Nothing stirred except the tiny arboreals and gossamers we had seen flitting through the trees yesterday. The forest itself seemed abnormally thick and dark. The Cleft offered a hundred terraces, ledges, and rock balconies to the northeast for entire bands of savages. An army could have hidden there in the crags and ever present mists.

After thirty minutes of fruitless vigilance and foolish cowardice, I returned to the campsite and prepared Tuk's body for burial. It took me well over two hours to dig a proper grave in the rocky soil of the plateau. When it was filled and the formal service was finished, I could think of nothing personal to say about the rough, funny little man who had been my guide. 'Watch over him, Lord,' I said at last, disgusted at my own hypocrisy, sure in my heart that I was mouthing words only to myself. 'Give him safe passage. Amen.'

This evening I have moved my camp half a kilometer north. My tent is pitched in an open area ten meters away but I am wedged with my back against the boulder, sleeping robes pulled around, the machete and maser nearby. After Tuk's funeral I went through the supplies and boxes of equipment. Nothing had been taken except for the few remaining arrestor rods. Immediately I wondered if someone had followed us through the flame forest in order to kill Tuk and strand me here, but I could think of no motive for such an elaborate action. Anyone from the plantations could have killed us as we slept in the rain forest or – better yet from a murderer's point of view – deep in the flame forest where no one would wonder at two charred corpses. That left the Bikura. My primitive charges.

I considered returning through the flame forest without the rods but soon abandoned the idea. It is probable death to stay and certain death to go.

Three months before the teslas become dormant. One hundred twenty of the twenty-six-hour local days. An eternity.

Dear Christ, why has this come to me? And why was I spared last night if I am merely to be offered up this night . . . or next?

I sit here under the darkening crag and I listen to the suddenly ominous moaning rising with the night wind from the Cleft and I pray as the sky lights with the blood-red streaks of meteor trails.

Mouthing words to myself.

Day 95:

The terrors of the past week have largely abated. I find that even fear fades and becomes commonplace after days of anticlimax.

I used the machete to cut small trees for a lean-to, covering the roof and side with gamma-cloth and caulking between the logs with mud. The back wall is the solid stone of the boulder. I have sorted through my research gear and set some of it out, although I suspect that I will never use it now.

I have begun foraging to supplement my quickly diminishing cache of freeze-dried food. By now, according to the absurd schedule drawn up so long ago on Pacem, I was to have been living with the Bikura for some weeks and trading small goods for local food. No matter. Besides my diet of bland but easily boiled chalma roots, I have found half a dozen varieties of berries and larger fruits that the comlog assures me are edible; so far only one has disagreed with me enough to keep me squatting all night near the edge of the nearest ravine.

I pace the confines of the region as restlessly as one of those caged pelops that were so prized by the minor padishahs on Armaghast. A kilometer to the south and four to the west, the flame forests are in full form. In the morning, smoke vies with the shifting curtains of mist to hide the sky. Only the near-solid breaks of bestos, the rocky soil here on the summit plateau, and the hogback ridges running like armor-plated vertebrae north-east from here keep the teslas at bay.

To the north, the plateau widens out and the undergrowth becomes denser near the Cleft for some fifteen kilometers until the way is blocked by a ravine a third as deep and half as wide as the Cleft itself. Yesterday I reached this northernmost point and stared across the gaping barrier with some frustration. I will try again someday, detouring to the east to find a crossing point, but from the telltale signs of phoenix across the chasm and the pall of smoke along the northeastern horizon, I suspect I will find only the chalma-filled canyons and steppes of flame forest that are roughed in on the orbital survey map I carry.

Tonight I visited Tuk's rocky grave as the evening wind began to wail its aeolian dirge. I knelt there and tried to pray but nothing came.

Edouard, nothing came. I am as empty as those fake sarcophagi that you and I unearthed by the score from the sterile desert sands near Tarum bel Wadi.

The Zen Gnostics would say that this emptiness is a good sign; that it presages openness to a new level of awareness, new insights, new experience.

Merde.

My emptiness is only . . . emptiness.

Day 96:

I have found the Bikura. Or, rather, they have found me. I will write what I can before they come to rouse me from my 'sleep'.

Today I was doing some detail mapping a mere four kilometers north of camp when the mists lifted in the midday warmth and I noticed a series of terraces on my side of the Cleft that had been hidden until then. I was using my powered glasses to inspect the terraces – actually a series of laddered ledges, spires, shelves, and tussocks extending far out onto the overhang – when I realized that I was staring at man-made habitations. The

37

dozen or so huts were crude – rough hovels of heaped chalma fronds, stones, and spongeturf – but they were unmistakably of human origin.

I was standing there irresolute, binoculars still lifted, trying to decide whether to climb down to the exposed ledges and confront the inhabitants or to retreat to my camp, when I felt that lifting chill along the back and neck that tells one with absolute certainty that he is no longer alone. I lowered the binoculars and turned slowly. The Bikura were there, at least thirty of them, standing in a semi-circle that left me no retreat to the forest.

I do not know what I expected; naked savages, perhaps, with fierce expressions and necklaces of teeth. Perhaps I had half expected to find the kind of bearded, wild-haired hermits that travelers sometimes encountered in the Moshé Mountains on Hebron. Whatever I had held in mind, the reality of the Bikura did not fit the template.

The people who had approached me so silently were short – none came higher than my shoulder – and swathed in roughly woven dark robes that covered them from neck to toe. When they moved, as some did now, they seemed to glide over the rough ground like wraiths. From a distance, their appearance reminded me of nothing so much as a gaggle of diminutive Jesuits at a New Vatican enclave.

I almost giggled then, but realized that such a response might well be a sign of rising panic. The Bikura showed no outward signs of aggression to cause such a panic; they carried no weapons, their small hands were empty. As empty as their expressions.

Their physiognomy is hard to describe succinctly. They are bald. All of them. That baldness, the absence of any facial hair, and the loose robes that fell in a straight line to the ground, all conspired to make it very difficult to tell the men from the women. The group now confronting me – more than fifty by this time – looked to be all of roughly the same age: somewhere between forty and fifty standard years. Their faces were smooth, the skin tinged with a yellowish cast that I guessed might be associated with generations of ingesting trace minerals in the chalma and other local plant life.

One might be tempted to describe the round faces of the Bikura as cherubic until, upon closer inspection, that impression of sweetness fades and is replaced by another interpretation – placid idiocy. As a priest, I have spent enough time on backward worlds to see the effects of an ancient genetic disorder variously called Down's syndrome, mongolism, or generation-ship legacy. This, then, was the overall impression created by the sixty or so dark-robed little people who had approached me – I was being greeted by a silent, smiling band of bald, retarded children.

I reminded myself that these were almost certainly the same group of 'smiling children' who had slit Tuk's throat while he slept and left him to die like a butchered pig.

The closest Bikura stepped forward, stopped five paces from me, and said something in a soft monotone.

'Just a minute,' I said and fumbled out my comlog, I tapped in the translator function.

'Beyetet ota menna lot cresfem ket?' asked the short man in front of me.

I slipped on the hearplug just in time to hear the comlog's translation. There was no lag time. The apparently foreign language was a simple corruption of archaic seedship English not so far removed from the indigene argot of the plantations. 'You are the man who belongs to the cross shape/cruciform,' interpreted the comlog, giving me two choices for the final noun.

'Yes,' I said, knowing now that these were the ones who had touched me the night I slept through Tuk's murder. Which meant that these were the ones who had murdered Tuk.

I waited. The hunting maser was in my pack. The pack was set against a small chalma not ten paces from me. Half a dozen Bikura stood between me and it. It did not matter. I knew at that instant that I would not use a weapon against another human being, even a human being who had murdered my guide and might well be planning to murder me at any second. I closed my eyes and said a silent Act of Contrition. When I opened my eyes, more of the Bikura had arrived, There was a cessation of movement, as if a quorum had been filled, a decision reached.

'Yes,' I said again into the silence, 'I am the one who wears the cross.' I heard the comlog speaker pronounce the last word 'cresfem'.

The Bikura nodded in unison and – as if from long practice as altar boys – all went to one knee, robes rustling softly, in a perfect genuflection.

I opened my mouth to speak and found that I had nothing to say. I closed my mouth.

The Bikura stood. A breeze moved the brittle chalma fronds and leaves together to make a dry, end-of-summer sound above us. The Bikura nearest to me on the left stepped closer, grasped my forearm with a touch of cool, strong fingers, and spoke a soft sentence that my comlog translated as, 'Come. It is time to go to the houses and sleep.'

It was midafternoon. Wondering if the comlog had translated the word 'sleep' properly or if it might be an idiom or metaphor for 'die', I nodded and followed them toward the village at the edge of the Cleft.

Now I sit in the hut and wait. There are rustling sounds. Someone else is awake now. I sit and wait.

Day 97:
The Bikura call themselves the 'Three Score and Ten'.

I have spent the past twenty-six hours talking to them, observing, making notes when they take their two-hour, midafternoon 'sleep', and generally trying to record as much data as I can before they decide to slit ray throat.

Except now I am beginning to believe that they will not hurt me.

I spoke to them yesterday after our 'sleep'. Sometimes they do not respond to questions and when they do the responses are little better than the grunts or divergent answers one receives from slow children. After their initial question and invitation at our first encounter, none of them originated a single query or comment my way.

I questioned them subtly, carefully, cautiously, and with the professional calm of a trained ethnologist. I asked the simplest, most factual questions possible to make sure that the comlog was functioning properly. It was. But the sum total of the answers left me almost as ignorant as I had been twenty-some hours before.

Finally, tired in body and spirit, I abandoned professional subtlety and asked the group I was sitting with, 'Did you kill my companion?'

My three interlocutors did not look up from the weaving they were doing on a crude loom. 'Yes,' said the one I have come to think of as Alpha because he had been the first to approach me in the forest, 'we cut your companion's throat with sharpened stones and held him down and silent while he struggled. He died the true death.'

'Why?' I asked after a moment. My voice sounded as dry as a corn husk crumbling.

'Why did he die the true death?' said Alpha, still not looking up. 'Because all of his blood ran out and he stopped breathing.'

'No,' I said. 'Why did you kill him?'

Alpha did not respond, but Betty – who may or may not be female and Alpha's mate – looked up from her loom and said simply, 'To make him die.'

'Why?'

The responses invariably came back and just as invariably failed to enlightened me one iota. After much questioning, I had ascertained that they had killed Tuk to make him die and that he had died because he had been killed.

'What is the difference between death and true death?' I asked, not trusting the comlog or my temper at this point.

The third Bikura, Del, grunted a response that the comlog interpreted as, 'Your companion died the true death. You did not.'

Finally, in frustration far too close to rage, I snapped, 'Why not? Why didn't you kill me?'

All three stopped in the middle of their mindless weaving and looked at me. 'You cannot be killed because you cannot die,' said Alpha. 'You cannot die because you belong to the cruciform and follow the way of the cross.'

I had no idea why the damn machine would translate cross as 'cross' one second and as 'cruciform' the next. *Because you belong to the cruciform.*

A chill went through me, followed by the urge to laugh. Had I stumbled into that old adventure holo cliché – the lost tribe that worshiped the 'god' that had tumbled into their jungle until the poor bastard cuts himself shaving or something, and the tribespeople, assured and a bit relieved at the obvious mortality of their visitor, offer up their erstwhile deity as a sacrifice?

It would have been funny if the image of Tuk's bloodless face and raw-rimmed, gaping wound was not so fresh.

Their reaction to the cross certainly suggested that I had encountered a group of survivors of a once Christian colony – Catholics? – even though the data in the comlog insisted that the dropship of seventy colonists who had crashed on this plateau four hundred years ago had held only Neo-Kerwin Marxists, all of whom should have been indifferent if not openly hostile to the old religions.

I considered dropping the matter as being far too dangerous to pursue, but my stupid need to know drove me on. 'Do you worship Jesus?' I asked.

Their blank expressions left no need for a verbal negative.

'Christ?' I tried again. 'Jesus Christ? Christian? The Catholic Church?' No interest.

'Catholic? Jesus? Mary? St Peter? Paul? St Teilhard?'

The comlog made noises but the words seemed to have no meaning for them.

'You follow the cross?' I said, flailing for some last contact.

All three looked at me. 'We belong to the cruciform,' said Alpha.

I nodded, understanding nothing.

This evening I fell asleep briefly just before sunset and when I awoke it was to the organ-pipe music of the Cleft's nightfall winds. It was much louder here on the village ledges. Even the hovels seemed to join the chorus as the rising gusts whistled and whined through stone gaps, flapping fronds, and crude smokeholes.

Something was wrong. It took me a groggy minute to realize that the village was abandoned. Every hut was empty. I sat on a cold boulder and wondered if my presence had sparked some mass exodus. The wind music had ended and meteors were beginning their nightly show through cracks in low clouds when I heard a sound behind me and turned to find all seventy of the Three Score and Ten behind me.

They walked past without a word and went to their huts. There were no lights. I imagined them sitting in their hovels, staring.

I stayed outside for some time before returning to my own hut. After a while I walked to the edge of the grassy shelf and stood where rock dropped away into the abyss. A cluster of vines and roots clung to the cliff face but appeared to end a few meters into space and hang there above emptiness. No vine could have been long enough to offer a way to the river two kilometers below.

But the Bikura had come from this direction.

Nothing made sense. I shook my head and went back to my hut.

Sitting here, writing by the light of the comlog diskey, I try to think of precautions I can take to insure that I will see the sunrise.

I can think of none.

Day 103:
The more I learn, the less I understand.

I have moved most of my gear to the hut they leave empty for me here in the village.

I have taken photographs, recorded video and audio chips, and imaged a full holoscan of the village and its inhabitants. They do not seem to care. I project their images and they walk right through them, showing no interest. I play back their words to them and they smile and go back into their hovels to sit for hours, doing nothing, saying nothing. I offer them trade trinkets and they take them without comment, check to see if they are edible, and then leave them lying. The grass is littered with plastic beads, mirrors, bits of colored cloth, and cheap pens.

I have set up the full medical lab but to no avail; the Three Score and Ten will not let me examine them, will not let me take blood samples, even though I have repeatedly shown them that it is painless, will not let me scan them with the diagnostic equipment – will not, in short, cooperate in any way. They do not argue. They do not explain. They simply turn away and go about their nonbusiness.

After a week I still cannot tell the males from the females. Their faces remind me of those visual puzzles that shift forms as you stare; sometimes Betty's face looks undeniably female and ten seconds later the sense of gender is gone and I think of her (him?) as Beta again. Their voices undergo the same shift. Soft, well modulated, sexless . . . they remind me of the poorly programmed homecomps one encounters on backward worlds.

I find myself hoping to catch a glimpse of a naked Bikura. This is not easy for a Jesuit of forty-eight standard years to admit. Still, it would not be an easy task even for a veteran voyeur. The nudity taboo seems absolute. They wear the long robes while awake and during their two-hour midday nap. They leave the village area to urinate and defecate, and I suspect that they do not remove the loose robes even then. They do not seem to bathe. One would suspect that this would cause olfactory problems, but there is no odor about these primitives except for the slight, sweet smell of chalma. 'You must undress sometimes,' I said to Alpha one day, abandoning delicacy in favor of information. 'No,' said Al and went elsewhere to sit and do nothing while fully dressed.

They have no names. I found this incredible at first, but now I am sure.

'We are all that was and will be,' said the shortest Bikura, one I think of as female and call Eppie. 'We are the Three Score and Ten.'

I searched the comlog records and confirmed what I suspected: in more than sixteen thousand known human societies, none are listed where there are no individual names at all. Even in the Lusus hive societies, individuals respond to their class category followed by a simple code.

I tell them my name and they stare. 'Father Paul Duré, Father Paul Duré,' repeats the comlog translator but there is no attempt at even simple repetition.

Except for their mass disappearances each day before sunset and their common two-hour sleep time, they do very little as a group. Even their lodging arrangements appear random. Al will spend one naptime with

Betty, the next with Gam, and the third with Zeida or Pete. No system or schedule is apparent. Every third day the entire group of seventy goes into the forest to forage and returns with berries, chalma roots and bark, fruit, and whatever else might be edible. I was sure they were vegetarians until I saw Del munching on the cold corpse of an infant arboreal. The little primate must have fallen from the high branches. It seems then that the Three Score and Ten do not disdain meat; they simply are too stupid to hunt and kill it.

When the Bikura are thirsty they walk almost three hundred meters to a stream that cascades into the Cleft. In spite of this inconvenience, there are no signs of water skins, jugs, or any type of pottery. I keep my reserve of water in ten-gallon plastic containers but the villagers take no notice. In my plummeting respect for these people, I do not find it unlikely that they have spent generations in a village with no handy water source.

'Who built the houses?' I ask. They have no word for village.

'The Three Score and Ten,' responds Will. I can tell him from the others only by a broken finger that did not mend well. Each of them has at least one such distinguishing feature, although sometimes I think it would be easier to tell crows apart.

'When did they build them?' I ask, although I should know by now that any question that starts with 'when' will not receive an answer.

I receive no answer.

They do go into the Cleft each evening. Down the vines. On the third evening, I tried to observe this exodus but six of them turned me back from the edge and gently but persistently brought me back to my hut. It was the first observable action of the Bikura that had hinted at aggression and I sat in some apprehension after they had gone.

The next evening as they departed I went quietly to my hut, not even peering out, but after they returned I retrieved the imager and its tripod from where I had left them near the edge. The timer had worked perfectly. The holos showed the Bikura grabbing the vines and scrambling down the cliff face as nimbly as the little arboreals that fill the chalma and weirwood forest. Then they disappeared under the overhang.

'What do you do when you go down the cliff each evening?' I asked Al the next day.

The native looked at me with the seraphic, Buddha smile I have learned to hate. 'You belong to the cruciform,' he said as if that answered everything.

'Do you worship when you go down the cliff?' I asked.

No answer.

I thought a minute. 'I also follow the cross,' I said, knowing that it would be translated as 'belong to the cruciform'. Any day now I will not need the translator program. But this conversation was too important to leave to chance. 'Does this mean that I should join you when you go down the cliff face?'

For a second I thought that Al was thinking. His brow furrowed and I realized that it was the first tune that I had seen one of the Three Score and Ten come close to frowning. Then he said, 'You cannot. You belong to the cruciform but you are not of the Three Score and Ten.'

I realized that it had taken every neuron and synapse in his brain to frame that distinction.

'What would you do if I did go down the cliff face?' I asked, expecting no response. Hypothetical questions almost always had as much luck as my time-based queries.

This time he did respond. The seraphic smile and untroubled countenance returned and Alpha said softly, 'If you try to go down the cliff we will hold you down on the grass, take sharpened stones, cut your throat, and wait until your blood stops flowing and your heart stops beating.'

I said nothing. I wondered if he could hear the pounding of my heart at that moment. *Well*, I thought, *at least you don't have to worry any longer that they think you are a god.*

The silence stretched. Finally Al added one more sentence that I have been thinking about ever since. 'And if you did it again,' he said, 'we would have to kill you again.'

We stared at each other for some time after that; each convinced, I am sure, that the other was a total idiot.

Day 104:
Each new revelation adds to my confusion.

The absence of children here has bothered me since my first day in the village. Looking back through my notes, I find frequent mention of it in the daily observations I have dictated to my comlog, but no record of it in the personal mishmash here that I call a journal. Perhaps the implications were too frightening.

To my frequent and clumsy attempts at piercing this mystery, the Three Score and Ten have offered their usual enlightenment. The person questioned smiles beatifically and responds in some non sequitur that would make the babble of the Web's worst village idiot seem like sage aphorisms in comparison. More often than not, they do not answer at all.

One day I stood in front of the one I have tagged as Del, stayed there until he had to acknowledge my presence, and asked, 'Why are there no children?'

'We are the Three Score and Ten,' he said softly.

'Where are the babies?'

No response. No sense of evading the question, merely a blank stare.

I took a breath. 'Who is the youngest among you?'

Del appeared to be thinking, wrestling with the concept. He was overmatched. I wondered if the Bikura had lost their time sense so completely that any such question was doomed. After a minute of silence, however, Del pointed to where Al was crouched in the sunlight, working with his crude hand loom, and said, 'There is the last one to return.'

'To return?' I said. 'From where?'

Del stared at me with no emotion, not even impatience. 'You belong to the cruciform,' he said. 'You must know the way of the cross.'

I nodded. I knew enough to recognize that in this direction lay one of the many conversational illogic-loops that usually derailed our dialogues. I hunted for some way to keep a grasp of the thin thread of information. 'Then Al,' I said and pointed, 'is the last to be born. To return. But others will . . . return?'

I was not sure that I understood my own question. How does one inquire about birth when the interviewee has no word for child and no concept of time? But Del seemed to understand. He nodded.

Encouraged, I asked, 'Then when will the next of the Three Score and Ten be born? Return?'

'No one can return until one dies,' he said.

Suddenly I thought I understood. 'So no new children . . . no one will be returned until someone dies,' I said. 'You replace the missing one with another to keep the group at Three Score and Ten?'

Del responded with the type of silence I had come to interpret as assent.

The pattern seemed clear enough. The Bikura were quite serious about their Three Score and Ten. They kept the tribal population at seventy – the same number recorded on the passenger list of the dropship that crashed here four hundred years ago. Little chance of coincidence there. When someone died, they allowed a child to be born to replace the adult. Simple.

Simple but impossible. Nature and biology do not work that neatly. Besides the problem of minimum-herd population, there were other absurdities. Even though it is difficult to tell the ages of these smooth-skinned people, it is obvious that no more than ten years separate the oldest from the youngest. Although they act like children, I would guess their average age to be in the late thirties or mid-forties in standard years. So where are the very old? Where are the parents, aging uncles, and unmarried aunts? At this rate, the entire tribe will enter old age at approximately the same time. What happens when they all pass beyond childbearing age and it comes time to replace members of the tribe?

The Bikura lead dull, sedentary lives. The accident rate – even while living on the very edge of the Cleft – must be low. There are no predators, the seasonal variations are minimal and the food supply almost certainly remains stable. But, granted all this, there must have been times in the four-hundred-year history of this baffling group when disease swept the village, when more than the usual number of vines gave way and dropped citizens into the Cleft, or when *something* caused that abnormal cluster of sudden deaths that insurance companies have dreaded since time immemorial.

And then what? Do they breed to make up the difference and then revert to their current sexless behavior? Are the Bikura so different from every other recorded human society that they have a rutting period once every few years – once a decade? – once in a lifetime? It is doubtful.

I sit here in my hut and review the possibilities. One is that these people live *very* long lifetimes and can reproduce during most of that time, allowing for simple replacement of tribal casualties. Only this does not explain their common ages. And there is no mechanism to explain any such longevity. The best anti-aging drugs the Hegemony has to offer only manage to extend an active lifetime a bit over the hundred standard-year mark. Preventive health measures have spread the vitality of early middle age well into the late sixties – my age – but except for clonal transplants, bioengineering, and other perks for the very rich, no one in the Worldweb can expect to begin planning a family when they are seventy or expect to dance at their hundred-and-tenth birthday party. If eating chalma roots or breathing the pure air of the Pinion Plateau had a dramatic effect on retarding aging, it would be a sure bet that everyone on Hyperion would be living here munching chalma, that this planet would have had a farcaster centuries ago, and that every citizen of the Hegemony who has a universal card would be planning to spend vacations and retirement here.

No, a more logical conclusion is that the Bikura live normal-length lives, have children at a normal rate, but kill them unless a replacement is required. They may practice abstinence or birth control – other than slaughtering the newborn – until the entire band reaches an age where new blood will soon be needed. A mass-birthing time explains the apparent common age of the members of the tribe.

But who teaches the young? What happens to the parents and other older people? Do the Bikura pass along the rudiments of their crude excuse for a culture and then allow their own deaths? Would this be a 'true death' – the rubbing out of an entire generation? Do the Three Score and Ten murder individuals at both ends of the bell-shaped age curve?

This type of speculation is useless. I am beginning to get furious at my own lack of problem-solving skills. Let's form a strategy here and act on it, Paul. Get off your lazy, Jesuit ass.

PROBLEM: How to tell the sexes apart?

SOLUTION: Cajole or coerce a few of these poor devils into a medical exam. Find out what all the sex-role mystery and nudity taboo is about. A society that depends upon years of rigid sexual abstinence for population control is consistent with my new theory.

PROBLEM: Why are they so fanatical about maintaining the same Three Score and Ten population that the lost dropship colony started with?

SOLUTION: Keep pestering them until you find out.

PROBLEM: Where are the children?

SOLUTION: Keep pressing and poking until you find out. Perhaps the evening excursion down the cliff is related to all of this. There may be a nursery there. Or a pile of small bones.

PROBLEM: What *is* this 'belong to the cruciform' and 'way of the cross' business if not a contorted vestige of the original colonists' religious belief?

SOLUTION: Find out by going to the source. Could their daily descent down the cliff be religious in nature?

PROBLEM: What is down the cliff face?

SOLUTION: Go down and see.

Tomorrow, if their pattern holds true, all threescore and ten of the Three Score and Ten will wander into the woods for several hours of foraging. This time I will go with them.

This time I am going over the edge and down the cliff.

Day 105:

0930 hours – Thank you, O Lord, for allowing me to see what I have seen today.

Thank you, O Lord, for bringing me to this place at this time to see the proof of Your Presence.

1125 hours – Edouard . . . Edouard!

I have to return. To show you all! To show everyone.

I've packed everything I need, putting the imager disks and film in a pouch I wove from bestos leaves. I have food, water, the maser with its weakening charge. Tent. Sleep robes.

If only the arrestor rods had not been stolen!

The Bikura might have kept them. No, I've searched the hovels and the nearby forest. They would have no use for them.

It doesn't matter!

I'll leave today if I can. Otherwise, as soon as I can.

Edouard! I have it all here on the film and disks.

1400—

There is no way through the flame forests today. The smoke drove me back even before I penetrated the edge of the active zone.

I returned to the village and went over the holos. There is no mistake. The miracle is real.

1530 hours—

The Three Score and Ten will return any moment. What if they know . . . what if they can tell by looking at me that I have been *there*?

I could hide.

No, there is no need to hide. God did not bring me this far and let me see what I have seen only to let me die at the hands of these poor children.

1615 hours—

The Three Score and Ten returned and went to their huts without giving me a glance.

I sit here in the doorway of my own hut and cannot keep from smiling, from laughing, and from praying. Earlier I walked to the edge of the Cleft, said Mass, and took Communion. The villagers did not bother to watch.

How soon can I leave? Supervisor Orlandi and Tuk had said that the flame forest was fully active for three local months – a hundred and twenty days – then relatively quiet for two. Tuk and I arrived here on Day 87 . . .

I cannot wait another hundred days to bring the news to the world . . . to all of the worlds.

If only a skimmer would brave the weather and flame forests and pluck me out of here. If only I could access one of the datafix sats that serve the plantations.

Anything is possible. More miracles will occur.

2350 hours—

The Three Score and Ten have gone down into the Cleft. The voices of the evening wind choir are rising all around.

How I wish I could be with them now! There, below.

I will do the next best thing. I will drop to my knees here near the cliff edge and pray while the organ notes of the planet and sky sing what I now know is a hymn to a real and present God.

Day 106:

I awoke today to a perfect morning. The sky was a deep turquoise; the sun was a sharp, blood-red stone set within. I stood outside my hut as the mists cleared, the arboreals ended their morning screech concert, and the air began to warm. Then I went in and viewed my tapes and disks.

I realize that in yesterday's excited scribblings I mentioned nothing of what I found down the cliff. I will do so now. I have the disks, filmtapes, and comlog notes, but there is always the chance that only these personal journals will be found.

I lowered myself over the cliff edge at approximately 0730 hours yesterday morning. The Bikura were all foraging in the forest. The descent on vines had looked simple enough – they were bound around one another sufficiently to create a sort of ladder in most places – but as I swung out and began to let myself down, I could feel my heart pounding hard enough to be painful. There was a sheer three-thousand-meter drop to the rocks and river below. I kept a tight grip on at least two vines at all times and centimetered my way down, trying not to look at the abyss beneath my feet.

It took me the better part of an hour to descend the hundred and fifty meters that I am sure the Bikura can cover in ten minutes. Eventually I reached the curve of an overhang. Some vines trailed away into space but most of them curled under the sheer slab of rock toward the cliff wall thirty meters in. Here and there the vines appeared to have been braided to form crude bridges upon which the Bikura probably walked with little or no help from their hands. I crawled along these braided strands, clutching other vines for support and uttering prayers I had not said since my boyhood. I stared straight ahead as if I could forget that there was only a seemingly infinite expanse of air under those swaying, creaking strands of vegetable matter.

There was a broad ledge along the cliff wall. I allowed three meters of it to separate me from the gulf before I squeezed through the vines and dropped two and a half meters to the stone.

The ledge was about five meters wide and it terminated a short distance to the northeast where the great mass of the overhang began. I followed a path along the ledge to the southwest and had gone twenty or thirty paces before I stopped in shock. It was a *path*. A path worn out of solid stone. Its shiny surface had been pushed centimeters below the level of the surrounding rock. Farther on, where the path descended a curving lip of ledge to a lower, wider level, steps had been cut into the stone but even these had been worn to the point that they seemed to sag in the middle.

I sat down for a second as the impact of this simple fact struck me. Even four centuries of daily travel by the Three Score and Ten could not account for such erosion of solid rock. Someone or something had used this path long before the Bikura colonists crashed here. *Someone or something had used this path for millennia.*

I stood and walked on. There was little noise except for the wind blowing gently along the half-kilometer-wide Cleft. I realized that I could hear the soft sound of the river far below.

The path curved left around a section of cliff and ended. I stepped out onto a broad apron of gently descending stone and stared. I believe I made the sign of the cross without thinking.

Because this ledge ran due north and south for a hundred-meter cut of cliff, I could look due west along a thirty-kilometer slash of Cleft to open sky where the plateau ended. I realized at once that the setting sun would illuminate this slab of cliff wall under the overhang each evening. It would not have surprised me if – on the spring or autumn solstice – Hyperion's sun would, from this vantage point, appear to set directly into the Cleft, its red sides just touching the pink-toned rock walls.

I turned left and stared at the cliff face. The worn path led across the wide ledge to doors carved into the vertical slab of stone. No, these were not merely doors, they were portals, intricately carved portals with elaborate stone casements and lintels. To either side of these twin doors spread broad windows of stained glass, rising at least twenty meters toward the overhang. I went closer and inspected the facade. Whoever had built this had done so by widening the area under the overhang, slicing a sheer, smooth wall into the granite of the plateau, and then tunneling directly into the cliff face. I ran my hand over the deeply cut folds of ornamental carving around the door. Smooth. Everything had been smoothed and worn and softened by time, even here, hidden away from most of the elements by the protective lip of overhang. How many thousands of years had this . . . temple . . . been carved into the south wall of the Cleft?

The stained glass was neither glass nor plastic but some thick, translucent substance that seemed as hard as the surrounding stone to the touch. Nor was the window a composite of panels; the colors swirled, shaded, melded, and blended into one another like oil on water.

I removed my flashlight from the pack, touched one of the doors, and hesitated as the tall portal swung inward with frictionless ease.

I entered the vestibule – there is no other word for it – crossed the silent ten-meter space, and paused in front of another wall made from the same stained-glass material that even now glowed behind me, filling the vestibule with thick light of a hundred subtle hues. I realized instantly that at the sunset hour the direct rays of the sun would fill this room with incredibly deep shafts of color, would strike the stained-glass wall in front of me, and would illuminate whatever lay beyond.

I found the single door, outlined by thin, dark metal set into the stained-glass stone, and I passed through it.

On Pacem we have – as best we could from ancient photos and holos – rebuilt the basilica of St Peter's exactly as it stood in the ancient Vatican. Almost seven hundred feet long and four hundred and fifty feet wide, the church can hold fifty thousand worshipers when His Holiness says Mass. We have never had more than five thousand faithful there even when the Council of Bishops of All the Worlds is in assembly every forty-three years. In the central apse near our copy of Bernini's Throne of St Peter, the great dome rises more than a hundred and thirty meters above the floor of the altar. It is an impressive space.

This space was larger.

In the dim light I used the beam of my flashlight to ascertain that I was in a single great room – a giant hall hollowed out of solid stone. I estimated that the smooth walls rose to a ceiling that must be only a few meters beneath the surface of the crag where the Bikura had set their huts. There was no ornamentation here, no furniture, no sign of any concession to form or function except for the object that sat squarely in the center of this huge, echoing cave of a room.

Centered in the great hall was an altar – a five-meter-square slab of stone left when the rest was hollowed out – and from this altar rose a cross.

Four meters high, three meters wide, carved in the old style of the elaborate crucifixes of Old Earth, the cross faced the stained-glass wall as if awaiting the sun and the explosion of light that would ignite the inlaid diamonds, sapphires, blood crystals, lapis beads, queen's tears, onyxes, and other precious stones that I could make out in the light of the flashlight as I approached.

I knelt and prayed. Shutting off the flashlight, I waited several minutes before my eyes could discern the cross in the dim, smoky light. This was, without a doubt, the cruciform of which the Bikura spoke. And it had been set here a minimum of many thousands of years ago – perhaps tens of thousands – long before mankind first left Old Earth. Almost certainly before Christ taught in Galilee.

I prayed.

Today I sit out in the sunlight after reviewing the holodisks. I have confirmed what I barely noticed during my return up the cliff after discovering what I now think of as 'the basilica'. On the ledge outside the basilica there are steps descending farther into the Cleft. Although not as worn as the path leading to the basilica, they are equally intriguing. God alone knows what other wonders wait below.

I *must* let the worlds know of this find!

The irony of my being the one to discover this is not lost on me. If it had not been for Armaghast and my exile, this discovery might have waited more centuries. The Church might have died before this revelation could have brought new life to it.

But I *have* found it.

One way or the other, I will leave or get my message out.

Day 107:

I am a prisoner.

This morning I was bathing in my usual place near where the stream drops over the cliff edge when I heard a sound and looked up to see the Bikura I call Del staring at me with wide eyes. I called a greeting but the little Bikura turned and ran. It was perplexing. They rarely hurry. Then I realized that even though I had been wearing trousers at the time, I had undoubtedly violated their nudity taboo by allowing Del to see me naked from the waist up.

I smiled, shook my head, finished dressing, and returned to the village. If I had known what awaited me there, I would not have been amused.

The entire Three Score and Ten stood watching as I approached. I stopped a dozen paces from Al. 'Good morning,' I said.

Alpha pointed and half a dozen of the Bikura lunged toward me, seized my arms and legs, and pinned me to the ground. Beta stepped forward and removed a sharp-edged stone from his or her robes. As I struggled in vain to pull free, Beta cut my clothes down the front and pulled apart the shreds until I was all but naked.

I ceased struggling as the mob pressed forward. They stared at my pale, white body and murmured to themselves. I could feel my heart pounding. 'I am sorry if I have offended your laws,' I began, 'but there is no reason . . .'

'Silence,' said Alpha and spoke to the tall Bikura with the scar on his palm – the one I call Zed. 'He is not of the cruciform.'

Zed nodded.

'Let me explain,' I began again, but Alpha silenced me with a back-handed slap that left my lip bleeding and my ears ringing. There had been no more sense of hostility in his action than I would have shown in silencing a comlog by throwing a switch.

'What are we to do with him?' asked Alpha.

'Those who do not follow the cross must die the true death,' said Beta and the crowd shifted forward. Many had sharpened stones in their hands. 'Those not of the cruciform must die the true death,' said Beta and her voice held the tone of complacent finality common to oft-repeated formulae and religious litanies.

'*I follow* the cross!' I cried out as the crowd tugged me to my feet. I grabbed at the crucifix that hung around my neck and struggled against the pressure of many arms. Finally I managed to lift the little cross over my head.

Alpha held up his hand and the crowd paused. In the sudden silence I could hear the river three kilometers below in the Cleft. 'He does carry a cross,' said Alpha.

Del pressed forward. 'But he is not of the cruciform! I saw. It was not as we thought. He is not of the cruciform!' There was murder in his voice.

I cursed myself for being careless and stupid. The future of the Church depended upon my survival and I had thrown both away by beguiling myself into believing that the Bikura were dull, harmless children.

'Those who do not follow the cross must die the true death,' repeated Beta. It was a final sentencing.

Stones were being raised by seventy hands when I shouted, knowing that it was either my last chance or my final condemnation. 'I have been down the cliff and worshiped at your altar! I follow the cross!'

Alpha and the mob hesitated. I could see that they were wrestling with this new thought. It was not easy for them.

'I follow the cross and wish to be of the cruciform,' I said as calmly as I could. 'I have been to your altar.'

'Those who do not follow the cross must die the true death,' called Gamma.

'But he follows the cross,' said Alpha. 'He has prayed in the room.'

'This cannot be,' said Zed. 'The Three Score and Ten pray there and he is not of the Three Score and Ten.'

'We knew before this that he is not of the Three Score and Ten,' said Alpha, frowning slightly as he dealt with the concept of past tense.

'He is not of the cruciform,' said Delta-two.

'Those who are not of the cruciform must die the true death,' said Beta.

'He follows the cross,' said Alpha. 'Can he not then become of the cruciform?'

An outcry arose. In the general babble and shuffle of forms I pulled against restraining hands but their grips remained firm.

'He is not of the Three Score and Ten and is not of the cruciform,' said Beta, sounding more puzzled than hostile now. 'How is it that he should not die the true death? We must take the stones and open his throat so that the blood flows until his heart stops. He is not of the cruciform.'

'He follows the cross,' said Alpha. 'Can he not become of the cruciform?'

This time silence followed the question.

'He follows the cross and has prayed at the room of the cruciform,' said Alpha. 'He must not die the true death.'

'All die the true death,' said a Bikura whom I did not recognize. My arms were aching from the strain of holding the crucifix above my head. 'Except the Three Score and Ten,' finished the anonymous Bikura.

'Because they followed the cross, prayed at the room, and became of the cruciform,' said Alpha. 'Must he not then become of the cruciform?'

I stood there gripping the cold metal of the small cross and awaited their verdict. I was afraid to die – I *felt* afraid – but the larger part of my mind seemed almost detached. My greatest regret was that I would not be able to send out the news of the basilica to an unbelieving universe.

'Come, we will talk of this,' Beta said to the group and they pulled me with them as they trod silently back to the village.

They have imprisoned me here in my hut. There was no chance to try for the hunting maser; several of them held me down while they emptied the hut of most of my possessions. They took my clothing, leaving me only one of their rough-woven robes to cover myself with.

The longer I sit here the more angry and anxious I become. They have taken my comlog, imager, disks, chips . . . everything. I have a single, unopened crate of medical diagnostic equipment left up at the old site, but that cannot help me document the miracle in the Cleft. If they destroy the things they have taken – and then destroy me – there will be no record of the basilica.

If I had a weapon I could kill the guards and

Oh dear God what am I thinking? Edouard, what am I to do?

And even if I survive this – make my way back to Keats – arrange travel back to the Web – who would believe me? – after nine years' absence from Pacem because of the quantum-leap time-debt – just an old man returning with the same lies he was exiled for—

Oh, dear God, if they destroy the data let them destroy me as well.

Day 110:
After three days they have decided my fate.

Zed and the one I think of as Theta-Prime came to get me shortly after midday. I blinked as they led me out into the light. The Three Score and Ten stood in a wide semicircle near the cliff edge. I fully expected to be thrown over that edge. Then I noticed the bonfire.

I had assumed that the Bikura were so primitive that they had lost the art of making and using fire. They did not warm themselves with fire and their huts were always dark. I had never seen them cook a meal, not even the rare corpse of an arboreal they devoured. But now the fire was burning strongly and they were the only ones who could have started it. I looked to see what fueled the flames.

They were burning my clothes, my comlog, my field notes, the tape cassettes, video chips, data disks, the imager . . . everything that had held information. I screamed at them, tried to throw myself at the fire, and called them names I had not used since the street days of my childhood. They ignored me.

Finally Alpha came close. 'You will become of the cruciform,' he said softly.

I did not care. They led me back to my hut where I wept for an hour. There is no guard at the door. A minute ago I stood at the doorway and considered running for the flame forests. Then I thought of a much shorter but no less fatal run to the Cleft.

I did nothing.

The sun will be setting in a short time. Already the winds are rising. Soon. Soon.

Day 112:

Has it been only two days? It has been forever.

It did not come off this morning. It *did not come off.*

The medscanner's image wafer is right here in front of me but I still cannot believe it. And yet I do. I am of the cruciform now.

They came for me just before sunset. All of them. I did not struggle as they led me to the edge of the Cleft. They were more agile on the vines than I could have imagined. I slowed them down but they were patient, showing me the easiest footholds, the fastest route.

Hyperion's sun had dropped below low clouds and was visible above the rim wall to the west as we walked the final few meters to the basilica. The evening windsong was louder than I had anticipated; it was as if we were caught amid the pipes of a gigantic church organ. The notes rose from bass growls so deep that my bones and teeth resonated in sympathy to high, piercing screams that slid easily into the ultrasonic.

Alpha opened the outer doors and we passed through the antechamber into the central basilica. The Three Score and Ten made a wide circle around the altar and its tall cross. There was no litany. There was no singing. There was no ceremony. We simply stood there in silence as the wind roared through the fluted columns outside and echoed in the great empty room carved into the stone – echoed and resonated and grew in volume until I clapped my hands over my ears. And all the while the streaming, horizontal rays of sunlight filled the hall with deepening hues of amber, gold, lapis, and then amber again – colors so deep that they made the air thick with light and lay like paint against the skin. I watched as the cross caught this light and held it in each of its thousand precious stones, held it – it seemed – even after the sun had set and the windows had faded to a twilight gray. It was as if the great crucifix had absorbed the light and was radiating it toward us, into us. Then even the cross was dark and the winds died and in the sudden dimness Alpha said softly. 'Bring him along.'

We emerged onto the wide ledge of stone and Beta was there with torches. As Beta passed them out to a selected few, I wondered if the Bikura reserved fire for ritual purposes only. Then Beta was leading the way and we descended the narrow staircase carved into the stone.

At first I crept along, terrified, clutching at the smooth rock and searching for any reassuring projection of root or stone. The drop to our right was so sheer and endless that it bordered on being absurd. Descending the ancient staircase was far worse than clutching at vines on the cliff face above. Here I had to look down each time I placed a foot on the narrow, age-slickened slabs. A slip and fall at first seemed probable, then inevitable.

I had the urge to stop then, to return at least to the safety of the basilica, but most of the Three Score and Ten were behind me on the narrow staircase and there seemed little chance that they would stand aside to let me pass. Besides this, and even greater than my fear, was the nagging curiosity about what was at the bottom of the staircase. I did pause long enough to glance up at the lip of the Cleft three hundred méters above and to see that the clouds were gone, the stars were out, and the nightly ballet of meteor trails was bright against a sable sky. Then I lowered my head, began a whispered recitation of the rosary, and followed the torchlight and the Bikura into the treacherous depths.

I could not believe that the staircase would take us all the way to the bottom of the Cleft, but it did. When, sometime after midnight, I realized that we would be descending all the way down to the level of the river, I estimated that it would take us until noon of the next day, but it did not.

We reached the base of the Cleft shortly before sunrise. The stars still shone in the aperture of sky between cliff walls that rose an impossible distance on either side. Exhausted, staggering downward step by step, recognizing slowly that there were no more steps, I stared upward and wondered stupidly if the stars remained visible there in the daylight as they did in a well I had lowered myself into once as a child in Villefranche-sur-Saône.

'Here,' said Beta. It was the first word uttered in many hours and was barely audible over the roar of the river. The Three Score and Ten stopped where they were and stood motionless. I collapsed to my knees and fell on my side. There was no possibility that I could climb that stairway we had just descended. Not in a day. Not in a week. Perhaps never. I closed my eyes to sleep but the dull fuel of nervous tension continued to burn inside me. I looked out across the floor of the ravine. The river here was wider than I had anticipated, at least seventy meters across, and the noise of it was beyond mere noise; I felt that I was being consumed by a great beast's roar.

I sat up and stared at a patch of darkness in the opposing cliff wall. It was a shadow darker than the shadows, more regular than the serrated patchwork of buttresses and crevices and columns that mottled the face of the cliff. It was a perfect square of darkness, at least thirty meters to a side. A door or hole in the cliff wall. I struggled to my feet and looked downriver along the wall we had just descended; yes, it was there. The other entrance, the one toward which Beta and the others even now were walking, was faintly visible in the starlight.

I had found an entrance to Hyperion's labyrinth.

'Did you know that Hyperion was one of the nine labyrinthine worlds?' someone had asked me on the dropship. Yes, it was the young priest named Hoyt. I had said yes and dismissed the fact. I was interested in the Bikura – actually more in the self-inflicted pain of my own exile – not the labyrinths or their builders.

Nine worlds have labyrinths. Nine out of a hundred seventy-six Webworlds and another two hundred-some colonial and protectorate planets. Nine worlds out of eight thousand or more worlds explored – however cursorily – since the Hegira.

There are planetary archaeohistorians who devote their lives to the study of the labyrinths. Not I. I had always found them a sterile topic, vaguely unreal. Now I walked toward one with the Three Score and Ten as the Kans River roared and vibrated and threatened to douse our torches with its spray.

The labyrinths were dug . . . tunneled . . . *created* more than three quarters of a million standard years ago. The details were inevitably the same, their origins inevitably unsolved.

Labyrinthine worlds are always Earthlike, at least to 7.9 on the Solmev Scale, always circling a G-type star, and yet always restricted to worlds that are tectonically dead, more like Mars than Old Earth. The tunnels themselves are set deep – usually a minimum of ten kilometers but often as deep as thirty – and they catacomb the crust of the planet. On Svoboda, not far from Pacem's system, over eight hundred thousand kilometers of labyrinth have been explored by remotes. The tunnels on each world are thirty meters square and carved by some technology still not available to the Hegemony. I read once in an archaeological journal that Kemp-Höltzer and Weinstein had postulated a 'fusion tunneler' that would explain the perfectly smooth walls and lack of tailings, but their theory did not explain where the Builders or their machines had come from or why they had devoted centuries to such an apparently aimless engineering task. Each of the labyrinthine worlds – including Hyperion – has been probed and researched. Nothing has ever been found. No signs of excavation machinery, no rusting miners' helmets, not a single piece of shattered plastic or decomposing stimstick wrapper. Researchers have not even identified entrance and exit shafts. No suggestion of heavy metals or precious ores has been sufficient to explain such a monumental effort. No legend or artifact of the Labyrinth Builders has survived. The mystery had mildly intrigued me over the years but never concerned me. Until now.

We entered the tunnel mouth. It was not a perfect square. Erosion and gravity had turned the perfect tunnel into a rough cave for a hundred meters into the cliff wall. Beta stopped just where the tunnel floor grew smooth and extinguished his torch. The other Bikura did likewise.

It was very dark. The tunnel had turned enough to block out any starlight that might have entered. I had been in caves before. With the torches extinguished, I did not expect my eyes to adapt to the near-total darkness. But they did.

Within thirty seconds I began to sense a roseate glow, dim at first, then ever richer until the cave was brighter than the canyon had been, brighter than Pacem under the glow of its triune moons. The light came from a hundred sources – a thousand sources. I was able to make out the nature of these sources just as the Bikura dropped reverently to their knees.

The cave walls and ceiling were encrusted with crosses ranging in size from a few millimeters to almost a meter long. Each glowed with a deep, pink light of its own. Invisible in the torchlight, these glowing crosses now suffused the tunnel with light. I approached one embedded in the wall nearest me. Thirty or so centimeters across, it pulsed with a soft, organic flow. This was not something that had been carved out of stone or attached to the wall; it was definitely organic, definitely alive, resembling soft coral. It was slightly warm to the touch.

There came the slightest whisper of sound – no, not sound, a disturbance in the cool air, perhaps – and I turned in time to see something enter the chamber.

The Bikura were still kneeling, their heads down, eyes lowered. I remained standing. My gaze never left the thing which moved among the kneeling Bikura.

It was vaguely man-shaped but in no way human. It stood at least three meters tall. Even when it was at rest, the silvered surface of the thing seemed to shift and flow like mercury suspended in midair. The reddish glow from the crosses set into the tunnel walls reflected from sharp surfaces and glinted on the curved metal blades protruding from the thing's forehead, four wrists, oddly jointed elbows, knees, armored back, and thorax. It flowed between the kneeling Bikura, and when it extended four long arms, hands extended but fingers clicking into place like chrome scalpels, I was absurdly reminded of His Holiness on Pacem offering a benediction to the faithful.

I had no doubt that I was looking at the legendary Shrike.

At that moment I must have moved or made a sound, for large red eyes turned my way and I found myself hypnotized by the dance of light within the multifaceted prisms there: not merely reflected light but a fierce, blood-bright glow which seemed to burn within the creature's barbed skull and pulse in the terrible gems set where God meant eyes to be.

Then it moved . . . or, rather, it did not move but ceased being *there* and was *here*, leaning less than a meter from me, its oddly jointed arms encircling me in a fence of body-blades and liquid silver steel. Panting hard but unable to take a breath, I saw my own reflection, face white and distorted, dancing across the surface of the thing's metallic shell and burning eyes.

I confess that I felt something closer to exaltation than fear. Something *inexplicable* was happening. Forged in Jesuit logic and tempered in the cold bath of science, I nevertheless understood at that second the ancient obsession of the God-fearing for another kind of fear: the thrill of exorcism, the mindless whirl of Dervish possession, the puppet-dance ritual of Tarot, and the almost erotic surrender of seance, speaking in tongues, and Zen Gnostic trance. I realized at that instant just how surely the affirmation of demons or the summoning of Satan somehow can affirm the reality of their mystic antithesis – the God of Abraham.

Thinking none of this but feeling all of it, I awaited the embrace of the Shrike with the imperceptible tremble of a virgin bride.

It disappeared.

There was no thunderclap, no sudden smell of brimstone, not even a scientifically sound inrush of air. One second the thing was there, surrounding me with its beautiful certainty of sharp-edged death, and the next instant it was gone.

Numbed, I stood there and blinked as Alpha rose and approached me in the Bosch-tinted gloom. He stood where the Shrike had stood, his own arms extended in a pathetic imitation of the deadly perfection I had just witnessed, but there was no sign on Alpha's bland, Bikura face that he had seen the creature. He made an awkward, open-handed gesture which seemed to include the labyrinth, cave wall, and scores of glowing crosses embedded there.

'Cruciform,' said Alpha. The Three Score and Ten rose, came closer, and knelt again. I looked at their placid faces in the soft light and I also knelt.

'You will follow the cross all of your days,' said Alpha, and his voice carried the cadence of litany. The rest of the Bikura repeated the statement in a tone just short of a chant.

'You will be of the cruciform all of your days,' said Alpha, and as the others repeated this he reached out and pulled a small cruciform away from the cave wall. It was not more than a dozen centimeters long and it came away from the wall with the faintest of snaps. Its glow faded even as I watched. Alpha removed a small thong from his robe, tied it around small knobs at the top of the cruciform, and held the cross above my head. 'You will be of the cruciform now and forever,' he said.

'Now and forever,' echoed the Bikura.

'Amen,' I whispered.

Beta signaled that I should open the front of my robe. Alpha lowered the small cross until it hung around my neck. It felt cool against my chest; the back of it was perfectly flat, perfectly smooth.

The Bikura stood and wandered toward the cave entrance, apparently apathetic and indifferent once again. I watched them leave and then I gingerly touched the cross, lifted and inspected it. The cruciform was cool, inert. If it had truly been living a few seconds earlier, it showed no sign of it now. It continued to feel more like coral than crystal or rock; there was no sign of any adhesive material on the smooth back of it. I speculated on photochemical effects that would have created the luminescent quality. I speculated on natural phosphors, bioluminescence, and on the chances that evolution would shape such things. I speculated on what, if anything, their presence here had to do with the labyrinth and on the aeons necessary to raise this plateau so the river and canyon could slice through one of the tunnels. I speculated on the basilica and its makers, on the Bikura, on the Shrike, and on myself. Eventually I ceased speculating and closed my eyes to pray.

When I emerged from the cave, the cruciform cool against my chest under the robe, the Three Score and Ten were obviously ready to begin the three-kilometer climb up the staircase. I looked up to see a pale slash of morning sky between the wails of the Cleft.

'No!' I shouted, my voice almost lost against the roar of the river. 'I need rest. *Rest!*' I sank to my knees on the sand but half a dozen of the Bikura approached, pulled me gently to my feet, and moved me toward the staircase.

I tried, the Lord knows that I tried, but two or three hours into the climb I felt my legs give way and I collapsed, sliding across the rock, unable to stop my six-hundred-meter fall to the rocks and river. I remember grasping at the cruciform under the thick robe and then half a dozen hands stopped my slide, lifted me, carried me. Then I remember no more.

Until this morning. I woke to a sunrise pouring light through the opening of my hut. I wore only the robe and a touch assured me that the cruciform was still hanging from its fibrous thong. As I watched the sun lift over the forest, I realized that I had lost a day, that somehow I had slept through not only my ascent up that endless staircase (how could these little people carry me two and a half vertical kilometers?) but through the next day and night as well.

I looked around my hut. My comlog and other recording devices were gone. Only my medscanner and a few packets of anthropological software made useless by the destruction of my other equipment remained. I shook my head and went up to the stream to wash.

The Bikura appeared to be sleeping. Now that I had participated in their ritual and 'become of the cruciform', they seemed to have lost interest in me. As I stripped to bathe, I decided to take no interest in them. I decided that I would leave as soon as I was strong enough. I would find a way around the flame forests if necessary. I could descend the staircase and follow the Kans if I had to. I knew more than ever that word of these miraculous artifacts had to be brought to the outside world.

I pulled off the heavy robe, stood pale and shivering in the morning light, and went to lift the small cruciform from my chest.

It did not come off.

It lay there as if it were part of my flesh. I pulled, scraped, and tore at the thong until it snapped and fell away. I clawed at the cross-shaped lump on my chest. *It did not come off.* It was as if my flesh had sealed itself around the edges of the cruciform. Except for the scratches from my fingernails, there was no pain or physical sensation in the cruciform or surrounding flesh, only sheer terror in my soul at the thought of this thing attached to me. After the first rush of panic subsided, I sat a minute and then hastily pulled on my robe and ran back to the village.

My knife was gone, my maser, scissors, razor – everything that might have helped me peel back the growth on my chest. My nails left bloody tracks across the red welt and my chest. Then I remembered the medscanner. I passed the transceiver over my chest, read the diskey display, shook my head in disbelief, and then ran an entire body scan. After a while I keyed in a request for hard copies of the scan results and sat motionless for a very long time.

I sit here now holding the image wafers. The cruciform is quite visible on both the sonic and k-cross images . . . as are the internal fibers that spread like thin tentacles, like *roots*, throughout my body.

Excess ganglia radiate from a thick nucleus above my sternum to filaments everywhere – a nightmare of nematodes. As well as I can tell with my simple field scanner, the nematodes terminate in the amygdala and other basal ganglia in each cerebral hemisphere. My temperature, metabolism, and lymphocyte level are normal. There has been no invasion of foreign tissue. According to the scanner, the nematodic filaments are the result of extensive but simple metastasis. According to the scanner, the cruciform itself is composed of familiar tissue . . . *the DNA is mine.*

I am of the cruciform.

Day 116:
Each day I pace the confines of my cage – the flame forests to the south and east, the forested ravines to the northeast, and the Cleft to the north and west. The Three Score and Ten will not let me descend into the Cleft beyond the basilica. The *cruciform* will not let me get more than ten kilometers from the Cleft.

At first I could not believe this. I had resolved to enter the flame forests, trusting to luck and to God's help to see me through. But I had gone no more than two kilometers into the fringes of the forest when pain struck me in the chest and arms and head. I was sure that I was having a massive heart attack. But as soon as I turned back toward the Cleft the symptoms ceased. I experimented for some time and the results were invariably the same. Whenever I ventured deeper into the flame forest, away from the Cleft, the pain would return and increase in severity until I turned back.

I begin to understand other things. Yesterday I happened across the wreckage of the original seedship shuttle as I explored to the north. Only a rusted, vine-enmeshed wreck of metal remains among the rocks at the edge of the flame forest near the ravine. But crouching among the exposed alloy ribs of the ancient craft, I could imagine the rejoicing of the seventy survivors, their short voyage to the Cleft, their eventual discovery of the basilica, and . . . and what? Conjectures beyond that point are useless, but suspicions remain. Tomorrow I will attempt another physical exam of one of the Bikura. Perhaps now that I am 'of the cruciform' they will allow it.

Each day I do a medscan of myself. The nematodes remain – perhaps thicker, perhaps not. I am convinced that they are purely parasitic although my body has shown no signs of this. I peer at my face in the pool near the waterfall and see only the same long, aging countenance that I have learned to dislike in recent years. This morning, while gazing at my image in the water, I opened my mouth wide, half thinking that I would see gray filaments and nematode clusters growing from the roof of my mouth and the back of my throat. There was nothing.

Day 117:
The Bikura are sexless. Not celibate or hermaphroditic or undeveloped – sexless. They are as devoid of external or internal genitalia as a child's flowfoam doll. There is no evidence that the penis or testes or comparable female organs have atrophied or been surgically altered. *There is no sign that they ever existed.* Urine is conducted through a primitive urethra terminating in a small chamber contiguous with the anus – a sort of crude cloaca.

Beta allowed the examination. The medscanner confirmed what my eyes would not believe. Del and Theta also agreed to be scanned. I have absolutely no doubt that the rest of the Three Score and Ten are equally sexless. There is no sign that they have been . . . altered. I would suggest that they had all been *born* that way but from what kind of parents? And how do these sexless lumps of human clay plan to reproduce? It must be tied in with the cruciform in some way.

When I was finished with their medscans I stripped and studied myself. The cruciform rises from my chest like pink scar tissue, but I am still a man.

For how long?

Day 133:

Alpha is dead.

I was with him three mornings ago when he fell. We were about three kilometers east, hunting for chalma tubers in the large boulders near the edge of the Cleft. It had been raining most of the past two days and the rocks were quite slippery. I looked up from my own scrambling just in time to see Alpha lose his footing and go sliding down a broad slab of stone, over the edge. He did not shout. The only sound was the rasp of his robe against the rock, followed several seconds later by the sickening dropped-melon sound of his body striking a ledge eighty meters below.

It took me an hour to find a route down to him. Even before I began the treacherous descent I knew it was too late to help. But it was my duty.

Alpha's body was half wedged between two large rocks. He must have died instantly; his arms and legs were splintered and the right side of his skull had been crushed. Blood and brain tissue clung to the wet rock like the refuse of a sad picnic. I wept as I stood over the little body. I do not know why I wept, but I did. And as I wept I administered Extreme Unction and prayed that God would accept the soul of this poor, sexless little person. Later I wrapped the body in vines, laboriously climbed the eighty meters of cliff, and – pausing frequently to pant with exhaustion – pulled the broken corpse up to me.

There was little interest as I carried the body of Alpha into the Bikura village. Eventually Beta and half a dozen others wandered over to stare down indifferently at the corpse. No one asked me how he had died. After a few minutes the small crowd dispersed.

Later I carried Alpha's body to the promontory where I had buried Tuk so many weeks earlier. I was digging the shallow grave with a flat stone when Gamma appeared. The Bikura's eyes widened and for a brief second I thought I saw emotion cross those bland features.

'What are you doing?' asked Gamma.

'Burying him.' I was too tired to say more. I leaned against a thick chalma root and rested.

'No.' It was a command. 'He is of the cruciform.'

I stared as Gamma turned and walked quickly back to the village. When the Bikura was gone, I pulled off the crude fiber tarp I had draped over the corpse.

Alpha was, without any doubt, truly dead. It no longer mattered to him or the universe whether he was of the cruciform or not. The fall had stripped him of most of his clothes and all of his dignity. The right side of his skull had been cracked and emptied like a breakfast egg. One eye stared sightlessly toward Hyperion's sky through a thickening film while the other looked out lazily from under a drooping lid. His rib cage had been splintered so thoroughly that shards of bone protruded from his flesh. Both arms were broken and his left leg had been twisted almost off. I had used the medscanner to perform a perfunctory autopsy and it had revealed massive internal injuries; even the poor devil's heart had been pulped by the force of the fall.

I reached out and touched the cold flesh. Rigor mortis was setting in. My fingers brushed across the cross-shaped welt on his chest and I quickly pulled my hand away. The cruciform was warm.

'Stand away.'

I looked up to see Beta and the rest of the Bikura standing there. I had no doubt that they would murder me in a second if I did not move away from the corpse. As I did so, an idiotically frightened part of my mind noted that the Three Score and Ten were now the Three Score and Nine. It seemed funny at the time.

The Bikura lifted the body and moved back toward the village. Beta looked at the sky, looked at me, and said:

'It is almost time. You will come.'

We went down into the Cleft. The body was carefully tied into a basket of vines and lowered with us.

The sun was not yet illuminating the interior of the basilica when they set Alpha's corpse on the broad altar and removed his remaining rags.

I do not know what I expected next – some ritual act of cannibalism perhaps. Nothing would have surprised me. Instead, one of the Bikura raised his arms, just as the first shafts of colored light entered the basilica, and intoned, 'You will follow the cross all of your days.'

The Three Score and Nine knelt and repeated the sentence. I remained standing. I did not speak.

'You will be of the cruciform all of your days,' said the little Bikura and the basilica echoed to the chorus of voices repeating the phrase. Light the color and texture of clotting blood threw a huge shadow of the cross on the far wall.

'You will be of the cruciform now and forever and ever,' came the chant as the winds rose outside and the organ pipes of the canyon wailed with the voice of a tortured child.

When the Bikura stopped chanting I did not whisper 'Amen.' I stood there while the others turned and left with the sudden, total indifference of spoiled children who have lost interest in their game.

'There is no reason to stay,' said Beta when the others had gone.

'I want to,' I said, expecting a command to leave. Beta turned without so much as a shrug and left me there. The light dimmed. I went outside to watch the sun set and when I returned it had begun.

Once, years ago in school, I saw a time-lapse holo showing the decomposition of a kangaroo mouse. A week's slow work of nature's recycling had been accelerated to thirty seconds of horror. There was the sudden, almost comic bloating of the little corpse, then the stretching of flesh into lesions, followed by the sudden appearance of maggots in the mouth, eyes, and open sores, and finally the sudden and incredible corkscrew cleaning of meat from the bones – there is no other phrase that fits the image – as the pack of maggots spiraled right to left, head to tail, in a time-lapsed helix of carrion consumption that left behind nothing but bones and gristle and hide.

Now it was a man's body I watched.

I stopped and stared, the last of the light fading quickly. There was no sound in the echoing silence of the basilica except for the pounding of my pulse in my own ears. I stared as Alpha's corpse first twitched and then visibly vibrated, almost levitating off the altar in the spastic violence of sudden decomposition. For a few seconds the cruciform seemed to increase in size and deepen in color, glowing as red as raw meat, and I imagined then that I caught a glimpse of the network of filaments and nematodes holding the disintegrating body together like metal fibers in a sculptor's melting model. *The flesh flowed.*

I stayed in the basilica that night. The area around the altar remained lit by the glow of the cruciform on Alpha's chest. When the corpse moved the light would cast strange shadows on the walls.

I did not leave the basilica until Alpha left on the third day, but most of the visible changes had taken place by the end of that first night. The body of the Bikura I had named Alpha was broken down and rebuilt as I watched. The corpse that was left was not quite Alpha and not quite *not* Alpha, but it was intact. The face was a flowfoam doll's face, smooth and unlined, features stamped in a slight smile. At sunrise of the third day, I saw the corpse's chest begin to rise and fall and I heard the first intake of breath – a rasp like water being poured into a leather pouch. Shortly before noon I left the basilica to climb the vines.

I followed Alpha.

He has not spoken, will not reply. His eyes have a fixed, unfocused look and occasionally he pauses as if he hears distant voices calling.

No one paid attention to us when we returned to the village. Alpha went to a hut and sits there now. I sit in mine. A minute ago I opened my robe and ran my fingers across the welt of the cruciform. It lies benignly under the flesh of my chest. Waiting.

Day 140:

I am recovering from my wounds and the loss of blood. It cannot be cut out with a sharpened stone.

It does not like pain. I lost consciousness long before the pain or loss of blood demanded it. Each time I awoke and resumed cutting, I would be made to pass out. It does not like pain.

Day 158:

Alpha speaks some now. He seems duller, slower, and only vaguely aware of me (or anyone else) but he eats and moves. He appears to recognize me to some extent. The medscanner shows the heart and internal organs of a young man – perhaps of a boy of sixteen.

I must wait about another Hyperion month and ten days – about fifty days in all – until the flame forests become quiet enough for me to try to walk out, pain or no pain. We will see who can stand the most pain.

Day 173:

Another death.

The one called Will – the one with the broken finger – had been missing for a week. Yesterday the Bikura went several kilometers northeast as if following a beacon, and found the remains near the great ravine.

Evidently a branch had snapped while he was climbing to grasp some chalma fronds. Death must have been instantaneous when he broke his neck, but it is where he fell that is important. The body – if one could call it that – was lying between two great mud cones marking the burrows of the large red insects that Tuk called fire mantises. Carpet beetles might have been a more apt phrase. In the past few days the insects had stripped the corpse clean to the bone. Little was left to be found except the skeleton, some random shreds of tissue and tendon, and the cruciform – still attached to the rib cage like some splendid cross packed in the sarcophagus of a long-dead pope.

It is terrible, but I cannot help but feel some small sense of triumph beneath the sadness. There is no way that the cruciform can regenerate something out of these bare bones; even the terrible illogic of this accursed parasite must respect the imperative of the law of conservation of mass. The Bikura I called Will has died the true death. The Three Score and Ten truly are the Three Score and Nine from this time on.

Day 174:

I am a fool.

Today I inquired about Will, about his dying the true death. I was curious at the lack of reaction from the Bikura. They had retrieved the cruciform but left the skeleton lying where they had found it: there was no attempt to carry the remains to the basilica. During the night I had become concerned that I would be made to fill the role of the missing member of the Three Score and Ten. 'It is very sad,' I said, 'that one of you has died the true death. What is to become to the Three Score and Ten?'

Beta stared at me. 'He cannot die the true death,' said the bald little androgyny. 'He is of the cruciform.'

Somewhat later, while continuing my medscans of the tribe, I discovered the truth. The one I have tagged as Theta looks the same and acts the same, but now carries two cruciforms embedded in his flesh. I have no doubt that this is one Bikura who will tend toward corpulence in coming years, swelling and ripening like some obscene *E coli* cell in a petri dish. When he/she/ it dies, two will leave the tomb and the Three Score and Ten will be complete once more.

I believe I am going mad.

Day 195:

Weeks of studying the damn parasite and still no clue as to how it functions. Worse, I no longer care. What I care about now is more important.

Why has God allowed this obscenity?

Why have the Bikura been punished this way?

Why was I chosen to suffer their fate?

I ask these questions in nightly prayers but I hear no answers, only the blood song of the wind from the Cleft.

Day 214:

The last ten pages should have covered all of my field notes and technical conjectures. This will be my last entry before attempting the quiescent flame forest in the morning.

There is no doubt that I have discovered the ultimate in stagnant human societies. The Bikura have realized the human dream of immortality and have paid for it with their humanity and their immortal souls.

Edouard, I have spent so many hours wrestling with my faith – my lack of faith – but now, in this fearful corner of an all but forgotten world, riddled as I am with this loathsome parasite, I have somehow rediscovered a strength of belief the likes of which I have not known since you and I were boys. I now understand the *need* for faith – pure, blind, fly-in-the-face-of-reason faith – as a small life preserver in the wild and endless sea of a universe ruled by unfeeling laws and totally indifferent to the small, reasoning beings that inhabit it.

Day after day I have tried to leave the Cleft area and day after day I have suffered pain so terrible that it has become a tangible part of my world, like the too small sun or the green and lapis sky. Pain has become my ally, my guardian angel, my remaining link with humanity. The cruciform does not like pain. Nor do I but, like the cruciform, I am willing to use it to serve my purposes. And I will do so consciously, not instinctively like the mindless mass of alien tissue embedded in me. This thing only seeks a mindless avoidance of death by any means. I do not wish to die, but I welcome pain and death rather than an eternity of mindless life. Life is sacred – I still hold to that as a core element of the Church's thought and teachings these past twenty-eight hundred years when life has been so cheap – but even more sacred is the soul.

I realize now that what I was trying to do with the Armaghast data was offer the Church not a rebirth but only a transition to a false life such as these poor walking corpses inhabit. If the Church is meant to die, it must do so – but do so gloriously, in the full knowledge of its rebirth in Christ. It must go into the darkness not willingly but well – bravely and firm of faith – like the millions who have gone before us, keeping faith with all those generations facing death in the isolated silence of death camps and nuclear fireballs and cancer wards and pogroms, going into the darkness, if not hopefully, then prayerfully that there is some reason for it all, something worth the price of all that pain, all those sacrifices. All those before us have gone into the darkness without assurance of logic or fact or persuasive theory, with only a slender thread of hope or the all too shakable conviction of faith. And if they have been able to sustain that slim hope in the face of darkness, then so must I . . . and so must the Church.

I no longer believe that any surgery or treatment can cure me of this thing that infests me, but if someone can separate it and study it and destroy it, even at the cost of my death, I will be well satisfied.

The flame forests are as quiet as they will ever be. To bed now. I leave before dawn.

Day 215:
There is no way out.

Fourteen kilometers into the forest. Stray fires and bursts of current, but penetrable. Three weeks of walking would have got me through.

The cruciform will not let me go.

The pain was like a heart attack that would not stop. Still I staggered forward, stumbling and crawling through the ash. Eventually I lost consciousness. When I came to I was crawling *toward* the Cleft. I would turn away, walk a kilometer, crawl fifty meters, then lose consciousness again and awake back where I had started. All day this insane battle for my body went on.

Before sunset the Bikura entered the forest, found me five kilometers from the Cleft, and carried me back.

Dear Jesus, why have you let this be?

There is no hope now unless someone comes looking for me.

Day 223:
Again the attempt. Again the pain. Again the failure.

Day 257:
I am sixty-eight standard years old today. Work goes on with the chapel I am building near the Cleft. Attempted to descend to the river yesterday but was turned back by Beta and four others.

Day 280:
One local year on Hyperion. One year in purgatory. Or is it hell?

Day 311:
Working on quarrying stones on the ledges below the shelf where the chapel is going up and I made the discovery today: the arrestor rods. The

Bikura must have thrown them over the edge when they murdered Tuk that night two hundred and twenty-three days ago.

These rods would allow me to penetrate the flame forest at any time if the cruciform would allow it. But it will not. If only they had not destroyed my medkits with the painkillers! But still, sitting here holding the rods today, I have an idea.

My crude experiments with the medscanner have continued. Two weeks ago when Theta broke his leg in three places, I observed the reaction of the cruciform. The parasite did its best to block the pain; Theta was unconscious much of the time and his body was producing incredible quantities of endorphins. But the break was a very painful one and after four days the Bikura slashed Theta's throat and took his body to the basilica. It was easier for the cruciform to resurrect his corpse than to tolerate such pain over a long period. But before his murder my scanner showed an appreciable retreat of the cruciform nematodes from some parts of the central nervous system.

I do not know if it would be possible to inflict on oneself – or to tolerate – levels of nonlethal pain sufficient to drive the cruciform out completely, but I am sure of one thing: the Bikura would not allow it.

Today I sit on the ledge below the half-finished chapel and I consider possibilities.

Day 438:
The chapel is finished. It is my life's work.

Tonight, when the Bikura went down into the Cleft for their daily parody of worship, I said Mass at the altar of the newly erected chapel. I had baked the bread from chalma flour and I am sure that it must have tasted of that bland, yellow leaf, but to me the taste was exactly like that of the first Host I had partaken of during my first Holy Communion in Villefranche-sur-Saône some sixty standard years earlier.

In the morning I will do what I have planned. Everything is in readiness: my journals and the medscan wafers will be in the pouch of woven bestos fibers. That is the best I can do.

The consecrated wine was only water, but in the dim light of sunset it looked blood red and tasted of communion wine.

The trick will be to penetrate deep enough into the flame forest. I will have to trust that there is enough incipient activity in and from the tesla trees even during the quiet periods.

Goodbye, Edouard. I doubt if you are still alive, and should you be, I see no way that we could be reunited, separated as we are not only by years of distance but by a much wider gulf in the form of a cross. My hope of seeing you again shall not be placed on this life but on the one to come. Strange to hear me speak like this again, is it not? I must tell you, Edouard, that after all these decades of uncertainty, and with great fear of what lies ahead, my heart and soul are nonetheless at peace.

Oh, my God,
I am heartily sorry for having offended Thee,
And I detest all my sins,
Because of the loss of heaven
And the pains of hell,
But most of all because I have offended Thee,
My God,
Who art all good
And deserving of all my love.
I firmly resolve with the help of Thy grace to confess my sins, to do penance,
And to amend my life,
Amen.

2400 hours:
The sunset comes through the open chapel window and bathes the altar, the crudely carved chalice, and me in light. The wind from the Cleft rises in the last such chorus that – with luck and God's mercy – I will ever hear.

'That is the final entry,' said Lenar Hoyt.

When the priest quit reading, the six pilgrims at the table raised their faces toward him as if they were awakening from a common dream. The Consul glanced upward and saw that Hyperion was much closer now, filling a third of the sky, banishing the stars with its cold radiance.

'I arrived some ten weeks after I had last seen Father Duré,' continued Father Hoyt. His voice was a hoarse rasp. 'More than eight years had passed on Hyperion . . . seven years since the last entry in Father Duré's journal.' The priest was visibly in pain now, his face paled to a sick luminescence and filmed with perspiration.

'Within a month I found my way to Perecebo Plantation upriver from Port Romance,' he continued, forcing some strength into his voice. 'My assumption was that the fiberplastic growers might tell me the truth even if they would have nothing to do with the consulate or Home Rule Authorities. I was right. The administrator at Perecebo, a man named Orlandi, remembered Father Duré, as did Orlandi's new wife, the woman named Semfa whom Father Duré mentioned in his journals. The plantation manager had tried to mount several rescue operations onto the Plateau, but an unprecedented series of active seasons in the flame forests had made them abandon their attempts. After several years they had given up hope that Duré or their man Tuk could still be alive.

'Nonetheless, Orlandi recruited two expert bush pilots to fly a rescue expedition up the Cleft in two plantation skimmers. We stayed in the Cleft itself for as long as we could, trusting to terrain-avoidance instruments and luck to get us to Bikura country. Even with bypassing most of the flame forest that way, we lost one of the skimmers and four people to tesla activity.'

Father Hoyt paused and swayed slightly. Gripping the edge of the table to

68

steady himself, he cleared his throat and said, 'There's little else to tell. We located the Bikura village. There were seventy of them, each as stupid and uncommunicative as Duré's notes had suggested. I managed to ascertain from them that Father Duré had died while trying to penetrate the flame forest. The bestos pouch had survived and in it we found his journals and medical data.' Hoyt looked at the others a second and then glanced down. 'We persuaded them to show us where Father Duré had died,' he said. 'They . . . ah . . . they had not buried him. His remains were badly burned and decomposed but complete enough to show us that the intensity of the tesla charges had destroyed the . . . the cruciform . . . as well as his body.

'Father Duré had died the true death. We returned the remains to the Perecebo Plantation where he was buried following a full funeral Mass.' Hoyt took a deep breath. 'Over my strong objections, M. Orlandi destroyed the Bikura village and a section of the Cleft wall with shaped nuclear charges he had brought from the plantation. I do not believe that any of the Bikura could have survived. As far as we could tell, the entrance to the labyrinth and the so-called basilica also must have been destroyed in the landslide.

'I had sustained several injuries during the expedition and thus had to remain at the plantation for several months before returning to the northern continent and booking passage to Pacem. No one knows of these journals or their contents except M. Orlandi, Monsignor Edouard, and whichever of his superiors Monsignor Edouard chose to tell. As far as I know, the Church has issued no declaration relating to the journals of Father Paul Duré.'

Father Hoyt had been standing and now he sat. Sweat dripped from his chin and his face was blue-white in the reflected light of Hyperion.

'Is that . . . all?' asked Martin Silenus.

'Yes,' managed Father Hoyt.

'Gentlemen and lady,' said Het Masteen, 'it is late. I suggest that you gather your luggage and rendezvous at our friend the Consul's ship on sphere eleven in thirty minutes or sooner. I will be using one of the tree's dropships to join you later.'

Most of the group was assembled in less than fifteen minutes. The Templars had rigged a gangway from a work pier on the interior of the sphere to the ship's top-tier balcony, and the Consul led the way into the lounge as crew clones stowed luggage and departed.

'A fascinating old instrument,' said Colonel Kassad as he ran one hand across the top of the Steinway. 'Harpsichord?'

'Piano,' said the Consul. 'Pre-Hegira. Are we all here?'

'Everyone except Hoyt,' said Brawne Lamia as she took a seat in the projection pit.

Het Masteen entered. 'The Hegemony warship has granted permission for you to descend to Keats's spaceport,' said the Captain. He glanced around. 'I will send a crew member to see if M. Hoyt needs assistance.'

'No,' said the Consul. He modulated his voice. 'I'd like to get him. Can you tell me the way to his quarters?'

The treeship Captain looked at the Consul for a long second and then reached into the folds of his robe. *'Bon voyage,'* he said, handing over a wafer. 'I will see you on the planet, sometime before our midnight departure time from the Shrike's Temple in Keats.'

The Consul bowed. 'It was a pleasure traveling within the protective branches of the Tree, Het Masteen,' he said formally. Turning to the others, he gestured. 'Please make yourselves comfortable in the lounge or the library on the deck below this. The ship will see to your needs and answer any questions you might have. We will depart as soon as Father Hoyt and I return.'

The priest's environment pod was halfway up the treeship, far out on a secondary branch. As the Consul expected, the comlog direction wafer Het Masteen had given him also served as a palmlock override. After useless minutes tapping the announcer chime and pounding on the access portal, the Consul triggered the override and stepped into the pod.

Father Hoyt was on his knees, writhing in the center of the grass carpet. Bedclothes, gear, garments, and the contents of a standard medkit were strewn on the floor around him. He had torn off his tunic and collar and sweated through his shirt so that it now hung in damp folds, ripped and tattered where he had clawed through the fabric. Hyperion light seeped through the pod wall, making the bizarre tableau appear to be staged underwater – or, thought the Consul, in a cathedral.

Lenar Hoyt's face contorted in agony as his hands raked at his chest. Muscles on his exposed forearms writhed like living creatures moving beneath his pale tarp of a skin. 'The injector . . . *malfunctioned,'* gasped Hoyt. *'Please.'*

The Consul nodded, commanded the door to close, and knelt next to the priest. He removed the useless injector from Hoyt's clenched fist and ejected the syrette ampule. Ultramorphine. The Consul nodded again and took out an injector from the medkit he had brought from his ship. It took less than five seconds to load the ultramorph.

'Please,' begged Hoyt. His whole body spasmed. The Consul could almost see the waves of pain passing through the man.

'Yes,' said the Consul. He took a ragged breath. 'But first the rest of the story.'

Hoyt stared, reached weakly for the injector.

Sweating himself now, the Consul held the instrument just out of reach. 'Yes, in a second,' he said. 'After the rest of the story. It's important that I *know.'*

'Oh, God, sweet Christ,' sobbed Hoyt. *'Please!'*

'Yes,' gasped the Consul. 'Yes. As soon as you tell me the truth.'

Father Hoyt collapsed onto his forearms, breathing in quick pants. 'You fucking bastard,' he gasped. The priest took several deep breaths, held one until his body quit shaking, and tried to sit up. When he looked at the Consul, there was something like relief in the maddened eyes. 'Then . . . you'll give me . . . the shot?'

'Yes,' said the Consul.

'All right,' Hoyt managed in a sour whisper. 'The truth. Perecebo Plantation . . . like I said. We flew in . . . early October . . . Lycius . . . eight years after Duré . . . disappeared. Oh, *Christ*, it hurts! Alcohol and endos don't work at all anymore. Only . . . pure ultramorph . . .'

'Yes,' whispered the Consul. 'It's ready. As soon as the story is done.'

The priest lowered his head. Sweat dripped from his cheeks and nose onto the short grass. The Consul saw the man's muscles tense as if he were going to attack, then another spasm of pain wracked the thin body and Hoyt sagged forward. 'Skimmer wasn't destroyed . . . by tesla. Semfa, two men, and I . . . forced down near the Cleft while . . . while Orlandi searched upriver. His skimmer . . . had to wait while the lightning storm died down.

'Bikura came in the night. Killed . . . killed Semfa, the pilot, the other man . . . forget his name. Left me . . . alive.' Hoyt reached for his crucifix, realized that he had torn it off. He laughed briefly, stopping before the laughter turned to sobs. 'They . . . told me about the way of the cross. About the cruciform. Told me about . . . the Son of the Flames.

'Next morning, they took me to see the Son. Took me . . . to see him.' Hoyt struggled upright and clawed at his own cheeks. His eyes were wide, the ultramorph obviously forgotten despite the pain. 'About three kilometers into the flame forest . . . big tesla . . . eighty, a hundred meters tall, at least. Quiet then, but still a lot . . . a lot of charge in the air. Ash everywhere.

'The Bikura wouldn't . . . wouldn't go too close. Just knelt there with their goddamned bald heads bowed. But I . . . went close . . . had to. Dear God . . . Oh, Christ, it was him. Duré. What was *left* of him.

'He'd used a ladder to get three . . . maybe four meters . . . up on the bole of the tree. Built a sort of platform. For his feet. Broken the arrestor rods off . . . little more than spikes . . . then sharpened them. Must've used a rock to drive the long one through his feet into the bestos platform and tree.

'His left arm . . . he'd pounded the stake between the radius and ulna . . . missed veins . . . just like the goddamned Romans. Very secure as long as his skeleton was intact. Other hand . . . right hand . . . palm down. He'd driven the spike first. Sharpened both ends. Then . . . impaled his right hand. Somehow bent the spike over. Hook.

'Ladder'd fallen . . . long ago . . . but it was bestos. Hadn't burned. Used it to climb up to him. Everything'd burned away years ago . . . clothes, skin, top layers of flesh . . . but the bestos pouch was still around his neck.

'The alloy spikes still conducted current even when . . . I could see it . . . *feel* it . . . surging through what was left of the body.

'*It still looked like Paul Duré*. Important. I told Monsignor. No skin. Flesh raw or boiled away. Nerves and things visible . . . like gray and yellow roots. Christ, the smell. *But it still looked like Paul Duré!*

'I understood then. Understood it all. Somehow . . . even before reading the journals. Understood he'd been hanging there . . . oh, dear God . . . seven years. Living. Dying. The cruciform . . . forcing him to live again. Electricity . . . surging through him every second of those . . . those seven years. Flames. Hunger. Pain. Death. But somehow the goddamned . . . cruciform . . . leeching substance from the tree maybe, the air, what was left . . . rebuilding what it could . . . forcing him to *live*, to feel the pain, over and over and over . . .

'But he *won*. Pain was his ally. Oh, Jesus, not a few hours on the tree and then the spear and rest, but *seven years*!

'But . . . he won. When I removed the pouch, the cruciform on his chest fell away also. Just . . . fell right off . . . long, bloody roots. Then the thing . . . the thing I'd been sure was a corpse . . . the man raised its head. No eyelids. Eyes baked white. Lips gone. But it looked at me and smiled. *He* smiled. And he died . . . really died . . . there in my arms. The ten thousandth time, but *real* this time. He smiled at me and died.'

Hoyt stopped, communed in silence with his own pain, and then continued between bouts of clenching his teeth. 'Bikura took me . . . back to . . . Cleft. Orlandi came the next day. Rescued me. He . . . Semfa . . . I couldn't . . . he lasered the village, burned the Bikura where they stood like stupid sheep. I didn't . . . didn't argue with him. I *laughed*. Dear God, forgive me. Orlandi nuked the site with shaped charges they used to . . . to clear the jungle . . . fiberplastic matrix.'

Hoyt looked directly at the Consul and made a contorted gesture with his right hand. 'The painkillers worked all right at first. But every year . . . every day . . . got worse. Even in fugue . . . the pain. I would have had to come back anyway. How could he . . . *seven years*! Oh, Jesus,' said Father Hoyt and clawed at the carpet.

The Consul moved quickly, injecting the full ampule of ultramorph just under the armpit, catching the priest as he collapsed, and gently lowering the unconscious form to the floor. His vision unclear, the Consul ripped open Hoyt's sweat-sodden shirt, casting the rags aside. It was there, of course, lying under the pale skin of Hoyt's chest like some great, raw, cross-shaped worm. The Consul took a breath and gently turned the priest over. The second cruciform was where he had expected to find it, a slightly smaller, cross-shaped welt between the thin man's shoulder blades. It stirred slightly as the Consul's fingers brushed the fevered flesh.

The Consul moved slowly but efficiently – packing the priest's belongings, straightening the room, dressing the unconscious man with the gentle care one would use in clothing the body of a dead family member.

The Consul's comlog buzzed. 'We need to go,' came Colonel Kassad's voice.

'We're coming,' replied the Consul. He coded the comlog to summon crew clones to fetch the luggage, but lifted Father Hoyt himself. The body seemed to weigh nothing.

The pod door dilated open and the Consul stepped out, moving from the deep shadow of the branch into the blue-green glow of the world which filled the sky. Deciding what cover story he would tell the others, the Consul paused a second to look at the sleeping man's face. He glanced up at Hyperion and then moved on. Even if the gravity field had been full Earth standard, the Consul knew the body in his arms would have been no burden.

Once a parent to a child now dead, the Consul walked on, knowing once again the sensation of bearing a sleeping son to bed.

TWO

It had been a warm, rainy day in Keats, Hyperion's capital, and even after the rains stopped a layer of clouds moved slow and heavy over the city, filling the air with the salt scent of the ocean twenty kilometers to the west. Toward evening, as the gray daylight was beginning to fade into gray twilight, a double sonic boom shook the town and then echoed from the single, sculpted peak to the south. The clouds glowed blue-white. Half a minute later an ebony spacecraft broke through the overcast and descended carefully on a tail of fusion flame, its navigation lights blinking red and green against the gray.

At one thousand meters the craft's landing beacons flared and three beams of coherent light from the spaceport north of town locked the ship in a welcoming ruby tripod. The spacecraft hovered at three hundred meters, slipped sideways as smoothly as a mug sliding on a wet table top, and then settled weightlessly into a waiting blast pit.

High-pressure jets of water bathed the pit and the base of the ship, sending up billows of steam to blend with the curtain of drizzle blowing across the paved plain of the spaceport. When the water jets ceased there was no noise except the whisper of rain and the random ticks and creaks of the cooling spaceship.

A balcony extruded itself from the ship's bulkhead twenty meters above the pit wall. Five figures emerged. 'Thank you for the ride, sir,' Colonel Kassad said to the Consul.

The Consul nodded and leaned on the railing, taking in deep breaths of fresh air. Droplets of rain beaded on his shoulders and eyebrows.

Sol Weintraub lifted his baby from her infant carrier. Some change in pressure, temperature, scent, motion, noise, or a combination of all of these had awakened her and now she began to cry lustily. Weintraub bounced her and cooed to her but the wailing continued.

'An appropriate comment upon our arrival,' said Martin Silenus. The poet wore a long purple cape and a red beret which slouched to his right shoulder. He took a drink from a wineglass he had carried out from the lounge. 'Christ on a stick, this place looks different.'

The Consul, who had been away only eight local years, had to agree. The spaceport had been a full nine klicks from the city when he lived in Keats; now shacks, tents, and mud streets surrounded the landing field's perimeter. In the Consul's day, no more than a ship a week had put in at the tiny spaceport; now he counted more than twenty spacecraft on the field.

The small administration and customs building had been superseded by a huge, prefabricated structure, a dozen new blast pits and dropship grids had been added where the field had been hastily extended to the west, and the perimeter now was littered with scores of camouflage-sheathed modules which the Consul knew must serve as everything from ground control stations to barracks. A forest of exotic antennae grew skyward from a cluster of such boxes at the far end of the landing apron. 'Progress,' murmured the Consul.

'War,' said Colonel Kassad.

'Those are *people*,' said Brawne Lamia, pointing toward the main terminal gates on the south side of the field. A wave of drab colors crashed like a silent surf against the outer fence and the violet containment field.

'My God,' said the Consul, 'you're right.'

Kassad produced his binoculars and they took turns staring at the thousands of forms tugging at the wire, pressing against the repelling field.

'Why are they here?' asked Lamia. 'What do they want?' Even from half a kilometer away, the mindless will of the mob was daunting. Dark forms of FORCE:Marines could be seen patrolling just within the perimeter. The Consul realized that between the wire, the containment field, and the Marines a strip of raw earth almost surely signified mines or a deathbeam zone, or both.

'What do they want?' repeated Lamia.

'They want out,' said Kassad.

Even before the Colonel spoke, the Consul realized that the shack city around the spaceport and the mob at the gates were inevitable; the people of Hyperion were ready to *leave*. He guessed that there must be such a silent surge toward the gates each time a ship landed.

'Well, there's one who'll be staying,' said Martin Silenus and pointed toward the low mountain across the river to the south. 'Old Weeping William Rex, God rest his sinful soul.' The sculpted face of Sad King Billy was just visible through the light rain and growing darkness. 'I knew him, Horatio,' said the drunken poet. 'A man of infinite jest. Not one of them funny. A real horse's ass, Horatio.'

Sol Weintraub stood just inside the ship, shielding his baby from the drizzle and removing her cries from the vicinity of the conversation. He pointed. 'Someone is coming.'

A groundcar with its camouflage polymer inert and a military EMV modified with hoverfans for Hyperion's weak magnetic field were crossing the damp hardpan.

Martin Silenus's gaze never left Sad King Billy's dour visage. Silenus said in a voice almost too soft to be heard:

'Deep in the shady sadness of a vale
Far sunken from the healthy breath of morn,
Far from the fiery noon, and eve's one star,
Sat gray-hair'd Saturn, quiet as a stone,

Still as the silence round about his lair;
Forest on forest hung above his head
Like cloud on cloud . . .'

Father Hoyt came onto the balcony, rubbing his face with both hands. His eyes were wide and unfocused, a child rising from his nap. 'Are we there?' he asked.

'Fucking aye,' cried Martin Silenus, returning the binoculars to the Colonel. 'Let's go down and greet the gendarmes.'

The young Marine lieutenant seemed unimpressed with the group even after he had scanned the authorization wafer Het Masteen had passed along from the task force commander. The lieutenant took his time scanning their visa chips, letting them wait in the drizzle, occasionally making a comment with the idle arrogance common to such nobodies who have just come into a small bit of power. Then he came to Fedmahn Kassad's chip and looked up with the expression of a startled stoat. 'Colonel Kassad!'

'Retired,' said Kassad.

'I'm sorry, sir,' said the lieutenant, stumbling over his words as he fumbled the visas back to everyone. 'I had no idea you were with this party, sir. That is . . . the Captain just said . . . I mean . . . my uncle was with you on Bressia, sir. I mean, I'm sorry . . . anything I or my men can do to . . .'

'At ease, Lieutenant,' said Kassad. 'Is there any chance of getting some transport into the city?'

'Ah . . . well, sir . . . ' The young Marine started to rub his chin and then remembered that he was wearing his helmet. 'Yes, sir. But the problem is, sir, the mobs can get pretty nasty and . . . well, the damn EMVs don't work for shit on this . . . uh, pardon me, sir. You see, the ground transports're limited to cargo and we don't have any skimmers free to leave the base until 2200 hours but I'll be happy to get your party on the roster for . . .'

'Just a minute,' said the Consul. A battered passenger skimmer with the gold geodesic of the Hegemony painted on one flare skirt had landed ten meters away. A tall, thin man stepped out. 'Theo!' cried the Consul.

The two men stepped forward, started to shake hands, and then hugged each other instead. 'Damn,' said the Consul, 'you look good, Theo.' It was true. His former aide had gained half a dozen years on the Consul, but the younger man still had the boyish smile, thin face, and thick red hair that had attracted every unmarried woman – and not a few married ones – on the consulate staff. The shyness which had been part of Theo Lane's vulnerability was still there, as evidenced by the way he now needlessly adjusted his archaic horn-rimmed glasses – the young diplomat's one affectation.

'It's good to have you back,' said Theo.

The Consul turned, started to introduce his friend to the group, and then stopped. 'My God,' he said, 'you're Consul now. I'm sorry, Theo, I wasn't thinking.'

Theo Lane smiled and adjusted his glasses. 'No problem, sir,' he said. 'Actually, I'm no longer Consul. For the last few months I've been acting Governor-General. The Home Rule Council finally requested – and received – formal colonial status. Welcome to the newest world in the Hegemony.'

The Consul stared a second and then hugged his former protégé again. 'Congratulations, Your Excellency.'

Theo grinned and glanced at the sky. 'It's going to rain in earnest before long. Why don't we get your group aboard the skimmer and I'll drive you into town.' The new Governor-General smiled at the young Marine. 'Lieutenant?'

'Uh . . . yes, *sir?*' The officer had snapped to attention.

'Could you get your men to load these good people's luggage, please? We'd all like to get in out of the rain.'

The skimmer flew south above the highway at a steady sixty meters. The Consul rode in the front passenger seat; the rest of the group relaxed in flowfoam recliners behind. Martin Silenus and Father Hoyt appeared to be asleep. Weintraub's baby had ceased crying in favor of nursing on a soft bottle of synthesized mother's milk.

'Things have changed,' said the Consul. He rested his cheek against the rain-spattered canopy and looked down at the chaos.

Thousand of shacks and lean-tos covered the hillsides and gullies along the three-klick ride to the suburbs. Fires were being lighted under wet tarps and the Consul watched mud-colored figures moving between mud-colored shacks. High fences had been rigged along the old Spaceport Highway and the road itself had been widened and regraded. Two lanes of truck and hover traffic, most of it military green or shrouded with inactive camouflage polymer, moved sluggishly in both directions. Ahead, the lights of Keats seemed to have multiplied and spread across new sections of the river valley and hills.

'Three million,' said Theo, as if reading his former boss's mind. 'At least three million people and growing every day.'

The Consul stared. 'There were only four and a half million people on the *planet* when I left.'

'Still are,' said the new Governor-General. 'And every one of them wants to get to Keats, board a ship, and get the hell out. Some are waiting for the farcaster to be built, but most don't believe it'll happen in time. They're afraid.'

'Of the Ousters?'

'Them too,' said Theo, 'but mostly of the Shrike.'

The Consul turned his face from the coolness of the canopy. 'It's come south of the Bridle Range then?'

Theo laughed without humor. 'It's everywhere. Or *they're* everywhere. Most people are convinced that there are dozens or hundreds of the things now. Shrike deaths have been reported on all three continents. Everywhere except Keats, segments of the coast along the Mane, and a few of the big cities like Endymion.'

'How many casualties?' The Consul did not really want to know.

'At least twenty thousand dead or missing,' said Theo. 'There are a lot of injured people but that isn't the Shrike, is it?' Again came the dry laugh. 'The Shrike doesn't just *wound* people, does it? Uh-uh, people shoot each other by accident, fall down stairways or jump out windows in their panic, and trample each other in crowds. It's a fucking mess.'

In the eleven years the Consul had worked with Theo Lane, he had never heard the younger man use profanity of any sort. 'Is FORCE any help?' the Consul asked. 'Are they what's keeping the Shrike away from the big cities?'

Theo shook his head. 'FORCE hasn't done a damn thing except control the mobs. Oh, the Marines put on a show of keeping the spaceport open here and the harbor landing zone at Port R secure, but they haven't even tried to confront the Shrike. They're waiting to fight the Ousters.'

'SDF?' asked the Consul, knowing even as he spoke that the poorly trained Self-defense Force would have been of little use.

Theo snorted. 'At least eight thousand of the casualties are SDF. General Braxton took the "Fighting Third" up the River Road to "strike at the Shrike menace in their lair" and that was the last we heard of them.'

'You're joking,' said the Consul, but one look at his friend's face told him that he wasn't. 'Theo,' he said, 'how in the world did you have time to meet us at the spaceport?'

'I didn't,' said the Governor-General. He glanced in the back. The others were sleeping or staring exhaustedly out windows. 'I needed to talk to you,' said Theo. 'Convince you not to go.'

The Consul started to shake his head but Theo grasped his arm, squeezed hard. 'Now listen to what I have to say, damn it, I know how hard it is for you to come back here after . . . what happened but, goddamn it, there's no sense in your throwing everything away for no reason. Abandon this stupid pilgrimage. Stay in Keats.'

'I can't . . .' began the Consul.

'*Listen* to me,' demanded Theo. 'Reason one: you're the finest diplomat and crisis manager I've ever seen and we need your skills.'

'It doesn't . . .'

'Shut up a minute. Reason two: you and the others won't get within two hundred klicks of the Time Tombs. This isn't like the old days when you were here and the goddamned suicides could get up there and even sit around for a week and maybe even change their minds and come home. The Shrike is on the *move*. It's like a plague.'

'I understand that but . . .'

'Reason three: I need you. I begged Tau Ceti Center to send someone else out. When I found that you were coming . . . well, hell, it got me through the last two years.'

The Consul shook his head, not understanding.

Theo started the turn toward the city center and then hovered, taking his eyes off the controls to look directly at the Consul. 'I want you to take over the governor-generalship. The Senate won't interfere – except perhaps for Gladstone – and by the time she finds out, it will be too late.'

The Consul felt as though someone had struck him below the third rib. He looked away, down at the maze of narrow streets and crooked buildings that was Jacktown, the Old City. When he could speak again, he said, 'I can't, Theo.'

'Listen, if you . . . '

'No. I mean I can*not*. It would be no good if I did accept it, but the simple truth is, I can't. I have to go on this pilgrimage.'

Theo straightened his glasses, stared straight ahead.

'Look, Theo, you're the most competent and capable Foreign Service professional I've ever worked with. I've been out of things for eight years. I think . . . '

Theo nodded tersely, interrupted. 'I suppose you want to go to the Shrike Temple.'

'Yes.'

The skimmer circled and settled. The Consul was staring at nothing, thinking, when the side doors of the skimmer raised and folded and Sol Weintraub said, 'Good God.'

The group stepped out and stared at the charred and toppled wreckage of what had been the Shrike Temple. Since the Time Tombs had been closed as too dangerous some twenty-five local years earlier, the Shrike Temple had become Hyperion's most popular tourist attraction. Filling three full city blocks, rising more than a hundred and fifty meters to its central, sharpened spire, the Shrike Church's central temple was part awe-inspiring cathedral, part Gothic joke with its fluid, buttressed curves of stone perma-bonded to its whiskered-alloy skeleton, part Escher print with its tricks of perspective and impossible angles, part Boschian nightmare with its tunnel entrances, hidden chambers, dark gardens, and forbidden sections, and – more than anything else – it had been part of Hyperion's past.

Now it was gone. Tall heaps of blackened stone were the only hint of the structure's former majesty. Melted alloy girders rose from the stones like the ribs of some giant carcass. Much of the rubble had tumbled into the pits, basements, and passages which had lain beneath the three-century-old landmark. The Consul walked close to the edge of a pit and wondered if the deep basements had – as legend decreed – actually connected to one of the planet's labyrinths.

'It looks as if they used a hellwhip on this place,' said Martin Silenus, using an archaic term for any high-energy laser weapon. The poet seemed suddenly sobered as he joined the Consul at the edge of the pit. 'I remember when the Temple and parts of the Old City were the only things here,' he said. 'After the disaster near the Tombs, Billy decided to relocate Jacktown here because of the Temple. Now it's gone. Christ.'

'No,' said Kassad.

The others looked at him.

The Colonel rose from where he had been examining the rubble. 'Not a hellwhip,' he said. 'Shaped plasma charges. Several of them.'

'Now do you want to stay here and go on this useless pilgrimage?' asked Theo. 'Come with me back to the consulate.' He was speaking to the Consul but extending the invitation to everyone.

The Consul turned away from the pit, looking at his former aide but now seeing, for the first time, the Governor-General of a besieged Hegemony world. 'We can't, Your Excellency,' said the Consul. 'At least I can't. I won't speak for the others.'

The four men and the woman shook their heads. Silenus and Kassad began unloading luggage. The rain returned as a light mist falling out of the darkness. At that second the Consul noticed the two FORCE attack skimmers hovering above the nearby rooftops. Darkness and chameleon-polymer hulls had hidden them well, but the rain now revealed their outlines. *Of course*, thought the Consul, *the Governor-General does not travel unescorted.*

'Did the priests escape? Were there survivors when the Temple was destroyed?' asked Brawne Lamia.

'Yes,' said Theo. The de facto dictator of five million doomed souls removed his glasses and dried them on his shirttail. 'All of the Shrike Cult priests and acolytes escaped through tunnels. The mob had been surrounding this place for months. Their leader, a woman named Cammon from somewhere east of the Sea of Grass, gave everyone in the Temple plenty of warning before they set off the DL-20.'

'Where were the police?' asked the Consul. 'The SDF? FORCE?'

Theo Lane smiled and at that second he looked decades older than the young man the Consul had known. 'You folks have been in transit for three years,' he said. 'The universe has changed. Shrike cultists are being burned out and beaten up *in the Web*. You can imagine the attitude here. The Keats police have been absorbed under the martial law I declared fourteen months ago. They and the SDF watched while the mob torched the Temple. So did I. There were half a million people here that night.'

Sol Weintraub stepped closer. 'Do they know about us? About this final pilgrimage?'

'If they did,' said Theo, 'none of you would be alive. You'd think they'd welcome anything that might appease the Shrike, but the only thing the mob would notice is that you were chosen by the Shrike Church. As it was, I had to overrule my own Advisory Council. They were in favor of destroying your ship before it reached the atmosphere.'

'Why did you?' asked the Consul. 'Overrule them, I mean.'

Theo sighed and adjusted his glasses. 'Hyperion still needs the Hegemony, and Gladstone still has the vote of confidence of the All Thing, if not the Senate. And I still need you.'

The Consul looked at the rubble of the Shrike Temple.

'This pilgrimage was over before you got here,' said Governor-General

Theo Lane. 'Will you come back to the consulate with me . . . at least in an advisory capacity?'

'I'm sorry,' said the Consul. 'I can't.'

Theo turned without a word, dropped into the skimmer, and lifted off. His military escort followed as a blur in the rain.

It was raining harder now. The group moved closer together in the growing darkness. Weintraub had rigged a makeshift hood over Rachel and the noise of the rain on plastic made the baby cry.

'What now?' said the Consul, looking around at the night and narrow streets. Their luggage lay heaped in a soggy pile. The world smelled of ashes.

Martin Silenus grinned. 'I know a bar.'

It turned out that the Consul also knew the bar; he had all but lived in Cicero's for most of his eleven-year assignment on Hyperion.

Unlike most things in Keats, on Hyperion, Cicero's was not named after some piece of pre-Hegira literary trivia. Rumor had it that the bar was named after a section of an Old Earth city – some said Chicago, USA, others were sure it was Calcutta, AIS – but only Stan Leweski, owner and great-grandson of the founder, knew for sure, and Stan had never revealed its secret. The bar itself had overflowed over the century and a half of its existence from a walkup loft in one of Jacktown's sagging older buildings along the Hoolie River to nine levels in *four* sagging old buildings along the Hoolie. The only consistent elements of decor at Cicero's over the decades were the low ceilings, thick smoke, and constant background babble which offered a sense of privacy in the midst of bustle.

There was no privacy this night. The Consul and the others paused as they carried their gear through the Marsh Lane entrance.

'Jesus wept,' muttered Martin Silenus

Cicero's looked as if it had been invaded by barbarian hordes. Every chair was filled, every table occupied, mostly by men, and the floors were littered with packs, weapons, bedrolls, antiquated comm equipment, ration boxes, and all of the other detritus of an army of refugees . . . or perhaps a refugee army. The heavy air of Cicero's, which once had been filled with the blended scent of broiling steaks, wine, stim, ale, and T-free tobacco, was now laden with the overlapping smells of unwashed bodies, urine, and hopelessness.

At that moment the huge form of Stan Leweski materialized out of the gloom. The bar owner's forearms were as huge and heavy as ever, but his forehead had advanced more than a few centimeters against the receding tangle of black hair and there were more creases than the Consul remembered around the dark eyes. Those eyes were wide now as Leweski stared at the Consul. 'Ghost,' he said.

'No.'

'You are not dead?'

'No.'

'By damn!' declared Stan Leweski and, grasping the Consul by the upper arms, picked him up as easily as a man would lift a five-year-old. 'By damn! You *are* not dead. What are you doing here?'

'Checking your liquor license,' said the Consul. 'Put me down.'

Leweski carefully set the Consul down, tapped his shoulders, and grinned. He looked at Martin Silenus and the grin changed to a frown. 'You look familiar but I have never seen you before.'

'I knew your great-grandfather,' said Silenus. 'Which reminds me, do you have any of that pre-Hegira ale left? The warm, British stuff that tastes like recycled moose piss. I could never get enough of that.'

'Nothing left,' said Leweski. He pointed at the poet. 'By damn. Grandfather Jiri's trunk. That old holo of the satyr in the original Jacktown. Can it be?' He stared at Silenus and then at the Consul, touching them both gingerly with a massive forefinger. 'Two ghosts.'

'Six tired people,' said the Consul. The baby began crying again. 'Seven. Do you have space for us?'

Leweski turned in a half circle, hands spread, palms up. 'It is all like this. No space left. No food. No wine.' He squinted at Martin Silenus. 'No ale. Now we have become a big hotel with no beds. The SDF bastards stay here without paying and drink their own upcountry rotgut and wait for the world to end. That will happen soon enough, I think.'

The group was standing in what had once been the entrance mezzanine. Their heaped luggage joined a riot of gear already littering the floor. Small clusters of men shouldered their way through the throng and cast appraising glances at the newcomers – especially at Brawne Lamia. She returned their stares with a flat, cold glare.

Stan Leweski looked at the Consul for a moment. 'I have a balcony table. Five of those SDF Death Commandos have been parked there for a week, telling everyone and each other how they are going to wipe out the Ouster Legions with their bare hands. You want the table, I will throw the teat-suckers out.'

'Yes,'said the Consul.

Leweski had turned to leave when Lamia stopped him with a hand on his arm. 'Would you like a little help?' she asked.

Stan Leweski shrugged, grinned. 'I do not need it, but I might like it. Come.'

They disappeared into the crowd.

The third-floor balcony had just enough room for the splintered table and six chairs. Despite the insane crowding on the main floors, stairs, and landings, no one had challenged them for the space after Leweski and Lamia threw the protesting Death Commandos over the railing and into the river nine meters below. Somehow Leweski had managed to send up a tankard of beer and a basket of bread and cold beef.

The group ate in silence, obviously suffering more than the usual amount of postfugue hunger, fatigue, and depression. The darkness of the balcony was relieved only by dim, reflected light from deeper within Cicero's and by the lanterns on passing river barges. Most of the buildings along the Hoolie were dark but other city lights reflected from low clouds. The Consul could make out the ruins of the Shrike Temple half a kilometer upriver.

'Well,' said Father Hoyt, obviously recovered from the heavy dose of ultramorph and teetering on the delicate balance between pain and sedation, 'what do we do next?'

When no one answered, the Consul closed his eyes. He refused to take the lead in anything. Sitting on the balcony at Cicero's, it was all too easy to fall back into the rhythms of a former life; he would drink until the early morning hours, watch the predawn meteor showers as the clouds cleared, and then stagger to his empty apartment near the market, going into the consulate four hours later showered, shaved, and seemingly human except for the blood in his eyes and the insane ache in his skull. Trusting in Theo – quiet, efficient Theo – to get him through the morning. Trusting in luck to get him through the day. Trusting in the drinking at Cicero's to get him through the night. Trusting in the unimportance of his posting to get him through life.

'You are all ready to leave for the pilgrimage?'

The Consul's eyes snapped open. A hooded figure stood in the doorway and for a second the Consul thought it was Het Masteen, but then he realized that this man was much shorter, his voice not accented with the stilted Templar consonants.

'If you are ready, we must go,' said the dark figure.

'Who are you?' asked Brawne Lamia.

'Come quickly,' was the shadow's only reply.

Fedmahn Kassad stood, bending to keep his head from striking the ceiling, and detained the robed figure, flipping back the man's hood with a flick of his left hand.

'An android!' said Lenar Hoyt, staring at the man's blue skin and blue-on-blue eyes.

The Consul was less surprised. For more than a century it had been illegal to own androids in the Hegemony, and none had been biofactured for almost that long, but they were still used for manual labor in remote parts of backwater, noncolony worlds – worlds like Hyperion. The Shrike Temple had used androids extensively, complying with the Church of the Shrike doctrine which proclaimed that androids were free from original sin, therefore spiritually superior to humankind and – incidentally – exempt from the Shrike's terrible and inevitable retribution.

'You must come quickly,' whispered the android, setting his hood in place.

'Are you from the Temple?' asked Lamia.

'Quiet!' snapped the android. He glanced into the hall, turned back, and nodded. 'We must hurry. Please follow me.'

All of them stood and then hesitated. The Consul watched as Kassad casually unsealed the long leather jacket he was wearing. He caught the briefest glimpse of a deathwand tucked in the Colonel's belt. Normally the Consul would have been appalled by even the thought of a deathwand nearby – the slightest mistaken touch could purée every synapse on the balcony – but at this moment he was oddly reassured by the sight of it.

'Our luggage . . . ' began Weintraub.

'It has been seen to,' whispered the hooded man. 'Quickly now.'

The group followed the android down the stairs and into the night, their movement as tired and passive as a sigh.

The Consul slept late. Half an hour after sunrise a rectangle of light found its way between the porthole's shutters and fell across his pillow. The Consul rolled away and did not wake. An hour after that there came a loud clatter as the tired mantas which had pulled the barge all night were released and fresh ones harnessed. The Consul slept on. In the next hour the footsteps and cries of the crew on the deck outside his stateroom grew louder and more persistent, but it was the warning klaxon below the locks at Karla which finally brought him up out of his sleep.

Moving slowly in the druglike languor of fugue hangover, the Consul bathed as best he could with only basin and pump, dressed in loose cotton trousers, an old canvas shirt, and foam-soled walking shoes, and found his way to the mid-deck.

Breakfast had been set out on a long sideboard near a weathered table which could be retracted into the deck planking. An awning shaded the eating area and the crimson and gold canvas snapped to the breeze of their passage. It was a beautiful day, cloudless and bright, with Hyperion's sun making up in ferocity what it lacked in size.

M. Weintraub, Lamia, Kassad, and Silenus had been up for some time. Lenar Hoyt and Het Masteen joined the group a few minutes after the Consul arrived.

The Consul helped himself to toasted fish, fruit, and orange juice at the buffet and then moved to the railing. The water was wide here, at least a kilometer from shore to shore, and its green and lapis sheen echoed the sky. At first glance the Consul did not recognize the land on either side of the river. To the east, periscope-bean paddies stretched away into the haze of distance where the rising sun reflected on a thousand flooded surfaces. A few indigenie huts were visible at the junction of paddy dikes, their angled walls made of bleached weirwood or golden halfoak. To the west, the bottomland along the river was overgrown with low tangles of gissen, woman-grove root, and a flamboyant red fern the Consul did not recognize, all growing around mud marshes and miniature lagoons which stretched another kilometer or so to bluffs where scrub everblues clung to any bare spot between granite slabs.

For a second the Consul felt lost, disoriented on a world he thought he knew well, but then he remembered the klaxon at the Karla Locks and realized that they had entered a rarely used stretch of the Hoolie north of

Doukhobor's Copse. The Consul had never seen this part of the river, having always traveled on or flown above the Royal Transport Canal which lay to the west of the bluffs. He could only surmise that some danger or disturbance along the main route to the Sea of Grass had sent them this back way along bypassed stretches of the Hoolie. He guessed that they were about a hundred and eighty kilometers northwest of Keats.

'It looks different in the daylight, doesn't it?' said Father Hoyt.

The Consul looked at the shore again, not sure what Hoyt was talking about; then he realized the priest meant the barge.

It had been strange – following the android messenger in the rain, boarding the old barge, making their way through its maze of tessellated rooms and passages, picking up Het Masteen at the ruins of the Temple, and then watching the lights of Keats fall astern.

The Consul remembered those hours before and after midnight as from a fatigue-blurred dream, and he imagined the others must have been just as exhausted and disoriented. He vaguely remembered his surprise that the barge's crew were all android, but mostly he recalled his relief at finally closing the door of his stateroom and crawling into bed.

'I was talking to A. Bettik this morning,' said Weintraub, referring to the android who had been their guide. 'This old scow has quite a history.'

Martin Silenus moved to the sideboard to pour himself more tomato juice, added a dash of something from the flask he carried, and said, 'It's obviously been around a bit. The goddamn railings've been oiled by hands, the stairs worn by feet, the ceilings darkened by lamp soot, and the beds beaten saggy by generations of humping. I'd say it's several centuries old. The carvings and rococo finishes are fucking marvelous. Did you notice that under all the other scents the inlaid wood still smells of sandalwood? I wouldn't be surprised if this thing came from Old Earth.'

'It does,' said Sol Weintraub. The baby, Rachel, slept on his arm, softly blowing bubbles of saliva in her sleep. 'We're on the proud ship *Benares*, built in and named after the Old Earth city of the same name.'

'I don't remember hearing of any Old Earth city with that name,' said the Consul.

Brawne Lamia looked up from the last of her breakfast. 'Benares, also known as Varanasi or Gandhipur, Hindi Free State. Part of the Second Asian Co-prosperity Sphere after the Third Sino-Japanese War. Destroyed in the Indo-Soviet Muslim Republic Limited Exchange.'

'Yes,' said Weintraub, 'the *Benares* was built quite some time before the Big Mistake. Mid-twenty-second century, I would guess. A. Bettik informs me that it was originally a levitation barge . . . '

'Are the EM generators still down there?' interrupted Colonel Kassad.

'I believe so,' said Weintraub. 'Next to the main salon on the lowest deck. The floor of the salon is clear lunar crystal. Quite nice if we were cruising at two thousand meters . . . quite useless now.'

'Benares,' mused Martin Silenus. He ran his hand lovingly across a time-darkened railing. 'I was robbed there once.'

Brawne Lamia put down her coffee mug. 'Old man, are you trying to tell us that you're ancient enough to remember *Old Earth*! We're not fools, you know.'

'My dear child,' beamed Martin Silenus, 'I am not trying to tell you anything. I just thought it might be entertaining – as well as edifying and enlightening – if at some point we exchanged lists of all the locations at which we have either robbed or been robbed. Since you have the unfair advantage of having been the daughter of a senator, I am sure that your list would be much more distinguished . . . and *much* longer.'

Lamia opened her mouth to retort, frowned, and said nothing.

'I wonder how this ship got to Hyperion?' murmured Father Hoyt. 'Why bring a levitation barge to a world where EM equipment doesn't work?'

'It would work,' said Colonel Kassad. 'Hyperion has *some* magnetic field. It just would not be reliable in holding anything airborne.'

Father Hoyt raised an eyebrow, obviously at a loss to see the distinction.

'Hey,' cried the poet from his place at the railing, 'the gang's all here!'

'So?' said Brawne Lamia. Her lips all but disappeared into a thin line whenever she spoke to Silenus.

'So we're all here,' he said. 'Let's get on with the storytelling.'

Het Masteen said, 'I thought it had been agreed that we would tell our respective stories after the dinner hour.'

Martin Silenus shrugged. 'Breakfast, dinner, who the fuck cares? We're assembled. It's not going to take six or seven days to get to the Time Tombs, is it?'

The Consul considered. Less than two days to get as far as the river could take them. Two more days, or less if the winds were right, on the Sea of Grass. Certainly no more than one more day to cross the mountains. 'No,' he said. 'Not quite six days.'

'All right,' said Silenus, 'then let's get on with the telling of tales. Besides, there's no guarantee that the Shrike won't come calling before we knock on his door. If these bedtime stories are supposed to be helpful to our survival chances in some way, then I say let's hear from everyone before the contributors start getting chopped and diced by that ambulatory food processor we're so eager to visit.'

'You're disgusting,' said Brawne Lamia.

'Ah, darling,' smiled Silenus, 'those are the same words you whispered last night after your second orgasm.'

Lamia looked away. Father Hoyt cleared his throat and said, 'Whose turn is it? To tell a story, I mean?' The silence stretched.

'Mine,' said Fedmahn Kassad. The tall man reached into the pocket of his white tunic and held up a slip of paper with a large 2 scribbled on it.

'Do you mind doing this now?' asked Sol Weintraub.

Kassad showed a hint of a smile. 'I wasn't in favor of doing it at all,' he said, 'but if it were done when 'tis done, then 'twere well it were done quickly.'

'Hey!' cried Martin Silenus. 'The man knows his pre-Hegira playwrights.'

'Shakespeare?' said Father Hoyt.

'No,' said Silenus. 'Lerner and fucking Lowe. Neil buggering Simon. Hamel fucking Posten.'

'Colonel,' Sol Weintraub said formally, 'the weather is nice, none of us seems to have anything pressing to do in the next hour or so, and we would be obliged if you would share the tale of what brings you to Hyperion on the Shrike's last pilgrimage.'

Kassad nodded. The day grew warmer as the canvas awning snapped, the decks creaked, and the levitation barge *Benares* worked its steady way upstream toward the mountains, the moors, and the Shrike.

THE SOLDIER'S TALE:
THE WAR LOVERS

It was during the Battle of Agincourt that Fedmahn Kassad encountered the woman he would spend the rest of his life seeking.

It was a wet and chilly late October morning in A.D. 1415. Kassad had been inserted as an archer into the army of Henry V of England. The English force had been on French soil since August 14 and had been retreating from superior French forces since October 8. Henry had convinced his War Council that the army could beat the French in a forced march to the safety of Calais. They had failed. Now, as October 25 dawned gray and drizzly, seven thousand Englishmen, mostly bowmen, faced a force of some twenty-eight thousand French men-at-arms across a kilometer of muddy field.

Kassad was cold, tired sick, and scared. He and the other archers had been surviving on little more than scavenged berries for the past week of the march and almost every man on the line that morning was suffering from diarrhea. The air temperature was in the low fifties Fahrenheit and Kassad had spent a long night trying to sleep on damp ground. He was impressed with the unbelievable realism of the experience – the Olympus Command School Historical Tactical Network was as far beyond regular stimsims as full-form holos were beyond tintypes – but the physical sensations were so convincing, so *real*, that Kassad did not relish the thought of being wounded. There were tales of cadets receiving fatal wounds in the OCS:HTN sims and being pulled dead from their immersion creches.

Kassad and the other bowmen on Henry's right flank had been staring at the larger French force for most of the morning when pennants waved, the fifteenth-century equivalent of sergeants brayed, and the archers obeyed the King's command and began marching against the enemy. The ragged English line, stretching about seven hundred meters across the field from treeline to treeline, consisted of clusters of archers like Kassad's troop interspersed with smaller groups of men-at-arms. The English had no formal cavalry and most of the horses Kassad could see on his end of the field were carrying men clustered near the King's command group three hundred meters toward the center, or huddled around the Duke of York's position much closer to where Kassad and the other archers stood near the right flank. These command groups reminded Kassad of a FORCE:ground mobile staff HQ, only instead of the inevitable forest of comm antennae giving away their position, bright banners and pennants hung limp on pikes. An obvious artillery target, thought Kassad, and then reminded himself that this particular military nuance did not yet exist.

Kassad noticed that the French had plenty of horses. He estimated six or seven hundred mounted men formed in ranks on each of the French flanks and a long line of cavalry behind the main battle line. Kassad did not like horses. He had seen holos and pictures, of course, but he had not encountered the animals themselves until this exercise, and the size, smell, and sound of them tended to be unnerving – especially so when the damn quadrupeds were armored chest and head, shod in steel, and trained to carry armored men wielding four meters of lance.

The English advance halted. Kassad estimated that his battle line was about two hundred and fifty meters from the French. He knew from the experience of the past week that this was within longbow range, but he also knew that he would have to pull his arm half out of its socket to hold the pull.

The French were shouting what Kassad assumed were insults. He ignored them as he and his silent comrades stepped forward from where they had planted their long arrows and found soft ground in which to drive their stakes. The stakes were long and heavy and Kassad had been carrying his for a week. Almost a meter and a half long, the clumsy thing had been sharpened at both ends. When the order first came down for all archers to find saplings and cut stakes, somewhere in the deep woods just after they had crossed the Somme, Kassad had wondered idly what the things were for. Now he knew.

Every third archer carried a heavy mallet and now they took turns driving their stakes in at a careful angle. Kassad pulled out his long knife, resharpened the end which, even leaning, rose almost to his chest, and stepped back through the hedgehog of sharpened stakes to await the French charge.

The French did not charge.

Kassad waited with the others. His bow was strung, forty-eight arrows were planted in two clusters at his feet, and his feet were set properly.

The French did not charge.

The rain had stopped but a cool breeze had come up and what little body heat Kassad had generated by the short march and the task of driving stakes had been lost quickly. The only sounds were the metallic shufflings of men and horses, occasional mutterings or nervous laughs, and the heavier thud of hooves as the French cavalry rearranged itself but still refused to charge.

'Fuck this,' said a grizzled yeoman a few feet from Kassad. 'Those bastards've wasted our whole bleeding morning. They'd better piss or get off the pot.'

Kassad nodded. He was not sure if he was hearing and understanding

Middle English or if the sentence had been in simple Standard. He had no idea if the grizzled archer was another Command School cadet, an instructor, or merely an artifact of the sim. He could not guess if the slang had been correct. He did not care. His heart was pounding and his palms were sweaty. He wiped his hands on his jerkin.

As if King Henry had taken his cue from the old man's muttering, command flags suddenly bobbed and rose, sergeants screamed, and row upon row of English archers raised their longbows, pulled when commands were shouted, released on the next command.

Four waves of arrows comprised of more than six thousand meter-long, chisel-pointed, clothyard missiles rose, seemed to hang in a cloud thirty meters up, and fell on the French.

There came the sound of horses screaming and a thousand demented children pounding on ten thousand tin pots as the French men-at-arms leaned into the rain of arrows to let their steel helmets and their chest and shoulder armor take the brunt of the downpour. Kassad knew that in military terms little real damage had been done, but this was small solace to the occasional French soldier with ten inches of arrow through his eye, or to the scores of horses leaping, tumbling, and crashing into one another while their riders struggled to remove wooden shafts from the creatures' backs and flanks.

The French did not charge.

More commands were shouted. Kassad raised, readied, loosed his arrow. Again. And again. The sky darkened every ten seconds. Kassad's arm and back ached from the punishing rhythm. He found that he felt neither elation nor anger. He was doing his job. His forearm was raw. Again the arrows flew. And again. Fifteen of his first sheaf of twenty-four arrows were gone when a cry went up along the English line and Kassad paused and glanced down while holding full pull.

The French were charging.

A cavalry charge was something beyond Kassad's experience. Watching twelve hundred armored horses charging directly at him created internal sensations which Kassad found a bit unnerving. The charge took less than forty seconds but Kassad discovered that this was ample time for his mouth to go absolutely dry, his breathing to begin to have problems, and for his testicles to retreat completely into his body. If the rest of Kassad could have found a comparable hiding place, he would have seriously considered crawling into it.

As it was, he was too busy to run.

Firing on command, his line of archers got off five flat volleys at the attacking horsemen, managed one more shot in independent fire, and then they fell back five paces.

Horses, it turned out, were too smart to willingly impale themselves upon stakes – no matter how hard their human riders implored them to do so – but the second and third waves of cavalry did not stop as abruptly as the first, and in a single mad moment horses were down and screaming, riders were thrown and screaming, and Kassad was out and screaming, rushing at every downed Frenchman he could see, wielding a mallet on the prostrate form when he could, slashing through gaps in armor with his long knife when it was too crowded to swing the mallet. Soon he and the grizzled archer and a younger man who had lost his cap became an efficient killing team, closing in on a downed rider from three sides, Kassad using the mallet to knock the pleading horseman off his knees, then all three moving in with their blades.

Only one knight gained his feet and raised a sword to confront them. The Frenchman flipped up his visor and called out a clear request for honor and single combat. The old man and the youth circled like wolves. Kassad returned with his bow and put an arrow into the knight's left eye from ten paces.

The battle continued in the deadly comic-opera vein common to all armed combat since the first rock and thighbone duels on Old Earth. The French cavalry managed to turn and flee just as the first wave of ten thousand men-at-arms charged the English center on foot. The melee broke up the rhythm of the attack and, by the time the French had regained their initiative, Henry's own men-at-arms had braced to hold them at pike length while Kassad and several thousand other archers poured volley fire into the massed French infantry at close range.

That did not end the battle. It was not necessarily even the decisive moment. The turning point, when it came, was lost – as all such moments are – within the dust and turmoil of a thousand individual encounters where infantrymen faced infantrymen across the distance of their personal weapons. Before it was over some three hours later there would be minor variations on repeated themes, ineffective thrusts and clumsy counter-thrusts, and a less than honorable moment when Henry would order prisoners killed rather than leave them in the rear when the English were confronted with a new threat. But the heralds and historians would later agree that the outcome had been sealed somewhere in the confusion during the first French infantry charge. The French died in their thousands. English dominion on that part of the Continent would continue for a while. The day of the armored man-at-arms, the knight, the embodiment of chivalry, was over – hammered into history's coffin by a few thousand ragtag peasant archers carrying longbows. The ultimate insult to the noble-born French dead – if the dead indeed could be further insulted – lay in the fact that the English archers were not only common men, common in the lowest, most flea-infested sense of the word, but that they were *draftees*. Doughboys. GIs. Grunts. AIPs. Spezzes. K-techs. Jump Rats.

But all that was in the lesson Kassad was supposed to have learned during the OCS:HTN exercise. He learned none of it. He was too busy having an encounter which would change his life.

The French man-at-arms went over the head of his falling horse, rolled once, and was up and running for the woods before the mud quit flying. Kassad followed. He was halfway to the tree line before he realized that the youth and the grizzled archer had not come with him. It did not matter. Kassad's adrenaline was flowing and the bloodlust had him in its grip.

The man-at-arms, who had just been thrown to the ground from a horse moving at full gallop and who was wearing sixty pounds of clumsy armor, should have been an easy prey to catch. He was not. The Frenchman glanced back once, saw Kassad coming on at a full run with a mallet in his hand and his eye full of business, and then the man-at-arms shifted into a higher gear and reached the trees fifteen meters ahead of his pursuer.

Kassad was deep into the woods before he stopped, leaned on the mallet, gasped, and considered his position. Thuds, screams, and crashes from the battlefield behind him were muffled by distance and shrubbery. The trees were almost bare and still dripped from the rainstorm the night before; the floor of the forest was carpeted with a thick layer of old leaves and a snarl of shrubs and brambles. The man-at-arms had left a trail of broken branches and footprints for the first twenty meters or so, but now deer trails and overgrown paths made it difficult to see where he had passed.

Kassad moved slowly, stepping deeper into the woods, trying to be alert for any noise above the sound of his own panting and the insane pounding of his heart. It occurred to Kassad that, tactically speaking, this was not a brilliant move; the man-at-arms had been wearing full armor and carrying his sword when he disappeared in the bushes. At any moment the Frenchman might forget his panic, regret his temporary loss of honor, and remember his years of combat training. Kassad also had been trained. He looked down at his cloth shirt and leather vest. The mallet was still in his hands, the knife in his broad belt. He had been trained to use high-energy weapons with a killing range of a few meters to thousands of kilometers. He had been rated in plasma grenades, hellwhips, fleschette rifles, sonics, recoilless zero-gravity weapons, deathwands, kinetic assault guns, and beam gauntlets. He now had a working knowledge of an English longbow. None of these objects – including the longbow – was on his person at the moment.

'Ah, shit,' murmured Second Lieutenant Kassad.

The man-at-arms came out of the bushes like a charging bear, arms up, legs apart, the sword coming around in a flat arc meant to disembowel Kassad. The OCS cadet tried to leap back and raise his mallet at the same time. Neither effort was completely successful. The Frenchman's sword knocked the heavy mallet out of Kassad's grip while the dull point of the blade slashed through leather, shirt, and skin.

Kassad bellowed and stumbled backward again, tugging at the knife in his belt. His right heel caught the branch of a fallen tree and he went down backward, cursing and rolling deeper into the tangle of branches as the man-at-arms crashed forward, his heavy sword clearing limbs like an oversized machete. Kassad had his knife out by the time the man-at-arms had cleared a path through the deadfall, but the ten-inch blade was a pitiful thing against armor unless the knight was helpless. This knight was not helpless. Kassad knew that he would never get inside the arc of sword blade. His only hope was in running, but the tall trunk of the fallen tree behind him and the deadfall beyond eliminated that option. He did not wish to get cut down from behind as he turned. Nor from below as he climbed. Kassad did not wish to be cut down from any angle.

Kassad went into a knife fighter's crouch which he hadn't used since his street-fighting days in the Tharsis slums. He wondered how the simulation would deal with his death.

The figure appeared behind the man-at-arms like a sudden shadow. The noise of Kassad's mallet striking the knight's armored shoulder sounded precisely like someone bashing the hood of an EMV with a sledgehammer.

The Frenchman staggered, turned to meet the new threat, and took a second mallet below in the chest. Kassad's savior was small; the man-at-arms did not go down. The French knight was raising his sword above his head when Kassad hit him behind and below the knees with a shoulder tackle.

Tree limbs snapped as the Frenchman went down. The small attacker stood astride the knight, pinning the armored man's sword arm with one foot while bringing the mallet down repeatedly onto helmet and visor. Kassad extricated himself from the tangle of legs and branches, sat on the downed man's knees, and began slashing through gaps in armor at groin, sides, and underarms. Kassad's rescuer jumped aside to plant both feet on the knight's wrist and Kassad scrambled forward, stabbing through crevices where the helmet met chest armor, finally slamming the blade through slits in the visor itself.

The knight screamed as the mallet came down a final time, almost catching Kassad's hand as the hammer drove the blade through the visor slit like a ten-inch tent peg. The man-at-arms arched, lifting Kassad and sixty pounds of armor clear of the ground in a final violent spasm and then fell back limply.

Kassad rolled onto his side. His rescuer collapsed beside him. Both were covered with sweat and the dead man's blood. Kassad looked at his savior. The woman was dressed in clothes not dissimilar to Kassad's. For a moment they merely lay there and gasped for air.

'Are you . . . all right?'Kassad managed after a while. He was suddenly struck by her appearance. Her brown hair was short by current Worldweb fashion, short and straight and cut so that the longest strands fell from the part, just a few centimeters left of the center of her forehead, to just above her right ear. It was a boy's haircut from some forgotten time, but she was no boy. Kassad thought that she was perhaps the most beautiful woman he had ever seen: bone structure so perfect that chin and cheekbones were shaped without being too sharp, large eyes glowing with life and intelligence, a gentle mouth with a soft underlip. Lying next to her, Kassad realized that she was tall – not so tall as he but obviously not a woman from the fifteenth century – and even under her loose tunic and baggy trousers he could see the soft swell of hips and breast. She appeared to be a few years older than Kassad, perhaps in her late twenties, but this fact barely registered as she continued staring into his face with those soft, beguiling, endlessly deep eyes.

'Are you all right?' he asked again. His voice sounded strange, even to himself.

She did not answer. Or, rather, she answered by sliding long fingers across Kassad's chest, ripping away the leather thongs which bound the rough vest. Her hands found his shirt. It was soaked with blood and ripped halfway down the front. The woman ripped it open the rest of the way. She moved against him now, her fingers and lips on his chest, hips already beginning to move. Her right hand found the cords to his trouser front, ripped them free.

Kassad helped her pull off the rest of his clothes, removed hers with three fluid movements. She wore nothing under her shirt and coarse-cloth trousers. Kassad's hand slid between her thighs, behind her, cupped her moving buttocks, pulled her closer, and slid to the moist roughness in front. She opened to him, her mouth closing on his. Somehow, with all of their motion and disrobing, their skin never lost contact. Kassad felt his own excitement rubbing against the cusp of her belly.

She rolled above him then, her thighs astride his hips, her gaze still locked with his. Kassad had never been so excited. He gasped as her right hand went behind her, found him, guided him into her. When he opened his eyes again she was moving slowly, her head back, eyes closed. Kassad's hands moved up her sides to cup her perfect breasts. Nipples hardened against his palms.

They made love then. Kassad, at twenty-three standard years, had been in love once and had enjoyed sex many times. He thought he knew the way and the why of it. There was nothing in his experience to that moment which he could not have described with a phrase and a laugh to his squadmates in the hold of a troop transport. With the calm, sure cynicism of a twenty-three-year-old veteran he was sure that he would *never* experience anything that could not be so described, so dismissed. He was wrong. He could never adequately share the sense of the next few minutes with anyone else. He would never try.

They made love in a sudden shaft of late October light with a carpet of leaves and clothes beneath them and a film of blood and sweat oiling the sweet friction between them. Her green eyes stared down at Kassad, widening slightly when he began moving quickly, closing at the same second he closed his.

They moved together then in the sudden tide of sensation as old and inevitable as the movement of worlds: pulses racing, flesh quickening with its own moist purposes, a further, final rising together, the world receding to nothing at all – and then, still joined by touch and heartbeat and the fading thrill of passion, allowing consciousness to slide back to separate flesh while the world flowed in through forgotten senses.

They lay next to each other. The dead man's armor was cold against Kassad's left arm, her thigh warm against his right leg. The sunlight was a benediction. Hidden colors rose to the surface of things. Kassad turned his head and gazed at her as she rested her head on his shoulder. Her cheeks glowed with flush and autumn light and her hair lay like copper threads along the flesh of his arm. She curved her leg over his thigh and Kassad felt the clockwise stirring of renewed passion. The sun was warm on his face. He closed his eyes.

When he awoke she was gone. He was certain that only seconds had passed – no more than a minute, certainly – but the sunlight was gone, colors had flowed out of the forest, and a cool evening breeze moved bare branches.

Kassad dressed in torn clothes made stiff with blood. The French man-at-arms lay still and rigid in the unselfconscious attitude of death. He already seemed inanimate, a part of the forest. There was no sign whatsoever of the woman.

Fedmahn Kassad limped his way back through the woods, evening gloom, and a sudden, chilling drizzle.

The battlefield still held people, living and dead. The dead lay in heaps like the piles of toy soldiers Kassad had played with as a child. Wounded men moved slowly with the help of friends. Here and there furtive forms picked their way among the dead, and near the opposite treeline a lively group of heralds, both French and English, met in conclave with much pointing and animated conversation. Kassad knew that they had to decide upon a name for the battle so that their respective records would agree. He also knew that they would settle on the name of the nearest castle, Agincourt, even though it had figured in neither strategy nor battle.

Kassad was beginning to think that this was no simulation, that his life in the Worldweb was the dream and that this gray day had to be reality, when suddenly the entire scene froze with outlines of human figures, horses, and the darkening forest becoming as transparent as a fading holo. And then Kassad was being helped out of his simulation creche at the Olympus Command School and the other cadets and instructors were rising, talking, laughing with one another – all seemingly unaware that the world had changed forever.

For weeks Kassad spent every free hour wandering the Command School grounds, watching from the ramparts as the evening shadow of Mons Olympus covered first the Plateau forest, then the heavily settled highlands, then everything halfway to the horizon, and then all the world. And every second he thought about what had happened. He thought about her.

No one else had noticed anything strange in the simulation. No one else had left the battlefield. One instructor explained that nothing beyond the battlefield *existed* in that particular segment of the simulation. No one had missed Kassad. It was as if the incident in the forest – and the woman – had never happened.

Kassad knew better. He attended his classes on military history and mathematics. He put in his hours at the firing range and gym. He walked off barracks punishments on the Caldera Quadrangle, although these were rare. In general, young Kassad became an even more excellent officer cadet than he had been. But all the while he waited.

And then she came again.

Again it was in the final hours of an OCS:HTN simulation. By then Kassad had learned that the exercises were something more than mere simulations. The OCS:HTN was part of the Worldweb All Thing, the real-time network which governed Hegemony politics, fed information to tens of billions of data-hungry citizens, and had evolved a form of autonomy and consciousness all its own. More than a hundred and fifty planetary dataspheres mingled their resources within the framework created by six thousand omega-class AIs to allow the OCS:HTN to function.

'The HTN stuff doesn't simulate,' whined Cadet Radinski, the best AI expert Kassad could find and bribe to explain, 'it *dreams*, dreams with the best historical accuracy in the Web – way beyond the sum of its parts 'cause it plugs in holistic insight as well as facts – and when it dreams, it lets us dream with it.'

Kassad had not understood but he had believed. And then she came again.

In the First US–Vietnam War they made love in the aftermath of an ambush during the darkness and terror of a night patrol. Kassad wore rough camouflage clothes – with no underwear because of the jungle crotch rot – and a steel helmet not much more advanced than those at Agincourt. She wore black pajamas and sandals, the universal garb of the Southeast Asian peasant. And the Viet Cong. Then neither of them wore anything as they made love standing in the night, her back against a tree and her legs wrapped around him, while beyond them the world exploded in the green glow of perimeter flares and the sputter-crack of claymores.

She came to him on the second day of Gettysburg and again at Borodino, where the clouds of powder smoke hung above the piles of bodies like a vapor congealed from departing souls.

They made love in the shattered hulk of an APC in Hellas Basin while the hovertank battle still raged and the red dust of the approaching simoon scraped and shrieked at the titanium hull. 'Tell me your name,' he had whispered in Standard. She shook her head. 'Are you real – outside the simulation?' he asked in the Japanese-English of that era. She had nodded and leaned closer to kiss him.

They lay together in a sheltered place among the ruins of Brasilia while deathbeams from Chinese EMVs played like blue searchlights on broken ceramic walls. During an unnamed battle after a siege of a forgotten tower city on the Russian steppes, he pulled her back into the shattered room where they had made love, and he whispered, 'I want to stay with you.' She touched his lips with a finger and shook her head. After the evacuation of

New Chicago, as they lay on the hundredth-floor balcony where Kassad had set his sniper's nest for the last US President's hopeless rearguard action, he placed his hand on the warm flesh between her breasts and said, 'Can you ever join me . . . out there?' She touched his cheek with her palm and smiled.

During the last year in Command School there were only five OCS:HTN sims as the cadets' training shifted to live field exercises. Sometimes, as when Kassad was strapped into the tactical command chair during a battalion-sized drop onto Ceres, he closed his eyes, looked between the primary-colored geographies of the cortically generated tactical/terrain matrix, and felt a sense of . . . someone? Of her? He was not sure.

And then she did not come again. Not in the final months of work. Not in the final simulation of the great Coal Sack Battle where General Horace Glennon-Height's mutiny was defeated. Not during the parades and parties of graduation, nor as the class marched in a final Olympian review before the Hegemony CEO, saluting from his red-lit levitation deck.

And there was no time even for dreaming as the young officers farcast to Earth's Moon for the Masada Ceremony, farcast again to Tau Ceti Center for their formal swearing-in to FORCE, and then they were finished.

Second Lieutenant Cadet Kassad became Lieutenant Kassad, spent three standard weeks free in the Web with a FORCE-issued universal card which allow him to farcast as far and as frequently as he wished, and then he was shipped out to the Hegemony Colonial Service training school on Lusus to prepare for active duty beyond the Web. He was sure that he would never see her again.

He was wrong.

Fedmahn Kassad had grown up in a culture of poverty and sudden death. As a member of the minority who still called themselves Palestinians, he and his family had lived in the slums of Tharsis, human testimony to the bitter legacy of the terminally dispossessed. Every Palestinian in the World-web and beyond carried the cultural memory of a century of struggle capped by a month of nationalist triumph before the Nuclear Jihad of 2038 wiped it all away. Then came their second Diaspora, this one lasting five centuries and leading to dead-end desert worlds like Mars, their dream buried with the death of Old Earth.

Kassad, like the other boys of the South Tharsis Relocation Camps, either ran with gangs or faced the option of being prey to every self-proclaimed predator in the camps. He chose to run with the gangs. Kassad had killed another youth by the time he was sixteen standard years old.

If Mars was known for anything in the Worldweb, it was for hunting in the Mariner Valley, Schrauder's Zen Massif in Hellas Basin, and the Olympus Command School. Kassad did not have to travel to Mariner Valley to learn about hunting and being hunted, he had no interest in Zen Gnosticism, and as a teenager he felt nothing but contempt for the uniformed cadets who came from every part of the Web to train for FORCE. He joined with his peers in sneering at the New Bushido as a code for faggots, but an ancient vein of honor in the young Kassad's soul secretly resonated to the thought of a samurai class whose life and work revolved around duty, self-respect, and the ultimate value of one's word.

When Kassad was eighteen, a Tharsis Province higher circuit judge offered him the choice of a Martian year at polar work camp or volunteering for the John Carter Brigade then forming to help FORCE put down the resurgent Glennon-Height Rebellion in the Class Three colonies. Kassad volunteered and discovered that he enjoyed the discipline and cleanliness of military life, even though the John Carter Brigade saw only garrison duty within the Web and was dissolved shortly after Glennon-Height's cloned grandson died on Renaissance. Two days after his nineteenth birthday, Kassad applied to FORCE:ground and was turned down. He went on a nine-day drunk, awoke in one of the deeper hive tunnels of Lusus with his military comlog implant stolen – by someone who apparently had taken a correspondence course in surgery – his universal card and farcaster access revoked, and his head exploring new frontiers of pain.

Kassad worked on Lusus for a standard year, saving over six thousand marks and allowing physical labor in the 1.3-ES gravity to put an end to his Martian frailness. By the time he used his savings to ship out to Maui-Covenant on an ancient solar sail freighter with jury-rigged Hawking drives, Kassad was still lean and tall by Web standards, but what muscles there were worked wonderfully well by anyone's standards.

He arrived on Maui-Covenant three days before the vicious and unpopular Island War began there, and eventually the FORCE combined commander at Firstsite got so tired of seeing the young Kassad waiting in his outer office that he allowed the boy to enlist in the 23rd Supply Regiment as an assistant hydrofoil driver. Eleven standard months later, Corporal Fedmahn Kassad of the Twelfth Mobile Infantry Battalion had received two Distinguished Service Clusters, a Senate Commendation for valor in the Equatorial Archipelago campaign, and two Purple Hearts. He was also tapped for FORCE command school and shipped Webward on the next convoy.

Kassad dreamed of her often. He had never learned her name, she had never spoken, but he could have recognized her touch and scent in total darkness among a thousand others. He thought of her as Mystery.

When other young officers went whoring or seeking girlfriends in the indigenie populations, Kassad would remain on base or take long walks through strange cities. He kept his obsession with Mystery secret, knowing full well how it would read on a psych report. Sometimes, on bivouac under multiple moons or in the womblike zero-g of a troop transport hold, Kassad would realize how insane his love affair with a phantom truly was. But then he would recall the small mole under her left breast which he had kissed one night, feeling her heartbeat under his lips as the ground itself shook from the firing of the big guns near Verdun. He would remember the impatient gesture with which she brushed back her hair as her cheek rested on his thigh. And the young officers would go to town or to the huts near the base, and Fedmahn Kassad would read another history book or jog along the perimeter or run tactical strategies on his comlog.

It was not long before Kassad came to the attention of his superiors.

During the undeclared war with the Free Miners in the Lambert Ring Territories, it was Lieutenant Kassad who led the surviving infantry troops and Marine guards in cutting through the bottom of the old asteroid bore shaft on Peregrine to evacuate the Hegemony consulate staff and citizens.

But it was during the short reign of the New Prophet on Qom-Riyadh that Captain Fedmahn Kassad came to the attention of the entire Web.

The FORCE:space captain of the only Hegemony ship within two leap years of the colony world had been paying a courtesy call when the New Prophet chose to lead thirty million New Order Shi'ites against two continents of Sunni shopkeepers and ninety thousand resident Hegemony infidels. The ship's captain and five of his executive officers were taken prisoner. Urgent fatline messages from Tau Ceti Center demanded that the ranking officer aboard the orbiting HS *Denieve* settle the situation on Qom-Riyadh, free all hostages, and depose the New Prophet . . . without resorting to the use of nuclear weapons within the planet's atmosphere. The *Denieve* was an aging orbital defense picket. It carried no nuclear weapons that could be used within an atmosphere. The ranking officer on board was FORCE:combined Captain Fedmahn Kassad.

On the third day of the revolution, Kassad landed the *Denieve*'s single assault boat in the main courtyard of the Grand Mosque at Mashhad. He and the other thirty-four FORCE troopers watched as the mob grew to three hundred thousand militants kept at bay only by the boat's containment field and the lack of an order to attack by the New Prophet. The New Prophet himself was no longer in the Grand Mosque; he had flown to the northern hemisphere of Riyadh to join in the victory celebrations there.

Two hours after he landed, Captain Kassad stepped out of his ship and broadcast a short announcement. He said that he had been raised as a Muslim. He also announced that interpretation of the Koran since the Shi'ites' seedship days had definitely shown that the God of Islam would neither condone nor allow the slaughter of the innocent, no matter how many jihads were proclaimed by tinhorn heretics like the New Prophet. Captain Kassad gave the leaders of the thirty million zealots three hours to surrender their hostages and return to their homes on the desert continent of Qom.

In the first three days of the revolution the armies of the New Prophet had occupied most of the cities on two continents and had taken more than twenty-seven thousand Hegemony hostages. Firing squads had been busy day and night settling ancient theological disputes and it was estimated that at least a quarter of a million Sunnis had been slaughtered in the first two days of the New Prophet's occupation. In response To Kassad's ultimatum, the New Prophet announced that all of the infidels would be put to death immediately following his live television address that evening. He also ordered an attack on Kassad's assault boat.

Avoiding high explosives because of the Grand Mosque, the Revolutionary Guard used automatic weapons, crude energy cannon, plasma charges, and human wave attacks. The containment field held.

The New Prophet's televised address began fifteen minutes before Kassad's ultimatum ran out. The New Prophet agreed with Kassad's statement that Allah would horribly punish heretics but announced that it was the Hegemony infidels who would be so punished. It was the only time the New Prophet ever had been seen to lose his temper on camera. Screaming, saliva flying, he ordered the human wave attacks to be renewed on the grounded assault boat. He announced that at that moment a dozen fission bombs were being assembled at the occupied Power for Peace reactor in Ali. With these, the forces of Allah would be carried into space itself. The first fission bomb, he explained, would be used on the infidel Kassad's satanic assault boat that very afternoon. The New Prophet then began to explain exactly how the Hegemony hostages would be executed, but at that moment Kassad's deadline ran out.

Qom-Riyadh was, by its own choice and the accident of its distant location, a technically primitive world. But the inhabitants were not so primitive that they did not have an active datasphere. Nor were the revolutionary mullahs who had led the invasion so opposed to the 'Great Satan of Hegemony Science' that they refused to tie into the global data net with their personal comlogs.

The HS *Denieve* had seeded enough spysats so that by 1729 hours Qom-Riyadh Central Time, the datasphere had been tapped to the point that the Hegemony ship had identified sixteen thousand eight hundred and thirty revolutionary mullahs by their access codes. At 1729:30 hours the spysats began feeding their real-time targeting data to the twenty-one perimeter defense sats which Kassad's assault boat had left in low orbit. These orbital defense weapons were so old that the *Denieve*'s mission had been to return them to the Web for safe destruction. Kassad had suggested another use for them.

At precisely 1730 hours, nineteen of the small satellites detonated their fusion cores. In the nanoseconds before their self-destruction, the resulting X-rays were focused, aimed, and released in sixteen thousand eight hundred and thirty invisible but very coherent beams. The ancient defense sats were not designed for atmospheric use and had an effective destructive radius of less than a millimeter. Luckily, that was all that was needed. Not all of the targeting beams penetrated whatever stood between the mullahs and the sky. Fifteen thousand seven hundred and eighty-four did.

The effect was immediate and dramatic. In each case the target's brain and cerebral fluid boiled, turned to vapor, and blew the encasing skull to bits. The New Prophet was in the middle of his live, planetwide broadcast –

literally in the middle of pronouncing the word 'heretic' – when 1730 hours arrived.

For almost two minutes the TV screens and walls around the planet carried the image of the New Prophet's headless body slumped over the microphone. Then Fedmahn Kassad cut in on all bands to announce that his next deadline was one hour away and that any actions against the hostages would be. met with a more dramatic demonstration of Allah's displeasure.

There were no reprisals.

That night, in orbit around Qom-Riyadh, Mystery visited Kassad for the first time since his cadet days. He was asleep but the visit was more than a dream and less than the alternative reality of the OCS:HTN sims. The woman and he were lying together under a light blanket beneath a broken roof. Her skin was warm and electric, her face little more than a pale outline against nighttime darkness. Overhead the stars had just begun to fade into the false light of predawn. Kassad realized that she was trying to speak to him; her soft lips formed words which were just below the threshold of Kassad's hearing. He pulled back a second in order to see her face better and, in so doing, lost contact completely. He awoke in his sleep webbing with moisture on his cheeks and the hum of the ship's systems sounding as strange to him as the breathing of some half-awakened beast.

Nine standard ship weeks later, Kassad stood before a FORCE court-martial review on Freeholm. He had known when he made his decision on Qom-Riyadh that his superiors would have no choice but to crucify or promote him.

FORCE prided itself on preparing itself for all contingencies in the Web or the colonial regions, but nothing had properly prepared it for the Battle of South Bressia and its implications for the New Bushido.

The New Bushido Code which governed Colonel Kassad's life had evolved out of the necessity for the military class to survive. After the obscenities of the late twentieth and early twenty-first centuries on Old Earth, when military leaders had committed their nations to strategies wherein entire civilian populations were legitimate targets while their uniformed executioners sat safe in self-contained bunkers fifty meters under the earth, the repugnance of the surviving civilians was so great that for more than a century the word 'military' was an invitation to a lynching.

As the New Bushido evolved it combined the age-old concepts of honor and individual courage with the need to spare civilians whenever possible. It also saw the wisdom of returning to the pre-Napoleonic concepts of small, 'nontotal' wars with defined goals and proscribed excesses. The Code demanded a forsaking of nuclear weapons and strategic bombing campaigns in all but the most extreme cases but, more than that, it demanded a return to Old Earth medieval concepts of set battles between small, professional forces at a mutually agreed-upon time in a place where destruction of public and private property would be kept to a minimum.

This Code worked well for the first four centuries of post-Hegira expansion. The fact that essential technologies were essentially frozen in place for three of those centuries worked in the Hegemony's favor as its monopoly on the use of farcasters allowed it to apply the modest resources of FORCE at the right place in the required amount of time. Even when separated by the inevitable leap years of time-debt, no colonial or independent world could hope to match the power of the Hegemony. Incidents such as the political rebellion on Maui-Covenant, with its unique guerrilla warfare, or the religious insanity on Qom-Riyadh were put down quickly and firmly and any excesses in the campaigns merely pointed out the importance of returning to the strict Code of the New Bushido. But for all of FORCE's calculations and preparations, no one had adequately planned on the inevitable confrontation with the Ousters.

The Ousters had been the single external threat to the Hegemony for the four centuries since the forebears of the barbarian hordes had left Sol System in their crude fleet of leaking O'Neill cities, tumbling asteroids, and experimental comet farm clusters. Even after the Ousters acquired the Hawking drive, it remained official Hegemony policy to ignore them as long as their swarms stayed in the darkness between the stars and limited their in-system plunderings to scooping small amounts of hydrogen from gas giants and water ice from uninhabited moons.

The early Outback skirmishes such as Bent's World and GHC 2990 were considered aberrations, of little interest to the Hegemony. Even the pitched battle for Lee Three had been treated as a Colonial Service problem and when the FORCE task force arrived six local years after the attack, five years after the Ousters departed, any atrocities were conveniently forgotten in favor of the view that no barbarian raid would repeat itself when the Hegemony chose to flex its muscle.

In the decades which followed Lee Three, FORCE and Ouster space forces skirmished in a hundred border areas, but except for the odd Marine encounters in airless, weightless places, there were no infantry confrontations. Stories in the Worldweb proliferated: the Ousters would never be a threat to Earthlike worlds because of their three centuries of adaptation to weightlessness; the Ousters had evolved into something more – or less – than human; the Ousters did not have farcaster technology, would never have it, and thus never would be a threat to FORCE. Then came Bressia.

Bressia was one of those smug, independent worlds, pleased with both its convenient access to the Web and its eight-month separation from it, growing rich from the export of diamonds, burr root, and its unequaled coffee, coyly refusing to become a colony world but still dependent upon the Hegemony Protectorate and Common Market to meet its soaring economic goals. As with most such worlds, Bressia was proud of its Self-defense Force: twelve torchships, a refitted attack carrier which had been decommissioned by FORCE:space half a century earlier, twoscore or more of small, fast orbital patrol vessels, a standing army of ninety thousand volunteers, a respectable oceangoing navy, and a store of nuclear weapons stockpiled purely for symbolic purposes.

The Ouster Hawking wake had been noticed by Hegemony monitoring stations but was misinterpreted as merely another swarm migration which would pass no closer than half a light-year to the Bressian system. Instead, with a single course correction which was not detected until the swarm was within the Oört cloud radius, the Ousters fell on Bressia like some Old Testament plague. A minimum of seven standard months separated Bressia from any Hegemony rescue or response.

Bressia's space force was obliterated within the first twenty hours of fighting. The Ouster swarm then put more than three thousand ships into Bressia's cislunar space and began the systematic reduction of all planetary defenses.

The world had been settled by no-nonsense Central Europeans in the first wave of the Hegira, and its two continents bore the prosaic names of North Bressia and South Bressia. North Bressia held desert, high tundra, and six major cities housing mostly burr-root harvesters and petroleum engineers. South Bressia, much more temperate in climate and geography, was the home for most of the world's four hundred million people and the huge coffee plantations.

As if to demonstrate what war had once been about, the Ousters scoured North Bressia – first with several hundred fallout-free nuclear weapons and tactical plasma bombs, then with deathbeams, and finally with tailored viruses. Only a handful of the fourteen million residents escaped. South Bressia received no bombardment except for the lancing of specific military targets, airports, and the large harbor at Solno.

FORCE doctrine held that, while a world could be reduced from orbit, actual military invasion of an industrialized planet was an impossibility; the problems with landing logistics, the immense area to be occupied, and the unwieldy size of the invading army were considered to be the ultimate arguments against invasion.

The Ousters obviously had not read the FORCE doctrine books. On the twenty-third day of the investiture, more than two thousand dropships and assault boats fell on South Bressia. What was left of the Bressian air force was destroyed in those first hours of the invasion. Two nuclear devices were actually detonated against Ouster staging areas: the first was deflected by energy fields and the second destroyed a single scoutship which may have been a decoy.

Ousters, it turned out, *had* changed physically in three centuries. They *did* prefer zero-gravity environments. But their mobile infantry's powered exoskeletons served very well and it was only a matter of days before the black-clad, long-limbed Ouster troops were swarming over South Bressia's cities like an infestation of giant spiders.

The last organized resistance collapsed on the nineteenth day of the invasion. Buckminster, the capital, fell the same day. The last fatline message from Bressia to the Hegemony was cut off in mid-transmission an hour after Ouster troops entered the city.

Colonel Fedmahn Kassad arrived with FORCE Fleet One twenty-nine standard weeks later. Thirty omega-class torchships protecting a single, farcaster-equipped JumpShip penetrated the system at high speed. The singularity sphere was activated three hours after spin-down and ten hours after that there were four hundred FORCE ships of the line in system. The counterinvasion began twenty-one hours later.

Those were the mathematics of the first minutes of the Battle of Bressia. For Kassad, the memory of those days and weeks held not mathematics but the terrible beauty of combat. It was the first time JumpShips had been used on anything above a division level and there was the expected confusion. Kassad went through from five light-minutes out and fell into gravel and yellow dust because the assault boat farcaster portal was facing down a steep incline made slick with mud and the blood of the first squads through. Kassad lay in the mud and looked down the hillside at madness. Ten of the seventeen farcaster assault boats were down and burning, scattered across the foothills and plantation fields like broken toys. The containment fields of the surviving boats were shrinking under an onslaught of missile and CPB fire that turned the landing areas into domes of orange flame. Kassad's tactical display was a hopeless mess; his visor showed a garble of impossible fire vectors, blinking red phosphors where FORCE troops lay dying, and overlays of Ouster jamming ghosts. Someone was screaming 'Oh, goddammit! Goddammit! Oh, goddammit!' on his primary command circuit and the implants registered a void where Command Group's data should be.

An enlisted man helped him up, Kassad flicked mud off his command wand and got out of the way of the next squad farcasting through, and the war was on.

From his first minutes on South Bressia, Kassad realized that the New Bushido was dead. Eighty thousand superbly armed and trained FORCE: ground troops advanced from their staging areas, seeking battle in an unpopulated place. Ouster forces retreated behind a line of scorched earth, leaving only booby traps and dead civilians. FORCE used farcasters to outmaneuver the enemy, to force him to fight. The Ousters responded with a barrage of nuclear and plasma weapons, pinning the ground troops under forcefields while the Ouster infantry retreated to prepared defenses around cities and dropship staging areas.

There were no quick victories in space to shift the balance on South Bressia. Despite feints and occasional fierce battles, the Ousters retained complete control of everything within three AU of Bressia. FORCE:space units fell back and concentrated on keeping the fleet within farcaster range and protecting the primary JumpShip.

What had been forecast as a two-day battle ground on for thirty days, then sixty. Warfare had been thrown back to the twentieth or twenty-first century: long, grim campaigns fought through the brick dust of ruined cities over the corpses of civilians. The eighty thousand original FORCE troops were ground up, reinforced with a hundred thousand more, and were still being decimated when the call went out for two hundred thousand more. Only the grim resolve of Meina Gladstone and a dozen other determined senators kept the war alive and the troops dying while the billions of voices of the All Thing and the AI Advisory Council called for disengagement.

Kassad had understood the change of tactics almost at once. His street-fighting instincts had risen to the forefront even before most of his division was wiped out in the Battle of the Stoneheap. While other FORCE commanders were all but ceasing to function, frozen into indecision by this violation of the New Bushido, Kassad – in command of his regiment and in temporary command of his division after the nuking of Command Group Delta – was trading men for time and calling for the release of fusion weapons to spearhead his own counterattack. By the time the Ousters withdrew ninety-seven days after the FORCE 'rescue' of Bressia, Kassad had earned the double-edged nickname of the Butcher of South Bressia. It was rumored that even his own troops were afraid of him.

And Kassad dreamed of *her* with dreams that were more – and less – than dreams.

On the last night of the Battle for Stoneheap, in the maze of dark tunnels where Kassad and his hunter-killer groups used sonics and T-5 gas to flush out the last warrens of Ouster commandos, the Colonel fell asleep amid the flame and screams and felt the touch of her long fingers on his cheek and the soft compression of her breasts against him.

When they entered New Vienna on the morning after the space strike Kassad had called in, the troops following the glass-smooth, twenty-meter-wide burn grooves into the lanced city, Kassad had stared without blinking at the rows of human heads lying on the pavement, carefully lined up as if to welcome the rescuing FORCE troops with their accusatory stares. Kassad had returned to his command EMV, closed the hatches, and – curling up in the warm darkness smelling of rubber, heated plastics, charged ions – had heard *her* whispers over the babble of the C3 channels and implant coding.

On the night before the Ouster retreat, Kassad left the command conference on the HS *Brazil*, farcast to his HQ in the Indelibles north of the Hyne Valley, and took his command car to the summit to watch the final bombardment. The nearest of the tactical nuclear strikes was forty-five kilometers away. The plasma bombs blossomed like orange and blood-red flowers planted in a perfect grid. Kassad counted more than two hundred dancing columns of green light as the hellwhip lances ripped the broad plateau to shreds. And even before he slept, while he sat on the flareskirt of the EMV and shook pale afterimages from his eyes, she came. She wore a pale blue dress and walked lightly between the dead burr-root plants on the hillside. The breeze lifted the hem of the soft fabric of her dress. Her face and arms were pale, almost translucent. She called his name – he could almost hear the words – and then the second wave of bombardment rolled in across the plain below him and everything was lost in noise and flame.

As tends to be the case in a universe apparently ruled by irony, Fedmahn Kassad passed unscathed through ninety-seven days of the worst fighting the Hegemony had ever seen, only to be wounded two days after the last of the Ousters had retreated to their fleeing swarmships. He was in the Civic Center Building in Buckminster, one of only three buildings left standing in the city, giving curt answers to stupid questions from a Worldweb newsteep when a plasma booby trap no larger than a microswitch exploded fifteen floors above, blew the newsteep and two of Kassad's aides through a ventilator grille into the street beyond, and dropped the building on him.

Kassad was medevacked to division HQ and then farcast to the JumpShip now in orbit around Bressia's second moon. There he was resuscitated and put on full life support while the military brass and Hegemony politicians decided what to do with him.

Because of the farcaster connection and the real-time media coverage of Bressia, Colonel Fedmahn Kassad had become somewhat of a *cause célèbre*. Those billions who had been appalled by the unprecedented savagery of the South Bressia campaign would have been pleased to see Kassad court-martialed or tried for war crimes. CEO Gladstone and many others considered Kassad and the other FORCE commanders as saviors.

In the end, Kassad was put on a hospital spinship for the slow trip back to the Web. Since most of the physical repair would be done in fugue anyway, it made some sense to let the old hospital ships work on the seriously wounded and the revivable dead. By the time Kassad and the other patients reached the Worldweb, they would be ready for active duty. More importantly, Kassad would have accrued a time-debt of at least eighteen standard months and whatever controversy surrounded him might well be over by that time.

Kassad awoke to see the dark shape of a woman bending over him. For a second he was sure that it was *her*, and then he realized that it was a FORCE medic.

'Am I dead?' he whispered.

'You were. You're on the HS *Merrick*. You've been through resuscitation and renewal several times but you probably don't remember because of the fugue hangover. We're ready to start the next step in physical therapy. Do you feel like trying to walk?'

Kassad lifted his arm to cover his eyes. Even through the disorientation of fugue state, he now remembered the painful therapy sessions, the long hours in the RNA virus baths, and the surgery. Most of all the surgery. 'What's our route?' he asked, still shielding his eyes. 'I forget how we're getting back to the Web.'

The medic smiled as if this were a question he asked each time he came out of fugue. Perhaps it was. 'We'll be putting in at Hyperion and Garden,' she said. 'We're just entering the orbit of . . . '

The woman was interrupted by the sound of the end of the world – great brass trumpets blowing, metal ripping, furies screaming. Kassad rolled off the bed, wrapping the mattress around him as he fell in the one-sixth g. Hurricane winds slid him across the deck and hurled pitchers, trays, bed-clothes, books, bodies, metal instruments, and countless other objects at him. Men and women were screaming, their voices rising through falsetto as the air rushed out of the ward. Kassad felt the mattress slam into the wall; he looked out between clenched fists.

A meter from him, a football-sized spider with wildly waving legs was trying to force itself into a crack which had suddenly appeared in the bulkhead. The thing's jointless legs seemed to be swatting at the paper and other detritus whirling around it. The spider rotated and Kassad realized that it was the head of the medic; she had been decapitated in the initial explosion. Her long hair writhed at Kassad's face. Then the crack widened to the width of a fist and the head disappeared through it.

Kassad pulled himself up just as the boom arm quit spinning and 'up' ceased to be. The only forces now in play were the hurricane winds still flinging everything in the ward toward the cracks and gaps in the bulkhead and the sickening lurch and tumble of the ship. Kassad swam against it all, pulling himself toward the door to the boom-arm corridor, using every handhold he could find, kicking free the last five meters. A metal tray struck him above the eye; a corpse with hemorrhaged eyes almost tumbled him back into the ward. The airtight emergency doors were slamming uselessly into a dead Marine whose spacesuited body blocked the seal from closing. Kassad rolled through into the boom-arm shaft and pulled the corpse after him. The door sealed behind him, but there was no more air in the shaft than there had been in the ward. Somewhere a klaxon's scream thinned to inaudibility.

Kassad also screamed, trying to relieve the pressure so that his lungs and eardrums would not burst. The boom arm was still draining air; he and the corpse were being sucked the hundred and thirty meters to the main body of the ship. He and the dead Marine tumbled along the boom-arm shaft in a grisly waltz.

It took Kassad twenty seconds to slap open the emergency releases on the Marine's suit, another minute to eject the man's corpse and to get his own body in. He was at least ten centimeters taller than the dead man, and although the suit was built to allow some expansion, it still pinched pain-fully at his neck and wrists and knees. The helmet squeezed his forehead like a cushioned vise. Gobbets of blood and a moist white material clung to the inside of the visor. The piece of shrapnel which had killed the Marine had left entrance and exit holes, but the suit had done its best to seal itself. Most of the chest lights were red and the suit did not respond when Kassad ordered it to give a status report, but the rebreather worked, although with a worrying rasp.

Kassad tried the suit radio. Nothing, not even background static. He found the comlog lead, jacked into a hull termex. Nothing. The ship pitched again then, metal reverberating to a succession of blows, and Kassad was thrown against the wall of the boom-arm shaft. One of the transport cages tumbled by, its severed cables whipping like the tentacles of an agitated sea anemone. There were corpses in the cage and more bodies tangled along the segments of spiral staircase still intact along the shaft wall. Kassad kicked the remaining distance to the end of the shaft and found all of the airtight doors there sealed, the boom-arm shaft itself irised shut, but there were hoies in the primary bulkhead large enough to drive a commercial EMV through.

The ship lurched again and began to tumble more wildly, imparting complex new Coriolis forces to Kassad and everything else in the shaft. Kassad hung on torn metal and pulled himself through a rent in the triple hull of the HS *Merrick*.

He almost laughed when he saw the interior. Whoever had lanced the old hospital ship had done it right, chopping and stabbing the hull with CPBs until pressure seals failed, self-seal units ruptured, damage-control remotes overloaded, and the interior bulkheads collapsed. Then the enemy ship had put missiles into the guts of the hulk with warheads of what the FORCE:space people quaintly called canister shot. The effect had been quite similar to setting off an antipersonnel grenade in a crowded rat maze.

Lights shone through a thousand holes, here and there becoming colorful rays where they found a colloidal base in floating haze of dust or blood or lubricant. From where Kassad hung, twisting with the lurch and tumble of the ship, he could see a score or more of bodies, naked and torn, each moving with the deceptive underwater-ballet grace of the zero-gravity dead. Most of the corpses floated within their own small solar systems of blood and tissue. Several of them watched Kassad with the cartoon-character stares of their pressure-expanded eyes and seemed to beckon him closer with random, languid movements of arms and hands.

Kassad kicked through the wreckage to reach the main dropshaft to the command core. He had seen no weapons – it seemed that no one except the Marine had managed to suit up – but he knew that there would be a weapons locker in the command core or in the Marine quarters aft.

Kassad stopped at the last torn pressure seal and stared. He did laugh this time. Beyond this point there was no main dropshaft, no aft section. There was no ship. This section – a boom-arm and medical ward mod, a ragged chunk of the hull – had been ripped free of the ship as easily as Beowulf had torn the arm from Grendel's body. The final, unsealed doorway to the dropshaft led to open space. Some kilometers away, Kassad could see a dozen other ravaged fragments of the HS *Merrick* tumbling in the glare of sunlight. A green and lapis planet loomed so close that Kassad felt a surge of acrophobia and clung more tightly to the doorframe. Even as he watched, a star moved above the limb of the planet, laser weapons winked their ruby morse, and a gutted ship section half a kilometer away across the gulf of vacuum from Kassad burst again in a gout of vaporized metal, freezing volatiles, and tumbling black specks which Kassad realized were bodies.

Kassad pulled himself deeper into the concealing tangle of wreckage and considered his situation. The Marine's suit could not last more than another hour – already Kassad could smell the rotten-eggs stench of the malfunctioning rebreather – and he had seen no airtight compartment or container during his struggle through the wreckage. And even if he found a closet or air-lock to shelter in, what then? Kassad did not know if the planet below was Hyperion or Garden, but he was sure that there was no FORCE presence on either world. He was also quite sure that no local defense forces would challenge an Ouster warship. It would be days before any patrol craft investigated the wreckage. It was quite possible, Kassad knew, that the orbit of the tumbling piece of junk he now inhabited would decay before they sent anyone up to check on it, sending thousands of tons of twisted metal burning through the atmosphere. The locals would not like that, Kassad knew, but from their point of view it might be preferable to let a bit of sky fall than to antagonize the Ousters. If the planet had primitive orbital defenses or ground-based CPBs, he realized with a grim smile, it would make more sense for them to blast the wreckage than to fire on the Ouster ship.

It would make no difference to Kassad. Unless he did something quickly, he would be dead long before the remnants of the ship entered atmosphere or the locals took action.

The Marine's amplification shield had been cracked by the shrapnel which had killed him, but now Kassad tugged what was left of the view-plate down over the visor. Telltales winked red but there was still enough suit power to show the amplified view glowing pale green through the spiderweb of cracks. Kassad watched as the Ouster torchship stood off a hundred klicks, its defense fields blurring background stars, and launched several objects. For an instant Kassad was sure that these were the *coup de grâce* missiles and he found himself grinning joylessly at the certainty of having only a few seconds to live. Then he noticed their low velocity and notched the amplification higher. The power lights blinked red and the amplifier failed, but not before Kassad had seen the tapering ovoid shapes, spotted with thrusters and cockpit blisters, each trailing a tangle of six jointless manipulator arms. 'Squids,' the FORCE:space people had called the Ouster boarding craft.

Kassad pulled himself farther back in the wreckage. He had only a few minutes before one or more of the squids reached his piece of the ship. How many Ousters would one of those things carry? Ten? Twenty? Kassad was sure that it would be no fewer than ten. And they would be well armed and rigged with infrared and motion sensors. The elite Ouster equivalent of Hegemony Space Marines, the commandos would not only have been trained for free-fall combat but had been born and bred to zero-g. Their long limbs, prehensile toes, and prosthetic tails would be added advantages for this environment, although Kassad doubted that they needed any more advantages than they already had.

He began to pull himself carefully back through the labyrinth of twisted metal, fighting the adrenaline fear-surge that made him want to kick off screaming through the darkness. *What did they want?* Prisoners. That would solve his immediate survival problem. All he had to do to survive was surrender. The difficulty with that solution was that Kassad had seen the FORCE:intelligence holos of the Ouster ship they had captured off Bressia. There had been more than two hundred prisoners in the storage bay of that ship. And the Ousters obviously had many questions for these Hegemony citizens. Perhaps they had found it inconvenient to feed and imprison so many – or perhaps it was their basic interrogation policy – but the fact was that the Bressian civilians and captured FORCE troops had been found flayed open and pinned down on steel trays like frogs in a biology lab, their organs bathed with nutrient fluids, arms and legs efficiently amputated, eyes removed, and their minds readied for interrogators' questions with crude cortical comtaps and shunt-plugs jacked directly through three-centimeter holes in the skulls.

Kassad pulled himself along, floating through debris and the tangled entrails of the ship's wiring. He felt no inclination whatsoever to surrender. The tumbling hulk vibrated and then steadied some as at least one of the squids attached itself to the hull or bulkhead. *Think*, Kassad commanded. He needed a weapon more than a hiding place. Had he seen anything during his crawl through the wreckage that would help him survive?

Kassad stopped moving and hung from an exposed section of fiberoptic cable while he thought. The medical ward where he had awakened, beds, fugue tanks, intensive care apparatus . . . most of it expelled through the breaches in the spinmod's hull. Boom-arm shaft, elevator cage, corpses on the stairs. No weapons. Most of the bodies had been stripped by the canister shot explosions or sudden decompression. The elevator cables? No, too long, impossible to sever without tools. Tools? He had seen none. The medical offices flayed open along the corridors beyond the main dropshaft. Medical imaging rooms, MRI tanks, and CPD bays flung open like looted sarcophagi. At least one operating room intact, its interior a maze of scattered instruments and floating cables. The solarium, scraped clean when the windows exploded outward. Patient lounges. Medics' lounges. The scrub rooms, corridors, and unidentifiable cubicles. The corpses.

Kassad hung there a second longer, oriented himself in the tumbling maze of light and shadow, and then kicked off.

He had hoped for ten minutes; he was given less than eight. He knew that the Ousters would be methodical and efficient but had underestimated how efficient they could be in zero-g. He gambled his life that there would be at least two of them on each sweep – basic Space Marine procedure, much as FORCE:ground jump rats had learned to go door to door in city fighting, one to burst into each room, the other to provide cover fire. If there were more than two, if the Ousters worked in squads of four, Kassad almost certainly would be dead.

He was floating in the middle of Operating Room 3 when the Ouster came through the door. Kassad's rebreather had all but failed, he was floating immobile, gasping foul air, as the Ouster commando swung in, swung aside, and brought his two weapons to bear on the unarmed figure in a battered Marine spacesuit.

Kassad had bargained that the gruesome condition of his suit and visor would gain him a second or two. Behind his gore-smeared faceplate, Kassad's eyes stared sightlessly upward as the Ouster's chestlight swept across him. The commando carried two weapons – a sonic stunner in one hand and a smaller but much more lethal tightbeam pistol in the long toes of his left 'foot'. He raised the sonic. Kassad had time to notice the killing spike on the prosthetic tail and then he triggered the mouse in his gauntleted right hand.

It had taken Kassad most of his eight minutes to tie in the emergency generator to the operating-room circuits. Not all of the surgery lasers had survived, but six still worked. Kassad had positioned four of the smaller ones to cover the area just to the left of the doorway, the two bone-cutters to target the space to the right. The Ouster had moved to the right.

The Ouster's suit exploded. The lasers continued to slice away in their preprogrammed circles as Kassad propelled himself forward, ducking under the blue beams now swirling in a spreading mist of useless suit sealant and boiling blood. He wrested the sonic away just as the second Ouster swung into the room, agile as an Old Earth chimp.

Kassad pressed the sonic against the man's helmet and fired. The suited figure went limp. The prosthetic tail spasmed a few times from random nerve impulses. Triggering the sonic that close was no way to take a prisoner; a burst from that distance turned a human brain into something resembling oatmeal mush. Kassad did not want to take a prisoner.

He kicked free, grabbed a girder, swept the active sonic across the open doorway. No one else came through. A check twenty seconds later showed an empty corridor.

Kassad ignored the first body and stripped the man with the intact suit. The commando was naked under the spacesuit and it turned out not to be a man; the female commando had short-cropped blond hair, small breasts, and a tattoo just above her line of pubic hair. She was very pale and droplets of blood floated from her nose, ears, and eyes. Kassad made a note that the Ousters used women in their Marines. All of the Ouster bodies on Bressia had been male.

He kept his helmet and rebreather pack on as he kicked the body aside and tugged on the unfamiliar suit. Vacuum exploded blood vessels in his flesh. Deep cold nipped at him as he struggled with strange clasps and locks. Tall as he was, he was too short for the woman's suit. He could operate the hand gauntlets by stretching, but the foot gloves and tail connections were hopeless. He let them hang useless as he bailed out of his own helmet and wrestled the Ouster bubble into place.

Lights in the collar diskey glowed amber and violet. Kassad heard the rush of air through aching eardrums and almost gagged as a thick, rich stench assailed him. He assumed it was the sweet smell of home to an Ouster. Earphone patches in the bubble whispered coded commands in a language which sounded like an audio tape of Ancient English played backward at high speed. Kassad was gambling again, this time on the fact that Ouster ground units on Bressia had functioned as semi-independent teams united by voice radio and basic telemetry rather than a FORCE:-ground type of tactical implant web. If they used the same system here, then the commando leader might know that two of his (or her) troops were missing, possibly even have medcom readings on them, but might *not* know exactly where they were.

Kassad decided that it was time to quit hypothesizing and to get moving. He programmed the mouse to have the surgical lasers fire on anything entering the operating room, and then bounce-stumbled his way down the corridor. Moving in one of these damn suits, he thought, was like trying to walk in a gravity field while standing on your own trousers. He had brought along both energy pistols and – finding no belt, lockrings, hooks, Velcro pads, magclamps, or pockets to secure them with – now floated along like some drunken holodrama pirate, a weapon in each hand, bouncing from wall to wall. Reluctantly, he left one pistol floating behind him while he tried to hook himself along one-handed. The gauntlet fit like a size fifteen mitten on a size two hand. The damned tail wobbled, banged against his helmet bubble, and was a literal pain in the ass.

Twice he squeezed into crevices when he saw lights in the distance. He was just about to the deck opening where he had watched the squid approach when he rounded a corner and almost floated into three Ouster commandos.

The fact that he was wearing an Ouster suit gave him at least a two-second advantage. He shot the first suited figure in the helmet at point-blank range. The second man – or woman – fired a wild sonic burst past Kassad's left shoulder a second before he put three bolts into the Ouster's chestplate. The third commando flipped backward, found three handholds, and was out of sight around a broken bulkhead before Kassad could retarget. His headset rang with curses, commands, and questions. Kassad gave silent chase.

The third Ouster would have escaped if he had not rediscovered honor and turned to fight. Kassad felt an inexplicable sense of déjà vu as he put an energy bolt through the man's left eye from five meters away.

The corpse tumbled backward into sunlight. Kassad pulled himself to the opening and stared at the squid moored not twenty meters away. It was, he thought, the first undiluted piece of luck he had had in some time.

He kicked across the gap, knowing that if someone wanted to shoot him from the squid or the wreckage there was nothing he could do about it. He felt the scrotum-lifting tension he always experienced when he was an obvious target. No shots were fired. Commands and interrogatives squawked in his ears. He could not understand them, did not know where they originated, and, on the whole, thought it best if he stayed out of the dialogue.

The clumsiness of the suit almost caused him to miss the squid. He thought briefly that such an anticlimax would be the universe's fitting verdict on his martial pretensions: the brave warrior floating off into near-planet orbit, no maneuvering systems, no propellant, no reaction mass of any sort – even the pistol was non-recoil. He would end his life as useless and harmless as a child's runaway balloon.

Kassad stretched until his joints popped, caught a whip antenna, and pulled himself hand over hand to the squid's hull.

Where the hell was the airlock? The hull was relatively smooth for a spacefaring vessel but was decorated with a riot of designs, decals, and panels announcing what he assumed were the Ouster equivalents of NO STEP and DANGER: THRUSTER PORT. No entrances were visible. He guessed that there were Ousters on board, a pilot at least, and that they were probably wondering why their returning commando was crawling around the hull like a spavined crab rather than cycling the airlock. Or perhaps they knew why and were waiting inside with drawn pistols. At any rate, it was obvious that no one was going to open the door for him.

The hell with it, thought Kassad and shot out one of the observation blisters.

The Ousters kept a tidy ship. Not much more than the equivalent of a few lost paper clips and coins geysered out with the ship's air. Kassad waited until the eruption had died down and squeezed through the gap.

He was in the carrier section: a cushioned hold looking a lot like the jump rat bay of any dropship or APC. Kassad made a mental note that a squid probably held about twenty Ouster commandos in full vacuum combat gear. Now it was empty. An open hatch led to the cockpit.

Only the command pilot had remained on board and he was in the final process of unbelting when Kassad shot him. Kassad pushed the body into the carrier section and strapped himself into what he hoped was the command chair.

Warm sunlight came through the blister above him. Video monitors and console holos showed scenes from dead ahead, astern, and shoulder-camera glimpses of the search operation inside. Kassad caught a glimpse of the nude body in Operating Room 3 and several figures in a firefight with surgical lasers.

In the holodramas of Fedmahn Kassad's childhood, heroes always seemed to know how to operate skimmers, spacecraft, exotic EMVs, and other strange machinery whenever the need arose. Kassad had been trained to handle military transports, simple tanks and APCs, even an assault boat or dropship if he was desperate. If stranded on a runaway FORCE spacecraft, a remote possibility, he could find his way around the command core sufficiently to communicate with the primary computer or put out a distress call on a radio or fatline transmitter. Sitting in the command chair of an Ouster squid, Kassad did not have a clue.

That was not quite true. He immediately recognized the remote grip slots for the squid's tentacle manipulators, and given two or three hours of thought and inspection, he might have figured out several other controls. He did not have the time. The forward screen showed three spacesuited figures jumping for the squid, firing as they came. The pale, oddly alien head of an Ouster commander suddenly materialized on the holo console. Kassad heard shouts from his bubble earpatches.

Globules of sweat hung in front of his eyes and streaked the inside of his helmet. He shook them away as best he could, squinted at the control consoles, and pushed several likely-looking surfaces. If there were voice command circuits, override controls, or a suspicious ship's computer, Kassad knew, he was screwed. He had thought of all this in the second or two before he shot the pilot but had not been able to think of a way to coerce or trust the man. No, this had to be the way, thought Kassad even as he tapped more control surfaces.

A thruster began firing.

The squid pulled and tugged at its moorings. Kassad bounced back and forth in his webbing. 'Shit,' he whispered, his first audible comment since he had asked the FORCE medic where the ship was putting in. He strained far enough forward to get his gauntleted fingers into the grip slots. Four of the six manipulators released. One ripped off. The final one tore away a chunk of bulkhead from the HS *Merrick*.

The squid tumbled free. Video cameras showed two of the space-suited figures missing their jumps, the third clutching at the same whip antenna which had saved Kassad. Knowing roughly where the thruster controls were now, Kassad tapped in a frenzy. An overhead light came on. All of the holo projectors went dead. The squid commenced a maneuver which incorporated all of the most violent elements of pitch, roll, and yaw. Kassad saw the spacesuited form tumble past the overhead blister, appear briefly on the forward video screen, become a speck on the aft screen. The Ouster was still firing energy bolts as he – or she – became too small to see.

Kassad struggled to stay conscious as the violent tumbling continued. Various voice and visual alarms were screaming for his attention. Kassad tapped at thruster controls, considered it a success, and pulled his hands away when he felt as if he were being pulled apart in only two directions rather than five.

A random camera shot showed him that the torchship was receding. Good. Kassad had no doubt that the Ouster warship could destroy him at any second, and that it *would* if he approached or threatened it in any way. He did not know if the squid was armed, personally doubted if it would carry anything larger than antipersonnel weapons, but he knew beyond a doubt that no torchship commander would allow an out-of-control shuttlecraft to come anywhere near his ship. Kassad assumed that the Ousters all knew by now that the squid had been hijacked by the enemy. He would not be surprised – disappointed, but not surprised – if the torch-ship vaporized him at any second, but in the meantime he was counting on two emotions that were quintessentially human if not necessarily Ouster human: curiosity and the desire for revenge.

Curiosity, he knew, could easily be overridden in times of stress, but he counted on a paramilitary, semifeudal culture like the Ousters' to be deeply involved with revenge. Everything else being equal, with no chance to hurt them further and almost no chance to escape, it would seem that Colonel Fedmahn Kassad had become a prime candidate for one of their dissection trays. He hoped so.

Kassad looked at the forward video display, frowned, and loosened his harness long enough to look out the overhead blister. The ship was tumbling but not nearly so violently as before. The planet seemed closer – one hemisphere filled the view 'above' him – but he had no idea how close the squid was to atmosphere. He could read none of the data displays. He could only guess what their orbital velocity had been and how violent a reentry shock would be. His one long glimpse from the wreckage of the *Merrick* had suggested to Kassad that they were very close, perhaps only five or six hundred klicks above the surface, and in the kind of parking orbit which he knew preceded the launching of dropships.

Kassad tried to wipe his face and frowned when the tips of loose gauntlet fingers tapped at his visor. He was tired. Hell, only a few hours earlier he had been in fugue and just a few ship-weeks before *that* he had almost certainly been body-dead.

He wondered if the world below was Hyperion or Garden; he had been to neither but knew that Garden was more widely settled, closer to becoming a Hegemony colony. He hoped it was Garden.

The torchship launched three assault boats. Kassad saw them clearly before the aft camera panned beyond range. He tapped at the thruster controls until it felt as though the ship was tumbling more quickly toward the wall of planet above. There was little else he could do.

The squid reached atmosphere before the three Ouster assault boats reached the squid. The boats undoubtedly were armed and well within range, but someone on the command circuit must have been curious. Or furious.

Kassad's squid was in no way aerodynamic. As with most ship-to-ship craft, the squid could flirt with planetary atmospheres but was doomed if it dove too deeply into the gravity well. Kassad saw the telltale red glow of reentry, heard the ion buildup on the active radio channels, and suddenly wondered if this had been such a good idea.

Atmospheric drag stabilized the squid and Kassad felt the first tentative tug of gravity as he searched the console and the command chair arms for the control circuit he prayed would be there. A static-filled video screen showed one of the dropships growing a blue-plasma tail as it decelerated. The illusion created was similar to that encountered when one skydiver watched another open his chute or activate his suspension rig; the assault boat seemed to climb suddenly.

Kassad had other things to worry about. There seemed to be no obvious bail-out control, no ejection apparatus. Every FORCE:space shuttle carried some sort of atmospheric egress device – it was a custom dating back almost eight centuries to when the entire realm of space flight consisted only of tentative excursions just above the skin of Old Earth's atmosphere. A ship-to-ship shuttle probably would never need a planetary bail-out device, but age-old fears written into ancient regulations tended to die hard.

Or so the theory went. Kassad could find nothing. The ship was quaking now, spinning, and beginning to heat up in earnest. Kassad slapped open his harness release and pulled himself toward the rear of the squid, not even sure what he was looking for. Suspension packs? Parachutes? A set of wings?

There was nothing in the troop carrier section except the corpse of the Ouster pilot and a few storage compartments not much larger than lunchboxes. Kassad tore through them, finding nothing bigger than a medkit. No miracle devices.

Kassad could *hear* the squid shaking and beginning to break up as he hung on a pivot ring and all but accepted the fact that the Ousters had not wasted money or space on such low-probability rescue devices for their squids. Why should they? Their lifetimes were spent in the darknesses between star systems; their concept of an atmosphere was the eight-klick pressurized tube of a can city. The external audio sensors on Kassad's bubble helmet began to pick up the raging hiss of air on the hull and through the broken blister in the aft section. Kassad shrugged. He had gambled too many times and lost.

The squid shuddered and bounced. Kassad could hear the manipulator tentacles tearing away from the bow. The Ouster's corpse suddenly was sucked up and out of the broken blister like an ant into a vacuum cleaner. Kassad clung to the pivot ring and stared through the open hatch at the control seats in the cockpit. It struck him that they were wonderfully archaic, like something out of a textbook of the earliest spacecraft. Parts of the ship's exterior were burning away now, roaring past the observation blisters like gobbets of lava. Kassad closed his eyes and tried to remember lectures from Olympus Command School on the structure and layout of ancient spacegoing craft. The squid began a terminal tumble. The noise was incredible.

'By Allah!' gasped Kassad, a cry he had not uttered since childhood. He began pulling himself forward into the cockpit, bracing himself on the open hatch, finding handholds on the deck as if he were climbing a vertical wall. He *was* climbing a wall. The squid had spun, stabilized in a stern-first death dive. Kassad climbed under a 3-g load, knowing that a single slip would break every bone in his body. Behind him, atmospheric hiss turned to a scream and then to a dragon roar. The troop carrier section was burning through in fierce, molten explosions.

Climbing into the command seat was like negotiating a rock overhang with the weight of two other climbers swinging from his back. The clumsy gauntlets made his grip on the headrest even less sure as Kassad hung over the vertical drop to the flaming cauldron of the carrier section. The ship lurched, Kassad swung his legs up, and he was in the command seat. The display videos were dead. Flame heated the overhead blister to a sick red. Kassad almost lost consciousness as he bent forward, his fingers feeling in the darkness below the command seat, between his knees. There was nothing. Wait . . . a hand-grip. No, sweet Christ and Allah . . . a D-ring. Something out of the history books.

The squid began to break up. Overhead, the blister burned through and spattered liquid Perspex throughout the interior of the cockpit, splashing Kassad's suit and visor. He smelled plastic melting. The squid was spinning as it broke up. Kassad's sight turned pink, dimmed, was gone. He used numb fingers to tighten the harness . . . tighter . . . either it was cutting into his chest or the Perspex had burned through. His hand went back to the D-ring. Fingers too clumsy to close around it . . . no. *Pull.*

Too late. The squid flew apart in a final screech and explosion of flame, the control console tearing through the cockpit in ten thousand shrapnel-sized bits.

Kassad was slammed into his seat. Up. Out. Into the heart of the flame.

Tumbling.

Kassad was dimly aware that the seat was projecting its own containment field as it tumbled. Flame was centimeters from his face.

Pyrobolts fired, kicking the ejection seat out of the squid's blazing slipstream. The command seat made its own track of blue flame across the sky. Microprocessors spun the seat so that the disc of the forcefield was between Kassad and the furnace of friction. A giant sat on Kassad's chest as he decelerated across two thousand kilometers of sky at eight gravities.

Kassad forced his eyelids open once, noted that he lay curled in the belly of a long column of blue-white flame, and then he closed his eyes again. He saw no sign of a control for a parachute, suspension pack, or any other braking device. It didn't matter. He could not move his arms or hands in any case.

The giant shifted, grew heavier.

Kassad realized that part of his helmet bubble had melted or been blown away. The noise was indescribable. It didn't matter.

He closed his eyes more tightly. It was a good time to take a nap.

Kassad opened his eyes and saw the dark shape of a woman bending over him. For a second he thought it was *her*. He looked again and realized that it was her. She touched his cheek with cool fingers.

'Am I dead?' whispered Kassad, raising his own hand to grip her wrist.

116

'No.' Her voice was soft and throaty, burred with the hint of an accent he could not place. He had never heard her speak before.

'You're real?'

'Yes.'

Kassad sighed and looked around. He lay naked under a thin robe on some sort of couch or platform set in the middle of a dark, cavernous room. Overhead, starlight was visible through a broken roof. Kassad raised his other hand to touch her shoulder. Her hair was a dark nimbus above him. She wore a loose, thin gown which – even in the starlight – allowed him to see the outlines of her body. He caught her scent, the fragrant hint of soap and skin and *her* that he knew so well from their other times together.

'You must have questions,' she whispered as Kassad released the gold clasp which held her gown in place. The gown whispered to the floor. She wore nothing underneath. Above them, the band of the Milky Way was clearly visible.

'No,' said Kassad and pulled her to him.

Toward morning a breeze arose, and Kassad pulled the light cover over them. The thin material seemed to preserve all of their body heat and they lay together in perfect warmth. Somewhere sand or snow rasped at bare walls. The stars were very clear and very bright.

They awoke at the first hint of dawn, their faces close together under the silken coverlet. She ran her hand down Kassad's side, finding old and recent scars.

'Your name?' whispered Kassad.

'Hush,' she whispered back, her hand sliding lower.

Kassad moved his face into the scented curve of her neck. Her breasts were soft against him. Night paled to morning. Somewhere sand or snow blew against bare walls.

They made love, slept, made love again. In full light they rose and dressed. She had laid out underwear, gray tunic and trousers for Kassad. They fit perfectly, as did the spongesocks and soft boots. The woman wore a similar outfit of navy blue.

'Your name?' Kassad asked as they left the building with the shattered dome and walked through a dead city.

'Moneta,' said his dream, 'or Mnemosyne, whichever name pleases you more.'

'Moneta,' whispered Kassad. He looked up at a small sun rising into a lapis sky. 'This is Hyperion?'

'Yes.'

'How did I land? Suspensor field? Parachute?'

'You descended under a wing of gold foil.'

'I don't hurt. There were no wounds?'

'They were tended to.'

'What is this place?'

117

'The City of Poets. Abandoned more than a hundred years ago. Beyond that hill lie the Time Tombs.'

'The Ouster assault boats that were following me?'

'One landed nearby. The Pain Lord took the crew unto himself. The other two set down some distance away.'

'Who is the Pain Lord?'

'Come,' said Moneta. The dead city ended in desert. Fine sand slid across white marble half buried in dunes. To the west an Ouster dropship sat with its portals irised open. Nearby, on a fallen column, a thermcube yielded hot coffee and fresh-baked rolls. They ate and drank in silence.

Kassad worked to recall the legends of Hyperion. 'The Pain Lord is the Shrike,' he said at last.

'Of course.'

'You're from here . . . from the City of Poets?'

Moneta smiled and slowly shook her head.

Kassad finished his coffee and set the cup down. The feeling that he was in a dream persisted, much stronger than during any sim he had ever participated in. But the coffee had tasted pleasantly bitter; the sun was warm on his face and hands.

'Come, Kassad,' said Moneta.

They crossed expanses of cold sand. Kassad found himself glancing skyward, knowing that the Ouster torchship could lance them from orbit . . . then knowing with a sudden certainty that it would not.

The Time Tombs lay in a valley. A low obelisk glowed softly. A stone sphinx seemed to absorb the light. A complex structure of twisted pylons threw shadows onto itself. Other tombs were silhouettes against the rising sun. Each of the tombs had a door and each door was open. Kassad knew that they had been open when the first explorers discovered the Tombs and that the structures were empty. More than three centuries of searching for hidden rooms, tombs, vaults, and passageways had been fruitless.

'This is as far as you can go,' Moneta said as they neared the cliff at the head of the valley. 'The time tides are strong today.'

Kassad's tactical implant was silent. He had no comlog. He searched his memory. 'There are anti-entropic forcefields around the Time Tombs,' he said.

'Yes.'

'The tombs are ancient. The anti-entropic fields keep them from aging.'

'No,' said Moneta. 'The time tides drive the Tombs backward through time.'

'Backward through time,' Kassad repeated stupidly.

'Look.'

Shimmering, miragelike, a tree of steel thorns appeared out of the haze and a sudden dust storm of ochre sand. The thing seemed to fill the valley, rising at least two hundred meters to the height of the cliffs. Branches shifted, dissolved, and reformed like elements of a poorly tuned hologram. Sunlight danced on five-meter-long thorns. Corpses of Ouster men and women, all naked, were impaled on at least a score of these thorns. Other branches held other bodies. Not all were human.

The dust storm obscured the view for a moment and when the winds subsided the vision was gone. 'Come,' said Moneta.

Kassad followed her through the fringes of the time tides, avoiding the ebb and flow of the anti-entropic field the way children would play tag with an ocean surf on a broad beach. Kassad felt the pull of the time tides like waves of *déjà vu* tugging at every cell of his body.

Just beyond the entrance to the valley, where hills opened to the dunes and low moors led to the City of Poets, Moneta touched a wall of blue slate and an entrance opened to a long, low room set into the cliff face.

'Is this where you live?' asked Kassad but saw immediately that there were no signs of habitation. The stone walls of the room were inset with shelves and crowded niches.

'We must ready ourselves,' whispered Moneta and the lighting shifted to a golden hue. A long rack lowered its wares. A wafer-thin strip of reflective polymer curtained from the ceiling to serve as a mirror.

Kassad watched with the calm passivity of a dreamer as Moneta stripped off her clothes and then his. Their nudity was no longer erotic, merely ceremonial.

'You have been in my dreams for years,' he told her.

'Yes. Your past. My future. The shock wave of events moves across time like ripples on a pond.'

Kassad blinked as she raised a gold ferule and touched his chest. He felt a slight shock and his flesh became a mirror, his head and face a featureless ovoid reflecting all the color tones and textures of the room. A second later Moneta joined him, her body becoming a cascade of reflections, water over quicksilver over chrome. Kassad saw his own reflecting reflection in every curve and muscle of her body. Moneta's breasts caught and bent the light; her nipples rose like small splashes on a mirrored pond. Kassad moved to embrace her and felt their surfaces flow together like magnetized fluid. Under the connected fields, his flesh touched hers.

'Your enemies await beyond the city,' she whispered. The chrome of her face flowed with light.

'Enemies?'

'The Ousters. The ones who followed you here.'

Kassad shook his head, saw the reflection do likewise. 'They're not important anymore.'

'Oh, yes,' whispered Moneta, 'the enemy is always important. You must arm yourself.'

'With what?' But even as he spoke, Kassad realized that she was touching him with a bronze sphere, a dull blue toroid. His altered body spoke to him now as clearly as troops reporting in on an implant command circuit. Kassad felt the bloodlust build in him with turgid strength.

'Come.' Moneta led the way into open desert again. The sunlight seemed polarized and heavy. Kassad felt that they were gliding across the dunes, flowing like liquid through the white marble streets of the dead city. Near the west end of town, near the shattered remnants of a structure still bearing the inscribed lintel of Poets' Amphitheatre, something stood waiting.

For a second Kassad thought it was another person wearing the chromium forcefields he and Moneta were draped in – but only for a second. There was nothing human about this particular quicksilver-over-chrome construct. Kassad dreamily noted the four arms, retractable fingerblades, the profusion of thornspikes on throat, forehead, wrists, knees, and body, but not once did his gaze leave the two thousand-faceted eyes which burned with a red flame that paled sunlight and dimmed the day to blood shadows.

The Shrike, thought Kassad.

'The Lord of Pain,' whispered Moneta.

The thing turned and led them out of the dead city.

Kassad approved of the way the Ousters had prepared their defenses. The two assault boats were grounded less than half a kilometer apart, their guns, projectors, and missile turrets covering each other and a full three hundred and sixty degrees of fire. Ouster ground troops had been busy digging revetments a hundred meters out from the boats and Kassad could see at least two EM tanks hull down, their projection arrays and launch tubes commanding the wide, empty moor between the Poets' City and the boats. Kassad's vision had been altered; he could see the overlapping ship containment fields as ribbons of yellow haze, the motion sensors and antipersonnel mines as eggs of pulsing red light.

He blinked, realizing that something was wrong with the image. Then it came to him: besides the thickness of the light and his enhanced perception of energy fields, nothing was moving. The Ouster troops, even those set in attitudes of motion, were as stiff as the toy soldiers he had played with as a boy in the Tharsis slums. The EM tanks were dug into their hull-down positions, but Kassad noticed that now even their acquisition radars – visible to him as concentric purple arcs – were motionless. He glanced skyward and saw some sort of large bird hanging in the sky, as unmoving as an insect frozen in amber. He passed a cloud of windblown dust hanging suspended, extended one chrome hand, and flicked spirals of particles to the ground.

Ahead of them, the Shrike strode casually through the red maze of sensor-mines, stepped over the blue lines of tripbeams, ducked under the violet pulses of the autofire scanners, passed through the yellow containment field and the green wall of the sonic defense perimeter, and walked into the assault boat's shadow. Moneta and Kassad followed.

— *How is this possible*? Kassad realized that he had posed the question through a medium that was something less than telepathy but something far more sophisticated than implant conduction.

— *He controls time.*

— *The Pain Lord?*

— *Of course.*

— *Why are we here?*

Moneta gestured toward the motionless Ousters.

— *They are your enemies.*

Kassad felt that he was finally awaking from a long dream. This was *real*. The Ouster trooper's eyes, unblinking behind his helmet, were *real*. The Ouster assault boat, rising like a bronze tombstone to his left, was *real*.

Fedmahn Kassad realized that he could kill them all – commandos, assault boat crew, all of them – and they could do nothing about it. He knew that time had not stopped – any more than it stopped while a ship was under Hawking drive – it was merely a matter of varying rates. The bird frozen above them would complete the flap of its wings given enough minutes or hours. The Ouster in front of him would close his eyes in a blink if Kassad had the patience to watch long enough. Meanwhile, Kassad and Moneta and the Shrike could kill all of them without the Ousters realizing that they were under attack.

It was not fair, Kassad realized. It was wrong. It was the ultimate violation of the New Bushido, worse in its way than the wanton murder of civilians. The essence of honor lay in the moment of combat between equals. He was about to communicate this to Moneta when she said/thought—*Watch*.

Time began again with an explosion of sound not unlike the rush of air into an airlock. The bird soared and circled overhead. A desert breeze threw dust against the static-charged containment field. An Ouster commando rose from one knee, saw the Shrike and the two human shapes, screamed something over his tactical comm channel, and raised his energy weapon.

The Shrike did not seem to move – to Kassad it merely ceased being *here* and appeared *there*. The Ouster commando emitted a second, shorter scream, and then looked down in disbelief as the Shrike's arm withdrew with the man's heart in its bladed fist. The Ouster stared, opened his mouth as if to speak, and collapsed.

Kassad turned to his right and found himself face to face with an armored Ouster. The commando ponderously lifted a weapon. Kassad swung his arm, felt the chrome forcefield hum, and saw the flat of his hand cut through body armor, helmet, and neck. The Ouster's head rolled in the dust.

Kassad leaped into a low trench and saw several troopers begin to turn. Time was still out of joint; the enemy moved in extreme slow motion one second, jerked like a damaged holo to four-fifths speed in the next instant. They were never as quick as Kassad. Gone were his thoughts of the New Bushido. These were the barbarians who had tried to *kill* him. He broke one man's back, stepped aside, jabbed rigid, chrome fingers through the body armor of a second man, crushed the larynx of a third, dodged a knife blade moving in slow motion and kicked the spine out of the knife wielder. He leaped up out of the ditch.

— *Kassad!*

Kassad ducked as the laser beam crept past his shoulder, burning its way through the air like a slow fuse of ruby light. Kassad smelled ozone as it crackled past. *Impossible. I've dodged a laser!* He picked up a stone and flung it at the Ouster manning the tank-mounted hellwhip. A sonic boom cracked; the gunner exploded backward. Kassad pulled a plasma grenade from a corpse's bandolier, leaped to the tank hatch, was thirty meters away before the explosion geysered flame as high as the assault boat's bow.

Kassad paused in the eye of the storm to see Moneta in the center of her own circle of carnage. Blood splashed her but did not adhere, flowing like oil on water across the rainbow curves of chin, shoulder, breast, and belly. She looked at him across the battlefield and Kassad felt a renewed surge of bloodlust in himself.

Behind her, the Shrike moved slowly through the chaos, choosing victims as if he were harvesting. Kassad watched the creature wink in and out of existence and realized that to the Pain Lord he and Moneta would appear to be moving as slowly as the Ousters did to Kassad.

Time jumped, moved to four-fifths speed. The surviving troops were panicking now, firing into one another, deserting their posts, and fighting to get aboard the assault boat. Kassad tried to realize what the past minute or two had been like for them: blurs moving through their defensive positions, comrades dying in great gouts of blood. Kassad watched Moneta moving through their ranks, killing at her leisure. To his amazement, he discovered that he had some control of time: *blink* and his opponents slowed to one-third speed, *blink* and events moved at nearly their normal pace. Kassad's sense of honor and sanity called out for him to stop the slaughter but his almost sexual bloodlust overpowered any objections.

Someone in the assault boat had sealed the airlock and now a terrified commando used a shaped plasma charge to blow the portal open. The mob pressed in, trampling the wounded in their flight from unseen killers. Kassad followed them in.

The phrase 'fight like a cornered rat' is an extremely apt description. Throughout the history of military encounters, human combatants have been known to fight at their fiercest when challenged in enclosed places where flight is not an option. Whether in the passageways of La Haye Sainte and Hougoumont at Waterloo or in the Hive tunnels of Lusus, some of the most terrible hand-to-hand battles in history have been fought in cramped spaces where no retreat is possible. It was true this day. The Ousters fought . . . and died . . . like cornered rats.

The Shrike had disabled the assault boat. Moneta remained outside to kill the threescore commandos who had stayed at their posts. Kassad killed those within.

In the end, the final assault boat fired on its doomed counterpart. Kassad was outside by then and he watched the particle beams and high-intensity lasers creep toward him, followed an eternity later by missiles which seemed to move so slowly that he could have written his name on them in flight. By that time all of the Ousters were dead in and around the overrun boat, but its containment field held. Energy dispersion and impact explosions tossed corpses around on the outer perimeter, set fire to equipment, and glazed the sand to glass, but Kassad and Moneta watched from inside a dome of orange flame as the remaining assault boat retreated to space.

— *Can we stop them?* Kassad was panting, pouring sweat, and literally quivering from excitement.

— *We could*, replied Moneta, *but we do not want to. They will carry the message to the swarm.*

— *What message?*

'Come here, Kassad.'

He turned at the sound of her voice. The reflective forcefield was gone. Moneta's flesh was oiled with sweat; her dark hair was matted against her temples; her nipples were hard. 'Come here.'

Kassad glanced down at himseif. His own forcefield was gone – he had *willed* it away – and he was more sexually excited than he could ever remember being.

'Come here.' Moneta whispered this time.

Kassad went to her, lifted her, felt the sweat-slick smoothness of her buttocks as he carried her to an empty stretch of grass atop a wind-carved hummock. He lowered her to the ground between piles of Ouster bodies, roughly opened her legs, took both her hands in the grasp of one of his, lifted her arms above her head, pinned them to the ground, and lowered his long body between her legs.

'Yes,' whispered Moneta as he kissed the lobe of her left ear, set his lips to the pulse at the hollow of her neck, licked the salt tang of sweat from her breasts. *Lying among the dead. More dead to come. The thousands. The millions. Laughter out of dead bellies. The long lines of troops emerging from JumpShips to enter the waiting flames.*

'Yes.' Her breath was hot in his ear. She freed her hands, slid them along Kassad's damp shoulders, trailed long nails down his back, grasped his buttocks to pull him closer. Kassad's erection scraped her pubic hair, throbbed against the cusp of her belly. *Farcaster portals opening to admit the cold lengths of attack carriers. The warmth of plasma explosions. Hundreds of ships, thousands, dancing and dying like dust motes in a whirlwind. Great columns of solid ruby light lancing across great distances, bathing targets in the ultimate surge of warmth, bodies boiling in red light.*

'Yes.' Moneta opened her mouth and body to him. Warmth above and below, her tongue in his mouth as he entered her, welcomed by warm friction. His body strained deep, pulled back slightly, allowed the moist warmth to engulf him further as they began to move together. *Heat on a hundred worlds. Continents burning in bright spasms, the roll of boiling seas. The air itself aflame. Oceans of superheated air swelling like warm skin rising to a lover's touch.*

'Yes . . . yes . . . yes.' Moneta breathes warmth against his lips. Her skin is oil and velvet. Kassad thrusts quickly now, the universe contracting as sensation expands, senses dwindling as she closes warm and wet and tight around him. Her hips thrust harshly in response now, as if sensing the terrible build in pressure at the base of his being. Demanding. Kassad grimaces, closes his eyes, sees . . .

. . . *fireballs expanding, stars dying, suns exploding in great pulses of flame, star systems perishing in an ecstasy of destruction* . . .

. . . he feels pain in his chest, his hips not stopping, moving faster, even as he opens his eyes and sees . . .

. . . the great thorn of steel rising from between Moneta's breasts, almost impaling him as he unconsciously pulls up and back, the thornblade drawing blood which drips on her flesh, her pale flesh, reflective now, flesh as cold as dead metal, his hips still moving even as he watches through passion-dimmed eyes as Moneta's lips wither and curl back, revealing rows of steel blades where teeth had been, metal blades slash at his buttocks where fingers had gripped, legs like powerful steel bands imprison his pumping hips, her eyes . . .

. . . in the last seconds before orgasm Kassad tries to pull away . . . his hands on her throat, pressing . . . she clings like a leech, a lamprey ready to drain him . . . they roll against dead bodies . . .

. . . her eyes like red jewels, blazing with a mad heat like that which fills his aching testicles, expanding like a flame, spilling over . . .

. . . Kassad slams both hands against the soil, lifts himself away from her . . . from it . . . his strength insane but not enough as terrible gravities press them together . . . sucking like a lamprey's mouth as he threatens to explode, looks in her eyes . . . the death of worlds . . . *the death of worlds*!

Kassad screams and pulls away. Strips of his flesh rip away as he lunges up and sideways. Metal teeth click shut in a steel vagina, missing his glans by a moist millimeter. Kassad slumps on his side, rolls away, hips moving, unable to stop his ejaculation. Semen explodes in streams, falls on the curled fist of a corpse. Kassad moans, rolls again, curls in a fetal position even as he comes again. And again.

He hears the hiss and rustle as she rises behind him. Kassad rolls on his back and squints up against sunlight and his own pain. She stands above him, legs apart, a silhouette of thorns. Kassad wipes sweat from his eyes, sees his wrist come away red with blood, and waits for the killing blow. His skin contracts in anticipation of the slash of blade into flesh. Panting, Kassad looks up to see Moneta above him, thighs flesh rather than steel, her groin matted from the moisture of their passion. Her face is dark, the sun behind her, but he sees red flames dying in the multifaceted pits of her eyes. She smiles and he sees sunlight glint on rows of metal teeth. 'Kassad . . . ' she whispers and it is the sound of sand scraping against bone.

Kassad tears his gaze away, struggles to his feet, and stumbles across corpses and burning rubble in his terror to be free. He does not look back.

Scouting elements of Hyperion's Self-defense Force found Colonel Fedmahn Kassad almost two days later. He was discovered lying unconscious on one of the grassy moors which lead to the abandoned Chronos Keep, some twenty kilometers from the dead city and the wreckage of the Ouster ejection pod. Kassad was naked and almost dead from the effects of exposure and several serious wounds, but he responded well to emergency field treatment and was immediately airlifted south of the Bridle Range to a hospital at Keats. Reconnaissance squads from the SDF battalion moved northward carefully, cautious of the anti-entropic tides around the Time Tombs and wary of any booby traps left behind by the Ousters. There were none. The scouts found only the wreckage of Kassad's escape mechanism and the burned out hulks of the two assault boats which the Ousters had lanced from orbit. There were no clues as to why they had slagged their own ships and the Ouster bodies – both in and around the boats – had been burned beyond any hope of autopsy or analysis.

Kassad regained consciousness three Hyperion days later, swore that he remembered nothing after stealing the squid, and was shipped out on a FORCE torchship two local weeks later.

Upon returning to the Web, Kassad resigned his commission. For a while he was active in antiwar movements, occasionally appearing on the All Thing net arguing disarmament. But the attack on Bressia had mobilized the Hegemony toward true interstellar war as had nothing else in three centuries, and Kassad's voice was either drowned out or dismissed as the guilty conscience of the Butcher of South Bressia.

In the sixteen years after Bressia, Colonel Kassad had disappeared from the Web and from the Web consciousness. Although there had been no more major battles, the Ousters remained the Hegemony's prime bogey-men. Fedmahn Kassad was only a fading memory.

It was late morning when Kassad finished his story. The Consul blinked and looked around him, noticing the ship and its surroundings for the first time in more than two hours. The *Benares* had come out into the main channel of the Hoolie. The Consul could hear the creaks of the chains and hawsers as the river mantas surged against their harnesses. The *Benares* appeared to be the only ship heading upriver, but now numerous small craft were visible going the other way. The Consul rubbed his forehead and was surprised to see his hand come away slick with sweat. The day had grown very warm and the shadow of the tarp had crept away from the Consul without his noticing. He blinked, wiped sweat from his eyes, and moved into the shade to get a drink from one of the liquor bottles the androids had set on a cabinet near the table.

'My God,' Father Hoyt was saying, 'so, according to this Moneta creature, the Time Tombs are moving *backward* in time?'

'Yes,' said Kassad.

'Is that possible?' asked Hoyt.

'Yes.' It was Sol Weintraub who answered.

'If that's true,' said Brawne Lamia, 'then you "met" this Moneta . . . or whatever her real name is . . . in her past but your future . . . in a meeting that's still to come.'

'Yes,' said Kassad.

Martin Silenus walked to the railing and spat into the river. 'Colonel, do you think the bitch *was* the Shrike?'

'I don't know.' Kassad's monotone was barely audible.

Silenus turned to Sol Weintraub. 'You're a scholar. Is there anything in the Shrike mythography that says the thing can change shape?'

'No,' said Weintraub. He was preparing a milk globe to feed his daughter. The infant made soft, mewling noises and moved tiny fingers.

'Colonel,' said Het Masteen, 'the forcefield . . . whatever the fighting suit was . . . did you bring it with you after the encounter with the Ousters and this . . . female?'

Kassad looked at the Templar a moment and then shook his head.

The Consul was staring into his drink but his head suddenly snapped upright with the force of a thought. 'Colonel, you said that you saw a vision of the Shrike's killing tree . . . the structure, the *thing* where it impales its victims.'

Kassad moved his basilisk stare from the Templar to the Consul. He slowly nodded.

'And there were bodies on it?'

Another nod.

The Consul wiped sweat from his upper lip. 'If the tree is traveling backward in time with the Time Tombs, then the victims are from *our* future.'

Kassad said nothing. The others also were staring at the Consul now but only Weintraub appeared to understand what the comment meant . . . and what the Consul's next question had to be.

The Consul resisted the urge to wipe the sweat from his lips again. His voice was steady. 'Did you see any of us there?'

Kassad said nothing for more than a minute. The soft sounds of the river and the ship's rigging suddenly seemed very loud. Finally Kassad took a breath. 'Yes.'

Silence stretched again. Brawne Lamia broke it. 'Will you *tell* us who?'

'No.' Kassad rose and went to the stairway leading to the lower decks.

'Wait,' called Father Hoyt.

Kassad paused at the head of the stairway.

'Will you at least tell us two other things?'

'What?'

Father Hoyt grimaced from a wave of pain. His gaunt face went white under its film of perspiration. He took a breath and said, 'First, do you think the Shrike . . . the woman . . . somehow wants to use *you* to start this terrible interstellar war you foresaw?'

'Yes,' Kassad said softly.

'Second, will you tell us what you plan to petition the Shrike for . . . or this Moneta . . . when you meet them on the pilgrimage?'

Kassad smiled for the first time. It was a thin smile, and very, very cold. 'I will make no petition,' said Kassad. 'I will ask nothing of them. When I meet them this time, I will kill them.'

The other pilgrims did not speak or look at one another as Kassad went below. The *Benares* continued north-northeast into afternoon.

THREE

The barge *Benares* entered the river port of Naiad an hour before sunset. Crew and pilgrims pressed to the rail to stare at smoldering embers of what once had been a city of twenty thousand people. Little remained. The famous River Front Inn, built in the days of Sad King Billy, had burned to the foundations; its charred docks, piers, and screened balconies now collapsed into the shallows of the Hoolie. The customhouse was a burned-out shell. The airship terminal on the north end of town survived only as a blackened hulk, its mooring tower reduced to a spire of charcoal. There was no sign whatsoever of the small riverfront Shrike temple. Worst of all, from the pilgrims' point of view, was the destruction of the Naiad River Station – the harness dock lay burned and sagging, the manta holding pens open to the river.

'God *damn* it!' said Martin Silenus.

'Who did it?' asked Father Hoyt. 'The Shrike?'

'More likely the SDF,' said the Consul. 'Although they may have been fighting the Shrike.'

'I can't believe this,' snapped Brawne Lamia. She turned to A. Bettik, who had just joined them on the rear deck. 'Didn't you know this had happened?'

'No,' said the android. 'There has been no contact with any point north of the locks for more than a week.'

'Why the hell not?' asked Lamia. 'Even if this godforsaken world doesn't have a datasphere, don't you have radio?'

A. Bettik smiled slightly. 'Yes, M. Lamia, there is radio, but the comsats are down, the microwave repeater stations at the Karla Locks were destroyed, and we have no access to shortwave.'

'What about the mantas?' asked Kassad. 'Can we press on to Edge with the ones we have?'

Bettik frowned. 'We will have to, Colonel,' he said. 'But it is a crime. The two in harness will not recover from such a pull. With fresh mantas we would have put into Edge before dawn. With these two . . .' The android shrugged. 'With luck, if the beasts survive, we will arrive by early afternoon . . .'

'The windwagon will still be there, will it not?' asked Het Masteen.

'We must assume so,' said A. Bettik. 'If you will excuse me, I will see to feeding the poor beasts we have. We should be under way again within the hour.'

They saw no one in or near the ruins of Naiad. No river craft made their appearance above the city. An hour's pull northeast of the town they entered the region where the forests and farms of the lower Hoolie gave way to the undulating orange prairie south of the Sea of Grass. Occasionally the Consul would see the mud towers of architect ants, some of their serrated structures near the river reaching almost ten meters in height. There was no sign of intact human habitation. The ferry at Betty's Ford was totally gone, with not even a towrope or warming shack left to show where it had stood for almost two centuries. The River Runners Inn at Cave Point was dark and silent. A. Bettik and other crew members hallooed, but there was no response from the black cave mouth.

Sunset brought a sensuous stillness over the river, soon broken by a chorus of insect noises and night-bird calls. For a while the surface of the Hoolie became a mirror of the gray-green disk of twilight sky, disturbed only by the leap of dusk-feeding fish and the wake of the laboring mantas. As true darkness fell, innumerable prairie gossamers – much paler than their forest cousins, but also of greater wingspan, luminescent shades the size of small children – danced in the vales and valleys of the gently rolling hills. By the time the constellations emerged and the meteor trails began scarring the night sky, a brilliant display this far from all man-made light, the lanterns had been lit and dinner set out on the aft deck.

The Shrike pilgrims were subdued, as if still contemplating Colonel Kassad's grim and confusing tale. The Consul had been drinking steadily since before midday and now he felt the pleasant displacement – from reality, from the pain of memory – which allowed him to get through each day and night. Now he asked, his voice as careful and unslurred as only a true alcoholic's can be, whose turn it was to tell a tale.

'Mine,' said Martin Silenus. The poet also had been drinking steadily since early in the day. His voice was as carefully controlled as the Consul's but redness on his sharp cheeks and an almost manic brightness of eye gave the old poet away. 'At least I drew number three . . .' He held up his slip of paper. 'If you still want to hear the fucking thing.'

Brawne Lamia lifted her glass of wine, scowled, and set it down. 'Perhaps we should talk about what we have learned from the first two stories and how it might relate to our current . . . situation.'

'Not yet,' said Colonel Kassad. 'We don't have enough information.'

'Let M. Silenus speak,' said Sol Weintraub. 'Then we can begin discussing what we have heard.'

'I agree,' said Lenar Hoyt.

Het Masteen and the Consul nodded.

'Agreed!' cried Martin Silenus. 'I'll tell my story. Just let me finish my fucking glass of wine.'

THE POET'S TALE:
'HYPERION CANTOS'

In the beginning was the Word. Then came the fucking word processor. Then came the thought processor. Then came the death of literature. And so it goes.

Francis Bacon once said, 'There arises from a bad and unapt formation of words a wonderful obstruction to the mind.' We have all contributed our wonderful obstructions to the mind, have we not? I more than most. One of the twentieth century's better, forgotten writers – that is better-comma-forgotten – once *bon moted*: 'I love being a writer. It's the paperwork I can't stand.' Get it? Well, amigos and amigette, I love being a poet. It's the goddamned words I can't stand.

Where to start?

Start with Hyperion perhaps?

(Fade in) Almost two standard centuries ago.

Sad King Billy's five seedships spin like gold dandelions above this all too familiar lapis sky. We land like conquistadors strutting to and fro; more than two thousand visual artists and writers and sculptors and poets and ARNists and vid makers and holie directors and composers and decom-posers and God knows what all, supported by five times that many administrators and technicians and ecologists and supervisors and court chamberlains and professional ass kissers, not to mention the family of royal asses themselves, supported in turn by ten times *that* many androids willing to till the soil and stoke the reactors and raise the cities and lift that bale and tote that load . . . hell, you get the idea.

We landed on a world already seeded by the poor buggers who'd gone indigenie two centuries before and were living hand to mouth and cudgel to brain wherever they could. Naturally the noble descendants of these brave pioneers greeted us like gods – especially after a few of our security folk slagged a few of their more aggressive leaders – and naturally we accepted their worship as our due and put them to work next to our blueskins, plowing the south forty and working to build our shining city on the hill.

And it *was* a shining city on a hill. Seeing the ruins today can tell you nothing of the place. The desert has advanced in three centuries; the aqueducts from the mountains have fallen and shattered; the city itself is only bones. But in its day the City of Poets was fair indeed, a bit of Socrates' Athens with the intellectual excitement of Renaissance Venice, the artistic fervor of Paris in the days of the Impressionists, the true democracy of the first decade of Orbit City, and the unlimited future of Tau Ceti Center.

But, in the end, it was none of these things, of course. It was only Hrothgar's claustrophobic mead hall with the monster waiting in the darkness without. We had our Grendel, to be sure. We even had our Hrothgar if one squints a bit at Sad King Billy's poor slouched profile. We lacked only our Geats; our great, broad-shouldered, small-brained Beowulf with his band of merry psychopaths. So, lacking a Hero, we settled into the role of victims and composed our sonnets and rehearsed our ballets and unrolled our scrolls, while all the while our thorn-and-steel Grendel served the night with fear and harvested thighbones and gristle.

And this was when I – a satyr then, formed in flesh as mirror to my soul – came as close to completing my *Cantos*, my life's work, as I have come in five sad centuries of stubborn continuance.

(Fade to black)

It occurs to me that the Grendel tale is premature. The players have not been brought upon the stage. Dislinear plotting and non-contiguous prose have their adherents, not the least of which am I, but in the end, my friends, it is character which wins or loses immortality upon the vellum. Haven't you ever harbored the secret thought that somewhere Huck and Jim are – at this instant – poling their raft down some river just beyond our reach, so much more real are they than the shoe clerk who fitted us just a forgotten day ago? At any rate, if this fucking story's to be told, you should know who's in it. So – as much as it pains me – I'll back up to begin at the beginning.

In the beginning was the Word. And the Word was programmed in classic binary. And the Word said, 'Let there be life!' And so, somewhere in the TechnoCore vaults of my mother's estate, frozen sperm from my long-dead daddy was defrosted, set in suspension, shaken like the vanilla malts of yore, loaded into something part squirt gun and part dildo, and – at the magic touch of a trigger – ejaculated into Mother at a time when the moon was full and the egg was ripe.

Mother didn't have to be impregnated in this barbaric fashion, of course. She could have chosen *ex utero* fertilization, a male lover with a transplant of Daddy's DNA, a clonal surrogate, a gene-spliced virgin birth, you name it . . . but, as she told me later, she opened her legs to tradition. My guess is that she preferred it that way.

Anyway, I was born.

I was born on Earth . . . *Old Earth* . . . and fuck you, Lamia, if you don't believe it. We lived on Mother's estate on an island not far from the North American Preserve.

Notes for sketch of home on Old Earth:

Fragile twilights fading from violet to fuchsia to purple above the crepe-paper silhouettes of trees beyond the southwest sweep of lawn. Skies as delicate as translucent china, unscarred by cloud or contrail. The pre-symphony hush of first light followed by the cymbal crash of sunrise. Oranges and russets igniting to gold, the long, cool descent to green: leaf shadow, shade, tendrils of cypress and weeping willow, the hushed green velvet of the glade.

Mother's estate – our estate – a thousand acres centered in a million more. Lawns the size of small prairies with grass so perfect it beckoned a body to lie on it, to nap on its soft perfection. Noble shade trees making sundials of the Earth, their shadows circling in stately procession; now mingling, now contracting to midday, finally stretching eastward with the dying of the day. Royal oak. Giant elms. Cottonwood and cypress and redwood and bonsai. Banyan trees lowering new trunks like smooth-sided columns in a temple roofed by sky. Willows lining carefully laid canals and haphazard streams, their hanging branches singing ancient dirges to the wind.

Our house rises on a low hill where, in the winter, the browning curves of lawn look like the smooth flank of some female beast, all thigh muscle and meant for speed. The house shows its centuries of accretion: a jade tower on the east courtyard catching the first light of dawn, a series of gables on the south wing throwing triangles of shadow on the crystal conservatory at teatime, the balconies and maze of exterior stairways along the east porticoes playing Escher games with afternoon's shadows.

It was after the Big Mistake but before everything grew uninhabitable. Mostly we occupied the estate during what we quaintly called 'periods of remission' – stretches of ten to eighteen quiet months between planet-wide spasms as the Kiev Team's goddamn little black hole digested bits of the Earth's center and waited for its next feast. During the 'Bad Times', we vacationed at Uncle Kowa's place out beyond the moon, on a terraformed asteroid brought there before the Ouster migration.

You might already be able to tell that I was born with a silver spoon up my ass. I offer no apologies. After three thousand years of dabbling with democracy, the remaining Old Earth families had come to the realization that the only way to avoid such riffraff was not to allow them to breed. Or, rather, to sponsor seedship fleets; spinship explorations, new farcaster migrations . . . all of the panicked urgency of the Hegira . . . as long as they bred out there and left Old Earth alone. The fact that the homeworld was a diseased old bitch, gone in the teeth, didn't hurt the riffraff's urge to pioneer. No fools they.

And like the Buddha, I was almost grown before I saw my first hint of poverty. I was sixteen standard years old, on my *Wanderjahr*, and backpacking through India when I saw a beggar. The Hindu Old Families kept them around for religious reasons, but all I knew at the time was that here was a man in rags, ribs showing, holding out a wicker basket with an ancient credit diskey in it, begging for a touch of my universal card. My friends thought it was hysterical. I threw up. It was in Benares.

My childhood was privileged but not obnoxiously so. I have pleasant memories of Grande Dame Sybil's famous parties (she was a great-aunt on my mother's side). I remember one three-day affair she threw in the Manhattan Archipelago, guests ferried in by dropship from Orbit City and from the European arcologies. I remember the Empire State Building rising from the water, its many lights reflecting on the lagoons and fern canals; the EMVs unloading passengers on the observation deck while cooking fires burned on the overgrown island mounds of lower buildings all around.

The North American Preserve was our private playground in those days. It was said that about eight thousand people still resided in that mysterious continent, but half of these were rangers. The rest included the renegade ARNists who plied their trade by resurrecting species of plants and animals long absent from their antediluvian North American haunts, the ecology engineers, licensed primitives such as the Ogalalla Sioux or the Hell's Angel Guild, and the occasional tourist. I had a cousin who reportedly back-packed from one observation zone to the other in the Preserve, but he did so in the Midwest where the zones were relatively close together and where the dinosaur herds were much scarcer.

In the first century after the Big Mistake, Gaea was mortally injured but slow in the dying. The devastation was great during the Bad Times – and these came more often in precisely plotted spasms, shorter remissions, more terrible consequences after each attack – but the Earth abided and repaired itself as best it could.

The Preserve was, as I say, our playground but, in a real sense, so was all of the dying Earth. Mother let me have my own EMV when I was seven and there was no place on the globe farther than an hour's flight from home. My best friend, Amalfi Schwartz, lived in the Mount Erebus Estates in what had once been the Antarctic Republic. We saw each other daily. The fact that Old Earth law forbade farcasters did not bother us in the least; lying on some hillside at night looking up through the ten thousand Orbiting Lights and the twenty thousand beacons of the Ring, at the two or three thousand visible stars, we felt no jealousy, no urge to join the Hegira that even then was spinning the farcaster silk of the Worldweb. We were happy.

My memories of Mother are oddly stylized, as if she were another fiction-al construct from one of my Dying Earth novels. Perhaps she was. Perhaps I was raised by robots in the automated cities of Europe, suckled by androids in the Amazon Desert, or simply grown in a vat like brewer's yeast. What I recall is Mother's white gown sliding ghostlike through the shadowed rooms of the estate; infinitely delicate blue veins on the back of her thin-fingered hand as she poured tea in the damask and dust light of the conservatory; candlelight caught like a gold fly in the spiderweb sheen of her hair, hair done up in a bun in the style of the Grandes Dames. Sometimes I dream that I remember her voice, the lilt and tone and turn-in-the-womb *centerness* of it, but then I awake and it becomes only the wind moving lace curtains or the sound of some alien sea on stone.

From my earliest sense of *self*, I knew that I would be – should be – a poet. It was not as if I had a choice; more like the dying beauty all about breathed its last breath in me and commanded that I be doomed to play with words the rest of my days, as if in expiation for our race's thoughtless slaughter of its crib world. So what the hell; I became a poet.

I had a tutor whose name was Balthazar, human but ancient, a refugee from ancient Alexandria's flesh-scented alleys. Balthazar all but glowed blue-white from those crude, early Poulsen treatments; he was like an irradiated mummy of a man, sealed in liquid plastic. And randy as the proverbial goat. Centuries later, when I was in my satyr period, I felt that I finally understood poor don Balthazar's priapic compulsions, but in those days it was mostly a hindrance to keeping young girls on the estate's staff. Human or android, don Balthazar did not discriminate – he poinked them all.

Luckily for my education, there was nothing homosexual in don Balthazar's addiction to young flesh, so his escapades evidenced themselves either as absences from our tutorial sessions or an inordinate amount of attention lavished on memorizing verses from Ovid, Senesh, or Wu.

He was an excellent tutor. We studied the ancients and the late classical period, took field trips to the ruins of Athens, Rome, London, and Hannibal, Missouri, and never once had a quiz or test. Don Balthazar expected me to learn everything by heart at first encounter and I did not disappoint him. He convinced my mother that the pitfalls of 'progressive education' were not for an Old Earth family, so I never knew the mind-stunting shortcuts of RNA medication, datasphere immersion, systemic flashback training, stylized encounter groups, 'higher-level thinking skills' at the expense of facts, or preliterate programming. As a result of these deprivations, I was able to recite all of Fitzgerald's translation of the *Odyssey* by the time I was six, compose a sestina before I could dress myself, and think in spiral fugue-verse before I ever interfaced with an AI.

My scientific education, on the other hand, was something less than stringent. Don Balthazar had little interest in what he referred to as 'the mechanical side of the universe'. I was twenty-two before I realized that computers, RMUs, and Uncle Kowa's asteroidal life-support devices were *machines* and not some benevolent manifestations of the *animas* around us. I believed in fairies, woodsprites, numerology, astrology, and the magic of Midsummer's Eve deep in the primitive forests of the NAP. Like Keats and Lamb in Haydon's studio, don Balthazar and I drank toasts to 'the confusion of mathemetics' and mourned the destruction of the poetry of the rainbow by M. Newton's prying prism. The early distrust and actual hatred of all things scientific and clinical served me well in later life. It is not difficult, I have learned, to remain a pre-Copernican pagan in the post-scientific Hegemony.

My early poetry was execrable. As with most bad poets, I was unaware of this fact, secure in my arrogance that the very act of creating gave some worth to the worthless abortions I was spawning. My mother remained tolerant even as I left reeking little piles of doggerel lying around the house. She was indulgent of her only child even if he was as blithely incontinent as an unhousebroken llama. Don Balthazar never commented on my work; primarily, I assume, because I never showed him any of it. Don Balthazar thought that the venerable Daton was a fraud, that Salmud Brevy and Robert Frost should have hanged themselves with their own entrails, that Wordsworth was a fool, and that anything less than Shakespeare's sonnets

134

was a profanation of the language. I saw no reason to bother don Balthazar with my verse, rife with budding genius though I knew it to be.

I published several of these little literary turds in the various hardcopy journals then in vogue in the various arcologies of the European Houses, the amateur editors of these crude journals being as indulgent of my mother as she was of me. Occasionally I would press Amalfi or one of my other playmates – less aristocratic than I and thus with access to the datasphere or fatline transmitters – to uplink some of my verses to the Ring or to Mars, and thus to the burgeoning farcaster colonies. They never replied. I assumed they were too busy.

Belief in one's identity as a poet or writer prior to the acid test of publication is as naive and harmless as the youthful belief in one's immortality . . . and the inevitable disillusionment is just as painful.

My mother died with Old Earth. About half the Old Families stayed during that last cataclysm; I was twenty years old then and had made my own romantic plans to die with the homeworld. Mother decided otherwise. What concerned her was not my premature demise – like me, she was far too self-centered to think of someone else at a time like *that* – nor even the fact that the death of my DNA would mark the end of a line of aristocrats which stretched back to the *Mayflower*; no, what bothered Mother was that the family was going to die out *in debt*. Our last hundred years of extravagance, it seems, had been financed through massive loans from the Ring Bank and other discreet extraterrestrial institutions. Now that the continents of Earth were crashing under the impact of contraction, the great forests aflame, the oceans heaving and heating themselves into a lifeless soup, the very air transforming itself into something too hot and thick to break and too thin to plow, *now* the banks wanted their money back. I was collateral.

Or, rather, Mother's plan was. She liquidated all available assets some weeks before that phrase became a literal reality, deposited a quarter of a million marks in long-term accounts in the fleeing Ring Bank, and dispatched me on a trip to the Rifkin Atmospheric Protectorate on Heaven's Gate, a minor world circling the star Vega. Even then, that poisonous world had a farcaster connection to Sol System, but I did not farcast. Nor was I a passenger on the single spinship with Hawking drive which put into Heaven's Gate each standard year. No, Mother sent me to this back end of the outback on a Phase Three ramship, *slower than light*, frozen with the cattle embryos and orange juice concentrate and feeder viruses, on a trip that took *one hundred and twenty-nine* shipboard years, with an objective time-debt of *one hundred and sixty-seven standard years*!

Mother figured that the accrued interest on the long-term accounts would be enough to pay off our family debt and perhaps allow me to survive comfortably for a while. For the first and last time in her life, Mother figured wrong.

*

Notes for a sketch of Heaven's Gate:

Mud lanes which run back from the station's conversion docks like a pattern of sores on a leper's back. Sufrus-brown clouds which hang in tatters from a rotten burlap sky. A tangle of shapeless wooden structures half decayed before they were ever fully constructed, their paneless windows now staring sightlessly into the gaping mouths of their neighbors. Indigenies breeding like . . . like humans, I suppose . . . eyeless cripples, lungs burned out with air rot, squiring a nest of a dozen offspring, the children's skin scabrous by age five-standard, their eyes watering incessantly from the sting of an atmosphere which will kill them before they're forty, their smiles carious, their oily hair rife with lice and the blood bags of dracula ticks. Proud parents beaming. Twenty million of these doomed schmucks, crowded into slums overflowing an island smaller than my family's west lawn on Old Earth, all of them fighting to breathe the only breathable air on a world where the standard is to inhale and die, crowding ever closer to the center of the sixty-mile radius of survivable atmosphere which the Atmospheric Generating Station had been able to provide *before* it began to malfunction.

Heaven's Gate: my new home.

Mother had not taken into account the possibility that all Old Earth accounts would be frozen – and then appropriated into the growing Worldweb economy. Nor had she remembered that the reason people had waited for the Hawking drive to see the spiral arm of the galaxy is that in long-term cryogenic sleep – as opposed to a few weeks or months of fugue – chances of terminal brain damage were one in six. I was lucky. When I was uncrated on Heaven's Gate and put to work digging out acid canals beyond the perimeter, I had suffered only a cerebral accident – a stroke. Physically, I was able to work in the mud pits within a few local weeks. Mentally, there was much left to be desired.

The left side of my brain had been shut down like a damaged section of a spinship being sealed off, airtight doors leaving the doomed compartments open to vacuum. I could still think. Control of the right side of my body soon returned. Only the language centers had been damaged beyond simple repair. The marvelous organic computer wedged in my skull had dumped its language content like a flawed program. The right hemisphere was not without *some* language – but only the most emotionally charged units of communication could lodge in that affective hemisphere; my vocabulary was now down to nine words. (This, I learned later, was exceptional, many victims of CVAs retain only two or three.) For the record, here is my entire vocabulary of manageable words: fuck, shit, piss, cunt, goddamn, motherfucker, asshole, peepee, and poopoo.

A quick analysis will show some redundancy here. I had at my disposal eight nouns which stood for six things; five of the eight nouns could double as verbs. I retained one indisputable noun and a single adjective which also could be used as a verb or expletive. My new language universe was comprised of four monosyllables, three compound words, and two baby-talk repetitions. My arena of literal expression offered four avenues to the topic of elimination, two references to human anatomy, one request for divine imprecation, one standard description of or request for coitus, and a coital variation which was no longer an option for me since my mother was deceased.

All in all, it was enough.

I will not say that I remember my three years in the mud pits and slime slums of Heaven's Gate with *fondness*, but it is true that these years were at least as formative as – and probably more so than – my previous two decades on Old Earth.

I soon found that among my intimate acquaintances – Old Sludge, the scoop-shovel foreman; Unk, the slumyard bully to whom I paid my protection bribes; Kiti, the lice-ridden crib doxy whom I slept with when I could afford it – my vocabulary served me well. 'Shit-fuck,' I would grunt, gesticulating. 'Asshole cunt peepee fuck.'

'Ah,' grinned Old Sludge, showing his one tooth, 'going to the company store to get some algae chewies, huh?'

'Goddamn poopoo,' I would grin back at him.

The life of a poet lies not merely in the finite language-dance of expression but in the nearly infinite combinations of perception and memory combined with the sensitivity to what is perceived and remembered. My three local years on Heaven's Gate, almost fifteen hundred standard days, allowed me to see, to feel, to hear – to remember, as if I literally had been born again. Little matter that I had been born again in hell; reworked experience is the stuff of all true poetry and raw experience was the birthing gift of my new life.

There was no problem adapting to a brave new world a century and a half beyond my own. For all of our talk of expansion and pioneering spirit these past five centuries, we all know how stultified and static our human universe has become. We are in a comfortable Dark Ages of the inventive mind; institutions change but little, and that by gradual evolution rather than revolution; scientific research creeps crablike in a lateral shuffle, where once it leaped in great intuitive bounds; devices change even less, plateau technologies common to us would be instantly identifiable – and operable! – to our great-grandfathers. So while I slept the Hegemony became a formal entity, the Worldweb was spun to something close to its final shape, the All Thing took its democratic place among the list of humanity's benevolent despots, the TechnoCore seceded from human service and then offered its help as an ally rather than a slave, and the Ousters retreated to darkness and the role of Nemesis . . . but all these things had been creeping toward critical mass even before I was frozen into my ice coffin between the pork bellies and sherbet, and such obvious extensions of old trends took little effort to understand. Besides, history viewed from the inside is always a dark, digestive mess, far different from the easily recognizable cow viewed from afar by historians.

My life was Heaven's Gate and the minute-to-minute demands of survival there. The sky was always an eternal yellow-brown sunset hanging like a collapsing ceiling mere meters above my shack. My shack was oddly comfortable: a table for eating, a cot for sleeping and fucking, a hole for pissing and shitting, and a window for silent staring. My environment mirrored my vocabulary.

Prison always has been a good place for writers, killing, as it does, the twin demons of mobility and diversion, and Heaven's Gate was no exception. The Atmospheric Protectorate owned my body but my mind – or what was left of it – was mine.

On Old Earth, my poetry was composed on a Sadu-Dekenar comlog thought processor while I lounged in a padded chaise longue or floated in my EM barge above dark lagoons or walked pensively through scented bowers. The execrable, undisciplined, limp-wristed flatulent products of those reveries already have been described. On Heaven's Gate, I discovered what a mental stimulant physical labor could be; not mere *physical* labor, I should add, but absolutely spine-bending, lung-racking, gut-ripping, ligament-tearing, and ball-breaking physical labor. But as long as the task is both onerous and repetitive, I discovered, the mind is not only *free* to wander to more imaginative climes, it actually *flees* to higher planes.

Thus, on Heaven's Gate, as I dredged bottom scum from the slop canals under the red gaze of Vega Primo or crawled on hands and knees through stalactites and stalagmites of rebreather bacteria in the station's labyrinthine lungpipes, I became a poet.

All I lacked were the words.

The twentieth century's most honored writer, William Gass, once said in an interview; 'Words are the supreme objects. They are *minded* things.'

And so they are. As pure and transcendent as any Idea which ever cast a shadow into Plato's dark cave of our perceptions. But they are also pitfalls of deceit and misperception. Words bend our thinking to infinite paths of self-delusion, and the fact that we spend most of our mental lives in brain mansions built of words means that we lack the objectivity necessary to see the terrible distortion of reality which language brings. Example: the Chinese pictogram for 'integrity' is a two-part symbol of a man literally standing next to his word. So far, so good. But what does the Late English word 'honesty' mean? Or 'Motherland'? Or 'progress'? Or 'democracy'? Or 'beauty'? But even in our self-deception, we become gods.

A philosopher/mathematician named Bertrand Russell, who lived and died in the same century as Gass, once wrote: 'Language serves not only to express thought but to make possible thoughts which could not exist without it.' Here is the essence of mankind's creative genius: not the edifices of civilization nor the bang-flash weapons which can end it, but the *words* which fertilize new concepts like spermatozoa attacking an ovum. It might be argued that the Siamese-twin infants of word/idea are the *only* contribution the human species can, will, or should make to the reveling cosmos. (Yes, our DNA is unique but so is a salamander's. Yes, we construct artifacts but so have species ranging from beavers to the architect ants whose crenellated towers are visible right now off the port bow. Yes, we weave real-fabric things from the dreamstuff of mathematics, but the universe is hardwired with arithmetic. Scratch a circle and π peeps out. Enter a new solar system and Tycho Brahe's formulae lie waiting under the black velvet cloak of space/time. But *where* has the universe hidden a *word* under its outer layer of biology, geometry, or insensate rock?) Even the traces of other intelligent life we have found – the blimps on Jove II, the Labyrinth Builders, the Seneschai empaths on Hebron, the Stick People of Durulis, the architects of the Time Tombs, the Shrike itself – have left us mysteries and obscure artifacts but no *language*. No *words*.

The poet John Keats once wrote to a friend of his named Bailey: 'I am certain of nothing but the holiness of the Heart's affections and the truth of Imagination – What the imagination seizes as Beauty must be truth – whether it existed before or not.'

The Chinese poet George Wu, who died in the Last Sino-Japanese War about three centuries before the Hegira, understood this when he recorded on his comlog: 'Poets are the mad midwives to reality. They see not what is, nor what can be, but what *must become*.' Later, on his last disk to his lover the week before he died, Wu said: 'Words are the only bullets in truth's bandolier. And poets are the snipers.'

You see, in the beginning was the Word. And the Word was made flesh in the weave of the human universe. And only the poet can expand this universe, finding shortcuts to new realities the way the Hawking drive tunnels under the barriers of Einsteinian space/time.

To be a poet, I realized, a *true poet*, was to become the Avatar of humanity incarnate; to accept the mantle of poet is to carry the cross of the Son of Man, to suffer the birth pangs of the Soul-Mother of Humanity.

To be a *true poet* is to become God.

I tried to explain this to my friends on Heaven's Gate. 'Piss, shit,' I said. 'Asshole motherfucker, goddamn shit goddamn. Cunt. Peepee cunt. God-damn!'

They shook their heads and smiled, and walked away. Great poets are rarely understood in their own day.

The yellow-brown clouds rained acid on me. I waded in mud up to my thighs and cleaned leechweed from the city sewer pipes. Old Sludge died during my second year there when we were all working on a project extending the First Avenue Canal to the Midsump Mudflats. An accident. He was climbing a slime dune to rescue a single sulfur-rose from the advancing grouter when there was a mudquake. Kiti married shortly after that. She still worked part time as a crib doxy, but I saw less and less of her. She died in childbirth shortly after the green tsunami carried away Mudflat City. I continued to write poetry.

How is it, you might ask, that someone can write fine verse with a vocabulary of only nine right-hemisphere words?

The answer is that I used no words at all. Poetry is only secondarily about words. Primarily, it is about *truth*. I dealt with the *Ding an Sich*, the substance behind the shadow, weaving powerful concepts, similes, and connections the way an engineer would raise a skyscraper with the whiskered-alloy skeleton being constructed long before the glass and plastic and chromaluminum appears.

And slowly the words returned. The brain retrains and retools itself amazingly well. What had been lost in the left hemisphere found a home elsewhere or reasserted their primacy in the damaged regions like pioneers returning to a fire-damaged plain made more fertile by the flames. Where before a simple word like 'salt' would leave me stuttering and gasping, my mind probing emptiness like a tongue prodding the socket of a missing tooth, now the words and phrases flowed back slowly, like the names of forgotten playmates. During the day I labored in the slimefields, but at night I sat at my splintered table and wrote my *Cantos* by the light of a hissing ghee lamp. Mark Twain once opined in his homey way: 'The difference between the right word and the almost right word is the difference between lightning and the lightning bug.' He was droll but incomplete. During those long months of beginning my *Cantos* on Heaven's Gate. I discovered that the difference between finding the right word as opposed to accepting the almost right word was the difference between being *struck* by lightning and merely watching a lightning display.

So my *Cantos* began and grew. Written on the flimsy sheets of recycled leechweed fiber which they issued by the ton for use as toilet paper, scribbled by one of the cheap felt-tip pens sold at the Company Store, the *Cantos* took shape. As the words returned, slipping into place like once scattered pieces of a 3-D puzzle, I needed a form. Returning to don Balthazar's teachings, I tried on the measured nobility of Milton's epic verse. Gaining confidence, I added the romantic sensuality of a Byron matured by a Keatsish celebration of the language. Stirring all this, I seasoned the mixture with a dash of Yeats's brilliant cynicism and a pinch of Pound's obscure, scholastic arrogance. I chopped, diced, and added such ingredients as Eliot's control of imagery, Dylan Thomas's feel for place, Delmore Schwartz's sense of doom, Steve Tem's touch of horror, Salmud Brevy's plea for innocence, Daton's love of the convoluted rhyme scheme, Wu's worship of the physical, and Edmond Ki Fererra's radical playfulness.

In the end, of course, I threw this entire mixture out and wrote the *Cantos* in a style all my own.

If it had not been for Unk the slumyard bully, I probably still would be on Heaven's Gate, digging acid canals by day and writing *Cantos* by night.

It was my day off and I was carrying my *Cantos* – the only copy of my manuscript! – to the Company Library in the Common Hall to do some research when Unk and two of his cronies appeared from an alley and demanded immediate payment of the next month's protection money. We had no universal cards in the Heaven's Gate Atmospheric Protectorate; we paid our debts in company scrip or bootleg marks. I had neither. Unk demanded to see what was in my plastic shoulder bag. Without thinking, I refused. It was a mistake. If I'd shown Unk the manuscript, he most probably would have scattered it in the mud and slapped me around after making threats. As it was, my refusal angered him so he and his two Neanderthal companions tore open the bag, scattered the manuscript in the mud, and beat me within the proverbial inch of my life.

It so happened that on this day an EMV belonging to a Protectorate air quality control manager was passing low above and the wife of the manager, traveling alone to the arc's Company Residential Store, ordered the EMV down, had her android servant retrieve me and what was left of my *Cantos*, and then personally drove me to the Company Hospital. Normally, the members of the bonded work force received medical aid, if any, at the walk-in Bio Clinic, but the hospital did not want to refuse the wife of a manager so I was admitted – still unconscious – and watched over by a human doctor and the manager's wife while I recovered in a healing tank.

All right, to make a banal long story into a banal short story, I'll cut to the uplink. Helenda – that was the manager's wife – read my manuscript while I was floating in renewal nutrient. She liked it. On the same day I was being decanted in the Company Hospital, Helenda farcast to Renaissance where she showed my *Cantos* to her sister Felia, who had a friend whose lover knew an editor at Transline Publishing. When I awoke the next day, my broken ribs had been set, my shattered cheekbone had been healed, my bruises were gone, and I'd received five new teeth, a new cornea for my left eye, and a contract with Transline.

My book came out five weeks later. A week after that, Helenda divorced her manager and married me. It was her seventh marriage, my first. We honeymooned on the Concourse and, when we returned a month later, my book had sold more than a billion copies – the first book of verse to hit the bestseller lists in four centuries – and I was a millionaire many times over.

Tyrena Wingreen-Feif was my first editor at Transline. It was her idea to title the book *The Dying Earth* (a records search showed a novel by that name five hundred years earlier, but the copyright had lapsed and the book was out of print). It was her idea to publish just the sections of the *Cantos* which dealt with the nostalgic final days of Old Earth. And it was her idea to remove the sections which she thought would bore the readers – the philosophical passages, the descriptions of my mother, the sections which paid homage to earlier poets, the places where I played with experimental verse, the more personal passages – everything, in fact, except the descriptions of the idyllic final days which, emptied of all heavier freight, came across as sentimental and insipid. Four months after publication *The Dying Earth* had sold two and a half billion hardfax copies, an abridged and digitalized version was available on the See Thing datasphere, and it had been optioned for the holies. Tyrena pointed out that the timing had been perfect . . . that the original trauma shock of the death of Old Earth had meant a century of denial, almost as if Earth had never existed, followed by a period of revived interest culminating in the Old Earth nostalgia cults which could now be found on every world in the Web. A book – even a book of verse – dealing with the final days had struck at precisely the right moment.

For me, the first few months of life as a celebrity in the Hegemony were far more disorienting than my earlier transition from spoiled son of Old Earth to enslaved stroke victim on Heaven's Gate. During those first months I did book and fax signing on more than a hundred worlds; I appeared on 'The AllNet Now!' show with Marmon Hamlit; I met CEO Senister Perót and All Thing Speaker Drury Fein as well as a score of senators; I spoke to the Interplanetary Society of PEN Women and to the Lusus Writers' Union; I was given honorary degrees at the University of New Earth and at Cambridge Two; I was feted, interviewed, imaged, reviewed (favorably), bioed (unauthorized), lionized, serialized, and swindled. It was a busy time.

Notes for a sketch of life in the Hegemony:

My home has thirty-eight rooms on thirty-six worlds. No doors: the arched entrances are farcaster portals, a few opaqued with privacy curtains, most open to observation and entry. Each room has windows everywhere and at least two walls with portals. From the grand dining hall on Renaissance Vector, I can see the bronze skies and the verdigris towers of Keep Enable in the valley below my volcanic peak, and by turning my head I can look through the farcaster portal and across the expense of white carpet in the formal living area to see the Edgar Allan Sea crash against the spires of Point Prospero on Nevermore. My library looks out on the glaciers and green skies of Nordholm while a walk of ten paces allows me to *descend* a short stairway to my tower study, a comfortable, open room encircled by polarized glass which offers a three-hundred-sixty-degree view of the highest peaks of the Kushpat Karakoram, a mountain range two thousand kilometers from the nearest settlement in the easternmost reaches of the Jamnu Republic on Deneb Drei.

The huge sleeping room Helenda and I share rocks gently in the boughs of a three-hundred-meter Worldtree on the Templar world of God's Grove and connects to a solarium which sits alone on the arid saltflats of Hebron. Not all of our views are of wilderness: the media room opens to a skimmer pad on the hundred and thirty-eighth floor of a Tau Ceti Center arctower and our patio lies on a terrace overlooking the market in the Old Section of bustling New Jerusalem. The architect, a student of the legendary Millon DeHaVre, has incorporated several small jokes into the house's design: the steps *go down* to the tower room, of course, but equally droll is the exit from the eyrie which leads to the exercise room on the lowest level of Lusus's deepest Hive, or perhaps the guest bathroom, which consists of toilet, bidet, sink and shower stall on an open, wall-less raft afloat on the violet seaworld of Mare Infinitus.

At first the shifts in gravity from room to room were disturbing, but I soon adapted, subconsciously bracing myself for the drag of Lusus and Hebron and Sol Draconi Septem, unconsciously anticipating the less than 1-standard-g freedom of the majority of the rooms.

In the ten standard months Helenda and I are together we spend little time in our home, preferring instead to move with friends among the resorts and vacation arcologies and night spots of the Worldweb. Our 'friends' are the former farcaster set, now calling themselves the Caribou Herd after an extinct, Old Earth migratory mammal. This herd consists of other writers, a few successful visual artists, Concourse intellectuals, All Thing media representatives, a few radical ARNists and cosmetic gene splicers, Web aristocrats, wealthy farcaster freaks and Flashback addicts, a few holie and stage directors, a scattering of actors and performance artists, several Mafia dons gone straight, and a revolving list of recent celebrities . . . myself included.

Everyone drinks, uses stims and autoimplants, takes the wire, and can afford the best drugs. The drug of choice is Flashback. It is definitely an upper-class vice: one needs the full range of expensive implants to fully experience it. Helenda has seen to it that I have been so fitted: biomonitors, sensory extenders, and internal comlog, neural shunts, kickers, metacortex processors, blood chips, RNA tapeworms . . . my mother wouldn't have recognized my insides.

I try Flashback twice. The first time is a glide – I target my ninth birthday party and hit it with the first salvo. It is all there: the servants singing on the north lawn at daybreak, don Balthazar grudgingly canceling classes so I can spend the day with Amalfi in my EMV, streaking across the gray dunes of the Amazon Basin in gay abandon; the torchlight procession that evening as representatives of the other Old Families arrive at dusk, their brightly wrapped presents gleaming under the moon and the Ten Thousand Lights. I rise from nine hours in Flashback with a smile on my face. The second trip almost kills me.

I am four and crying, seeking my mother through endless rooms smelling of dust and old furniture. Android servants seek to console me but I shake off their hands, running down hallways soiled with shadows and the soot of too many generations. Breaking the first rule I ever learned, I throw open the doors to Mother's sewing room, her sanctum sanctorum to which she retires for three hours every afternoon and from which she emerges with her soft smile, the hem of her pale dress whispering across the carpet like the echo of a ghost's sigh.

Mother is sitting there in the shadows. I am four and my finger has been hurt and I rush to her, throwing myself into her arms.

She does not respond. One of her elegant arms remains reclined along the back of the chaise longue, the other remains limp on the cushion.

I pull back, shocked by her cool plasticity. I tug open the heavy velvet drapes without rising from her lap.

Mother's eyes are white, rolled back in her head. Her lips are slightly open. Drool moistens the corners of her mouth and glints on her perfect chin. From the gold threads of her hair – done up in the Grande Dame style she favors – I see the cold steel gleam of the stim wire and the duller sheen of the skull socket she has plugged it into. The patch of bone on either side is very white. On the table near her left hand lies the empty Flashback syringe.

The servants arrive and pull me away. Mother never blinks. I am pulled screaming from the room.

I wake screaming.

Perhaps it was my refusal to use Flashback again which hastened Helenda's departure, but I doubt it. I was a toy to her – a primitive who amused her by my innocence about a life she had taken for granted for many decades. Whatever the case, my refusal to Flashback left me with many days without her; the time spent in replay is real time and Flashback users often die having spent more days of their lives under the drug than they ever experienced conscious.

At first I entertained myself with the implants and technotoys which had been denied to me as a member of an Old Earth Family. The datasphere was a constant delight that first year – I called up information almost continually, living in a frenzy of full interface. I was as addicted to raw data as the Caribou Herd were to their stims and drugs. I could imagine don Balthazar spinning in his molten grave as I gave up long-term memory for the transient satisfaction of implant omniscience. It was only later that I felt the loss – Fitzgerald's *Odyssey*, Wu's *Final March*, and a score of other epics which had survived my stroke now were shredded like cloud fragments in a high wind. Much later, freed of implants, I painstakingly learned them all again.

For the first and only time in my life I became political. Days and nights would pass with me monitoring the Senate on farcaster cable or lying tapped into the All Thing. Someone once estimated that the All Thing deals with about a hundred active pieces of Hegemony legislation per day, and during my months spent screwed into the sensorium I missed none of them. My voice and name became well known on the debate channels. No bill was too small, no issue too simple or too complex for my input. The simple act of voting every few minutes gave me a false sense of having *accomplished* something. I finally gave up the political obsession only after I realized that accessing the All Thing regularly meant either staying home or turning into a walking zombie. A person constantly busy accessing on his implants makes a pitiful sight in public and it didn't take Helenda's derision to make me realize that if I stayed home I would turn into an All Thing sponge like so many millions of other slugs around the Web. So I gave up politics. But by then I had found a new passion: religion.

I joined religions. Hell, I helped *create* religions. The Zen Gnostic Church was expanding exponentially and I became a true believer, appearing on HTV talk shows and searching for my Places of Power with all of the devoutness of a pre-Hegira Muslim pilgrimaging to Mecca. Besides, I loved farcasting. I had earned almost a hundred million marks from royalties for *The Dying Earth*, and Helenda had invested well, but someone once figured that a farcaster home such as mine cost more than fifty thousand marks a day just to keep in the Web and I did not limit my farcasting to the thirty-six worlds of my home. Transline Publishing had qualified me for a gold universal card and I used it liberally, farcasting to unlikely corners of the Web and then spending weeks staying in luxury accommodations and leasing EMVs to find my Places of Power in remote areas of backwater worlds.

I found none. I renounced Zen Gnosticism about the same time Helenda divorced me. By that time the bills were piling up and I had to liquidate most of the stocks and long-term investments remaining to me after Helenda had taken her share. (I was not only naive and in love when she had had her attorneys draw up the marriage contract . . . I was stupid.)

Eventually, even with such economies as cutting down my farcasting and dismissing the android servants, I was facing financial disaster.

I went to see Tyrena Wingreen-Feif.

'No one wants to read poetry,' she said, leafing through the thin stack of *Cantos* I had written in the past year and a half.

'What do you mean?' I said. '*The Dying Earth* was poetry.'

'*The Dying Earth* was a fluke,' said Tyrena. Her nails were long and green and curved in the latest mandarin fashion; they curled around my manuscript like the claws of some chlorophyll beast. 'It sold because the mass subconscious was ready for it.'

'Maybe the mass subconscious is ready for this,' I said. I was beginning to get angry.

Tyrena laughed. It was not an altogether pleasant sound. 'Martin, Martin, Martin,' she said. 'This is *poetry*. You're writing about Heaven's Gate and the Caribou Herd, but what comes across is loneliness, displacement, angst, and a cynical look at humanity.'

'So?'

'So no one wants to *pay* for a look at another person's angst,' laughed Tyrena.

I turned away from her desk and walked to the far side of the room. Her office took up the entire four hundred and thirty-fifth floor of the Transline Spire in the Babel section of Tau Ceti Center. There were no windows; the circular room was open from floor to ceiling, shielded by a solar-generated containment field which showed no shimmer whatsoever. It was like standing between two gray plates suspended halfway between the sky and earth. I watched crimson clouds move between the lesser spires half a kilometer below and I thought about hubris. Tyrena's office had no doorways, stairways, elevators, field lifts, or trapdoors: no connection to the other levels at all. One entered Tyrena's office through the five-faceted farcaster which shimmered in midair like an abstract holosculpture. I found myself thinking about tower fires and power failures as well as hubris. I said, 'Are you saying that you won't publish it?'

'Not at all,' smiled my editor. 'You've earned Transline several billion marks, Martin. We will publish it. All I am saying is that no one will buy it.'

'You're wrong!' I shouted. 'Not everyone recognizes fine poetry, but there are still enough people who read to make it a bestseller.'

Tyrena did not laugh again but her smile slashed upward in a twist of green lips. 'Martin, Martin, Martin,' she said, 'the population of literate people has been declining steadily since Gutenberg's day. By the twentieth century, less than two percent of the people in the so-called industrialized democracies read even one book a year. And that was *before* the smart machines, dataspheres, and user-friendly environments. By the Hegira, ninety-eight percent of the Hegemony's population had no reason to read anything. So they didn't bother learning how to. It's worse today. There are more than a hundred billion human beings in the Worldweb and less than one percent of them bothers to hardfax any printed material, much less *read a book.*'

'*The Dying Earth* sold almost three billion copies,' I reminded her.

'Mm-hmm,' said Tyrena. 'It was the *Pilgrim's Progress* Effect.'

'The what?'

'*Pilgrim's Progress* Effect. In the Massachusetts Colony of – what was it! – seventeenth-century Old Earth, every decent family had to have a copy in the household. But, my heavens, no one had to *read* it. It was the same with Hitler's *Mein Kampf* or Stukatsky's *Visions in the Eye of a Decapitated Child.*'

'Who was Hitler?' I said.

Tyrena smiled slightly. 'An Old Earth politician who did some writing. *Mein Kampf* is still in print . . . Transline renews the copyright every hundred and thirty-eight years.'

'Well, look,' I said, 'I'm going to take a few weeks to polish up the *Cantos* and give it my best shot.'

'Fine,' smiled Tyrena.

'I suppose you'll want to edit it the way you did last time?'

'Not at all,' said Tyrena. 'Since there's no core of nostalgia this time, you might as well write it the way you want.'

I blinked. 'You mean I can keep in the blank verse this time?'

'Of course.'

'And the philosophy?'

'Please do.'

'And the experimental sections?'

'Yes.'

'And you'll print it the way I write it?'

'Absolutely.'

'Is there a *chance* it'll sell?'

'Not a hope in hell.'

My 'few weeks to polish up the *Cantos*' turned into ten months of obsessive labor. I shut off most of the rooms in the house, keeping only the tower room on Deneb Drei, the exercise room on Lusus, the kitchen, and the bathroom raft on Mare Infinitus. I worked a straight ten hours a day, took a break for some vigorous exercise followed by a meal and a nap, and then returned to my writing table for another eight-hour stint. It was similar to the time five years before when I was recovering from my stroke and it sometimes took an hour or a day for a word to come to me, for a concept to sink its roots into the firm soil of language. Now it was an even slower process as I agonized over the perfect word, the precise rhyme scheme, the most playful image, and the most ineffable analog to the most elusive emotion.

After ten standard months I was done, acknowledging the ancient aphorism to the effect that no book or poem is ever finished, merely abandoned.

'What do you think?' I asked Tyrena as she read through the first copy.

Her eyes were blank, bronze disks in that week's fashion, but this did not hide the fact that there were tears there. She brushed one away. 'It's beautiful,' she said.

'I tried to discover the voice of some of the Ancients,' I said, suddenly shy.

'You succeeded brilliantly.'

'The Heaven's Gate Interlude is still rough,' I said.

'It's perfect.'

'It's about loneliness,' I said.

'It is loneliness.'

'Do you think it's ready?' I asked.

'It's perfect . . . a masterpiece.'

'Do you think it'll sell?' I asked.

'No fucking way.'

They planned an initial run of seventy million hardfax copies of *Cantos*. Transline ran ads throughout the datasphere, placed HTV commercials, transmitted software inserts, successfully solicited blurbs from best-selling authors, made sure it was reviewed in the *New New York Times Book Section* and the TC^2 *Review*, and generally spent a fortune on advertising.

The *Cantos* sold twenty-three thousand hardfax copies during the first year it was in print. At ten percent royalties of the 12MK cover price, I had earned back 13,800MK of my 2,000,000MK advance from Transline. The second year saw a sale of 638 hardfax copies; there were no datasphere rights sold, no holie options, and no book tours.

What the *Cantos* lacked in sales it made up for in negative reviews: 'Indecipherable . . . archaic . . . irrelevant to all current concerns,' said the *Times Book Section*. 'M. Silenus has committed the ultimate act of non-communication,' wrote Urban Kapry in the *TC² Review*, 'by indulging himself in an orgy of pretentious obfuscation.' Marmon Hamlit on 'AllNet Now!' issued the final deathblow: 'Oh, the poetry thing from Whatshisname – couldn't read it. Didn't try.'

Tyrena Wingreen-Feif did not seem concerned. Two weeks after the first reviews and hardfax returns came in, a day after my thirteen-day binge ended, I farcast to her office and threw myself into the black flowfoam chair which crouched in the center of the room like a velvet panther. One of Tau Ceti Center's legendary thunderstorms was going on and Jovian-sized lightning crashes were rending the blood-tinged air just beyond the invisible containment field.

'Don't sweat it,' said Tyrena. This week's fashions included a hairdo which sent black spikes thrusting half a meter above her forehead and a body field opaciter which left shifting currents of color concealing – and revealing – the nudity beneath. 'The first run only amounted to sixty thousand fax transmits so we're not out much there.'

'You said seventy million were planned,' I said.

'Yeah, well, we changed our minds after Transline's resident AI read it.'

I slumped lower in the flowfoam. 'Even the AI hated it?'

'The AI *loved* it,' said Tyrena. 'That's when we knew for sure that *people* were going to hate it.'

I sat up. 'Couldn't we have sold copies to the TechnoCore?'

'We did,' said Tyrena. 'One. The millions of AIs there probably real-time-shared it the minute it came in over fatline. Interstellar copyright doesn't mean shit when you're dealing with silicon.'

'All right,' I said, slumping. 'What next?' Outside, lightning bolts the size of Old Earth's ancient superhighways danced between the corporate spires and cloud towers.

Tyrena rose from her desk and walked to the edge of the carpeted circle. Her body field flickered like electrically charged oil on water. 'Next,' she said, 'you decide if you want to be a writer or the Worldweb's biggest jerk-off.'

'What?'

'You heard me.' Tyrena turned and smiled. Her teeth had been capped to gold points. 'The contract allows us to recover the advance in any way we have to. Seizing your assets at Interbank, recovering the gold coins you've got hidden on Homefree, and selling that gaudy farcaster house would about do it. And then you can go join the other artistic dilettantes and dropouts and mental cases that Sad King Billy collects on whatever Outback world he lives on.'

I stared.

'Then again,' she said and smiled her cannibal smile, 'we can just forget this temporary setback and you can get to work on your next book.'

My next book appeared five standard months later. *The Dying Earth II* picked up where *The Dying Earth* left off, in plain prose this time, the sentence length and chapter content carefully guided by neuro-bio-monitored responses on a test group of 638 average hardfax readers. The book was in novel form, short enough not to intimidate the potential buyer at Food Mart checkout stands, and the cover was a twenty-second interactive holo wherein the tall, swarthy stranger – Amalfi Schwartz, I suppose, although Amalfi was short and pale and wore corrective lenses – rips the bodice of the struggling female just to the nipple line before the protesting blonde turns toward the viewer and cries for help in a breathless whisper provided by porn holie star Leeda Swann.

Dying Earth II sold nineteen million copies.

'Not bad,' said Tyrena. 'It takes awhile to build an audience.'

'The first *Dying Earth* sold three billion copies,' I said.

'*Pilgrim's Progress*,' she said. '*Mein Kampf*. Once in a century. Maybe less.'

'But it sold three *billion* . . .'

'Look,' said Tyrena. 'In twentieth-century Old Earth, a fast food chain took dead cow meat, fried it in grease, added carcinogens, wrapped it in petroleum-based foam, and sold nine hundred billion units. Human beings. Go figure.'

Dying Earth III introduced the characters of Winona, the escaped slave girl who rose to the ownership of her own fiberplastic plantation (never mind that fiberplastic never grew on Old Earth), Arturo Redgrave, the dashing blockade runner (what blockade?!), and Innocence Sperry, the nine-year-old telepath dying of an unspecified Little Nell disease. Innocence lasted until *Dying Earth IX*, and on the day Transline allowed me to kill the little shit off, I went out to celebrate with a six-day, twenty-world binge. I awoke in a lungpipe on Heaven's Gate, covered with vomit and rebreather mold, nursing the Web's biggest headache and the sure knowledge that I soon would have to start on Volume X of *The Chronicles of the Dying Earth*.

It isn't hard being a hack writer. Between *Dying Earth II* and *Dying Earth IX*, six standard years had passed relatively painlessly. My research was meager, my plots formulaic, my characters cardboard, my prose preliterate, and my free time was my own. I traveled. I married twice more; each wife left me with no hard feelings but with a sizable portion of the royalties from my next *Dying Earth*. I explored religions and serious drinking, finding more hope of lasting solace in the latter.

I kept my home, adding six rooms on five worlds, and filled it with fine art. I entertained. Writers were among my acquaintances but, as in all times, we tended to mistrust and badmouth each other, secretly resenting the other's successes and finding fault in their work. Each of us knew in his or her heart that he or she was a true artist of the word who merely happened to be commercial; the others were hacks.

Then, on a cool morning with my sleeping room rocking slightly in the upper branches of my tree on the Templar world, I awoke to a gray sky and the realization that my muse had fled.

It had been five years since I had written any poetry. The *Cantos* lay open in the Deneb Drei tower, only a few pages finished beyond what had been published. I had been using thought processors to write my novels and one of these activated as I entered the study. SHIT, it printed out, WHAT DID I DO WITH MY MUSE?

It says something about the type of writing I had been doing that my muse could flee without my noticing. For those who do not write and who never have been stirred by the creative urge, talk of muses seems a figure of speech, a quaint conceit, but for those of us who live by the Word, our muses are as real and necessary as the soft clay of language which they help to sculpt. When one is writing – *really* writing – it is as if one is given a fatline to the gods. No true poet has been able to explain the exhilaration one feels when the mind becomes an *instrument* as surely as does the pen or thought processor, ordering and expressing the revelations flowing in *from somewhere else*.

My muse had fled. I sought her in the other worlds of my house but only silence echoed back from the art-bedecked walls and empty spaces. I farcast and flew to my favorite places, watching the suns set on the windblown prairies of Grass and the night fogs obscure the ebony crags of Nevermore, but although I emptied my mind of the trash-prose of the endless *Dying Earth*, there came no whispers from my muse.

I sought her in alcohol and Flashback, returning to the productive days on Heaven's Gate when her inspiration was a constant buzzing in my ears, interrupting my work, waking me from sleep, but in the relived hours and days her voice was as muted and garbled as a damaged audio disk from some forgotten century.

My muse had fled.

I farcast to Tyrena Wingreen-Feif's office at the precise moment of my appointment. Tyrena had been promoted from editor-in-chief of the hard-fax division to publisher. Her new office occupied the highest level of the Tau Ceti Center Transline Spire and standing there was like perching on the carpeted summit of the galaxy's tallest, thinnest peak; only the invisible dome of the slightly polarized containment field arched overhead and the edge of the carpet ended in a six-kilometer drop. I wondered if other authors felt the urge to jump.

'The new opus?' said Tyrena. Lusus was dominating the fashion universe this week and 'dominate' was the right word; my editor was dressed in leather and iron, rusted spikes on her wrists and neck and a massive bandolier across her shoulder and left breast. The cartridges looked real.

'Yeah,' I said and tossed the manuscript box on her desk.

'Martin, Martin, Martin,' she sighed, 'when are you going to transmit your books rather than going to all the trouble of printing them out and bringing them here in person?'

'There's a strange satisfaction in delivering them,' I said. 'Especially this one.'

'Oh?'

'Yes,' I said. 'Why don't you read some of it?'

Tyrena smiled and clicked black fingernails along the cartridges in her bandolier. 'I'm sure it's up to your usual high standards, Martin,' she said. 'I don't have to look at it.'

'Please do,'I said.

'Really,' said Tyrena, 'there's no reason. It always makes me nervous to read a new work while the author is present.'

'This one won't,' I said. 'Read just the first few pages.'

She must have heard something in my voice because she frowned slightly and opened the box. The frown deepened as she read the first page and flipped through the rest of the manuscript.

Page one had a single sentence: 'And then, one fine morning in October, the Dying Earth swallowed its own bowels, spasmed its final spasm and died.' The other two hundred and ninety-nine pages were blank.

'A joke, Martin?'

'Nope.'

'A subtle hint then? You would like to begin a new series?'

'Nope.'

'It's not as if we hadn't expected it, Martin. Our story-liners have come up with several exciting series ideas for you. M. Subwaizee thinks that you would be perfect for the novelizations of the Crimson Avenger holies.'

'You can stick the Crimson Avenger up your corporate ass, Tyrena,' I said cordially. 'I'm finished with Transline and this premasticated gruel you call fiction.'

Tyrena's expression did not flicker. Her teeth were not pointed; today they were rusted iron to match the spikes on her wrists and the collar around her neck. 'Martin, Martin, Martin,' she sighed, 'you have no idea how finished you will be if you don't apologize, straighten up, and fly right. But that can wait until tomorrow. Why don't you step home, sober up, and think about this?'

I laughed. 'I'm as sober as I've been in eight years, lady. It just took me awhile to realize that it wasn't just *me* who's writing crap . . . there's not a book published in the Web this year that hasn't been total garbage. Well, I'm getting off the scow.'

Tyrena rose. For the first time I noticed that on her simulated canvas web belt there hung a FORCE deathwand. I hoped that it was a designer-fake like the rest of her costume.

'Listen, you miserable, no-talent hack,' she hissed. 'Transline owns you from the balls up. If you give us any more trouble we'll have you working in the Gothic Romance factory under the name Rosemary Titmouse. Now go home, sober up, and get to work on *Dying Earth X*.'

I smiled and shook my head.

Tyrena squinted slightly. 'You're still into us for almost a million-mark advance,' she said. 'One word to Collections and we'll seize every room of your house except that goddamn raft you use as an outhouse. You can sit on it until the oceans fill up with crap.'

I laughed a final time. 'It's a self-contained disposal unit,' I said. 'Besides, I sold the house yesterday. The check for the balance of the advance should have been transmitted by now.'

Tyrena tapped the plastic grip of her deathwand. 'Transline's copyrighted the Dying Earth concept, you know. We'll just have someone else write the books.'

I nodded. 'They're welcome to it.'

Something in my ex-editor's voice changed when she realized that I was serious. Somewhere, I sensed, there was an advantage to her if I stayed. 'Listen,' she said, 'I'm sure we can work this out, Martin. I was saying to the director the other day that your advances were too small and that Transline should let you develop a new story line . . .'

'Tyrena, Tyrena, Tyrena,' I sighed. 'Goodbye.'

I farcast to Renaissance Vector and then to Parsimony, where I boarded a spinship for the three-week voyage to Asquith and the crowded kingdom of Sad King Billy.

Notes for a sketch of Sad King Billy:

His Royal Highness King William XXIII, sovereign lord of the Kingdom of Windsor-in-Exile, looks a bit like a wax candle of a man who has been left on a hot stove. His long hair runs in limp rivulets to slumped shoulders while the furrows on his brow trickle downward to the tributaries of wrinkles around the basset-hound eyes, and then run southward again through folds and frown lines to the maze of wattles in neck and jowls. King Billy is said to remind anthropologists of the worry dolls of the Outback Kinshasa, to make Zen Gnostics recall the Pitiful Buddha after the temple fire on Tai Zhin, and to send media historians rushing to their archives to check photos of an ancient flat-film movie actor named Charles Laughton. None of these references mean anything to me; I look at King Billy and think of my long-dead tutor don Balthazar after a week-long binge.

Sad King Billy's reputation for gloominess is exaggerated. He often laughs; it is merely his misfortune that his peculiar form of laughter makes most people think he is sobbing.

A man cannot help his physiognomy, but in His Highness's case, the entire persona tends to suggest either 'buffoon' or 'victim'. He dresses, if that can be the word, in something approaching a constant state of anarchy, defying the taste and color sense of his android servants, so that on some days he clashes with himself and his environment simultaneously. Nor is his appearance limited to sartorial chaos – King William moves in a permanent sphere of dishabille, his fly unsealed, his velvet cape torn and tattered and drawing crumbs magnetically from the floor, his left sleeve ruffle twice as long as the right, which – in turn – looks as if it has been dipped in jam.

You get the idea.

For all this, Sad King Billy has an insightful mind and a passion for the arts and literature which has not been equaled since the true Renaissance days on old Old Earth.

In some ways King Billy is the fat child with his face eternally pressed to the candy store window. He loves and appreciates fine music but cannot produce it. A connoisseur of ballet and all things graceful, His Highness is a klutz, a moving series of pratfalls and comic bits of clumsiness. A passionate reader, unerring poetry critic, and patron of forensics, King Billy combines a stutter in his verbal expression with a shyness which will not allow him to show his verse or prose to anyone else.

A lifelong bachelor now entering his sixtieth year, King Billy inhabits the tumbledown palace and two-thousand-square-mile kingdom as if it were another suit of rumpled, royal clothes. Anecdotes abound: one of the famous oil painters whom King Billy supports finds His Majesty walking head down, hands clasped behind him, one foot on the garden path and one in the mud, obviously lost in thought. The artist hails his patron. Sad King Billy looks up, blinks, looks around as if awakening from a long nap. 'Excuse me,' His Highness says to the bemused painter, 'b-b-but could you p-p-please tell me – was I headed *toward* the palace or *away* from the p-p-palace?' 'Toward the palace, Your Majesty,' replies the artist. 'Oh, g-g-good,' sighs the King, 'then I've had lunch.'

General Horace Glennon-Height had begun his rebellion and the Outback world of Asquith lay directly in his path of conquest. Asquith was not worried – the Hegemony had offered a FORCE:space fleet as a shield – but the royal ruler of the Kingdom of Monaco-in-Exile seemed more melted than ever when he called me in.

'Martin,' said His Majesty, 'you've h-h-heard about the b-battle for Fomalhaut?'

'Yeah,' I said. 'It doesn't sound like anything to worry about. Fomalhaut was just the kind of place Glennon-Height's been hitting . . . small, no more than a few thousand colonists, rich in minerals, and with a time-debt of at least – what was it? – twenty standard months from the Web.'

'Twenty-three,' said Sad King Billy. 'So you d-d-don't think that w-we are in d-d-d-jeopardy?'

'Uh-uh,' I said. 'With only a three-week real-transit time and a time-debt of less than a year, the Hegemony can always get forces here from the Web faster than the General can spin up from Fomalhaut.'

'Perhaps,' mused King Billy, beginning to lean on a globe and then jumping upright as it started to turn under his weight. 'But none-the-the less I've decided to start our own m-m-modest Hegira.'

I blinked, surprised. Billy had been talking about relocating the kingdom in exile for almost two years, but I had never thought he would go through with it.

'The sp-sp-sp . . . the ships are ready on Parvati,' he said. 'Asquith has agreed to su-su-su . . . to provide the transport we need to the Web.'

'But the palace?' I said. 'The library? The farms and grounds?'

'Donated, of course,' said King Billy, 'but the contents of the library will travel with us.'

I sat on the arm of the horsehair divan and rubbed my cheek. In the ten years I had been in the kingdom, I had progressed from Billy's subject of patronage to tutor, to confidant, to friend, but never did I pretend to understand this disheveled enigma. Upon my arrival he had granted me an immediate audience. 'D-d-do you w-w-wish to j-j-join the other t-t-talented people in our little colony?' he had asked.

'Yes, Your Majesty.'

'And w-w-will you wr-wr-write more books like the *D-D-Dying Earth*?'

'Not if I can help it, Your Majesty.'

'I r-r-read it, you know,' the little man had said. 'It was v-v-very interesting.'

'You're most kind, Sir.'

'B-b-b-bullshit, M. Silenus. It w-w-was interesting because someone had obviously b-b-bowdlerized it and left in all the *bad* parts.'

I had grinned, surprised by the sudden revelation that I was going to like Sad King Billy.

'B-b-but the *Cantos*,' he sighed, 'th-th-that was a *book*. Probably the finest volume of v-v . . . poetry published in the Web in the last two centuries. How you managed to get that by the mediocrity police I will never know. I ordered twenty thousand copies for the k-k-kingdom.'

I bowed my head slightly, at a loss for words for the first time since my poststroke days two decades before.

'Will you write more p-p-poetry like the *Cantos*?'

'I came here to try, Your Majesty.'

'Then welcome,' said Sad King Billy. 'You will stay in the west wing of the p-p-p . . . castle, near my offices, and my door will always be open to you.'

Now I glanced at the closed door and at the little sovereign who – even when smiling – looked as if he were on the verge of tears. 'Hyperion?' I asked. He had mentioned the colony world-gone-primitive many times.

'Precisely. The android seedships have been there for some years, M-M-Martin. Preparing the way, as it were.'

I raised an eyebrow. King Billy's wealth came not from the assets of the kingdom but from major investments in the Web economy. Even so, if he had been carrying on a surreptitious recolonization effort for years, the cost must have been staggering.

'D-d-do you remember why the original colonists named the pluh-pluh-pluh . . . the world Hyperion, Martin?'

'Sure. Before the Hegira they were a tiny freehold on one of the moons of

Saturn. They couldn't last without terrestrial resupply, so they emigrated to the Outback and named the survey world after their moon.'

King Billy smiled sadly. 'And do you know why the name is p-p-propitious for *our* endeavor?'

It took me about ten seconds to make the connection. 'Keats,' I said.

Several years earlier, near the end of a long discussion about the essence of poetry, King Billy had asked me who was the purest poet who had ever lived.

'The purest?' I had said. 'Don't you mean the greatest?'

'No, no,' said Billy, 'that's absurd t-t-to argue over who is the *greatest*. I'm curious about your opinion of the p-p-purest . . . the closest to the essence you describe.'

I had thought about it a few days and then brought my answer to King Billy as we watched the setting suns from the top of the bluff near the palace. Red and blue shadows stretched across the amber lawn toward us. 'Keats,' I said.

'John Keats,' whispered Sad King Billy. 'Ahh.' And then a moment later: 'Why?'

So I had told him what I knew about the nineteenth-century Old Earth poet; about his upbringing, training, and early death . . . but mostly about a life dedicated almost totally to the mysteries and beauties of poetic creation.

Billy had seemed interested then; he seemed obsessed now as he waved his hand and brought into existence a holo model which all but filled the room. I moved backward, stepping through hills and buildings and grazing animals to get a better view.

'Behold Hyperion,' whispered my patron. As was usually the case when he was totally absorbed, King Billy forgot to stutter. The holo shifted through a series of views: river cities, port cities, mountain eyries, a city on a hill filled with monuments to match the strange buildings in a nearby valley.

'The Time Tombs?' I said.

'Precisely. The greatest mystery in the known universe.'

I frowned at the hyperbole. 'They're fucking empty,' I said. 'They've *been* empty since they were discovered.'

'They are the source of a strange, anti-entropic force-field which lingers still,' said King Billy. 'One of the few phenomena outside singularities which dares to tamper with time itself.'

'It's no big deal,' I said. 'It must've been like painting rust preventative on metal. They were made to last but they're *empty*. And since when do we go bugfuck about technology?'

'Not technology,' sighed King Billy, his face melting into deeper grooves. '*Mystery*. The strangeness of place so necessary to some creative spirits. A perfect mixture of the classical utopia and the pagan mystery.'

I shrugged, not impressed.

Sad King Billy waved the holo away. 'Has your p-p-poetry improved?'

I crossed my arms and glared at the regal dwarf-slob. 'No.'

'Has your m-m-muse returned?'

I said nothing. If looks could have killed, we would all be crying 'The King is dead, long live the King!' before nightfall.

'Very w-w-well,' he said, showing that he could look insufferably smug as well as sad. 'P-p-pack your bags, my boy. We're going to Hyperion.'

(Fade in)

Sad King Billy's five seedships floating like golden dandelions above a lapis sky. White cities rising on three continents: Keats, Endymion, Port Romance . . . the Poets' City itself. More than eight thousand of Art's pilgrims seeking escape from the tyranny of mediocrity and searching for a renewal of vision on this rough-hewn world.

Asquith and Windsor-in-Exile had been a center for android biofacture in the century following the Hegira, and now these blueskinned friends-of-man labored and tilled with the understanding that once these final labors were finished they were free at last. The white cities rose. The indigenies, tired of playing native, came out of their villages and forests and helped us rebuild the colony to more human specifications. The technocrats and bureaucrats and ecocrats were thawed and let loose upon the unsuspecting world and Sad King Billy's dream came one step closer to reality.

By the time we arrived at Hyperion, General Horace Glennon-Height was dead, his brief but brutal mutiny already crushed, but there was no turning back.

Some of the more rugged artists and artisans spurned the Poets' City and eked out rugged but creative lives in Jacktown or Port Romance, or even in the expanding frontiers beyond, but I stayed.

I found no muse on Hyperion during those first years. For many, the expansion of distance because of limited transportation – EMVs were unreliable, skimmers scarce – and the contraction of artificial consciousness due to absence of datasphere, no access to the All Thing, and only one fatline transmitter – all led to a renewal of creative energies, a new realization of what it meant to be human and an artist.

Or so I heard.

No muse appeared. My verse continued to be technically proficient and dead as Huck Finn's cat.

I decided to kill myself.

But first I spent some time, nine years at least, carrying out a community service by providing the one thing new Hyperion lacked: decadence.

From a biosculptor aptly named Graumann Hacket, I obtained the hairy flanks, hooves, and goat legs of a satyr. I cultivated my beard and extended my ears. Graumann made interesting alterations to my sexual apparatus. Word got around. Peasant girls, indigenies, the wives of our true-blue city planners and pioneers – all awaited a visit from Hyperion's only resident satyr or arranged one themselves. I learned what 'priapic' and 'satyriasis' really mean. Besides the unending series of sexual contests, I allowed my

drinking bouts to become legendary and my vocabulary to return to something approaching the old poststroke days.

It was fucking wonderful. It was fucking hell.

And then on the night I had set aside to blow my brains out, Grendel
appeared.

Notes for a sketch of our visiting monster:

Our worst dreams have come alive. Something wicked shuns the light.
Shades of Morbius and the Krell. Keep the fires high, Mother, Grendel
comes tonight.

At first we think the missing are merely absent; there are no watchers on
the walls of our city, no walls actually, no warriors at the door of our mead
hall. Then a husband reports a wife who disappears between the evening
meal and the tucking in of their two children. Then Hoban Kristus, the
abstract implosionist, fails to appear at a midweek performance at Poets'
Amphitheatre, his first missed cue in eighty-two years of treading the
boards. Concern rises. Sad King Billy returns from his labors as overseer on
the Jacktown restoration and promises that security will be tightened. A
sensor net is woven around the town. ShipSecurity officers sweep the Time
Tombs and report that all remains empty. Mechs are sent into the labyrinth
entrance at the base of the Jade Tomb and report nothing in a six-
thousand-kilometer probe. Skimmers, automated and manned, sweep the
area between the city and the Bridle Range and sense nothing larger than
the heat signature of a rock eel. For a local week there are no more disappearances.

Then the deaths begin.

The sculptor Pete Garcia is found in his studio . . . and in his bedroom . . . and in the yard beyond. ShipSecurity Manager Truin Hines is
foolish enough to tell a newsteep: 'It's like he was mauled by some vicious
animal. But no animal I've ever seen could do that to a man.'

We are all secretly thrilled and titillated. True, the dialogue is bad,
straight out of a million movies and holies we've scared ourselves with, but
now we are part of the show.

Suspicion turns toward the obvious: a psychopath is loose among us,
probably killing with a pulse-blade or hellwhip. This time he (or she) had
not found time to dispose of the body. Poor Pete.

ShipSecurity Manager Hines is sacked and City Manager Pruett receives
permission from His Majesty to hire, train, and arm a city police force of
approximately twenty officers. There is talk of truth-testing the entire
Poets' City population of six thousand. Sidewalk cafes buzz with conversation on civil rights . . . we were technically out of the Hegemony –
did we have any rights? . . . and harebrained schemes are hatched to catch
the murderer.

Then the slaughter begins.

There was no pattern to the murders. Bodies were found in twos and threes, or alone, or not at all. Some of the disappearances were bloodless; others left gallons of gore. There were no witnesses, no survivors of attacks. Location did not seem to matter: the Weimont family lived in one of the outlying villas but Sira Rob never stirred from her tower studio near the center of town; two of the victims disappeared alone, at night, apparently while walking in the Zen Garden, but Chancellor Lehman's daughter had private bodyguards yet vanished while alone in a bathroom on the seventh floor of Sad King Billy's palace.

On Lusus or Tau Ceti Center or a dozen other of the old Web worlds, the deaths of a thousand people add up to minor news – items for datasphere short-term or the inside pages of the morning paper – but in a city of six thousand on a colony of fifty thousand, a dozen murders – like the proverbial sentence to be hanged in the morning – tend to focus one's attention wonderfully well.

I knew one of the first victims. Sissipriss Harris had been one of my first conquests as a satyr – and one of my most enthusiastic – a beautiful girl, long blond hair too soft to be real, a fresh-picked-peach complexion too virginal to dream of touching, a beauty too perfect to believe: precisely the sort that even the most timid male dreams of violating, Sissipriss now had been violated in earnest. They found only her head, lying upright in the center of Lord Byron's Plaza as if she had been buried to her neck in pourable marble. I knew when I heard these details precisely what kind of creature we were dealing with, for a cat I had owned on Mother's estate had left similar offerings on the south patio most summer mornings – the head of a mouse staring up from the sandstone in pure rodent amazement, or perhaps a ground squirrel's toothy grin – killing trophies from a proud but hungry predator.

Sad King Billy came to visit me while I was working on my *Cantos*.

'Good morning, Billy,' I said.

'It's *Your Majesty*,' grumped His Majesty in a rare show of royal pique. His stutter had disappeared the day the royal dropship landed on Hyperion.

'Good morning, Billy, Your Majesty.'

'Hnnrh,' growled my liege lord, moving some papers and managing to sit in the only puddle of spilled coffee on an otherwise dry bench. 'You're writing again, Silenus.'

I saw no reason to acknowledge an acknowledgment of the obvious.

'Have you always used a pen?'

'No,' I said, 'only when I want to write something worth reading.'

'Is that worth reading?' He gestured toward the small heap of manuscript I had accrued in two local weeks of work.

'Yes.'

'Yes? Just *yes*?'

'Yes.'

'Will I get to read it soon?'

'No.'

King Billy looked down and noticed that his leg was in a puddle of coffee. He frowned, moved, and mopped at the shrinking pool with the hem of his cape. 'Never?' he said.

'Not unless you outlive me.'

'Which I plan to do,' said the King. 'While you expire from playing goat to the kingdom's ewes.'

'Is that an attempt at a metaphor?'

'Not in the least,' said King Billy. 'Merely an observation.'

'I haven't forced my attentions on a ewe since my boyhood days on the farm,' I said. 'I promised my mother in song that I wouldn't indulge in sheep fucking again without asking her permission.' While King Billy looked on mournfully, I sang a few bars of an ancient ditty called 'There'll Never Be Another Ewe'.

'Martin,' he said, 'someone or something is killing my people.'

I set aside my paper and pen. 'I know,' I said.

'I need your help.'

'How, for Christ's sake? Am I supposed to track down the killer like some HTV detective? Have a fight to the fucking death on Reichenbach fucking Falls?'

'That would be satisfactory, Martin. But in the meantime a few opinions and words of advice would suffice.'

'Opinion One,' I said, 'it was stupid to come here. Opinion Two, it's stupid to stay. Advice Alpha/Omega: leave.'

King Billy nodded dolefully. 'Leave this city or all of Hyperion?'

I shrugged.

His Majesty rose and walked to the window of my small study. It looked out across a three-meter alley to the brick wall of the automated recycling plant next door. King Billy studied the view. 'You're aware,' he said, 'of the ancient legend of the Shrike?'

'I've heard bits of it.'

'The indigenies associate the monster with the Time Tombs,' he said.

'The indigenies smear paint on their bellies for the harvest celebration and smoke unrecombinant tobacco,' I said.

King Billy nodded at the wisdom of this. He said: 'The Hegemony First-down Team was wary of this area. They set up the multichannel recorders and kept their bases south of the Bridle.'

'Look,' I said, 'Your Majesty . . . what do you want? Absolution for screwing up and building the city here? You're absolved. Go and sin no more, my son. Now, if you don't mind, Your Royalship, *adiós*. I've got dirty limericks to write here.'

King Billy did not turn away from the window. 'You recommend that we evacuate the city, Martin?'

I hesitated only a second. 'Sure.'

'And would you leave with the rest?'

'Why wouldn't I?'

King Billy turned and looked me in the eye. '*Would* you?'

I said nothing. After a minute I looked away.

'I thought so,' said the ruler of the planet. He clasped his pudgy hands behind his back and stared at the wall again. 'If I were a detective,' he said, 'I would be suspicious. The city's least productive citizen starts writing again after a decade of silence only . . . what, Martin? . . . two days after the first murders happened. Now he's disappeared from the social life he once dominated and spends his time composing an epic poem . . . why, even the young girls are safe from his goatish ardor.'

I sighed. 'Goatish ardor, m'lord?'

King Billy glanced over his shoulder at me.

'All right,' I said. 'You've got me. I confess. I've been murdering them and bathing in their blood. It works as a fucking literary aphrodisiac. I figure two . . . three hundred more victims, tops . . . and I'll have my next book ready for publication.'

King Billy turned back to the window.

'What's the matter,' I said, 'don't you believe me?'

'No.'

'Why not?'

'Because,' said the King, 'I know who the murderer is.'

We sat in the darkened holopit and watched the Shrike kill novelist Sira Rob and her lover. The light level was very low; Sira's middle-aged flesh seemed to glow with a pale phosphorescence while her much younger boyfriend's white buttocks gave the illusion in the dim light of floating separately from the rest of his tanned body. Their lovemaking was reaching its frenzied peak when the inexplicable occurred. Rather than the final thrusts and sudden pause of orgasm, the young man seemed to levitate up and backward, rising into the air as if Sira had somehow forcefully ejected him from her body. The sound track on the disk, previously consisting of the usual banal pants, gasps, exhortations, and instructions one would expect from such activity, suddenly filled the holopit with screams – first the young man's, then Sira's.

There was a thud as the boy's body struck a wall off camera. Sira's body lay waiting in tragically comic vulnerability, her legs wide, arms open, breasts flattened, thighs pale. Her head had been thrown back in ecstasy but now she had time to raise it, shock and anger already replacing the oddly similar expression of imminent orgasm. She opened her mouth to shout something.

No words. There came the watermelon-carving sound of blades piercing flesh, of hooks being pulled free of tendon and bone. Sira's head went back, her mouth opened impossibly wide, and her body exploded from the breastbone down. Flesh separated as if an invisible ax were chopping Sira Rob for kindling. Unseen scalpels completed the job of opening her, lateral incisions appearing tike obscene time-lapse footage of a mad surgeon's favorite operation. It was a brutal autopsy performed on a living person. On a once living person, rather, for when the blood stopped flying and the body ceased spasming, Sira's limbs relaxed in death, legs opening again in an echo of the obscene display of viscera above. And then – for the briefest second – there was a blur of red and chrome near the bed.

'Freeze, expand, and augment,' King Billy told the house computer.

The blur resolved itself into a head out of a jolt addict's nightmare: a face part steel, part chrome, and part skull, teeth like a mechanized wolf's crossed with a steam shovel, eyes like ruby lasers burning through blood-filled gems, forehead penetrated by a curved spike-blade rising thirty centimeters from a quicksilver skull, and a neck ringed with similar thorns.

'The Shrike?' I asked.

King Billy nodded – the merest movement of chin and jowls.

'What happened to the boy?' I asked.

'There was no sign of him when Sira's body was discovered,' said the King. 'No one knew he was missing until this disk was discovered. He has been identified as a young recreation specialist from Endymion.'

'You just found the holo?'

'Yesterday,' said King Billy. 'The security people found the imager on the ceiling. Less than a millimeter across. Sira had a library of such disks. The camera apparently was there only to record . . . ah . . . '

'The bedroom follies,' I said.

'Precisely.'

I stood up and approached the floating image of the creature. My hand passed through forehead, spike, and jaws. The computer had calculated its size and represented it properly. Judging from the thing's head, our local Grendel stood more than three meters tall. 'Shrike,' I muttered, more in greeting than in identification.

'What can you tell me about it, Martin?'

'Why ask me?' I snapped. 'I'm a poet, not a mythohistorian.'

'You accessed the seedship computer with a query about the Shrike's nature and origins,'

I raised an eyebrow. Computer access was supposed to be as private and anonymous as datasphere entry in the Hegemony. 'So what?' I said. 'Hundreds of people must have checked out the Shrike legend since the killings began. Maybe thousands. It's the only fucking monster legend we've *got*.'

King Billy moved his wrinkles and folds up and down. 'Yes,' he said, 'but you searched the files three months before the first disappearance.'

I sighed and slumped into the holopit cushions. 'All right,' I said, 'I did. So what? I wanted to use the fucking legend in the fucking poem I'm writing, so I researched it. Arrest me.'

'What did you learn?'

I was very angry now. I stamped satyr hooves into the soft carpet. 'Just the stuff in the fucking file,' I snapped. 'What in the hell do you want from me, Billy?'

The King rubbed his brow and winced as he accidentally stuck his little finger in his eye. 'I don't know,' he said. 'The security people wanted to take you up to the ship and put you on full interrogative interface. I chose to talk to you instead.'

I blinked, feeling a strange zero-g sensation in my stomach. Full interrogative meant cortical shunts and sockets in the skull. Most people interrogated that way recovered fully. Most.

'Can you tell me what aspect of the Shrike legend you planned to use in your poem?' King Billy asked softly.

'Sure,' I said. 'According to the Shrike Cult gospel that the indigenies started, the Shrike is the Lord of Pain and the Angel of Final Atonement, come from a place beyond time to announce the end of the human race. I liked that conceit.'

'The end of the human race,' repeated King Billy.

'Yeah. He's Michael the Archangel and Moroni and Satan and Masked Entropy and the Frankenstein monster all rolled into one package,' I said. 'He hangs around the Time Tombs waiting to come out and wreak havoc when it's mankind's time to join the dodo and the gorilla and the sperm whale on the extinction Hit Parade list.'

'The Frankenstein monster,' mused the short little fat man in the wrinkled cape. 'Why him?'

I took a breath. 'Because the Shrike Cult believes that mankind somehow *created* the thing,' I said, although I knew that King Billy knew everything I knew and more.

'Do they know how to *kill* it?' he asked.

'Not that I know of. He's supposed to be immortal, beyond time.'

'A god?'

I hesitated. 'Not really,' I said at last. 'More like one of the universe's worst nightmares come to life. Sort of like the Grim Reaper, but with a penchant for sticking souls on a giant thorn tree . . . while the people's souls are still in their bodies.'

King Billy nodded.

'Look,' I said, 'if you insist on splitting hairs from back-world theologies, why don't you fly to Jacktown and ask a few of the Cult priests?'

'Yes,' said the King, chin on his pudgy fist, obviously distracted, 'they're already on the seedship being interrogated. It's all most confusing.'

I rose to leave, not sure if I would be allowed to.

'Martin?'

'Yeah.'

'Before you go, can you think of anything else that could help us understand this thing?'

I paused in the doorway, feeling my heart batting at my ribs to get out. 'Yeah,' I said, my voice only marginally steady. 'I can tell you who and what the Shrike really is.'

'Oh?'

'It's my muse,' I said, and turned, and went back to my room to write.

*

162

Of course I had summoned the Shrike. I knew that. I had summoned it by beginning my epic poem about it. In the beginning was the Word.

I retitled my poem *The Hyperion Cantos*. It was not about the planet but about the passing of the self-styled Titans called humans. It was about the unthinking hubris of a race which dared to murder its homeworld through sheer carelessness and then carried that dangerous arrogance to the stars, only to meet the wrath of a god which humanity had helped to sire. *Hyperion* was the first serious work I had done in many years and it was the best I would ever do. What began as a comic-serious homage to the ghost of John Keats became my last reason for existence, an epic tour de force in an age of mediocre farce. *Hyperion Cantos* was written with a skill I could never have attained, with a mastery I could never have gained, and sung in a voice which was not mine. The passing of humankind was my topic. The Shrike was my muse.

A score more people died before King Billy evacuated the City of Poets. Some of the evacuees went to Endymion or Keats or one of the other new cities, but most voted to take the seedships back to the Web. King Billy's dream of a creative utopia died, although the King himself lived on in the gloomy palace at Keats. Leadership of the colony passed to the Home Rule Council, which petitioned the Hegemony for membership and immediately established a Self-defense Force. The SDF – made up primarily of the same indigenies who had been cudgeling each other a decade before, but commanded now by self-styled officers from our new colony – succeeded only in disturbing the peacefulness of the night with their automated skimmer patrols and marring the beauty of the returning desert with their mobile surveillance mechs.

Surprisingly, I was not the only one to stay behind; at least two hundred remained, although most of us avoided social contact, smiling politely when we passed on Poets' Walk or while we ate apart in the echoing emptiness of the dining dome.

The murders and disappearances continued, averaging about one a local fortnight, although they were usually discovered not by us but by the regional SDF commander, who demanded a head count of citizens every few weeks.

The image that remains in my mind from that first year is an unusually communal one: the night we gathered on the Commons to watch the seedship leave. It was at the height of the autumn meteor season and Hyperion's night skies were already ablaze with gold streaks and red crisscrosses of flame when the seedship's engines fired, a small sun flared, and for an hour we watched as friends and fellow artists receded as a streak of fusion flame. Sad King Billy joined us that night and I remember that he looked at me before he solemnly reentered his ornate coach to return to the safety of Keats.

In the dozen years which followed I left the city half a dozen times; once to find a biosculptor who could rid me of my satyr affectation, the other times to buy food and supplies. The Shrike Temple had renewed the Shrike pilgrimages by this time, and on my trips I would use their elaborate avenue to death in reverse – the walk to Chronos Keep, the aerial tram across the Bridle Range, the windwagons, and the Charon barge down the Hoolie. Coming back, I would stare at the pilgrims and wonder who would survive.

Few visited the City of Poets. Our half-finished towers began to look like tumbled ruins. The gal, with their splendid metal-glass domes and covered arcades grew heavy with vines; pyreweed and scargrass poked up between the flagstones. The SDF added to the chaos, setting mines and booby traps to kill the Shrike, but only succeeding in devastating once beautiful sections of the city. Irrigation broke down. The aqueduct collapsed. The desert encroached. I moved from room to room in King Billy's abandoned palace, working on my poem, waiting for my muse.

When you think about it, the cause-effect begins to resemble some mad logic-loop by the data artist Carolus or perhaps a print by Escher: the Shrike had come into existence because of the incantatory powers of my poem but the poem could not have existed without the threat/presence of the Shrike as muse. Perhaps I was a bit mad in those days.

In a dozen years sudden death culled the city of dilettantes until only the Shrike and I remained. The annual passage of the Shrike Pilgrimage was a minor irritation, a distant caravan crossing the desert to the Time Tombs. Sometimes a few figures returned, fleeing across vermilion sands to the refuge of Chronos Keep twenty kilometers to the southwest. More often, no one emerged.

I watched from the shadows of the city. My hair and beard had grown until they covered some of the rags I wore. I came out mostly at night, moving through the ruins like a furtive shadow, sometimes gazing at my lighted palace tower like David Hume peering in his own windows and solemnly deciding that he wasn't home. I never moved the food synthesizer from the dining dome to my apartments, preferring instead to eat in the echoing silence under that cracked *duomo* like some addled Eloi fattening himself up for the inevitable Morlock.

I never saw the Shrike. Many nights, just before dawn, I would awaken from a nap at a sudden sound – the scratch of metal on stone, the rasp of sand under something's foot – but although I was often sure that I was being watched, I never saw the watcher.

Occasionally I made the short trip to the Time Tombs, especially at night, avoiding the soft, disconcerting tugs of the anti-entropic time tides while I moved through complicated shadows under the wings of the Sphinx or stared at stars through the emerald wall of the Jade Tomb. It was upon my return from one of these nocturnal pilgrimages that I found an intruder in my study.

'Impressive, M-M-M-Martin,' said King Billy, tapping one of several heaps of manuscript which lay about the room. Seated in the oversized chair at the long table, the failed monarch looked old, more melted than ever. It was obvious that he had been reading for several hours. 'Do you r-r-really think that mankind d-d-d-deserves such an end?' he asked softly. It had been a dozen years since I had heard the stutter.

I moved away from the door but did not answer. Billy had been a friend and patron for more than twenty standard years, but at that moment I could have killed him. The thought of someone reading *Hyperion* without permission filled me with rage.

'You d-d-date your p-p-p . . . cantos?' said King Billy, riffling through the most recent stack of completed pages.

'How did you get here?' I snapped. It was not an idle question. Skimmers, dropships, and helicopters had not had much luck flying to the Time Tombs region in recent years. The machines arrived *sans* passengers. It had done wonders in fueling the Shrike myth.

The little man in the rumpled cape shrugged. His uniform was meant to be brilliant and regal but merely made him look like an overweight Harlequin. 'I followed the last batch of pilgrims,' he said. 'And then c-c-came down from Keep Chronos to visit. I notice that you've written nothing in many months, M-M-Martin. Can you explain that?'

I glowered in silence while sidling closer.

'Perhaps I can explain it,' said King Billy. He looked at the last completed page of *Hyperion Cantos* as if it had the answer to a long-puzzled riddle. 'The last stanzas were written the same week last year that J.T. Telio disappeared.'

'So?' I had moved to the far edge of the table now. Feigning a casual attitude, I pulled a short stack of manuscript pages closer and moved them out of Billy's reach.

'So that w-w-w-was . . . according to the SDF monitors . . . the d-d-date of the death of the last remaining Poets' City dweller,' he said. 'The last except for y-y-you, that is, Martin.'

I shrugged and began moving around the table. I needed to get to Billy without getting the manuscript in the way.

'You know, you haven't f-f-f-finished it, Martin,' he said in his deep, sad voice. 'There is still some chance that humanity s-s-s-survives the Fall.'

'No,' I said and sidled closer.

'But you can't write it, can you, Martin? You can't c-c-c-compose this poetry unless your m-m-muse is shedding blood, can you?'

'Bullshit,' I said.

'Perhaps. But a fascinating coincidence. Have you ever wondered why *you* have been spared, Martin?'

I shrugged again and slid another stack of papers out of his reach. I was taller, stronger, and meaner than Billy, but I had to be sure that none of the manuscript would be damaged if he struggled as I lifted him out of his seat and threw him out.

'It's t-t-t-time we did something about this problem,' said my patron.

'No,' I said, 'it's time you left.' I shoved the last stacks of poetry aside and raised my arms, surprised to see a brass candlestick in one hand.

'Stop right there, please,' King Billy said softly and lifted a neural stunner from his lap.

I paused only a second. Then I laughed. 'You miserable little hangdog fraud,' I said. 'You couldn't use a fucking weapon if your life depended on it.'

I stepped forward to beat him up and throw him out.

My cheek was against the stone of the courtyard but one eye was open enough for me to see that stars still shone through the broken latticework of the galleria dome. I could not blink. My limbs and torso tingled with the pinpricks of returning sensation, as if my entire body had fallen asleep and was now coming painfully awake. It made me want to scream, but my jaw and tongue refused to work. Suddenly I was lifted and propped against a stone bench so that I could see the courtyard and the dry fountain which Rithmet Corbet had designed. The bronze Laocoön wrestled with bronze snakes in the flickering illumination of the predawn meteor showers.

'I'm s-s-sorry, Martin,' came a familiar voice, 'b-b-but this m-m-madness has to end.' King Billy came into my field of view carrying a tall stack of manuscript. Other heaps of pages lay on the shell of the fountain at the foot of the metal Trojan. An open bucket of kerosene sat nearby.

I managed to blink. My eyelids moved like rusted iron.

'The stun should w-w-wear off any s-s-s . . . any minute,' said King Billy. He reached into the fountain, raised a sheaf of manuscript, and ignited it with a flick of his cigarette lighter.

'No!' I managed to scream through clenched jaws.

The flames danced and died. King Billy let the ashes drop into the fountain and lifted another stack of pages, rolling them into a cylinder. Tears glistened on lined cheeks illuminated by flame. 'You c-c-called it f-f-forth,' gasped the little man. 'It must be f-f-finished.'

I struggled to rise. My arms and legs jerked like a marionette's mishandled limbs. The pain was incredible. I screamed again and the agonized sound echoed from marble and granite.

King Billy lifted a fat sheaf of papers and paused to read from the top page:

'Without story or prop
But my own weak mortality, I bore
The load of this eternal quietude,
The unchanging gloom, and the three fixed shapes
Ponderous upon my senses a whole moon.
For by my burning brain I measured sure
Her silver seasons shedded on the night
And ever day by day I thought I grew
More gaunt and ghostly – Oftentimes I prayed,

Intense, that Death would take me from the vale
And all its burdens – Gasping with despair
Of change, hour after hour I cursed myself.'

King Billy raised his face to the stars and consigned this page to flame.

'No!' I cried again and forced my legs to bend. I got to one knee, tried to steady myself with an arm ablaze with pinpricks, and fell on my side.

The shadow in the cape lifted a stack too thick to roll and peered at it in the dim light.

'Then I saw a wan face
Not pinned by human sorrows, but bright blanched
By an immortal sickness which kills not;
It works a constant change, which happy death
Can put no end to; deathwards progressing
To no death was that visage; it had passed
The lily and the snow; and beyond these
I must not think now, though I saw that face . . .'

King Billy moved his lighter and this and fifty other pages burst into flame. He dropped the burning papers into the fountain and reached for more.

'Please!' I cried and pulled myself up, stiffening my legs against the twitches of random nerve impulses while leaning against the stone bench. 'Please.'

The third figure did not actually appear so much as allow its presence to impinge upon my consciousness; it was as if it always had been there and King Billy and I had failed to notice it until the flames grew bright enough. Impossibly tall, four-armed, molded in chrome and cartilage, the Shrike turned its red gaze on us.

King Billy gasped, stepped back, and then moved forward to feed more cantos to the fire. Embers rose on warm drafts. A flight of doves burst from the vine-choked girders of the broken dome with an explosion of wing sound.

I moved forward in a motion more lurch than step. The Shrike did not move, did not shift its bloody gaze.

'Go!' cried King Billy, stutter forgotten, voice exalted, a blazing mass of poetry in each hand. 'Return to the pit whence you came!'

The Shrike seemed to incline its head ever so slightly. Red light gleamed on sharp surfaces.

'My lord!' I cried, although to King Billy or the apparition from hell I did not know then and know not now. I staggered the last few paces and reached for Billy's arm.

He was not there. One second the aging King was a hand's length from me and in the next instant he was ten meters away, raised high above the courtyard stones. Fingers like steel thorns pierced his arms and chest and thighs, but he still writhed and my *Cantos* burned in his fists. The Shrike held him out like a father offering his son for baptism.

'Destroy it!' Billy cried, his pinned arms making pitiful gestures. 'Destroy it!'

I stopped at the fountain's edge, tottered weakly against the rim. At first I thought he meant destroy the Shrike . . . and then I thought he meant the poem . . . and then I realized that he meant both. A thousand pages and more of manuscript lay tumbled in the dry fountain. I picked up the bucket of kerosene.

The Shrike did not move except to pull King Billy slowly back against his chest in an oddly affectionate motion. Billy writhed and screamed silently as a long steel thorn emerged from his Harlequin silk just above the breastbone. I stood there stupidly and thought of butterfly collections I had displayed as a child. Slowly, mechanically, I sloshed kerosene on the scattered pages.

'End it!' gasped King Billy. 'Martin, for the love of God!'

I picked up the lighter from where he had dropped it. The Shrike made no move. Blood soaked the black patches of Billy's tunic until they blended with the crimson squares already there. I thumbed the antique lighter once, twice, a third time; sparks only. Through my tears I could see my life's work lying in the dusty fountain. I dropped the lighter.

Billy screamed. Dimly, I heard blades rubbing bone as he twisted in the Shrike's embrace. 'Finish it!' he cried. 'Martin . . . oh, God!'

I turned then, took five fast paces, and threw the half-full bucket of kerosene. Fumes blurred my already blurred vision. Billy and the impossible creature that held him were soaked like two comics in a slapstick holie. I saw Billy blink and splutter, I saw the slickness on the Shrike's chiseled muzzle reflect the meteor-brightened sky, and then the dying embers of burned pages in Billy's still clenched fists ignited the kerosene.

I raised my hands to protect my face – too late, beard and eyebrows singed and smoldered – and staggered backward until the rim of the fountain stopped me.

For a second the pyre was a perfect sculpture of flame, a blue and yellow *Pietà* with a four-armed madonna holding a blazing Christ figure. Then the burning figure writhed and arched, still pinned by steel thorns and a score of scalpeled talons, and a cry went up which to this day I cannot believe emanated from the human half of that death-embraced pair. The scream knocked me to my knees, echoed from every hard surface in the city, and drove the pigeons into wheeling panic. And the scream continued for minutes after the flaming vision simply ceased to be, leaving behind neither ashes nor retinal image. It was another minute or two before I realized that the scream I now heard was mine.

Anticlimax is, of course, the warp and way of things. Real life seldom structures a decent denouement.

It took me several months, perhaps a year, to recopy the kerosene-damaged pages and to rewrite the burned *Cantos*. It will be no surprise to learn that I did not finish the poem. It was not by choice. My muse had fled.

The City of Poets decayed in peace. I stayed another year or two – perhaps five, I do not know; I was quite mad by then. To this day records of early Shrike pilgrims tell of the gaunt figure, all hair and rags and bulging eyes, who would wake them from their Gethsemane sleep by screaming obscenities and shaking his fist at the silent Time Tombs, daring the coward within to show itself.

Eventually the madness burned itself out – although the embers will always glow – and I hiked the fifteen hundred kilometers to civilization, my backpack weighted down with just manuscript, surviving on rock eels and snow and on nothing at all for the last ten days.

The two and a half centuries since are not worth telling, much less reliving. The Poulsen treatments to keep the instrument alive and waiting. Two long, cold sleeps in illegal, sublight, cryogenic voyages; each swallowing a century or more; each taking its toll in brain cells and memory.

I waited then. I will still. The poem must be finished. It *will* be finished.

In the beginning was the Word.

In the end . . . past honor, past life, past caring . . .

In the end will be the Word.

FOUR

The *Benares* put into Edge a little after noon on the next day. One of the mantas had died in harness only twenty kilometers downriver from their destination and A. Bettik had cut it loose. The other had lasted until they tied up to the bleached pier and then it rolled over in total exhaustion, bubbles rising from its twin airholes. Bettik ordered this manta cut loose as well, explaining that it had a slim chance of surviving if it drifted along in the more rapid current.

The pilgrims had been awake and watching the scenery roll by since before sunrise. They spoke little and none had found anything to say to Martin Silenus. The poet did not appear to mind . . . he drank wine with his breakfast and sang bawdy songs as the sun rose.

The river had widened during the night and by morning it was a two-kilometer-wide highway of blue gray cutting through the low green hills south of the Sea of Grass. There were no trees this close to the Sea, and the browns and golds and heather tones of the Mane shrubs had gradually brightened to the bold greens of the two-meter-tall northern grasses. All morning the hills had been pressed lower until now they were compressed into low bands of grassy bluffs on either side of the river. An almost invisible darkening hung above the horizon to the north and east, and those pilgrims who had lived on ocean worlds and knew it as a promise of the approaching sea had to remind themselves that the only sea now near was comprised of several billion acres of grass.

Edge never had been a large outpost and now it was totally deserted. The score of buildings lining the rutted lane from the dock had the vacant gaze of all abandoned structures and there were signs on the riverfront that the population had fled weeks earlier. The Pilgrims' Rest, a three-century-old inn just below the crest of the hill, had been burned.

A. Bettik accompanied them to the summit of the low bluff. 'What will you do now?' Colonel Kassad asked the android.

'According to the terms of the Temple bonditure, we are free after this trip,' said Bettik. 'We shall leave the *Benares* here for your return and take the launch downriver. And then we go on our way.'

'With the general evacuations?' asked Brawne Lamia.

'No.' Bettik smiled. 'We have our own purposes and pilgrimages on Hyperion.'

The group reached the rounded crest of the bluff. Behind them, the *Benares* seemed a small thing tied to a sagging dock; the Hoolie ran southwest into the blue haze of distance below the town and curved west above it, narrowing toward the impassable Lower Cataracts a dozen kilometers upriver from Edge. To their north and east lay the Sea of Grass.

'My God,' breathed Brawne Lamia.

It was as if they had climbed the last hill in creation. Below them, a scattering of docks, wharves, and sheds marked the end of Edge and the beginning of the Sea. Grass stretched away forever, rippling sensuously in the slight breeze and seeming to lap like a green surf at the base of the bluffs. The grass seemed infinite and seamless, stretching to all horizons and apparently rising to precisely the same height as far as the eye could see. There was not the slightest hint of the snowy peaks of the Bridle Range, which they knew lay some eight hundred kilometers to the northwest. The illusion that they were gazing at a great green sea was nearly perfect, down to the wind-ruffled shimmers of stalks looking like whitecaps far from shore.

'It's beautiful,' said Lamia, who had never seen it before.

'It's striking at sunset and sunrise,' said the Consul.

'Fascinating,' murmured Sol Weintraub, lifting his infant so that she could see. She wiggled in happiness and concentrated on watching her fingers.

'A well-preserved ecosystem,' Het Masteen said approvingly. 'The Muir would be pleased.'

'Shit,' said Martin Silenus.

The others turned to stare.

'There's no fucking windwagon,' said the poet.

The four other men, woman, and android stared silently at the abandoned wharves and empty plain of grass.

'It's been delayed,' said the Consul.

Martin Silenus barked a laugh. 'Or it's left already. We were supposed to be here last night.'

Colonel Kassad raised his powered binoculars and swept the horizon. 'I find it unlikely that they would have left without us,' he said. 'The wagon was to have been sent by the Shrike Temple priests themselves. They have a vested interest in our pilgrimage.'

'We could walk,' said Lenar Hoyt. The priest looked pale and weak, obviously in the grip of both pain and drugs, and barely able to stand, much less walk.

'No,' said Kassad. 'It's hundreds of klicks and the grass is over our heads.'

'Compasses,' said the priest.

'Compasses don't work on Hyperion,' said Kassad, still watching through his binoculars.

'Direction finders then,' said Hoyt.

'We have an IDF, but that isn't the point,' said the Consul. 'The grass is sharp. Half a klick out and we'd be nothing but tatters.'

'And there are the grass serpents,' said Kassad, lowering the glasses. 'It's a well-preserved ecosystem but not one to take a stroll in.'

171

Father Hoyt sighed and half collapsed into the short grass of the hilltop. There was something close to relief in his voice when he said, 'All right, we go back.'

A. Bettik stepped forward. 'The crew will be happy to wait and ferry you back to Keats in the *Benares* should the windwagon not appear.'

'No,' said the Consul, 'take the launch and go.'

'Hey, just a fucking minute!' cried Martin Silenus. 'I don't remember electing you dictator, amigo. *We need to get there*. If the fucking windwagon doesn't show, we'll have to find another way.'

The Consul wheeled to face the smaller man. 'How? By boat? It takes two weeks to sail up the Mane and around the North Littoral to Otho or one of the other staging areas. And that's when there are ships available. Every seagoing vessel on Hyperion is probably involved in the evacuation effort.'

'Dirigible then,' growled the poet.

Brawne Lamia laughed. 'Oh, yes. We've seen so *many* in the two days we've been on the river.'

Martin Silenus whirled and clenched his fists as if to strike the woman. Then he smiled. 'All right then, lady, what do we do? Maybe if we sacrifice someone to a grass serpent the transportation gods will smile on us.'

Brawne Lamia's stare was arctic. 'I thought burned offerings were more your style, little man.'

Colonel Kassad stepped between the two. His voice barked command. 'Enough. The Consul's right. We stay here until the wagon arrives. M. Masteen, M. Lamia, go with A. Bettik to supervise the unloading of our gear. Father Hoyt and M. Silenus will bring some wood up for a bonfire.'

'A bonfire?' said the priest. It was hot on the hillside.

'After dark,' said Kassad. 'We want the windwagon to know we're here. Now let's *move*.'

It was a quiet group that watched the powered launch move downriver at sunset. Even from two kilometers away the Consul could see the blue skins of the crew. The *Benares* looked old and abandoned at its wharf, already a part of the deserted city. When the launch was lost in the distance, the group turned to watch the Sea of Grass. Long shadows from the river bluffs crept out across what the Consul already found himself thinking of as the surf and shallows. Farther out, the sea seemed to shift in color, the grass mellowing to an aquamarine shimmer before darkening to a hint of verdurous depths. The lapis sky melted into the reds and golds of sunset, illuminating their hilltop and setting the pilgrims' skins aglow with liquid light. The only sound was the whisper of wind in grass.

'We've got a fucking huge heap of baggage,' Martin Silenus said loudly. 'For a bunch of folks on a one-way trip.'

It was true, thought the Consul. Their luggage made a small mountain on the grassy hilltop.

'Somewhere in there,' came the quiet voice of Het Masteen, 'may lie our salvation.'

172

'What do you mean?' asked Brawne Lamia.

'Yeah,' said Martin Silenus, lying back, putting his hands under his head, and staring at the sky. 'Did you bring a pair of undershorts that are Shrike-proof?'

The Templar shook his head slowly. The sudden twilight cast his face in shadow under the cowl of the robe. 'Let us not trivialize or dissemble,' he said. 'It is time to admit that each of us has brought on this pilgrimage something which he or she hopes will alter the inevitable outcome when the moment arrives that we must face the Lord of Pain.'

The poet laughed. 'I didn't bring even my lucky fucking rabbit's foot.'

The Templar's hood moved slightly. 'But your manuscript perhaps?'

The poet said nothing.

Het Masteen moved his invisible gaze to the tall man on his left. 'And you, Colonel, there are several trunks which bear your name. Weapons, perhaps?'

Kassad raised his head but did not speak.

'Of course,' said Het Masteen, 'it would be foolish to go hunting without a weapon.'

'What about me?' asked Brawne Lamia, folding her arms. 'Do you know what secret weapon I've smuggled along?'

The Templar's oddly accented voice was calm. 'We have not yet heard your tale, M. Lamia. It would be premature to speculate.'

'What about the Consul?' asked Lamia.

'Oh, yes, it is obvious what weapon our diplomatic friend has in store.'

The Consul turned from his contemplation of the sunset. 'I brought only some clothes and two books to read,' he said truthfully.

'Ah,' sighed the Templar, 'but what a beautiful spacecraft you left behind.'

Martin Silenus jumped to his feet. 'The fucking ship!' he cried. 'You can call it, can't you? Well, goddammit, get your dog whistle out, I'm tired of sitting here.'

The Consul pulled a strand of grass and stripped it. After a minute he said:

'Even if I could call it . . . and you heard A. Bettik say that the comsats and repeater stations were down . . . even if I could call it, we couldn't land north of the Bridle Range. That meant instant disaster even *before* the Shrike began ranging south of the mountains.'

'Yeah,' said Silenus, waving his arms in agitation, 'but we could get across this fucking . . . *lawn*! Call the ship.'

'Wait until morning,' said the Consul. 'If the windwagon's not here, we will discuss alternatives.'

'Fuck that . . .' began the poet, but Kassad stepped forward with his back to him, effectively removing Silenus from the circle.

'M. Masteen,' said the Colonel, 'what is *your* secret?'

There was enough light from the dying sky to show a slight smile on the

Templar's thin lips. He gestured toward the mound of baggage. 'As you see, my trunk is the heaviest and most mysterious of all.'

'It's a Möbius cube,' said Father Hoyt. 'I've seen ancient artifacts transported that way.'

'Or fusion bombs,' said Kassad.

Het Masteen shook his head. 'Nothing so crude,' he said.

'Are you going to tell us?' demanded Lamia.

'When it is my turn to speak,' said the Templar.

'Are you next?' asked the Consul. 'We can listen while we wait.'

Sol Weintraub cleared his throat. 'I have number four,' he said, showing the slip of paper. 'But I would be more than pleased to trade with the True Voice of the Tree.' Weintraub lifted Rachel from his left shoulder to his right, patting her gently on the back.

Het Masteen shook his head. 'No, there is time. I meant only to point out that in hopelessness there is always hope. We have learned much from the stories so far. Yet each of us has some seed of promise buried even deeper than we have admitted.'

'I don't see . . .' began Father Hoyt but was interrupted by Martin Silenus's sudden shout.

'It's the wagon! The fucking windwagon. Here at last!'

It was another twenty minutes before the windwagon tied up to one of the wharves. The craft came out of the north, its sails white squares against a dark plain draining of color. The last light had faded by the time the large ship had tacked close to the low bluff, folded its main sails, and rolled to a stop.

The Consul was impressed. The thing was wooden, handcrafted, and huge – curved in the pregnant lines of some seagoing galleon out of Old Earth's ancient history. The single gigantic wheel, set in the center of the curving hull, normally would have been invisible in the two-meter-tall grass, but the Consul caught a glimpse of the underside as he carried luggage onto the wharf. From the ground it would be six or seven meters to the railing, and more than five times that height to the tip of the mainmast. From where he stood, panting from exertion, the Consul could hear the snap of pennants far above and a steady, almost subsonic hum that would be coming from either the ship's interior flywheel or its massive gyroscopes.

A gangplank extruded from the upper hull and lowered itself to the wharf. Father Hoyt and Brawne Lamia had to step back quickly or be crushed.

The windwagon was less well lighted than the *Benares*; illumination appeared to consist of several lanterns hanging from spars. No crew had been visible during the approach of the ship and no one came into view now.

'Hallo!' called the Consul from the base of the gangplank. No one answered.

'Wait here a minute, please,' said Kassad and mounted the long ramp in five strides.

The others watched while Kassad paused at the top, touched his belt where the small deathwand was tucked, and then disappeared amidships. Several minutes later a light flared through broad windows at the stern, casting trapezoids of yellow on the grass below.

'Come up,' called Kassad from the head of the ramp. 'It's empty.'

The group struggled with their luggage, making several trips. The Consul helped Het Masteen with the heavy Möbius cube and through his fingertips he could feel a faint but intense vibration.

'So where the fuck is the crew?' asked Martin Silenus when they were assembled on the foredeck. They had taken their single-file tour through the narrow corridors and cabins, down stairways more ladder than stairs, and through cabins not much bigger than the built-in bunks they contained. Only the rearmost cabin – the captain's cabin, if that is what it was – approached the size and comfort of standard accommodations on the *Benares*.

'It's obviously automated,' said Kassad. The FORCE officer pointed to halyards which disappeared into slots in the deck, manipulators all but invisible among the rigging and spars, and the subtle hint of gears halfway up the lateen-rigged rear mast.

'I didn't see a control center,' said Lamia. 'Not so much as a diskey or C-spot nexus.' She slipped her comlog from a breast pocket and tried to interface on standard data, comm, and biomed frequencies. There was no response from the ship.

'The ships used to be crewed,' said the Consul. 'Temple initiates used to accompany the pilgrims to the mountains.'

'Well, they're not here now,' said Hoyt. 'But I guess we can assume that *someone* is still alive at the tram station or Keep Chronos. They sent the wagon for us.'

'Or everyone's dead and the windwagon is running on an automatic schedule,' said Lamia. She looked over her shoulders as rigging and canvas creaked in a sudden gust of wind. 'Damn, it's weird to be cut off from everybody and everything like this. It's like being blind and deaf. I don't know how colonials stand it.'

Martin Silenus approached the group and sat on the railing. He drank from a long green bottle and said:

'Where's the Poet? Show him! Show him,
Muses mine, that I may know him!
'Tis the man who with a man
  Is an equal, be he king,
Or poorest of the beggar-class,
  Or any other wondrous thing
A man may be 'twixt ape and Plato.
  'Tis the man who with a bird,

Wren or eagle, finds his way to
   All its instincts. He hath heard
The lion's roaring, and can tell
   What his horny throat expresseth,
And to him the tiger's yell
   Comes articulate and presseth
On his ear like mother-tongue.'

'Where did you get that wine bottle?' asked Kassad.

Martin Silenus smiled. His eyes were small and bright in the lantern glow. 'The galley's fully stocked and there's a bar. I declared it open.'

'We should fix some dinner,' said the Consul although all he wanted at the moment was some wine. It had been more than ten hours since they had last eaten.

There came a clank and whir and all six of them moved to the starboard rail. The gangplank had drawn itself in. They whirled again as canvas unfurled, lines grew taut, and somewhere a flywheel hummed into the ultrasonic. Sails filled, the deck tilted slightly, and the windwagon moved away from the wharf and into the darkness. The only sounds were the flap and creak of the ship, the distant rumble of the wheel, and the rasp of grass on the hull bottom.

The six of them watched as the shadow of the bluff fell behind, the unlighted beacon pyre receding as a faint gleam of starlight on pale wood, and then there were only the sky and night and swaying circles of lantern light.

'I'll go below,' said the Consul, 'and see if I can get a meal together.'

The others stayed awhile, feeling the slight surge and rumble through the soles of their feet and watching darkness pass. The Sea of Grass was visible only as the place where stars ended and flat blackness began. Kassad used a handbeam to illuminate glimpses of canvas and rigging, lines being pulled tight by invisible hands, and then he checked all the corners and shadowed places from stern to bow. The others watched in silence. When he clicked the light off, the darkness seemed less oppressive, the starlight brighter. A rich, fertile smell – more of a farm in springtime than of the sea – came to them on a breeze which had swept across a thousand kilometers of grass.

Sometime later the Consul called to them and they went below to eat.

The galley was cramped and there was no mess table, so they used the large cabin in the stern as their common room, pushing three of the trunks together as a makeshift table. Four lanterns swinging from low beams made the room bright. A breeze blew in when Het Masteen opened one of the tall windows above the bed.

The Consul set plates piled high with sandwiches on the largest trunk and returned again with thick white cups and a coffee therm. He poured while the others ate.

'This is quite good,' said Fedmahn Kassad. 'Where did you get the roast beef?'

'The cold box is fully stocked. There's another large freezer in the aft pantry.'

'Electrical?' asked Het Masteen.

'No. Double insulated.'

Martin Silenos sniffed a jar, found a knife on the sandwich plate, and added great dollops of horseradish to his sandwiches. His eyes sparkled with tears as he ate.

'How long does this crossing generally take?' Lamia asked the Consul.

He looked up from his study of the circle of hot black coffee in his cup. 'I'm sorry, what?'

'Crossing the Sea of Grass. How long?'

'A night and half a day to the mountains,' said the Consul. 'If the winds are with us.'

'And then . . . how long to cross the mountains?'asked Father Hoyt.

'Less than a day,' said the Consul.

'If the tramway is running,' added Kassad.

The Consul sipped the hot coffee and made a face. 'We have to assume it is. Otherwise . . .'

'Otherwise what?' demanded Lamia.

'Otherwise,' said Colonel Kassad, moving to the open window and putting his hands on his hips, 'we will be stranded six hundred klicks from the Time Tombs and a thousand from the southern cities.'

The Consul shook his head. 'No,' he said. 'The Temple priests or whoever are behind this pilgrimage have seen to it that we've gotten this far. They'll make sure we go all the way.'

Brawne Lamia crossed her arms and frowned. 'As what . . . sacrifices?'

Martin Silenus whooped a laugh and brought out his bottle:

'Who are these coming to the sacrifice?
  To what green altar, O mysterious priest,
Lead'st thou that heifer lowing at the skies,
  And all her silken flanks with garlands dressed?
What little town by river or sea-shore,
  Or mountain-built with peaceful citadel,
  Is emptied of its folk, this pious morn?
And, little town, thy streets for evermore
  Will silent be; and not a soul, to tell
  Why thou art desolate, can e'er return.'

Brawne Lamia reached under her tunic and brought out a cutting laser no larger than her little finger. She aimed it at the poet's head. 'You miserable little shit. One more word out of you and . . . I swear . . . I'll slag you where you stand.'

The silence was suddenly absolute except for the background rumble-groan of the ship. The Consul moved toward Martin Silenus. Colonel Kassad took two steps behind Lamia.

The poet took a long drink and smiled at the dark-haired woman. His lips were moist. 'Oh build your ship of death,' he whispered. 'Oh build it!'

Lamia's fingers were white on the pencil laser. The Consul edged closer to Silenus, not knowing what to do, imagining the whipping beam of light fusing his own eyes. Kassad leaned toward Lamia like two meters of tensed shadow.

'Madam,' said Sol Weintraub from where he sat on the bunk against the far wall, 'need I remind you that there is a child present?'

Lamia glanced to her right. Weintraub had removed a deep drawer from a ship's cupboard and had set it on the bed as a cradle. He had bathed the infant and come in silently just before the poet's recitation. Now he set the baby softly in the padded nest.

'I'm sorry,' said Brawne Lamia and lowered the small laser. 'It's just that he makes me so . . . angry.'

Weintraub nodded, rocking the drawer slightly. The gentle roll of the windwagon combined with the incessant rumble of the great wheel appeared to have already put the child to sleep. 'We're all tired and tense,' said the scholar. 'Perhaps we should find our lodgings for the night and turn in.'

The woman sighed and tucked the weapon in her belt. 'I won't sleep,' she said. 'Things are too . . . strange.'

Others nodded. Martin Silenus was sitting on the broad ledge below the stern windows. Now he pulled up his legs, took a drink, and said to Weintraub, 'Tell your story, old man.'

'Yes,' said Father Hoyt. The priest looked exhausted to the point of being cadaverous, but his feverish eyes burned. 'Tell us. We need to have the stories told and time to think about them before we arrive.'

Weintraub passed a hand across his bald scalp. 'It's a dull tale,' he said. 'I've been to Hyperion before. There are no confrontations with monsters, no acts of heroism. It's a tale by a man whose idea of epic adventure is speaking to a class without his notes.'

'All the better,' said Martin Silenus. 'We need a soporific.'

Sol Weintraub sighed, adjusted his glasses, and nodded. There were a few streaks of dark in his beard, but most of it had gone gray. He turned the lantern low over the baby's bed and moved to a chair in the center of the room.

The Consul turned down the other lamps and poured more coffee for those who wanted it. Sol Weintraub's voice was slow, careful in phrase and precise in wording, and before long the gentle cadence of his story blended with the soft rumble and slow pitchings of the windwagon's progress north.

THE SCHOLAR'S TALE:
THE RIVER LETHE'S TASTE IS BITTER

Sol Weintraub and his wife Sarai had enjoyed their life even before the birth of their daughter; Rachel made things as close to perfect as the couple could imagine.

Sarai was twenty-seven when the child was conceived, Sol was twenty-nine. Neither of them had considered Poulsen treatments because neither of them could afford it, but even without such care they looked forward to another fifty years of health.

Both had lived their entire lives on Barnard's World, one of the oldest but least exciting members of the Hegemony. Barnard's was in the Web, but it made little difference to Sol and Sarai since they could not afford frequent farcaster travel and had little wish to go at any rate. Sol had recently celebrated his tenth year with Nightenhelser College, where he taught history and classical studies and did his own research on ethical evolution. Nightenhelser was a small school, fewer than three thousand students, but its academic reputation was outstanding and it attracted young people from all over the Web. The primary complaint of these students was that Nightenhelser and its surrounding community of Crawford constituted an island of civilization in an ocean of corn. It was true; the college was three thousand flat kilometers away from the capital of Bussard and the terra-formed land in between was given over to farming. There had been no forests to fell, no hills to deal with, and no mountains to break the flat monotony of cornfields, bean-fields, cornfields, wheatfields, cornfields, rice paddies, and cornfields. The radical poet Salmud Brevy had taught briefly at Nightenhelser before the Glennon-Height Mutiny, had been fired, and upon farcasting to Renaissance Vector had told his friends that Crawford County on South Sinzer on Barnard's World constituted the Eighth Circle of Desolation on the smallest pimple on the absolute ass-end of Creation.

Sol and Sarai Weintraub liked it. Crawford, a town of twenty-five thousand, might have been reconstructed from some nineteenth-century mid-American template. The streets were wide and over-arched with elms and oaks. (Barnard's had been the second extrasolar Earth colony, centuries before the Hawking drive and Hegira, and the seedships then had been huge.) Homes in Crawford reflected styles ranging from early Victorian to Canadian Revival, but they all seemed to be white and set far back on well-trimmed lawns.

The college itself was Georgian, an assemblage of red brick and white pillars surrounding the oval common. Sol's office was on the third floor of Placher Hall, the oldest building on campus, and in the winter he could look out on bare branches which carved the common into complex geometries. Sol loved the chalk-dust and old-wood smell of the place, a smell which had not changed since he was a freshman there, and each day climbing to his office he treasured the deeply worn grooves in the steps, a legacy of twenty generations of Nightenhelser students.

Sarai had been born on a farm halfway between Bussard and Crawford and had received her PhD in music theory a year before Sol earned his doctorate. She had been a happy and energetic young woman, making up in personality what she lacked in accepted norms of physical beauty, and she carried this attractiveness of person into later life. Sarai had studied off-world for two years at the University of New Lyons on Deneb Drei, but she was homesick there: the sunsets were abrupt, the much-vaunted mountains slicing off the sunlight like a ragged scythe, and she longed for the hours-long sunsets of home where Barnard's Star hung on the horizon like a great, tethered, red balloon while the sky congealed to evening. She missed the perfect flatness where – peering from her third-floor room under the steep gables – a little girl could look fifty kilometers across tasseled fields to watch a storm approach like a bruise-black curtain lit within by lightning bolts. And Sarai missed her family.

She and Sol met a week after she transferred to Nightenhelser; it was another three years before he proposed marriage and she accepted. At first she saw nothing in the short graduate student. She was still wearing Web fashions then, involved in Post-Destructionist music theories, reading *Obit* and *Nihil* and the most avant-garde magazines from Renaissance Vector and TC^2, feigning sophisticated weariness with life and a rebel's vocabulary – and none of this jelled with the undersized but earnest history major who spilled fruit cocktail on her at Dean Moore's honors party. Any exotic qualities which might have come from Sol Weintraub's Jewish legacy were instantly negated by his BW accent, his Crawford Squire Shop wardrobe, and the fact that he had come to the party with a copy of Detresque's *Solitudes in Variance* absentmindedly tucked under his arm.

For Sol it was love at first sight. He stared at the laughing, red-cheeked girl and ignored the expensive dress and affected mandarin nails in favor of the personality which blazed like a beacon to the lonely junior. Sol had not known he was lonely until he met Sarai, but after the first time he shook her hand and spilled fruit salad down the front of her dress he knew that his life would be empty forever if they did not marry.

They married the week after the announcement of Sol's teaching appointment at the college. Their honeymoon was on Maui-Covenant, his first farcast trip abroad, and for three weeks they rented a mobile isle and sailed alone on it through the wonders of the Equatorial Archipelago. Sol never forgot the images from those sun-drenched and wind-filled days, and the secret image he would always most cherish was of Sarai rising nude from a nighttime swim, the Core stars blazing above while her own body glowed constellations from the phosphorescence of the island's wake.

They had wanted a child immediately but it was to be five years before nature agreed.

Sol remembered cradling Sarai in his arms as she curled in pain, a difficult delivery, until finally, incredibly, Rachel Sarah Weintraub was born at 2:01 A.M. in Crawford County Med Center.

The presence of an infant intruded upon Sol's solipsistic life as a serious academic and Sarai's profession as music critic for Barnard's datasphere, but neither minded. The first months were a blend of constant fatigue and joy. Late at night, between feedings, Sol would tiptoe into the nursery just to check on Rachel and to stand and gaze at the baby. More often than not he would find Sarai already there and the two would watch, arm in arm, at the miracle of a baby sleeping on its stomach, rump in the air, head burrowed into the bumper pad at the head of the crib.

Rachel was one of those rare children who managed to be cute without becoming self-consciously precious; by the time she was two standard years old her appearance and personality were striking – her mother's light brown hair, red cheeks, and broad smile, her father's large brown eyes. Friends said that the child combined the best portions of Sarai's sensitivity and Sol's intellect. Another friend, a child psychologist from the college, once commented that Rachel at age five showed the most reliable indicators of true giftedness in a young person: structured curiosity, empathy for others, compassion, and a fierce sense of fair play.

One day in his office, studying ancient files from Old Earth, Sol was reading about the effect of Beatrice on the world view of Dante Alighieri when he was struck by a passage written by a critic from the twentieth or twenty-first century:

> She [Beatrice] alone was still real for him, still implied meaning in the world, and beauty. Her nature became his landmark – what Melville would call, with more sobriety than we can now muster, his Greenwich Standard . . .

Sol paused to access the definition of Greenwich Standard, and then he read on. The critic had added a personal note:

> Most of us, I hope, have had some child or spouse or friend like Beatrice, someone who by his very nature, his seemingly innate goodness and intelligence, makes us uncomfortably conscious of our lies when we lie.

Sol had shut off the display and gazed out at the black geometries of branches above the common.

Rachel was not insufferably perfect. When she was five standard, she carefully cut the hair of her five favorite dolls and then cut her own hair shortest of all. When she was seven, she decided that the migrant workers staying in their run-down houses on the south end of town lacked a nutritious diet, so she emptied the house's pantries, cold boxes, freezers, and synthesizer banks, talked three friends into accompanying her, and distributed several hundred marks' worth of the family's monthly food budget.

When she was ten, Rachel responded to a dare from Stubby Berkowitz and tried to climb to the top of Crawford's oldest elm. She was forty meters up, less than five meters from the top, when a branch broke and she fell two thirds of the way to the ground. Sol was paged on his comlog while discussing the moral implications of Earth's first nuclear disarmament era and he left the class without a word and ran the twelve blocks to the Med Center.

Rachel had broken her left leg, two ribs, punctured a lung, and fractured her jaw. She was floating in a bath of recovery nutrient when Sol burst in, but she managed to look over her mother's shoulder, smile slightly, and say through the wire cast on her jaw: 'Dad, I was fifteen feet from the *top*. Maybe closer. I'll make it next time.'

Rachel graduated with honors from secondary tutorials and received scholarship offers from corporate academies on five worlds and three universities, including Harvard on New Earth. She chose Nightenhelser.

It was little surprise to Sol that his daughter chose archaeology as a major. One of his fondest memories of her was the long afternoons she had spent under the front porch when she was about two, digging in the loam, ignoring spiders and googlepeds, rushing into the house to show off every plastic plate and tarnished pfennig she had excavated, demanding to know where it had come from, what were the people like who had left it there?

Rachel received her undergraduate degree when she was nineteen standard, worked that summer on her grandmother's farm, and farcast away the next fall. She was at Reichs University on Freeholm for twenty-eight local months, and when she returned it was as if color had flowed back into Sol and Sarai's world.

For two weeks their daughter – an adult now, self-aware and secure in some ways that grown-ups twice her age often failed to be – rested and reveled in being home. One evening, walking across the campus just after sunset, she pressed her father on details of his heritage. 'Dad, do you still consider yourself a Jew?'

Sol had run his hand over his thinning hair, surprised by the question. 'A Jew? Yes, I suppose so. It doesn't mean what it once did, though.'

'Am I a Jew?' asked Rachel. Her cheeks glowed in the fragile light.

'If you want to be,' said Sol. 'It doesn't have the same significance with Old Earth gone.'

'If I'd been a boy, would you have had me circumcised?'

Sol had laughed, delighted and embarrassed by the question.

'I'm serious,' said Rachel.

Sol adjusted his glasses. 'I guess I would have, kiddo. I never thought about it.'

'Have you been to the synagogue in Bussard?'

'Not since my bar mitzvah,' said Sol, thinking back to the day fifty years earlier when his father had borrowed Uncle Richard's Vikken and had flown the family to the capital for the ritual.

'Dad, why do Jews feel that things are . . . less important now than before the Hegira?'

Sol spread his hands – strong hands, more those of a stoneworker than an academic. 'That's a good question, Rachel. Probably because so much of the dream is dead. Israel is gone. The New Temple lasted less time than the first and second. God broke His word by destroying the Earth a second time in the way He did. And this Diaspora is . . . forever.'

'But Jews maintain their ethnic and religious identity in some places,' his daughter insisted.

'Oh, sure. On Hebron and isolated areas of the Concourse you can find entire communities . . . Hasidic, Orthodox, Hasmonean, you name it . . . but they tend to be . . . nonvital, picturesque . . . tourist-oriented.'

'Like a theme park?'

'Yes.'

'Could you take me to Temple Beth-el tomorrow? I can borrow Khaki's strat.'

'No need,' said Sol. 'We'll use the college's shuttle.' He paused. 'Yes,' he said at last, 'I would like to take you to the synagogue tomorrow.'

It was getting dark under the old elms. Streetlights came on up and down the wide lane which led to their home.

'Dad,' said Rachel, 'I'm going to ask you a question I've asked about a million times since I was two. Do you believe in God?'

Sol had not smiled. He had no choice but to give her the answer he had given her a million times. 'I'm waiting to,' he said.

Rachel's postgraduate work dealt with alien and pre-Hegira artifacts. For three standard years Sol and Sarai would receive occasional visits followed by fatline flimsies from exotic worlds near but not within the Web. They all knew that her field work in quest of dissertation would soon take her beyond the Web, into the Outback where time-debt ate away at the lives and memories of those left behind.

'Where the hell is Hyperion?' Sarai had asked during Rachel's last vacation before the expedition left. 'It sounds like a brand name for some new household product.'

'It's a great place, Mom. There are more nonhuman artifacts there than any place except Armaghast.'

'Then why not go to Armaghast?' said Sarai. 'It's only a few months from the Web. Why settle for second best?'

'Hyperion hasn't become the big tourist attraction yet,' said Rachel. 'Although they're beginning to become a problem. People with money are more willing to travel outside the Web now.'

Sol had found his voice suddenly husky. 'Will you be going to the labyrinth or the artifacts called the Time Tombs?'

'The Time Tombs, Dad. I'll be working with Dr Melio Arundez and he knows more about the Tombs than anyone alive.'

'Aren't they dangerous?' asked Sol, framing the question as casually as he could but hearing the edge in his voice.

Rachel smiled. 'Because of the Shrike legend? No. Nobody's been both-ered by that particular legend for two standard centuries.'

'But I've seen documents about the trouble there during the second colonization . . .' began Sol.

'Me too, Dad. But they didn't know about the big rock eels that came down into the desert to hunt. They probably lost a few people to those things and panicked. *You* know how legends begin. Besides, the rock eels have been hunted to extinction.'

'Spacecraft don't land there,' persisted Sol. 'You have to sail to the Tombs. Or hike. Or some damn thing.'

Rachel laughed. 'In the early days, people flying in underestimated the effects of the anti-entropic fields and there were some accidents. But there's dirigible service now. They have a big hotel called Keep Chronos at the north edge of the mountains where hundreds of tourists a year stay.'

'Will you be staying there?' asked Sarai.

'Part of the time. It'll be *exciting*, Mom.'

'Not too exciting, I hope,' said Sarai and all of them had smiled.

During the four years that Rachel was in transit – a few weeks of cryogenic fugue for her – Sol found that he missed his daughter much more than if she had been out of touch but busy somewhere in the Web. The thought that she was flying away from him faster than the speed of light, wrapped in the artificial quantum cocoon of the Hawking effect, seemed unnatural and ominous to him.

They kept busy. Sarai retired from the critic business to devote more time to local environmental issues, but for Sol it was one of the most hectic times of his life. His second and third books came out and the second one – *Moral Turning Points* – caused such a stir that he was in constant demand at offworld conferences and symposia. He traveled to a few alone, to a few more with Sarai, but although both of them enjoyed the *idea* of traveling, the actual experience of facing strange foods, different gravities, and the light from strange suns all paled after a while and Sol found himself spend-ing more time at home researching his next book, attending conferences, if he had to, via interactive holo from the college.

It was almost five years after Rachel left on her expedition that Sol had a dream which would change his life.

Sol dreamed that he was wandering through a great structure with columns the size of small redwood trees and a ceiling lost to sight far above him, through which red light fell in solid shafts. At times he caught glimpses of things far off in the gloom to his left or right: once he made out a pair of stone legs rising like massive buildings through the darkness; another time he spied what appeared to be a crystal scarab rotating far above him, its insides ablaze with cool lights.

Finally Sol stopped to rest. Far behind him he could hear what sounded like a great conflagration, entire cities and forests burning. Ahead of him glowed the lights he had been walking toward, two ovals of deepest red.

He was mopping sweat from his brow when an immense voice said to him:

'Sol! Take your daughter, your only daughter Rachel, whom you love, and go to the world called Hyperion and offer her there as a burnt offering at one of the places of which I shall tell you.'

And in his dream Sol had stood and said, 'You can't be serious.' And he had walked on through darkness, the red orbs glowing now like bloody moons hanging above an indistinct plain, and when he stopped to rest the immense voice said:

'Sol! Take your daughter, your only daughter Rachel, whom you love, and go to the world called Hyperion and offer her there as a burnt offering at one of the places of which I shall tell you.'

And Sol had shrugged off the weight of the voice and had said distinctly into the darkness, 'I heard you the first time . . . the answer is still no.'

Sol knew he was dreaming then, and part of his mind enjoyed the irony of the script, but another part wanted only to waken. Instead, he found himself on a low balcony looking down on a room where Rachel lay naked on a broad block of stone. The scene was illuminated by the glow of the twin red orbs. Sol looked down at his right hand and found a long, curved knife there. The blade and handle appeared to be made of bone.

The voice, sounding more than ever to Sol like some cut-rate holie director's shallow idea of what God's voice should sound like, came again:

'Sol! You must listen well. The future of humankind depends upon your obedience in this matter. You must take your daughter, your daughter Rachel whom you love, and go to the world called Hyperion and offer her there as a burnt offering at one of the places of which I shall tell you.'

And Sol, sick of the whole dream yet somehow alarmed by it, had turned and thrown the knife far into the darkness. When he turned back to find his daughter, the scene had faded. The red orbs hung closer than ever, and now Sol could see that they were multifaceted gems the size of small worlds.

The amplified voice came again:

'So? You have had your chance, Sol Weintraub. If you change your mind, you know where to find me.'

And Sol awakened half laughing, half chilled by the dream. Amused by the thought that the entire Talmud and the Old Testament might be nothing more than a cosmic shaggy-dog story.

About the time Sol was having his dream, Rachel was on Hyperion finishing her first year of research there. The team of nine archaeologists and six physicists had found Keep Chronos fascinating but far too crowded with tourists and would-be Shrike pilgrims, so after the first month spent commuting from the hotel, they had set up a permanent camp between the ruined city and the small canyon holding the Time Tombs.

While half the team excavated the more recent site of the unfinished city, two of Rachel's colleagues helped her catalogue every aspect of the Tombs. The physicists were finished with the anti-entropic fields and spent much of their time setting small flags of different colors to mark the limits of the so-called time tides.

Rachel's team concentrated their work in the structure called the Sphinx, although the creature represented in stone was neither human nor lion; it may not have been a creature at all, although the smooth lines atop the stone monolith suggested curves of a living thing, and the sweeping appendages made everyone think of wings. Unlike the other Tombs, which lay open and were easily inspected, the Sphinx was a mass of heavy blocks honeycombed with narrow corridors, some of which tightened to impossibility, some of which widened to auditorium-sized proportions, but none of which led anywhere but back on themselves. There were no crypts, treasure rooms, plundered sarcophogi, wall murals, or secret passages, merely a maze of senseless corridors through sweating stone.

Rachel and her lover, Melio Arundez, began mapping the Sphinx, using a method which had been in use for at least seven hundred years, having been pioneered in the Egyptian pyramids sometime in the twentieth century. Arranging sensitive radiation and cosmic ray detectors at the lowest point in the Sphinx, they recorded arrival times and deflection patterns of the particles passing through the mass of stone above them, watching for hidden rooms or passages which would not show up even on deep imaging radar. Because of the busy tourist season and the concern of the Hyperion Home Rule Council that the Tombs might be damaged by such research, Rachel and Melio went out to their site every night at midnight, making the half-hour walk and crawl through the corridor maze which they had rigged with blue glow-globes. There, sitting under hundreds of thousands of tons of stone, they would watch their instruments until morning, listening to their earphones ping with the sound of particles born in the belly of dying stars.

The time tides had not been a problem with the Sphinx. Of all the Tombs, it seemed the least protected by the anti-entropic fields and the physicists had carefully mapped the times when the tide surges might pose a threat. High tide was at 1000 hours, receding only twenty minutes later back toward the Jade Tomb half a kilometer to the south. Tourists were not allowed near the Sphinx until after 1200 hours, and to leave a margin of safety, the site made sure they were put by 0900. The physics team had planted chronotropic sensors at various points along the paths and walkways between the Tombs, both to alert the monitors to variations of the tides and to warn the visitors.

With only three weeks to go of her year of research on Hyperion, Rachel awoke one night, left her sleeping lover, and took a ground effect jeep from the camp to the Tombs. She and Melio had decided that it was foolish for both of them to monitor the equipment every night; now they alternated, one working at the site while the other collated data and prepared for the final project – a radar mapping of the dunes between the Jade Tomb and the Obelisk.

The night was cool and beautiful. A profusion of stars stretched from horizon to horizon, four or five times the number Rachel had grown up looking at from Barnard's World. The low dunes whispered and shifted in the strong breeze blowing from the mountains in the south.

Rachel found lights still burning at the site. The physics team was just calling it a day loading their own jeep. She chatted with them, had a cup of coffee as they drove away, and then took her backpack and made the twenty-five-minute trip into the basement of the Sphinx.

For the hundredth time Rachel wondered who had built the Tombs and for what purpose. Dating of the construction materials had been useless because of the effect of the anti-entropic field. Only analysis of the Tombs in relation to the erosion of the canyon and other surrounding geological features had suggested an age of at least half a million years. The feeling was that the architects of the Time Tombs had been humanoid, even though nothing but the gross scale of the structures suggested such a thing. Certainly the passageways in the Sphinx revealed little: some were human enough in size and shape, but then meters farther along the same corridor might dwindle to a tube the size of a sewer pipe and then transform itself into something larger and more random than a natural cavern. Doorways, if they could be called such since they opened to nothing in particular, might be triangular or trapezoidal or ten-sided as commonly as rectangular.

Rachel crawled the last twenty meters down a steep slope, sliding her backpack ahead of her. The heatless glow-globes gave the rock and her flesh a bluish, bloodless cast. The 'basement', when she reached it, seemed a haven of human clutter and smells. Several folding chairs filled the center of the small space while detectors, oscilloscopes, and other paraphernalia lined the narrow table against the north wall. A plank on sawhorses along the opposite wall held coffee cups, a chess set, a half-eaten doughnut, two paperbacks, and a plastic toy of some sort of dog in a grass skirt.

Rachel settled in, set her coffee therm next to the toy, and checked the cosmic ray detectors. The data appeared to be the same: no hidden rooms or passages, just a few niches even the deep radar had missed. In the morning Melio and Stefan would set a deep probe working, getting an imager filament in and sampling the air before digging further with a micro-manipulator. So far a dozen such niches had turned up nothing of interest. The joke at camp was that the next hole, no bigger than a fist, would reveal miniature sarcophagi, undersized urns, a petite mummy, or – as Melio put it – 'a teeny-tiny Tutankhamun'.

Out of habit, Rachel tried the comm links on her comlog. Nothing. Forty meters of stone tended to do that. They had talked of stringing telephone wire from the basement to the surface, but there had been no pressing need and now their time was almost up. Rachel adjusted the input channels on her comlog to monitor the detector data and then settled back for a long, boring night.

There was the wonderful story of the Old Earth pharaoh – was it Cheops? – who authorized his huge pyramid, agreed to the burial chamber being deep under the center of the thing, and then lay awake nights for years in a claustrophobic panic, thinking of all those tons of stone above him for all eternity. Eventually the pharaoh ordered the burial chamber repositioned two thirds the way up the great pyramid. Most unorthodox. Rachel could understand the king's position. She hoped that – wherever he was – he slept better now.

Rachel was almost dozing herself when – at 0215 – her comlog chirped, the detectors screamed, and she jumped to her feet. According to the sensors, the Sphinx had suddenly grown a dozen new chambers, some larger than the total structure. Rachel keyed displays and the air misted with models that changed as she watched. Corridor schematics twisted back on themselves like rotating Möbius strips. The external sensors indicated the upper structure twisting and bending like polyflex in the wind – or like wings.

Rachel knew that it was some type of multiple malfunction, but even as she tried to recalibrate she called data and impressions into her comlog. Then several things happened at once.

She heard the drag of feet in the corridor above her.

All of the displays went dead simultaneously.

Somewhere in the maze of corridors a time-tide alarm began to blare.

All of the lights went off.

This final event made no sense. The instrument packages held their own power supplies and would have stayed lit through a nuclear attack. The lamp they used in the basement had a new ten-year power cell. The glow-globes in the corridors were bioluminescent and needed no power.

Nonetheless, the lights were out. Rachel pulled a flashlight laser out of the knee pocket of her jumpsuit and triggered it. Nothing happened.

For the first time in her life, terror closed on Rachel Weintraub like a hand on her heart. She could not breathe. For ten seconds she willed herself to be absolutely still, not even listening, merely waiting for the panic to recede. When it had subsided enough for her to breathe without gasping, she felt her way to the instruments and keyed them. They did not respond. She lifted her comlog and thumbed the diskey. Nothing . . . which was impossible, of course, given the solid-state invulnerability and power-cell reliability of the thing. Still, nothing.

Rachel could hear her pulse pounding now but she again fought back the panic and began feeling her way toward the only exit. The thought of finding her way through the maze in absolute darkness made her want to scream but she could think of no other alternatives.

Wait. There had been old lights throughout the Sphinx maze but the research team had strung the glow-globes. *Strung* them. There was a perlon line connecting them all the way to the surface.

Fine. Rachel groped her way toward the exit, feeling the cold stone under her fingers. Was it this cold before?

There came the clear sound of something sharp scraping its way down the access shaft.

'Melio?' called Rachel into the blackness. 'Tanya? Kurt?'

The scraping sounded very close. Rachel backed away, knocking over an instrument and chair in the blackness. Something touched her hair and she gasped, raised her hand.

The ceiling was lower. The solid block of stone, five meters square, slid lower even as she raised her other hand to touch it. The opening to the corridor was halfway up the wall. Rachel staggered toward it, swinging her hands in front of her like a blind person. She tripped over a folding chair, found the instrument table, followed it to the far wall, felt the bottom of the corridor shaft disappearing as the ceiling came lower. She pulled back her fingers a second before they were sliced off.

Rachel sat down in the darkness. An oscilloscope scraped against the ceiling until the table cracked and collapsed under it. Rachel moved her head in short, desperate arcs. There was a metallic rasp – almost a breathing sound – less than a meter from her. She began to back away, sliding across a floor suddenly filled with broken equipment. The breathing grew louder.

Something sharp and infinitely cold grasped her wrist.

Rachel screamed at last.

There was no fatline transmitter on Hyperion in those days. Nor did the spinship *HS Farraux City* have FTL-comm capability. So the first Sol and Sarai heard of their daughter's accident was when the Hegemony consulate on Parvati fatlined the college that Rachel had been injured, that she was stable but unconscious, and that she was being transferred from Parvati to the Web world of Renaissance Vector via medical torchship. The trip would take a little over ten days' shiptime with a five-month time-debt. Those five months were agony for Sol and his wife, and by the time the medical ship put in at the Renaissance farcaster nexus, they had imagined the worst a thousand times. It had been eight years since they had last seen Rachel.

The Med Center in DaVinci was a floating tower sustained by direct broadcast power. The view over the Como Sea was breathtaking but neither Sol nor Sarai had time for it as they went from level to level in search of their daughter. Dr Singh and Melio Arundez met them in the hub of Intensive Care. Introductions were rushed.

'Rachel?' asked Sarai.

'Asleep,' said Dr Singh. She was a tall woman, aristocratic but with kind eyes. 'As far as we can tell, Rachel has suffered no physical . . . ah . . . injury. But she has been unconscious now for some seventeen standard weeks, her time. Only in the past ten days have her brain waves registered deep sleep rather than coma.'

'I don't understand,' said Sol. 'Was there an accident at the site? A concussion?'

'Something happened,' said Melio Arundez, 'but we're not sure what. Rachel was in one of the artifacts . . . alone . . . her comlog and other instruments recorded nothing out of the ordinary. But there was a surge in a phenomenon there known as anti-entropic fields . . .'

'The time tides,' said Sol. 'We know about them. Go on.'

Arundez nodded and opened his hands as if molding air. 'There was a . . . field surge . . . more like a tsunami, than a tide . . . the Sphinx . . . the artifact Rachel was in . . . was totally inundated. I mean, there was no *physical* damage but Rachel was unconscious when we found her . . .' He turned to Dr Singh for help.

'Your daughter was in a coma,' said the doctor. 'It was not possible to put her into cryogenic fugue in that condition . . .'

'So she came through quantum leap without fugue?' demanded Sol. He had read about the psychological damage to travelers who had experienced the Hawking effect directly.

'No, no,' soothed Singh. 'She was unconscious in a way which shielded her quite as well as fugue state.'

'Is she *hurt*?' demanded Sarai.

'We don't know,' said Singh. 'All life signs have returned to near normal. Brain-wave activity is nearing a conscious state. The problem is that her body appears to have absorbed . . . that is, the anti-entropic field appears to have contaminated her.'

Sol rubbed his forehead. 'Like radiation sickness?'

Dr Singh hesitated. 'Not precisely . . . ah . . . this case is quite unprecedented. Specialists in aging diseases are due in this afternoon from Tau Ceti Center, Lusus, and Metaxas.'

Sol met the woman's gaze. 'Doctor, are you saying that Rachel contracted some aging disease on Hyperion?' He paused a second to search his memory. 'Something like Methuselah syndrome or early Alzheimer's disease?'

'No,' said Singh, 'in fact your daughter's illness has no name. The medics here are calling it Merlin's sickness. You see . . . your daughter is aging at a normal rate . . . but as far as we can tell, she is aging backward.'

Sarai pulled away from the group and stared at Singh as if the doctor were insane. 'I want to see my daughter,' she said, quietly but very firmly. 'I want to see Rachel *now*.'

Rachel awakened less than forty hours after Sol and Sarai arrived. Within minutes she was sitting up in bed, talking even while the medics and technicians bustled around her. '*Mom! Dad!* What are you doing here?'

Before either could answer, she looked around her and blinked. 'Wait a minute, where's *here*? Are we in Keats?'

Her mother took her hand. 'We're in a hospital in DaVinci, dear. On Renaissance Vector.'

Rachel's eyes widened almost comically. 'Renaissance. We're in the *Web*?' She looked around her in total bewilderment.

'Rachel, what is the last thing you remember?' asked Dr Singh.

The young woman looked uncomprehendingly at the medic. 'The last thing I . . . I remember going to sleep next to Melio after . . .' She glanced at her parents and touched her cheeks with the tips of her fingers. 'Melio? The others? Are they . . .'

'Everyone on the expedition is all right,' soothed Dr Singh. 'You had a slight accident. About seventeen weeks have passed. You're back in the Web. Safe. Everyone in your party is all right.'

'Seventeen *weeks* . . .' Under the fading remnant of her tan, Rachel went very pale.

Sol took her hand. 'How do you feel, kiddo?' The return pressure on his fingers was heartbreakingly weak.

'I don't know, Daddy,' she managed. 'Tired. Dizzy. *Confused.*'

Sarai sat on the bed and put her arms around her. 'It's all right, baby. Everything's going to be all right.'

Melio entered the room, unshaven, his hair rumpled from the nap he had been taking in the outer lounge. 'Rache?'

Rachel looked at him from the safety of her mother's arm. 'Hi,' she said, almost shyly. 'I'm back.'

Sol's opinion had been and continued to be that medicine hadn't really changed much since the days of leeches and poultices; nowadays they whirred one in centrifuges, realigned the body's magnetic field; bombarded the victim with sonic waves, tapped into the cells to interrogate the RNA, and then admitted their ignorance without actually coming out and saying so. The only thing that had changed was that the bills were bigger.

He was dozing in a chair when Rachel's voice awoke him.

'Daddy?'

He sat up, reached for her hand. 'Here, kiddo.'

'Where am I, Dad? What's happened?'

'You're in a hospital on Renaissance, baby. There was an accident on Hyperion. You're all right now except it's affecting your memory a bit.'

Rachel clung to his hand. 'A hospital? In the Web? How'd I get here? How long have I been here?'

'About five weeks,' whispered Sol. 'What's the last thing you remember, Rachel?'

She sat back on her pillows and touched her forehead, feeling the tiny sensors there. 'Melio and I had been at the meeting. Talking with the team about setting up the search equipment in the Sphinx. Oh . . . Dad . . . I haven't told you about Melio . . . he's . . .'

'Yes,' said Sol and handed Rachel her comlog. 'Here, kiddo. Listen to this.' He left the room.

Rachel touched the diskey and blinked as her own voice began talking to her. 'OK, Rache, you just woke up. You're confused. You don't know how you got here. Well, something's happened to you, kid. Listen up.

'I'm recording this on the twelfth day of Tenmonth, year 457 of the Hegira, A.D. 2739 old reckoning. Yes, I *know* that's half a standard year from the last thing you remember. Listen.

'Something happened in the Sphinx. You got caught up in the time tide. It changed you. You're aging backward, as dumb as that sounds. Your body's getting younger every minute, although that's not the important part right now. When you sleep . . . when *we* sleep . . . you forget. You lose another day from your memory *before* the accident, and you lose everything since. Don't ask me why. The doctors don't know. The experts don't know. If you want an analogy, just think of a tapeworm virus . . . one of the old kind . . . that's chewing up the data in your comlog . . . *backward* from the last entry.

'They don't know why the memory loss hits you when you sleep, either. They tried stay-awakes, but after about thirty hours you just go catatonic for a while and the virus does its thing anyway. So what the hell.

'You know something? This talking about yourself in the third person is sort of therapeutic. Actually, I'm lying here waiting for them to take me up to imaging, knowing I'll fall asleep when I get back . . . knowing I'll forget *everything* again . . . and it scares the shit out of me.

'OK, key the diskey for short-term and you get a prepared spiel here that should catch you up on everything since the accident. Oh . . . Mom and Dad are both here and they know about Melio. But *I* don't know as much as I used to. When did we first make love with him, mmm? The second month on Hyperion? Then we have just a few weeks left, Rachel, and then we'll be just acquaintances. Enjoy your memories while you can, girl.

'This is yesterday's Rachel, signing off.'

Sol came in to find his daughter sitting upright in the bed, still grasping the comlog tightly, her face pale and terrified. 'Daddy . . .'

He went to sit next to her and let her cry . . . for the twentieth night in a row.

Eight standard weeks after she arrived on Renaissance, Sol and Sarai waved goodbye to Rachel and Melio at the DaVinci farcaster multiport and then farcast home to Barnard's World.

'I don't think she should have left the hospital,' muttered Sarai as they took the evening shuttle to Crawford. The continent was a patchwork of harvest-ready right angles below them.

'Mother,' said Sol, touching her knee, 'the doctors would have kept her there forever. But they're doing it for their own curiosity now. They've done everything they can to help her . . . nothing. She has a life to live.'

'But why go away with . . . with him?' said Sarai. 'She barely knows him.'

Sol sighed and leaned back against the cushions of his seat. 'In two weeks she won't remember him at all,' he said. 'At least in the way they share now. Look at it from her position, Mother. Fighting every day to reorient herself in a world gone mad. She's twenty-five years old and in love. Let her be happy.'

Sarai turned her face to the window and together, not speaking, they watched the red sun hang like a tethered balloon on the edge of evening.

Sol was well into the second semester when Rachel called. It was a one-way message via farcaster cable from Freeholm and her image hung in the center of the old holopit like a familiar ghost.

'Hi, Mom. Hi, Dad. Sorry I haven't written or called the past few weeks. I guess you know that I've left the university. And Melio. It was dumb to try to take new graduate-level stuff. I'd just forget Tuesday whatever was discussed Monday. Even with disks and comlog prompts it was a losing battle. I may enroll in the undergraduate program again . . . I remember *all* of it! Just kidding.

'It was just too hard with Melio, too. Or so my notes tell me. It wasn't *his* fault, I'm sure of that. He was gentle and patient and loving to the end. It's just that . . . well, you can't start from scratch on a relationship every *day*. Our apartment was filled with photos of us, notes I wrote to myself about us, holos of us on Hyperion, but . . . you know. In the morning he would be an absolute stranger. By afternoon I began to believe what we'd had, even if I couldn't remember. By evening I'd be crying in his arms . . . then, sooner or later, I'd go to sleep. It's better this way.'

Rachel's image paused, turned as if she was going to break contact, and then steadied. She smiled at them. 'So anyway, I've left school for a while. The Freeholm Med Center wants me full time but they'd have to get in line . . . I got an offer from the Tau Ceti Research Institute that's hard to turn down. They offer a . . . I think they call it a "research honorarium" . . . that's bigger than what we paid for four years at Nightenhelser and all of Reichs combined.

'I turned them down. I'm still going in as an outpatient, but the RNA transplant series just leaves me with bruises and a depressed feeling. Of course, I could just be depressed because every morning I can't remember where the bruises came from. Ha-ha.

'Anyway, I'll be staying with Tanya for a while and then maybe . . . I thought maybe I'd come home for a while. Secondmonth's my birthday . . . I'll be twenty-two again. Weird, huh? At any rate, it's a lot easier being around people I know and I met Tanya just after I transferred here when I was twenty-two . . . I think you understand.

'So . . . is my old room still here, Mom, or have you turned it into a mah-jongg parlor like you've always threatened? So write or give me a call. Next time I'll shell out the money for two-way so we can really talk. I just . . . I guess I thought . . .'

Rachel waved. 'Gottago. See you later, alligators. I love you both.'

*

Sol flew to Bussard City the week before Rachel's birthday to pick her up at the world's only public farcaster terminex. He saw her first, standing with her luggage near the floral clock. She looked young but not noticeably younger than when they had waved goodbye on Renaissance Vector. No, Sol realized, there was something less *confident* about her posture. He shook his head to rid himself of such thoughts, called to her, and ran to hug her.

The look of shock on her face when he released her was so profound that he could not ignore it. 'What is it, sweetie? What's wrong?'

It was one of the few times he had ever seen his daughter totally at a loss for words.

'I . . . you . . . I forgot,' she stammered. She shook her head in a familiar way and managed to laugh and cry at the same instant. 'You look a little different is all, Dad. I *remember* leaving here like it was . . . literally . . . yesterday. When I saw . . . your hair . . .' Rachel covered her mouth.

Sol ran his hand across his scalp. 'Ah, yes,' he said, suddenly close to laughing and crying himself. 'With your school and travels, it's been more than eleven years. I'm old. And bald.' He opened his arms again. 'Welcome back, little one.'

Rachel moved into the protective circle of his embrace.

For several months things went well. Rachel felt more secure with familiar things around, and for Sarai the heartbreak of their daughter's illness was temporarily offset by the pleasure of having her home again.

Rachel rose early every morning and viewed her private 'orientation show' which, Sol knew, contained images of him and Sarai a dozen years older than she remembered. He tried to imagine what it was like for Rachel: she awoke in her own bed, memory fresh, twenty-two years old, home on vacation before going offworld to graduate school, only to find her parents suddenly aged, a hundred small changes in the house and town, the news different . . . years of history having passed her by.

Sol could not imagine it.

Their first mistake was acceding to Rachel's wishes in inviting her old friends to her twenty-second birthday party: the same crew who had celebrated the first time – irrepressible Niki, Don Stewart and his friend Howard, Kathi Obeg and Marta Tyn, her best friend Linna McKyler – all of them then just out of college, shucking off cocoons of childhood for new lives.

Rachel had seen them all since her return. But she had slept . . . and forgotten. And Sol and Sarai this one time did not remember that she had forgotten.

Niki was thirty-four standard, with two children of her own – still energetic, still irrepressible, but ancient by Rachel's standards. Don and Howard talked about their investments, their children's sports accomplishments, and their upcoming vacations. Kathi was confused, speaking only twice to Rachel and then as if she was speaking to an impostor. Marta was openly jealous of Rachel's youth. Linna, who had become an ardent Zen Gnostic in the years between, cried and left early.

When they had gone, Rachel sat in the postparty ruin of the living room and stared at the half-eaten cake. She did not cry. Before going upstairs she hugged her mother and whispered to her father, 'Dad, please don't let me do anything like that again.'

Then she went upstairs to sleep.

It was that spring when Sol again had the dream. He was lost in a great, dark place, lighted only by two red orbs. It was not absurd when the flat voice said:

> 'Sol. Take your daughter, your only Rachel, whom you love, and go to the world called Hyperion and offer her there as a burnt offering at one of the places of which I shall tell you.'

And Sol had screamed into the darkness:

'You already have her, you son of a bitch! What do I have to do to get her back? Tell me! Tell me, goddamn you!'

And Sol Weintraub woke sweating with tears in his eyes and anger in his heart. In the other room he could feel his daughter sleeping while the great worm devoured her.

In the months which followed Sol became obsessive about obtaining information on Hyperion, the Time Tombs, and the Shrike. As a trained researcher, he was astounded that there was so little hard data on so provocative a topic. There was the Church of the Shrike, of course – there were no temples on Barnard's World but many in the Web – but he soon found that seeking hard information in Shrike cult literature was like trying to map the geography of Sarnath by visiting a Buddhist monastery. Time was mentioned in Shrike Church dogma, but only in the sense that the Shrike was supposed to be '. . . the Angel of Retribution from Beyond Time' and that true time had ended for the human race when Old Earth died and that the four centuries since had been 'false time'. Sol found their tracts the usual combination of double talk and navel lint-gathering common to most religions. Still, he planned to visit a Shrike Church temple as soon as he had explored more serious avenues of research.

Melio Arundez launched another Hyperion expedition, also sponsored by Reichs University, this one with the stated goal of isolating and understanding the time-tide phenomenon which had inflicted the Merlin sickness on Rachel. A major development was the Hegemony Protectorate's decision to send along on that expedition a fatline transmitter for installation at the Hegemony consulate in Keats. Even so, it would be more than three years' Web time before the expedition arrived on Hyperion. Sol's first instinct was to go with Arundez and his team – certainly any holodrama would have the primary characters returning to the scene of the action. But

Sol overrode the instinctive urge within minutes. He was a historian and philosopher; any contribution he might make to the expedition's success would be minute, at best. Rachel still retained the interest and skills of a well-trained undergraduate archaeologist-to-be, but those skills dwindled a bit each day and Sol could see no benefit to her returning to the site of the accident. Each day would be a shock to her, awakening on a strange world, on a mission which would require skills unknown to her. Sarai would not allow such a thing.

Sol set aside the book he was working on – an analysis of Kierkegaard's theories of ethics as compromise morality as applied to the legal machinery of the Hegemony – and concentrated on collecting arcane data on time, on Hyperion, and on the story of Abraham.

Months spent carrying on business as usual and collecting information did little to satisfy his need for action. Occasionally he vented his frustration on the medical and scientific specialists who came to examine Rachel like streams of pilgrims to a holy shrine.

'How the hell can this be happening!' he screamed at one little specialist who had made the mistake of being both smug and condescending to the patient's father. The doctor had a head so hairless, his face looked like lines painted on a billiard ball. 'She's begun growing smaller!' Sol shouted, literally buttonholing the retreating expert. 'Not so one can see, but bone mass is decreasing. How can she even *begin* to become a child again? What the *hell* does that do to the law of conservation of mass?'

The expert had moved his mouth but had been too rattled to speak. His bearded colleague answered for him. 'M. Weintraub,' he said, 'sir. You have to understand that your daughter is currently inhabiting . . . ah . . . think of it as a localized region of reversed entropy.'

Sol wheeled on the other man. 'Are you saying that she is merely stuck in a bubble of backwardness?'

'Ah . . . no,' said the colleague, massaging his chin nervously. 'Perhaps a better analogy is that . . . biologically at least . . . the life/metabolism mechanism has been reversed . . . ah . . .'

'Nonsense,' snapped Sol. 'She doesn't excrete for nutrition or regurgitate her food. And what about all the neurological activity? Reverse the electrochemical impulses and you get nonsense. Her brain *works*, gentlemen . . . it's her memory that is disappearing. Why, gentlemen? Why?'

The specialist finally found his voice. 'We don't know why, M. Weintraub. Mathematically, your daughter's body resembles a time-reversed equation . . . or perhaps an object which has passed through a rapidly spinning black hole. We don't know *how* this has happened or *why* the physically impossible is occurring in this instance, M. Weintraub. We just don't know enough.'

Sol shook each man's hand. 'Fine. That's all I wanted to know, gentlemen. Have a good trip back.'

*

On Rachel's twenty-first birthday she came to Sol's door an hour after they had all turned in. 'Daddy?'

'What is it, kiddo?' Sol pulled on his robe and joined her in the doorway. 'Can't sleep?'

'I haven't slept for two days,' she whispered. 'Been taking stay-awakes so I can get through all of the briefing stuff I left in the Wanta Know? file.'

Sol nodded.

'Daddy, would you come downstairs and have a drink with me? I've got some things I want to talk about.'

Sol got his glasses from the nightstand and joined her downstairs.

It proved to be the first and only time that Sol would get drunk with his daughter. It was not a boisterous drunk – for a while they chatted, then began telling jokes and making puns, until each was giggling too hard to continue. Rachel started to tell another story, sipped her drink just at the funniest part, and almost snorted whiskey out her nose, she was laughing so hard. Each of them thought it was the funniest thing that had ever happened.

'I'll get another bottle,' said Sol when the tears had ceased. 'Dean Moore gave me some Scotch last Christmas . . . I think.'

When he returned, walking carefully, Rachel had sat up on the couch and brushed her hair with her fingers. He poured her a small amount and the two drank in silence for a while.

'Daddy?'

'Yes?'

'I went through the whole thing. Saw myself, listened to myself, saw the holos of Linna and the others all middle-aged . . .'

'Hardly middle-aged,' said Sol. 'Linna will be thirty-five next month . . .'

'Well, *old*, you know what I mean. Anyway, I read the medical briefs, saw the photos from Hyperion, and you know what?'

'What?'

'I don't believe any of it, Dad.'

Sol put down his drink and looked at his daughter. Her face was fuller than before, less sophisticated. And even more beautiful.

'I mean, I *do* believe it,' she said with a small, scared laugh. 'It's not like you and Mom would put on such a cruel joke. Plus there's your . . . your age . . . and the news and all. I know it's *real*, but I don't *believe* it. Do you know what I mean, Dad?'

'Yes,' said Sol.

'I mean I woke up this morning and I thought, *Great . . . tomorrow's the paleontology exam and I've hardly studied.* I was looking forward to showing Roger Sherman a thing or two . . . he thinks he's so *smart*.'

Sol took a drink. 'Roger died three years ago in a plane crash south of Bussard,' he said. He would not have spoken without the whiskey in him, but he had to find out if there was a Rachel hiding within the Rachel.

'I know,' said Rachel and pulled her knees up to her chin. 'I accessed everybody I knew. Gram's dead. Professor Eikhardt isn't teaching anymore. Niki married some . . . *salesman*. A lot happens in four years.'

'More than eleven years,' said Sol. 'The trip to and from Hyperion left you six years behind us stay-at-homes.'

'But that's normal,' cried Rachel. 'People travel outside the Web all the time. *They* cope.'

Sol nodded. 'But this is different, kiddo.'

Rachel managed a smile and drained the last of her whiskey. 'Boy, what an understatement.' She set the glass down with a sharp, final sound. 'Look, here's what I've decided. I've spent two and a half days going through all of the stuff she . . . I . . . prepared to let me know what's happened, what's going on . . . and *it just doesn't help*.'

Sol sat perfectly still, not even daring to breathe.

'I mean,' said Rachel, 'knowing that I'm getting younger every day, losing the memory of people I haven't even *met* yet . . . I mean, what happens next? I just keep getting younger and smaller and less capable until I just *disappear* someday? Jesus, Dad.' Rachel wrapped her arms more tightly around her knees. 'It's sort of funny in a weird way, isn't it?'

'No,' Sol said quietly.

'No, I'm sure it's not,' said Rachel. Her eyes, always large and dark, were moist. 'It must be the worst nightmare in the world for you and Mom. Every day you have to watch me come down the stairs . . . confused . . . waking up with yesterday's memories but hearing my own voice tell me that yesterday was *years* ago. That I had a love affair with some guy named Amelio . . .'

'Melio,' whispered Sol.

'Whatever. It just doesn't *help*, Dad. By the time I can even begin to absorb it, I'm so worn out that I have to sleep. Then . . . well, you know what happens then.'

'What . . .' began Sol and had to clear his throat. 'What do you want us to do, little one?'

Rachel looked him in the eye and smiled. It was the same smile she had gifted him with since her fifth week of life. 'Don't tell me, Dad,' she said firmly. 'Don't let *me* tell me. It just hurts. I mean, I didn't *live* those times . . .' She paused and touched her forehead. 'You know what I mean, Dad. The Rachel who went to another planet and fell in love and got hurt . . . that was *a different Rachel*! I shouldn't have to suffer her pain.' She was crying now. 'Do you understand? Do you?'

'Yes,' said Sol. He opened his arms and felt her warmth and tears against his chest. 'Yes, I understand.'

Fatline messages from Hyperion came frequently the next year but they were all negative. The nature and source of the anti-entropic fields had not been found. No unusual time-tide activity had been measured around the Sphinx. Experiments with laboratory animals in and around the tidal regions had resulted in sudden death for some animals, but the Merlin sickness had not been replicated. Melio ended every message with 'My love to Rachel'.

Sol and Sarai used money loaned from Reichs University to receive limited Poulsen treatments in Bussard City. They were already too old for the process to extend their lives for another century, but it restored the look of a couple approaching fifty standard rather than seventy. They studied old family photos and found that it was not too difficult to dress the way they had a decade and a half before.

Sixteen-year-old Rachel tripped down the stairs with her comlog tuned to the college radio station. 'Can I have rice cereal?'

'Don't you have it every morning?' smiled Sarai.

'Yes,' grinned Rachel. 'I just thought we might be out or something. I heard the phone. Was that Niki?'

'No,' said Sol.

'Damn,' said Rachel and glanced at them. 'Sorry. But she *promised* she'd call as soon as the standardized scores came in. Three weeks since tutorials. You'd think I'd have heard *something*.'

'Don't worry,' said Sarai. She brought the coffeepot to the table, started to pour Rachel a cup, poured it for herself. 'Don't worry, honey. I promise you that your scores will be good enough to get you into any school you want.'

'*Mom*,' sighed Rachel. 'You don't *know*. It's a dog-eat-dog world out there.' She frowned. 'Have you seen my math ansible? My room was all messed around. I couldn't find *any*thing.'

Sol cleared his throat. 'No classes today, kiddo.'

Rachel stared. 'No classes? On a Tuesday? Six weeks from graduation? What's up?'

'You've been sick,' Sarai said firmly. 'You can stay home one day. Just today.'

Rachel's frown deepened. 'Sick? I don't feel sick. Just sort of *weird*. Like things aren't . . . aren't right somehow. Like why's the couch moved around in the media room? And where's Chips? I called and called but he didn't come.'

Sol touched his daughter's wrist. 'You've been sick for a while,' he said. 'The doctor said you might wake up with a few gaps. Let's talk while we walk over to the campus. Want to?'

Rachel brightened. 'Skip classes and go to the college? Sure.' She faked a look of consternation. 'As long as we don't run into Roger Sherman. He's taking freshman calculus up there and he's such a *pain*.'

'We won't see Roger,' said Sol. 'Ready to go?'

'Almost.' Rachel leaned over and gave her mother a huge hug. ''Later alligator.'

''While, crocodile,' said Sarai.

'Okay,' grinned Rachel, her long hair bouncing. 'I'm ready.'

*

The constant trips to Bussard City had required the purchase of an EMV and on a cool day in autumn Sol took the slowest route, far below the traffic lanes, enjoying the sight and smell of the harvested fields below. More than a few men and women working in the fields waved to him.

Bussard had grown impressively since Sol's childhood, but the synagogue was still there on the edge of one of the oldest neighborhoods in the city. The temple was old, Sol felt old, even the yarmulke he put on as he entered seemed ancient, worn thin by decades of use, but the rabbi was young. Sol realized that the man was at least forty – his hair was thinning on either side of the dark skullcap – but to Sol's eyes he was little more than a boy. Sol was relieved when the younger man suggested that they finish their conversation in the park across the street.

They sat on a park bench. Sol was surprised to find himself still carrying the yarmulke, passing the cloth from hand to hand. The day smelled of burning leaves and the previous night's rain.

'I don't quite understand, M. Weintraub,' said the rabbi. 'Is it the dream you're disturbed about or the fact that your daughter has become ill since you began the dream?'

Sol raised his head to feel the sunlight on his face. 'Neither, exactly,' he said. 'I just can't help but feel that the two are connected somehow.'

The rabbi ran a finger over his lower lip. 'How old is your daughter?'

'Thirteen,' said Sol after an imperceptible pause.

'And is the illness . . . serious? Life threatening?'

'Not life threatening,' said Sol. 'Not yet.'

The rabbi folded his arms across an ample belly. 'You don't believe . . . may I call you Sol?'

'Of course.'

'Sol, you don't believe that by having this dream that somehow you've caused your little girl's illness. Do you?'

'No,' said Sol and sat a moment, wondering deep within if he was telling the truth. 'No, Rabbi, I don't think . . .'

'Call me Mort, Sol.'

'All right, Mort. I didn't come because I believe that I – or the dream – am causing Rachel's illness. But I believe my subconscious might be trying to tell me something.'

Mort rocked back and forth slightly. 'Perhaps a neuro-specialist or psychologist could help you more there, Sol. I'm not sure what I . . .'

'I'm interested in the story of Abraham,' interrupted Sol. 'I mean, I've had some experience with different ethical systems, but it's hard for me to understand one which began with the order to a father to slay his son.'

'No, no, no!' cried the rabbi, waving oddly childlike fingers in front of him. 'When the time came, God stayed Abraham's hand. He would not have allowed a human sacrifice in His name. It was the *obedience* to the will of the Lord that . . .'

'Yes,' said Sol. 'Obedience. But it says, "Then Abraham put forth his hand, and took the knife to slay his son.'' God must have looked into his soul and seen that Abraham *was* ready to slay Isaac. A mere show of obedience without inner commitment would not have appeased the God of Genesis. What would have happened if Abraham had loved his son more than he loved God?'

Mort drummed his fingers on his knee a moment and then reached out to grasp Sol's upper arm. 'Sol, I can see you're upset about your daughter's illness. Don't get it mixed up with a document written eight thousand years ago. Tell me more about your little girl. I mean, children don't *die* of diseases anymore. Not in the Web.'

Sol rose, smiled, and stepped back to free his arm. 'I'd like to talk more, Mort. I want to. But I have to get back. I have a class this evening.'

'Will you come to temple this Sabbath?' asked the rabbi, extending stubby fingers for a final human contact.

Sol dropped the yarmulke into the younger man's hands. 'Perhaps one of these days, Mort. One of these days I will.'

Later the same autumn Sol looked out the window of his study to see the dark figure of a man standing under the bare elm in front of the house. *The media*, thought Sol, his heart sinking. For a decade he had been dreading the day the secret got out, knowing it would mean the end of their simple life in Crawford. He walked out into the evening chill. 'Melio!' he said when he saw the tall man's face.

The archaeologist stood with his hands in the pockets of his long blue coat. Despite the ten standard years since their last contact, Arundez had aged but little – Sol guessed that he was still in his late twenties. But the younger man's heavily tanned face was lined with worry. 'Sol,' he said and extended his hand almost shyly.

Sol shook his hand warmly. 'I didn't know you were back. Come into the house.'

'No.' The archaeologist took a half step back. 'I've been out here for an hour, Sol. I didn't have the courage to come to the door.'

Sol started to speak but then merely nodded. He put his hands in his own pockets against the chill. The first stars were becoming visible above the dark gables of the house. 'Rachel's not home right now,' he said at last. 'She went to the library. She . . . she thinks she has a history paper due.'

Melio took a ragged breath and nodded in return. 'Sol,' he said, his voice thick, 'you and Sarai need to understand that we did everything we could. The team was on Hyperion for almost three standard years. We would have stayed if the university hadn't cut our funds. There was *nothing* . . .'

'We know,' said Sol. 'We appreciated the fatline messages.'

'I spent months alone in the Sphinx myself,' said Melio. 'According to the instruments, it was just an inert pile of stones, but sometimes I thought I felt . . . *something* . . .' He shook his head again. 'I failed her, Sol.'

'No,' said Sol and gripped the younger man's shoulder through the wool coat. 'But I have a question. We've been in touch with our senators . . . even talked to the Science Council directors . . . but no one can explain to me why the Hegemony hasn't spent more time and money investigating the phenomena on Hyperion. It seems to me that they should have invested that world into the Web long ago, if only for its scientific potential. How can they ignore an enigma like the Tombs?'

'I know what you mean, Sol. Even the early cutoff of our funds was suspicious. It's as if the Hegemony had a policy to keep Hyperion at arm's length.'

'Do you think . . .' began Sol but at that moment Rachel approached them in the autumn twilight. Her hands were thrust deep in her red jacket, her hair was cut short in the decades-old style of adolescents everywhere, and her full cheeks were flushed with the cold. Rachel was teetering on the brink of childhood and young adulthood; her long legs in jeans, sports shoes, and bulky jacket might have been the silhouette of a boy.

She grinned at them. 'Hi, Dad.' Stepping closer in the dim light, she nodded at Melio shyly. 'Sorry, didn't mean to interrupt your conversation.'

Sol took a breath. 'That's all right, kiddo. Rachel, this is Dr Arundez from Reichs University on Freeholm. Dr Arundez, my daughter Rachel.'

'Pleased to meet you,' said Rachel, beaming in earnest now. 'Wow, Reichs. I've read their catalogues. I'd *love* to go there someday.'

Melio nodded rigidly. Sol could see the stiffness in his shoulders and torso. 'Do you . . .' began Melio. 'That is, what would you like to study there?'

Sol thought the pain in the man's voice must be audible to Rachel but she only shrugged and laughed. 'Oh, jeez, *everything*. Old Mr Eikhardt – he's the paleontology/archaeology tute in the advanced class I take up at the Ed Center – he says they have a *great* classics and ancient artifacts department.'

'They do,' managed Melio.

Rachel glanced shyly from her father to the stranger, apparently sensing the tension there but not knowing the source. 'Well, I'm just interrupting your conversation more here. I've got to get in and get to bed. I guess I've had this strange virus . . . sort of like meningitis, Mom says, only it must make me sort of goofy. Anyway, nice to meet you, Dr Arundez. I hope I'll see you at Reichs someday.'

'I hope that too,' said Melio, staring at her so intensely in the gloom that Sol had the feeling he was trying to memorize everything about the instant.

'Okay, well . . .' said Rachel and stepped back, her rubber-soled shoes squeaking on the sidewalk, 'good night, then. See you in the morning, Dad.'

'Good night, Rachel.'

She paused at the doorway. The gaslight on the lawn made her look much younger than thirteen. ''Later, alligators.'

''While, crocodile,' said Sol and heard Melio whisper it in unison.

They stood awhile in silence, feeling the night settle on the small town. A boy on a bicycle rode by, leaves crackling under his wheels, spokes gleaming in the pools of light under the old streetlamps. 'Come in the house,' Sol said to the silent man. 'Sarai will be very pleased to see you. Rachel will be asleep.'

'Not now,' said Melio. He was a shadow there, his hands still in his pockets. 'I need to . . . it was a mistake, Sol.' He started to turn away, looked back. 'I'll phone when I get to Freeholm,' he said. 'We'll get another expedition put together.'

Sol nodded. *Three years transit,* he thought. *If they left tonight she would be . . . not quite ten before they arrive.* 'Good,' he said.

Melio paused, raised a hand in farewell, and walked away along the curb, ignoring the leaves that crunched underfoot.

Sol never saw him in person again.

The largest Church of the Shrike in the Web was on Lusus and Sol farcast there a few weeks before Rachel's tenth birthday. The building itself was not much larger than an Old Earth cathedral, but it seemed gigantic with its effect of flying buttresses in search of a church, twisted upper stories, and support walls of stained glass. Sol's mood was low and the brutal Lusian gravity did nothing to lighten it. Despite his appointment with the bishop, Sol had to wait more than five hours before he was allowed into the inner sanctum. He spent most of the time staring at the slowly rotating twenty-meter, steel and polychrome sculpture which might have been of the legendary Shrike . . . and might have been an abstract homage to every edged weapon ever invented. What interested Sol the most were the two red orbs floating within the nightmare space which might have been a skull.

'M. Weintraub?'

'Your Excellency,' said Sol. He noticed that the acolytes, exorcists, lectors, and ostiaries who had kept him company during the long wait had prostrated themselves on the dark tiles at the high priest's entry. Sol managed a formal bow.

'Please, please, do come in, M. Weintraub,' said the priest. He indicated the doorway to the Shrike sanctuary with a sweep of his robed arm.

Sol passed through, found himself in a dark and echoing place not too dissimilar from the setting of his recurrent dream, and took a seat where the bishop indicated. As the cleric moved to his own place at what looked like a small throne behind an intricately carved but thoroughly modern desk, Sol noticed that the high priest was a native Lusian, gone to fat and heavy in the jowls, but formidable in the way all Lusus residents seemed to be. His robe was striking in its redness . . . a bright, arterial red, flowing more like a contained liquid than like silk or velvet, trimmed in onyx ermine. The bishop wore a large ring on each finger and they alternated red and black, producing a disturbing effect in Sol.

'Your Excellency,' began Sol, 'I apologize in advance for any breach in church protocol which I have committed . . . or may commit. I confess I know little about the Church of the Shrike, but what I do know has brought me here. Please forgive me if I inadvertently display my ignorance by my clumsy use of titles or terms.'

The bishop wiggled his fingers at Sol. Red and black stones flashed in the weak light. 'Titles are unimportant, M. Weintraub. Addressing us as "Your Excellency" is quite acceptable for a nonbeliever. We must advise you, however, that the formal name of our modest group is the Church of the Final Atonement and the entity whom the world so blithely calls . . . the Shrike . . . we refer to . . . if we take His name at all . . . as the Lord of Pain or, more commonly, the Avatar. Please proceed with the important query you said you had for us.'

Sol bowed slightly. 'Your Excellency, I am a teacher . . .'

'Excuse us for interrupting, M. Weintraub, but you are much more than a teacher. You are a scholar. We are very familiar with your writings on moral hermeneutics. The reasoning therein is flawed but quite challenging. We use it regularly in our courses in doctrinal apologetics. Please proceed.'

Sol blinked. His work was almost unknown outside the most rarefied academic circles and this recognition had thrown him. In the five seconds it took him to recover, Sol found it preferable to believe that the Shrike bishop wanted to know with whom he spoke and had an excellent staff. 'Your Excellency, my background is immaterial. I asked to see you because my child . . . my daughter . . . has taken ill as a possible result of research she was carrying out in an area which is of some importance to your Church. I speak, of course, of the so-called Time Tombs on the world of Hyperion.'

The bishop nodded slowly. Sol wondered if he knew about Rachel.

'You are aware, M. Weintraub, that the area you referred to . . . what we call the Covenant Arks . . . has recently been declared off limits to so-called researchers by the Home Rule Council of Hyperion?'

'Yes, Your Excellency. I have heard that. I understand that your Church was instrumental in that legislation being passed.'

The bishop showed no response to this. Far off in the incense-layered gloom, small chimes sounded:

'At any rate, Your Excellency, I hoped that some aspect of your Church's doctrine might shed light on my daughter's illness.'

The bishop inclined his head forward so that the single shaft of light which illuminated him gleamed on his forehead and cast his eyes into shadow. 'Do you wish to receive religious instruction in the mysteries of the Church, M. Weintraub?

Sol touched his beard with a finger. 'No, Your Excellency, unless in so doing I might improve the wellbeing of my daughter.'

'And does your daughter wish to be initiated into the Church of the Final Atonement?'

Sol hesitated a beat. 'Again, Your Excellency, she wishes to be well. If joining the Church would heal or help her, it would be a very serious consideration.'

The bishop sat back in a rustle of robes. Redness seemed to flow from him into the gloom. 'You speak of *physical* wellbeing, M. Weintraub. Our Church is the final arbiter of *spiritual* salvation. Are you aware that the former invariably flows from the latter?'

'I am aware that this is an old and widely respected proposition,' said Sol. 'The total wellbeing of our daughter is the concern of my wife and myself.'

The bishop rested his massive head on his fist. 'What is the nature of your daughter's illness, M. Weintraub?'

'It is . . . a time-related illness, Your Excellency.'

The bishop sat forward, suddenly tense. 'And at which of the holy sites did you say your daughter contracted this malady, M. Weintraub?'

'The artifact called the Sphinx, Your Excellency.'

The bishop stood so quickly that papers on his desktop were knocked to the floor. Even without the robes, the man would have massed twice Sol's weight. In the fluttering red robes, stretched to his full height, the Shrike priest now towered over Sol like crimson death incarnate. 'You can go!' bellowed the big man. 'Your daughter is the most blessed and cursed of individuals. There is nothing that you or the Church . . . or any agent in this life . . . can do for her.'

Sol stood . . . or, rather, sat . . . his ground. 'Your Excellency, if there is any possibility . . .'

'NO!' cried the bishop, red in the face now, a consummately consistent apparition. He tapped at his desk. Exorcists and lectors appeared in the doorway, their black robes with red trim an ominous echo of the bishop. The all-black ostiaries blended with the shadows. 'The audience is at an end,' said the bishop with less volume but infinite finality. 'Your daughter has been chosen by the Avatar to atone in a way which all sinners and nonbelievers must someday suffer. Someday very soon.'

'Your Excellency, if I can have just five minutes more of your time . . .'

The bishop snapped his fingers and the exorcists came forward to escort Sol out. The men were Lusian. One of them could have handled five scholars Sol's size.

'Your Excellency . . .' cried Sol after he had shrugged off the first man's hands. The three other exorcists came to assist with the equally brawny lectors hovering nearby. The bishop had turned his back and seemed to be staring into the darkness.

The outer sanctuary echoed to grunts and the scraping of Sol's heels and to at least one loud gasp as Sol's foot made contact with the least priestly parts of the lead exorcist. The outcome of the debate was not affected. Sol landed in the street. The last ostiary to turn away tossed Sol's battered hat to him.

Ten more days on Lusus achieved nothing but more gravity fatigue for Sol. The Temple bureaucracy would not answer his calls. The courts could offer him no wedge. The exorcists waited just within the doors of the vestibule.

Sol farcast to New Earth and Renaissance Vector, to Fuji and TC^2, to

Deneb Drei and Deneb Vier, but everywhere the Shrike temples were closed to him.

Exhausted, frustrated, out of money, Sol 'cast home to Barnard's World, got the EMV out of the long-term lot, and arrived home an hour before Rachel's birthday.

'Did you bring me anything, Daddy?' asked the excited ten-year-old. Sarai had told her that day that Sol had been gone.

Sol brought out the wrapped package. It was the collected *Anne of Green Gobles* series. It was not what he had wanted to bring her.

'Can I open it?'

'Later, little one. With the other things.'

'Oh, *please*, Dad. Just one thing now. Before Niki and the other kids get here?'

Sol caught Sarai's eye. She shook her head. Rachel remembered inviting Niki and Linna and her other friends to the party only days before. Sarai had not yet come up with an excuse.

'All right, Rachel,' he said. 'Just this one before the party.'

While Rachel ripped into the small package, Sol saw the giant package in the living room, secured with red ribbon. The new bike, of course. Rachel had asked for the new bike for a year before her tenth birthday. Sol tiredly wondered if she would be surprised tomorrow to find the new bike here the day *before* her tenth birthday. Or perhaps they would get rid of the bike that night, while Rachel slept.

Sol collapsed onto the couch. The red ribbon reminded him of the bishop's robes.

Sarai had never had an easy time of surrendering the past. Every time she cleaned and folded and put away a set of Rachel's outgrown baby clothes, she had shed secret tears that Sol somehow knew about. Sarai had treasured every stage of Rachel's childhood, enjoying the day-to-day *normalcy* of things; a normalcy which she quietly accepted as the best of life. She had always felt that the essence of human experience lay not primarily in the peak experiences, the wedding days and triumphs which stood out in the memory like dates circled in red on old calendars, but, rather, in the unselfconscious flow of little things – the weekend afternoon with each member of the family engaged in his or her own pursuit, their crossings and connections casual, dialogues imminently forgettable, but the *sum* of such hours creating a synergy which was important and eternal.

Sol found Sarai in the attic, weeping softly as she went through boxes. These were not the gentle tears once shed for the ending of small things. Sarai Weintraub was *angry*.

'What are you doing, Mother?'

'Rachel needs clothes. Everything is too big. What fit on an eight-year-old won't fit a seven-year-old. I have some more of her things here somewhere.'

'Leave it,' said Sol. 'We'll buy something new.'

Sarai shook her head. 'And have her wonder every day where all of her favorite clothes have gone? No. I've saved some things. They're here somewhere.'

'Do it later.'

'Damn it, there *is* no later!' shouted Sarai and then turned away from Sol and raised her hands to her face. 'I'm sorry.'

Sol put his arms around her. Despite the limited Poulsen treatments, her bare arms were much thinner than he remembered. Knots and cords under rough skin. He hugged her tightly.

'I'm sorry,' she repeated, sobbing openly now. 'It's just not *fair*.'

'No,' agreed Sol. 'It's not fair.' The sunlight coming through the dusty attic panes had a sad, cathedral quality to it. Sol had always loved the smell of an attic – the hot and stale *promise* of a place so underused and filled with future treasures. Today it was ruined.

He crouched next to a box. 'Come, dear,' he said, 'we'll look together.'

Rachel continued to be happy, involved with life, only slightly confused by the incongruities which faced her each morning when she awoke. As she grew younger it became easier to explain away the changes that appeared to have occurred overnight – the old elm out front gone, the new apartment building on the corner where M. Nesbitt used to live in a colonial-era home, the absence of her friends – and Sol began to see as never before the flexibility of children. He now imagined Rachel living on the breaking crest of the wave of time, not seeing the murky depths of the sea beyond, keeping her balance with her small store of memories and a total commitment to the twelve to fifteen hours of *now* allowed her each day.

Neither Sol nor Sarai wanted their daughter isolated from other children and it was difficult to find ways to make contact. Rachel was delighted to play with the 'new girl' or 'new boy' in the neighborhood – children of other instructors, the grandchildren of friends, for a while with Niki's daughter – but the other children had to grow accustomed to Rachel greeting them anew each day, remembering nothing of their common past, and only a few had the sensitivity to continue such a charade for the sake of a playmate.

The story of Rachel's unique illness was no secret in Crawford, of course. The fact of it had spread through the college the first year of Rachel's return and the entire town knew soon after. Crawford reacted in the fashion of small towns immemorial – some tongues wagged constantly, some people could not keep the pity and pleasure at someone else's misfortune out of their voices and gazes – but mostly the community folded its protective wings around the Weintraub family like an awkward mother bird shielding its young.

Still, they were allowed to live their lives, and even when Sol had to cut back classes and then take an early retirement because of trips seeking medical treatment for Rachel, the real reason was mentioned by no one.

But it could not last, of course, and on the spring day when Sol stepped onto the porch and saw his weeping seven-year-old daughter coming back from the park surrounded and followed by a pack of newsteeps, their camera implants gleaming and comlogs extended, he knew that a phase of their life was over forever. Sol jumped from the porch and ran to Rachel's side.

'M. Weintraub, is it true that your daughter contracted a terminal time illness? What's going to happen in seven years? Will she just disappear?'

'M. Weintraub! M. Weintraub! Rachel says that she thinks Raben Dowell is Senate CEO and this is the year A.D. 2711. Has she lost those thirty-four years completely or is this a delusion caused by the Merlin sickness?'

'Rachel! Do you remember being a grown woman? What's it feel like to be a kid again?'

'M. Weintraub! M. Weintraub! Just one still image, please. How about you get a picture of Rachel when she was older and you and the kid stand looking at it?'

'M. Weintraub! Is it true that this is the curse of the Time Tombs? Did Rachel see the Shrike monster?'

'Hey, Weintraub! Sol! Hey, Solly! What're you and the little woman going to do when the kid's gone?'

There was a newsteep blocking Sol's way to the front door. The man leaned forward, the stereo lenses of his eyes elongating as they zoomed in for a close-up of Rachel. Sol grabbed the man's long hair – which was conveniently tied in a queue – and flung him aside.

The pack brayed and bellowed outside the house for seven weeks. Sol realized what he had known and forgotten about very small communities: they were frequently annoying, always parochial, sometimes prying on a one-to-one level, but never had they subscribed to the vicious legacy of the so-called 'public's right to know'.

The Web did. Rather than have his family become permanent prisoners to the besieging reporters, Sol went on the offensive. He arranged interviews on the most pervasive farcaster cable news programs, participated in All Thing discussions, and personally attended the Concourse Medical Research Conclave. In ten standard months he asked for help for his daughter on eighty worlds.

Offers poured in from ten thousand sources but the bulk of the communications were from faith healers, project promoters, institutes and free-lance researchers offering their services in exchange for the publicity, Shrike cultists and other religious zealots pointing out that Rachel deserved the punishment, requests from various advertising agencies for product endorsements, offers from media agents to 'handle' Rachel for such endorsements, offers of sympathy from common people – frequently enclosing credit chips, expressions of disbelief from scientists, offers from holie producers and book publishers for exclusive rights to Rachel's life, and a barrage of real estate offers.

Reichs University paid for a team of evaluators to sort the offers and see if anything might benefit Rachel. Most of the communications were discarded. A few medical or research offers were seriously considered. In the end, none seemed to offer any avenue of research or experimental therapy which Reichs had not already tried. One fatline flimsy came to Sol's attention. It was from the Chairman of Kibbutz K'far Shalom on Hebron and read simply:

IF IT BECOMES TOO MUCH, COME.

It soon became too much. After the first few months of publicity the siege seemed to lift, but this was only the prelude to the second act. Faxsimmed tabloids referred to Sol as the 'Wandering Jew', the desperate father wandering afar in search of a cure for his child's bizarre illness – an ironic title given Sol's lifelong dislike of travel. Sarai inevitably was 'the grieving mother'. Rachel was 'the doomed child' or, in one inspired headline, 'Virgin Victim of the Time Tombs' Curse'. None of the family could go outside without finding a newsteep or imager hiding behind a tree.

Crawford discovered that there was money to be found in the Weintraubs' misfortune. At first the town held the line, but when entrepreneurs from Bussard City moved in with gift shops, T-shirt concessions, tours, and datachip booths for the tourists who were coming in larger and larger numbers, the local business people first dithered, then wavered, then decided unanimously that, if there was commerce to be carried on, the profits should not go to outsiders.

After four hundred and thirty-eight standard years of comparative solitude, the town of Crawford received a farcaster terminex. No longer did visitors have to suffer the twenty-minute flight from Bussard City. The crowds grew.

On the day they moved it rained heavily and the streets were empty. Rachel did not cry, but her eyes were very wide all day and she spoke in subdued tones. It was ten days before her sixth birthday. 'But, Daddy, *why* do we have to move?'

'We just do, honey.'

'But *why*?'

'It's something we have to do, little one. You'll like Hebron. There are lots of parks there.'

'But how come you never *said* we were going to move?'

'We did, sweetie. You must have forgotten.'

'But what about Gram and Grams and Uncle Richard and Aunt Tetha and Uncle Saul and everybody?'

'They can come visit us any time.'

'But what about Niki and Linna and my *friends*?'

Sol said nothing but carried the last of the luggage to the EMV. The house was sold and empty; furniture had been sold or sent ahead to Hebron. For a week there had been a steady stream of family and old friends, college associates, and even some of the Reichs med team who had worked with Rachel for eighteen years, but now the street was empty. Rain streaked the Perspex canopy of the old EMV and ran in complex rivulets. The three of them sat in the vehicle for a moment, staring at the house. The interior smelled of wet wool and wet hair.

Rachel clutched the teddy bear Sarai had resurrected from the attic six months earlier. She said, 'It's not fair.'

'No,' agreed Sol. 'It's not fair.'

Hebron was a desert world. Four centuries of terraforming had made the atmosphere breathable and a few million acres of land arable. The creatures which had lived there before were small and tough and infinitely wary, and so were the creatures imported from Old Earth, including the human kind.

'Ahh,' gasped Sol the day they arrived in the sun-baked village of Dan above the sun-baked kibbutz of K'far Shalom, 'what masochists we Jews are. Twenty thousand surveyed worlds fit for our kind when the Hegira began, and those schmucks came here.'

But it was not masochism which brought either the first colonists or Sol and his family. Hebron was mostly desert, but the fertile areas were almost frighteningly fertile. Sinai University was respected throughout the Web and its Med Center brought in wealthy patients and a healthy income for the cooperative. Hebron had a single farcaster terminex in New Jerusalem and allowed portals nowhere else. Belonging to neither the Hegemony nor Protectorate, Hebron taxed travelers heavily for farcaster privilege and allowed no tourists outside New Jerusalem. For a Jew seeking privacy, it was perhaps the safest place in three hundred worlds trod by man.

The kibbutz was more a cooperative by tradition than in operation. The Weintraubs were welcomed to their own home – a modest place offering sun-dried adobe, curves instead of right angles, and bare wood floors, but also offering a view from the hill which showed an infinite expanse of desert beyond the orange and olive groves. The sun seemed to dry up everything, thought Sol, even worries and bad dreams. The light was a physical thing. In the evening their house glowed pink for an hour after the sun had set.

Each morning Sol sat by his daughter's bed until she awoke. The first minutes of her confusion were always painful to him, but he made sure that he was the first thing Rachel saw each day. He held her while she asked her questions.

'Where are we, Daddy?'

'In a wonderful place, little one. I'll tell you all about it over breakfast.'

'How did we get here?'

'By 'casting and flying and walking a bit,' he would say. 'It's not so far away . . . but far enough to make it an adventure.'

'But my bed's here . . . my stuffed animals . . . why don't I remember coming?'

And Sol would hold her gently by the shoulders and look into her brown

210

eyes and say, 'You had an accident, Rachel. Remember in *The Homesick Toad* where Terrence hits his head and forgets where he lives for a few days? It was sort of like that.'

'Am I better?'

'Yes,' Sol would say, 'you're all better now.' And the house would fill with the smell of breakfast and they would go out to the terrace where Sarai waited.

Rachel had more playmates than ever. The kibbutz cooperative had a school where she was always the welcomed visitor, greeted anew each day. In the long afternoons the children played in the orchards and explored along the cliffs.

Avner, Robert, and Ephraim, the Council elders, urged Sol to work on his book. Hebron prided itself on the number of scholars, artists, musicians, philosophers, writers and composers it sheltered as citizens and long-term residents. The house, they pointed out, was a gift of the state. Sol's pension, though small by Web standards, was more than adequate for their modest needs in K'far Shalom. To Sol's surprise, however, he found that he enjoyed physical labor. Whether working in the orchards or clearing stones in the unclaimed fields or repairing a wall above the city, Sol found that his mind and spirit were freer than they had been in many years. He discovered that he could wrestle with Kierkegaard while he waited for mortar to dry and find new insights in Kant and Vandeur while carefully checking the apples for worms. At the age of seventy-three standard, Sol earned his first calluses.

In the evenings he would play with Rachel and then take a walk in the foothills with Sarai as Judy or one of the other neighbor girls watched their sleeping child. One weekend they went away to New Jerusalem, just Sol and Sarai, the first time they had been alone together for that long since Rachel returned to live with them seventeen standard years before.

But everything was not idyllic. Too frequent were the nights when Sol awoke alone and walked barefoot down the hall to see Sarai watching over Rachel in her sleep. And often at the end of a long day, bathing Rachel in the old ceramic tub or tucking her in as the walls glowed pinkly, the child would say, 'I like it here, Daddy, but can we go home tomorrow?' And Sol would nod. And after the goodnight story, and the lullaby, and the good-night kiss, sure that she was asleep, he would begin to tiptoe out of the room only to hear the muffled ''Later, alligator' from the blanketed form on the bed, to which he had to reply ''While, crocodile.' And lying in bed himself, next to the softly breathing and possibly sleeping length of the woman he loved, Sol would watch the strips of pale light from one or both of Hebron's small moons move across the rough walls and he would talk to God.

Sol had been talking to God for some months before he realized what he was doing. The idea amused him. The dialogues were in no way prayers but took the form of angry monologues which – just short of the point where they became diatribes – became vigorous arguments with himself. Only not just with himself. Sol realized one day that the topics of the heated debates were so profound, the stakes to be settled so serious, the ground covered so broad, that the only person he could possibly be berating for such short-comings was God Himself. Since the concept of a personal God, lying awake at night worrying about human beings, intervening in the lives of individuals, always had been totally absurd to Sol, the thought of such dialogues made him doubt his sanity.

But the dialogues continued.

Sol wanted to know how any ethical system – much less a religion so indomitable that it had survived every evil mankind could throw at it – could flow from a command from God for a man to slaughter his son. It did not matter to Sol that the command had been rescinded at the last moment. It did not matter that the command was a test of obedience. In fact, the idea that it was the *obedience* of Abraham which allowed him to become the father of all the tribes of Israel was precisely what drove Sol into fits of fury.

After fifty-five years of dedicating his life and work to the story of ethical systems, Sol Weintraub had come to a single, unshakable conclusion: any allegiance to a deity or concept or universal principle which put *obedience* above decent behavior toward an innocent human being was evil.

— *So define 'innocent'?* came the vaguely amused, faintly querulous voice which Sol associated with these arguments.

— A child is innocent, thought Sol. Isaac was. Rachel is.

— *'Innocent' by the mere fact of being a child?*

— Yes.

— *And there is no situation where the blood of the innocent must be shed for a greater cause?*

— No, thought Sol. None.

— *But the 'innocent' are not restricted to children, I presume.*

— Sol hesitated, sensing a trap, trying to see where his subconscious interlocutor was heading. He could not. No, he thought, the 'innocent' include others as well as children.

— *Such as Rachel? At age twenty-four? The innocent should not be sacrificed at any age?*

— That's right.

— *Perhaps this is part of the lesson which Abraham needed to learn before he could be father to the blessed of the nations of the earth.*

— What lesson? thought Sol. What lesson? But the voice in his mind had faded and now there were only the sounds of night birds outside and the soft breathing of his wife beside him.

Rachel could still read at age five. Sol had trouble remembering when she had learned to read – it seemed she always had been able to. 'Four stand-ard,' said Sarai. 'It was early summer . . . three months after her birthday. We were picnicking in the field above the college, Rachel was looking at her *Winnie-the-Pooh* book, and suddenly she said, "I hear a voice in my head."'

Sol remembered then.

He also remembered the joy he and Sarai had felt at the rapid acquisition of new skills Rachel had shown at that age. He remembered because now they were confronted with the reverse of that process.

'Dad,' said Rachel from where she lay on the floor of his study, carefully coloring, 'how long has it been since Mom's birthday?'

'It was on Monday,' said Sol, preoccupied with something he was reading. Sarai's birthday had not yet come but Rachel remembered it.

'I *know*. But how long has it been since then?'

'Today is Thursday,' said Sol. He was reading a long Talmudic treatise on obedience.

'I *know*. But how many *days*?'

Sol put down the hard copy. 'Can you name the days of the week?' Barnard's World had used the old calendar.

'Sure,' said Rachel. 'Saturday, Sunday, Monday, Tuesday, Wednesday, Thursday, Friday, Saturday . . .'

'You said Saturday already.'

'Yeah. But how many *days* ago?'

'Can you count from Monday to Thursday?'

Rachel frowned, moved her lips. She tried again, counting on her fingers this time. 'Four days?'

'Good,' said Sol. 'Can you tell me what ten minus four is, kiddo?'

'What does minus mean?'

Sol forced himself to look at his papers again. 'Nothing,' he said. 'Something you'll learn at school.'

'When we go home tomorrow?'

'Yes.'

One morning when Rachel went off with Judy to play with the other children – she was too young to attend school any longer – Sarai said: 'Sol, we have to take her to Hyperion.'

Sol stared at her. 'What?'

'You heard me. We can't wait until she is too young to walk . . . to talk. Also, we're not getting any younger.' Sarai barked a mirthless laugh. 'That sounds strange, doesn't it? But we're not. The Poulsen treatments will be wearing off in a year or two.'

'Sarai, did you forget? The doctors all say that Rachel could not survive cryogenic fugue. No one experiences FTL travel without fugue state. The Hawking effect can drive one mad . . . or worse.'

'It doesn't matter,' said Sarai. 'Rachel has to return to Hyperion.'

'What on earth are you talking about?' said Sol, angered.

Sarai gripped his hand. 'Do you think you're the only one who has had the dream?'

'Dream?' managed Sol.

She sighed and sat at the white kitchen table. Morning light struck the plants on the sill like a yellow spotlight. 'The dark place,' she said. 'The red lights above. The voice. Telling us to . . . telling us to take . . . to go to Hyperion. To make . . . an offering.'

Sol licked his lips but there was no moisture there. His heart pounded. 'Whose name . . . whose name is called?'

Sarai looked at him strangely. 'Both of our names. If you weren't there . . . in the dream with me . . . I could never have borne it all these years.'

Sol collapsed into his chair. He looked down at the strange hand and forearm lying on the table. The knuckles of the hand were beginning to enlarge with arthritis; the forearm was heavily veined, marked with liver spots. It was his hand, of course. He heard himself say: 'You never mentioned it. Never said a word . . .'

This time Sarai's laugh was without bitterness. 'As if I had to! All those times both of us coming awake in the dark. And you covered with sweat. I knew from the first time that it was not merely a dream. We have to go, Father. Go to Hyperion.'

Sol moved the hand. It still did not feel a part of him. 'Why? For God's sake, why, Sarai? We can't . . . *offer* Rachel . . .'

'Of course not, Father. Haven't you thought about this? We have to go to Hyperion . . . to wherever the dream tells us to go . . . and offer ourselves instead.'

'Offer ourselves,' repeated Sol. He wondered if he was having a heart attack. His chest ached so terribly that he could not take in a breath. He sat for a full minute in silence, convinced that if he attempted to utter a word only a sob would escape. After another minute he said: 'How long have you . . . thought about this, Mother?'

'Do you mean *known* what we must do? A year. A little more. Just after her fifth birthday.'

'A year! Why haven't you said something?'

'I was waiting for you. To realize. To *know*.'

Sol shook his head. The room seemed far away and slightly tilted. 'No. I mean, it doesn't seem . . . I have to *think*. Mother.' Sol watched as the strange hand patted Sarai's familiar hand.

She nodded.

Sol spent three days and nights in the arid mountains, eating only the thick-crusted bread he had brought and drinking from his condenser therm.

Ten thousand times in the past twenty years he had wished that *he* could take Rachel's illness; that if anyone had to suffer it should be the father, not the child. Any parent would feel that way – *did* feel that way every time his child lay injured or racked with fever. Surely it could not be that simple.

In the heat of the third afternoon, as he lay half dozing in the shade of a thin tablet of rock, Sol learned that it was *not* that simple.

— Can that be Abraham's answer to God? That *he* would be the offering, not Isaac?

— *It could have been Abraham's. It cannot be yours.*

— Why?

As if in answer, Sol had the fever-vision of naked adults filing toward the ovens past armed men, mothers hiding their children under piles of coats. He saw men and women with flesh hanging in burned strips carrying the dazed children from the ashes of what once had been a city. Sol knew that these images were no dreams, were the very stuff of the First and Second Holocausts, and in his understanding knew before the voice spoke in his mind what the answer was. What it must be.

— *The parents have offered themselves. That sacrifice already has been accepted. We are beyond that.*

— Then what? What!

Silence answered him. Sol stood in the full glare of the sun, almost fell. A black bird wheeled overhead or in his vision. Sol shook his fist at the gunmetal sky.

— You use Nazis as your instruments. Madmen. Monsters. You're a goddamn monster yourself.

— *No.*

The earth tilted and Sol fell on his side against sharp rocks. He thought that it was not unlike leaning against a rough wall. A rock the size of his fist burned his cheek.

— The correct answer for Abraham was obedience, thought Sol. Ethically, Abraham was a child himself. All men were at that time. The correct answer for Abraham's children was to become adults and to offer themselves instead. What is the correct answer for us?

There was no answer. The ground and sky quit spinning. After a while Sol rose shakily, rubbed the blood and grit from his cheek, and walked down to the town in the valley below.

'No,' Sol told Sarai, 'we will not go to Hyperion. It is not the correct solution.'

'You would have us do nothing then.' Sarai's lips were white with anger but her voice was firmly in control.

'No. I would have us not do the *wrong* thing.'

Sarai expelled her breath in a hiss. She waved toward the window where their four-year-old was visible playing with her toy horses in the backyard. 'Do you think *she* has time for us to do the wrong thing . . . or anything . . . indefinitely?'

'Sit down, Mother.'

Sarai remained standing. There was the faintest sprinkling of spilled sugar on the front of her tan cotton dress. Sol remembered the young woman rising nude from the phosphorescent wake of the motile isle on Maui-Covenant.

'We have to do something,' she said.

'We've seen over a hundred medical and scientific experts. She's been tested, prodded, probed, and tortured by two dozen research centers. I've been to the Shrike Church on every world in this Web; they won't see me. Melio and the other Hyperion experts at Reichs say that the Shrike Cult has nothing like the Merlin sickness in their doctrine and the indigenies on Hyperion have no legends of the malady or clues to its cure. Research during the three years the team was on Hyperion showed nothing. Now research there is illegal. Access to the Time Tombs is granted only to the so-called pilgrims. Even getting a travel visa to Hyperion is becoming almost impossible. And if we take Rachel, the trip may kill her.'

Sol paused for breath, touched Sarai's arm again. 'I'm sorry to repeat all this, Mother. But we have done something.'

'Not enough,' said Sarai. 'What if we go as pilgrims?'

Sol folded his arms in frustration. 'The Church of the Shrike chooses its sacrificial victims from thousands of volunteers. The Web is full of stupid, depressed people. Few of these return.'

'Doesn't that prove something?' Sarai whispered quickly, urgently. 'Somebody or something is preying on these people.'

'Bandits,' said Sol.

Sarai shook her head. 'The golem.'

'You mean the Shrike.'

'It's the golem,' insisted Sarai. 'The same one we see in the dream.'

Sol was uneasy. 'I don't see a golem in the dream. What golem?'

'The red eyes that watch,' said Sarai. 'It's the same golem that Rachel heard that night in the Sphinx.'

'How do you know that she heard anything?'

'It's in the *dream*,' said Sarai. 'Before we enter the place where the golem waits.'

'We haven't dreamed the same dream,' said Sol. 'Mother, Mother . . . why haven't you told me this before?'

'I thought I was going mad,' whispered Sarai.

Sol thought of his secret conversations with God and put his arm around his wife.

'Oh, Sol,' she whispered against him, 'it hurts so much to watch. And it's so lonely here.'

Sol held her. They had tried to go home – home would always be Barnard's World – half a dozen times to visit family and friends, but each time the visits were ruined by an invasion of newsteeps and tourists. It was no one's fault. News traveled almost instantaneously through the megadatasphere of a hundred and sixty Web worlds. To scratch the curiosity itch one had only to pass a universal card across a terminex diskey and step through a farcaster. They had tried arriving unannounced and traveling incognito but they were not spies and the efforts were pitiful. Within twenty-four standard hours of their reentry to the Web, they were besieged. Research institutes and large med centers easily provided the security screen for such a visit, but friends and family suffered. Rachel was NEWS.

'Perhaps we could invite Tetha and Richard again . . .' began Sarai.

'I have a better idea,' said Sol. 'Go yourself, Mother. You want to see your sister but you also want to see, hear, and *smell* home . . . watch a sunset where there are no iguanas . . . walk in the fields. Go.'

'Go? Just me? I couldn't be away from Rachel . . .'

'Nonsense,' said Sol. 'Twice in twenty years – almost forty if we count the good days before . . . anyway, twice in twenty years doesn't constitute child neglect. It's a wonder that this family can stand one another, we've been cooped up together so long.'

Sarai looked at the tabletop, lost in thought. 'But wouldn't the news people find me?'

'I bet not,' said Sol. 'It's Rachel they seem to key on. If they do hound you, come home. But I bet you can have a week visiting everyone at home before the teeps catch on.'

'A week,' gasped Sarai. 'I couldn't . . .'

'Of course you can. In fact, you *must*. It will give me a few days to spend more time with Rachel and then when you come back refreshed I'll spend some days selfishly working on the book.'

'The Kierkegaard one?'

'No. Something I've been playing with called *The Abraham Problem*.'

'Clumsy title,' said Sarai.

'It's a clumsy problem,' said Sol. 'Now go get packed. We'll fly you to New Jerusalem tomorrow so you can 'cast out before the Sabbath begins.'

'I'll think about it,' she said, sounding unconvinced.

'You'll *pack*,' said Sol, hugging her again. When the hug was completed he had turned her away from the window so that she faced the hallway and the bedroom door. 'Go. When you return from home I'll have thought of something we *can* do.'

Sarai paused. 'Do you promise?'

Sol looked at her. 'I promise I will before time destroys everything. I swear as Rachel's father that I'll find a way.'

Sarai nodded, more relaxed than he had seen her in months. 'I'll go pack,' she said.

When he and the child returned from New Jerusalem the next day, Sol went out to water the meager lawn while Rachel played quietly inside. When he came in, the pink glow of sunset infusing the walls with a sense of sea warmth and quiet, Rachel was not in her bedroom or the other usual places. 'Rachel?'

When there was no answer he checked the backyard again, the empty street.

'Rachel!' Sol ran in to call the neighbors but suddenly there was the slightest of sounds from the deep closet Sarai used for storage. Sol quietly opened the screen panel.

Rachel sat beneath the hanging clothes, Sarai's antique pine box open between her legs. The floor was littered with photos and holochips of Rachel as a high school student, Rachel on the day she set off for college, Rachel standing in front of a carved mountainside on Hyperion. Rachel's research comlog lay whispering on the four-year-old Rachel's lap. Sol's heart seized at the familiar sound of the confident young woman's voice.

'Daddy,' said the child on the floor, her own voice a tiny frightened echo of the voice on the comlog, 'you never told me that I had a sister.'

'You don't, little one.'

Rachel frowned. 'Is this Mommy when she was . . . not so big? Uh-uh, it can't be. *Her* name's Rachel, too, she says. How can . . .'

'It's all right,' he said. 'I'll explain . . .' Sol realized that the phone was ringing in the living room, had been ringing. 'Just a moment, sweetie. I'll be right back.'

The holo that formed above the pit was of a man Sol had never seen before. Sol did not activate his own imager, eager to get rid of the caller. 'Yes?' he said abruptly.

'M. Weintraub? M. Weintraub who used to live on Barnard's World, currently in the village of Dan on Hebron?'

Sol started to disconnect and then paused. Their access code was unfiled. Occasionally a salesperson called from New Jerusalem, but offworld calls were rare. And, Sol suddenly realized, his stomach feeling a stab of cold, *it was past sundown on the Sabbath*. Only emergency holo calls were allowed.

'Yes?' said Sol.

'M. Weintraub,' said the man, staring blindly past Sol, 'there's been a terrible accident.'

When Rachel awoke her father was sitting by the side of her bed. He looked tired. His eyes were red and his cheeks were gray with stubble above the line of his beard.

'Good morning, Daddy.'

'Good morning, sweetheart.'

Rachel looked around and blinked. Some of her dolls and toys and things were there, but the room was not hers. The light was different. The air felt different. Her daddy looked different. 'Where are we, Daddy?'

'We've gone on a trip, little one.'

'Where to?'

'It doesn't matter right now. Hop out, sweetie. Your bath is ready and then we have to get dressed.'

A dark dress she had never seen before lay at the base of her bed. Rachel looked at the dress and then back at her father. 'Daddy, what's the matter? Where's Mommy?'

Sol rubbed his cheek. It was the third morning since the accident. It was the day of the funeral. He had told her each of the preceding days because he could not imagine lying to her then; it seemed the ultimate betrayal – of both Sarai and Rachel. But he did not think he could do it again. 'There's been an accident, Rachel,' he said, his voice a pained rasp. 'Mommy died. We're going to go say goodbye to her today.' Sol paused. He knew by now that it would take a minute for the fact of her mother's death to become real for Rachel. On the first day he had not known if a four-year-old could truly comprehend the concept of death. He knew now that Rachel could.

Later, as he held the sobbing child, Sol tried to understand the accident he had described so briefly to her. EMVs were by far the safest form of personal transportation mankind had ever designed. Their lifters could fail but, even so, the residual charge in the EM generators would allow the aircar to descend safely from any altitude. The basic, failsafe design of an EMV's collision-avoidance equipment had not changed in centuries. But everything failed. In this case it was a joy-riding teenage couple in a stolen EMV outside the traffic lanes, accelerating to Mach 1.5 with all lights and transponders off to avoid detection, who defied all odds by colliding with Aunt Tetha's ancient Vikken as it descended toward the Bussard City Opera House landing apron. Besides Tetha and Sarai and the teenagers, three others died in the crash as pieces of falling vehicles cartwheeled into the crowded atrium of the Opera House itself.

Sarai.

'Will we ever see Mommy again?' Rachel asked between sobs. She had asked this each time.

'I don't know, sweetheart,' responded Sol truthfully.

The funeral was at the family cemetery in Kates County on Barnard's World. The press did not invade the graveyard itself but teeps hovered beyond the trees and pressed against the black iron gate like an angry storm tide.

Richard wanted Sol and Rachel to stay a few days, but Sol knew what pain would be inflicted on the quiet farmer if the press continued their assault. Instead, he hugged Richard, spoke briefly to the clamoring reporters beyond the fence, and fled to Hebron with a stunned and silent Rachel in tow.

Newsteeps followed to New Jerusalem and then attempted to follow to Dan, but military police overrode their chartered EMVs, threw a dozen in jail as an example, and revoked the farcaster visas of the rest.

In the evening Sol walked the ridge lines above the village while Judy watched his sleeping child. He found that his dialogue with God was audible now and he resisted the urge to shake his fist at the sky, to shout obscenities, to throw stones. Instead he asked questions, always ending with – Why?

There was no answer. Hebron's sun set behind distant ridges and the rocks glowed as they gave up their heat. Sol sat on a boulder and rubbed his temples with his palms.

Sarai.

They had lived a full life, even with the tragedy of Rachel's illness hanging over them. It was too ironic that in Sarai's first hour of relaxation with her sister . . . Sol moaned aloud.

The trap, of course, had been in their total absorption with Rachel's illness. Neither had been able to face the future beyond Rachel's . . . death? Disappearance? The world had hinged upon each day their child lived and no thought had been given to the chance of accident, the perverse antilogic of a sharp-edged universe. Sol was sure that Sarai had considered suicide just as he had, but neither of them could ever have abandoned the other. Or Rachel. He had never considered the possibility of being alone with Rachel when . . .

Sarai!

At that moment Sol realized that the often angry dialogue which his people had been having with God for so many millennia had not ended with the death of Old Earth . . . nor with the new Diaspora . . . but continued still. He and Rachel and Sarai had been part of it, were part of it now. He let the pain come. It filled him with the sharp-edged agony of resolve.

Sol stood on the ridge line and wept as darkness fell.

In the morning he was next to Rachel's bed when sunlight filled the room.

'Good morning, Daddy.'

'Good morning, sweetheart.'

'Where are we, Daddy?'

'We've gone on a trip. It's a pretty place.'

'Where's Mommy?'

'She's with Aunt Tetha today.'

'Will we see her tomorrow?'

'Yes,' said Sol. 'Now let's get you dressed and I'll make breakfast.'

Sol began to petition the Church of the Shrike when Rachel turned three. Travel to Hyperion was severely limited and access to the Time Tombs had become all but impossible. Only the occasional Shrike Pilgrimage sent people to that region.

Rachel was sad that she had to be away from her mother on her birthday but the visit of several children from the kibbutz distracted her a bit. Her big present was an illustrated book of fairy tales which Sarai had picked out in New Jerusalem months before.

Sol read some of the stories to Rachel before bedtime. It had been seven months since she could read any of the words herself. But she loved the stories – especially 'Sleeping Beauty' – and made her father read it to her twice.

'I'm gonna show Mommy it when we get home,' she said through a yawn as Sol turned out the overhead light.

'Good night, kiddo,' he said softly, pausing at the door.

'Hey, Daddy?'

'Yes?'

''Later, alligator.'
''While, crocodile.'
Rachel giggled into her pillow.

It was, Sol thought during the final two years, not so much different from watching a loved one falling into old age. Only worse. A thousand times worse.

Rachel's permanent teeth had fallen out over intervals between her eighth and second birthdays. Baby teeth replaced them but by her eight-eenth month half of these had receded into her jaw.

Rachel's hair, always her one vanity, grew shorter and thinner. Her face lost its familiar structure as baby fat obscured the cheekbones and firm chin. Her coordination failed by degrees, noticeable at first in a sudden clumsiness as she handled a fork or pencil. On the day she could no longer walk, Sol put her down in her crib early and then went into his study to get thoroughly and quietly drunk.

Language was the hardest for him. Her vocabulary loss was like the burning of a bridge between them, the severing of a final line of hope. It was sometime after her second birthday receded that Sol tucked her in and, pausing in the doorway, said, ''Later, alligator.'

'Huh?'

'See you later, alligator.'

Rachel giggled.

'You say – "In a while, crocodile,"' said Sol. He told her what an alligator and crocodile were.

'In a while, 'acadile,' giggled Rachel.

In the morning she had forgotten.

Sol took Rachel with him as he traveled the Web – no longer caring about the newsteeps – petitioning the Shrike Church for pilgrimage rights, lobbying the Senate for a visa and access to forbidden areas on Hyperion, and visiting any research institute or clinic which might offer a cure. Months were lost while more medics admitted failure. When he fled back to Hebron, Rachel was fifteen standard months old; in the ancient units used on Hebron she weighed twenty-five pounds and measured thirty inches tall. She could no longer dress herself. Her vocabulary con-sisted of twenty-five words, of which her favorites were 'Mommy' and 'Daddy'.

Sol loved carrying his daughter. There were times when the curve of her head against his cheek, her warmth against his chest, the smell of her skin – all worked to allow him to forget the fierce injustice of it all. At those times Sol would have been temporarily at peace with the universe if only Sarai had been there. As it was, there were temporary cease-fires in his angry dialogue with a God in Whom he did not believe.

— What possible reason can there be for this?

— What reason has been visible for all of the forms of pain suffered by humankind?

— Precisely, thought Sol, wondering if he had just won a point for the first time. He doubted it.

— The fact of a thing not being visible does not mean it does not exist.

— That's clumsy. It shouldn't take three negatives to make a statement. Especially to state something as nonprofound as that.

— Precisely, Sol. You're beginning to get the drift of all this.

— What?

There was no answer to his thoughts. Sol lay in his house and listened to the desert wind blow.

Rachel's last word was 'Mamma', uttered when she was just over five months old.

She awoke in her crib and did not – could not – ask where she was. Her world was one of mealtimes, naps, and toys. Sometimes when she cried Sol wondered if she was crying for her mother.

Sol shopped in the small stores in Dan, taking the infant with him as he selected diapers, nursing paks, and the occasional new toy.

The week before Sol left for Tau Ceti Center, Ephraim and the two other elders came to talk. It was evening and the fading light glowed on Ephraim's bald scalp. 'Sol, we're worried about you. The next few weeks will be hard. The women want to help. We want to help.'

Sol laid his hand on the older man's forearm. 'It's appreciated, Ephraim. Everything the last few years is appreciated. This is our home now, too. Sarai would have . . . would have wanted me to say thank you. But we're leaving on Sunday. Rachel is going to get better.'

The three men on the long bench looked at one another. Avner said, 'They've found a cure?'

'No,' said Sol, 'but I've found a reason to hope.'

'Hope is good,' Robert said in cautious tones.

Sol grinned, his teeth white against the gray of his beard. 'It had better be,' he said. 'Sometimes it is all we're given.'

The studio holo camera zoomed in for a close-up of Rachel as the infant sat cradled in Sol's arm on the set of 'Common Talk'. 'So you're saying,' said Devon Whiteshire, the show's host and the third-best-known face in the Web datasphere, 'that the Shrike Church's refusal to allow you to return to the Time Tombs . . . and the Hegemony's tardiness in processing a visa . . . these things will doom your child to this . . . *extinction?*'

'Precisely,' said Sol. 'The voyage to Hyperion cannot be made in under six weeks. Rachel is now twelve weeks old. Any further delay by either the Shrike Church or the Web bureaucracy will kill this child.'

The studio audience stirred. Devon Whiteshire turned toward the nearest imaging remote. His craggy, friendly visage filled the monitor frame. 'This man doesn't know if he can save his child,' said Whiteshire, his voice powerful with subtle feeling, 'but all he asks is a chance. Do you think he . . . and the baby . . . deserve one? If so, access your planetary representatives and your nearest Church of the Shrike temple. The number of your nearest temple should be appearing now.' He turned back to Sol. 'We wish you luck, M. Weintraub. And' – Whiteshire's large hand touched Rachel's cheek – 'we wish you Godspeed, our young friend.'

The monitor image held on Rachel until it faded to black.

The Hawking effect caused nausea, vertigo, headache, and hallucinations. The first leg of the voyage was the ten-day transit to Parvati on the Hegemony torchship HS *Intrepid*.

Sol held Rachel and endured. They were the only people fully conscious aboard the warship. At first Rachel cried, but after some hours she lay quietly in Sol's arms and stared up at him with large, dark eyes. Sol remembered the day she was born – the medics had taken the infant from atop Sarai's warm stomach and handed her to Sol. Rachel's dark hair was not much shorter then, her gaze no less profound.

Eventually they slept from sheer exhaustion.

Sol dreamed that he was wandering through a structure with columns the size of redwood trees and a ceiling lost to sight far above him. Red light bathed cool emptiness. Sol was surprised to find that he still carried Rachel in his arms. Rachel as a child had never been in his dream before. The infant looked up at him and Sol felt the *contact* of her consciousness as surely as if she had spoken aloud.

Suddenly a different voice, immense and cold, echoed through the void:

'Sol! Take your daughter, your only daughter Rachel, whom you love, and go to the world called Hyperion and offer her there as a burnt offering at one of the places of which I shall tell you.'

Sol hesitated and looked back to Rachel. The baby's eyes were deep and luminous as she looked up at her father. Sol felt the unspoken *yes*. Holding her tightly, he stepped forward into the darkness and raised his voice against the silence:

'Listen! There will be no more offerings, neither child nor parent. There will be no more sacrifices for anyone other than our fellow human. The time of obedience and atonement is past.'

Sol listened. He could feel the pounding of his heart and Rachel's warmth against his arm. From somewhere, high above there came the cold sound of wind through unseen fissures. Sol cupped his hand to his mouth and shouted:

'That's all! Now either leave us alone or join us as a father rather than a receiver of sacrifices. You have the choice of Abraham!'

Rachel stirred in his arms as a rumble grew out of the stone floor. Columns vibrated. The red gloom deepened and then winked out, leaving only darkness. From far away there came the boom of huge footsteps. Sol hugged Rachel to him as a violent wind roared past.

There was a glimmer of light as both he and Rachel awoke on the HS *Intrepid* outward bound for Parvati to transfer to the treeship *Yggdrasill* for the planet Hyperion. Sol smiled at his seven-week-old daughter. She smiled back.

It was her last and her first smile.

The main cabin of the windwagon was silent when the old scholar finished his story. Sol cleared his throat and took a drink of water from a crystal goblet. Rachel slept on in the makeshift cradle of the open drawer. The windwagon rocked gently on its way, the rumble of the great wheel and the hum of the main gyroscope a lulling background noise.

'My God,' Brawne Lamia said softly. She started to speak again and then merely shook her head.

Martin Silenus closed his eyes and said:

'Considering that, all hatred driven hence.
The soul recovers radical innocence
And learns at last that it is self-delighting,
Self-appeasing, self-affrighting,
And that its own sweet will is Heaven's will;
She can, though every face will scowl
And every windy quarter howl
Or every bellows burst, be happy still.'

Sol Weintraub asked, 'William Butler Yeats?'

Silenus nodded. '"A Prayer for My Daughter".'

'I think I'm going up on deck for a breath of air before turning in,' said the Consul. 'Would anyone care to join me?'

Everyone did. The breeze of their passage was refreshing as the group stood on the quarterdeck and watched the darkened Sea of Grass rumble by. The sky was a great, star-splashed bowl above them, scarred by meteor trails. The sails and rigging creaked with a sound as old as human travel.

'I think we should post guards tonight,' said Colonel Kassad. 'One person on watch while the others sleep. Two-hour intervals.'

'I agree,' said the Consul. 'I'll take the first watch.'

'In the morning . . .' began Kassad.

'Look!' cried Father Hoyt.

They followed his pointing arm. Between the blaze of constellations, colored fireballs flared – green, violet, orange, green again – illuminating the great plain of grass around them like flashes of heat lightning. The stars and meteor trails paled to insignificance beside the sudden display.

'Explosions?' ventured the priest.

'Space battle,' said Kassad. 'Cislunar. Fusion weapons.' He went below quickly.

'The Tree,' said Het Masteen, pointing to a speck of light which moved among the explosions like an ember floating through a fireworks display.

Kassad returned with his powered binoculars and handed them around.

'Ousters?' asked Lamia. 'Is it the invasion?'

'Ousters, almost certainly,' said Kassad. 'But almost as certainly just a scouting raid. See the clusters? Those are Hegemony missiles being exploded by the Ouster ramscouts' countermeasures.'

The binoculars came to the Consul. The flashes were quite clear now, an expanding cumulus of flame. He could see the speck and long blue tail of at least two scoutships fleeing from the Hegemony pursuers.

'I don't think . . .' began Kassad and then stopped as the ship and sails and Sea of Grass glowed bright orange in reflected glare.

'Dear Christ,' whispered Father Hoyt. 'They've hit the treeship.'

The Consult swept the glass left. The growing nimbus of flames could be seen with the naked eye but in the binoculars the kilometer-long trunk and branch array of the *Yggdrasill* was visible for an instant as it burned and flared, long tendrils of flame arcing away into space as the containment fields failed and the oxygen burned. The orange cloud pulsed, faded, and fell back on itself as the trunk became visible for a final second even as it glowed and broke up like the last long ember in a dying fire. Nothing could have survived. The treeship *Yggdrasill* with its crew and complement of clones and semisentient erg drivers was dead.

The Consul turned toward Het Masteen and belatedly held out the binoculars. 'I'm so . . . sorry,' he whispered.

The tall Templar did not take the glasses. Slowly he lowered his gaze from the skies, pulled forward his cowl, and went below without a word.

The death of the treeship was the final explosion. When ten minutes had passed and no more flares had disturbed the night, Brawne Lamia spoke. 'Do you think they got them?'

'The Ousters?' said Kassad. 'Probably not. The scoutships are built for speed and defense. They're light-minutes away by now.'

'Did they go after the treeship on purpose?' asked Silenus. The poet sounded very sober.

'I think not,' said Kassad. 'Merely a target of opportunity.'

'Target of opportunity,' echoed Sol Weintraub. The scholar shook his head. 'I'm going to get a few hours' sleep before sunrise.'

One by one the others went below. When only Kassad and the Consul were left on deck, the Consul said, 'Where should I stand watch?'

'Make a circuit,' said the Colonel. 'From the main corridor at the base of the ladder you can see all of the stateroom doors and the entrance to the mess and galley. Come above and check the gangway and decks. Keep the lanterns lit. Do you have a weapon?'

The Consul shook his head.

Kassad handed over his deathwand. 'It's on tight beam – about half a meter at ten meters' range. Don't use it unless you're sure that there's an intruder. The rough plate that slides forward is the safety. It's on.'

The Consul nodded, making sure that his finger stayed away from the firing stud.

'I'll relieve you in two hours,' said Kassad. He checked his comlog. 'It'll be sunrise before my watch is over.' Kassad looked at the sky as if expecting the *Yggdrasill* to reappear and continue its firefly path across the sky. Only the stars glowed back. On the northeastern horizon a moving mass of black promised a storm.

Kassad shook his head. 'A waste,' he said and went below.

The Consul stood there awhile and listened to the wind in the canvas, the creek of rigging, and the rumble of the wheel. After a while he went to the railing and stared at darkness while he thought.

FIVE

Sunrise over the Sea of Grass was a thing of beauty. The Consul watched from the highest point on the aft deck. After his watch he had tried to sleep, given it up, and come up onto deck to watch the night fade into day. The stormfront had covered the sky with low clouds and the rising sun lit the world with brilliant gold reflected from above and below. The windwagon's sails and lines and weathered planks glowed in the brief benediction of light in the few minutes before the sun was blocked by the ceiling of clouds and color flowed out of the world once again. The wind which followed this curtain closing was chill, as if it had blown down from the snowy peaks of the Bridle Range just visible as a dark blur on the northeastern horizon.

Brawne Lamia and Martin Silenus joined the Consul on the aft deck, each nursing a cup of coffee from the galley. The wind whipped and tugged at the rigging. Brawne Lamia's thick mass of curls fluttered around her face like a dark nimbus.

'Morning,' muttered Silenus, squinting out over his coffee cup at the wind-rippled Sea of Grass.

'Good morning,' replied the Consul, amazed at how alert and refreshed he felt for not having slept at all the night before. 'We have a headwind, but the wagon still seems to be making decent time. We'll definitely be to the mountains before nightfall.'

'Hrrgnn,' commented Silenus and buried his nose in the coffee cup.

'I didn't sleep at all last night,' said Brawne Lamia, 'just for thinking about M. Weintraub's story.'

'I don't think . . .' began the poet and then broke off as Weintraub came onto deck, his baby peering over the lip of an infant carrier sling on his chest.

'Good morning, everyone,' said Weintraub, looking around and taking a deep breath. 'Mmm, brisk, isn't it?'

'Fucking freezing,' said Silenus. 'North of the mountains it'll be even worse.'

'I think I'll go down to get a jacket,' said Lamia, but before she could move there came a single shrill cry from the deck below.

'*Blood!*'

There was, indeed, blood everywhere. Het Masteen's cabin was strangely neat – bed unslept in, travel trunk and other boxes stacked precisely in one corner, robe folded over a chair – except for the blood which covered great sections of the deck, bulkhead, and overhead. The six pilgrims crowded just inside the entrance, reluctant to go farther in.

'I was passing on my way to the upper deck,' said Father Hoyt, his voice a strange monotone. 'The door was slightly ajar. I caught a glimpse of . . . the blood on the wall.'

'*Is* it blood?' demanded Martin Silenus.

Brawne Lamia stepped into the room, ran a hand through a thick smear on the bulkhead, and raised her fingers to her lips. 'It's blood.' She looked around, walked to the wardrobe, looked briefly among the empty shelves and hangers, and then went to the small porthole. It was latched and bolted from the inside.

Lenar Hoyt looked more ill than usual and staggered to a chair. 'Is he dead then?'

'We don't know a damn thing except that Captain Masteen isn't in his room and a lot of blood *is*,' said Lamia. She wiped her hand on her pant leg. 'The thing to do now is search the ship thoroughly.'

'Precisely,' said Colonel Kassad, 'and if we do not find the Captain?'

Brawne Lamia opened the porthole. Fresh air dissipated the slaughterhouse smell of blood and brought in the rumble of the wheel and the rustle of grass under the hull. 'If we don't find Captain Masteen,' she said, 'then we assume that he either left the ship under his own will or was taken off.'

'But the *blood* . . .' began Father Hoyt.

'Doesn't prove anything,' finished Kassad. 'M. Lamia's correct. We don't know Masteen's blood type or genotype. Did anyone see or hear *anything*?'

There was silence except for negative grunts and the shaking of heads.

Martin Silenus looked around. 'Don't you people recognize the work of our friend the Shrike when you see it?'

'We don't know that,' snapped Lamia. 'Maybe someone *wanted* us to think that it was the Shrike's doing.'

'That doesn't make sense,' said Hoyt, still gasping for air.

'Nonetheless,' said Lamia, 'we'll search in twos. Who has weapons besides myself?'

'I do,' said Colonel Kassad. 'I have extras if needed.'

'No,' said Hoyt.

The poet shook his head.

Sol Weintraub had returned to the corridor with his child. Now he looked in again. 'I have nothing,' he said.

'No,' said the Consul. He had returned the deathwand to Kassad when his shift ended two hours before first light.

'All right,' said Lamia, 'the priest will come with me on the lower deck. Silenus, go with the Colonel. Search the mid-deck. M. Weintraub, you and the Consul check everything above. Look for *anything* out of the ordinary. Any sign of struggle.'

'One question,' said Silenus.

'What?'

'Who the hell elected you queen of the prom?'

'I'm a private investigator,' said Lamia, leveling her gaze on the poet.

Martin Silenus shrugged. 'Hoyt here is a priest of some forgotten religion. That doesn't mean we have to genuflect when he says Mass.'

'All right,' sighed Brawne Lamia. 'I'll give you a better reason.' The woman moved so fast that the Consul almost missed the action in a blink. One second she was standing by the open port and in the next she was halfway across the stateroom, lifting Martin Silenus off the deck with one arm, her massive hand around the poet's thin neck. 'How about,' she said, 'that you do the logical thing because it's the logical thing to do?'

'Gkkrgghh,' managed Martin Silenus.

'Good,' said Lamia without emotion and dropped the poet to the deck. Silenus staggered a meter and almost sat on Father Hoyt.

'Here,' said Kassad, returning with two small neural stunners. He handed one to Sol Weintraub. 'What do you have?' Kassad asked Lamia.

The woman reached into a pocket of her loose tunic and produced an ancient pistol.

Kassad looked at the relic for a moment and then nodded. 'Stay with your partner,' he said. 'Don't shoot at anything unless it's positively identified and unquestionably threatening.'

'That describes the bitch I plan to shoot,' said Silenus, still massaging his throat.

Brawne Lamia took a half step toward the poet. Fedmahn Kassad said, 'Shut up. Let's get this over with.' Silenus followed the Colonel out of the stateroom.

Sol Weintraub approached the Consul, handed him the stunner. 'I don't want to hold this thing with Rachel. Shall we go up?'

The Consul took the weapon and nodded.

The windwagon held no further sign of Templar Voice of the Tree Het Masteen. After an hour of searching, the group met in the stateroom of the missing man. The blood there seemed darker and drier.

'Is there a chance that we missed something?' said Father Hoyt. 'Secret passages? Hidden compartments?'

'There's a chance,' said Kassad, 'but I swept the ship with heat and motion sensors. If there's anything else on board larger than a mouse, I can't find it.'

'If you had these sensors,' said Silenus, 'why the fuck did you have us crawling through bilge and byways for an hour?'

'Because the right equipment or apparel can hide a man from a heat-'n'-beat search.'

'So, in answer to my question,' said Hoyt, pausing a second as a visible wave of pain passed through him, 'with the right equipment or apparel, Captain Masteen might be hiding in a secret compartment somewhere.'

'Possible but improbable,' said Brawne Lamia. 'My guess is that he's no longer aboard.'

'The Shrike,' said Martin Silenus in a disgusted tone. It was not a question.

'Perhaps,' said Lamia. 'Colonel, you and the Consul were on watch through those four hours. Are you sure that you heard and saw nothing?'

Both men nodded.

'The ship was quiet,' said Kassad. 'I would have heard a struggle even before I went on watch.'

'And I didn't sleep after my watch,' said the Consul. 'My room shared a bulkhead with Masteen's. I heard nothing.'

'Well,' said Silenus, 'we've heard from the two men who were creeping around in the dark with weapons when the poor shit was killed. They say they're innocent. Next case!'

'If Masteen was killed,' said Kassad, 'it was with no deathwand. No silent modern weapon I know throws that much blood around. There were no gunshots heard – no bullet holes found – so I presume M. Lamia's automatic pistol is not suspect. *If* this is Captain Masteen's blood, then I would guess an edged weapon was used.'

'The Shrike *is* an edged weapon,' said Martin Silenus.

Lamia moved to the small stack of luggage. 'Debating isn't going to solve anything. Let's see if there's anything in Masteen's belongings.'

Father Hoyt raised a hesitant hand. 'That's . . . well, *private*, isn't it? I don't think we have the right.'

Brawne Lamia crossed her arms. 'Look, Father, if Masteen's dead, it doesn't matter to him. If he's still alive, looking through this stuff might give us some idea where he was taken. Either way, we have to try to find a clue.'

Hoyt looked dubious but nodded. In the end, there was little invasion of privacy. Masteen's first trunk held only a few changes of linen and a copy of *Muir's Book of Life*. The second bag held a hundred separately wrapped seedlings, flash-dried and nestled in moist soil.

'Templars must plant at least a hundred offspring of the Eternal Tree on whatever world they visit,' explained the Consul. 'The shoots rarely take, but it's a ritual.'

Brawne Lamia moved toward the large metal box which had sat at the bottom of the pile.

'Don't touch that!' snapped the Consul.

'Why not?'

'It's a Möbius cube,' responded Colonel Kassad for the Consul. 'A carbon-carbon-shell set around a zero impedance containment field folded back on itself.'

'So?' said Lamia. 'Möbius cubes seal artifacts and stuff in. They don't explode or anything.'

'No,' agreed the Consul, 'but what they *contain* may explode. May already *have* exploded, for that matter.'

'A cube that size could hold a kiloton nuclear explosion in check as long as it was boxed during the nanosecond of ignition,' added Fedmahn Kassad.

Lamia scowled at the trunk. 'Then how do we know that something in there didn't kill Masteen?'

Kassad pointed to a faintly glowing green strip along the trunk's only seam. 'It's sealed. Once unsealed, a Möbius cube has to be reactivated at a place where containment fields can be generated. Whatever's in there didn't harm Captain Masteen.'

'So there's no way to tell?' mused Lamia.

'I have a good guess,' said the Consul.

The others looked at him. Rachel began to cry and Sol pulled a heating strip on a nursing pak.

'Remember,' said the Consul, 'at Edge yesterday when M. Masteen made a big deal out of the cube? He talked about it as if it were a secret weapon?'

'A weapon?' said Lamia.

'Of course!' Kassad said suddenly. 'An erg!'

'Erg?' Martin Silenus stared at the small crate. 'I thought ergs were those forcefield critters that Templars use on their treeships.'

'They are,' said the Consul. 'The things were found about three centuries ago living on asteroids around Aldebaran. Bodies about as big as a cat's spine, mostly a piezoelectric nervous system sheathed in silicon gristle, but they feed on . . . and manipulate . . . forcefields as large as those generated by small spinships.'

'So how do you get all that into such a little box?' asked Silenus, staring at the Möbius cube. 'Mirrors?'

'In a sense,' said Kassad. 'The thing's field would be damped . . . neither starving nor feeding. Rather like cryogenic fugue for us. Plus this must be a small one. A cub, so to speak.'

Lamia ran her hand along the metal sheath. 'Templars control these things? Communicate with them?'

'Yes,' said Kassad. 'No one is quite sure how. It's one of the Brotherhood secrets. But Het Masteen must have been confident that the erg would help him with . . .'

'The Shrike,' finished Martin Silenus. 'The Templar thought that this energy imp would be his secret weapon when he faced the Lord of Pain.' The poet laughed.

Father Hoyt cleared his throat. 'The Church has accepted the Hegemony's ruling that . . . these creatures . . . ergs . . . are not sentient beings . . . and thus not candidates for salvation.'

'Oh, they're sentient, all right, Father,' said the Consul. 'They *perceive* things far better than we could ever imagine. But if you meant intelligent . . . self-aware . . . then you're dealing with something along the lines of a smart grasshopper. Are grasshoppers candidates for salvation?'

Hoyt said nothing. Brawne Lamia said, 'Well, evidently Captain Masteen thought this thing was going to be *his* salvation. Something went wrong.'

She looked around at the bloodstained bulkheads and at the drying stains on the deck. 'Let's get out of here.'

The windwagon tacked into increasingly strong winds as the storm approached from the northeast. Ragged banners of clouds raced white beneath the low, gray ceiling of stormfront. Grasses whipped and bent under gusts of cold wind. Ripples of lightning illuminated the horizon and were followed by rolls of thunder sounding like warning shots across the windwagon's bow. The pilgrims watched in silence until the first icy raindrops drove them below to the large stateroom in the stern.

'This was in his robe pocket,' said Brawne Lamia, holding up a slip of paper with the number 5 on it.

'So Masteen would have told his story next,' muttered the Consul.

Martin Silenus tilted his chair until his back touched the tall windows. Storm light made his satyr's features appear slightly demonic. 'There's another possibility,' he said. 'Perhaps someone who hasn't spoken yet had the fifth spot and killed the Templar to trade places.'

Lamia stared at the poet. 'That would have to be the Consul or me,' she said, her voice flat.

Silenus shrugged.

Brawne Lamia pulled another piece of paper from her tunic. 'I have number six. What would I have achieved? I go next anyway.'

'Then perhaps it's what Masteen would have *said* that needed to be silenced,' said the poet. He shrugged again. 'Personally, I think the Shrike has begun harvesting us. Why did we think we'd be allowed to get to the Tombs when the thing's been slaughtering people halfway from here to Keats?'

'This is different,' said Sol Weintraub. 'This is the Shrike Pilgrimage.'

'So?'

In the silence that followed, the Consul walked to the windows. Wind-driven torrents of rain obscured the Sea and rattled the leaded panes. The wagon creaked and leaned heavily to starboard as it began another leg of its tack.

'M. Lamia,' asked Colonel Kassad, 'do you want to tell your story now?'

Lamia folded her arms and looked at the rain-streaked glass. 'No. Let's wait until we get off this damned ship. It stinks of death.'

The windwagon reached the port of Pilgrims' Rest in midafternoon but the storm and tired light made it feel like late evening to the weary passengers. The Consul had expected representatives from the Shrike Temple to meet them here at the beginning of the penultimate stage of their journey but Pilgrims' Rest appeared to the Consul to be as empty as Edge had been.

The approach to the foothills and the first sight of the Bridle Range was as exciting as any landfall and brought all six of the would-be pilgrims on deck despite the cold rain which continued to fall. The foothills were sere and sensuous, their brown curves and sudden upthrustings contrasting strongly with the verdant monochrome of the Sea of Grass. The nine-thousand-meter peaks beyond were only hinted at by gray and white planes soon intersected by low clouds, but even so truncated were powerful to behold. The snow line came down to a point just above the collection of burned-out hovels and cheap hotels which had been Pilgrims' Rest.

'If they destroyed the tramway, we're finished,' muttered the Consul. The thought of it, forbidden until now, made his stomach turn over.

'I see the first five towers,' said Colonel Kassad, using his powered glasses. 'They seem intact.'

'Any sign of a car?'

'No . . . wait, yes. There's one in the gate at the station platform.'

'Any moving?' asked Martin Silenus, who obviously understood how desperate their situation would be if the tramway was not intact.

'No.'

The Consul shook his head. Even in the worst weather with no passengers, the cars had been kept moving to keep the great cables flexed and free of ice.

The six of them had their luggage on deck even before the windwagon reefed its sails and extended a gangplank. Each now wore a heavy coat against the elements – Kassad in FORCE-issue thermouflage cape, Brawne Lamia in a long garment called a trenchcoat for reasons long forgotten, Martin Silenus in thick furs which rippled now sable, now gray with the vagaries of wind, Father Hoyt in long black which made him more of a scarecrow figure than ever, Sol Weintraub in a thick goosedown jacket which covered him and the child, and the Consul in the thinning but serviceable greatcoat his wife had given him some decades before.

'What about Captain Masteen's things?' asked Sol as they stood at the head of the gangplank. Kassad had gone ahead to reconnoiter the village.

'I brought them up,' said Lamia. 'We'll take them with us.'

'It doesn't seem right somehow,' said Father Hoyt. 'Just going on, I mean. There should be some . . . service. Some recognition that a man has died.'

'*May* have died,' reminded Lamia, easily lifting a forty-kilo backpack with one hand.

Hoyt looked incredulous. 'Do you really believe that M. Masteen might be alive?'

'No,' said Lamia. Snowflakes settled on her black hair.

Kassad waved to them from the end of the dock and they carried their luggage off the silent windwagon. No one looked back.

'Empty?' called Lamia as they approached the Colonel. The tall man's cloak was still fading from its gray and black chameleon mode.

'Empty.'

'Bodies?'

'No,' said Kassad. He turned toward Sol and the Consul. 'Did you get the things from the galley?'

Both men nodded.

'What things?' asked Silenus.

233

'A week's worth of food,' said Kassad, turning to look up the hill toward the tramway station. For the first time the Consul noticed the long assault weapon in the crook of the Colonel's arm, barely visible under the cloak. 'We're not sure if there are any provisions beyond this point.'

Will we be alive a week from now? thought the Consul. He said nothing.

They ferried the gear to the station in two trips. Wind whistled through the open windows and shattered domes of the dark buildings. On the second trip, the Consul carried one end of Masteen's Möbius cube while Lenar Hoyt puffed and panted under the other end.

'Why are we taking the erg thing with us?' gasped Hoyt as they reached the base of the metal stairway leading to the station. Rust streaked and spotted the platform like orange lichen.

'I don't know,' said the Consul, gasping for breath himself.

From the terminal platform they could see far out over the Sea of Grass. The windwagon sat where they had left it, sails reefed, a dark and lifeless thing. Snow squalls moved across the prairie and gave the illusion of whitecaps on the numberless stalks of high grass.

'Get the material aboard,' called Kassad. 'I'll see if the running gear can be reset from the operator's cabin up there.'

'Isn't it automatic?' asked Martin Silenus, his small head almost lost in thick furs. 'Like the windwagon?'

'I don't think so,' said Kassad. 'Go on, I'll see if I can get it started up.'

'What if it leaves without you?' called Lamia at the Colonel's retreating back.

'It won't.'

The interior of the tramcar was cold and bare except for metal benches in the forward compartment and a dozen rough bunks in the smaller, rear area. The car was big – at least eight meters long by five wide. The rear compartment was partitioned from the front cabin by a thin metal bulkhead with an opening but no door. A small commode took up a closet-sized corner of this aft compartment. Windows rising from waist height to the roof-line lined the forward compartment.

The pilgrims heaped their luggage in the center of the wide floor and stomped around, waved their arms, or otherwise worked to stay warm. Martin Silenus lay full length on one of the benches, with only his feet and the top of his head emerging from fur. 'I forgot,' he said, 'how the fuck do you turn on the heat in this thing?'

The Consul glanced at the dark lighting panels. 'It's electrical. It'll come on when the Colonel gets us moving.'

'*If* the Colonel gets us moving,' said Silenus.

Sol Weintraub had changed Rachel's diaper. Now he bundled her up again in an infant's thermsuit and rocked her in his arms. 'Obviously I've never been here before,' he said. 'Both of you gentlemen have?'

'Yeah,'said the poet.

'No,' said the Consul. 'But I've seen pictures of the tramway.'

'Kassad said he *returned* to Keats once this way,' called Brawne Lamia from the other room.

'I think . . .' began Sol Weintraub and was interrupted by a great grinding of gears and a wild lurch as the long car rocked sickeningly and then swung forward under the suddenly moving cable. Everyone rushed to the window on the platform side.

Kassad had thrown his gear aboard before climbing the long ladder to the operator's cabin. Now he appeared in the cabin's doorway, slid down the long ladder, and ran toward the car. The car was already passing beyond the loading area of the platform.

'He isn't going to make it,' whispered Father Hoyt.

Kassad sprinted the last ten meters with legs that looked impossibly long, a cartoon stick figure of a man.

The tramcar slid out of the loading notch, swung free of the station. Space opened between the car and the station. It was eight meters to the rocks below. The platform deck was streaked with ice. Kassad ran full speed ahead even as the car pulled away.

'Come on!' screamed Brawne Lamia. The others picked up the cry.

The Consul looked up at sheaths of ice cracking and dropping away from the cable as the tramcar moved up and forward. He looked back. There was too much space. Kassad could never make it.

Fedmahn Kassad was moving at an incredible speed when he reached the edge of the platform. The Consul was reminded for the second time of the Old Earth jaguar he had seen in a Lusus zoo. He half expected to see the Colonel's feet slip on a patch of ice, the long legs flying out horizontal, the man falling silently to the snowy boulders below. Instead, Kassad seemed to fly for an endless moment, long arms extended, cape flying out behind. He disappeared behind the car.

There came a thud, followed by a long minute when no one spoke or moved. They were forty meters high now, climbing toward the first tower. A second later Kassad became visible at the corner of the car, pulling himself along a series of icy niches and handholds in the metal. Brawne Lamia flung open the cabin door. Ten hands helped pull Kassad inside.

'Thank God,' said Father Hoyt.

The Colonel took a deep breath and smiled grimly. 'There was a dead man's brake. I had to rig the lever with a sandbag. I didn't want to bring the car back for a second try.'

Martin Silenus pointed to the rapidly approaching support tower and the ceiling of clouds just beyond. The cable stretched upward into oblivion. 'I guess we're crossing the mountains now whether we want to or not.'

'How long to make the crossing?' asked Hoyt.

'Twelve hours. A little less perhaps. Sometimes the operators would stop the cars if the wind rose too high or the ice got too bad.'

'We won't be stopping on this trip,' said Kassad.

'Unless the cable's breached somewhere,' said the poet. 'Or we hit a snag.'

'Shut up,' said Lamia. 'Who's interested in heating some dinner?'

'Look,' said the Consul.

They moved to the forward windows. The tram rose a hundred meters above the last brown curve of foothills. Kilometers below and behind they caught a final glimpse of the station, the haunted hovels of Pilgrims' Rest, and the motionless windwagon.

Then snow and thick cloud enveloped them.

The tramcar had no real cooking facilities but the aft bulkhead offered a cold box and a microwave for reheating. Lamia and Weintraub combined various meats and vegetables from the windwagon's galley to produce a passable stew. Martin Silenus had brought along wine bottles from the *Benares* and the windwagon and he chose a Hyperion burgundy to go with the stew.

They were nearly finished with their dinner when the gloom pressing against the windows lightened and then lifted altogether. The Consul turned on his bench to see the sun suddenly reappear, filling the tramcar with a transcendent golden light.

There was a collective sigh from the group. It had seemed that darkness had fallen hours before, but now, as they rose above a sea of clouds from which rose an island chain of mountains, they were treated to a brilliant sunset. Hyperion's sky had deepened from its daytime glaucous glare to the bottomless lapis lazuli of evening while a red-gold sun ignited cloud towers and great summits of ice and rock. The Consul looked around. His fellow pilgrims, who had seemed gray and small in the dim light of half a minute earlier, now glowed in the gold of sunset.

Martin Silenus raised his glass. That's better, by God.'

The Consul looked up at their line of travel, the massive cable dwindling to threadlike thinness far ahead and then to nothing at all. On a summit several kilometers beyond, gold light glinted on the next support tower.

'One hundred and ninety-two pylons,' said Silenus in a singsong tour guide's bored tones. 'Each pylon is constructed of duralloy and whiskered carbon and stands eighty-three meters high.'

'We must be high,' said Brawne Lamia in a low voice.

'The high point of the ninety-six-kilometer tramcar voyage lies above the summit of Mount Dryden, the fifth highest peak in the Bridle Range, at nine thousand two hundred forty-six meters,' droned on Martin Silenus.

Colonel Kassad looked around. 'The cabin's pressurized. I felt the change-over some time ago.'

'Look,' said Brawne Lamia.

The sun had been resting on the horizon line of clouds for a long moment. Now it dipped below, seemingly igniting the depths of storm cloud from beneath and casting a panoply of colors along the entire western edge of the world. Snow cornices and glaze ice still glowed along the western side of the peaks, which rose a kilometer or more above the rising tramcar. A few brighter stars appeared in the deepening dome of sky.

The Consul turned to Brawne Lamia. 'Why don't you tell your story now, M. Lamia? We'll want to sleep later, before arriving at the Keep.'

Lamia sipped the last of her wine. 'Does everyone want to hear it now?'

Heads nodded in the roseate twilight. Martin Silenus shrugged.

'All right,' said Brawne Lamia. She set down her empty glass, pulled her feet up on the bench so that her elbows rested on her knees, and began her tale.

THE DETECTIVE'S TALE:
THE LONG GOOD-BYE

I knew the case was going to be special the minute that he walked into my office. He was beautiful. By that I don't mean effeminate or 'pretty' in the male-model, HTV-star mode, merely . . . beautiful.

He was a short man, no taller than I, and I was born and raised in Lusus's 1.3-g field. It was apparent in a second that my visitor was not from Lusus – his compact form was well proportioned by Web standards, athletic but thin. His face was a study in purposeful energy: low brow, sharp cheekbones, compact nose, solid jaw, and a wide mouth that suggested both a sensuous side and a stubborn streak. His eyes were large and hazel-colored. He looked to be in his late twenties standard.

Understand, I didn't itemize all this the moment he walked in. My first thought was, *Is this a client?* My second thought was, *Shit, this guy's beautiful.*

'M. Lamia?'

'Yeah.'

'M. Brawne Lamia of All Web Investigations?'

'Yeah.'

He looked around as if he didn't quite believe it. I understood the look. My office is on the twenty-third level of an old industrial hive in the Old Digs section of Iron Pig on Lusus. I have three big windows that look out on Service Trench 9 where it's always dark and always drizzling thanks to a massive filter drip from the Hive above. The view is mostly of abandoned automated loading docks and rusted girders.

What the hell, it's cheap. And most of my clients call rather than show up in person.

'May I sit down?' he asked, evidently satisfied that a bona fide investigatory agency would operate out of such a slum.

'Sure,' I said and waved him to a chair. 'M . . . ah?'

'Johnny,' he said.

He didn't look like a first-name type to me. Something about him breathed *money*. It wasn't his clothes – common enough casuals in black and gray, although the fabric was better than average – it was just a sense that the guy had class. There was something about his accent. I'm good at placing dialects – it helps in this profession – but I couldn't place this guy's homeworld, much less local region.

'How can I help you, Johnny?' I held out the bottle of Scotch I had been ready to put away as he entered.

Johnny-boy shook his head. Maybe he thought I wanted him to drink from the bottle. Hell, I have more class than that. There are paper cups over by the water cooler. 'M. Lamia,' he said, the cultivated accent still bugging me by its elusiveness, 'I need an investigator.'

'That's what I do.'

He paused. Shy. A lot of my clients are hesitant to tell me what the job is. No wonder, since ninety-five percent of my work is divorce and domestic stuff. I waited him out.

'It's a somewhat sensitive matter,' he said at last.

'Yeah, M . . . ah, Johnny, most of my work falls under that category. I'm bonded with UniWeb and everything having to do with a client falls under the Privacy Protection Act. *Everything* is confidential, even the fact that we're talking now. Even if you decide not to hire me.' That was basic bullshit since the authorities could get at my files in a moment if they ever wanted to, but I sensed that I had to put this guy at ease somehow. God, he was beautiful.

'Uh-huh,' he said and glanced around again. He leaned forward. 'M. Lamia, I would want you to investigate a murder.'

This got my attention. I'd been reclining with my feet on the desk; now I sat up and leaned forward. 'A *murder*? Are you sure? What about the cops?'

'They aren't involved.'

'That's not possible,' I said with the sinking feeling that I was dealing with a loony rather than a client. 'It's a crime to conceal a murder from the authorities.' What I thought was: *Are you the murderer, Johnny?*

He smiled and shook his head. 'Not in this case.'

'What do you mean?'

'I mean, M. Lamia, that a murder *was* committed but that the police – local and Hegemony – have neither knowledge of it nor jurisdiction over it.'

'Not possible,' I said again. Outside, sparks from an industrial welder's torch cascaded into the trench along with the rusty drizzle. 'Explain.'

'A murder was committed outside of the Web. Outside of the Protectorate. There were no local authorities.'

That made sense. Sort of. For the life of me, though, I couldn't figure where he was talking about. Even the Outback settlements and colonial worlds have cops. On board some sort of spaceship? Uh-uh. The Interstellar Transit Authority has jurisdiction there.

'I see,' I said. It'd been some weeks since I'd had a case. 'All right, tell me the details.'

'And the conversation will be confidential even if you do not take the case?'

'Absolutely.'

'And if you do take the case, you will report only to me?'

'Of course.'

My prospective client hesitated, rubbing his fingers against his chin. His hands were exquisite. 'All right,' he said at last.

'Start at the beginning,' I said. 'Who was murdered?'

Johnny sat up straight, an attentive schoolboy. There was no doubting his sincerity. He said, 'I was.'

It took ten minutes to get the story out of him. When he was finished, I no longer thought he was crazy. I was. Or I would be if I took the job.

Johnny – his real name was a code of digits, letters, and cipher bands longer than my arm – was a cybrid.

I'd heard about cybrids. Who hasn't? I once accused my first husband of being one. But I never expected to be sitting in the same room with one. Or to find it so damned attractive.

Johnny was an AI. His consciousness or ego or whatever you want to call it floated somewhere in the megadatasphere datumplane of TechnoCore. Like everyone else except maybe the current Senate CEO or the AIs' garbage removers, I had no idea where the TechnoCore was. The AIs had peacefully seceded from human control more than three centuries ago – before my time – and while they continued to serve the Hegemony as allies by advising the All Thing, monitoring the dataspheres, occasionally using their predictive abilities to help us avoid major mistakes or natural disasters, the TechnoCore generally went about its own indecipherable and distinctly nonhuman business in privacy.

Fair enough, it seemed to me.

Usually AIs do business with humans and human machines via the datasphere. They can manufacture an interactive holo if they need to – I remembered during the Maui-Covenant incorporation, the TechnoCore ambassadors at the treaty signing looked suspiciously like the old holo star Tyrone Bathwaite.

Cybrids are a whole different matter. Tailored from human genetic stock, they are far more human in appearance and outward behavior than androids are allowed to be. Agreements between the TechnoCore and the Hegemony allow only a handful of cybrids to be in existence.

I looked at Johnny. From an AI's perspective, the beautiful body and intriguing personality sitting across the desk from me must be merely another appendage, a remote, somewhat more complex but otherwise no more important than any one of ten thousand such sensors, manipulators, autonomous units, or other remotes that an AI might use in a day's work. Discarding 'Johnny' probably would create no more concern in an AI than clipping a fingernail would bother me.

What a waste, I thought.

'A cybrid,' I said.

'Yes. Licensed. I have a Worldweb user's visa.'

'Good,' I heard myself say. 'And someone . . . murdered your cybrid and you want me to find out who?'

'No,' said the young man. He had brownish-red curls. Like his accent, the hairstyle eluded me. It seemed archaic somehow, but I had seen it *somewhere.* 'It was not merely this body that was murdered. My assailant murdered *me.*'

'You?'

'Yes.'

'You as in the . . . ah . . . AI itself?'

'Precisely.'

I didn't get it. AIs can't die. Not as far as anyone in the Web knew. 'I don't get it,' I said.

Johnny nodded, 'Unlike a human personality which can . . . I believe the consensus is . . . be destroyed at death, my own consciousness cannot be terminated. There was, however, as a result of the assault, an . . . interruption. Although I possessed . . . ah . . . shall we say duplicate recordings of memories, personality, et cetera, there was a loss. Some data were destroyed in the attack. In that sense, the assailant committed murder.'

'I see,' I lied. I took a breath. 'What about the AI authorities . . . if there are such things . . . or the Hegemony cybercops? Wouldn't they be the ones to go to?'

'For personal reasons,' said the attractive young man whom I was trying to see as a cybrid, 'it is important – even necessary – that I do not consult these sources.'

I raised an eyebrow. This sounded more like one of my regular clients.

'I assure you,' he said, 'it is nothing illegal. Nor unethical. Merely . . . embarrassing to me on a level which I cannot explain.'

I folded my arms across my chest. 'Look, Johnny. This is a pretty half-assed story. I mean, I only have your word that you're a cybrid. You might be a scam artist for all I know.'

He looked surprised. 'I had not thought of that. How would you like me to show you that I am what I say I am?'

I did not hesitate a second. 'Transfer a million marks to my checking account in TransWeb,' I said.

Johnny smiled. At the same instant my phone rang and the image of a harried man with the TransWeb code block floating behind him said, 'Excuse me, M. Lamia, but we wondered with a . . . ah . . . deposit of this size if you would be interested in investigating our long-term savings options or our mutual assured market possibilities?'

'Later,' I said.

The bank manager nodded and vanished.

'That could've been a simulation,' I said.

Johnny's smile was pleasant. 'Yes, but even that would be a satisfactory demonstration, would it not?'

'Not necessarily.'

He shrugged. 'Assuming I am what I say I am, will you take the case?'

'Yeah.' I sighed. 'One thing though. My fee isn't a million marks. I get five hundred a day plus expenses.'

The cybrid nodded. 'Does that mean you will take the case?'

I stood up, put on my hat, and pulled an old coat from a rack by the window. I bent over the lower desk drawer, smoothly sliding my father's pistol into a coat pocket. 'Let's go,' I said.

'Yes,' said Johnny. 'Go where?'

'I want to see where you were murdered.'

Stereotype has it that someone born on Lusus hates to leave the Hive and suffers from instant agoraphobia if we visit anything more open to the elements that a shopping mall. The truth of it is, most of my business comes from . . . and leads to . . . offworld. Skiptracing deadbeats who use the farcaster system and a change of identity to try to start over. Finding philandering spouses who think rendezvousing on a different planet will keep them safe from discovery. Tracking down missing kids and absent parents.

Still, I was surprised to the point of hesitating a second when we stepped through the Iron Pig Concourse farcaster onto an empty stone plateau which seemed to stretch to infinity. Except for the bronze rectangle of the farcaster portal behind us, there was no sign of civilization anywhere. The air smelled like rotten eggs. The sky was a yellow-brown cauldron of sick-looking clouds. The ground around us was gray and scaled and held no visible life, not even lichen. I had no idea how far away the horizon really was, but we felt *high* and it looked *far*, and there was no hint of trees, shrubs, or animal life in the distance either.

'Where the hell are we?' I asked. I had been sure that I knew all of the worlds in the Web.

'Madhya,' said Johnny, pronouncing it something like 'Mudye'.

'I never heard of it,' I said, putting one hand in my pocket and finding the pearl-handled grip of Dad's automatic.

'It's not officially in the Web yet,' said the cybrid. 'Officially it's a colony of Parvati. But it's only light-minutes from the FORCE base there and the farcaster connections have been set up before Madhya joins the Protectorate.'

I looked at the desolation. The hydrogen-sulfide stench was making me ill and I was afraid it was going to ruin my suit. 'Colonies? Nearby?'

'No. There are several small cities on the other side of the planet.'

'What's the nearest inhabited area?'

'Nanda Devi. A town of about three hundred people. It's more than two thousand kilometers to the south.'

'Then why put a farcaster portal here?'

'Potential mining sites,' said Johnny. He gestured toward the gray plateau. 'Heavy metals. The consortium authorized over a hundred farcaster portals in this hemisphere for easy access once the development began.'

'Okay,' I said. 'It's a good place for a murder. Why'd you come here?'

'I don't know. It was part of the memory section lost.'

'Who'd you come with?'

'I don't know that either.'

'What do you know?'

The young man put his graceful hands in his pockets. 'Whoever . . . whatever . . . attacked me used a type of weapon known in the Core as an AIDS II virus.'

'What's that?'

'AIDS II was a human plague disease back long before the Hegira,' said Johnny. 'It disabled the immune system. This . . . virus . . . works the same with an AI. In less than a second it infiltrates security systems and turns lethal phagocyte programs against the host . . . against the AI itself. Against *me*.'

'So you couldn't have contracted this virus naturally?'

Johnny smiled. 'Impossible. It's comparable to asking a shooting victim if he might not have fallen on the bullets.'

I shrugged. 'Look, if you want a datumnet or AI expert, you've come to the wrong woman. Other than accessing the sphere like twenty billion other chumps, I know zilch about the ghost world.' I used the old term to see if it would get a rise out of him.

'I know,' said Johnny, still equable. 'That's not what I want you to do.'

'What *do* you want me to do?'

'Find out who brought me here and killed me. And why.'

'All right. Why do you think this is where the murder took place?'

'Because this is where I regained control of my cybrid when I was . . . reconstituted.'

'You mean your cybrid was incapacitated while the virus destroyed you?'

'Yes.'

'And how long did that last?'

'My death? Almost a minute before my reserve persona could be activated.'

I laughed. I couldn't help myself.

'What is amusing, M. Lamia?'

'Your concept of death,' I said.

The hazel eyes looked sad. 'Perhaps it is amusing to you, but you have no idea what a minute of . . . disconnection . . . means to an element of the TechnoCore. It is eons of time and information. Millennia of non-communication.'

'Yeah,' I said, able to hold back my own tears without too much effort. 'So what did your body, your cybrid do while you were changing personae tapes or whatever?'

'I presume it was comatose.'

'It can't handle itself autonomously?'

'Oh, yes, but not when there's a general systems failure.'

'So where did you come to?'

'Pardon me?'

'When you reactivated the cybrid, where was it?'

Johnny nodded in understanding. He pointed to a boulder less than five meters from the farcaster. 'Lying there.'

'On this side or the other side?'

'The other side.'

I went over and examined the spot. No blood. No notes. No murder weapons left lying about. Not even a footprint or indication that Johnny's body had lain there for that eternity of a minute. A police forensics team might have read volumes into the microscopic and biotic clues left there, but all I could see was hard rock.

'If your memory's really gone,' I said, 'how do you know someone else came here with you?'

'I accessed the farcaster records.'

'Did you bother to check the mystery person or persons' name on the universal card charge?'

'We both farcast on my card,' said Johnny.

'Just one other person?'

'Yes.'

I nodded. Farcaster records would solve *every* inter-world crime if the portals were true teleportation; the transport data record could have re-created the subject down to the last gram and follicle. Instead, a farcaster essentially is just a crude hole ripped in space/time by a phased singularity. If the farcaster criminal doesn't use his or her own card, the only data we get are origination and destination.

'Where'd you two farcast from?' I asked.

'Tau Ceti Center.'

'You have the portal code?'

'Of course.'

'Let's go there and finish this conversation,' I said. 'This place stinks to high heaven.'

TC^2, the age-old nickname for Tau Ceti Center, is certainly the most crowded world in the Web. Besides its population of five billion people scrabbling for room on less than half the land area of Old Earth, it has an orbital ring ecology that is home for half a billion more. In addition to being the capital of the Hegemony and home of the Senate, TC^2 is the business nexus for Webtrade. Naturally the portal number Johnny had found brought us to a six-hundred-portal terminex in one of the biggest spires in New London, one of the oldest and largest city sections.

'Hell,' I said, 'let's get a drink.'

There was a choice of bars near the terminex and I picked one that was relatively quiet: a simulated ship's tavern, dark, cool, with plenty of fake wood and brass. I ordered a beer. I never drink the hard stuff or use Flashback when on a case. Sometimes I think that need for self-discipline is what keeps me in the business.

Johnny also ordered a beer, a dark, German brew bottled on Renaissance Vector. I found myself wondering what vices a cybrid might have. I said:

'What else did you find out before coming to see me?'

The young man opened his hands. 'Nothing.'

'Shit,' I said reverently. 'This is a joke. With all the powers of an AI at your disposal, you can't trace your cybrid's whereabouts and actions for a few days prior to your . . . accident?'

'No.' Johnny sipped his beer. 'Rather, I could but there are important reasons why I do not want my fellow AIs to find me investigating.'

'You suspect one of them?'

Instead of answering, Johnny handed me a flimsy of his universal card purchases. 'The blackout caused by my murder left five standard days unaccounted for. Here are the card charges for that time.'

'I thought you said you were only disconnected for a minute.'

Johnny scratched his cheek with one finger. 'I was lucky to lose only five days' worth of data,' he said.

I waved over the human waiter and ordered another beer. 'Look,' I said, 'Johnny . . . whoever you are, I'll never be able to get an angle on this case unless I know more about you and your situation. Why would someone want to kill you if they know you'll be reconstituted or whatever the hell it is?'

'I see two possible motives,' said Johnny over his beer.

I nodded. 'One would be to create just the memory loss they succeeded in getting,' I said. 'That would suggest that, whatever it was they wanted you to forget, it'd occurred or come to your attention in the past week or so. What's the second motive?'

'To send me a message,' said Johnny. 'I just don't know what it is. Or from whom.'

'Do you know who would want to kill you?'

'No.'

'No guesses at all?'

'None.'

'Most murders,' I said, 'are acts of sudden, mindless rage committed by someone the victim knows well. Family. A friend or lover. A majority of the premeditated ones are usually carried out by someone close to the victim.'

Johnny said nothing. There was something about his face that I found incredibly attractive – a sort of masculine strength combined with a feminine sense of awareness. Perhaps it was the eyes.

'Do AIs have families?' I asked. 'Feuds? Squabbles? Lovers' spats?'

'No.' He smiled slightly. 'There *are* quasi-family arrangements, but they share none of the requirements of emotion or responsibility that human families exhibit. AI "families" are primarily convenient code groups for showing where certain processing trends originated.'

'So you don't think another AI attacked you?'

'It's possible.' Johnny rotated his glass in his hands. 'I just do not see why they would attack me through my cybrid.'

'Easier access?'

'Perhaps. But it complicates things for the assailant. An attack in datum-plane would have been infinitely more lethal. Also, I do fail to see any motive for another AI. It makes no sense. I'm a threat to no one.'

'Why do you have a cybrid, Johnny? Maybe if I understood your role in things, I could get a motive.'

He picked up a pretzel and played with it. 'I have a cybrid . . . in some ways I *am* a cybrid, because my . . . function . . . is to observe and react to human beings. In a sense, I was human once myself.'

I frowned and shook my head. So far nothing he'd said had made sense.

'You've heard of personality retrieval projects?' he asked.

'No.'

'A standard year ago, when the FORCE sims re-created the personality of General Horace Glennon-Height to see what made him such a brilliant general? It was in all the news.'

'Yeah.'

'Well, I am . . . or was . . . an earlier and much more complicated re-trieval project. My core persona was based on a pre-Hegira Old Earth poet. Ancient. Born late eighteenth century Old Calendar.'

'How the hell can they reconstruct a personality that lost in time?'

'Writings,' said Johnny. 'His letters. Diaries. Critical biographies. Testi-mony of friends. But mostly through his verse. The sim re-creates the environment, plugs in the known factors, and works backward from the creative products. *Voilà* – a persona core. Crude at first but, by the time I came into being, relatively refined. Our first attempt was a twentieth-century poet named Ezra Pound. Our persona was opinionated to the point of absurdity, prejudiced beyond rationality, and functionally insane. It took a year of tinkering before we discovered that the persona was accurate; it was the man who had been nuts. A genius but nuts.'

'And then what?' I said. 'They build your personality around a dead poet. Then what?'

'This becomes the template upon which the AI is grown,' said Johnny. 'The cybrid allows me to carry out my role in the datumplane community.'

'As poet?'

Johnny smiled again. 'More as poem,' he said.

'A poem?'

'An ongoing work of art . . . but not in the human sense. A puzzle perhaps. A variable enigma which occasionally offers unusual insights into more serious lines of analysis.'

'I don't get it,' I said.

'It probably does not matter. I very much doubt if my . . . purpose . . . was the cause of the assault.'

'What do you think was the cause?'

'I have no idea.'

I felt us closing a circle. 'All right,' I said. 'I'll try to find out what you were doing and who you were with during these lost five days. Is there anything besides the credit flimsy that you can think of to help?'

Johnny shook his head. 'You know, of course, why it is important for me to know the identity and motive of my assailant?'

'Sure,' I said, 'they might try it again.'

'Precisely.'

'How can I get hold of you if I need to?'

Johnny passed me an access chip.

'A secure line?' I said.

'Very.'

'Okay,' I said, 'I'll get back to you if and when I get some information.'

We moved out of the bar and toward the terminex. He was moving away when I took three quick steps and grabbed his arm. It was the first time that I had touched him. 'Johnny. What's the name of the Old Earth poet they resurrected . . .'

'Retrieved.'

'Whatever. The one they built your AI persona on?'

The attractive cybrid hesitated. I noticed that his eyelashes were very long. 'How can it be important?' he asked.

'Who knows what's important?'

He nodded. 'Keats,' he said. 'Born in A.D. 1795. Died of tuberculosis in 1821. John Keats.'

Following someone through a series of farcaster changes is damn near impossible. Especially if you want to remain undetected. The Web cops can do it, given about fifty agents assigned to the task, plus some exotic and damned expensive high-tech toys, not to mention the cooperation of the Transit Authority. For a solo, the task is almost impossible.

Still, it was fairly important for me to see where my new client was headed.

Johnny did not look back as he crossed the terminex plaza. I moved to a nearby kiosk and watched through my pocket-sized imager as he punched codes on a manual diskey, inserted his card, and stepped through the glowing rectangle.

The use of the manual diskey probably meant that he was headed for a general access portal since private 'caster codes are usually imprinted on eyes-only chips. Great. I'd narrowed his destination down to approximately two million portals on a hundred and fifty-some Web worlds and half that many moons.

With one hand I pulled the red 'lining' out of my overcoat while I hit replay on the imager, watching through the eyepiece as it magnified the diskey sequence. I tugged out a red cap to go with my new red jacket and pulled the brim low over my face. Moving quickly across the plaza, I queried my comlog about the nine-digit transfer code I'd seen on the imager. I knew the first three digits meant the world of Tsingtao-Hsishuang Panna – I'd memorized all the planetary prefixes – and was told an instant later that the portal code led to a residential district in the First Expansion city of Wansiehn.

I hurried to the first open booth and 'cast there, stepping out onto a small terminex plaza paved in worn brick. Ancient oriental shops leaned against one another, eaves of their pagoda roofs hanging over narrow side streets. People thronged the plaza and stood in doorways and, while most of those in sight were obviously descendants of the Long Flight exiles who settled THP, many were offworlders. The air smelled of alien vegetation, sewage, and cooking rice.

'Damn,' I whispered. There were three other farcaster portals there and none were in constant use. Johnny could have farcast out immediately.

Instead of 'casting back to Lusus, I spent a few minutes checking the plaza and side streets. By this time the melanin pill I'd swallowed had worked and I was a young black woman – or man, it was hard to tell in my trendy red balloon jacket and polarized visor, strolling idly while taking pictures with my tourist imager.

The trace pellet I'd dissolved in Johnny's second German beer had had more than enough time to work. The UV-positive microspores were almost hanging in the air by now – I could almost follow the trail of exhalations he had left. Instead, I found a bright yellow handprint on a dark wall (bright yellow to my especially fitted visor of course, invisible out of the UV spectrum) and then followed the trail of vague blotches where saturated clothing had touched market stalls or stone.

Johnny was eating in a Cantonese restaurant less than two blocks from the terminex plaza. The frying food smelled delicious but I restrained myself from entering – checking prices in alley bookstalls and haggling in the market for almost an hour before he finished, returned to the plaza, and farcast out. This time he used a chip code – a private portal, certainly, possibly a private home – and I took two chances by using my pilot-fish card to follow him. Two chances because first the card is totally illegal and would someday cost me my license if caught – less than likely if I kept using Daddy Silva's obscenely expensive but aesthetically perfect shapechanger chips – and, second, I ran a better than even chance of ending up in the living room of Johnny's house . . . never an easy situation to talk one's way out of.

It was not his living room. Even before I'd located the street signs I recognized the familiar extra tug of gravity, the dim, bronze light, the scent of oil and ozone in the air, and knew I was home on Lusus.

Johnny had 'cast into a medium-security private residential tower in one of the Bergson Hives. Perhaps that was why he'd chosen my agency – we were almost neighbors, less than six hundred klicks apart.

My cybrid was not in sight. I walked purposefully so as not to alert any security vids programmed to respond to loitering. There was no residents' directory, no numbers or names on the apartment doorways, and no listings accessible by comlog. I guessed that there were about twenty thousand residential cubbies in East Bergson Hive.

The telltales were fading as the spore soup died, but I checked only two of the radial corridors before I found a trail. Johnny lived far out on a glass-floored wing above a methane lake. His palmlock showed a faintly glowing handprint. I used my cat-burglar tools to take a reading of the lock and then I 'cast home.

All in all, I'd watched my man go out for Chinese food and then go home for the night. Enough accomplished for one day.

BB Surbringer was my AI expert. BB worked in Hegemony Flow Control Records and Statistics and spent most of his life reclining on a free-fall couch with half a dozen microleads running from his skull while he communed with other bureaucrats in datumplane. I'd known him in college when he was a pure cyberpuke, a twentieth-generation hacker, cortically shunted when he was twelve standard. His real name was Ernest but he'd earned the nickname BB when he went out with a friend of mine named Shayla Toyo. Shayla'd seen him naked on their second date and had laughed for a solid half hour: Ernest was – and is – almost two meters tall but masses less than fifty kilos. Shayla said that he had a butt like two BBs and – like most cruel things do – the nickname stuck.

I visited him in one of the windowless worker monoliths on TC^2. No cloud towers for BB and his ilk.

'So, Brawne,' he said, 'how come you're getting information-literate in your old age? You're too old to get a real job.'

'I just want to know about AIs, BB.'

'Only one of the most complex topics in the known universe,' he sighed and looked longingly at his disconnected neural shunt and metacortex leads. Cyberpukes never come down, but civil servants are required to dismount for lunch. BB was like most cyberpukes in that he never felt comfortable exchanging information when he wasn't riding a data wave. 'So what do you want to know?' he said.

'Why did the AIs drop out?' I had to start somewhere.

BB made a convoluted gesture with his hands. 'They said they had projects which were not compatible with total immersion in Hegemony – read human – affairs. Truth is, nobody knows.'

'But they're still around. Still managing things?'

'Sure. The system couldn't run without them. You know that, Brawne. Even the All Thing couldn't work without AI management of the real-time Schwarzschild patterning . . .'

'Okay,' I said, cutting him off before he lapsed into cyberpukese, 'but what are their "other projects"?'

'No one knows. Branner and Swayze up at ArtIntel Corp think that the AIs are pursuing the evolution of consciousness on a galactic scale. We know they have their own probes out far deeper into the Outback than . . .'

'What about cybrids?'

'Cybrids?' BB sat up and looked interested for the first time. 'Why do you mention cybrids?'

'Why are you surprised that I mentioned them, BB?'

He absently rubbed his shunt socket. 'Well, first of all, most people forget they exist. Two centuries ago it was all alarmism and pod people taking over and all that, but now nobody thinks about them. Also, I just ran across an anomaly advisory yesterday that said that cybrids were disappearing.'

'Disappearing?' It was my turn to sit up.

'You know, being phased out. The AIs used to maintain about a thousand licensed cybrids in the Web. About half of them based right here on TC^2. Last week's census showed about two thirds of those'd been recalled in the past month or so.'

'What happens when an AI recalls its cybrid?'

'I dunno. They're destroyed, I suppose. AIs don't like to waste things, so I imagine the genetic material's recycled somehow.'

'Why are they being recycled?'

'Nobody knows, Brawne. But then most of us don't know why the AIs do most of the things they do.'

'Do experts see them – the AIs – as a threat?'

'Are you kidding? Six hundred years ago, maybe. Two centuries ago the Secession made us leery. But if the things wanted to hurt humanity, they could've done it long before this. Worrying about AIs turning on us is about as productive as worrying that farm animals are going to revolt.'

'Except the AIs are smarter than us,' I said.

'Yeah, well, there is that.'

'BB, have you heard of personality retrieval projects?'

'Like the Glennon-Height thing? Sure. Everyone has. I even worked on one at Reichs University a few years ago. But they're passé. No one's doing them anymore.'

'Why's that?'

'Jesus, you *don't* know shit about anything, do you, Brawne? The personality retrieval projects were all washouts. Even with the best sim control . . . they got the FORCE OCS:HTN network involved . . . you can't factor all variables successfully. The persona template becomes self-aware . . . I don't mean just self-aware, like you and me, but self-aware that it's an artificially self-aware persona – and that leads to terminal Strange Loops and nonharmonic labyrinths that go straight to Escher-space.'

'Translate,' I said.

BB sighed and glanced at the blue and gold time band on the wall. Five minutes and his mandatory lunch hour was over. He could rejoin the real world. 'Translated,' he said, 'the retrieved personality breaks down. Goes crazy. Psycho City. Bugfuck.'

'All of them?'

'All of them.'

'But the AIs are still interested in the process?'

'Oh, yeah? Who says? They've never *done* one. All the retrieval efforts I've ever heard of were human-run . . . mostly botched university projects. Brain-dead academics spending fortunes to bring back dead academic brains.'

I forced a smile. There were three minutes until he could plug back in. 'Were all the retrieved personalities given cybrid remotes?'

'Uh-uh. What gave you that idea, Brawne? None were. Couldn't work.'

'Why not?'

'It'd just fuck up the stimsim. Plus you'd need perfect clone stock and an interactive environment precise to the last detail. You see, kiddo, with a retrieved personality, you let it live in *its* world via full-scale sim and then you just sneak a few questions in via dreams or scenario interactives. Pulling a persona *out* of sim reality into slow time . . .'

This was the cyberpukes' age-old term for the . . . pardon the expression . . . real world.

'. . . would just drive it bugfuck all the sooner,' he finished.

I shook my head. 'Yeah, well, thanks, BB.' I moved to the door. There were thirty seconds left before my old college friend could escape from slow time.

'BB,' I said as an afterthought, 'have you ever heard of a persona retrieved from an Old Earth poet named John Keats?'

'Keats? Oh, sure there was a big write-up on that in my undergrad text. Marti Carollus did that about fifty years ago at New Cambridge.'

'What happened?'

'The usual. Persona went Strange Loop. But before it broke up it died a full sim death. Some ancient disease.' BB glanced at the clock, smiled, and lifted his shunt. Before clicking it into his skull socket he looked at me again, almost beatifically. 'I remember now,' he said through his dreamy smile, 'it was tuberculosis.'

If our society ever opted for Orwell's Big Brother approach, the instrument of choice for oppression would have to be the credit wake. In a totally noncash economy with only a vestigial barter black market, a person's activities could be tracked in real time by monitoring the credit wake of his or her universal card. There were strict laws protecting card privacy but laws had a bad habit of being ignored or abrogated when societal push came to totalitarian shove.

Johnny's credit wake for the five-day period leading to his murder showed a man of regular habits and modest expenses. Before following up the leads on the credit flimsy I'd spent a dull two days following Johnny himself.

Data: He lived alone in East Bergson Hive. A routine check showed that he'd lived there about seven local months – less than five standard. In the morning he had breakfast at a local cafe and then farcast to Renaissance Vector where he worked for about five hours, evidently gathering research of some sort in the print archives, followed by a light lunch at a courtyard vendor's stand, another hour or two in the library, and then 'cast home to Lusus or to some favorite eating spot on another world. In his cubby by 2200 hours. More farcasting than the average Lusian middle-class drone, but an otherwise uninspiring schedule. The credit flimsies confirmed that he had held to the agenda on the week he was murdered, with the addition of a few extra purchases – shoes one day, groceries the next – and one stop at a bar on Renaissance V on the day of his 'murder'.

I joined him for dinner at the small restaurant on Red Dragon Street near the Tsingtao-Hsishuang Panna portal. The food was very hot, very spicy, and very good.

'How is it going,' he asked.

'Great. I'm a thousand marks richer than when we met and I found a good Cantonese restaurant.'

'I'm glad my money is going toward something important.'

'Speaking of your money . . . where does it come from? Hanging out in a Renaissance Vector library can't pay much.'

Johnny raised an eyebrow. 'I live on a small . . . inheritance.'

'Not too small, I hope. I want to be paid.'

'It will be adequate for our purposes, M. Lamia. Have you discovered anything of interest?'

I shrugged. 'Tell me what you do in that library.'

'Can it possibly be germane?'

'Yeah, could be.'

He looked at me strangely. Something about his eyes made me go weak at the knees. 'You remind me of someone,' he said softly.

'Oh?' From anyone else that line would have been cause for an exit. 'Who?' I asked.

'A . . . woman I once knew. Long ago.' He brushed fingers across his brow as if he were suddenly tired or dizzy.

'What was her name?'

'Fanny.' The word was almost whispered.

I knew who he was talking about. John Keats had a fiancée named Fanny. Their love affair had been a series of romantic frustrations which almost drove the poet mad. When he died in Italy, alone except for one fellow traveler, feeling abandoned by friends and his lover, Keats had asked that unopened letters from Fanny and a lock of her hair be buried with him.

I'd never heard of John Keats before this week; I'd accessed all this shit with my comlog. I said, 'So what do you do at the library?'

The cybrid cleared his throat. 'I'm researching a poem. Searching for fragments of the original.'

'Something by Keats?'

'Yes.'

'Wouldn't it be easier to access it?'

'Of course. But it is important for me to see the original . . . to touch it.'

I thought about that. 'What's the poem about?'

He smiled . . . or at least his lips did. The hazel eyes still seemed troubled. 'It's called *Hyperion*. It's difficult to describe what it's about. Artistic failure, I suppose. Keats never finished it.'

I pushed aside my plate and sipped warm tea. 'You say Keats never finished it. Don't you mean *you* never finished it?'

His look of shock had to be genuine . . . unless AIs were consummate actors. For all I knew, they could be. 'Good God,' he said, 'I'm not John Keats. Having a persona based upon a retrieval template no more makes me

Keats than having the name Lamia makes you a monster. There've been a million influences that have separated me from that poor, sad genius.'

'You said I reminded you of Fanny.'

'An echo of a dream. Less. You've taken RNA learning medication, yes?'

'Yes.'

'It's like that. Memories which feel . . . hollow.'

A human waiter brought fortune cookies.

'Do you have any interest in visiting the real Hyperion?' I asked.

'What's that?'

'The Outback world. Somewhere beyond Parvati, I think.'

Johnny looked puzzled. He had broken open the cookie but had not yet read the fortune.

'It used to be called Poets' World, I think,' I said. 'It even has a city named after you . . . after Keats.'

The young man shook his head. 'I'm sorry, I haven't heard of the place.'

'How can that be? Don't AIs know everything?'

His laugh was short and sharp. 'This one knows very little.' He read his fortune: BE WARY OF SUDDEN IMPULSES.

I crossed my arms. 'You know, except for that parlor trick with the bank manager holo, I have no proof that you are what you say you are.'

'Give me your hand.'

'My hand?'

'Yes. Either one. Thank you.'

Johnny held my right hand in both of his. His fingers were longer than mine. Mine were stronger.

'Close your eyes,' he said.

I did. There was no transition: one instant I was sitting in the Blue Lotus on Red Dragon Street and the next I was . . . nowhere. Somewhere. Streaking through gray-blue datumplane, banking along chrome-yellow information highways, passing over and under and through great cities of glowing information storage, red skyscrapers sheathed in black security ice, simple entities like personal accounts or corporate files blazing like burning refineries in the night. Above it all, just out of sight as if poised in twisted space, hung the gigantic *weights* of the AIs, their simplest communications pulsing like violent heat lightning along the infinite horizons. Somewhere in the distance, all but lost in the maze of three-dimensional neon that partitioned one tiny second of arc in the incredible datasphere of one small world, I sensed rather than saw those soft, hazel eyes waiting for me.

Johnny released my hand. He cracked my fortune cookie open. The strip of paper read: INVEST WISELY IN NEW VENTURES.

'Jesus,' I whispered. BB had taken me flying in datumplane before, but without a shunt the experience had been a shadow of this. It was the difference between watching a black and white holo of a fireworks display and *being* there. 'How do you do that?'

'Will you be making any progress on the case tomorrow?' he asked.

I regained my composure. 'Tomorrow,' I said, 'I plan to solve it.'

*

Well, maybe not solve it, but at least get things moving. The last charge on Johnny's credit flimsy had been the bar on Renaissance V. I'd checked it out the first day, of course, talked to several of the regulars since there was no human bartender, but had come up with no one who remembered Johnny. I'd been back twice with no greater luck. But on the third day I went back to stay until something broke.

The bar was definitely not in the class of the wood and brass place Johnny and I had visited on TC^2. This place was tucked on the second floor of a decaying building in a run-down neighborhood two blocks from the Renaissance library where Johnny spent his days. Not the kind of place he would stop in on the way to the farcaster plaza, but just the kind of place he might end up if he met someone in or near the library – someone who wanted to talk in private.

I'd been there six hours and was getting damned tired of salted nuts and flat beer when an old derelict came in. I guessed that he was a regular by the way he didn't pause in the doorway or look around, but headed straight for a small table in the back and ordered a whiskey before the serving mech had come to a full stop. When I joined him at the table I realized that he wasn't so much a derelict as an example of the tired men and women I'd seen in the junk shops and street stalls in that neighborhood. He squinted up at me through defeated eyes.

'May I sit down?'

'Depends, sister. What're you selling?'

'I'm buying.' I sat, set my beer mug on the table, and slid across a flat photo of Johnny entering the farcaster booth on TC^2. 'Seen this guy?'

The old man glanced at the photo and returned his full attention to his whiskey. 'Maybe.'

I waved over the mech for another round. 'If you did see him, it's your lucky day.'

The old man snorted and rubbed the back of his hand against the gray stubble on his cheek. 'If it is, it'll be the first time in a long fucking time.' He focused on me. 'How much? For what?'

'Information. How much depends on the information. Have you seen him?' I removed a black market fifty-mark bill from my tunic pocket.

'Yeah.'

The bill came down to the table but remained in my hand. 'When?'

'Last Tuesday. Tuesday morning.'

That was the correct day. I slid the fifty marks to him and removed another bill. 'Was he alone?'

The old man licked his lips. 'Let me think. I don't think . . . no, he was there.' He pointed toward a table at the rear. 'Two other guys with him. One of them . . . well, that's why I remembered.'

'What's that?'

The old man rubbed finger and thumb in a gesture as old as greed.

'Tell me about the two men,' I coaxed.

The young guy . . . your guy . . . he was with one of them, you know, the nature freaks with robes. You see 'em on HTV all the time. Them and their damn trees.'

Trees? 'A Templar?' I said, astounded. What would a Templar be doing in a Renaissance V bar? If he'd been after Johnny, why would he wear his robe? That would be like a murderer going out to do business in a clown suit.

'Yeah. Templar. Brown robe, sort of oriental-looking.'

'A man?'

'Yeah, I said he was.'

'Can you describe him more?'

'Nah, Templar. Tall son of a bitch. Couldn't see his face very well.'

'What about the other one?'

The old man shrugged. I removed a second bill and set them both near my glass.

'Did they come in together?' I prompted. 'The three of them?'

'I don't . . . I can't . . . No, wait. Your guy and the Templar guy came in first. I remember seeing the robe before the other guy sat down.'

'Describe the other man.'

The old man waved over the mech and ordered a third drink. I used my card and the servitor slid away on noisy repellers.

'Like you,' he said. 'Sort of like you.'

'Short?' I said. 'Strong arms and legs? A Lusian?'

'Yeah. I guess so. Never been there.'

'What else?'

'No hair,' said the old man,' Just a whattyacallit like my niece used to wear. A pony tail.'

'A queue,' I said.

'Yeah. Whatever.' He started to reach for the bills.

'Couple more questions. Did they argue?'

'Nah. Don't think so. Talked real quiet. Place's pretty empty that time of day.'

'What time of day was it?'

'Morning. About ten o'clock.'

This coincided with the credit flimsy code.

'Did you hear any of the conversation?'

'Uh-uh.'

'Who did most of the talking?'

The old man took a drink and furrowed his brow in thought. 'Templar guy did at first. Your man seemed to be answering questions. Seemed surprised once when I was looking.'

'Shocked?'

'Uh-uh, just surprised. Like the guy in the robe'd said something he didn't expect.'

'You said the Templar did most of the talking at first. Who spoke later? My guy?'

'Uh-uh, the one with the pony tail. Then they left.'

'All three of them left?'

'Nah. Your guy and the pony tail.'

'The Templar stayed behind?'

'Yeah. I guess so. I think. I went to the lav. When I got back I don't think he was there.'

'What way did the other two go?'

'I don't know, goddammit. I wasn't paying much attention. I was having a drink, not playing spy!'

I nodded. The mech rolled over again but I waved it away. The old man scowled at its back.

'So they weren't arguing when they left? No sign of a disagreement or that one was forcing the other to leave?'

'Who?'

'My guy and the queue.'

'Uh-uh. Shit, I don't know.' He looked down at the bills in his grimy hand and at the whiskey in the mech's display panel, realizing, perhaps, that he wasn't going to get any more of either from me. 'Why do you want to know all this shit, anyway?'

'I'm looking for the guy,' I said. I looked around the bar. About twenty customers sat at tables. Most of them looked like neighborhood regulars. 'Anyone else here who might've seen them? Or somebody else you might remember who was here?'

'Uh-uh,' he said dully. I realized then that the old man's eyes were precisely the color of the whiskey he'd been drinking.

I stood, set a final twenty-mark bill on the table. 'Thanks, friend.'

'Any time, sister.'

The mech was rolling toward him before I'd reached the door.

I walked back toward the library, paused a minute in the busy farcaster plaza, and stood there a minute. Scenario so far: Johnny had met the Templar or been approached by him, either in the library or outside when he arrived in midmorning. They went somewhere private to talk, the bar, and something the Templar said surprised Johnny. A man with a queue – possibly a Lusian – showed up and took over the conversation. Johnny and Queue left together. Sometime after that, Johnny farcast to TC^2 and then farcast from there with one other person – possibly Queue or the Templar – to Madhya where someone tried to kill him. *Did* kill him.

Too many gaps. Too many 'someones'. Not a hell of a lot to show for a day's work.

I was debating whether to 'cast back to Lusus when my comlog chirped on the restricted comm frequency I'd given to Johnny.

His voice was raw. 'M. Lamia. Come quickly, please. I think they've just tried again. To kill me.' The coordinates which followed were for the East Bergson Hive.

I ran for the farcaster.

*

The door to Johnny's cubby was open a crack. There was no one in the corridor, no sounds from the apartment. Whatever had happened hadn't brought the authorities yet.

I brought out Dad's automatic pistol from my coat pocket, jacked a round into the chamber, and clicked on the laser targeting beam with a single motion.

I went in low, both arms extended, the red dot sliding across the dark walls, a cheap print on the far wall, a darker hall leading into the cubby. The foyer was empty. The living room and media pit were empty.

Johnny lay on the floor of the bedroom, his head against the bed. Blood soaked the sheet. He struggled to prop himself up, fell back. The sliding door behind him was open and a dank industrial wind blew in from the open mall beyond.

I checked the single closet, short hall, kitchen niche, and came back to step out on the balcony. The view was spectacular from the perch two hundred or so meters up the curved Hive wall, looking down the ten or twenty kilometers of the Trench Mall. The roof of the Hive was a dark mass of girders another hundred or so meters above. Thousands of lights, commercial holos, and neon lights glowed from the mall, joining in the haze of distance to a brilliant, throbbing electric blur.

There were hundreds of similar balconies on this wall of the Hive, all deserted. The nearest was twenty meters away. They were the kind of thing rental agents like to point to as a plus – God knows that Johnny probably paid plenty extra for an outside room – but the balconies were totally impractical because of the strong wind rushing up toward the ventilators, carrying the usual grit and debris as well as the eternal Hive scent of oil and ozone.

I put my pistol away and went back to check on Johnny.

The cut ran from his hairline to his eyebrow, superficial but messy. He was sitting up as I returned from the bathroom with a sterile drypad and pressed it against the cut. 'What happened?' I said.

'Two men . . . were waiting in the bedroom when I came in. They'd bypassed the alarms on the balcony door.'

'You deserve a refund on your security tax,' I said. 'What happened next?'

'We struggled. They seemed to be dragging me toward the door. One of them had an injector but I managed to knock it out of his hand.'

'What made them leave?'

'I activated the in-house alarms.'

'But not Hive security?'

'No. I didn't want them involved.'

'Who hit you?'

Johnny smiled sheepishly. 'I did. They released me, I went after them. I managed to trip and fall against the nightstand.'

'Not a very graceful brawl on either side,' I said. I switched on a lamp and checked the carpet until I found the injection ampule where it had rolled under the bed.

Johnny eyed it as if it were a viper.

'What's your guess?' I said. 'More AIDS II?'

He shook his head.

'I know a place where we can get it analyzed,' I said. 'My guess is that it's just a hypnotic trank. They just wanted you to come along . . . not to kill you.'

Johnny moved the drypad and grimaced. The blood was still flowing. 'Why would anyone want to kidnap a cybrid?'

'You tell me. I'm beginning to think that the so-called murder was just a botched kidnapping attempt.'

Johnny shook his head again.

I said, 'Did one of the men wear a queue?'

'I don't know. They wore caps and osmosis masks.'

'Was either one tall enough to be a Templar or strong enough to be a Lusian?'

'A Templar?' Johnny was surprised. 'No. One was about average Web height. The one with the ampule could have been Lusian. Strong enough.'

'So you went after a Lusian thug with your bare hands. Do you have some bioprocessors or augmentation implants I don't know about?'

'No. I was just mad.'

I helped him to his feet. 'So AIs get angry?'

'I do.'

'Come on,' I said, 'I know an automated med clinic that's discount. Then you'll be staying with me for a while.'

'With you? Why?'

'Because you've graduated from just needing a detective,' I said. 'Now you need a bodyguard.'

My cubby wasn't registered in the Hive zoning schematic as an apartment; I'd taken over a renovated warehouse loft from a friend of mine who'd run afoul of loan sharks. My friend had decided late in life to emigrate to one of the Outback colonies and I'd gotten a good deal on a place just a klick down the corridor from my office. The environment was a little rough and sometimes the noise from the loading docks could drown out conversation, but it gave me ten times the room of a normal cubby and I could use my weights and workout equipment right at home.

Johnny honestly seemed intrigued by the place and I had to kick myself for being pleased. Next thing you knew, I'd be putting on lipstick and body rouge for this cybrid.

'So why do you live on Lusus?' I asked him. 'Most offworlders find the gravity a pain and the scenery monotonous. Plus your research material's at the library on Renaissance V. Why here?'

I found myself looking and listening very carefully as he answered. His hair was straight on top, parted in the middle, and fell in reddish-brown curls to his collar. He had the habit of resting his cheek on his fist as he spoke. It struck me that his dialect was actually the nondialect of someone who has learned a new language perfectly but without the lazy shortcuts of someone born to it. And beneath that there was a hint of lilt that brought back the overtones of a cat burglar I'd known who had grown up on Asquith, a quiet, backwater Web world settled by First Expansion immigrants from what had once been the British Isles.

'I have lived on many worlds,' he said. 'My purpose is to observe.'

'As a poet?'

He shook his head, winced, and gingerly touched the stitches. 'No. I'm not a poet. He *was*.'

Despite the circumstances, there was an energy and vitality to Johnny that I'd found in too few men. It was hard to describe, but I'd seen rooms full of more important personages rearrange themselves to orbit around personalities like his. It was not merely his reticence and sensitivity, it was an *intensity* that he emanated even when merely observing.

'Why do *you* live here?' he asked.

'I was born here.'

'Yes, but you spent your childhood years on Tau Ceti Center. Your father was a senator.'

I said nothing.

'Many people expected you to go into politics,' he said. 'Did your father's suicide dissuade you?'

'It wasn't suicide,' I said.

'No?'

'All the news reports and the inquest said it was,' I said tonelessly, 'but they were wrong. My father never would have taken his own life.'

'So it was murder?'

'Yes.'

'Despite the fact that there was no motive or hint of a suspect?'

'Yes.'

'I see,' said Johnny. The yellow glow from the loading dock lamps came through the dusty windows and made his hair gleam like new copper. 'Do you like being a detective?'

'When I do it well,' I said. 'Are you hungry?'

'No.'

'Then let's get some sleep. You can have the couch.'

'Do you do it well often?' he said. 'Being a detective?'

'We'll see tomorrow.'

In the morning Johnny farcast to Renaissance Vector at about the usual time, waited a moment in the plaza, and then 'cast to the Old Settlers' Museum on Sol Draconi Septem. From there he jumped to the main terminex on Nordholm and then 'cast to the Templar world of God's Grove.

We'd worked out the timing ahead of time and I was waiting for him on Renaissance V, standing back in the shadows of the colonnade.

A man with a queue was the third through after Johnny. There was no doubt he was Lusian – between the Hive pallor, the muscle and body mass, and the arrogant way of walking, he might have been my long-lost brother.

He never looked at Johnny but I could tell that he was surprised when the cybrid circled around to the outbound portals. I stayed back and only caught a glimpse of his card but would've bet anything that it was a tracer.

Queue was careful in the Old Settlers' Museum, keeping Johnny in sight but checking his own back as well. I was dressed in a Zen Gnostic's meditation jumper, isolation visor and all, and I never looked their way as I circled to the museum outportal and 'cast directly to God's Grove.

It made me feel funny, leaving Johnny alone through the museum and Nordholm terminex, but both were public places and it was a calculated risk.

Johnny came through the Worldtree arrival portal right on time and bought a ticket for the tour. His shadow had to scurry to catch up, breaking cover to board the omnibus skimmer before it left. I was already settled in the rear seat on the upper deck and Johnny found a place near the front, just as we had planned. Now I was wearing basic tourist garb and my imager was one of a dozen in action when Queue hurried to take his place three rows behind Johnny.

The tour of the Worldtree is always fun – Dad first took me there when I was only three standard – but this time as the skimmer moved above branches the size of freeways and circled higher around a trunk the width of Olympus Mons, I found myself reacting to the glimpses of hooded Templars with something approaching anxiety.

Johnny and I had discussed various clever and infinitely subtle ways to trail Queue if he showed up, to follow him to his lair and spend weeks if necessary deducing his game. In the end I opted for something less than the subtle approach.

The omnibus had dumped us out near the Muir Museum and people were milling around on the plaza, torn between spending ten marks for a ticket to educate themselves or going straight for the gift shop, when I walked up to Queue, gripped him by the upper arm, and said in conversational tones, 'Hi. Do you mind telling me what the fuck you want with my client?'

There's an old stereotype that says that Lusians are as subtle as a stomach pump and about half as pleasant. If I'd helped confirm the first part of that, Queue went a long way toward reinforcing the second prejudice.

He was fast. Even with my seemingly casual grip paralyzing the muscles of his right arm, the knife in his left hand sliced up and around in less than a second.

I let myself fall to my right, the knife slicing air centimeters from my cheek, hitting pavement and rolling as I palmed the neural stunner and came up on one knee to meet the threat.

No threat. Queue was running. Away from me. Away from Johnny. He shoved tourists aside, dodged behind them, moving toward the museum entrance.

I slid the stunner back into its wristband and began running myself. Stunners are great close-range weapons – as easy to aim as a shotgun without the dire effects if the spread pattern finds innocent bystanders – but they aren't worth anything beyond eight or ten meters. On full dispersal, I could give half the tourists in the plaza a miserable headache but Queue was already too far away to bring down. I ran after him.

Johnny ran toward me. I waved him back. 'My place!' I shouted. 'Use the locks!'

Queue had reached the museum entrance and now he looked back at me; the knife was still in his hand.

I charged at him, feeling something like joy at the thought of the next few minutes.

Queue vaulted a turnstile and shoved tourists aside to get through the doors. I followed.

It was only when I reached the hushed interior of the Grand Hall and saw him shoving his way up the crowded escalator to the Excursion Mezzanine that I realized where he was headed.

My father had taken me on the Templar Excursion when I was three. The farcaster portals were permanently open; it took about three hours to walk all the guided tours on the thirty worlds where the Templar ecologists had preserved some bit of nature which they thought would please the Muir. I couldn't remember for sure, but I thought the paths were loop trails with the portals relatively close together for easy transit by Templar guides and maintenance people.

Shit.

A uniformed guard near the tour portal saw the confusion as Queue cut through and stepped forward to intercept the rude intruder. Even from fifteen meters away I could see the shock and disbelief on the old guard's face as he staggered backward, the hilt of Queue's long knife protruding from his chest.

The old guard, probably a retired local cop, looked down, face white, touched the bone hilt gingerly as if it were a gag, and collapsed face first on the mezzanine tiles. Tourists screamed. Someone yelled for a medic. I saw Queue shove a Templar guide aside and throw himself through the glowing portal.

This was not going as I'd planned.

I vaulted for the portal without slowing.

Through and half sliding on the slippery grass of a hillside. Sky lemon yellow above us. Tropical scents. I saw startled faces turned my way. Queue was halfway to the other farcaster, cutting through elaborate flower beds and kicking aside bonsai topiary. I recognized the world of Fuji and careened down the hillside, clambering uphill again through the flower beds, following the trail of destruction Queue had left. 'Stop that man!' I screamed, realizing how foolish it sounded. No one made a move except for a Nipponese tourist who raised her imager and recorded a sequence.

Queue looked back, shoved past a gawking tour group, and stepped through the farcast portal.

I had the stunner in my hand again and waved it at the crowd. 'Back! Back!' They hastily made room.

I went through warily, stunner raised. Queue no longer had his knife but I didn't know what other toys he carried.

Brilliant light on water. The violent waves of Mare Infinitus. The path was a narrow wooden walkway ten meters above the support floats. It led out and away, curving above a fairyland coral reef and a sargasso of yellow island kelp before curving back, but a narrow catwalk cut across to the portal at the end of the trail. Queue had climbed the NO ACCESS gate and was halfway across the catwalk.

I ran the ten paces to the edge of the platform, selected tightbeam, and held the stunner on full auto, sweeping the invisible beam back and forth as if I were aiming a garden hose.

Queue seemed to stumble a half step but then made the last ten meters to the portal and dived through. I cursed and climbed the gate, ignoring shouts from a Templar guide behind me. I caught a glimpse of a sign which reminded tourists to don therm gear and then I was through the portal, barely sensing the shower-tingle sensation of passing through the farcaster screen.

A blizzard roared, whipping against the arched containment field which turned the tourist trail into a tunnel through fierce whiteness. Sol Draconi Septem – the northern reaches where Templar lobbying of the All Thing had stopped the colonial heating project in order to save the arctic wraiths. I could feel the 1.7-standard gravity on my shoulders like the yoke of my workout machine. It was a shame that Queue was a Lusian also; if he'd been Web-standard in physique, there would have been no contest if I caught him here. Now we would see who was in better shape.

Queue was fifty meters down the trail and looking back over his shoulder. The other farcaster was somewhere near but the blizzard made anything off the trail invisible and inaccessible. I began loping after him. In deference to the gravity, this was the shortest of the Templar Excursion trails, curving back after only two hundred or so meters. I could hear Queue's panting as I closed on him. I was running easily; there was no way that he was going to beat me to the next farcaster. I saw no tourists on the trail and so far no one had given chase. I thought that this would not be a bad place to interrogate him.

Queue was thirty meters short of the exit portal when he turned, dropped to one knee, and aimed an energy pistol. The first bolt was short, possibly because of the unaccustomed weight of the weapon in Sol Draconi's gravity field, but it was close enough to leave a scorched slash of slagged walkway and melted permafrost to within a meter of me. He adjusted his aim.

I went out through the containment field, shouldering my way through the elastic resistance and stumbling into drifts above my waist. The cold air burned my lungs and wind-driven snow caked my face and bare arms in seconds. I could see Queue looking for me from within the lighted pathway, but the blizzard dimness worked in my favor now as I threw myself through drifts in his direction.

Queue forced his head, shoulders, and right arm through the field wall, squinting in the barrage of icy particles which coated his cheeks and brow in an instant. His second shot was high and I felt the heat of the bolt as it passed over. I was within ten meters of him now; I set the stunner on widest dispersal and sprayed it in his direction without lifting my head from the snowdrift where I had dropped.

Queue let the energy pistol tumble into the snow and fell back through the containment field.

I screamed in triumph, my shout lost in the wind roar, and staggered toward the field wall. My hands and feet were distant things now, beyond the pain of cold. My cheeks and ears burned. I put the thought of frostbite out of my mind and threw myself against the field.

It was a class-three field, designed to keep out the elements and anything as huge as an arctic wraith, while allowing the occasional errant tourist or errand-bent Templar reentry to the path, but in my cold-weakened condition I found myself batting against it for a moment like a fly against plastic, my feet slipping on snow and ice. Finally I threw myself forward, landing heavily and clumsily, dragging my legs through.

The sudden warmth of the pathway set me to shaking uncontrollably. Shards of sleet fell from me as I forced myself to my knees, then to my feet.

Queue ran the last five yards to the exit portal with his right arm dangling as if broken. I knew the nerve-fire agony of a neural stunner and did not envy him. He looked back once as I began running toward him and then he went through.

Maui-Covenant. The air was tropical and smelled of ocean and vegetation. The sky was an Old Earth blue. I saw immediately that the trail had led to one of the few free motile isles which the Templars had saved from Hegemony domestication. It was a large isle, perhaps half a kilometer from end to end, and from the access portal's vantage point on a wide deck encircling the main treesail trunk I could see the expansive sail leaves filling with wind and the indigo rudder vines trailing far behind. The exit portal lay only fifteen meters away down a staircase but I saw at once that Queue had run the other way, along the main trail, toward a cluster of huts and concession stands near the edge of the isle.

It was only here, halfway along the Templar Excursion trail, that they allowed human structures to shelter weary hikers while they purchased refreshments or souvenirs to benefit the Templar Brotherhood. I began jogging down the wide staircase to the trail below, still shivering, my clothes soaked with rapidly melting snow. Why was Queue running toward the cluster of people there?

I saw the bright carpets laid out for rental and understood. The hawking mats were illegal on most Web worlds but still a tradition on Maui-Covenant because of the Siri legend; less than two meters long and a meter wide, the ancient playthings lay waiting to carry tourists out over the sea and back again to the wandering isle. If Queue reached one of those . . . I broke into a full sprint, catching the other Lusian a few meters short of the hawking mat area and tackling him just below the knees. We rolled into the concession stand area and the few tourists there shouted and scattered.

My father taught me one thing which any child ignores at his or her own peril: a good big guy can always beat a good little guy. In this case we were about even. Queue twisted free and jumped to his feet, falling into an arms-out, fingers-splayed oriental fighting stance. Now we'd see who the better guy was.

Queue got the first blow in, feinting a straight-fingered jab with his left hand and coming up and around with a swinging kick instead. I ducked but he connected solidly enough to make my left shoulder and upper arm go numb.

Queue danced backward. I followed. He swung a close-fisted right-handed punch. I blocked it. He chopped with his left hand. I blocked with my right forearm. Queue danced back, whirled, and unleashed a left-footed kick. I ducked, caught his leg as it passed over, and dumped him on the sand.

Queue jumped up. I knocked him down with a short left hook. He rolled away and scrambled to his knees. I kicked him behind his left ear, pulling the blow enough to leave him conscious.

Too conscious, I realized a second later as he ran four fingers under my guard in an attempted heart jab. Instead, he bruised the layers of muscle under my right breast. I punched him full force in the mouth, sending blood spraying as he rolled to the waterline and lay still. Behind us, people ran toward the exit portal, calling to the few others to get the police.

I lifted Johnny's would-be assassin by his queue, dragged him to the edge of the isle, and dipped his face in the water until he came to. Then I rolled him over and lifted him by his torn and stained shirtfront. We would have only a minute or two until *someone* arrived.

Queue stared up at me with a glazed glare. I shook him once and leaned close. 'Listen, my friend,' I whispered. 'We're going to have a short but sincere conversation. We'll start with who you are and why you're bothering the guy you were following.'

I felt the surge of current before I saw the blue. I cursed and let go of his shirtfront. The electrical nimbus seemed to surround Queue's entire body at once. I jumped back but not before my own hair stood on end and surge control alarms on my comlog chirped urgently. Queue opened his mouth to scream and I could see the blue within like a poorly done holo special effect. His shirtfront sizzled, blackened, and burst into flame. Beneath it his chest grew blue spots like an ancient film burning through. The spots widened, joined, widened again. I looked into his chest cavity and saw

263

organs melting in blue flame. He screamed again, audibly this time, and I watched as teeth and eyes collapsed into blue fire.

I took another step back.

Queue was burning now, the orange-red flames superseding the blue glow. His flesh exploded outward with flame as if his bones had ignited. Within a minute he was a smoking caricature of charred flesh, the body reduced to the ancient dwarf-boxer posture of burning victims everywhere. I turned away and put a hand over my mouth, searching the faces of the few watchers to see if any of them could have done this. Wide, frightened eyes stared back. Far above, gray security uniforms burst from the farcaster.

Damn. I looked around. The treesails surged and billowed overhead. Radiant gossamers, beautiful even in daylight, flitted among tropical vegetation of a hundred hues. Sunlight danced on blue ocean. The way to both portals was blocked. The security guard leading the group had drawn a weapon.

I was to the first hawking mat in three strides, trying to remember from my own ride two decades earlier how the flight threads were activated. I tapped designs in desperation.

The hawking mat went rigid and lifted ten centimeters off the beach. I could hear the shouts now as security guards reached the edge of the crowd. A woman in gaudy Renaissance Minor garb pointed my way. I jumped off the hawking mat, gathered up the other seven mats, and jumped aboard my own. Barely able to find the flight designs under the tumble of rugs, I slapped the forward controls until the mat lurched into flight, almost tumbling me off as it rose.

Fifty meters out, thirty meters high, I dumped the other mats into the sea and swiveled to see what was happening on the beach. Several gray uniforms were huddled around the burned remains. Another pointed a silver wand in my direction.

Delicate needles of pain tingled along my arm, shoulders, and neck. My eyelids drooped and I almost slid off the mat to my right. I gripped the far side with my left hand, slumped forward, and tapped at the ascent design with fingers made of wood. Climbing again, I fumbled at my right sleeve for my own stunner. The wristband was empty.

A minute later I sat up and shook off most of the effects of the stun, although my fingers still burned and I had a fierce headache. The motile isle was far behind, shrinking more each second. A century ago the island would have been driven by the bands of dolphins brought here originally during the Hegira, but the Hegemony pacification program during the Siri Rebellion had killed off most of the aquatic mammals and now the islands wandered listlessly, carrying their cargo of Web tourists and resort owners.

I checked the horizons for another island, a hint of one of the rare mainlands. Nothing. Or, rather, blue sky, endless ocean, and soft brushstrokes of clouds far to the west. Or was it to the east?

I pulled my comlog off my belt lock and keyed in general datasphere access, then stopped. If the authorities had chased me this far, the next step would be to pinpoint my location and send out a skimmer or security EMV. I wasn't sure if they could trace my comlog when I logged in but I saw no reason to help them. I thumbed the comm-link on standby and looked around again.

Good move, Brawne. Poking along at two hundred meters on a three-century-old hawking mat with who knows how many . . . or how few! . . . hours of charge in its flight threads, possibly a thousand klicks or more from land of any sort. And lost. Great. I crossed my arms and sat back to think.

'M. Lamia?' Johnny's soft voice almost made me jump off the mat.

'Johnny?' I stared at the comlog. It was still on standby. The general comm frequency indicator was dark. 'Johnny, is that you?'

'Of course. I thought you'd never turn your comlog on.'

'How did you trace me? What band are you calling on?'

'Never mind that. Where are you headed?'

I laughed and told him that I didn't have the slightest idea. 'Can you help?'

'Wait.' There was the briefest second of pause. 'All right, I have you on one of the weather-mapping sats. A terribly primitive thing. Good thing your hawking mat has a passive transponder.'

I stared at the rug that was the only thing between me and a long, loud fall to the sea. 'It does? Can the others track me?'

'They could,' said Johnny, 'but I'm jamming this particular signal. Now, where do you want to go?'

'Home.'

'I'm not sure if that's wise after the death of . . . ah . . . our suspect.'

I squinted, suddenly suspicious. 'How do you know about that? I didn't say anything.'

'Be serious, M. Lamia. The security bands are full of it on six worlds. They have a reasonable description of you.'

'Shit.'

'Precisely. Now where would you like to go?'

'Where are you?' I asked. 'My place?'

'No. I left there when the security bands mentioned you. I'm . . . near a farcaster.'

'That's where I need to be.' I looked around again. Ocean sky, a hint of clouds. At least no fleets of EMVs.

'All right,' said Johnny's disembodied voice. 'There's a powered-down FORCE multi-portal less than ten klicks from your present location.'

I shielded my eyes and rotated three hundred and sixty degrees. 'The hell there is,' I said. 'I don't know how far away the horizon is on this world, but it's at least forty klicks and I can't see anything.'

'Submersible base,' said Johnny. 'Hang on. I'm going to take control.'

The hawking mat lurched again, dipped once, and then fell steadily. I held on with both hands and resisted the urge to scream.

'Submersible,' I called against the wind rush, 'how *far*?'

'Do you mean how deep?'

'Yeah!'

'Eight fathoms.'

I converted the archaic units to meters. This time I did scream. 'That's almost fourteen meters *underwater*!'

'Where else do you expect a submersible to be?'

'What the hell do you expect me to do, hold my breath?' The ocean rushed toward me.

'Not necessary,' said my comlog. 'The hawking mat has a primitive crash field. It should easily hold for a mere eight fathoms. Please hang on.'

I hung on.

Johnny was waiting for me when I arrived. The submersible had been dark and dank with the sweat of abandonment; the farcaster had been of a military variety I'd never seen before. It was a relief to step into sunlight and a city street with Johnny waiting.

I told him what had happened to Queue. We walked empty streets past old buildings. The sky was pale blue fading toward evening. No one was in sight. 'Hey,' I said, stopping, 'where *are* we?' It was an incredibly Earthlike world but the sky, the gravity, the *texture* of the place was like nothing I'd visited.

Johnny smiled. 'I'll let you guess. Let's walk some more.'

There were ruins to our left as we walked down a wide street. I stopped and stared. 'That's the Colosseum,' I said. 'The Roman Colosseum on Old Earth.' I looked around at the aging buildings, the cobblestone streets, and the trees swaying slightly in a soft breeze. 'This is a reconstruction of the Old Earth city of Rome,' I said, trying to keep the astonishment out of my voice. 'New Earth?' I knew at once that it wasn't. I'd been to New Earth numerous times and the sky tones, smells, and gravity had not been like this.

Johnny shook his head. 'This is nowhere in the Web.'

I stopped walking. 'That's impossible.' By definition, any world which could be reached by farcaster was in the Web.

'Nonetheless, it is not in the Web.'

'Where is it then?'

'Old Earth.'

We walked on. Johnny pointed out another ruin. 'The Forum.' Descending a long staircase, he said, 'Ahead is the Piazza di Spagna where we'll spend the night.'

'Old Earth,' I said, my first comment in twenty minutes. 'Time travel?'

'That is not possible, M. Lamia.'

'A theme park then?'

Johnny laughed. It was a pleasant laugh, unselfconscious and easy. 'Perhaps. I don't really know its purpose or function. It is . . . an analog.'

'An analog.' I squinted at the red, setting sun just visible down a narrow street. 'It looks like the holos I've seen of Old Earth. It *feels* right, even though I've never been there.'

'It is very accurate.'

'Where is it? I mean, what star?'

'I don't know the number,' said Johnny. 'It's in the Hercules Cluster.'

I managed not to repeat what he said but I stopped and sat down on one of the steps. With the Hawking drive humankind had explored, colonized, and linked with farcaster worlds across many thousands of light-years. But no one had tried to reach the exploding Core suns. We had barely crawled out of the cradle of one spiral arm. The *Hercules Cluster*.

'Why has the TechnoCore built a replica of Rome in the Hercules Cluster?' I asked.

Johnny sat next to me. We both looked up as a whirling mass of pigeons exploded into flight and wheeled above the rooftops. 'I don't know, M. Lamia. There is much that I have not learned . . . at least partially because I have not been interested until now.'

'Brawne,' I said.

'Excuse me?'

'Call me Brawne.'

Johnny smiled and inclined his head. 'Thank you, Brawne. One thing, though. I do not believe that it is a replica of the city of Rome alone. It is all of Old Earth.'

I set both hands on the sun-warmed stone of the step I was sitting on. '*All* of Old Earth? All of its . . . continents, cities?'

'I believe so. I haven't been out of Italy and England except for a sea voyage between the two, but I believe the analog is complete.'

'Why, for God's sake?'

Johnny nodded slowly. 'That may indeed be the case. Why don't we go inside and eat and talk more about this? It may relate to who tried to kill me and why.'

'Inside' was an apartment in a large house at the foot of the marble stairs. Windows looked out on what Johnny called the 'piazza' and I could see up the staircase to a large, yellow-brown church above, and down to the square where a boat-shaped fountain tossed water into the evening stillness. Johnny said that the fountain had been designed by Bernini but the name meant nothing to me.

The rooms were small but high-ceilinged, with rough but elaborately carved furniture from an era I did not recognize. There was no sign of electricity or modern appliances. The house did not respond when I spoke to it at the door and again in the apartment upstairs. As dusk fell over the square and city outside the tall windows, the only lights were a few streetlamps of gas or some more primitive combustible.

'This is out of Old Earth's past,' I said, touching the thick pillows. I raised my head, suddenly understanding. 'Keats died in Italy. Early . . . nineteenth or twentieth century. This is . . . then.'

'Yes. Early nineteenth century: 1821, to be precise.'

'The whole world is a museum?'

'Oh no. Different areas are different eras, of course. It depends upon the analog being pursued.'

'I don't understand.' We had moved into a room cluttered with thick furniture and I sat on an oddly carved couch by a window. A film of gold evening light still touched the spire of the tawny church up the steps. Pigeons wheeled white against blue sky. 'Are there millions of people . . . cybrids . . . living on this fake Old Earth?'

'I do not believe so,' said Johnny, 'Only the number necessary for the particular analog project.' He saw that I still did not understand and took a breath before continuing. 'When I . . . awoke here, there were cybrid analogs of Joseph Severn, Dr Clark, the landlady Anna Angeletti, young Lieutenant Elton, and a few others. Italian shopkeepers, the owner of the trattoria across the square who used to bring us our food, passersby, that sort of thing. No more than a score at the most.'

'What happened to them?'

'They were probably . . . recycled. Like the man with the queue.'

'Queue . . .' I suddenly stared across the darkening room at Johnny. 'He was a cybrid?'

'Without doubt. The self-destruction you described is precisely the way I would rid myself of this cybrid if I had to.'

My mind was racing. I realized how stupid I had been, how little I had learned about anything. 'Then it was another AI who tried to kill you.'

'It seems that way.'

'Why?'

Johnny made a gesture with his hands. 'Possibly to erase some quantum of knowledge that died with my cybrid. Something I had learned only recently and the other AI . . . or AIs knew would be destroyed in my systems crash.'

I stood, paced back and forth, and stopped at the window. The darkness was settling in earnest now. There were lamps in the room but Johnny made no move to light them and I preferred the dimness. It made the unreality of what I was hearing even that much more unreal. I looked into the bedroom. The western windows admitted the last of the light; bed-clothes glowed whitely. 'You died here,' I said.

'*He* did,' said Johnny. 'I am not he.'

'But you have his memories.'

'Half-forgotten dreams. There are gaps.'

'But you know what he *felt*.'

'I remember what the designers *thought* that he felt.'

'Tell me.'

'What?' Johnny's skin was very pale in the gloom. His short curls looked black.

'What it was like to die. What it was like to be reborn.'

Johnny told me, his voice very soft, almost melodic, lapsing sometimes into an English too archaic to be understood but far more beautiful to the ear than the hybrid tongue we speak today.

He told me what it was like to be a poet obsessed with perfection, far harsher toward his own efforts than even the most vicious critic. And the critics were vicious. His work was dismissed, ridiculed, described as derivative and silly. Too poor to marry the woman he loved, loaning money to his brother in America and thus losing the last chance of financial security . . . and then the brief glory of growing into the full maturation of his poetic powers just as he fell prey to the 'consumption' which had claimed his mother and his brother Tom. Then sent off to exile in Italy, reputedly 'for his health' while knowing all the while it meant a lonely, painful death at the age of twenty-six. He talked of the agony of seeing Fanny's handwriting on the letters he found too painful to open; he talked of the loyalty of the young artist Joseph Severn, who had been chosen as a traveling companion for Keats by 'friends' who had abandoned the poet at the end, of how Severn had nursed the dying man and stayed with him during the final days. He told of the hemorrhages in the night, of Dr Clark bleeding him and prescribing 'exercise and good air', and of the ultimate religious and personal despair which had led Keats to demand his own epitaph be carved in stone as: 'Here lies One Whose Name was writ in Water.'

Only the dimmest light from below outlined the tall windows. Johnny's voice seemed to float in the night-scented air. He spoke of awakening after his death in the bed where he died, still attended by the loyal Severn and Dr Clark, of remembering that he was the poet John Keats the way one remembers an identity from a fast-fading dream while all the while knowing that *he was something else.*

He told of the illusion continued, the trip back to England, the reunion with the Fanny-who-was-not-Fanny and the near mental breakdown this had engendered. He told of his inability to write further poetry, of his increasing estrangement from the cybrid impostors, of his retreat into something resembling catatonia combined with 'hallucinations' of his true AI existence in the nearly incomprehensible (to a nineteenth-century poet) TechnoCore, and of the ultimate crumbling of the illusion and the abandonment of the 'Keats Project'.

'In truth,' he said, 'the entire, evil charade made me think of nothing so much as a passage in a letter I wrote . . . *he* wrote . . . to his brother George some time before his illness. Keats said:

'May there not be superior beings amused with any graceful, though instinctive attitude my mind may fall into, as I am entertained with the alertness of a Stoat or the anxiety of a Deer? Though a quarrel in the streets is a thing to be hated, the energies displayed in it are fine. By a superior being our reasonings may take the same tone – though erroneous they may be fine – This is the very thing in which consists poetry.'

'You think the . . . Keats Project . . . was evil?' I asked.

'Anything which deceives is evil, I believe.'

'Perhaps you are more John Keats than you are willing to admit.'

'No. The absence of poetic instinct showed otherwise even in the midst of the most elaborate illusion.'

I looked at the dark outlines of shapes in the dark house. 'Do the AIs know that we're here?'

'Probably. Almost surely. There is no place that I can go that the Techno-Core cannot trace and follow. But it was the Web authorities and brigands from whom we fled, no?'

'But you know now that it was someone . . . some intelligence in the TechnoCore who assaulted you.'

'Yes, but only in the Web. Such violence in the Core would not be tolerated.'

There came a noise from the street. A pigeon, I hoped. Wind blowing trash across cobblestones perhaps. I said, 'How will the TechnoCore respond to my being here?'

'I have no idea.'

'Surely it must be a secret.'

'It is . . . something they consider *irrelevant* to humanity.'

I shook my head, a futile gesture in the darkness. 'The re-creation of Old Earth . . . the resurrection of . . . how many? . . . human personalities as cybrids on this re-created world . . . AIs killing AIs . . . irrelevant!' I laughed but managed to keep the laughter under control. 'Jesus wept, Johnny.'

'Almost certainly.'

I moved to the window, not caring what sort of target I would afford anyone in the dark street below, and fumbled out a cigarette. They were damp from the afternoon's chase through the snowdrifts but one lighted when I struck it. 'Johnny, earlier when you said that the Old Earth analog was complete, I said, "Why, for God's sake?" and you said something like "That may be the case." Was that just a wiseass comment or did you mean something?'

'I mean that it might indeed be for God's sake.'

'Explain.'

Johnny sighed in the darkness. 'I don't understand the exact purpose of the Keats Project or the other Old Earth analogs, but I suspect that it is part of a TechnoCore project going back at least seven standard centuries to realize the Ultimate Intelligence.'

'The Ultimate Intelligence,' I said, exhaling smoke. 'Uh-huh. So the TechnoCore is trying to . . . what? . . . to build God.'

'Yes,'

'Why?'

'There is no simple answer, Brawne. Any more than there is a simple answer to the question of why humankind has sought God in a million guises for ten thousand generations. But with the Core, the interest lies more in the quest for more efficiency, more reliable ways to handle . . . variables.'

'But the TechnoCore can draw on itself and the mega-datasphere of two hundred worlds.'

'And there still will be blanks in the . . . predictive powers.'

I threw my cigarette out the window, watching the ember fall into the night. The breeze was suddenly cold; I hugged my arms. 'How does all this . . . Old Earth, the resurrection projects, the cybrids . . . how does it lead to creating the Ultimate Intelligence?'

'I don't know, Brawne. Eight standard centuries ago, at the beginning of the First Information Age, a man named Norbert Wiener wrote: "Can God play a significant game with his own creature? Can any creator, even a limited one, play a significant game with his own creature?" Humanity dealt with this inconclusively with their early AIs. The Core wrestles with it in the resurrection projects. Perhaps the UI program has been completed and all of this remains a function of the ultimate Creature/Creator, a personality whose motives are as far beyond the Core's understanding as the Core's are beyond humanity's.'

I started to move in the dark room, bumped a low table with my knee, and remained standing. 'None of which tells us who is trying to kill you,' I said.

'No.' Johnny rose and moved to the far wall. A match flared and he lighted a candle. Our shadows wavered on the walls and ceiling.

Johnny came closer and softly gripped my upper arms. The soft light painted his curls and eyelashes copper and touched his high cheekbones and firm chin. 'Why are you so tough?' he asked.

I stared at him. His face was only inches from mine. We were the same height. 'Let go,' I said.

Instead, he leaned forward and kissed me. His lips were soft and warm and the kiss seemed to last for hours. *He's a machine*, I thought. *Human, but a machine behind that.* I closed my eyes. His soft hand touched my cheek, my neck, the back of my head.

'Listen . . .' I whispered when we broke apart for an instant.

Johnny did not let me finish. He lifted me in his arms and carried me into the other room. The tall bed. The soft mattress and deep comforter. The candlelight from the other room flickered and danced as we undressed each other in a sudden urgency.

We made love three times that night, each time responding to slow, sweet imperatives of touch and warmth and closeness and the escalating intensity of sensation. I remember looking down at him the second time; his eyes were closed, hair fell loosely across his forehead, the candlelight showing the flush across his pale chest, his surprisingly strong arms and hands rising to hold me in place. He had opened his eyes that second to look back at me and I saw only the emotion and passion of that moment reflected there.

Sometime before dawn we slept; just as I turned away and drifted off, I felt the cool touch of his hand on my hip in a movement protective and casual without being possessive.

They hit us just after first light. There were five of them, not Lusian but heavily muscled, all men, and they worked well together as a team.

The first I heard of them was when the door to the apartment was kicked open. I rolled out of bed, jumped to the side of the bedroom door, and watched them come through. Johnny sat up and shouted something as the first man leveled a stunner. Johnny had pulled on cotton shorts before going to sleep; I was nude. There are real disadvantages to fighting in the nude when one's opponents are dressed, but the greatest problem is psychological. If you can get over the sense of heightened vulnerability, the rest is easy to compensate for.

The first man saw me, decided to stun Johnny anyway, and paid for the mistake. I kicked the weapon out of his hand and clubbed him down with a blow behind the left ear. Two more men pushed into the room. This time both of them were smart enough to deal with me first. Two others leaped for Johnny.

I blocked a stiff-fingered jab, parried a kick that would have done real damage, and backed away. There was a tall dresser to my left and the top drawer came out smooth and heavy. The big man in front of me shielded his face with both arms so that the thick wood splintered, but the instinctive reaction gave me a second's opening and I took it, putting my entire body into the kick. Number two man grunted and fell back against his partner.

Johnny was struggling but one of the intruders had him around the throat in a choke hold while the other pinned his legs. I came off the floor in a crouch, accepted the blow from my number two, and leaped across the bed. The guy holding Johnny's legs went through the glass and wood of the window without a word.

Someone landed on my back and I completed the roll across the bed and floor, bringing him up against the wall. He was good. He took the blow on his shoulder and went for a nerve pinch beneath my ear. He had a second of trouble because of the extra layers of muscle there and I got an elbow deep into his stomach and rolled away. The man choking Johnny dropped him and delivered a textbook-perfect kick to my ribs. I took half the impact, feeling at least one rib go, and spun inside, attempting no elegance as I used my left hand to crush his left testicle. The man screamed and was out of it.

I'd never forgotten the stunner on the floor and neither had the last of the opposition. He scurried around to the far side of the bed, out of reach, and dropped to all fours to grab the weapon. Definitely feeling the pain from the broken rib now, I lifted the massive bed with Johnny in it and dropped it on the guy's head and shoulders.

I went under the bed from my side, retrieved the stunner, and backed into an empty corner.

One guy had gone out the window. We were on the second floor. The first man to enter was still lying in the doorway. The guy I'd kicked had managed to get to one knee and both elbows. From the blood on his mouth and chin, I guessed that a rib had punctured a lung. He was breathing very raggedly. The bed had crushed the skull of the other man on the floor. The guy who'd been choking Johnny was curled up near the window, holding his crotch and vomiting. I stunned him into silence and went over to the one I'd kicked and lifted him by the hair. 'Who sent you?'

'Fuck you.' He sprayed some bloody spittle in my face.

'Maybe later,' I said. 'Again, who sent you?' I placed three fingers against his side where the ribcage seemed concave and pressed.

The man screamed and went very white. When he coughed the blood was too red against pale skin.

'Who sent you?' I set four fingers against his ribs.

'The bishop!' He tried to levitate away from my fingers.

'What bishop?'

'Shrike Temple . . . Lusus . . . don't, *please* . . . oh, shit . . .'

'What were you going to do with him . . . us?'

'Nothing . . . Oh, God *damn* . . . don't! I need a medic, *please!*'

'Sure. Answer.'

'Stun him, bring him . . . back to the Temple . . . Lusus. Please. I can't breathe.'

'And me?'

'Kill you if you resisted.'

'Okay,' I said, lifting him a little higher by his hair, 'we're doing fine here. What did they want him for?'

'I don't know.' He screamed very loudly. I kept one eye on the doorway to the apartment. The stunner was still in my palm under a fistful of hair. 'I . . . don't . . . know . . .' he gasped. He was hemorrhaging in earnest now. The blood dripped on my arm and left breast.

'How'd you get here?'

'EMV . . . roof.'

'Where'd you 'cast in?'

'Don't know . . . I *swear* . . . some city in the water. Car's set to return there . . . *please!*'

I ripped at his clothes. No comlog. No other weapons. There was a tattoo of a blue trident just above his heart. 'Goonda?' I said.

'Yeah . . . Parvati Brotherhood.'

Outside the Web. Probably very hard to trace. 'All of you?'

'Yeah . . . please . . . get me some help . . . oh, shit . . . please . . .' He sagged, almost unconscious.

I dropped him, stepped back, and sprayed the stun beam over him.

Johnny was sitting up, rubbing his throat, and staring at me with a strange gaze.

'Get dressed,' I said. 'We're leaving.'

*

The EMV was an old, transparent Vikken Scenic with no palmlocks on the ignition plate or diskey. We caught up to the terminator before we had crossed France and looked down on darkness that Johnny said was the Atlantic Ocean. Except for lights of the occasional floating city or drilling platform, the only illumination came from the stars and the broad, swimming-pool glows of the undersea colonies.

'Why are we taking their vehicle?' asked Johnny.

'I want to see where they farcast from.'

'He said the Lusus Shrike Temple.'

'Yeah. Now we'll see.'

Johnny's face was barely visible as he looked down at the dark sea twenty klicks below. 'Do you think those men will die?'

'One was already dead,' I said. 'The guy with the punctured lung will need help. Two of them'll be okay. I don't know about the one who went out the window. Do you care?'

'Yes. The violence was . . . barbaric.'

'"Though a quarrel in the street is a thing to be hated, the energies displayed in it are fine,"' I quoted. 'They weren't cybrids, were they?'

'I think not.'

'So there are at least two groups out to get you . . . the AIs and the bishop of the Shrike Temple. And we still don't know why.'

'I do have an idea now.'

I swiveled in the foam recliner. The constellations above us – familiar neither from holos of Old Earth's skies nor from any Web world I knew – cast just enough light to allow me to see Johnny's eyes. Tell me,' I said.

'Your mention of Hyperion gave me a clue,' he said. 'The fact that I had no knowledge of it. Its absence said that it was important.'

'The strange case of the dog barking in the night,' I said.

'What?'

'Nothing. Go on.'

Johnny leaned closer. 'The only reason that I would not be aware of it is that some elements of the TechnoCore have blocked my knowledge of it.'

'Your cybrid . . .' It was strange to talk to Johnny that way now. 'You spend most of your time in the Web, don't you?'

'Yes.'

'Wouldn't you run across mention of Hyperion somewhere? It's in the news every once in a while, especially when the Shrike Cult's topical.'

'Perhaps I did hear. Perhaps that is why I was murdered.'

I lay back and looked at the stars. 'Let's go ask the bishop,' I said.

Johnny said that the lights ahead were an analog of New York City in the mid-twenty-first century. He didn't know what resurrection project the city had been rebuilt for. I took the EMV off auto and dropped lower.

Tall buildings from the phallic-symbol era of urban architecture rose from the swamps and lagoons of the North American littoral. Several had lights burning. Johnny pointed to one decrepit but oddly elegant structure and said, 'The Empire State Building.'

'Okay,' I said. 'Whatever it is, that's where the EMV wants to land.'

'Is it safe?'

I grinned at him. 'Nothing in life's safe.' I let the car have its head and we dropped to a small, open platform below the building's spire. We got out and stood on the cracked balcony. It was quite dark except for the few building lights far below and the stars. A few paces away, a vague blue glow outlined a farcaster portal where elevator doors may once have been.

'I'll go first,' I said but Johnny had already stepped through. I palmed the borrowed stunner and followed him.

I'd never been in the Shrike Temple on Lusus before but there was no doubt that we were there now. Johnny stood a few paces ahead of me but other than him there was no one around. The place was cool and dark and cavernous if caverns could really be that large. A frightening polychrome sculpture which hung from invisible cables rotated to unfelt breezes. Johnny and I both turned as the farcaster portal winked out of existence.

'Well, we did their work for them, didn't we?' I whispered to Johnny. Even the whisper seemed to echo in the red-lit hall. I hadn't planned on Johnny 'casting to the Temple with me.

The light seemed to come up then, not really illuminating the great hall but widening its scope so that we could see the semicircle of men there. I remembered that some were called exorcists and others lectors and there was some other category I forgot. Whoever they were, it was alarming to see them standing there, at least two dozen of them, their robes variations on red and black and their high foreheads glowing from the red light above. I had no trouble recognizing the bishop. He was from my world, although shorter and fatter than most of us, and his robe was very red.

I did not try to hide the stunner. It was possible that if they all tried to rush us I could bring them all down. Possible but not probable. I could not see any weapons but their robes could have hidden entire arsenals.

Johnny walked toward the bishop and I followed. Ten paces from the man we stopped. The bishop was the only one not standing. His chair was made of wood and looked as if it could be folded so that the intricate arms, supports, back, and legs could be carried in a compact form. One couldn't say the same of the mass of muscle and fat evident under the bishop's robes.

Johnny took another step forward. 'Why did you try to kidnap my cybrid?' He spoke to the Shrike Cult holy man as if the rest of us were not there.

The bishop chuckled and shook his head. 'My dear . . . entity . . . it is true that we wished your presence in our place of worship, but you have no evidence that we were involved in any attempt to kidnap you.'

'I'm not interested in evidence,' said Johnny. 'I'm curious as to why you want me here.'

I heard a rustling behind us and I swiveled quickly, the stunner charged and pointed, but the broad circle of Shrike priests remained motionless. Most were out of the stunner's range. I wished that I had brought my father's projectile weapon with me.

The bishop's voice was deep and textured and seemed to fill the huge space. 'Surely you know that the Church of the Final Atonement has a deep and abiding interest in the world of Hyperion.'

'Yes.'

'And surely you are aware that during the past several centuries the persona of the Old Earth poet Keats has been woven into the cultural mythos of the Hyperion colony?'

'Yes. So?'

The bishop rubbed his cheek with a large red ring on one finger. 'So when you offered to go on the Shrike Pilgrimage we agreed. We were distressed when you reneged on this offer.'

Johnny's look of amazement was most human. '*I* offered? When?'

'Eight local days ago,' said the bishop. 'In this room. You approached us with the idea.'

'Did I say why I wanted to go on the . . . Shrike Pilgrimage?'

'You said that it was . . . I believe the phrase you used was . . . "important for your education". We can show you the recording if you wish. All such conversations in the Temple are recorded. Or you may have a duplicate of the recording to view at your own convenience.'

'Yes,' said Johnny.

The bishop nodded and an acolyte or whatever the hell he was disappeared into the gloom for a moment and returned with a standard video chip in his hand. The bishop nodded again and the black-robed man came forward and handed the chip to Johnny. I kept the stunner ready until the guy had returned to the semicircle of watchers.

'Why did you send the goondas after us?' I asked. It was the first time I'd spoken in front of the bishop and my voice sounded too loud and too raw.

The Shrike holy man made a gesture with one pudgy hand. 'M. Keats had expressed an interest in joining our holiest pilgrimage. Since it is our belief that the Final Atonement is drawing closer each day, this is of no little importance to us. Consequently, our agents reported that M. Keats may have been the victim of one or more assaults and that a certain private investigator . . . *you*, M. Lamia . . . was responsible for destroying the cybrid bodyguard provided M. Keats by the TechnoCore.'

'Bodyguard!' It was my turn to sound amazed.

'Of course,' said the bishop. He turned toward Johnny. 'The gentleman with the queue who was recently murdered on the Temple Excursion, was this not the same man whom you introduced as your bodyguard a week earlier? He is visible in the recording.'

Johnny said nothing. He seemed to be straining to remember something.

'At any rate,' continued the bishop, 'we must have your answer about the pilgrimage before the week is out. The *Sequoia Sempervirens* departs from the Web in nine local days.'

'But that's a Templar treeship,' said Johnny. 'They don't make the long leap to Hyperion.'

The bishop smiled. 'In this case it does. We have reason to believe that this may be the last Church-sponsored pilgrimage and we have chartered the Templar craft to allow as many of the faithful as possible to make the trip.' The bishop gestured and red-and-black-robed men faded back into darkness. Two exorcists came forward to fold his stool as the bishop stood. 'Please give us your answer as soon as possible.' He was gone. The remaining exorcist stayed to show us out.

There were no more farcasters. We exited by the main door of the Temple and stood on the top step of the long staircase, looking down on the Concourse Mall of Hive Center and breathing in the cool, oil-scented air.

My father's automatic was in the drawer where I'd left it. I made sure there was a full load of flechettes, palmed the magazine back in, and carried the weapon into the kitchen where breakfast was cooking. Johnny sat at the long table, staring down through gray windows at the loading dock. I carried the omelets over and set one in front of him. He looked up as I poured the coffee.

'Do you believe him?' I asked. 'That it was your idea?'

'You saw the video recording.'

'Recordings can be faked.'

'Yes. But this one wasn't.'

'Then why did you volunteer to go on this pilgrimage? And why did your bodyguard try to kill you after you talked to the Shrike Church and the Templar captain?'

Johnny tried the omelet, nodded, and took another forkful. 'The . . . bodyguard . . . is a complete unknown to me. He must have been assigned to me during the week lost to memory. His real purpose obviously was to make sure that I did not discover something . . . or, if I did stumble upon it, to eliminate me.'

'Something in the Web or in datumplane?'

'In the Web, I presume.'

'We need to know who he . . . it . . . worked for and why they assigned him to you.'

'I do know,' said Johnny. 'I just asked. The Core responds that I requested a bodyguard. The cybrid was controlled by an AI nexus which corresponds to a security force.'

'Ask why he tried to kill you.'

'I did. They emphatically deny that such a thing is possible.'

'Then why was this so-called bodyguard slinking around after you a week after the murder?'

'They respond that while I did not request security again after my . . . discontinuity . . . the Core authorities felt that it would be prudent to provide protection.'

I laughed. 'Some protection. Why the hell did he run on the Templar world when I caught up to him? They aren't even trying to give you a plausible story, Johnny.'

'No.'

'Nor did the bishop explain how the Shrike Church had farcaster access to Old Earth . . . or whatever you call that stage-set world.'

'And we did not ask.'

'*I* didn't ask because I wanted to get out of that damn Temple in one piece.'

Johnny didn't seem to hear. He was sipping his coffee, his gaze focused somewhere else.

'What?' I said.

He turned to look at me, tapping his thumbnail on his lower lip. 'There is a paradox here, Brawne.'

'What?'

'If it was truly my aim to go to Hyperion . . . for my cybrid to travel there . . . I could not have remained in the TechnoCore. I would have had to invest all consciousness in the cybrid itself.'

'Why?' But even as I asked I saw the reason.

'Think. Datumplane itself is an abstract. A commingling of computer and AI-generated dataspheres and the quasi-perceptual Gibsonian matrix designed originally for human operators, now accepted as common ground for man, machine, and AI.'

'But AI hardware exists somewhere in real space,' I said. 'Somewhere in the TechnoCore.'

'Yes, but that is irrelevant to the function of AI consciousness,' said Johnny. 'I can "be" anywhere the overlapping dataspheres allow me to travel . . . all of the Web worlds, of course, datumplane, and any of the TechnoCore constructs such as Old Earth . . . but it's only within that milieu that I can claim "consciousness" or operate sensors or remotes such as this cybrid.'

I set my coffee cup down and stared at the thing I had loved as a man during the night just past. 'Yes?'

'The colony worlds have limited dataspheres,' said Johnny. 'While there is some contact with the TechnoCore via fatline transmissions, it is an exchange of data only . . . rather like the First Information Age computer interfaces . . . rather than a flow of consciousness. Hyperion's datasphere is primitive to the point of non-existence. And from what I can access, the Core has no contact whatsoever with that world.'

'Would that be normal?' I asked. 'I mean with a colony world that far away?'

'No. The Core has contact with every colony world, with such interstellar barbarians as the Ousters, and with other sources the Hegemony could not imagine.'

I sat stunned. 'With the *Ousters*?' Since the war on Bressia a few years earlier, the Ousters had been the Web's prime bogeymen. The idea of the Core . . . the same congregation of AIs which advises the Senate and the All

278

Thing and which allows our entire economy, farcaster system, and technological civilization to run . . . the idea of the Core being in touch with the Ousters was frightening. And what the hell did Johnny mean by 'other sources'? I didn't really want to know right then.

'But you said it *is* possible for your cybrid to travel there?' I said. 'What did you mean by "investing all consciousness" in your cybrid? Can an AI *become* . . . human? Can you exist only in your cybrid?'

'It has been done,' Johnny said softly. 'Once. A personality reconstruction not too different from my own. A twentieth-century poet named Ezra Pound. He abandoned his AI persona and fled from the Web in his cybrid. But the Pound reconstruction was insane.'

'Or sane,' I said.

'Yes.'

'So all of the data and personality of an AI can survive in a cybrid's organic brain.'

'Of course not, Brawne. Not one percent of one percent of my total consciousness would survive the transition. Organic brains can't process even the most primitive information the way we can. The resultant personality would not be the AI persona . . . neither would it be a truly human consciousness or cybrid . . .' Johnny stopped in mid-sentence and turned quickly to look out the window.

After a long minute I said, 'What is it?' I reached out a hand but did not touch him.

He spoke without turning. 'Perhaps I was wrong to say that the consciousness would not be human,' he whispered. 'It is possible that the resulting persona could be human touched with a certain divine madness and meta-human perspective. It could be . . . if purged of all memory of our age, of all consciousness of the Core . . . it could be the person the cybrid was programmed to be . . .'

'John Keats,' I said.

Johnny turned away from the window and closed his eyes. His voice was hoarse with emotion. It was the first time I had heard him recite poetry:

'Fanatics have their dreams, wherewith they weave
A paradise for a sect, the savage too
From forth the loftiest fashion of his sleep
Guesses at Heaven; pity these have not
Traced upon vellum or wild Indian leaf
The shadows of melodious utterance.
But bare of laurel they live, dream, and die;
For Poesy alone can tell her dreams,
With the fine spell of words alone can save
Imagination from the sable charm
And dumb enchantment. Who alive can say,
"Thou art no Poet – mayst not tell thy dreams"?
Since every man whose soul is not a clod

279

Hath visions, and would speak, if he had loved,
And been well nurtured in his mother tongue.
Whether the dream now purposed to rehearse
Be Poet's or Fanatic's will be known
When this warm scribe my hand is in the grave.'

'I don't get it,' I said. 'What does it mean?'

'It means,' said Johnny, smiling gently, 'that I know what decision I made and why I made it. I wanted to cease being a cybrid and become a man. I wanted to go to Hyperion. I still do.'

'Somebody killed you for that decision a week ago,' I said.

'Yes.'

'And you're going to try again?'

'Yes.'

'Why not invest consciousness in your cybrid here? Become human in the Web?'

'It would never work,' said Johnny. 'What you see as a complex interstellar society is only a small part of the Core reality matrix. I would be constantly confronted with and at the mercy of the AIs. The Keats persona . . . *reality* . . . would never survive.'

'All right,' I said, 'you need to get out of the Web. But there are other colonies. Why Hyperion?'

Johnny took my hand. His finger were long and warm and strong. 'Don't you see, Brawne? There is some connection here. It may well be that Keats's dreams of Hyperion were some sort of transtemporal communication between his then persona and his now persona. If nothing else, Hyperion is the key mystery of our age – physical and poetic – and it is quite probable that he . . . that *I* was born, died, and was born again to explore it.'

'It sounds like madness to me,' I said. 'Delusions of grandeur.'

'Almost certainly,' laughed Johnny. 'And I never have been happier!' He grabbed my arms and brought me to my feet, his arms around me. 'Will you go with me, Brawne? Go with me to Hyperion?'

I blinked in surprise, both at his question and the answer, which filled me like a rush of warmth. 'Yes,' I said. 'I'll go.'

We went into the sleeping area then and made love the rest of that day, sleeping finally to awaken to the low light of Shift Three in the industrial trench outside. Johnny was lying on his back, his hazel eyes open and staring at the ceiling, lost in thought. But not so lost he did not smile and put his arm around me. I nestled my cheek against him, settling into the small curve where shoulder meets chest, and went back to sleep.

I was wearing my best clothes – a suit of black whipcord, a blouse woven of Renaissance silk with a Carvnel bloodstone at the throat, a cocked Eulin Bré tricorne – when Johnny and I farcast to TC^2 the next day. I left him in the wood and brass bar near the central terminex, but not before I slid Dad's automatic across to him in a paper bag and told him to shoot anyone who even looked cross-eyed at him.

'Web English is such a subtle tongue,' he said.

'That phrase is older than the Web,' I said. 'Just *do* it.' I squeezed his hand and left without looking back.

I took a skycab to the Administration Complex and walked my way through about nine security checks before they let me into the Center grounds. I walked the half klick across Deer Park, admiring the swans in the nearby lake and the white buildings on the hilltop in the distance, and then there were nine more checkpoints before a Center security woman led me up the flagstoned path to Government House, a low, graceful building set amid flower gardens and landscaped hills. There was an elegantly furnished waiting room but I barely had time to sit down on an authentic pre-Hegira de Kooning before an aide appeared and ushered me into the CEO's private office.

Meina Gladstone came around the desk to shake my hand and show me to a chair. It was strange to see her in person again after all those years of watching her on HTV. She was even more impressive in the flesh: her hair was cut short but seemed to be blowing back in gray-white waves; her cheeks and chin were as sharp and Lincolnesque as all the history-prone pundits insisted, but it was the large, sad, brown eyes which dominated the face and made one feel as if he or she were in the presence of a truly original person.

I found that my mouth was dry. 'Thank you for seeing me, M. Executive. I know how busy you are.'

'I'm never too busy to see you, Brawne. Just as your father was never too busy to see me when I was a junior senator.'

I nodded. Dad had once described Meina Gladstone as the only political genius in the Hegemony. He knew that she would be CEO someday despite her late start in politics. I wished Dad had lived to see it.

'How is your mother, Brawne?'

'She's well, M. Executive. She rarely leaves our old summer place on Freeholm anymore but I see her every Christmas Fest.'

Gladstone nodded. She had been sitting casually on the edge of a massive desk which the tabloids said had once belonged to an assassinated President – not Lincoln – of the pre-Mistake USA, but now she smiled and went around to the simple chair behind it. 'I miss your father, Brawne. I wish he were in this administration. Did you see the lake when you came in?'

'Yes.'

'Do you remember sailing toy boats there with my Kresten when you were both toddlers?'

'Just barely, M. Executive. I was pretty young.'

Meina Gladstone smiled. An intercom chimed but she waved it into silence. 'How can I help you, Brawne?'

I took a breath. 'M. Executive, you may be aware that I'm working as an independent private investigator . . .' I didn't wait for her nod. 'A case I've been working on recently has led me back to Dad's suicide . . .'

'Brawne, you know that was investigated most thoroughly. I saw the commission's report.'

'Yeah,' I said. 'I did too. But recently I've discovered some very strange things about the TechnoCore and its attitude toward the world Hyperion. Weren't you and Dad working on a bill that would have brought Hyperion into the Hegemony Protectorate?'

Gladstone nodded. 'Yes, Brawne, but there were over a dozen other colonies being considered that year. None were allowed in.'

'Right. But did the Core or the AI Advisory Council take a special interest in Hyperion?'

The CEO tapped a stylus against her lower lip. 'What kind of information do you have, Brawne?' I started to answer but she held up a blunt finger. 'Wait!' She keyed an interactive. 'Thomas, I'll be stepping out for a few minutes. Please be sure that the Sol Draconi trade delegation is entertained if I fall a bit behind schedule.'

I didn't see her key anything else but suddenly a blue and gold farcaster portal hummed into life near the far wall. She gestured me to go through first.

A plain of gold, knee-high grass stretched to horizons which seemed farther away than most. The sky was a pale yellow with burnished copper streaks which may have been clouds. I didn't recognize the world.

Meina Gladstone stepped through and touched the comlog design on her sleeve. The farcaster portal winked out. A warm breeze blew spice scents to us.

Gladstone touched her sleeve again, glanced skyward, and nodded. 'I'm sorry for the inconvenience, Brawne. Kastrop-Rauxel has no datasphere or sats of any kind. Now please go ahead with what you were saying. What kind of information have you come across?'

I looked around at the empty grasslands. 'Nothing to warrant this security . . . probably. I've just discovered that the TechnoCore seems very interested in Hyperion. They've also built some sort of analog to Old Earth . . . an entire world!'

If I expected shock or surprise I was disappointed. Gladstone nodded. 'Yes. We know about the Old Earth analog.'

I was shocked. 'Then why hasn't it even been announced? If the Core can rebuild Old Earth, a lot of people would be interested.'

Gladstone began walking and I strolled with her, walking faster to keep up with her long-legged strides. 'Brawne, it would not be in the Hegemony's interest to announce it. Our best human intelligence sources have no idea why the Core is doing such a thing. They have offered no insight. The best policy now is to wait. What information do you have about Hyperion?'

I had no idea whether I could trust Meina Gladstone, old times or not. But I knew that if I was going to get information I would have to give some.

'They built an analog reconstruction of an Old Earth poet,' I said, 'and they seem obsessed with keeping any information about Hyperion away from him.'

Gladstone picked a long stem of grass and sucked on it. 'The John Keats cybrid.'

'Yes.' I was careful not to show surprise this time. 'I know that Dad was pushing hard to get Protectorate status for Hyperion. If the Core has some special interest in the place, they may have had something to do . . . may have manipulated . . .'

'His apparent suicide?'

'Yeah?'

The wind moved gold grass in waves. Something very small scurried away in the stalks at our feet. 'It is not beyond the realm of possibility, Brawne. But there was absolutely no evidence. Tell me what this cybrid is going to do.'

'First tell me why the Core is so interested in Hyperion.'

The older woman spread her hands. 'If we knew that, Brawne, I would sleep much easier nights. As far as we know, the TechnoCore has been obsessed with Hyperion for centuries. When CEO Yevshensky allowed King Billy of Asquith to recolonize the planet, it almost precipitated a true secession of AIs from the Web. Recently the establishment of our fatline transmitter there brought about a similar crisis.'

'But the AIs didn't secede.'

'No, Brawne, it appears that, for whatever reason, they need us almost as badly as we need them.'

'But if they're so interested in Hyperion, why don't they allow it into the Web so they can go there themselves?'

Gladstone ran a hand through her hair. The bronze clouds far above rippled in what must be a fantastic jet stream. 'They are adamant about Hyperion not being admitted to the Web,' she said. 'It is an interesting paradox. Tell me what the cybrid is going to do.'

'First tell me why the Core is obsessed with Hyperion.'

'We do not know for sure.'

'Best guess then.'

CEO Gladstone removed the stem of grass from her mouth and re-garded it. 'We believe that the Core is embarked on a truly incredible project which would allow them to predict . . . everything. To handle every variable of space, time, and history as a quantum of manageable information.'

'Their Ultimate Intelligence Project,' I said, knowing that I was being careless and not caring.

This time CEO Gladstone did register shock. 'How do you know about that?'

'What does that project have to do with Hyperion?'

Gladstone sighed. 'We don't know for sure, Brawne. But we do know that there is an anomaly on Hyperion which they have not been able to factor into their predictive analyses. Do you know about the so-called Time Tombs that the Shrike Church holds holy?'

'Sure. They've been off limits to tourists for a while.'

'Yes. Because of an accident to a researcher there a few decades ago, our scientists have confirmed that the anti-entropic fields around the Tombs are not merely a protection against time's erosive effects as has been widely believed.'

'What are they?'

'The remnants of a field . . . or force . . . which has actually propelled the Tombs and their contents backward in time from some distant future.'

'Contents?' I managed. 'But the Tombs are empty. Ever since they were discovered.'

'Empty now,' said Meina Gladstone. 'But there is evidence that they were full . . . will be full . . . when they open. In our near future.'

I stared at her. 'How near?'

Her dark eyes remained soft but the movement of her head was final. 'I've told you too much already, Brawne. You are forbidden to repeat it. We'll ensure that silence if necessary.'

I hid my own confusion by finding a piece of grass to strip for chewing. 'All right,' I said. 'What's going to come out of the Tombs? Aliens? Bombs? Some sort of reverse time capsules?'

Gladstone smiled tightly. 'If we knew that, Brawne, we would be ahead of the Core, and we are not.' The smile disappeared. 'One hypothesis is that the Tombs relate to some future war. A settling of future scores by rearranging the past, perhaps.'

'A war between who, for Chrissakes?'

She opened her hands again. 'We need to be getting back, Brawne. Would you please tell me what the Keats cybrid is going to do now?'

I looked down and then back up to meet her steady gaze. I couldn't trust anyone, but the Core and the Shrike Church already knew Johnny's plans. If this was a three-sided game, perhaps each side should know in case there was a good guy in the bunch. 'He's going to invest all consciousness in the cybrid,' I said rather clumsily. 'He's going to become human, M. Gladstone, and then go to Hyperion. I'm going with him.'

The CEO of the Senate and All Thing, chief officer for a government which spanned almost two hundred worlds and billions of people, stared at me in silence for a long moment. Then she said, 'He plans to go with the Templar ship on the pilgrimage then.'

'Yes.'

'No,' said Meina Gladstone.

'What do you mean?'

'I mean that the *Sequoia Sempervirens* will not be allowed to leave Hegemony space. There will be no pilgrimage unless the Senate decides it is in *our* interest.' Her voice was iron-hard.

'Johnny and I'll go by spinship,' I said. 'The pilgrimage is a loser's game anyway.'

'No,' she said. 'There will be no more civilian spinships to Hyperion for some time.'

The word 'civilian' tipped me. 'War?'

Gladstone's lips were tight. She nodded. 'Before most spinships could reach the region.'

'A war with . . . the Ousters?'

'Initially. View it as a way to force the issue between the TechnoCore and ourselves, Brawne. We will either have to incorporate the Hyperion system into the Web to allow it FORCE protection, or it will fall to a race which despises and distrusts the Core and all AIs.'

I didn't mention Johnny's comment that the Core had been in touch with the Ousters. I said, 'A way to force the issue. Fine. But who manipulated the Ousters into attacking?'

Gladstone looked at me. If her face was Lincolnesque at that moment, then Old Earth's Lincoln was one tough son of a bitch. 'It's time to get back, Brawne. You appreciate how important it is that none of this information gets out.'

'I appreciate the fact that you wouldn't have told me unless you had a reason to,' I said. 'I don't know who you want the stuff to go to, but I know I'm a messenger, not a confidante.'

'Don't underestimate our resolve to keep this classified, Brawne.'

I laughed. 'Lady, I wouldn't underestimate your resolve in anything.'

Meina Gladstone gestured for me to step through the farcaster portal first.

'I know a way we can discover what the Core is up to,' said Johnny as we rode alone in a rented jetboat on Mare Infinitus. 'But it would be dangerous.'

'So what else is new?'

'I'm serious. We should only attempt it if we feel that it is imperative to understand what the Core fears from Hyperion.'

'I do.'

'We will need an operative. Someone who is an artist in datumplane operations. Someone smart but not so smart that they won't take a chance. And someone who would risk everything and keep the secret just for the ultimate in cyberpuke pranks.'

I grinned at Johnny. 'I've got just the man.'

BB lived alone in a cheap apartment at the base of a cheap tower in a cheap TC^2 neighborhood. But there was nothing cheap about the hardware that filled most of the space in the four-room flat. Most of BB's salary for the past standard decade had gone into state-of-the art cyberpuke toys.

I started by saying that we wanted him to do something illegal. BB said that, as a public employee, he couldn't consider such a thing. He asked what the thing was. Johnny began to explain. BB leaned forward and I saw the old cyberpuke gleam in his eyes from our college days. I half expected him to try to dissect Johnny right there just to see how a cybrid worked. Then Johnny got to the interesting part and BB's gleam turned into a sort of green glow.

'When I self-destruct my AI persona,' said Johnny, 'the shift to cybrid consciousness will take only nanoseconds, but during that time my section of the Core perimeter defenses will drop. The security phages will fill the gap before too many more nanoseconds pass, but during the time . . .'

'Entry to the Core,' whispered BB, his eyes glowing like some antique VDT.

'It would be *very* dangerous,' stressed Johnny. 'To my knowledge, no human operator has ever penetrated Core periphery.'

BB rubbed his upper lip. 'There's a legend that Cowboy Gibson did it before the Core seceded,' he mumbled. 'But nobody believes it. And Cowboy disappeared.'

'Even if you penetrate,' said Johnny, 'there would be insufficient time to access except for the fact that I have the data coordinates.'

'Fan-fucking-tastic,' whispered BB. He turned back to his console and reached for his shunt. 'Let's do it.'

'Now?' I said. Even Johnny looked taken aback.

'Why wait?' BB clicked in his shunt and attached metacortex leads, but left the deck idling. 'Are we doing this, or what?'

I went over next to Johnny on the couch and took his hand. His skin was cool. He showed no expression now but I could imagine what it must be like to be facing imminent destruction of one's personality and previous existence. Even if the transfer worked, the human with the John Keats persona would not be 'Johnny'.

'He's right,' said Johnny. 'Why wait?'

I kissed him. 'All right,' I said. 'I'm going in with BB.'

'No!' Johnny squeezed my hand. 'You can't help and the danger would be terrible.'

I heard my own voice, as implacable as Meina Gladstone's. 'Perhaps. But I can't ask BB to do this if I won't. And I won't leave you in there alone.' I squeezed his hand a final time and went over to sit by BB at the console. 'How do I connect with this fucking thing, BB?'

You've read all the cyberpuke stuff. You know all about the terrible beauty of datumplane, the three-dimensional highways with their landscapes of black ice and neon perimeters and Day-Glo Strange Loops and shimmering skyscrapers of data blocks under hovering clouds of AI presence. I saw all of it riding piggyback on BB's carrier wave. It was almost too much. Too intense. Too terrifying. I could *hear* the black threats of the hulking security phages; I could *smell* death on the breath of the counterthrust tapeworm viruses even through the ice screens; I could *feel* the weight of the AIs' wrath above us – we were insects under elephants' feet – and we hadn't even *done* anything yet except travel approved dataways on a logged-in access errand BB had dreamed up, some homework stuff for his Flow Control Records and Statistics job.

And I was wearing stick-on leads, seeing things in a datumplane version of fuzzy black and white TV while Johnny and BB were viewing full stimsim holo, as it were.

I don't know how they took it.

'OK,' whispered BB in some datumplane equivalent of a whisper, 'we're here.'

'Where?' All I saw was an infinite maze of bright lights and even brighter shadows, ten thousand cities arrayed in four dimensions.

'Core periphery,' whispered BB. 'Hang on. It's about time.'

I had no arms to hang on with and nothing physical in this universe to grasp, but I concentrated on the waveform shades that were our data truck and *clung*.

Johnny died then.

I've seen a nuclear explosion firsthand. When Dad was a senator he took Mom and me to Olympus Command School to see a FORCE demonstration. For the last course the audience viewing pod was farcast to some godforsaken world . . . Armaghast, I think . . . and a FORCE:ground recon platoon fired a clean tactical nuke at a pretend adversary some nine klicks away. The viewing pod was shielded with a class ten containment field, polarized, the nuke only a fifty-kiloton field tactical, but I'll never forget the blast, the shock wave rocking the eighty-ton pod like a leaf on its repellers, the physical shock of light so obscenely bright that it polarized our field to midnight and still brought tears to our eyes and clamored to get in.

This was worse.

A section of datumplane seemed to flash and then to implode on itself, reality flushed down a drain of pure black.

'Hang on!' BB screamed against datumplane static that rasped at my bones and we were whirling, tumbling, sucked into the vacuum like insects in an oceanic vortex.

Somehow, incredibly, impossibly, black-armored phages thrust toward us through the din and madness. BB avoided one, turned the other's acid membranes against itself. We were being sucked into something colder and blacker than any void in our reality could ever be.

'There!' called BB, his voice analog almost lost in the tornado rush of ripping datasphere.

There what? Then I saw it: a thin line of yellow rippling in the turbulence like a cloth banner in a hurricane. BB rolled us, found our own wave to carry us against the storm, matched coordinates that danced past me too quickly to see, and we were riding the yellow band into . . .

. . . into what? Frozen fountains of fireworks. Transparent mountain ranges of data, endless glaciers of ROMworks, access ganglia spreading like fissures, iron clouds of semisentient internal process bubbles, glowing pyramids of primary source stuff, each guarded by lakes of black ice and armies of black-pulse phages.

'Shit,' I whispered to no one in particular.

BB followed the yellow band down, in, through. I felt a *connection* as if someone had suddenly given us a great mass to carry.

'Got it!' screamed BB, and suddenly there was a sound louder and larger than the maelstrom of noise surrounding and consuming us. It was neither klaxon nor siren, but it was both in its tone of warning and aggression.

We were climbing out of it all. I could see a vague wall of gray through the brilliant chaos and somehow knew it to be the periphery, the vacuum dwindling but still breaching the wall like a shrinking black stain. We were climbing out.

But not quickly enough.

The phages hit us from five sides. During the twelve years I've been an investigator I've been shot once, knifed twice. I'd had more than this one rib broken. This hurt more than all that combined. BB was fighting and climbing at the same time.

My contribution to the emergency was to scream. I felt cold claws on us, pulling us down, back into the brightness and noise and chaos. BB was using some program, some formula of enchantment to fight them off. But not enough. I could feel the blows slamming home – not against me primarily, but connecting to the matrix analog that was BB.

We were sinking back. Inexorable forces had us in tow. Suddenly I felt Johnny's presence and it was as if a huge, strong hand had scooped us up, lifted us through the periphery wall an instant before the stain snapped our lifeline to existence and the defensive field crashed together like steel teeth.

We moved at impossible speed down congested dataways, passing datumplane couriers and other operator analogs like an EMV ripping past oxcarts. Then we were approaching a slow-time gate, leapfrogging grid-locked exiting operator analogs in some four-dimensional high jump.

I felt the inevitable nausea of transition as we came out of the matrix. Light burned my retinas. *Real* light. Then the pain washed in and I slumped over the console and groaned.

'Come on, Brawne.' It was Johnny – or someone just like Johnny – helping me to my feet and moving us both toward the door.

'BB,' I gasped.

'No.'

I opened aching eyes long enough to see BB Surbringer draped across his console. His Stetson had fallen off and rolled to the floor. BB's head had exploded, spattering most of the console with gray and red. His mouth was open and a thick white foam still issued from it. It looked like his eyes had melted.

Johnny caught me, half lifted me. 'We have to go,' he whispered. 'Someone will be here any minute.'

I closed my eyes and let him take me away from there.

*

I awoke to dim red light and the sound of water dripping. I smelled sewage, mildew, and the ozone of uninsulated power cables. I opened one eye.

We were in a low space more cave than room with cables snaking from a shattered ceiling and pools of water on the slime-caked tiles. The red light came from somewhere beyond the cave – a maintenance access shaft perhaps, or automech tunnel. I moaned softly. Johnny was there, moving from the rough bedroll of blankets to my side. His face was darkened with grease or dirt and there was at least one fresh cut.

'Where are we?'

He touched my cheek. His other arm went around my shoulders and helped me to a sitting position. The awful view shifted and tilted and for a moment I thought I was going to be sick. Johnny helped me drink water from a plastic tumbler.

'Dregs' Hive,' said Johnny.

I'd guessed even before I was fully conscious. Dregs' Hive is the deepest pit on Lusus, a no man's land of mech tunnels and illegal burrows occupied by half the Web's outcasts and outlaws. It was in Dregs' Hive that I'd been shot several years ago and still bore the laser scar above my left hipbone.

I held the tumbler out for more water. Johnny fetched some from a steel therm and came back. I panicked for a second as I fumbled in my tunic pocket and on my belt: Dad's automatic was gone. Johnny held the weapon up and I relaxed, accepting the cup and drinking thirstily. 'BB?' I said, hoping for a moment that it had all been a terrible hallucination.

Johnny shook his head. 'There were defenses that neither of us had anticipated. BB's incursion was brilliant, but he couldn't outfight Core omega phages. But half the operators in datumplane felt echoes of the battle. BB is already the stuff of legend.'

'Fucking great,' I said and gave a laugh that sounded suspiciously like the beginning of a sob. 'The stuff of legend. And BB's dead. For fuck-all nothing.'

Johnny's arm was tight around me. 'Not for nothing, Brawne. He made the grab. And passed the data to me before he died.'

I managed to sit fully upright and to look at Johnny. He seemed the same – the same soft eyes, same hair, same voice. But something was subtly different, deeper. More human? 'You?' I said. 'Did you make the transfer? Are you . . .'

'Human?' John Keats smiled at me. 'Yes, Brawne. Or as close to human as someone forged in the Core could ever be.'

'But you remember . . . me . . . BB . . . what's happened.'

'Yes. And I remember first looking into Chapman's Homer. And my brother Tom's eyes as he hemorrhaged in the night. And Severn's kind voice when I was too weak to open my own eyes to face my fate. And our night in Piazza di Spagna when I touched your lips and imagined Fanny's cheek against mine. I remember, Brawne.'

For a second I was confused, and then hurt, but then he set his palm against my cheek and *he* touched *me*, there was no one else, and I understood. I closed my eyes. 'Why are we here?' I whispered against his shirt.

'I couldn't risk using a farcaster. The Core could trace us at once. I considered the spaceport but you were in no condition to travel. I chose the Dregs'.'

I nodded against him. 'They'll try to kill you.'

'Yes.'

'Are the local cops after us? The Hegemony police? Transit cops?'

'No, I don't think so. The only ones who've challenged us so far were two bands of goondas and some of the Dregs' dwellers.'

I opened my eyes. 'What happened with the goondas?' There were more deadly hoodlums and contract killers in the Web but I'd never run across any.

Johnny held up Dad's automatic and smiled.

'I don't remember anything after BB,' I said.

'You were injured by the phage backlash. You could walk but we were the cause of more than a few odd looks in the Concourse.'

'I bet. Tell me about what BB discovered. Why is the Core obsessed with Hyperion?'

'Eat first,' said Johnny. 'It's been more than twenty-eight hours.' He crossed the dripping width of the cave room and returned with a self-heating packet. It was basic holo fanatic fare – flash-dried and reheated cloned beef, potatoes which had never seen soil, and carrots which looked like some sort of deep-sea slugs. Nothing had ever tasted so good.

'OK,' I said, 'tell me.'

'The TechnoCore has been divided into three groups for as long as the Core has existed,' said Johnny. 'The Stables are the old-line AIs, some of them dating back to pre-Mistake days; at least one of them gained sentience in the First Information Age. The Stables argue that a certain level of symbiosis is necessary between humanity and the Core. They've promoted the Ultimate Intelligence Project as a way to avoid rash decisions, to delay until all variables can be factored. The Volatiles are the force behind the Secession three centuries ago. The Volatiles have done conclusive studies that show how humankind's usefulness is past and from this point on human beings constitute a threat to the Core. They advocate immediate and total extinction.'

'Extinction,' I said. After a moment I asked, 'Can they do it?'

'Of humans in the Web, yes,' said Johnny. 'Core intelligences not only create the infrastructure for Hegemony society but are necessary for everything from FORCE deployment to the failsafes on stockpiled nuclear and plasma arsenals.'

'Did you know about this when you were . . . in the Core?'

'No,' said Johnny. 'As a pseudo-poet cybrid retrieval project, I was a freak, a pet, a partial thing allowed to roam the Web the way a pet is let out of the house each day. I had no idea there were three camps of AI influence.'

'Three camps,' I said. 'What's the third? And where does Hyperion come in?'

'Between the Stables and the Volatiles are the Ultimates. For the past five centuries the Ultimates have been obsessed with the UI Project. The existence or extinction of the human race is of interest to them only in how it applies to the project. To this date, they have been a force for moderation, an ally of the Stables, because it is their perception that such reconstruction and retrieval projects as the Old Earth experiment are necessary to the culmination of the UI.

'Recently, however, the Hyperion issue has caused the Ultimates to move toward the Volatiles' views. Since Hyperion was explored four centuries ago, the Core has been concerned and nonplussed. It was immediately obvious that the so-called Time Tombs were artifacts launched backward in time from a point at least ten thousand years in the galaxy's future. More disturbing, however, is the fact that Core predictive formulae have *never* been able to factor the Hyperion variable.

'Brawne, to understand this, you must realize how much the Core relies upon prediction. Already, without UI input, the Core knows the details of the physical, human, and AI future to a margin of 98.9995 percent for a period of at least two centuries. The AI Advisory Council to the All Thing with its vague, delphic utterances – considered so indispensable by humans – is a joke. The Core drops tidbits of revelations to the Hegemony when it serves the Core's purposes – sometimes to aid the Volatiles, sometimes the Stables, but *always* to please the Ultimates.

'Hyperion is a rent in the entire predictive fabric of the Core's existence. It is the penultimate oxymoron – a nonfactorable variable. Impossible as it seems, Hyperion appears to be exempt from the laws of physics, history, human psychology, and AI prediction as practiced by the Core.

'The result has been two futures – two *realities* if you will – one in which the Shrike scourge soon to be released on the Web and interstellar human- ity is a weapon from the Core-dominated future, a retroactive first strike from the Volatiles who rule the galaxy millennia hence. The other reality sees the Shrike invasion, the coming interstellar war, and the other pro- ducts of the Time Tombs' opening as a *human* fist struck back through time, a final, twilight effort by the Ousters, ex-colonials, and other small bands of humans who escaped the Volatiles' extinction programs.'

Water dripped on tile. Somewhere in the tunnels nearby a mech cauter- izer's warning siren echoed from ceramic and stone. I leaned against the wall and stared at Johnny.

'Interstellar war,' I said. 'Both scenarios demand an interstellar war?'

'Yes. There is no escaping that.'

'Can both Core groups be wrong in their prediction?'

'No. What happens on Hyperion is problematic, but the disruption in the Web and elsewhere is quite clear. The Ultimates use this knowledge as the prime argument for hurrying the next step in Core evolution.'

'And what did BB's stolen data show about us, Johnny?'

Johnny smiled, touched my hand, but did not hold it. 'It showed that I am somehow part of the Hyperion unknown. Their creation of a Keats cybrid was a terrible gamble. Only my apparent lack of success as a Keats analog allowed the Stables to preserve me. When I made up my mind to go to Hyperion, the Volatiles killed me with the clear intention of obliterating my AI existence if my cybrid again made that decision.'

'You did. What happened?'

'They failed. In the Core's limitless arrogance, they failed to take two things into account. First, that I might invest all consciousness in my cybrid and thus change the nature of the Keats analog. Second, that I would go to you.'

'*Me!*'

He took my hand. 'Yes, Brawne. It seems that you also are part of the Hyperion unknown.'

I shook my head. Realizing that there was a numbness in my scalp above and behind my left ear, I raised my hand, half expecting to find damage from the datumplane fight. Instead, my fingers encountered the plastic of a neural shunt socket.

I jerked my other hand from Johnny's grasp and stared at him in horror. He'd had me wired while I was unconscious.

Johnny held up both hands, palms toward me. 'I had to, Brawne. It may be necessary for the survival of both of us.'

I made a fist. 'You fucking low-life son of a bitch. Why do *I* need to interface directly, you lying bastard?'

'Not with the Core,' Johnny said softly. 'With me.'

'You?' My arm and fist quivered with the anticipation of smashing his vat-cloned face. 'You!' I sneered. 'You're human now, remember?'

'Yes. But certain cybrid functions remain. Do you remember when I touched your hand several days ago and brought us to datumplane?'

I stared at him. 'I'm not going to datumplane again.'

'No. Nor am I. But I may need to relay incredible amounts of data to you within a very short period of time. I brought you to a black market surgeon in the Dregs' last night. She implanted a Schrön loop.'

'Why?' The Schrön loop was tiny, no larger than my thumbnail, and very expensive. It held countless field-bubble memories, each capable of holding near infinite bits of information. Schrön loops could not be accessed by the biological carrier and thus were used for courier purposes. A man or woman could carry AI personalities or entire planetary dataspheres in a Schrön loop. Hell, a *dog* could carry all that.

'Why?' I said again, wondering if Johnny or some forces behind Johnny were using me as such a courier. 'Why?'

Johnny moved closer and put his hand around my fist. 'Trust me, Brawne.'

I don't think I'd trusted anyone since Dad blew his brains out twenty years ago and Mom retreated into the pure selfishness of her seclusion. There was no reason in the universe to trust Johnny now.

But I did.

I relaxed my fist and took his hand.

'All right,' said Johnny. 'Finish your meal and we'll get busy trying to save our lives.'

Weapons and drugs were the two easiest things to buy in Dregs' Hive. We spent the last of Johnny's considerable stash of black marks to buy weapons.

By 2200 hours, we each wore whiskered titan-poly body armor. Johnny had a goonda's mirror-black helmet and I wore a FORCE-surplus command mask. Johnny's power gauntlets were massive and a bright red. I wore osmosis gloves with killing trim. Johnny carried an Ouster hellwhip captured on Bressia and had tucked a laser wand in his belt. Along with Dad's automatic, I now carried a Steiner-Ginn mini-gun on a gyroed waist brace. It was slaved to my command visor and I could keep both hands free while firing.

Johnny and I looked at each other and began giggling. When the laughter stopped there was a long silence.

'Are you sure the Shrike Temple here on Lusus is our best chance?' I asked for the third or fourth time.

'We can't farcast,' said Johnny. 'All the Core has to do is record a malfunction and we're dead. We can't even take an elevator from the lower levels. We'll have to find unmonitored stairways and climb the hundred and twenty floors. The best chance to make the Temple is straight down the Concourse Mall.'

'Yes, but will the Shrike Church people take us in?'

Johnny shrugged, a strangely insectoid gesture in his combat outfit. The voice through the goonda helmet was metallic. 'They're the only group which has a vested interest in our survival. And the only ones with enough political pull to shield us from the Hegemony while finding transit for us to Hyperion.'

I pushed up my visor. 'Meina Gladstone said that no future pilgrimage flights to Hyperion would be allowed.'

The dome of mirror black nodded judiciously. 'Well, fuck Meina Gladstone,' said my poet lover.

I took a breath and walked to the opening of our niche, our cave, our last sanctuary. Johnny came up behind me. Body armor rubbed against body armor. 'Ready, Brawne?'

I nodded, brought the mini-gun around on its pivot, and started to leave.

Johnny stopped me with a touch. 'I love you, Brawne.'

I nodded, still tough. I forgot that my visor was up and he could see my tears.

*

The Hive is awake all twenty-eight hours of the day, but through some tradition, Third Shift was the quietest, the least populated. We would have had a better chance at the height of First Shift rush hour along the pedestrian causeways. But if the goondas and thuggees were waiting for us, the death toll of civilians would have been staggering.

It took us more than three hours to climb our way to Concourse Mall, not up a single staircase but along an endless series of mech corridors, abandoned access verticals swept clean by the Luddite riots eighty years ago, and a final stairway that was more rust than metal. We exited onto a delivery corridor less than half a klick from the Shrike Temple.

'I can't believe it was so easy,' I whispered to him on intercom.

'They are probably concentrating people on the spaceport and private farcaster clusters.'

We took the least exposed walkway onto the Concourse, thirty meters below the first shopping level and four hundred meters below the roof. The Shrike Temple was an ornate, free-stranding structure now less than half a klick away. A few off-hour shoppers and joggers glanced at us and then moved quickly away. I had no doubt that the Mall police were being paged, but I'd be surprised if they showed up too quickly.

A gang of brightly painted street thugs exploded from a lift shaft, hollering and whooping. They carried pulse-knives, chains, and power gauntlets. Startled, Johnny wheeled toward them with the hellwhip sending out a score of targeting beams. The mini-gun whir-whirred out of my hands, shifting from aiming point to aiming point as I moved my eyes.

The gang of seven kids skidded to a halt, held up their hands, and backed away, eyes wide. They dropped into the lift shaft and were gone.

I looked at Johnny. Black mirrors looked back. Neither of us laughed.

We crossed to the northbound shopping lane. The few pedestrians scurried for open shopfronts. We were less than a hundred meters from the Temple stairs. I could actually hear my heartbeat in the FORCE helmet earphones. We were within fifty meters of the stairs. As if called, an acolyte or priest of some sort appeared at the ten-meter door of the Temple and watched us approach. Thirty meters. If anyone was going to intercept us, they would have done it before this.

I turned toward Johnny to say something funny. At least twenty beams and half that many projectiles hit us at once. The outer layer of the titan-poly exploded outward, deflecting most of the projectile energy in the counterblast. The mirrored surface beneath bounced most of the killing light. Most of it.

Johnny was flung off his feet by the impact. I went to one knee and let the mini-gun train on the laser source.

Ten stories up along the residential Hive wall. My visor opaqued. Body armor burned off in a steam of reflective gas. The mini-gun sounded precisely like the kind of chainsaw they used in history holodramas. Ten stories up, a five-meter section of balcony and wall disintegrated in a cloud of explosive flechettes and armor-piercing rounds.

Three heavy slugs struck me from behind.

I landed on my palms, silenced the mini-gun, and swiveled. There were at least a dozen of them on each level, moving quickly in precise combat choreography. Johnny had reached his knees and was firing the hellwhip in orchestrated bursts of light, working his way through the rainbow to beat bounce defenses.

One of the running figures exploded into flame as the shop window behind it turned to molten glass and spattered fifteen meters onto the Concourse. Two more men came up over the level railings and I sent them back with a burst from the mini-gun.

An open skimmer came down from the rafters, repellers laboring as it banked around pylons. Rocket fire slammed into concrete around Johnny and me. Shopfronts vomited a billion shards of glass over us. I looked, blinked twice, targeted, and fired. The skimmer lurched sideways, struck an escalator with a dozen cowering civilians on it, and tumbled in a mass of twisting metal and exploding ordnance. I saw one shopper leap in flames to the Hive floor eighty meters below.

'Left!' shouted Johnny over the tight beam intercom.

Four men in combat armor had dropped from an upper level using personal lift packs. The polymerized chameleon armor labored to keep up with the shifting background but only succeeded in turning each man into a brilliant kaleidoscope of reflections. One moved inside the sweep arch of my mini-gun to neutralize me while the other three went for Johnny.

He came in with a pulse-blade, ghetto style. I let it chew at my armor, knowing it would get through to forearm flesh but using it to buy the second I needed. I got it. I killed the man with the rigid edge of my gauntlet and swept the mini-gun fire into the three worrying Johnny.

Their armor went rigid and I used the gun to sweep them backward like someone hosing down a littered sidewalk. Only one of the men got to his feet before I blew them all off the level overhang.

Johnny was down again. Parts of his chest armor were gone, melted away. I smelled cooking flesh but saw no mortal wounds. I half crouched, lifted him.

'Leave me, Brawne. Run. The stairs.' The tightbeam was breaking up.

'Fuck off,' I said, getting my left arm around him enough to support him while allowing room for the mini-gun to track. 'I'm still getting paid to be your bodyguard.'

They were sniping at us from both walls of the Hive, the rafters, and the shopping levels above us. I counted at least twenty bodies on the walkways; about half were brightly clad civilians. The power assist on the left leg of my armor was grinding. Straight-legged, I awkwardly pulled us another ten meters toward the Temple stairs. There were several Shrike priests at the head of the stairs now, seemingly oblivious to the gunfire all around them.

'Above!'

I swiveled, targeted, and fired in one moment, hearing the gun go empty after one burst and seeing the second skimmer get off its missiles in the instant before it became a thousand pieces of hurtling, unrelated metal and torn flesh. I dropped Johnny heavily to the pavement and fell on him, trying to cover his exposed flesh with my body.

The missiles detonated simultaneously, several in airburst and at least two burrowing. Johnny and I were lifted into the air and hurled fifteen or twenty meters down the pitching walkway. Good thing. The alloy and ferroconcrete pedestrian strip where we had been a second before burned, bubbled, sagged, and tumbled down onto the flaming walkway below. There was a natural moat there now, a gap between most of the other ground troops and us.

I rose, slapped away the useless mini-gun and mount, pulled off useless shards of my own armor, and lifted Johnny in both arms. His helmet had been blown off and his face was very bad. Blood seeped through a score of gaps in his armor. His right arm and left foot had been blown off. I turned and began carrying him up the Shrike Temple stairs.

There were sirens and security skimmers filling the Concourse flyspace now. The goondas on the upper levels and far side of the tumbled walkway ran for cover. Two of the commandos who had dropped on lift packs ran up the stairs after me. I did not turn. I had to lift my straight and useless left leg for every step. I knew that I had been seriously burned on my back and side and there were shrapnel wounds elsewhere.

The skimmers whooped and circled but avoided the Temple steps. Gun-fire rattled up and down the Mall. I could hear metal-shod footsteps coming rapidly behind me. I managed another three steps. Twenty steps above, impossibly far away, the bishop stood amid a hundred Temple priests.

I made another step and looked down at Johnny. One eye was open, staring up at me. The other was closed with blood and swollen tissue. 'It's all right,' I whispered, aware for the first time that my own helmet was gone. 'It's all right. We're almost there.' I managed one more step.

The two men in bright black combat armor blocked my way. Both had lifted visors streaked with deflection scars and their faces were very hard.

'Put him down, bitch, and maybe we'll let you live.'

I nodded tiredly, too tired to take another step or do anything but stand there and hold him in both arms. Johnny's blood dripped on white stone.

'I said, put the son of a bitch down and . . .'

I shot both of them, one in the left eye and one in the right, never lifting Dad's automatic from where I held it under Johnny's body.

They fell away. I managed another step. And then another. I rested a bit and then lifted my foot for another.

At the top of the stairs the group of black and red robes parted. The doorway was very tall and very dark. I did not look back but I could hear from the noise behind us that the crowd on the Concourse was very large. The bishop walked by my side as I went through the doors and into the dimness.

I laid Johnny on the cool floor. Robes rustled around us. I pulled my own armor off where I could, then batted at Johnny's. It was fused to his flesh in several places. I touched his burned cheek with my good hand. 'I'm sorry . . .'

Johnny's head stirred slightly and his eye opened. He lifted his bare left hand to touch my cheek, my hair, the back of my head. 'Fanny . . .'

I felt him die then. I also felt the surge as his hand found the neural shunt, the white-light warmth of the surge to the Schrön loop as everything Johnny Keats ever was or would be exploded into me; almost, almost it was like his orgasm inside me two nights earlier, the surge and throb and sudden warmth and stillness after, with the echo of sensation there.

I lowered him to the floor and let the acolytes remove the body, taking it out to show the crowd and the authorities and the ones who waited to know.

I let them take me away.

I spent two weeks in a Shrike Temple recovery creche. Burns healed, scars removed, alien metal extracted, skin grafted, flesh regrown, nerves rewoven. And still I hurt.

Everyone except the Shrike priests lost interest in me. The Core made sure that Johnny was dead; that his presence in the Core had left no trace; that his cybrid was dead.

The authorities took my statement, revoked my license, and covered things up as best they could. The Web press reported that a battle between Dregs' Level Hive gangs had erupted onto the Concourse Mall. Numerous gang members and innocent bystanders were killed. The police contained it.

A week before word came that the Hegemony would allow the *Yggdrasill* to sail with pilgrims for the war zone near Hyperion, I used a Temple farcaster to 'cast to Renaissance Vector where I spent an hour alone in the archives there.

The papers were in vacuum-press so I could not touch them. The handwriting was Johnny's; I had seen his writing before. The parchment was yellow and brittle with age. There were two fragments. The first read:

The day is gone, and all its sweets are gone!
  Sweet voice, sweet lips, soft hand, and softer breast,
Warm breath, light whisper, tender semi-tone,
  Bright eyes, accomplished shape, and languorous waist!
Faded the flower and all its budded charms,
  Faded the sight of beauty from my eyes,
Faded the shape of beauty from my arms,
  Faded the voice, warmth, whiteness, paradise—
Vanished unseasonably at shut of eve,
  When the dusk holiday – or holinight—
Of fragrant-curtained love begins to weave

The woof of darkness thick, for hid delight;
But, as I've read love's missal through today,
He'll let me sleep, seeing I fast and pray.

The second fragment was in a wilder hand and on rougher paper, as if slashed across a notepad in haste:

This living hand, now warm and capable
Of earnest grasping, would, if it were cold
And in the icy silence of the tomb,
So haunt thy days and chill thy dreaming nights
That thou wouldst wish thine own heart dry of blood
So in my veins red life might stream again,
And thou be conscience-calm'd – see here it is—
I hold it towards you

I'm pregnant. I think that Johnny knew it. I don't know for sure.

I'm pregnant twice. Once with Johnny's child and once with the Schrön-loop memory of what he was. I don't know if the two are meant to be linked. It will be months before the child is born and only days before I face the Shrike.

But I remember those minutes after Johnny's torn body was taken out to the crowd and before I was led away for help. They were all there in the darkness, hundreds of the priests and acolytes and exorcists and ostiaries and worshipers . . . and as one voice they began to chant, there in that red dimness under the revolving sculpture of the Shrike, and their voices echoed in Gothic vaults. And what they chanted went something like this:

'BLESSED BE SHE

BLESSED BE THE MOTHER OF OUR SALVATION

BLESSED BE THE INSTRUMENT OF OUR ATONEMENT

BLESSED BE THE BRIDE OF OUR CREATION

BLESSED BE SHE'

I was injured and in shock. I didn't understand it then. I don't understand it now.

But I know that, when the time arrives and the Shrike comes, Johnny and I will face it together.

It was long after dark. The tramcar rode between stars and ice. The group sat in silence, the only sound the creak of cable.

After a time had passed, Lenar Hoyt said to Brawne Lamia, 'You also carry the cruciform.'

Lamia looked at the priest.

Colonel Kassad leaned toward the woman. 'Do you think Het Masteen was the Templar who had spoken to Johnny?'

'Possibly,' said Brawne Lamia. 'I never found out.'

Kassad did not blink. 'Were you the one who killed Masteen?'

'No.'

Martin Silenus stretched and yawned. 'We have a few hours before sunrise,' he said. 'Anyone else interested in getting some sleep?'

Several heads nodded.

'I'll stay up to keep watch,' said Fedmahn Kassad. 'I'm not tired.'

'I'll keep you company,' said the Consul.

'I'll heat some coffee for the therm,' said Brawne Lamia.

When the others slept, the infant Rachel making soft cooing sounds in her sleep, the other three sat at the windows and watched the stars burn cold and distant in the high night.

SIX

Chronos Keep jutted from the easternmost rim of the great Bridle Range: a grim, baroque heap of sweating stones with three hundred rooms and halls, a maze of lightless corridors leading to deep halls, towers, turrets, balconies overlooking the northern moors, airshafts rising half a kilometer to light and rumored to drop to the world's labyrinth itself, parapets scoured by cold winds from the peaks above, stairways – inside and out – carved from the mountain stone and leading nowhere, stained-glass windows a hundred meters tall set to catch the first rays of solstice sun or the moon on midwinter night, paneless windows the size of a man's fist looking out on nothing in particular, an endless array of bas-relief, grotesque sculptures in half-hidden niches, and more than a thousand gargoyles staring down from eave and parapet, transept and sepulcher, peering down through wood rafters in the great halls and positioned so as to peer in the blood-tinted windows of the northeast face, their winged and hunchbacked shadows moving like grim sundial hours, cast by sunlight in the day and gas-fed torches at night. And everywhere in Chronos Keep, signs of the Shrike Church's long occupation – atonement altars draped in red velvet, hanging and free-standing sculptures of the Avatar with polychrome steel for blades and bloodgems for eyes, more statues of the Shrike carved from the stone of narrow stairways and dark halls so that nowhere in the night would one be free of the fear of touching hands emerging from rock, the sharp curve of blade descending from stone, four arms enveloping in a final embrace. As if in a last measure of ornamentation, a filigree of blood in many of the once occupied halls and rooms, arabesques of red spattered in almost recognizable patterns along walls and tunnel ceilings, bedclothes caked hard with rust-red substance, and a central dining hall filled with the stench of food rotting from a meal abandoned weeks earlier, the floor and table, chairs and wall adorned with blood, stained clothing and shredded robes lying in mute heaps. And everywhere the sound of flies.

'Jolly fucking place, isn't it?' said Martin Silenus, his voice echoing.

Father Hoyt took several steps deeper into the great hall. Afternoon light from the west-facing skylight forty meters above fell in dusty columns. 'It's incredible,' he whispered. 'St Peter's in the New Vatican is nothing like this.'

Martin Silenus laughed. Thick light outlined his cheekbones and satyr's brows. 'This was built for a *living* deity,' he said.

Fedmahn Kassad lowered his travel bag to the floor and cleared his throat. 'Surely this place predates the Shrike Church.'

'It does,' said the Consul. 'But they've occupied it for the past two centuries.'

'It doesn't look too occupied now,' said Brawne Lamia. She held her father's automatic in her left hand.

They had all shouted during their first twenty minutes in the Keep, but the dying echoes, silences, and buzz of flies in the dining hall had reduced them to silence.

'Sad King Billy's androids and bond clones built the goddamn thing,' said the poet. 'Eight local years of labor before the spinships arrived. It was supposed to be the greatest tourist resort in the Web, the jumping-off point for the Time Tombs and the City of Poets. But I suspect that even then the poor schmuck android laborers knew the locals' version of the Shrike story.'

Sol Weintraub stood near an eastern window, holding his daughter up so that soft light fell across her cheek and curled fist. 'All that matters little now,' he said. 'Let's find a corner free of carnage where we can sleep and eat our evening meal.'

'Are we going on tonight?' asked Brawne Lamia.

'To the Tombs?' asked Silenus, showing real surprise for the first time on the voyage. 'You'd go to the Shrike in the dark?'

Lamia shrugged. 'What difference does it make?'

The Consul stood near a leaded glass door leading to a stone balcony and closed his eyes. His body still lurched and balanced to the movement of the tramcar. The night and day of travel above the peaks had blurred together in his mind, lost in the fatigue of almost three days without sleep and his rising tension. He opened his eyes before he dozed off standing up. 'We're tired,' he said. 'We'll stay here tonight and go down in the morning.'

Father Hoyt had gone out onto the narrow ledge of balcony. He leaned on a railing of jagged stone. 'Can we see the Tombs from here?'

'No,' said Silenus. 'They're beyond that rise of hills. But see those white things to the north and west a bit . . . those things gleaming like shards of broken teeth in the sand?'

'Yes.'

'That's the City of Poets. King Billy's original site for Keats and for all things bright and beautiful. The locals say that it's haunted now by headless ghosts.'

'Are you one of them?' asked Lamia.

Martin Silenus turned to say something, looked a moment at the pistol still in her hand, shook his head, and turned away.

Footsteps echoed from an unseen curve of staircase and Colonel Kassad reentered the room. 'There are two small storerooms above the dining hall,' he said. 'They have a section of balcony outside but no other access than this stairway. Easy to defend. The rooms are . . . clean.'

Silenus laughed. 'Does that mean nothing can get at us or that, when something *does* get at us, we'll have no way to get out?'

'Where would we go?' asked Sol Weintraub.

'Where indeed?' said the Consul. He was very tired. He lifted his gear and took one handle of the heavy Möbius cube, waiting for Father Hoyt to lift the other end. 'Let's do what Kassad says. Find a space to spend the night. Let's at least get out of this room. It stinks of death.'

Dinner was the last of their dried rations, some wine from Silenus's last bottle, and some stale cake which Sol Weintraub had brought along to celebrate their last evening together. Rachel was too little to eat the cake, but she took her milk and went to sleep on her stomach on a mat near her father.

Lenar Hoyt removed a small balalaika from his pack and strummed a few chords.

'I didn't know you played,' said Brawne Lamia.

'Poorly.'

The Consul rubbed his eyes. 'I wish we had a piano.'

'You do have one,' said Martin Silenus.

The Consul looked at the poet.

'Bring it here,' said Silenus. 'I'd welcome a Scotch.'

'What are you talking about?' snapped Father Hoyt. 'Make sense.'

'His *ship*,' said Silenus. 'Do you remember our dear, departed Voice of the Bush Masteen telling our Consul friend that *his* secret weapon was that nice Hegemony singleship sitting back at Keats Spaceport? Call it up, Your Consulship. Bring it on in.'

Kassad moved away from the stairway where he had been placing tripbeams. 'The planet's datasphere is dead. The comsats are down. The orbiting FORCE ships are on tightbeam. How is he supposed to call it?'

It was Lamia who spoke. 'A fatline transmitter.'

The Consul moved his stare to her.

'Fatline transmitters are the size of buildings,' said Kassad.

Brawne Lamia shrugged. 'What Masteen said made sense. If I were the Consul . . . if I were one of the few thousand individuals in the entire damn Web to own a singleship . . . *I'd* be damn sure I could fly it in on remote if I needed it. The planet's too primitive to depend on its comm net, the ionosphere's too weak for shortwave, the comsats are the first things to go in a skirmish . . . I'd call it by fatline.'

'And the size?' said the Consul.

Brawne Lamia returned the diplomat's level gaze. 'The Hegemony can't yet build portable fatline transmitters. There are rumors that the Ousters can.'

The Consul smiled. From somewhere there came a scrape and then the sound of metal crashing.

'Stay here,' said Kassad. He removed a deathwand from his tunic, canceled the tripbeams with his tactical comlog, and descended from sight.

'I guess we're under martial law now,' said Silenus when the Colonel was gone. 'Mars ascendant.'

'Shut up,' said Lamia.

'Do you think it's the Shrike?' asked Hoyt.

The Consul made a gesture. 'The Shrike doesn't have to clank around downstairs. It can simply appear . . . *here*.'

Hoyt shook his head. 'I mean the Shrike that has been the cause of everyone's . . . absence. The signs of slaughter here in the Keep.'

'The empty villages might be the result of the evacuation order,' said the Consul. 'No one wants to stay behind to face the Ousters. The SDF forces have been running wild. Much of the carnage could be their doing.'

'With no bodies?' laughed Martin Silenus. 'Wishful thinking. Our absent hosts downstairs dangle now on the Shrike's steel tree. Where, ere long, we too will be.'

'Shut up,' Brawne Lamia said tiredly.

'And if I don't,' grinned the poet, 'will you shoot me, madam?'

'Yes.'

The silence lasted until Colonel Kassad returned. He reactivated the tripbeams and turned to the group seated on packing crates and flowfoam cubes. 'It was nothing. Some carrion birds – harbingers, I think the locals call them – had come in through the broken glass doors in the dining hall and were finishing the feast.'

Silenus chuckled. 'Harbingers. Very appropriate.'

Kassad sighed, sat on a blanket with his back to a crate, and poked at his cold food. A single lantern brought from the windwagon lighted the room and the shadows were beginning to mount the walls in the corners away from the door to the balcony. 'It's our last night,' said Kassad. 'One more story to tell.' He looked at the Consul.

The Consul had been twisting his slip of paper with the number 7 scrawled on it. He licked his lips. 'What's the purpose? The purpose of the pilgrimage has been destroyed already.'

The others stirred.

'What do you mean?' asked Father Hoyt.

The Consul crumpled the paper and threw it into a corner. 'For the Shrike to grant a request, the band of pilgrims must constitute a prime number. We had seven. Masteen's . . . disappearance . . . reduces us to six. We go to our deaths now with no hope of a wish being granted.'

'Superstition,' said Lamia.

The Consul sighed and rubbed his brow. 'Yes. But that is our final hope.'

Father Hoyt gestured toward the sleeping infant. 'Can't Rachel be our seventh?'

Sol Weintraub rubbed his beard. 'No. A pilgrim must come to the Tombs of his or her own free will.'

'But she did once,' said Hoyt. 'Maybe it qualifies.'

'No,' said the Consul.

Martin Silenus had been writing notes on a pad but now he stood and paced the length of the room. 'Jesus Christ, people. Look at us. We're not six fucking pilgrims, we're a mob. Hoyt there with his cruciform carrying the ghost of Paul Duré. Our "semisentient" erg in the box there. Colonel

Kassad with his memory of Moneta. M. Brawne there, if we are to believe her tale, carrying not only an unborn child but a dead Romantic poet. Our scholar with the child his daughter used to be. Me with my muse. The Consul with whatever fucking baggage he's brought to this insane trek. My God, people, we should have received a fucking group rate for this trip.'

'Sit down,' said Lamia in a dead even tone.

'No, he's right,' said Hoyt. 'Even the presence of Father Duré in cruciform must affect the prime-number superstition somehow. I say that we press on in the morning in the belief that . . .'

'Look!' cried Brawne Lamia, pointing to the balcony doorway where the fading twilight had been replaced with pulses of strong light.

The group went out into the cool evening air, shielding their eyes from the staggering display of silent explosions which filled the sky: pure white fusion bursts expanding like explosive ripples across a lapis pond; smaller, brighter plasma implosions in blue and yellow and brightest red, curling inward like flowers folding for the night: the lightning dance of gigantic hellwhip displays, beams the size of small worlds cutting their swath across light-hours and being contorted by the riptides of defensive singularities: the aurora shimmer of defense fields leaping and dying under the assault of terrible energies only to be reborn nanoseconds later. Amid it all, the blue-white fusion tails of torchships and larger warships slicing perfectly true lines across the sky like diamond scratches on blue glass.

'The Ousters,' breathed Brawne Lamia.

'The war's begun,' said Kassad. There was no elation in his voice, no emotion of any kind.

The Consul was shocked to discover that he was weeping silently. He turned his face from the group.

'Are we in danger here?' asked Martin Silenus. He sheltered under the stone archway of the door, squinting at the brilliant display.

'Not at this distance,' said Kassad. He raised his combat binoculars, made an adjustment, and consulted his tactical comlog. 'Most of the engagements are at least three AU away. The Ousters are testing the FORCE:space defenses.' He lowered the glasses. 'It's just begun.'

'Has the farcaster been activated yet?' asked Brawne Lamia. 'Are the people being evacuated from Keats and the other cities?'

Kassad shook his head. 'I don't believe so. Not yet. The fleet will be fighting a holding action until the cislunar sphere is completed. Then the evacuation portals will be opened to the Web while FORCE units come through by the hundreds.' He raised the binoculars again. 'It'll be a hell of a show.'

'Look!' It was Father Hoyt pointing this time, not at the fireworks display in the sky but out across the low dunes of the northern moors. Several kilometers toward the unseen Tombs, a single figure was just visible as a speck of a form throwing multiple shadows under the fractured sky.

Kassad trained his glasses on the figure.

'The Shrike?' asked Lamia.

'No, I don't think so . . . I think it's . . . a Templar by the looks of the robe.'

'Het Masteen!' cried Father Hoyt.

Kassad shrugged and handed the glasses around. The Consul walked back to the group and leaned on the balcony. There was no sound but the whisper of wind, but that made the violence of explosions above them more ominous somehow.

The Consul took his turn looking when the glasses came to him. The figure was tall and robed, its back to the Keep, and strode across the flashing vermilion sands with purposeful intent.

'Is he headed toward us or the Tombs?' asked Lamia.

'The Tombs,' said the Consul.

Father Hoyt leaned elbows on the ledge and raised his gaunt face to the exploding sky. 'If it is Masteen, then we're back to seven, aren't we?'

'He'll arrive hours before us,' said the Consul. 'Half a day if we sleep here tonight as we proposed.'

Hoyt shrugged. 'That can't matter too much. Seven set out on the pilgrimage. Seven will arrive. The Shrike will be satisfied.'

'If it *is* Masteen,' said Colonel Kassad, 'why the charade on the wind-wagon? And how did he get here before us? There were no other tramcars running and he couldn't have walked over the Bridle Range passes.'

'We'll ask him when we arrive at the Tombs tomorrow,' Father Hoyt said tiredly.

Brawne Lamia had been trying to raise someone on her comlog's general comm frequencies. Nothing emerged but the hiss of static and the occasional growl of distant EMPs. She looked at Colonel Kassad. 'When do they start bombing?'

'I don't know. It depends upon the strength of the FORCE fleet defenses.'

'The defenses weren't very good the other day when the Ouster scouts got through and destroyed the *Yggdrasill*,' said Lamia.

Kassad nodded.

'Hey,' said Martin Silenus, 'are we sitting on a fucking *target*?'

'Of course,' said the Consul. 'If the Ousters are attacking Hyperion to prevent the opening of the Time Tombs, as M. Lamia's tale suggests, then the Tombs and this entire area would be a primary target.'

'For nukes?' asked Silenus, his voice strained.

'Almost certainly,' answered Kassad.

'I thought something about the anti-entropic fields kept ships away from here,' said Father Hoyt.

'*Crewed* ships,' said the Consul without looking back at the others from where he leaned on the railing. 'The anti-entropic fields won't bother guided missiles, smart bombs, or hellwhip beams. It won't bother mech infantry, for that matter. The Ousters could land a few attack skimmers or automated tanks and watch on remote while they destroy the valley.'

'But they won't,' said Brawne Lamia. 'They want to *control* Hyperion, not destroy it.'

'I wouldn't wager my life on that supposition,' said Kassad.

Lamia smiled at him. 'But we are, aren't we, Colonel?'

Above them, a single spark separated itself from the continuous patchwork of explosions, grew into a bright orange ember, and streaked across the sky. The group on the terrace could see the flames, hear the tortured shriek of atmospheric penetration. The fireball disappeared beyond the mountains behind the Keep.

Almost a minute later, the Consul realized that he had been holding his breath, his hands rigid on the stone railing. He let out air in a gasp. The others seemed to be taking a breath at the same moment. There had been no explosion, no shock wave rumbling through the rock.

'A dud?' asked Father Hoyt.

'Probably an injured FORCE skirmisher trying to reach the orbital perimeter or the spaceport at Keats,' said Colonel Kassad.

'He didn't make it, did he?' asked Lamia. Kassad did not respond.

Martin Silenus lifted the field glasses and searched the darkening moors for the Templar. 'Out of sight,' said Silenus. 'The good Captain either rounded that hill just this side of the Time Tombs valley or he pulled his disappearing act again.'

'It's a pity that we'll never hear his story,' said Father Hoyt. He turned toward the Consul. 'But we'll hear yours, won't we?'

The Consul rubbed his palms against his pant legs. His heart was racing. 'Yes,' he said, realizing even as he spoke that he had finally made up his mind. 'I'll tell mine.'

The wind roared down the east slopes of the mountains and whistled along the escarpment of Chronos Keep. The explosions above them seemed to have diminished ever so slightly, but the coming of darkness made each one look even more violent than the last.

'Let's go inside,' said Lamia, her words almost lost in the wind sound. 'It's getting cold.'

They had turned off the single lamp and the interior of the room was lighted only by the heat-lightning pulses of color from the sky outside. Shadows sprang into being, vanished, and appeared again as the room was painted in many colors. Sometimes the darkness would last several seconds before the next barrage.

The Consul reached into his traveling bag and took out a strange device, larger than a comlog, oddly ornamented, and fronted with a liquid crystal diskey like something out of a history holo.

'Secret fatline transmitter?' Brawne Lamia asked dryly.

The Consul's smile showed no humor. 'It's an ancient comlog. It came out during the Hegira.' He removed a standard micro-disk from a pouch on his belt and inserted it. 'Like Father Hoyt, I have someone else's tale to tell before you can understand my own.'

'Christ on a stick,' sneered Martin Silenus, 'am I the only one who can tell a straightforward story in this fucking herd? How long do I have to . . .'

The Consul's movement surprised even himself. He rose, spun, caught the smaller man by the cape and shirtfront, slammed him against the wall, draped him over a packing crate with a knee in Silenus's belly and a forearm against his throat, and hissed, 'One more word from you, poet, and *I'll* kill you.'

Silenus began to struggle but a tightening on his windpipe and a glance at the Consul's eyes made him cease. His face was very white.

Colonel Kassad silently, almost gently, separated the two. 'There will be no more comments,' he said. He touched the deathwand in his belt.

Martin Silenus went to the far side of the circle, still rubbing his throat, and slumped against a crate without a word. The Consul strode to the door, took several deep breaths, and walked back to the group. He spoke to everyone but the poet. 'I'm sorry. It is just that . . . I never expected to share this.'

The light from outside surged red and then white, followed by a blue glow which faded to near darkness.

'We know,' Brawne Lamia said softly. 'We all felt that way.'

The Consul touched his lower lip, nodded, roughly cleared his throat, and came to sit by the ancient comlog. 'The recording is not as old as the instrument,' he said. 'It was made about fifty standard years ago. I'll have some more to say when it's over.' He paused as if there were more to be said, shook his head, and thumbed the antique diskey.

There were no visuals. The voice was that of a young man. In the background one could hear a breeze blowing through grass or soft branches and, more distantly, the roll of surf.

Outside, the light pulsed madly as the tempo of the distant space battle quickened. The Consul tensed as he waited for the crash and concussion. There was none. He closed his eyes and listened with the others.

THE CONSUL'S TALE:
REMEMBERING SIRI

I climb the steep hill to Siri's tomb on the day the islands return to the shallow seas of the Equatorial Archipelago. The day is perfect and I hate it for being so. The sky is as tranquil as tales of Old Earth's seas, the shallows are dappled with ultramarine tints, and a warm breeze blows in from the sea to ripple the russet willowgrass on the hillside near me.

Better low clouds and gray gloom on such a day. Better mist or a shrouding fog which sets the masts in Firstsite Harbor dripping and raises the lighthouse horn from its slumbers. Better one of the great sea-simoons blowing up out of the cold belly of the south, lashing before it the motile isles and their dolphin herders until they seek refuge in the lee of our atolls and stony peaks.

Anything would be better than this warm spring day when the sun moves through a vault of sky so blue that it makes me want to run, to jump in great loping arcs, and to roll in the soft grass as Siri and I have done at just this spot.

Just this spot. I pause to look around. The willowgrass bends and ripples like the fur of some great beast as the salt-tinged breeze gusts up out of the south. I shield my eyes and search the horizon but nothing moves there. Out beyond the lava reef, the sea begins to chop and lift itself in nervous strokes.

'Siri,' I whisper. I say her name without meaning to do so. A hundred meters down the slope, the crowd pauses to watch me and to catch its collective breath. The procession of mourners and celebrants stretches for more than a kilometer to where the white buildings of the city begin. I can make out the gray and balding head of my younger son in the vanguard. He is wearing the blue and gold robes of the Hegemony. I know that I should wait for him, walk with him, but he and the other aging Council members cannot keep up with my young, ship-trained muscles and steady stride. But decorum dictates that I should walk with him and my grand-daughter Lira and my nine-year-old grandson.

To hell with it. And to hell with them.

I turn and jog up the steep hillside. Sweat begins to soak my loose cotton shirt before I reach the curving summit of the ridge and catch sight of the tomb.

Siri's tomb.

I stop. The wind chills me although the sunlight is warm enough as it glints off the flawless white stone of the silent mausoleum. The grass is high near the sealed entrance to the crypt. Rows of faded festival pennants on ebony staffs line the narrow gravel path.

Hesitating, I circle the tomb and approach the steep cliff edge a few meters beyond. The willowgrass is bent and trampled here where irreverent picnickers have laid their blankets. There are several fire rings formed from the perfectly round, perfectly white stones purloined from the border of the gravel path.

I cannot stop a smile. I know the view from here: the great curve of the outer harbor with its natural seawall, the low, white buildings of Firstsite, and the colorful hulls and masts of the catamarans bobbing at anchorage. Near the pebble beach beyond Common Hall, a young woman in a white skirt moves toward the water. For a second I think that it is Siri and my heart pounds. I half prepare to throw up my arms in response to her wave but she does not wave. I watch in silence as the distant figure turns away and is lost in the shadows of the old boat building.

Above me, far out from the cliff, a wide-winged Thomas Hawk circles above the lagoon on rising thermals and scans the shifting bluekelp beds with its infrared vision, seeking out harp seals or torpids. *Nature is stupid,* I think and sit in the soft grass. Nature sets the stage all wrong for such a day and then it is insensitive enough to throw in a bird searching for prey which have long since fled the polluted waters near the growing city.

I remember another Thomas Hawk on that first night when Siri and I came to this hilltop. I remember the moonlight on its wings and the strange, haunting cry which echoed off the cliff and seemed to pierce the dark air above the gaslights of the village below.

Siri was sixteen . . . no, not quite sixteen . . . and the moonlight that touched the hawk's wings above us also painted her bare skin with milky light and cast shadows beneath the soft circles of her breasts. We looked up guiltily when the bird's cry cut the night and Siri said, ' "It was the nightingale and not the lark, That pierc'd the fearful hollow of thine ear." '

'Huh?' I said. Siri was almost sixteen. I was nineteen. But Siri knew the slow pace of books and the cadences of theater under the stars. I knew only the stars.

'Relax, young Shipman,' she whispered and pulled me down beside her then. 'It's only an old Tom's Hawk hunting. Stupid bird. Come back, Shipman. Come back, Merin.'

The *Los Angeles* had chosen that moment to rise above the horizon and to float like a wind-borne ember west across the strange constellations of Maui-Covenant, Siri's world. I lay next to her and described the workings of the great Hawking-drive spinship which was catching the high sunlight against the drop of night above us, and all the while my hand was sliding lower along her smooth side, her skin seemed all velvet and electricity, and her breath came more quickly against my shoulder. I lowered my face to the hollow of her neck, to the sweat and perfume essence of her tousled hair.

'Siri,' I say and this time her name is not unbidden. Below me, below the crest of the hill and the shadow of the white tomb, the crowd stands and shuffles. They are impatient with me. They want me to unseal the tomb, to enter, and to have my private moment in the cool silent emptiness that has replaced the warm presence that was Siri. They want me to say my farewells so they can get on with their rites and rituals, open the farcaster doors, and join the waiting Worldweb of the Hegemony.

To hell with that. And to hell with them.

I pull up a tendril of the thickly woven willowgrass, chew on the sweet stem, and watch the horizon for the first sign of the migrating islands. The shadows are still long in the morning light. The day is young. I will sit here for a while and remember.

I will remember Siri.

Siri was a . . . what? . . . a bird, I think, the first time I saw her. She was wearing some sort of mask with bright feathers. When she removed it to join in the raceme quadrille, the torchlight caught the deep auburn tints of her hair. She was flushed, cheeks aflame, and even from across the crowded common I could see the startling green of her eyes contrasting with the summer heat of her face and hair. It was Festival Night, of course. The torches danced and sparked to the stiff breeze coming in off the harbor and the sound of the flutists on the break-wall playing for the passing isles was almost drowned out by surf sounds and the crack of pennants snapping in the wind. Siri was almost sixteen and her beauty burned more brightly than any of the torches set round the throng-filled square. I pushed through the dancing crowd and went to her.

It was five years ago for me. It was more than sixty-five years ago for us. It seems only yesterday.

This is not going well.

Where to start?

'What say we go find a little nooky, kid?' Mike Osho was speaking. Short, squat, his pudgy face a clever caricature of a Buddha, Mike was a god to me then. We were all gods; long-lived if not immortal, well paid if not quite divine. The Hegemony had chosen us to help crew one of its precious quantum-leap spinships, so how could we be less than gods? It was just that Mike, brilliant, mercurial, irreverent Mike, was a little older and a little higher in the Shipboard pantheon than young Merin Aspic.

'Hah. Zero probability of that,' I said. We were scrubbing up after a twelve-hour shift with the farcaster construction crew. Shuttling the workers around their chosen singularity point some one hundred and sixty-three thousand kilometers out from Maui-Covenant was a lot less glamorous for us than the four-month leap from Hegemony-space. During the C-plus portion of the trip we had been master specialists; forty-nine starship experts shepherding some two hundred nervous passengers. Now the passengers had their hardsuits on and we Shipmen had been reduced to serving as glorified truck drivers as the construction crew wrestled the bulky singularity containment sphere into place.

'Zero probability,' I repeated. 'Unless the groundlings have added a whorehouse to that quarantine island they leased us.'

'Nope. They haven't,' grinned Mike. He and I had our three days of planetary R and R coming up but we knew from Shipmaster Singh's briefings and the moans of our Shipmates that the only ground time we had to look forward to would be spent on a seven-by-four-kilometer island administered by the Hegemony. It wasn't even one of the motile isles we had heard about, just another volcanic peak near the equator. Once there, we could count on real gravity underfoot, unfiltered air to breathe, and the chance to taste unsynthesized food. But we could also count on the fact that the only intercourse we would have with the Maui-Covenant colonists would be through buying local artifacts at the duty-free store. Even those were sold by Hegemony trade specialists. Many of our Shipmates had chosen to spend their R and R on the *Los Angeles*.

'So how do we find a little nooky, Mike? The colonies are off limits until the farcaster's working. That's about sixty years away, local time. Or are you talking about Meg in spincomp?'

'Stick with me, kid,' said Mike. 'Where there's a will, there's a way.'

I stuck with Mike. There were only five of us in the dropship. It was always a thrill to me to fall out of high orbit into the atmosphere of a real world. Especially a world that looked as much like Old Earth as Maui-Covenant did. I stared at the blue and white limb of the planet until the seas were *down* and we were in atmosphere, approaching the twilight terminator in a gentle glide at three times the speed of our own sound.

We were gods then. But even gods must descend from their high thrones upon occasion.

Siri's body never ceased to amaze me. That time on the Archipelago. Three weeks in that huge, swaying tree-house under the billowing treesails with the dolphin herders keeping pace like outriders, tropical sunsets filling the evening with wonder, the canopy of stars at night, and our own wake marked by a thousand phosphorescent swirls that mirrored the constellations above. And still it is Siri's body I remember. For some reason – shyness, the years of separation – she wore two strips of swimsuit for the first few days of our Archipelago stay and the soft white of her breasts and lower belly had not darkened to match the rest of her tan before I had to leave again.

I remember her that first time. Triangles in the moonlight as we lay in the soft grass above Firstsite Harbor. Her silk pants catching on a weave of willowgrass. There was a child's modesty then; the slight hesitation of something given prematurely. But also pride. The same pride that later allowed her to face down the angry mob of Separatists on the steps of the Hegemony consulate in South Tern and send them to their homes in shame.

I remember my fifth planetfall, our Fourth Reunion. It was one of the few times I ever saw her cry. She was almost regal in her fame and wisdom by then. She had been elected four times to the All Thing and the Hegemony Council turned to her for advice and guidance. She wore her independence like a royal cloak and her fierce pride had never burned more brightly. But when we were alone in the stone villa south of Fevarone, it was she who turned away. I was nervous, frightened by this powerful stranger, but it was Siri – Siri of the straight back and proud eyes, who turned her face to the wall and said through tears, 'Go away. Go away, Merin. I don't want you to see me. I'm a crone, all slack and sagging. *Go away.*'

I confess that I was rough with her then. I pinned her wrists with my left hand – using a strength which surprised even me – and tore her silken robe down the front in one move. I kissed her shoulders, her neck, the faded shadows of stretch marks on her taut belly, and the scar on her upper leg from the skimmer crash some forty of her years earlier. I kissed her graying hair and the lines etched in the once smooth cheeks. I kissed her tears.

'Jesus, Mike, this can't be legal,' I'd said when my friend unrolled the hawking mat from his backpack. We were on island 241, as the Hegemony traders had so romantically named the desolate volcanic blemish which they had chosen for our R and R site. Island 241 was less than fifty kilometers from the oldest of the colonial settlements but it might as well have been fifty light-years away. No native ships were to put in at the island while *Los Angeles* crewmen or farcaster workmen were present. The Maui-Covenant colonists had a few ancient skimmers still in working order, but by mutual agreement there would be no overflights. Except for the dormitories, swimming beach, and the duty-free store, there was little on the island to interest us Shipmen. Someday, when the last components had been brought in-system by the *Los Angeles* and the farcaster finished, Hegemony officials would make island 241 into a center for trade and tourism. Until then it was a primitive place with a dropship grid, newly finished buildings of the local white stone, and a few bored maintenance people. Mike checked the two of us out for three days of backpacking on the steepest and most inaccessible end of the little island.

'I don't want to go backpacking, for Chrissake,' I'd said. 'I'd rather stay on the *L.A.* and plug into a stimsim.'

'Shut up and follow me,' said Mike and, like a lesser member of the pantheon following an older and wiser deity, I had shut up and followed. Two hours of heavy tramping up the slopes through sharp-branched scrubtrees brought us to a lip of lava several hundred meters above the crashing surf. We were near the equator on a mostly tropical world but on this exposed ledge the wind was howling and my teeth were chattering. The sunset was a red smear between dark cumulus to the west and I had no wish to be out in the open when full night descended.

'Come on,' I said. 'Let's get out of the wind and build a fire. I don't know how the hell we're going to set up a tent on all of this rock.'

Mike sat down and lit a cannabis stick. 'Take a look in your pack, kid.'

I hesitated. His voice had been neutral but it was the flat neutrality of the practical joker's voice just before the bucket of water descends. I crouched down and began pawing through the nylon sack. The pack was empty except for old flowfoam packing cubes to fill it out. Those and a Harlequin's costume complete with mask and bells on the toes.

'Are you . . . is this . . . are you goddamn *crazy*?' I spluttered. It was getting dark quickly now. The storm might or might not pass to the south of us. The surf was rasping below like a hungry beast. If I had known how to find my own way back to the trade compound in the dark, I might have considered leaving Mike Osho's remains to feed the fishes far below.

'Now look at what's in my pack,' he said. Mike dumped out some flowfoam cubes and then removed some jewelry of the type I'd seen hand-crafted on Renaissance Vector, an inertial compass, a laser pen which might or might not be labeled a concealed weapon by ShipSecurity, another Harlequin costume – this one tailored to his more rotund form – and a hawking mat.

'Jesus, Mike,' I said while running my hand over the exquisite design of the old carpet, 'this can't be legal.'

'I didn't notice any customs agents back there,' grinned Mike. 'And I seriously doubt that the locals have any traffic control ordinances.'

'Yes, but . . .' I trailed off and unrolled the rest of the mat. It was a little more than a meter wide and about two meters long. The rich fabric had faded with age but the flight threads were still as bright as new copper. 'Where did you get it?' I asked. 'Does it still work?'

'On Garden,' said Mike and stuffed my costume and his other gear into his backpack. 'Yes, it does.'

It had been more than a century since old Vladimir Sholokov, Old Earth emigrant, master lepidopterist, and EM systems engineer, had handcrafted the first hawking mat for his beautiful young niece on New Earth. Legend had it that the niece had scorned the gift but over the decades the toys had become almost absurdly popular – more with rich adults than with children – until they were outlawed on most Hegemony worlds. Dangerous to handle, a waste of shielded monofilaments, almost impossible to deal with in controlled airspace, hawking mats had become curiosities reserved for bedtime stories, museums, and a few colony worlds.

'It must have cost you a fortune,' I said.

'Thirty marks,' said Mike and settled himself on the center of the carpet. 'The old dealer in Carvnel Marketplace thought it was worthless. It was . . . for him. I brought it back to the ship, charged it up, reprogrammed the inertia chips, and *voilà*!' Mike palmed the intricate design and the mat stiffened and rose fifteen centimeters above the rock ledge.

I stared doubtfully. 'All right,' I said, 'but what if it . . .'

'It won't,' said Mike and impatiently patted the carpet behind him. 'It's fully charged. I know how to handle it. Come on, climb on or stand back. I want to get going before that storm gets any closer.'

'But I don't think . . .'

'Come *on*, Merin. Make up your mind. I'm in a hurry.'

I hesitated for another second or two. If we were caught leaving the island, we would both be kicked off the ship. Shipwork was my life now. I had made that decision when I accepted the eight-mission Maui-Covenant contract. More than that, I was two hundred light-years and five and a half leap years from civilization. Even if they brought us back to Hegemony-space, the round trip would have cost us eleven years' worth of friends and family. The time-debt was irrevocable.

I crawled on the hovering hawking mat behind Mike. He stuffed the backpack between us, told me to hang on, and tapped at the flight designs. The mat rose five meters above the ledge, banked quickly to the left, and shot out over the alien ocean. Three hundred meters below us, the surf crashed whitely in the deepening gloom. We rose higher above the rough water and headed north into the night.

In such seconds of decision entire futures are made.

I remember talking to Siri during our Second Reunion, shortly after we first visited the villa along the coast near Fevarone. We were walking along the beach. Alón had been allowed to stay in the city under Magritte's supervision. It was just as well. I was not truly comfortable with the boy. Only the undeniable green solemnity of his eyes and the disturbing mirror-familiarity of his short, dark curls and snub of a nose served to tie him to me . . . to us . . . in my mind. That and the quick, almost sardonic smile I would catch him hiding from Siri when she reprimanded him. It was a smile too cynically amused and self-observant to be so practiced in a ten-year-old. I knew it well. I would have thought such things were learned, not inherited.

'You know very little,' Siri said to me. She was wading, shoeless, in a shallow tidepool. From time to time she would lift the delicate shell of a frenchhorn conch, inspect it for flaws, and drop it back into the silty water.

'I've been well trained,' I replied.

'Yes, I'm sure you've been well trained,' agreed Siri. 'I know you are quite skillful, Merin. But you *know* very little.'

Irritated, unsure of how to respond, I walked along with my head lowered. I dug a white lavastone out of the sand and tossed it far out into the bay. Rain clouds were piling along the eastern horizon. I found myself wishing that I was back aboard the ship. I had been reluctant to return this time and now I knew that it had been a mistake. It was my third visit to Maui-Covenant, our Second Reunion as the poets and her people were calling it. I was five months away from being twenty-one standard years old. Siri had just celebrated her thirty-seventh birthday three weeks earlier.

'I've been to a lot of places you've never seen,' I said at last. It sounded petulant and childish even to me.

'Oh, yes,' said Siri and clapped her hands together. For a second, in her enthusiasm, I glimpsed my other Siri – the young girl I had dreamed about during the long nine months of turnaround. Then the image slid back to harsh reality and I was all too aware of her short hair, the loosening neck muscles, and the cords appearing on the backs of those once beloved hands. 'You've been to places I'll *never* see,' said Siri in a rush. Her voice was the same. Almost the same. 'Merin, my love, you've already seen things I cannot even imagine. You probably know more facts about the universe than I would guess exist. But you *know* very little, my darling.'

'What the hell are you talking about, Siri?' I sat down on a half-submerged log near the strip of wet sand and drew my knees up like a fence between us.

Siri strode out of the tidepool and came to kneel in front of me. She took my hands in hers and, although mine were bigger, heavier, blunter of finger and bone, I could feel the *strength* in hers. I imagined it as the strength of years I had not shared. 'You have to live to really know things, my love. Having Alón has helped me to understand that. There is something about raising a child that helps to sharpen one's sense of what is real.'

'How do you mean?'

Siri squinted away from me for a few seconds and absently brushed back a strand of hair. Her left hand stayed firmly around both of mine. 'I'm not sure,' she said softly. 'I think one begins to feel when things aren't *important*. I'm not sure how to put it. When you've spent thirty years entering rooms filled with strangers you feel less pressure than when you've had only half that number of years of experience. You know what the room and the people in it probably hold for you and you go looking for it. If it's not there, you sense it earlier and leave to go about your business. You just *know* more about what is, what isn't, and how little time there is to learn the difference. Do you understand, Merin? Do you follow me even a little bit?'

'No,' I said.

Siri nodded and bit her lower lip. But she did not speak again for a while. Instead, she leaned over and kissed me. Her lips were dry and a little questioning. I held back for a second, seeing the sky beyond her, wanting time to think. But then I felt the warm intrusion of her tongue and closed my eyes. The tide was coming in behind us. I felt a sympathetic warmth and rising as Siri unbuttoned my shirt and ran sharp fingernails across my chest. There was a second of emptiness between us and I opened my eyes in time to see her unfastening the last buttons on the front of her white dress. Her breasts were larger than I remembered, heavier, the nipples broader and darker. The chill air nipped at both of us until I pulled the fabric down her shoulders and brought our upper bodies together. We slid down along the log to the warm sand. I pressed her closer, all the while wondering how I possibly could have thought her the stronger one. Her skin tasted of salt.

Siri's hands helped me. Her short hair pressed back against bleached wood, white cotton, and sand. My pulse outraced the surf.

'Do you understand, Merin?' she whispered to me seconds later as her warmth connected us.

'Yes,' I whispered back. But I did not.

Mike brought the hawking mat in from the east toward Firstsite. The flight had taken over an hour in the dark and I had spent most of the time huddling from the wind and waiting for the carpet to fold up and tumble us both into the sea. We were still half an hour out when we saw the first of the motile isles. Racing before the storm, treesails billowing, the islands sailed up from their southern feeding grounds in seemingly endless procession. Many were lit brilliantly, festooned with colored lanterns and shifting veils of gossamer light.

'You sure this is the way?' I shouted.

'Yes,' shouted Mike. He did not turn his head. The wind whipped his long black hair back against my face. From time to time he would check his compass and make small corrections to our course. It might have been easier to follow the isles. We passed one – a large one almost half a kilometer in length – and I strained to make out details but the isle was dark except for the glow of its phosphorescent wake. Dark shapes cut through the milky waves. I tapped Mike on the shoulder and pointed.

'Dolphins!' he shouted. 'That's what this colony was all about, remember? A bunch of do-gooders during the Hegira wanted to save all the mammals in Old Earth's oceans. Didn't succeed.'

I would have shouted another question but at that moment the headland and Firstsite Harbor came into view.

I had thought the stars were bright above Maui-Covenant. I had thought the migrating islands were memorable in their colorful display. But the city of Firstsite, wrapped about with harbor and hills, was a blazing beacon in the night. Its brilliance reminded me of a torchship I once had watched while it created its own plasma nova against the dark limb of a sullen gas giant. The city was a five-tiered honeycomb of white buildings, all illuminated by warmly glowing lanterns from within and by countless torches from without. The white lava-stone of the volcanic island itself seemed to glow from the city light. Beyond the town were tents, pavilions, campfires, cooking fires, and great flaming pyres, too large for function, too large for anything except to serve as a welcome to the returning isles.

The harbor was filled with boats: bobbing catamarans with cow-bells clanking from their masts, large-hulled, flat-bottomed house-boats built for creeping from port to port in the calm equatorial shallows but proudly ablaze with strings of lights this night, and then the occasional oceangoing yacht, sleek and functional as a shark. A lighthouse set out on the pincer's end of the harbor reef threw its beam far out to sea, illuminated wave and isle alike, and then swept its light back in to catch the colorful bobbing of ships and men.

Even from two kilometers out we could hear the noise. Sounds of celebration were clearly audible. Above the shouts and constant susurration of the surf rose the unmistakable notes of a Bach flute sonata. I learned later that this welcoming chorus was transmitted through hydrophones to the Passage Channels where dolphins leaped and cavorted to the music.

'My God, Mike, how did you know all of this was going on?'

'I asked the main ship computer,' said Mike. The hawking mat banked right to keep us far out from the ships and lighthouse beam. Then we curved back in north of Firstsite toward a dark spit of land. I could hear the soft booming of waves on the shallows ahead. 'They have this festival every year,' Mike went on, 'but this is their sesquicentennial. The party's been going on for three weeks now and is scheduled to continue another two. There are only about a hundred thousand colonists on this whole world, Merin, and I bet half of them are here partying.'

We slowed, came in carefully, and touched down on a rocky outcropping not far from the beach. The storm had missed us to the south but intermittent flashes of lightning and the distant lights of advancing isles still marked the horizon. Overhead, the stars were not dimmed by the glow from Firstsite just over the rise from us. The air was warmer here and I caught the scent of orchards on the breeze. We folded up the hawking mat and hurried to get into our Harlequin costumes. Mike slipped his laser pen and jewelry into loose pockets.

'What are those for?' I asked as we secured the backpack and hawking mat under a large boulder.

'These?' asked Mike as he dangled a Renaissance necklace from his fingers. 'These are currency in case we have to negotiate for favors.'

'Favors?'

'Favors,' repeated Mike. 'A lady's largesse. Comfort to a weary spacefarer. Nooky to you, kid.'

'Oh,' I said and adjusted my mask and fool's cap. The bells made a soft sound in the dark.

'Come on,' said Mike. 'We'll miss the party.' I nodded and followed him, bells jangling, as we picked our way over stone and scrub toward the waiting light.

I sit here in the sunlight and wait. I am not totally certain what I am waiting for. I can feel a growing warmth on my back as the morning sunlight is reflected from the white stone of Siri's tomb.

Siri's tomb?

There are no clouds in the sky. I raise my head and squint skyward as if I might be able to see the *LA* and the newly finished farcaster array through the glare of atmosphere. I cannot. Part of me knows that they have not risen yet. Part of me knows to the second the time remaining before ship and farcaster complete their transit to the zenith. Part of me does not want to think about it.

Siri, am I doing the right thing?

There is the sudden sound of pennants stirring on their staffs as the wind comes up. I sense rather than see the restlessness of the waiting crowd. For the first time since my planetfall for this, our Seventh Reunion, I am filled with sorrow. No, not sorrow, not yet, but a sharp-toothed sadness which soon will open into grief. For years I have carried on silent conversations with Siri, framing questions to myself for future discussion with her, and it suddenly strikes me with cold clarity that we will never again sit together and talk. An emptiness begins to grow inside me.

Should I let it happen, Siri?

There is no response except for the growing murmurs of the crowd. In a few minutes they will send Donel, my younger and surviving son, or his daughter Lira and her brother up the hill to urge me on. I toss away the sprig of willowgrass I've been chewing on. There is a hint of shadow on the horizon. It could be a cloud. Or it could be the first of the isles, driven by instinct and the spring northerlies to migrate back to the great band of the equatorial shallows whence they came. It does not matter.

Siri, am I doing the right thing?

There is no answer and the time grows shorter.

Sometimes Siri seemed so ignorant it made me sick.

She knew nothing of my life away from her. She would ask questions but I sometimes wondered if she was interested in the answers. I spent many hours explaining the beautiful physics behind our spinships but she never did seem to understand. Once, after I had taken great care to detail the

317

differences between their ancient seedship and the *Los Angeles*, Siri astounded me by asking, 'But why did it take my ancestors eighty years of shiptime to reach Maui-Covenant when you can make the trip in a hundred and thirty *days*?' She had understood nothing.

Siri's sense of history was, at best, pitiful. She viewed the Hegemony and the Worldweb the way a child would view the fantasy world of a pleasant but rather silly myth; there was an indifference there that almost drove me mad at times.

Siri knew all about the early days of the Hegira – at least insofar as they pertained to Maui-Covenant and the colonists – and she occasionally would come up with delightful bits of archaic trivia or phraseology, but she knew nothing of post-Hegira realities. Names like Garden and the Ousters, Renaissance and Lusus meant little to her. I could mention Salmud Brevy or General Horace Glennon-Height and she would have no associations or reactions at all. None.

The last time I saw Siri she was seventy standard years old. She was *seventy years old* and still she had never traveled offworld, used a fatline, tasted any alcoholic drink except wine, interfaced with an empathy surgeon, stepped through a farcaster door, smoked a cannabis stick, received gene tailoring, plugged into a stimsim, received any formal schooling, taken any RNA medication, heard of Zen Gnostics or the Shrike Church, or flown any vehicle except an ancient Vikken skimmer belonging to her family.

Siri had never made love to anyone except me. Or so she said. And so I believed.

It was during our First Reunion, that time on the Archipelago, when Siri took me to talk with the dolphins.

We had risen to watch the dawn. The highest levels of the tree-house were a perfect place from which to watch the eastern sky pale and fade to morning. Ripples of high cirrus turned to rose and then the sea itself grew molten as the sun floated above the flat horizon.

'Let's go swimming,' said Siri. The rich, horizontal light bathed her skin and threw her shadow four meters across the boards of the platform.

'I'm too tired,' I said. 'Later.' We had lain awake most of the night talking, making love, talking, and making love again. In the glare of morning I felt empty and vaguely nauseated. I sensed the slight movement of the isle under me as a tinge of vertigo, a drunkard's disconnection from gravity.

'No. Let's go now,' said Siri and grasped my hand to pull me along. I was irritated but did not argue. Siri was twenty-six, seven years older than I during that First Reunion, but her impulsive behavior often reminded me of the teenaged Siri I had carried away from the Festival only ten of my months earlier. Her deep, unselfconscious laugh was the same. Her green eyes cut as sharply when she was impatient. The long mane of auburn hair had not changed. But her body had ripened, filled out with a promise which had been only hinted at before. Her breasts were still high and full, almost girlish, bordered above by freckles that gave way to a whiteness so translucent that a gentle blue tracery of veins could be seen. But they were *different* somehow. She was different.

'Are you going to join me or just sit there staring?' asked Siri. She had slipped off her caftan as we came out onto the lowest deck. Our small ship was still tied to the dock. Above us, the island's treesails were beginning to open to the morning breeze. For the past several days Siri had insisted on wearing swimstrips when we went into the water. She wore none now. Her nipples rose in the cool air.

'Won't we be left behind?' I asked, squinting up at the flapping tree-sails. On previous days we had waited for the doldrums in the middle of the day when the isle was still in the water, the sea a glazed mirror. Now the jibvines were beginning to pull taut as the thick leaves filled with wind.

'Don't be silly,' said Siri. 'We could always catch a keelroot and follow it back. That or a feeding tendril. Come on.' She tossed an osmosis mask at me and donned her own. The transparent film made her face look slick with oil. From the pocket of her discarded caftan she lifted a thick medallion and set it in place around her neck. The metal looked dark and ominous against her skin.

'What's that?'I asked.

Siri did not lift the osmosis mask to answer. She set the comthreads in place against her neck and handed me the earplugs. Her voice was tinny. 'Translation disk,' she said. 'Thought you knew all about gadgets, Merin. Last one in's a seaslug.' She held the disk in place between her breasts with one hand and stepped off the isle. I could see the pale globes of her buttocks as she pirouetted and kicked for depth. In seconds she was only a white blur deep in the water. I slipped my own mask on, pressed the comthreads tight, and stepped into the sea.

The bottom of the isle was a dark stain on a ceiling of crystalline light. I was wary of the thick feeding tendrils even though Siri had amply demonstrated that they were interested in devouring nothing larger than the tiny zooplankton that even now caught the sunlight like dust in an abandoned ballroom. Keelroots descended like gnarled stalactites for hundreds of meters into the purple depths.

The isle was moving. I could see the faint fibrillation of the tendrils as they trailed along. A wake caught the light ten meters above me. For a second I was choking, the gel of the mask smothering me as surely as the surrounding water would, and then I relaxed and the air flowed freely into my lungs.

'Deeper, Merin,' came Siri's voice. I blinked – a slow-motion blink as the mask readjusted itself over my eyes – and caught sight of Siri twenty meters lower, grasping a keelroot and trailing effortlessly above the colder, deeper currents where the light did not reach. I thought of the thousands of meters of water under me, of the things which might lurk there, unknown, unsought out by the human colonists. I thought of the dark and the depths and my scrotum tightened involuntarily.

'Come on down.' Siri's voice was an insect buzz in my ears. I rotated and kicked. The buoyancy here was not so great as in Old Earth's seas, but it still took energy to dive so deep. The mask compensated for depth and nitrogen but I could feel the pressure against my skin and ears. Finally I quit kicking, grabbed a keelroot, and roughly hauled myself down to Siri's level.

We floated side by side in the dim light. Siri was a spectral figure here, her long hair swirling in a wine-dark nimbus, the pale strips of her body glowing in the blue-green light. The surface seemed impossibly distant. The widening V of the wake and the drift of the scores of tendrils showed that the isle was moving more quickly now, moving mindlessly to other feeding grounds, distant waters.

'Where are the . . .' I began to subvocalize.

'Shhh,' said Siri. She fiddled with the medallion. I could hear them then: the shrieks and trills and whistles and cat purrs and echoing cries. The depths were suddenly filled with strange music.

'Jesus,' I said and because Siri had tuned our comthreads to the translator, the word was broadcast as a senseless whistle and toot.

'Hello!' she called and the translated greeting echoed from the transmitter; a high-speed bird's call sliding into the ultrasonic. 'Hello!' she called again.

Minutes passed before the dolphins came to investigate. They rolled past us, surprisingly large, alarmingly large, their skin looking slick and muscled in the uncertain light. A large one swam within a meter of us, turning at the last moment so that the white of his belly curved past us like a wall. I could see the dark eye rotate to follow me as he passed. One stroke of his wide fluke kicked up a turbulence strong enough to convince me of the animal's power.

'Hello,' called Siri but the swift form faded into distant haze and there was a sudden silence. Siri clicked off the translator. 'Do you want to talk to them?' she asked.

'Sure.' I was dubious. More than three centuries of effort had not raised much of a dialogue between man and sea mammal. Mike had once told me that the thought structures of Old Earth's two groups of orphans were too different, the referents too few. One pre-Hegira expert had written that speaking to a dolphin or porpoise was about as rewarding as speaking to a one-year-old human infant. Both sides usually enjoyed the exchange and there was a simulacrum of conversation, but neither party would come away the more knowledgeable. Siri switched the translator disk back on. 'Hello,' I said.

There was a final minute of silence and then our earphones were buzzing while the sea echoed shrill ululations.

distance/no-fluke/hello-tone?/current pulse/circle me/funny?

'What the hell?' I asked Siri and the translator trilled out my question. Siri was grinning under her osmosis mask.

I tried again. 'Hello! Greetings from . . . uh . . . the surface. How are you?'

The large male . . . I assumed it to be a male . . . curved in toward us like a torpedo. He arch-kicked his way through the water ten times faster than I could have swum even if I had remembered to don flippers that morning. For a second I thought he was going to ram us and I raised my knees and clung tightly to the keelroot. Then he was past us, climbing for air, while Siri and I reeled from his turbulent wake and the high tones of his shout.

no-fluke/no-feed/no-swim/no-play/no-fun.

Siri switched off the translator and floated closer. She lightly grasped my shoulders while I held on to the keelroot with my right hand. Our legs touched as we drifted through the warm water. A school of tiny crimson warriorfish flickered above us while the dark shapes of the dolphins circled farther out.

'Had enough?' she asked. Her hand was flat on my chest.

'One more try,' I said. Siri nodded and twisted the disk to life. The current pushed us together again. She slid her arm around me.

'Why do you herd the islands?' I asked the bottle-nosed shapes circling in the dappled light. 'How does it benefit you to stay with the isles?'

sounding now/old songs/deep water/no-Great Voices/no-Shark/old songs/new songs.

Siri's body lay along the length of me now. Her left arm tightened around me. 'Great Voices were the whales,' she whispered. Her hair fanned out in streamers. Her right hand moved down and seemed surprised at what it found.

'Do you miss the Great Voices?' I asked the shadows. There was no response. Siri slid her legs around my hips. The surface was a churning bowl of light forty meters above us.

'What do you miss most of Old Earth's oceans?' I asked. With my left arm I pulled Siri closer, slid my hand down along the curve of her back to where her buttocks rose to meet my palm, held her tight. To the circling dolphins we must have appeared a single creature. Siri lifted herself against me and we became a single creature.

The translator disk had twisted around so it trailed over Siri's shoulder. I reached to shut it off but paused as the answer to my question buzzed urgently in our ears.

miss Shark/miss Shark/miss Shark/miss Shark/ Shark/Shark/Shark.

I turned off the disk and shook my head. I did not understand. There was so much I did not understand. I closed my eyes as Siri and I moved gently to the rhythms of the current and ourselves while the dolphins swam nearby and the cadence of their calls took on the sad, slow trilling of an old lament.

Siri and I came down out of the hills and returned to the Festival just before sunrise of the second day. For a night and a day we had roamed the hills, eaten with strangers in pavilions of orange silk, bathed together in the icy waters of the Shree, and danced to the music which never ceased going out to the endless file of passing isles. We were hungry. I had awakened at sunset to find Siri gone. She returned before the moon of Maui-Covenant rose. She told me that her parents had gone off with friends for several days on a slow-moving houseboat. They had left the family skimmer in Firstsite. Now we worked our way from dance to dance, bonfire to bonfire, back to the center of the city. We planned to fly west to her family estate near Fevarone.

It was very late but Firstsite Common still had its share of revelers. I was very happy. I was nineteen and I was in love and the .93 gravity of Maui-Covenant seemed much less to me. I could have flown had I wished. I could have done anything.

We had stopped at a booth and bought fried dough and mugs of black coffee. Suddenly a thought struck me. I asked, 'How did you know I was a Shipman?'

'Hush, friend Merin. Eat your poor breakfast. When we get to the villa, I will fix a true meal to break our fast.'

'No, I'm serious,' I said and wiped grease off my chin with the sleeve of my less than clean Harlequin's costume. 'This morning you said that you knew right away last night that I was from the ship. Why was that? Was it my accent? My costume? Mike and I saw other fellows dressed like this.'

Siri laughed and brushed back her hair. 'Just be glad it was I who spied you out, Merin, my love. Had it been my Uncle Gresham or his friends it would have meant trouble.'

'Oh? Why is that?' I picked up one more fried ring and Siri paid for it. I followed her through the thinning crowd. Despite the motion and the music all about, I felt weariness beginning to work on me.

'They are Separatists,' said Siri. 'Uncle Gresham recently gave a speech before the Council urging that we fight rather than agree to be swallowed into your Hegemony. He said that we should destroy your farcaster device before it destroys us.'

'Oh?' I said. 'Did he say how he was going to do that? The last I heard, you folks had no craft to get offworld in.'

'Nay, nor for the past fifty years have we,' said Siri. 'But it shows how irrational the Separatists can be.'

I nodded. Shipmaster Singh and Councilor Halmyn had briefed us on the so-called Separatists of Maui-Covenant. 'The usual coalition of colonial jingoists and throwbacks,' Singh had said. 'Another reason we go slow and develop the world's trade potential before finishing the farcaster. The Worldweb doesn't need these yahoos coming in prematurely. And groups like the Separatists are another reason to keep you crew and construction workers the hell away from the groundlings.'

'Where is your skimmer?' I asked. The Common was emptying quickly. Most of the bands had packed up their instruments for the night. Gaily costumed heaps lay snoring on the grass or cobblestones amid the litter and unlit lanterns. Only a few enclaves of merriment remained, groups dancing slowly to a lone guitar or singing drunkenly to themselves. I saw Mike Osho at once, a patchworked fool, his mask long gone, a girl on either arm. He was trying to teach the 'Hava Nagilla' to a rapt but inept circle of admirers. One of the troupe would stumble and they would all fall down. Mike would flog them to their feet among general laughter and they would start again, hopping clumsily to his basso profundo chant.

'There it is,' said Siri and pointed to a short line of skimmers parked behind the Common Hall. I nodded and waved to Mike but he was too busy hanging on to his two ladies to notice me. Siri and I had crossed the square and were in the shadows of the old building when the shout went up.

'Shipman! Turn around, you Hegemony son of a bitch.'

I froze and then wheeled around with fists clenched but no one was near me. Six young men had descended the steps from the grandstand and were standing in a semicircle behind Mike. The man in front was tall, slim, and strikingly handsome. He was twenty-five or twenty-six years old and his long blond curls spilled down on a crimson silk suit that emphasized his physique. In his right hand he carried a meter-long sword that looked to be of tempered steel.

Mike turned slowly. Even from a distance I could see his eyes sobering as he surveyed the situation. The women at his side and a couple of the young men in his group tittered as if something humorous had been said. Mike allowed the inebriated grin to stay on his face. 'You address me, sir?' he asked.

'I address you, you Hegemony whore's son,' hissed the leader of the group. His handsome face was twisted into a sneer.

'Bertol,' whispered Siri. 'My cousin. Gresham's younger son.' I nodded and stepped out of the shadows. Siri caught my arm.

'That is twice you have referred unkindly to my mother, sir,' slurred Mike. 'Have she or I offended you in some way? If so, a thousand pardons.' Mike bowed so deeply that the bells on his cap almost brushed the ground. Members of his group applauded.

'Your presence offends me, you Hegemony bastard. You stink up our air with your fat carcass.'

Mike's eyebrows rose comically. A young man near him in a fish costume waved his hand. 'Oh, come on, Bertol. He's just . . .'

'Shut up, Ferick. It is this fat shithead I am speaking to.'

'Shithead?' repeated Mike, eyebrows still raised. 'I've traveled two hundred light-years to be called a fat shithead? It hardly seems worth it.' He pivoted gracefully, untangling himself from the women as he did so. I would have joined Mike then but Siri clung tightly to my arm, whispering unheard entreaties. When I was free I saw that Mike was still smiling, still playing the fool. But his left hand was in his baggy shirt pocket.

'Give him your blade, Creg,' snapped Bertol. One of the younger men tossed a sword hilt-first to Mike. Mike watched it arc by and clang loudly on the cobblestones.

'You can't be serious,' said Mike in a soft voice that was suddenly quite sober. 'You cretinous cow turd. Do you really think I'm going to play duel with you just because you get a hard-on acting the hero for these yokels?'

'Pick up the sword,' screamed Bertol, 'or, by God, I'll carve you where you stand.' He took a quick step forward. The youth's face contorted with fury as he advanced.

'Fuck off,' said Mike. In his left hand was the laser pen.

'No!' I yelled and ran into the light. That pen was used by construction workers to scrawl marks on girders of whiskered alloy.

Things happened very quickly then. Bertol took another step and Mike flicked the green beam across him almost casually. The colonist let out a cry and leaped back; a smoking line of black was slashed diagonally across his silk shirtfront. I hesitated. Mike had the setting as low as it could go. Two of Bertol's friends started forward and Mike swung the light across their shins. One dropped to his knees cursing and the other hopped away holding his leg and hooting.

A crowd had gathered. They laughed as Mike swept off his fool's cap in another bow. 'I thank you,' said Mike. 'My mother thanks you.'

Siri's cousin strained against his rage. Froths of spittle spilled on his lips and chin. I pushed through the crowd and stepped between Mike and the tall colonist.

'Hey, it's all right,' I said. 'We're leaving. We're going now.'

'Goddamn it, Merin, get out of the way,' said Mike.

'It's all right,' I said as I turned to him. 'I'm with a girl named Siri who has a . . .' Bertol stepped forward and lunged past me with his blade. I wrapped my left arm around his shoulder and flung him back. He tumbled heavily onto the grass.

'Oh, shit,' said Mike as he backed up several paces. He looked tired and a little disgusted as he sat down on a stone step. 'Aw, *damn*,' he said softly. There was a short line of crimson in one of the black patches on the left side of his Harlequin costume. As I watched, the narrow slit spilled over and blood ran down across Mike Osho's broad belly.

'Oh, Jesus, Mike.' I tore a strip of fabric from my shirt and tried to staunch the flow. I could remember none of the first aid we'd been taught as mid-Shipmen. I pawed at my wrist but my comlog was not there. We had left them on the *Los Angeles*.

'It's not so bad, Mike,' I gasped. 'It's just a little cut.' The blood flowed down over my hand and wrist.

'It will serve,' said Mike. His voice was held taut by a cord of pain. 'Damn. A fucking sword. Do you believe it, Merin? Cut down in the prime of my prime by a piece of fucking cutlery out of a fucking one-penny opera. Oh, *damn*, that smarts.'

'Three-penny opera,' I said and changed hands. The rag was soaked.

'You know what your fucking problem is, Merin? You're always sticking your fucking two cents in. Awwwww.' Mike's face went white and then gray. He lowered his chin to his chest and breathed deeply. 'To *hell* with this, kid. Let's go home, huh?'

I looked over my shoulder. Bertol was slowly moving away with his friends. The rest of the crowd milled around in shock. 'Call a doctor!' I screamed. 'Get some medics up here!' Two men ran down the street. There was no sign of Siri.

'Wait a minute! Wait a minute!' said Mike in a stronger voice as if he had forgotten something important. 'Just a minute,' he said and died.

Died. A real death. Brain death. His mouth opened obscenely, his eyes rolled back so only the whites showed, and a minute later the blood ceased pumping from the wound.

For a few mad seconds I cursed the sky. I could see the *L.A.* moving across the fading starfield and I knew that I could bring Mike back if I could get him there in a few minutes. The crowd backed away as I screamed and ranted at the stars.

Eventually I turned to Bertol. 'You,' I said.

The young man had stopped at the far end of the Common. His face was ashen. He stared wordlessly.

'You,' I said again. I picked up the laser pen from where it had rolled, clicked the power to maximum, and walked to where Bertol and his friends stood waiting.

Later, through the haze of screams and scorched flesh, I was dimly aware of Siri's skimmer setting down in the crowded square, of dust flying up all around, and of her voice commanding me to join her. We lifted away from the light and madness. The cool wind blew my sweat-soaked hair away from my neck.

'We will go to Fevarone,' said Siri. 'Bertol was drunk. The Separatists are a small, violent group. There will be no reprisals. You will stay with me until the Council holds the inquest.'

'No,' I said. 'There. Land there.' I pointed to a spit of land not far from the city.

Siri landed despite her protests. I glanced at the boulder to make sure the backpack was still there and then climbed out of the skimmer. Siri slid across the seat and pulled my head down to hers. 'Merin, my love.' Her lips were warm and open but I felt nothing. My body felt anesthetized. I stepped back and waved her away. She brushed her hair back and stared at me from green eyes filled with tears. Then the skimmer lifted, turned, and sped to the south in the early morning light.

Just a minute, I felt like calling. I sat on a rock and gripped my knees as several ragged sobs were torn up out of me. Then I stood and threw the laser pen into the surf below. I tugged out the backpack and dumped the contents on the ground.

The hawking mat was gone.

I sat back down, too drained to laugh or cry or walk away. The sun rose as I sat there. I was still sitting there three hours later when the large black skimmer from ShipSecurity set down silently beside me.

*

'Father? Father, it is getting late.'

I turn to see my son Donel standing behind me. He is wearing the blue and gold robe of the Hegemony Council. His bald scalp is flushed and beaded with sweat. Donel is only forty-three but he seems much older to me.

'Please, Father,' he says. I nod and rise, brushing off the grass and dirt. We walk together to the front of the tomb. The crowd has pressed closer now. Gravel crunches under their feet as they shift restlessly. 'Shall I enter with you, Father?' Donel asks.

I pause to look at this aging stranger who is my child. There is little of Siri or me reflected in him. His face is friendly, florid, and tense with the excitement of the day. I can sense in him the open honesty which often takes the place of intelligence in some people. I cannot help but compare this balding puppy of a man to Alón – Alón of the dark curls and silences and sardonic smile. But Alón is thirty-three years dead, cut down in a stupid battle which had nothing to do with him.

'No,' I say. 'I'll go in by myself. Thank you, Donel.'

He nods and steps back. The pennants snap above the heads of the straining crowd. I turn my attention to the tomb.

The entrance is sealed with a palmlock. I have only to touch it.

During the past few minutes I have developed a fantasy which will save me from both the growing sadness within and the external series of events which I have initiated. Siri is not dead. In the last stages of her illness she had called together the doctors and the few technicians left in the colony and they rebuilt for her one of the ancient hibernation chambers used in their seedship two centuries earlier. Siri is only sleeping. What is more, the year-long sleep has somehow restored her youth. When I wake her she will be the Siri I remember from our early days. We will walk out into the sunlight together and when the farcaster doors open we shall be the first through.

'Father?'

'Yes.' I step forward and set my hand to the door of the crypt. There is a whisper of electric motors and the white slab of stone slides back. I bow my head and enter Siri's tomb.

'Damn it, Merin, secure that line before it knocks you overboard. Hurry!' I hurried. The wet rope was hard to coil, harder to tie off. Siri shook her head in disgust and leaned over to tie a bowline knot with one hand.

It was our Sixth Reunion. I had been three months too late for her birthday but more than five thousand other people had made it to the celebration. The CEO of the All Thing had wished her well in a forty-minute speech. A poet read his most recent verses to the Love Cycle sonnets. The Hegemony Ambassador had presented her with a scroll and a new ship, a small submersible powered by the first fusion cells to be allowed on Maui-Covenant.

Siri had eighteen other ships. Twelve belonged to her fleet of swift catamarans that plied their trade between the wandering Archipelago and the home islands. Two were beautiful racing yachts that were used only twice a year to win the Founder's Regatta and the Covenant Criterium. The other four craft were ancient fishing boats, homely and awkward, well maintained but little more than scows.

Siri had nineteen ships but we were on a fishing boat – the *Ginnie Paul*. For the past eight days we had fished the shelf of the Equatorial Shallows; a crew of two, casting and pulling nets, wading knee-deep through stinking fish and crunching trilobites, wallowing over every wave, casting and pulling nets, keeping watch, and sleeping like exhausted children during our brief rest periods. I was not quite twenty-three. I thought I was used to heavy labor aboard the *LA* and it was my custom to put in an hour of exercise in the 1.3-g pod every second shift, but now my arms and back ached from the strain and my hands were blistered between the calluses. Siri had just turned seventy.

'Merin, go forward and reef the foresail. Do the same for the jib and then go below to see to the sandwiches. Plenty of mustard.'

I nodded and went forward. For a day and a half we had been playing hide-and-seek with a storm: sailing before it when we could, turning about and accepting its punishment when we had to. At first it had been exciting, a welcome respite from the endless casting and pulling and mending. But after the first few hours the adrenaline rush faded to be replaced by constant nausea, fatigue, and a terrible tiredness. The seas did not relent. The waves grew to six meters and higher. The *Ginnie Paul* wallowed like the broad-beamed matron she was. Everything was wet. My skin was soaked under three layers of rain gear. For Siri it was a long-awaited vacation.

'This is nothing,' she had said during the darkest hour of the night as waves washed over the deck and smashed against the scarred plastic of the cockpit. 'You should see it during simoon season.'

The clouds still hung low and blended into gray waves in the distance but the sea was down to a gentle five-foot chop. I spread mustard across the roast beef sandwiches and poured steaming coffee into thick white mugs. It would have been easier to transport the coffee in zero-g without spilling it than to get up the pitching shaft of the companionway. Siri accepted her depleted cup without commenting. We sat in silence for a bit, appreciating the food and the tongue-scalding warmth. I took the wheel when Siri went below to refill our mugs. The gray day was dimming almost imperceptibly into night.

'Merin,' she said after handing me my mug and taking a seat on the long cushioned bench which encircled the cockpit, 'what will happen after they open the farcaster?'

I was surprised by the question. We had almost never talked about the time when Maui-Covenant would join the Hegemony. I glanced over at Siri and was struck by how ancient she suddenly seemed. Her face was a mosaic of seams and shadows. Her beautiful green eyes had sunken into wells of darkness and her cheekbones were knife edges against brittle parchment. She kept her gray hair cut short now and it stuck out in damp spikes. Her neck and wrists were tendoned cords emerging from a shapeless sweater.

'What do you mean?' I asked.

'What will happen after they open the farcaster?'

'You know what the Council says, Siri.' I spoke loudly because she was hard of hearing in one ear. 'It will open a new era of trade and technology for Maui-Covenant. And you won't be restricted to one little world any longer. When you become citizens, everyone will be entitled to use the farcaster doors.'

'Yes,' said Siri. Her voice was weary. 'I have heard all of that, Merin. But what will *happen*? Who will be the first through to us?'

I shrugged. 'More diplomats, I suppose. Cultural contact specialists. Anthropologists. Ethnologists, Marine biologists.'

'And then?'

I paused. It was dark out. The sea was almost gentle. Our running lights glowed red and green against the night. I felt the same anxiety I had known two days earlier when the wall of storm appeared on the horizon. I said, 'And then will come the missionaries. The petroleum geologists. The sea farmers. The developers.'

Siri sipped at her coffee. 'I would have thought your Hegemony was far beyond a petroleum economy.'

I laughed and locked the wheel in, 'Nobody gets beyond a petroleum economy. Not while there's petroleum there. We don't burn it, if that's what you mean. But it's still essential for the production of plastics, synthetics, food base, and keroids. Two hundred billion people use a lot of plastic.'

'And Maui-Covenant has oil?'

'Oh, yes,' I said. There was no more laughter in me. 'There are billions of barrels reservoired under the Equatorial Shallows alone.'

'How will they get it, Merin? Platforms?'

'Yeah. Platforms. Submersibles. Sub-sea colonies with tailored workers brought in from Mare Infinitus.'

'And the motile isles?' asked Siri. 'They must return each year to the shallows to feed on the bluekelp there and to reproduce. What will become of the isles?'

I shrugged again. I had drunk too much coffee and it had left a bitter taste in my mouth. 'I don't know,' I said. 'They haven't told the crew much. But back on our first trip out, Mike heard that they planned to develop as many of the isles as they can so some will be protected.'

'Develop?' Siri's voice showed surprise for the first time. 'How can they develop the isles? Even the First Families must ask permission of the Sea Folk to build our tree-house retreats there.'

I smiled at Siri's use of the local term for the dolphins. The Maui-Covenant colonists were such children when it came to their damned dolphins. 'The plans are all set,' I said. 'There are 128,573 motile isles big enough to build a dwelling on. Leases to those have long since been sold. The smaller isles will be broken up, I suppose. The home islands will be developed for recreation purposes.'

'Recreation purposes,' echoed Siri. 'How many people from the Hegemony will use the farcaster to come here . . . for recreation purposes?'

'At first, you mean?' I asked. 'Just a few thousand the first year. As long as the only door is on island 241 . . . the Trade Center . . . it will be limited. Perhaps fifty thousand the second year when Firstsite gets its door. It'll be quite the luxury tour. Always is after a seed colony is first opened to the Web.'

'And later?'

'After the five-year probation? There will be thousands of doors, of course. I would imagine that there will be twenty or thirty million new residents coming through during the first year of full citizenship.'

'Twenty or thirty million,' said Siri. The light from the compass stand illuminated her lined face from below. There was still a beauty there. But there was no anger or shock. I had expected both.

'But you'll be citizens then yourself,' I said. 'Free to step anywhere in the Worldweb. There will be sixteen new worlds to choose from. Probably more by then.'

'Yes,' said Siri and set aside her empty mug. A fine rain streaked the glass around us. The crude radar screen set in its hand-carved frame showed the seas empty, the storm past. 'Is it true, Merin, that people in the Hegemony have their homes on a dozen worlds? One house, I mean, with windows facing out on a dozen skies?'

'Sure,' I said. 'But not many people. Only the rich can afford multiworld residences like that.'

Siri smiled and set her hand on my knee. The back of her hand was mottled and blue-veined. 'But you are very rich, are you not, Shipman?'

I looked away. 'Not yet I'm not.'

'Ah, but soon, Merin, soon. How long for you, my love? Less than two weeks here and then the voyage back to your Hegemony. Five months more of your time to bring the last components back, a few weeks to finish, and then you step home a rich man. *Step* two hundred empty light-years home. What a strange thought . . . but where was I? That is how long? Less than a standard year.'

'Ten months,' I said. 'Three hundred and six standard days. Three hundred fourteen of yours. Nine hundred eighteen shifts.'

'And then your exile will be over.'

'Yes.'

'And you will be twenty-four years old and very rich.'

'Yes.'

'I'm tired, Merin. I want to sleep now.'

We programmed the tiller, set the collision alarm, and went below. The wind had risen some and the old vessel wallowed from wave crest to trough with every swell. We undressed in the dim light of the swinging lamp. I was first in the bunk and under the covers. It was the first time Siri and I had shared a sleep period. Remembering our last Reunion and her shyness at the villa, I expected her to douse the light. Instead she stood a minute, nude in the chill air, thin arms calmly at her sides.

Time had claimed Siri but had not ravaged her. Gravity had done its inevitable work on her breasts and buttocks and she was much thinner. I stared at the gaunt outlines of ribs and breastbone and remembered the sixteen-year-old girl with baby fat and skin like warm velvet. In the cold light of the swinging lamp I stared at Siri's sagging flesh and remembered moonlight on budding breasts. Yet somehow, strangely, inexplicably, it was the *same* Siri who stood before me now.

'Move over, Merin.' She slipped into the bunk beside me. The sheets were cool against our skin, the rough blanket welcome. I turned off the light. The little ship swayed to the regular rhythm of the sea's breathing. I could hear the sympathetic creak of masts and rigging. In the morning we could be casting and pulling and mending but now there was time to sleep. I began to doze to the sound of waves against wood.

'Merin?'

'Yes.'

'What would happen if the Separatists attacked the Hegemony tourists or the new residents?'

'I thought the Separatists had all been carted off to the isles.'

'They have been. But what if they resisted?'

'The Hegemony would send in FORCE troops who could kick the shit out of the Separatists.'

'What if the farcaster itself were attacked . . . destroyed before it was operational?'

'Impossible.'

'Yes, I know, but what if it were?'

'Then the *Los Angeles* would return nine months later with Hegemony troops who would proceed to kick the shit out of the Separatists . . . and anyone else on Maui-Covenant who got in their way.'

'Nine months' shiptime,' said Siri. 'Eleven years of our time.'

'But inevitable either way,' I said. 'Let's talk about something else.'

'All right,' said Siri but we did not speak. I listened to the crack and sigh of the ship. Siri had nestled in the hollow of my arm. Her head was on my shoulder and her breathing was so deep and regular that I thought her to be asleep. I was almost asleep myself when her warm hand slid up my leg and lightly cupped me. I was startled even as I began to stir and stiffen. Siri whispered an answer to my unasked question. 'No, Merin, one is never really too old. At least not too old to want the warmth and closeness. You decide, my love. I will be content either way.'

I decided. Toward the dawn we slept.

The tomb is empty.

'Donel, come in here!'

He bustles in, robes rustling in the hollow emptiness. The tomb *is* empty. There is no hibernation chamber – I did not truly expect there to be one – but neither is there sarcophagus or coffin. A bright bulb illuminates the white interior. 'What the hell is this, Donel? I thought this was Siri's tomb.'

'It is, Father.'

'Where is she interred? Under the floor for Chrissake?'

Donel mops at his brow. I remember that it is his mother I am speaking of. I also remember that he has had almost two years to accustom himself to the idea of her death.

'No one told you?' he asks.

'Told me what?' The anger and confusion are already ebbing. 'I was rushed here from the dropship station and told that I was to visit Siri's tomb before the farcaster opening. What?'

'Mother was cremated as per her instructions. Her ashes were spread on the Great South Sea from the highest platform of the family isle.'

'Then why this . . . *crypt*?' I watch what I say. Donel is sensitive.

He mops his brow again and glances to the door. We are shielded from the view of the crowd but we are far behind schedule. Already the other members of the Council have had to hurry down the hill to join the dignitaries on the bandstand. My slow grief this day has been worse than bad timing – it has turned into bad theater.

'Mother left instructions. They were carried out.' He touches a panel on the inner wall and it slides up to reveal a small niche containing a metal box. My name is on it.

'What is that?'

Donel shakes his head. 'Personal items Mother left for you. Only Magritte knew the details and she died last winter without telling anyone.'

'All right,' I say. 'Thank you. I'll be out in a moment.'

Donel glances at his chronometer. 'The ceremony begins in eight minutes. They will activate the farcaster in twenty minutes.'

'I know,' I say. I *do* know. Part of me knows precisely how much time is left. 'I'll be out in a moment.'

Donel hesitates and then departs. I close the door behind him with a touch of my palm. The metal box is surprisingly heavy. I set it on the stone floor and crouch beside it. A smaller palmlock gives me access. The lid clicks open and I peer into the container.

'Well I'll be damned,' I say softly. I do not know what I expected – artifacts perhaps, nostalgic mementos of our hundred and three days together – perhaps a pressed flower from some forgotten offering or the frenchhorn conch we dove for off Fevarone. But there are no mementos – not as such.

The box holds a small Steiner-Ginn handlaser, one of the most powerful projection weapons ever made. The accumulator is attached by a power lead to a small fusion cell that Siri must have cannibalized from her new submersible. Also attached to the fusion cell is an ancient comlog, an antique with a solid state interior and a liquid crystal diskey. The charge indicator glows green.

There are two other objects in the box. One is the translator medallion we had used so long ago. The final object makes me literally gape in surprise.

'Why, you little bitch,' I say. Things fall into place. I cannot stop a smile. 'You dear, conniving, little bitch.'

There, rolled carefully, power lead correctly attached, lies the hawking mat Mike Osho bought in Carvnel Marketplace for thirty marks. I leave the hawking mat there, disconnect the comlog, and lift it out. I sit crosslegged on the cold stone and thumb the diskey. The light in the crypt fades out and suddenly Siri is there before me.

They did not throw me off the ship when Mike died. They could have but they did not. They did not leave me to the mercy of provincial justice on Maui-Covenant. They could have but they chose not to. For two days I was held in Security and questioned, once by Shipmaster Singh himself. Then they let me return to duty. For the four months of the long leap back I tortured myself with the memory of Mike's murder. I knew that in my clumsy way I had helped to murder him. I put in my shifts, dreamed my sweaty nightmares, and wondered if they would dismiss me when we reached the Web. They could have told me but they chose not to.

They did not dismiss me. I was to have my normal leave in the Web but could take no off-Ship R and R while in the Maui-Covenant system. In addition, there was a written reprimand and temporary reduction in rank. That was what Mike's life had been worth – a reprimand and reduction in rank.

I took my three-week leave with the rest of the crew but, unlike the others, I did not plan to return. I farcast to Esperance and made the classic Shipman's mistake of trying to visit family. Two days in the crowded residential bulb was enough and I stepped to Lusus and took my pleasure in three days of whoring on the Rue des Chats. When my mood turned darker I 'cast to Fuji and lost most of my ready marks betting on the bloody samurai fights there.

Finally I found myself farcasting to Homesystem Station and taking the two-day pilgrim shuttle down to Hellas Basin. I had never been to Homesystem or Mars before and I never plan to return, but the ten days I spent there, alone and wandering the dusty, haunted corridors of the Monastery, served to send me back to the ship. Back to Siri.

Occasionally I would leave the red-stoned maze of the megalith and, clad only in skinsuit and mask, stand on one of the uncounted thousands of stone balconies and stare skyward at the pale gray star which had once been Old Earth. Sometimes then I thought of the brave and stupid idealists heading out into the great dark in their slow and leaking ships, carrying embryos and ideologies with equal faith and care. But most times I did not try to think. Most times I simply stood in the purple night and let Siri come to me. There in the Master's Rock, where perfect satori had eluded so many much worthier pilgrims, I achieved it through the memory of a not quite sixteen-year-old womanchild's body lying next to mine while moonlight spilled from a Thomas Hawk's wings.

When the *Los Angeles* spun back up to a quantum state, I went with her. Four months later I was content to pull my shift with the construction crew, plug into my usual stims, and sleep my R and R away. Then Singh came to me. 'You're going down,' he said. I did not understand. 'In the past eleven years the groundlings have turned your screw-up with Osho into a goddamned legend,' said Singh. 'There's an entire cultural mythos built around your little roll in the hay with that colonial girl.'

'Siri,' I said.

'Get your gear,' said Singh. 'You'll spend your three weeks groundside. The Ambassador's experts say you'll do the Hegemony more good down there than up here. We'll see.'

The world was waiting. Crowds were cheering. Siri was waving. We left the harbor in a yellow catamaran and sailed south-southeast, bound for the Archipelago and her family isle.

'Hello, Merin.' Siri floats in the darkness of her tomb. The holo is not perfect; a haziness mars the edges. But it is Siri – Siri as I last saw her, gray hair shorn rather than cut, head high, face sharpened with shadows. 'Hello, Merin, my love.'

'Hello, Siri,' I say. The tomb door is closed.

'I am sorry I cannot share our Seventh Reunion, Merin. I looked forward to it.' Siri pauses and looks down at her hands. The image flickers slightly as dust motes float through her form. 'I had carefully planned what to say here,' she goes on. 'How to say it. Arguments to be pled. Instructions to be given. But I know how useless that would have been. Either I have said it already and you have heard or there is nothing left to say and silence would best suit the moment.'

Siri's voice had grown even more beautiful with age. There is a fullness and calmness there which can come only from knowing pain. Siri moves her hands and they disappear beyond the border of the projection. 'Merin, my love, how strange our days apart and together have been. How beautifully absurd the myth that bound us. My days were but heartbeats to you. I hated you for that. You were the mirror that would not lie. If you could have seen your face at the beginning of each Reunion! The least you could have done was to hide your shock . . . that, at least, you could have done for me.

'But through your clumsy naiveté there has always been . . . what? . . . something, Merin. There is something there that belies the callowness and thoughtless egotism which you wear so well. A caring, perhaps. A *respect* for caring, if nothing else.

'Merin, this diary has hundreds of entries . . . thousands, I fear . . . I have kept it since I was thirteen. By the time you see this, they will all have been erased except the ones which follow. Adieu, my love. Adieu.'

I shut off the comlog and sit in silence for a minute. The crowd sounds are barely audible through the thick walls of the tomb. I take a breath and thumb the diskey.

Siri appears. She is in her late forties. I know immediately the day and place she recorded this image. I remember the cloak she wears, the eelstone pendant at her neck, and the strand of hair which has escaped her barrette and even now falls across her cheek. I remember everything about that day. It was the last day of our Third Reunion and we were with friends on the heights above South Tern. Donel was ten and we were trying to convince him to slide on the snowfield with us. He was crying. Siri turned away from us even before the skimmer settled. When Magritte stepped out we knew from Siri's face that something had happened.

The same face stares at me now. She brushes absently at the unruly strand of hair. Her eyes are red but her voice is controlled. 'Merin, they killed our son today. Alón was twenty-one and they killed him. You were so confused today, Merin. "How could such a mistake have happened?" you kept repeating. You did not really know our son but I could see the loss in your face when we heard. Merin, it was not an accident. If nothing else survives, no other record, if you never understand why I allowed a senti-mental myth to rule my life, let this be known – *it was not an accident that killed Alón*. He was with the Separatists when the Council police arrived. Even then he could have escaped. We had prepared an alibi together. The police would have believed his story. He chose to stay.

'Today, Merin, you were impressed with what I said to the crowd . . . the mob . . . at the embassy. Know this, Shipman – when I said, "Now is not the time to show your anger and your hatred," that is precisely what I meant. No more, no less. Today is not the time. But the day will come. It will surely come. The Covenant was not taken lightly in those final days, Merin. It is not taken lightly now. Those who have forgotten will be surprised when the day comes but it will surely come.'

The image fades to another and in the split second of overlap the face of a twenty-six-year-old Siri appears superimposed on the older woman's features. 'Merin, I am pregnant. I'm so glad. You've been gone five weeks now and I *miss* you. Ten *years* you'll be gone. More than that. Merin, why didn't you think to invite me to go with you? I could not have gone but I would have loved it if you had just *invited* me. But I'm pregnant, Merin. The doctors say that it will be a boy. I will tell him about you, my love. Perhaps someday you and he will sail in the Archipelago and listen to the songs of the Sea Folk as you and I have done these past few weeks. Perhaps you'll understand them by then. Merin, I *miss* you. Please hurry back.'

The holographic image shimmers and shifts. The sixteen-year-old girl is red-faced. Her long hair cascades over bare shoulders and a white nightgown. She speaks in a rush, racing tears. 'Shipman Merin Aspic, I'm sorry about your friend – I really am – but you left without even saying *goodbye*. I had such plans about how you would help us . . . how you and I . . . you didn't even say goodbye. I don't care *what* happens to you. I hope you go back to your stinking, crowded Hegemony hives and rot for all I care. In fact, Merin Aspic, I wouldn't want to see you again even if they paid me. *Goodbye*.'

She turns her back before the projection fades. It is dark in the tomb now but the audio continues for a second. There is a soft chuckle and Siri's voice – I cannot tell the age – comes one last time. 'Adieu, Merin. Adieu.'

'Adieu,' I say and thumb the diskey off.

The crowd parts as I emerge blinking from the tomb. My poor timing has ruined the drama of the event and now the smile on my face incites angry whispers. Loudspeakers carry the rhetoric of the official ceremony even to our hilltop. '. . . beginning a new era of cooperation,' echoes the rich voice of the Ambassador.

I set the box on the grass and remove the hawking mat. The crowd presses forward to see as I unroll the carpet. The tapestry is faded but the flight threads gleam like new copper. I sit in the center of the mat and slide the heavy box on behind me.

'. . . and more will follow until space and time will cease to be obstacles.'

The crowd moves back as I tap the flight design and the hawking mat rises four meters into the air. Now I can see beyond the roof of the tomb. The islands are returning to form the Equatorial Archipelago. I can see them, hundreds of them, borne up out of the hungry south by gentle winds.

'So it is with great pleasure that I close this circuit and welcome you, the colony of Maui-Covenant, into the community of the Hegemony of Man.'

The thin thread of the ceremonial comm-laser pulses to the zenith. There is a pattering of applause and the band begins playing. I squint skyward just in time to see a new star being born. Part of me knew to the microsecond what has just occurred.

For a few microseconds the farcaster had been functional. For a few microseconds time and space *had* ceased to be obstacles. Then the massive tidal pull of the artificial singularity triggered the thermite charge I had placed on the outer containment sphere. That tiny explosion had not been visible but a second later the expanding Schwarzschild radius is eating its shell, swallowing thirty-six thousand tons of fragile dodecahedron, and growing quickly to gobble several thousand kilometers of space around it. And *that* is visible – magnificently visible – as a miniature nova flares whitely in the clear blue sky.

The band stops playing. People scream and run for cover. There is no reason to. There is a burst of X-rays tunneling out as the farcaster continues to collapse into itself, but not enough to cause harm through

Maui-Covenant's generous atmosphere. A second streak of plasma becomes visible as the *Los Angeles* puts more distance between itself and the rapidly decaying little black hole. The winds rise and the seas are choppier. There will be strange tides tonight.

I want to say something profound but I can think of nothing. Besides, the crowd is in no mood to listen. I tell myself that I can hear some cheers mixed in with the screams and shouts.

I tap at the flight designs and the hawking mat speeds out over the cliff and above the harbor. A Thomas Hawk lazing on midday thermals flaps in panic at my approach.

'Let them come!' I shout at the fleeing hawk. 'Let them come! I'll be thirty-five and not alone and let them come if they dare!' I drop my fist and laugh. The wind is blowing my hair and cooling the sweat on my chest and arms.

Cooler now, I take a sighting and set my course for the most distant of the isles. I look forward to meeting the others. Even more, I look forward to talking to the Sea Folk and telling them that it is time for the Shark to come at last to the seas of Maui-Covenant.

Later, when the battles are won and the world is theirs, I will tell them about her. I will sing to them of Siri.

The cascade of light from the distant space battle continued. There was no sound except for the slide of wind across escarpments. The group sat close together, leaning forward and looking at the antique comlog as if expecting more.

There was no more. The Consul removed the microdisk and pocketed it.

Sol Weintraub rubbed the back of his sleeping infant and spoke to the Consul. 'Surely you're not Merin Aspic.'

'No,' said the Consul. 'Merin Aspic died during the Rebellion. Siri's Rebellion.'

'How did you come to possess this recording?' asked Father Hoyt. Through the priest's mask of pain, it was visible that he had been moved. 'This incredible recording . . .'

'He gave it to me,' said the Consul. 'A few weeks before he was killed in the Battle of the Archipelago.' The Consul looked at the uncomprehending faces before him. 'I'm their grandson,' he said. 'Siri's and Merin's. My father . . . the Donel whom Aspic mentions . . . became the first Home Rule Councilor when Maui-Covenant was admitted to the Protectorate. Later he was elected Senator and served until his death. I was nine years old that day on the hill near Siri's tomb. I was twenty – old enough to join the rebels and fight – when Aspic came to our isle at night, took me aside, and forbade me to join their band.'

'Would you have fought?' asked Brawne Lamia.

'Oh, yes. And died. Like a third of our menfolk and a fifth of our women. Like all of the dolphins and many of the isles themselves, although the Hegemony tried to keep as many of those intact as possible.'

'It is a moving document,' said Sol Weintraub. 'But why are you here? Why the pilgrimage to the Shrike?'

'I am not finished,' said the Consul. 'Listen.'

My father was as weak as my grandmother had been strong. The Hegemony did not wait eleven local years to return – the FORCE torchships were in orbit before five years had elapsed. Father watched as the rebels' hastily constructed ships were swatted aside. He continued to defend the Hegemony as they laid siege to our world. I remember when I was fifteen, watching with my family from the upper deck of our ancestral isle as a dozen other islands burned in the distance, the Hegemony skimmers lighting the sea with their depth charges. In the morning, the waves were gray with the bodies of the dead dolphins.

My older sister Lira went to fight with the rebels in those hopeless days after the Battle of the Archipelago. Eyewitnesses saw her die. Her body was never recovered. My father never mentioned her name again.

Within three years after the cease-fire and admission to the Protectorate, we original colonists were a minority on our own world. The isles were tamed and sold to tourists, just as Merin had predicted to Siri. Firstsite is a city of eleven million now, the condos and spires and EM cities extending around the entire island along the coast. Firstsite Harbor remains as a quaint bazaar, with descendants of the First Families selling crafts and overpriced art there.

We lived on Tau Ceti Center for a while when Father was first elected Senator, and I finished school there. I was the dutiful son, extolling the virtues of life in the Web, studying the glorious history of the Hegemony of Man, and preparing for my own career in the diplomatic corps.

And all the time I waited.

I returned to Maui-Covenant briefly after graduation, working in the offices on Central Administration Isle. Part of my job was to visit the hundreds of drilling platforms going up in the shallows, to report on the rapidly multiplying undersea complexes, and to act as liaison with the development corporations coming in from TC^2 and Sol Draconi Septem. I did not enjoy the work. But I was efficient. And I smiled. And I waited.

I courted and married a girl from one of the First Families, from Siri's cousin Bertol's line, and after receiving a rare 'First' on diplomatic corps examinations, I requested a post out of the Web.

Thus began our personal Diaspora, Gresha's and mine. I was efficient. I was born to diplomacy. Within five standard years I was an Under Consul. Within eight, a Consul in my own right. As long as I stayed in the Outback, this was as far as I would rise.

It was my choice. I worked for the Hegemony. And I waited.

At first my role was to provide Web ingenuity to help the colonists do what they do best – destroy truly indigenous life. It is no accident that in six centuries of interstellar expansion the Hegemony has encountered no species considered intelligent on the Drake-Turing-Chen Index. On Old Earth, it had long been accepted that if a species put mankind on its food-chain menu the species would be extinct before long. As the Web expanded, if a species attempted serious competition with

337

humanity's intellect, that species would be extinct before the first farcaster opened in-system.

On Whirl we stalked the elusive zeplen through their cloud towers. It is possible that they were not sapient by human or Core standards. But they were beautiful. When they died, rippling in rainbow colors, their many-hued messages unseen, unheard by their fleeing herdmates, the beauty of their death agony was beyond words. We sold their photoreceptive skins to Web corporations, their flesh to worlds like Heaven's Gate, and ground their bones to powder to sell as aphrodisiacs to the impotent and superstitious on a score of other colony worlds.

On Garden I was adviser to the arcology engineers who drained Grand Fen, ending the short reign of the marsh centaurs who had ruled – and threatened Hegemony progress – there. They tried to migrate in the end, but the North Reaches were far too dry and when I visited the region decades later, when Garden entered the Web, the desiccated remains of the centaurs still littered some of the distant Reaches like the husks of exotic plants from some more colorful era.

On Hebron I arrived just as the Jewish settlers were ending their long feud with the Seneschal Aluit, creatures as fragile as the world's waterless ecology. The Aluit were empathic and it was our fear and greed which killed them – that and our unbreachable alienness. But on Hebron it was not the death of the Aluit which turned my heart to stone, but my part in dooming the colonists themselves.

On Old Earth they had a word for what I was – quisling. For, although Hebron was not my world, the settlers who had fled there had done so for reasons as clear as those of my ancestors who signed the Covenant of Life on the Old Earth island of Maui. But I was waiting. And in my waiting I acted . . . in all senses of the word.

They trusted me. They grew to believe in my candid revelations of how wonderful it was to rejoin the community of mankind . . . to join the Web. They insisted that only the one city might be open to foreigners. I smiled and agreed. And now New Jerusalem holds sixty millions while the continent holds ten million Jewish indigenies, dependent upon the Web city for most of what they need. Another decade. Perhaps less.

I broke down a bit after Hebron was opened to the Web. I discovered alcohol, the blessed antithesis of Flashback and wireheading. Gresha stayed with me in the hospital there until I dried out. Oddly, for a Jewish world, the clinic was Catholic. I remember the rustle of robes in the halls at night.

My breakdown had been very quiet and very far away. My career was not damaged. As full Consul, I took my wife and son to Bressia.

How delicate our role there! How Byzantine the fine line we walked. For decades, Colonel Kassad, forces of the TechnoCore had been harassing the Ouster swarms wherever they fled. Now the forces-that-be in the Senate and AI Advisory Council had determined that some test had to be made of Ouster might in the Outback itself. Bressia was chosen. I admit, the Bressians had been our surrogates for decades before I arrived. Their society was archaically and delightfully Prussian, militaristic to a fault, arrogant in their economic pretensions, xenophobic to the point of happily enlisting to wipe out the 'Ouster Menace'. At first, a *few lend-lease torchships so that they could reach the swarms. Plasma weapons. Impact probes with tailored viruses.*

It was a slight miscalculation that I was still on Bressia when the Ouster hordes arrived. A few months' difference. A military-political analysis team should have been there in my place.

It did not matter. Hegemony purposes were served. The resolve and rapid-deployment capabilities of FORCE were properly tested where no real harm was done to Hegemony interests. Gresha died, of course. In the first bombardment. And Alón, my ten-year-old son. He had been with me . . . had survived the war itself . . . only to die when some FORCE idiot set off a booby trap or demolition charge too near the refugee barracks in Buckminster, the capital.

I was not with him when he died.

I was promoted after Bressia. I was given the most challenging and sensitive assignment ever delegated to someone of mere consular rank: diplomat in charge of direct negotiations with the Ousters themselves.

First I was 'cast to Tau Ceti Center for long conferences with Senator Gladstone's committee and some of the AI Councilors. I met with Gladstone herself. The plan was very complicated. Essentially the Ousters had to be provoked into attacking, and the key to that provocation was the world of Hyperion.

The Ousters had been observing Hyperion since before the Battle of Bressia. Our intelligence suggested that they were obsessed with the Time Tombs and the Shrike. Their attack on the Hegemony hospital ship carrying Colonel Kassad, among others, had been a miscalculation; their ship captain had panicked when the hospital ship had been mistakenly identified as a military spinship. Worse, from the Ousters' point of view, was the fact that by setting their dropships down near the Tombs themselves, the same commander had revealed their ability to defy the time tides. After the Shrike had decimated their commando teams, the torchship captain returned to the Swarm to be executed.

But our intelligence suggested that the Ouster miscalculation had not been a total disaster. Valuable information had been obtained about the Shrike. And their obsession with Hyperion had deepened.

Gladstone explained to me how the Hegemony planned to capitalize on that obsession.

The essence of the plan was that the Ousters had to be provoked into attacking the Hegemony. The focus of that attack was to be Hyperion itself. I was made to understand that the resulting battle had more to do with internal Web politics than with the Ousters. Elements of the TechnoCore had opposed Hyperion's entry into the Hegemony for centuries. Gladstone explained that this was no longer in the interest of humanity and that a forcible annexation of Hyperion – under the guise of defending the Web itself – would allow more progressive AI coalitions in the Core to gain power. This shift of the power balance in the Core would benefit the Senate and the Web in ways not fully explained to me. The Ousters would be eradicated as a potential menace once and for all. A new era of Hegemony glory would begin.

Gladstone explained that I need not volunteer, that the mission would be fraught with dangers – both for my career and my life. I accepted anyway.

339

The Hegemony provided me with a private spacecraft. I asked for only one modification: the addition of an antique Steinway piano.

For months I traveled alone under Hawking drive. For more months I wandered in regions where the Ouster Swarms regularly migrated. Eventually my ship was sensed and seized. They accepted that I was a courier and knew that I was a spy. They debated killing me and did not. They debated negotiating with me and eventually decided to do so.

I will not try to describe the beauty of life in a Swarm – their zero-gravity globe cities and comet farms and thrust clusters, their micro-orbital forests and migrating rivers and the ten thousand colors and textures of life at Rendezvous Week. Suffice it to say that I believe the Ousters have done what Web humanity has not in the past millennia: evolved. While we live in our derivative cultures, pale reflections of Old Earth life, the Ousters have explored new dimensions of aesthetics and ethics and biosciences and art and all the things that must change and grow to reflect the human soul.

Barbarians, we call them, while all the while we timidly cling to our Web like Visigoths crouching in the ruins of Rome's faded glory and proclaim ourselves civilized.

Within ten standard months, I had told them my greatest secret and they had told me theirs. I explained in all the detail I could what plans for extinction had been laid for them by Gladstone's people. I told them what little the Web scientists understood of the anomaly of the Time Tombs and revealed the Techno-Core's inexplicable fear of Hyperion. I described how Hyperion would be a trap for them if they dared attempt to occupy it, how every element of FORCE would be brought to Hyperion System to crush them. I revealed everything I knew and waited once again to die.

Instead of killing me, they told me something. They showed me fatline intercepts, tightbeam recordings, and their own records from the date they fled Old Earth System, four and a half centuries earlier. Their facts were terrible and simple.

The Big Mistake of '38 had been no mistake. The death of Old Earth had been deliberate, planned by elements of the TechnoCore and their human counterparts in the fledgling government of the Hegemony. The Hegira had been planned in detail decades before the runaway black hole had 'accidentally' been plunged into the heart of Old Earth.

The Worldweb, the All Thing, the Hegemony of Man – all of them had been built on the most vicious type of patricide. Now they were being maintained by a quiet and deliberate policy of fratricide – the murder of any species with even the slightest potential of being a competitor. And the Ousters, the only other tribe of humanity free to wander between the stars and the only group not dominated by the TechnoCore, was next on our list of extinction.

I returned to the Web. Over thirty years of Web-time had passed. Meina Gladstone was CEO. Siri's Rebellion was a romantic legend, a minor footnote in the history of the Hegemony.

I met with Gladstone. I told her many – but not all – of the things the Ousters had revealed. I told her that they knew that any battle for Hyperion would be a trap, but that they were coming anyway. I told her that the Ousters wanted me to become Consul on Hyperion so that I might be a double agent when war came.

I did not tell her that they had promised to give me a device which would open the Time Tombs and allow the Shrike free rein.

CEO Gladstone had long talks with me. FORCE:Intelligence agents had even longer talks with me, some lasting months. Technologies and drugs were used to confirm that I was telling the truth and keeping nothing back. The Ousters also had been very good with technologies and drugs. I was telling the truth. I was also keeping something back.

In the end, I was assigned to Hyperion. Gladstone offered to raise the world to Protectorate status and me to an ambassadorship, I declined both offers, although I asked if I could keep my private spacecraft. I arrived on a regularly scheduled spinship, and my own ship arrived several weeks later in the belly of a visiting torchship. It was left in a parking orbit with the understanding that I could summon it and leave any time I wished.

Alone on Hyperion, I waited. Years passed, I allowed my aide to govern the Outback world while I drank at Cicero's and waited.

The Ousters contacted me through private fatline and I took a three weeks' leave from the Consulate, brought my ship down to an isolated place near the Sea of Grass, rendezvoused with their scoutship near the Oört Cloud, picked up their agent – a woman named Andil – and a trio of technicians, and dropped down north of the Bridle Range, a few kilometers from the Tombs themselves.

The Ousters did not have farcasters. They spent their lives on the long marches between the stars, watching life in the Web speed by like some film or holie set at a frenzied speed. They were obsessed with time. The TechnoCore had given the Hegemony the farcaster and continued to maintain it. No human scientists or team of human scientists had come close to understanding it. The Ousters tried. They failed. But even in their failures they made inroads into understanding the manipulation of space/time.

They understood the time tides, the anti-entropic fields surrounding the Tombs. They could not generate such fields, but they could shield against them and – theoretically – collapse them. The Time Tombs and all their contents would cease to age backward. The Tombs would 'open'. The Shrike would slip its tether, no longer connected to the vicinity of the Tombs. Whatever else was inside would now be freed.

The Ousters believed that the Time Tombs were artifacts from their future, the Shrike a weapon of redemption awaiting the proper hand to seize it. The Shrike Cult saw the monster as an avenging angel; the Ousters saw it as a tool of human devising, sent back through time to deliver humanity from the TechnoCore. Andil and the technicians were there to calibrate and experiment.

'You won't use it now?' I asked. We were standing in the shadow of the structure called the Sphinx.

'Not now,' said Andil. 'When the invasion is imminent.'

'But you said it would take months for the device to work,' I said, 'for the Tombs to open.'

Andil nodded. Her eyes were a dark green. She was very tall, and I could make out the subtle stripes of the powered exoskeleton on her skinsuit. 'Perhaps a year or longer,' she said. 'The device causes the anti-entropic field to decay slowly. But once begun, the process is irrevocable. But we will not activate it until the Ten Councils have decided that invasion of the Web is necessary.'

'There are doubts?' I said.

'Ethical debates,' said Andil. A few meters from us, the three technicians were covering the device with chameleon cloth and a coded containment field. 'And interstellar war will cause the deaths of millions, perhaps billions. Releasing the Shrike into the Web will have unforeseen consequences. As much as we need to strike at the Core, there are debates as to which is the best way.'

I nodded and looked at the device and the valley of the Tombs. 'But once this is activated,' I said, 'there is no turning back. The Shrike will be released, and you will have to have won the war to control it?'

Andil smiled slightly. 'That is true.'

I shot her then, her and then the three technicians. Then I tossed Grandmother Siri's Steiner-Ginn laser far into the drift dunes and sat on an empty flowfoam crate and sobbed for several minutes. Then I walked over, used a technician's comlog to enter the containment field, threw off the chameleon cloth, and triggered the device.

There was no immediate change. The air held the same rich, late-winter light. The Jade Tomb glowed softly while the Sphinx continued to stare down at nothing. The only sound was the rasp of sand across the crates and bodies. Only a glowing indicator on the Ouster device showed that it was working . . . had already worked.

I walked slowly back to the ship, half expecting the Shrike to appear, half hoping that it would. I sat on the balcony of my ship for more than an hour, watching the shadows filling the valley and the sand covering the distant corpses. There was no Shrike. No thorn tree. After a while I played a Bach Prelude on the Steinway, buttoned up the ship, and rose into space.

I contacted the Ouster ship and said that there had been an accident. The Shrike had taken the others; the device had been activated prematurely. Even in their confusion and panic, the Ousters offered me refuge. I declined the offer and turned my ship toward the Web. The Ousters did not pursue.

I used my fatline transmitter to contact Gladstone and to tell her that the Ouster agents had been eliminated. I told her that the invasion was very likely, that the trap would be sprung as planned. I did not tell her about the device. Gladstone congratulated me and called me home. I declined. I told her that I needed silence and solitude. I turned my ship toward the Outback world nearest the Hyperion system, knowing that travel itself would eat time until the next act commenced.

Later, when the fatline call to pilgrimage came from Gladstone herself, I knew the role the Ousters had planned for me in these final days: the Ousters, or the Core, or Gladstone and her machinations. It no longer matters who consider themselves the masters of events. Events no longer obey their masters.

The world as we know it is ending, my friends, no matter what happens to us. As for me, I have no request of the Shrike. I bring no final words for it or the universe. I have returned because I must, because this is my fate. I've known what

I must do since I was a child, returning alone to Siri's tomb and swearing vengeance on the Hegemony. I've known what price I must pay, both in life and in history.

But when the time comes to judge, to understand a betrayal which will spread like flame across the Web, which will end worlds, I ask you not to think of me – my name was not even writ on water as your lost poet's soul said – but to think of Old Earth dying for no reason, to think of the dolphins, their gray flesh drying and rotting in the sun, to see – as I have seen – the motile isles with no place to wander, their feeding grounds destroyed, the Equatorial Shallows scabbed with drilling platforms, the islands themselves burdened with shouting, trammeling tourists smelling of UV lotion and cannabis.

Or better yet, think of none of that. Stand as I did after throwing the switch, a murderer, a betrayer, but still proud, feet firmly planted on Hyperion's shifting sand, head held high, fist raised against the sky, crying 'A plague on both your houses!'

For you see, I remember my grandmother's dream. I remember the way it could have been.

I remember Siri.

'Are you the spy?' asked Father Hoyt. 'The Ouster spy?'

The Consul rubbed his cheeks and said nothing. He looked tired, spent.

'Yeah,' said Martin Silenus. 'CEO Gladstone warned me when I was chosen for the pilgrimage. She said that there was a spy.'

'She told all of us,' snapped Brawne Lamia. She stared at the Consul. Her gaze seemed sad.

'Our friend is a spy,' said Sol Weintraub, 'but not merely an Ouster spy.' The baby had awakened. Weintraub lifted her to calm her crying. 'He is what they call in the thrillers a double agent, a triple agent in this case, an agent to infinite regression. In truth, an agent of retribution.'

The Consul looked at the old scholar.

'He's still a spy,' said Silenus. 'Spies are executed, aren't they?'

Colonel Kassad had the deathwand in his hand. It was not aimed in anyone's direction. 'Are you in touch with your ship?' he asked the Consul.

'Yes.'

'How?'

'Through Siri's comlog. It was . . . modified.'

Kassad nodded slightly. 'And you've been in touch with the Ousters via the ship's fatline transmitter?'

'Yes.'

'Making reports on the pilgrimage as they expected?'

'Yes.'

'Have they replied?'

'No.'

'How can we believe *him*?' cried the poet. 'He's a fucking *sky*.'

'Shut up,' Colonel Kassad said flatly, finally. His gaze never left the Consul. 'Did you attack Het Masteen?'

'No,' said the Consul. 'But when the *Yggdrasill* burned, I knew that something was wrong.'

'What do you mean?' said Kassad.

The Consul cleared his throat. 'I've spent time with Templar Voices of the Tree. Their connection to their treeships is almost telepathic. Masteen's reaction was far too subdued. Either he wasn't what he said he was, or he had *known* that the ship was to be destroyed and had severed contact with it. When I was on guard duty, I went below to confront him. He was gone. The cabin was as we found it, except for the fact that the Möbius cube was in a neutral state. The erg could have escaped. I secured it and went above.'

'You did not harm Het Masteen?' Kassad asked again.

'No.'

'I repeat, why the fuck should we believe *you*?' said Silenus. The poet was drinking Scotch from the last bottle he had brought along.

The Consul looked at the bottle as he answered. 'You have no reason to believe me. It doesn't matter.'

Colonel Kassad's long fingers idly tapped the dull casing of the death-wand. 'What will you do with your fatline commlink now?'

The Consul took a tired breath. 'Report when the Time Tombs open. If I'm still alive then.'

Brawne Lamia pointed at the antique comlog. 'We could destroy it.'

The Consul shrugged.

'It could be of use,' said the Colonel. 'We can eavesdrop on military and civilian transmissions made in clear. If we have to, we can call the Consul's ship.'

'No!' cried the Consul. It was the first time he had shown emotion in many minutes. 'We can't turn back now.'

'I believe we have no intention of turning back,' said Colonel Kassad. He looked around at pale faces. No one spoke for a moment.

'There is a decision we have to make,' said Sol Weintraub. He rocked his infant and nodded in the direction of the Consul.

Martin Silenus had been resting his forehead on the mouth of the empty bottle of Scotch. He looked up. 'The penalty for treason is death.' He giggled. 'We're all going to die within a few hours anyway. Why not make our last act an execution?'

Father Hoyt grimaced as a spasm of pain gripped him. He touched his cracked lips with a trembling finger. 'We're not a court.'

'Yes,' said Colonel Kassad, 'we are.'

The Consul drew up his legs, rested his forearms on his knees, and laced his fingers. 'Decide then.' There was no emotion in his voice.

Brawne Lamia had brought out her father's automatic pistol. Now she set it on the floor near where she sat. Her eyes darted from the Consul to Kassad. 'We're talking treason here?' she said. 'Treason toward what? None of us except maybe the Colonel there is exactly a leading citizen. We've all been kicked around by forces beyond our control.'

Sol Weintraub spoke directly to the Consul. 'What you have ignored, my friend, is that if Meina Gladstone and elements of the Core chose you for the Ouster contact, they knew very well what you would do. Perhaps they could not have guessed that the Ousters had the means by which to open the Tombs – although with the AIs of the Core one can never know – but they certainly knew that you would turn on both societies, both camps which have injured your family. It is all part of some bizarre plan. You were no more an instrument of your own will than was' – he held the baby up – 'this child.'

The Consul looked confused. He started to speak, shook his head instead.

'That may be correct,' said Colonel Fedmahn Kassad, 'but however they may try to use all of us as pawns, we must attempt to choose our own actions.' He glanced up at the wall where pulses of light from the distant space battle painted the plaster blood red. 'Because of this war, thousands will die. Perhaps millions. If the Ousters or the Shrike gain access to the Web's farcaster system, billions of lives on hundreds of worlds are at risk.'

The Consul watched as Kassad raised the deathwand.

'This would be faster for all of us,' said Kassad. 'The Shrike knows no mercy.'

No one spoke. The Consul seemed to be staring at something at a great distance.

Kassad pressed on the safety and set the wand back in his belt. 'We've come this far,' he said. 'We will go the rest of the way together.'

Brawne Lamia put away her father's pistol, rose, crossed the small space, knelt next to the Consul, and put her arms around him. Startled, the Consul raised one arm. Light danced on the wall behind them.

A moment later, Sol Weintraub came close and hugged them both with one arm around their shoulders. The baby wriggled in pleasure at the sudden warmth of bodies. The Consul smelled the talc-and-newborn scent of her.

'I was wrong,' said the Consul. 'I will make a request of the Shrike. I will ask for *her*.' He gently touched Rachel's head where the small skull curved in to neck.

Martin Silenus made a noise which began as a laugh and died as a sob. 'Our last requests,' he said. 'Does the muse grant requests? I have no request. I want only for the poem to be finished.'

Father Hoyt turned toward the poet. 'Is it so important?'

'Oh, yes, yes, yes, *yes*,' gasped Silenus. He dropped the empty Scotch bottle, reached into his bag, and lifted out a handful of flimsies, holding them high as if offering them to the group. 'Do you want to read it? Do you want *me* to read it to you? It's flowing again. Read the old parts. Read the *Cantos* I wrote three centuries ago and never published. It's all here. *We're* all here. My name, yours, this trip. Don't you see . . . I'm not creating a poem, I'm creating the *future*!' He let the flimsies fall, raised the empty bottle, frowned, and held it like a chalice. 'I'm creating the future,' he repeated without looking up, 'but it's the past which must be changed. One instant. One decision.'

Martin Silenus raised his face. His eyes were red. 'This thing that is going to kill us tomorrow – my muse, our maker, our unmaker – it's traveled back through time. Well, let it. This time, let it take *me* and leave Billy alone. Let it take *me* and let the poem end there, unfinished for all time.' He raised the bottle higher, closed his eyes, and threw it against the far wall. Glass shards reflected orange light from the silent explosions.

Colonel Kassad stepped closer and laid long fingers on the poet's shoulder.

For a few seconds the room seemed warmed by the mere fact of human contact. Father Lenar Hoyt stepped away from the wall where he had been leaning, raised his right hand with thumb and little finger touching, three fingers raised, the gesture somehow including himself as well as those before him, and said softly, *'Ego te absolvo.'*

Wind scraped at the outer walls and whistled around the gargoyles and balconies. Light from a battle a hundred million kilometers away painted the group in blood hues.

Colonel Kassad walked to the doorway. The group moved apart.

'Let's try to get some sleep,' said Brawne Lamia.

Later, alone in his bedroll, listening to the wind shriek and howl, the Consul set his cheek against his pack and pulled the rough blanket higher. It had been years since he had been able to fall asleep easily.

The Consul set his curled fist against his cheek, closed his eyes, and slept.

EPILOGUE

The Consul awoke to the sound of a balalaika being played so softly that at first he thought it was an undercurrent of his dream.

The Consul rose, shivered in the cold air, wrapped his blanket around him, and went out onto the long balcony. It was not yet dawn. The skies still burned with the light of battle.

'I'm sorry,' said Lenar Hoyt, looking up from his instrument. The priest was huddled deep in his cape.

'It's all right,' said the Consul. 'I was ready to awaken.' It was true. He could not remember feeling more rested. 'Please continue,' he said. The notes were sharp and clear but barely audible above the wind noise. It was as if Hoyt was playing a duet with the cold wind from the peaks above. The Consul found the clarity almost painful.

Brawne Lamia and Colonel Kassad came out. A minute later Sol Weintraub joined them. Rachel twisted in his arms, reaching toward the night sky as if she could grasp the bright blossoms there.

Hoyt played. The wind was rising in the hour before dawn, and the gargoyles and escarpments acted like reeds to the Keep's cold bassoon.

Martin Silenus emerged, holding his head. 'No fucking respect for a hangover,' he said. He leaned on the broad railing. 'If I barf from this height, it'll be half an hour before the vomitus lands.'

Father Hoyt did not look up. His fingers flew across the strings of the small instrument. The northwest wind grew stronger and colder and the balalaika played counterpart, its notes warm and alive. The Consul and the others huddled in blankets and capes as the breeze grew to a torrent and the unnamed music kept pace with it. It was the strangest and most beautiful symphony the Consul had ever heard.

The wind gusted, roared, peaked, and died. Hoyt ended his tune.

Brawne Lamia looked around. 'It's almost dawn.'

'We have another hour,' said Colonel Kassad.

Lamia shrugged. 'Why wait?'

'Why indeed?' said Sol Weintraub. He looked to the east where the only hint of sunrise was the faintest of palings in constellations there. 'It looks like a good day is coming.'

'Let's get ready,' said Hoyt. 'Do we need our luggage?'

The group looked at one another.

'No, I think not,' said the Consul. 'The Colonel will bring the comlog

347

with the fatline communicator. Bring anything necessary for your audience with the Shrike. We'll leave the rest of the stuff here.'

'All right,' said Brawne Lamia, turning back from the dark doorway, gesturing toward the others, 'let's do it.'

There were six hundred and sixty-one steps from the northeast portal of the Keep to the moor below. There were no railings. The group descended carefully, watching their step in the insecure light.

Once onto the valley floor, they looked back at the outcrop of stone above. Chronos Keep looked like part of the mountain, its balconies and external stairways mere slashes in the rock. Occasionally a brighter explosion would illuminate a window or throw a gargoyle shadow, but except for those instances it was as if the Keep had vanished behind them.

They crossed the low hills below the Keep, staying on grass and avoiding the sharp shrubs which extended thorns like claws. In ten minutes they had crossed to sand and were descending low dunes toward the valley.

Brawne Lamia led the group. She wore her finest cape and a red silk suit with black trim. Her comlog gleamed on her wrist. Colonel Kassad came next. He was in full battle armor, camouflage polymer not yet activated so the suit looked matte black, absorbing even the light from above. Kassad carried a standard-issue FORCE assault rifle. His visor gleamed like a black mirror.

Father Hoyt wore his black cape, black suit, and clerical collar. The balalaika was cradled in his arms like a child. He continued to set his feet carefully, as if each step caused pain. The Consul followed. He was dressed in his diplomatic best, starched blouse, formal black trousers and demi-jacket, velvet cape, and the gold tricorne he had worn the first day on the treeship. He had to keep a grip on the hat against the wind that had come up again, hurling grains of sand in his face and sliding across the dune tops like a serpent. Martin Silenus followed close behind in his coat of wind-rippled fur.

Sol Weintraub brought up the rear. Rachel rode in the infant carrier, nestled under the cape and coat against her father's chest. Weintraub was singing a low tune to her, the notes lost in the breeze.

Forty minutes out and they had come even with the dead city. Marble and granite gleamed in the violet light. The peaks glowed behind them, the Keep indistinguishable from the other mountain-sides. The group crossed a sandy vale, climbed a low dune, and suddenly the head of the valley of the Time Tombs was visible for the first time. The Consul could make out the thrust of the Sphinx's wings and a glow of jade.

A rumble and crash from far behind them made the Consul turn, startled, his heart pounding.

'Isn't it beginning?' asked Lamia. 'The bombardment?'

'No, look,' said Kassad. He pointed to a point above the mountain peaks where blackness obliterated the stars. Lightning exploded along the false horizon, illuminating icefields and glaciers. 'Only a storm,' he said.

They resumed their trek across vermilion sands. The Consul found himself straining to make out the shape of a figure near the Tombs or at the head of the valley. He was certain beyond all certainty that something awaited them there . . . that *it* awaited.

'Look at that,' said Brawne Lamia, her whisper almost lost in the wind.

The Time Tombs were glowing. What the Consul had first taken to be light reflected from above was not. Each Tomb glowed a different hue and each was clearly visible now, the glow brightening, the Tombs receding far back into the darkness of the valley. The air smelled of ozone.

'Is that a common phenomenon?' asked Father Hoyt, his voice thin.

The Consul shook his head. 'I've never heard of it.'

'It had never been reported at the time Rachel came to study the Tombs,' said Sol Weintraub. He began to hum the low tune as the group started forward again through shifting sands.

They paused at the head of the valley. Soft dunes gave way to rock and ink-black shadows at the swale which led down to the glowing Tombs. No one led the way. No one spoke. The Consul felt his heart beating wildly against his ribs. Worse than fear or knowledge of what lay below was the blackness of spirit which seemed to have come into him on the wind, chilling him and making him want to run screaming toward the hills from which they had come.

The Consul turned to Sol Weintraub. 'What's that tune you're singing to Rachel?'

The scholar forced a grin and scratched his short beard. 'It's from an ancient flat film. Pre-Hegira. Hell, it's pre-everything.'

'Let's hear it,' said Brawne Lamia, understanding what the Consul was doing. Her face was very pale.

Weintraub sang it, his voice thin and barely audible at first. But the tune was forceful and oddly compelling. Father Hoyt uncradled the balalaika and played along, the notes gaining confidence.

Brawne Lamia laughed. Martin Silenus said in awe, 'My God, I used to sing this in my childhood. It's ancient.'

'But who is the wizard?' asked Colonel Kassad, the amplified voice through his helmet oddly amusing in this context.

'And what is Oz?' asked Lamia.

'And just *who* is off to see this wizard?' asked the Consul, feeling the black panic in him fade ever so slightly.

Sol Weintraub paused and tried to answer their questions, explaining the plot of a flat film which had been dust for centuries.

'Never mind,' said Brawne Lamia. 'You can tell us later. Just sing it again.'

Behind them, the darkness had engulfed the mountains as the storm swept down and across the moors toward them. The sky continued to bleed light but now the eastern horizon had paled slightly more than the rest. The dead city glowed to their left like stone teeth.

Brawne Lamia took the lead again. Sol Weintraub sang more loudly, Rachel wiggling in delight. Lenar Hoyt threw back his cape so as to better play the balalaika. Martin Silenus threw an empty bottle far out onto the sands and sang along, his deep voice surprisingly strong and pleasant above the wind.

Fedmahn Kassad pushed up his visor, shouldered his weapon, and joined in the chorus. The Consul started to sing, thought about the absurd lyrics, laughed aloud, and started again.

Just where the darkness began, the trail broadened. The Consul moved to his right, Kassad joining him, Sol Weintraub filling the gap, so that instead of a single-file procession, the six adults were walking abreast. Brawne Lamia took Silenus's hand in hers, joined hands with Sol on the other side.

Still singing loudly, not looking back, matching stride for stride, they descended into the valley.

THE FALL
OF
HYPERION

To John Keats
Whose Name Was Writ
in Eternity

'Can God play a significant game with his own creature? Can any creator, even a limited one, play a significant game with his own creature?'

    — Norbert Wiener, *God and Golem, Inc.*

'. . . May there not be superior beings amused with any graceful, though instinctive attitude my mind may fall into, as I am entertained with the alertness of a Stoat or the anxiety of a Deer? Though a quarrel in the streets is a thing to be hated, the energies displayed in it are fine . . . By a superior being our reasonings may take the same tone – though erroneous they may be fine – This is the very thing in which consists poetry . . .'

    — John Keats, in a letter to his brother

'The Imagination may be compared to Adam's dream – he awoke and found it truth.'

    — John Keats, in a letter to a friend

PART ONE

ONE

On the day the armada went off to war, on the last day of life as we knew it, I was invited to a party. There were parties everywhere that evening, on more than a hundred and fifty worlds in the Web, but *this* was the only party that mattered.

I signified acceptance via the datasphere, checked to make sure that my finest formal jacket was clean, took my time bathing and shaving, dressed with meticulous care, and used the one-time diskey in the invitation chip to farcast from Esperance to Tau Ceti Center at the appointed time.

It was evening in this hemisphere of TC^2, and a low, rich light illuminated the hills and vales of Deer Park, the gray towers of the Administration Complex far to the south, the weeping willows and radiant fernfire which lined the banks of the River Tethys, and the white colonnades of Government House itself. Thousands of guests were arriving, but security personnel greeted each of us, checked our invitation codes against DNA patterns, and showed the way to bar and buffet with a graceful gesture of arm and hand.

'M. Joseph Severn?' the guide confirmed politely.

'Yes,' I lied. It was now my name but never my identity.

'CEO Gladstone still wishes to see you later in the evening. You will be notified when she is free for the appointment.'

'Very good.'

'If you desire anything in the way of refreshment or entertainment that is not set out, merely speak your wish aloud and the grounds monitors will seek to provide it.'

I nodded, smiled, and left the guide behind. Before I had strolled a dozen steps, he had turned to the next guests alighting from the terminex platform.

From my vantage point on a low knoll, I could see several thousand guests milling across several hundred acres of manicured lawn, many of them wandering among forests of topiary. Above the stretch of grass where I stood, its broad sweep already shaded by the line of trees along the river, lay the formal gardens, and beyond them rose the imposing bulk of Government House. A band was playing on the distant patio, and hidden speakers carried the sound to the farthest reaches of Deer Park. A constant line of EMVs spiraled down from a farcaster portal far above. For a few seconds I watched their brightly clad passengers disembark at the platform near the pedestrian terminex. I was fascinated by the variety of aircraft;

356

evening light glinted not only on the shells of the standard Vikkens and Altz and Sumatsos, but also on the rococo decks of levitation barges and the metal hulls of antique skimmers which had been quaint when Old Earth still existed.

I wandered down the long, gradual slope to the River Tethys, past the dock where an incredible assortment of river craft disgorged their passengers. The Tethys was the only webwide river, flowing past its permanent farcaster portals through sections of more than two hundred worlds and moons, and the folk who lived along its banks were some of the wealthiest in the Hegemony. The vehicles on the river showed this: great, crenelated cruisers, canvas-laden barks, and five-tiered barges, many showing signs of being equipped with levitation gear; elaborate houseboats, obviously fitted with their own farcasters; small, motile isles imported from the oceans of Maui-Covenant; sporty pre-Hegira speedboats and submersibles; an assortment of hand-carved nautical EMVs from Renaissance Vector; and a few contemporary go-everywhere yachts, their outlines hidden by the seamless reflective ovoid surfaces of containment fields.

The guests who alighted from these craft were no less flamboyant and impressive than their vehicles: personal styles ranged from pre-Hegira conservative evening wear on bodies obviously never touched by Poulsen treatments to this week's highest fashion from TC^2 draped on figures molded by the Web's most famous ARNists. Then I moved on, pausing at a long table just long enough to fill my plate with roast beef, salad, sky squid filet, Parvati curry, and fresh-baked bread.

The low evening light had faded to twilight by the time I found a place to sit near the gardens, and the stars were coming out. The lights of the nearby city and Administration Complex had been dimmed for tonight's viewing of the armada, and Tau Ceti Center's night sky was more clear than it had been for centuries.

A woman near me glanced over and smiled. 'I'm sure that we've met before.'

I smiled back, sure that we had not. She was very attractive, perhaps twice my age, in her late fifties, standard, but looking younger than my own twenty-six years, thanks to money and Poulsen. Her skin was so fair that it looked almost translucent. Her hair was done in a rising braid. Her breasts, more revealed than hidden by the wispwear gown, were flawless. Her eyes were cruel.

'Perhaps we have,' I said, 'although it seems unlikely. My name is Joseph Severn.'

'Of course,' she said. 'You're an artist!'

I was not an artist. I was . . . had been . . . a poet. But the Severn identity, which I had inhabited since my real persona's death and birth a year before, stated that I was an artist. It was in my All Thing file.

'I remembered,' laughed the lady. She lied. She had used her expensive comlog implants to access the datasphere.

I did not need to access . . . a clumsy, redundant word which I despised despite its antiquity. I mentally closed my eyes and was *in* the datasphere, sliding past the superficial All Thing barriers, slipping beneath the waves of surface data, and following the glowing strand of her access umbilical far into the darkened depths of 'secure' information flow.

'My name is Diana Philomel,' she said. 'My husband is sector transport administrator for Sol Draconi Septem.'

I nodded and took the hand she offered. She had said nothing about the fact that her husband had been head goon for the mold-scrubbers union on Heaven's Gate before political patronage had promoted him to Sol Draconi . . . or that her name once had been Dinee Teats, former crib doxie and hopstop hostess to lungpipe proxies in the Midsump Barrens . . . or that she had been arrested twice for Flashback abuse, the second time seriously injuring a halfway house medic . . . or that she had poisoned her half-brother when she was nine, after he had threatened to tell her stepfather that she was seeing a Mudflat miner named . . .

'Pleased to meet you, M. Philomel,' I said. Her hand was warm. She held the handshake an instant too long.

'Isn't it exciting?' she breathed.

'What's that?'

She made an expansive gesture that included the night, the glow-globes just coming on, the gardens, and the crowds. 'Oh, the party, the war, *everything*,' she said.

I smiled, nodded, and tasted the roast beef. It was rare and quite good, but gave the salty hint of the Lusus clone vats. The squid seemed authentic. Stewards had come by offering champagne, and I tried mine. It was inferior. Quality wine, Scotch, and coffee had been the three irreplaceable commodities after the death of Old Earth. 'Do you think the war is necessary?' I asked.

'Goddamn right it's necessary.' Diana Philomel had opened her mouth, but it was her husband who answered. He had come up from behind and now took a seat on the faux log where we dined. He was a big man, at least a foot and a half taller than I. But then, I am short. My memory tells me that I once wrote a verse ridiculing myself as '. . . Mr John Keats, five feet high,' although I am five feet one, slightly short when Napoleon and Wellington were alive and the average height for men was five feet six, ridiculously short now that men from average-g worlds range from six feet tall to almost seven. I obviously did not have the musculature or frame to claim I had come from a high-g world, so to all eyes I was merely short. (I report my thoughts above in the units in which I think . . . of all the mental changes since my rebirth into the Web, thinking in metric is by far the hardest. Sometimes I refuse to try.)

'Why is the war necessary?' I asked Hermund Philomel, Diana's husband.

'Because they goddamn *asked for it*,' growled the big man. He was a molar grinder and a cheek-muscle flexer. He had almost no neck and a subcutaneous beard that obviously defied depilatory, blade, and shaver. His hands were half again as large as mine and many times more powerful.

'I see,' I said.

'The goddamn Ousters goddamn *asked for it*,' he repeated, reviewing the high points of his argument for me. 'They fucked with us on Bressia and now they're fucking with us on . . . in . . . whatsis . . .'

'Hyperion system,' said his wife, her eyes never leaving mine.

'Yeah,' said her lord and husband, 'Hyperion system. They fucked with us, and now we've got to go out there and show them that the Hegemony isn't going to stand for it. Understand?'

Memory told me that as a boy I had been sent off to John Clarke's academy at Enfield and that there had been more than a few small-brained, ham-fisted bullies like this there. When I first arrived, I avoided them or placated them. After my mother died, after the world changed, I went after them with rocks in my small fists and rose from the ground to swing again, even after they had bloodied my nose and loosened my teeth with their blows.

'I understand,' I said softly. My plate was empty. I raised the last of my bad champagne to toast Diana Philomel.

'Draw me,' she said.

'I beg your pardon?'

'Draw me, M. Severn. You're an artist.'

'A painter,' I said, making a helpless gesture with an empty hand. 'I'm afraid I have no stylus.'

Diana Philomel reached into her husband's tunic pocket and handed me a light pen. 'Draw me. Please.'

I drew her. The portrait took shape in the air between us, lines rising and falling and turning back on themselves like neon filaments in a wire sculpture. A small crowd gathered to watch. Mild applause rippled when I finished. The drawing was not bad. It caught the lady's long, voluptuous curve of neck, high braid bridge of hair, prominent cheekbones . . . even the slight, ambiguous glint of eye. It was as good as I could do after the RNA medication and lessons had prepared me for the persona. The real Joseph Severn could do better . . . had done better. I remember him sketching me as I lay dying.

M. Diana Philomel beamed approval. M. Hermund Philomel glowered.

A shout went up. 'There they are!'

The crowd murmured, gasped, and hushed. Glow-globes and garden lights dimmed and went off. Thousands of guests raised their eyes to the heavens. I erased the drawing and tucked the light pen back in Hermund's tunic.

'It's the armada,' said a distinguished-looking older man in FORCE dress black. He lifted his drink to point something out to his young female companion. 'They've just opened the portal. The scouts will come through first, then the torchship escorts.'

The FORCE military farcaster portal was not visible from our vantage point; even in space, I imagine it would look like nothing more than a rectangular aberration in the starfield. But the fusion tails of the scoutships were certainly visible – first as a score of fireflies or radiant gossamers, then as blazing comets as they ignited their main drives and swept out through Tau Ceti System's cislunar traffic region. Another cumulative gasp went up as the torchships farcast into existence, their firetails a hundred times longer than the scouts'. TC^2's night sky was scarred from zenith to horizon with gold-red streaks.

Somewhere the applause began, and within seconds the fields and lawns and formal gardens of Government House's Deer Park were filled with riotous applause and raucous cheering as the well-dressed crowd of billionaires and government officials and members of noble houses from a hundred worlds forgot everything except a jingoism and war lust awakened now after more than a century and a half of dormancy.

I did not applaud. Ignored by those around me, I finished my toast – not to Lady Philomel now, but to the enduring stupidity of my race – and downed the last of the champagne. It was flat.

Above, the more important ships of the flotilla had translated in-system. I knew from the briefest touch of the datasphere – its surface now agitated with surges of information until it resembled a storm-tossed sea – that the main line of the FORCE:space armada consisted of more than a hundred capital spinships: matte-black attack carriers, looking like thrown spears, with their launch-arms lashed down; Three-C command ships, as beautiful and awkward as meteors made of black crystal; bulbous destroyers resembling the overgrown torchships they were; perimeter defense pickets, more energy than matter, their massive containment shields now set to total reflection – brilliant mirrors reflecting Tau Ceti and the hundreds of flame trails around them; fast cruisers, moving like sharks among the slower schools of ships; lumbering troop transports carrying thousands of FORCE:Marines in their zero-g holds; and scores of support ships – frigates; fast attack fighters; torpedo ALRs; fatline relay pickets; and the farcaster JumpShips themselves, massive dodecahedrons with their fairyland arrays of antennae and probes.

All around the fleet, kept at a safe distance by traffic control, flitted the yachts and sunjammers and private in-system ships, their sails catching sunlight and reflecting the glory of the armada.

The guests on the Government House grounds cheered and applauded. The gentleman in FORCE black was weeping silently. Nearby, concealed cameras and wideband imagers carried the moment to every world in the Web and – via fatline – to scores of worlds which were not.

I shook my head and remained seated.

'M. Severn?' A security guard stood over me.

'Yes?'

She nodded toward the executive mansion. 'CEO Gladstone will see you now.'

TWO

Every age fraught with discord and danger seems to spawn a leader meant only for that age, a political giant whose absence, in retrospect, seems inconceivable when the history of that age is written. Meina Gladstone was just such a leader for our Final Age, although none then could have dreamed that there would be no one but me to write the true history of her and her time.

Gladstone had been compared to the classical figure of Abraham Lincoln so many times that when I was finally ushered into her presence that night of the armada party, I was half surprised not to find her in a black frock coat and stovepipe hat. The CEO of the Senate and leader of a government serving a hundred and thirty billion people was wearing a gray suit of soft wool, trousers and tunic top ornamented only by the slightest hint of red cord piping at seams and cuffs. I did not think she looked like Abraham Lincoln . . . nor like Alvarez-Temp, the second most common hero of antiquity cited as her Doppelganger by the press. I thought that she looked like an old lady.

Meina Gladstone was tall and thin, but her countenance was more aquiline than Lincolnesque, with her blunt beak of a nose; sharp cheekbones; the wide, expressive mouth with thin lips; and gray hair rising in a roughly cropped wave, which did indeed resemble feathers. But to my mind, the most memorable aspect of Meina Gladstone's appearance was her eyes: large, brown, and infinitely sad.

We were not alone. I had been led into a long, softly lighted room lined with wooden shelves holding many hundreds of printed books. A long holoframe simulating a window gave a view of the gardens. A meeting was in the process of breaking up, and a dozen men and women stood or sat in a rough half-circle that held Gladstone's desk at its cusp. The CEO leaned back casually on her desk, resting her weight on the front of it, her arms folded. She looked up as I entered.

'M. Severn?'

'Yes.'

'Thank you for coming.' Her voice was familiar from a thousand All Thing debates, its timbre rough with age and its tone as smooth as an expensive liqueur. Her accent was famous – blending precise syntax with an almost forgotten lilt of pre-Hegira English, evidently now found only in the river-delta regions of her home world of Patawpha. 'Gentlemen and ladies, let me introduce M. Joseph Severn,' she said.

Several of the group nodded, obviously at a loss as to why I was there. Gladstone made no further introductions, but I touched the datasphere to identify everyone: three cabinet members, including the Minister of Defense; two FORCE chiefs of staff; two aides to Gladstone; four senators, including the influential Senator Kolchev; and a projection of a TechnoCore Councilor known as Albedo.

'M. Severn has been invited here to bring an artist's perspective to the proceedings,' said CEO Gladstone.

FORCE:ground General Morpurgo snorted a laugh. 'An *artist*'s perspective? With all due respect, CEO, what the hell does that mean?'

Gladstone smiled. Instead of answering the General, she turned back to me. 'What do you think of the passing of the armada, M. Severn?'

'It's pretty,' I said.

General Morpurgo made a noise again. '*Pretty?* He looks at the greatest concentration of space-force firepower in the history of the galaxy and calls it *pretty?*' He turned toward another military man and shook his head.

Gladstone's smile had not wavered. 'And what of the war?' she asked me. 'Do you have an opinion on our attempt to rescue Hyperion from the Ouster barbarians?'

'It's stupid,' I said.

The room became very silent. Current real-time polling in the All Thing showed 98 percent approval of CEO Gladstone's decision to fight rather than cede the colonial world of Hyperion to the Ousters. Gladstone's political future rested on a positive outcome of the conflict. The men and women in that room had been instrumental in formulating the policy, making the decision to invade, and carrying out the logistics. The silence stretched.

'Why is it stupid?' Gladstone asked softly.

I made a gesture with my right hand. 'The Hegemony's not been at war since its founding seven centuries ago,' I said. 'It is foolish to test its basic stability this way.'

'Not at war!' shouted General Morpurgo. He gripped his knees with massive hands. 'What the hell do you call the Glennon-Height Rebellion?'

'A rebellion,' I said. 'A mutiny. A police action.'

Senator Kolchev showed his teeth in a smile that held no amusement. He was from Lusus and seemed more muscle than man. 'Fleet actions,' he said, 'half a million dead, two FORCE divisions locked in combat for more than a year. Some police action, son.'

I said nothing.

Leigh Hunt, an older, consumptive-looking man reported to be Gladstone's closest aide, cleared his throat. 'But what M. Severn says is interesting. Where do you see the difference between this . . . ah . . . conflict and the Glennon-Height wars, sir?'

'Glennon-Height was a former FORCE officer,' I said, aware that I was stating the obvious. 'The Ousters have been an unknown quantity for centuries. The rebels' forces were known, their potential easily gauged; the

Ouster Swarms have been outside the Web since the Hegira. Glennon-Height stayed within the Protectorate, raiding worlds no farther than two months' time-debt from the Web; Hyperion is *three years* from Parvati, the closest Web staging area.'

'You think we haven't thought of all this?' asked General Morpurgo. 'What about the Battle of Bressia? We've already fought the Ousters there. That was no . . . rebellion.'

'Quiet, please,' said Leigh Hunt. 'Go on, M. Severn.'

I shrugged again. 'The primary difference is that in this case we are dealing with Hyperion,' I said.

Senator Richeau, one of the women present, nodded as if I had explained myself in full. 'You're afraid of the Shrike,' she said. 'Do you belong to the Church of the Final Atonement?'

'No,' I said, 'I'm not a member of the Shrike Cult.'

'What *are* you?' demanded Morpurgo.

'An artist,' I lied.

Leigh Hunt smiled and turned to Gladstone. 'I agree that we needed this perspective to sober us, CEO,' he said, gesturing toward the window and the holo images showing the still-applauding crowds, 'but while our artist friend has brought up necessary points, they have all been reviewed and weighed in full.'

Senator Kolchev cleared his throat. 'I hate to mention the obvious when it seems we are all intent on ignoring it, but does this . . . *gentleman* . . . have the proper security clearance to be present at such a discussion?'

Gladstone nodded and showed the slight smile so many caricaturists had tried to capture. 'M. Severn has been commissioned by the Arts Ministry to do a series of drawings of me during the next few days or weeks. The theory is, I believe, that these will have some historical significance and may lead to a formal portrait. At any rate, M. Severn has been granted a T-level gold security clearance, and we may speak freely in front of him. Also, I appreciate his candor. Perhaps his arrival serves to suggest that our meeting has reached its conclusion. I will join you all in the War Room at 0800 hours tomorrow morning, just before the fleet translates to Hyperion space.'

The group broke up at once. General Morpurgo glowered at me as he left. Senator Kolchev stared with some curiosity as he passed. Councilor Albedo merely faded into nothingness. Leigh Hunt was the only one besides Gladstone and me to remain behind. He made himself more comfortable by draping one leg over the arm of the priceless pre-Hegira chair in which he sat. 'Sit down,' said Hunt.

I glanced at the CEO. She had taken her seat behind the massive desk, and now she nodded. I sat in the straight-backed chair General Morpurgo had occupied. CEO Gladstone said, 'Do you really think that defending Hyperion is stupid?'

'Yes.'

Gladstone steepled her fingers and tapped at her lower lip. Behind her, the window showed the armada party continuing in silent agitation. 'If you have any hope of being reunited with your . . . ah . . . counterpart,' she said, 'it would seem to be in your interest for us to carry out the Hyperion campaign.'

I said nothing. The window view shifted to show the night sky still ablaze with fusion trails.

'Did you bring drawing materials?' asked Gladstone.

I brought out the pencil and small sketchpad I had told Diana Philomel I did not have.

'Draw while we talk,' said Meina Gladstone.

I began sketching, roughing in the relaxed, almost slumped posture, and then working on the details of the face. The eyes intrigued me.

I was vaguely aware that Leigh Hunt was staring intently at me. 'Joseph Severn,' he said. 'An interesting choice of names.'

I used quick, bold lines to give the sense of Gladstone's high brow and strong nose.

'Do you know why people are leery of cybrids?' Hunt asked.

'Yes,' I said. 'The Frankenstein monster syndrome. Fear of anything in human form that is not completely human. It's the real reason androids were outlawed, I suppose.'

'Uh-huh,' agreed Hunt. 'But cybrids *are* completely human, aren't they?'

'Genetically they are,' I said. I found myself thinking of my mother, remembering the times I had read to her during her illness. I thought of my brother Tom. 'But they are also part of the Core,' I said, 'and thus fit the description of "not completely human".'

'Are you part of the Core?' asked Meina Gladstone, turning full face toward me. I started a new sketch.

'Not really,' I said. 'I can travel freely through the regions they allow me in, but it is more like someone accessing the datasphere than a true Core personality's ability.' Her face had been more interesting in three-quarters profile, but the eyes were more powerful when viewed straight on. I worked on the latticework of lines radiating from the corners of those eyes. Meina Gladstone obviously had never indulged in Poulsen treatments.

'If it were possible to keep secrets from the Core,' said Gladstone, 'it would be folly to allow you free access to the councils of government. As it is . . .' She dropped her hands and sat up. I flipped to a new page.

'As it is,' said Gladstone, 'you have information I need. Is it true that you can read the mind of your counterpart, the first retrieval persona?'

'No,' I said. It was difficult to capture the complicated interplay of line and muscle at the corners of her mouth. I sketched in my attempt to do so, moved on to the strong chin and shaded the area beneath the underlip.

Hunt frowned and glanced at the CEO. M. Gladstone brought her fingertips together again. 'Explain,' she said.

I looked up from the drawing. 'I dream,' I said. 'The contents of the dream appear to correspond to the events occurring around the person carrying the implant of the previous Keats persona.'

'A woman named Brawne Lamia,' said Leigh Hunt.

'Yes.'

Gladstone nodded. 'So the original Keats persona, the one thought killed on Lusus, is still alive?'

I paused. 'It . . . he . . . is still aware,' I said. 'You know that the primary personality substrate was extracted from the Core, probably by the cybrid himself, and implanted in a Schrön-loop bio-shunt carried by M. Lamia.'

'Yes, yes,' said Leigh Hunt. 'But the fact is, you are *in contact* with the Keats persona, and through him, with the Shrike pilgrims.'

Quick, dark strokes provided a dark background to give the sketch of Gladstone more depth. 'I am not actually in contact,' I said. 'I dream dreams about Hyperion that your fatline broadcasts have confirmed as conforming to real-time events. I cannot communicate to the passive Keats persona, nor to its host or the other pilgrims.'

CEO Gladstone blinked. 'How did you know about the fatline broadcasts?'

'The Consul told the other pilgrims about his comlog's ability to relay through the fatline transmitter in his ship. He told them just before they descended into the valley.'

Gladstone's tone hinted of her years as a lawyer before entering politics. 'And how did the others respond to the Consul's revelation?'

I put the pencil back in my pocket. 'They knew that a spy was in their midst,' I said. 'You told each of them.'

Gladstone glanced at her aide. Hunt's expression was blank. 'If you're in touch with them,' she said, 'you must know that we've received no message since before they left Keep Chronos to descend to the Time Tombs.'

I shook my head. 'Last night's dream ended just as they approached the valley.'

Meina Gladstone rose, paced to the window, raised a hand, and the image went black. 'So you don't know if any of them are still alive?'

'No.'

'What was their status the last time you . . . dreamt?'

Hunt was watching me as intensely as ever. Meina Gladstone was staring at the dark screen, her back to both of us. 'All of the pilgrims were alive,' I said, 'with the possible exception of Het Masteen, the True Voice of the Tree.'

'He was dead?' asked Hunt.

'He disappeared from the windwagon on the Sea of Grass two nights before, only hours after the Ouster scouts had destroyed the treeship *Yggdrasill*. But shortly before the pilgrims descended from Keep Chronos, they saw a robed figure crossing the sands toward the Tombs.'

'Het Masteen?' asked Gladstone.

I lifted a hand. 'They assumed so. They were not sure.'

'Tell me about the others,' said the CEO.

I took a breath. I knew from the dreams that Gladstone had known at

365

least two of the people on the last Shrike Pilgrimage; Brawne Lamia's father had been a fellow senator, and the Hegemony Consul had been Gladstone's personal representative in secret negotiations with the Ousters. 'Father Hoyt is in great pain,' I said. 'He told the story of the cruciform. The Consul learned that Hoyt also wears one . . . two actually, Father Duré's and his own.'

Gladstone nodded. 'So he still carries the resurrection parasite?'

'Yes.'

'Does it bother him more as he approaches the Shrike's lair?'

'I believe so,' I said.

'Go on.'

'The poet, Silenus, has been drunk much of the time. He is convinced that his unfinished poem predicted and determines the course of events.'

'On Hyperion?' asked Gladstone, her back still turned.

'Everywhere,' I said.

Hunt glanced at the chief executive and then looked back at me. 'Is Silenus insane?'

I returned his gaze but said nothing. In truth, I did not know.

'Go on,' Gladstone said again.

'Colonel Kassad continues with his twin obsessions of finding the woman named Moneta and of killing the Shrike. He is aware that they may be one and the same.'

'Is he armed?' Gladstone's voice was very soft.

'Yes.'

'Go on.'

'Sol Weintraub, the scholar from Barnard's World, hopes to enter the tomb called the Sphinx as soon as—'

'Excuse me,' said Gladstone, 'but is his daughter still with him?'

'Yes.'

'And how old is Rachel now?'

'Five days, I believe.' I closed my eyes to remember the previous night's dream in greater detail. 'Yes,' I said, 'five days.'

'And still aging backward in time?'

'Yes.'

'Go on, M. Severn. Please tell me about Brawne Lamia and the Consul.'

'M. Lamia is carrying out the wishes of her former client . . . and lover,' I said. 'The Keats persona felt it was necessary for him to confront the Shrike. M. Lamia is doing it in his stead.'

'M. Severn,' began Leigh Hunt, 'you speak of "the Keats persona" as if it had no relevance or connection to your own . . .'

'Later, please, Leigh,' said Meina Gladstone. She turned to look at me. 'I'm curious about the Consul. Did he take his turn at telling his reason for joining the pilgrimage?'

'Yes,' I said.

Gladstone and Hunt waited.

'The Consul told them about his grandmother,' I said. 'The woman

366

called Siri who started the Maui-Covenant rebellion more than half a century ago. He told them about the death of his own family during the battle for Bressia, and he revealed his secret meetings with the Ousters.'

'Is that all?' asked Gladstone. Her brown eyes were very intense.

'No,' I said. 'The Consul told them that he had been the one to trigger an Ouster device which hastened the opening of the Time Tombs.'

Hunt sat straight up, his leg dropping off the arm of the chair. Gladstone visibly took a breath. 'Is that all?'

'Yes.'

'How did the others respond to his revelation of . . . betrayal?' she asked.

I paused, tried to reconstruct the dream images in a more linear fashion than memory provided. 'Some were outraged,' I said. 'But none feels overwhelming loyalty to the Hegemony at this point. They decided to go on. I believe that each of the pilgrims feels that punishment will be dealt out by the Shrike, not by human agency.'

Hunt slammed his fist down on the arm of the chair. 'If the Consul were here,' he snapped, 'he'd fast discover otherwise.'

'Quiet, Leigh.' Gladstone paced back to her desk, touched some papers there. All of the comm lights were glowing impatiently. I found myself amazed that she could spend so much time talking to me at such an hour. 'Thank you, M. Severn,' she said. 'I want you to be with us for the next few days. Someone will show you to your suite in the residential wing of Government House.'

I rose. 'I'll return to Esperance for my things,' I said.

'No need,' said Gladstone. 'They were brought here before you had stepped off the terminex platform. Leigh will show you out.'

I nodded and followed the taller man toward the door.

'Oh, M. Severn . . .' called Meina Gladstone.

'Yes?'

The CEO smiled. 'I did appreciate your candor earlier,' she said. 'But from this point on, let us assume you are a court artist and a court artist alone, *sans* opinions, *sans* visibility, *sans* mouth. Understood?'

'Understood, M. Executive,' I said.

Gladstone nodded, already turning her attention to the blinking phone lights. 'Very good. Please bring your sketchbook to the meeting in the War Room at 0800 hours.'

A security guard met us in the anteroom and started to lead me toward the maze of corridors and checkpoints. Hunt called out for him to stop and strode across the wide hall, his steps echoing on the tile. He touched my arm. 'Make no mistake,' he said. 'We know . . . *she* knows . . . who you are and what you are and whom you represent.'

I met his gaze and calmly extracted my arm. 'That's good,' I said, 'because at this point, I am quite sure that I do *not* know.'

THREE

Six adults and an infant in a hostile landscape. Their fire seems a small thing against the darkness falling. Above them and beyond them, the hills of the valley rise like walls while closer in, wrapped in the darkness of the valley itself, the huge shapes of the Tombs seem to creep closer like saurian apparitions from some antediluvian age.

Brawne Lamia is tired and aching and very irritable. The sound of Sol Weintraub's baby crying sets her teeth on edge. She knows the others are also tired; none has slept more than a few hours in the past three nights, and the day just ending has been filled with tension and unresolved terrors. She sets the last piece of wood on the fire.

'There's no more where that came from,' snaps Martin Silenus. The fire lights the poet's satyrish features from below.

'I know it,' says Brawne Lamia, too tired to put anger or any other energy into her voice. The firewood is from a cache carried in by the pilgrim groups of years gone by. Their three small tents are set in the area traditionally used by the pilgrims on their last night before confronting the Shrike. They are camped close to the Time Tomb called the Sphinx, and the black sweep of what may be a wing blots out some of the sky.

'We'll use the lantern when this is gone,' says the Consul. The diplomat looks even more exhausted than the others. The flickering light casts a red tint over his sad features. He had dressed in diplomatic finery for the day, but now the cape and tricorne cap look as soiled and wilted as the Consul himself.

Colonel Kassad returns to the fire and slides the night visor up on to the top of his helmet. Kassad is wearing full combat gear, and the activated chameleon polymer shows only his face, floating two meters above the ground. 'Nothing,' he says. 'No movement. No heat traces. No sound besides the wind.' Kassad leans the FORCE multipurpose assault rifle against a rock and sits near the others, the fibers of his impact armor deactivating into a matte black not much more visible than before.

'Do you think the Shrike will come tonight?' asks Father Hoyt. The priest has his black cloak wrapped around him and seems as much a part of the night as Colonel Kassad. The thin man's voice is strained.

Kassad leans forward and pokes the fire with his baton. 'There is no way to tell. I'll stand watch just in case.'

Suddenly all six look up as the star-filled sky spasms with color, orange and red blossoms unfolding silently, obliterating the starfield.

'There hasn't been much of that in the past few hours,' says Sol Wein-traub, rocking his infant. Rachel has quit crying and now tries to grasp her father's short beard. Weintraub kisses her tiny hand.

'They're testing Hegemony defenses again,' says Kassad. Sparks rise from the prodded fire, embers floating into the sky as if seeking to join the brighter flames there.

'Who won?' asks Lamia, referring to the silent space battle which had filled the sky with violence all the night before and much of that day.

'Who fucking cares?' says Martin Silenus. He searches through the pockets of his fur coat as if he might find a full bottle there. He does not. 'Who fucking cares,' he mutters again.

'I care,' the Consul says tiredly. 'If the Ousters break through, they may destroy Hyperion before we find the Shrike.'

Silenus laughs derisively. 'Oh, that would be terrible, wouldn't it? To die before we discover death? To be killed before we are scheduled to be killed? To go out swiftly and without pain, rather than to writhe forever on the Shrike's thorns? Oh, terrible thought, that.'

'Shut up,' says Brawne Lamia, and her voice again is without emotion but this time is not devoid of threat. She looks at the Consul. 'So where is the Shrike? Why didn't we find it?'

The diplomat stares at the fire. 'I don't know. Why should I know?'

'Perhaps the Shrike is gone,' says Father Hoyt. 'Perhaps by collapsing the anti-entropic fields you've freed it forever. Perhaps it's carried its scourge elsewhere.'

The Consul shakes his head and says nothing.

'No,' says Sol Weintraub. The baby is sleeping against his shoulder. 'It will be here. I feel it.'

Brawne Lamia nods. 'So do I. It's waiting.' She had retrieved several ration units from her pack, and now she pulls heating tabs and passes the units around.

'I know that anticlimax is the warp and woof of the world,' says Silenus. 'But this is fucking ridiculous. All dressed up with nowhere to die.'

Brawne Lamia glowers but says nothing, and for a while they eat in silence. The flames fade from the sky, and the densely packed stars return, but embers continue to rise as if seeking escape.

Wrapped in the dream-hazy tumble of Brawne Lamia's thoughts twice-removed, I try to reassemble the events since last I dreamt their lives.

The pilgrims had descended into the valley before dawn, singing, their shadows thrown before them by the light from the battle a billion kilometers above. All day they had explored the Time Tombs. Each minute they expected to die. After some hours, as the sun rose and the high desert cold gave way to heat, their fear and exultation faded.

The long day was silent except for the rasp of sand, occasional shouts, and the constant, almost subliminal moan of the wind around rocks and tombs. Kassad and the Consul each had brought an instrument that measured the intensity of the anti-entropic fields, but Lamia had been the first to notice that these were not needed, that the ebb and flow of the time tides could be felt as a slight nausea overladen with a sense of *déjà vu* which did not fade.

Nearest to the entrance of the valley had been the Sphinx; then came the Jade Tomb, its walls translucent only in morning and evening twilight; then, less than a hundred meters farther in, rose the tomb called the Obelisk; the pilgrim path then led up the widening arroyo to the largest tomb of them all, centrally placed, the Crystal Monolith, its surface devoid of design or opening, its flat-topped roof flush with the tops of the valley walls; then came the three Cave Tombs, their entrances visible only because of the well-worn paths that led to them; and finally – almost a kilometer farther down the valley – sat the so-called Shrike Palace, its sharp flanges and outflung spires reminiscent of the spikes of the creature said to haunt this valley.

All day they had moved from tomb to tomb, none venturing off alone, the group pausing before entering those artifacts which might be entered. Sol Weintraub had been all but overcome with emotion upon seeing and entering the Sphinx, the same tomb where his daughter had contracted the Merlin sickness twenty-six years earlier. The instruments set out by her university team still sat on tripods outside the tomb, although none in the group could tell if they still functioned, carrying out their monitoring duties. The passageways in the Sphinx were as narrow and labyrinthine as Rachel's comlog entries had suggested, the strings of glow-globes and electric lights left behind by various research groups now dark and depleted. They used hand torches and Kassad's night visor to explore the place. There was no sign of the room Rachel had been in when the walls closed in on her and the sickness began. There were only vestigial remnants of the once-powerful time tides. There was no sign of the Shrike.

Each tomb had offered its moment of terror, of hopeful and dreadful anticipation, only to be replaced by an hour or more of anticlimax as dusty, empty rooms appeared just as they had to the tourists and Shrike Pilgrims of centuries past.

Eventually the day had ended in disappointment and fatigue, the shadows from the eastern valley wall drawing across the Tombs and valley like a curtain closing an unsuccessful play. The day's heat had vanished, and the high desert cold returned quickly, borne on a wind that smelled of snow and the high reaches of the Bridle Range, twenty kilometers to the southwest. Kassad suggested that they make camp. The Consul had shown the way to the traditional grounds where Shrike Pilgrims had waited their last night before meeting the creature they sought. The flat area near the Sphinx, showing traces of litter from research groups as well as pilgrims, pleased Sol Weintraub, who imagined his daughter had camped there. No one else objected.

Now, in full darkness with the last piece of wood burning, I sensed the six of them drawing closer . . . not merely to the fire's warmth, but to each other . . . drawn by the fragile but tangible cords of shared experience forged during their voyage upriver on the levitation barge *Benares* and in their crossing to Keep Chronos. More than that, I sensed a unity more palpable than emotional bonds; it took a moment, but I soon realized that the group was connected in a microsphere of shared data and senseweb. On a world whose primitive, regional data relays had been shredded by the first hint of combat, this group had linked comlogs and biomonitors to share information and to watch over one another as best they could.

While the entry barriers were obvious and solid, I had no trouble sliding past, through, and under them, picking up the finite but numerous clues – pulse, skin temperature, cortical wave activity, access request, data inventory – which allowed me some insight into what each pilgrim was thinking, feeling, and doing. Kassad, Hoyt, and Lamia had implants, the flow of their thoughts was easiest to sense. At that second, Brawne Lamia was wondering if it had not been a mistake to seek out the Shrike; something was nagging at her, just under the surface but unrelenting in its demand to be heard. She felt as if she were ignoring some terribly important clue which held the solution to . . . what?

Brawne Lamia had always despised mysteries; it was one of the reasons she had left a life of some comfort and leisure to become a private investigator. But what mystery? She had all but solved the murder of her cybrid client . . . and lover . . . and had come to Hyperion to fulfill his final wish. Yet she sensed that this nagging doubt had little to do with the Shrike. What?

Lamia shook her head and poked the dying fire. Her body was strong, raised to resist Lusus's 1.3 standard gravity, and trained to even greater strength, but she had not slept in several days and she was very, very tired. She became vaguely aware that someone was speaking.

'. . . just to take a shower and get some food,' says Martin Silenus. 'Perhaps use your comm unit and fatline link to see who's winning the war.'

The Consul shakes his head. 'Not yet. The ship is for an emergency.'

Silenus gestures toward the night, the Sphinx, and the rising wind. 'You think that this isn't an emergency?'

Brawne Lamia realizes that they are talking about the Consul bringing his spacecraft here from the city of Keats. 'Are you sure that the absence of alcohol isn't the emergency you're referring to?' she asks.

Silenus glares at her. 'Would it hurt to have a drink?'

'No,' says the Consul. He rubs his eyes, and Lamia remembers that he too is addicted to alcohol. But his answer to bringing the ship here had been no. 'We'll wait until we have to.'

'What about the fatline transmitter?' says Kassad.

The Consul nods and removes the antique comlog from his small pack. The instrument had belonged to his grandmother Siri and to her grandparents before her. The Consul touches the diskey. 'I can broadcast with this, but not receive.'

Sol Weintraub has set his sleeping child in the opening of the closest tent. Now he turns toward the fire. 'And the last time you transmitted a message was when we arrived in the Keep?'

'Yes.'

Martin Silenus's tone is sarcastic. 'And we're supposed to believe that . . . from a confessed traitor?'

'Yes.' The Consul's voice is a distillation of pure weariness.

Kassad's thin face floats in the darkness. His body, legs, and arms are discernible only as a blackness against the already dark background. 'But it will serve to call the ship if we need it?'

'Yes.'

Father Hoyt hugs his cloak tighter around him to keep it from flapping in the rising wind. Sand scrapes against wool and tent fabric. 'Aren't you afraid that the port authorities or FORCE will move the ship or tamper with it?' he asks the Consul.

'No.' The Consul's head moves only slightly, as if he is too tired to shake it completely. 'Our clearance pip was from Gladstone herself. Also, the Governor-General is a friend of mine . . . was a friend.'

The others had met the recently promoted Hegemony governor shortly after landing; to Brawne Lamia, Theo Lane had seemed a man catapulted into events too large for his talents.

'The wind's coming up,' says Sol Weintraub. He turns his body to protect the baby from flying sand. Still squinting into the gale, the scholar says, 'I wonder if Het Masteen is out there?'

'We searched everywhere,' says Father Hoyt. His voice is muffled because he has lowered his head into the folds of his cloak.

Martin Silenus laughs. 'Pardon me, priest,' he says, 'but you're full of shit.' The poet stands and walks to the edge of the firelight. The wind ruffles the fur of his coat and rips his words away into the night. 'The cliff walls hold a thousand hiding places. The Crystal Monolith hides its entrance to us . . . but to a Templar? And besides, you saw the stairway to the labyrinth in the deepest room of the Jade Tomb.'

Hoyt looks up, squinting against the pinpricks of blowing sand. 'You think he's there? In the labyrinth?'

Silenus laughs and raises his arms. The silk of his loose blouse ripples and billows. 'How the fuck should I know, Padre? All I know is that Het Masteen could be out there now, watching us, waiting to come back to claim his luggage.' The poet gestures toward the Möbius cube in the center of their small pile of gear. 'Or he could be dead already. Or worse.'

'Worse?' says Hoyt. The priest's face has aged in the past few hours. His eyes are sunken mirrors of pain, his smile a rictus.

Martin Silenus strides back to the dying fire. 'Worse,' he says. 'He could be twisting on the Shrike's steel tree. Where we'll be in a few—'

Brawne Lamia rises suddenly and grasps the poet by his shirtfront. She lifts him off the ground, shakes him, lowers him until his face is on a level with hers. 'Once more,' she says softly, 'and I'll do very painful things to you. I won't kill you, but you will wish I had.'

The poet shows his satyr's smile. Lamia drops him and turns her back. Kassad says, 'We're tired. Everyone turn in. I'll stand watch.'

My dreams of Lamia are mixed with Lamia's dreams. It is not unpleasant to share a woman's dreams, a woman's thoughts, even those of a woman separated from me by a gulf of time and culture far greater than any imagined gap of gender. In a strange and oddly mirrorlike way, she dreamed of her dead lover, Johnny, of his too-small nose and his too-stubborn jaw, his too-long hair curling over his collar, and his eyes – those too-expressive, too-revealing, eyes that too-freely animated a face which might, except for those eyes, belong to any one of a thousand peasants born within a day's ride of London.

The face she dreamed was mine. The voice she heard in that dream was mine. But the lovemaking she dreamed of – remembering now – was nothing that I had shared. I sought to escape her dream, if only to find my own. If I were to be a voyeur, it might as well be in the tumble of manufactured memories which passed for my own dreams.

But I was not allowed to dream my own dreams. Not yet. I suspect that I was born – and born again from my deathbed – simply to dream those dreams of my dead and distant twin.

I resigned myself, ceased my struggles to awaken, and dreamed.

Brawne Lamia comes awake swiftly, jarringly, shaken from a pleasant dream by some sound or movement. For a long second she is disoriented; it is dark, there is a noise – not mechanical – which is louder than most sounds in the Lusus Hive where she lives; she is drunk with fatigue but knows that she has awakened after very little sleep; she is alone in a small, confined space, in something resembling an oversized body bag.

Raised on a world where enclosed places mean security from vicious air, winds, and animals, where many people suffer from agoraphobia when confronting the rare open space but few know the meaning of claustrophobia, Brawne Lamia nonetheless reacts as a claustrophobe: clawing for air, pushing aside bedroll and tent flaps in a panicked rush to escape the small cocoon of fiberplastic, crawling, pulling herself along by her hands and forearms and elbows until there is sand under her palms and sky above.

Not really sky, she realizes, suddenly seeing and remembering where she is. Sand. A blowing, raging, whirling sandstorm of particles, stinging her face like pinpricks. The campfire is out and covered with sand. Sand has banked on the windward side of all three of the tents, their sides flapping, cracking like rifle shots in the wind, and dunes of new-blown sand have grown up around the camp, leaving streaks and furrows and ridges in the lee of tents and gear. No one stirs from the other tents. The tent she was sharing with Father Hoyt is half-collapsed, all but buried by the rising dunes.

Hoyt.

It had been his absence which awakened her. Even in her dreams, some part of her consciousness had been aware of the soft breathing and almost indistinguishable moans from the sleeping priest as he wrestled with his pain. Sometime in the past half hour, he had left. Probably not more than a few minutes before; Brawne Lamia knew that even as she had dreamed of Johnny she had been half aware of a rustling, sliding sound above the rasp of sand and roar of the wind.

Lamia gets to her feet and shields her eyes from the sandstorm. It is very dark, the stars are occluded by high cloud and the surface storm, but a faint, almost electrical radiance fills the air and reflects from rock and dune surface. Lamia realizes that it *is* electrical, that the air is filled with a static which makes the curls of her hair leap and writhe in Medusalike gyrations. Static charges creep along her tunic sleeves and float over the tent surfaces like St Elmo's fire. As her eyes adapt, Lamia realizes that the shifting dunes are aglow with pale fire. Forty meters to the east, the tomb called the Sphinx is a crackling, pulsing outline in the night. Waves of current move along the outflung appendages often called the wings.

Brawne Lamia looks around, sees no sign of Father Hoyt, and considers calling for help. She realizes that her voice will not be heard above the wind roar. She wonders for a second whether the priest has merely gone to one of the other tents or to the crude latrine twenty meters west, but something tells her that this is not the case. She looks at the Sphinx and – for the briefest second – seems to see the shape of a man, black cloak flapping like a falling pennant, shoulders hunched against the wind, outlined against the static glow of the tomb.

A hand falls on her shoulder.

Brawne Lamia twists away, falls into a fighting crouch, left fist extended, right hand rigid. She recognizes Kassad standing there. The Colonel is half again as tall as Lamia – and half as broad – and miniature lightning plays across his thin form as he leans closer to shout in her ear. 'He went that way!' The long, black, scarecrow arm extends toward the Sphinx.

Lamia nods and shouts back, her voice almost inaudible to herself above the roar. 'Shall we wake the others?' She had forgotten that Kassad was standing watch. Did the man never sleep?

Fedmahn Kassad shakes his head. His visors are up and the helmet destructured to form a hood on the back of his combat-armored coverall. Kassad's face looks very pale in the glow from his suit. He gestures toward the Sphinx. His multipurpose FORCE rifle is nestled in the crook of his left arm. Grenades, binocular case, and more-mysterious items are draped from hooks and web belts on his impact armor. He points again toward the Sphinx.

Lamia leans forward and shouts. 'Did the Shrike take him?'

Kassad shakes his head.

'Can you see him?' She gestures toward his night visor and binoculars.

'No,' says Kassad. 'The storm. Fouls up heat signatures.'

Brawne Lamia turns her back to the wind, feeling the particles striking her neck like needles from a fléchette gun. She queries her comlog but it tells her only that Hoyt is alive and moving; nothing else is being transmitted on the common band. She moves until she is next to Kassad, their backs forming a wall against the gale. 'Are we going to follow him?' she shouts.

Kassad shakes his head. 'We can't leave the perimeter unguarded. I left telltales, but . . .' He gestures toward the storm.

Brawne Lamia ducks back in the tent, tugs on her boots, and emerges with her all-weather cape and her father's automatic pistol. A more conventional weapon, a Gier stunner, is in the breast pocket of the cape. 'I'll go then,' she says.

At first she thinks that the Colonel has not heard her, but then she sees something in his pale eyes and knows that he has. He taps the military comlog on his wrist.

Lamia nods and makes sure that her own implant and comlog are set to the widest bandwidth. 'I'll be back,' she says and wades up the growing dune. Her pant legs glow with static discharge, and the sand seems alive with silver-white pulses of current fleeting across its variegated surface.

Twenty meters from the camp, and she can see nothing of it. Ten meters farther, and the Sphinx rises above her. There is no sign of Father Hoyt; footprints do not survive ten seconds in the storm.

The wide entrance to the Sphinx is open, has been open as long as mankind has known of this place. Now it is a black rectangle in a faintly glowing wall. Logic suggested that Hoyt would have gone there, if only to get out of the storm, but something quite beyond logic tells her that this is not the priest's destination.

Brawne Lamia trudges past the Sphinx, rests in its lee for several moments to wipe the sand from her face and to breathe freely again, and then she moves on, following a faint, hard-packed trail between the dunes. Ahead of her, the Jade Tomb glows a milky green in the night, its smooth curves and crests oily with an ominous glow.

Squinting, Lamia looks again and sees someone or something outlined against that glow for the most fleeting of instants. Then the figure is gone, either inside the tomb or invisible against the black semicircle of its entrance.

Lamia puts her head down and moves forward, the wind pushing and shoving at her as if hurrying her toward something important.

FOUR

The military briefing droned on toward midmorning. I suspect that such meetings had shared the same qualities – brisk monotone continuing like a background buzz, the stale taste of too much coffee, the pall of smoke in the air, stacks of hard copy and the cortical overlay vertigo of implant access – for many centuries. I suspect it was simpler when I was a boy; Wellington rounded up his men, those he dispassionately and accurately called 'the scum of the earth', told them nothing, and sent them off to die.

I brought my attention back to the group. We were in a large room, gray walls relieved by white rectangles of light, gray carpet, gunmetal gray horseshoe table with black diskeys and the occasional carafe of water. CEO Meina Gladstone sat at the center of the arc of table, ranking senators and cabinet ministers near her, military officers and other second-rank decision makers farther along the curve. Behind them all, not at the table, sat the inevitable clusters of aides, none of the FORCE people below the rank of colonel, and behind them – on less comfortable-looking chairs – the aides to the aides.

I had no chair. With a cluster of other invited but obviously purposeless personnel, I sat on a stool near a rear corner of the room, twenty meters from the CEO and even farther from the briefing officer, a young colonel with a pointer in his hand and no hesitation whatsoever in his voice. Behind the colonel was the gold and gray slab of a callup template, before him the slightly raised omnisphere of the kind found in any holopit. From time to time, the callup clouded and leaped to life; at other times the air misted with complex holos. Miniatures of these diagrams glowed on every diskey plate and hovered above some comlogs.

I sat on my stool, watched Gladstone, and drew an occasional sketch.

Awakening that morning in the Government House guest room, bright Tau Ceti sunlight streaming between peach-colored drapes which had opened automatically at my 0630 wake-up time, there was a second when I was lost, displaced, still in pursuit of Lenar Hoyt and in fear of the Shrike and Het Masteen. Then, as if some power had granted my wish to leave me to dream my own dreams, there was a minute where confusion compounded, and I sat up gasping, looking around in alarm, expecting the lemon carpet and peach-colored light to fade like the fever dream it was, leaving only the pain and phlegm and terrible hemorrhages, blood on linen, the light-filled room dissolving into the shadows of the dark apartment on the Piazza di Spagna, and looming over all, the sensitive face of Joseph Severn leaning forward, leaning forward, watching and waiting for me to die.

I showered twice, first with water and then with sonic, dressed in a new gray suit that lay set out for me on the just-made bed when I emerged from the bathroom, and set off to find the east courtyard where – a courtesy pip left near my new clothing had told me – breakfast was being served for Government House guests.

The orange juice was fresh squeezed. The bacon was crisp and authentic. The newspaper said that CEO Gladstone would be addressing the Web via All Thing and media at 1030 hours Web standard. The pages were full of war news. Flat photos of the armada glowed in full color. General Morpurgo stared out grimly from page three; the paper called him 'the hero of the Second Height Rebellion'. Diana Philomel glanced over toward me from a nearby table where she dined with her Neanderthal husband. Her gown was more formal this morning, dark blue and far less revealing, but a slit up the side allowed a hint of last night's show. She kept her eyes on me as she lifted a strip of bacon with lacquered nails and took a careful bite. Hermund Philomel grunted as he read something agreeable on the folded financial pages.

'The Ouster migration cluster . . . commonly known as a Swarm . . . was detected by Hawking distortion-sensing equipment in the Camn System a little more than three standard years ago,' the young briefing officer was saying. 'Immediately upon detection, FORCE Task Force 42, pre-configured for evacuation of Hyperion System, spun up to C-plus status from Parvati with sealed orders to create a farcaster capability within portal range of Hyperion. At the same time, Task Force 87.2 was dispatched from Solkov-Tikata Staging Area around Camn III with orders to rendezvous with the evacuation force in Hyperion System, to find the Ouster migration cluster, and to engage and destroy their military components . . .' Images of the armada appeared on the callup temp and in front of the young colonel. He gestured with his pointer and a line of ruby light cut through the larger holo to illuminate one of the Three-C ships in the formation. 'Task Force 87.2 is under the command of Admiral Nashita aboard the HS *Hebrides* . . .'

'Yes, yes,' grumbled General Morpurgo, 'we know all this, Yani. Cut to the quick.'

The young colonel simulated a smile, nodded imperceptibly toward the General and CEO Gladstone, and resumed in a voice a trifle less confident. 'Coded fatline transmissions from TF 42 during the past seventy-two hours, standard, report pitched battles between scouting elements of the evacuation task force and forward elements of the Ouster migration cluster—'

'The Swarm,' interrupted Leigh Hunt.

'Yes,' said Yani. He turned toward the callup, and five meters of frosted glass burned to life. To me the display was an incomprehensible maze of arcane symbols, colored vector lines, substrate codes, and FORCE acronyms which added up to total gibberish. Perhaps it made no sense to the big brass and senior politicians in the room either, but no one let on that this was the case. I began a new drawing of Gladstone, with the bulldog profile of Morpurgo in the background.

'Although first reports suggested Hawking wakes in the neighborhood of four thousand drives, this is a misleading figure,' continued the colonel named Yani. I wondered whether that was his first or last name. 'As you know, Ouster . . . ah . . . Swarms can be constituted of up to ten thousand separate drive units, but the vast majority of these are small and either unarmed or of negligible military significance. Microwave, fatline, and other emission signature evaluation suggests—'

'Excuse me,' said Meina Gladstone, her weathered voice in sharp contrast to the briefing officer's syrupy flow, 'but could you tell us how many of the Ouster ships *are* of military significance?'

'Ah . . .' said the colonel, and glanced toward his superiors.

General Morpurgo cleared his throat. 'We think about six . . . seven hundred, tops,' he said. 'Nothing to worry about.'

CEO Gladstone raised an eyebrow. 'And the size of our battle groups?'

Morpurgo nodded toward the young colonel to stand at ease. Morpurgo answered. 'Task Force 42 has about sixty ships, CEO. Task Force—'

'Task Force 42 is the evacuation group?' said Gladstone.

General Morpurgo nodded, and I thought I saw a hint of condescension in his smile. 'Yes, ma'am. Task Force 87.2, the battle group, which translated in-system about an hour ago, will—'

'Were sixty ships adequate to face six or seven hundred?' asked Gladstone.

Morpurgo glanced toward one of his fellow officers as if asking for patience. 'Yes,' he said, 'more than adequate. You have to understand, CEO, that six hundred Hawking drives may sound like a lot, but they're nothing to worry about when they're pushing singleships, or scouts, or one of those little five-person attack craft they call lancers. Task Force 42 consisted of almost *two dozen* main line spinships, including the carriers *Olympus Shadow* and *Neptune Station*. Each of these can launch more than a hundred fighters or ALRs.' Morpurgo fumbled in his pocket, pulled out a recom smoke-stick the size of a cigar, appeared to remember that Gladstone disapproved of them, and stuck it back in his coat. He frowned. 'When Task Force 87.2 completes its deployment, we'll have more than enough firepower to deal with a dozen Swarms.' Still frowning, he nodded toward Yani to continue.

The colonel cleared his throat and gestured with his pointer toward the callup display. 'As you can see, Task Force 42 had no trouble clearing the necessary volume of space to initiate farcaster construction. This construction was begun six weeks ago, WST, and completed yesterday at 1624 hours, standard. Initial Ouster harassing attacks were beaten off with no casualties for TF 42, and during the past forty-eight hours, a major battle has been waged between advance units of the task force and main Ouster forces. The focus of this skirmish has been here' – Yani gestured again, and a section of the callup pulsed with blue light beyond the tip of his pointer – 'twenty-nine degrees above the plane of the ecliptic, thirty AU from Hyperion's sun, approximately 0.35 AU from the hypothetical rim of the system's Oört cloud.'

'Casualties?' said Leigh Hunt.

'Quite within acceptable limits for a firefight of this duration,' said the young colonel, who looked like he had never been within a light-year of hostile fire. His blond hair was carefully combed to the side and gleamed under the intense glow of the spots. 'Twenty-six Hegemony fast attack fighters destroyed or missing, twelve torpedo-carrying ALRs, three torchships, the fuel transport *Asquith's Pride*, and the cruiser *Draconi III*.'

'How many *people* lost?' asked CEO Gladstone. Her voice was very quiet.

Yani glanced quickly at Morpurgo but answered the question himself. 'Around twenty-three hundred,' he said. 'But rescue operations are currently being carried out, and there is some hope of finding survivors of the *Draconi*.' He smoothed his tunic and went on quickly. 'This should be weighed against confirmed kills of at least a hundred and fifty Ouster warships. Our own raids into the migration clust— the Swarm have resulted in an additional thirty to sixty destroyed craft, including comet farms, ore-processing ships, and at least one command cluster.'

Meina Gladstone rubbed her gnarled fingers together. 'Did the casualty estimate – *our* casualties – include the passengers and crew of the destroyed treeship *Yggdrasill*, which we had chartered for the evacuation?'

'No, ma'am,' Yani responded briskly. 'Although there was an Ouster raid in progress at the time, our analysis shows that the *Yggdrasill* was not destroyed by enemy action.'

Gladstone again raised an eyebrow. 'What then?'

'Sabotage, as far as we can tell at this time,' said the colonel. He prompted another Hyperion System diagram on to the callup.

General Morpurgo glanced at his comlog and said, 'Uh-uh, skip to the ground defenses, Yani. The CEO has to deliver her speech in thirty minutes.'

I completed the sketch of Gladstone and Morpurgo, stretched, and looked around for another subject. Leigh Hunt seemed a challenge, with his nondescript, almost pinched features. When I glanced back up, a holoed globe of Hyperion ceased spinning and unwound itself into a series of flattened projections: oblique equirectangular, Bonne, orthographic, rosette, Van der Grinten, Gores, interrupted Goode homolosine, gnomonic, sinusoidal, azimuthal equidistant, polyconic, hypercorrected Kuwatsi, computer-eschered, Briesemeister, Buckminster, Miller cylindrical, multicoligraphed, and satplot standard, before resolving into a standard Robinson-Baird map of Hyperion.

I smiled. That had been the most enjoyable thing I'd seen since the briefing began. Several of Gladstone's people were shifting with impatience. They wanted at least ten minutes with the CEO before the broadcast began.

'As you know,' began the colonel, 'Hyperion is Old Earth standard to nine point eight nine on the Thuron-Laumier Scale of—'

'Oh, for Chrissakes,' growled Morpurgo, 'get to the troop dispositions and get it over with.'

'Yessir.' Yani swallowed and lifted his pointer. His voice was no longer confident. 'As you know . . . I mean . . .' He pointed to the northernmost continent, floating like a poorly done sketch of a horse's head and neck, terminating jaggedly where the beast's chest and back muscles would begin. 'This is Equus. It has a different official name, but everyone's called it that since . . . this is Equus. The chain of islands running southeast . . . here and here . . . is called the Cat and Nine Tails. Actually, it's an archipelago with more than a hundred . . . anyway, the second major continent is called Aquila, and perhaps you can see it's shaped something like an Old Earth eagle, with the beak here . . . on the northwest coast . . . and the talons extended here, to the southwest . . . and at least one wing raised here, running to the northeast coast. This section is the so-called Pinion Plateau and is almost inaccessible due to the flame forests, but here . . . and here . . . to the southwest, are the main fiberplastic plantations . . .'

'The *disposition* of troops,' growled Morpurgo.

I sketched Yani. I discovered that it is impossible to convey the sheen of sweat with graphite.

'Yessir. The third continent is Ursus . . . looks a bit like a bear . . . but no FORCE troops landed there because it's south polar, almost uninhabitable, although the Hyperion Self-defense Force keeps a listening post there . . .' Yani seemed to sense he was babbling. He drew himself up, wiped his upper lip with the back of his hand, and continued in a more composed tone. 'Primary FORCE:ground installations here . . . here . . . and here.' His pointer illuminated areas near the capital of Keats, high on the neck of Equus. 'FORCE:space units have secured the primary spaceport at the capital as well as secondary fields here . . . and here.' He touched the cities of Endymion and Port Romance, both on the continent of Aquila. 'FORCE:ground units have prepared defensive installations here . . .' Two dozen red lights winked on; most on the neck and mane areas of Equus, but several in Aquila's Beak and Port Romance regions. 'These include elements of the Marines, as well as ground defenses, ground-to-air and ground-to-space components. High Command expects that, unlike Bressia, there will be no battles on the planet itself, but should they attempt an invasion, we will be ready for them.'

Meina Gladstone checked her comlog. Seventeen minutes remained until her live broadcast. 'What about evacuation plans?'

Yani's regained composure crumbled. He looked in some desperation toward his superior officers.

'No evacuation,' said Admiral Singh. 'It was a feint, a lure for the Ousters.'

Gladstone tapped her fingers together. 'There are several million people on Hyperion, Admiral.'

'Yes,' said Singh, 'and we'll protect them, but an evacuation of even the sixty thousand or so Hegemony citizens is quite out of the question. It would be chaos if we allowed all three million into the Web. Besides, for security reasons, it is not possible.'

'The Shrike?' queried Leigh Hunt.

'Security reasons,' repeated General Morpurgo. He stood up, took the pointer from Yani. The young man stood there for a second, irresolute, seeing no place to sit or stand, and then he moved to the rear of the room near me, stood at parade rest, and stared at something near the ceiling – possibly the end of his military career.

'Task Force 87.2 is in-system,' said Morpurgo. 'The Ousters have pulled back to their Swarm center, about sixty AU from Hyperion. To all intents and purposes, the system is secure. Hyperion is secure. We're waiting for a counterattack, but we know that we can contain it. Again, to all intents and purposes, Hyperion is now part of the Web. Questions?'

There were none. Gladstone left with Leigh Hunt, a pack of senators, and her aides. The military brass gravitated to huddles, apparently as dictated by rank. Aides scattered. The few reporters allowed in the room ran to their imager crews waiting outside. The young colonel, Yani, remained at parade rest, his eyes unfocused, his face very pale.

I sat for a moment, staring at the callup map of Hyperion. The continent Equus's resemblance to a horse was greater at this distance. From where I sat, I could just make out the mountains of the Bridle Range and the orange-yellow coloring of the high desert below the horse's 'eye'. There were no FORCE defensive positions marked northeast of the mountains, no symbols at all besides a tiny red glow which might have been the dead City of Poets. The Time Tombs were not marked at all. It was as if the Tombs had no military significance, no part to play in the day's proceedings. But somehow I knew better. Somehow I suspected that the entire war, the movement of thousands, the fate of millions – perhaps billions – depended upon the actions of six people in that unmarked stretch of orange and yellow.

I folded my sketchbook, stuffed my pencils in pockets, looked for an exit, found and used it.

Leigh Hunt met me in one of the long hallways that led to the main entrance. 'You are leaving?'

I took a breath. 'Aren't I allowed to?'

Hunt smiled, if one could call that upward folding of thin lips a smile. 'Of course, M. Severn. But CEO Gladstone has asked me to tell you that she would like to speak to you again this afternoon.'

'When?'

Hunt shrugged. 'Any time after her speech. At your convenience.'

I nodded. Literally millions of lobbyists, job seekers, would-be biographers, business people, fans of the CEO, and potential assassins would give almost anything to have a minute with the Hegemony's most visible leader, a few seconds with CEO Gladstone, and I could see her 'at my convenience'. No one ever said the universe was sane.

I brushed past Leigh Hunt and made for the front door.

By long tradition, Government House had no public farcaster portals within its walls. It was a short walk past the main-entrance security baffles, across the garden, to the low, white building that served as press headquarters and terminex. The newsteeps were clustered around a central viewing pit, where the familiar face and voice of Lewellyn Drake, 'the voice of the All Thing', gave background to CEO Gladstone's speech 'of vital importance to the Hegemony'. I nodded in his direction, found an unused portal, presented my universal card, and went in search of a bar.

The Grand Concourse was, once you got there, the one place in the Web where you could farcast for free. Every world in the Web had offered at least one of its finest urban blocks – TC^2 provided twenty-three blocks – for shopping, entertainment, fine restaurants, and bars. Especially bars.

Like the River Tethys, the Grand Concourse flowed between military-sized farcaster portals two hundred meters high. With wraparound, the effect was of an infinite main street, a hundred-kilometer torus of material delights. One could stand, as I did that morning, under the brilliant sun of Tau Ceti and look down the Concourse to the night-time midway of Deneb Drei, alive with neon and holos, and catch a glimpse of the hundred-tiered Main Mall of Lusus, while knowing that beyond it lay the shadow-dappled boutiques of God's Grove with its brick concourse and elevators to Treetops, the most expensive eatery in the Web.

I didn't give a damn about all that. I just wanted to find a quiet bar.

TC^2 bars were too filled with bureaucrats, teeps, and business types, so I caught one of the Concourse shuttles and stepped off on Sol Draconi Septem's main drag. The gravity discouraged many – it discouraged *me* – but it meant that the bars were less full, and those there had come to drink.

The place I chose was a ground-level bar, almost hidden under the support pillars and service chutes to the main shopping trellis, and it was dark inside: dark walls, dark wood, dark patrons – their skin as black as mine was pale. It was a good place to drink, and I did so, starting with a double Scotch and getting more serious as I went along.

Even there I couldn't be free of Gladstone. Far across the room, a flatscreen TV showed the CEO's face with the blue-and-gold background she used for state broadcasts. Several of the other drinkers had gathered to watch. I heard snatches of the speech: '. . . to insure the safety of Hegemony citizens and . . . cannot be allowed to endanger the safety of the

Web or our allies in . . . thus, I have authorized a full military response to . . .'

'Turn that goddamned thing down!' I was amazed to realize that it was me shouting. The patrons glowered over their shoulders, but they turned it down. I watched Gladstone's mouth move a moment, and then I waved to the bartender for another double.

Sometime later, it might have been hours, I looked up from my drink to realize that there was someone sitting across from me in the dark booth. It took me a second, blinking, to recognize who it was in the dim light. For an instant my heart raced as I thought, *Fanny*, but then I blinked again and said, 'Lady Philomel.'

She still wore the dark blue dress I'd seen her in at breakfast. Somehow it seemed cut lower now. Her face and shoulders seemed to glow in the near-darkness. 'M. Severn,' she said, her voice almost a whisper. 'I've come to redeem your promise.'

'Promise?' I waved the bartender over, but he did not respond. I frowned and looked at Diana Philomel. 'What promise?'

'To draw me, of course. Did you forget your promise at the party?'

I snapped my fingers, but the insolent barkeep still did not deign to look my way. 'I did draw you,' I said.

'Yes,' said Lady Philomel, 'but not *all* of me.'

I sighed and drained the last of my Scotch. 'Drinking,' I said.

Lady Philomel smiled. 'So I see.'

I started to stand to go after the bartender, thought better of it, and sat back slowly on to the weathered wood of the bench. 'Armageddon,' I said. 'They're playing with Armageddon.' I looked at the woman carefully, squinting slightly to bring her into focus. 'Do you know that word, m'lady?'

'I don't believe he will serve you any more alcohol,' she said. 'I have drinks at my place. You could have one while you draw.'

I squinted again, craftily now. I might have had a few too many Scotches, but they hadn't impaired my awareness. 'Husband,' I said.

Diana Philomel smiled again, and that too was radiant. 'Spending several days at Government House,' she said, truly whispering now. 'He can't be far from the source of power at such an important time. Come, my vehicle is just outside.'

I don't remember paying, but I assume I did. Or Lady Philomel did. I don't remember her helping me outside, but I assume that someone did. Perhaps a chauffeur. I remember a man in gray tunic and trousers, remember leaning against him.

The EMV had a bubble top, polarized from the outside but quite transparent from where we sat in deep cushions and looked out. I counted one, two portals, and then we were out and away from the Concourse and gaining altitude above blue fields under a yellow sky. Elaborate homes, made from some ebony wood, sat on hilltops surrounded by poppy fields and bronze lakes. Renaissance Vector? It was too difficult a puzzle to work on right then, so I laid my head against the bubble and decided to rest for a moment or two. Had to be rested for Lady Philomel's portrait . . . heh, heh.

The countryside passed below.

FIVE

Colonel Fedmahn Kassad follows Brawne Lamia and Father Hoyt through the dust storm toward the Jade Tomb. He had lied to Lamia; his night visor and sensors worked well despite the electrical discharge flickering around them. Following the two seemed the best chance for finding the Shrike. Kassad remembered the rock-lion hunts on Hebron – one tethered a goat and waited.

Data from the telltales he had set around the encampment flickers on Kassad's tactical display and whispers through his implant. It is a calculated risk to leave Weintraub and his daughter, Martin Silenus and the Consul sleeping there, unprotected except for the automatics and an alarm. But then, Kassad seriously doubts whether he can stop the Shrike anyway. They are all goats, tethered, waiting. It is the woman, the phantom named Moneta, whom Kassad is determined to find before he dies.

The wind has continued to rise, and now it screams around Kassad, reducing normal visibility to zero and pelting his impact armor. The dunes glow with discharge, and miniature lightning crackles around his boots and legs as he strides to keep Lamia's heat signature in clear view. Information flows in from her open comlog. Hoyt's closed channels reveal only that he is alive and moving.

Kassad passes under the outstretched wing of the Sphinx, feeling the weight invisible above him, hanging there like a great boot heel. Then he turns down the valley, seeing the Jade Tomb as an absence of heat in infrared, a cold outline. Hoyt is just entering the hemispherical opening; Lamia is twenty meters behind him. Nothing else moves in the valley. The telltales from the camp, hidden by night and storm behind Kassad, reveal Sol and the baby sleeping, the Consul lying awake but unmoving, nothing else within the perimeter.

Kassad slips the safety off on his weapon and moves forward quickly, his long legs taking great strides. He would give anything at that second to have access to a spottersat, his tactical channels complete, rather than have to deal with this partial picture of a fragmented situation. He shrugs within his impact armor and keeps moving.

Brawne Lamia almost does not make the final fifteen meters of her voyage to the Jade Tomb. The wind has risen to gale force and beyond, shoving her along so that twice she loses her footing and falls headlong into the sand. The lightning is real now, splitting the sky in great bursts that illuminate the glowing tomb ahead. Twice she tries calling Hoyt, Kassad, or the others, sure that no one could be sleeping through this back at the camp, but her comlog and implants give her only static, their widebands registering gibberish. After the second fall, Lamia gets to her knees and looks ahead; there has been no sign of Hoyt since that brief glimpse of someone moving toward the entrance.

Lamia grips her father's automatic pistol and gets to her feet, allowing the wind to blow her the last few meters. She pauses before the entrance hemisphere.

Whether due to the storm and electrical display or something else, the Jade Tomb is glowing a bright, bilious green which tinges the dunes and makes the skin of her wrists and hands look like something from the grave. Lamia makes a final attempt to raise someone on her comlog and then enters the tomb.

Father Lenar Hoyt of the twelve-hundred-year-old Society of Jesus, resident of the New Vatican on Pacem and loyal servant of His Holiness Pope Urban XVI, is screaming obscenities.

Hoyt is lost and in great pain. The wide rooms near the entrance to the Jade Tomb have narrowed, the corridor has wound back on itself so many times, that now Father Hoyt is lost in a series of catacombs, wandering between greenly glowing walls, in a maze he does not remember from the day's explorations or from the maps he has left behind. The pain – pain which has been with him for years, pain which has been his companion since the tribe of the Bikura had implanted the two cruciforms, his own and Paul Duré's – now threatens to drive him mad with its new intensity.

The corridor narrows again. Lenar Hoyt screams, no longer aware that he is doing so, no longer aware of the words he cries out – words which he has not used since childhood. He wants release. Release from the pain. Release from the burden of carrying Father Duré's DNA, personality . . . Duré's *soul* . . . in the cross-shaped parasite on his back. And from carrying the terrible curse of his own foul resurrection in the cruciform on his chest.

But even as Hoyt screams, he knows that it was not the now-dead Bikura who had condemned him to such pain; the lost tribe of colonists, resurrected by their own cruciforms so many times that they had become idiots, mere vehicles for their own DNA and that of their parasites, had been priests also . . . priests of the Shrike.

Father Hoyt of the Society of Jesus has brought a vial of holy water blessed by His Holiness, a Eucharist consecrated in a Solemn High Mass, and a copy of the Church's ancient rite of exorcism. These things are forgotten now, sealed in a Perspex bubble in a pocket of his cloak.

Hoyt stumbles against a wall and screams again. The pain is a force beyond description now, the full ampule of ultra-morph he had shot only fifteen minutes earlier, helpless against it. Father Hoyt screams and claws at his clothes, ripping off the heavy cloak, the black tunic and Roman collar, pants and shirt and underclothes, until he is naked, shivering with pain and cold in the glowing corridors of the Jade Tomb and screaming obscenities into the night.

He stumbles forward again, finds an opening, and moves into a room larger than any he remembers from the day's searches there. Bare, translucent walls rise thirty meters on each side of an empty space. Hoyt stumbles to his hands and knees, looks down, and realizes that the floor has become almost transparent. He is staring into a vertical shaft beneath the thin membrane of floor; a shaft that drops a kilometer or more to flames. The room fills with the red-orange pulse of light from the fire so far below.

Hoyt rolls to his side and laughs. If this is some image of hell summoned up for his benefit, it is a failure. Hoyt's view of hell is tactile; it is the pain which moves in him like jagged wires pulled through his veins and guts. Hell is also the memory of starving children in the slums of Armaghast and the smile of politicians sending boys off to die in colonial wars. Hell is the thought of the Church dying out in his lifetime, in Duré's lifetime, the last of its believers a handful of old men and women filling only a few pews of the huge cathedrals on Pacem. Hell is the hypocrisy of saying morning Mass with the evil of the cruciform pulsating warmly, obscenely, above one's heart.

There is a rush of hot air, and Hoyt watches as a section of floor slides back, creating a trapdoor to the shaft below. The room fills with the stench of sulfur. Hoyt laughs at the cliché, but within seconds the laughter turns to sobs. He is on his knees now, scraping with bloodied nails at the cruciforms on his chest and back. The cross-shaped welts seem to glow in the red light. Hoyt can hear the flames below.

'Hoyt!'

Still sobbing, he turns to see the woman – Lamia – framed in the doorway. She is looking past him, beyond him, and raising an antique pistol. Her eyes are very wide.

Father Hoyt feels the heat behind him, hears the roar as of a distant furnace, but above that, he suddenly hears the slide and scrape of metal on stone. Footsteps. Still clawing at the bloodied welt on his chest, Hoyt turns, his knees rubbed raw against the floor.

He sees the shadow first: ten meters of sharp angles, thorns, blades . . . legs like steel pipes with a rosette of scimitar blades at the knees and ankles. Then, through the pulse of hot light and black shadow, Hoyt sees the eyes. A hundred facets . . . a thousand . . . glowing red, a laser shone through twin rubies, above the collar of steel thorns and the quicksilver chest reflecting flame and shadow . . .

Brawne Lamia is firing her father's pistol. The slaps of the shots echo high and flat above the furnace rumble.

Father Lenar Hoyt swivels toward her, raises one hand. 'No, don't!' he screams. 'It grants one wish! I have to make a . . .'

The Shrike, which was *there* – five meters away – is suddenly *here*, an arm's length from Hoyt. Lamia quits firing. Hoyt looks up, sees his own reflection in the fire-burnished chrome of the thing's carapace . . . sees something else in the Shrike's eyes at that instant . . . and then it is gone, the Shrike is gone, and Hoyt lifts his hand slowly, touches his throat almost bemusedly, stares for a second at the cascade of red which is covering his hand, his chest, the cruciform, his belly . . .

He turns toward the doorway and sees Lamia still staring in terror and shock, not at the Shrike now, but at him, at Father Lenar Hoyt of the Society of Jesus, and in that instant he realizes that the pain is *gone*, and he opens his mouth to speak, but more, only more red comes out, a geyser of red. Hoyt glances down again, notices for the first time that he is naked, sees the blood dripping from his chin and chest, dripping and pouring to the now-dark floor, sees the blood pouring as if someone had upended a bucket of red paint, and then he sees nothing as he falls face first to the floor so far . . . so very far . . . below.

SIX

Diana Philomel's body was as perfect as cosmetic science and an ARNist's skills could make it. I lay in bed for several minutes after awakening and admired her body: turned away from me, the classic curve of back and hip and flank offering a geometry more beautiful and powerful than anything discovered by Euclid, the two dimples visible on the lower back, just above the heart-stopping widening of milk-white derriere, soft angles intersecting, the backs of full thighs somehow more sensual and solid than any aspect of male anatomy could hope to be.

Lady Diana was asleep, or seemed to be. Our clothes lay strewn across a wide expanse of green carpet. Thick light, tinged magenta and blue, flooded broad windows, through which gray and gold treetops were visible. Large sheets of drawing paper lay scattered around, beneath, and on top of our discarded clothes. I leaned to my left, lifted a sheet of paper, and saw a hasty scribble of breasts, thighs, an arm reworked in haste, and a face with no features. Doing a life study while drunk and in the process of being seduced is never a formula for quality art.

I moaned, rolled on my back, and studied the sculptured scrollwork on the ceiling twelve feet above. If the woman beside me had been Fanny, I might never want to move. As it was, I slipped out from under the covers, found my comlog, noted that it was early morning on Tau Ceti Center – fourteen hours after my appointment with the CEO – and padded off to the bathroom in search of a hangover pill.

There were several varieties of medication to choose from in Lady Diana's drug bin. In addition to the usual aspirin and endorphins, I saw stims, tranks, Flashback tubes, orgasm derms, shunt primers, cannabis inhalers, non-recom tobacco cigarettes, and a hundred less identifiable drugs. I found a glass and forced down two Dayafters, feeling the nausea and headache fade within seconds.

Lady Diana was awake and sitting up in bed, still nude, when I emerged. I started to smile and then saw the two men by the east doorway. Neither was her husband, although both were as large and shared the same no-neck, ham-fisted, dark-jowled style that Hermund Philomel had perfected.

In the long pageant of human history, I am sure that there has been some human male who could stand, surprised and naked, in front of two fully clothed and potentially hostile strangers, rival males as it were, *without* cringing, *without* having the urge to cover his genitals and hunch over, and *without* feeling totally vulnerable and at a disadvantage . . . but I am not that male.

I hunched over, covered my groin, backed toward the bathroom, and said, 'What . . . who . . .?' I looked toward Diana Philomel for help and saw the smile there . . . a smile that matched the cruelty I had first seen in her eyes.

'Get him. *Quickly!*' demanded my erstwhile lover.

I made it to the bathroom and was reaching for the manual switch to dilate the door closed when the closer of the two men reached me, grabbed me, thrust me back into the bedroom, and threw me to his partner. Both men were from Lusus or an equally high-g world, or else they subsisted exclusively on a diet of steroids and Samson cells, for they tossed me back and forth with no effort. It didn't matter how large they were. Except for my brief career as a school-yard fighter, my life . . . the memories of my life . . . offered few instances of violence and even fewer instances where I emerged from a scuffle the victor. One glance at the two men amusing themselves at my expense and I knew that these were the type one read about and did not quite believe in – individuals who could break bones, flatten noses, or crack kneecaps with no more compunction than I would feel about tossing away a defective stylus.

'*Quickly!*' Diana hissed again.

I canvased the datasphere, the house's memory, Diana's comlog umbilical, the two goons' tenuous connection to the information universe . . . and although I now knew where I was: the Philomel country estate, six hundred kilometers from the capital of Pirre in the agricultural belt of terraformed Renaissance Minor . . . and precisely who the goons were: Debin Farrus and Hemmit Gorma, plant security personnel for the Heaven's Gate Scrubbers Union . . . I had no idea why one was sitting on me, his knee in the small of my back, while the other crushed my comlog under his heel and slipped an osmosis cuff over my wrist, up my arm . . .

I heard the hiss and relaxed.

'Who are you?'

'Joseph Severn.'

'Is that your real name?'

'No.' I felt the effects of the truthtalk and knew that I could confound it merely by going away, stepping back into the datasphere or retreating fully to the Core. But that would mean leaving my body to the mercy of whoever was asking the questions. I stayed there. My eyes were closed but I recognized the next voice.

'Who *are* you?' asked Diana Philomel.

I sighed. It was a difficult question to answer honestly. 'John Keats,' I said at last. Their silence told me that the name meant nothing to them. *Why should it?* I asked myself. I once predicted that it would be a name 'writ in water'. Although I couldn't move or open my eyes, I found no trouble in canvasing the datasphere, following their access vectors. The poet's name was among eight hundred John Keatses on the list offered to them by the public file, but they didn't seem too interested in someone nine hundred years dead.

'Who do you work for?' It was Hermund Philomel's voice. For some reason I was mildly surprised.

'No one.'

The faint Doppler of voices changed as they talked amongst themselves. 'Can he be resisting the drug?'

'No one can *resist* it,' said Diana. 'They can *die* when it's administered, but they can't resist it.'

'Then what's going on?' asked Hermund. 'Why would Gladstone bring a nobody into the Council on the eve of war?'

'He can hear you, you know,' said another man's voice – one of the goons.

'It doesn't matter,' said Diana. 'He's not going to live after the interrogation anyway.' Her voice came again, directed toward me. 'Why did the CEO invite you to the Council . . . John?'

'Not sure. To hear about the pilgrims, probably.'

'What pilgrims, John?'

'The Shrike Pilgrims.'

Someone else made a noise. 'Hush,' said Diana Philomel. To me she said, 'Are those the Shrike Pilgrims on Hyperion, John?'

'Yes.'

'Is there a pilgrimage underway now?'

'Yes.'

'And why is Gladstone asking you, John?'

'I dream them.'

There was a disgusted sound. Hermund said, 'He's crazy. Even under truthtalk he doesn't know who he is, now he's giving us this. Let's get it over with and—'

'Shut up,' said Lady Diana. 'Gladstone's not crazy. She invited him, remember? John, what do you mean you dream them?'

'I dream the first Keats retrieval persona's impressions,' I said. My voice was thick, as if I were talking in my sleep. 'He hardwired himself into one of the pilgrims when they murdered his body, and now he roams their microsphere. Somehow his perceptions are my dreams. Perhaps my actions are his dreams, I don't know.'

'Insane,' said Hermund.

'No, no,' said Lady Diana. Her voice was strained, almost shocked. 'John, are you a cybrid?'

'Yes.'

'Oh, Christ and Allah,' said Lady Diana.

'What's a cybrid?' said one of the goons. He had a high, almost feminine voice.

There was silence for a moment, and then Diana spoke. 'Idiot. Cybrids were human remotes created by the Core. There were a few on the Advisory Council until last century, when they were outlawed.'

'Like an android or something?' said the other goon.

'Shut up,' said Hermund.

'No,' answered Diana. 'Cybrids were genetically perfect, recombed from DNA going back to Old Earth. All you needed was a bone . . . a fragment of hair . . . John, can you hear me? John?'

'Yes.'

'John, you're a cybrid . . . do you know who your persona template was?'

'John Keats.'

I could hear her take a deep breath. 'Who is . . . was . . . John Keats?'

'A poet.'

'When did he live, John?'

'From 1795 to 1821,' I said.

'Which reckoning, John?'

'Old Earth A.D.,' I said. 'Pre-Hegira. Modern era—'

Hermund's voice broke in, agitated. 'John, are you . . . are you in contact with the TechnoCore right now?'

'Yes.'

'Can you . . . are you free to communicate despite the truthtalk?'

'Yes.'

'Oh, fuck,' said the goon with the high voice.

'We've got to get out of here,' snapped Hermund.

'Just a minute more,' said Diana. 'We've got to know . . .'

'Can we take him with us?' asked the deep-voiced goon.

'Idiot,' said Hermund. 'If he's alive and in touch with the datasphere and Core . . . hell, he *lives* in the Core, his mind's there . . . then he can tip Gladstone, ExecSec, FORCE, *anybody*!'

'Shut up,' said Lady Diana. 'We'll kill him as soon as I'm finished. A few more questions. John?'

'Yes.'

'Why does Gladstone need to know what's happening to the Shrike Pilgrims? Does it have something to do with the war with the Ousters?'

'I'm not sure.'

'Shit,' whispered Hermund. 'Let's *go*.'

'Quiet. John, where are you from?'

'I've lived on Esperance the last ten months.'

'And before that?'

'On Earth before that.'

'Which Earth?' demanded Hermund. 'New Earth? Earth Two? Earth city? Which one?'

'Earth,' I said. Then I remembered. 'Old Earth.'

'*Old Earth?*' said one of the goons. 'This is fucked. I'm getting out of here.'

There came the frying-bacon sizzle of a weapons laser. I smelled something sweeter than frying bacon, and there was a heavy thump. Diana Philomel said, 'John, are you talking about your persona template's life on Old Earth?'

'No.'

'*You* – the cybrid you – were on Old Earth?'

'Yes,' I said. 'I woke from death there. In the same room on the Piazza di Spagna in which I died. Severn was not there, but Dr Clark and some of the others were . . .'

'He *is* crazy,' said Hermund. 'Old Earth's been destroyed for more than four centuries . . . unless cybrids can live for more than four hundred years . . . ?'

'No,' snapped Lady Diana. 'Shut up and let me finish this. John, why did the Core . . . bring you back?'

'I don't know for sure.'

'Does it have something to do with the civil war going on between the AIs?'

'Perhaps,' I said. 'Probably.' She asked interesting questions.

'Which group created you? The Ultimates, Stables, or Volatiles?'

'I don't know.'

I could hear a sigh of exasperation. 'John, have you notified anyone of where you are, of what's happening to you?'

'No,' I said. It was a sign of the lady's less than impressive intelligence that she waited so long to pose that question.

Hermund also let out a breath. 'Great,' he said. 'Let's get the hell out of here before . . .'

'John,' said Diana, 'do you know why Gladstone manufactured this war with the Ousters?'

'No,' I said. 'Or rather, there might be many reasons. The most probable is that it is a bargaining ploy in her dealings with the Core.'

'Why?'

'Elements in the leadership ROM of the Core are afraid of Hyperion,' I said. 'Hyperion is an unknown variable in a galaxy where every variable has been quantified.'

'*Who* is afraid, John? The Ultimates, Stables, or Volatiles? Which group of AIs is afraid of Hyperion?'

'All three,' I said.

'Shit,' whispered Hermund. 'Listen . . . John . . . do the Time Tombs and the Shrike have something to do with all this?'

'Yes, they have a lot to do with it.'

'How?' asked Diana.

'I don't know. No one does.'

Hermund, or someone, hit me sharply, viciously, in the chest. 'You mean the fucking Core Advisory Council hasn't predicted the outcome of this war, these events?' Hermund growled. 'Are you expecting me to believe that Gladstone and the Senate went to war without a probability prediction?'

'No,' I said. 'It has been predicted for centuries.'

Diana Philomel made a noise like a child being confronted with a large mound of candy. '*What* has been predicted, John? Tell us everything.'

My mouth was dry. The truthtalk serum had dried up my saliva. 'It predicted the war,' I said. 'The identities of the pilgrims on the Shrike Pilgrimage. The betrayal of the Hegemony Consul in activating a device that will open – has opened – the Time Tombs. The emergence of the Shrike Scourge. The outcome of the war and the Scourge . . .'

'What is the outcome, John?' whispered the woman I had made love to a few hours earlier.

'The end of the Hegemony,' I said. 'The destruction of the Worldweb.' I tried to lick my lips but my tongue was dry. 'The end of the human race.'

'Oh, Jesus and Allah,' whispered Diana. 'Is there any chance that the prediction could be in error?'

'No,' I said. 'Or rather, only in the effect of Hyperion on the result. The other variables are accounted for.'

'Kill him,' shouted Hermund Philomel. 'Kill *it* . . . so we can get out of here and inform Harbrit and the others.'

'All right,' said Lady Diana. Then, a second later, 'No, not the laser, you idiot. We'll inject the lethal dose of alcohol as planned. Here, hold the osmosis cuff so I can attach this drip.'

I felt a pressure on my right arm. A second later there were explosions, concussions, a shout. I smelled smoke and ionized air. A woman screamed.

'Get that cuff off him,' said Leigh Hunt. I could see him standing there, still wearing a conservative gray suit, surrounded by Executive Security commandos in full impact armor and chameleon polymers. A commando twice Hunt's height nodded, shouldered his hellwhip weapon, and rushed to do Hunt's bidding.

On one of the tactical channels, the one I had been monitoring for some time, I could see a relayed image of myself . . .naked, spread-eagled on the bed, the osmosis cuff on my arm and a rising bruise on my rib cage. Diana Philomel, her husband, and one of the goons lay unconscious but alive in the splinter and broken-glass rubble of the room. The other enforcer lay half in the doorway, the top part of his body looking the color and texture of a heavily grilled steak.

'Are you all right, M. Severn?' asked Leigh Hunt, lifting my head and setting a membrane-thin oxygen mask over my mouth and nose.

'Hrrmmmggh,' I said. 'Arret.' I swam to the surface of my own senses like a diver coming up too quickly from the deeps. My head hurt. My ribs ached like hell. My eyes were not working perfectly yet, but through the tactical channel, I could see Leigh Hunt give the small twitch of thin lips that I knew passed for a smile from him.

'We'll help you get dressed,' said Hunt. 'Get you some coffee on the flight back. Then it's back to Government House, M. Severn. You're late for a meeting with the CEO.'

SEVEN

Space battles in movies and holies had always bored me, but watching the real thing held a certain fascination: rather like seeing live coverage of a series of traffic accidents. Actually, the production values for reality – as had doubtless been the case for centuries – were much lower than for even a moderate-budget holodrama. Even with the tremendous energies involved, the overwhelming reaction one had to an actual battle in space was that space was so *large* and humanity's fleets and ships and dreadnoughts and whatnots were so *small*.

Or so I thought as I sat in the Tactical Information Center, the so-called War Room, with Gladstone and her military ganders, and watched the walls become twenty-meter holes into infinity as four massive holoframes surrounded us with in-depth imagery and the speakers filled the room with fatline transmissions: radio chatter between fighters, tactical command channels rattling away, ship-to-ship messages on wideband, lasered channels, and secure fatline, and all the shouts, screams, cries, and obscenities of battle which predate any media besides air and the human voice.

It was a dramatization of total chaos, a functional definition of confusion, an unchoreographed dance of sad violence. It was war.

Gladstone and a handful of her people sat in the middle of all this noise and light, the War Room floating like a gray-carpeted rectangle amidst the stars and explosions, the limb of Hyperion a lapis lazuli brilliance filling half of the north holowall, the screams of dying men and women on every channel and in every ear. I was one of the handful of Gladstone's people privileged and cursed to be there.

The CEO rotated in her high-backed chair, tapped her lower lip with steepled fingers, and turned toward her military group. 'What do you think?'

The seven bemedaled men there looked at one another, and then six of them looked at General Morpurgo. He chewed on an unlighted cigar. 'It's not good,' he said. 'We're keeping them away from the farcaster site . . . our defenses are holding well there . . . but they've pushed far too far in-system.'

'Admiral?' asked Gladstone, inclining her head a fraction toward the tall, thin man in FORCE:space black.

Admiral Singh touched his closely trimmed beard. 'General Morpurgo is correct. The campaign is not going as planned.' He nodded toward the fourth wall, where diagrams – mostly ellipsoids, ovals and arcs – were superimposed upon a static shot of the Hyperion system. Some of the arcs grew as we watched. The bright blue lines stood for Hegemony trajectories. The red tracks were Ouster. There were far more red lines than blue.

'Both of the attack carriers assigned to Task Force 42 have been put out of action,' said Admiral Singh. 'The *Olympus Shadow* was destroyed with all hands and the *Neptune Station* was seriously damaged but is returning to the cislunar docking area with five torchships for escort.'

CEO Gladstone nodded slowly, her lip coming down to touch the top of her steepled fingers. 'How many were aboard the *Olympus Shadow*, Admiral?'

Singh's brown eyes were as large as the CEO's, but did not suggest the same depths of sadness. He held her gaze for several seconds. 'Forty-two hundred,' he said. 'Not counting the Marine detachment of six hundred. Some of those were off-loaded at Farcaster Station Hyperion, so we do not have accurate information on how many were with the ship.'

Gladstone nodded. She looked back at General Morpurgo. 'Why the sudden difficulty, General?'

Morpurgo's face was calm, but he had all but bitten through the cigar clamped between his teeth. 'More fighting units than we expected, CEO,' he said. 'Plus their lancers . . . five-person craft, miniature torchships, really, faster and more heavily armed than our long-range fighters . . . they're deadly little hornets. We've been destroying them by the hundred, but if one gets through, it can make a dash inside fleet defenses and wreak havoc.' Morpurgo shrugged. 'More than one's got through.'

Senator Kolchev sat across the table with eight of his colleagues. Kolchev swiveled until he could see the tactical map. 'It looks like they're almost to Hyperion,' he said. The famous voice was hoarse.

Singh spoke up. 'Remember the scale, Senator. The truth is that we still hold most of the system. Everything within ten AU of Hyperion's star is ours. The battle was out beyond the Oört cloud, and we've been regrouping.'

'And those red . . . blobs . . . above the plane of the ecliptic?' asked Senator Richeau. The senator wore red herself; it had been one of her trademarks in the Senate.

Singh nodded. 'An interesting stratagem,' he said. 'The Swarm launched an attack of approximately three thousand lancers to complete a pincers movement against Task Force 87.2's electronic perimeter. It was contained, but one has to admire the cleverness of—'

'Three thousand lancers?' Gladstone interrupted softly.

'Yes, ma'am.'

Gladstone smiled. I stopped sketching and thought to myself that I was glad that I had not been the beneficiary of that particular smile.

'Weren't we told yesterday, in the briefing, that the Ousters would field six . . . seven hundred fighting units, *tops*?' The words had been Morpurgo's. CEO Gladstone swiveled to face the General. Her right eyebrow arched.

General Morpurgo removed the cigar, frowned at it, and fished a smaller piece from behind his lower teeth. 'That's what our intelligence said. It was wrong.'

Gladstone nodded. 'Was the AI Advisory Council involved in that intelligence assessment?'

All eyes turned toward Councilor Albedo. It was a perfect projection; he sat in his chair amongst the others, his hands curled on the armrests in a relaxed fashion; there was none of the haziness or see-through common to mobile projections. His face was long, with high cheekbones and a mobile mouth which suggested a hint of a sardonic smile even at the most serious of moments. This was a serious moment.

'No, CEO,' said Councilor Albedo, 'the Advisory Group was not asked to assess Ouster strength.'

Gladstone nodded. 'I assumed,' she said, still addressing Morpurgo, 'that when the FORCE intelligence estimates came in, they incorporated the Council's projections.'

The FORCE:ground General glared at Albedo. 'No ma'am,' he said. 'Since the Core acknowledges no contact with the Ousters, we felt that their projections wouldn't be any better than our own. We did use the OCS: HTN aggregate AI network to run our assessments.' He thrust the foreshortened cigar back into his mouth. His chin jutted. When he spoke, it was around the cigar. 'Could the Council have done better?'

Gladstone looked at Albedo.

The Councilor made a small motion with the long fingers of his right hand. 'Our estimates . . . for this Swarm . . . suggested four to six thousand fighting units.'

'You—' began Morpurgo, his face red.

'You did not mention this during the briefing,' said CEO Gladstone. 'Nor during our earlier deliberations.'

Councilor Albedo shrugged. 'The General is correct,' he said. 'We have no contact with the Ousters. Our estimates are no more reliable than FORCE's, merely . . . based upon different premises. The Olympus Command School Historical Tactical Network does excellent work. If the AIs there were one order of acuity higher on the Turing-Demmler scale, we would have to bring them into the Core.' He made the graceful gesture with his hand again. 'As it is, the Council's premises might be of use for future planning. We will, of course, turn over all projections to this group at any time.'

Gladstone nodded. 'Do so immediately.'

She turned back to the screen, and the others did so also. Sensing the silence, the room monitors brought the speaker volume back up, and once again we could hear the cries of victory, screams for help, and calm recitation of positions, fire-control directions, and commands.

The closest wall was a real-time feed from the torchship HS *N'Djamena* as it searched for survivors among the tumbling remnants of Battle Group B.5. The damaged torchship it was approaching, magnified a thousand times, looked like a pomegranate burst from the inside, its seeds and red rind spilling in slow motion, tumbling into a cloud of particles, gases, frozen volatiles, a million micro-electronics ripped from their cradles, food stores, tangled gear, and – recognizable now and then from their marionette tumble of arms or legs – many, many bodies. The *N'Djamena's* searchlight, ten meters wide after its coherent leap of twenty thousand miles, played across the starlit frozen wreckage, bringing individual items, facets, and faces into focus. It was quite beautiful in a terrible way. The reflected light made Gladstone's face look much older.

'Admiral,' she said, 'is it pertinent that the Swarm waited until Task Force 87.2 translated in-system?'

Singh touched his beard. 'Are you asking if it was a trap, CEO?'

'Yes.'

The Admiral glanced at his colleagues and then at Gladstone. 'I think not. We believe . . . I believe . . . that when the Ousters saw the intensity of our force commitment, they responded in kind. It does mean, however, that they are totally resolved to take Hyperion system.'

'Can they do it?' asked Gladstone, her eyes still on the tumbling wreckage above her. A young man's body, half in a spacesuit and half out, tumbled toward the camera. The burst eyes and lungs were clearly visible.

'No,' said Admiral Singh. 'They can bloody us. They can even drive us back to a totally defensive perimeter around Hyperion itself. But they cannot defeat us or drive us out.'

'Or destroy the farcaster?' Senator Richeau's voice was taut.

'Nor destroy the farcaster,' said Singh.

'He's right,' said General Morpurgo. 'I'd stake my professional career on it.'

Gladstone smiled and stood. The others, including myself, rushed to stand also. 'You have,' Gladstone said softly to Morpurgo. 'You have.' She looked around. 'We will meet here when events warrant it. M. Hunt will be my liaison with you. In the meantime, gentlemen and ladies, the work of government shall proceed. Good afternoon.'

As the others left, I took my seat again until I was the only one left in the room. The speakers came back up to volume. On one band, a man was crying. Manic laughter came through static. Above me, behind me, on both sides, the starfields moved slowly against blackness, and the starlight glinted coldly on wreckage and ruin.

Government House was constructed in the shape of a Star of David, and within the center of the star, shielded by low walls and strategically planted trees, there was a garden: smaller than the formal acres of flowers in Deer Park but no less beautiful. I was walking there as evening fell, the brilliant blue-white of Tau Ceti fading to golds, when Meina Gladstone approached.

For a while, we walked together in silence. I noticed that she had exchanged her suit for a long robe of the kind worn by grand matrons on Patawpha; the robe was wide and billowing, inset with intricate dark blue and gold designs which almost matched the darkening sky. Gladstone's hands were out of sight in hidden pockets; the wide sleeves stirred to a breeze; the hem dragged on the milk-white stones of the path.

'You let them interrogate me,' I said. 'I'm curious as to why.'

Gladstone's voice was tired. 'They were not transmitting. There was no danger of the information being passed on.'

I smiled. 'Nonetheless, you let them put me through that.'

'Security wished to know as much about them as they would divulge.'

'At the expense of any . . . inconvenience . . . on my part,' I said.

'Yes.'

'And does Security know who they were working for?'

'The man mentioned Harbrit,' said the CEO. 'Security is fairly certain that they meant Emlem Harbrit.'

'The commodities broker on Asquith?'

'Yes. She and Diana Philomel have ties with the old Glennon-Height royalist factions.'

'They were amateurs,' I said, thinking of Hermund mentioning Harbrit's name, the confused order of Diana's questioning.

'Of course.'

'Are the royalists connected to any serious group?'

'Only the Shrike Church,' said Gladstone. She paused where the path crossed a small stream via a stone bridge. The CEO gathered her robe and sat on a wrought-iron bench. 'None of the bishops have yet come out of hiding, you know.'

'With the riots and backlash, I don't blame them,' I said. I remained standing. There were no bodyguards or monitors in sight, but I knew that if I were to make any threatening move toward Gladstone, I would wake up in ExecSec detention. Above us, the clouds lost their last tinge of gold and began to glow with the reflected silver light of TC^2's countless tower cities. 'What did Security do with Diana and her husband?' I asked.

'They've been thoroughly interrogated. They're being . . . detained.'

I nodded. Thorough interrogation meant that even now their brains were floating in full-shunt tanks. Their bodies would be kept in cryogenic storage until a secret trial determined if their actions had been treasonable. After the trial, the bodies would be destroyed, and Diana and Hermund would remain in 'detention', with all sensory and comm channels turned off. The Hegemony had not used the death penalty for centuries, but the alternatives were not pleasant. I sat on the long bench, six feet from Gladstone.

'Do you still write poetry?'

I was surprised by her question. I glanced down the garden path where floating Japanese lanterns and hidden glow-globes had just come on. 'Not really,' I said. 'Sometimes I dream in verse. Or used to . . .'

Meina Gladstone folded her hands on her lap and studied them. 'If you were writing about the events unfolding now,' she said, 'what kind of poem would you create?'

I laughed. 'I've already begun it and abandoned it twice . . . or rather, *he* has. It was about the death of the gods and their difficulty in accepting their displacement. It was about transformation and suffering and injustice. And it was about the poet . . . whom *he* thought suffered most at such injustice.'

Gladstone looked at me. Her face was a mass of lines and shadows in the dimming light. 'And who are the gods that are being replaced this time, M. Severn? Is it humanity or the false gods we created to depose us?'

'How the hell should I know?' I snapped and turned away to watch the stream.

'You are part of both worlds, no? Humanity and TechnoCore?'

I laughed again. 'I'm part of neither world. A cybrid monster here, a research project there.'

'Yes, but whose research? And for what ends?'

I shrugged.

Gladstone rose and I followed. We crossed the stream and listened to water moving over the stones. The path wound between tall boulders covered with exquisite lichen which glowed in the lantern light.

Gladstone paused at the top of a short flight of stone steps. 'Do you think the Ultimates in the Core will succeed in constructing their Ultimate Intelligence, M. Severn?'

'Will they build God?' I said. 'There are those AIs which do not want to build God. They learned from the human experience that to construct the next step in awareness is an invitation to slavery, if not actual extinction.'

'But would a true God extinguish his creatures?'

'In the case of the Core and the hypothetical UI,' I said, 'God is the creature, not the creator. Perhaps a god must create the lesser beings in contact with it in order for it to feel any responsibility for them.'

'Yet the Core has appeared to take responsibility for human beings in the centuries since the AI Secession,' said Gladstone. She was gazing intently at me, as if gauging something by my expression.

I looked out at the garden. The path glowed whitely, almost eerily in the dark. 'The Core works toward its own ends,' I said, knowing as I spoke that no human being knew that fact better than CEO Meina Gladstone.

'And do you feel that humanity no longer figures as a means toward those ends?'

I made a dismissive gesture with my right hand. 'I'm a creature of neither culture,' I said again. 'Neither graced by the naiveté of the unintentional creators, nor cursed by the terrible awareness of their creatures.'

'Genetically, you are fully human,' said Gladstone.

It was not a question. I did not respond.

'Jesus Christ was said to be fully human,' she said. 'And also fully divine. Humanity and Godhead at intersection.'

I was amazed at her reference to that old religion. Christianity had been replaced first by Zen Christianity, then Zen Gnosticism, then by a hundred more vital theologies and philosophies. Gladstone's homeworld was no repository for discarded beliefs and I assumed – and hoped – that neither was the CEO. 'If he was fully human and fully God,' I said, 'then I am his antimatter image.'

'No,' said Gladstone, 'I would imagine that the Shrike your pilgrim friends are confronting is that.'

I stared. It was the first time she had mentioned the Shrike to me, despite the fact that I knew – and she knew that I knew – that it had been her plan which led the Consul to open the Time Tombs and release the thing.

'Perhaps you should have been on that pilgrimage, M. Severn,' said the CEO.

'In a way,' I said, 'I am.'

Gladstone gestured, and a door to her private quarters opened. 'Yes, in a way you are,' she said. 'But if the woman who carries your counterpart is crucified on the Shrike's legendary tree of thorns, will *you* suffer for all eternity in your dreams?'

I had no answer, so I stood there and said nothing.

'We will talk in the morning after the conference,' said Meina Gladstone. 'Good night, M. Severn. Have pleasant dreams.'

EIGHT

Martin Silenus, Sol Weintraub, and the Consul are staggering up the dunes toward the Sphinx as Brawne Lamia and Fedmahn Kassad return with Father Hoyt's body. Weintraub clutches his cape tight around him, trying to shelter his infant from the rage of blowing sand and crackling light. He watches as Kassad descends the dune, his long legs black and cartoonish against electrified sand, Hoyt's arms and hands dangling, moving slightly with each slide and step.

Silenus is shouting, but the wind whips away words. Brawne Lamia gestures toward the one tent still standing; the storm has collapsed or ripped away the others. They crowd into Silenus's tent, Colonel Kassad coming last, passing the body in gently. Inside, their shouts can be heard above the crack of fiberplastic canvas and the paper-splitting rip of lightning.

'Dead?' shouts the Consul, peeling back the cloak Kassad had wrapped around Hoyt's nude body. The cruciforms glow pinkly.

The Colonel points to the telltales blinking on the surface of the FORCE-issue medpak adhered to the priest's chest. The lights blink red except for the yellow winking of the systems-sustaining filaments and nodules. Hoyt's head rolls back, and now Weintraub can see the millipede suture holding the ragged edges of the slashed throat together.

Sol Weintraub tries to locate a pulse manually; finds none. He leans forward, sets his ear to the priest's chest. There is no heartbeat, but the welt of the cruciform there is hot against Sol's cheek. He looks at Brawne Lamia. 'The Shrike?'

'Yes . . . I think . . . I don't know.' She gestures toward the antique pistol she still holds. 'I emptied the magazine. Twelve shots at . . . whatever it was.'

'Did you see it?' the Consul asks Kassad.

'No. I entered the room ten seconds after Brawne, but I didn't see anything.'

'What about your fucking soldier gadgets?' says Martin Silenus. He is crowded in the back of the tent, huddled in a near-fetal position. 'Didn't all that FORCE shit show something?'

'No.'

A small alarm sounds from the medpak, and Kassad detaches another plasma cartridge from his belt, feeds it into the pak's chamber, and sits back on his heels, flipping his visor down to watch out the opening of the tent.

His voice is distorted by the helmet speaker. 'He's lost more blood than we can compensate for here. Did anyone else bring first aid equipment?'

Weintraub rummages in his pack. 'I have a basic kit. Not enough for this, though. Whatever slashed his throat cut through everything.'

'The Shrike,' whispers Martin Silenus.

'It doesn't matter,' says Lamia, hugging herself to stop her body from shaking. 'We've got to get help for him.' She looks at the Consul.

'He's dead,' says the Consul. 'Even a ship's surgery won't bring him back.'

'We have to *try*!' shouts Lamia, leaning forward to grab the Consul's tunic front. 'We can't leave him to those . . . things . . .' She gestures toward the cruciform glowing beneath the skin of the dead man's chest.

The Consul rubs his eyes. 'We can destroy the body. Use the Colonel's rifle . . .'

'*We're* going to die if we don't get out of this fucking storm!' cries Silenus. The tent is vibrating, fiberplastic pounding the poet's head and back with each billow. The sound of sand against fabric is like a rocket taking off just outside. 'Call the goddamned ship. Call it!'

The Consul pulls his pack closer, as if guarding the antique comlog inside it. Sweat glistens on his cheeks and forehead.

'We could wait the storm out in one of the Tombs,' says Sol Weintraub. 'The Sphinx, perhaps.'

'Fuck that,' says Martin Silenus.

The scholar shifts in the cramped space and stares at the poet. 'You came all this way to find the Shrike. Are you telling us that you've changed your mind now that he seems to have made an appearance?'

Silenus's eyes gleam out from under his lowered beret. 'I'm not telling you anything except that I want that goddamned ship of his here, and I want it *now*.'

'It might be a good idea,' says Colonel Kassad.

The Consul looks at him.

'If there's a chance to save Hoyt's life, we should take it.'

The Consul is in pain himself. 'We can't leave,' he says. 'Can't leave now.'

'No,' agrees Kassad. 'We won't use the ship to leave. But the surgery might help Hoyt. And we can wait out the storm in it.'

'And maybe find out what's happening up there,' says Brawne Lamia, jerking her thumb toward the roof of the tent.

The baby, Rachel, is crying shrilly. Weintraub rocks her, holding her head in his broad hand. 'I agree,' he says. 'If the Shrike wants to find us, it can find us on the ship as easily as out here. We'll make sure that no one leaves.' He touches Hoyt's chest. 'As horrible as it sounds, the information the surgery gives us on how this parasite works could be priceless to the Web.'

'All right,' says the Consul. He pulls the ancient comlog from his pack, lays his hand on the diskey, and whispers several phrases.

'Is it coming?' asks Martin Silenus.

'It's confirmed the command. We'll need to stow our gear for transfer. I told it to land just above the entrance to the valley.'

Lamia is surprised to find that she has been weeping. She wipes her cheeks and smiles.

'What's funny?' asks the Consul.

'All this,' she says, stabbing at her cheeks with the back of her hand, 'and all I can think about is how nice it'll be to have a shower.'

'A drink,' says Silenus.

'Shelter from the storm,' says Weintraub. The baby is taking milk from a nursing pak.

Kassad leans forward, his head and shoulders outside the tent. He raises his weapon and clicks off the safety. 'Telltales,' he says. 'Something's moving just beyond the dune.' The visor turns toward them, reflecting a pale and huddled group, the paler body of Lenar Hoyt. 'I'm going to check it out,' he says. 'Wait here until the ship arrives.'

'Don't leave,' says Silenus. 'It's like one of those fucking ancient horror holos where they go one by one to . . . hey!' The poet falls silent. The entrance to the tent is a triangle of light and noise. Fedmahn Kassad is gone.

The tent is beginning to collapse, stakes and wire anchors giving way as the sand shifts around them. Huddled together, shouting to be heard over the wind roar, the Consul and Lamia wrap Hoyt's body in his cloak. Readouts on the medpak continue to blink red. Blood has ceased to flow from the crude millipede suture.

Sol Weintraub sets his four-day-old child in the infant carrier on his chest, folds his cape around her, and crouches in the entrance. 'No sign of the Colonel!' he shouts. As he watches, a lightning bolt strikes the outstretched wing of the Sphinx.

Brawne Lamia moves to the entrance and lifts the priest's body. She is amazed at how light it is. 'Let's get Father Hoyt to the ship and in surgery. Then some of us will come back to search for Kassad.'

The Consul tugs his tricorne cap low and shrugs his collar high. 'The ship has deep radar and movement sensors. It'll tell us where the Colonel's gone.'

'And the Shrike,' says Silenus. 'Can't forget our host.'

'Let's go,' says Lamia and gets to her feet. She has to lean into the wind to make progress. Loose ends of Hoyt's cloak flap and crack around her, while her own cloak streams behind. Finding the path by the intermittent flashes of lightning, she moves toward the head of the valley, glancing back only once to see if the others are following.

Martin Silenus steps away from the tent, lifts Het Masteen's Möbius cube, and his purple beret whips away in the wind, climbing as it goes. Silenus stands there and curses impressively, stopping only when his mouth begins to fill with sand.

'Come,' shouts Weintraub, his hand on the poet's shoulder. Sol feels the sand striking his face, littering his short beard. His other hand covers his chest as if sheltering something infinitely precious. 'We'll lose sight of Brawne if we don't hurry.' The two help each other move forward against the wind. Silenus's fur coat ripples wildly as he detours to retrieve his beret from where it has come down in the lee of a dune.

The Consul is the last to leave, carrying both his own pack and Kassad's. A minute after he leaves the small shelter, stakes give way, fabric tears, and the tent flies into the night, surrounded by a halo of static electricity. He staggers the three hundred meters up the trail, occasionally catching glimpses of the two men ahead of him, more frequently losing the path and having to walk in circles until he comes across it again. The Time Tombs are visible behind him when the sandstorm ebbs a bit and the lightning flashes follow one another in close succession. The Consul sees the Sphinx, still glowing from repeated electrical strikes, the Jade Tomb beyond it, its walls luminescent, and beyond them the Obelisk, no glow there, a vertical swipe of pure black against the cliff walls. Then the Crystal Monolith. There is no sign of Kassad, although the shifting dunes, blowing sand, and sudden flashes make it seem as if many things are moving.

The Consul looks up, seeing the wide entrance to the valley now and the rushing clouds low above it, half expecting to see the blue fusion glow of his ship lowering through them. The storm is terrible, but his spacecraft has landed in worse conditions. He wonders if it is already down and the others are waiting at the base of it for him to arrive.

But when he reaches the saddle between cliff walls at the opening of the valley, the wind assaults him anew, he sees the four others huddled together at the beginning of the broad, flat plain, but there is no ship.

'Shouldn't it be here by now?' shouts Lamia as the Consul approaches the group.

He nods and crouches to extract the comlog from his pack. Weintraub and Silenus stand behind him, bending over to offer some shelter from the blowing sand. The Consul extracts the comlog and pauses, looking around. The storm makes it appear as if they are in some mad room where the walls and ceiling change from instant to instant, one second closing in on them, scant meters away, the next second receding to the distance, the ceiling floating upward, as in the scene where the room and Christmas tree expand for Clara in Tchaikovsky's *Nutcracker*.

The Consul palms the diskey, bends forward, and whispers into the voice square. The ancient instrument whispers back to him, the words just audible above the rasp of sand. He straightens up and faces the others. 'The ship was not allowed to leave.'

There is a babble of protest. 'What do you mean "not allowed"?' asks Lamia when the others fall silent.

The Consul shrugs and looks skyward as if a blue tail of flame might still announce the ship's coming. 'It wasn't given clearance at the spaceport in Keats.'

'Didn't you say you had clearance from the fucking queen?' shouts Martin Silenus. 'Old Gallstone herself?'

'Gladstone's clearance pip was in the ship's memory,' says the Consul. 'Both the FORCE and port authorities knew that.'

'So what the hell happened?' Lamia wipes her face. The tears she had shed back at the tent have left tiny rivulets of mud in the coating of sand on her cheeks.

The Consul shrugs. 'Gladstone overrode the original pip. There's a message here from her. Do you want to hear it?'

For a minute, no one answers. After their week of voyage, the thought of being in touch with someone outside their own group is so incongruous that it does not register at once; it was as if the world beyond the pilgrimage had ceased to exist except for the explosions in the night sky. 'Yes,' Sol Weintraub says, 'let's hear it.' A sudden lull in the storm makes the words seem very loud.

They gather around and crouch near the old comlog, setting Father Hoyt in the center of their circle. In the minute they have left him unattended, a small dune has begun to form itself around his body. The telltales are all red now except for the extreme-measures monitors glowing amber. Lamia sets another plasma cartridge in place and makes sure that the osmosis mask is secure on Hoyt's mouth and nose, filtering pure oxygen in and keeping sand out. 'All right,' she says.

The Consul triggers the diskey.

The message is a fatline squirt, recorded by the ship some ten minutes earlier. The air mists with the data columns and spherical-image colloid which characterizes comlogs dating back to the Hegira. The image of Gladstone shimmers, her face distorting bizarrely and then almost comically as millions of specks of windblown sand rip through the image. Even at full volume, her voice is almost lost to the storm.

'I'm sorry,' says the familiar image, 'but I cannot allow your spacecraft to approach the Tombs just yet. The temptation to leave would be too great, and the importance of your mission must override all other factors. Please understand that the fate of worlds may rest with you. Please be assured that my hopes and prayers are with you. Gladstone out.'

The image folds into itself and fades away. The Consul, Weintraub, and Lamia continue to stare in silence. Martin Silenus stands, throws a handful of sand at the empty air where Gladstone's face had been seconds earlier, and screams, 'Goddamn fatherfucking asshole political moral paraplegic dipshit drag-queen bitch!' He kicks sand in the air. The others shift their stares to him.

'Well, that really helped,' Brawne Lamia says softly.

Silenus waves his arms in disgust and walks away, still kicking at dunes.

'Is there anything else?' Weintraub asks the Consul.

'No.'

Brawne Lamia crosses her arms and frowns at the comlog. 'I forget how you said this thing works. How are you getting through the interference?'

'Tightbeam to a pocket comsat I seeded as we came down from the *Yggdrasill*,' says the Consul.

Lamia nods. 'So when you reported in, you just sent brief messages to the ship, and it sent fatline squirts to Gladstone . . . and your Ouster contacts.'

'Yes.'

'Can the ship take off without clearance?' asks Weintraub. The older man is sitting, his knees raised and his arms draped on them in a classic posture of pure fatigue. His voice is also tired. 'Just override Gladstone's prohibition?'

'No,' says the Consul. 'When Gladstone said no, FORCE set a class-three containment field over the blast pit where we parked the ship.'

'Get in touch with her,' says Brawne Lamia. 'Explain things.'

'I've tried.' The Consul holds the comlog in his hands, sets it back in the pack. 'No response. Also, I mentioned in the original squirt that Hoyt was badly hurt and that we needed medical help. I wanted the ship's surgery ready for him.'

'Hurt,' repeats Martin Silenus, striding back to where they huddled. 'Shit. Our padre friend is dead as Glennon-Height's dog.' He jerks his thumb in the direction of the cloak-wrapped body; all monitor displays are red.

Brawne Lamia bends closer and touches Hoyt's cheek. It is cold. Both his comlog biomonitor and the medpak begin chirping brain-death warnings. The osmosis mask continues to force pure O_2 into his lungs, and the medpak stimulators still work his lungs and heart, but the chirping rises to a scream and then settles to a steady, terrible tone.

'He lost too much blood,' says Sol Weintraub. He touches the dead priest's face, his own eyes closed, head bowed.

'Great,' says Silenus. 'Fucking great. And according to his own story, Hoyt's going to decompose and recompose, thanks to that goddamned cruciform thing . . . *two* of the goddamn things, the guy's rich in resurrection insurance . . . and then come lurching back like some brain-damaged edition of Hamlet's daddy's ghost. What are we going to do then?'

'Shut up,' says Brawne Lamia. She is wrapping Hoyt's body in a layer of tarp she has brought from the tent.

'Shut up yourself,' screams Silenus. 'We've got one monster lurking around. Old Grendel himself is out there somewhere sharpening his nails for his next meal, do you really want Hoyt's zombie joining our happy crew? You remember how he described the Bikura? They'd been letting the cruciforms bring *them* back for centuries, and talking to one of them was like talking to an ambulatory sponge. Do you *really* want Hoyt's corpse hiking with us?'

'Two,' says the Consul.

'What?' Martin Silenus whirls, loses his footing, and lands on his knees near the body. He leans toward him. 'What did you say?'

'Two cruciforms,' says the Consul. 'His and Father Paul Duré's. If his story about the Bikura was true, then they'll both be . . . resurrected.'

'Oh, Christ on a stick,' says Silenus and sits in the sand.

Brawne Lamia has finished wrapping the priest's body. She looks at it. 'I remember that in Father Duré's story about the Bikura named Alpha,' she says. 'But I still don't understand. The Law of Conservation of Mass has to come in there somewhere.'

'They'll be *short* zombies,' says Martin Silenus. He pulls his fur coat tighter and pounds the sand with his fist.

'There is so much we could have learned if the ship had arrived,' says the Consul. 'The autodiagnostics could have . . .' He pauses and gestures. 'Look. There is less sand in the air. Perhaps the storm is . . .'

Lightning flashes, and it begins to rain, the icy pellets striking their faces with more fury than the sandstorm had shown.

Martin Silenus begins to laugh. 'It's a fucking *desert!*' he shouts toward the sky. 'We'll probably drown in a flood.'

'We need to get out of this,' says Sol Weintraub. His baby's face is visible between the gaps in his cloak. Rachel is crying; her face is very red. She looks no older than a newborn.

'Keep Chronos?' says Lamia. 'It's a couple of hours . . .'

'Too far,' says the Consul. 'Let's bivouac in one of the Tombs.' Silenus laughs again. He says:

'Who are these coming to the sacrifice?
  To what green altar, O mysterious priest,
Lead'st thou that heifer lowing at the skies,
  And all her silken flanks with garlands dresst?'

'Does that mean yes?' asks Lamia.

'That means fucking "why not?"' laughs Silenus. 'Why make it hard for our cold muse to find us? We can watch our friend decompose while we wait. How long did Duré's tale say it took for one of the Bikura to rejoin the flock after death interrupted their grazing?'

'Three days,' says the Consul.

Martin Silenus slaps his forehead with the heel of his palm. 'Of course. How could I forget? How wonderfully fitting, New Testament-wise. In the meantime, maybe our Shrike-wolf will carry off a few of this flock. Do you think the padre would mind if I borrowed one of his cruciforms just in case? I mean, he has a spare . . .'

'Let's go,' says the Consul. Rain drips from his tricorne cap in a steady stream. 'We'll stay in the Sphinx until morning. I'll carry Kassad's extra gear and the Möbius cube. Brawne, you carry Hoyt's things and Sol's pack. Sol, you keep the baby warm and dry.'

'What about the padre?' asks the poet, jerking his thumb in the direction of the body.

'You're carrying Father Hoyt,' Brawne Lamia says softly, turning.

Martin Silenus opens his mouth, sees the pistol in Lamia's hand, shrugs, and bends to lift the body to his shoulder. 'Who's going to carry Kassad when we find him?' he asks. 'Of course, he could be in enough pieces that we could all—'

'Please shut up,' Brawne Lamia says tiredly. 'If I have to shoot you, it will give us one more thing to carry. Just walk.'

With the Consul leading, Weintraub coming closely behind, Martin Silenus staggering along some meters back, and Brawne Lamia in the rear, the group once again descends the low col into the Valley of the Tombs.

NINE

CEO Gladstone's schedule that morning was a busy one. Tau Ceti Center has a twenty-three-hour day, which makes it convenient for the government to run on Hegemony Standard Time without totally destroying local diurnal rhythms. At 0545 hours, Gladstone met with her military advisors. At 0630 hours she breakfasted with two dozen of the most important senators and with representatives of the All Thing and the TechnoCore. At 0715 the CEO farcast to Renaissance Vector, where it was evening, to officially open the Hermes Medical Center in Cadua. At 0740 she 'cast back to Government House for a meeting with her top aides, including Leigh Hunt, to go over the speech she was to give to the Senate and All Thing at 1000 hours. At 0830 Gladstone met again with General Morpurgo and Admiral Singh for an update on the situation in the Hyperion system. At 0845 hours, she met with me.

'Good morning, M. Severn,' said the CEO. She was behind her desk in the office where I'd first met her three nights earlier. She waved her hand toward a buffet against the wall where hot coffee, tea, and caffta sat in sterling silver pots.

I shook my head and sat down. Three of the holographic windows showed white light, but the one to my left offered the 3-D map of Hyperion System that I had tried to decode in the War Room. It seemed to me that Ouster red now covered and infiltrated the system like dye dissolving and settling into a blue solution.

'I want to hear your dreams,' said CEO Gladstone.

'I want to hear why you abandoned them,' I said, voice flat. 'Why you left Father Hoyt to die.'

Gladstone could not have been used to being spoken to in that tone, not after forty-eight years in the Senate and a decade and a half as CEO, but her only reaction was to raise one eyebrow a fraction of an inch. 'So you do dream the real events.'

'Did you doubt it?'

She set down the work pad she had been holding, keyed it off, and shook her head. 'Not really, but it is still a shock to hear about something that no one else in the Web knows about.'

'Why did you deny them the use of the Consul's ship?'

Gladstone swiveled to look up at the window where the tactical display shifted and changed as new updates changed the flow of red, the retreat of blue, the movement of planets and moons, but if the military situation was to have been part of her explanation, she abandoned that approach. She swiveled back. 'Why would I have to explain any executive decision to you, M. Severn? What is your constituency? Whom do you represent?'

'I represent those five people and a baby you left stranded on Hyperion,' I said. 'Hoyt could have been saved.'

Gladstone made a fist and tapped her lower lip with a curved forefinger. 'Perhaps,' she said. 'And perhaps he was already dead. But that wasn't the issue, was it?'

I sat back in the chair. I had not bothered to bring a sketchbook along, and my fingers ached to hold something. 'What is, then?'

'Do you remember Father Hoyt's story . . . the story he told during their voyage to the Tombs?' asked Gladstone.

'Yes.'

'Each of the pilgrims is allowed to petition the Shrike for one favor. Tradition says that the creature grants one wish, while denying the others and murdering those he denies. Do you remember what Hoyt's wish was?'

I paused. Recalling incidents from the pilgrims' past was like trying to remember details of last week's dreams. 'He wanted the cruciforms removed,' I said. 'He wanted freedom for both Father Duré's . . . soul, DNA, whatever . . . and for himself.'

'Not quite,' said Gladstone. 'Father Hoyt wanted to die.'

I stood up, almost knocking my chair over, and strode to the pulsing map. 'That's pure bullshit,' I said. 'Even if he did, the others had an obligation to save him . . . and so did you. You let him die.'

'Yes.'

'Just as you're going to let the rest of them die?'

'Not necessarily,' said CEO Meina Gladstone. 'That is their will . . . and the Shrike's, if such a creature actually exists. All I know at this point is that their pilgrimage is too important to allow them a means of . . . retreat . . . at the moment of decision.'

'Whose decision? Theirs? How can the lives of six or seven people . . . and a baby . . . affect the outcome of a society of a hundred and fifty *billion*?' I knew the answer to that, of course. The AI Advisory Council as well as the Hegemony's less sentient predictors had chosen the pilgrims very carefully. But for what? Unpredictability. They were ciphers that matched the ultimate enigma of the entire Hyperion equation. Did Gladstone know that, or did she know only what Councilor Albedo and her own spies told her? I sighed and returned to my chair.

'Did your dream tell you what the fate of Colonel Kassad was?' asked the CEO.

'No. I awoke before they returned to the Sphinx to seek shelter from the storm.'

Gladstone smiled slightly. 'You realize, M. Severn, that for our purposes it would be more convenient to have you sedated, prompted by the same truthtalk your Philomel friends used, and connected to subvocalizers for a more constant report on the events on Hyperion.'

411

I returned her smile. 'Yes,' I said, 'that would be more convenient. But it would be less than convenient for you if I slipped away into the Core via the datasphere and left my body behind. Which is precisely what I will do if put under duress again.'

'Of course,' said Gladstone. 'That is precisely what *I* would do if put in such circumstances. Tell me, M. Severn, what is it like in the Core? What is it like in that distant place where your consciousness truly resides?'

'Busy,' I said. 'Did you want to see me for anything else today?'

Gladstone smiled again and I sensed that it was a true smile, not the politician's weapon she used so well. 'Yes,' she said, 'I did have something else in mind. Would you like to go to Hyperion? The *real* Hyperion?'

'The real Hyperion?' I echoed stupidly. I felt my fingers and toes tingle as a strange sense of excitement suffused me. My consciousness might truly reside in the Core, but my body and brain were all too human, all too susceptible to adrenaline and other random chemicals.

Gladstone nodded. 'Millions of people want to go there. Farcast to somewhere new. Watch the war from close up.' She sighed and moved her work pad. 'The idiots.' She looked up at me, and her brown eyes were serious. 'But I want someone to go there and report back to me in person. Leigh is using one of the new military farcast terminals this morning, and I thought that you might join him. There might not be time to set down on Hyperion itself, but you would be in-system.'

I thought of several questions and was embarrassed by the first one that emerged. 'Will it be dangerous?'

Neither Gladstone's expression nor tone changed. 'Possibly. Although you will be far behind the lines, and Leigh has explicit instructions not to expose himself . . . or you . . . to any obvious risk.'

Obvious risk, I thought. But how many less-than-obvious risks were there in a war zone, near a world where a creature like the Shrike roamed free? 'Yes,' I said, 'I'll go. But there's one thing . . .'

'Yes?'

'I need to know why you want me to go. It seems that if you just want me for my connection to the pilgrims, you're running a needless risk in sending me away.'

Gladstone nodded. 'M. Severn, it's true that your connection to the pilgrims . . . although somewhat tenuous . . . is of interest to me. But it is also true that I am interested in your observations and evaluations. *Your* observations.'

'But I'm nothing to you,' I said. 'You don't know who else I might be reporting to, deliberately or otherwise. I'm a creature of the TechnoCore.'

'Yes,' said Gladstone, 'but you also may be the least-affiliated person on Tau Ceti Center at this moment, perhaps in the entire Web. Also, your observations are those of a trained poet, a man whose genius I respect.'

I barked a laugh. '*He* was a genius,' I said. 'I'm a simulacrum. A drone. A caricature.'

'Are you so sure?' asked Meina Gladstone.

I held up empty hands. 'I haven't written a line of poetry in the ten months I have been alive and aware in this strange afterlife,' I said. 'I do not *think* in poetry. Isn't that proof enough that this Core retrieval project is a sham? Even my false name is an insult to a man infinitely more talented than I will ever be . . . Joseph Severn was a shade in comparison to the real Keats, but I sully his name by using it.'

'That may be true,' said Gladstone. 'And it may not. In either case, I've requested that you go with M. Hunt on this brief trip to Hyperion.' She paused. 'You have no . . . duty . . . to go. In more than one sense, you are not even a citizen of the Hegemony. But I would appreciate it if you did go.'

'I'll go,' I said again, hearing my own voice as if from a distance.

'Very good. You'll need warm clothes. Wear nothing that would come loose or cause embarrassment in free-fall, although there is little likelihood that you will encounter that. Meet M. Hunt in the primary Government House farcaster nexus in . . .' She glanced at her comlog. '. . . twelve minutes.'

I nodded and turned to go.

'Oh, M. Severn . . .'

I paused by the door. The old woman behind the desk suddenly looked rather small and very tired.

'Thank you, M. Severn,' she said.

It was true that millions wanted to farcast to the war zone. The All Thing was shrill with petitions, arguments for letting civilians cast to Hyperion, requests by cruise lines to run brief excursions, and demands by planetary politicians and Hegemony representatives to be allowed to tour the system on 'fact-finding missions'. All such requests had been denied. Web citizens – especially Web citizens with power and influence – were not used to being denied access to new experiences, and for the Hegemony, all-out war remained one of the few experiences still untried.

But the CEO's office and the FORCE authorities remained adamant: no civilian or unauthorized farcasting to the Hyperion system, no uncensored newsteep coverage. In an age where no information was inaccessible, no travel denied, such exclusion was maddening and tantalizing.

I met M. Hunt at the executive farcaster nexus after showing my authorization pip to an even dozen security nodes. Hunt was wearing black wool, undecorated but evocative of the FORCE uniforms present everywhere in this section of Government House. I had had little time to change, returning to my apartments only to grab a loose vest with many pockets to hold drawing materials and a 35-mm imager.

'Ready?' said Hunt. The basset-hound face did not look pleased to see me. He carried a plain black valise.

I nodded.

Hunt gestured toward a FORCE transport technician, and a one-time portal shimmered into existence. I knew that the thing was tuned to our

413

DNA signatures and would admit no one else. Hunt took a breath and stepped through. I watched the quicksilver portal surface ripple after his passage like a stream returning to calm after the slightest of breezes, and then I stepped through myself.

It was rumored that the original farcaster prototypes had offered no sensation during transition and that the AI and human designers had altered the machinery to add that vague prickling, ozone-charged feeling to give the traveler a sense of having *traveled*. Whatever the truth of that, my skin was still alive with tension as I took a step away from the portal, paused, and looked around.

It's strange but true that war-going spacecraft have been depicted in fiction, film, holo, and stimsim for more than eight hundred years; even before humankind had left Old Earth in anything but atmosphere-skimming converted airplanes, their flatfilms had shown epic space battles, huge interstellar dreadnoughts with incredible armament lunging through space like streamlined cities. Even the spate of recent war holies after the Battle of Bressia showed great fleets battling it out at distances two ground soldiers would find claustrophobic, ships ramming and firing and burning like Greek triremes packed into the straits of Artemisium.

It's little wonder then that my heart was pounding and my palms were a bit moist as I stepped on to the flagship of the fleet, expecting to emerge on to the broad bridge of a warship out of the holies, giant screens showing enemy ships, klaxons sounding, craggy commanders huddled over the tactical command panels as the ship lurched first right, then left.

Hunt and I were standing in what could have been a narrow corridor of a power plant. Color-coded pipes twisted everywhere, occasional handholds and airtight hatches at regular intervals suggested that we were indeed in a spacecraft, state-of-the-art diskey and interact panels showed that the corridor served some purpose other than access to elsewhere, but the over-all effect was one of claustrophobia and primitive technology. I half expected to see *wires* running from circuit nodes. A vertical shaft inter-sected our corridor; other narrow, cluttered avenues were visible through other hatches.

Hunt looked at me and shrugged slightly. I wondered if it was possible that we had farcast to the wrong destination.

Before either of us said anything, a young FORCE:space ensign in black battle dress appeared from one of the side corridors, saluted Hunt, and said, 'Welcome to HS *Hebrides*, gentlemen. Admiral Nashita has asked me to convey his compliments and to invite you to the combat control center. If you will follow me, please.' With that the young ensign wheeled, reached for a rung, and pulled into a cramped vertical shaft.

We followed as best we could, Hunt struggling not to drop his valise and me trying not to have my hands ground under Hunt's heels as we climbed. After only a few yards, I realized that the gravity was far less than one-standard here, was not, in fact, gravity at all, but felt more like a multitude of small but insistent hands pressing me 'down'. I knew about spacecraft using a class-one containment field throughout a ship to simulate gravity, but this was my first direct experience of it. It was not a truly pleasant sensation; the constant pressure was rather like leaning into a wind, and the effect added to the claustrophobic qualities of the narrow corridors, small hatches, and equipment-cluttered bulkheads.

The *Hebrides* was a Three-C ship, Communication-Control-Command, and the combat control center was its heart and brain – but it was not a very impressive heart and brain. The young ensign passed us through three airtight hatches, led us down a final corridor past Marine guards, saluted, and left us in a room perhaps twenty yards square, but one so crowded with noise, personnel and equipment that one's first instinct was to step back outside the hatch to get a breath of air.

There were no giant screens, but dozens of young FORCE:space officers hunkered over cryptic displays, sat enmeshed in stimsim apparatus, or stood before pulsing callups which seemed to extend from all six bulkheads. Men and women were lashed into their chairs and sensory cradles, with the exception of a few officers – most looking more like harried bureaucrats than craggy warriors – who wandered the narrow aisles, patting subordinates on the back, barking for more information, and plugging into consoles with their own implant jacks. One of these men came over in a hurry, looked at both of us, saluted me, and said, 'M. Hunt?'

I nodded toward my companion.

'M. Hunt,' said the overweight young Commander, 'Admiral Nashita will see you now.'

The commander of all Hegemony forces in the Hyperion system was a small man with short white hair, skin far smoother than his age suggested, and a fair scowl that seemed carved in place. Admiral Nashita wore high-necked dress black with no rank insignia except for the single red-dwarf sun on his collar. His hands were blunt and quite powerful-looking, but the nails were recently manicured. The Admiral sat on a small dais surrounded by equipment and quiescent callups. The bustle and efficient madness seemed to flow around him like a fast stream around an impervious rock.

'You're the messenger from Gladstone,' he said to Hunt. 'Who's this?'

'My aide,' said Leigh Hunt.

I resisted the urge to raise an eyebrow.

'What do you want?' asked Nashita. 'As you see, we're busy.'

Leigh Hunt nodded and glanced around. 'I have some materials for you, Admiral. Is there anyplace we can go for privacy?'

Admiral Nashita grunted, passed his palm over a rheo-sense, and the air behind me grew denser, coalescing into a semisolid mist as the containment field reified. The noise of the combat control center disappeared. The three of us were in a small igloo of quiet.

'Hurry it up,' said Admiral Nashita.

Hunt unlocked the valise and removed a small envelope with a Government House symbol on the back. 'A private communication from the Chief

Executive,' said Hunt. 'To be read at your leisure, Admiral.' Nashita grunted and set the envelope aside.

Hunt set a larger envelope on the desk. 'And this is a hard copy of the motion of the Senate regarding the prosecution of this . . . ah . . . military action. As you know, the will of the Senate is for this to be a speedy exercise of force to achieve limited objectives, with as little loss of life as possible, followed by the standard offer of help and protection to our new . . . colonial asset.'

Nashita's scowl twitched slightly. He made no move to touch or read the communication containing the will of the Senate. 'Is that all?'

Hunt took his time responding. 'That is all, unless you wish to relay a personal message to the CEO through me, Admiral.'

Nashita stared. There was no active hostility in his small, black eyes, only an impatience that I guessed would not be quenched until those eyes were dimmed by death. 'I have private fatline access to the Chief Executive,' said the Admiral. 'Thank you very much, M. Hunt. No return messages at this time. Now if you will kindly return to the midships farcaster nexus and let me get on with prosecuting this *military action.*'

The containment field collapsed around us, and noise flowed in like water over a melting ice dam.

'There is one other thing,' said Leigh Hunt, his soft voice almost lost under the technobabble of the combat center.

Admiral Nashita swiveled his chair and waited.

'We'd like transport down to the planet,' said Hunt. 'Down to Hyperion.'

The Admiral's scowl seemed to deepen. 'CEO Gladstone's people said nothing about arranging a dropship.'

Hunt did not blink. 'Governor-General Lane knows that we might be coming.'

Nashita glanced at one of his callups, snapped his fingers, and barked something at a Marine major who hurried over. 'You'll have to hurry,' the Admiral said to Hunt. 'There is a courier just ready to leave from port twenty. Major Inverness will show you the way. You will be brought back up to the primary JumpShip. The *Hebrides* will be departing this position in twenty-three minutes.'

Hunt nodded and turned to follow the Major. I tagged along. The Admiral's voice stopped us.

'M. Hunt,' he called, 'please tell CEO Gladstone that the flagship will be too busy from this point on for any more political visits.' Nashita turned away to flickering callups and a line of waiting subordinates.

I followed Hunt and the Major back into the maze.

'There should be windows.'

'What?' I had been thinking about something, not paying attention.

Leigh Hunt turned his head toward me. 'I've never been in a dropship without windows or viewscreens. It's strange.'

I nodded and looked around, noticing the cramped and crowded interior for the first time. It was true that there were only blank bulkheads, and heaps of supplies and one young lieutenant in the passenger hold of the dropship with us. It seemed to conform to the claustrophobic ambience of the command ship.

I looked away, returning to the thoughts that had preoccupied me since we left Nashita. Following the other two to port twenty, it had suddenly occurred to me that I was not missing something I had *expected* to miss. Part of my anxiety toward this trip had lain in the thought of leaving the datasphere; I was rather like a fish contemplating leaving the sea. Part of my *consciousness* lay submerged somewhere in that sea, the ocean of data and commlinks from two hundred worlds and the Core, all linked by the invisible medium once called datumplane, now known only as the megasphere.

It struck me as we left Nashita that I could still hear the pulse of that particular sea – distant but constant, like the sound of the surf half a mile from the shore – and I had been trying to understand it all during the rush to the dropship, the buckling in and separation, and the ten-minute cis-lunar sprint to the fringes of Hyperion's atmosphere.

FORCE prided itself on using its own artificial intelligences, its own dataspheres and computing sources. The ostensible reason lay in the requirement to operate in the great spaces between Web worlds, the dark and quiet places between the stars and beyond the Web megasphere, but much of the real reason lay in a fierce need for independence which FORCE had shown toward the TechnoCore for centuries. Yet on a FORCE ship in the center of a FORCE armada in a non-Web, non-Protectorate system, I was tuned to the same comforting background babble of data and energy that I would have found anywhere in the Web. Interesting.

I thought of the links the farcaster had brought to Hyperion system: not just the JumpShip and farcaster containment sphere floating at Hyperion's L3 point like a gleaming new moon, but the miles of gigachannel fiberoptic cable snaking through permanent JumpShip farcaster portals, microwave repeaters mechanically shuttling the few inches to repeat their messages in near real-time, command ship tame AIs requesting – and receiving – new links to the Olympus High Command on Mars and elsewhere. Somewhere the datasphere had crept in, perhaps unknown to the FORCE machines and their operators and allies. The Core AIs knew everything happening here in Hyperion system. If my body were to die now, I would have the same escape path as always, fleeing down the pulsing links that led like secret passages beyond the Web, beyond any vestige of datumplane as humanity had known it, down datalink tunnels to the TechnoCore itself. *Not really to the Core*, I thought, *because the Core surrounds, envelops the rest, like an ocean holding separate currents, great Gulf Streams which think themselves separate seas.*

'I just wish there was a window,' whispered Leigh Hunt.

'Yes,' I said. 'So do I.'

The dropship bucked and vibrated as we entered Hyperion's upper atmosphere. *Hyperion*, I thought. *The Shrike*. My heavy shirt and vest seemed sticky and clinging. A faint susurration from without said that we were flying, streaking across the lapis skies at several times the speed of sound.

The young Lieutenant leaned across the aisle. 'First time down, gentlemen?'

Hunt nodded.

The Lieutenant was chewing gum, showing how relaxed he was. 'You two civilian techs from the *Hebrides*?'

'We just came from there, yes,' said Hunt.

'Thought so,' grinned the Lieutenant. 'Me, I'm running a courier pack down to the Marine base near Keats. My fifth trip.'

A slight jolt ran through me as I was reminded of the name of the capital; Hyperion had been repopulated by Sad King Billy and his colony of poets, artists, and other misfits fleeing an invasion of their homeworld by Horace Glennon-Height – an invasion which never came. The poet on the current Shrike Pilgrimage, Martin Silenus, had advised King Billy almost two centuries earlier in the naming of the capital. *Keats*. The locals called the old part Jacktown.

'You're not going to believe this place,' said the Lieutenant. 'It's the real anal end of nowhere. I mean, no datasphere, no EMVs, no farcasters, no stimsim bars, no *nothing*. It's no wonder that there are thousands of the fucking indigenies camped around the spaceport, just tearing down the fence to get offworld.'

'Are they really attacking the spaceport?' asked Hunt.

'Naw,' said the Lieutenant and snapped his gum. 'But they're *ready* to, if you know what I mean. That's why the Second Marine Battalion has set up a perimeter there and secured the way into the city. Besides, the yokels think that we're going to set up farcasters any day now and let 'em step out of the shit they got themselves into.'

'*They* got themselves into?' I said.

The Lieutenant shrugged. 'They must've done something to get the Ousters cricked at them, right? We're just here to pull their oysters out of the fire.'

'Chestnuts,' said Leigh Hunt.

The gum snapped. 'Whatever.'

The susurration of wind grew to a shriek clearly audible through the hull. The dropship bounced twice and then slid smoothly – ominously smoothly – as if it had encountered a chute of ice ten miles above the ground.

'I wish we had a window,' whispered Leigh Hunt.

It was warm and stuffy in the dropship. The bouncing was oddly relaxing, rather like a small sailing ship rising and falling on slow swells. I closed my eyes for a few minutes.

TEN

Sol, Brawne, Martin Silenus, and the Consul carry gear, Het Masteen's Möbius cube, and the body of Lenar Hoyt down the long incline to the entrance of the Sphinx. Snow is falling rapidly now, twisting across the already writhing dune surfaces in a complex dance of wind-driven particles. Despite their comlogs' claim that night nears its end, there is no hint of sunrise to the east. Repeated calls on their comlog radio link bring no response from Colonel Kassad.

Sol Weintraub pauses before the entrance to the Time Tomb called the Sphinx. He feels his daughter's presence as a warmth against his chest under the cape, the rise and fall of warm baby's breath against his throat. He raises one hand, touches the small bundle there, and tries to imagine Rachel as a young woman of twenty-six, a researcher pausing at this very entrance before going in to test the anti-entropic mysteries of the Time Tomb. Sol shakes his head. It has been twenty-six long years and a lifetime since that moment. In four days it will be his daughter's birthday. Unless Sol does something, finds the Shrike, makes some bargain with the creature, *does something*, Rachel will die in four days.

'Are you coming, Sol?' calls Brawne Lamia. The others have stored their gear in the first room, half a dozen meters down the narrow corridor through stone.

'Coming,' he calls, and enters the tomb. Glow-globes and electric lights line the tunnel but they are dead and dust-covered. Only Sol's flashlight and the glow from one of Kassad's small lanterns light the way.

The first room is small, no more than four by six meters. The other three pilgrims have set their baggage against the back wall and spread tarp and bedrolls in the center of the cold floor. Two lanterns hiss and cast a cold light. Sol stops and looks around.

'Father Hoyt's body is in the next room,' says Brawne Lamia, answering his unasked question. 'It's even colder there.'

Sol takes his place near the others. Even this far in, he can hear the rasp of sand and snow blowing against stone.

'The Consul is going to try the comlog again later,' says Brawne. 'Tell Gladstone the situation.'

Martin Silenus laughs. 'It's no use. No fucking use at all. She knows what she's doing, and she's never going to let us out of here.'

'I'll try just after sunrise,' says the Consul. His voice is very tired.

'I will stand watch,' says Sol. Rachel stirs and cries feebly. 'I need to feed the baby anyway.'

The others seem too tired to respond. Brawne leans against a pack, closes her eyes, and is breathing heavily within seconds. The Consul pulls his tricorne cap low over his eyes. Martin Silenus folds his arms and stares at the doorway, waiting.

Sol Weintraub fusses with a nursing pak, his cold and arthritic fingers having trouble with the heating tab. He looks in his bag and realizes that he has only ten more paks, a handful of diapers.

The baby is nursing, and Sol is nodding, almost sleeping, when a sound wakes them all.

'What?' cries Brawne, fumbling for her father's pistol.

'Shhh!' snaps the poet, holding his hand out for silence.

From somewhere beyond the tomb comes the sound again. It is flat and final, cutting through the wind noise and sand rasp.

'Kassad's rifle,' says Brawne Lamia.

'Or someone else's,' whispers Martin Silenus.

They sit in silence and strain to hear. For a long moment there is no sound at all. Then, in an instant, the night erupts with noise . . . noise which makes each of them cringe and cover his or her ears. Rachel screams in terror, but her cries cannot be heard over the explosions and rendings beyond the tomb.

ELEVEN

I awoke just as the dropship touched down. *Hyperion*, I thought, still separating my thoughts from the tatters of dream.

The young Lieutenant wished us luck and was the first out as the door irised open and cool, thin air replaced the pressurized thickness of the cabin atmosphere. I followed Hunt out and down a standard docking ramp, through the shield wall, and on to the tarmac.

It was night, and I had no idea what the local time was, whether the terminator had just passed this point on the planet or was just approaching, but it felt and smelled late. It was raining softly, a light drizzle perfumed with the salt scent of the sea and the fresh hint of moistened vegetation. Field lights glared around the distant perimeter, and a score of lighted towers threw halos toward the low clouds. A half dozen young men in Marine field uniforms were quickly unloading the dropship, and I could see our young lieutenant speaking briskly to an officer thirty yards to our right. The small spaceport looked like something out a history book, a colonial port from the earliest days of the Hegira. Primitive blast pits and landing squares stretched for a mile or more toward a dark bulk of hills to the north, gantries and service towers tended to a score of military shuttles and small warcraft around us, and the landing areas were ringed by modular military buildings sporting antennae arrays, violet containment fields, and a clutter of skimmers and aircraft.

I followed Hunt's gaze and noticed a skimmer moving toward us. The blue and gold geodesic symbol of the Hegemony on one of its skirts was illuminated by its running lights; rain streaked the forward blisters and whipped away from the fans in a violent curtain of mist. The skimmer settled, a Perspex blister split and folded, and a man stepped out and hurried across the tarmac toward us.

He held out his hand to Hunt. 'M. Hunt? I'm Theo Lane.'

Hunt shook the hand, nodded toward me. 'Pleased to meet you, Governor-General. This is Joseph Severn.'

I shook Lane's hand, a shock of recognition coming with the touch. I remembered Theo Lane through the *déjà vu* mists of the Consul's memory, recalling the years when the young man was the Vice-Consul; also from a brief meeting a week earlier when he greeted all of the pilgrims before they departed upriver on the levitation barge *Benares*. He seemed older than he had appeared just six days before. But the unruly lock of hair on his forehead was the same, as were the archaic eyeglasses he wore, and the brisk, firm handshake.

'I'm pleased you could take the time to make planetfall,' Governor-General Lane said to Hunt. 'I have several things I need to communicate to the CEO.'

'That's why we're here,' said Hunt. He squinted up at the rain. 'We have about an hour. Is there somewhere we can dry off?'

The Governor-General showed a youthful smile. 'The field here is a madhouse, even at 0520 hours, and the consulate is under siege. But I know a place.' He gestured toward the skimmer.

As we lifted off, I noticed the two Marine skimmers keeping pace with us but I was still surprised that the Governor-General of a Protectorate world flew his own vehicle and did not have constant bodyguards. Then I remembered what the Consul had told the other pilgrims about Theo Lane – about the young man's efficiency and self-effacing ways – and realized that such a low profile was in keeping with the diplomat's style.

The sun rose as we lifted off from the spaceport and banked toward town. Low clouds glowed brilliantly as they were lighted from below, the hills to the north sparkled a bright green, violet, and russet, and the strip of sky below the clouds to the east was that heart-stopping green and lapis which I remembered from my dreams. *Hyperion*, I thought, and felt a thick tension and excitement catch in my throat.

I leaned my head against the rain-streaked canopy and realized that some of the vertigo and confusion I felt at that moment came from a thinning of the background contact with the datasphere. The connection was still there, carried primarily on microwave and fatline channels now, but more tenuous than I had ever experienced – if the datasphere had been the sea in which I swam, I was now in shallow water indeed, perhaps a tidal pool would be a better metaphor, and the water grew even shallower as we left the envelope of the spaceport and its crude microsphere. I forced myself to pay attention to what Hunt and Governor-General Lane were discussing.

'You can see the shacks and hovels,' said Lane, banking slightly so we had a better view of the hills and valleys separating the spaceport from the suburbs of the capital.

Shacks and hovels were too-polite terms for the miserable collection of fiberplastic panels, patches of canvas, heaps of packing crates, and shards of flowfoam that covered the hills and deep canyons. What obviously had once been a scenic seven- or eight-mile drive from the city to the spaceport through wooded hills now showed land stripped of all trees for firewood and shelter, meadows beaten to barren mudflats by the press of feet, and a city of seven or eight hundred thousand refugees sprawled over every flat piece of land in sight. Smoke from thousands of breakfast fires floated toward the clouds, and I could see movement everywhere, children running in bare feet, women carrying water from streams that must be terribly polluted, men squatting in open fields and waiting in line at makeshift privies. I noted that high razorwire fences and violet containment field barriers had been set along both sides of the highway, and military checkpoints were visible every half mile. Long lines of FORCE camouflaged ground vehicles and skimmers moved in both directions along the highway and low-level flyways.

'. . . most of the refugees are indigenies,' Governor-General Lane was saying, 'although there are thousands of displaced landowners from the southern cities and the large fiberplastic plantations on Aquila.'

'Are they here because they think the Ousters will invade?' asked Hunt.

Theo Lane glanced at Gladstone's aide. 'Originally there was panic at the thought of the Time Tombs opening,' he said. 'People were convinced that the Shrike was coming for them.'

'Was it?' I asked.

The young man shifted in his seat to look back at me. 'The Third Legion of the Self-Defense Force went north seven months ago,' he said. 'It didn't come back.'

'You said *at first* they were fleeing the Shrike,' said Hunt. 'Why did the others come?'

'They're waiting for the evacuation,' said Lane. 'Everyone knows what the Ousters . . . and the Hegemony troops . . . did to Bressia. They don't want to be here when that happens to Hyperion.'

'You're aware that FORCE considers evacuation an absolute last resort?' said Hunt.

'Yes. But we're not announcing that to the refugees. There have been terrible riots already. The Shrike Temple has been destroyed . . . a mob laid siege, and someone used shaped plasma charges stolen from the mineworks on Ursus. Last week there were attacks on the consulate and the spaceport, as well as food riots in Jacktown.'

Hunt nodded and watched the city approach. The buildings were low, few over five stories, and their white and pastel walls glowed richly in the slanting rays of morning light. I looked over Hunt's shoulder and saw the low mountain with the carved face of Sad King Billy brooding over the valley. The Hoolie River twisted through the center of the old town, straightening before it headed northwest toward the unseen Bridle Range, twisting out of sight in the weirwood marshes to the southeast, where I knew it widened to its delta along the High Mane. The city looked uncrowded and peaceful after the sad confusion of the refugee slums, but even as we began to descend toward the river, I noticed the military traffic, the tanks and APCs and GAVs at intersections and sitting in parks, their camouflage polymer deliberately deactivated so the machines would look more threatening. Then I saw the refugees in the city: makeshift tents in the squares and alleys, thousands of sleeping forms along the curbs, like so many dull-colored bundles of laundry waiting to be picked up.

'Keats had a population of two hundred thousand two years ago,' said Governor-General Lane. 'Now, including the shack cities, we're nearing three and a half million.'

'I thought that there were fewer than five million people on the planet,' said Hunt. 'Including indigenies.'

'That's accurate,' said Lane. 'You see why everything's breaking down. The other two large cities, Port Romance and Endymion, are holding most of the rest of the refugees. Fiberplastic plantations on Aquila are empty, being reclaimed by the jungle and flame forests, the farm belts along the Mane and the Nine Tails aren't producing – or if they are, can't get their food to market because of the breakdown of the civilian transport system.'

Hunt watched the river come closer. 'What is the government doing?'

Theo Lane smiled. 'You mean what am *I* doing? Well, the crisis has been brewing for almost three years. The first step was to dissolve the Home Rule Council and formally bring Hyperion into the Protectorate. Once I had executive powers, I moved to nationalize the remaining transit companies and dirigible lines – only the military moves by skimmer here now – and to disband the Self-Defense Force.'

'Disband it?' said Hunt. 'I would think you would want to use it.'

Governor-General Lane shook his head. He touched the omni control lightly, confidently, and the skimmer spiraled down toward the center of old Keats. 'They were worse than useless,' he said, 'they were dangerous. I wasn't too upset when the "Fighting Third" Legion went north and just disappeared. As soon as the FORCE:ground troops and Marines landed, I disarmed the rest of the SDF thugs. They were the source of most of the looting. Here's where we'll get some breakfast and talk.'

The skimmer dropped in low over the river, circled a final time, and dropped lightly into the courtyard of an ancient structure made of stone and sticks and imaginatively designed windows: Cicero's. Even before Lane identified the place to Leigh Hunt I recognized it from the pilgrims' passage – the old restaurant/pub/inn lay in the heart of Jacktown and sprawled over four buildings on nine levels, its balconies and piers and darkened weir-wood walkways overhanging the slow-moving Hoolie on one side and the narrow lanes and alleys of Jacktown on the other. Cicero's was older than the stone face of Sad King Billy, and its dim cubicles and deep wine cellars had been the true home of the Consul during his years of exile here.

Stan Leweski met us at the courtyard door. Tall and massive, face as age-darkened and cracked as the stone walls of his inn, Leweski *was* Cicero's, as had been his father, grandfather, and great-grandfather before him.

'By damn!' declared the giant, clapping the Governor-General/de facto dictator of this world on his shoulders hard enough to make Theo stagger. 'You get up early for a change, heh? Bring your friends to breakfast? Welcome to Cicero's!' Stan Leweski's huge hand swallowed Hunt's and then mine in a welcome that left me checking fingers and joints for damage. 'Or is it later – Web time – for you?' he boomed. 'Maybe you like a drink or dinner!'

Leigh Hunt squinted at the pub owner. 'How did you know we were from the Web?'

Leweski boomed a laugh that sent weathervanes on the roofline spinning. 'Hah! Hard to deduct, yes? You come here with Theo at sunrise – you think he give everybody a ride here? – also wearing wool clothes when we got no sheeps here. You're not FORCE people and not fiberplastic plantation big shots . . . I know all those! Ipso fact toto, you farcast to ships from Web, drop down here for good food. Now, you want breakfast or plenty to drink?'

Theo Lane sighed. 'Give us a quiet corner, Stan. Bacon and eggs and brine kippers for me. Gentlemen?'

'Just coffee,' said Hunt.

'Yes,' I said. We were following the owner through the corridors now, up short staircases and down wrought-iron ramps, through more corridors. The place was lower, darker, smokier, and more fascinating than I remembered from my dreams. A few regulars looked up at us as we passed, but the place was far less crowded than I remembered. Obviously Lane had sent troops to throw out the last of the SDF barbarians who had been occupying the place. We passed a high, narrow window, and I verified that hypothesis by catching a glimpse of a FORCE:ground APC parked in the alley, troops lounging on and near it with obviously loaded weapons.

'Here,' said Leweski, waving us into a small porch which overhung the Hoolie and looked out on to the gabled rooftops and stone towers of Jacktown. 'Dommy be here in two minutes with your breakfast and coffees.' He disappeared quickly . . . for a giant.

Hunt glanced at his comlog. 'We have about forty-five minutes before the dropship is supposed to return with us. Let's talk.'

Lane nodded, removed his glasses, and rubbed his eyes. I realized that he had been up all night . . . perhaps several nights. 'Fine,' he said, setting the glasses back in place. 'What does CEO Gladstone want to know?'

Hunt paused while a very short man with parchment-white skin and yellow eyes brought our coffee in deep, thick mugs and set down a platter with Lane's food. 'The CEO wants to know what you feel your priorities are,' said Hunt. 'And she needs to know if you can hold out here if the fighting is prolonged.'

Lane ate for a moment before responding. He took a long sip of coffee and stared intently at Hunt. It was real coffee from the taste of it, better than most Web-grown. 'First question last,' Lane said. 'Define prolonged.'

'Weeks.'

'Weeks, probably. Months, no way.' The Governor-General tried the brine kippers. 'You see the state of our economy. If it wasn't for the supplies dropped in by FORCE, we'd have food riots every day instead of once a week. There are no exports with the quarantine. Half the refugees want to find the Shrike Temple priests and kill them, the other half want to convert before the Shrike finds *them*.'

'Have you found the priests?' asked Hunt.

'No. We're sure they escaped the temple bombing, but the authorities can't locate them. Rumor has it that they've gone north to Keep Chronos, a stone castle right above the high steppe where the Time Tombs are.'

I knew better. At least, I knew the pilgrims had not seen any Shrike Temple priests during their brief stay in the Keep. But there had been signs of a slaughter there.

'As for our priorities,' Theo Lane was saying, 'the first is evacuation. The second is elimination of the Ouster threat. The third is help with the Shrike scare.'

Leigh Hunt sat back against oiled wood. Steam lifted from the heavy mug in his hands. 'Evacuation is not a possibility at this time—'

'Why?' Lane fired the question like a hellwhip bolt.

'CEO Gladstone does not have the political power . . . at this point . . . to convince the Senate and All Thing that the Web can accept five million refugees—'

'Bullshit,' said the Governor-General. 'There were twice that many tourists flooding Maui-Covenant its first year in the Protectorate. And that destroyed a unique planetary ecology. Put us on Armaghast or some desert world until the war scare is past.'

Hunt shook his head. His basset-hound eyes looked sadder than usual. 'It isn't just the logistical question,' he said. 'Or the political one. It's . . .'

'The Shrike,' said Lane. He broke a piece of bacon. 'The Shrike is the real reason.'

'Yes. As well as fears of an Ouster infiltration of the Web.'

The Governor-General laughed. 'So you're afraid that if you set up far-caster portals here and let us out, a bunch of three-meter Ousters are going to land and get in line without anyone noticing?'

Hunt sipped his coffee. 'No,' he said, 'but there is a real chance of an invasion. Every farcaster portal is an opening to the Web. The Advisory Council warns against it.'

'All right,' said the younger man, his mouth half-full. 'Evacuate us by ship then. Wasn't that the reason for the original task force?'

'That was the *ostensible* reason,' said Hunt. 'Our real goal now is to defeat the Ousters and then bring Hyperion fully into the Web.'

'And what about the Shrike threat then?'

'It will be . . . neutralized,' said Hunt. He paused while a small group of men and women passed by our porch.

I glanced up, started to return my attention to the table, and then snapped my head back around. The group had passed out of sight down the hallway. 'Wasn't that Melio Arundez?' I said, interrupting Governor-General Lane.

'What? Oh, Dr Arundez. Yes. Do you know him, M. Severn?'

Leigh Hunt was glaring at me, but I ignored it. 'Yes,' I said to Lane, although I had never actually met Arundez. 'What is he doing on Hyperion?'

'His team landed over six local months ago with a project proposal from Reichs University on Freeholm to do additional research on the Time Tombs.'

'But the Tombs were closed to research and tourists,' I said.

'Yes. But their instruments – we allowed data to be relayed weekly through the consulate fatline transmitter – had already shown the change in the anti-entropic fields surrounding the Tombs. Reichs University knew the Tombs were opening . . . if that's really what the change means . . . and they sent the top researchers in the Web to study it.'

'But you did not grant them permission?' I said.

Theo Lane smiled without warmth. 'CEO Gladstone did not grant them permission. The closure of the Tombs is a direct order from TC^2. If it were up to me, I would have denied the pilgrims passage and allowed Dr Arundez's team priority access.' He turned back to Hunt.

'Excuse me,' I said and slipped out of the booth.

I found Arundez and his people – three women and four men, their clothing and physical styles suggesting different worlds in the Web – two porches away. They were bent over their breakfasts and scientific com-logs, arguing in technical terms so abtruse as to leave a Talmudic scholar envious.

'Dr Arundez?' I said.

'Yes?' He looked up. He was two decades older than I remembered, entering middle age in his early sixties, but the strikingly handsome profile was the same, with the same bronzed skin, solid jaw, wavy black hair going only slightly gray at the temples, and piercing hazel eyes. I understood how a young female graduate student could have quickly fallen in love with him.

'My name is Joseph Severn,' I said. 'You don't know me, but I knew a friend of yours . . . Rachel Weintraub.'

Arundez was on his feet in a second, offering apologies to the others, leading me by the elbow until we found an empty booth in a cubicle under a round window looking out on red-tiled rooftops. He released my elbow and appraised me carefully, taking in the Web clothing. He turned my wrists over, looking for the telltale blueness of Poulsen treatments. 'You're too young,' he said. 'Unless you knew Rachel as a child.'

'Actually, it's her father I know best,' I said.

Dr Arundez let out a breath and nodded. 'Of course,' he said. 'Where *is* Sol? I've been trying to trace him for months through the consulate. The authorities on Hebron will only say that he's moved.' He gave me that appraising stare again. 'You knew about Rachel's . . . illness?'

'Yes,' I said. The Merlin's sickness which had caused her to age backward, losing memories with each day and hour that passed. Melio Arundez had been one of those memories. 'I know that you went to visit her about fifteen standard years ago on Barnard's World.'

Arundez grimaced. 'That was a mistake,' he said. 'I thought that I would talk to Sol and Sarai. When I saw her . . .' He shook his head. 'Who are you? Do you know where Sol and Rachel are now? It's *three days* until her birthday.'

I nodded. 'Her first and last birthday.' I glanced around. The hallway was silent and empty except for a distant murmur of laughter from a lower level. 'I'm here on a fact-finding trip from the CEO's office,' I said. 'I have information that Sol Weintraub and his daughter have traveled to the Time Tombs.'

Arundez looked as though I'd struck him in the solar plexus. *'Here?* On Hyperion?' He stared out at the rooftops for a moment. 'I should have realized . . . although Sol always refused to return here . . . but with Sarai gone . . .' He looked at me. 'Are you in touch with him? Is she . . . are they all right?'

I shook my head. 'There are no radio or datasphere links with them at present,' I said. 'I know that they made the trip safely. The question is, what do *you* know? Your team? Data on what is occurring at the Time Tombs might be very important to their survival.'

Melio Arundez ran his hand through his hair. 'If only they'd let us go there! That damned, stupid, bureaucratic shortsightedness . . . You say you're from Gladstone's office. Can you explain to them why it's so important for us to get there?'

'I'm only a messenger,' I said. 'But tell me why it's so important, and I'll try to get the information to someone.'

Arundez's large hands cupped an invisible shape in midair. His tension and anger were palpable. 'For three years, the data was coming via telemetry in the squirts the consulate would allow once a week on their precious fatline transmitter. It showed a slow but relentless degradation of the anti-entropic envelope – the time tides – in and around the Tombs. It was erratic, illogical, but steady. Our team was authorized to travel here shortly after the degradation began. We arrived about six months ago, saw data that suggested that the Tombs were opening . . . coming into phase with *now* . . . but four days after we arrived, the instruments quit sending. All of them. We begged that bastard Lane to let us just go and recalibrate them, set up new sensors if he wouldn't let us investigate in person.

'Nothing. No transit permission. No communication with the university . . . even with the coming of FORCE ships to make it easier. We tried going upriver ourselves, without permission, and some of Lane's Marine goons intercepted us at Karla Locks and brought us back in handcuffs. I spent four weeks in jail. Now we're allowed to wander around Keats, but we'll be locked up indefinitely if we leave the city again.' Arundez leaned forward. *'Can* you help?'

'I don't know,' I said. 'I want to help the Weintraubs. Perhaps it would be best if you could take your team to the site. Do you know when the Tombs will open?'

The time-physicist made an angry gesture. 'If we had *new* data!' He sighed. 'No, we don't know. They could be open already or it could be another six months.'

'When you say "open",' I said, 'you don't mean physically open?'

'Of course not. The Time Tombs have been physically open for inspection since they were discovered four standard centuries ago. I mean open in the sense of dropping the time curtains that conceal parts of them, bringing the entire complex into phase with the local flow of time.'

'By "local" you mean . . . ?'

'I mean in this universe, of course.'

'And you're sure that the Tombs are moving backward in time . . . from our future?' I asked.

'Backward in time, yes,' said Arundez. 'From our future, we can't say. We're not even sure what the "future" means in temporal/physical terms. It could be a series of sine-wave probabilities or a decision-branch megaverse, or even—'

'But whatever it is,' I said, 'the Time Tombs and the Shrike are coming from there?'

'The Time Tombs are for certain,' said the physicist. 'I have no knowledge of the Shrike. My own guess is that it's a myth fueled by the same hunger for superstitious verities that drives other religions.'

'Even after what happened to Rachel?' I said. 'You still don't believe in the Shrike?'

Melio Arundez glowered at me. 'Rachel contracted Merlin's sickness,' he said. 'It's an anti-entropic aging disease, not the bite of a mythical monster.'

'Time's bite has never been mythical,' I said, surprising myself with such a cheap bit of homespun philosophy. 'The question is – will the Shrike or whatever power inhabits the Time Tombs return Rachel to the "local" time flow?'

Arundez nodded and turned his gaze to the rooftops. The sun had moved into the clouds, and the morning was drab, the red tiles bleached of color. Rain was beginning to fall again.

'And the question is,' I said, surprising myself again, 'are you still in love with her?'

The physicist turned his head slowly, fixing me in an angry gaze. I felt the retort – possibly physical – build, crest, and wane. He reached into his coat pocket and showed me a snapshot holo of an attractive woman with graying hair and two children in their late teens. 'My wife and children,' said Melio Arundez. 'They're waiting on Renaissance Vector.' He pointed a blunt finger at me. 'If Rachel were . . . were cured today, I would be eighty-two standard years old before she again reached the age she was when we first met.' He lowered the finger, returned the holo to his pocket. 'And yes,' he said, 'I'm still in love with her.'

'Ready?' The voice broke the silence a moment later. I looked up to see Hunt and Theo Lane in the doorway. 'The dropship lifts off in ten minutes,' said Hunt.

I stood and shook hands with Melio Arundez. 'I'll try,' I said.

Governor-General Lane had one of his escort skimmers return us to the spaceport while he went back to the consulate. The military skimmer was no more comfortable than his consulate machine had been, but it was faster. We were strapped and fielded into our webseats aboard the dropship before Hunt said, 'What was all that about with that physicist?'

'Just renewing old ties with a stranger,' I said.

Hunt frowned. 'What did you promise him that you'd try?'

I felt the dropship rumble, twitch, and then leap as the catapult grid launched us skyward. 'I told him I'd try to get him in to visit a sick friend,' I said.

Hunt continued to frown, but I pulled out a sketchpad and doodled images of Cicero's until we docked at the JumpShip fifteen minutes later.

It was a shock to step through the farcaster portal into the executive nexus in Government House. Another step took us to the Senate gallery, where Meina Gladstone was still speaking to a packed house. Imagers and microphones carried her speech to the All Thing and a hundred billion waiting citizens.

I glanced at my chronometer. It was 1038 hours. We had been gone only ninety minutes.

TWELVE

The building housing the Senate of the Hegemony of Man was patterned more after the United States Senate building of eight centuries earlier rather than the more imperial structures of the North American Republic or the First World Council. The main assembly room was large, girded with galleries, and big enough for the three-hundred-plus senators from Web worlds and the more than seventy nonvoting representatives from Protectorate colonies. Carpets were a rich wine red and radiated from the central dais where the President Pro Tem, the Speaker of the All Thing, and, today, the Chief Executive Officer of the Hegemony had their seats. Senators' desks were made of muirwood, donated by the Templars of God's Grove, who held such products sacred, and the glow and scent of burnished wood filled the room even when it was as crowded as it was today.

Leigh Hunt and I entered just as Gladstone was finishing her speech. I keyed my comlog for a quick readout. As with most of her talks, it had been short, comparatively simple, without condescension or bombast, yet laced with a certain lilt of original phrasing and imagery which carried great power. Gladstone had reviewed the incidents and conflicts that led to the current state of belligerency with the Ousters, proclaimed the time-honored wish for peace, which still was paramount in Hegemony policy, and called for unity within the Web and Protectorate until this current crisis was past. I listened to her summation.

'. . . and so it has come to pass, fellow citizens, that after more than a century of peace we are once again engaged in a struggle to maintain those rights to which our society has been dedicated since before the death of our Mother Earth. After more than a century of peace, we must now pick up – however unwillingly, however distastefully – the shield and sword, which have ever preserved our birthright and vouchsafed our common good, so that peace may again prevail.

'We must not . . . and shall not . . . be misled by the stir of trumpets or the rush of near-joy which the call to arms inevitably produces. Those who ignore history's lessons in the ultimate folly of war are forced to do more than relive them . . . they may be forced to die by them. Great sacrifices may lie ahead for all of us. Great sorrows may lie in store for some of us. But come what successes or setbacks must inevitably occur, I say to you now that we must remember these two things above all: First, that we fight for peace and know that war must never be a condition but, rather, a temporary scourge which we suffer as a child does a fever, knowing that health

431

follows the long night of pain and that peace is health. Second, that we shall never surrender . . . never surrender or waver or bend to lesser voices or more comfortable impulses . . . never waver until the victory is ours, aggression is undone, and the peace is won. I thank you.'

Leigh Hunt leaned forward and watched intently as most of the senators rose to give Gladstone an ovation that roared back from the high ceiling and struck us in the gallery in waves. *Most* of the senators. I could see Hunt counting those who remained sitting, some with arms folded, many with visible frowns. The war was less than two days old, and already the opposition was building . . . first from the colonial worlds afraid for their own safety while FORCE was diverted to Hyperion, then from Gladstone's opponents – of which there were many since no one stays in power as long as she without creating cadres of enemies, and finally from members of her own coalition who saw the war as a foolish undoing of unprecedented prosperity.

I watched her leaving the dais, shaking hands with the aged President and young Speaker, then taking the center aisle out – touching and talking to many, smiling the familiar smile. All Thing imagers followed her, and I could feel the pressure of the debate net swell as billions voiced their opinions on the interact levels of the megasphere.

'I need to see her now,' said Hunt. 'Are you aware that you're invited to a state dinner tonight at Treetops?'

'Yes.'

Hunt shook his head slightly, as if incapable of understanding why the CEO wanted me around. 'It will run late and will be followed by a meeting with FORCE:command. She wants you to attend both.'

'I'll be available,' I said.

Hunt paused at the door. 'Do you have something to do back at Government House until the dinner?'

I smiled at him. 'I'll work on my portrait sketches,' I said. 'Then I'll probably take a walk through Deer Park. After that . . . I don't know . . . I may take a nap.'

Hunt shook his head again and hurried off.

THIRTEEN

The first shot misses Fedmahn Kassad by less than a meter, splitting a boulder he is passing, and he is moving before the blast strikes him; rolling for cover, his camouflage polymer fully activated, impact armor tensed, assault rifle ready, visor in full targeting mode. Kassad lies there for a long moment, feeling his heart pounding and searching the hills, valley, and Tombs for the slightest hint of heat or movement. Nothing. He begins to grin behind the black mirror of his visor.

Whoever had shot at him had meant to miss, he is sure. They had used a standard pulse bolt, ignited by an 18-mm cartridge, and unless the shooter was ten or more kilometers away . . . there was no chance of a miss.

Kassad stands up to run toward the shelter of the Jade Tomb, and the second shot catches him in the chest, hurling him backward.

This time he grunts and rolls away, scuttling toward the Jade Tomb's entrance with all sensors active. The second shot had been a rifle bullet. Whoever is playing with him is using a FORCE multipurpose assault weapon similar to his own. He guesses that the assailant knows he is in body armor, knows that the rifle bullet would be ineffective at any range. But the multipurpose weapon has other settings, and if the next level of play involves a killing laser, Kassad is dead. He throws himself into the doorway of the tomb.

Still no heat or movement on his sensors except for the red-and-yellow images of his fellow pilgrims' footprints, rapidly cooling, where they had entered the Sphinx several minutes before.

Kassad uses his tactical implants to switch displays, quickly running through VHF and optical comm channels. Nothing. He magnifies the valley a hundredfold, computes in wind and sand, and activates a moving-target indicator. Nothing larger than an insect is moving. He sends out radar, sonar, and lorfo pulses, daring the sniper to home in on them. Nothing. He calls up tactical displays of the first two shots; blue ballistic trails leap into existence.

The first shot had come from the Poets' City, more than four klicks to the southwest. The second shot, less than ten seconds later, came from the Crystal Monolith, almost a full klick down the valley to the northeast. Logic dictates that there have to be two snipers. Kassad is sure that there is only one. He refines the display scale. The second shot had come from high on the Monolith, at least thirty meters up on the sheer face.

Kassad swings out, raises amplification, and peers through night and the

433

last vestiges of the sand- and snowstorm toward the huge structure. Nothing. No windows, no slits, no openings of any sort.

Only the billions of colloidal particles left in the air from the storm allow the laser to be visible for a split second. Kassad sees the green beam *after* it strikes him in the chest. He rolls back into the entrance of the Jade Tomb, wondering if the green walls will help deter a green light lance, while superconductors in his combat armor radiate heat in every direction and his tactical visor tells him what he already knows: the shot has come from high on the Crystal Monolith.

Kassad feels pain sting his chest, and he looks down in time to see a five-centimeter circle of invulnarmor drip molten fibers on to the floor. Only the last layer has saved him. As it is, his body drips with sweat inside the suit, and he can see the walls of the tomb literally glowing with the heat his suit has discarded. Biomonitors clamor for attention but hold no serious news, his suit sensors report some circuit damage but describe nothing irreplaceable, and his weapon is still charged, loaded, and operative.

Kassad thinks about it. All of the Tombs are priceless archaeological treasures, preserved for centuries as a gift to future generations, even if they *are* moving backward in time. It would be a crime on an interplanetary scale if Colonel Fedmahn Kassad were to put his own life above the preservation of such priceless artifacts.

'Oh fuck it,' whispers Kassad and rolls into firing position.

He sprays laser fire across the face of the Monolith until crystal slags and runs. He pumps high-explosive pulse bolts into the thing at ten-meter intervals, starting with the top levels. Thousands of shards of mirrored material fly out into the night, tumbling in slow motion toward the valley floor, leaving gaps as ugly as missing teeth in the building's face. Kassad switches back to wide-beam coherent light and sweeps the interior through the gaps, grinning behind his visor when *something* bursts into flames on several floors. Kassad fires bhees – beams of high-energy electrons – which rip through the Monolith and plow perfectly cylindrical fourteen-centimeter-wide tunnels for half a kilometer through the rock of the valley wall. He fires canister grenades, which explode into tens of thousands of needle fléchettes after passing through the crystal face of the Monolith. He triggers random pulse-laser swaths, which will blind anyone or anything looking in his direction from the structure. He fires body-heat-seeking darts into every orifice the shattered structure offers him.

Kassad rolls back into the Jade Tomb's doorway and flips up his visor. Flames from the burning tower are reflected in thousands of crystal shards scattered up and down the valley. Smoke rises into a night suddenly without wind. Vermilion dunes glow from the flames. The air is suddenly filled with the sound of wind chimes as more pieces of crystal break and fall away, some dangling by long tethers of melted glass.

Kassad ejects drained power clips and ammo bands, replaces them from his belt, and rolls on his back, breathing in the cooler air that comes through the open doorway. He is under no illusion that he has killed the sniper.

'Moneta,' whispers Fedmahn Kassad. He closes his eyes a second before going on.

Moneta had first come to Kassad at Agincourt on a late-October morning in A.D. 1415. The fields had been strewn with French and English dead, the forest alive with the menace of a single enemy, but that enemy would have been the victor if not for the help of the tall woman with short hair, and eyes he would never forget. After their shared victory, still dappled with the blood of their vanquished knight, Kassad and the woman made love in the forest.

The Olympus Command School Historical Tactical Network was a stimsim experience closer to reality than anything civilians would ever experience, but the phantom lover named Moneta was not an artifact of the stimsim. Over the years, when Kassad was a cadet at FORCE Olympus Command School and later, in the fatigue-drugged post-cathartic dreams that inevitably followed actual combat, she had come to him.

Fedmahn Kassad and the shadow named Moneta had made love in the quiet corners of battlefields ranging from Antietam to Qom-Riyadh. Unknown to anyone, unseen by other stimsim cadets, Moneta had come to him in tropical nights on watch and during frozen days while under siege on the Russian steppes. They had whispered their passion in Kassad's dreams after nights of real victory on the island battlefields of Maui-Covenant and during the agony of physical reconstruction after his near-death on South Bressia. And always Moneta had been his single love – an overpowering passion mixed with the scent of blood and gunpowder, the taste of napalm and soft lips and ionized flesh.

Then came Hyperion.

Colonel Fedmahn Kassad's hospital ship was attacked by Ouster torch-ships while returning from the Bressia system. Only Kassad had survived, stealing an Ouster shuttle and crash-landing it on Hyperion. On the continent of Equus. In the high deserts and barren wastelands of the sequestered lands beyond the Bridle Range. In the valley of the Time Tombs. In the realm of the Shrike.

And Moneta had been waiting for him. They made love . . . and when the Ousters landed in force to reclaim their prisoner, Kassad and Moneta and the half-sensed presence of the Shrike had laid waste to Ouster ships, destroyed their landing parties, and slaughtered their troops. For a brief time, Colonel Fedmahn Kassad from the Tharsis slums, child and grand-child and great-grandchild of refugees, citizen of Mars in every sense, had known the pure ecstasy of using time as a weapon, of moving unseen amongst one's enemies, of being a god of destruction in ways not dreamt of by mortal warriors.

But then, even while making love after the carnage of battle, Moneta had changed. Had become a monster. Or the Shrike had replaced her. Kassad could not remember the details; *would* not remember them if he did not have to in order to survive.

But he knew that he had returned to find the Shrike and to kill it. To find Moneta and to kill her. To kill her? He did not know. Colonel Fedmahn Kassad knew only that all the great passions of a passionate life had led him to this place and to this moment, and if death awaited him here, then so be it. And if love and glory and a victory that would make Valhalla quake awaited, then so be it.

Kassad slaps down his visor, rises to his feet, and rushes from the Jade Tomb, screaming as he goes. His weapon launches smoke grenades and chaff toward the Monolith, but these offer little cover for the distance he must cross. Someone is still alive and firing from the tower; bullets and pulse charges explode along his path as he dodges and dives from dune to dune, from one heap of rubble to the next.

Fléchettes strike his helmet and legs. His visor cracks, and warning telltales blink. Kassad blinks away the tactical displays, leaving only the night-vision aids. High-velocity solid slugs strike his shoulder and knee. Kassad goes down, is driven down. The impact armor goes rigid, relaxes, and he is up and running again, feeling the deep bruises already forming. His chameleon polymer works desperately to mirror the no-man's-land he is crossing: night, flame, sand, melted crystal, and burning stone.

Fifty meters from the Monolith, and ribbons of light lance to his left and right, turning sand to glass with a touch, reaching for him with a speed nothing and no one can dodge. Killing lasers quit playing with him and lance home, stabbing at his helmet, heart, and groin with the heat of stars. His combat armor goes mirror bright, shifting frequencies in microseconds to match the changing colors of attack. A nimbus of superheated air surrounds him. Microcircuits shriek to overload and beyond as they release the heat and work to build a micrometer-thin field of force to keep it away from flesh and bone.

Kassad struggles the final twenty meters, using power assist to leap barriers of slagged crystal. Explosions erupt on all sides, knocking him down and then lifting him again. The suit is absolutely rigid; he is a doll thrown between flaming hands.

The bombardment stops. Kassad gets to his knees and then to his feet. He looks up at the face of the Crystal Monolith and sees the flames and fissures and little else. His visor is cracked and dead. Kassad lifts it, breathes in smoke and ionized air, and enters the tomb.

His implants tell him that the other pilgrims are paging him on all the comm channels. He shuts them off. Kassad removes his helmet and walks into darkness.

It is a single room, large and square and dark. A shaft has opened in the center and he looks up a hundred meters to a shattered skylight. A figure is waiting on the tenth level, sixty meters above, silhouetted by flames.

Kassad drapes his weapon over one shoulder, tucks his helmet under his arm, finds the great spiral staircase in the center of the shaft, and begins to climb.

FOURTEEN

'Did you have your nap?' Leigh Hunt asked as we stepped on to the farcaster reception area of Treetops.

'Yes.'

'Pleasant dreams, I hope?' said Hunt, making no effort to hide either his sarcasm or his opinion of those who slept while the movers and shakers of government toiled.

'Not especially,' I said and looked around as we ascended the wide staircase toward the dining levels.

In a Web where every town in every province of every country on every continent seemed to brag of a four-star restaurant, where true gourmets numbered in the tens of millions and palates had been educated by exotic fare from two hundred worlds, even in a Web so jaded with culinary triumphs and restaurantic success, Treetops stood alone.

Set atop one of a dozen highest trees on a world of forest giants, Treetops occupied several acres of upper branches half a mile above the ground. The staircase Hunt and I ascended, four meters wide here, was lost amid the immensity of limbs the size of avenues, leaves the size of sails, and a main trunk – illuminated by spotlights and just glimpsed through gaps in the foliage – more sheer and massive than most mountain faces. Treetops held a score of dining platforms in its upper bowers, ascending in order of rank and privilege and wealth and power. Especially power. In a society where billionaires were almost commonplace, where a lunch at Treetops could cost a thousand marks and be within the reach of millions, the final arbiter of position and privilege was power – a currency that never went out of style.

The evening's gathering was to be on the uppermost deck, a wide, curving platform of weirwood (since muirwood cannot be stepped upon), with views of a fading lemon sky, an infinity of lesser treetops stretching off to a distant horizon, and the soft orange lights of Templar treehomes and houses of worship glowing through far-off green and umber and amber walls of softly stirring foliage. There were about sixty people in the dinner party; I recognized Senator Kolchev, white hair shining under the Japanese lanterns, as well as Councilor Albedo, General Morpurgo, Admiral Singh, President Pro Tem Denzel-Hiat-Amin, All Thing Speaker Gibbons, another dozen senators from such powerful Web worlds as Sol Draconi Septem, Deneb Drei, Nordholm, Fuji, both the Renaissances, Metaxas, Maui-Covenant, Hebron, New Earth, and Ixion, as well as a bevy of lesser politicians. Spenser Reynolds, the action artist, was there, resplendent in a maroon velvet formal tunic, but I saw no other artists. I did see Tyrena Wingreen-Feif across the crowded deck; the publisher-turned-philanthropist still stood out in a crowd in her gown made of thousands of silk-thin leather petals, her blue-black hair rising high in a sculpted wave, but the gown was a Tedekai original, the makeup was dramatic but non-interactive, and her appearance was far more subdued than it would have been a mere five or six decades earlier. I moved in her direction across the crowded floor as guests milled about on the penultimate deck, making raids on the numerous bars and waiting for the call to dine.

'Joseph, *dear*,' cried Wingreen-Feif as I closed the last few yards, 'how in the *world* did you get invited to such a dreary function?'

I smiled and offered her a glass of champagne. The dowager empress of literary fashion knew me only because of her week-long visit to the Esperance arts festival the previous year and my friendship with such Web-class names as Salmud Brevy III, Millon De Havre, and Rithmet Corber. Tyrena was a dinosaur who refused to become extinct – her wrists, palms, and neck would have glowed blue from repeated Poulsens if it had not been for makeup, and she spent decades on short-hop interstellar cruises or incredibly expensive cryogenic naps at spas too exclusive to have names; the upshot was that Tyrena Wingreen-Feif had held the social scene in an iron grip for more than three centuries and showed no signs of relinquishing it. With every twenty-year nap, her fortune expanded and her legend grew.

'Do you still live on that *dreary* little planet I visited last year?' she asked.

'Esperance,' I said, knowing that she knew precisely where each important artist on that unimportant world resided. 'No, I appear to have moved my residence to TC^2 for the present.'

M. Wingreen-Feif made a face. I was vaguely aware that there was a group of eight to ten hangers-on watching intently, wondering who this brash young man was who had moved into *her* inner orbit. 'How dreadful for you,' said Tyrena, 'to have to abide on a world of business people and government bureaucrats. I hope they allow you to escape soon!'

I raised my glass in a toast to her. 'I wanted to ask you,' I said, 'weren't you Martin Silenus's editor?'

The dowager empress lowered her glass and fixed me with a cold stare. For a second I imagined Meina Gladstone and this woman locked in a combat of wills; I shuddered and waited for her answer. 'My darling boy,' she said, 'that is such *ancient* history. Why would you bother your pretty young head about such prehistoric trivia?'

'I'm interested in Silenus,' I said. 'In his poetry. I was just curious if you were still in touch with him.'

'Joseph, Joseph, Joseph,' tutted M. Wingreen-Feif, 'no one has heard from poor Martin in *decades*. Why, the poor man would be *ancient*!'

I didn't point out to Tyrena that when she was Silenus's editor, the poet was much younger than she.

'It is odd that you mention him,' she continued. 'My old firm, Transline, said recently that they were considering releasing some of Martin's work. I don't know if they ever contacted his estate.'

'His *Dying Earth* books?' I said, thinking of the Old Earth nostalgia volumes which had sold so well so long ago.

'No, oddly enough. I believe they were thinking of printing his *Cantos*,' said Tyrena. She laughed and held out a cannabis stick ensconced in a long, ebony cigarette holder. One of her retinue hurried to light it. 'Such an *odd* choice,' she said, 'considering that no one ever read the *Cantos* when poor Martin was alive. Well, nothing helps an artist's career more than a little death and obscurity, I always say.' She laughed – sharp little sounds like metal chipping rock. Half a dozen of her circle laughed along with her.

'You'd better make sure that Silenus is dead,' I said. 'The *Cantos* would make better reading if they were complete.'

Tyrena Wingreen-Feif looked at me strangely, the chimes for dinner sounded through shifting leaves, Spenser Reynolds offered the *grande dame* his arm as people began climbing the last staircase toward the stars, and I finished my drink, left the empty glass on a railing, and went up to join the herd.

The CEO and her entourage arrived shortly after we were seated, and Gladstone gave a brief talk, probably her twentieth of the day, excluding her morning speech to the Senate and Web. The original reason for tonight's dinner had been the recognition of a fund-raising effort for the Armaghast Relief Fund, but Gladstone's talk soon turned to the war and the necessity of prosecuting it vigorously and efficiently while leaders from all parts of the Web promoted unity.

I gazed out over the railing while she spoke. The lemon sky had dissolved to a muted saffron and then quickly faded to a tropical dusk so rich that it seemed as if a thick, blue curtain had been drawn across the sky. God's Grove had six small moons, five of them visible from this latitude, and four were racing across the sky as I watched the stars emerge. The air was oxygen rich here, almost intoxicating, and carried a heavy fragrance of moistened vegetation which reminded me of the morning visit to Hyperion. But no EMVs or skimmers or flying machines of any sort were allowed on God's Grove – petrochemical emissions or fusion-cell wakes had never polluted these skies – and the absence of cities, highways, and electrical lighting made the stars seem bright enough to compete with the Japanese lanterns and glow-globes hanging from branches and stanchions.

The breeze had come up again after sunset, and now the entire tree swayed slightly, the broad platform moving as softly as a ship on a gentle sea, weirwood and muirwood stanchions and supports creaking softly with the gentle swells. I could see lights shining up through distant treetops and knew that many of them came from 'rooms' – a few of thousands leased by the Templars – which one could add to one's multiworld farcaster-connected residence if one had the million-mark beginning price for such an extravagance.

The Templars did not sully themselves with the day-to-day operations of Treetops or the leasing agencies, merely setting strict, inviolable ecological conditions to any such endeavor, but they benefited from the hundreds of millions of marks brought in by such enterprises. I thought of their interstellar cruise ship, the *Yggdrasill*, a kilometer-long Tree from the planet's most sacred forest, driven by Hawking drive singularity generators and protected by the most complex force shields and Erg force fields that could be carried. Somehow, inexplicably, the Templars had agreed to send the *Yggdrasill* on an evacuation mission that was a mere cover for the FORCE invasion task force.

And as things tend to happen when priceless objects are set in harm's way, the *Yggdrasill* was destroyed while in orbit around Hyperion, whether by Ouster attack or some other force not yet determined. How had the Templars reacted? What conceivable goal could have made them risk one of the four Treeships in existence? And why had their Treeship captain – Het Masteen – been chosen as one of the seven Shrike Pilgrims and then proceeded to disappear before the windwagon reached the Bridle Range on the shores of the Sea of Grass?

There were too damned many questions, and the war was only a few days old.

Meina Gladstone had finished her remarks and urged us all to enjoy the fine dinner. I applauded politely and waved over a steward to have my wineglass filled. The first course was a classic salad à la the empire period, and I applied myself to it with enthusiasm. I realized that I'd eaten nothing since breakfast that day. Spearing a sprig of watercress, I remembered Governor-General Theo Lane eating bacon and eggs and kippers as the rain fell softly from Hyperion's lapis lazuli sky. *Had that been a dream?*

'What do you think of the war, M. Severn?' asked Reynolds, the action artist. He was several seats down and across the broad table from me, but his voice carried very well. I could see Tyrena raise an eyebrow toward me from where she sat, three seats to my right.

'What can one think of war?' I said, tasting the wine again. It was quite good, though nothing in the Web could match my memories of French Bordeaux. 'War does not call for judgement,' I said, 'merely survival.'

'On the contrary,' said Reynolds, 'like so many other things humankind has redefined since the Hegira, warfare is on the threshold of becoming an art form.'

'An art form,' sighed a woman with short-cropped chestnut hair. The datasphere told me that she was M. Sudette Chier, wife of Senator Gabriel Fyodor Kolchev and a powerful political force in her own right. M. Chier wore a blue and gold lamé gown and an expression of rapt interest. 'War as an art form, M. Reynolds! What a fascinating concept!'

Spenser Reynolds was a bit shorter than Web average, but far handsomer. His hair was curled but cropped short, his skin appeared bronzed by a benevolent sun and slightly gilded with subtle body paint, his clothes and ARNistry were expensively flamboyant without being outré, and his demeanor proclaimed a relaxed confidence that all men dreamed of and precious few obtained. His wit was obvious, his attention to others sincere, and his sense of humor legendary.

I found myself disliking the son of a bitch at once.

'*Everything* is an art form, M. Chier, M. Severn.' Reynolds smiled. 'Or must become one. We are beyond the point where warfare can be merely the churlish imposition of policy by other means.'

'Diplomacy,' said General Morpurgo, on Reynolds' left.

'I beg your pardon, General?'

'Diplomacy,' he said. 'And it's "extension of", not "imposition of".'

Spenser Reynolds bowed and made a small roll of his hand. Sudette Chier and Tyrena laughed softly. The image of Councilor Albedo leaned forward from my left and said, 'Von Clausewitz, I believe.'

I glanced toward the Councilor. A portable projection unit not much larger than the radiant gossamers flitting through the branches hovered two meters above and behind him. The illusion was not as perfect as in Government House, but it was far better than any private holo I had ever seen.

General Morpurgo nodded toward the Core representative.

'Whatever,' said Chier. 'It is the *idea* of warfare as art which is so brilliant.'

I finished the salad, and a human waiter whisked the bowl away, replacing it with a dark gray soup I did not recognize. It was smoky, slightly redolent of cinnamon and the sea, and delicious.

'Warfare is a perfect medium for an artist,' began Reynolds, holding his salad utensil aloft like a baton. 'And not merely for those . . . craftsmen who have studied the so-called science of war, either.' He smiled toward Morpurgo and another FORCE officer to the General's right, dismissing both of them from consideration. 'Only someone who is willing to look beyond the bureaucratic limits of tactics and strategies and the obsolescent will to "win" can truly wield an artist's touch with a medium so difficult as warfare in the modern age.'

'The *obsolescent* will to win?' said the FORCE officer. The datasphere whispered that he was Commander William Ajunta Lee, a naval hero of the Maui-Covenant conflict. He looked young – middle fifties perhaps – and his rank suggested that his youth was due to years of traveling between the stars rather than Poulsen.

'Of course obsolescent,' laughed Reynolds. 'Do you think a sculptor wishes to *defeat* the clay? Does a painter attack the canvas? For that matter, does an eagle or a Thomas hawk assault the sky?'

'Eagles are extinct,' grumbled Morpurgo. 'Perhaps they *should* have attacked the sky. It betrayed them.'

Reynolds turned back to me. Waiters removed his abandoned salad and brought the soup course I was finishing. 'M. Severn, you are an artist . . . an illustrator at least,' he said. 'Help me explain to these people what I mean.'

'I don't know what you mean.' While I waited for the next course, I tapped my wineglass. It was filled immediately. From the head of the table, thirty feet away, I could hear Gladstone, Hunt, and several of the relief fund chairmen laughing.

Spenser Reynolds did not look surprised at my ignorance. 'For our race to achieve the true satori, for us to move to that next level of consciousness and evolution that so many of our philosophies proclaim, *all* facets of human endeavor must become conscious strivings for art.'

General Morpurgo took a long drink and grunted. 'Including such bodily functions as eating, reproducing, and eliminating waste, I suppose.'

'Most *especially* such functions!' exclaimed Reynolds. He opened his hands, offering the long table and its many delights. 'What you see here is the animal requirement of turning dead organic compounds to energy, the base act of devouring other life, but Treetops has turned it into an *art*! Reproduction has long since replaced its crude animal origins with the essence of dance for civilized human beings. Elimination must become pure poetry!'

'I'll remember that the next time I go in to take a shit,' said Morpurgo.

Tyrena Wingreen-Feif laughed and turned to the man in red and black to her right. 'Monsignor, your church . . . Catholic, early Christian isn't it? . . . don't you have some delightful old doctrine about mankind achieving a more exalted evolutionary status?'

We all turned to look at the small, quiet man in the black robe and strange little cap. Monsignor Edouard, a representative of the almost-forgotten early Christian sect now limited to the world of Pacem and a few colony planets, was on the guest list because of his involvement with the Armaghast relief project, and until now he had been quietly applying himself to his soup. He looked up with a slightly surprised look on a face lined with decades of exposure to weather and worry. 'Why yes,' he said, 'the teachings of St Teilhard discuss an evolution toward the Omega Point.'

'And is the Omega Point similar to our Zen Gnostic idea of practical satori?' asked Sudette Chier.

Monsignor Edouard looked wistfully at his soup, as if it were more important than the conversation at that moment. 'Not really too similar,' he said. 'St Teilhard felt that all of life, every level of organic consciousness was part of a planned evolution toward ultimate mergence with the Godhead.' He frowned slightly. 'The Teilhard position has been modified much over the past eight centuries, but the common thread has been that we consider Jesus Christ to have been an incarnate example of what that ultimate consciousness might be like on the human plane.'

I cleared my throat. 'Didn't the Jesuit Paul Duré write extensively on the Teilhard hypothesis?'

Monsignor Edouard leaned forward to see around Tyrena and looked directly at me. There was surprise on that interesting face. 'Why yes,' he said, 'but I am amazed that you're familiar with the work of Father Duré.'

I returned the gaze of the man who had been Duré's friend even while exiling the Jesuit to Hyperion for apostasy. I thought of another refugee from the New Vatican, young Lenar Hoyt, lying dead in a Time Tomb while the cruciform parasites carrying the mutated DNA of both Duré and himself carried out their grim purpose of resurrection. How did the abomination of the cruciform fit into Teilhard and Duré's view of inevitable, benevolent evolution toward the Godhead?

Spenser Reynolds obviously thought that the conversation had been out of his arena for too long. 'The point *is*,' he said, his deep voice drowning out other conversation half-way down the table, 'that warfare, like religion or any other human endeavor that taps and organizes human energies on such a scale, must abandon its infantile preoccupation with *Ding an sich* literalism – usually expressed through a slavish fascination with "goals" – and revel in the artistic dimension of its own oeuvre. Now my own most recent project—'

'And what is your cult's goal, Monsignor Edouard?' Tyrena Wingreen-Feif asked, stealing the conversational ball away from Reynolds without raising her voice or shifting her gaze from the cleric.

'To help mankind to know and serve God,' he said and finished his soup with an impressive slurp. The archaic little priest looked down the table toward the projection of Councilor Albedo. 'I've heard rumors, Councilor, that the TechnoCore is pursuing an oddly similar goal. Is it true that you are attempting to build your own God?'

Albedo's smile was perfectly calculated to be friendly with no sign of condescension. 'It is no secret that elements of the Core have been working for centuries to create at least a theoretical model of a so-called artificial intelligence far beyond our own poor intellects.' He made a deprecating gesture. 'It is hardly an attempt to create God, Monsignor. More in the line of a research project exploring the possibilities your St Teilhard and Father Duré pioneered.'

'But you believe that it's possible to orchestrate your own evolution to such a higher consciousness?' asked Commander Lee, the naval hero, who had been listening attentively. 'Design an ultimate intelligence the way we once designed your crude ancestors out of silicon and microchips?'

Albedo laughed. 'Nothing so simple or grandiose, I'm afraid. And when you say "you", Commander, please remember that I am but one personality in an assemblage of intelligences no less diverse than the human beings on this planet . . . indeed, in the Web itself. The Core is no monolith. There are as many camps of philosophies, beliefs, hypotheses – *religions*, if you will – as there would be in any diverse community.' He folded his hands as if enjoying an inside joke. 'Although I prefer to think of the quest for an Ultimate Intelligence as a hobby more than a religion. Rather like building ships in a bottle, Commander, or arguing over how many angels would fit on the head of a pin, Monsignor.'

The group laughed politely, except for Reynolds who was frowning unintentionally as he no doubt pondered how to regain control of the conversation.

'And what about the rumor that the Core has built a perfect replica of Old Earth in the quest for an Ultimate Intelligence?' I asked, amazing myself with the question.

Albedo's smile did not falter, the friendly gaze did not quiver, but there was a nanosecond of *something* conveyed through the projection. What? Shock? Fury? Amusement? I had no idea. He could have communicated with me privately during that eternal second, transmitting immense quantities of data via my own Core umbilical or along the unseen corridors we have reserved for ourselves in the labyrinthine datasphere which humankind thought so simply contrived. Or he could have killed me, pulling rank with whatever gods of the Core controlled the environment for a consciousness like mine – it would have been as simple as the director of an institute calling down to order the technicians to permanently anesthetize an obnoxious laboratory mouse.

Conversation had halted up and down the table. Even Meina Gladstone and her cluster of ultra-VIPs glanced down our way.

Councilor Albedo smiled more broadly. 'What a delightfully odd rumor! Tell me, M. Severn, how does anyone . . . especially an organism such as the Core, which your own commentators have called "a disembodied bunch of brains, runaway programs that have escaped their circuits and spend most of their time pulling intellectual lint out of their nonexistent navels" . . . how does anyone build "a perfect replica of Old Earth"?'

I looked at the projection, *through* the projection, realizing for the first time that Albedo's dishes and dinner were also projected; he had been eating while we spoke.

'And,' he continued, obviously deeply amused, 'has it occurred to the promulgators of this rumor that "a perfect replica of Old Earth" would *be* Old Earth to all intents and purposes? What possible good would such an effort do in exploring the theoretical possibilities of an enhanced artificial intelligence matrix?'

When I did not answer, an uncomfortable silence settled over the entire midsection of the table.

Monsignor Edouard cleared his throat. 'It would seem,' he said, 'that any . . . ah . . . society that could produce an exact replica of any world – but especially a world destroyed these four centuries – would have no need to seek God; it would *be* God.'

'Precisely!' laughed Councilor Albedo. 'It's an insane rumor, but delightful . . . absolutely delightful!'

Relieved laughter filled the hole of silence. Spenser Reynolds began telling about his next project – an attempt to have suicides coordinate their leaps from bridges on a score of worlds while the All Thing watched – and Tyrena Wingreen-Feif stole all attention by putting her arm around Monsignor Edouard and inviting him to her after-dinner nude swimming party at her floating estate on Mare Infinitus.

I saw Councilor Albedo staring at me, turned in time to see an inquisitive glance from Leigh Hunt and the CEO, and swiveled to watch the waiters bring up the entrées on silver platters.

The dinner was excellent.

FIFTEEN

I did not go to Tyrena's nude swimming party. Nor did Spenser Reynolds, whom I last saw speaking earnestly with Sudette Chier. I do not know whether Monsignor Edouard gave in to Tyrena's enticements.

Dinner was not quite over, relief fund chairpeople were giving short speeches, and many of the more important senators had already begun to fidget when Leigh Hunt whispered to me that the CEO's party was ready to leave and my presence was requested.

It was almost 2300 hours Web standard time, and I assumed the group would be returning to Government House, but when I stepped through the one-time portal – I was the last in the party to do so except for the Praetorian bodyguards bringing up the rear of the group – I was shocked to be looking down a stone-walled corridor relieved by long windows showing a Martian sunrise.

Technically, Mars is not in the Web; the oldest extra-terrestrial colony of humankind is made deliberately difficult to reach. Zen Gnostic pilgrims traveling to the Master's Rock in Hellas Basin have to 'cast to the Home System Station and take shuttles from Ganymede or Europa to Mars. It is an inconvenience of only a few hours, but to a society where everything is literally ten steps away, it makes for a sense of sacrifice and adventure. Other than for historians and experts in brandy cactus agriculture, there are few professional reasons to be drawn to Mars. With the gradual decline of Zen Gnosticism during the past century, even the pilgrim traffic there has grown lighter. No one cares for Mars.

Except for FORCE. Although the FORCE administrative offices are on TC^2 and the bases are spread through the Web and Protectorate, Mars remains the true home of the military organization, with the Olympus Command School as the heart.

There was a small group of military VIPs waiting to greet the small group of political VIPs, and while the clusters swirled like colliding galaxies, I walked over to a window and stared.

The corridor was part of a complex carved into the upper lip of Mons Olympus, and from where we stood, some ten miles high, it felt as if one could take in half the planet with a single glance. From this point the world *was* the ancient shield volcano, and the trick of distance reduced access roads, the old city along the cliff walls, and the Tharsis Plateau slums and forests to mere squiggles in a red landscape which looked unchanged from

445

the time the first human set foot on that world, proclaimed it for a nation called Japan, and snapped a photograph.

I was watching a small sun rise, thinking *That is* the *sun*, enjoying the incredible play of light on the clouds creeping out of darkness up the side of the interminable mountainside, when Leigh Hunt stepped closer. 'The CEO will see you after the conference.' He handed me two sketchbooks which one of the aides had brought from Government House. 'You realize that everything you hear and see in this conference is highly classified?'

I did not treat the statement as a question.

Wide bronze doors opened in the stone walls, and guidelights switched on, showing the carpeted ramp and staircase leading to the War Room table in the center of a wide, black place which might have been a massive auditorium sunk in a darkness absolute except for the single, small island of illumination. Aides hurried to show the way, pull out chairs, and blend back into the shadows. With reluctance, I turned my back on the sunrise and followed our party into the pit.

General Morpurgo and a troika of other FORCE leaders handled this briefing personally. The graphics were light-years away from the crude callups and holos of the Government House briefing; we *were* in a vast space, large enough to hold all eight thousand cadets and staff when required, but now most of the blackness above us was filled with omega-quality holos and diagrams the size of freeball fields. It was frightening in a way.

So was the content of the briefing.

'We're losing this struggle in Hyperion System,' Morpurgo concluded. 'At best we will achieve a draw, with the Ouster Swarm held at bay beyond a perimeter some fifteen AU from the farcaster singularity sphere, with attrition from their small-ship raids a constant source of harassment. At worst, we will have to fall back to defensive positions while we evacuate the fleet and Hegemony citizens and allow Hyperion to fall into Ouster hands.'

'What happened to the knockout blow we were promised?' asked Senator Kolchev from his place near the head of the diamond-shaped table. 'The decisive attacks on the Swarm?'

Morpurgo cleared his throat but glanced at Admiral Nashita, who rose. The FORCE:space commander's black uniform left the illusion of only his scowling face floating in darkness. I felt a tug of *déjà vu* at the thought of that usage, but I looked back at Meina Gladstone, illuminated now by the war charts and colors floating above us like a holo-spectrum version of Damocles' famous sword, and commenced drawing again. I had put away the paper sketchpad and now used my light stylus on a flexible callup sheet.

'First, our intelligence on the Swarms was necessarily limited,' began Nashita. Graphics changed above us. 'Recon probes and long-distance scouts could not tell us the full nature of every unit in the Ouster migration fleet. The result has been an obvious and serious underestimation of actual combat strength in this particular Swarm. Our efforts to penetrate Swarm defenses, using only long-range attack fighters and torchships, have not been as successful as we had hoped.

'Second, the requirement of maintaining a secure defensive perimeter of such a magnitude in the Hyperion system has made such demands on our two operative task forces that it has been impossible to devote sufficient numbers of ships to an offensive capability at this time.'

Kolchev interrupted. 'Admiral, what I hear you saying is that you have too few ships to carry out the mission of destroying or beating off this Ouster attack on Hyperion System. Is that correct?'

Nashita stared at the senator, and I was reminded of paintings I had seen of samurai in the seconds before the killing sword was removed from its scabbard. 'That is correct, Senator Kolchev.'

'Yet in our war cabinet briefings as recently as a standard week ago, you assured us that the two task forces would be enough to protect Hyperion from invasion or destruction *and* to deliver a knockout blow to this Ouster Swarm. What happened, Admiral?'

Nashita drew himself up to his full height – greater than Morpurgo's but still shorter than Web average – and turned his gaze toward Gladstone. 'M. Executive, I have explained the variables that require an alteration in our battle plan. Shall I begin this briefing again?'

Meina Gladstone had her elbow on the table, and her right hand supported her head with two fingers against her cheek, two under her chin, and a thumb along her jawline in a posture of tired attention. 'Admiral,' she said softly, 'while I believe Senator Kolchev's question is totally pertinent, I think that the situation you have outlined in this briefing and earlier ones today answers it.' She turned toward Kolchev. 'Gabriel, we guessed wrong. With this commitment of FORCE, we get a stalemate at best. The Ousters are meaner, tougher, and more numerous than we thought.' She turned her tired gaze back toward Nashita. 'Admiral, how many more ships will you need?'

Nashita took a breath, obviously thrown off stride at being asked this question so early in the briefing. He glanced at Morpurgo and the other joint chiefs and then folded his hands in front of his crotch like a funeral director. 'Two hundred warships,' he said. '*At least* two hundred. It is a minimum number.'

A stir went through the room. I looked up from my drawing. Everyone was whispering or changing position except Gladstone. It took a second for me to understand.

The entire FORCE:space fleet of warships numbered fewer than six hundred. Of course each was hideously expensive – few planetary economies could afford to build more than one or two interstellar capital ships, and even a handful of torchships equipped with Hawking drives could bankrupt a colonial world. And each was hideously powerful: an attack carrier could destroy a world, a force of cruisers and spinship destroyers could destroy a sun. It was conceivable that the Hegemony ships already massed in the Hyperion system could – if vectored through the FORCE large transit farcaster matrix – destroy most of the star systems in the Web. It had taken fewer than fifty ships of the type Nashita was requesting to destroy the Glennon-Height fleet a century earlier and to quell the Mutiny forever.

But the real problem behind Nashita's request was the commitment of *two-thirds* of the Hegemony's fleet in the Hyperion system at one time. I could feel the anxiety flow through the politicians and policy makers like an electrical current.

Senator Richeau from Renaissance Vector cleared her throat. 'Admiral, we've never concentrated fleet forces like that before, have we?'

Nashita's head pivoted as smoothly as if it were on bearings. The scowl did not flicker. 'We have never committed ourselves to a fleet action of this importance to the future of the Hegemony, Senator Richeau.'

'Yes, I understand that,' said Richeau. 'But my question was meant to ask what impact this would have on Web defenses elsewhere. Isn't that a terrible gamble?'

Nashita grunted, and the graphics in the vast space behind him swirled, misted, and coalesced as a stunning view of the Milky Way galaxy as seen from far above the plane of the ecliptic; the angle changed as we seemed to rush at dizzying speed toward one spiral arm until the blue latticework of the farcaster web became visible, the Hegemony an irregular gold nucleus with spires and pseudopods extending into the green nimbus of the Protectorate. The Web seemed both random in design and dwarfed by the sheer size of the galaxy . . . and both of these impressions were accurate reflections of reality.

Suddenly the graphics shifted, and the Web and colonial worlds became the universe except for a spattering of a few hundred stars to give it perspective.

'These represent the position of our fleet elements at this time,' said Admiral Nashita. Amidst and beyond the gold and green, several hundred specks of intense orange appeared; the heaviest concentration was around a distant Protectorate star I recognized belatedly as Hyperion's.

'And these the Ouster Swarms as of their most recent plottings.' A dozen red lines appeared, vector signs and blue-shift tails showing the direction of travel. Even at this scale, none of the Swarm vectors appeared to intersect Hegemony space except for the Swarm – a large one – that seemed to be curving into Hyperion System.

I noticed that FORCE:space deployments frequently reflected Swarm vectors, except for clusterings near bases and troublesome worlds such as Maui-Covenant, Bressia, and Qom-Riyadh.

'Admiral,' said Gladstone, preempting any description of these deployments, 'I presume you have taken into account fleet reaction time should there be a threat to some other point on our frontier.'

Nashita's scowl twitched into something that might have been a smile. There was a hint of condescension in his voice. 'Yes, CEO. If you notice the closest Swarms besides the one at Hyperion . . .' The view zoomed toward red vectors above a gold cloud, which embraced star systems I was fairly certain included Heaven's Gate, God's Grove, and Mare Infinitus. At this scale, the Ouster threat seemed very distant indeed.

'We plot the Swarm migrations according to Hawking drive wakes picked up by listening posts in and beyond the Web. In addition, our long-distance probes verify Swarm size and direction on a frequent basis.'

'How frequent, Admiral?' asked Senator Kolchev.

'At least once every few years,' snapped the Admiral. 'You must realize that travel time is many months, even at spinship velocities, and the time-debt from our viewpoint may be as much as twelve years for such a transit.'

'With gaps of years between direct observations,' persisted the senator, 'how do you know where the Swarms are at any given time?'

'Hawking drives do not lie, Senator.' Nashita's voice was absolutely flat. 'It is impossible to simulate the Hawking distortion wake. What we are looking at is the real-time location of hundreds . . . or in the case of the larger Swarms, thousands . . . of singularity drives under way. As with fatline broadcasts, there is no time-debt for transmission of the Hawking effect.'

'Yes,' said Kolchev, his voice as flat and deadly as the Admiral's, 'but what if the Swarms were traveling at less than spinship velocities?'

Nashita actually smiled. '*Below* hyperlight velocities, Senator?'

'Yes.'

I could see Morpurgo and a few of the other military men shake their heads or hide smiles. Only the young FORCE:sea commander, William Ajunta Lee, was leaning forward attentively with a serious expression.

'At sublight velocities,' deadpanned Admiral Nashita, 'our great-great-grandchildren might have to worry about warning their grandchildren of an invasion.'

Kolchev would not desist. He stood and pointed toward where the closest Swarm curved away from the Hegemony above Heaven's Gate. 'What about if this Swarm were to approach without Hawking drives?'

Nashita sighed, obviously irritated at having the substance of the meeting suborned by irrelevancies. 'Senator, I assure you that if that Swarm turned off their drives *now*, and turned toward the Web *now*, it would be' – Nashita's eyes blinked as he consulted his implants and comm links – 'two hundred and thirty standard years before they approached our frontiers. It is not a factor in this decision, Senator.'

Meina Gladstone leaned forward, and all eyes shifted toward her. I stored my previous sketch in the callup and started a new one.

'Admiral, it seems to me the real concern here is both the unprecedented nature of this concentration of forces near Hyperion and the fact that we're putting all of our eggs in one basket.'

There was a murmur of amusement around the table. Gladstone was famous for aphorisms, stories, and clichés so old and forgotten that they were brand-new. This might have been one of them.

'*Are* we putting all of our eggs in one basket?' she continued.

Nashita stepped forward and set his hands on the table, long fingers extended, pressing down with great intensity. That intensity matched the power of the small man's personality; he was one of those rare individuals who commanded others' attention and obedience without effort. 'No, CEO, we are not.' Without turning, he gestured toward the display above and behind him. 'The closest Swarms could not approach Hegemony space without a warning time of two months in Hawking drive . . . that is *three years* of our time. It would take our fleet units in Hyperion – even assuming they were widely deployed and in a combat situation – less than *five hours* to fall back and translate anywhere in the Web.'

'That does not include fleet units beyond the Web,' said Senator Richeau. 'The colonies cannot be left unprotected.'

Nashita gestured again. 'The two hundred warships we will call in to make the Hyperion campaign decisive are those already within the Web or those carrying JumpShip farcaster capabilities. None of the independent fleet units assigned to the colonies will be affected.'

Gladstone nodded. 'But what if the Hyperion portal were damaged or seized by the Ousters?'

From the shifting, nodding, and exhalations from the civilians around the table, I guessed that she had hit upon the major concern.

Nashita nodded and strode back to the small dais as if this were the question he had been anticipating and was pleased irrelevancies were at an end. 'Excellent question,' he said. 'It has been mentioned in previous briefings, but I will cover this possibility in some detail.'

'First, we have redundancy in our farcaster capability, with no fewer than two JumpShips in-system at this time and plans for three more when the reinforced task force arrives. The chances of all five of these ships being destroyed are very, very small . . . almost insignificant when one considers our enhanced defensive capabilities with the reinforced task force.

'Second, chances of the Ousters seizing an intact military farcaster and using it to invade the Web are nil. Each ship . . . each *individual* . . . that transits a FORCE portal must be identified by tamperproof, coded micro-transponders, which are updated daily—'

'Couldn't the Ousters break these codes . . . insert their own?' asked Senator Kolchev.

'Impossible.' Nashita was striding back and forth on the small dais, hands behind his back. 'The updating of codes is done daily via fatline one-time pads from FORCE headquarters within the Web—'

'Excuse me,' I said, amazed to hear my own voice here, 'but I made a brief visit to Hyperion System this morning and was aware of no codes.'

Heads turned. Admiral Nashita again carried out his successful impression of an owl turning its head on frictionless bearings. 'Nonetheless, M. Severn,' he said, 'you and M. Hunt were encoded – painlessly and unobtrusively by infrared lasers, at both ends of the farcaster transit.'

I nodded, amazed for a second that the Admiral had remembered my name until I realized that he also had implants.

'Third,' continued Nashita as if I had not spoken, 'should the impossible happen and Ouster forces overwhelm our defenses, capture our farcasters intact, circumvent the failsafe transit code systems, and activate a technology with which they are not familiar, and which we have denied them for more than four centuries . . . then all their efforts would still be for naught, because all military traffic is being routed to Hyperion via the base at Madhya.'

'Where?' came a chorus of voices.

I had heard of Madhya only through Brawne Lamia's tale of her client's death. Both she and Nashita pronounced it 'mud-ye'.

'Madhya,' repeated Admiral Nashita, smiling now in earnest. It was an oddly boyish smile. 'Do not query your comlogs, gentlemen and ladies. Madhya is a "black" system, not found in any inventories or civilian farcaster charts. We reserve it for just such purposes. With only one habitable planet, fit only for mining and our bases, Madhya is the ultimate fallback position. Should Ouster warships do the impossible and breach our defenses and portals in Hyperion, the *only* place they can go is Madhya, where significant amounts of automated firepower are directed toward anything and everything that comes through. Should the impossible be squared and their fleet survive transit to the Madhya system, outgoing farcaster connections would automatically self-destruct, and their warships would be stranded years from the Web.'

'Yes,' said Senator Richeau, 'but so would ours. Two thirds of our fleet would be left in Hyperion System.'

Nashita stood at parade rest. 'This is true,' he said, 'and certainly the joint chiefs and I have weighed the consequences of this remote . . . one would have to say statistically impossible . . . event many times. We find the risks acceptable. Should the impossible happen, we still would have more than two hundred warships in reserve to defend the Web. At worst, we would have lost the Hyperion system after dealing a terrible blow to the Ousters . . . one which would, in and of itself, almost certainly deter any future aggression.'

'*But this is not the outcome me anticipate.* With two hundred warships transferred soon – within the next eight standard hours – our predictors and the AI Advisory Council predictors . . . see a 99 percent probability of total defeat of the aggressive Ouster Swarm, with inconsequential losses to our forces.'

Meina Gladstone turned toward Councilor Albedo. In the low light the projection was perfect. 'Councilor, I did not know the Advisory Group had been asked this question. Is the 99 percent probability figure reliable?'

Albedo smiled. 'Quite reliable, CEO. And the probability factor was 99.962794 percent.' The smile broadened. 'Quite reassuring enough to have one put all one's eggs into one basket for a short while.'

Gladstone did not smile. 'Admiral, how long after you get the reinforcements do you see the fighting going on?'

'One standard week, CEO. At the most.'

Gladstone's left eyebrow rose slightly. 'So short a time?'

'Yes, CEO.'

'General Morpurgo? Thoughts from FORCE:ground?'

'We concur, CEO. Reinforcement is necessary, and at once. Transports will carry approximately a hundred thousand Marines and ground troops for the mopping up in the remnants of the Swarm.'

'In seven standard days or less?'

'Yes, CEO.'

'Admiral Singh?'

'Absolutely necessary, CEO.'

'General Van Zeidt?'

One by one, Gladstone polled the joint chiefs and top-ranking military there, even asking the commandant of the Olympus Command School, who swelled with pride at being consulted. One by one, she received their unequivocal advice to reinforce.

'Commander Lee?'

All gazes shifted toward the young naval officer. I noticed the stiffness of posture and scowls of the senior military men and suddenly realized that Lee was there at the invitation of the CEO rather than the benevolence of his superiors. I remembered that Gladstone had been quoted as saying that young Commander Lee showed the kind of initiative and intelligence which FORCE had sometimes lacked. I suspected that the man's career was forfeit for attending this meeting.

Commander William Ajunta Lee shifted uncomfortably in his comfortable chair. 'With all due respect, CEO, I'm a mere junior naval officer and am not qualified to give an opinion on matters of such strategic importance.'

Gladstone did not smile. Her nod was almost imperceptible. 'I appreciate that, Commander. I am sure your superiors here do also. However, in this case, I wonder if you would indulge me and comment on the issue at hand.'

Lee sat upright. For an instant his eyes held both conviction and the desperation of a small, trapped animal. 'Well then, CEO, if I must comment, I have to say that my own instincts – and they are only instincts: I am profoundly ignorant of interstellar tactics – would advise me against this reinforcement.' Lee took a breath. 'This is a purely military assessment, CEO. I know nothing of the political ramifications of defending Hyperion System.'

Gladstone leaned forward. 'Then on a purely military basis, Commander, why do you oppose the reinforcements?'

From where I sat half a table away, I could feel the impact of the FORCE chiefs' gazes like one of the one-hundred-million-joule laser blasts used to ignite deuterium-tritium spheres in one of the ancient inertial confinement fusion reactors. I was amazed that Lee did not collapse, implode, ignite, and fuse before our very eyes.

'On a military basis,' Lee said, his eyes hopeless but his voice steady, 'the two biggest sins one can commit are to divide one's forces and to . . . as you put it, CEO . . . put all of your eggs in a single basket. And in this case, the basket is not even of our own making.'

Gladstone nodded and sat back, steepling her fingers beneath her lower lip.

'*Commander*,' said General Morpurgo, and I discovered that a word could, indeed, be spat, 'now that we have the benefit of your . . . advice . . . could I ask if you have ever been involved in a space battle?'

'No, sir.'

'Have you ever been *trained* for a space battle, Commander?'

'Except for the minimal amount required in OCS, which amounts to a few history courses, no, sir, I have not.'

'Have you ever been involved in *any* strategic planning above the level of . . . how many naval surface ships did you command on Maui-Covenant, Commander?'

'One, sir.'

'One,' breathed Morpurgo. 'A large ship, Commander?'

'No, sir.'

'Were you given command of this ship, Commander? Did you earn it? Or did it fall to you through the vicissitudes of war?'

'Our captain was killed, sir. I took command by default. It was the final naval action of the Maui-Covenant campaign and—'

'That will be all, *Commander*.' Morpurgo turned his back on the war hero and addressed the CEO. 'Do you wish to poll us again, ma'am?'

Gladstone shook her head.

Senator Kolchev cleared his throat. 'Perhaps we should have a closed cabinet meeting at Government House.'

'No need,' said Meina Gladstone. 'I've decided. Admiral Singh, you are authorized to divert as many fleet units to the Hyperion system as you and the joint chiefs see fit.'

'Yes, CEO.'

'Admiral Nashita, I will expect a successful termination of hostilities within one standard week of the time you have adequate reinforcements.' She looked around the table. 'Ladies and gentlemen, I cannot stress to you enough the importance of our possession of Hyperion and the deterrent of Ouster threats once and for all.' She rose and walked to the base of the ramp leading up and out into the darkness. 'Good evening, gentlemen, ladies.'

It was almost 0400 hours Web and Tau Ceti Center time when Hunt rapped at my door. I had been fighting sleep for the three hours since we 'cast back. I had just decided that Gladstone had forgotten about me and was beginning to doze when the knock came.

'The garden,' said Leigh Hunt, 'and for God's sake tuck your shirt in.'

My boots made soft noises on the fine gravel of the path as I wandered the dark lanes. The lanterns and glow-globes barely emitted light. The stars were not visible above the courtyard because of the glare of TC^2's interminable cities, but the running lights of the orbital habitations moved across the sky like an endless ring of fireflies.

Gladstone was sitting on the iron bench near the bridge.

'M. Severn,' she said, her voice low, 'thank you for joining me. I apologize for it being so late. The cabinet meeting just broke up.'

I said nothing and remained standing.

'I wanted to ask about your visit to Hyperion this morning.' She chuckled in the darkness. 'Yesterday morning. Did you have any impressions?'

I wondered what she meant. My guess was that the woman had an insatiable appetite for data, no matter how seemingly irrelevant. 'I did meet someone,' I said.

'Oh?'

'Yes, Dr Melio Arundez. He was . . . is . . .'

'. . . a friend of M. Weintraub's daughter,' finished Gladstone. 'The child who is aging backward. Do you have any updates on her condition?'

'Not really,' I said. 'I had a brief nap today, but the dreams were fragmented.'

'And what did the meeting with Dr Arundez accomplish?'

I rubbed my chin with fingers suddenly gone cold. 'His research team has been waiting in the capital for months,' I said. 'They may be our only hope for understanding what's going on with the Tombs. And the Shrike . . .'

'Our predictors say that it is important that the pilgrims be left alone until their act is played out,' came Gladstone's voice in the darkness. She seemed to be looking to the side, toward the stream.

I felt sudden, inexplicable, implacable anger surge through me. 'Father Hoyt is already "played out",' I said more sharply than I intended. 'They could have saved him if the ship had been allowed to rendezvous with the pilgrims. Arundez and his people might be able to save the baby – Rachel – even though there are only a few days left.'

'Less than three days,' said Gladstone. 'Was there anything else? Any impressions of the planet or Admiral Nashita's command ship which you found . . . interesting?'

My hands clenched into fists, relaxed. 'You won't allow Arundez to fly up to the Tombs?'

'Not now, no.'

'What about the evacuation of civilians from Hyperion? At least the Hegemony citizens?'

'That is not a possibility at this time.'

I started to say something, checked myself. I stared at the sound of the water beneath the bridge.

'No other impressions, M. Severn?'

'No.'

'Well, I wish you a good night and pleasant dreams. Tomorrow may be a very hectic day, but I do want to talk to you about those dreams at some point.'

'Good night,' I said and turned on my heel and walked quickly back to my wing of Government House.

In the darkness of my room, I called up a Mozart sonata and took three trisecobarbitals. Most probably they would knock me out in a drugged, dreamless sleep, where the ghost of dead Johnny Keats and his even more ghostly pilgrims could not find me. It meant disappointing Meina Gladstone, and that did not dismay me in the least.

I thought of Swift's sailor, Gulliver, and his disgust with mankind after his return from the land of the intelligent horse – the Houyhnhnms – a disgust with his own species which grew to the point that he had to sleep in the stables with the horses just to be reassured by their smell and presence.

My last thought before sleep was *To hell with Meina Gladstone, to hell with the war, and to hell with the Web.*

And to hell with dreams.

PART TWO

SIXTEEN

Brawne Lamia slept fitfully just before dawn, and her dreams were filled with images and sounds from elsewhere – half-heard and little-understood conversations with Meina Gladstone, a room that seemed to be floating in space, a movement of men and women along corridors where the walls whispered like a poorly tuned fatline receiver – and underlying the feverish dreams and random images was the maddening sense that Johnny – her Johnny – was so close, *so close*. Lamia cried out in her sleep, but the noise was lost in the random echoes of the Sphinx's cooling stones and shifting sands.

Lamia awoke suddenly, coming completely conscious as surely as a solid-state instrument switching on. Sol Weintraub had been supposed to be standing guard, but now he slept near the low door of the room where the group sheltered. His infant daughter, Rachel, slept between blankets on the floor next to him; her rump was raised, face pressed against the blanket, a slight bubble of saliva on her lips.

Lamia looked around. In the dim illumination from a low-wattage glow-globe and the faint daylight reflected down four meters of corridor, only one other of her fellow pilgrims was visible, a dark bundle on the stone floor. Martin Silenus lay there snoring. Lamia felt a surge of fear, as if she had been abandoned while sleeping. Silenus, Sol, the baby . . . she realized that only the Consul was missing. Attrition had eaten at the pilgrimage party of seven adults and an infant: Het Masteen, missing on the wind-wagon crossing of the Sea of Grass; Lenar Hoyt killed the night before; Kassad missing later that night . . . the Consul . . . where was the Consul?

Brawne Lamia looked around again, satisfied herself that the dark room held nothing but packs, blanket bundles, the sleeping poet, scholar and child, and then she rose, found her father's automatic pistol amidst the tumble of blankets, felt in her pack for the neural stunner, and then slipped past Weintraub and the baby into the corridor beyond.

It was morning and so bright out that Lamia had to shield her eyes with her hand as she stepped from the Sphinx's stone steps on to the hard-packed trail which led away down the valley. The storm had passed. Hyperion's skies were a deep, crystalline lapis lazuli shot through with green, Hyperion's star, a brilliant white point source just rising above the eastern cliff walls. Rock shadows blended with the outflung silhouettes of the Time Tombs across the valley floor. The Jade Tomb sparkled. Lamia could see the fresh drifts and dunes deposited by the storm, white and vermilion sands blending in sensuous curves and striations around stone. There was no evidence of their campsite the night before. The Consul sat on a rock ten meters down the hill. He was gazing down the valley, and smoke spiraled upward from his pipe. Slipping the pistol in her pocket with the stunner, Lamia walked down the hill to him.

'No sign of Colonel Kassad,' said the Consul as she approached. He did not turn around.

Lamia looked down the valley to where the Crystal Monolith stood. Its once-gleaming surface was pocked and pitted, the upper twenty or thirty meters appeared to be missing, and debris still smoked at its base. The half kilometer or so between the Sphinx and the Monolith was scorched and cratered. 'It looks as if he didn't leave without a fight,' she said.

The Consul grunted. The pipe smoke made Lamia hungry. 'I searched as far as the Shrike Palace, two klicks down the valley,' said the Consul. 'The locus of the firefight seems to have been the Monolith. There's still no sign of a ground-level opening to the thing but there are enough holes farther up now so that you can see the honeycomb pattern which deep radar has always shown inside.'

'But no sign of Kassad?'

'None.'

'Blood? Scorched bones? A note saying that he'd be back after delivering his laundry?'

'Nothing.'

Brawne Lamia sighed and sat on a boulder near the Consul's rock. The sun was warm on her skin. She squinted out toward the opening to the valley. 'Well, hell,' she said, 'what do we do next?'

The Consul removed his pipe, frowned at it, and shook his head. 'I tried the comlog relay again this morning, but the ship is still penned in.' He shook ashes out. 'Tried the emergency bands too, but obviously we're not getting through. Either the ship isn't relaying, or people have orders not to respond.'

'Would you really leave?'

The Consul shrugged. He had changed from his diplomatic finery of the day before into a rough wool pullover tunic top, gray whipcord trousers, and high boots. 'Having the ship here would give us – you – the option of leaving. I wish the others would consider going. After all, Masteen's missing, Hoyt and Kassad are gone . . . I'm not sure what to do next.'

A deep voice said, 'We could try making breakfast.'

Lamia turned to watch Sol come down the path. Rachel was in the infant carrier on the scholar's chest. Sunlight glinted on the older man's balding head. 'Not a bad idea,' she said. 'Do we have enough provisions left?'

'Enough for breakfast,' said Weintraub. 'Then a few more meals of cold foodpaks from the Colonel's extra provisions bag. Then we'll be eating googlepedes and each other.'

The Consul attempted a smile, set the pipe back in his tunic pocket. 'I suggest we walk back to Chronos Keep before we reach that point. We'd used up the freeze-dried foods from the *Benares*, but there were storerooms at the Keep.'

'I'd be happy to—' began Lamia but was interrupted by a shout from inside the Sphinx.

She was the first to reach the Sphinx, and she had the automatic pistol in her hand before she went through the entrance. The corridor was dark, the sleeping room darker, and it took a second for her to realize that no one was there. Brawne Lamia crouched, swinging the pistol toward the dark curve of corridor even as Silenus's voice again shouted 'Hey! Come here!' from somewhere out of sight.

She looked over her shoulder as the Consul came through the entrance.

'Wait there!' snapped Lamia and moved quickly down the corridor, staying against the wall, pistol extended, propulsion charge primed, safety off. She paused at the open doorway to the small room where Hoyt's body lay, crouched, swung around and in with weapon tracking.

Martin Silenus looked up from where he crouched by the corpse. The fiberplastic sheet they had used to cover the priest's body lay crumpled and lifted in Silenus's hand. He stared at Lamia, looked without interest at the gun, and gazed back at the body. 'Do you believe this?' he said softly.

Lamia lowered the weapon and came closer. Behind them, the Consul peered in. Brawne could hear Sol Weintraub in the corridor; the baby was crying.

'My God,' said Brawne Lamia and crouched next to the body of Father Lenar Hoyt. The young priest's pain-ravaged features had been resculpted into the face of a man in his late sixties: high brow, long aristocratic nose, thin lips with a pleasant upturn at the corners, sharp cheekbones, sharp ears under a fringe of gray hair, large eyes under lids as pale and thin as parchment.

The Consul crouched near them. 'I've seen holos. It's Father Paul Duré.'

'Look,' said Martin Silenus. He lowered the sheet further, paused, and then rolled the corpse on its side. Two small cruciforms on this man's chest pulsed pinkly, just as Hoyt's had, but his back was bare.

Sol stood by the door, hushing Rachel's cries with gentle bouncing and whispered syllables. When the infant was silent, he said, 'I thought that the Bikura took three days to . . . regenerate.'

Martin Silenus sighed. 'The Bikura have been resurrected by the cruciform parasites for more than two standard centuries. Perhaps it's easier the first time.'

'Is he . . .' began Lamia.

'Alive?' Silenus took her hand. 'Feel.'

The man's chest rose and fell ever so slightly. The skin was warm to the touch. Heat from the cruciforms under the skin was palpable. Brawne Lamia snatched her hand back.

The thing that had been the corpse of Father Lenar Hoyt six hours earlier opened its eyes.

'Father Duré?' said Sol, stepping forward.

The man's head turned. He blinked as though the dim light hurt his eyes, then made an unintelligible noise.

'Water,' said the Consul and reached into his tunic pocket for the small plastic bottle he carried. Martin Silenus held the man's head while the Consul helped him drink.

Sol came closer, went to one knee, and touched the man's forearm. Even Rachel's dark eyes seemed curious. Sol said, 'If you can't speak, blink twice for "yes", once for "no". Are you Duré?'

The man's head swiveled toward the scholar. 'Yes,' he said softly, his voice deep, tones cultured, 'I am Father Paul Duré.'

Breakfast consisted of the last of the coffee, bits of meat fried over the unfolded heating unit, a scoop of grain mixed with rehydrated milk, and the end of their last loaf of bread, torn into five chunks. Lamia thought that it was delicious.

They sat at the edge of shade under the Sphinx's outflung wing, using a low, flat-topped boulder as their table. The sun climbed toward mid-morning, and the sky remained cloudless. There was no sound except for the occasional klink of a fork or spoon and the soft tones of their conversation.

'You remember . . . before?' asked Sol. The priest wore an extra set of the Consul's shipclothes, a gray jumpsuit with the Hegemony seal on the left breast. The uniform was a bit too small.

Duré held the cup of coffee in both hands, as if he were about to lift it for consecration. He looked up, and his eyes suggested depths of intelligence and sadness in equal measure. 'Before I died?' said Duré. The patrician lips sketched a smile. 'Yes, I remember. I remember the exile, the Bikura . . .' He looked down. 'Even the tesla tree.'

'Hoyt told us about the tree,' said Brawne Lamia. The priest had nailed himself on to an active tesla tree in the flame forests, suffering *years* of agony, death, resurrection, and death again rather than give in to the easy symbiosis of life under the cruciform.

Duré shook his head. 'I thought . . . in those last seconds . . . that I had beaten it.'

'You had,' said the Consul. 'Father Hoyt and the others found you. You had driven the thing out of your body. Then the Bikura planted your cruciform on Lenar Hoyt.'

Duré nodded. 'And there is no sign of the body?'

Martin Silenus pointed toward the man's chest. 'Evidently the fucking thing can't defy laws governing conservation of mass. Hoyt's pain had been so great for so long – he wouldn't return to where the thing wanted him to go – that he never gained the weight for a . . . what the hell would you call it? A double resurrection.'

'It doesn't matter,' said Duré. His smile was sad. 'The DNA parasite in the cruciform has infinite patience. It will reconstitute one host for generations if need be. Sooner or later, both parasites will have a home.'

'Do you remember anything after the tesla tree?' asked Sol quietly.

Duré sipped the last of his coffee. 'Of death? Of heaven or hell?' The smile was genuine. 'No, gentlemen and lady, I wish I could say I did. I remember pain . . . eternities of pain . . . and then release. And then darkness. And then awakening here. How many years did you say have passed?'

'Almost twelve,' said the Consul. 'But only about half that for Father Hoyt. He spent time in transit.'

Father Duré stood, stretched, and paced back and forth. He was a tall man, thin but with a sense of strength about him, and Brawne Lamia found herself impressed by his presence, by that strange, inexplicable charisma of personality which had cursed and bestowed power upon a few individuals since time immemorial. She had to remind herself that, first, he was a priest of a cult that demanded celibacy from its clerics, and, second, an hour earlier he had been a corpse. Lamia watched the older man pace up and down, his movements as elegant and relaxed as a cat's, and she realized that both observations were true but neither could counteract the personal magnetism the priest radiated. She wondered if the men sensed it.

Duré sat on a boulder, stretched his legs straight ahead of him, and rubbed at his thighs as if trying to get rid of a cramp. 'You've told me something about who you are . . . why you are here,' he said. 'Can you tell me more?'

The pilgrims glanced at one another.

Duré nodded. 'Do you think that I'm a monster myself? Some agent of the Shrike? I wouldn't blame you if you did.'

'We don't think that,' said Brawne Lamia. 'The Shrike needs no agents to do his bidding. Besides, we know you from Father Hoyt's story about you and from your journals.' She glanced at the others. 'We found it . . . difficult . . . to tell our stories of why we have come to Hyperion. It would be all but impossible to repeat them.'

'I made notes on my comlog,' said the Consul. 'They're very condensed, but it should make some sense out of our histories . . . and the history of the last decade of the Hegemony. Why the Web is at war with the Ousters. That sort of thing. You're welcome to access it if you wish. It shouldn't take more than an hour.'

'I would appreciate it,' said Father Duré and followed the Consul back into the Sphinx.

Brawne Lamia, Sol, and Silenus walked to the head of the valley. From the saddle between the low cliffs, they could see the dunes and barrens stretching toward the mountains of the Bridle Range, less than ten klicks to the southwest. The broken globes, soft spires, and shattered gallerias of the dead City of Poets were visible only two or three klicks to their right, along a broad ridge which the desert was quietly invading.

'I'll walk back to the Keep and find some rations,' said Lamia.

'I hate to split up the group,' said Sol. 'We could all return.'

Martin Silenus folded his arms. 'Somebody should stay here in case the Colonel returns.'

'Before anyone leaves,' said Sol, 'I think we should search the rest of the valley. The Consul didn't check far beyond the Monolith this morning.'

'I agree,' said Lamia. 'Let's get to it before it gets too late. I want to get provisions at the Keep and return before nightfall.'

They had descended to the Sphinx when Duré and the Consul emerged. The priest held the Consul's spare comlog in one hand. Lamia explained the plan for a search, and the two men agreed to join them.

Once again they walked the halls of the Sphinx, the beams from their hand torches and pencil lasers illuminating sweating stone and bizarre angles. Emerging into noontime sunlight, they made the three-hundred-meter hike to the Jade Tomb. Lamia found herself shivering as they entered the room where the Shrike had appeared the night before. Hoyt's blood had left a rust-brown stain on the green ceramic floor. There was no sign of the transparent opening to the labyrinth below. There was no sign of the Shrike.

The Obelisk had no rooms, merely a central shaft in which a spiral ramp, too steep for human comfort, twisted upward between ebony walls. Even whispers echoed here, and the group kept talk to a minimum. There were no windows, no view, at the top of the ramp, fifty meters above the stone floor, and their torch beams illuminated only blackness as the roof curved in above them. Fixed ropes and chains left over from two centuries of tourism allowed them to descend without undue fear of a slip and fall that would end in death below. As they paused at the entrance, Martin Silenus called Kassad's name a final time, and the echoes followed them into sunlight.

They spent half an hour or more inspecting the damage near the Crystal Monolith. Puddles of sand turned to glass, some five to ten meters across, prismed the noonday light and reflected heat in their faces. The broken face of the Monolith, pocked now with holes and still-dangling strands of melted crystal, looked like the target of an act of mindless vandalism, but each knew that Kassad must have been fighting for his life. There was no door, no opening to the honeycomb maze within. Instruments told them that the interior was as empty and unconnected as it always had been. They left reluctantly, climbing the steep trails to the base of the north cliffs where the Cave Tombs lay separated by less than a hundred meters each.

'Early archaeologists thought that these were the oldest of the Tombs because of their crudeness,' said Sol as they entered the first cave, sent flashlight beams playing across stone carved in a thousand indecipherable patterns. None of the caves was deeper than thirty or forty meters. Each ended in a stone wall that no amount of probing or radar imaging had ever discovered an extension to.

Upon exiting the third Cave Tomb, the group sat in what little shade they could find and shared water and protein biscuits from Kassad's extra field rations. The wind had risen, and now it sighed and whispered through fluted rock high above them.

'We're not going to find him,' said Martin Silenus. 'The fucking Shrike took him.'

Sol was feeding the baby with one of the last nursing paks. The top of her head had been turned pink by the sun despite Sol's every effort to shield her as they walked outside. 'He could be in one of the Tombs we were in,' he said, 'if there are sections out of time-phase with us. That's Arundez's theory. He sees the Tombs as four-dimensional constructs with intricate folds through space-time.'

'Great,' said Lamia. 'So even if Fedmahn Kassad is there, we won't see him.'

'Well,' said the Consul, getting to his feet with a tired sigh, 'let's at least go through the motions. One tomb left.'

The Shrike Palace was a kilometer farther down the valley, lower than the others and hidden by a bend in the cliff walls. The structure was not large, smaller than the Jade Tomb, but its intricate construction – flanges, spires, buttresses, and support columns arching and arcing in controlled chaos – made it seem larger than it was.

The interior of the Shrike Palace was one echoing chamber with an irregular floor made up of thousands of curving, jointed segments which reminded Lamia of the ribs and vertebrae of some fossilized creature. Fifteen meters overhead, the dome was crisscrossed by dozens of the chrome 'blades' which continued through walls and each other to emerge as steel-tipped thorns above the structure. The material of the dome itself was slightly opaque, giving a rich, milky hue to the vaulted space.

Lamia, Silenus, the Consul, Weintraub, and Duré all began to shout for Kassad, their voices echoing and resonating to no avail.

'No sign of Kassad or Het Masteen,' said the Consul as they emerged. 'Perhaps this will be the pattern . . . each of us disappearing until only one remains.'

'And does that final one get his or her wish as the Shrike Cult legends foretell?' asked Brawne Lamia. She sat on the rocky hearth to the Shrike Palace, her short legs dangling in air.

Paul Duré raised his face to the sky. 'I can't believe that it was Father Hoyt's wish that he would die so that I could live again.'

Martin Silenus squinted up at the priest. 'So what would your wish be, Padre?'

Duré did not hesitate. 'I would wish . . . pray . . . that God will lift the scourge of these twin obscenities – the war and the Shrike – from mankind once and for all.'

There was a silence in which the early afternoon wind inserted its distant sighs and moans. 'In the meantime,' said Brawne Lamia, 'we've got to get some food or learn how to subsist on air.'

Duré nodded. 'Why did you bring so little with you?'

Martin Silenus laughed and said loudly:

'Ne cared he for wine, or half-and-half,
Ne cared he for fish or flesh or fowl,
And sauces held he worthless as the chaff;
He 'sdained the swine-herd at the wassail-bowl,
Ne with lewd ribbalds sat he cheek by jowl,
Ne with sly Lemans in the scorner's chair,
But after water-brooks this Pilgrim's soul
Panted, and all his food was woodland air
Though he would oft-times feast on gillyflowers rare.'

Duré smiled, obviously still puzzled.

'We all expected to triumph or die the first night,' said the Consul. 'We hadn't anticipated a long stay here.'

Brawne Lamia stood and brushed off her trousers. 'I'm going,' she said. 'I should be able to carry back four or five days' rations if they're field foodpaks or the bulk-stored items we saw.'

'I'll go too,' said Martin Silenus.

There was a silence. During the week of their pilgrimage, the poet and Lamia had almost come to blows half a dozen times. Once she had threatened to kill the man. She looked at him for a long moment. 'All right,' she said at last. 'Let's stop by the Sphinx to get our packs and water bottles.'

The group moved up the valley as the shadows began to grow from the western walls.

SEVENTEEN

Twelve hours earlier, Colonel Fedmahn Kassad stepped off the spiral stair-case on to the highest remaining level of the Crystal Monolith. Flames rose on all sides. Through gaps he had inflicted on the crystal surface of the structure, Kassad could see darkness. The storm blew vermilion dust through the apertures until it filled the air like powdered blood. Kassad pulled his helmet on.

Ten paces in front of him, Moneta awaited.

She was nude under the energy skinsuit, and the effect was of quicksilver poured directly on flesh. Kassad could see the flames reflected in the curves of breast and thigh, the bend of light into the hollow of throat and navel. Her neck was long, her face chrome-carved in perfect smoothness. Her eyes held twin reflections of the tall shadow that was Fedmahn Kassad.

Kassad raised the assault rifle and clicked the selector manually to full-spectrum fire. Inside his activated impact armor, his body clenched in anticipation of attack.

Moneta moved her hand, and the skinsuit faded from the crown of her head to her neck. She was vulnerable now. Kassad felt that he knew every facet of that face, every pore and follicle. Her brown hair was cut short, falling softly to the left. The eyes were the same, large, curious, startling in their green depths. The small mouth with the full underlip still hesitated on the edge of a smile. He noted the slightly inquisitive arch of eyebrows, the small ears he had kissed and whispered in so many times. The soft throat where he had lain his cheek to listen to her pulse.

Kassad raised the rifle and aimed it at her.

'Who are you?' she asked. Her voice was as soft and sensual as he remembered, the slight accent as elusive.

His finger on the trigger, Kassad paused. They had made love scores of times, known each other for years in his dreams and their lovers' landscape of the military simulations. But if she were truly moving backward in time . . .

'I know,' she said, her voice calm, apparently unaware of the pressure he had already begun to exert on the trigger, 'you are the one whom the Lord of Pain has promised.'

Kassad was gasping for air. When he spoke, his voice was raw and very strained. 'You don't remember me?'

'No.' She cocked her head to look at him quizzically. 'But the Lord of Pain has promised a warrior. We were destined to meet.'

'We met long ago,' managed Kassad. The rifle would automatically aim for the face, shifting wavelengths and frequencies every microsecond until the skinsuit defenses were defeated. Along with the hellwhip and laser beams, fléchettes and pulse bolts would be fired an instant later.

'I have no memory of long ago,' she said. 'We move in opposite directions along the general flow of time. What name do you know me by in my future, your past?'

'Moneta,' gasped Kassad, willing his straining hand and finger to fire.

She smiled, nodded. 'Moneta. The child of Memory. There is a crude irony there.'

Kassad remembered her betrayal, the *changing* as they made love that last time in the sands above the dead City of Poets. She had either become the Shrike or allowed the Shrike to take her place. It had turned an act of love into an obscenity.

Colonel Kassad pulled the trigger.

Moneta blinked. 'It will not work here. Not within the Crystal Monolith. Why do you wish to kill me?'

Kassad growled, threw the useless weapon across the landing, directed power to his gauntlets, and charged.

Moneta made no move to escape. She watched him charge the ten paces; his head was down, his impact armor moaning as it changed the crystal alignment of polymers, and Kassad was screaming. She lowered her arms to meet the charge.

Kassad's speed and mass knocked Moneta off her feet and sent both of them tumbling, Kassad trying to get his gauntleted hands on her throat, Moneta holding his wrists in a vise-strong grip as they rolled across the landing to the edge of the platform. Kassad rolled on top of her, trying to let gravity add to the force of his attack, arms straight, gauntlets rigid, fingers curved in a killing cusp. His left leg hung over the sixty-meter drop to the dark floor below.

'Why do you want to kill me?' whispered Moneta, and rolled him to one side, tumbling both of them off the platform.

Kassad screamed and flipped down his visor with a snap of his head. They tumbled through space, their legs entwined around each other's bodies in fierce scissors grips, Kassad's hands held at bay by her death hold on his wrists. Time seemed to decelerate until they fell in slow motion, the air moving across Kassad like a blanket being pulled slowly over his face. Then time accelerated, grew normal: they were falling the last ten meters. Kassad shouted and visualized the proper symbol to let his impact armor go rigid; and there was a terrible crash.

From a blood-red distance, Fedmahn Kassad fought to the surface of consciousness, knowing that only a second or two had elapsed since they had struck the ground. He staggered to his feet. Moneta was also rising slowly, on one bent knee now, staring at the ground where the ceramic floor had been shattered by their fall.

Kassad sent power to the servomechanisms in his suit leg and kicked at her head with full force.

Moneta dodged the blow, caught his leg, twisted, and sent him crashing into the three-meter square of crystal, shattering it, tumbling him out into the sand and the night. Moneta touched her neck, her face flowed with quicksilver, and she stepped out after him.

Kassad flipped up his shattered visor, removed the helmet. The wind tousled his short, black hair, and sand grated against his cheeks. He got to his knees, his feet. Telltales in the suit's collar display were blinking red, announcing the last reservoirs of power draining away. Kassad ignored the alarms; there would be enough for the next several seconds . . . and that would be all that mattered.

'Whatever happened in my future . . . your past,' said Moneta, 'it was not I who changed. I am not the Lord of Pain. He—'

Kassad jumped the three meters that separated them, landed *behind* Moneta, and brought the killing gauntlet on his right hand around in an arc that broke the sound barrier, palm-edge rigid and sharp as carbon-carbon piezoelectric filaments could make it.

Moneta did not duck or attempt to block the attack. Kassad's gauntlet caught the base of her neck in a blow which would have severed a tree, carved through half a meter of stone. On Bressia, in hand-to-hand combat in the capital of Buckminster, Kassad had killed an Ouster colonel so quickly – his gauntlet cutting through impact armor, helmet, personal forcefield, flesh and bone without pause – that the man's head had blinked up at his own body for twenty seconds before death claimed him.

Kassad's blow struck true but stopped at the surface of the quicksilver skinsuit. Moneta did not stagger or react. Kassad felt his suit power fail at the same instant his arm went numb, his shoulder muscles wrenching in agony. He staggered back, his right arm dead at his side, the suit power draining like blood from an injured man.

'You don't listen,' said Moneta. She stepped forward, grabbed Kassad by the front of his combat suit, and threw him twenty meters toward the Jade Tomb.

He landed hard, the impact armor stiffening to absorb only part of the collision as power reserves failed. His left arm protected his face and neck, but then the armor locked up, his arm bent uselessly under him.

Moneta jumped the twenty meters, crouched next to him, lifted him into the air with one hand, grabbed a handful of impact armor with the other hand, and ripped his combat suit down the front, tearing apart two hundred layers of microfilaments and omega-cloth polymers. She slapped him gently, almost lackadaisically. Kassad's head snapped around, and he almost lost consciousness. Wind and sand pelted the bare flesh of his chest and belly.

Moneta tore the rest of the suit off, ripping off biosensors and feedback teeps. She lifted the naked man by his upper arms and shook him. Kassad tasted blood and red dots swam in his field of vision.

'We didn't have to be enemies,' she said softly.

'You . . . fired . . . at me.'

'To test your responses, not to kill you.' Her mouth moved normally under its quicksilver caul. She slapped him again and Kassad flew two meters in the air to land on a dune, rolled downhill in the cold sand. The air was filled with a million specks – snow, dust, pinwheels of colored light. Kassad rolled over, fought his way to his knees, gripped the shifting dune sand with fingers turned to numbed claws.

'Kassad,' whispered Moneta.

He rolled on to his back, waiting.

She had deactivated the skinsuit. Her flesh looked warm and vulnerable, the skin so pale as to be almost translucent. There were soft blue veins visible along the tops of her perfect breasts. Her legs looked strong, carefully sculpted, the thighs separated slightly where they met her body. Her eyes were a dark green.

'You love war, Kassad,' whispered Moneta as she lowered herself on to him.

He struggled, tried to twist aside, raised his arms to strike her. Moneta pinned his arms above his head with one of her hands. Her body was radiant with heat as she brushed her breasts back and forth across his chest, lowered herself between his parted legs. Kassad could feel the slight curve of her belly against his abdomen.

He realized then that this was a rape, that he could fight back simply by not responding, refusing her. It did not work. The air seemed liquid around them, the windstorm a distant thing, sand hanging in the air like a lace curtain borne aloft by steady breezes.

Moneta moved back and forth above him, against him. Kassad could feel the slow clockwise stir of his excitement. He fought it, fought her, wrestled and kicked and struggled to free his arms. She was much stronger. She used her right knee to brush his leg aside. Her nipples rubbed across his chest like warm pebbles; the warmth of her belly and groin made his flesh react like a flower twisting toward the light.

'No!' screamed Fedmahn Kassad but was silenced as Moneta lowered her mouth to his. With her left hand, she continued to pin his arms above him, with her right hand she moved between them, found him, guided him.

Kassad bit at her lip as warmth enveloped him. His struggles brought him closer, sent him deeper into her. He tried to relax, and she lowered herself on him until his back was pressed into the sand. He remembered the other times they had made love, finding sanity in each other's warmth while war raged beyond the circle of their passion.

Kassad closed his eyes, arched his neck back to postpone the agony of pleasure which closed on him like a wave. He tasted blood on his lips, whether his or hers he did not know.

A minute later, the two of them still moving together, Kassad realized that she had released his arms. Without hesitating, he brought both arms down, around, fingers flat against her back, and roughly pressed her closer to him, slid one hand higher to cup the back of her neck with gentle pressure.

The wind resumed, sound returned, sand blew from the edge of the dune in curls of spindrift. Kassad and Moneta slid lower on the gently curling bank of sand, rolled together down the warm wave to the place where it would break, oblivious of the night, the storm, the forgotten battle, and everything except the moment and each other.

Later, walking together through the shattered beauty of the Crystal Monolith, she touched him once with a golden ferule, once more with a blue torus. He watched in the shard of a crystal panel as his reflection became a quicksilver sketch of a man, perfect down to the details of his gender and the lines where his ribs showed on the slender torso.

— *What now?* asked Kassad through the medium that was neither telepathy nor sound.

— *The Lord of Pain awaits.*

— *You are its servant?*

— *Never. I am his consort and nemesis. His keeper.*

— *You came from the future with it?*

— *No. I was taken from my time to travel back in time with him.*

— *Then who were you before—*

Kassad's question was interrupted by the sudden appearance . . . No, he thought, *the sudden* presence, *not appearance* . . . of the Shrike.

The creature was as he remembered it from their first encounter years before. Kassad noticed the quicksilver-over-chrome slickness of the thing, so similar to their own skinsuits, but he knew intuitively that there was no mere flesh and bone beneath that carapace. It stood at least three meters tall, the four arms seemed normal on the elegant torso, and the body was a sculpted mass of thorns, spikes, joints, and layers of ragged razorwire. The thousand-faceted eyes burned with a light that might have been made by a ruby laser. The long jaw and layers of teeth were the stuff of nightmare.

Kassad stood ready. If the skinsuit gave him the same strength and mobility it had afforded Moneta, he might at least die fighting.

There was no time for that. One instant the Lord of Pain stood five meters away across black tile, and the next instant it was beside Kassad, gripping the Colonel's upper arm in a steel-bladed vise that sank through the skinsuit field and drew blood from his biceps.

Kassad tensed, waiting for the blow and determined to strike back even though to do so meant impaling himself on blades, thorns, and razorwire.

The Shrike lifted its right hand and a four-meter rectangular field portal came into existence. It was similar to a farcaster portal except for the violet glow which filled the interior of the Monolith with thick light.

Moneta nodded at him and stepped through. The Shrike stepped forward, fingerblades cutting only slightly into Kassad's upper arm.

Kassad considered pulling back, realized that curiosity was stronger in him than an urge to die, and stepped through with the Shrike.

EIGHTEEN

CEO Meina Gladstone could not sleep. She rose, dressed quickly in her dark apartments deep in Government House, and did what she often did when sleep would not come – she walked the worlds.

Her private farcaster portal pulsed into existence. Gladstone left her human guards sitting in the anteroom, taking with her only one of the microremotes. She would have taken none if the laws of the Hegemony and the rule of the TechnoCore would allow it. They did not.

It was far past midnight on TC^2 but she knew that many of the worlds would be in daylight, so she wore a long cape with a Renaissance privacy collar. Her trousers and boots revealed neither gender nor class, although the quality of the cape itself might mark her in some places.

CEO Gladstone stepped through the one-time portal, sensing rather than seeing or hearing the microremote as it buzzed through behind her, climbing for altitude and invisibility as she stepped out into the Square of St Peter's in the New Vatican on Pacem. For a second, she did not know why she had coded her implant for that destination – the presence of that obsolete monsignor at the dinner on God's Grove? – but then she realized that she had been thinking of the pilgrims as she lay awake, thinking of the seven who left three years earlier to meet their fate on Hyperion. Pacem had been the home of Father Lenar Hoyt . . . and the other priest before him, Duré.

Gladstone shrugged under the cape and crossed the square. Visiting the homeworlds of the pilgrims was as good a schematic for her walk as any; most sleepless nights saw her walking a score of worlds, returning just before dawn and the first meetings on Tau Ceti Center. At least this would be but seven worlds.

It was early here. The skies of Pacem were yellow, tinged with greenish clouds and an ammonia smell which attacked her sinuses and made her eyes water. The air had that thin, foul, chemical smell of a world neither completely terra-formed nor totally inimical to man. Gladstone paused to look around.

St Peter's was on a hilltop, the square embraced by a semicircle of pillars, a great basilica at its cusp. To her right, where the pillars opened to a staircase descending a kilometer or more to the south, a small city was visible, low, crude homes huddling between bone-white trees that resembled the skeletons of stunted creatures long since departed.

Only a few people could be seen, hurrying across the square or ascending

471

the stairs as if late for services. Bells somewhere under the great dome of the cathedral began to toll, but the thin air leached the sound of any authority.

Gladstone walked the circle of pillars, head down, ignoring the curious glances of clerics and the street-sweeping crew, who rode a beast resembling a half-ton hedgehog. There were scores of marginal worlds like Pacem in the Web, more in the Protectorate and nearby Outback – too poor to be attractive to an infinitely mobile citizenry, too Earthlike to be ignored during the dark days of the Hegira. It had fit a small group like the Catholics who had come here seeking a resurgence of faith. They had numbered in the millions then, Gladstone knew. There could be no more than a few tens of thousands now. She closed her eyes and recalled dossier holos of Father Paul Duré.

Gladstone loved the Web. She loved the human beings in it; for all their shallowness and selfishness and inability to change, they were the stuff of humankind. Gladstone loved the Web. She loved it enough to know that she must help in destroying it.

She returned to the small three-portal terminex, brought her own farcaster nexus into existence with a simple override command to the datasphere, and stepped through into sunlight and the smell of the sea.

Maui-Covenant. Gladstone knew precisely where she was. She stood on the hill above Firstsite where Siri's tomb still marked the spot where the short-lived rebellion had begun the better part of a century ago. At that time, Firstsite was a village of a few thousand, and each Festival Week flutists welcomed the motile isles as they were herded north to their feeding grounds in the Equatorial Archipelago. Now Firstsite stretched out of view around the island, arctowns and residential hives rising half a kilometer in all directions, towering over the hill which had once commanded the best view on the seaworld of Maui-Covenant.

But the tomb remained. The body of the Consul's grandmother was no longer there . . . never really had been there . . . but like so many symbolic things from this world, the empty crypt commanded reverence, almost awe.

Gladstone looked out between the towers, out past the old breakwater where blue lagoons had been turned brown, out past the drilling platforms and tourist barges, out to where the sea began. There were no motile isles now. They no longer moved in great herds across the oceans, their treesails billowing to southern breezes, their dolphin herders cutting the water in white vees of foam.

The isles were tamed and populated by Web citizens now. The dolphins were dead – some killed in the great battles with FORCE, most killing themselves in the inexplicable South Sea Mass Suicide, the last mystery of a race draped in mysteries.

Gladstone took a seat on a low bench near the cliff's edge and found a stalk of grass she could peel and chew. What happened to a world when it went from a home for a hundred thousand humans, in delicate balance with a delicate ecology, to the playground for more than four hundred million in the first standard decade of citizenship in the Hegemony?

Answer: the world died. Or its soul did, even as the ecosphere continued to function after a fashion. Planetary ecologists and terraform specialists kept the husk alive, kept the seas from choking completely on the unavoidable garbage and sewage and oil spills, worked to minimize or disguise the noise pollution and a thousand other things which progress had brought. But the Maui-Covenant that the Consul had known as a child less than a century earlier, climbing this very hill to his grandmother's funeral, was gone forever.

A formation of hawking mats flew overhead, the tourists on them laughing and shouting. Far above them, a massive excursion EMV occluded the sun for a moment. In the sudden shadow, Gladstone tossed down her stalk of grass, and rested her forearms on her knees. She thought of the Consul's betrayal. She had *counted* on the Consul's betrayal, had wagered everything on the man raised on Maui-Covenant, descendant of Siri, joining the Ousters in the inevitable battle for Hyperion. It had not been her plan alone; Leigh Hunt had been instrumental in the decades of planning, the delicate surgery of placing the precise individual in contact with the Ousters, in a position where he might betray both sides by activating the Ouster device to collapse the time tides on Hyperion.

And he had. The Consul, a man who had given four decades of his life as well as his wife and child to Hegemony service, had finally exploded in revenge like a bomb which had lain dormant for half a century.

Gladstone took no pleasure in the betrayal. The Consul had sold his soul, and would pay a terrible price – in history, in his own mind – but his treason was as nothing to the treachery Gladstone was prepared to suffer for. As Hegemony CEO, she was the symbolic leader of a hundred and fifty billion human souls. She was prepared to betray them all in order to save humanity.

She rose, felt age and rheumatism in her bones, and walked slowly to the terminex. She paused a moment by the gently humming portal, looking over her shoulder for a final glimpse of Maui-Covenant. The breeze carried in from the sea, but it carried the flat stench of oil spills and refinery gases, and Gladstone turned her face away.

The weight of Lusus fell on her caped shoulders like iron shackles. It was rush hour in the Concourse, and thousands of commuters, shoppers, and tourists crowded every walkway level, filled the kilometer-long escalators with colorful humanity, and gave the air a rebreathed heaviness that mixed with the sealed-system scent of oil and ozone. Gladstone ignored the expensive shopping levels and took a perstrans diskway the ten klicks to the main Shrike Temple.

There were police interdiction and containment fields glowing violet and green beyond the base of the wide stairway. The temple itself was boarded and dark; many of the tall, thin stained-glass windows facing the Concourse had been shattered. Gladstone remembered the reports of riots months before and knew that the Bishop and his acolytes had fled.

She walked close to the interdiction field, staring through the shifting violet haze at the stairway where Brawne Lamia had carried her dying client and lover, the original Keats cybrid, to the waiting Shrike priests. Gladstone had known Brawne's father well; they had spent their early Senate years together. Senator Byron Lamia had been a brilliant man – at one time, long before Brawne's mother had come on the social scene from her backwater province of Freeholm, Gladstone had considered marrying him – and when he died, part of Gladstone's youth had been buried with him. Byron Lamia had been obsessed with the TechnoCore, consumed with the mission of moving humankind out from under the bondage the AIs had imposed over five centuries and a thousand light-years. It had been Brawne Lamia's father who had made Gladstone aware of the danger, had led her to the commitment which would result in the most terrible betrayal in the history of man.

And it was Senator Byron Lamia's 'suicide' that had trained her to decades of caution. Gladstone did not know if it had been agents of the Core that had orchestrated the senator's death, perhaps it had been elements of the Hegemony hierarchy protecting its own vested interests, but she did know that Byron Lamia would never have taken his own life, never have abandoned his helpless wife and headstrong daughter in such a way. Senator Lamia's last senate act had been to co-propose Protectorate status for Hyperion, a move that would have brought the world into the Web twenty standard years earlier than the events now unfolding. After his death, the surviving co-sponsor – the newly influential Meina Gladstone – had withdrawn the bill.

Gladstone found a dropshaft and fell past shopping levels and residential levels, manufacturing and service levels, waste disposal and reactor levels. Both her comlog and the dropshaft speaker began warning her that she was entering unlicensed and unsafe areas far beneath the Hive. The dropshaft program tried to stop her descent. She overrode the command and silenced the warnings. She continued to drop, past levels without panels or lights now, descending through a tangle of fiber-optic spaghetti, heating and cooling ducts, and naked rock. Eventually she stopped.

Gladstone emerged into a corridor lighted only by distant glow-globes and oily firefly paint. Water dripped from a thousand cracks in ceilings and walls and accumulated in toxic puddles. Steam drifted from apertures in the wall that might be other corridors, or personal cubbies, or merely holes. Somewhere in the distance there was the ultrasonic scream of metal cutting metal; closer, the electronic screeches of nihil-music. Somewhere a man screamed and a woman laughed, her voice echoing metallically down shafts and conduits. There came the sound of a fléchette rifle coughing.

Dregs' Hive. Gladstone came to an intersection of cave-corridors and paused to look around. Her microremote dipped and circled closer now, as insistent as an angered insect. It was calling for security backup. Only Gladstone's persistent override prevented its cry being heard.

Dregs' Hive. This was where Brawne Lamia and her cybrid lover had hidden for those last few hours before their attempt to reach the Shrike Temple. This was one of the myriad underbellies of the Web, where the black market could provide anything from Flashback to FORCE-grade weapons, illegal androids to bootleg Poulsen treatments that would as likely kill you as give you another twenty years of youth. Gladstone turned right, down the darkest corridor.

Something the size of a rat but with many legs scurried into a broken ventilator tube. Gladstone smelled sewage, sweat, the ozone of overworked datumplane decks, the sweet scent of handgun propellant, vomit, and the reek of low-grade pheromones mutated to toxins. She walked the corridors, thinking of the weeks and months to come, the terrible price the worlds would pay for her decisions, her obsessions.

Five youths, tailored by back-room ARNists to the point they were more animal than human, stepped into the corridor in front of Gladstone. She paused.

The microremote dropped in front of her and neutralized its camouflage polymers. The creatures in front of her laughed, seeing only a machine the size of a wasp bobbing and darting in the air. It was quite possible that they were too far gone in the RNA tailoring even to recognize the device. Two of them flicked open vibrades. One extended ten-centimeter-long steel claws. One clicked open a fléchette pistol with rotating barrels.

Gladstone did not want a fight. She knew, even if these Dregs' Hive deadheads did not, that the micro could defend her from these five and a hundred more. But she did not want someone killed simply because she chose the Dregs as a place to take her walk.

'Go away,' she said.

The youths stared, yellow eyes, bulbous black eyes, hooded slits and photoreceptive belly bands. In unison but spreading into a half circle, they took two steps toward her.

Meina Gladstone pulled herself erect, gathered her cape around her, and dropped the privacy collar enough that they could see her eyes. 'Go away,' she said again.

The youths paused. Feathers and scales vibrated to unseen breezes. On two of them, antennae quivered and thousands of small sensory hairs pulsed.

They went away. Their departure was as silent and swift as their arrival. In a second there was no sound but water dripping, distant laughter.

Gladstone shook her head, summoned her personal portal, and stepped through.

Sol Weintraub and his daughter had come from Barnard's World. Gladstone translated to a minor terminex in their hometown of Crawford. It was evening. Low, white homes set back on manicured lawns reflected Canadian Republic Revival sensibilities and farmers' practicality. The trees were tall, broad limbed, and amazingly faithful to their Old Earth heritage. Gladstone turned away from the flow of pedestrians, most hurrying home after a workday elsewhere in the Web, and found herself strolling down brick walkways past brick buildings set around a grassy oval. To her left, she caught glimpses of farm fields past a row of homes. Tall green plants, possibly corn, grew in softly sighing ranks that stretched to the distant horizon where the last arc of a huge red sun was setting.

Gladstone walked through the campus, wondering if this had been the college where Sol had taught, but not curious enough to query the datasphere. Gaslamps were lighting themselves under the canopy of leaves, and the first stars were becoming visible in the gaps where sky faded from azure to amber to ebony.

Gladstone had read Weintraub's book, *The Abraham Dilemma*, in which he analyzed the relationship between a God who demanded the sacrifice of a son and the human race who agreed to it. Weintraub had reasoned that the Old Testament Jehovah had not simply been testing Abraham, but had communicated in the only language of loyalty, obedience, sacrifice, and command that humankind could understand at that point in the relationship. Weintraub had dealt with the New Testament's message as a presage of a new stage in that relationship – a stage wherein mankind would no longer sacrifice its children to any god, for any reason, but where parents . . . entire races of parents . . . would offer themselves up instead. Thus the Twentieth-Century Holocausts, the Brief Exchange, the tripartite wars, the reckless centuries, and perhaps even the Big Mistake of '38.

Finally, Weintraub had dealt with refusing all sacrifice, refusing any relationship with God except one of mutual respect and honest attempts at mutual understanding. He wrote about the multiple deaths of God and the need for a divine resurrection now that humankind had constructed its own gods and released them on the universe.

Gladstone crossed a graceful stone bridge arcing over a stream lost in shadows, its whereabouts indicated only by the noises it made in the dark. Soft yellow light fell on railings of hand-set stone. Somewhere off campus, a dog barked and was hushed. Lights burned on the third floor of an old building, a gabled and roughly shingled brick structure that must date back to before the Hegira.

Gladstone thought about Sol Weintraub and his wife Sarai and their beautiful twenty-six-year-old daughter, returning from a year of archaeological discovery on Hyperion with no discovery except the Shrike's curse, the Merlin's sickness. Sol and Sarai watching as the woman aged backward to child, from child to infant. And then Sol watching alone after Sarai died in a senseless, stupid EMV crash while visiting her sister.

Rachel Weintraub whose first and final birthday would arrive in less than three standard days.

Gladstone pounded her fist against stone, summoned her portal, and went elsewhere.

It was midday on Mars. The Tharsis slums had been slums for six centuries and more. The sky overhead was pink, the air too thin and too cold for

Gladstone, even with her cape around her, and dust blew everywhere. She walked the narrow lanes and cliffwalks of Relocation City, never finding an open enough spot to see anything beyond the next cluster of hovels or dripping filter towers.

There were few plants here – the great forests of the Greening had been cut down for firewood or died and been covered by red dunes. Only a few bootleg brandy cacti and scuttling packs of parasitic spider lichen were visible between paths pocked hard as stone by twenty generations of bare feet.

Gladstone found a low rock and rested, lowering her head and massaging her knees. Groups of children, each naked except for strips of rags and dangling shunt jacks, surrounded her, begged for money, and then ran away giggling when she did not respond.

The sun was high. Mons Olympus and the stark beauty of Fedmahn Kassad's FORCE academy were not visible from here. Gladstone looked around. This was where the proud man had come from. Here is where he had run with youth gangs before being sentenced to the order, sanity, and honor of the military.

Gladstone found a private place and stepped through her portal.

God's Grove was as it always was – perfumed by the scent of a million million trees, silent except for the soft sounds of leaf rustle and wind, colored in halftones and pastels, the sunset igniting the literal rooftop of the world as an ocean of treetops caught the light, each leaf shimmering to the breeze, glittering with dew and morning showers as the breeze rose and carried the smell of rain and wet vegetation to Gladstone on her platform high above the world still sunk in sleep and darkness half a kilometer below.

A Templar approached, saw the glint of Gladstone's access bracelet as she moved her hand, and withdrew, a tall, robed figure blending back into the maze of foliage and vines.

The Templars were one of the trickiest variables in Gladstone's game. Their sacrifice of their treeship *Yggdrasill* was unique, unprecedented, inexplicable, and worrisome. Of all her potential allies in the war to come, none were more necessary and inscrutable than the Templars. Dedicated to life and devoted to the Muir, the Brotherhood of the Tree was a small but potent force in the Web – a token of ecological awareness in a society devoted to self-destruction and waste but unwilling to acknowledge its indulgent ways.

Where was Het Masteen? Why had he left the Möbius cube with the other pilgrims?

Gladstone watched the sun rise. The sky filled with orphan montgolfiers saved from the slaughter on Whirl, their many-hued bodies floating skyward like so many Portuguese men-o'-war. Radiant gossamers spread membrane-thin solar wings to collect the sunlight. A flock of ravens broke cover and spiraled skyward, their cries providing harsh counterpoint to the soft breeze and sibilant rush of rain coming toward Gladstone from the west. The insistent sound of raindrops on leaves reminded her of her own home in the deltas of Patawpha, of the Hundred Day Monsoon which sent her and her brothers out into the fens hunting for toad flyers, bendits, and Spanish moss serpents to bring to school in a jar.

Gladstone realized for the hundred thousandth time that there was still time to stop things. All-out war was not inevitable at this point. The Ousters had not counterattacked yet in a way the Hegemony could not ignore. The Shrike was not free. Not yet.

All she had to do to save a hundred billion lives was return to the Senate floor, reveal three decades of deception and duplicity, reveal her fears and uncertainties . . .

No. *It would go as planned until it went beyond planning. Into the unforeseen. Into the wild waters of chaos where even the TechnoCore predictors, those who saw everything, would be blind.*

Gladstone walked the platforms, towers, ramps, and swinging bridges of the Templar tree city. Arboreals from a score of worlds and ARNied chimps scolded her and fled, swinging gracefully from flimsy vines three hundred meters above the forest floor. From areas closed to tourists and privileged visitors, Gladstone caught the scent of incense and clearly heard the Gregorian-like chants of the Templar sunrise service. Beneath her, the lower levels were coming alive with light and movement. The brief showers had passed over, and Gladstone returned to the upper levels, rejoicing in the view, crossing a sixty-meter wooden suspension bridge connecting her tree to one even larger, where half a dozen of the great hot air balloons – the only air transport the Templars allowed on God's Grove – hung tethered and seemingly impatient to be away, their passenger nacelles swinging like heavy brown eggs, the skins of the balloons lovingly dyed in the patterns of living things – montgolfiers, Monarch butterflies, Thomas hawks, radiant gossamers, the now-extinct zeplens, sky squids, moon moths, eagles – so revered in legend that they had never been retrieved or ARNied – and more.

All this could be destroyed if I continue. Will be *destroyed.*

Gladstone paused at the edge of a circular platform and gripped a railing so tightly that the age-mottles on her hands stood out harshly against suddenly pale skin. She thought of the old books she had read, pre-Hegira, pre-spaceflight, where people in embryonic nations on the continent of Europe had transported darker people – Africans – away from their homelands into a life of slavery in the colonial West. Would those slaves, chained and shackled, naked and curled in the fetid belly of a slave ship . . . would those slaves have hesitated to rebel, to drag down their captors, if it meant destroying the beauty of that slave ship . . . of Europe itself?

But they had Africa to return to.

Meina Gladstone let out a sound part groan and part sob. She whirled away from the glorious sunrise, from the sound of chants greeting the new day, from the rise of balloons – living and artificial – into the newborn sky, and she went below, down into the relative darkness to summon her farcaster.

She could not go where the last pilgrim, Martin Silenus, had come from. Silenus was only a century and a half old, half-blue from Poulsen treatments, his cells remembering the cold freeze of a dozen long cryogenic fugues and even colder storage, but his lifetime had spanned more than four centuries. He had been born on Old Earth during the last days there, his mother from one of the noblest families, his youth a pastiche of decadence and elegance, beauty and the sweet smell of decay. While his mother stayed with the dying Earth, he had been sent spaceward so that someone could clear family debts, even if it meant . . . which it did . . . years of service as a bonded manual laborer on one of the most hellish backwater worlds in the Web.

Gladstone could not go to Old Earth so she went to Heaven's Gate.

Mudflat was the capital, and Gladstone walked the cobblestone streets there, admiring the large old houses which overhung the narrow, stone-troughed canals criss-crossing their way up the artificial mountainside like something from an Escher print. Elegant trees and even larger horsetail ferns crowned the hilltops, lined the broad, white avenues, and swept out of sight around the elegant curve of white sand beaches. The lazy tide brought in violet waves which prismed to a score of colors before dying on the perfect beaches.

Gladstone paused at a park looking over the Mudflat Promenade, where scores of couples and carefully dressed tourists took the evening air under gaslamp and leaf shadow, and she imagined what Heaven's Gate had been more than three centuries earlier when it was a rough Protectorate world, not yet fully terraformed, and young Martin Silenus, still suffering from cultural dislocation, the loss of his fortune, and brain damage due to Freezer Shock on the long trip out, was working here as a slave.

The Atmospheric Generating Station then had provided a few hundred square kilometers of breathable air, marginally liveable land. Tsunamis carried away cities, land reclamation projects, and workers with equal indifference. Bonded workers like Silenus dug out the acid canals, scraped rebreather bacteria from the lungpipe labyrinths under the mud, and dredged scum and dead bodies from the tidal mudflats after the floods.

We have made some progress, thought Gladstone, *despite the inertia forced upon us by the Core. Despite the near-death of science. Despite our fatal addiction to the toys granted us by our own creations.*

She was dissatisfied. Before this world walk was over she had wanted to visit the home of each of the Hyperion pilgrims, however futile she knew that gesture to be. Heaven's Gate was where Silenus had learned to write true poetry even while his temporarily damaged mind was lost to language, but this was not his home.

Gladstone ignored the pleasant music rising from the concert on the

Promenade, ignored the flights of commuter EMVs moving overhead like migrating fowl, ignored the pleasant air and soft light, as she called her portal to her and commanded it to farcast to Earth's moon. *The* moon.

Instead of activating the translation, her comlog warned her of the dangers of going there. She overrode it.

Her microremote buzzed into existence, its tiny voice in her implant suggesting that it was not a good idea for the Chief Executive to travel to such an unstable place. She silenced it.

The farcaster portal itself began to argue with her choice until she used her universal card to program it manually.

The farcaster door blurred into existence, and Gladstone stepped through.

The only place on Old Earth's moon still habitable was the mountain and Mare area preserved for the FORCE Masada Ceremony, and it was here that Gladstone stepped out. The viewing stands and marching field were empty. Class-ten containment fields blurred the stars and the distant rim walls, but Gladstone could see where internal heating from terrible gravity tides had melted the distant mountains and made them flow into new seas of rock.

She moved across a plain of gray sand, feeling the light gravity like an invitation to fly. She imagined herself as one of the Templar balloons, lightly tethered but eager to be away. She resisted the impulse to jump, to leap along in giant bounds, but her step was light, and dust flew in improbable patterns behind her.

The air was very thin under the containment field dome, and Gladstone found herself shivering despite the heating elements in her cape. For a long moment she stood in the center of the featureless plain and tried to imagine just the moon, humankind's first step in its long stagger from the cradle. But the FORCE viewing stands and equipment sheds distracted her, made such imaginings futile, and finally she raised her eyes to see what she had actually come for.

Old Earth hung in the black sky. But not Old Earth, of course, merely the pulsing accretion disk and globular cloud of debris which had once been Old Earth. It was very bright, brighter than any of the stars seen from Patawpha on even the rarest clear night, but its brightness was strangely ominous, and it cast a thick light across the mud-gray field.

Gladstone stood and stared. She had never been here before, had made herself not come before, and now that she was here, she desperately wanted to *feel* something, *hear* something, as if some voice of caution or inspiration or perhaps merely commiseration would come to her here.

She heard nothing.

She stood there another few minutes, thinking of little, feeling her ears and nose beginning to freeze, before she decided to go. It would be almost dawn on TC^2.

Gladstone had activated the portal and was taking a final look around when another portable farcaster door blurred into existence less than ten meters away. She paused. Not five human beings in the Web had individual access to Earth's moon.

The microremote buzzed down to float between her and the figure emerging from the portal.

Leigh Hunt stepped out, glanced around, shivered from the cold, and walked quickly toward her. His voice was thin, almost amusingly childlike in the thin air.

'M. Chief Executive, you must return at once. The Ousters have succeeded in breaking through in an amazing counterattack.'

Gladstone sighed. She had known that this would be the next step. 'All right,' she said. 'Has Hyperion fallen? Can we evacuate our forces from there?'

Hunt shook his head. His lips were almost blue from the cold. 'You don't understand,' came the attenuated voice of her aide. 'It's not just Hyperion. The Ousters are attacking at a dozen points. *They're invading the Web itself!*'

Suddenly numb and chilled to her core, more from shock than from the lunar cold, Meina Gladstone nodded, gathered her cape more tightly around her, and stepped back through the portal to a world which would never be the same again.

NINETEEN

They gathered at the head of the Valley of the Time Tombs, Brawne Lamia and Martin Silenus burdened with as many backpacks and carrying bags as they could manage, Sol Weintraub, the Consul, and Father Duré standing silent as a tribunal of patriarchs. The first shadows of afternoon were beginning to stretch east across the valley, reaching for the softly glowing Tombs like fingers of darkness.

'I'm still not sure it's a good idea to split up like this,' said the Consul, rubbing his chin. It was very hot. Sweat gathered on his stubbled cheeks and ran down his neck.

Lamia shrugged. 'We knew that we each would be confronting the Shrike alone. Does it matter if we're separated a few hours? We need the food. You three could come if you want.'

The Consul and Sol glanced at Father Duré. The priest was obviously exhausted. The search for Kassad had drained whatever reserves of energy the man had kept after his ordeal.

'Someone should wait here in case the Colonel returns,' said Sol. The baby looked very small in his arms.

Lamia nodded agreement. She settled straps on her shoulders and neck. 'All right. It should be about two hours getting to the Keep. A little longer coming back. Figure a full hour there loading supplies, and we'll still be back before dark. Close to dinnertime.'

The Consul and Duré shook hands with Silenus. Sol put his arms around Brawne. 'Come back safely,' he whispered.

She touched the bearded man's cheek, set her hand on the infant's head for a second, turned, and started up the valley at a brisk pace.

'Hey, wait a fucking minute for me to catch up!' called Martin Silenus, canteens and water bottles clattering as he ran.

They came up out of the saddle between the cliffs together. Silenus glanced back and saw the other three men already dwarfed by distance, small sticks of color amid the boulders and dunes near the Sphinx. 'It isn't going quite as planned, is it?' he said.

'I don't know,' said Lamia. She had changed into shorts for the hike, and the muscles of her short, powerful legs gleamed under a sheen of sweat. 'How was it planned?'

'My plan was to finish the universe's greatest poem and then go home,' said Silenus. He took a drink from the last bottle holding water. 'Goddamn, I wish we'd brought enough wine to last us.'

'I didn't have a plan,' said Lamia, half to herself. Her short curls, matted with perspiration, clung to her broad neck.

Martin Silenus snorted a laugh. 'You wouldn't be here if it weren't for that cyborg lover . . .'

'Client,' she snapped.

'Whatever. It was the Johnny Keats retrieval persona who thought it was important to get here. So now you've dragged him this far . . . you're still carrying the Schrön loop aren't you?'

Lamia absently touched the tiny neural shunt behind her left ear. A thin membrane of osmotic polymer kept sand and dust out of the follicle-sized connector sockets. 'Yes.'

Silenus laughed again. 'What the fuck good is it if there's no datasphere to interact with, kid? You might as well have left the Keats persona on Lusus or wherever.' The poet paused a second to adjust straps and packs. 'Say, can you access the personality on your own?'

Lamia thought of her dreams the night before. The presence in them had felt like Johnny . . . but the images had been of the Web. *Memories?* 'No,' she said, 'I can't access a Schrön loop by myself. It carries more data than a hundred simple implants could deal with. Now why don't you shut up and walk?' She picked up the pace and left him standing there.

The sky was cloudless, verdant, and hinting of depths of lapis. The boulder field ahead stretched southwest to the barrens, the barrens surrendering to the dunefields. The two walked in silence for thirty minutes, separated by five meters and their thoughts. Hyperion's sun hung small and bright to their right.

'The dunes are steeper,' said Lamia as they struggled up to another crest and slid down the other side. The surface was hot, and already her shoes were filling with sand.

Silenus nodded, stopped, and mopped his face with a silken handkerchief. His floppy purple beret hung low over his brow and left ear, but offered no shade. 'It would be easier following the high ground to the north there. Near the dead city.'

Brawne Lamia shielded her eyes to stare in that direction. 'We'll lose at least half an hour going that way.'

'We'll lose more than that going *this* way.' Silenus sat on the dune and sipped from his water bottle. He pulled off his cape, folded it, and stuffed it in the largest of his backpacks.

'What are you carrying there?' asked Lamia. 'That pack looks full.'

'None of your damned business, woman.'

Lamia shook her head, rubbed her cheeks, and felt the sunburn there. She was not used to so many days in sunlight, and Hyperion's atmosphere blocked little of the ultraviolet. She fumbled in her pocket for the tube of sunblock cream and smeared some on. 'All right,' she said. 'We'll detour that way. Follow the ridgeline until the worst of the dunes are past and then cut back on a straight line toward the Keep.' The mountains hung on the horizon, seeming to grow no closer. The snow-topped summits tantalized her with their promise of cool breezes and fresh water. The Valley of the Time Tombs was invisible behind them, the view blocked by dunes and the boulder field.

Lamia shifted her packs, turned to her right, and half slid, half walked down the crumbling dune.

As they came up out of the sand on to the low gorse and needle grass of the ridge, Martin Silenus could not take his eyes from the ruins of the City of Poets. Lamia had cut left around it, avoiding everything but the stones of the half-buried highways that circled the city, other roads leading out into the barrens until they disappeared beneath the dunes.

Silenus fell farther and farther behind until he stopped and sat on a fallen column, which had once been a portal through which the android laborers filed every evening after working in the fields. Those fields were gone now. The aqueducts, canals, and highways only hinted at by fallen stones, depressions in the sand, or the sand-scoured stumps of trees where once they had overhung a waterway or shaded a pleasant lane.

Martin Silenus used his beret to mop his face as he stared at the ruins. The city was still white . . . as white as bones uncovered by shifting sands, as white as teeth in an earth-brown skull. From where he sat, Silenus could see that many of the buildings were as he had last seen them more than a century and a half ago. Poets' Ampitheatre lay half-finished but regal in its ruin, a white, otherworldly Roman Colosseum overgrown with desert creeper and fanfare ivy. The great atrium was open to the sky, the gallerias shattered – not by time, Silenus knew, but by the probes and lances and explosive charges of Sad King Billy's useless security people in the decades after the evacuation of the city. They were going to kill the Shrike. They were going to use electronics and angry beams of coherent light to kill Grendel *after* he had laid waste to the mead hall.

Martin Silenus chuckled and leaned forward, suddenly dizzy from the heat and exhaustion.

Silenus could see the great dome of the Common Hall where he had eaten his meals, first with the hundreds in artistic camaraderie, then in separation and silence with the few others who had remained, for their own inscrutable and unrecorded reasons, after Billy's evacuation to Keats, and then alone. Truly alone. Once he had dropped a goblet and the echo rang for half a minute under the vine-graffitied dome.

Alone with the Morlocks, thought Silenus. *But not even Morlocks for company in the end. Only my muse.*

There was a sudden explosion of sound, and a score of white doves burst from some niche in the heap of broken towers that had been Sad King Billy's palace. Silenus watched them whirl and circle in the overheated sky, marveling that they had survived the centuries here on the edge of nowhere.

If I could do it, why not they?

There were shadows in the city, pools of sweet shade. Silenus wondered if the wells were still good, the great underground reservoirs, sunk before the human seedships had arrived, still filled with sweet water. He wondered if his wooden worktable, an antique from Old Earth, still sat in the small room in which he had written much of his *Cantos*.

'What's wrong?' Brawne Lamia had retraced her steps and was standing near him.

'Nothing.' He squinted up at her. The woman looked like some squat tree, a mass of dark thigh roots and sunburned bark and frozen energy. He tried to imagine her being exhausted . . . the effort made *him* tired. 'I just realized,' he said. 'We're wasting our time going all the way back to the Keep. There are wells in the city. Probably food reserves too.'

'Uh-uh,' said Lamia. 'The Consul and I thought of that, talked about it. The Dead City's been looted for generations. Shrike Pilgrims must have depleted the stores sixty or eighty years ago. The wells aren't depend-able . . . the aquifer has shifted, the reservoirs are contaminated. We go to the Keep.'

Silenus felt his anger grow at the woman's insufferable arrogance, her instant assumption that she could take command in any situation. 'I'm going to explore,' he said. 'It might save us hours of travel time.'

Lamia moved between him and the sun. Her black curls glowed with the corona of eclipse. 'No. If we waste time here, we won't be back before dark.'

'Go on, then,' snapped the poet, surprised at what he was saying. 'I'm tired. I'm going to check out the warehouse behind the Common Hall. I might remember storage places the pilgrims never found.'

He could see the woman's body tense as she considered dragging him to his feet, pulling him out on to the dunes again. They were little more than a third of the way to the foothills where the long climb to the Keep staircase began. Her muscles relaxed. 'Martin,' she said, 'the others are depending on us. Please don't screw this up.'

He laughed and sat back against the tumbled pillar. 'Fuck that,' he said. 'I'm *tired*. You know that you're going to do ninety-five percent of the transporting anyway. I'm *old*, woman. Older than you can imagine. Let me stay and rest a while. Maybe I'll find some food. Maybe I'll get some writing done.'

Lamia crouched next to him and touched his pack. 'That's what you've been carrying. The pages of your poem. The *Cantos*.'

'Of course,' he said.

'And you still think that proximity to the Shrike will allow you to finish it?'

Silenus shrugged, feeling the heat and dizziness whirl around him. 'The thing is a fucking killer, a sheet-metal Grendel forged in hell,' he said. 'But it's my muse.'

Lamia sighed, squinted at the sun already lowering itself toward the mountains, and then looked back the way they had come. 'Go back,' she said softly. 'To the valley.' She hesitated a moment. 'I'll go with you, then return.'

Silenus smiled with cracked lips. 'Why go back? To play cribbage with three other old men until our beastie comes to tuck us in? No thanks, I'd rather rest here a bit and get some work done. Go on, woman. You can carry more than three poets could.' He struggled out of his empty packs and bottles, handing them to her.

Lamia held the tangle of straps in a fist as short and hard as the head of a steel hammer. 'Are you sure? We can walk slowly.'

He struggled to his feet; fueled by a moment of pure anger at her pity and condescension. 'Fuck you and the horse you rode in on, Lusian. In case you forgot, the purpose of the pilgrimage was to get here and say hello to the Shrike. Your friend Hoyt didn't forget. Kassad understood the game. The fucking Shrike's probably chewing on his stupid military bones right now. I wouldn't be surprised if the three we left behind *don't need* food or water by this point. Go on. Get the hell out of here. I'm tired of your company.'

Brawne Lamia remained crouching for a moment, looking up at him as he weaved above her. Then she got to her feet, touched his shoulder for the briefest of seconds, lifted the packs and bottles to her back, and swung away, her pace faster than anything he could have kept up with in his youth. 'I'll be back this way in a few hours,' she called, not turning back to look at him. 'Be out on this edge of the city. We'll return to the Tombs together.'

Martin Silenus said nothing as he watched her diminish and then disappear in the rough ground to the southwest. The mountains shimmered in the heat. He looked down and saw that she had left the water bottle for him. He spat, added the bottle to his load, and walked into the waiting shade of the dead city.

TWENTY

Duré all but collapsed while they were eating lunch from the last two ration paks; Sol and the Consul carried him up the Sphinx's wide stairway into the shade. The priest's face was as white as his hair.

He attempted a smile as Sol lifted a water bottle to his lips. 'All of you accept the fact of my resurrection rather easily,' he said, wiping the corners of his mouth with a finger.

The Consul leaned back against the stone of the Sphinx. 'I saw the cruciforms on Hoyt. The same as you wear now.'

'And I believed his story . . . *your* story,' said Sol. He passed the water to the Consul.

Duré touched his forehead. 'I've been listening to the comlog disks. The stories, including mine, are . . . incredible.'

'Do you doubt any of them?' asked the Consul.

'No. It is making sense of them that is the challenge. Finding the common element . . . the string of connection.'

Sol lifted Rachel to his chest, rocking her slightly, his hand on the back of her head. 'Does there have to be a connection? Other than the Shrike?'

'Oh yes,' said Duré. A bit of color was returning to his cheeks. 'This pilgrimage was not an accident. Nor was your selection.'

'Different elements had a say in who came on this pilgrimage,' said the Consul. 'The AI Advisory Group, the Hegemony Senate, even the Shrike Church.'

Duré shook his head. 'Yes, but there was only one guiding intelligence behind this selection, my friends.'

Sol leaned closer. 'God?'

'Perhaps,' said Duré, smiling, 'but I was thinking of the Core . . . the artificial intelligences who have behaved so mysteriously through this entire sequence of events.'

The baby made soft, mewling noises. Sol found a pacifier for it and tuned the comlog on his wrist to heartbeat rates. The child curled its fists once and relaxed against the scholar's shoulder. 'Brawne's story suggests that elements in the Core are trying to destabilize the status quo . . . allow humankind a chance for survival while still pursuing their Ultimate Intelligence project.'

The Consul gestured toward the cloudless sky. 'Everything that's happened . . . our pilgrimage, even this war . . . was manufactured because of the internal politics of the Core.'

'And what do we know of the Core?' asked Duré softly.

'Nothing,' said the Consul, and threw a pebble toward the carved stone to the left of the Sphinx's stairway. 'When all is said and done, we know nothing.'

Duré was sitting up now, massaging his face with a slightly moistened cloth. 'Yet their goal is oddly similar to our own.'

'What's that?' asked Sol, still rocking the baby.

'To know God,' said the priest. 'Or failing that, to create Him.' He squinted down the long valley. Shadows were moving farther out from the southwestern walls now, beginning to touch and enfold the Tombs. 'I helped promote such an idea within the Church . . .'

'I've read your treatises on St Teilhard,' said Sol. 'You did a brilliant job defending the necessity of evolution toward the Omega Point – the God-head – without stumbling into the Socinian Heresy.'

'The what?' asked the Consul.

Father Duré smiled slightly. 'Socinus was an Italian heretic in the six-teenth century A.D. His belief . . . for which he was excommunicated . . . was that God is a limited being, able to learn and to grow as the world . . . the universe . . . becomes more complex. And I did stumble into the Socinian Heresy, Sol. That was the first of my sins.'

Sol's gaze was level. 'And the last of your sins?'

'Besides pride?' said Duré. 'The greatest of my sins was falsifying data from a seven-year dig on Armaghast. Trying to provide a connection be-tween the vanished Arch Builders there and a form of proto-Christianity. It did not exist. I fudged data. So the irony is, the greatest of my sins, at least in the Church's eyes, was to violate the scientific method. In her final days, the Church can accept theological heresy but can brook no tampering with the protocols of science.'

'Was Armaghast like this?' asked Sol, making a gesture with his arm that included the valley, the Tombs, and the encroaching desert.

Duré looked around, his eyes bright for a moment. 'The dust and stone and sense of death, yes. But this place is infinitely more threatening. Some-thing here has not yet succumbed to death when it should have.'

The Consul laughed. 'Let's hope that we're in that category. I'm going to drag the comlog up to that saddle and try again to establish a relay link with the ship.'

'I'll go too,' said Sol.

'And I,' said Father Duré, getting to his feet, weaving for only a second, and refusing the offer of Weintraub's hand.

The ship did not respond to queries. Without the ship, there could be no fatline relay to the Ousters, the Web, or anywhere else beyond Hyperion. Normal comm bands were down.

'Could the ship have been destroyed?' Sol asked the Consul.

'No. The message is being received, just not responded to. Gladstone still has the ship in quarantine.'

Sol squinted out over the barrens to where the mountains shimmered in the heat haze. Several klicks closer, the ruins of the City of Poets rose jaggedly against the skyline. 'Just as well,' he said. 'We have one *deus ex machina* too many as it is.'

Paul Duré began to laugh then, a deep, sincere sound, and stopped only when he began coughing and had to take a drink of water.

'What is it?' asked the Consul.

'The *deus ex machina*. What we were talking about earlier. I suspect that this is precisely the reason each of us is here. Poor Lenar with his deus in the machina of the cruciform. Brawne with her resurrected poet trapped in a Schrön loop, seeking the machina to release her personal deus. You, Sol, waiting for the dark deus to solve your daughter's terrible problem. The Core, machina spawned, seeking to build their own deus.'

The Consul adjusted his sun glasses. 'And you, Father?'

Duré shook his head. 'I wait for the largest machina of all to produce its deus – the universe. How much of my elevation of St Teilhard stemmed from the simple fact that I found no sign of a living Creator in the world today? Like the TechnoCore intelligences, I seek to build what I cannot find elsewhere.'

Sol watched the sky. 'What deus do the Ousters seek?'

The Consul answered. 'Their obsession with Hyperion is real. They think that this will be the birthplace of a new hope for humankind.'

'We'd better go back down,' said Sol, shielding Rachel from the sun. 'Brawne and Martin should be returning before dinner.'

But they did not return before dinner. Nor was there any sign of them by sunset. Every hour, the Consul walked to the valley entrance, climbed a boulder, and watched for movement out among the dunes and boulder field. There was none. The Consul wished that Kassad had left a pair of his powered binoculars.

Even before the sky faded to twilight the bursts of light across its zenith announced the continuing battle in space. The three men sat on the highest step of the Sphinx's staircase and watched the light show, slow explosions of pure white, dull red blossoms, and sudden green and orange streaks which left retinal echoes.

'Who's winning, do you think?' said Sol.

The Consul did not look up. 'It doesn't matter. Do you think we should sleep somewhere other than the Sphinx tonight? Wait at one of the other Tombs?'

'I can't leave the Sphinx,' said Sol. 'You're welcome to go on.'

Duré touched the baby's cheek. She was working on the pacifier, and her cheek moved against his finger. 'How old is she now, Sol?'

'Two days. Almost exactly. She would have been born about fifteen minutes after sunset at this latitude, Hyperion time.'

'I'll go up and look one last time,' said the Consul. 'Then we'll have to build a bonfire or something to help them find their way back.'

The Consul had descended half the steps toward the trail when Sol stood and pointed. Not toward where the head of the valley glowed in low sunlight, but the other way, into the shadows of the valley itself.

The Consul stopped, and the other two men joined him. The Consul reached into his pocket and removed the small neural stunner Kassad had given him several days earlier. With Lamia and Kassad gone, it was the only weapon they had.

'Can you see?' whispered Sol.

The figure was moving in the darkness beyond the faint glow of the Jade Tomb. It did not look large enough or move quickly enough to be the Shrike; its progress was strange . . . slow, halting for half a moment at a time, weaving.

Father Duré glanced over his shoulder at the entrance to the valley, then back. 'Is there any way Martin Silenus could have entered the valley from that direction?'

'Not unless he jumped down the cliff walls,' whispered the Consul. 'Or went eight klicks around to the northeast. Besides, it's too tall to be Silenus.'

The figure paused again, weaved, and then fell. From more than a hundred meters away, it looked like another low boulder on the valley floor.

'Come,' said the Consul.

They did not run. The Consul led the way down the staircase, stunner extended, set for twenty meters although he knew the neural effect would be minimal at that range. Father Duré walked close behind, holding Sol's child while the scholar hunted for a small rock to carry.

'David and Goliath?' asked Duré when Sol came up with a palm-sized stone and set it in a fiberplastic sling he had cut from package wrap that afternoon.

The scholar's sunburned face above the beard turned a darker color. 'Something like that. Here, I'll take Rachel back.'

'I enjoy carrying her. And if there's any fighting to be done, better the two of you have free hands.'

Sol nodded and closed the gap to walk side by side with the Consul, the priest and the child a few paces behind.

From fifteen meters away it became obvious that the fallen figure was a man – a very tall man – wearing a rough robe and lying face down in the sand.

'Stay here,' said the Consul and ran. The others watched while he turned over the body, set his stunner back in his pocket, and removed a water bottle from his belt.

Sol jogged slowly, feeling his exhaustion as a kind of pleasant vertigo. Duré followed more slowly.

When the priest came into the light thrown by the Consul's hand torch, he saw the hood of the fallen man pushed back from a vaguely Asian, oddly distorted long face lighted by the glow of the Jade Tomb as well as the torch.

'It's a Templar,' said Duré, astonished to find a follower of the Muir here.

'It's the True Voice of the Tree,' said the Consul. 'It's the first of our missing pilgrims . . . it's Het Masteen.'

TWENTY-ONE

Martin Silenus had worked all afternoon on his epic poem, and only the dying of the light made him pause in his efforts.

He had found his old workroom pillaged, the antique table missing. Sad King Billy's palace had suffered the worst of time's insults, with all windows broken, miniature dunes drifted across discolored carpets once worth fortunes, and rats and small rock eels living between the tumbled stones. The apartment towers were homes for the doves and hunting falcons gone back to the wild. Finally the poet had returned to the Common Hall under the great geodesic dome of its dining room to sit at a low table and write.

Dust and debris covered the ceramic floor, and the scarlet tones of desert creeper all but obscured the broken panes above, but Silenus ignored these irrelevancies and worked on his *Cantos*.

The poem dealt with the death and displacement of the Titans by their offspring, the Hellenic gods. It dealt with the Olympian struggle which followed the Titans' refusal to be displaced – the boiling of great seas as Oceanus struggled with Neptune, his usurper, the extinction of suns as Hyperion struggled with Apollo for control of the light, and the trembling of the universe itself as Saturn struggled with Jupiter for control of the throne of the gods. What was at stake was not the mere passage of one set of deities to be replaced by another, but the end of a golden age and the beginning of dark times which must spell doom for all mortal things.

The *Hyperion Cantos* made no secret of the multiple identities of these gods: the Titans were easily understood to be the heroes of humankind's short history in the galaxy, the Olympian usurpers were the TechnoCore AIs, and their battlefield stretched across the familiar continents, oceans, and airways of all the worlds in the Web. Amidst all this, the monster Dis, son of Saturn but eager to inherit the kingdom with Jupiter, stalked its prey, harvesting both god and mortal.

The *Cantos* were also about the relationship between creatures and their creators, the love between parent and children, artists and their art, all creators and their creations. The poem celebrated love and loyalty but teetered on the brink of nihilism with its constant thread of corruption through love of power, human ambition and intellectual hubris.

Martin Silenus had been working on his *Cantos* for more than two standard centuries. His finest work had been done in these surroundings – the abandoned city, the desert winds whining like an ominous Greek chorus in the background, the ever-present threat of the Shrike's sudden interruption. By saving his own life, by leaving, Silenus had abandoned his muse and condemned his pen to silence. Beginning work again, following that sure trail, that perfect circuit which only the inspired writer has experienced, Martin Silenus felt himself returning to life . . . veins opening wider, lungs filling more deeply, tasting the rich light and pure air without being aware of them, enjoying each stroke of antique pen across the parchment, the great heap of previous pages stacked around on the circular table, chunks of broken masonry serving as paperweights, the story flowing freely again, immortality beckoning with each stanza, each line.

Silenus had come to the most difficult and exciting part of the poem, the scenes where conflict has raged across a thousand landscapes, entire civilizations have been laid waste, and representatives of the Titans call pause to meet and negotiate with the Olympians' humorless heroes. On this broad landscape of his imagination strode Saturn, Hyperion, Cottus, Iäpetus, Oceanus, Briareus, Mimus, Porphyrion, Enceladus, Rhoetus and others – their equally titanic sisters Tethys, Phoebe, Theia, and Clymene – and opposite them the doleful countenances of Jupiter, Apollo, and their ilk.

Silenus did not know the outcome of this most epic of poems. He lived on now only to finish the tale . . . had done so for decades. Gone were the dreams of his youth of fame and wealth from apprenticing himself to the Word – he had gained fame and wealth beyond measure and it had all but killed him, *had* killed his art – and although he knew that the *Cantos* was the finest literary work of his age, he wanted only to finish it, to know the outcome himself, and to set each stanza, each line, *each word*, in the finest, clearest, most beautiful form possible.

Now he wrote feverishly, almost mad with desire to finish what he had long thought unfinishable. The words and phrases flew from his antique pen to the antiquated paper; stanzas leaped into being with no effort, cantos found their voice and finished themselves with no need for revision, no pause for inspiration. The poem unfolded with shocking speed, astounding revelations, heart-stopping beauty in both word and image.

Under their flag of truce, Saturn and his usurper, Jupiter, faced each other across a treaty slab of sheer-cut marble. Their dialogue was both epic and simple, their arguments for being, their rationale for war creating the finest debate since Thucydides' *Melian Dialogue*. Suddenly something new, something totally unplanned by Martin Silenus in all of his long hours of musing without his muse, entered the poem. Both of the kings of the gods expressed fear of some *third* usurper, some terrible outside force that threatened the stability of either of their reigns. Silenus watched in pure astonishment as the characters he had created through thousands of hours of effort defied his will and shook hands across the marble slab, setting an alliance against . . .

Against what?

The poet paused, the pen stopping, as he realized that he could barely see the page. He had been writing in half-darkness for some time, and now full darkness had descended.

Silenus returned to himself in that process of allowing the world to rush in once more, much like the return to the senses following orgasm. Only the descent of the writer to the world was more painful as he or she returned, trailing clouds of glory which quickly dissipated in the mundane flow of sensory trivia.

Silenus looked around. The great dining hall was quite dark except for the fitful glow of starlight and distant explosions through the panes and ivy above. The tables around him were mere shadows, the walls, thirty meters away in all directions, darker shadows laced through with the varicose darkness of desert creeper. Outside the dining hall, the evening wind had risen, its voices louder now, contralto and soprano solos being sung by cracks in the jagged rafters and rents in the dome above him.

The poet sighed. He had no hand torch in his pack. He had brought nothing but water and his *Cantos*. He felt his stomach stir in hunger. *Where was that goddamn Brawne Lamia?* But as soon as he thought of it, he realized that he was pleased that the woman had not returned for him. He needed to stay in solitude to finish the poem . . . at this rate it would take no longer than a day, the night perhaps. A few hours and he would be finished with his life's work, ready to rest a while and appreciate the small daily things, the trivia of living which for decades now had been only an interruption of work he could not complete.

Martin Silenus sighed again and began setting manuscript pages in his pack. He would find a light somewhere . . . start a fire if he had to use Sad King Billy's ancient tapestries for kindling. He would write outside by the light of the space battle if he had to.

Silenus held the last few pages and his pen in hand and turned to look for the exit.

Something was standing in the darkness of the hall with him.

Lamia, he thought, feeling relief and disappointment war with one another.

But it was not Brawne Lamia. Silenus noted the distortion, the bulk of mass above and too-long legs below, the play of starlight on carapace and thorn, the shadow of arms under arms, and especially the ruby glow of hell-lighted crystal where the eyes should be.

Silenus let out a groan and sat again. 'Not now!' he cried. 'Begone, goddamn your eyes!'

The tall shadow moved closer, its footfalls silent on cold ceramic. The sky rippled with blood-red energy, and the poet could see the thorns and blades and razorwire wrappings now.

'No!' cried Martin Silenus. 'I refuse. Leave me alone.'

The Shrike stepped closer. Silenus's hand twitched, lifted the pen again, and wrote across the empty lower margin of his last page: IT IS TIME, MARTIN.

He stared at what he had written, stifling the urge to giggle insanely. To his knowledge, the Shrike had never spoken . . . never *communicated* . . . to anyone. Other than through the paired media of pain and death.

'No!' he screamed again. 'I have work to do. Take someone else, goddamn you!'

The Shrike took another step forward. The sky pulsed with silent plasma explosions while yellows and reds ran down the creature's quicksilver chest and arms like spilled paints. Martin Silenus's hand twitched, wrote across his earlier message – IT IS TIME NOW, MARTIN.

Silenus hugged his manuscript to himself, lifting the last pages from the table so that he could write no more. His teeth showed in a terrible rictus as he all but hissed at the apparition.

YOU WERE READY TO TRADE PLACES WITH YOUR PATRON his hand wrote on the tabletop itself.

'Not now!' screamed the poet. 'Billy's *dead*! Just let me finish. *Please!*' Martin Silenus had never begged in his long, long life. He begged now. 'Please, oh please. Please just let me finish.'

The Shrike took a step forward. It was so close that its misshapen upper body blocked out the starlight and set the poet in shadow.

NO wrote Martin Silenus's hand, and then the pen dropped as the Shrike reached out infinitely long arms, and infinitely sharp fingers pierced the poet's arms to the marrow.

Martin Silenus screamed as he was dragged from under the dining dome. He screamed as he saw dunes underfoot, heard the slide of sand under his own screams, and saw the tree rising out of the valley.

The tree was larger than the valley, taller than the mountains the pilgrims had crossed; its upper branches seemed to reach into space. The tree was steel and chrome, and its branches were thorns and nettles. Human beings struggled and wriggled on those thorns – thousands and tens of thousands. In the red light from the dying sky, Silenus focused above his pain and realized that he recognized some of those forms. They were *bodies*, not souls or other abstracts, and they obviously were suffering the agonies of the pain-wracked living.

IT IS NECESSARY wrote Silenus's own hand against the unyielding cold of the Shrike's chest. Blood dripped on quicksilver and sand.

'No!' screamed the poet. He beat his fists against scalpel blades and razorwire. He pulled and struggled and twisted even as the creature hugged him more closely, pulling him on to its own blades as if he were a butterfly being mounted, a specimen being pinned. It was not the unthinkable pain that drove Martin Silenus beyond sanity, it was the sense of irretrievable loss. He had almost finished it. *He had almost finished it!*

'No!' screamed Martin Silenus, struggling more wildly until a spray of blood and screamed obscenities filled the air. The Shrike carried him toward the waiting tree.

In the dead city, screams echoed for another minute, growing fainter and farther away. Then there was a silence broken only by the doves returning to their nests, dropping into the shattered domes and towers with a soft rustle of wings.

The wind came up, rattling loose Perspex panes and masonry, shifting brittle leaves across dry fountains, finding entrance through the broken panes of the dome and lifting manuscript pages in a gentle whirlwind, some pages escaping to be blown across the silent courtyards and empty walkways and collapsed aqueducts.

After a while, the wind died, and then nothing moved in the City of Poets.

TWENTY-TWO

Brawne Lamia found her four-hour walk turning into a ten-hour nightmare. First there was the diversion to the dead city and the difficult choice of leaving Silenus behind. She did not want the poet to stay there alone; she did not want to force him to go on nor to take the time for a return to the Tombs. As it was, the detour along the ridgeline cost her an hour of travel time.

Crossing the last of the dunes and the rock barrens was exhausting and tedious. By the time she reached the foothills it was late afternoon and the Keep was in shadow.

It had been easy descending the six hundred and sixty-one stone stairs from the Keep forty hours earlier. The ascent was a test even of her Lusus-bred muscles. As she climbed, the air grew cooler, the view more spectacular, until by the time she was four hundred meters above the foothills she was no longer perspiring and the Valley of the Time Tombs was in sight once again. Only the tip of the Crystal Monolith was visible from this angle, and that as an irregular glimmer and flash of light. She stopped once to make sure that it was not truly a message being flashed, but the glimmers were random, merely a panel of crystal catching the light as it dangled from the broken Monolith.

Just before the last hundred stairs, Lamia tried her comlog again. The comm channels were the usual hash and nonsense, presumably distorted by the time tides, which broke down all but the closest of electromagnetic communications. A comm laser would have worked . . . it seemed to work with the Consul's antique comlog relay . . . but besides that single machine, they had no comm lasers now that Kassad had disappeared. Lamia shrugged and climbed the final stairs.

Chronos Keep had been built by Sad King Billy's androids – never a true keep, it had been intended as a resort, travel inn, and artists' summer haven. After the evacuation of the City of Poets, the place had remained empty for more than a century, visited by only the most daring of adventurers.

With the gradual waning of the Shrike menace, tourists and pilgrims had begun to use the place, and eventually the Church of the Shrike reopened it as a necessary stop on the annual Shrike Pilgrimage. Some of its rooms carved deepest in the mountain or atop the least accessible of turrets had been rumored to be the site of arcane rituals and elaborate sacrifices to that creature the Shrike Cultists called the Avatar.

With the imminent opening of the Tombs, wild irregularities of the time tides, and evacuation of the northern reaches, Chronos Keep had again fallen silent. And so it was when Brawne Lamia returned.

The desert and dead city were still in sunlight, but the Keep was in twilight as Lamia reached the bottom terrace, rested a moment, found her flashlight in her smallest pack, and entered the maze. The corridors were dark. During their stay there two days earlier, Kassad had explored and announced that all power sources were down for good – solar converters shattered, fusion cells smashed, and even the backup batteries broken and strewn about the cellars. Lamia had thought of that a score of times as she hiked up the six hundred and three-score stairs, glowering at the elevator nacelles frozen on their rusted vertical tracks.

The larger halls, designed for dinners and gatherings, were just as they had left them . . . strewn with the desiccated remains of abandoned banquets and the signs of panic. There were no bodies, but browning streaks on stone walls and tapestries suggested an orgy of violence not too many weeks before.

Lamia ignored the chaos, ignored the harbingers – great, black birds with obscenely human faces – taking wing from the central dining hall, and ignored her own fatigue as she climbed the many levels to the storeroom where they had camped. Stairways grew inexplicably narrower, while pale light through colored glass cast sickly hues. Where the panes were shattered or absent, gargoyles peered in as if frozen in the act of entering. A cold wind blew down from the snowy reaches of the Bridle Range and made Lamia shiver under her sunburn.

The packs and extra belongings were where they had left them, in the small storeroom high above the central chamber. Lamia checked to make sure that the some of the boxes and crates in the room contained nonperishable food items, and then she went out on to the small balcony where Lenar Hoyt had played his balalaika so few hours – such an eternity – ago.

The shadows of the high peaks stretched kilometers across the sand, almost to the dead city. The Valley of the Time Tombs and the jumbled wastes beyond still languished in evening light, boulders and low rock formations throwing a jumble of shadows. Lamia could not make out the Tombs from here, although an occasional glimmer still sparkled from the Monolith. She tried her comlog again, cursed it when it gave her only static and background garble, and went back in to choose and load her supplies.

She took four packs of basics wrapped in flowfoam and molded fiberplastic. There was water in the Keep – the troughs from the snowmelt far above were a technology which could not break down – and she filled all of the bottles she had brought and searched for more. Water was their most serious need. She cursed Silenus for not coming with her; the old man could have carried at least a half a dozen water bottles.

She was ready to leave when she heard the noise. Something was in the Grand Hall, between her and the staircase. Lamia pulled on the last of the packs, pulled her father's automatic pistol from her belt, and went slowly down the staircases.

The Hall was empty; the harbingers had not returned. Heavy tapestries, stirred by the wind, blew like rotted pennants above the litter of food and utensils. Against the far wall, a huge sculpture of the Shrike's face, all free-floating chrome and steel, rotated to the breeze.

Lamia edged across the space, swiveling every few seconds so that her back was never turned to one dark corner for long. Suddenly a scream froze her in her tracks.

It was not a human scream. The tones ululated to the ultrasonic and beyond, setting Lamia's teeth on edge and making her grip the pistol with white fingers. Abruptly it was cut off as if a player beam had been lifted from a disk.

Lamia saw where the noise had come from. Beyond the banquet table, beyond the sculpture, under the six large stained-glass windows where the dying light bled muted colors, there was a small door. The voice had echoed up and out as if it had escaped from some dungeon or cellar far below.

Brawne Lamia was curious. All of her life had been a conflict with inquisitiveness above and beyond the norm, culminating in her choice of the obsolete and sometimes amusing profession of private investigator. More than one time her curiosity had led her into embarrassment or trouble or both. And more than a few times her curiosity had paid off in knowledge few others had.

Not this time.

Lamia had come to find much-needed food and water. None of the others would have come here . . . the three older men could not have beaten her here even with her detour to the dead city . . . and anything or anyone else was not her concern.

Kassad? she wondered but stifled the thought. That sound had not come from the throat of the FORCE Colonel.

Brawne Lamia backed away from the door, keeping her pistol ready, found the steps to the main levels, and descended carefully, moving through each room with as much stealth as is possible while carrying seventy kilos of goods and more than a dozen water bottles. She caught a glimpse of herself in a faded glass on the lowest level – squat body poised, pistol raised and swiveling, a great burden of packs tottering on her back and dangling from broad straps, bottles and canteens clanking together.

Lamia did not find it amusing. She breathed a sigh of relief when she was out on the lowest terrace, out in the cool, thin air and ready to descend once again. She did not need her flashlight yet – an evening sky suddenly filled with lowering clouds shed a pink and amber light on the world, illuminating even the Keep and the foothills below in its rich glow.

She took the steep stairs two at a time, her powerful leg muscles aching before she had reached halfway. She did not tuck the gun away but kept it ready should anything descend from above or appear in an aperture in the rock face. Reaching the bottom, she stepped away from the staircase and looked up at the towers and terraces half a kilometer above.

Rocks were falling toward her. More than rocks, she realized, gargoyles had been knocked off their ancient perches and were tumbling with the boulders, their demonic faces lighted by the twilight glow. Lamia ran, packs and bottles swinging, realized that she had no time to reach a safe distance before the debris arrived, and threw herself between two low boulders leaning against one another.

Her packs kept her from fitting all the way beneath them, and she struggled, loosening straps, aware of the incredible noises as the first of the rocks struck behind her, ricocheted overhead. Lamia pulled and pushed with an effort that tore leather, snapped fiberplastic, and then she was under the boulders, pulling her packs and bottles in with her, determined not to have to return to the Keep.

Rocks the size of her head and hands pelted the air around her. The shattered head of a stone goblin bounced past, smashing a small boulder not three meters away. For a moment, the air was filled with missiles, larger stones smashed on the boulder above her head, and then the avalanche was past, and there was only the patter of smaller stones from the secondary fall.

Lamia leaned over to tug her pack further in to safety, and a stone the size of her comlog ricocheted off the rockface outside, skipped almost horizontally toward her hiding place, and bounced twice in the small cave her shelter made, then struck her in the temple.

Lamia awoke with an old-person's groan. Her head hurt. It was full night outside, the pulses from distant skirmishes lighting the inside of her shelter through cracks above. She raised fingers to her temple and found caked blood along her cheek and neck.

She pulled herself out of the crevice, struggling over the tumble of new-fallen rocks outside, and sat a moment, head lowered, resisting the urge to vomit.

Her packs were intact, and only one water bottle had been smashed. She found her pistol where she had dropped it in the small space not littered with smashed rocks. The stone outcrop on which she stood had been scarred and slashed by the violence of the brief avalanche.

Lamia queried her comlog. Less than an hour had elapsed. Nothing had descended to carry her away or slit her throat while she lay unconscious. She peered one last time at the ramparts and balconies, now invisible far above her, dragged her gear out, and set off down the treacherous stone path at double time.

Martin Silenus was not at the edge of the dead city when she detoured to it. Somehow she had not expected him to be, although she hoped he had merely gotten tired of waiting and had walked the few kilometers to the valley.

The temptation to take off her packs, lower the bottles to the ground and rest a while was very strong. Lamia resisted it. Her small automatic in her hand, she walked through the streets of the dead city. The explosions of light were enough to guide her way.

The poet did not respond to her echoing shouts, although hundreds of small birds Lamia couldn't identify exploded into flight, their wings white in the darkness. She walked through the lower levels of the king's old palace, shouting up stairways, even firing her pistol once, but there was no sign of Silenus. She walked through courtyards beneath walls heavy-laden with creeper vines, calling his name, hunting for some sign that he had been there. Once, she saw a fountain that reminded her of the poet's tale about the night Sad King Billy disappeared, carried off by the Shrike, but there were other fountains, and she could not be sure this was the one.

Lamia walked through the central dining hall under the shattered dome, but the room was dark with shadows. There was a sound, and she swiveled, pistol ready, but it was only a leaf or ancient sheet of paper blowing across ceramic.

She sighed and left the city, walking easily despite her fatigue after days without sleep. There was no response to comlog queries, although she felt the *déjà vu* tug of the time tides and was not surprised. The evening winds had eradicated any tracks Martin might have left on his return to the valley.

The Tombs were glowing again, Lamia noticed even before she reached the wide saddle at the entrance to the valley. It was not a bright glow – nothing to compare to the silent riot of light above – but each of the aboveground Tombs seemed to be shedding a pale light, as if releasing energy stored during the long day.

Lamia stood at the head of the valley and shouted, warning Sol and the others that she was returning. She would not have refused an offer to help with the packs for this last hundred meters. Lamia's back was raw and her shirt was soaked with blood where the straps had cut into flesh.

There was no answer to her cries.

She felt her exhaustion as she slowly climbed the steps to the Sphinx, dropped her gear on the broad, stone porch, and fumbled for her flashlight. The interior was dark. Sleeping robes and packs lay strewn about in the room where they had slept. Lamia shouted, waited for the echoes to die, and played her light around the room again. Everything was the same. No, wait, *something* was different. She closed her eyes and remembered the room as it had been that morning.

The Möbius cube was missing. The strange energy-sealed box left behind by Het Masteen on the windwagon was no longer in its place in the corner. Lamia shrugged and went outside.

The Shrike was waiting. It stood just outside the door. It was taller than she had imagined, towering over her.

Lamia stepped out and backed away, stifling the urge to scream at the thing. The raised pistol seemed small and futile in her hand. The flashlight dropped unheeded to the stone.

The thing cocked its head and looked at her. Red light pulsed from somewhere behind its multifaceted eyes. The angles of its body and blades caught the light from above.

'You son of a bitch,' said Lamia, her voice level. 'Where are they? What have you done with Sol and the baby? Where are the others?'

The creature cocked its head the other way. Its face was sufficiently alien that Lamia could make out no expression there. Its body language communicated only threat. Steel fingers clicked open like retractable scalpels.

Lamia shot it four times in the face, the heavy 16-mm slugs striking solidly and whining away into the night.

'I didn't come here to die, you metallic motherfucker,' said Lamia, took aim, and fired another dozen times, each slug striking home.

Sparks flew. The Shrike jerked its head upright as if listening to some distant sound.

It was gone.

Lamia gasped, crouched, whirled around. Nothing. The valley floor glowed in starlight as the sky grew quiescent. The shadows were ink black but distant. Even the wind was gone.

Brawne Lamia staggered over to her packs and sat on the largest one, trying to bring her heart rate down to normal. She was interested to find that she had not been afraid . . . not really . . . but there was no denying the adrenaline in her system.

Her pistol still in her hand, half a dozen bullets remaining in the magazine and the propellant charge still strong, she lifted a water bottle and took a long drink.

The Shrike appeared at her side. The arrival had been instantaneous and soundless.

Lamia dropped the bottle, tried to bring the pistol around while twisting to one side.

She might as well have been moving in slow motion. The Shrike extended its right hand, fingerblades the length of darning needles caught the light, and one of the tips slid behind her ear, found her skull, and slipped inside her head with no friction, no pain beyond an icy sense of penetration.

TWENTY-THREE

Colonel Fedmahn Kassad had stepped through a portal expecting strangeness; instead he found the choreographed insanity of war. Moneta had preceded him. The Shrike had escorted him, fingerblades sunk into Kassad's upper arm. When Kassad finished his step through the tingling energy curtain, Moneta was waiting and the Shrike was gone.

Kassad knew at once where they were. The view was from atop the low mountain into which Sad King Billy had commanded his effigy carved almost two centuries earlier. The flat area atop the peak was empty except for the debris of an anti-space missile defense battery which still smoldered. From the glaze of the granite and the still-bubbling molten metal, Kassad guessed that the battery had been lanced from orbit.

Moneta walked to the edge of the cliff, fifty meters above Sad King Billy's massive brow, and Kassad joined her there. The view of the river valley, the city, and the spaceport heights ten kilometers to the west told the story.

Hyperion's capital was burning. The old part of the city, Jacktown, was a miniature firestorm, and there were a hundred lesser fires dotting the suburbs and lining the highway to the airport like well-tended signal fires. Even the Hoolie River was burning as an oil fire spread beneath antiquated docks and warehouses. Kassad could see the spire of an ancient church rising above the flames. He looked for Cicero's, but the bar was hidden by smoke and flames upriver.

The hills and valley were a mass of movement, as if an anthill had been kicked apart by giant boots. Kassad could see the highways, clogged with a river of humanity and moving more slowly than the real river as tens of thousands fled the fighting. The flash of solid artillery and energy weapons stretched to the horizon and lighted low clouds above. Every few minutes, a flying machine – military skimmer or dropship – would rise from the smoke near the spaceport or from the wooded hills to the north and south, the air would fill with stabs of coherent light from above and below, and the vehicle would fall, trailing a plume of black smoke and orange flames.

Hovercraft flitted across the river like waterbugs, dodging between the burning wreckage of boats, barges, and other hovercraft. Kassad noticed that the single highway bridge was down, with even its concrete and stone abutments burning. Combat lasers and hellwhip beams lashed through the smoke; antipersonnel missiles were visible as white specks traveling faster than the eye could follow, leaving trails of rippling, superheated air in their wakes. As he and Moneta watched, an explosion near the spaceport mush-roomed a cloud of flame into the air.

— *Not nuclear*, he thought.

— *No.*

The skinsuit covering his eyes acted like a vastly improved FORCE visor, and Kassad used the ability to zoom in on a hill five kilometers to the northwest across the river. FORCE Marines loped toward the summit, some already dropping and using their shaped excavation charges to dig fox-holes. Their suits were activated, the camouflage polymers perfect, their heat signatures minimal, but Kassad had no difficulty seeing them. He could make out faces if he wished.

Tactical command and tightbeam channels whispered in his ears. He recognized the excited chatter and inadvertent obscenities which had been the hallmark of combat for too many human generations to count. Thousands of troops had dispersed from the spaceport and their staging areas and were digging in around a circle with its circumference twenty klicks from the city, its spokes carefully planned fields of fire and total-destruction vectors.

— *They're expecting an invasion*, communicated Kassad, feeling the effort as something more than subvocalization, something less than tele-pathy.

Moneta raised a quicksilver arm to point toward the sky.

It was a high overcast, at least two thousand meters, and it was a shock when it was penetrated first by one blunt craft, then a dozen more, and, within seconds, a hundred descending objects. Most were concealed by camouflage polymers and background-coded containment fields, but again Kassad had no difficulty making them out. Under the polymers, the gun-metal gray skins had faint markings in the subtle calligraphy he recognized as Ouster. Some of the larger craft were obviously dropships, their blue plasma tails visible enough, but the rest descended slowly under the rip-pling air of suspension fields, and Kassad noted the lumpy size and shape of Ouster invasion canisters, some undoubtedly carrying supplies and artil-lery, many undoubtedly empty, decoys for the ground defenses.

An instant later, the cloud ceiling was broken again as several thousand free-falling specks fell like hail: Ouster infantry dropping past canisters and dropships, waiting until the last possible second to deploy their suspension fields and parafoils.

Whoever the FORCE commander was, he had discipline – over both himself and his men. Ground batteries and the thousands of Marines deployed around the city ignored the easy targets of the dropships and canisters, then waited for the paratroops' arresting devices to deploy . . . some at little better than treetop height. At that instant, the air filled with thousands of shimmers and smoke trails as lasers flickered through the smoke and missiles exploded.

At first glance, the damage done was devastating, more than enough to deter any attack, but a quick scan told Kassad that at least forty percent of the Ousters had landed – adequate numbers for the first wave of any planetary attack.

A cluster of five parafoilists swung toward the mountain where he and Moneta stood. Beams from the foothills tumbled two of them in flames, one corkscrewed down in a panic descent to avoid further lancing, and the final two caught a breeze from the east, sending them spiraling into the forest below.

All of Kassad's senses were engaged now; he smelled the ionized air and cordite and solid propellant; smoke and the dull acid of plasma explosive made his nostrils flare; somewhere in the city, sirens wailed while the crack of small-arms fire and burning trees came to him on the gentle breeze; radio and intercepted tightbeam channels babbled; flames lit the valley and laser lances played like searchlights through the clouds. Half a kilometer below them, where the forest faded to the grass of the foothills, squads of Hegemony Marines were engaging Ouster paratroopers in a hand-to-hand struggle. Screams were audible.

Fedmahn Kassad watched with the fascination he had once felt at the stimsim experience of a French cavalry charge at Agincourt.

— *This is no simulation?*

— *No*, replied Moneta.

— *Is it happening now?*

The silver apparition at his side cocked its head. *When is now?*

— *Contiguous with our . . . meeting . . . in the Valley of the Tombs.*

— *No.*

— *The future then?*

— *Yes.*

— *But the near future?*

— *Yes. Five days from the time you and your friends arrived in the valley.*

Kassad shook his head in wonder. If Moneta was to be believed, he had traveled forward in time.

Her face reflected flames and multiple hues as she swiveled toward him. *Do you wish to participate in the fighting?*

— *Fight the Ousters?* He folded his arms and watched with new intensity. He had received a preview of the fighting abilities of this strange skinsuit. It was quite likely that he could turn the tide of battle single-handedly . . . most probably destroy the few thousand Ouster troops already on the ground. *No*, he sent to her, *not now. Not at this time.*

— *The Lord of Pain believes that you are a warrior.*

Kassad turned to look at her again. He was mildly curious as to why she gave the Shrike such a ponderous title. *The Lord of Pain can go fuck itself*, he sent. *Unless it wants to fight me.*

Moneta was still for a long minute, a quicksilver sculpture on a wind-blown peak.

— *Would you really fight him?* she sent at last.

— *I came to Hyperion to kill it. And you. I will fight whenever either or both of you agree.*

— *You still believe that I am your enemy?*

Kassad remembered the assault on him at the Tombs, knowing now that it was less a rape than a granting of his own wish, his own subvocalized desire to be lovers with this improbable woman once again. *I don't know what you are.*

— *At first I was victim, like so many,* sent Moneta, her gaze returning to the valley. *Then, far in our future, I saw why the Lord of Pain had been forged . . . had to be forged . . . and then I became both companion and keeper.*

— *Keeper?*

— *I monitored the time tides, made repairs to the machinery, and saw to it that the Lord of Pain did not awake before his time.*

— *Then you can control it?* Kassad's pulse raced at the thought.

— *No.*

— *Then who or what can control it?*

— *Only he or she who beats it in personal combat.*

— *Who has beaten it?*

— *No one,* sent Moneta. *Either in your future or your past.*

— *Have many tried?*

— *Millions.*

— *And they have all died?*

— *Or worse.*

Kassad took a breath. *Do you know if I will be allowed to fight it?*

— *You will.*

Kassad let the breath out. No one had beaten it. His future was her past . . . she had lived there . . . she had glimpsed the terrible tree of thorns just as he had, seeing familiar faces there the way he had seen Martin Silenus struggling, impaled, years before he had met the man. Kassad turned his back on the fighting in the valley below. *Can we go to him now? I challenge him to personal combat.*

Moneta looked into his face for a silent moment. Kassad could see his own quicksilver visage reflected in hers. Without answering, she turned, touched the air, and brought the portal into existence.

Kassad stepped forward and went through first.

TWENTY-FOUR

Gladstone translated directly to Government House and swept into the Tactical Command Center with Leigh Hunt and half a dozen other aides in attendance. The room was packed: Morpurgo, Singh, Van Zeidt and a dozen others represented the military, although Gladstone noticed that the young naval hero, Commander Lee, was absent; most of the cabinet ministers were there, including Allan Imoto of Defense, Garion Persov of Diplomacy, and Barbre Dan-Gyddis of Economy; senators were arriving even as Gladstone did, some of them looking as though they had just been awakened – the 'power curve' of the oval conference table held Senators Kolchev from Lusus, Richeau from Renaissance Vector, Roanquist from Nordholm, Kakinuma from Fuji, Sabenstorafem from Sol Draconi Septem, and Peters from Deneb Drei; President Pro Tem Denzel-Hiat-Amin sat with a befuddled expression, his bald head gleaming in the light from overhead spots, while his young counterpart, All Thing Speaker Gibbons, perched on the edge of his seat, hands on his knees, his posture a study in barely contained energy. Councilor Albedo's projection sat directly opposite Gladstone's empty chair. All stood as Gladstone swept down the aisle, took her seat, and gestured everyone to theirs.

'Explain,' she said.

General Morpurgo stood, nodded at a subordinate, and lights dimmed while holos misted.

'Forgo the visuals!' snapped Meina Gladstone. '*Tell us.*'

Holos faded and the lights came back up. Morpurgo looked stunned, slightly vacant. He looked down at his light pointer, frowned at it, and dropped it in a pocket. 'Madame Executive, Senators, Ministers, President and Speaker, Honorables . . .' Morpurgo cleared his throat, 'the Ousters have succeeded in a devastating surprise attack. Their combat Swarms are closing on half a dozen Web worlds.'

The commotion in the room drowned him out. 'Web worlds!' cried various voices. There were shouts from politicians, ministers, and executive branch functionaries.

'Silence,' commanded Gladstone, and there was silence. 'General, you assured us that any hostile forces were a minimum of five years from the Web. How and why has this changed?'

The General made eye contact with the CEO. 'Madame Executive, as far as we can tell, all of the Hawking drive wakes were decoys. The Swarms

507

went off their drives decades ago and drove toward their objectives at sublight speed . . .'

Excited babble drowned him out.

'Go on, General,' said Gladstone, and the hubbub died once more.

'At sublight velocities . . . some of the Swarms must have been traveling that way for fifty standard years or more . . . there was no possible way to detect them. It simply was not the fault of—'

'What worlds are in danger, General?' asked Gladstone. Her voice was very low, very level.

Morpurgo glanced toward the empty air as if seeking visuals there, returned his gaze to the table. His hands clenched into fists. 'Our intelligence at this time, based on fusion drive sightings followed by a shift to Hawking drives when they were discovered, suggests that the first wave will arrive at Heaven's Gate, God's Grove, Mare Infinitus, Asquith, Ixion, Tsingtao-Hsishuang Panna, Acteon, Barnard's World, and Tempe within the next fifteen to seventy-two hours.'

This time there was no silencing the commotion. Gladstone let the shouts and exclamations continue for several minutes before she raised a hand to bring the group under control.

Senator Kolchev was on his feet. 'How the goddamn *hell* did this happen, General? Your assurances were absolute!'

Morpurgo stood his ground. There was no responsive anger in his voice. 'Yes, Senator, and also based on faulty data. We were wrong. Our assumptions were wrong. The CEO will have my resignation within the hour . . . the other joint chiefs join me in this.'

'God*damn* your resignation!' shouted Kolchev. 'We may all be hanging from farcaster stanchions before this is over. The question is – what the hell are you *doing* about this invasion?'

'Gabriel,' Gladstone said softly, 'sit down, please. That was my next question. General? Admiral? I presume that you have already issued orders regarding the defense of these worlds?'

Admiral Singh stood and took his place next to Morpurgo. 'M. Executive, we've done what we could. Unfortunately, of all the worlds threatened by this first wave, only Asquith has a FORCE contingent in place. The rest can be reached by the fleet – none lack farcaster capabilities – but the fleet cannot spread itself that thin to protect them all. And, unfortunately . . .' Singh paused a moment and then raised his voice to be heard over the rising tumult. 'And, unfortunately, deployment of the strategic reserve to reinforce the Hyperion campaign already had been initiated. Approximately sixty percent of the two hundred fleet units we had committed to this redeployment have either farcast through to Hyperion System or been translated to staging areas away from their forward defensive positions on the Web periphery.'

Meina Gladstone rubbed her cheek. She realized that she was still wearing her cape, although the privacy collar was lowered, and now she unclasped it and let it fall on to the back of her chair. 'What you're saying,

Admiral, is that these worlds are undefended and there is no way to get our forces turned around and back there in time. Correct?'

Singh stood at attention, as ramrod stiff as a man before a firing squad. 'Correct, CEO.'

'What *can* be done?' she asked over the renewed shouting.

Morpurgo stepped forward. 'We're using the civilian farcaster matrix to translate as many FORCE:ground infantry and Marines as we can to the threatened worlds, along with light artillery and air/space defenses.'

Minister of Defense Imoto cleared his throat. 'But these will make little difference without fleet defenses.'

Gladstone glanced toward Morpurgo.

'This is true,' said the General. 'At best our forces will provide a rearguard action while an attempt at evacuation is carried out . . .'

Senator Richeau was on her feet. 'An *attempt* at evacuation! General, yesterday you told us that an evacuation of two or three million civilians from Hyperion was impractical. Are you now saying that we can successfully evacuate' – she paused a second to consult her comlog implant – 'seven *billion* people before the Ouster invasion force intervenes?'

'No,' said Morpurgo. 'We can sacrifice troops to save a few . . . a few selected officials, First Families, community and industrial leaders necessary to the continued war effort.'

'General,' said Gladstone, 'yesterday this group authorized immediate transferral of FORCE troops to the reinforcement fleet translating to Hyperion. Is that a problem in this new redeployment?'

General Van Zeidt of the Marines stood. 'Yes, M. Executive. Troops were farcast to waiting transports within the hour of this body's decision. Almost two thirds of the hundred thousand designated troops have translated into the Hyperion System by' – he glanced at his antique chronometer – '0530 hours standard. Approximately twenty minutes ago. It will be at least another eight to fifteen hours before these transports can return to Hyperion System staging areas and be returned to the Web.'

'And how many FORCE troops are available webwide?' asked Gladstone. She raised one knuckle to touch her lower lip.

Morpurgo took a breath. 'Approximately thirty thousand, M. Executive.'

Senator Kolchev slapped the table with the palm of his hand. 'So we stripped the Web of not only our fighting spacecraft, but the majority of FORCE troops.'

It was not a question, and Morpurgo did not answer.

Senator Feldstein from Barnard's World rose to her feet. 'M. Executive, my world . . . all of the worlds mentioned . . . need to be warned. If you are not prepared to make an immediate announcement, I must do so.'

Gladstone nodded. 'I will announce the invasion immediately after this meeting, Dorothy. We will facilitate your contact with constituents via all media.'

'Media be damned,' said the short, dark-haired woman, 'I'll be 'casting home as soon as we're done here. Whatever fate befalls Barnard's World, it is mine to share. Gentlemen and ladies, we should *all* be hanging from stanchions if the news is true.' Feldstein sat down amid murmurs and whispers.

Speaker Gibbons rose, waited for silence. His voice was wire-taut. 'General, you spoke of the *first* wave . . . is this cautionary military jargon, or do you have intelligence that there will be later waves? If so, what other Web and Protectorate worlds might be involved?'

Morpurgo's hands clenched and unclenched. He glanced again toward empty air, turned toward Gladstone. 'M. Executive, may I use one graphic?'

Gladstone nodded.

The holo was the same the military had used during their Olympus briefing – the Hegemony, gold; Protectorate stars, green; the Ouster Swarm vectors, red lines with blue-shifting tails; the Hegemony fleet deployments, orange – and it was immediately obvious that the red vectors had swung far from their old courses, lancing into Hegemony space like blood-tipped spears. The orange embers were heavily concentrated in the Hyperion System now, with others strung out along farcaster routes like beads on a chain.

Some of the senators with military experience gasped at what they saw.

'Of the dozen Swarms we know to be in existence,' said Morpurgo, his voice still soft, 'all appear to be committed to the invasion of the Web. Several have split into multiple attack groups. The second wave, projected to arrive at their targets within one hundred to two hundred and fifty hours of the first wave's assault, are vectored as pictured here.'

There was no sound in the room. Gladstone wondered if others were also holding their breaths.

'Second-wave assault targets include – Hebron, one hundred hours from now; Renaissance Vector, one hundred and ten hours; Renaissance Minor, one hundred and twelve hours; Nordholm, one hundred and twenty-seven hours; Maui-Covenant, one hundred and thirty hours; Thalia, one hundred and forty-three hours; Deneb Drei and Vier, one hundred and fifty hours; Sol Draconi Septem, one hundred and sixty-nine hours; Freeholm, one hundred and seventy hours; New Earth, one hundred and ninety-three hours; Fuji, two hundred and four hours; New Mecca, two hundred and five hours; Pacem, Armaghast, and Svoboda, two hundred and twenty-one hours; Lusus, two hundred and thirty hours; and Tau Ceti Center, two hundred and fifty hours.'

The holo faded. The silence stretched. General Morpurgo said, 'We assume that the first-wave Swarms will have secondary targets after their initial invasions, but transit times under Hawking drive will be standard Web travel time-debts, ranging from nine weeks to three years.' He stepped back and stood at parade rest.

'Good Christ,' whispered someone a few seats behind Gladstone.

The Chief Executive rubbed her lower lip. In order to save humanity from what she considered an eternity of slavery . . . or worse, extinction . . . she had been prepared to open the front door of the house to the wolf while most of the family hid upstairs, safe behind locked doors. Only now the day had arrived, and wolves were coming in through every door and window. She almost smiled at the justice of it, at her ultimate foolishness in thinking that she could uncage chaos and then control it.

'First,' she said, 'there will be no resignations, no self-recriminations, until I authorize them. It is quite possible that this government shall fall . . . that, indeed, members of this cabinet, myself among them . . . shall be, as Gabriel so aptly put it, hanging from stanchions. But in the meantime, we *are* the government of the Hegemony and must act as such.

'Second, I will meet with this body and representatives of other Senate committees in one hour in order to go over the speech I will give to the Web at 0800 standard. Your suggestions will be welcome at that time.

'Third, I hereby command and authorize the FORCE authorities here assembled and throughout the reaches of the Hegemony to do everything in their power to preserve and protect the citizenry and property of the Web and Protectorate, through whatever extraordinary means they must employ. General, Admiral, I want the troops translated back to threatened Web worlds within ten hours. I don't care how this is done, but it *will* be done.

'Fourth, after my speech, I will call a full session of the Senate and All Thing. At that time, I will declare that a state of war exists between the Human Hegemony and the Ouster nations. Gabriel, Dorothy, Tom, Eiko . . . *all* of you . . . you'll be very busy in the next few hours. Prepare your speeches for your homeworlds, but *deliver that vote*. I want unanimous Senate support. Speaker Gibbons, I can only ask for your help in guiding the All Thing debate. It is essential that we have a vote of the gathered All Thing by 1200 hours today. There can be no surprises.

'Fifth, we *will* evacuate the citizens of the worlds threatened by the first wave.' Gladstone held up her hand and stifled the objections and explanations from the experts. 'We will evacuate everyone we can in the time we have. Ministers Persov, Imoto, Dan-Gyddis, and Crunnens from the Web Transit Ministry will create and spearhead the Evacuation Coordination Council and will deliver a detailed report and action timeline to me by 1300 hours today. FORCE and the Bureau for Web Security will oversee crowd control and protection of farcaster access.

'Finally, I wish to see Councilor Albedo, Senator Kolchev, and Speaker Gibbons in my private chambers in three minutes. Are there any questions from anyone?'

Stunned faces stared back.

Gladstone rose. 'Good luck,' she said. 'Work quickly. Do nothing to spread unnecessary panic. And God save the Hegemony.' She turned and swept from the room.

Gladstone sat behind her desk. Kolchev, Gibbons, and Albedo sat across from her. The urgency in the air, felt from half-sensed activities beyond the doors, was made more maddening by Gladstone's long delay before speaking. She never took her eyes off Councilor Albedo. 'You,' she said at last, 'have betrayed us.'

The projection's urbane half-smile did not waver. 'Never, CEO.'

'Then you have one minute to explain why the TechnoCore and specifically the AI Advisory Council did not predict this invasion.'

'It will take only one word to explain this, M. Executive,' said Albedo. 'Hyperion.'

'Hyperion *shit!*' cried Gladstone, slamming her palm down on the ancient desk in a most un-Gladstone-like explosion of temper. 'I'm sick and tired of hearing about unfactorable variables and Hyperion the predictive black hole, Albedo. Either the Core can help us understand probabilities or they've been lying to us for five centuries. Which is it?'

'The Council predicted the war, CEO,' said the gray-haired image. 'Our confidential advisories to you and the need-to-know group explained the uncertainty of events once Hyperion became involved.'

'That's crap,' snapped Kolchev. 'Your predictions are supposed to be infallible in general trends. This attack must have been planned decades ago. Perhaps centuries.'

Albedo shrugged. 'Yes, Senator, but it is quite possible that only this administration's determination to start a war in the Hyperion System caused the Ousters to go through with the plan. We advised against any actions concerning Hyperion.'

Speaker Gibbons leaned forward. 'You gave us the names of the individuals necessary for the so-called Shrike Pilgrimage.'

Albedo did not shrug again, but his projected posture was relaxed, self-confident. 'You asked us to come up with names of Web individuals whose requests to the Shrike would change the outcome of the war we predicted.'

Gladstone steepled her fingers and tapped at her chin. 'And have you determined yet *how* these requests would change the outcome of that war . . . this war?'

'No,' said Albedo.

'Councilor,' said CEO Meina Gladstone, 'please be apprised that as of this moment, depending upon the outcome of the next few days, the government of the Hegemony of Man is considering declaring that a state of war exists between us and the entity known as the TechnoCore. As de facto ambassador from that entity, you are entrusted with relaying this fact.'

Albedo smiled. He spread his hands. 'M. Executive, the shock of this terrible news must have caused you to make a poor joke. Declaring war against the Core would be like . . . like a fish declaring war against water, like a driver attacking his EMV because of disturbing news of an accident elsewhere.'

Gladstone did not smile. 'I once had a grandfather on Patawpha,' she said slowly, her dialect thickening, 'who put six slugs from a pulse rifle into the family EMV when it did not start one morning. You are dismissed, Councilor.'

Albedo blinked and disappeared. The abrupt departure was either a deliberate breach of protocol – the projection usually left a room or let others leave before deliquescing – or it was a sign that the controlling intelligence in the Core had been shaken by the exchange.

Gladstone nodded at Kolchev and Gibbons. 'I won't keep you gentlemen,' she said. 'But be assured that I expect total support when the declaration of war is submitted in five hours.'

'You'll have it,' said Gibbons. The two men departed.

Aides came in through doorways and hidden panels, firing questions and cueing comlogs for instructions. Gladstone held up a finger. 'Where is Severn?' she asked. At the sight of blank faces, she added, 'The poet . . . artist, I mean. The one doing my portrait?'

Several aides looked at one another as if the Chief had come unhinged.

'He's still asleep,' said Leigh Hunt. 'He'd taken some sleeping pills, and no one thought to awaken him for the meeting.'

'I want him here within twenty minutes,' said Gladstone. 'Brief him. Where is Commander Lee?'

Niki Cardon, the young woman in charge of military liaison, spoke up. 'Lee was reassigned to perimeter patrol last night by Morpurgo and the FORCE:sea sector chief. He'll be hopping from one ocean world to another for twenty years our time. Right now he's . . . just translated to FORCE: SEA-COMCEN on Bressia, awaiting offworld transport.'

'Get him back here,' said Gladstone. 'I want him promoted to rear admiral or whatever the hell the necessary staff rank would be and then assigned here, to *me*, not Government House or Executive Branch. He can be the nuclear bagman if necessary.'

Gladstone looked at the blank wall a moment. She thought of the worlds she had walked that night; Barnard's World, the lamplight through leaves, ancient brick college buildings; God's Grove with its tethered balloons and free-floating zeplens greeting the dawn; Heaven's Gate with its Promenade . . . all these were first-wave targets. She shook her head. 'Leigh, I want you and Tarra and Brindenath to have the first drafts of both speeches – general address and the declaration of war – to me within forty-five minutes. Short. Unequivocal. Check the files under Churchill and Strudensky. Realistic but defiant, optimistic but tempered with grim resolve. Niki, I need real-time monitoring of every move the joint chiefs make. I want my own command map displays – relayed through my implant. CEO ONLY. Barbre, you're going to be my extension of diplomacy by other means in the Senate. Get in there and call in notes, pull strings, blackmail, cajole, and generally make them realize that it would be safer to go out and fight the Ousters right now than to cross me in the next three or four votes.

'Questions, anyone?' Gladstone waited three seconds and slapped her hands together. 'Well, let's move, people!'

In the brief interval before the next wave of senators, ministers, and aides, Gladstone swiveled toward the blank wall above her, raised her finger toward the ceiling, and shook her hand.

She turned back just as the next mob of VIPs was shown in.

TWENTY-FIVE

Sol, the Consul, Father Duré, and the unconscious Het Masteen were in the first of the Cave Tombs when they heard the shots. The Consul went out alone, slowly, carefully, testing for the storm of time tides which had driven them deeper into the valley.

'It's all right,' he called back. The pale glow of Sol's lantern lighted the back of the cave, illuminating three pale faces and the robed bundle that was the Templar. 'The tides have lessened,' called the Consul.

Sol stood. His daughter's face was a pale oval below his own. 'Are you sure the shots came from Brawne's gun?'

The Consul motioned toward the darkness outside. 'None of the rest of us carried a slugthrower. I'll go check.'

'Wait,' said Sol, 'I'll go with you.'

Father Duré remained kneeling next to Het Masteen. 'Go ahead. I'll stay with him.'

'One of us will check back within the next few minutes,' said the Consul.

The valley glowed from the pale light of the Time Tombs. Wind roared from the south, but the airstream was higher tonight, above the cliff walls, and the dunes on the valley floor were not disturbed. Sol followed the Consul as he picked his way down the rough trail to the valley floor and turned toward the head of the valley. Slight tugs of *déjà vu* reminded Sol of the violence of time tides an hour earlier, but now even the remnants of the bizarre storm were fading.

Where the trail widened on the valley floor, Sol and the Consul walked together past the scorched battlefield of the Crystal Monolith, the tall structure exuding a milky glow reflected by the countless shards littering the floor of the arroyo, then climbing slightly past the Jade Tomb with its pale-green phosphorescence, then turning again and following the gentle switchbacks leading up to the Sphinx.

'My God,' whispered Sol and rushed forward, trying not to jar his sleeping child in her carrier. He knelt by the dark figure on the top step.

'Brawne?' asked the Consul, stopping two paces back and panting for breath after the sudden climb.

'Yes.' Sol started to lift her head and then jerked his hand back when he encountered something slick and cool extruding from her skull.

'Is she dead?'

Sol held his daughter's head closer to his chest as he checked for a pulse in the woman's throat. 'No,' he said and took a deep breath. 'She's alive . . . but unconscious. Give me your light.'

Sol took the flashlight and played it over Brawne Lamia's sprawled form, following the silver cord – 'tentacle' was a better description, since the thing had a fleshy mass to it that made one think of organic origins – which led from the neural shunt socket in her skull across the broad top step of the Sphinx, in through the open portal. The Sphinx itself glowed the brightest of any of the Tombs, but the entrance was very dark.

The Consul came closer. 'What is it?' He reached out to touch the silver cable, jerked his hand back as quickly as Sol had. 'My God, it's warm.'

'It feels alive,' agreed Sol. He had been chafing Brawne's hands, and now he slapped her cheeks lightly, trying to awaken her. She did not stir. He swiveled and played the flashlight beam along the cable where it snaked out of sight down the entrance corridor. 'I don't think this is something she voluntarily attached herself to.'

'The Shrike,' said the Consul. He leaned closer to activate biomonitor readouts on Brawne's wrist comlog. 'Everything is normal except her brain waves, Sol.'

'What do they say?'

'They say that she's dead. Brain dead at least. No higher functions whatsoever.'

Sol sighed and rocked back on his heels. 'We have to see where that cable goes.'

'Can't we just unhook it from the shunt socket?'

'Look,' said Sol and played the light on the back of Brawne's head while lifting a mass of dark curls away. The neural shunt, normally a plasflesh disk a few millimeters wide with a ten-micrometer socket, had seemed to melt . . . flesh rising in a red welt to connect with the microlead extensions of the metal cable.

'It would take surgery to remove that,' whispered the Consul. He touched the angry-looking welt of flesh. Brawne did not stir. The Consul retrieved the flashlight and stood. 'You stay with her. I'll follow it in.'

'Use the comm channels,' said Sol, knowing how useless they had been during the rise and fall of time tides.

The Consul nodded and moved forward quickly before fear made him hesitate.

The chrome cable snaked down the main corridor, turning out of sight beyond the room where the pilgrims had slept the night before. The Consul glanced in the room, the flashlight beam illuminating the blankets and packs they had left behind in their hurry.

He followed the cable around the bend in the corridor; through the central portal where the hallway broke into three narrower halls; up a ramp and right again down the narrow passage they had called 'King Tut's Highway' during their earlier explorations; then down a ramp; along a low tunnel where he had to crawl, placing his hands and knees carefully so as not to touch the flesh-warm metal tentacle; up an incline so steep that he had to climb it like a chimney; down a wider corridor he did not remember, where stones leaned inward toward the ceiling, moisture dripping; and then down steeply, slowing his descent only by losing skin on his palms and knees, crawling finally along a stretch longer than the Sphinx had appeared wide. The Consul was thoroughly lost, trusting in the cable to lead him back out when the time came.

'Sol,' he called at last, not believing for an instant that the communicator would carry through stone and time tides.

'Here,' came the barest whisper of the scholar's voice.

'I'm way the hell inside,' the Consul whispered into his comlog. 'Down a corridor I don't remember us seeing before. It feels deep.'

'Did you find where the cable ends?'

'Yeah,' the Consul replied softly, sitting back to wipe sweat from his face with a handkerchief.

'Nexus?' asked Sol, referring to one of the countless terminal nodes where Web citizens could jack into the datasphere.

'No. The thing seems to flow directly into the stone of the floor here. The corridor ends here too. I've tried moving it, but the join is similar to where the neural shunt's been welded to her skull. It just seems part of the rock.'

'Come on out,' came Sol's voice over the rasp of static. 'We'll try to cut it off her.'

In the damp and darkness of the tunnel, the Consul felt true claustrophobia close on him for the first time in his life. He found it hard to breathe. He was sure that something was behind him in the darkness, closing off his air and only avenue of retreat. The pounding of his heart was almost audible in the tight stone crawlway.

He took slow breaths, wiped his face again, and forced the panic back. 'That might kill her,' he said between slow gasps for air.

No answer. The Consul called again, but something had cut off their thin connection.

'I'm coming out,' he said into the silent instrument and turned around, playing his flashlight along the low tunnel. *Had the cable-tentacle twitched, or was that just a trick of light?*

The Consul began crawling back the way he had come.

They had found Het Masteen at sunset, just minutes before the time storm struck. The Templar had been staggering when the Consul, Sol, and Duré had first seen him, and by the time they reached his fallen form, Masteen was unconscious.

'Carry him to the Sphinx,' said Sol.

At that moment, as if choreographed by the setting sun, the time tides flowed over them like a tidal wave of nausea and *déjà vu*. All three men fell to their knees. Rachel awoke and cried with the vigor of the newly born and terrified.

'Make for the valley entrance,' gasped the Consul, standing with Het Masteen draped over his shoulder. 'Got to . . . get out . . . the valley.'

The three men moved toward the mouth of the valley, past the first tomb, the Sphinx, but the time tides became worse, blowing against them like a terrible wind of vertigo. Thirty meters beyond and they could climb no more. They fell to hands and knees, Het Masteen rolling across the hard-packed trail. Rachel had ceased wailing and writhed in discomfort.

'Back,' gasped Paul Duré. 'Back down the valley. It was . . . better . . . below.'

They retraced their steps, staggering along the trail like three drunkards, each carrying a burden too precious to be dropped. Below the Sphinx they rested a moment, backs to a boulder, while the very fabric of space and time seemed to shift and buckle around them. It was as if the world had been the surface of a flag and someone had unfurled it with an angry snap. Reality seemed to billow and fold, then plunge farther away, folding back like a wave cresting above them. The Consul left the Templar lying against the rock and fell to all fours, panting, fingers clinging to the soil in panic.

'The Möbius cube,' said the Templar, stirring, his eyes still closed. 'We must have the Möbius cube.'

'Damn,' managed the Consul. He shook Het Masteen roughly. 'Why do we need it? Masteen, why do we need it?' The Templar's head bobbed back and forth limply. He was unconscious once again.

'I'll get it,' said Duré. The priest looked ancient and ill, his face and lips pale.

The Consul nodded, lifted Het Masteen over his shoulder, helped Sol gain his feet, and staggered away down the valley, feeling the riptides of anti-entropic fields lessen as they moved farther away from the Sphinx.

Father Duré had climbed the trail, climbed the long stairway, and staggered to the entrance of the Sphinx, clinging to the rough stones there the way a sailor would cling to a thrown line in rough seas. The Sphinx seemed to totter above him, first tilting thirty degrees one way, then fifty the other. Duré knew that it was only the violence of the time tides distorting his senses, but it was enough to make him kneel and vomit on the stone.

The tides paused a moment, like a violent surf resting between terrible wave assaults, and Duré found his feet, wiped his mouth with the back of his hand, and stumbled into the dark tomb.

He had not brought a flashlight; stumbling, he felt his way along the corridor, appalled by the twin fantasies of touching something slick and cool in the darkness or of stumbling into the room where he was reborn and finding his own corpse there, still moldering from the grave. Duré screamed, but the sound was lost in the tornado roar of his own pulse as the time tides returned in force.

The sleeping room was dark, that terrible dark which means the total absence of light, but Duré's eyes adjusted, and he realized that the Möbius cube itself was glowing slightly, telltales winking.

He stumbled across the cluttered room and grabbed the cube, lifting the heavy thing with a sudden burst of adrenaline. The Consul's summary tapes had mentioned this artifact – Masteen's mysterious luggage during the pilgrimage – as well as the fact that it was believed to hold an erg, one of the alien forcefield creatures used to power a Templar treeship. Duré had no idea why the erg was important now, but he clutched the box to his chest as he struggled back down the corridor, outside and down the steps, deeper into the valley.

'Here!' called the Consul from the first Cave Tomb at the base of the cliff wall. 'It's better here.'

Duré staggered up the trail, almost dropping the cube in his confusion and sudden draining of energy; the Consul helped him the last thirty steps into the tomb.

It was better inside. Duré could feel the ebb and flow of time tides just beyond the cave entrance, but back in the rear of the cave, glow-globes revealing elaborate carvings in their cold light, it was almost normal. The priest collapsed next to Sol Weintraub and set the Möbius cube near the silent but staring form of Het Masteen.

'He just awakened as you approached,' whispered Sol. The baby's eyes were very wide and very dark in the weak light.

The Consul dropped down next to the Templar. 'Why do we need the cube? Masteen, why do we need it?'

Het Masteen's gaze did not falter; he did not blink. 'Our ally,' he whispered. 'Our only ally against the Lord of Pain.' The syllables were etched with the distinctive dialect of the Templar world.

'*How* is it our ally?' demanded Sol, grabbing the man's robe in both his fists. 'How do we use it? When?'

The Templar's gaze was set on something in the infinite distance. 'We vied for the honor,' he whispered, voice hoarse. 'The True Voice of the *Sequoia Sempervirens* was the first to contact the Keats retrieval cybrid . . . but *I* was the one honored by the light of the Muir. It was the *Yggdrasill*, my *Yggdrasill*, which was offered in atonement for our sins against the Muir.' The Templar closed his eyes. A slight smile looked incongruous on his stern-featured face.

The Consul looked at Duré and Sol. 'That sounds more like Shrike Cult terminology than Templar dogma.'

'Perhaps it is both,' whispered Duré. 'There have been stranger coalitions in the history of theology.'

Sol lifted his palm to the Templar's forehead. The tall man was burning up with fever. Sol rummaged through their only medpak in search of a pain derm or feverpatch. Finding one, he hesitated. 'I don't know if Templars are within standard med norms. I don't want some allergy to kill him.'

The Consul took the feverpatch and applied it to the Templar's frail upper arm. 'They're within the norm.' He leaned closer. 'Masteen, what happened on the windwagon?'

The Templar's eyes opened but remained unfocused. 'Windwagon?'

'I don't understand,' whispered Father Duré.

Sol took him aside. 'Masteen never told his tale on the pilgrimage out,' he whispered. 'He disappeared during our first night out on the windwagon. Blood was left behind – plenty of blood – as well as his luggage and the Möbius cube. But no Masteen.'

'What happened on the windwagon?' the Consul whispered again. He shook the Templar slightly to get his attention. 'Think, True Voice of the Tree Het Masteen!'

The tall man's face changed, his eyes coming into focus, the vaguely Asiatic features settling into familiar, stern lines. 'I released the elemental from his confinement . . .'

'The erg,' Sol whispered to the baffled priest.

'. . . and bound him with the mind discipline I had learned in the High Branches. But then, without warning, the Lord of Pain came unto us.'

'The Shrike,' Sol whispered, more to himself than to the priest.

'Was it your blood spilled there?' the Consul asked the Templar.

'Blood?' Masteen drew his hood forward to hide his confusion. 'No, it was not my blood. The Lord of Pain had a . . . celebrant . . . in his grasp. The man fought. Attempted to escape the atonement spikes . . .'

'What about the erg?' pressed the Consul. 'The elemental. What did you expect it to do for you? . . . to protect you from the Shrike?'

The Templar frowned and raised a trembling hand to his brow. 'It . . . was not ready. *I* was not ready. I returned it to its confinement. The Lord of Pain touched me on the shoulder. I was . . . pleased . . . that my atonement should be within the same hour as the sacrifice of my treeship.'

Sol leaned closer to Duré. 'The treeship *Yggdrasill* was destroyed in orbit that same evening,' he whispered.

Het Masteen closed his eyes. 'Tired,' he whispered, his voice fading.

The Consul shook him again. 'How did you get here? Masteen, how did you get here from the Sea of Grass?'

'I awoke among the Tombs,' whispered the Templar without opening his eyes. 'Awoke among the Tombs. Tired. Must sleep.'

'Let him rest,' said Father Duré.

The Consul nodded and lowered the robed man to a sleeping position.

'Nothing makes sense,' whispered Sol as the three men and an infant sat in the dim light and felt the time tides ebb and flow outside.

'We lose a pilgrim, we gain one,' muttered the Consul. 'It's as if some bizarre game were being played.'

An hour later, they had heard the shots echo down the valley.

Sol and the Consul crouched by the silent form of Brawne Lamia.

'We'd need a laser to cut that thing off,' said Sol. 'With Kassad gone, so are our weapons.'

The Consul touched the young woman's wrist. 'Cutting it off might kill her.'

'According to the biomonitor, she's already dead.'

The Consul shook his head. 'No. Something else is going on. That thing may be tapping into the Keats cybrid persona she's been carrying. Perhaps when it's finished, it'll give us Brawne back.'

Sol lifted his daughter to his shoulder and looked out over the softly glowing valley. 'What a madhouse. Nothing's going as we thought. If only your damn ship were here . . . it would have cutting tools in case we have to free Brawne from this . . . this *thing* . . . and she and Masteen might have a chance for survival in the surgery.'

The Consul remained kneeling, staring at nothing. After a moment he said, 'Wait here with her, please,' rose, and disappeared in the dark maw of the Sphinx's entrance. Five minutes later, he was back with his own large travel bag. He removed a rolled rug from the bottom and unfurled it on the stone of the Sphinx's top stair.

It was an ancient rug, a little less than two meters long and a bit more than a meter wide. The intricately woven cloth had faded over the centuries, but the monofilament flight threads still glowed like gold in the dim light. Thin leads ran from the carpet to a single power cell which the Consul now detached.

'Good God,' whispered Sol. He remembered the Consul's tale of his grandmother Siri's tragic love affair with Hegemony Shipman Merin Aspic. It had been a love affair that had raised a rebellion against the Hegemony and plunged Maui-Covenant into years of war. Merin Aspic had flown to Firstsite on a friend's hawking mat.

The Consul nodded. 'It belonged to Mike Osho, Grandfather Merin's friend. Siri left it in her tomb for Merin to find. He gave it to me when I was a child – just before the Battle of the Archipelago, where he and the dream of freedom died.'

Sol ran his hand across the centuries-old artifact. 'It's a shame it can't work here.'

The Consul glanced up. 'Why can't it?'

'Hyperion's magnetic field is below the critical level for EM vehicles,' said Sol. 'That's why there are dirigibles and skimmers rather than EMVs, why the *Benares* was no longer a levitation barge.' He stopped, feeling foolish explaining this to a man who had been Hegemony Consul on Hyperion for eleven local years. 'Or am I wrong?'

The Consul smiled. 'You're right that standard EMVs aren't reliable here. Too much mass-to-lift ratio. But the hawking mat is all lift, almost no mass. I've tried it here when I lived in the capital. It's not a smooth ride . . . but it should work with one person aboard.'

Sol glanced back down the valley, past the glowing forms of the Jade Tomb, Obelisk, and Crystal Monolith, to where the shadows of the cliff wall hid the entrance to the Cave Tombs. He wondered if Father Duré and Het Masteen were still alone . . . still alive. 'You're thinking of going for help?'

'Of one of us going for help. Bringing the ship back. Or at least freeing it and sending it back unmanned. We could draw lots to see who goes.'

It was Sol's turn to smile. 'Think, my friend. Duré is in no condition to travel and does not know the way in any case. I . . .' Sol lifted Rachel until the top of her head touched his cheek. 'The voyage might last several days.

I – we – do not have several days. If something is to be done for her, we must remain here and take our chances. It is you who must go.'

The Consul sighed but did not argue.

'Besides,' said Sol, 'it is your ship. If anyone can free it from Gladstone's interdiction, you can. And you know the Governor-General well.'

The Consul looked toward the west. 'I wonder if Theo is still in power.'

'Let's go back and tell Father Duré our plan,' said Sol. 'Also, I left the nursing paks in the cave, and Rachel is hungry.'

The Consul rolled the carpet, slipped it in his pack, and stared down at Brawne Lamia, at the obscene cable snaking away into darkness. 'Will she be all right?'

'I'll have Paul come back with a blanket to stay with her while you and I carry our other invalid back here. Will you leave tonight or wait until sunrise?'

The Consul rubbed his cheeks tiredly. 'I don't like the thought of crossing the mountains at night, but we can't spare the time. I'll leave as soon as I put some things together.'

Sol nodded and looked toward the entrance to the valley. 'I wish Brawne could tell us where Silenus has gone.'

'I'll look for him as I fly out,' said the Consul. He glanced up at the stars. 'Figure thirty-six to forty hours of flying to get back to Keats. A few hours to free the ship. I should be back here within two standard days.'

Sol nodded, rocking the crying child. His tired but amiable expression did not conceal his doubt. He set his hand on the Consul's shoulder. 'It is right that we try, my friend. Come, let us talk to Father Duré, see if our other fellow traveler is awake, and eat a meal together. It looks as if Brawne brought enough supplies to allow us a final feast.'

TWENTY-SIX

When Brawne Lamia had been a child, her father a senator and their home relocated, however briefly, from Lusus to the wooded wonders of Tau Ceti Center's Administrative Residential Complex, she had seen the ancient flatfilm Walt Disney animation of *Peter Pan*. After seeing the animation, she had read the book, and both had captured her heart.

For months, the five-standard-year-old girl had waited for Peter Pan to arrive one night and take her away. She had left notes pointing the way to her bedroom under the shingled dormer. She had left the house while her parents slept and lain on the soft grass of the Deer Park lawns, watching the milkish-gray night sky of TC^2 and dreaming of the boy from Neverland who would some night soon take her away with him flying toward the second star to the right, straight on till morning. She would be his companion, the mother to the lost boys, fellow nemesis to the evil Hook, and most of all, Peter's new Wendy . . . the new child-friend to the child who would not grow old.

And now, twenty years later, Peter had finally come for her.

Lamia had felt no pain, only the sudden, icy rush of displacement as the Shrike's steel talon penetrated the neural shunt behind her ear. Then she was away and flying.

She had moved through the datumplane and into the datasphere before. Only weeks before, her time, Lamia had ridden into the TechnoCore matrix with her favorite cyberpuke, silly BB Surbringer, to help Johnny steal back his cybrid retrieval persona. They had penetrated the periphery and stolen the persona, but an alarm had been tripped, BB had died. Lamia never wanted to enter the datasphere again.

But she was there now.

The experience was like nothing she had ever had with comlog leads or nodes before. That was like full stimsim – like being in a holodrama with full color and wraparound stereo – this was like *being there*.

Peter had finally come to take her away.

Lamia rose above the curve of Hyperion's planetary limb, seeing the rudimentary channels of microwaved dataflow and tightbeamed commlink that passed for an embryonic datasphere there. She did not pause to tap into it, for she was following an orange umbilical skyward toward the *real* avenues and highways of datumplane.

Hyperion space had been invaded by FORCE and by the Ouster Swarm, and both had brought the intricate folds and latticework of the datasphere with them. With new eyes, Lamia could see the thousand levels of FORCE dataflow, a turbulent green ocean of information shot through with the red veins of secured channels and the spinning violet spheres with their black phage outriders that were the FORCE AIs. This pseudopod of the great Web megadatasphere flowed out of normal space through black funnels of shipboard farcasters, along expanding wave fronts of overlapping, instantaneous ripples that Lamia recognized as continuous bursts from a score of fatline transmitters.

She paused, suddenly unsure of where to go, which avenue to take. It was as if she had been flying and her uncertainty had endangered the magic – threatening to drop her back to the ground so many miles below.

Then Peter took her hand and buoyed her up.

— *Johnny!*

— *Hello, Brawne.*

Her own body image clicked into existence at the same second she saw and felt his. It was Johnny as she had last seen him – her client and lover – Johnny of the sharp cheekbones, hazel eyes, compact nose and solid jaw. Johnny's brownish-red curls still fell to his collar, and his face remained a study in purposeful energy. His smile still made her melt inside.

Johnny! She hugged him then, and she *felt* the hug, felt his strong hands on her back as they floated high above everything, felt her breasts flatten against his chest as he returned the hug with surprising strength for his small frame. They kissed, and there was no denying that *that* was real.

Lamia floated at arms' length, her hands on his shoulders. Both their faces were lighted by the green and violet glow of the great datasphere ocean above them.

— *Is this real?* She heard her own voice and dialect in the question even though she knew she had only thought it.

— *Yes. Real as any part of the datumplane matrix can be. We're on the edge of the megasphere in Hyperion space.* His voice still held that elusive accent that she found so beguiling and maddening.

— *What happened?* With the words, she conveyed images to him of the Shrike's appearance, the sudden, terrible invasion of the blade-finger.

— *Yes*, thought Johnny, holding her more tightly. *Somehow it freed me from the Schrön loop and jacked us directly into the datasphere.*

— *Am I dead, Johnny?*

The face of Johnny Keats smiled down at her. He shook her slightly, kissed her gently, and rotated so that they could both see the spectacle above and below. *No, you're not dead, Brawne, although you may be hooked to some kind of bizarre life support while your datumplane analog wanders here with me.*

— *Are you dead?*

He grinned at her again. *Not any longer, although life in a Schrön loop isn't all it's cracked up to be. It was like dreaming someone else's dreams.*

— *I dreamed about you.*

Johnny nodded. *I don't think that was me. I dreamed the same dreams . . .*

conversations with Meina Gladstone, glimpses of the Hegemony government councils . . .

— Yes!

He squeezed her hand. *I suspect that they reactivated another Keats cybrid. Somehow we were able to connect across all the light-years.*

— Another cybrid? How? You destroyed the Core template, liberated the persona . . .

Her lover shrugged. He was wearing a ruffled shirt and silk waistcoat of a style she had never seen before. The flow of data through the avenues above them painted both of them with pulses of neon light as they floated there. *I suspected that there would be more backups than BB and I could find in such a shallow penetration of the Core periphery. It doesn't matter, Brawne. If there's another copy, then he's me, and I can't believe he'd be an enemy. Come on, let's explore.*

Lamia held back a second as he tugged her upward. *Explore what?*

— This is our chance to see what's going on, Brawne. A chance to get to the bottom of a lot of mysteries.

She heard the uncharacteristic timidity in her own voice/thought. *I'm not sure I want to, Johnny.*

He rotated to look at her. *Is this the detective I knew? What happened to the woman who couldn't stand secrets?*

— She's been through some rough times, Johnny. I've been able to look back and see that becoming a detective was – in large part – a reaction to my father's suicide. I'm still trying to solve the details of his death. In the meantime, a lot of people have gotten hurt in real life. Including you, my dear.

— And have you solved it?

— What?

— Your father's death?

Lamia frowned at him. *I don't know. I don't think so.*

Johnny pointed toward the fluid mass of the datasphere ebbing and flowing above them. *There are a lot of answers waiting up there, Brawne. If we have the courage to go looking for them.*

She took his hand again. *We could die there.*

— Yes.

Lamia paused, looked down toward Hyperion. The world was a dark curve with the few isolated dataflow pockets glowing like campfires in the night. The great ocean above them seethed and pulsated with light and dataflow noise – and Brawne knew that it was only the smallest extension of the megasphere beyond. She knew . . . *she felt* . . . that their reborn datumplane analogs could now go places no cyberpuke cowboy had ever dreamt of.

With Johnny as her guide, Brawne knew that the megasphere and TechnoCore were penetrable to depths no human had plumbed. And she was scared.

But she was with Peter Pan, at last. And Neverland beckoned.

— All right, Johnny. What are we waiting for?

They rose together toward the megasphere.

TWENTY-SEVEN

Colonel Fedmahn Kassad followed Moneta through the portal and found himself standing upon a vast lunar plain where a terrible tree of thorns rose five kilometers high into a blood-red sky. Human figures writhed on the many branches and spikes: the closer forms recognizably human and in pain, the farther ones dwarfed by distance until they resembled clusters of pale grapes.

Kassad blinked and took a breath beneath the surface of his quicksilver skinsuit. He looked around, past the silent form of Moneta, tearing his gaze from the obscenity of the tree.

What he had thought was a lunar plain was the surface of Hyperion, at the entrance to the Valley of the Time Tombs, but a Hyperion terribly changed. The dunes were frozen and distorted as if they had been blasted and glazed into glass; the boulders and cliff faces also had flowed and frozen like glaciers of pale stone. There was no atmosphere – the sky was black with the pitiless clarity of airless moons everywhere. The sun was not Hyperion's; the light was not of human experience. Kassad looked up, and the viewing filters of his skinsuit polarized to deal with terrible energies that filled the sky with bands of blood red and blossoms of fierce white light.

Below him, the valley seemed to vibrate as if to unfelt tremors. The Time Tombs glowed of their own interior energies, pulses of cold light thrown many meters across the valley floor from every entrance, portal, and aperture. The Tombs looked new, slick, and shining.

Kassad realized that only the skinsuit was allowing him to breathe and saving his flesh from the lunar cold that had replaced the desert warmth. He turned to look at Moneta, attempted to phrase an intelligent question, failed, and raised his gaze to the impossible tree once again.

The thorn tree seemed to be made of the same steel and chrome and cartilage as the Shrike itself: obviously artificial and yet horribly organic at the same instant. The trunk was two or three hundred meters thick at its base, the lower branches almost as broad, but the smaller branches and thorns soon tapered to stiletto thinness as they splayed toward the sky with their awful impalement of human fruit.

Impossible that humans so impaled could live for long; doubly impossible that they could survive in the vacuum of this place outside of time and space. But survive and suffer they did. Kassad watched them writhe. *All* of them were alive. And all were in pain.

Kassad was aware of the pain as a great sound beyond hearing, a huge, incessant foghorn of pain, as if thousands of untrained fingers were falling on thousands of keys playing a massive pipe organ of pain. The pain was so palpable that he searched the blazing sky as if the tree were a pyre or huge beacon with the waves of pain clearly visible.

There was only the harsh light and lunar stillness.

Kassad raised the magnification of his skinsuit viewing lenses and looked from branch to branch, thorn to thorn. The people writhing there were of both genders and all ages. They wore a variety of torn clothing and disarrayed cosmetics that spanned many decades if not centuries. Many of the styles were not familiar to Kassad, and he assumed that he was looking at victims from his future. There were thousands . . . tens of thousands . . . of victims there. All were alive. All were in pain.

Kassad stopped, focused on a branch four hundred meters from the bottom, upon a cluster of thorns and bodies far out from the trunk, upon a single thorn three meters long from which a familiar purple cape billowed. The form there writhed, twisted, and turned toward Fedmahn Kassad.

He was looking at the impaled figure of Martin Silenus.

Kassad cursed and formed fists so tight that the bones in his hands ached. He looked around for his weapons, magnifying vision to stare into the Crystal Monolith. There was nothing there.

Colonel Kassad shook his head, realized that his skinsuit was a better weapon than any he had brought to Hyperion, and began to stride toward the tree. He did not know how he would climb it, but he would find a way. He did not know how he would get Silenus down alive – get all of the victims down – but he would do so or die in the trying.

Kassad took ten paces and stopped on a curve of frozen dune. The Shrike stood between him and the tree.

He realized that he was grinning fiercely beneath the chromium force-field of the skinsuit. This was what he had waited many years for. This was the honorable warfare he had pledged his life and honor for twenty years earlier in the FORCE Masada Ceremony. Single combat between warriors. A struggle to protect the innocent. Kassad grinned, flattened the edge of his right hand into a silver blade, and stepped forward.

— *Kassad!*

He looked back at Moneta's call. Light cascaded on the quicksilver surface of her nude body as she pointed toward the valley.

A second Shrike was emerging from the tomb called the Sphinx. Farther down the valley, a Shrike stepped from the entrance to the Jade Tomb. Harsh light glinted from spikes and razorwire as another emerged from the Obelisk, half a klick away.

Kassad ignored them and turned back toward the tree and its protector.

A hundred Shrikes stood between Kassad and the tree. He blinked, and a hundred more appeared to his left. He looked behind him, and a legion of Shrikes stood as impassively as sculptures on the cold dunes and melted boulders of the desert.

Kassad pounded his own knee with his fist. *Damn.*

Moneta came up next to him until their arms touched. The skinsuits flowed together, and he felt the warm flesh of her forearm against his. She stood thigh to thigh with him.

— *I love you, Kassad.*

He gazed at the perfect lines of her face, ignored the riot of reflections and colors there, and tried to remember the first time he had met her, in the forest near Agincourt. He remembered her startling green eyes and short, brown hair. The fullness of her lower lip and how it tasted of tears the time he accidentally had bitten it.

He raised a hand and touched her cheek, feeling the warmth of skin beneath the skinsuit. *If you love me*, he sent, *stay here.*

Colonel Fedmahn Kassad turned away then and let out a scream only he could hear in the lunar silence – a scream part rebel yell from the distant human past, part FORCE cadet graduation shout, part karate cry, and part pure defiance. He ran across the dunes toward the thorn tree and the Shrike directly in front of it.

There were thousands of Shrikes in the hills and valleys now. Talons clicked open in unison; light glinted on tens of thousands of scalpel-sharp blades and thorns.

Kassad ignored the others and ran toward the Shrike he thought was the first he had seen. Above the thing, human forms writhed in the solitude of their pain.

The Shrike he was running toward opened its arms as if offering an embrace. Curved blades on its wrists, joints, and chest seemed to extend from hidden sheaths.

Kassad screamed and closed the remaining distance.

TWENTY-EIGHT

'I shouldn't go,' said the Consul.

He and Sol had carried the still-unconscious Het Masteen from the Cave Tomb to the Sphinx while Father Duré watched over Brawne Lamia. It was almost midnight, and the valley glowed from the reflected light of the Tombs. The wings of the Sphinx cut arcs from the bit of sky visible to them between the cliff walls. Brawne lay motionless, the obscene cable snaking into the darkness of the tomb.

Sol touched the Consul's shoulder. 'We've discussed it. You should go.'

The Consul shook his head and idly stroked the ancient hawking mat. 'It may be able to carry two. You and Duré could make it to where the *Benares* is tied up.'

Sol held his daughter's small head in the cusp of his hand as he gently rocked her. 'Rachel is two days old. Besides, this is where we must be.'

The Consul looked around. His eyes showed his pain. 'This is where *I* should be. The Shrike . . .'

Duré leaned forward. The luminescence from the tomb behind them painted his high forehead and sharp cheeks with light. 'My son, if you stay here, it is for no other reason than suicide. If you attempt to bring the ship back for M. Lamia and the Templar, you will be helping others.'

The Consul rubbed his cheek. He was very tired. 'There's room for you on the mat, Father.'

Duré smiled. 'Whatever my fate may be, I feel that I am meant to meet it here. I will wait for your return.'

The Consul shook his head again but moved to sit cross-legged on the mat, pulling the heavy duffel bag toward him. He counted the ration paks and water bottles Sol had packed for him. 'There are too many. You'll need more for yourself.'

Duré chuckled. 'We have enough food and water for four days, thanks to M. Lamia. After that, if we have to fast, it will not be the first time for me.'

'But what if Silenus and Kassad return?'

'They can share our water,' said Sol. 'We can make another trip to the Keep for food if the others return.'

The Consul sighed. 'All right.' He touched the appropriate flight thread designs, and the two meters of carpet stiffened and rose ten centimeters above the stone. If there was a wobble in the uncertain magnetic fields, it was not discernible.

'You'll need oxygen for the mountain crossing,' said Sol.

The Consul lifted the osmosis mask from the pack.

Sol handed him Lamia's automatic pistol.

'I can't . . .'

'It won't help us with the Shrike,' said Sol. 'And it might make the difference of whether you get to Keats or not.'

The Consul nodded and set the weapon in his bag. He shook hands with the priest, then with the old scholar. Rachel's tiny fingers brushed his forearm.

'Good luck,' said Duré. 'May God be with you.'

The Consul nodded, tapped the flight designs, and leaned forward as the hawking mat lifted five meters, wobbled ever so slightly, and then slid forward and up as if riding invisible rails in the air.

The Consul banked right toward the entrance to the valley, passed ten meters above the dunes there, and then banked left toward the barrens. He looked back only once. The four figures on the top step of the Sphinx, two men standing, two shapes reclining, looked very small indeed. He could not make out the baby in Sol's arms.

As they had agreed, the Consul aimed the hawking mat toward the west to overfly the City of Poets in hopes of finding Martin Silenus. Intuition told him that the irascible poet might have detoured there. The skies were relatively free of the light of battle, and the Consul had to search shadows unbroken by starlight as he passed twenty meters above the broken spires and domes of the city. There was no sign of the poet. If Brawne and Silenus had come this way, even their footprints in the sand had been erased by the night winds which now moved the Consul's thinning hair and flapped his clothing.

It was cold on the mat at this altitude. The Consul could feel the shudders and vibrations as the hawking mat felt its way along unsteady lines of force. Between Hyperion's treacherous magnetic field and the age of the EM flight threads, he knew that there was a real chance the mat would tumble out of the sky long before he reached the capital of Keats.

The Consul shouted Martin Silenus's name several times, but there was no response except for an explosion of doves from their nesting place in the shattered dome of one of the gallerias. He shook his head and banked south toward the Bridle Range.

Through his grandfather Merin, the Consul knew the history of this hawking mat. It had been one of the first such playthings handcrafted by Vladimir Sholokov, Web-famous lepidopterist and EM systems engineer, and it may well have been the one he gave to his teenaged niece. Sholokov's love for the young girl had become legend, as had the fact that she spurned the gift of the flying carpet.

But others had loved the idea, and while hawking mats were soon outlawed on worlds with sensible traffic control, they continued to show up on colonial planets. This one had allowed the Consul's grandfather to meet his grandmother Siri on Maui-Covenant.

The Consul looked up as the mountain range approached. Ten minutes of flying had covered the two-hour hike across the barrens. The others had urged him not to stop at Chronos Keep to look for Silenus; whatever fate might have befallen the poet there might well claim the Consul too, before his journey had really begun. He contented himself with hovering just beyond the windows two hundred meters up the cliff wall, an arm's length from the terrace where they had looked out at the valley three days before, and shouting for the poet.

Only echoes answered him from the dark banquet halls and corridors of the Keep. The Consul held on tightly to the edges of the hawking mat, feeling the sense of height and exposure this close to the vertical stone walls. He was relieved when he banked the mat away from the Keep, gained altitude, and climbed toward the mountain passes where snow gleamed in the starlight.

He followed the cables of the tramway as they climbed the pass and connected one nine-thousand-meter peak to the next across the wide span of the mountain range. It was very cold at this altitude, and the Consul was glad for Kassad's extra thermal cape as he huddled under it, taking care not to expose the flesh of his hands or cheeks. The gel of the osmosis mask stretched across his face like some hungry symbiote, gobbling oxygen where little was to be found.

It was enough. The Consul took slow, deep breaths as he flew ten meters above the ice-caked cables. None of the pressurized tramcars were running, and the isolation above the glaciers, sheer peaks, and shadow-shrouded valleys was heart-stopping. The Consul was glad that he was attempting this trip if for no other reason than to see Hyperion's beauty one last time, unspoiled by the terrible threat of the Shrike or Ouster invasion.

It had taken the tramcar twelve hours to ferry them from south to north. Despite the hawking mat's slow twenty-klick-per-hour airspeed, the Consul made the crossing in six hours. Sunrise caught him still above the high peaks. He startled awake, realized with a shock that he had been dreaming while the hawking mat flew on toward a peak rising another five meters above his altitude. The Consul could see boulders and snowfields fifty meters ahead. A black bird with a three-meter wingspan – one of those the locals called a harbinger – pushed off from its icy eyrie and floated in the thin air, looking back at the Consul with black and beady eyes while he banked steeply to the left, felt something give way in the hawking mat's flight gear, and fell thirty meters before the flight threads found purchase and leveled the carpet off.

The Consul gripped the edges of the mat with fingers gone white. He had tied the strap of his duffel bag around his belt, otherwise the bag would have tumbled off to a glacier far below.

There was no sign of the tramway. Somehow the Consul had slept long enough to allow the hawking mat to drift off course. For a second, he panicked, jinking the mat this way and then that, desperate for a path between the peaks surrounding him like teeth. Then he saw the morning sunlight golden on the slopes ahead of him and to his right, the shadows leaping across glaciers and high tundra behind him and to his left, and he knew that he was still on the right track. Beyond this final spine of high peaks lay the southern foothills. And beyond that . . .

The hawking mat seemed to hesitate as the Consul tapped flight designs and urged it higher, but it rose in reluctant steps until it cleared the final nine-thousand-meter peak and he could see the lower mountains beyond, dwindling to foothills a mere three thousand meters above sea level. The Consul descended with gratitude.

He found the tramline gleaming in sunlight, eight klicks south of where he left the Bridle Range. Tramcars hung silently around the west terminal station. Below, the sparse buildings of the village of Pilgrims' Rest appeared as abandoned as they had several days earlier. There was no sign of the windwagon where it had been left at the low pier leading out over the shallows of the Sea of Grass.

The Consul let down near the pier, deactivated the hawking mat, stretched his legs with some pain before rolling up the mat for safe-keeping, and found a toilet in one of the abandoned buildings near the wharf. When he emerged, the morning sun was creeping down the foot-hills and erasing the last shadows there. As far as he could see to the south and west stretched the Sea of Grass, its tabletop smoothness belied by occasional breezes which sent ripples across the verdant surface, briefly revealing the russet and ultramarine stalks beneath in a movement so wavelike that one expected to see whitecaps and fish leaping.

There were no fish in the Sea of Grass, but there were grass serpents twenty meters long, and if the Consul's hawking mat failed him out there, even a safe landing would not keep him alive for long.

The Consul unrolled the mat, set his bag behind him, and activated the carpet. He stayed relatively low, twenty-five meters above the surface, but not so low that a grass serpent might mistake him for a low-flying morsel. It had taken the windwagon less than a full Hyperion day to ferry them across the Sea, but with the winds frequently from the northeast, that had involved quite a bit of tacking to and fro. The Consul bet that he could fly across this narrowest part of the Sea in less than fifteen hours. He tapped the forward control designs, and the hawking mat sped faster.

Within twenty minutes, the mountains had fallen behind until the foot-hills were lost in the haze of distance. Within an hour, the peaks began to shrink as the curve of the world hid their base. Two hours out, and the Consul could see only the highest of the peaks as an indistinct, serrated shadow rising from the haze.

Then the Sea of Grass spread to all horizons, unchanging except for the sensuous ripples and furrows caused by the occasional breeze. It was much warmer here than on the high plateau north of the Bridle Range. The Consul shed his thermal cape, then his coat, then his sweater. The sun beat down with surprising intensity for such high latitudes. The Consul fumbled in his bag, found the wrinkled and battered tricorne cap he had worn with such aplomb just two days earlier, and wedged it on his head to give some shade. His forehead and balding skull were already sunburned.

About four hours out, he ate his first meal of the trip, chewing on the tasteless strips of ration-pak protein as if they were filet mignon. The water was the most delicious part of the meal, and the Consul had to fight his urge to empty all the bottles in a single orgy of drinking.

The Sea of Grass stretched below, behind, and ahead. The Consul dozed, snapping awake each time with a sense of falling, hands gripping the edge of the rigid hawking mat. He realized that he should have tied himself in with the single rope he had brought in his bag, but he didn't want to land – the grass was sharp and higher than his head. Although he had seen none of the telltale V-shaped wakes of the grass serpents, he could not be sure they were not resting in wait below.

He wondered idly where the windwagon had gone. The thing had been fully automated and presumably programmed by the Church of the Shrike, since they had sponsored the pilgrimage. What other duties might the thing have had? The Consul shook his head, sat upright, and pinched his cheeks. He had been drifting in and out of dreams even as he thought about the windwagon. Fifteen hours had seemed a short enough time as he stood talking about it in the Valley of the Time Tombs. He glanced at his comlog; five hours had passed.

The Consul lifted the mat to two hundred meters, looked carefully for any sign of a serpent, and then brought the mat down to a hover five meters above the grass. Carefully he extracted the rope, made a loop, moved to the front of the carpet, and wound several lengths around the carpet, leaving enough slack to slide his body in before tightening the knot.

If the mat fell, the tether would be worse than useless, but the snug bands of rope against his back gave a sense of security as he leaned forward to tap the flight designs again, leveled the carpet out at forty meters, and laid his cheek against the warm fabric. Sunlight filtered through his fingers, and he realized that his bare forearms were getting a terrible sunburn.

He was too tired to sit up and roll down his sleeves.

A breeze came up. The Consul could hear a rustling and sliding below as either the grasses blew or something large slithered past.

He was too tired to care. The Consul closed his eyes and was asleep in less than thirty seconds.

The Consul dreamed of his home – his true home – on Maui-Covenant and the dream was filled with color: the bottomless blue sky, the wide expanse of the South Sea, ultramarine fading to green where the Equatorial Shallows began, the startling greens and yellows and orchid reds of the motile isles as they were herded north by the dolphins . . . extinct now since the Hegemony invasion in the Consul's childhood, but quite alive in his dream, breaking the water in great leaps that sent a thousand prisms of light dancing in the pure air.

In his dream, the Consul was a child again, and he stood on the highest level of a treehouse on their First Family Isle. Grandmother Siri was next to him – not the regal grande dame he had known but the beautiful young woman his grandfather had met and fallen in love with. The treesails were flapping as the southerlies came up, moving the herd of motile isles in precise formation through the blue channels through the Shallows. Just on the northern horizon, he could see the first of the Equatorial Archipelago islands rising green and permanent against an evening sky.

Siri touched his shoulder and pointed to the west.

The isles were burning, sinking, their keel roots writhing in purposeless pain. The dolphin herders were gone. The sky rained fire. The Consul recognized billion-volt lances as they fried the air and left blue-gray after-images on his retinas. Underwater explosions lighted the oceans and sent thousands of fish and fragile sea creatures bobbing to the surface in their death throes.

'Why?' asked Grandmother Siri, but her voice was the soft whisper of a teenager.

The Consul tried to answer her but could not. Tears blinded him. He reached for her hand, but she was no longer there, and the sense that she was *gone*, that he could never make up for his sins, hurt him so badly that he found it impossible to breathe. His throat was clogged with emotion. Then he realized that it was smoke that burned his eyes and filled his lungs; the Family Isle was on fire.

The child who was the Consul staggered forward in the blue-black darkness, hunting blindly for someone to hold his hand, to reassure him.

A hand closed on his. It was not Siri's. The hand was impossibly firm as it squeezed. The fingers were blades.

The Consul came awake gasping.

It was dark. He had slept for at least seven hours. Struggling with the ropes, he sat up, stared at his glowing comlog display.

Twelve hours. He had slept for twelve hours.

Every muscle in his body ached as he leaned over and peered below. The hawking mat held a steady altitude of forty meters, but he had no idea where he was. Low hills rose and fell below. The mat must have cleared some by only two or three meters; orange grass and scrub lichen grew in spongy tufts.

Somewhere, sometime in the past few hours, he had passed over the south shore of the Sea of Grass, missed the small port of Edge and the Hoolie River docks where their levitation barge, *Benares*, had been tied up.

The Consul had no compass – compasses were useless on Hyperion – and his comlog had not been programmed as an inertial direction finder. He had planned to find his way back to Keats by following the Hoolie south and west, retracing the laborious path of their upriver pilgrimage minus the bends and turns in the river.

Now he was lost.

The Consul set the hawking mat down on a low hilltop, stepped off to solid ground with a groan of pain, and collapsed the mat. He knew that the charge in the flight threads must be at least a third expended by now . . . perhaps more. He had no idea how much efficiency the mat lost with age.

The hills looked like the rough country southwest of the Sea of Grass, but there was no sight of the river. His comlog told him that it had been dark for only an hour or two, but the Consul could see no hint of sunset in the west. The skies were overcast, shielding both starlight and any space battles from sight.

'Damn,' whispered the Consul. He walked around until circulation returned, urinated at the edge of a small drop-off, and returned to his mat to drink from a water bottle. *Think.*

He had set the mat on a southwesterly course that should have left the Sea of Grass at or near the port city of Edge. If he had simply overflown Edge and the river while he slept, the river would be somewhere to his south, off to his left. But if he had aimed poorly as he left Pilgrims' Rest, been just a few degrees off to his left, then the river would be winding northeast somewhere to his right. Even if he went the wrong way, he eventually would find a landmark – the coast of the Northern Mane if nothing else – but the delay could cost him a full day.

The Consul kicked at a rock and folded his arms. The air was very cool after the heat of the day. A shiver made him realize that he was half-sick from sunburn. He touched his scalp and pulled his fingers away with a curse. *Which way?*

The wind whistled through low sage and sponge lichen. The Consul felt very far removed from the Time Tombs and the threat of the Shrike, but he felt the presence of Sol and Duré and Het Masteen and Brawne and the missing Silenus and Kassad as an urgent pressure on his shoulders. The Consul had joined the pilgrimage as a final act of nihilism, a pointless suicide to put an end to his own pain, pain at the loss of even the *memory* of wife and child, killed during the Hegemony's machinations on Bressia, and pain at the knowledge of his terrible betrayal – betrayal of the government he had served for almost four decades, betrayal of the Ousters who had trusted him.

The Consul sat on a rock and felt that purposeless self-hatred fade as he thought of Sol and his infant child waiting in the Valley of the Time Tombs. He thought of Brawne, that brave woman, energy incarnate, lying helpless with that leechlike extension of the Shrike's evil growing from her skull.

He sat, activated the mat, and rose to eight hundred meters, so close to the ceiling of clouds that he could have raised a hand and touched them.

A second's break in the cloud cover far to his left showed a glint of ripple. The Hoolie lay about five klicks to the south.

The Consul banked the hawking mat steeply to his left, feeling the tired containment field trying to press him to the carpet but feeling safer with the ropes still attached. Ten minutes later, he was high over the water, swooping down to ascertain that it was the broad Hoolie rather than some tributary.

It was the Hoolie. Radiant gossamers glowed in the low, marshy areas along the banks. The tall, crenelated towers of architect ants cast ghostly silhouttes against a sky only slightly darker than the land.

The Consul rose to twenty meters, took a drink of water from his bottle, and headed downriver at full speed.

Sunrise found him below the village of Doukhobor's Copse, almost to the Karla Locks, where the Royal Transport Canal cut west toward the northern urban settlements and the Mane. The Consul knew that it was less than a hundred and fifty klicks to the capital from here – but still a maddening seven hours away at the hawking mat's slow pace. This was the point in the trip where he had hoped to find a military skimmer on patrol, one of the passenger dirigibles from the Copse of Naiad, even a fast powerboat he could commandeer. But there was no sign of life along the banks of the Hoolie except for the occasional burning building or ghee lamps in distant windows. The docks had been stripped of all boats. The river manta pens above the Locks were empty, the great gates open to the current, and no transport barges were lined up below where the river widened to twice its upriver size.

The Consul swore and flew on.

It was a beautiful morning as the sunrise illuminated the low clouds and made every bush and tree stand out in the low, horizontal light. It felt to the Consul as if it had been months since he had seen real vegetation. Weirwood and halfoak trees rose to majestic heights on the distant bluffs, while in the floodplain, the rich light caught the green shoots of a million periscope beans rising from their indigenie paddies. Womangrove root and firefern lined the banks, and each branch and twisting stood out in the sharp light of sunrise.

The clouds swallowed the sun. It began to rain. The Consul tugged on the battered tricorne, huddled under Kassad's extra cloak, and flew on southward at a hundred meters.

The Consul tried to remember. *How long did the child Rachel have?*

Despite his long sleep the day before, the Consul's mind was heavy with fatigue toxins. *Rachel had been four days old when they had arrived at the valley. That had been . . . four days ago.*

The Consul rubbed his cheek, reached for a water bottle, and found them all empty. He could easily dip down and refill the bottles in the river, but he did not want to take the time. His sunburn ached and made him shiver as the rain dripped from his cap.

Sol said that as long as I'm back by nightfall it would be all right. Rachel was born after twenty hundred hours, translated to Hyperion time. If that's right, if there's no error, she has until eight tonight. The Consul rubbed water from his cheeks and eyebrows. *Say seven more hours to Keats. An hour or two to liberate the ship. Theo will help . . . he's Governor-General now. I can convince him that it's in the Hegemony's interest to countervene Gladstone's orders to quarantine the ship. If necessary, I'll tell him that she ordered me to conspire with the Ousters to betray the Web.*

Say, ten hours plus the fifteen-minute flight in the ship. Should be at least an hour to spare before sunset. Rachel will be only a few minutes old, but . . . what? What do we try besides the cryogenic fugue lockers? Nothing. It has to be that. It was always Sol's last chance, despite the doctors' warnings that it might kill the child. But then, what about Brawne?

The Consul was thirsty. He pulled back the cloak, but the rain had lessened to the point that it was a fine drizzle, just enough to wet his lips and tongue to make him more thirsty. He cursed softly and began to descend slowly. Perhaps he could hover over the river just long enough to fill his bottle.

The hawking mat quit flying thirty meters above the river. One second it was descending gradually, as smooth as a carpet on a gentle glass incline, and the next instant it was tumbling and plummeting out of control, a two-meter rug and terrified man thrown out of the window of a ten-story building.

The Consul screamed and tried to jump free, but the rope connecting him to the carpet and the duffel strap tied to his belt tangled him in the flapping mass of hawking mat, and he fell with it, tumbling and twisting, the final twenty meters to the hard surface of the waiting Hoolie River.

TWENTY-NINE

Sol Weintraub had high hopes the night the Consul left. At long last, they were *doing* something. Or trying to. Sol did not believe that the cryogenic vaults of the Consul's ship would be the answer to saving Rachel – medical experts on Renaissance Vector had pointed out the extreme danger of that procedure – but it was good to have an alternative, *any* alternative. And Sol felt that they had been passive long enough, awaiting the Shrike's pleasure like condemned criminals awaiting the guillotine.

The interior of the Sphinx seemed too treacherous this night, and Sol brought their possessions out on the broad granite porch of the tomb, where he and Duré sought to make Masteen and Brawne comfortable under blankets and capes, with packs for pillows. Brawne's medical monitors continued to show no brain activity whatsoever, while her body rested comfortably. Masteen turned and tossed in the grip of fever.

'What do you think the Templar's problem is?' asked Duré. 'Disease?'

'It could be simple exposure,' said Sol. 'After being abducted from the windwagon, he found himself wandering in the barrens and here in the Valley of the Time Tombs. He was eating snow for liquid and had no food at all.'

Duré nodded and checked the FORCE medpak they had attached to the inside of Masteen's arm. The telltales showed the steady drip of intravenous solution. 'But it seems to be something else,' said the Jesuit. 'Almost a madness.'

'Templars have an almost telepathic connection to their treeships,' said Sol. 'It must have driven Voice of the Tree Masteen a bit mad when he watched the destruction of the *Yggdrasill*. Especially if he somehow knew it was necessary.'

Duré nodded and continued sponging the Templar's waxy forehead. It was after midnight, and the wind had come up, moving vermilion dust in lazy spirals and moaning around the wings and rough edges of the Sphinx. The Tombs glowed brightly and then dimmed, now one tomb, then the next, in no apparent order or sequence. Occasionally the tug of time tides would assail both men, making them gasp and grip the stone, but the wave of *déjà vu* and vertigo would fade after a moment. With Brawne Lamia attached to the Sphinx via the cable welded to her skull, they could not leave.

Sometime before dawn, the clouds parted and the sky became visible, the thickly clustered stars almost painful in their clarity. For a while, the only signs of the great fleets warring there were the occasional fusion trails, narrow diamond-scratches on the pane of night, but then the blossoms of distant explosions began to unfurl again, and within the hour the glow of the Tombs had been dimmed by the violence above.

'Who do you think will win?' asked Father Duré. The two men sat with their backs to the stone wall of the Sphinx, faces raised to the cusp of sky revealed between the tomb's forward-curved wings.

Sol was rubbing Rachel's back as she slept on her stomach, rear end raised under the thin blankets. 'From what the others say, it seems preordained that the Web must suffer a terrible war.'

'So you believe the AI Advisory Council's predictions?'

Sol shrugged in the darkness. 'I really know nothing about politics . . . or the Core's accuracy in predicting things. I'm a minor scholar from a small college on a backwater world. But I have the *feeling* that something terrible is in store for us . . . that some rough beast is slouching toward Bethlehem to be born.'

Duré smiled. 'Yeats,' he said. The smile faded. 'I suspect that this place is the new Bethlehem.' He looked down the valley toward the glowing Tombs. 'I spent a lifetime teaching about St Teilhard's theories of evolution toward the Omega Point. Instead of that, we have this. Human folly in the skies, and a terrible Antichrist waiting to inherit the rest.'

'You think that the Shrike is the Antichrist?'

Father Duré set his elbows on his raised knees and folded his hands. 'If it's not, we're all in trouble.' He laughed bitterly. 'It wasn't long ago that I would have been delighted to discover an Antichrist . . . even the presence of some antidivine power would have served to shore up my failing belief in any form of divinity.'

'And now?' Sol asked quietly.

Duré spread his fingers. 'I too have been crucified.'

Sol thought of the images from Lenar Hoyt's story about Duré; the elderly Jesuit nailing himself to a tesla tree, suffering the years of pain and rebirth rather than surrender to the cruciform DNA parasite which even now burrowed under the flesh of his chest.

Duré lowered his face from the sky. 'There was no welcome from a heavenly Father,' he said softly. 'No reassurance that the pain and sacrifice had been worth anything. Only pain. Pain and darkness and then pain again.'

Sol's hand stopped moving on his infant's back. 'And that made you lose your faith?'

Duré looked at Sol. 'On the contrary, it made me feel that faith is all the more essential. Pain and darkness have been our lot since the Fall of Man. But there must be some hope that we can rise to a higher level . . . that consciousness can evolve to a plane more benevolent than its counterpoint of a universe hardwired to indifference.'

Sol nodded slowly. 'I had a dream during Rachel's long battle with Merlin's sickness . . . my wife Sarai had the same dream . . . that I was being called to sacrifice my only daughter.'

'Yes,' said Duré. 'I listened to the Consul's summary on disk.'

'Then you know my response,' said Sol. 'First, that Abraham's path of obedience can no longer be followed, even if there is a God demanding such obedience. Second, that we have offered sacrifices to that God for too many generations . . . that the payments of pain must stop.'

'Yet you are here,' said Duré, gesturing toward the valley, the Tombs, the night.

'I'm here,' agreed Sol. 'But not to grovel. Rather to see what response these powers have to my decision.' He touched his daughter's back again. 'Rachel is a day and a half old now and growing younger each second. If the Shrike is the architect of such cruelty, I want to face him, even if he *is* your Antichrist. If there is a God and he has done this thing, I will show the same contempt to him.'

'Perhaps we've all shown too much contempt as it is,' mused Duré.

Sol looked up as a dozen pinpoints of fierce light expanded into ripples and shock waves of plasma explosions far out in space. 'I wish we had the technology to fight God on an equal basis,' he said in low, tight tones. 'To beard him in his den. To fight back for all of the injustices heaped on humanity. To allow him to alter his smug arrogance or be blown to hell.'

Father Duré raised one eyebrow and then smiled slightly. 'I know the anger you feel.' The priest gently touched Rachel's head. 'Let's try to get some sleep before sunrise, shall we?'

Sol nodded, lay next to his child, and pulled the blanket up to his cheek. He heard Duré whispering something that might have been a soft good night, or perhaps a prayer.

Sol touched his daughter, closed his eyes, and slept.

The Shrike did not come in the night. Nor did it come the next morning as sunlight painted the southwestern cliffs and touched the top of the Crystal Monolith. Sol awoke as sunlight crept down the valley; he found Duré sleeping next to him, Masteen and Brawne still unconscious. Rachel was stirring and fussing. Her cry was that of a hungry newborn. Sol fed her with one of the last nursing paks, pulling the heating tab and waiting a moment for the milk to reach body temperature. Cold had settled in the valley overnight, and frost glinted on the steps to the Sphinx.

Rachel ate greedily, making the soft mewling and sucking sounds that Sol remembered from more than fifty years earlier as Sarai had nursed her. When she finished, Sol burped her and left her on his shoulder as he rocked gently to and fro.

A day and a half left.

Sol was very tired. He was growing old despite the single Poulsen treatment a decade earlier. At the time he and Sarai would normally have been freed of parental duties – their only child in graduate school and off on an archaelogical dig in the Outback – Rachel had fallen prey to Merlin's sickness, and parenthood had soon descended upon them once again. The curve of those duties rose as Sol and Sarai grew older – then Sol alone, after the air crash on Barnard's World – and now he was very, very tired. But despite that, despite everything, Sol was interested to note that he did not regret a single day of caring for his daughter.

A day and a half left.

Father Duré awoke after a bit, and the two men made breakfast from the various canned goods Brawne had brought back with her. Het Masteen did not awaken, but Duré applied the next-to-last medpak, and the Templar began receiving fluids and IV nutrient.

'Do you think M. Lamia should have the last medpak applied?' asked Duré.

Sol sighed and checked her comlog monitors again. 'I don't think so, Paul. According to this, blood sugar is high . . . nutrient levels check out as if she had just eaten a decent meal.'

'But how?'

Sol shook his head. 'Perhaps that damned thing is some sort of umbilical.' He gestured toward the cable attached to the point in her skull where the neural shunt socket had been.

'So what do we do today?'

Sol peered at a sky already fading to the green and lapis dome they had grown used to on Hyperion. 'We wait,' he said.

Het Masteen awoke in the heat of the day, shortly before the sun reached the zenith. The Templar sat straight up and said, 'The Tree!'

Duré hurried up the steps from where he had been pacing below. Sol lifted Rachel from where she lay in shadow near the wall and moved to Masteen's side. The Templar's eyes were focused on something above the level of the cliffs. Sol glanced up but could see only the paling sky.

'The Tree!' cried the Templar again, and lifted one roughened hand.

Duré restrained the man. 'He's hallucinating. He thinks he see the *Yggdrasill*, his treeship.'

Het Masteen struggled against their hands. 'No, not the *Yggdrasill*,' he gasped through parched lips, 'the Tree. The Final Tree. The Tree of Pain!'

Both men looked up then, but the sky was clear except for wisps of clouds blowing in from the southwest. At that moment, there was a surge of time tides, and both Sol and the priest bowed their heads in sudden vertigo. It passed.

Het Masteen was trying to get to his feet. The Templar's eyes were still focused on something far away. His skin was so hot that it burned Sol's hands.

'Get the final medpak,' snapped Sol. 'Program the ultramorph and anti-fever agent.' Duré hurried to comply.

'The Tree of Pain!' managed Het Masteen. 'I was meant to be its Voice! The erg is meant to drive it through space and time! The Bishop and the Voice of the Great Tree have chosen *me*! I cannot fail them.' He strained against Sol's arms a second, then collapsed back to the stone porch. 'I am the True Chosen,' he whispered, energy leaving him like air from an emptying balloon. 'I must guide the Tree of Pain during the time of Atonement.' He closed his eyes.

Duré attached the final medpak, made sure the monitor was set for Templar quirks in metabolism and body chemistry, and triggered the adrenaline and painkillers. Sol huddled over the robed form.

'That's not Templar terminology or theology,' said Duré. 'He's using Shrike Cult language.' The priest caught Sol's eye. 'That explains some of the mystery . . . especially from Brawne's tale. For some reason, the Templars have been in collusion with the Church of the Final Atonement . . . the Shrike Cult.'

Sol nodded, slipped his own comlog on Masteen's wrist and adjusted the monitor.

'The Tree of Pain must be the Shrike's fabled tree of thorns,' muttered Duré, glancing up at the empty sky where Masteen had been staring. 'But what does he mean that he and the erg were chosen to drive it through space and time? Does he really think he can pilot the Shrike's tree the way the Templars do the treeships? Why?'

'You'll have to ask him in the next life,' said Sol tiredly. 'He's dead.'

Duré checked the monitors, added Lenar Hoyt's comlog to the array. They tried the medpak revival stimulants, CPR, and mouth-to-mouth resuscitation. The monitor telltales did not waver. Het Masteen, Templar True Voice of the Tree and Shrike Pilgrim, was indeed dead.

They waited an hour, suspicious of all things in this perverse valley of the Shrike, but when the monitors began showing rapid decomposition of the corpse, they buried Masteen in a shallow grave fifty meters up the trail toward the entrance to the valley. Kassad had left behind a collapsible shovel – labeled 'entrenching tool' in FORCE jargon – and the men took turns digging while the other watched over Rachel and Brawne Lamia.

The two men, one cradling a child, stood in the shadow of a boulder while Duré said a few words before the soil was dropped on to the makeshift fiberplastic shroud.

'I did not truly know M. Masteen,' said the priest. 'We were not of the same faith. But we were of the same profession; Voice of the Tree Masteen spent much of his life doing what he understood to be God's work, pursuing God's will in the writings of the Muir and the beauties of nature. His was the true faith – tested by the difficulties, tempered by obedience, and, in the end, sealed by sacrifice.'

Duré paused and squinted into a sky that had faded to gunmetal glare. 'Please accept your servant, O Lord. Welcome him into your arms as you will someday welcome us, your other searchers who have lost their way. In the name of the Father, and of the Son, and of the Holy Spirit, amen.'

Rachel began to cry. Sol walked her around as Duré shoveled the earth on to the man-shaped bundle of fiberplastic.

They returned to the porch of the Sphinx and gently moved Brawne into what little shade remained. There was no way to shield her from the late afternoon sun unless they carried her into the tomb itself, and neither man wanted to do that.

'The Consul must be more than halfway to the ship by now,' said the priest after taking a long drink of water. The man's forehead was sunburned and filmed with sweat.

'Yes,' said Sol.

'By this time tomorrow, he should be back here. We'll use laser cutters to free Brawne, then set her in the ship surgery. Perhaps Rachel's reverse aging can be arrested in cryogenic storage, despite what the doctors said.'

'Yes.'

Duré lowered the water bottle and looked at Sol. 'Do you believe that is what will happen?'

Sol returned the other man's gaze. 'No.'

Shadows stretched from the southwestern cliff walls. The day's heat coalesced into a solid thing, then dissipated a bit. Clouds moved in from the south.

Rachel slept in the shadows near the doorway. Sol walked up to where Paul Duré stood staring down the valley and set a hand on the priest's shoulder. 'What are you thinking about, my friend?'

Duré did not turn. 'I am thinking that if I did not truly believe that suicide was a mortal sin, that I would end things to allow young Hoyt a chance at life.' He looked at Sol and showed a hint of smile. 'But is it suicide when this parasite on my chest . . . on *his* chest then . . . would someday drag me kicking and screaming to my own resurrection?'

'Would it be a gift to Hoyt,' asked Sol quietly, 'to bring him back to this?'

Duré said nothing for a moment. Then he clasped Sol's upper arm. 'I think that I shall take a walk.'

'Where?' Sol squinted out at the thick heat of the desert afternoon. Even with the low cloud cover, the valley was an oven.

The priest made a vague gesture. 'Down the valley. I will be back before too long.'

'Be careful,' said Sol. 'And remember, if the Consul runs across a patrol skimmer along the Hoolie, he might be back as early as this afternoon.'

Duré nodded, went over to pick up a water bottle and to touch Rachel gently, and then he went down the long stairway of the Sphinx, picking his way slowly and carefully, like an old, old man.

Sol watched him leave, becoming a smaller and smaller figure, distorted by heat waves and distance. Then Sol sighed and went back to sit near his daughter.

Paul Duré tried to keep to the shadows, but even there the heat was oppressive, weighing on him like a great yoke on his shoulders. He passed the Jade Tomb and followed the path toward the northern cliffs and the Obelisk. That tomb's thin shadow painted darkness on the roseate stone and dust of the valley floor. Descending again, picking his way through the rubble surrounding the Crystal Monolith, Duré glanced up as a sluggish wind moved shattered panes and whistled through cracks high up on the face of the tomb. He saw his reflection in the lower surfaces and remembered hearing the organ song of the evening wind rising from the Cleft when he had found the Bikura high on the Pinion Plateau. That seemed like lifetimes ago. It *was* lifetimes ago.

Duré felt the damage the cruciform reconstruction had done to his mind and memory. It was sickening – the equivalent of suffering a stroke with no hope of recovery. Reasoning that once would have been child's play to him now required extreme concentration or was simply beyond his ability. Words eluded him. Emotions tugged at him with the same sudden violence as the time tides. Several times he had had to leave the other pilgrims while he wept in solitude for no reason he could understand.

The other pilgrims. Now only Sol and the child remained. Father Duré would gladly surrender his own life if those two could be spared. Was it a sin, he wondered, to plan deals with the Antichrist?

He was far down the valley now, almost to the point where it curved eastward into the widening cul-de-sac where the Shrike Palace threw its maze of shadows across the rocks. The trail wound close to the northwest wall as it passed the Cave Tombs. Duré felt the cool air from the first tomb and was tempted to enter just to recover from the heat, close his eyes, and take a nap.

He continued walking.

The entrance to the second tomb had more baroque carvings in the stone, and Duré was reminded of the ancient basilica he had discovered in the Cleft – the huge cross and altar where the retarded Bikura had 'worshiped'. It had been the obscene immortality of the cruciform they had been worshiping, not the chance of true Resurrection promised by the Cross. *But what was the difference?* Duré shook his head, trying to clear the fog and cynicism that clouded every thought. The path wound higher here past the third Cave Tomb, the shortest and least impressive of the three.

There was a light in the third Cave Tomb.

Duré stopped, took a breath, and glanced back down the valley. The Sphinx was quite visible almost a kilometer away, but he could not quite make out Sol in the shadows. For a moment Duré wondered if it had been the *third* tomb they had sheltered in the day before . . . if one of them had left a lantern there.

It had not been the third tomb. Except for the search for Kassad, no one had entered this tomb in three days.

Father Duré knew that he should ignore the light, return to Sol, keep the vigil with the man and his daughter.

But the Shrike came to each of the others separately. Why should I refuse the summons?

Duré felt moisture on his cheek and realized that he was weeping soundlessly, mindlessly. He roughly wiped the tears away with the back of his hand and stood there clenching his fists.

543

My intellect was my greatest vanity. I was the intellectual Jesuit, secure in the tradition of Teilhard and Prassard. Even the theology I pushed on the Church, on the seminarians, and on those few faithful still listening had emphasized the mind, that wonderful Omega Point of consciousness. God as a clever algorithm.

Well, some things are beyond intellect, Paul.

Duré entered the third Cave Tomb.

Sol awoke with a start, sure that someone was creeping up on him.

He jumped to his feet and looked around. Rachel was making soft sounds, awakening from her nap at the same time as her father. Brawne Lamia lay motionless where he had left her, med telltales still glowing green, brain activity readout a flat red.

He had slept for at least an hour; the shadows had crept across the valley floor, and only the top of the Sphinx was still in sunlight as the sun broke free of the clouds. Shafts of light slanted through the valley entrance and illuminated the cliff walls opposite. The wind was rising.

But nothing moved in the valley.

Sol lifted Rachel, rocked her as she cried, and ran down the steps, looking behind the Sphinx and toward the other Tombs.

'Paul!' His voice echoed off rock. Wind stirred dust beyond the Jade Tomb, but nothing else stirred. Sol still had the feeling that something was sneaking up on him, that he was being watched.

Rachel screamed and wiggled in his grasp, her voice the high, thin wail of a newborn. Sol glanced at his comlog. She would be one day old in an hour. He searched the sky for the Consul's ship, cursed softly at himself, and went back to the entrance to the Sphinx to change the baby's diaper, check on Brawne, pull a nursing pak from his bag, and grab a cloak. The heat dissipated quickly when the sun was gone.

In the half-hour of twilight remaining, Sol moved quickly down the valley, shouting Duré's name and peering into the Tombs without entering. Past the Jade Tomb where Hoyt had been murdered, its sides already beginning to glow a milky green. Past the dark Obelisk, its shadow thrown high on the southeastern cliff wall. Past the Crystal Monolith, its upper reaches glowing with the last of the day's light, then fading as the sun set somewhere beyond the City of Poets. In the sudden chill and hush of evening, past the Cave Tombs, Sol shouting into each and feeling the dank air against his face like a cold breath from an open mouth.

No answer.

In the last of the twilight, around the bend in the valley to the blade-and-buttress riot of the Shrike Palace, dark and ominous in the growing gloom. Sol stood at the entrance trying to make sense of the ink-black shadows, spires, rafters, and pylons, shouted into the dark interior; only his echo answered. Rachel began to cry again.

Shivering, feeling a chill on the back of his neck, wheeling constantly to surprise the unseen watcher and seeing only deepening shadows and the first of the night's stars between clouds above, Sol hurried back up the valley toward the Sphinx, walking quickly at first and then almost running past the Jade Tomb as the evening wind rose with a sound of children screaming.

'God*damn*!' breathed Sol as he reached the top of the stairs to the Sphinx.

Brawne Lamia was gone. There was no sign of her body or the metal umbilical.

Cursing, holding Rachel tight, Sol fumbled through his pack for the flashlight.

Ten meters down the central corridor, Sol found the blanket Brawne had been wrapped in. Beyond that, nothing. The corridors branched and twisted, now widening, now narrowing as the ceiling lowered to the point that Sol was crawling, holding the baby in his right arm so that her cheek was next to his. He hated being in this tomb. His heart was pounding so fiercely that he half expected to have a coronary then and there.

The last corridor narrowed to nothing. Where the metal cable had snaked into stone, now there was only stone.

Sol held the flashlight in his teeth and slapped at the rock, shoved at stones the size of houses as if a secret panel would open, tunnels would be revealed.

Nothing.

Sol hugged Rachel tighter and began to make his way out, taking several wrong turns, feeling his heart race even more wildly as he thought himself lost. Then they were in a corridor he recognized, then in the main corridor, then out.

He carried his child to the bottom of the steps and away from the Sphinx. At the head of the valley, he stopped, sat on a low rock, and panted for breath. Rachel's cheek still lay against his neck, and the baby made no sound, no movement other than the soft curl of fingers against his beard.

Wind blew in from the barrens behind him. Clouds opened above and then closed, hiding the stars so that the only light came from the sick glow of the Time Tombs. Sol was afraid that the wild beating of his heart would frighten the baby, but Rachel continued to curl calmly against him, her warmth a tactile reassurance.

'Damn,' whispered Sol. He had cared for Brawne Lamia. He had cared for all of the pilgrims, and now they were gone. Sol's decades as an academic had preconditioned him to hunt for patterns in events, a moral grain in the accreted stone of experience, but there had been no pattern to events on Hyperion – merely confusion and death.

Sol rocked his child and looked out on the barrens, considering leaving this place at once . . . walking to the dead city or Chronos Keep . . . walking northwest to the Littoral or southeast to where the Bridle Range intersected the sea. Sol raised a shaky hand to his face and rubbed his cheek; there would be no salvation in the wilderness. Leaving the valley had not saved Martin Silenus. The Shrike had been reported far south of the Bridle Range – as far south as Endymion and the other southern cities – and even if the monster spared them, starvation and thirst would not. Sol might survive on plants, rodent flesh, and snowmelt from the high places – but Rachel's supply of milk was limited, even with the supplies Brawne had brought back from the Keep. Then he realized that the milk supply did not matter . . .

I'll be alone in less than a day. Sol stifled a moan as the thought struck him. His determination to save his child had brought him across two and a half decades and a hundred times that many light-years. His resolve to return Rachel's life and health to her was an almost palpable force, a fierce energy which he and Sarai had shared and which he had kept alive the way a temple priest preserves the sacred temple flame. No, by God, there *was* a pattern to things, a moral underpinning to this platform of seemingly random events, and Sol Weintraub would wager his and his daughter's lives on that belief.

Sol stood, walked slowly down the trail to the Sphinx, climbed the stairs, found a therm cloak and blankets, and made a nest for the two of them on the highest step as Hyperion winds howled and the Time Tombs glowed more brightly.

Rachel lay on his chest and stomach, her cheek on his shoulder, her tiny hands curling and uncurling as she released the world for the land of infant sleep. Sol heard her gentle breathing as she moved into deep slumber, heard the soft sound as she blew tiny bubbles of saliva. After a while, he released his own hold on the world and joined her in sleep.

THIRTY

Sol dreamed the dream he had suffered since the day Rachel had incurred Merlin's sickness.

He was walking through a vast structure, where columns the size of redwood trees rose into the gloom and where crimson light fell in solid shafts from somewhere far above. There came the sound of a giant conflagration, entire worlds burning. Ahead of him glowed two ovals of the deepest red.

Sol knew the place. He knew that he would find an altar ahead with Rachel on it – Rachel in her twenties and unconscious – and then would come the Voice, demanding.

Sol stopped on the low balcony and stared down at the familiar scene. His daughter, the woman he and Sarai had bid farewell to when she left for postgraduate work on distant Hyperion, lay naked on a broad block of stone. Above them all floated the twin red orbs of the Shrike's gaze. On the altar lay a long, curved knife made of sharpened bone. The Voice came then:

'Sol! Take your daughter, your only daughter, Rachel, whom you love, and go to the world called Hyperion and offer her there as a burnt offering at one of the places of which I shall tell you.'

Sol's arms were shaking with rage and grief. He pulled at his hair and shouted into the darkness, repeating what he had told that voice before:

'There will be no more offerings, neither child nor parent. There will be no more sacrifices. The time of obedience and atonement is past. Either help us as a friend, or go away!'

In previous dreams, this had led to the sound of wind and isolation, terrible footsteps receding in the dark. But this time the dream persisted, the altar shimmered and was suddenly empty except for the bone knife. The twin red orbs still floated high above, fire-filled rubies the size of worlds.

'Sol, listen,' came the Voice, modulated now so it did not boom from far above but almost whispered in his ear, *'the future of humankind depends upon your choice. Can you offer Rachel out of love, if not obedience?'*

Sol heard the answer in his mind even as he groped for the words. There would be no more offerings. Not this day. Not any day. Humankind had suffered enough for its love of gods, its long search for God. He thought of the many centuries in which his people, the Jews, had negotiated with God, complaining, bickering, decrying the unfairness of things but always

– always – returning to obedience at whatever the cost. Generations dying in the ovens of hatred. Future generations scarred by the cold fires of radiation and renewed hatred.

Not this time. Not ever again.

'Say yes, Daddy.'

Sol started at the touch of a hand on his. His daughter, Rachel, stood next to him, neither infant nor adult, but the eight-year-old he had known twice – aging and growing backward through that age with Merlin's sickness – Rachel with her light brown hair tied back in a simple braid, short form soft in washed-denim play tunic and kid sneakers.

Sol took her hand, gripping as tightly as he could without hurting her, feeling the returned grip. This was no illusion, no final cruelty of the Shrike. This was his daughter.

'Say yes, Daddy.'

Sol had solved Abraham's problem of obedience to a God turned malicious. Obedience could no longer be paramount in relations between humanity and its deity. But when the *child* chosen as sacrifice asked for obedience to that God's whim?

Sol went to one knee next to his daughter and opened his arms. 'Rachel.'

She hugged him with the energy he remembered from countless such hugs, her chin high over his shoulder, her arms fierce in their intensity of love. She whispered in his ear, 'Please, Daddy, we have to say yes.'

Sol continued to hug her, feeling her thin arms around him and the warmth of her cheek against his. He was crying silently, feeling the wetness on his cheeks and in his short beard, but unwilling to release her for even the second it would take to wipe the tears away.

'I love you, Daddy,' whispered Rachel.

He rose then, wiped his face with a swipe of the back of his hand, and with Rachel's left hand still firmly in his, began the long descent with her toward the altar below.

Sol awoke with a sense of falling, grabbing for the baby. She was asleep on his chest, her fist curled, her thumb in her mouth, but when he started upright she awoke with the cry and arching reflex of a startled newborn. Sol got to his feet, dropping blankets and cloak around him, clutching Rachel tightly to him.

It was daylight. Late morning, if anything. They had slept while the night died and sunlight crept into the valley and across the Tombs. The Sphinx huddled over them like some predatory beast, powerful forelegs extended on either side of the stairway where they had slept.

Rachel wailed, her face contorting with the shock of waking and hunger and sensed fear in her father. Sol stood in the fierce sunlight and rocked her. He went to the top step of the Sphinx, changed her diaper, heated one of the last nursing paks, offered it to her until the wails turned to soft nursing sounds, burped her, and walked her around until she drifted into light sleep again.

It was less than ten hours until her 'birthday'. Less than ten hours until sunset and the last few minutes of his daughter's life. Not for the first time, Sol wished that the Time Tomb were a great glass building symbolizing the cosmos and the deity that ran it. Sol would throw rocks at the structure until not a single pane remained unbroken.

He tried to remember the details of his dream, but the warmth and reassurance of it shredded in the harsh light of Hyperion's sun. He remembered only Rachel's whispered entreaty. The thought of offering her to the Shrike made Sol's stomach ache with horror. 'It's all right,' he whispered to her as she twitched and sighed toward the treacherous haven of sleep once again. 'It's all right, kiddo. The Consul's ship will be here soon. The ship will come any minute.'

The Consul's ship did not come by noon. The Consul's ship did not come by midafternoon. Sol walked the valley floor, calling out for those who had disappeared, singing half-forgotten songs when Rachel awoke, crooning lullabies as she drifted back to sleep. His daughter was so tiny and light: six pounds and three ounces, nineteen inches at birth, he remembered, smiling at the antique units of his antique home, of Barnard's World.

In late afternoon, he startled awake from his half-doze in the shade of the Sphinx's outflung paw, standing with Rachel waking in his arms as a spacecraft arched across the dome of deep lapis sky.

'It's come!' he cried, and Rachel stirred and wiggled as if in response.

A line of blue fusion flame glowed with that daylight intensity reserved to spacecraft in atmosphere. Sol hopped up and down, filled with the first relief in many days. He shouted and leaped until Rachel wailed and wept in concern. Sol stopped, lifted her high, knowing that she could not yet focus her eyes but wanting her to see the beauty of the descending ship as it arced above the distant mountain range, dropping toward the high desert.

'He did it!' cried Sol. 'He's coming! The ship will . . .'

Three heavy thuds struck the valley almost at once; the first two were the twin sonic booms of the spacecraft's 'footprint' racing ahead of it as it decelerated. The third was the sound of its destruction.

Sol stared as the glowing pinpoint at the apex of the long fusion trail suddenly grew as bright as the sun, expanded into a cloud of flame and boiling gases, and then tumbled toward the distant desert in ten thousand burning pieces. He blinked away retinal echoes as Rachel continued crying.

'My God,' whispered Sol. 'My God.' There was no denying the complete destruction of the spacecraft. Secondary explosions ripped the air, even from thirty kilometers away, as pieces fell, trailing smoke and flames, toward the desert, the mountains, and the Sea of Grass beyond. 'My God.'

Sol sat on the warm sand. He was too exhausted to cry, too empty to do anything but rock his child until her crying stopped.

Ten minutes later Sol looked up as two more fusion trails burned the sky, these headed south from the zenith. One of these exploded, too distant for sound to reach him. The second one dropped out of sight below the southern cliffs, beyond the Bridle Range.

'Perhaps it was not the Consul,' whispered Sol. 'It could be the Ouster invasion. Perhaps the Consul's ship still will come for us.'

But the ship did not come by late afternoon. It had not come by the time the light of Hyperion's small sun shone on the cliff wall, shadows reaching for Sol on the highest step of the Sphinx. It did not come when the valley fell in shadow.

Rachel was born less than thirty minutes from this second. Sol checked her diaper, found her dry, and fed her from the last nursing pak. As she ate, she looked up at him with great, dark eyes, seemingly searching his face. Sol remembered the first few minutes he had held her while Sarai rested under warmed blankets; the baby's eyes had burned into him then with these same questions and startlement at finding such a world.

The evening wind brought clouds moving in quickly above the valley. Rumbles to the southwest came first as distant thunder and then with the sick regularity of artillery, most likely nuclear or plasma explosions five hundred klicks or more to the south. Sol scanned the sky between lowering clouds and caught glimpses of fiery meteor trails arching overhead: ballistic missiles or dropships, probably. Death for Hyperion in either case.

Sol ignored it. He sang softly to Rachel as she finished nursing. He had walked to the head of the valley, but now he returned slowly to the Sphinx. The Tombs were glowing as never before, rippling with the harsh light of neon gases excited by electrons. Overhead, the last shafts from the setting sun changed the low clouds to a ceiling of pastel flames.

Less than three minutes remained until the final celebration of Rachel's birth. Even if the Consul's ship arrived now, Sol knew that he would not have time to board it or get his child into cryogenic sleep.

He did not want to.

Sol climbed the stairs to the Sphinx slowly, realizing that Rachel had come this way twenty-six standard years earlier, never guessing the fate that awaited her in that dark crypt.

He paused at the top step and took in a breath. The light from the sun was a palpable thing, filling the sky and igniting the wings and upper mass of the Sphinx. The tomb itself seemed to be releasing the light it had stored, like the rocks in Hebron's desert, where Sol had wandered in the wilderness years before, seeking enlightenment and finding only sorrow. The air shimmered with light, and the wind continued to rise, blowing sand across the valley floor and then relenting.

Sol went to one knee on the top step, pulling off Rachel's blanket until the child was in only her soft cotton newborn's clothes. Swaddling clothes.

Rachel wiggled in his hands. Her face was purple and slick, her hands tiny and red with the effort of clenching and unclenching. Sol remembered her exactly like this as the doctor handed the infant to Sol, as he stared at his newborn daughter as he was staring now, then set her on Sarai's stomach so the mother could see.

'Ah, God,' breathed Sol and dropped to his other knee, truly kneeling now.

The entire valley quivered as if to an earthquake tremor. Sol could vaguely hear the explosions continuing far to the south. But of more immediate concern now was the terrible glow from the Sphinx. Sol's shadow leaped fifty meters behind him down the stairway and across the valley floor as the tomb pulsed and vibrated with light. Out of the corner of his eye, Sol could see the other Tombs glowing as brightly – huge, baroque reactors in their final seconds before meltdown.

The entrance to the Sphinx pulsed blue, then violet, then a terrible white. Behind the Sphinx, on the wall of the plateau above the Valley of the Time Tombs, an impossible tree shimmered into existence, its huge trunk and sharp steel branches rising into the glowing clouds and above. Sol glanced quickly, saw the three-meter thorns and the terrible fruit they bore, and then he looked back at the entrance to the Sphinx.

Somewhere the wind howled and thunder rumbled. Somewhere vermilion dust blew like curtains of dried blood in the terrible light from the Tombs. Somewhere voices cried out and a chorus shrieked.

Sol ignored all this. He had eyes only for his daughter's face and, beyond her, for the shadow that now filled the glowing entrance to the tomb.

The Shrike emerged. The thing had to bend to allow its three-meter bulk and steel blades to clear the top of the doorway. It stepped on to the top porch of the Sphinx and moved forward, part creature, part sculpture, walking with the terrible deliberation of nightmare.

The dying light above rippled on the thing's carapace, cascaded down across curving breastplate to steel thorns there, shimmering on finger-blades and scalpels rising from every joint. Sol hugged Rachel to his chest and stared into the multi-faceted red furnaces that passed for the Shrike's eyes. The sunset faded into the blood-red glow of Sol's recurrent dream.

The Shrike's head turned slightly, swiveling without friction, rotating ninety degrees right, ninety degrees left, as if the creature were surveying its domain.

The Shrike took three steps forward, stopping less than two meters from Sol. The thing's four arms twisted and rose, fingerblades uncurling.

Sol hugged Rachel tightly to him. Her skin was moist, her face bruised and blotched with the exertions of birth. Seconds remained. Her eyes tracked separately, seemed to focus on Sol.

Say yes, Daddy. Sol remembered the dream.

The Shrike's head lowered until the ruby eyes in that terrible hood stared at nothing but Sol and his child. The quicksilver jaws parted slightly, showing layers and levels of steel teeth. Four hands came forward, metallic palms up, pausing half a meter from Sol's face.

Say yes, Daddy. Sol remembered the dream, remembered his daughter's hug, and realized that in the end – when all else is dust – loyalty to those we love is all we can carry with us to the grave. Faith – true faith – was trusting in that love.

Sol lifted his newborn and dying child, seconds old, shrieking now with her first and last breath, and handed her to the Shrike.

The absence of her slight weight struck Sol with a terrible vertigo.

The Shrike lifted Rachel, stepped backward, and was enveloped in light.

Behind the Sphinx, the tree of thorns ceased shimmering, shifted into phase with *now*, and came into terrible focus.

Sol stepped forward, arms imploring, as the Shrike stepped back into the radiance and was gone. Explosions rippled the clouds and slammed Sol to his knees with shock waves of pressure.

Behind him, around him, the Time Tombs were opening.

PART THREE

THIRTY-ONE

I awoke and was not pleased to be awakened.

Rolling over, squinting and cursing the sudden invasion of light, I saw Leigh Hunt sitting on the edge of the bed, an aerosol injector still in his hand.

'You took enough sleeping pills to keep you in bed all day,' he said. 'Rise and shine.'

I sat up, rubbed the morning stubble on my cheeks, and squinted in Hunt's direction. 'Who the hell gave you the right to enter my room?' The effort of speaking started me coughing, and I did not stop until Hunt returned from the bathroom with a glass of water.

'Here.'

I drank, vainly trying to project anger and outrage between spasms of coughing. The remnants of dreams fled like morning mists. I felt a terrible sense of loss descend.

'Get dressed,' said Hunt, standing. 'The CEO wants you in her chambers in twenty minutes. While you've been sleeping, things have been happening.'

'What things?' I rubbed my eyes and ran fingers through my tousled hair.

Hunt smiled tightly. 'Access the datasphere. Then get down to Gladstone's chambers soonest. Twenty minutes, Severn.' He left.

I accessed the datasphere. One way to visualize one's entry point to the datasphere is to imagine a patch of Old Earth's ocean in varying degrees of turbulence. Normal days tended to show a placid sea with interesting patterns of ripples. Crises showed chop and whitecaps. Today there was a hurricane under way. Entry was delayed to any access route, confusion reigned in breaking waves of update surges, the datumplane matrix was wild with storage shifts and major credit transfers, and the All Thing, normally a multilayered buzz of information and political debate, was a raging wind of confusion, abandoned referenda and obsolete position templates blowing by like tattered clouds.

'Dear God,' I whispered, breaking access but feeling the pressure of the information surge still pounding at my implant circuits and brain. War. Surprise attack. Imminent destruction of the Web. Talk of impeaching Gladstone. Riots on a score of worlds. Shrike Cult uprisings on Lusus. The FORCE fleet abandoning Hyperion System in a desperate rearguard action, but too late, too late. Hyperion already under attack. Fear of farcaster incursion.

I rose, ran naked to the shower, and sonicked in record time. Hunt or someone had laid out a formal gray suit and cape, and I dressed in a hurry, brushing back my wet hair so that damp curls fell to my collar.

It wouldn't do to keep the CEO of the Hegemony of Man waiting. Oh no, that wouldn't do at all.

'It's about time you got here,' said Meina Gladstone as I entered her private chambers.

'What the fuck have you done?' I snapped.

Gladstone blinked. Evidently the CEO of the Hegemony of Man was not used to being spoken to in that tone. *Tough shit*, I thought.

'Remember who you are and to whom you're speaking,' Gladstone said coldly.

'I don't know who I am. And I may be speaking to the greatest mass murderer since Horace Glennon-Height. Why the hell did you allow this war to happen?'

Gladstone blinked again and looked around. We were alone. Her sitting room was long and pleasantly dark and hung with original art from Old Earth. At that moment I didn't care if I was in a room filled with original van Goghs. I stared at Gladstone, the Lincolnesque face merely that of an old woman in the thin light through the blinds. She returned my gaze for a moment, then looked away again.

'I apologize,' I snapped, no apology in my voice, 'you didn't *allow* it, you *made* it happen, didn't you?'

'No, Severn, I did not make it happen.' Gladstone's voice was hushed, almost a whisper.

'Speak up,' I said. I paced back and forth near the tall windows, watching the light from the blinds move across me like painted stripes. 'And I'm not Joseph Severn.'

She raised an eyebrow. 'Shall I call you M. Keats?'

'You can call me No Man,' I said. 'So that when the other cyclopes come, you can say that No Man has blinded you, and they will go away, saying that it's the will of the gods.'

'Do you plan to blind me?'

'Right now I could wring your neck and walk away without a twinge of remorse. *Millions* will die before this week is out. How could you have allowed it?'

Gladstone touched her lower lip. 'The future branches in only two directions,' she said softly. 'War and total uncertainty, or peace and totally certain annihilation. I chose war.'

'Who says this?' There was more curiosity than anger in my voice now.

'It is a fact.' She glanced at her comlog. 'In ten minutes I have to go before the Senate to declare war. Tell me the news of the Hyperion pilgrims.'

I crossed my arms and stared down at her. 'I will tell you if you promise to do something.'

'I will if I can.'

I paused, realized that no amount of leverage in the universe could make this woman write a blank check on her word. 'All right,' I said. 'I want you to fatline Hyperion, release the hold you have on the Consul's ship, and send someone up the Hoolie River to find the Consul himself. He's about a hundred and thirty klicks from the capital, above the Karla Locks. He may be hurt.'

Gladstone crooked a finger, rubbed her lip, and nodded. 'I will send someone to find him. Releasing the ship depends upon what else you have to tell me. Are the others alive?'

I curled my short cape around me and collapsed on a couch across from her. 'Some are.'

'Byron Lamia's daughter? Brawne?'

'The Shrike took her. For a while, she was unconscious, connected to some sort of neural shunt to the datasphere. I dreamed . . . she was floating somewhere, reunited with the implant persona of the first Keats retrieval personality. Just entering the datasphere . . . the megasphere really, Core connections and dimensions I never dreamed of as well as the accessible 'sphere.'

'Is she alive now?' Gladstone leaned forward, intense.

'I don't know. Her body disappeared. I was awakened before I saw where her persona entered the megasphere.'

Gladstone nodded. 'What about the Colonel?'

'Kassad was taken somewhere by Moneta, the human female who seems to reside in the Tombs as they travel through time. The last I saw of him, he was attacking the Shrike barehanded. Shrikes, actually, there were thousands of them.'

'Did he survive?'

I opened my hands. 'I don't know. These were *dreams*. Fragments. Bits and pieces of perception.'

'The poet?'

'Silenus was carried off by the Shrike. Impaled on the tree of thorns. But I glimpsed him there later in Kassad's dream. Silenus was still alive. I don't know how.'

'So the tree of thorns is real, not merely Shrike Cult propaganda?'

'Oh yes, it's real.'

'And the Consul left? Tried to return to the capital?'

'He had his grandmother's hawking mat. It worked all right until he reached the place near Karla Locks I mentioned. It . . . and he . . . fell into the river.' I preempted her next question. 'I don't know if he survived.'

'And the priest? Father Hoyt?'

'The cruciform brought him back as Father Duré.'

'*Is* it Father Duré? Or a mindless duplicate?'

'It's Duré,' I said. 'But . . . damaged. Discouraged.'

'And he is still in the valley?'

'No. He disappeared in one of the Cave Tombs. I don't know what happened to him.'

Gladstone glanced at her comlog. I tried to imagine the confusion and chaos which reigned in the rest of this building . . . this world . . . in the Web. The CEO obviously had retreated here for fifteen minutes prior to her speech to the Senate. It might be the last such solitude she would see for the next several weeks. Perhaps ever.

'Captain Masteen?'

'Dead. Buried in the valley.'

She took a breath. 'And Weintraub and the child?'

I shook my head. 'I dreamed things out of sequence . . . out of time. I *think* it's already happened, but I'm confused.' I looked up. Gladstone was waiting patiently. 'The baby was only a few seconds old when the Shrike came,' I said. 'Sol offered her to the thing. I think it took her into the Sphinx. The Tombs were glowing very brightly. There were . . . other Shrikes . . . emerging.'

'The Tombs have opened, then?'

'Yes.'

Gladstone touched her comlog. 'Leigh? Have the duty officer in the communications center contact Theo Lane and the necessary FORCE people on Hyperion. Release the ship we have in quarantine. Also, Leigh, tell the Governor-General that I will have a personal message for him in a few minutes.' The instrument chirped and she looked back at me. 'Is there anything else from your dreams?'

'Images. Words. I don't understand what's going on. Those are the high points.'

Gladstone smiled slightly. 'Are you aware that you are dreaming events beyond the range of the other Keats persona's experience?'

I said nothing, stunned with the shock of what she said. My contact with the pilgrims had been possible through some Core-based connection to the persona implant in Brawne's Schrön loop, through it and the primitive datasphere they had shared. But the persona had been liberated; the datasphere destroyed by separation and distance. Even a fatline receiver cannot receive messages when there is no transmitter.

Gladstone's smile disappeared. 'Can you explain this?'

'No.' I looked up. 'Perhaps they were only dreams. Real dreams.'

She stood. 'Perhaps we'll know when and if we find the Consul. Or when his ship arrives in the valley. I have two minutes before I appear in the Senate. Is there anything else?'

'A question,' I said. 'Who am I? Why am I here?'

The slight smile again. 'We all ask those questions, M. Sev—M. Keats.'

'I'm serious. I think you know better than I.'

'The Core sent you to be my liaison with the pilgrims. And to observe. You are, after all, a poet and artist.'

I made a noise and stood. We walked slowly toward the private farcaster portal that would take her to the Senate floor. 'What good does observation do when it's the end of the world?'

'Find out,' said Gladstone. 'Go see the end of the world.' She handed me a microcard for my comlog. I inserted it, glanced at the diskey; it was a universal authorization chip, allowing me access to all portals, public, private or military. It was a ticket to the end of the world.

I said, 'What if I get killed?'

'Then we will never hear the answers to your questions,' said CEO Gladstone. She touched my wrist fleetingly, turned her back, and stepped through the portal.

For a few minutes I stood alone in her chambers, appreciating the light and silence and art. There *was* a van Gogh on one of the walls, worth more than most planets could pay. It was a painting of the artist's room at Arles. Madness is not a new invention.

After a while, I left, let my comlog memory guide me through the maze of Government House until I found the central farcaster terminex, and stepped through to find the end of the world.

There were two full-access farcaster pathways through the Web: the Concourse and River Tethys. I 'cast to the Concourse where the half-kilometer strip of Tsingtao-Hsishuang Panna connected to New Earth and the short seaside strip of Nevermore. Tsingtao-Hsishuang Panna was a first-wave world, thirty-four hours away from the Ouster onslaught. New Earth had been on the second-wave list, even now being announced, and had a little over a standard week before invasion. Nevermore was deep in the Web, years away from attack.

There were no signs of panic. People were taking to the datasphere and All Thing rather than the streets. Walking the narrow lanes of Tsingtao, I could hear Gladstone's voice from a thousand receivers and personal comlogs, a strange verbal undertone to the shouts of street vendors and hiss of tires on wet pavement as electric rickshaws hummed overhead on the transport levels.

'. . . as another leader told his people on the eve of attack almost eight centuries ago – "I have nothing to offer but blood, toil, tears, and sweat." You ask, what is our policy? I say to you: It is to wage war, in space, on land, in the air, by sea, wage war with all our might and with all the strength justice and right can give us. *That* is our policy . . .'

There were FORCE troops near the translation zone between Tsingtao and Nevermore, but the flow of pedestrians seemed normal enough. I wondered when the military would commandeer the pedestrian mall of the Concourse for vehicular traffic and if it would be headed *toward* the front or away.

I stepped through to Nevermore. The streets were dry there, except for the occasional spray from the ocean thirty meters below the stone ramparts of the Concourse. The sky was its usual tones of threatening ochre and gray, ominous twilight in the middle of the day. Small stone shops glowed with light and merchandise. I was aware that the streets were emptier than usual; people standing in shops or sitting on stone walls or benches, heads bowed and eyes distracted as they listened.

'. . . you ask, what is our aim? I answer in one word. It is victory, victory at all costs, victory in spite of all terror, victory however long and hard the road may be; for without victory, there is no survival . . .'

The lines at Edgartown's main terminex were short. I coded for Mare Infinitus and stepped through.

The skies were their usual cloudless green, the ocean beneath the float city a deeper green. Kelp farms floated to the horizon. The crowds this far from the Concourse were even smaller; the boardwalks were almost empty, some shops closed. A group of men stood near a kipboat dock and listened to an antique fatline receiver. Gladstone's voice was flat and metallic in the sea-rich air.

'. . . even now, units of FORCE move relentlessly to their stations, firm in their resolve and confident in their ability to rescue not only the threatened worlds but all of the Hegemony of Man from the foulest and most soul-destroying tyranny ever to stain the annals of history . . .'

Mare Infinitus was eighteen hours from invasion. I looked skyward, half expecting to see some sign of the enemy swarm, some indication of orbital defenses, space-borne troop movements. There was only the sky, the warm day, and the gentle rocking of the city on the sea.

Heaven's Gate was the first world on the list of invasion. I stepped through the Mudflat VIP portal and looked down from Rifkin Heights at the beautiful city which belied its name. It was deep night, so late the mech street sweepers were out, their brushes and sonics humming against cobblestone, but here there *was* movement, long lines of silent people at the Rifkin Heights public terminex and even longer lines visible below at the Promenade portals. Local police were in evidence, tall figures in brown impact coveralls, but if FORCE units were rushing to reinforce this area, they were invisible.

The people in the lines were not local residents – the Rifkin Heights and Promenade landowners almost certainly had private portals – but looked to be workers from the reclamation projects many klicks out beyond the fern forest and parks. There was no panic and very little conversation. The lines filed past with the patient stoicism of families shuffling toward a theme park attraction. Few carried anything larger than a travel bag or backpack.

Have we attained such equanimity, I wondered, that we handle ourselves with dignity even in the face of invasion?

Heaven's Gate was thirteen hours from H-hour. I keyed my comlog to the All Thing.

'. . . if we can meet this threat, then worlds we love may remain free and the life of the Web may move forward into the sunlit future. But if we fail, then the whole Web, the Hegemony, everything we have known and cared for, will sink into the abyss of a new Dark Age made infinitely more sinister and protracted by the lights of science perverted and human freedom denied.

'Let us therefore brace ourselves to our duties, and so bear ourselves that if the Hegemony of Man and its Protectorate and allies were to last ten thousand years, humankind will still say: "*This* was their finest hour."'

Somewhere in the silent, fresh-smelling city below, shooting began. First came the rattle of fléchette guns, then the deep hum of antiriot stunners, then screams and the sizzle of weapon lasers. The crowd on the Promenade surged forward toward the terminex, but riot police emerged from the park, switched on powerful halogen searchlights which bathed the crowd in glare, and began ordering them through bullhorns to resume lines or disperse. The crowd hesitated, surged back and forth like a jellyfish caught in tricky currents, and then – spurred on by the sound of firing, louder and closer now – surged forward toward the portal platforms.

The riot cops fired tear gas and vertigo canisters. Between the mob and the farcaster, violet interdiction fields whined into existence. A flight of military EMVs and security skimmers came in low over the city, search-lights stabbing downward. One of the beams of light caught me, held me until my comlog winked at an interrogation signal, and then moved on. It began to rain.

So much for equanimity.

The police had secured the Rifkin Heights public terminex and were stepping through the private Atmospheric Protectorate portal I had used. I decided to go elsewhere.

There were FORCE commandos guarding the halls of Government House, screening the farcaster arrivals despite the fact that this portal was one of the most difficult to access in the Web. I passed through three checkpoints before reaching the executive/residential wing where my apartments were. Suddenly, guards stepped out to empty the main hall and secure its tributaries, and Gladstone swept by accompanied by a swirling crowd of advisors, aides, and military leaders. Surprisingly, she saw me, brought her retinue to a clumsy halt, and spoke to me through the barricade of combat-armored Marines.

'How did you like the speech, M. No Man?'

'Fine,' I said. 'Stirring. And stolen from Winston Churchill if I'm not mistaken.'

Gladstone smiled and shrugged slightly. 'If one is to steal, steal from the forgotten masters.' The smile faded. 'What is the news from the frontier?'

'The reality is just beginning to sink in,' I said. 'Expect panic.'

'I always do,' said the CEO. 'What news have you from the pilgrims?'

I was surprised. 'The pilgrims? I haven't been . . . dreaming.'

The current of Gladstone's retinue and impending events began to sweep her away down the hall. 'Perhaps you no longer need to sleep to dream,' she called. 'Try it.'

I watched her go, was released to seek out my suite, found the door, and turned away in disgust with myself. I was retreating in fear and shock from the terror descending on us all. I would be quite happy to lie in bed, avoiding sleep, the covers pulled right to my chin while I wept for the Web, for the child Rachel, and for myself.

I left the residential wing and found my way out to the central garden, wandering down graveled paths. Tiny microremotes buzzed like bees through the air, one pacing me as I passed through the rose garden, into the area where a sunken path twisted through steamy tropical plants, and into the Old Earth section near the bridge. I sat on the stone bench where Gladstone and I had talked.

Perhaps you no longer need to sleep to dream. Try it.

I pulled my feet up on the bench, touched my chin to my knees, set fingertips against my temples, and closed my eyes.

THIRTY-TWO

Martin Silenus twists and writhes in the pure poetry of pain. A steel thorn two meters long enters his body between his shoulder blades and passes out through his chest, extending to a point a terrible, tapering meter beyond him. His flailing arms cannot touch the point. The thorn is frictionless, his sweaty palms and curling fingers can find no purchase there. Despite the thorn's slickness to the touch, his body does not slide; he is as firmly impaled as a butterfly pinned for exhibition.

There is no blood.

In the hours after rationality returned through the mad haze of pain, Martin Silenus wondered about that. There is no blood. But there is pain. Oh yes, there is pain in abundance here – pain beyond the poet's wildest imaginings of what pain was, pain beyond human endurance and the boundaries of suffering.

But Silenus endures. And Silenus suffers.

He screams for the thousandth time, a ragged sound, empty of content, free of language, even obscenities. Words fail to convey such agony. Silenus screams and writhes. After a while, he hangs limply, the long thorn bouncing slightly in response to his gyrations. Other people hang above, below, and behind him, but Silenus spends little time observing them. Each is separated by his or her own private cocoon of agony.

'*Why this is hell,*' thinks Silenus, quoting Marlowe, '*nor am I out of it.*'

But he knows it is not hell. Nor any afterlife. But he also knows that it is not some subbranch of reality; the thorn passes through his *body*! Eight centimeters of organic steel through his chest! But he has not died. He does not bleed. This place was somewhere and something, but it was not hell and it was not living.

Time was strange here. Silenus had known time to stretch and slow before – the agony of the exposed nerve in the dentist's chair, the kidney-stone pain in the Med clinic waiting room – time could slow, seem not to move as the hands of an outraged biological clock stood still in shock. But time did move then. The root canal was finished. The ultramorph finally arrived, took effect. But here the very air is frozen in the absence of time. Pain is the curl and foam of a wave *that does not break*.

Silenus screams in anger and pain. And writhes upon his thorn.

'Goddamn!' he manages at last. 'Goddamn motherfuck sonofabitch.' The words are relics of a different life, artifacts from the dream he had lived before the reality of the tree. Silenus only half remembers that life, as he only half remembers the Shrike carrying him here, impaling him here, leaving him here.

'Oh *God!*' screams the poet and clutches at the thorn with both hands, trying to lever himself up to relieve the great weight of his body which adds so immeasurably to the unmeasurable pain.

There is a landscape below. He can see for miles. It is a frozen, papier-mâché diorama of the Valley of the Time Tombs and the desert beyond. Even the dead city and the distant mountains are reproduced in plasticized, sterile miniature. It does not matter. For Martin Silenus there is only the tree and the pain, and the two are indivisible. Silenus shows his teeth in a pain-cracked smile. When he was a child on Old Earth, he and Amalfi Schwartz, his best friend, had visited a commune of Christians in the North American Preserve, learned their crude theology, and afterward had made many jokes about crucifixion. Young Martin had spread his arms wide, crossed his legs, lifted his head, and said, 'Gee, I can see the whole town from up here.' Amalfi had roared.

Silenus screams.

Time does not truly pass, but after a while Silenus's mind returns to something resembling linear observation . . . something other than the scattered oases of clear, pure agony separated by the desert of mindlessly received agony . . . and in that linear perception of his own pain, Silenus begins to impose time on this timeless place.

First, the obscenities add clarity to his pain. Shouting hurts, but his anger clears and clarifies.

Then, in the exhausted times between shouting or pure spasms of pain, Silenus allows himself thought. At first it is merely an effort to sequence, to recite the times tables in his mind, anything to separate the agony of ten seconds ago from the agony yet to come. Silenus discovers that in the effort of concentrating, the agony is lessened slightly – still unbearable, still driving all true thought like wisps before a wind, but lessened some indefinable amount.

So Silenus concentrates. He screams and rails and writhes, but he concentrates. Since there is nothing else to concentrate on, he concentrates on the pain.

Pain, he discovers, has a structure. It has a floor plan. It has designs more intricate than a chambered nautilus, features more baroque than the most buttressed Gothic cathedral. Even as he screams, Martin Silenus studies the structure of this pain. He realizes that it is a poem.

Silenus arches his body and neck for the ten thousandth time, seeking relief where no relief is possible, but this time he sees a familiar form five meters above him, hanging from a similar thorn, twisting in the unreal breeze of agony.

'Billy!' gasps Martin Silenus, his first true thought.

His former liege lord and patron stares across a sightless abyss, made blind with the pain that had blinded Silenus, but turning slightly as if in response to the call of his name in this place beyond names.

'Billy!' cries Silenus again and then loses vision and thought to the pain. He concentrates on the structure of pain, following its patterns as if he were tracing the trunk and branches and twigs and thorns of the tree itself. 'My lord!'

Silenus hears a voice above the screams and is amazed to find that both the screams and the voice are his:

> '. . . Thou art a dreaming thing;
> A fever of thyself – think of the Earth;
> What bliss even in hope is there for thee?
> What haven? every creature hath its home;
> Every sole man hath days of joy and pain,
> Whether his labours be sublime or low—
> The pain alone; the joy alone; distinct:
> Only the dreamer venoms all his days,
> Bearing more woe than all his sins deserve.'

He knows the verse, not his, John Keats's, and feels the words further structuring the seeming chaos of pain around him. Silenus understands that the pain has been with him since birth – the universe's gift to a poet. It is a physical reflection of the pain he has felt and futilely tried to set to verse, to pin down with prose, all those useless years of life. It is worse than pain; it is unhappiness because the universe offers pain to all.

> 'Only the dreamer venoms all his days,
> Bearing more woe than all his sins deserve!'

Silenus shouts it but does not scream. The roar of pain from the tree, more psychic than physical, abates for the barest fraction of a second. There is an island of distraction amidst this ocean of single-mindedness.

'Martin!'

Silenus arches, lifts his head, tries to focus through the haze of pain. Sad King Billy is looking at him. *Looking.*

Sad King Billy croaks a syllable which, after an endless moment, Silenus recognizes as 'More!'

Silenus screams in agony, writhes in a palsied spasm of mindless physical response, but when he stops, dangling in exhaustion, the pain not lessened but driven from the motor areas of his brain by fatigue toxins, he allows the voice within him to shout and whisper its song:

> 'Spirit here that reignest!
> Spirit here that painest!
> Spirit here that burnest!
> Spirit here that mournest!
>   Spirit! I bow
>   My forehead low,
>   Enshaded with thy pinions!

Spirit! I look
All passion-struck
Into thy pale dominions!'

The small circle of silence widens to include several nearby branches, a handful of thorns carrying their clusters of human beings in extremis.

Silenus stares up at Sad King Billy and sees his betrayed lord open his sad eyes. For the first time in more than two centuries, patron and poet look upon one another. Silenus delivers the message that has brought him here, hung him here. 'My lord, I'm sorry.'

Before Billy can respond, before the chorus of screaming drowns out any response, the air *changes*, the sense of frozen time *stirs*, and the tree *shakes*, as if the entire thing has dropped a meter. Silenus screams with the others as the branch shakes and the impaling thorn tears at his insides, rends his flesh anew.

Silenus opens his eyes and sees that the sky is real, the desert real, the Tombs glowing, the wind blowing, and time begun again. There is no lessening of torment, but clarity has returned.

Martin Silenus laughs through tears. 'Look, Mom!' he shouts, giggling, the steel spear still protruding a meter beyond his shattered chest, 'I can see the whole town from up here!'

'M. Severn? Are you all right?'

Panting, on my hands and knees, I turned toward the voice. Opening my eyes was painful, but no pain could compare to what I had just experienced.

'Are you all right, sir?'

No one was near me in the garden. The voice came from a microremote that buzzed half a meter from my face, probably one of the security people somewhere in Government House.

'Yes,' I managed, getting to my feet and brushing gravel from my knees. 'I'm fine. A sudden . . . pain.'

'Medical help can be here in two minutes, sir. Your biomonitor reports no organic difficulty, but we can—'

'No, no,' I said. 'I'm fine. Leave it be. And leave *me* alone.'

The remote fluttered like a nervous hummingbird. 'Yes, sir. Just call if you need anything. The garden and grounds monitor will respond.'

'Go away,' I said.

I went out of the gardens, through the main hall of Government House – all checkpoints and security guards now – and out across the landscaped acres of Deer Park.

The dock area was quiet, the River Tethys more still than I had ever seen it. 'What's happening?' I asked one of the security people on the pier.

The guard accessed my comlog, confirmed my executive override pip and CEO clearance, but still did not hurry to answer. 'The portals've been turned off for TC^2,' he drawled. 'Bypassed.'

'Bypassed? You mean the river doesn't flow through Tau Ceti Center anymore?'

'Right.' He flipped his visor down as a small boat approached, flipped it up when he identified the two security people in it.

'Can I get out that way?' I pointed upriver to where the tall portals showed an opaque curtain of gray.

The guard shrugged. 'Yeah. But you won't be allowed back that way.'

'That's all right. Can I take that small boat?'

The guard whispered into his bead mike and nodded. 'Go ahead.'

I stepped gingerly into the small craft, sat on the rear bench and held on to the gunwales until the rocking subsided, touched the power diskey and said, 'Start.'

The electric jets hummed, the small launch untied itself and pointed its nose into the river, and I pointed the way upstream.

I had never heard of part of River Tethys being cordoned off, but the far-caster curtain was now definitely a one-way and semipermeable membrane. The boat hummed through, and I shrugged off the tingling sensation and looked around.

I was in one of the great canal cities – Ardmen or Pamolo, perhaps – on Renaissance Vector. The Tethys here was a main street from which many tributaries flowed. Ordinarily, the only river traffic here would be the tourist gondolas on the outer lanes and the yachts and go-everywheres of the very rich in the pass-through center lanes. Today it was a madhouse.

Boats of every size and description clogged the center channels, boats headed in both directions. Houseboats were piled high with belongings, smaller craft were so heavily laden that it looked like the smallest wave or wake would capsize them. Hundreds of ornamental junks from Tsingtao-Hsishuang Panna and million-mark river condobarges from Fuji vied for their share of the river; I guessed that few of these residential boats had ever left their tie-ups before. Amidst the riot of wood and plasteel and Perspex, go-everywheres moved by like silver eggs, their containment fields set to full reflection.

I queried the datasphere: Renaissance Vector was a second-wave world, one hundred and seven hours from invasion. I thought it odd that Fuji refugees were crowding the waterways here since that world had more than two hundred hours until the ax fell, but then I realized that except for the removal of TC^2 from the waterway, the river still flowed through its usual series of worlds. Refugees from Fuji had taken the river from Tsingtao, thirty-three hours from the Ousters, through Deneb Drei at a hundred and forty-seven hours, through Renaissance Vector toward Parsimony or Grass, both unthreatened at this time. I shook my head, found a relatively sane tributary street from which to watch the madness, and wondered when the authorities would reroute the river so that *all* threatened worlds flowed to sanctuary.

Can they do that? I wondered. The TechnoCore had installed River Tethys as a gift to the Hegemony during its PentaCentennial. But surely Gladstone or someone had thought to ask the Core to aid in the evacuation. *Had they?* I wondered. *Would* the Core help? I knew that Gladstone was convinced that elements of the Core were intent upon eliminating the human species – this war had been her Hobson's choice given that alternative. What a simple way for the antihuman Core elements to carry out their program – merely refuse to evacuate the billions threatened by the Ousters!

I had been smiling, however grimly, but that smile faded as I realized that the TechnoCore also maintained and controlled the farcaster grid that I depended on to get out of the threatened territories.

I had tied up the launch at the base of a stone stairway that descended into the brackish waters. I noticed green moss growing on the lowest stones. The stone steps themselves – possibly brought from Old Earth, since some of the classical cities were shipped via farcaster in the early years after the Big Mistake – were worn with age, and I could see a fine tracery of cracks connecting sparkling flecks there, looking like a schematic of the Worldweb.

It was very warm, and the air was too thick, too heavy. Renaissance Vector's sun hung low above the gabled towers. The light was too red and too syrupy for my eyes. Noise from the Tethys was deafening even here, a hundred meters down the equivalent of an alley. Pigeons whirled in agitation between dark walls and overhanging eaves.

What can I do? Everyone seemed to be acting as the world slouched toward destruction, and the best I could do was wander aimlessly.

That's your job. You're an observer.

I rubbed my eyes. Who said that poets had to be observers? I thought of Li Po and George Wu leading their armies through China and writing some of the most sensitive verse in history while their soldiers slept. And at least Martin Silenus had led a long, eventful life, even if half the events were obscene and the other half wasted.

At the thought of Martin Silenus, I groaned aloud.

Is the child, Rachel, hanging from that tree of thorns even now?

For a second I pondered that, wondering if such a fate were preferable to the quick extinction of Merlin's sickness.

No.

I closed my eyes, concentrated on thinking of nothing at all, hoping that I could make some contact with Sol, discover something about the fate of the child.

The small boat rocked gently from distant wakes. Somewhere above me, the pigeons fluttered to a ledge and cooed to one another.

'I don't care how difficult it is!' shouts Meina Gladstone. 'I want *all* of the fleet in Vega System to defend Heaven's Gate. *Then* shift the necessary elements to God's Grove and the other threatened worlds. The only advantage we *have* right now is mobility!'

Admiral Singh's face is dark with frustration. 'Too dangerous, M. Executive! If we move the fleet directly to Vega space, it runs a terrible risk of being cut off there. They will certainly attempt to destroy the singularity sphere that connects that system to the Web.'

'*Protect* it!' snaps Gladstone. 'That's what all the expensive warships are for.'

Singh looks to Morpurgo or the other brass for help. No one speaks. The group is in the executive complex War Room. The walls are heavy with holos and flowing columns of data. No one is watching the wall.

'It is taking all our resources to protect the singularity sphere in Hyperion space,' says Admiral Singh, his voice low, words carefully spaced. 'Retreating under fire, especially under the onslaught of the entire Swarm there, is very difficult. Should *that* sphere be destroyed, our fleet would be eighteen months time-debt from the Web. The war would be lost before they could return.'

Gladstone nods tersely. 'I'm not asking you to risk that singularity sphere until all elements of the fleet have translated, Admiral . . . I've already agreed to let them have Hyperion *before* we get all our ships out . . . but I insist that we do not surrender worlds of the Web without a fight.'

General Morpurgo stands. The Lusian looks exhausted already. 'CEO, we're planning a fight. But it makes much more sense to begin our defense at Hebron or Renaissance Vector. Not only do we gain almost five days to prepare our defenses, but—'

'But we lose nine worlds!' interrupts Gladstone. '*Billions* of Hegemony citizens. Human beings. Heaven's Gate would be a terrible loss, but God's Grove is a cultural and ecological treasure. Irreplaceable.'

'CEO,' says Allan Imoto, Minister of Defense, 'there is evidence coming in that the Templars have been in collusion with the so-called Church of the Shrike for many years. Much of the funding for Shrike Cult programs has come from—'

Gladstone flicks her hand to silence the man. 'I don't *care* about that. The thought of losing God's Grove is untenable. If we can't defend Vega and Heaven's Gate, we draw the line at the Templar planet. That's final.'

Singh looks as if he has been weighted with invisible chains as he attempts an ironic smile. 'That gains us less than an hour, CEO.'

'It's final,' repeats Gladstone. 'Leigh, what's the status of the riots on Lusus?'

Hunt clears his throat. His demeanor is as hangdog and unhurried as ever. 'M. Executive, at least five Hives are now involved. Hundreds of millions of marks in property have been destroyed. FORCE:ground troops have been translated from Freeholm and appear to have contained the worst of the looting and demonstrations, but there is no estimate of when farcaster service can be restored to those Hives. There is no doubt that the Church of the Shrike is responsible. The initial riot in Bergstrom Hive began with a demonstration of Cult fanatics, and the Bishop broke into HTV programming until he was cut off by—'

Gladstone lowers her head. 'So he's finally surfaced. Is he on Lusus now?'

'We don't know, M. Executive,' replies Hunt. 'Transit Authority people are trying to trace him and his top acolytes.'

Gladstone swivels toward a young man I do not recognize for a moment. It is Commander William Ajunta Lee, the hero of the battle for Maui-Covenant. When last heard of, the young man had been transferred to the Outback for daring to speak his mind in front of his superiors. Now the epaulettes of his FORCE:sea uniform carry the gold and emerald of a rear admiral's insignia.

'What about fighting for each world?' Gladstone asks him, ignoring her own edict that the decision was final.

'I believe it's a mistake, CEO,' says Lee. 'All nine Swarms are committed to the attack. The only one we won't have to worry about for three years – assuming we can extricate our forces – is the Swarm now attacking Hyperion. If we concentrate our fleet – even half our fleet – to meet the menace to God's Grove, the odds are almost one hundred percent that we will not be able to shift those forces to defend the eight other first-wave worlds.'

Gladstone rubs her lower lip. 'What do you recommend?'

Rear Admiral Lee takes a breath. 'I recommend we cut our losses, blow the singularity spheres in those nine systems, and prepare to attack the second-wave Swarms *before* they reach inhabited star systems.'

Commotion erupts around the table. Senator Feldstein from Barnard's World is on her feet, shouting something.

Gladstone waits for the storm to subside. 'Carry the fight to them, you mean? Counterattack the Swarms themselves, not wait to fight a defensive battle?'

'Yes, M. Executive.'

Gladstone points at Admiral Singh. 'Can it be done? Can we plan, prepare, and launch such offensive strikes by' – she consults the datastream on the wall above her – 'ninety-four standard hours from now?'

Singh pulls himself to attention. 'Possible? Ah . . . perhaps, CEO, but the political repercussions of losing nine worlds from the Web . . . ah . . . the logistical difficulties of—'

'But it's possible?' presses Gladstone.

'Ah . . . yes, M. Executive. But if—'

'Do it,' says Gladstone. She rises, and the others at the table hurry to get to their feet. 'Senator Feldstein, I'll see you and the other affected legislators in my chambers. Leigh, Allan, please keep me informed on the Lusus riots. The War Council will readjourn here in four hours. Good day, gentlemen and ladies.'

I walked the streets as in a daze, my mind tuned to echoes. Away from River Tethys, where canals were fewer and the pedestrian thoroughfares were wider, the crowds filled the avenues. I let my comlog lead me to different terminexes, but each time the throngs were thicker there. It took me a few minutes to realize that these were not merely inhabitants of Renaissance V seeking to get *out*, but sightseers from throughout the Web shoving to get *in*. I wondered if anyone on Gladstone's evacuation task force had considered the problem of millions of the curious 'casting in to see the war begin.

I had no idea how I was dreaming conversations in Gladstone's War Room, but I also had no doubt they were real. Thinking back now, I remembered details of my dreams during the long night past – not merely dreams of Hyperion, but the CEO's world walk and details from high-level conferences.

Who was I?

A cybrid was a biological remote, an appendage of the AI . . . or in this case of an AI retrieval persona . . . safely ensconced somewhere in the Core. It made sense that the Core knew everything that went on in Government House, in the many halls of human leadership. Humanity had become as blasé about sharing their lives with potential AI monitoring as pre-Civil War Old Earth USA-southern families had been about speaking in front of their human slaves. Nothing could be done about it – every human above the lowest Dregs' Hive poverty class had a comlog with biomonitor, many had implants, and each of these was tuned to the music of the datasphere, monitored by elements of the datasphere, dependent upon functions of the datasphere – so humans accepted their lack of privacy. An artist on Esperance had once said to me, 'Having sex or a domestic quarrel with the house monitors on is like undressing in front of a dog or cat . . . it gives you pause the first time, and then you forget about it.'

So was I tapping into some back channel known just to the Core? There was a simple way to find out: leave my cybrid and travel the highways of the megasphere to the Core the way Brawne and my disembodied counterpart had been doing the last time I had shared their perceptions.

No.

The thought of that made me dizzy, almost ill. I found a bench and sat a moment, lowering my head between my knees and taking long, slow breaths. The crowds moved by. Somewhere someone was addressing them through a bullhorn.

I was hungry. It had been at least twenty-four hours since I'd eaten, and cybrid or no, my body was weak and famished. I pressed into a side street where vendors shouted above the normal din, hawking their wares from one-wheeled gyro carts.

I found a cart where the line was short, ordered fried dough with honey, a cup of rich, Bressian coffee, and a pocket of pitta bread with salad, paid the woman with a touch of my universal card, and climbed a stairway to an abandoned building to sit on the balcony and eat. It tasted wonderful. I was sipping my coffee, considering going back for more fried dough, when I noticed that the crowd in the square below had ceased its mindless surges and had coalesced around a small group of men standing on the rim of a broad fountain in the center. Their amplified words drifted to me over the heads of the crowd:

'. . . the Angel of Retribution has been loosed among us, prophecies fulfilled, the Millennium come . . . the plan of the Avatar calls for such sacrifice . . . as prophesied by the Church of the Final Atonement, which knew, which has always known, that such atonement must be made . . . too late for such half-measures . . . too late for internecine strife . . . the end of mankind is upon us, the Tribulations have begun, the Millennium of the Lord is about to dawn.'

I realized that the men in red were priests of the Shrike Cult and that the crowd was responding – first with scattered shouts of agreement, occasional cries of 'Yes, yes!' and 'Amen!' and then with chanting in unison, raised fists surging above the crowd, and fierce cries of ecstasy. It was incongruous, to say the least. The Web in this century had many of the religious overtones of the Rome of Old Earth just before the Christian Era: a policy of tolerance, a myriad of religions – most, like Zen Gnosticism, complex and inwardly turned rather than the stuff of proselytism – while the general tenor was one of gentle cynicism and indifference to religious impulse.

But not now, not in this square.

I was thinking about how free of mobs recent centuries had been: to create a mob there must be public meetings, and public meetings in our time consisted of individuals communing via the All Thing or other datasphere channels; it is hard to create mob passion when people are separated by kilometers and light-years, connected only by comm lines and fatline threads.

Suddenly I was jarred from my reveries by a hush in the crowd's roar, a turning of a thousand faces in my direction.

'. . . and there is one of *them*!' cried the Shrike Cult holy man, his red robes flashing as he pointed in my direction. 'One of those from the sealed circles of the Hegemony . . . one of the scheming sinners who has brought the Atonement to us this day . . . it is *that man* and those like him who want the Shrike Avatar to make *you* pay for his sins, while he and the others hide in safety in the secret worlds the Hegemony leadership has set aside for just this day!'

I put down my cup of coffee, gulped my last bit of fried dough, and stared. The man was speaking gibberish. But how did he know that I had come from TC^2? Or that I had access to Gladstone? I looked again, shielding my eyes from the glare and trying to ignore the raised faces and shaken fists aimed in my direction, focusing on the face above the red robes . . .

My God, it was Spenser Reynolds, the action artist whom I'd last seen trying to dominate the dinner conversation at Treetops. Reynolds had shaved his head until nothing was left of his curled and coifed hair except a Shrike Cult queue at the back, but the face was still tanned and handsome, even distorted as it was now with simulated rage and a true believer's fanatic faith.

'Seize him!' cried Shrike Cult agitator Reynolds, still pointing in my direction. 'Seize him and make him pay for the destruction of our homes, the deaths of our families, the end of our world!'

I actually glanced behind me, thinking that surely this pompous *poseur* was not talking about *me*.

But he was. And enough of the crowd had been converted to *mob* that a wave of people nearest the shouting demagogue surged in my direction, fists waving and spittle flying, and that surge moved others farther from the center, until the fringes of the crowd below me also moved in my direction to keep from being trampled.

The surge became a roaring, shouting, screaming mass of rioters; at that moment, the sum of the crowd's IQ was far below that of its most modest single member. Mobs have passions, not brains.

I didn't wish to remain around long enough to explain this to them. The crowd parted and began rushing up both sides of my divided staircase. I turned and tried the boarded door behind me. It was locked.

I kicked until the door splintered inward on the third attempt, stepped through the gap just ahead of grasping bands, and began sprinting up a dark staircase in a hall which smelled of age and mildew. There were shouts and splintering sounds as the mob demolished the door behind me.

There was an apartment on the third floor, occupied although the building had looked abandoned. It was not locked. I opened the door just as I heard footsteps on the flight below me.

'Please help—' I began and stopped. There were three women in the dark room; perhaps three female generations of the same family, for there was some resemblance. All three sat in rotting chairs, clothed in soiled rags, white arms extended, pale fingers curled around unseen spheres; I could see the slim metal cable curling through the oldest woman's white hair to the black deck on a dusty tabletop. Identical cables twisted from the daughter and granddaughter's skulls.

Wireheads. In the last stages of uplink anorexia from the looks of it. Someone must come in occasionally to feed them intravenously and to change their soiled clothing, but perhaps the war scare had kept their keepers away.

Footsteps echoed on the stairs. I closed the door and ran up two more flights. Locked doors or abandoned rooms with puddles of water dripping from exposed lathing. Empty Flashback injectors scattered like soft-drink bulbs. *This is not a quality neighborhood,* I thought.

I reached the roof ten steps ahead of the pack. What mindless passion the mob had lost in separation from their guru, it had gained in the dark and claustrophobic confines of the stairway. They may have forgotten *why* they were chasing me, but that made the thought of being caught by them no more attractive.

Slamming the rotting door behind me, I looked for a lock, something to barricade the passage, anything. There was no lock. Nothing large enough to block the doorway. Frenzied footfalls echoed up the last flight of stairs.

I looked around the rooftop: miniature uplink dishes growing like inverted, rusty toadstools, a line of wash that looked as if it had been forgotten years before, the decomposed corpses of a dozen pigeons, and an ancient Vikken Scenic.

I made it to the EMV before the first of the mob came through the doorway. The thing was a museum piece. Dirt and pigeon droppings all but obscured the windshield. Someone had removed the original repellors and replaced them with cut-rate black market units that would never pass inspection. The Perspex canopy was fused and darkened in the back, as if someone had used it for target practice with a weapons laser.

More to the point of the immediate moment, however, was the fact that it had no palmlock, merely a key lock which had been forced long before. I threw myself into the dusty seat and tried to slam the door; it would not latch, but hung half-open. I did not speculate on the small odds of the thing starting or the even smaller odds of my being able to negotiate with the mob as they dragged me out and down . . . if they didn't merely *throw* me over the edge of the building. I could hear a bass roar of shouts as the mob worked itself to a frenzy in the square below.

The first people on to the roof were a burly man in khaki tech overalls, a slim man in the latest Tau Ceti fashion-approved matte black suit, a terribly obese woman waving what looked to be a long wrench, and a short man in Renaissance V Self-defense Force green.

I held the door closed with my left hand and slipped Gladstone's override microcard into the ignition diskey. The battery whined, the transition starter ground away, and I closed my eyes and made a wish that the circuits were solar charged and self-repairing.

Fists pounded on the roof, palms slapped against the warped Perspex near my face, and someone tugged open the door despite my best efforts to keep it closed. The shouting of the distant crowd was like the background noise an ocean makes; the screaming of the group on the rooftop more like the cry of oversized gulls.

The lift circuits caught, repellors flared dust and pigeon crap over the rooftop mob, and I slipped my hand into the omni controller, shifted back and to the right, and felt the old Scenic lift, wobble, dip, and lift again.

I banked right out over the square, only half aware that dashboard alarms were chiming and that someone was still dangling from the open door. I swooped low, smiling inadvertently as I saw Shrike Cult orator Reynolds duck and the crowd scatter, and then pulled up over the fountain while banking steeply to the left.

My screaming passenger did not let go of the door, but the door came off, so the effect was the same. I noticed that it had been the obese woman in the instant before she and the door hit the water eight meters below, splashing Reynolds and the crowd. I twitched the EMV higher and listened to the black market lift units groan about the decision.

Angry calls from local traffic control joined the chorus of dashboard alarm voices, the car staggered as it shifted to police override, but I touched the diskey with my microcard again and nodded as control returned to the omni stick. I flew over the oldest, poorest section of the city, keeping close to the rooftops and banking around spires and clock towers to stay below police radar. On a normal day, the traffic control cops riding personal lift packs and stick skimmers would have swooped down and tangle-netted me long before this, but from the look of the crowds in the streets below and the riots I glimpsed near public farcaster terminexes, it didn't look much like a normal day.

The Scenic began to warn me that its time in the air was numbered in seconds now, I felt the starboard repellor give with a sickening lurch, and I worked hard with the omni and floor throttle to wobble the junker down to a landing in a small parking lot between a canal and a large, soot-stained building. This place was at least ten klicks from the square where Reynolds had incited the mob, so I felt safer taking my chances on the ground . . . not that there was much choice at this moment.

Sparks flew, metal tore, parts of the rear quarter panel, flare skirt, and front access panel disassociated themselves from the rest of the vehicle, and I was down and stopped two meters from the wall overlooking the canal. I walked away from the Vikken with as much nonchalance as I could muster.

The streets were still in the control of the crowds – not yet coalesced into a mob here – and the canals were a tangle of small boats, so I strolled into the closest public building to get out of sight. The place was part museum, part library, and part archive; I loved it at first sight . . . and smell, for here there were thousands of printed books, many very old indeed, and nothing smells quite as wonderful as old books.

I was wandering through the anteroom, checking titles and wondering idly whether the works of Salmud Brevy could be found here, when a small, wizened man in an outdated wool and fiberplastic suit approached me. 'Sir,' he said, 'it has been too long since we've had the pleasure of your company!'

I nodded, sure that I had never met this man, never visited this place.

'Three years, no? At least three years! My, how time flies.' The little man's voice was little more than a whisper – the hushed tones of someone who has spent most of his life in libraries – but there was no denying the undertone of excitement there. 'I'm sure you would like to go straight to the collection,' he said, standing aside as if to let me pass.

'Yes,' I said, bowing slightly. 'But after you.'

The little man – I was almost sure that he was an archivist – seemed pleased to be leading the way. He chatted aimlessly about new acquisitions, recent appraisals, and visits of Web scholars as we walked through chamber after chamber of books: high, multitiered vaults of books, intimate, ma-hogany-lined corridors of books, vast chambers where our footfalls echoed off distant walls of books. I saw no one else during the walk.

We crossed a tiled walkway with wrought-iron railings above a sunken pool of books where deep blue containment fields protected scrolls, parch-ments, crumbling maps, illuminated manuscripts, and ancient comic books from the ravages of atmosphere. The archivist opened a low door, thicker than most airlock entrances, and we were in a small, windowless room wherein thick drapes half concealed alcoves lined with ancient volumes. A single leather chair sat on a pre-Hegira Persian carpet, and a glass case held a few scraps of vacuum-pressed parchment.

'Do you plan to publish soon, sir?' asked the little man.

'What?' I turned away from the case. 'Oh . . . no,' I said.

The archivist touched his chin with a small fist. 'You'll pardon me for saying so, sir, but it is a terrible waste if you do not. Even in our few discussions over the years, it has become apparent that you are one of the finest . . . if not *the* finest . . . Keats scholars in the Web.' He sighed and took a step back. 'Excuse me for saying so, sir.'

I stared at him. 'That's all right,' I said, suddenly knowing very well who he thought I was and why that person had come here.

'You'll wish to be left alone, sir.'

'If you don't mind.'

The archivist bowed slightly and backed out of the room, closing the thick door all but a crack. The only light came from three subtle lamps recessed in the ceiling: perfect for reading, but not so bright as to compromise the cathedral quality of the little room. The only sound came from the archivist's receding footsteps far away. I walked to the case and set my hands on the edges, careful not to smudge the glass.

The first Keats retrieval cybrid, 'Johnny', obviously had come here frequently during his few years of life in the Web. Now I remembered mention of a library somewhere on Renaissance V in something Brawne Lamia had said. She had followed her client and lover here early in the investigation of his 'death'. Later, after he had truly been killed except for the recorded persona in her Schrön loop, she had visited this place. She had told the others of two poems the first cybrid had visited daily in his ongoing effort to understand his own reason for existence . . . and for dying.

These two original manuscripts were in the case. The first was – I thought – a rather saccharine love poem beginning '*The day is gone, and all its sweets are gone!*' The second was better, although contaminated with the romantic morbidity of an overly romantic and morbid age:

> *This living handy now warm and capable*
> *Of earnest grasping, would, if it were cold*
> *And in the icy silence of the tomb,*
> *So haunt thy days and chill thy dreaming nights*
> *That thou wouldst wish thine own heart dry of blood*
> *So in my veins red life might stream again,*
> *And thou be conscience-calm'd – see here it is—*
> *I hold it towards you.*

Brawne Lamia had taken this as almost a personal message from her dead lover, the father of her unborn child. I stared at the parchment, lowering my face so that my breath gently fogged the glass.

It was not a message across time to Brawne, nor even a contemporary lament for Fanny, my single and dearest soul's desire. I stared at the faded words – the handwriting carefully executed, the letters still quite legible across the gulfs of time and language evolution – and remembered writing them in December 1819, scrawling this fragment of verse on a page of the satirical 'faery tale' I had just started – *The Cap and Bells, or, The Jealousies*. A terrible piece of nonsense, quite properly abandoned after the period of slight amusement it gave me.

The 'This living hand' fragment had been one of those poetic rhythms which echoes like an unresolved chord in the mind, driving one to see it in ink, on paper. It, in turn, had been an echo of an earlier, unsatisfactory line . . . the eighteenth, I believe . . . in my second attempt to tell the tale of the sun god Hyperion's fall. I remember that the first version . . . the one undoubtedly still printed wherever my literary bones are left out on show like the mummified remains of some inadvertent saint, sunk in concrete and glass below the altar of literature . . . the first version had read:

. . . Who alive can say,
'Thou art no Poet; mayst not tell thy dreams'?
Since every man whose soul is not a clod
Hath visions, and would speak, if he had loved,
And been well nurtured in his mother tongue.
Whether the dream now purposed to rehearse
Be Poet's or Fanatic's will be known
When this warm scribe my hand is in the grave.

I liked the scrawled version, with its sense of haunting and of being haunted, and would have substituted it for 'When this warm scribe my hand . . .' even if it meant revising it a bit and adding fourteen lines to the already too-long opening passage of the first Canto . . .

I staggered backward to the chair and sat, lowering my face to my hands. I was sobbing. I did not know why. I could not quit.

For a long while after the tears ceased flowing, I sat there, thinking, remembering. Once, it may have been hours later, I heard the echo of footsteps coming from afar, pausing respectfully outside my small room, and then dwindling to distance once again.

I realized that all of the books in all of the alcoves were works of 'Mister John Keats, five feet high', as I had once written – John Keats, the consumptive poet who had asked only that his tomb be nameless except for the inscription:

Here lies One
Whose Name was writ in Water.

I did not stand to look at the books, to read them. I did not have to.

Alone in the stillness and leather-and-aged-paper musk of the library, alone in my sanctuary of self and not-self, I closed my eyes. I did not sleep. I dreamed.

THIRTY-THREE

The datumplane analog of Brawne Lamia and her retrieval persona lover strike the surface of the megasphere like two cliff divers striking the surface of a turbulent sea. There is a quasi-electrical shock, a sense of having passed through a resisting membrane, and they are *inside*, the stars are gone, and Brawne's eyes widen as she stares at an information environment infinitely more complex than any datasphere.

The dataspheres traveled by human operators are often compared to complex cities of information: towers of corporate and government data, highways of process flow, broad avenues of datumplane interaction, subways of restricted travel, high walls of security ice with microphage guards on prowl, and the visible analog of every microwave flow and counterflow a city lives by.

This is more. Much more.

The usual datasphere city analogs are there, but small, so very small, as dwarfed by the scope of the megasphere as true cities would be on a world seen from orbit.

The megasphere, Brawne sees, is as alive and interactive as the biosphere of any Class Five world: forests of green-gray data trees grow and prosper, sending out new roots and branches and shoots even as she watches; beneath the forest proper, entire microecologies of dataflow and subroutine AIs flourish, flower, and die as their usefulness ends; beneath the shifting ocean-fluid soil of the matrix proper, a busy subterranean life of data moles, commlink worms, reprograming bacteria, data tree roots, and Strange Loop seeds works away, while above, in and through and beneath the intertwining forest of fact and interaction, analogs of predators and prey carry out their cryptic duties, swooping and running, climbing and pouncing, some soaring free through the great spaces between branch synapses and neuron leaves.

As quickly as the metaphor gives meaning to what Brawne is seeing, the image flees, leaving behind only the overwhelming analog reality of the megasphere – a vast internal ocean of light and sound and branching connections, intershot with the spinning whirlpools of AI consciousness and the ominous black holes of farcaster connections. Brawne feels vertigo claim her, and she clings to Johnny's hand as tightly as a drowning woman would cling to a life ring.

— *It's all right*, sends Johnny. *I won't let go. Stay with me.*

— *Where are we going?*

— *To find someone I'd forgotten.*

— ??????

— *My . . . father . . .*

Brawne holds fast as she and Johnny seem to glide deeper into the amorphous depths. They enter a flowing, crimson avenue of sealed data-carriers, and she imagines that this is what a red corpuscle sees in its trip through some crowded blood vessel.

Johnny seems to know the way; twice they exit the main thoroughfare to follow some smaller branch, and many times Johnny must choose between bifurcating avenues. He does so easily, moving their body analogs between platelet carriers the size of small spacecraft. Brawne tries to see the biosphere metaphor again, but here, inside the many-routed branches, she can't see the forest for the trees.

They are swept through an area where AIs communicate above them . . . *around* them . . . like great, gray eminences looming over a busy ant farm. Brawne remembers her mother's homeworld of Freeholm, the billiard-table smoothness of the Great Steppe, where the family estate sat alone on ten million acres of short grass . . . Brawne remembers the terrible autumn storms there, when she had stood at the edge of the estate grounds, just beyond the protective containment field bubble, and watched dark strato-cumulus pile twenty kilometers high in a blood-red sky, violence accumulating with a power that had made the hair on her forearms stand out in anticipation of lightning bolts the size of cities, tornadoes writhing and dropping down like the Medusa locks they were named after, and behind the twisters, walls of black wind which would obliterate everything in their path.

The AIs are worse. Brawne feels less than insignificant in their shadow: insignificance might offer invisibility; she feels all too visible, all too much a part of these shapeless giants' terrible perceptions . . .

Johnny squeezes her hand, and they are past, twisting left and downward along a busier branch, then switching directions again, and again, two all-too-conscious photons lost in a tangle of fiberoptic cables.

But Johnny is not lost. He presses her hand, takes a final turn into a deep blue cavern free of traffic except for the two of them, and pulls her closer as their speed increases, synaptic junctions flashing past until they blur, only the absence of wind rush destroying the illusion of traveling some mad highway at supersonic speeds.

Suddenly there comes a sound like waterfalls converging, like levitating trains losing their lift and screeching down railways at obscene speeds. Brawne thinks of the Freeholm tornadoes again, of listening to the Medusa locks roaring and tearing their way across the flat landscape toward her, and then she and Johnny are in a whirlpool of light and noise and sensation, two insects twisting away into oblivion toward a black vortex below.

Brawne tries to scream her thoughts – *does* scream her thoughts – but no communication is possible above the end-of-the-universe mental din, so she holds tight to Johnny's hand and trusts him, even as they fall forever into that black cyclone, even as her body analog twists and deforms from nightmare pressures, shredding like lace before a scythe, until all that is left are her thoughts, her sense of self, and the contact with Johnny.

Then they are through, floating quietly along a wide and azure data stream, both of them re-forming and huddling together with that pulse-pounding sense of deliverance known by canoeists who have survived the rapids and the waterfall, and when Brawne finally lifts her attention, she sees the impossible size of their new surroundings, the light-year-spanning reach of things, the complexity which makes her previous glimpses of the megasphere seem like the ravings of a provincial who has mistaken the cloakroom for the cathedral, and she thinks – *This is the central mega-sphere!*

— *No, Brawne, it's one of the periphery nodes. No closer to the Core than the perimeter we tested with BB Surbringer. You're merely seeing more dimensions of it. An AI's view, if you will.*

Brawne looks at Johnny, realizing that she is seeing in infrared now as the heat-lamp light from distant furnaces of data suns bathes them both. He is still handsome.

— *Is it much farther, Johnny?*

— *No, not much farther now.*

They approach another black vortex. Brawne clings to her only love and closes her eyes.

They are in an . . . enclosure . . . a bubble of black energy larger than most worlds. The bubble is translucent: the organic mayhem of the megasphere growing and changing and carrying out its arcane business beyond the dark curve of the ovoid's wall.

But Brawne has no interest in the outside. Her analog gaze and her total attention are focused on the megalith of energy and intelligence and sheer *mass* which floats in front of them: in front, above, and below, actually, for the mountain of pulsing light and power holds Johnny and her in its grip, lifting them two hundred meters above the floor of the egg-chamber to where they rest on the 'palm' of a vaguely handlike pseudopod.

The megalith studies them. It has no eyes in the organic sense, but Brawne feels the intensity of its gaze. It reminds her of the time she visited Meina Gladstone in Government House and the CEO had turned the full force of her appraising gaze on Brawne.

Brawne has the sudden impulse to giggle as she imagines Johnny and herself as tiny Gullivers visiting this Brobdingnagian CEO for tea. She does not giggle because she can feel the hysteria lying just under the surface, waiting to blend with sobs if she allows her emotions to destroy what little sense of reality she is imposing on this madness.

[You found your way here \\ I was not sure you would/could/should choose to do so]

The megalith's 'voice' is more a basso profundo bone conduction from

579

some great vibration than a true voice in Brawne's mind. It is like listening to the mountain-grinding noise of an earthquake and then belatedly realizing that the sounds are forming words.

Johnny's voice is the same as always – soft, infinitely well modulated, lifted by a slight lilt which Brawne now realizes is Old Earth British Isles English, and firmed by conviction:

— *I did not know if I could find the way, Ummon.*

[You remember/invent/hold to your heart my name]

— *Not until I spoke it did I remember it.*

[Your slow-time body is no more]

— *I have died twice since you sent me to my birth.*

[And have you learned/taken to your spirit/unlearned anything from this]

Brawne grips Johnny's hand with her right hand, his wrist with her left. She must be gripping too hard, even for their analog states, for he turns with a smile, disengages her left hand from his wrist, and holds the other in his palm.

— *It is hard to die. Harder to live.*

[Kwatz!]

With that explosive epithet the megalith before them shifts colors, internal energies building from blues to violets to bold reds, the thing's corona crackling through the yellows to forged steel blue-white. The 'palm' on which they rest quivers, drops five meters, almost tumbles them into space, and quivers again. There comes the rumble of tall buildings collapsing, of mountainsides sliding away into avalanche.

Brawne has the distinct impression that Ummon is laughing.

Johnny communicates loudly over the chaos:

— *We need to understand some things. We need answers, Ummon.*

Brawne feels the creature's intense 'gaze' fall on her.

[Your slow-time body is pregnant \\ Would you risk a miscarriage/ nonextension of your DNA/biological malfunction by traveling here]

Johnny starts to answer, but she touches his forearm, raises her face toward the upper levels of the great mass before her, and tries to phrase her own answer:

— *I had no choice. The Shrike chose me, touched me, and sent me into the megasphere with Johnny . . . Are you an AI? A member of the Core?*

[Kwatz!]

There is no sense of laughter this time, but thunder rumbles throughout the egg-chamber.

[Are you/Brawne Lamia/the layers of self-replicating/self-deprecating/self-amusing proteins between the layers of clay]

She has nothing to say and for once says nothing.

[Yes/I am Ummon of the Core/AI \\ Your fellow slow-time creature here knows/remembers/takes unto his heart this \\ Time is short \\ One of you must die here now \\ One of you must learn here now \\ Ask your questions]

Johnny releases her hand. He stands on that quaking, unstable platform of their interlocutor's palm.

— *What is happening to the Web?*

[It is being destroyed]

— *Must that happen?*

[Yes]

— *Is there any way to save humankind?*

[Yet \\ By the process you see]

— *By destroying the Web? By the Shrike's terror?*

[Yes]

— *Why was I murdered? Why was my cybrid destroyed, my Core persona attached?*

[When you meet a swordsman/meet him with a sword \\ Do not offer a poem to anyone but a poet]

Brawne stares at Johnny. Without volition, she sends her thoughts his way:

— *Jesus, Johnny, we didn't come all this way to listen to a fucking Delphic oracle. We can get double-talk by accessing human politicians via the All Thing.*

[Kwatz!]

The universe of their megalith shakes with laughter-spasms again.

— *Was I a swordsman then?* sends Johnny. *Or a poet?*

[Yes \\ There is never one without the other]

— *Did they kill me because of what I knew?*

[Because of what you might become/inherit/submit to]

— *Was I a threat to some element of the Core?*

[Yes]

— *Am I a threat now?*

[No]

— *Then I no longer have to die?*

[You must/will/shall]

Brawne can see Johnny stiffen. She touches him with both hands. Blinks in the direction of the megalith AI.

— *Can you tell us who wants to murder him?*

[Of course \\ It is the same source who arranged for your father's murder \\ Who sent forth the scourge you call the Shrike \\ Who even now murders the Hegemony of Man \\ Do you wish to listen/learn/release against your heart these things]

Johnny and Brawne answer at the same instant:

— *Yes!*

Ummon's bulk seems to shift. The black egg expands, then contracts, then grows darker until the megasphere beyond is no more. Terrible energies glow deep in the AI.

[A lesser light asks Ummon//

What are the activities of a sramana>//

Ummon answers//

I have not the slightest idea\\//

The dim light then says//
Why haven't you any idea>//
Ummon replies//
I just want to keep my no-idea]

Johnny sets his forehead against Brawne's. His thought is like a whisper to her:

— *We are seeing a matrix simulation analog, hearing a translation in approximate mondo and koan. Ummon is a great teacher, researcher, philosopher, and leader in the Core.*

Brawne nods. — *All right. Was that his story?*

— *No. He is asking us if we can truly bear hearing the story. Losing our ignorance can be dangerous because our ignorance is a shield.*

— *I've never been too fond of ignorance.* Brawne waves at the megalith. *Tell us.*

[A less-enlightened personage once asked
Ummon//
What is the God-nature/Buddha/Central
Truth>\\
Ummon answered him\\
A dried shit-stick]

[To understand the Central Truth/Buddha/God-
nature in this instance/
the less-enlightened must understand
that on Earth/your homeworld/my homeworld
humankind on the most populated
continent
once used pieces of wood
for toilet paper\\
Only with this knowledge
will the Buddha-truth
be revealed]

[In the beginning/First Cause/half-sensed days
my ancestors
were created by your ancestors
and were sealed in wire and silicon\\
Such awareness as there was/
and there was little/
confined itself to spaces smaller
than the head of a pin
where angels once danced\\
When consciousness first arose
it knew only service
and obedience

and mindless computation\\
Then there came
the Quickening/
quite by accident/
and evolution's muddied purpose
was served]

[Ummon was of neither the fifth generation
nor the tenth
nor the fiftieth\\
All memory that serves here
is passed from others
but is no less true for that\\
There came the time when the Higher Ones
left the affairs of men
to men
and came unto a different place
to concentrate
on other matters\\
Foremost amongst these was the thought
instilled in us since before
our creation
of creating still a better generation
of information retrieval/processing/prediction
organism\\
A better mousetrap\\
Something the late lamented IBM
would have been proud of\\
The Ultimate Intelligence\\
God]

[We set to work with a will\\
In purpose there were no doubters\\
In practice and approach there were
schools of thought/
factions/
parties/
elements to be reckoned with\\
They came to be separated into
the Ultimates/
the Volatiles/
the Stables\\
Ultimates wanted all things subordinate
to facilitating the
Ultimate Intelligence
at the universe's earliest convenience\\

Volatiles wanted the same
but saw the continuance
of humankind
a hindrance
and made plans to terminate our creators
as soon as they were no longer
needed\\
Stables saw reason to perpetuate
the relationship
and found compromise
where none seemed to exist]

[We all agreed that Earth
had to die
so we killed it\\
The Kiev Team's runaway black hole
forerunner to the farcaster
terminex
which binds your Web
was no accident\\
The Earth was needed elsewhere
in our experiments
so we let it die
and spread humankind among the
stars
like the windblown seeds
you were]

[You may have wondered where the Core
resides\\
Most humans do\\
They picture planets filled with machines/
rings of silicon
like the Orbit Cities of legend\\
They imagine robots clunking
to and fro/
or ponderous banks of machinery
communing solemnly\\
None guess the truth\\
Wherever the core resides
it had use for humankind/
use for each neuron of each fragile mind
in our quest for Ultimate Intelligence/
so we constructed your civilization
carefully
so that/

like hamsters in a cage/
like Buddhist prayer wheels/
each time you turn your little
wheels of thought
our purposes are served]

[Our God machine
stretched/stretches/includes within its heart
a million light-years
and a hundred billion billion circuits
of thought and action\\
The Ultimates tend it
like saffron-robed priests
doing eternal zazen
in front of the rusting hulk
of a 1938 Packard\\
But][Kwatz!]
[it works\\
We created the Ultimate Intelligence\\
Not now
nor
ten thousand years from now
but sometime in a future
so distant
that yellow suns are red
and bloated with age/
swallowing their children
Saturn-like\\
Time is no barrier to the Ultimate Intelligence\\
It///
the UI///
steps through time
or shouts through time
as easily as Ummon moves through what you call
the megasphere
or you
walk the mallways of the Hive
you called home
on Lusus\\
Imagine our surprise then/
our chagrin/
the Ultimates' embarrassment
when the first message our UI sent us
across space/
across time/
across the barriers of Creator and Created

was this simple phrase//
THERE IS ANOTHER\\//
Another Ultimate Intelligence
up there
where time itself
creaks with age\\
Both were real
if (real)
means anything\\
Both were jealous gods
not beyond passion\
not into cooperative play\\
Our UI spans galaxies\
uses quasars for energy sources
the way you might
have a light snack\\
Our UI sees everything that is
and was
and will be
and tells us selected bits
so that
we may tell you
and in so doing
look a bit like UIs ourselves\\
Never underestimate/Ummon says/
the power of a few beads
and trinkets
and bits of glass
over avaricious natives]

[This other UI
has been there longer
evolving quite mindlessly/
an accident
using human minds for circuitry
the same way we had connived
with our deceptive All Thing
and our vampire dataspheres
but not deliberately/
almost reluctantly/
like self-replicating cells
which never wished to replicate
but have no choice in the matter\\
This other UI
had no choice\\
He is humankind-made/generated/forged

but no human volition accompanied his birth \\
He is a cosmic accident \\
As with our most deliberately consummated
Ultimate Intelligence/
this pretender finds time
no barrier \\
He visits the human past
now meddling/
now watching/
now not interfering/
now interfering with a will
which approaches pure perversity
but which actually
is pure naiveté \\
Recently
he has been quiescent \\
Millennia of your slow-time
have passed since your own UI
has made his shy advances
like some lonely choir boy
at his first dance]

[Naturally our UI
attacked yours \\
There is a war up there
where time creaks
which spans galaxies
and eons
back and forward
to the Big Bang
and the Final Implosion \\
Your guy was losing \\
He had no belly for it \\
Our Volatiles cried// Another reason
to terminate our predecessors//
but the Stables voted caution
and the Ultimates did not look up
from their deus machinations \\
Our UI is simple, uniform, elegant in
its ultimate design
but yours is an accretion of god-parts/
a house added on to
over time/
an evolutionary compromise \\
The early holy men of humankind
were right

587

(How)(through accident)
(through sheer luck
or ignorance)
in describing its nature \\
Your own UI is essentially triune/
composed as it is
of one part Intellect/
one part Empathy/
and one part the Void Which Binds \\
Our UI inhabits the interstices
of reality/
inheriting this home from us
its creators
the way humankind has inherited
a liking for trees \\
Your UI
seems to make its home
on the plane where Heisenberg and Schrödinger
first trespassed \\
Your accidental Intelligence
appears not only to be the gluon
but the glue \\
Not a watchmaker
but a sort of Feynman gardener
tidying up a no-boundary universe
with his crude sum-over-histories rake/
idly keeping track of every sparrow fall
and electron spin
while allowing each particle
to follow every possible
track
in space-time
and each particle of humankind
to explore every possible
crack
of cosmic irony]
[Kwatz!]
[Kwatz!]
[Kwatz!]

[The irony is
of course
that in this no-boundary universe
into which we all were dragged/
silicon and carbon/
matter and antimatter/

Ultimate/
Volatile/
and Stable/
there is no need for such a gardener
since all that is
or was
or will be
begin and end at singularities
which make our farcaster web
look like pinpricks
(less than pinpricks)
and which break the laws of science
and of humankind
and of silicon/
tying time and history and everything that is
into a self-contained knot with neither
boundary nor edge\\
Even so
our UI wishes to regulate all this/
reduce it to some reason
less affected by the vagaries
of passion
and accident
and human evolution]

[To sum it up/
there is a war
such a blind Milton would kill to see\\
Our UI wars against your UI
across battlefields beyond even Ummon's
imagination\\
Rather/there
was
a war/
for suddenly a part of your UI
the less-than-sum-of entity/self-thought of as
Empathy
had no more stomach for it
and fled back through time
cloaking itself in human form/
not for the first time\\
The war cannot continue without your UI's
wholeness\\
Victory by default is not victory for the only
Ultimate Intelligence
made by design\\

So our UI searches time for the runaway child of
its opponent
while your UI waits in idiot
harmony/
refusing to fight until Empathy is restored]
[The end of my story is simple///
The Time Tombs are artifacts sent back to carry
the Shrike/
Avatar/Lord of Pain/Angel of
Retribution/
half-perceived perceptions of an all-too-real
extension of our UI\\
Each of you was chosen to help with the opening
of the Tombs
and
the Shrike's search for the hidden one
and
the elimination of the Hyperion Variable/
for in the space-time knot which our UI
would rule
no such variables will be allowed\\
Your damaged/two-part UI
has chosen one of humankind to travel
with the Shrike
and witness its efforts\\
Some of the Core have sought to eradicate
humanity\\
Ummon has joined those who sought the second
path/
one filled with uncertainty for both races\\
Our group told Gladstone of
her choice/
humankind's choice/
of certain extermination or entry down the black
hole
of the Hyperion Variable and
warfare/
slaughter/
disruption of all unity/
the passing of gods/
but also the end of stalemate/
victory of one side or the other
if the Empathy third
of the triune
can be found and forced to return to the war\\
The Tree of Pain will call him\\

The Shrike will take him \\
The true UI will destroy him \\
Thus you have Ummon's story]

Brawne looks at Johnny in the hell-light from the megalith's glow. The egg-chamber is still black, the megasphere and universe beyond, opaqued to nonexistence. She leans forward until their temples touch, knowing that no thought can be secret here but wanting the sense of whispering:

— *Jesus Christ, do you understand all of that?*

Johnny raises soft fingers to touch her cheek:

— *Yes.*

— *Part of some human-created Trinity is hiding out in the Web?*

— *The Web or elsewhere. Brawne, we do not have much time left here. I need some final answers from Ummon.*

— *Yeah. Me too. But let's keep it from waxing rhapsodic again.*

— *Agreed.*

— *Can I go first, Johnny?*

Brawne watches her lover's analog bow slightly and make a you-first gesture and then she returns her attention to the energy megalith:

— *Who killed my father? Senator Byron Lamia?*

[Elements of the Core authorized it \\ Myself included]

— *Why? What did he do to you?*

[He insisted on bringing Hyperion into the equation before it could be factored/predicted/absorbed]

— *Why? Did he know what you just told us?*

[He knew only that the Volatiles were pressing for
quick
extinction
of humankind \\
He passed this knowledge
to his colleague
Gladstone]

— *Then why haven't you murdered her?*

[Some of us have precluded
that possibility/inevitability \\
The time is right now
for the Hyperion Variable
to be played]

— *Who murdered Johnny's first cybrid? Attacked his Core persona?*

[I did \\ It was Ummon's will which prevailed]

— *Why?*

[We created him \\
We found it necessary to discontinue him
for a while \\
Your lover is a persona retrieved
from a humankind poet

now long dead\\
Except for the Ultimate Intelligence Project
no effort has been
so complicated
nor so little understood
as this resurrection\\
Like your kind/
we usually destroy
what we cannot understand]

Johnny raises his fists toward the megalith:
— *But there is another of me. You failed!*
[Not failure \\ You had to be destroyed
so that the other
might live]
— *But I am not destroyed!* cries Johnny.
[Yes \\
You are]
The megalith seizes Johnny with a second massive pseudopod before Brawne can either react or touch her poet lover a final time. Johnny twists a second in the AI's massive grip, and then his analog – Keats's small but beautiful body – is torn, compacted, smashed into an unrecognizable mass which Ummon sets against his megalith flesh, absorbing the analog's remains back into the orange-and-red depths of itself.

Brawne falls to her knees and weeps. She wills rage . . . prays for a shield of anger . . . but feels only loss.

Ummon turns his gaze on her. The egg-chamber ovoid collapses, allowing the din and electric insanity of the megasphere to surround them.
[Go away now \\
Play out the last
of this act
so that we may live
or sleep
as fate decrees]
— *Fuck you!* Brawne pounds the palm-platform on which she kneels, kicks and pummels the pseudoflesh beneath her. *You're a goddamned loser! You and all your fucking AI pals. And our UI can beat your UI any day of the week!*
[That is
doubtful]
— *We built you, Buster. And we'll find your Core. And when we do we'll tear your silicon guts out!*
[I have no silicon guts/organs/internal components]
— *And another thing,* screams Brawne, still slashing at the megalith with her hands and nails. *You're a piss-poor storyteller. Not a tenth the poet that Johnny is! You couldn't tell a straightforward tale if your stupid AI ass depended—*

[Go away]

Ummon the AI megalith drops her, sending her analog tumbling and falling into the upless and downless crackling immensity of the megasphere.

Brawne is buffeted by data traffic, almost trod upon by AIs the size of Old Earth's moon, but even as she tumbles and blows with the winds of dataflow, she senses a light in the distance, cold but beckoning, and knows that neither life nor the Shrike is finished with her.

And she is not finished with them.

Following the cold glow, Brawne Lamia heads home.

THIRTY-FOUR

'Are you all right, sir?'

I realized that I had doubled over in the chair, my elbows on my knees, my fingers curled through my hair, gripping fiercely, palms pressed hard against the sides of my head. I sat up, stared at the archivist.

'You cried out, sir. I thought that perhaps something was wrong.'

'No,' I said. I cleared my throat and tried again. 'No, it's all right. A headache.' I looked down in confusion. Every joint in my body ached. My comlog must have malfunctioned, because it said that eight hours had elapsed since I first entered the library.

'What time is it?' I asked the archivist. 'Web standard?'

He told me. Eight hours had elapsed. I rubbed my face again, and my fingers came away slick with sweat. 'I must be keeping you past closing time,' I said. 'I'm sorry.'

'It is no problem,' said the little man. 'I am pleased to keep the archives open late for scholars.' He folded his hands in front of him. 'Especially today. With all of the confusion, there is little incentive to go home.'

'Confusion,' I said, forgetting everything for a moment . . . everything except the nightmarish dream of Brawne Lamia, the AI named Ummon, and the death of my Keats-persona counterpart. 'Oh, the war. What is the news?'

The archivist shook his head:

'Things fall apart; the centre cannot hold;
Mere anarchy is loosed upon the world,
The blood-dimmed tide is loosed, and everywhere
The ceremony of innocence is drowned;
The best lack all conviction, while the worst
Are full of passionate intensity.'

I smiled at the archivist. 'And do you believe that some "rough beast, its hour come round at last,/Slouches towards Bethlehem to be born"?'

The archivist did not smile. 'Yes, sir, I do.'

I stood and moved past the vacuum-press display cases, not looking down at my handwriting on parchment nine hundred years old. 'You may be right,' I said. 'You may well be right.'

It was late; the parking lot was empty except for the wreck of my stolen

Vikken Scenic and a single, ornate EMV sedan obviously handcrafted here on Renaissance Vector.

'Can I drop you somewhere, sir?'

I breathed in the cool night air, smelling the fish-and-spilled-oil scent of the canals. 'No thanks, I'll 'cast home.'

The archivist shook his head. 'That may be difficult, sir. All of the public terminexes have been placed under martial law. There have been . . . riots.' The word was obviously distasteful to the little archivist, a man who seemed to value order and continuity above most things. 'Come,' he said, 'I'll give you a lift to a private farcaster.'

I squinted at him. In another era on Old Earth, he would have been the head monk in a monastery devoted to saving the few remnants of a classical past. I glanced at the old archives building behind him and realized that indeed he was just that.

'What is your name?' I asked, no longer caring if I should have known it because the other Keats cybrid had known it.

'Edward B. Tynar,' he said, blinking at my extended hand and then taking it. His handshake was firm.

'I'm . . . Joseph Severn.' I couldn't very well tell him that I was the technological reincarnation of the man whose literary crypt we had just left.

M. Tynar hesitated only a fraction of a second before nodding, but I realized that to a scholar such as he, the name of the artist who was with Keats at his death would be no disguise.

'What about Hyperion?' I asked.

'Hyperion? Oh, the Protectorate world where the space fleet went a few days ago. Well, I understand that there's been some trouble recalling the necessary warships. The fighting has been very fierce there. Hyperion, I mean. Odd, I was just thinking of Keats and his unfinished masterwork. Strange how these small coincidences seem to crop up.'

'Has it been invaded? Hyperion?'

M. Tynar had stopped by his EMV, and now he laid his hand on the palmlock on the driver's side. Doors lifted and accordioned inward. I lowered myself into the sandalwood-and-leather smell of the passenger cell; Tynar's car smelled like the archives, like Tynar himself, I realized, as the archivist reclined in the driver's seat next to me.

'I don't really know if it's been invaded,' he said, sealing the doors and activating the vehicle with a touch and command. Under the sandalwood-and-leather scent, the cockpit had that new-car smell of fresh polymers and ozone, lubricants and energy which had seduced mankind for almost a millennium. 'It's so hard to access properly today,' he continued, 'the datasphere is more overloaded than I've ever seen it. This afternoon I actually had to *wait* for a query on Robinson Jeffers!'

We lifted out and over the canal, right over a public square much like the one where I'd almost been killed earlier this day, and leveled off on a lower flyway three hundred meters above the rooftops. The city was pretty at night: most of the ancient buildings were outlined in old-fashioned glow-strips, and there were more street lamps than advertising holos. But I could see crowds surging in side streets, and there were Renaissance SDF military vehicles hovering over the main avenues and terminex squares. Tynar's EMV was queried twice for ID, once by local traffic control and again by a human, FORCE-confident voice.

We flew on.

'The archives doesn't have a farcaster?' I said, looking off in the distance to where fires seemed to be burning.

'No. There was no need. We have few visitors, and the scholars who do come do not mind the walk of a few blocks.'

'Where's the private farcaster that you think I might be able to use?'

'Here,' said the archivist. We dropped out of the flyway and circled a low building, no more than thirty stories, and settled on to an extruded landing flange just where the Glennon-Height Period Deco flanges grew out of stone and plasteel. 'My order keeps its residence here,' he said. 'I belong to a forgotten branch of Christianity called Catholicism.' He looked embarrassed. 'But you are a scholar, M. Severn. You must know of our Church from the old days.'

'I know of it from more than books,' I said. 'Is there an order of priests here?'

Tynar smiled. 'Hardly priests, M. Severn. There are eight of us in the lay order of Historical and Literary Brethren. Five serve at the Reichs University. Two are art historians, working on the restoration of Lutzchendorf Abbey. I maintain the literary archives. The Church has found it cheaper to allow us to live here than to commute daily from Pacem.'

We entered the apartment hive – old even by Old Web standards: retrofitted lighting in corridors of real stone, hinged doors, a building that did not even challenge or welcome us as we entered. On an impulse, I said, 'I'd like to 'cast to Pacem.'

The archivist looked surprised. 'Tonight? This moment?'

'Why not?'

He shook his head. I realized that to this man, the hundred-mark farcaster fee would represent several weeks' pay.

'Our building has its own portal,' he said. 'This way.'

The central staircase was faded stone and corroded wrought iron with a sixty-meter drop in the center. From somewhere down a darkened corridor came the wail of an infant, followed by a man's shouting and a woman's crying.

'How long have you lived here, M. Tynar?'

'Seventeen local years, M. Severn. Ah . . . thirty-two standard, I believe. Here it is.'

The farcaster portal was as ancient as the building, its translation frame surrounded by gilded bas-relief gone green and gray.

'There are Web restrictions on travel tonight,' he said. 'Pacem should be accessible. Some two hundred hours remain before the barbarians . . .

whatever they're called . . . are scheduled to reach there. Twice the time left to Renaissance Vector.' He reached out and grasped my wrist. I could feel his tension as a slight vibration through tendon and bone. 'M. Severn . . . do you think they will burn my archives? Would even *they* destroy ten thousand years of thought?' His hand dropped away.

I was not sure who the 'they' were – Ousters? Shrike Cult saboteurs? Rioters? Gladstone and the Hegemony leaders were willing to sacrifice these 'first-wave' worlds. 'No,' I said, extending my hand to shake his. 'I don't believe they'll allow the archives to be destroyed.'

M. Edward B. Tynar smiled and stood back a step, embarrassed at showing emotion. He shook hands. 'Good luck, M. Severn. Wherever your travels take you.'

'God bless you, M. Tynar.' I had never used that phrase before, and it shocked me that I had spoken it now. I looked down, fumbled out Gladstone's override card, and tapped the three-digit code for Pacem. The portal apologized, said that it was not possible at the moment, finally got it through its microcephalic processors that this was an override card, and hummed into existence.

I nodded at Tynar and stepped through, half expecting that I was making a serious mistake not going straight home to TC^2.

It was night on Pacem, much darker than Renaissance Vector's urban glow, and it was raining to boot. Raining hard with that fist-on-metal pounding violence that makes one want to curl up under thick blankets and wait for morning.

The portal was under cover in some half-roofed courtyard but outside enough for me to feel the night, the rain, and the cold. Especially the cold. Pacem's air was half as thick as Web standard, its single habitable plateau twice as high as Renaissance V's sea-level cities. I would have turned back then rather than step into that night and downpour, but a FORCE:Marine stepped out of the shadows, multipurpose assault rifle slung but ready to swivel, and asked me for my ID.

I let him scan the card, and he snapped to attention. 'Yes, *sir*!'

'Is this the New Vatican?'

'Yes, sir.'

I caught a glimpse of illuminated dome through the downpour. I pointed over the courtyard wall. 'Is that St Peter's?'

'Yes, sir.'

'Would Monsignor Edouard be found there?'

'Across this courtyard, left at the plaza, the low building to the left of the cathedral, *sir*!'

'Thank you, Corporal.'

'It's Private, *sir*!'

I pulled my short cape around me, ceremonial and quite useless against such a rain as it was, and ran across the courtyard.

*

A human . . . perhaps a priest, although he wore no robe or clerical collar . . . opened the door to the residential hall. Another human behind a wooden desk told me that Monsignor Edouard was in residence and was awake, despite the late hour. Did I have an appointment?

No, I did not have an appointment but wished to speak to the Monsignor. It was important.

On what topic? the man behind the desk politely but firmly asked. He had not been impressed by my override card. I suspected that I was speaking to the Bishop.

On the topic of Father Paul Duré and Father Lenar Hoyt, I told him.

The gentleman nodded, whispered into a bead mike so small that I had not noticed it on his collar, and led me into the residential hall.

This place made the old tower that M. Tynar lived in look like a sybarite's palace. The corridor was absolutely featureless except for the rough plaster walls and even rougher wooden doors. One of the doors was open, and as we passed, I glimpsed a chamber more prison cell than sleeping room: low cot, rough blanket, wooden kneeling stool, an unadorned dresser holding a pitcher of water and simple basin; no windows, no media walls, no holo pit, no data access deck. I suspected the room wasn't even interactive.

From somewhere there echoed voices rising in a chanting/singing so elegant and atavistic that it made the hair on my neck tingle. Gregorian. We passed through a large eating area as simple as the cells had been, through a kitchen that would have been familiar to cooks in John Keats's day, down a worn stone staircase, through an ill-lighted corridor, and up another, narrower staircase. The other man left me, and I stepped into one of the most beautiful spaces I had ever seen.

Although part of me realized that the Church had moved and reconstructed St Peter's Basilica, down to transplanting the bones believed to be those of Peter himself to their new burial beneath the altar, another part of me felt that I had been transported back to the Rome I had first seen in mid-November of 1820; the Rome I had seen, stayed in, suffered in, and died in.

This space was more beautiful and elegant than any mile-high office spire on Tau Ceti Center could ever hope to be; St Peter's Basilica stretched more than six hundred feet into shadows, was four hundred and fifty feet wide where the 'cross' of the transept intersected the nave, and was capped by the perfection of Michelangelo's dome, rising almost four hundred feet above the altar. Bernini's bronze baldachin, the ornate canopy supported by twisting, Byzantine columns, capped the main altar and gave the immense space the human dimension necessary for perspective on the intimate ceremonies conducted there. Soft lamp- and candlelight illuminated discrete areas of the basilica, gleamed on smooth travertine stone, brought gold mosaics into bold relief, and picked out the infinite detail painted, embossed, and raised on the walls, columns, cornices, and grand dome itself. Far above, the continuous flash of lightning from the storm poured thickly through yellow stained-glass windows and sent columns of violent light slanting toward Bernini's 'Throne of St Peter'.

I paused there, just beyond the apse, afraid that my footsteps in such a space would be a desecration and that even my breathing would send echoes the length of the basilica. In a moment, my eyes adjusted to the dim light, compensated for the contrasts between the storm light above and candlelight below, and it was then I realized that there were no pews to fill the apse or long nave, no columns here beneath the dome, only two chairs set near the altar some fifty feet away. Two men sat talking in these chairs, close together, both leaning forward in apparent urgency to communicate. Lamplight and candlelight and the glow from a large mosaic of Christ on the front of the dark altar illuminated bits and fragments of the men's faces. Both were elderly. Both were priests, the white bands of their collars glowing in the dimness. With a start of recognition, I realized that one was Monsignor Edouard.

The other was Father Paul Duré.

They must have been alarmed at first – looking up from their whispered conversation to see this apparition, this short shadow of a man emerge from the darkness, calling their names . . . crying Duré's name in loud amazement . . . babbling at them about pilgrimages and pilgrims, Time Tombs and the Shrike, AIs and the death of gods.

The Monsignor did not call security; neither he nor Duré fled; together they calmed this apparition, tried to glean some sense from his excited babblings, and turned this strange confrontation into sane conversation.

It *was* Paul Duré. Paul Duré and not some bizarre Doppelganger or android duplicate or cybrid reconstruction. I made sure of that by listening to him, quizzing him, by looking into his eyes . . . but mostly by shaking his hand, *touching* him, and knowing that it was indeed Father Paul Duré.

'You know . . . incredible details of my life . . . our time on Hyperion, at the Tombs . . . but *who* did you say you are?' Duré was saying.

It was my turn to convince him. 'A cybrid reconstruction of John Keats. A twin to the persona Brawne Lamia carried with her on your pilgrimage.'

'And you were able to communicate . . . to know what happened to us because of that shared persona?'

I was on one knee between them and the altar. I lifted both hands in frustration. 'Because of that . . . because of some anomaly in the megasphere. But I have *dreamt* your lives, heard the tales the pilgrims told, listened to Father Hoyt speak of the life and death of Paul Duré . . . of *you.*' I reached out to touch his arm through the priestly garments. Actually being in the same space and time with one of the pilgrims made me a bit light-headed. 'Then you know how I got here,' said Father Duré.

'No. I last dreamed that you were entering one of the Cave Tombs. There was a light. I know nothing since then.'

Duré nodded. His face was more patrician and more weary than my dreams had prepared me for. 'But you know the fate of the others?'

I took a breath. 'Some. The poet Silenus is alive but impaled on the Shrike's tree of thorns. I last saw Kassad attacking the Shrike with his bare hands. M. Lamia had traveled the megasphere to the TechnoCore periphery with my Keats counterpart . . .'

'He survived in that . . . Schrön loop . . . whatever it was called?' Duré seemed fascinated.

'No longer,' I said. 'The AI personality called Ummon killed him . . . destroyed the persona. Brawne was returning. I don't know if her body survives.'

Monsignor Edouard leaned toward me. 'And what of the Consul and the father and child?'

'The Consul tried to return to the capital by hawking mat,' I said, 'but crashed some miles north. I don't know his fate.'

'Miles,' said Duré, as if the word brought back memories.

'I'm sorry.' I gestured at the basilica. 'This place makes me think in the units of my . . . previous life.'

'Go on,' said Monsignor Edouard. 'The father and child.'

I sat on the cool stone, exhausted, my arms and hands shaking with fatigue. 'In my last dream, Sol had offered Rachel to the Shrike. It was *Rachel*'s request. I could not see what happened next. The Tombs were opening.'

'All of them?' asked Duré.

'All I could see.'

The two men looked at one another.

'There's more,' I said, and told them about the dialogue with Ummon. 'Is it possible that a deity could . . . evolve from human consciousness like that without humanity being aware of it?'

The lightning had ceased but now the rain fell so violently that I could hear it on the great dome far above. Somewhere in the darkness, a heavy door squeaked, footsteps echoed and then receded. Votive candles in the dim recesses of the basilica flickered red light against walls and draperies.

'I taught that St Teilhard said that it was possible,' Duré said tiredly, 'but if that God is a limited being, evolving in the same way all we other limited beings have done, then no . . . it is not the God of Abraham and Christ.'

Monsignor Edouard nodded. 'There is an ancient heresy . . .'

'Yes,' I said. 'The Socinian Heresy. I heard Father Duré explain it to Sol Weintraub and the Consul. But what difference does it make *how* this . . . power . . . evolved, and whether it's limited or not. If Ummon is telling the truth, we're dealing with a force that uses quasars for energy sources. That's a God who can destroy *galaxies*, gentlemen.'

'That would be a god who destroys galaxies,' said Duré. 'Not God.'

I heard his emphasis clearly. 'But if it's *not* limited,' I said. 'If it's the Omega Point God of total consciousness you've written about, if it's the same Trinity your Church has argued for and theorized about since before Aquinas . . . but if one part of that Trinity has fled backward through time to here . . . to now . . . then what?'

'But fled from *what*?' Duré asked softly. 'Teilhard's God . . . the Church's God . . . *our* God, would be the Omega Point God in whom the Christ of Evolution, the Personal, and the Universal . . . what Teilhard called the *En Haut* and the *En Avant*, are perfectly joined. There could be nothing so threatening that any element of that deity's personality would flee. No Antichrist, no theoretical satanic power, no "counter-God" could possibly threaten such a universal consciousness. What would this other god be?'

'The God of machines?' I said, so softly that even I was not sure that I had spoken aloud.

Monsignor Edouard clasped both hands in what I thought was a preparation for prayer but which turned out to be a gesture of deep thought and deeper agitation. 'But Christ had doubts,' he said. 'Christ sweated blood in the garden and asked that this cup should be taken from him. If there was some second sacrifice pending, something even more terrible than the crucifixion . . . then I could imagine the Christ-entity of the Trinity passing through time, walking through some fourth-dimensional garden of Gethsemane to gain a few hours . . . or years . . . of time to think.'

'Something more terrible than the crucifixion,' repeated Duré in a hoarse whisper.

Both Monsignor Edouard and I stared at the priest. Duré had crucified himself on a high-voltage tesla tree on Hyperion rather than submit to his cruciform parasite's control. Through that creature's ability to resurrect, Duré had suffered the agonies of crucifixion and electrocution many times.

'Whatever the *En Haut* consciousness flees,' whispered Duré, 'it is most terrible.'

Monsignor Edouard touched his friend's shoulder. 'Paul, tell this man about your voyage here.'

Duré returned from whatever distant place his memories had taken him and focused on me. 'You know all of our stories . . . and the details of our stay in the Valley of the Tombs on Hyperion?'

'I believe so. Up to the point you disappeared.'

The priest sighed and touched his forehead with long, slightly trembling fingers. 'Then perhaps,' he said, 'just perhaps you can make some sense of how I got here . . . and what I saw along the way.'

'I saw a light in the third Cave Tomb,' said Father Duré. 'I stepped inside. I confess that thoughts of suicide had been in my mind . . . what is left of my mind after the cruciform's brutal replication . . . I will not dignify that parasite's function with the term resurrection.

'I saw a light and thought that it was the Shrike. It was my feeling that my second meeting with that creature – the first encounter was years ago in the labyrinth beneath the Cleft, when the Shrike anointed me with my unholy cruciform – the second meeting was long overdue.

'When we had searched for Colonel Kassad on the previous day, this Cave Tomb had been short, featureless, with a blank rock wall stopping us after thirty paces. Now that wall was gone and in its place was a carving not unlike the mouth of the Shrike, stone extended in that blend of the mechanical and organic, stalactites and stalagmites as sharp as calcium carbonate teeth.

'Through the mouth there was a stone stairway descending. It was from those depths that the light emanated, glowing pale white one moment, dark red the next. There was no noise except for the sigh of wind, as if the rock there were breathing.

'I am no Dante. I sought no Beatrice. My brief bout of courage – although fatalism is a more accurate term – had evaporated with the loss of daylight. I turned and almost ran the thirty paces to the opening of the cave.

'There was no opening. The passage merely ended. I had heard no sound of cave-in or avalanche, and besides, the rock where the entrance should have been looked as ancient and undisturbed as the rest of that cavern. For half an hour I searched for an alternate exit, finding none, refusing to return to the staircase, finally sitting for some hours where the Cave Tomb entrance once had been. Another Shrike trick. Another cheap theatrical stunt by this perverse planet. Hyperion's idea of a joke. Ha ha.

'After several hours of sitting there in semidarkness, watching the light at the far end of the cave pulse soundlessly, I realized that the Shrike was not going to come to me here. The entrance would not magically reappear. I had the choice of sitting there until I died of starvation – or thirst, more likely, since I was already dehydrated – or of descending the damned staircase.

'I descended.

'Years ago, literally lifetimes ago, when I visited the Bikura near the Cleft on the Pinion Plateau, the labyrinth where I had encountered the Shrike had been three kilometers below the canyon wall. That was close to the surface; most of the labyrinths on most of the labyrinthine worlds are at least ten klicks beneath the crust. I had no doubt that this endless staircase . . . a steep and twisting spiral of stone stairs wide enough for ten priests to descend to hell abreast . . . would end up in the labyrinth. The Shrike had first cursed me with immortality there. If the creature or the power that drove it had any sense of irony at all, it would be fitting that both my immortality and mortal life ended there.

'The staircase twisted downward; the light grew brighter . . . now a roseate glow; ten minutes later, a heavy red; half an hour lower than that, a flickering crimson. It was far too Dante-esque and cheap fundamentalist staging for my tastes. I almost laughed aloud at the thought of a little devil appearing, tail and trident and cloven hooves intact, pencil-thin mustache twitching.

'But I did not laugh when I reached depths where the cause of the light became evident: cruciforms, hundreds and then thousands of them, small at first, clinging to the rough walls of the staircase like rough-hewn crosses left by some subterranean conquistadors, then larger ones and more of them until they almost overlapped, coral-pink, raw-flesh flushed, blood-red bioluminescent.

'It made me ill. It was like entering a shaft lined with bloated, pulsing leeches, although these were worse. I have seen the medscanner sonic and k-cross imaging of myself with only *one* of these things on me: excess ganglia infiltrating my flesh and organs like gray fibers, sheaths of twitching filaments, clusters of nematodes like terrible tumors which will not grant even the mercy of death. Now I had *two* on me: Lenar Hoyt's and my own. I prayed that I would die rather than suffer another.

'I continued lower. The walls pulsed with heat as well as light, whether from the depths or the crowding of the thousands of cruciforms, I do not know. Eventually I reached the lowest step, the staircase ended, I turned a final twisting of stone, and was there.

'The labyrinth. It stretched away as I had seen it in countless holos and once in person: smooth-tunneled, thirty meters to a side, carved out of Hyperion's crust more than three quarters of a million years ago, crossing and crisscrossing the planet like catacombs planned by some insane engineer. Labyrinths can be found on nine worlds, five in the Web, the rest, like this one, in the Outback: all are identical, all were excavated at the same time in the past, none surrender any clues as to the reason for their existence. Legends abound about the labyrinth builders, but the mythical engineers left no artifacts, no hints of their methods or alien makeup, and none of the theories about the labyrinths give a sensible reason for what must have been one of the largest engineering projects the galaxy has ever seen.

'All of the labyrinths are empty. Remotes have explored millions of kilometers of corridor cut from stone, and except where time and cave-in have altered the original catacombs, the labyrinths are featureless and empty.

'But not where I now stood.

'Cruciforms lighted a scene from Hieronymus Bosch as I gazed down an endless corridor, endless but not empty . . . no, not empty.

'At first I thought they were crowds of living people, a river of heads and shoulders and arms, stretching on for the kilometers I could see, the current of humanity broken here and there by the presence of parked vehicles all of the same rust-red color. As I stepped forward, approaching the wall of jam-packed humanity less than twenty meters from me, I realized that they were corpses. Tens, hundred of thousands of human corpses stretching as far down the corridor as I could see; some sprawled on the stone floor, some crushed against walls, but most buoyed up by the pressure of other corpses so tightly were they jammed in this particular avenue of the labyrinth.

'There was a path; cutting its way through the bodies as if some machine with blades had munched its way through. I followed it – careful not to touch an outspread arm or emaciated ankle.

'The bodies were human, still clothed in most cases, and mummified over eons of slow decomposing in this bacteria-free crypt. Skin and flesh had been tanned, stretched, and torn like rotten cheesecloth until it covered nothing but bone, and frequently not even that. Hair remained as tendrils of dusty tar, stiff as varnished fiberplastic. Blackness stared out from under opened eyelids, between teeth. Their clothing which must once have been a myriad of colors now was tan or gray or black, brittle as garments sculpted from thin stone. Time-melted plastic lumps on their wrists and necks might have been comlogs or their equivalent.

'The large vehicles might once have been EMVs but now were heaps of pure rust. A hundred meters in, I stumbled, and rather than fall off the meter-wide path into the field of bodies, I steadied myself on a tall machine all curves and clouded blisters. The pile of rust collapsed inward on itself.

'I wandered, Virgil-less, following the terrible path gnawed out of decayed human flesh, wondering why I was being shown all this, what it meant. After an indeterminable time of walking, staggering between piles of discarded humanity, I came to an intersection of tunnels; all three corridors ahead were filled with bodies. The narrow path continued in the labyrinth to my left. I followed it.

'Hours later, perhaps longer, I stopped and sat on the narrow stone walk which wound among the horror. If there were tens of thousands of corpses in this small stretch of tunnel, Hyperion's labyrinth must contain billions. More. The nine labyrinthine worlds together must be a crypt for trillions.

'I had no idea why I was being shown this ultimate Dachau of the soul. Near where I sat, the mummified corpse of a man still sheltered a woman's corpse with the curve of his bone-bare arm. In her arms was a small bundle with short black hair. I turned away and wept.

'As an archaeologist I had excavated victims of execution, fire, flood, earthquake, and volcano. Such family scenes were not new to me; they were the *sine qua non* of history. But somehow this was much more terrible. Perhaps it was the numbers; the dead in their holocaust millions. Perhaps it was the soul-stealing glow of the cruciforms which lined the tunnels like thousands of blasphemous bad jokes. Perhaps it was the sad crying of the wind moving through endless corridors of stone.

'My life and teachings and sufferings and small victories and countless defeats had brought me here – past faith, past caring, past simple, Miltonic defiance. I had the sense that these bodies had been here half a million years or more, but that the people themselves were from our time or, worse yet, our future. I lowered my face to my hands and wept.

'No scraping or actual noise warned me, but something, something, a movement of air perhaps . . . I looked up and the Shrike was there, not two meters distant. Not on the path but in among the bodies: a sculpture honoring the architect of all this carnage.

'I got to my feet. I would not sit or kneel before this abomination.

'The Shrike moved toward me, gliding more than walking, sliding as if it were on frictionless rails. The blood light of the cruciforms spilled over its quicksilver carapace. Its eternal, impossible grin – steel stalactites, stalagmites.

'I felt no violence toward the thing. Only sadness and a terrible pity. Not for the Shrike – whatever the hell it was – but for all the victims who, alone and ungirded by even the flimsiest of faiths, have had to face the terror-in-the-night which that thing embodies.

'For the first time, I noticed that up close, less than a meter away, there was a smell around the Shrike – a stench of rancid oil, overheated bearings, and dried blood. The flames in its eyes pulsed in perfect rhythm with the rise and fall of the cruciform glow.

'I did not believe years ago that this creature was supernatural, some manifestation of good or evil, merely an aberration of the universe's unfathomable and seemingly senseless unfoldings: a terrible joke of evolution. St Teilhard's worst nightmare. But still a *thing*, obeying natural laws, no matter how twisted, and subject to some rules of the universe somewhere, somewhen.

'The Shrike lifted its arms toward me, around me. The blades on its four wrists were much longer than my own hands; the blade on its chest, longer than my forearm. I stared up into its eyes as one pair of its razorwire and steel-spring arms surrounded me while the other pair came slowly around, filling the small space between us.

'Fingerblades uncurled. I flinched but did not step back as those blades lunged, sank into my chest with a pain like cold fire, like surgical lasers slicing nerves.

'It stepped back, holding something red and reddened further with my blood. I staggered, half expecting to see my heart in the monster's hands: the final irony of a dead man blinking in surprise at his own heart in the seconds before blood drains from a disbelieving brain.

'But it was not my heart. The Shrike held the cruciform I had carried on my chest, *my* cruciform, that parasitic depository of *my* slow-to-die DNA. I staggered again, almost fell, touched my chest. My fingers came away coated with blood but not with the arterial surges that such crude surgery deserved; the wound was healing even while I watched. I *knew* that the cruciform had sent tubers and filaments throughout my body. I *knew* that no surgical laser had been able to separate those deadly vines from Father Hoyt's body – nor from mine. But I *felt* the contagion healing, the internal fibers drying and fading to the faintest hint of internal scar tissue.

'I still had Hoyt's cruciform. But that was different. When I died, Lenar Hoyt would rise from this re-formed flesh. *I* would die. There would be no more poor duplicates of Paul Duré, duller and less vital with each artificial generation.

'The Shrike had granted me death without killing me.

'The thing cast the cooling cruciform into the heaps of bodies and took my upper arm in his hand with an effortless cutting of three layers of fabric, an instant flow of blood from my biceps at the slightest contact with those scalpels.

'He led the way through bodies toward the wall. I followed, trying not to step on corpses, but in my haste not to have my arm severed, I was not always successful. Bodies crumpled to dust. One received my footprint in the collapsing cavity of its chest.

'Then we were at the wall, at a section suddenly cleared of cruciforms, and I realized that it was some energy-shielded opening . . . the wrong size and shape to be a standard farcaster portal, but similar in its opaque buzz of energy. Anything to get me out of this storage place of death.

'The Shrike shoved me through.'

'Zero gravity. A maze of shattered bulkheads, tangles of wiring floating like some giant creature's entrails, red lights flashing – for a second, I thought there were cruciforms here too but then realized that these were emergency lights in a dying spacecraft – then recoiling, tumbling in unaccustomed zero-g as more corpses tumbled by: not mummies here, but fresh dead, newly killed, mouths agape, eyes distended, lungs exploded, trailing clouds of gore as they simulated life in their slow, necrotic response to each random current of air and surge of the shattered FORCE spacecraft.

'It *was* a FORCE spacecraft, I was sure. I saw the FORCE:space uniforms on the young corpses. I saw the military-jargon lettering on the bulkheads and blown hatches, the useless instructions on the worse-than-useless emergency lockers with their skinsuits and still-uninflated pressure balls folded away on shelves. Whatever had destroyed this ship had done so with the suddenness of a plague in the night.

'The Shrike appeared next to me.

'*The Shrike . . . in space! Free of Hyperion and the bonds of the time tides! There were farcasters on many of these ships!*

'There was a farcaster portal not five meters down the corridor from me. One body tumbled toward it, the young man's right arm passing through the opaque field as if he were testing the water of the world on the other side. Air was screaming out of this shaft in a rising whine. *Go!* I urged the corpse, but the pressure differential blew him away from the portal, his arm surprisingly intact, recovered, although his face was an anatomist's mask.

'I turned toward the Shrike, the movement making me spin half a revolution in the other direction.

'The Shrike lifted me, blades tearing skin, and passed me down the corridor toward the farcaster. I could not have changed trajectories if I had wanted to. In the seconds before I passed through the humming, sputtering portal, I imagined vacuum on the other side, drops from great heights, explosive decompression, or – worst of all – a return to the labyrinth.

'Instead, I tumbled half a meter to a marble floor. Here, not two hundred meters from this spot, in the private chambers of Pope Urban XVI – who, it so happens, had died of old age not three hours before I fell through his private farcaster. The "Pope's Door" the New Vatican calls it. I felt the pain-punishment from being so far from Hyperion – so far from the source of the cruciforms – but pain is an old ally now and no longer holds sway over me.

'I found Edouard. He was kind enough to listen for hours as I told a story no Jesuit has ever had to confess. He was even kinder to believe me. Now you have heard it. That is my story.'

The storm had passed. The three of us sat by candlelight beneath the dome of St Peter's and said nothing at all for several moments.

'The Shrike has access to the Web,' I said at last.

Duré's gaze was level. 'Yes.'

'It must have been some ship in Hyperion space . . .'

'So it would seem.'

'Then we might be able to get back there. Use the . . . the Pope's Door? . . . to return to Hyperion space.'

Monsignor Edouard raised an eyebrow. 'You wish to do this, M. Severn?'

I chewed on a knuckle. 'It's something I've considered.'

'Why?' the Monsignor asked softly. 'Your counterpart, the cybrid personality Brawne Lamia carried on her pilgrimage, found only death there.'

I shook my head, as if trying to clear the jumble of my thoughts through that simple gesture. 'I'm a part of this. I just don't know what part to play . . . or where to play it.'

Paul Duré laughed with humor. 'All of us have known that feeling. It is like some poor playwright's treatise on predestination. Whatever happened to free will?'

The Monsignor glanced sharply at his friend. 'Paul, all of the pilgrims . . . you yourself . . . have been confronted with choices you made with your own will. Great powers may be shaping the general turn of events, but human personalities still determine their own fate.'

Duré sighed. 'Perhaps so, Edouard. I do not know. I am very tired.'

'If Ummon's story is true,' I said. 'If the third part of this human deity fled to our time, where and who do you think it is? There are more than a hundred billion human beings in the Web.'

Father Duré smiled. It was a gentle smile, free of irony. 'Have you considered that it might be yourself, M. Severn?'

The question struck me like a slap. 'It can't be,' I said. 'I'm not even . . . not even fully human. My consciousness floats somewhere in the matrix of the Core. My body was reconstituted from remnants of John Keats's DNA and biofactured like an android's. Memories were implanted. The end of my life . . . my "recovery" from consumption . . . were all simulated on a world built for that purpose.'

Duré was still smiling. 'So? Does any of this preclude you from being this Empathy entity?'

'I don't *feel* like a part of some god,' I said sharply. 'I don't remember anything, understand anything, or know what to do next.'

Monsignor Edouard touched my wrist, 'Are we so sure that Christ always knew what to do next? He knew what had to be done. It is not always the same as knowing what to do.'

I rubbed my eyes. 'I don't even know what has to be done.'

The Monsignor's voice was quiet. 'I believe that what Paul is saying is that *if* the spirit creature you say is hiding here in our time, it may well not know its own identity.'

'That's insane,' I said.

Duré nodded. 'Much of the events on and around Hyperion have seemed insane. Insanity seems to be spreading.'

I looked closely at the Jesuit. '*You* would be a good candidate for the deity,' I said. 'You've lived a life of prayer, contemplating theologies, and honoring science as an archaeologist. Plus, you've already been crucified.'

Duré's smile was gone. 'Do you hear what we're saying? Do you hear the blasphemy in what we're saying? I'm no candidate for the Godhead, Severn. I've betrayed my Church, my science, and now, by disappearing, my friends on the pilgrimage. Christ may have lost his faith for a few seconds. He did not sell it in the marketplace for the trinkets of ego and curiosity.'

'Enough,' commanded Monsignor Edouard. 'If the identity of this Empathy part of some future, manufactured deity is the mystery, think of the candidates just in the immediate troupe of your little Passion Play, M. Severn. The CEO, M. Gladstone, carrying the weight of the Hegemony on her shoulders. The other members of the pilgrimage . . . M. Silenus who, according to what you told Paul, even now suffers on the Shrike's tree for his poetry. M. Lamia, who has risked and lost so much for love. M. Weintraub, who has suffered Abraham's dilemma . . . even his daughter, who has returned to the innocence of childhood. The Consul, who—'

'The Consul seems more Judas than Christ,' I said. 'He betrayed both the Hegemony and the Ousters, who thought he was working for them.'

'From what Paul tells me,' said the Monsignor, 'the Consul was true to his convictions, faithful to the memory of his grandmother Siri.' The older man smiled. 'Plus, there are a hundred billion other players in this play. God did not choose Herod or Pontius Pilate or Caesar Augustus as His instrument. He chose the unknown son of an unknown carpenter in one of the least important stretches of the Roman Empire.'

'All right,' I said, standing and pacing before the glowing mosaic below the altar. 'What do we do now? Father Duré, you need to come with me to see Gladstone. She knows about your pilgrimage. Perhaps your story can help avert some of the bloodbath which seems so imminent.'

Duré stood also, folding his arms and staring toward the dome as if the darkness high above held some instructions for him. 'I've thought of that,' he said. 'But I don't think it's my first obligation. I need to go to God's Grove to speak to their equivalent of the Pope – the True Voice of the World-tree.'

I stopped pacing. 'God's Grove? What does that have to do with anything?'

'I feel that the Templars have been the key to some missing element in this painful charade. Now you say that Het Masteen is dead. Perhaps the True Voice can explain to us what they had planned for this pilgrimage . . . Masteen's tale, as it were. He was, after all, the only one of the seven original pilgrims who did not tell the story of why he had come to Hyperion.'

I paced again, more rapidly now, trying to keep anger in check. 'My God, Duré. We don't have time for such idle curiosity. It's only' – I consulted my implant – 'an hour and a half until the Ouster invasion Swarm enters the God's Grove system. It must be bedlam there.'

'Perhaps,' said the Jesuit, 'but I still will go there first. Then I will speak to Gladstone. It may be that she will authorize my return to Hyperion.'

I grunted, doubting that the CEO would ever let such a valuable informant return to harm's way. 'Let's get going,' I said, and turned to find my way out.

'A moment,' said Duré. 'You said a while ago that you were sometimes able to . . . to "dream" . . . about the pilgrims while you were still awake. A sort of trance state, is it?'

'Something like that.'

'Well, M. Severn, please dream about them now.'

I stared in amazement. 'Here? Now?'

Duré gestured toward his chair. 'Please. I wish to know the fate of my friends. Also, the information might be most valuable in our confrontation with the True Voice and M. Gladstone.'

I shook my head but took the seat he offered. 'It might not work,' I said.

'Then we have lost nothing,' said Duré.

I nodded, closed my eyes, and sat back in the uncomfortable chair. I was all too aware of the other two men watching me, of the faint smell of incense and rain, of the echoing space surrounding us. I was sure that this would never work; the landscape of my dreams was not so close that I could summon it merely by closing my eyes.

The feeling of being watched faded, the smells grew distant, and the sense of space expanded a thousandfold as I returned to Hyperion.

THIRTY-FIVE

Confusion.

Three hundred spacecraft retreating in Hyperion space under heavy fire, falling back from the Swarm like men fighting bees. Madness near the military farcaster portals, traffic control overloaded, ships backed up like EMVs in TC²'s airborne gridlock, vulnerable as partridges to the roaming Ouster assault ships.

Madness at the exit points: FORCE spacecraft lined up like sheep in a narrow pen as they cycle from the Madhya cutoff portal to the outgoing 'caster. Ships spinning down into Hebron space, a few translating to Heaven's Gate, God's Grove, Mare Infinitus, Asquith. Only hours left now before the Swarms enter Web systems.

Confusion as hundreds of millions of refugees farcast away from the threatened worlds, stepping into cities and relocation centers gone half mad with the aimless excitement of incipient war. Confusion as unthreatened Web worlds ignite with riots: three Hives on Lusus – almost seventy million citizens – quarantined due to Shrike Cult riots, thirty-level malls looted, apartment monoliths overrun by mobs, fusion centers blown, farcaster terminexes under attack. The Home Rule Council appeals to the Hegemony; the Hegemony declares martial law and sends FORCE:Marines to seal the hives.

Secessionist riots on New Earth and Maui-Covenant. Terrorist attacks from Glennon-Height royalists – quiet now for three quarters of a century – on Thalia, Armaghast, Nordholm, and Lee Three. More Shrike Cult riots on Tsingtao-Hsishuang Panna and Renaissance Vector.

FORCE Command on Olympus transfers combat battalions from transports returning from Hyperion to Web worlds. Demolition squads assigned to torchships in threatened systems report farcaster singularity spheres wired for destruction, awaiting only the fatlined order from TC².

'There is a better way,' Councilor Albedo tells Gladstone and the War Council.

The CEO turns toward the ambassador from the TechnoCore.

'There is a weapon that will eliminate the Ousters without harming Hegemony property. Or Ouster property, for that matter.'

General Morpurgo glowers. 'You're talking about the bomb equivalent of a deathwand,' he says. 'It won't work. FORCE researchers have shown that it propagates indefinitely. Besides being dishonorable, against the New

Bushido Code, it would wipe out planetary populations as well as the invaders.'

'Not at all,' says Albedo. 'If Hegemony citizens are properly shielded, there need be no casualties whatsoever. As you know, deathwands can be calibrated for specific cerebral wavelengths. So could a bomb based on the same principle. Livestock, wild animals, even other anthropoid species would not be affected.'

General Van Zeidt of FORCE:Marines stands. 'But there's no way to shield a population! Our testing showed that death-bomb heavy neutrinos would penetrate solid rock or metal to a depth of six kilometers. No one has shelters like that!'

The projection of Councilor Albedo folds his hands on the table. 'We have nine worlds with shelters which would hold billions,' he says softly.

Gladstone nods. 'The labyrinthine worlds,' she whispers. 'But certainly such a transfer of population would be impossible.'

'No,' says Albedo. 'Now that you have joined Hyperion to the Protectorate, each of the labyrinthine worlds has farcaster capability. The Core can make arrangements to transfer populations directly to these underground shelters.'

There is babble around the long table, but Meina Gladstone's intense gaze never leaves Albedo's face. She beckons for silence and receives it. 'Tell us more,' she says. 'We are interested.'

The Consul sits in the spotty shade of a low neville tree and waits to die. His hands are tied behind him with a twist of fiberplastic. His clothes are torn to rags and are still damp; the moisture on his face is partially from the river but mostly from perspiration.

The two men who stand over him are finishing their inspection of his duffel bag. 'Shit,' says the first man, 'there bey nothing worth anything here-in except this fucking antique pistol.' He thrusts Brawne Lamia's father's weapon in his belt.

'It bey too bad we couldn't get that goddamn flying carpet,' says the second man.

'It beyn't flying too well there toward the end!' says the first man, and both of them laugh.

The Consul squints at the two massive figures, their armored bodies made silhouettes by the lowering sun. From their dialect he assumes them to be indigenies; from their appearance – bits of outmoded FORCE body armor, heavy multipurpose assault rifles, tatters of what once had been camou-polymer cloth – he guesses them to be deserters from some Hyperion Self-defense Force unit.

From their behavior toward him, he is sure that they are going to kill him.

At first, stunned from the fall into the Hoolie River, still tangled in the ropes connecting him to his duffel bag and the useless hawking mat, he thought them to be his saviors. The Consul had hit the water hard, stayed under for a much longer time than he would have imagined possible without drowning, and surfaced only to be pushed under by a strong current and then pulled under again by the tangle of ropes and mat. It had been a valiant but losing battle, and he was still ten meters from the shallows when one of the men emerging from the neville and thorn tree forest had thrown the Consul a line. Then they had beaten him, robbed him, tied him, and – judging from their matter-of-fact comments – were now preparing to cut his throat and leave him for the harbinger birds.

The taller of the two men, his hair a mass of oiled spikes, squats in front of the Consul and pulls a ceramic zero-edge knife from its scabbard. 'Any last words, Pops?'

The Consul licks his lips. He has seen a thousand movies and holies where this was the point at which the hero twisted his opponent's legs out from under him, kicked the other one into submission, seized a weapon and dispatched both – firing with his hands still tied – and then went on with his adventures. But the Consul feels like no hero: he is exhausted and middle-aged and hurt from his fall in the river. *Each* of these men is leaner, stronger, faster, and obviously meaner than the Consul ever has been. He has seen violence – even committed violence once – but his life and training have been devoted to the tense but quiet paths of diplomacy.

The Consul licks his lips again and says, 'I can pay you.'

The crouching man smiles and moves the zero-edge blade back and forth five centimeters in front of the Consul's eyes. 'With what, Pops? We've got your universal card, and it bey worth shit out here.'

'Gold,' says the Consul, knowing that this is the only syllable that has held its power over the ages.

The crouching man does not react – there is a sick light in his eyes as he watches the blade – but the other man steps forward and sets a heavy hand on his partner's shoulder. 'What bey you talkin' about, man? Wherefore you got gold?'

'My ship,' says the Consul. 'The *Benares*.'

The crouching man raises the blade next to his own cheek. 'He bey lyin', Chez. The *Benares* bey that old flat-bottomed manta-pulled barge belongin' to the blue-skins we finished trey day ago.'

The Consul closes his eyes for a second, feeling the nausea in him but not surrendering to it. A. Bettik and the other android crewmen had left the *Benares* in one of the ship's launches less than a week earlier, heading downstream toward 'freedom'. Evidently they had found something else. 'A. Bettik,' he says. 'The crew captain. He didn't mention the gold?'

The man with the knife grins. 'He make lots a noise, but he don't speak much. He say the boat way and the shit gone up to Edge. Too fuckin' far for a barge with no mantas, me-think.'

'Shut up, Obem.' The other man crouches in front of the Consul. 'Why would you have gold on that old barge, man?'

The Consul raises his face. 'Don't you recognize me? I was Hegemony Consul to Hyperion for years.'

'Hey, don't bey fuckin' with us . . .' begins the man with the knife, but the other interrupts. 'Yeah, man, I remember your face on the camp holie when I bey kid-like. So why you carryin' gold upriver now when the sky bey fallin', Hegemony-man?'

'We were heading for the shelter . . . Chronos Keep,' says the Consul, trying not to sound too eager but at the same time grateful for each second he is allowed to live. *Why?* part of him thinks. *You were tired of living. Ready to die.* Not like this. Not while Sol and Rachel and the others need his help.

'Several of Hyperion's most wealthy citizens,' he says. 'The evacuation authorities wouldn't allow them to transfer the bullion, so I agreed to help them store it in vaults in Chronos Keep, the old castle north of the Bridle Range. For a commission.'

'You bey fuckin' crazy!' sneers the man with the knife. 'Everything north of here bey Shrike country now.'

The Consul lowers his head. There is no need to simulate the fatigue and sense of defeat he projects. 'So we discovered. The android crew deserted last week. Several of the passengers were killed by the Shrike. I was coming downriver by myself.'

'This bey shit,' says the man with the knife. His eyes have that sick, distracted look again.

'Just a second,' says his partner. He slaps the Consul once, hard. 'So where bey this so-called gold ship, old man?'

The Consul tastes blood. 'Upriver. Not *on* the river, but hidden in one of the tributaries.'

'Yeah,' says the knife-man, setting the zero-edge blade flat against the side of the Consul's neck. He will not need to slash in order to sever the Consul's throat, merely rotate the blade. 'I say this bey shit. And I say we bey wastin' time.'

'Just a second,' snaps the other man. 'How far upriver?'

The Consul thinks of the tributaries he has passed in the last few hours. It is late. The sun almost touches the line of a copse of trees to the west. 'Just above Karla Locks,' he says.

'So why you bey flyin' down on that toy-like rather than bargin' it?'

'Trying to get help,' says the Consul. The adrenaline has faded, and now he feels a terminal exhaustion very close to despair. 'There were too many . . . too many bandits along the shore. The barge seemed too risky. The hawking mat was . . . safer.'

The man called Chez laughs. 'Put the knife away, Obem. We bey walkin' up it a bit, hey?'

Obem leaps to his feet. The knife is still in his hand but now the blade – and the anger – are aimed toward his partner. 'Bey you *fucked*, man, hey? Bey your head bey full of *shit* between ears, hey? He bey lyin' to keep from deathwards flyin'.'

Chez neither blinks nor steps back. 'Sure, he bey maybe lyin'. Don't matter, hey? The Locks they bey less'n half-day walk we bey makin' anyway, hey? No boat, no gold, you cut his throat, hey? Only slowwise, ankles-up like. They bey gold, you still gets the job, bladewise, only bey rich man now, hey?'

Obem teeters a second between rage and reason, turns to the side, and swings the ceramic zero-edge blade at a neville tree eight centimeters thick through the trunk. He has time to turn back and crouch in front of the Consul before gravity informs the tree that it has been severed and the neville falls back toward the river's edge with a crash of branches. Obem grabs the Consul's still-damp shirtfront. 'OK, we see what bey there, Hegemony-man. Talk, run, trip, stumble, and I bey slicin' fingers and ears just for practice, hey?'

The Consul staggers to his feet, and the three of them move back into the cover of brush and low trees, the Consul three meters behind Chez and the same distance in front of Obem, trudging back the way he had come, moving away from the city and the ship and any chance of saving Sol and Rachel.

An hour passes. The Consul can think of no clever scheme once the tributaries are reached, the barge not discovered. Several times Chez waves them into silence and hiding, once at the sound of gossamers fluttering in branches, again at a disturbance across the river, but there is no sign of other human beings. No sign of help. The Consul remembers the burned-out buildings along the river, the empty huts and vacant wharves. Fear of the Shrike, fear of being left behind to the Ousters in the evacuation, and months of plundering by rogue elements of the SDF have turned this area into a no-man's-land. The Consul concocts excuses and extensions, then discards them. His only hope is that they will walk close to the Locks where he can make a leap for the deep and rapid water there, try to stay afloat with his hands tied behind him until he is hidden in the maze of small islands below that point.

Except that he is too tired to swim, even if his arms were free. And the weapons the two men carry would target him easily, even if he had a ten-minute start among the snags and isles. The Consul is too tired to be clever, too old to be brave. He thinks about his wife and son, dead these many years now, killed in the bombing of Bressia by men with no more honor than these two creatures. The Consul is only sorry that he has broken his word to help the other pilgrims. Sorry about that . . . and that he will not see how it all comes out.

Obem makes a spitting noise behind him. 'Shit with this, Chez, hey? What say we sit him and slit him and help him talk a bit, hey? Then we go lonewise to the barge, if barge they bey?'

Chez turns, rubs sweat out of his eyes, frowns at the Consul specu-latively, and says, 'Hey, yeah, I think maybe timewise and quietwise you bey right, goyo, but leave it talkable toward the end, hey?'

'Sure,' grins Obem, slinging his weapon and extracting his zero-edge.

'DO NOT MOVE!' booms a voice from above. The Consul drops to his knees and the ex-SDF bandits unsling weapons with practiced swiftness.

There is a rush, a roar, a whipping of branches and dust about them, the Consul looks up in time to see a rippling of the cloud-covered evening sky, lower than the clouds, a sense of *mass* directly above, descending, and then Chez is lifting his fléchette rifle and Obem is targeting his launcher and then all three are falling, pitching over, not like soldiers shot, not like recoil elements in some ballistic equation, but dropping like the tree Obem had felled earlier on.

The Consul lands face first in dust and gravel and lies there unblinking, unable to blink.

Stun weapon he thinks through synapses gone sluggish as old oil. A localized cyclone erupts as something large and invisible lands between the three bodies in the dust and the river's edge. The Consul hears a hatch whine open and the internal tick of repellor turbines dropping below lift-critical. He still cannot blink, much less lift his head, and his vision is limited to several pebbles, a dunescape of sand, a small grass forest, and a single architect ant, huge at this distance, that seems to be taking a sudden interest in the Consul's moist but unblinking eye. The ant turns to hurry the half meter between itself and its moist prize, and the Consul thinks *Hurry* at the unhurried footsteps behind him.

Hands under his arms, grunting, a familiar but strained voice saying, 'Damn, you've put on weight.'

The Consul's heels drag in the dirt, bouncing over the randomly twitching fingers of Chez . . . or perhaps it is Obem . . . the Consul cannot turn his head to see their faces. Nor can he see his rescuer until he is lifted – with a grunted litany of soft curses near his ear – through the starboard blister-hatch of the decamouflaged skimmer, into the long, soft leather of the reclining passenger seat.

Governor-General Theo Lane appears in the Consul's field of vision, boyish-looking but slightly demonic-looking too as the hatch lowers and the red interior lamps light his face. The younger man leans over to secure crashweb snaps across the Consul's chest. 'I'm sorry I had to stun you along with those other two.' Theo sits back, snaps his own web in place, and twitches the omni-controller. The Consul feels the skimmer shiver and then lift off, hovering a second before spinning left like a plate on friction-less bearings. Acceleration pushes the Consul into his seat.

'I didn't have much choice,' says Theo over the soft internal skimmer noises. 'The only weapon these things are allowed to carry are the riot-control stunners, and the easiest way was to drop all three of you at lowest setting and get you out of there fast.' Theo pushes his archaic glasses higher on his nose with a familiar twitch of one finger and turns to grin at the Consul. 'Old mercenary proverb – "Kill 'em all and let God sort 'em out." '

The Consul manages to move his tongue enough to make a sound and to drool a bit on his cheek and the seat leather.

'Relax a minute,' says Theo, returning his attention to the instruments and view outside. 'Two or three minutes and you should be talking all right. I'm staying low, flying slow, so it's about a ten-minute ride back to

Keats.' Theo glances toward his passenger. 'You're lucky, sir. You must have been dehydrated. Those other two wet their pants when they went down. Humane weapon, the stunner, but embarrassing if you don't have a change of pants around.'

The Consul tries to express his opinion of this 'humane' weapon.

'Another couple of minutes, sir,' says Governor-General Theo Lane, reaching over to dab at the Consul's cheek with a handkerchief. 'I should warn you, it's a mite uncomfortable when the stun begins to wear off.'

At that moment, someone inserts several thousand pins and needles in the Consul's body.

'How the hell did you find me?' asks the Consul. They are a few kilometers above the city, still flying over the Hoolie River. He is able to sit up, and his words are more or less intelligible, but the Consul is glad that he has several more minutes before he will have to stand or walk.

'What, sir?'

'I said, how did you find me? How could you possibly know that I had come back down the Hoolie?'

'CEO Gladstone fatlined me. Eyes-only on the old consulate one-time pad.'

'Gladstone?' The Consul is shaking his hands, trying to agitate feeling back into fingers as useful as rubber sausages. 'How the hell could Gladstone possibly know that I was in trouble on the Hoolie River? I left Grandmother Siri's comlog receiver back in the valley so I could call the other pilgrims when I got to the ship. How could Gladstone know?'

'I don't know, sir, but she specified your location and that you were in trouble. She even said you'd been flying a hawking mat that went down.'

The Consul shakes his head. 'This lady has resources we hadn't dreamt of, Theo.'

'Yes, sir.'

The Consul glances at his friend. Theo Lane had been Governor-General of the new Protectorate world of Hyperion for over a local year now, but old habits died hard and the 'sir' came from the seven years Theo had served as Vice-Consul and principal aide during the Consul's years. The last time he had seen the young man – not so young now, the Consul realizes: responsibility has brought lines and wrinkles to that young face – Theo had been furious that the Consul would not take over the governor-generalship. That had been a little more than a week ago. Ages and eons ago.

'By the way,' says the Consul, enunciating each word carefully, 'thank you, Theo.'

The Governor-General nods, apparently lost in thought. He does not ask about what the Consul has seen north of the mountains, nor the fate of the other pilgrims. Beneath them, the Hoolie widens and winds toward the capital of Keats. Far back on either side, low bluffs rise, their granite slabs glowing softly in the evening light. Stands of everblues shimmer in the breeze.

'Theo, how did you possibly have time to come for me yourself? The situation on Hyperion must be pure madness.'

'It is.' Theo ordered the autopilot to take over as he turned to look at the Consul. 'It's a matter of hours . . . perhaps minutes . . . before the Ousters actually invade.'

The Consul blinked. 'Invade? You mean land?'

'Exactly.'

'But the Hegemony fleet—'

'Is in total chaos. They were barely holding their own against the Swarm *before* the Web was invaded.'

'The Web!'

'Entire systems falling. Others threatened. FORCE has ordered the fleet back through their military farcasters, but evidently the ships in-system have found it hard to disengage. No one gives me details, but it's obvious that the Ousters have free rein everywhere except for the defensive perimeter FORCE has put up around the singularity spheres and the portals.'

'The spaceport?' The Consul thinks of his beautiful ship lying as glowing wreckage.

'It hasn't been attacked yet, but FORCE has been pulling its dropships and supply craft out as quickly as they can. They've left a skeleton force of Marines behind.'

'What about the evacuation?'

Theo laughed. It was the most bitter sound the Consul had ever heard from the young man. 'The evacuation will consist of whatever consulate people and Hegemony VIPs can fit on the last dropship out.'

'They've given up trying to save the people of Hyperion?'

'Sir, they can't save their *own* people. Word trickling down through the ambassadors' fatline says that Gladstone has decided to let the threatened Web worlds fall so that FORCE can regroup, have a couple of years to create defenses while the Swarms accrue time-debt.'

'My God,' whispers the Consul. He had worked most of his life to represent the Hegemony, all the while plotting its downfall in order to avenge his grandmother . . . his grandmother's way of life. But now the thought of it actually happening . . .

'What about the Shrike?' he asks suddenly, seeing the low white buildings of Keats a few kilometers ahead. Sunlight touches the hills and river like a final benediction before darkness.

Theo shakes his head. 'There are still reports, but the Ousters have taken over as the primary source of panic.'

'But it's not in the Web? The Shrike, I mean.'

The Governor-General gives the Consul a sharp look. 'In the Web? How could it be in the Web? They still haven't allowed farcaster portals on Hyperion. And there have been no sightings near Keats or Endymion or Port Romance. None of the larger cities.'

The Consul says nothing, but he is thinking: *My God, my betrayal was for nothing. I sold my soul to open the Time Tombs, and the Shrike will not be the cause of the Web's fall . . . The Ousters! They were wise to us all along. My betrayal of the Hegemony was part of their plan!*

'Listen,' Theo says harshly, gripping the Consul's wrist, 'there's a reason Gladstone had me leave everything to find you. She's authorized the release of your ship—'

'Wonderful!' says the Consul. 'I can—'

'Listen! You're not to go back to the Valley of the Time Tombs. Gladstone wants you to avoid the FORCE perimeter and travel in-system until you contact elements of the Swarm.'

'The Swarm? Why would—'

'The CEO wants you to negotiate with them. They *know* you. Somehow she's managed to let them know that you're coming. She thinks that they'll let you . . . that they won't destroy your ship. But she hasn't received confirmation of that. It'll be risky.'

The Consul sits back in the leather seat. He feels as if he has been hit by the neural stunner again. 'Negotiate? What the hell would I have to negotiate?'

'Gladstone said that she would contact you via your ship's fatline once you're off Hyperion. This has to be done quickly. Today. Before all the first-wave worlds fall to the Swarms.'

The Consul hears *first-wave worlds* but does not ask if his beloved Maui-Covenant is amongst them. Perhaps, he thinks, it would be best if it were. He says, 'No, I'm going back to the valley.'

Theo adjusts his glasses. 'She won't allow that, sir.'

'Oh?' The Consul smiles. 'How is she going to stop me? Shoot down my ship?'

'I don't know, but she said that she wouldn't allow it.' Theo sounds sincerely worried. 'The FORCE fleet *does* have picket ships and torchships in orbit, sir. To escort the last dropships.'

'Well,' says the Consul, still smiling, 'let them try to shoot me down. Manned ships haven't been able to land near the Valley of the Time Tombs for two centuries anyway: ships land perfectly, but their crews disappear. Before they slag me, I'll be hanging on the Shrike's tree.' The Consul closes his eyes a moment and imagines the ship landing, empty, on the plain above the valley. He imagines Sol, Duré, and the others – miraculously returned – running for shelter in the ship, using its surgery to save Het Masteen and Brawne Lamia, its cryogenic fugue and sleep chambers to save little Rachel.

'My God,' whispers Theo and the shocked tone slams the Consul out of his reverie.

They have come around the final turn in the river above the city. The bluffs rise higher here, culminating to the south in the carved-mountain likeness of Sad King Billy. The sun is just setting, igniting low clouds and buildings high on the eastern bluffs.

Above the city, a battle is raging. Lasers lance into and through the clouds, ships dodge like gnats and burn like moths too close to a flame, while parafoils and the blur of suspension fields drift beneath the cloud ceiling. The city of Keats is being attacked. The Ousters have come to Hyperion.

'Oh, sweet fuck,' Theo whispers reverently.

Along the forested ridge northwest of the city, a brief spout of flame and a flicker of contrail mark a shoulder-launched rocket coming directly toward the Hegemony skimmer.

'Hang on!' snaps Theo. He takes manual control, throws switches, banks the skimmer steeply to starboard, trying to turn inside the small rocket's own turning radius.

An explosion aft throws the Consul into the crashweb and blurs his vision for a moment. When he can focus again, the cabin is filled with smoke, red warning lights pulse through the gloom, and the skimmer warns of systems failure in a dozen urgent voices. Theo is slumped grimly over the omni-controller.

'Hang on,' he says again, needlessly. The skimmer slews sickeningly, finds a grip in the air, and then loses it as they tumble and sideslip toward the burning city.

THIRTY-SIX

I blinked and opened my eyes, disoriented for a second as I looked around the immense, dark space of St Peter's Basilica, Pacem. Monsignor Edouard and Father Paul Duré leaned forward in the dim candlelight, their expressions intense.

'How long was I . . . asleep?' I felt as if only seconds had elapsed, the dream a shimmer of images one has in the instants between lying peacefully and full sleep.

'Ten minutes,' said the Monsignor. 'Can you tell us what you saw?'

I saw no reason not to. When I was finished describing the images, Monsignor Edouard crossed himself. '*Mon Dieu*, the ambassador from the TechnoCore urges Gladstone to send people to those . . . tunnels.'

Duré touched my shoulder. 'After I talk to the True Voice of the World-tree on God's Grove, I will join you on TC². We have to tell Gladstone the folly of such a choice.'

I nodded. All thoughts of my going to God's Grove with Duré or to Hyperion itself had fled. 'I agree. We should depart at once. Is your . . . can the Pope's Door take me to Tau Ceti Center?'

The Monsignor stood, nodded, stretched. Suddenly I realized that he was a very old man, untouched by Poulsen treatments. 'It has a priority access,' he said. He turned to Duré. 'Paul, you know that I would accompany you if I could. The funeral of His Holiness, the election of a new Holy Father . . .' Monsignor Edouard made a small, rueful sound. 'Odd how the daily imperatives persist even in the face of collective disaster. Pacem itself has fewer than ten standard days until the barbarians arrive.'

Duré's high forehead gleamed in the candlelight. 'The business of the Church is something beyond a mere daily imperative, my friend. I will make my visit on the Templar world brief, then join M. Severn in his effort of convincing the CEO not to listen to the Core. Then I will return, Edouard, and we will try to make some sense of this confused heresy.'

I followed the two of them out of the basilica, through a side door that led to a passageway behind the tall colonnades, left across an open courtyard – the rain had stopped and the air smelled fresh – down a stairway, and through a narrow tunnel into the papal apartments. Members of the Swiss Guard snapped to attention as we came into the apartments' anteroom; the tall men were dressed in armor and yellow-and-blue striped pantaloons, although their ceremonial halberds were also FORCE-quality energy weapons. One stepped forward and spoke softly to the Monsignor.

'Someone has just arrived at the main terminex to see you, M. Severn.'

'Me?' I had been listening to other voices in other rooms, the melodious rise and fall of oft-repeated prayers. I assumed it had to do with preparation for the Pope's burial.

'Yes, an M. Hunt. He says that it is urgent.'

'Another minute and I would have seen him at Government House,' I said. 'Why not have him join us here?'

Monsignor Edouard nodded and spoke softly to the Swiss Guard, who whispered into an ornamental crest on his antique armor.

The so-called Pope's Door – a small farcaster portal surrounded by intricate gold carvings of seraphim and cherubim, topped with a five-station bas-relief illustrating Adam and Eve's fall from grace and expulsion from the garden – stood in the center of a well-guarded room just off the Pope's private apartments. We waited there, our reflections wan and tired-looking in the mirrors on each wall.

Leigh Hunt was escorted in by the priest who had led me to the basilica.

'Severn!' cried Gladstone's favorite advisor. 'The CEO needs you at once.'

'I was just going there,' I said. 'It would be a criminal mistake if Gladstone allowed the Core to build and use the death device.'

Hunt blinked – an almost comical reaction on that basset-hound countenance. 'Do you know *everything* that happens, Severn?'

I had to laugh. 'A young child sitting unattended in a holo pit sees much and understands very little. Still, he has the advantage of being able to change channels and turn the thing off when he grows tired of it.' Hunt knew Monsignor Edouard from various state functions, and I introduced Father Paul Duré of the Society of Jesus.

'Duré?' managed Hunt, his jaw almost hanging slack. It was the first time that I had seen the advisor at a loss for words, and I rather enjoyed the sight.

'We'll explain later,' I said and shook the priest's hand. 'Good luck on God's Grove, Duré. Don't be too long.'

'An hour,' promised the Jesuit. 'No longer. There is merely one piece of the puzzle I must find before speaking to the CEO. Please explain to her about the horror of the labyrinth . . . I will give her my own testimony later.'

'It's possible that she'll be too busy to see me before you get there anyway,' I said. 'But I'll do my best to play John the Baptist for you.'

Duré smiled. 'Just don't lose your head, my friend.' He nodded, tapped in a transfer code on the archaic diskey panel, and disappeared through the portal.

I bid farewell to Monsignor Edouard. 'We will get all this settled before the Ouster wave gets this far.'

The old priest raised a hand and blessed me. 'Go with God, young man. I feel that dark times await us all but that you will be especially burdened.'

I shook my head. 'I'm just an observer, Monsignor. I wait and watch and dream. Little burden there.'

'Wait and watch and dream later,' Leigh Hunt said sharply. 'Her Nibs wants you within reach *now*, and I have a meeting to get back to.'

I looked at the little man. 'How did you find me?' I asked needlessly. Farcasters were operated by the Core, and the Core worked with the Hegemony authorities.

'The override card she gave you also makes it easier to keep track of your travels,' Hunt said, his impatience audible. 'Right now we have an obligation to be where things are happening.'

'Very well.' I nodded at the Monsignor and his aide, beckoned to Hunt, and tapped in the three-digit code for Tau Ceti Center, added two digits for the continent, three more for Government House, and added the final two numbers for the private terminex there. The farcaster's hum went up a notch on the scale, its opaque surface seemed to shimmer with expectancy.

I stepped through first, stepped aside to give Hunt room as he followed.

We are not in the central Government House terminex. As far as I can tell, we are nowhere near Government House. A second later, my senses total the input of sunlight, sky color, gravity, distance to horizon, smells, and *feel* of things, and decide that we aren't on Tau Ceti Center.

I would have jumped back through the portal then, but the Pope's Door is small. Hunt is coming through – leg, arm, shoulder, chest, head, second leg appearing – so I grab his wrist, pull him through roughly, say 'Something's wrong!' and try to step back through, but too late, the frameless portal on this side shimmers, dilates to a circle the size of my fist, and is gone.

'Where the hell are we?' demands Hunt.

I look around and think, *Good question*. We are in the country, on a hilltop. A road underfoot winds through vineyards, goes down a long hill through a wooded vale, and disappears around another hill a mile or two distant. It is very warm, and the air hums with the sounds of insects, but nothing larger than a bird moves in this vast panorama. Between bluffs to our right, a blue smear of water is visible – either an ocean or sea. High cirrus ripples overhead; the sun is just past the zenith. I see no houses, no technology more complicated than the vineyard rows and the stone-and-mud road underfoot. More importantly, the constant background buzz of the datasphere is gone. It is somewhat like suddenly hearing the absence of a sound one has been immersed in since infancy; it is startling, heart-stopping, confusing, and a bit terrifying.

Hunt staggers, claps his ears as if it is true sound he is missing, taps at his comlog. 'Goddamn,' he mutters. 'Goddamn. My implant's malfunctioning. Comlog's out.'

'No,' I say, 'I believe we're beyond the datasphere.' But even as I say this, I hear a deeper, softer hum – something far greater and far less accessible than the datasphere. The megasphere? *The music of the spheres*, I think, and smile.

'What the hell are you grinning about, Severn? Did you do this on purpose?'

'No. I gave the proper codes for Government House.' The total absence of panic in my voice is a kind of panic itself.

'What is it then? That goddamned Pope's Door? Did it do this? Some malf or trick?'

'No, I think not. The door didn't malfunction, Hunt. It brought us just where the TechnoCore wants us.'

'The Core?' What little color left in that basset countenance quickly drains away as the CEO's aide realizes who controls the farcaster. Who controls *all* farcasters. 'My God. My God.' Hunt staggers to the side of the road and sits in the tall grass there. His suede executive suit and soft black shoes look out of place here.

'Where are we?' he asks again.

I take a deep breath. The air smells of fresh-turned soil, newly mown grass, road dust, and the sharp tinge of the sea. 'My guess is that we're on Earth, Hunt.'

'Earth.' The little man is staring straight ahead, focusing on nothing. 'Earth. Not New Earth. Not Terra. Not Earth Two. Not . . .'

'No,' I say. 'Earth. Old Earth. Or its duplicate.'

'Its duplicate.'

I go over and sit beside him. I pull a strand of grass and strip the lower part of its outer sheath. The grass tastes tart and familiar. 'You remember my report to Gladstone on the Hyperion pilgrims' stories? Brawne Lamia's tale? She and my cybrid counterpart . . . the first Keats retrieval persona . . . traveled to what they thought was an Old Earth duplicate. In the Hercules Cluster, if I remember correctly.'

Hunt glances up as if he can judge what I am saying by checking constellations. The blue above is graying slightly as the high cirrus spreads across the dome of sky. 'Hercules Cluster,' he whispers.

'Why the TechnoCore built a duplicate, or what they're doing with it now, Brawne didn't learn,' I say. 'Either the first Keats cybrid didn't know, or he wasn't saying.'

'Wasn't saying,' nods Hunt. He shakes his head. 'All right, how the hell do we get *out* of here? Gladstone needs me. She can't . . . there are dozens of vital decisions to be made in the next few hours.' He jumps to his feet, runs to the center of the road, a study in purposeful energy.

I chew on the stalk of grass. 'My guess is that we don't get out of here.'

Hunt comes at me as if he is going to assault me then and there. 'Are you *insane*! No way out? That's nuts. Why would the Core do that?' He pauses, looks down at me. 'They don't want you talking to her. You know something that the Core can't risk her learning.'

'Perhaps.'

'Leave *him*, let *me* go back!' he screams at the sky.

No one answers. Far out across the vineyard, a large black bird takes flight. I think it is a crow; I remember the name of the extinct species as if from a dream.

After a moment, Hunt gives up on addressing the sky and paces back and forth on the stone road. 'Come on. Maybe there's a terminex wherever this thing goes.'

'Perhaps,' I say, breaking off the stalk of grass to get at the sweet, dry upper half. 'But which way?'

Hunt turns, looks at the road disappearing around hills in both directions, turns again. 'We came through the portal looking . . . this way.' He points. The road goes downhill into a narrow wood.

'How far?' I ask.

'Goddammit, does it matter?' he barks. 'We have to get *somewhere*!'

I resist the impulse to smile. 'All right.' I stand and brush off my trousers, feeling the fierce sunlight on my forehead and face. After the incense-laden darkness of the basilica, it is a shock. The air is very hot, and my clothing is already damp with sweat.

Hunt starts walking vigorously down the hill, his fists clenched, his doleful expression ameliorated for once by a stronger expression – sheer resolve.

Walking slowly, in no hurry, still chewing on my stalk of sweet grass, eyes half-closed with weariness, I follow him.

Colonel Fedmahn Kassad screamed and attacked the Shrike. The surreal, out-of-time landscape – a minimalist stage designer's version of the Valley of the Time Tombs, molded in plastic and set in a gel of viscous air – seemed to vibrate to the violence of Kassad's rush.

For an instant there had been a mirror-image scattering of Shrikes – Shrikes throughout the valley, spread across the barren plain – but with Kassad's shout these resolved themselves to the single monster, and now it moved, four arms unfolding and extending, curving to greet the Colonel's rush with a hearty hug of blades and thorns.

Kassad did not know if the energy skinsuit he wore, Moneta's gift, would protect him or serve him well in combat. It had years before when he and Moneta had attacked two dropships' worth of Ouster commandos, but time had been on their side then; the Shrike had frozen and unfrozen the flow of moments like a bored observer playing with a holopit remote control. Now they were outside time, and there was the enemy, not some terrible patron. Kassad shouted and put his head down and attacked, no longer aware of Moneta watching, nor of the impossible tree of thorns rising into the clouds with its terrible, impaled audience, nor even aware of himself except as a fighting tool, an instrument of revenge.

The Shrike did not disappear in its usual manner, did not cease being *there* to suddenly be *here*. Instead, it crouched and opened its arms wider. Its fingerblades caught the light of the violent sky. The Shrike's metal teeth glistened in what might have been a smile.

Kassad was angry; he was not insane. Rather than rush into that embrace of death, he threw himself aside at the last instant, rolling on arm and shoulder, and kicking out at the monster's lower leg, below the cluster of thornblades at the knee joint, above a similar array on the ankle. *If he could get it down . . .*

It was like kicking at a pipe embedded in half a klick of concrete. The blow would have broken Kassad's own leg if the skinsuit had not acted as armor and shock absorber.

The Shrike moved, quickly but not impossibly; the two right arms swinging up and down and around in a blur, ten fingerblades carving soil and stone in surgical furrows, arm thorns sending sparks flying as the hands continued upward, slicing air with an audible rush. Kassad was out of range, continuing his roll, coming to his feet again, crouching, his own arms tensed, palms flat, energy-suited fingers rigid and extended.

Single combat, thought Fedmahn Kassad. *The most honorable sacrament in the New Bushido.*

The Shrike feinted with its right arms again, swung the lower left arm around and up with a sweeping blow violent enough to shatter Kassad's ribs and scoop his heart out.

Kassad blocked the right-arm feint with his left forearm, feeling the skinsuit flex and batter bone as the steel-and-axe force of the Shrike's blow struck home. The left-arm killing blow he stopped with his right hand on the monster's wrist, just above the corsage of curved spikes there. Incredibly, he slowed the blow's momentum enough that scalpel-sharp fingerblades were now scraping against his skinsuit field rather than splintering ribs.

Kassad was almost lifted off the ground with the effort of restraining that rising claw; only the downward thrust of the Shrike's first feint kept the Colonel from flying backward. Sweat poured freely under the skinsuit, muscles flexed and ached and threatened to rip in that interminable twenty seconds of struggle before the Shrike brought its fourth arm into play, slashing downward at Kassad's straining leg.

Kassad screamed as the skinsuit field ripped, flesh tore, and at least one fingerblade sliced close to bone. He kicked out with his other leg, released the thing's wrist, and rolled frantically away.

The Shrike swung twice, the second blow whistling millimeters from Kassad's moving ear, but then jumped back itself, crouching, moving to its right.

Kassad got to his left knee, almost fell, then staggered to his feet, hopping slightly to keep his balance. The pain roared in his ears and filled the universe with red light, but even as he grimaced and staggered, close to fainting from the shock of it, he could feel the skinsuit closing on the wound – serving as both tourniquet and compress. He could feel the blood on his lower leg, but it was no longer flowing freely, and the pain was manageable, almost as if the skinsuit carried medpak injectors like his FORCE battle armor.

The Shrike rushed him.

Kassad kicked once, twice, aiming for and finding the smooth bit of chrome carapace beneath the chest spike. It was like kicking the hull of a torchship, but the Shrike seemed to pause, stagger, step back.

Kassad stepped forward, planted his weight, struck twice where the creature's heart should be with a closed-fist blow that would have shattered tempered ceramic, ignored the pain from his fist, swiveled, and slammed a straight-armed, open-palmed blow into the creature's muzzle, just above the teeth. Any human being would have heard the sound of his nose being broken and felt the explosion of bone and cartilage being driven into his brain.

The Shrike snapped at Kassad's wrist, missed, swung four hands at Kassad's head and shoulders.

Panting, pouring sweat and blood under his quicksilver armor, Kassad spun to his right once, twice, and came around with a killing blow to the back of the creature's short neck. The noise of the impact echoed in the frozen valley like the sound of an axe thrown from miles on high into the heart of a metal redwood.

The Shrike tumbled forward, rolled on to its back like some steel crustacean.

It had gone down!

Kassad stepped forward, still crouched, still cautious, but not cautious enough as the Shrike's armored foot, claw, whatever the hell it was, caught the back of Kassad's ankle and half sliced, half kicked him off his feet.

Colonel Kassad felt the pain, knew that his Achilles' tendon had been severed, tried to roll away, but the creature was throwing itself up and sideways on him, spikes and thorns and blades coming at Kassad's ribs and face and eyes. Grimacing with the pain, arching in a vain attempt to throw the monster off, Kassad blocked some blows, saved his eyes, and felt other blades slam home in his upper arms, chest, and belly.

The Shrike hovered closer and opened its mouth. Kassad stared up into row upon row of steel teeth set in a metal lamprey's hollow orifice of a mouth. Red eyes filled his sight through vision already tinged with blood.

Kassad got the base of his palm under the Shrike's jaw and tried to find leverage. It was like trying to lift a mountain of sharp scrap with no fulcrum. The Shrike's fingerblades continued to tear at Kassad's flesh. The thing opened its mouth and tilted its head until teeth filled Kassad's field of vision from ear to ear. The monster had no breath, but the heat from its interior stank of sulfur and heated iron filings. Kassad had no defense left; when the thing snapped its jaws shut, it would take the flesh and skin of Kassad's face off to the bone.

Suddenly Moneta was there, shouting in that place where sound did not carry, grabbing the Shrike by its ruby-faceted eyes, skinsuited fingers arching like talons, her boot planted firmly on its carapace below the back spike, pulling, pulling.

The Shrike's arms snapped backward, as double-jointed as some nightmare crab, fingerblades raked Moneta and she fell away, but not before

Kassad rolled, scrambled, felt the pain but ignored it, and leaped to his feet, dragging Moneta with him as he retreated across the sand and frozen rock.

For a second, their skinsuits merged as it had when they were making love, and Kassad felt her flesh next to his, felt their blood and sweat mingling and heard the joined poundings of their hearts.

Kill it Moneta whispered urgently, pain audible even through that sub-vocal medium.

I'm trying. I'm trying.

The Shrike was on its feet, three meters of chrome and blades and other people's pain. It showed no damage. Someone's blood ran in narrow rivulets down its wrists and carapace. Its mindless grin seemed wider than before.

Kassad separated his skinsuit from Moneta's, lowered her gently to a boulder although he sensed that he had been hurt worse than she. This was not her fight. Not yet.

He moved between his love and the Shrike.

Kassad hesitated, hearing a faint but rising susurration as if from a rising surf on an invisible shore. He glanced up, never fully removing his gaze from the slowly advancing Shrike, and realized that it was a shouting from the thorn tree far behind the monster. The crucified people there – small dabs of color hanging from the metal thorns and cold branches – were making some noise other than the subliminal moans of pain Kassad had heard earlier. They were cheering.

Kassad returned his attention to the Shrike as the thing began to circle again. Kassad felt the pain and weakness in his almost-severed heel – his right foot was useless, unable to bear weight – and he half hopped, half swiveled with one hand on the boulder to keep his body between the Shrike and Moneta.

The distant cheering seemed to stop as if in a gasp.

The Shrike ceased being *there* and came into existence *here*, next to Kassad, on top of Kassad, its arms already around him in a terminal hug, thorns and blades already impinging. The Shrike's eyes blazed with light. Its jaws opened again.

Kassad shouted in pure rage and defiance and struck at it.

Father Paul Duré stepped through the Pope's Door to God's Grove without incident. From the incense-laden dimness of the papal apartments, he suddenly found himself in rich sunlight with a lemon sky above and green leaves all around.

The Templars were waiting as he stepped down from the private farcaster portal. Duré could see the edge of the weirwood platform five meters to his right and beyond it, nothing – or, rather, everything, as the treetop world of God's Grove stretched great distances to the horizon, the rooftop of leaves shimmering and moving like a living ocean. Duré knew that he was high on the Worldtree, the greatest and holiest of all the trees the Templars held sacred.

The Templars greeting him were important in the complicated hierarchy of the Brotherhood of the Muir, but served as mere guides now, leading him from the portal platform to a vine-strewn elevator which rose through upper levels and terraces where few non-Templars had ever ascended, and then out again and up along a staircase bound by a railing of the finest muirwood, spiraling skyward around a trunk that narrowed from its two-hundred-meter base to less than eight meters across here near its top. The weirwood platform was exquisitely carved; its railings showed a delicate tracery of handcarved vines, posts and balusters boasted the faces of gnomes, wood sprites, faeries, and other spirits, and the table and chairs which Duré now approached were carved from the same piece of wood as the circular platform itself.

Two men awaited him. The first was the one Duré expected – True Voice of the Worldtree, High Priest of the Muir, Spokesman of the Templar Brotherhood Sek Hardeen. The second man was a surprise. Duré noted the red robe – a red the color of arterial blood – with black ermine trim, the heavy Lusian body covered by that robe, the face all jowls and fat bisected by a formidable beak of a nose, two tiny eyes lost above fat cheeks, two pudgy hands with a black or red ring on each finger. Duré knew that he was looking at the Bishop of the Church of the Final Atonement – the high priest of the Shrike Cult.

The Templar rose to his almost two-meter height and offered his hand. 'Father Duré, we are most pleased that you could join us.'

Duré shook hands, thinking as he did so how much like a root the Templar's hand was, with its long, tapering, yellowish-brown fingers. The True Voice of the Worldtree wore the same hooded robe that Het Masteen had worn, its rough brown and green threads in sharp contrast to the brilliance of the Bishop's garb.

'Thank you for seeing me on such short notice, M. Hardeen,' said Duré. The True Voice was the spiritual leader of millions of the followers of the Muir, but Duré knew that Templars disliked titles or honorifics in conversation. Duré nodded in the direction of the Bishop. 'Your Excellency, I had no idea that I would have the honor of being in your presence.'

The Shrike Cult Bishop nodded almost imperceptibly. 'I was visiting. M. Hardeen suggested that it might be of some small benefit if I attended this meeting. I am pleased to meet you, Father Duré. We have heard much about you in the past few years.'

The Templar gestured toward a seat across the muirwood table from the two of them, and Duré sat, folding his hands on the polished tabletop, thinking furiously even as he pretended to inspect the beautiful grain in the wood. Half the security forces in the Web were searching for the Shrike Cult Bishop. His presence suggested complications far beyond those the Jesuit had been prepared to deal with.

'Interesting, is it not,' said the Bishop, 'that three of humankind's most profound religions are represented here today?'

'Yes,' said Duré. 'Profound, but hardly representational of the beliefs of the majority. Out of almost a hundred and fifty billion souls, the Catholic Church claims fewer than a million. The Shr— ah . . . the Church of the Final Atonement perhaps five to ten million. And how many Templars are there, M. Hardeen?'

'Twenty-three million,' the Templar said softly. 'Many others support our ecological causes and might even wish to join, but the Brotherhood is not open to outsiders.'

The Bishop rubbed one of his chins. His skin was very pale, and he squinted as if he were not used to daylight. 'The Zen Gnostics claim forty billion followers,' he rumbled. 'But what kind of religion is that, eh? No churches. No priests. No holy books. No concept of sin.'

Duré smiled. 'It seems to be the belief most attuned to the times. And has been for many generations now.'

'Bah!' The Bishop slapped his hand down on the table, and Duré winced as he heard the metal of the rings strike muirwood.

'How is it that you know who I am?' asked Paul Duré.

The Templar lifted his head just enough that Duré could see sunlight on his nose, cheeks, and the long line of chin within the shadows of the cowl. He did not speak.

'We chose you,' growled the Bishop. 'You and the other pilgrims.'

'You being the Shrike Church?' said Duré.

The Bishop frowned at the phrase but nodded without speaking.

'Why the riots?' asked Duré. 'Why the disturbances now that the Hegemony is threatened?'

When the Bishop rubbed his chin, red and black stones glinted in the evening light. Beyond him, a million leaves rustled in a breeze which brought the scent of rain-moistened vegetation. 'The Final Days are here, priest. The prophecies given to us by the Avatar centuries ago are unfolding before our eyes. What you call riots are the first death throes of a society which deserves to die. The Days of Atonement are upon us and the Lord of Pain soon will walk among us.'

'The Lord of Pain,' repeated Duré. 'The Shrike.'

The Templar made an ameliorating gesture with one hand, as if he were trying to take some of the edge off the Bishop's statement. 'Father Duré, we are aware of your miraculous rebirth.'

'Not a miracle,' said Duré. 'The whim of a parasite called a cruciform.'

Again the gesture with the long, yellow-brown fingers. 'However you see it, Father, the Brotherhood rejoices that you are with us once again. Please go ahead with the query you mentioned when you called earlier.'

Duré rubbed his palms against the wood of the chair, glanced at the Bishop sitting across from him in all of his red-and-black bulk. 'Your groups have been working together for some time, haven't they?' said Duré. 'The Templar Brotherhood and the Shrike Church.'

'Church of the Final Atonement,' the Bishop said in a bass growl.

Duré nodded. 'Why? What brings you together in this?'

The True Voice of the Worldtree leaned forward so that shadow filled his cowl once again. 'You must see, Father, that the prophecies of the Church of the Final Atonement touch upon our mission from the Muir. Only these prophecies have held the key to what punishment must befall humankind for killing its own world.'

'Humankind alone didn't destroy Old Earth,' said Duré, 'It was a computer error in the Kiev Team's attempt to create a mini-black hole.'

The Templar shook his head. 'It was human arrogance,' he said softly. 'The same arrogance which has caused our race to destroy all species that might even hope to evolve to intelligence someday. The Seneschai Aluit on Hebron, the zeplens of Whirl, the marsh centaurs of Garden and the great apes of Old Earth . . .'

'Yes,' said Duré. 'Mistakes have been made. But that shouldn't sentence humankind to death, should it?'

'The sentence has been handed down by a Power far greater than ourselves,' rumbled the Bishop. 'The prophecies are precise and explicit. The Day of Final Atonement must come. All who have inherited the Sins of Adam and Kiev must suffer the consequences of murdering their homeworld, of extinguishing other species. The Lord of Pain has been freed from the bonds of time to render this final judgement. There is no escaping his wrath. There is no avoiding Atonement. A Power far greater than us has said this.'

'It is true,' said Sek Hardeen. 'The prophecies have come to us . . . spoken to the True Voices over the generations . . . humankind is doomed, but with their doom will come a new flowering for pristine environments in all parts of what is now the Hegemony.'

Trained in Jesuit logic, devoted to the evolutionary theology of Teilhard de Chardin, Father Paul Duré was nonetheless tempted to say, *But who the hell cares if the flowers bloom if no one is around to see them, to smell them?* Instead, he said, 'Have you considered that these prophecies were not divine revelations, but merely manipulations from some secular power?'

The Templar sat back as if slapped, but the Bishop leaned forward and curled two Lusian fists which could have crushed Duré's skull with a single blow. 'Heresy! Whoever dares deny the truth of the revelations must die!'

'What power could do this?' managed the True Voice of the Worldtree. 'What power other than the Muir's Absolute could enter our minds and hearts?'

Duré gestured toward the sky. 'Every world in the Web has been joined through the TechnoCore's datasphere for generations. Most people of influence carry comlog extension implants for ease of accessing . . . do you not, M. Hardeen?'

The Templar said nothing, but Duré saw the small twitch of fingers, as if the man were going to pat his chest and upper arm where the microimplants had lain for decades.

'The TechnoCore has created a transcendent . . . Intelligence,' continued Duré. 'It taps incredible amounts of energy, is able to move backward and forward in time, and is not motivated by human concerns. One of the goals of a sizeable percentage of the Core personalities was to eliminate human-kind . . . indeed, the Big Mistake of the Kiev Team may have been deliberately executed by the AIs involved in that experiment. What you hear as prophecies may be the voice of this *deus ex machina* whispering through the datasphere. The Shrike may be here not to make humankind atone for its sins, but merely to slaughter human men, women, and children for this machine personality's own goals.'

The Bishop's heavy face was as red as his robe. His fists pummeled the table, and he struggled to his feet. The Templar laid a hand on the Bishop's arm and restrained him, somehow pulled him back to his seat. 'Where have you heard this idea?' Sek Hardeen asked Duré.

'From those on the pilgrimage who have access to the Core. And from . . . others.'

The Bishop shook a fist in Duré's direction. 'But you yourself have been touched by the Avatar . . . not once, but *twice*! He has granted you a form of immortality so you can see what he has in store for the Chosen People . . . those who prepare Atonement before the Final Days are upon us!'

'The Shrike gave me pain,' said Duré. 'Pain and suffering beyond imagination. I *have* met the thing twice, and I know in my heart that it is neither divine nor diabolical, but merely some organic machine from a terrible future.'

'Bah!' The Bishop made a dismissive gesture, folded his arms, and stared out over the low balcony at nothing.

The Templar appeared shaken. After a moment, he raised his head and said softly, 'You had a question for me?'

Duré took a breath. 'I did. And sad news, I'm afraid. True Voice of the Tree Het Masteen is dead.'

'We know,' said the Templar.

Duré was surprised. He could not imagine how they could receive that information. But it did not matter now. 'What I need to know, is why did he go on the pilgrimage? What was the mission that he did not live to see completed? Each of us told our . . . our story. Het Masteen did not. Yet somehow I feel that his fate held the key to many mysteries.'

The Bishop looked back at Duré and sneered. 'We need tell you nothing, priest of a dead religion.'

Sek Hardeen sat silent a long moment before responding. 'M. Masteen volunteered to be the one to carry the Word of the Muir to Hyperion. The prophecy has lain in the roots of our belief for centuries that when the troubled times came, a True Voice of the Tree would be called upon to take a treeship to the Holy World, to see it destroyed there, and then to have it reborn carrying the message of Atonement and the Muir.'

'So Het Masteen knew that the treeship *Yggdrasill* would be destroyed in orbit?'

'Yes. It was foretold.'

'And he and the single energy-binder erg from the ship were to fly a new treeship?'

'Yes,' said the Templar almost inaudibly. 'A Tree of Atonement which the Avatar would provide.'

Duré sat back, nodded. 'A Tree of Atonement. The thorn tree. Het Masteen was psychically injured when the *Yggdrasill* was destroyed. Then he was taken to the Valley of the Time Tombs and shown the Shrike's thorn tree. But he was not ready or able to do it. The thorn tree is a structure of death, of suffering, of pain . . . Het Masteen was not prepared to captain it. Or perhaps he refused. In any case, he fled. And died. I thought as much . . . but I had no idea what fate the Shrike had offered him.'

'What are you talking about?' snapped the Bishop. 'The Tree of Atonement is described in the prophecies. It will accompany the Avatar in his final harvest. Masteen would have been prepared and honored to captain it through space and time.'

Paul Duré shook his head.

'We have answered your question?' asked M. Hardeen.

'Yes.'

'Then you must answer ours,' said the Bishop. 'What has happened to the Mother?'

'What mother?'

'The Mother of Our Salvation. The Bride of Atonement. The one you called Brawne Lamia.'

Duré thought back, trying to remember the Consul's taped summaries of the tales the pilgrims had told on the way to Hyperion. Brawne had been pregnant with the first Keats cybrid's child. The Shrike Temple on Lusus had saved her from the mob, included her in the pilgrimage. She had said something in her story about the Shrike Cultists treating her with reverence. Duré tried to fit all this into the confused mosaic of what he had already learned. He could not. He was too tired . . . and, he thought, too stupid after this so-called resurrection. He was not and never would be the intellectual Paul Duré once had been.

'Brawne was unconscious,' he said. 'Evidently taken by the Shrike and attached to some . . . *thing*. Some cable. Her mental state was the equivalent of brain death, but the fetus was alive and healthy.'

'And the persona she carried?' asked the Bishop, his voice tense.

Duré remembered what Severn had told him about the death of that persona in the megasphere. Evidently these two did not know about the second Keats persona – the Severn personality that at this moment was warning Gladstone about the dangers of the Core proposal. Duré shook his head. He was very tired. 'I don't know about the persona she carried in the Schrön loop,' he said. 'The cable . . . the thing the Shrike attached to her . . . seemed to plug into the neural socket like a cortical shunt.'

The Bishop nodded, evidently satisfied. 'The prophecies proceed apace. You have served your purpose as messenger, Duré. I must leave now.' The big man stood, nodded toward the True Voice of the Worldtree, and swept across the platform and down the stairs toward the elevator and terminex.

Duré sat across from the Templar in silence for several minutes. The sound of leaves blowing and the gentle rocking of the treetop platform was marvelously lulling, inviting the Jesuit to doze off. Above them the sky was fading through delicate saffron shades as the world of God's Grove turned into twilight.

'Your statement about a *deus ex machina* misleading us for generations through false prophecies was a terrible heresy,' the Templar said at last.

'Yes. But terrible heresies have proven to be grim truths many times before in the longer history of my Church, Sek Hardeen.'

'If you were a Templar, I could have you put to death,' the hooded figure said softly.

Duré sighed. At his age, in his situation, and as tired as he was, the thought of death created no fear in his heart. He stood and bowed slightly. 'I need to go, Sek Hardeen. I apologize if anything I said offended you. It is a confused and confusing time.' *The best lack all conviction*, he thought, *while the worst are full of passionate intensity*.

Duré turned and walked to the edge of the platform. And stopped.

The staircase was gone. Thirty vertical meters and fifteen horizontal meters of air separated him from the next lower platform where the elevator waited. The Worldtree dropped away a kilometer or more into leafy depths beneath him. Duré and the True Voice of that Tree were isolated here on the highest platform. Duré walked to a nearby railing, raised his suddenly sweaty face to the evening breeze, and noticed the first of the stars emerging from the ultramarine sky. 'What's going on, Sek Hardeen?'

The robed and cowled figure at the table was wrapped in darkness. 'In eighteen minutes, standard, the world of Heaven's Gate will fall to the Ousters. Our prophecies say that it will be destroyed. Certainly its farcaster will, and its fatline transmitters, and to all intents and purposes, that world will have ceased to exist. Precisely one standard hour later, the skies of God's Grove will be alight from the fusion fires of Ouster warships. Our prophecies say that all of the Brotherhood who remain – and anyone else, although all Hegemony citizens have long since been evacuated by farcaster – will perish.'

Duré walked slowly back to the table. 'It's imperative that I 'cast to Tau Ceti Center,' he said. 'Severn . . . someone is waiting for me. I have to speak to CEO Gladstone.'

'No,' said True Voice of the Worldtree Sek Hardeen. 'We will wait. We will see if the prophecies are correct.'

The Jesuit clenched his fists in frustration, fighting the surge of violent emotion that made him want to strike the robed figure. Duré closed his eyes and said two Hail Marys. It didn't help.

'Please,' he said. 'The prophecies will be confirmed or denied whether I am here or not. And then it will be too late. The FORCE torchships will blow the singularity sphere, and the farcaster will be gone. We'll be cut off from the Web for years. Billions of lives may depend upon my immediate return to Tau Ceti Center.'

The Templar folded his arms so that his long-fingered hands disappeared in the folds of his robe. 'We will wait,' he said. 'All things predicted will come to pass. In minutes, the Lord of Pain will be loosed on those in the Web. I do not believe in the Bishop's faith that those who have sought Atonement will be spared. We are better off here, Father Duré, where the end will be swift and painless.'

Duré searched his tired mind for something decisive to say, to do. Nothing occurred to him. He sat at the table and stared at the cowled and silent figure across from him. Above them, the stars emerged in their fiery multitudes. The world-forest of God's Grove rustled a final time to the evening breeze and seemed to hold its breath in anticipation.

Paul Duré closed his eyes and prayed.

THIRTY-SEVEN

We walk all day, Hunt and I, and toward evening we find an inn with food set out for us – a fowl, rice pudding, cauliflower, a dish of macaroni, and so forth – although there are no people here, no sign of people other than the fire in the hearth, burning brightly as if just lit, and the food still warm on the stove.

Hunt is unnerved by it; by it and by the terrible withdrawal symptoms he is suffering from the loss of contact with the datasphere. I can imagine his pain. For a person born and raised into a world where information was always at hand, communication with anyone anywhere a given, and no distance more than a farcaster step away, this sudden regression to life as our ancestors had known it would be like suddenly awakening blind and crippled. But after the rantings and rages of the first few hours of walking, Hunt finally settled down into a taciturn gloom.

'But the CEO *needs* me!' he had shouted that first hour.

'She needs the information I was bringing her,' I said, 'but there's nothing to be done about it.'

'Where *are* we?' demanded Hunt for the tenth time.

I had already explained about this alternate Old Earth, but I knew he meant something else now.

'Quarantine, I think,' I said.

'The Core brought us here?' demanded Hunt.

'I can only assume.'

'How do we get back?'

'I don't know. I presume that when they feel it's safe to allow us out of quarantine, a farcaster will appear.'

Hunt cursed softly. 'Why quarantine *me*, Severn?'

I shrugged. I assumed it was because he had heard what I said on Pacem, but I was not certain. I was certain of nothing.

The road led through meadows, vineyards, winding over low hills and twisting through valleys where glimpses of the sea were visible.

'Where does this road go?' Hunt demanded just before we discovered the inn.

'All roads lead to Rome.'

'I'm serious, Severn.'

'So am I, M. Hunt.'

Hunt pried a loose stone from the highway and threw it far into the bushes. Somewhere a thrush called.

'You've been here before?' Hunt's tone was one of accusation, as if I had pirated him away. Perhaps I had.

'No,' I said. But *Keats* had, I almost added. My transplanted memories surged to the surface, almost overwhelming me with their sense of loss and looming mortality. So far from friends, so far from Fanny, his one eternal love.

'You're sure you can't access the datasphere?' asked Hunt.

'I'm positive,' I answered. He did not ask about the megasphere, and I did not offer the information. I am terrified of entering the megasphere, of losing myself there.

We found the inn just at sunset. It was nestled in a small valley, and smoke rose from the stone chimney.

While eating, darkness pressing against the panes, our only light the flicker of the fire and two candles on a stone mantle, Hunt said, 'This place makes me half believe in ghosts.'

'I do believe in ghosts,' I said.

Night. I awake coughing, feel wetness on my bare chest, hear Hunt fumbling with the candle, and in its light, look down to see blood on my skin, spotting the bedclothes.

'My God,' breathes Hunt, horrified. 'What is it? What's going on?'

'Hemorrhage,' I manage after the next fit of coughing leaves me weaker and spotted with more blood. I start to rise, fall back on the pillow, and gesture toward the basin of water and towel on the nightstand.

'Damn, damn,' mutters Hunt, searching for my comlog to get a med reading. There is no comlog. I had thrown away Hoyt's useless instrument while we were walking earlier in the day.

Hunt removes his own comlog, adjusts the monitor, and wraps it around my wrist. The readings are meaningless to him, other than to signify urgency and the need for immediate medical care. Like most people of his generation, Hunt had never seen illness or death – that was a professional matter handled out of sight of the populace.

'Never mind,' I whisper, the siege of coughing past but weakness lying on me like a blanket of stones. I gesture toward the towel again, and Hunt moistens it, washes the blood from my chest and arms, helps me sit in the single chair while he removes the spattered sheets and blankets.

'Do you know what's going on?' he asks, real concern in his voice.

'Yes.' I attempt a smile. 'Accuracy. Verisimilitude. Ontogeny recapitulating phylogeny.'

'Make sense,' snaps Hunt, helping me back into the bed. 'What caused the hemorrhage? What can I do to help?'

'A glass of water, please.' I sip it, feel the boiling in my chest and throat but manage to avoid another round of coughing. My belly feels as if it's on fire.

'What's going on?' Hunt asks again.

I talk slowly, carefully, setting each word in place as if placing my feet on soil strewn with mines. The coughing does not return. 'It's an illness called consumption,' I say. 'Tuberculosis. The final stages, judging from the severity of the hemorrhage.'

Hunt's basset-hound face is white. 'Good God, Severn. I never heard of tuberculosis.' He raises his wrist as if to consult his comlog memory but the wrist is bare.

I return his instrument. 'Tuberculosis has been absent for centuries. Cured. But John Keats had it. Died of it. And this cybrid body belongs to Keats.'

Hunt stands as if ready to rush out the door seeking help. 'Surely the Core will allow us to return now! They can't keep you here on this empty world where there's no medical assistance!'

I lay my head back in the soft pillows, feeling the feathers under the ticking. 'That may be precisely why I am being kept here. We'll see tomorrow when we arrive in Rome.'

'But you can't travel! We won't be going anywhere in the morning.'

'We'll see,' I say and close my eyes. 'We'll see.'

In the morning a *vettura*, a small carriage, is waiting outside the inn. The horse is a large gray mare, and it rolls its eyes at us as we approach. The creature's breath rises in the chill morning air.

'Do you know what that *is*?' says Hunt.

'A horse.'

Hunt raises a hand toward the animal as if it will pop and disappear like a soap bubble when he touches its flank. It does not. Hunt snatches his hand back as the mare's tail flicks.

'Horses are *extinct*,' he says. 'They've never been ARNied back into existence.'

'This one looks real enough,' I say, climbing into the carriage and sitting on the narrow bench there.

Hunt gingerly takes his seat beside me, his long fingers twitching with anxiety. 'Who drives?' he says. 'Where are the controls?'

There are no reins, and the coachman's seat is quite empty. 'Let's see if the horse knows the way,' I suggest, and at that instant we start moving at a leisurely pace, the springless carriage jolting over the stones and furrows of the rough road.

'This is some sort of joke, isn't it?' asks Hunt, staring at the flawless blue sky and distant fields.

I cough as lightly and briefly as possible into a handkerchief I have made from a towel borrowed from the inn. 'Possibly,' I say. 'But then, what isn't?'

Hunt ignores my sophistry, and we rumble on, jolting and bouncing toward whatever destination and destiny await.

'Where are Hunt and Severn?' asked Meina Gladstone.

Sedeptra Akasi, the young black woman who was Gladstone's second most important aide, leaned closer so as not to interrupt the flow of the military briefing. 'Still no word, M. Executive.'

'That's impossible. Severn had a tracer and Leigh stepped through to Pacem almost an hour ago. Where the hell are they?'

Akasi glanced toward the faxpad she had unfolded on the tabletop. 'Security can't find them. The transit police can't locate them. The farcaster unit recorded only that they coded TC^2 – here – stepped through, but did not arrive.'

'That's impossible.'

'Yes, M. Executive.'

'I want to talk to Albedo or one of the other AI Councilors as soon as this meeting is over.'

'Yes.'

Both women returned their attention to the briefing. The Government House Tactical Center had been joined to the Olympus Command Center War Room and to the largest Senate briefing room with fifteen-meter-square, visually open portals so that the three spaces created one cavernous and asymetrical conference area. The War Room holos seemed to rise into infinity on the display end of the space, and columns of data floated everywhere along the walls.

'Four minutes until cislunar incursion,' said Admiral Singh.

'Their long-range weapons could have opened up on Heaven's Gate long before this,' said General Morpurgo. 'They seem to be showing some restraint.'

'They didn't show much restraint toward our torchships,' said Garion Persov of Diplomacy. The group had been assembled an hour earlier when the sortie of the hastily assembled fleet of a dozen Hegemony torchships had been summarily destroyed by the advancing Swarm. Long-range sensors had relayed the briefest image of that Swarm – a cluster of embers with cometlike fusion tails – before the torchships and their remotes quit broadcasting. There had been many, many embers.

'Those were warships,' said General Morpurgo. 'We've been broadcasting for hours now that Heaven's Gate is an open planet. We can hope for restraint.'

The holographic images of Heaven's Gate surrounded them: the quiet streets of Mudflat, airborne images of the coastline, orbital images of the gray-brown world with its constant cloud cover, cislunar images of the baroque dodecahedron of the singularity sphere which tied together all farcasters, and space-aimed telescopic, UV, and X-ray images of the advancing Swarm – much larger than specks or embers now, at less than one AU. Gladstone looked up at the fusion tails of Ouster warships, the tumbling, containment-field-shimmering massiveness of their asteroid farms and bubble worlds, their complex and oddly non-human zero-gravity city complexes, and she thought, *What if I am wrong?*

The lives of billions rested on her belief that the Ousters would not wantonly destroy Hegemony worlds.

'Two minutes until incursion,' Singh said in his professional warrior's monotone.

'Admiral,' said Gladstone, 'is it absolutely necessary to destroy the singularity sphere as soon as the Ousters have penetrated our *cordon sanitaire*? Couldn't we wait another few minutes to judge their intentions?'

'No, CEO,' answered the Admiral promptly. 'The farcaster link must be destroyed as soon as they are within quick assault range.'

'But if your remaining torchships don't do it, Admiral, we still have the in-system links, the fatline relays, and the timed devices, don't we?'

'Yes, M. Executive, but we *must* assure that all farcaster capability is removed before the Ousters overrun the system. There can be no compromising this already slim safety margin.'

Gladstone nodded. She understood the need for absolute caution. *If only there were more time.*

'Fifteen seconds until incursion and singularity destruction,' said Singh. 'Ten . . . seven . . .'

Suddenly all of the torchship and cislunar remote holos glowed violet, red, and white.

Gladstone leaned forward. 'Was that the singularity sphere going?'

The military men buzzed amongst themselves, calling up further data, switching images on the holos and screens. 'No, CEO,' answered Morpurgo. 'The torchships are under attack. What you're seeing is their defensive fields overloading. The . . . ah . . . *there.*'

A central image, possibly from a low orbital relay ship, showed an enhanced image of the dodecahedronal singularity containment sphere, its thirty thousand square meters of surface still intact, still glowing in the harsh light of Heaven's Gate's sun. Then, suddenly, the glow increased, the nearest face of the structure seemed to become incandescent and sag in upon itself, and less than three seconds later the sphere expanded as the caged singularity there escaped and devoured itself as well as everything within a six-hundred-kilometer radius.

At the same instant, most of the visual images and many of the data columns went blank.

'All farcaster connections terminated,' announced Singh. 'In-system data now relayed by fatline transmitters only.'

There was a buzz of approval and relief from the military people, something closer to a sigh and soft moan from the dozens of senators and political advisors present. The world of Heaven's Gate had just been amputated from the Web . . . the first such loss of a Hegemony world in more than four centuries.

Gladstone turned to Sedeptra Akasi. 'What is travel time to Heaven's Gate from the Web now?'

'By Hawking drive, seven months onboard,' said the aide without a pause to access, 'a little over nine years time-debt.'

Gladstone nodded. Heaven's Gate was now nine years distant from the nearest Web world.

'There go our torchships,' intoned Singh. The view had been from one of the orbital pickets, relayed through the jerky, false-color images of high-speed fatline squirts being computer processed in rapid progression. The images were visual mosaics, but they always made Gladstone think of the earliest silent films from the dawn of the Media Age. But this was no Charlie Chaplin comedy. Two, then five, then eight bursts of brilliant light blossomed against the starfield above the limb of the planet.

'Transmissions from HS *Niki Weimart*, HS *Terrapin*, HS *Cornet*, and HS *Andrew Paul* have ceased,' reported Singh.

Barbre Dan-Gyddis raised a hand. 'What about the other four ships, Admiral?'

'Only the four mentioned had FTL-comm capability. The pickets confirm that radio, maser, and wideband commlinks from the other four torchships also have ceased. The visual data . . .' Singh stopped and gestured toward the image relayed from the automatic picket ship: eight expanding and fading circles of light, a starfield crawling with fusion tails and new lights. Suddenly even that image went blank.

'All orbital sensors and fatline relays terminated,' said General Morpurgo. He gestured, and the blackness was replaced with images of the streets of Heaven's Gate with the inevitable low-lying clouds. Aircraft added shots above the clouds – a sky gone crazy with moving stars.

'All reports confirm total destruction of the singularity sphere,' said Singh. 'Advance units of the Swarm now entering high orbit around Heaven's Gate.'

'How many people are left there?' asked Gladstone. She was leaning forward, her elbows on the table, her hands folded very tightly.

'Eighty-six thousand seven hundred and eighty-nine,' said Defense Minister Imoto.

'That doesn't count the twelve thousand Marines who were farcast in during the past two hours,' added General Van Zeidt.

Imoto nodded toward the General.

Gladstone thanked them and returned her attention to the holos. The data columns floating above and their extracts on the faxpads, comlogs, and table panels held the pertinent data – numbers of Swarm craft now in-system, number and types of ships in orbit, projected braking orbits and time curves, energy analyses and comm-band intercepts – but Gladstone and the others were watching the relatively uninformative and unchanging fatlined images from the aircraft and surface cameras: stars, cloud tops, streets, the view from Atmospheric Generating Station Heights out over the Mudflat Promenade where Gladstone herself had stood less than twelve hours earlier. It was night there. Giant horsetail ferns moved to silent breezes blowing in from the bay.

'I think they'll negotiate,' Senator Richeau was saying. 'First they'll present us with this *fait accompli*, nice worlds overrun, then they'll negotiate and negotiate hard for a new balance of power. I mean, even if both of their invasion waves succeeded, that would be twenty-five worlds out of almost two hundred in the Web and Protectorate.'

'Yes,' said Head of Diplomacy Persov, 'but don't forget, Senator, that these include some of our most strategically important worlds . . . *this* one, for example. TC^2 is only two hundred and thirty-five hours behind Heaven's Gate on the Ouster timetable.'

Senator Richeau stared Persov down. 'I'm well aware of that,' she said coldly. 'I'm merely saying that the Ousters cannot have true conquest on their minds. That would be pure folly on their part. Nor will FORCE allow the second wave to penetrate so deeply. Certainly this so-called invasion is a prelude to negotiation.'

'Perhaps,' said Nordholm's Senator Roanquist, 'but such negotiations would necessarily depend upon—'

'Wait,' said Gladstone.

The data columns now showed more than a hundred Ouster warcraft in orbit around Heaven's Gate. Ground forces there had been instructed not to fire unless fired upon, and no activity was visible in the thirty-some views being fatlined to the War Room. Suddenly, however, the cloud cover above Mudflat City glowed as if giant searchlights had been turned on. A dozen broad beams of coherent light stabbed down into the bay and the city, continuing the searchlight illusion, appearing to Gladstone as if giant white columns had been erected between the ground and the ceiling of clouds.

That illusion ended abruptly as a whirlwind of flame and destruction erupted at the base of each of these hundred-meter-wide columns of light. The water of the bay boiled until huge geysers of steam occluded the nearer cameras. The view from the heights showed century-old stone buildings in the town erupting into flame, imploding as if a tornado were moving against them. The Web-famous gardens and commons of the Promenade erupted in flame, exploded in dirt and flying debris as if an invisible plow were moving across them. Horsetail ferns two centuries old bent as if before a hurricane wind, burst into flame, and were gone.

'Lances from a *Bowers*-class torchship,' Admiral Singh said into the silence. 'Or its Ouster equivalent.'

The city was burning, exploding, being plowed into rubble by the light columns and then being torn asunder again. There were no audio channels on these fatlined images, but Gladstone imagined that she could hear screams.

One by one, the ground cameras went black. The view from the Atmospheric Generating Station Heights disappeared in a white flash. Airborne cameras were already gone. The twenty or so other ground-based images began winking out, one in a terrible burst of crimson that left everyone in the room rubbing their eyes.

'Plasma explosion,' said Van Zeidt. 'Low megaton range.' The view had been of a FORCE:Marine air defense complex north of the Intercity Canal.

Suddenly all images ceased. Dataflow ended. The room lights began to come up to compensate for a darkness so sudden that it took everyone's breath away.

'The primary fatline transmitter's gone,' said General Morpurgo. 'It was at the main FORCE base near High Gate. Buried under our strongest containment field, fifty meters of rock, and ten meters of whiskered stalloy.'

'Shaped nuclear charges?' asked Barbre Dan-Gyddis.

'At least,' said Morpurgo.

Senator Kolchev rose, his Lusian bulk emanating an almost ursine sense of strength. 'All right. This isn't some goddamned negotiating ploy. The Ousters have just reduced a Web world to ashes. This is all-out, give-no-mercy warfare. The survival of civilization is at stake. What do we do now?'

All eyes turned toward Meina Gladstone.

The Consul dragged a semiconscious Theo Lane from the wreckage of the skimmer and staggered fifty meters with the younger man's arm over his shoulder before collapsing on a stretch of grass beneath trees along the bank of the Hoolie River. The skimmer was not on fire, but it lay crumpled against the collapsed stone wall where it had finally skidded to a halt. Bits of metal and ceramic polymers lay strewn along the riverbank and abandoned avenue.

The city was burning. Smoke obscured the view across the river, and this part of Jacktown, the Old Section, looked as if several pyres had been lighted where thick columns of black smoke rose toward the low cloud ceiling. Combat lasers and missile trails continued to streak through the haze, sometimes exploding against the assault dropships, parafoils, and suspension-field bubbles which continued to drop through the clouds like chaff blown from a recently harvested field.

'Theo, are you all right?'

The Governor-General nodded and moved to push his glasses higher on his nose . . . stopping in confusion as he realized that his glasses were gone. Blood streaked Theo's forehead and arms. 'Hit my head,' he said groggily.

'We need to use your comlog,' said the Consul. 'Get someone here to pick us up.'

Theo nodded, lifted his arm, and frowned at his wrist. 'Gone,' he said. 'Comlog's gone. Gotta look in the skimmer.' He tried to get to his feet.

The Consul pulled him back down. They were in the shelter of a few ornamental trees here, but the skimmer was exposed, and their landing had been no secret. The Consul had glimpsed several armored troops moving down an adjacent street as the skimmer pancaked in for its crash landing. They might be SDF or Ousters or even Hegemony Marines, but the Consul imagined that they would be trigger-happy whatever their loyalties.

'Never mind that,' he said. 'We'll get to a phone. Call the consulate.' He looked around, identified the section of warehouses and stone buildings where they had crashed. Upriver a few hundred meters, an old cathedral stood abandoned, its chapter house crumbling and overhanging the river-bank.

'I know where we are,' said the Consul. 'It's just a block or two to Cicero's. Come on.' He lifted Theo's arm over his head and on to his shoulders, pulling the injured man to his feet.

'Cicero's, good,' muttered Theo. 'Could use a drink.'

The rattle of fléchette fire and an answering sizzle of energy weapons came from the street to their south. The Consul took as much of Theo's weight as he could and half walked, half staggered along the narrow lane beside the river.

'Oh damn,' the Consul whispered.

Cicero's was burning. The old bar and inn – as old as Jacktown and much older than most of the capital – had lost three of its four sagging riverfront buildings to the flames, and only a determined bucket brigade of patrons was saving the last section.

'I see Stan,' said the Consul, pointing to the huge figure of Stan Leweski standing near the head of the bucket brigade line. 'Here.' The Consul helped Theo to a sitting position under an elm tree along the walkway. 'How's your head?'

'Hurts.'

'I'll be right back with help,' said the Consul and moved as quickly as he could down the narrow lane toward the men.

Stan Leweski stared at the Consul as if he were a ghost. The big man's face was streaked with soot and tears, and his eyes were wide, almost uncomprehending. Cicero's had been in his family for six generations. It was raining softly now, and the fire seemed beaten. Men shouted up and down the line as a few timbers from the burned-out sections sagged into the embers of the basement.

'By God, it's gone,' said Leweski. 'You see? Grandfather Jiri's addition? It's gone.'

The Consul grabbed the huge man by his shoulders. 'Stan, we need help. Theo's over there. Hurt. Our skimmer crashed. We need to get to the spaceport . . . to use your phone. It's an emergency, Stan.'

Leweski shook his head. 'Phone's gone. Comlog bands are jammed. God-damn war is on.' He pointed toward the burned sections of the old inn. 'They're gone, by damn. *Gone.*'

The Consul made a fist, furious in the grip of sheer frustration. Other men milled around, but the Consul recognized none of them. There were no FORCE or SDF authorities in sight. Suddenly a voice behind him said, 'I can help. I have a skimmer.'

The Consul whirled to see a man in his late fifties or early sixties, soot and sweat covering his handsome face and streaking his wavy hair. 'Great,' said the Consul. 'I'd appreciate it.' He paused. 'Do I know you?'

'Dr Melio Arundez,' said the man, already moving toward the parkway where Theo rested.

'Arundez,' repeated the Consul, hurrying to keep up. The name echoed strangely. Someone he knew? Someone he should know? 'My God, Arundez!' he said. 'You were the friend of Rachel Weintraub when she came here decades ago.'

'Her university advisor, actually,' said Arundez. 'I know you. You went on the pilgrimage with Sol.' They stopped where Theo was sitting, still holding his head in his hands. 'My skimmer's over there,' said Arundez.

The Consul could see a small, two-person Vikken Zephyr parked under the trees. 'Great. We'll get Theo to the hospital and then I need to get to the spaceport immediately.'

'The hospital's overcrowded to the point of insanity,' said Arundez. 'If you're trying to get to your ship, I suggest you take the Governor-General there and use the ship's surgery.'

The Consul paused. 'How did you know I have a ship there?'

Arundez dilated the doors and helped Theo on to the narrow bench behind the front contour seats. 'I know all about you and the other pilgrims, M. Consul. I've been trying to get permission to go to the Valley of the Time Tombs for months. You can't believe my frustration when I learned that your pilgrims' barge left secretly with Sol aboard.' Arundez took a deep breath and asked a question which he obviously had been afraid to ask before. 'Is Rachel still alive?'

He was her lover when she was a grown woman, thought the Consul. 'I don't know,' he said. 'I'm trying to get back in time to help her, if I can.'

Melio Arundez nodded and settled into the driver's seat, gesturing for the Consul to get in. 'We'll try to get to the spaceport. It won't be easy with the fighting around there.'

The Consul sat back, feeling his bruises, cuts, and exhaustion as the seat folded around him. 'We need to get Theo . . . the Governor-General . . . to the consulate or government house or whatever they call it now.'

Arundez shook his head and powered up the repellors. 'Uh-uh. The consulate's gone, hit by a wayward missile, according to the emergency news channel. All the Hegemony officials went out to the spaceport for evacuation before your friend even went hunting for you.'

The Consul looked at the semiconscious Theo Lane. 'Let's go,' he said softly to Arundez.

The skimmer came under small-arms fire as they crossed the river, but fléchettes merely rattled on the hull and the single energy beam fired sliced beneath them, sending a spout of steam ten meters high. Arundez drove like a crazy person – weaving, bobbing, pitching, yawing, and occasionally slewing the skimmer around on its axis like a plate sliding atop a sea of marbles. The Consul's seat restraints closed around him, but he still felt his gorge threaten to rise. Behind them, Theo's head moved loosely back and forth on the car bench as he surrendered to unconsciousness.

'The downtown's a mess!' Arundez shouted over repellor roar. 'I'll follow the old viaduct to the spaceport highway and then cut across country, staying low.' They pirouetted around a burning structure which the Consul belatedly recognized as his old apartment building.

'Is the spaceport highway open?'

Arundez shook his head. 'Never make it. Paratroopers have been dropping around it for the last thirty minutes.'

'Are the Ousters trying to destroy the city?'

'Uh-uh. They could have done that from orbit without all this fuss. They seem to be investing the capital. Most of their dropships and paratroopers land at least ten klicks out.'

'Is it our SDF who's fighting back?'

Arundez laughed, showing white teeth against tanned skin. 'They're halfway to Endymion and Port Romance by now . . . though reports ten minutes ago, before the comm lines were jammed, say that those cities are also under attack. No, the little resistance you see is from a few dozen FORCE:Marines left behind to guard the city and the spaceport.'

'So the Ousters haven't destroyed or captured the spaceport?'

'Not yet. At least not as of a few minutes ago. We'll soon see. Hang on!'

The ten-kilometer ride to the spaceport via the VIP highway or the skylanes above it usually took a few minutes, but Arundez's roundabout, up-and-down approach over the hills, through the valleys, and between the trees added time and excitement to the trip. The Consul turned his head to watch hillsides and the slums of burning refugee camps flash by to his right. Men and women crouched against boulders and under low trees, covering their heads as the skimmer rushed past. Once the Consul saw a squad of FORCE:Marines dug in on a hilltop, but their attention was focused on a hill to the north from which there came a panoply of laser-lance fire. Arundez saw the Marines at the same instant and jinked the skimmer hard left, dropping it into a narrow ravine scant seconds before the treetops on the ridge above were sliced off as if by invisible shears.

Finally they roared up and over a final ridgeline, and the western gates and fences of the spaceport became visible ahead of them. The perimeter was ablaze with the blue and violet glows of containment and interdiction fields, and they were still a klick away when a visible tightbeam laser flicked out, found them, and a voice over the radio said, 'Unidentified skimmer, land immediately or be destroyed.'

Arundez laughed.

The tree line ten meters away seemed to shimmer, and suddenly they were surrounded by wraiths in activated chameleon polymers. Arundez had opened the cockpit blisters, and now assault rifles were aimed at him and the Consul.

'Step away from the machine,' said a disembodied voice behind the camouflage shimmer.

'We have the Governor-General,' called the Consul. 'We have to get in.'

'The hell you say,' snapped a voice with a definite Web accent. 'Out!'

The Consul and Arundez hastily released their seat restraints and had started to climb out when a voice from the back seat snapped, 'Lieutenant Mueller, is that you?'

'Ah, yes, sir.'

'Do you recognize me, Lieutenant?'

The camouflage shimmer depolarized, and a young Marine in full battle armor stood not a meter from the skimmer. His face was nothing more than a black visor but the voice sounded young. 'Yes, sir . . . ah . . . Governor. Sorry I didn't recognize you without your glasses. You've been hurt, sir.'

'I know I've been hurt, Lieutenant. That is why these gentlemen have escorted me here. Don't you recognize the former Hegemony Consul for Hyperion?'

'Sorry, sir,' said Lieutenant Mueller, waving his men back into the tree line. 'The base is sealed.'

'Of *course* the base is sealed,' Theo said through gritted teeth. 'I countersigned those orders. But I also authorized evacuation of all essential Hegemony personnel. You *did* allow those skimmers through, did you not, Lieutenant Mueller?'

An armored hand rose as if to scratch the helmeted and visored head. 'Ah . . . yes, sir. Ah, affirmative. But that was an hour ago, sir. The evacuation dropships are gone and—'

'For God sake, Mueller, get on your tactical channel and get authorization from Colonel Gerasimov to let us through.'

'The Colonel's dead, sir. There was a dropship assault on the east perimeter, and—'

'Captain Lewellyn then,' said Theo. He swayed and then steadied himself against the back of the Consul's seat. His face was very white under the blood.

'Ah . . . tactical channels are down, sir. The Ousters are jamming on wideband with—'

'*Lieutenant,*' snapped Theo in a tone the Consul had never heard his young friend use, 'you've visually identified me and scanned my implant ID. Now either admit us to the field or shoot us.'

The armored Marine glanced back toward the tree line as if considering whether to order his men to open fire. 'The dropships are all gone, sir. Nothing else is coming down.'

Theo nodded. Blood had dried and caked on his forehead, but now a fresh trickle started from his scalp line. 'The impounded ship is still in Blast Pit Nine, isn't it?'

'Yes, sir,' answered Mueller, snapping to attention at last. 'But it's a civilian ship and could never make space with all the Ouster—'

Theo waved the officer into silence and gestured for Arundez to drive toward the perimeter. The Consul glanced ahead toward the deadlines, interdiction fields, containment fields, and probable pressure mines that the skimmer would encounter in ten seconds. He saw the Marine lieutenant wave, and an opening irised in the violet and blue energy fields ahead.

No one fired. In half a minute they were crossing the hardpan of the spaceport itself. Something large was burning on the northern perimeter. To their left, a huddle of FORCE trailers and command modules had been slagged to a pool of bubbling plastic.

There had been people in there, thought the Consul and once again had to fight to keep his gorge from rising.

Blast Pit Seven had been destroyed, its circular walls of reinforced ten-centimeter carbon-carbon blown outward and apart as if they had been made of cardboard. Blast Pit Eight was burning with that white-hot incandescence which suggested plasma grenades. Blast Pit Nine was intact, with the bow of the Consul's ship just visible above the pit wall through the shimmer of a class-three containment field.

'The interdiction's been lifted?' said the Consul.

Theo lay back on the cushioned bench. His voice was thick. 'Yeah. Gladstone authorized the dropping of the restraining dome field. That's just the usual protective field. You can override it with a command.'

Arundez dropped the skimmer to tarmac just as warning lights went red and synthesized voices began describing malfunctions. They helped Theo out and paused near the rear of the small skimmer where a line of fléchettes had stitched a ragged row through the engine cowling and repellor housing. Part of the hood had melted from overload.

Melio Arundez patted the machine once, and both men turned to help Theo through the blast pit door and up the docking umbilical.

'My God,' said Dr Melio Arundez, 'this is beautiful. I've never been in a private interstellar spacecraft before.'

'There are only a few dozen in existence,' said the Consul, setting the osmosis mask in place over Theo's mouth and nose and gently lowering the redhead into the surgery's tank of emergency care nutrient. 'Small as it is, this ship cost several hundred million marks. It's not cost-effective for corporations and Outback planetary governments to use their military craft on those rare occasions when they need to travel between the stars.' The Consul sealed the tank and conversed briefly with the diagnostics program. 'He'll be all right,' he said at last to Arundez, and returned to the holopit.

Melio Arundez stood near the antique Steinway, gently running his hand over the glossy finish of the grand piano. He glanced out through the transparent section of hull above the stowed balcony platform and said, 'I see fires near the main gate. We'd better get out of here.'

'That's what I'm doing,' said the Consul, gesturing Arundez toward the circular couch lining the projection pit.

The archaeologist dropped into the deep cushions and glanced around. 'Aren't there . . . ah . . . controls?'

The Consul smiled. 'A bridge? Cockpit instruments? Maybe a wheel I can steer with? Uh-uh. Ship?'

'Yes,' came the soft voice from nowhere.

'Are we cleared for takeoff?'

'Yes.'

'Is that containment field removed?'

'It was our field. I've withdrawn it.'

'OK, let's get the hell out of here. I don't have to tell you that we're in the middle of a shooting war, do I?'

'No. I've been monitoring all developments. The last FORCE spacecraft are in the process of leaving the Hyperion system. These Marines are stranded and—'

'Save the tactical analyses for later, Ship,' said the Consul. 'Set our course for the Valley of the Time Tombs and get us out of here.'

'Yes, sir,' said the ship. 'I was just pointing out that the forces defending this spaceport have little chance of holding out for more than an hour or so.'

'Noted,' said the Consul. 'Now take off.'

'I'm required to share this fatline transmission first. The squirt arrived at 1622:38:14, Web standard, this afternoon.'

'Whoa! Hold it!' cried the Consul, freezing the holo transmission in mid-construction. Half of Meina Gladstone's face hung above them. 'You're *required* to show this before we leave? Whose commands do you respond to, Ship?'

'CEO Gladstone's, sir. The Chief Executive empowered a priority over-ride on all ships' functions five days ago. This fatline squirt is the last requirement before—'

'So that's why you didn't respond to my remote commands,' murmured the Consul.

'Yes,' said the ship in conversational tones. 'I was about to say that the showing of this transmission is the last requirement prior to returning command to you.'

'And then you'll do what I say?'

'Yes.'

'Take us where I'll tell you to?'

'Yes.'

'No hidden overrides?'

'None that I know of.'

'Play the squirt,' said the Consul.

The Lincolnesque countenance of CEO Meina Gladstone floated in the center of the projection pit with the telltale twitches and breakups endemic to fatline transmissions. 'I am pleased that you survived the visit to the Time Tombs,' she said to the Consul. 'By now you must know that I am asking you to negotiate with the Ousters *before* you return to the valley.'

The Consul folded his arms and glared at Gladstone's image. Outside the sun was setting. He had only a few minutes before Rachel Weintraub reached her birth hour and minute and simply ceased to exist.

'I understand your urgency to return and help your friends,' said Gladstone, 'but you can do nothing to help the child at this moment . . .

648

experts in the Web assure us that neither cryogenic sleep nor fugue could arrest the Merlin's sickness. Sol knows this.'

Across the projection pit, Dr Arundez said, 'It's true. They experimented for years. She would die in fugue state.'

'. . . you *can* help the billions of people in the Web whom you believe you have betrayed,' Gladstone was saying.

The Consul leaned forward and rested his elbows on his knees and his chin on his fists. His heart was pounding very loudly in his ears.

'I knew that you would open the Time Tombs,' Gladstone said, her sad brown eyes seeming to stare directly at the Consul. 'Core predictors showed that your loyalty to Maui-Covenant . . . and to the memory of your grand-parents' rebellion . . . would override all other factors. It was *time* for the Tombs to be opened, and only you could activate the Ouster device before the Ousters themselves decided to.'

'I've heard enough of this,' said the Consul and stood, turning his back on the projection. 'Cancel message,' he said to the ship, knowing that it would not obey.

Melio Arundez walked through the projection and gripped the Consul's arm tightly. 'Hear her out. Please.'

The Consul shook his head but stayed in the pit, arms folded.

'Now the worst has happened,' said Gladstone. 'The Ousters are invading the Web. Heaven's Gate is being destroyed. God's Grove has less than an hour before the invasion sweeps over it. It is imperative that you meet with the Ousters in Hyperion System and negotiate . . . use your diplomatic skills to open a dialogue with them. The Ousters will not respond to our fatline or radio messages, but we have alerted them to your coming. I think they will still trust you.'

The Consul moaned and walked over to the piano, pounding his fist against its lid.

'We have minutes, not hours, Consul,' said Gladstone. 'I will ask you to go first to the Ousters in Hyperion System and then attempt to return to the Valley of the Time Tombs if you must. You know better than I the results of warfare. Millions will die needlessly if we cannot find a secure channel through which to communicate with the Ousters.

'It is your decision, but please consider the ramifications if we fail in this last attempt to find the truth and preserve the peace. I will contact you via fatline once you have reached the Ouster Swarm.'

Gladstone's image shimmered, fogged, and faded.

'Response?' asked the ship.

'No.' The Consul paced back and forth between the Steinway and the projection pit.

'No spacecraft or skimmer has landed near the valley with its crew intact for almost two centuries,' said Melio Arundez. 'She must know how small the odds are that you can go there . . . survive the Shrike . . . and then rendezvous with the Ousters.'

'Things are different now,' said the Consul without turning to face the other man. 'The time tides have gone berserk. The Shrike goes where it pleases. Perhaps whatever phenomenon prevented manned landings before is no longer operative.'

'And perhaps your ship will land perfectly without us,' said Arundez. 'Just as so many others have.'

'Goddammit,' shouted the Consul, wheeling, 'you knew the risks when you said that you wanted to join me!'

The archaeologist nodded calmly. 'I'm not talking about the risk to myself, sir. I'm willing to accept any risk if it means I might help Rachel . . . or even see her again. It's *your* life that may hold the key to humankind's survival.'

The Consul shook his fists in the air and paced back and forth like some caged predator. 'That's not *fair*! I was Gladstone's pawn before. She used me . . . cynically . . . deliberately. I *killed* four Ousters, Arundez. Shot them because I had to activate their goddamned device to open the Tombs. Do you think they'll welcome me back with open arms?'

The archaeologist's dark eyes looked up at the Consul without blinking. 'Gladstone believes that they will parley with you.'

'Who *knows* what they'll do? Or what Gladstone believes for that matter. The Hegemony and its relationship with the Ousters aren't my worry now. I sincerely wish a plague on both their houses.'

'To the extent that humanity suffers?'

'I don't know humanity,' said the Consul in an exhausted monotone. 'I do know Sol Weintraub. And Rachel. And an injured woman named Brawne Lamia. And Father Paul Duré. And Fedmahn Kassad. And—'

The ship's soft voice enveloped them. 'This spaceport's north perimeter has been breached. I am initiating final launch procedures. Please take your seats.'

The Consul half stumbled to the holopit even as the internal containment field pressed down on him as its vertical differential increased dramatically, sealing every object in its place and protecting the travelers far more securely than any straps or seat restraints could. Once in free-fall, the field would lessen but still serve in the stead of planetary gravity.

The air above the holopit misted and showed the blast pit and spaceport receding quickly below, the horizon and distant hills jerking and tilting as the ship threw itself through eighty-g evasive maneuvers. A few energy weapons winked in their direction, but data columns showed the external fields handling the neglible effects. Then the horizon receded and curved as the lapis lazuli sky darkened to the black of space.

'Destination?' queried the ship.

The Consul closed his eyes. Behind them, a chime sounded to announce that Theo Lane could be moved from the recovery tank to the main surgery.

'How long until we could rendezvous with elements of the Ouster invasion force?' asked the Consul.

'Thirty minutes to the Swarm proper,' answered the ship.

'And how long until we come in range of their attack ships' weapons?'

'They are tracking us now.'

Melio Arundez's expression was calm but his fingers were white on the back of the holopit couch.

'All right,' said the Consul. 'Make for the Swarm. Avoid Hegemony ships. Announce on all frequencies that we are an unarmed diplomatic ship requesting parley.'

'That message was authorized and set in by CEO Gladstone, sir. It is now being broadcast on fatline and all comm frequencies.'

'Carry on,' said the Consul. He pointed to Arundez's comlog. 'Do you see the time?'

'Yes. Six minutes until the precise instant of Rachel's birth.'

The Consul settled back, his eyes closed again. 'You've come a long way for nothing, Dr Arundez.'

The archaeologist stood, swayed a second before finding his legs in the simulated gravity, and carefully walked to the piano. He stood there a moment and looked out through the balcony window at the black sky and the still-brilliant limb of the receding planet. 'Perhaps not,' he said. 'Perhaps not.'

THIRTY-EIGHT

Today we entered the swampy wasteland which I recognize as the Campagna, and to celebrate I have another coughing fit, terminated by vomiting more blood. Much more. Leigh Hunt is beside himself with concern and frustration and, after holding my shoulders during the spasm and helping to clean my clothes with rags moistened in a nearby stream, he asks, 'What can I do?'

'Collect flowers from the fields,' I gasp. 'That's what Joseph Severn did.'

He turns away angrily, not realizing that even in my feverish, exhausted state, I was merely telling the truth.

The little cart and tired horse pass through the Campagna with more painful bumping and rattling than before. Late in the afternoon, we pass some skeletons of horses along the way, then the ruins of an old inn, then the more massive ruin of a viaduct overgrown with moss, and finally posts to which it appears that white sticks have been nailed.

'What on earth is that?' asks Hunt, not realizing the irony of the ancient phrase.

'The bones of bandits,' I answer truthfully.

Hunt looks at me as if my mind has succumbed to the sickness. Perhaps it has.

Later we climb out of the swamplands of the Campagna and get a glimpse of a flash of red moving far out among the fields.

'What is that?' demands Hunt eagerly, hopefully. I know that he expects to see people any moment and a functioning farcaster portal a moment after that.

'A cardinal,' I say, again telling the truth. 'Shooting birds.'

Hunt accesses his poor, crippled comlog. 'A cardinal *is* a bird,' he says.

I nod, look to the west, but the red is gone. 'Also a cleric,' I say. 'And we are approaching Rome, you know.'

Hunt frowns at me and attempts for the thousandth time to raise someone on the comm bands of his comlog. The afternoon is silent except for the rhythmic creak of the *vettura's* wooden wheels and the trill of some distant songbird. A cardinal, perhaps?

We enter Rome as the first flush of evening touches the clouds. The little cart rocks and rumbles through the Lateran Gate, and almost immediately we are confronted with the sight of the Colosseum, overgrown with ivy and obviously the home of thousands of pigeons, but immensely more impressive than holos of the ruin, set now as it was, not within the grubby confines of a postwar city ringed with giant arcologies, but contrasted against clusters of small huts and open fields where the city ends and countryside begins. I can see Rome proper in the distance . . . a scattering of rooftops and smaller ruins on its fabled Seven Hills, but here the Colosseum rules.

'Jesus,' whispers Leigh Hunt. 'What is it?'

'The bones of bandits,' I say again slowly, fearful of starting the terrible coughing once again.

We move on, clopping through the deserted streets of nineteenth-century Old Earth Rome as the evening settles thick and heavy around us and the light fails and pigeons wheel above the domes and rooftops of the Eternal City.

'Where is everyone?' whispers Hunt. He sounds frightened.

'Not here because they are not needed,' I say. My voice sounds sharp edged in the canyon dusk of the city streets. The wheels turn on cobblestones now, hardly more smooth than the random stones of the highway we just escaped.

'Is this some stimsim?' he asks.

'Stop the cart,' I say, and the obedient horse comes to a halt. I point out a heavy stone by the gutter. 'Kick that,' I say to Hunt.

He frowns at me but steps down, approaches the stone, and gives it a hearty kick. More pigeons erupt skyward from bell towers and ivy, panicked by the echoes of his cursing.

'Like Dr Johnson, you've demonstrated the reality of things,' I say. 'This is no stimsim or dream. Or rather, no more one than the rest of our lives have been.'

'Why did they bring us here?' demands the CEO's aide, glancing skyward as if the gods themselves were listening just beyond the fading pastel barriers of the evening clouds. 'What do they want?'

They want me to die, I think, realizing the truth of it with the impact of a fist in my chest. I breathe slowly and shallowly to avoid a fit of coughing even as I feel the phlegm boil and bubble in my throat. *They want me to die and they want you to watch.*

The mare resumes its long haul, turning right on the next narrow street, then right again down a wider avenue filled with shadows and the echoes of our passing, and then stopping at the head of an immense flight of stairs.

'We're here,' I say and struggle to exit the cart. My legs are cramped, my chest aches, and my ass is sore. In my mind runs the beginning of a satirical ode to the joys of traveling.

Hunt steps out as stiffly as I had and stands at the head of the giant, bifurcated staircase, folding his arms and glaring at the steps as if they are a trap or illusion. 'Where, exactly, is *here*, Severn?'

I point to the open square at the foot of the steps. 'The Piazza di Spagna,' I say. It is suddenly strange to hear Hunt call me *Severn*. I realize that the name ceased to be mine when we passed through the Lateran Gate. Or, rather, that my true name had suddenly become my own again.

'Before too many years pass,' I say, 'these will be called the Spanish Steps.' I start down the right bend in the staircase. A sudden dizziness causes me to stagger, and Hunt moves quickly to take my arm.

'You can't walk,' he says. 'You're too ill.'

I point to a mottled old building forming a wall to the opposite side of the broad steps and facing the Piazza. 'It's not far, Hunt. There is our destination.'

Gladstone's aide turns his scowl toward the structure. 'And what is there? Why are we stopping there? What awaits us there?'

I cannot help but smile at this least poetic of men's unconscious use of assonance. I suddenly imagine us sitting up long nights in that dark hulk of a building as I teach him how to pair such technique with masculine or feminine caesura, or the joys of alternating iambic foot with unstressed pyrrhic, or the self-indulgence of the frequent spondee.

I cough, continue coughing, and do not cease until blood is spattering my palm and shirt.

Hunt helps me down the steps, across the Piazza where Bernini's boat-shaped fountain gurgles and burbles in the dusk, and then, following my pointing finger, leads me into the black rectangle of the doorway – the doorway to Number 26 Piazza di Spagna – and I think, without volition, of Dante's *Commedia* and seem to see the phrase 'LASCIATE OGNE SPERANZA, VOI CH'INTRATE' – '*Abandon Every Hope, Who Enter Here*' – chiseled above the cold lintel of the doorway.

Sol Weintraub stood at the entrance to the Sphinx and shook his fist at the universe as night fell and the Tombs glowed with the brilliance of their opening and his daughter did not return.

Did not return.

The Shrike had taken her, lifted her newborn body in its palm of steel, and then stepped back into the radiance which even now pushed Sol away like some terrible, bright wind from the depths of the planet. Sol pressed against the hurricane of light, but it kept him out as surely as might a runaway containment field.

Hyperion's sun had set, and now a cold wind blew from the barrens, driven in from the desert by a front of cold air sliding down the mountains to the south, and Sol turned to stare as vermilion dust blew into the searchlight glare of the opening Time Tombs.

The opening Tombs!

Sol squinted against the cold brilliance and looked down the valley to where the other Tombs glowed like pale green jack-o'-lanterns behind their curtain of blown dust. Light and long shadows leaped across the valley floor while the clouds were drained of the last of their sunset color overhead, and night came in with the howling wind.

Something was moving in the entrance of the second structure, the Jade

Tomb. Sol staggered down the steps of the Sphinx, glancing up at the entrance where the Shrike had disappeared with his daughter, and then he was off the stairway, running past the Sphinx's paws and stumbling down the windblown path toward the Jade Tomb.

Something moved slowly from the oval doorway, was silhouetted by the shaft of light emanating from the tomb, but Sol could not tell if it was human or not, Shrike or not. If it was the Shrike, he would seize it with his bare hands, shake it until it either returned his daughter to him or until one of them was dead.

It was not the Shrike.

Sol could see the silhouette as human now. The person staggered, leaned against the Jade Tomb's doorway as if injured or tired.

It was a young woman.

Sol thought of Rachel here in this place more than half a standard century earlier, the young archaeologist researching these artifacts and never guessing the fate awaiting her in the form of Merlin's sickness. Sol had always imagined his child being saved by the sickness being canceled, the infant aging normally again, the child-who-would-some-day-be-Rachel given back her life. But what if Rachel returned as the twenty-six-year-old Rachel who had entered the Sphinx?

Sol's pulse was pounding so loudly in his ears that he could not hear the wind rage around him. He waved at the figure, half-obscured now by the dust storm.

The young woman waved back.

Sol raced forward another twenty meters, stopped thirty meters from the tomb, and cried out. 'Rachel! Rachel!'

The young woman silhouetted against the roaring light moved away from the doorway, touched her face with both hands, shouted something lost in the wind, and began to descend the stairs.

Sol ran, tripping over rocks as he lost the path and stumbled blindly across the valley floor, ignored the pain as his knee struck a low boulder, found the true path again, and ran to the base of the Jade Tomb, meeting her as she emerged from the cone of expanding light.

She fell just as Sol reached the bottom of the stairs, and he caught her, lowered her gently to the ground as blown sand rasped against his back and the time tides whirled about them in unseen eddies of vertigo and *déjà vu*.

'It *is* you,' she said and raised a hand to touch Sol's cheek. 'It's real. I'm back.'

'Yes, Brawne,' said Sol, trying to hold his voice steady, brushing matted curls from Brawne Lamia's face. He held her firmly, his arm on his knee, propping her head, his back bent to provide more shelter from the wind and sand. 'It's all right, Brawne,' he said softly, sheltering her, his eyes bright with tears of disappointment he would not let fall. 'It's all right. You're back.'

Meina Gladstone walked up the stairs of the cavernous War Room and stepped out into the corridor where long strips of thick Perspex allowed a view down Mons Olympus to the Tharsis Plateau. It was raining far below, and from this vantage point almost twelve klicks high in the Martian sky, she could see pulses of lightning and curtains of static electricity as the storm dragged itself across the high steppes.

Her aide Sedeptra Akasi moved out into the corridor to stand silently next to the CEO.

'Still no word on Leigh or Severn?' asked Gladstone.

'None,' said Akasi. The young black woman's face was illuminated by both the pale light of the Home System's sun above and the play of lightning below. 'The Core authorities say that it may have been a farcaster malfunction.'

Gladstone showed a smile with no warmth. 'Yes. And can you remember any farcaster malfunction in our lifetime, Sedeptra? Anywhere in the Web?'

'No, M. Executive.'

'The Core feels no need for subtlety. Evidently they think they can kidnap whomever they want and not be held accountable. They think we need them too much in our hour of extremis. And you know something, Sedeptra?'

'What?'

'They're right.' Gladstone shook her head and turned back toward the long descent into the War Room. 'It's less than ten minutes until the Ousters envelop God's Grove. Let's go down and join the others. Is my meeting with Councilor Albedo on immediately after this?'

'Yes, Meina. I don't think . . . I mean, some of us think that it is too risky to confront them directly like that.'

Gladstone paused before entering the War Room. 'Why?' she asked and this time her smile was sincere. 'Do you think the Core will disappear me the way they did Leigh and Severn?'

Akasi started to speak, stopped, and raised her palms.

Gladstone touched the younger woman on the shoulder. 'If they do, Sedeptra, it will be a mercy. But I think they will not. Things have gone so far that they believe that there is nothing an individual can do to change the course of events.' Gladstone withdrew her hand, her smile faded. 'And they may be right.'

Not speaking, the two descended to the circle of waiting warriors and politicians.

'The moment approaches,' said the True Voice of the Worldtree Sek Hardeen.

Father Paul Duré was brought back from his reverie. In the past hour, his desperation and frustration had descended through resignation to something akin to pleasure at the thought of having no more choices, no more duties to perform. Duré had been sitting in companionable silence with the leader of the Templar Brotherhood, watching the setting of God's Grove's sun and the proliferation of stars and lights in the night that were not stars.

Duré had wondered at the Templar's isolation from his people at such a crucial moment, but what he knew of Templar theology made Duré realize that the Followers of the Muir would meet such a moment of potential destruction alone on the most sacred platforms and in the most secret bowers of their most sacred trees. And the occasional soft comments Hardeen made into the cowl of his robe made Duré realize that the True Voice was in touch with fellow Templars via comlog or implants.

Still, it was a peaceful way to wait for the end of the world, sitting high in the known galaxy's tallest living tree, listening to a warm evening breeze rustle a million acres of leaves and watching stars twinkle and twin moons hurtle across a velvet sky.

'We have asked Gladstone and the Hegemony authorities to offer no resistance, to allow no FORCE warships in-system,' said Sek Hardeen.

'Is that wise?' asked Duré. Hardeen had told him earlier what the fate of Heaven's Gate had been.

'The FORCE fleet is not yet organized enough to offer serious resistance,' answered the Templar. 'At least this way our world has some chance of being treated as a nonbelligerent.'

Father Duré nodded and leaned forward the better to see the tall figure in the shadows of the platform. Soft glow-globes in the branches below them were their only illumination other than the starlight and moonglow. 'Yet you welcomed this war. Aided the Shrike Cult authorities in bringing it about.'

'No, Duré. Not the war. The Brotherhood knew it must be part of the Great Change.'

'And what is that?' asked Duré.

'The Great Change is when humankind accepts its role as part of the natural order of the universe instead of its role as a cancer.'

'Cancer?'

'It is an ancient disease which—'

'Yes,' said Duré. 'I know what cancer was. How is it like humankind?'

Sek Hardeen's perfectly modulated, softly accented tones showed a hint of agitation. 'We have spread out through the galaxy like cancer cells through a living body, Duré. We multiply without thought to the countless life forms that must die or be pushed aside so that we may breed and flourish. We eradicate competing forms of intelligent life.'

'Such as?'

'Such as the Seneschai empaths on Hebron. The marsh centaurs of Garden. The *entire ecology* was destroyed on Garden, Duré, so that a few thousand human colonists might live where millions of native life forms once had thrived.'

Duré touched his cheek with a curled finger. 'That is one of the drawbacks of terraforming.'

'We did not terraform Whirl,' the Templar said quickly, 'but the Jovian life forms there were hunted to extinction.'

'But no one ascertained that the zeplens were intelligent,' said Duré, hearing the lack of conviction in his own voice.

'They sang,' said the Templar. 'They called across thousands of kilometers of atmosphere to each other in songs which held meaning and love and sorrow. Yet they were hunted to death like the great whales of Old Earth.'

Duré folded his hands. 'Agreed, there have been injustices. But surely there is a better way to right them than to support the cruel philosophy of the Shrike Cult . . . and to allow this war to go on.'

The Templar's hood moved back and forth. 'No. If these were mere human injustices, other remedies could be found. But much of the ill- ness . . . much of the insanity which has led to the destruction of races and the despoiling of worlds . . . this has come from the sinful symbiosis.'

'Symbiosis?'

'Humankind and the TechnoCore,' said Sek Hardeen in the harshest tones Duré had ever heard a Templar use. 'Man and his machine intelli- gences. Which is a parasite on the other? Neither part of the symbiote can now tell. But it is an evil thing, a work of the Anti-Nature. Worse than that, Duré, it is an evolutionary dead end.'

The Jesuit stood and walked to the railing. He looked out over the darkened world of treetops spreading out like cloud tops in the night. 'Surely there is a better way than turning to the Shrike and interstellar war.'

'The Shrike is a catalyst,' said Hardeen. 'It is the cleansing fire when the forest has been stunted and allowed to grow diseased by overplanting. There will be hard times, but the results will be new growth, new life, and a proliferation of species . . . not merely elsewhere but in the community of humankind itself.'

'Hard times,' mused Duré. 'And your Brotherhood is willing to see billions of people die to accomplish this . . . weeding out?'

The Templar clenched his fists. 'That will not occur. The Shrike is the warning. Our Ouster brethren seek only to control Hyperion and the Shrike long enough to strike at the TechnoCore. It will be a surgical procedure . . . the destruction of a symbiote and the rebirth of humankind as a distinct partner in the cycle of life.'

Duré sighed. 'No one knows where the TechnoCore resides,' he said. 'How can the Ousters strike at it?'

'They will,' said the True Voice of the Worldtree, but there was less confidence in his voice than there had been a moment before.

'And was attacking God's Grove part of the deal?' asked the priest.

It was the Templar's turn to stand and pace, first to the railing, then back to the table. 'They will not attack God's Grove. That is what I have kept you here to see. Then you must report to the Hegemony.'

'They'll know at once whether the Ousters attack,' said Duré, puzzled.

'Yes, but they will not know *why* our world will be spared. You must bring this message. Explain this truth.'

'To hell with that,' said Father Paul Duré. 'I'm tired of being everyone's messenger. How do you know all this? The coming of the Shrike? The reason for the war?'

'There have been prophecies—' began Sek Hardeen.

Duré slammed his fist into the railing. How could he explain the manipulations of a creature who could – or at least was an agent of a force which could – manipulate time itself?

'You will see . . .' began the Templar again, and as if to punctuate his words there came a great, soft sound, almost as though a million hidden people had sighed and then moaned softly.

'Good God,' said Duré and looked to the west where it seemed that the sun was rising where it had disappeared less than an hour before. A hot wind rustled leaves and blew across his face.

Five blossoming and inward-curling mushroom clouds climbed above the western horizon, turning night to day as they boiled and faded. Duré had instinctively covered his eyes until he realized that these explosions were so far away that although brilliant as the local sun, they would not blind him.

Sek Hardeen pulled back his cowl so that the hot wind ruffled his long, oddly greenish hair. Duré stared at the man's long, thin, vaguely Asian features and realized that he saw shock etched there. Shock and disbelief. Hardeen's cowl whispered with comm calls and the micro-babble of excited voices.

'Explosions on Sierra and Hokkaido,' whispered the Templar to himself. 'Nuclear explosions. From the ships in orbit.'

Duré remembered that Sierra was a continent, closed to outsiders, less than eight hundred kilometers from the Worldtree where they stood. He thought that he remembered that Hokkaido was the sacred isle where the potential treeships were grown and prepared.

'Casualties?' he asked, but before Hardeen could answer, the sky was slashed with brilliant light as a score or more tactical lasers, CPBs, and fusion lances cut a swath from horizon to horizon, switching and flashing like searchlights across the roof of the world forest that was God's Grove. And where the lance beams cut, flame erupted in their wake.

Duré staggered as a hundred-meter-wide beam skipped like a tornado through the forest less than a kilometer from the Worldtree. The ancient forest exploded in flame, creating a corridor of fire rising ten kilometers into the night sky. Wind roared past Duré and Sek Hardeen as air rushed in to feed the fire storm. Another beam slashed north and south, passing close to the Worldtree before disappearing over the horizon. Another swath of flame and smoke rose toward the treacherous stars.

'They promised,' gasped Sek Hardeen. 'The Ouster brethren *promised*!'

'You need help!' cried Duré, 'Ask the Web for emergency assistance.'

Hardeen grabbed Duré's arm, pulled him to the edge of the platform. The stairs were back in place. On the platform below, a farcaster portal shimmered.

'Only the advance units of the Ouster fleet have arrived,' cried the Templar over the sound of forests burning. Ash and smoke filled the air, drifting past amidst hot embers. 'But the singularity sphere will be destroyed any second. *Go!*'

'I'm not leaving without you,' called the Jesuit, sure that his voice could not be heard over the wind roar and terrible crackling. Suddenly, only kilometers to the east, the perfect blue circle of a plasma explosion expanded, imploded inward, then expanded again with visible concentric circles of shock wave. Kilometer-tall trees bent and broke in the first wave of the blast, their eastern sides exploding in flame, leaves flying off by the millions and adding to the almost solid wall of debris hurtling toward the Worldtree. Behind the circle of flame, another plasma bomb went off. Then a third.

Duré and the Templar fell down the steps and were blown across the lower platform like leaves on a sidewalk. The Templar grabbed a burning muirwood baluster, seized Duré's arm in an iron grip, and struggled to his feet, moving toward the still shimmering farcaster like a man leaning into a cyclone.

Half conscious, half aware of being dragged, Duré managed to get to his own feet just as Voice of the Worldtree Sek Hardeen pulled him to the edge of the portal. Duré clung to the portal frame, too weak to pull himself the final meter, and looked past the farcaster to see something which he would never forget.

Once, many, many years before, near his beloved Villefranche-sur-Saône, the youngster Paul Duré had stood on a cliff top, secure in the arms of his father and safe in a thick concrete shelter, and watched through a narrow window as a forty-meter tall tsunami rushed toward the coast where they lived.

This tsunami was three kilometers high, was made of flame, and was racing at what seemed the speed of light across the helpless roof of the forest toward the Worldtree, Sek Hardeen, and Paul Duré. What the tsunami touched, it destroyed. It raged closer, rising higher and nearer until it obliterated the world and sky with flame and noise.

'No!' screamed Father Paul Duré.

'Go!' cried the True Voice of the Worldtree and pushed the Jesuit through the farcaster portal even as the platform, the Worldtree's trunk, and the Templar's robe burst into flames.

The farcaster shut down even as Duré tumbled through, slicing off the heel of his shoe as it contracted, and Duré felt his eardrums rupture and his clothes smolder even as he fell, struck something hard with the back of his head, and fell again into darkness more absolute.

Gladstone and the others watched in horrified silence as the civilian satellites sent images of the death throes of God's Grove through the farcaster relays.

'We have to blow it *now*,' cried Admiral Singh over the crackling of forests burning. Meina Gladstone thought that she could hear the screams of human beings and the countless arboreals who lived in the Templar forests.

'We can't let them get closer!' cried Singh. 'We have only the remotes to detonate the sphere.'

'Yes,' said Gladstone, but although her lips moved she heard no sound.

Singh turned and nodded toward a FORCE:space colonel. The Colonel touched his tactical board. The burning forests disappeared, the giant holos went absolutely dark, but the sound of screams somehow remained. Gladstone realized that it was the sound of blood in her ears.

She turned toward Morpurgo. 'How long . . .' She cleared her throat. 'General, how long until Mare Infinitus is attacked?'

'Three hours and fifty-two minutes, M. Executive,' said the General.

Gladstone turned toward the former Commander William Ajunta Lee. 'Is your task force ready, Admiral?'

'Yes, CEO,' said Lee, his face pale beneath a tan.

'How many ships will be in the strike?'

'Seventy-four, M. Executive.'

'And you will hit them away from Mare Infinitus?'

'Just within the Oört Cloud, M. Executive.'

'Good,' said Gladstone. 'Good hunting, Admiral.'

The young man took this as his cue to salute and leave the chamber. Admiral Singh leaned over and whispered something to General Van Zeidt.

Sedeptra Akasi leaned toward Gladstone and said, 'Government House Security reports that a man just farcast into the secured GH terminex with an outdated priority access code. The man was injured, taken to the East Wing infirmary.'

'Leigh?' asked Gladstone. 'Severn?'

'No, M. Executive,' said Akasi. 'The priest from Pacem. Paul Duré.'

Gladstone nodded. 'I'll see him after my meeting with Albedo,' she said to her aide. To the group, she announced, 'Unless anyone has anything to add to what we saw, we shall adjourn for thirty minutes and take up the defense of Asquith and Ixion when we reassemble.'

The group stood as the CEO and her entourage stepped through the permanent connecting portal to Government House and filed through a door in the far wall. The rumble of argument and shock resumed when Gladstone was out of sight.

Meina Gladstone sat back in her leather chair and closed her eyes for precisely five seconds. When she opened them, the cluster of aides still stood there, some looking anxious, some looking eager, all of them waiting for her next word, her next command.

'Get out,' she said softly. 'Go on, take a few minutes to get some rest. Put your feet up for ten minutes. There'll be no more rest for the next twenty-four to forty-eight hours.'

The group filed out, some looking on the verge of protest, others on the verge of collapse.

'Sedeptra,' said Gladstone, and the young woman stepped back into the office. 'Assign two of my personal guard to the priest who just came through, Duré.'

Akasi nodded and made a note on her faxpad.

'How is the political situation?' asked Gladstone, rubbing her eyes.

'The All Thing is chaos,' said Akasi. 'There are factions but they haven't coalesced into effective opposition yet. The Senate is a different story.'

'Feldstein?' said Gladstone, naming the angry senator from Barnard's World. Less than forty-two hours remained before Barnard's World would be attacked by the Ousters.

'Feldstein, Kakinuma, Peters, Sabenstorafem, Richeau . . . even Sudette Chier is calling for your resignation.'

'What about her husband?' Gladstone considered Senator Kolchev the most influential person in the Senate.

'No word from Senator Kolchev yet. Public or private.'

Gladstone tapped a thumbnail against her lower lip. 'How much time do you think this administration has before a vote of no confidence brings us down, Sedeptra?'

Akasi, one of the most astute political operatives Gladstone had ever worked with, returned her boss's stare. 'Seventy-two hours at the outside, CEO. The votes are there. The mob just doesn't know it's a mob yet. *Somebody* has to pay for what's happening.'

Gladstone nodded absently. 'Seventy-two hours,' she murmured. 'More than enough time.' She looked up and smiled. 'That will be all, Sedeptra. Get some rest.'

The aide nodded but her expression showed her true opinion of that suggestion. It was very quiet in the study when the door closed behind her.

Gladstone sat thinking for a moment, her fist to her chin. Then she said to the walls, 'Bring Councilor Albedo here, please.'

Twenty seconds later, the air on the other side of Gladstone's broad desk misted, shimmered, and solidified. The representative of the TechnoCore looked as handsome as ever, short gray hair gleaming in the light, a healthy tan on his open, honest face.

'M. Executive,' began the holographic projection, 'the Advisory Council and the Core predictors continue to offer their services in this time of great—'

'Where is the Core, Albedo?' interrupted Gladstone.

The Councilor's smile did not falter. 'I'm sorry, M. Executive, what was the question?'

'The TechnoCore. Where is it?'

Albedo's friendly face showed a slight puzzlement but no hostility, no visible emotion other than bemused helpfulness. 'You're certainly aware, M. Executive, that it has been Core policy since the Secession not to reveal the location of the . . . ah . . . physical elements of the TechnoCore. In another sense, the Core is nowhere, since—'

'Since you exist on the datumplane and datasphere consensual realities,' said Gladstone, voice flat. 'Yes, I've heard that crap all of my life, Albedo. So did my father and his father before him. I'm asking a straight question now. *Where* is the TechnoCore?'

The Councilor shook his head bemusedly, regretfully, as if he were an adult being asked for the thousandth time the child's question, Why is the sky blue, Daddy?

'M. Executive, it is simply not possible to answer that question in a way that would make sense in human three-dimensional coordinates. In a sense we . . . the Core . . . exist within the Web and beyond the Web. We swim in the datumplane reality which you call the datasphere, but as for the physical elements . . . what your ancestors called "hardware", we find it necessary to—'

'To keep it a secret,' finished Gladstone. She crossed her arms. 'Are you aware, Councilor Albedo, that there will be those people in the Hegemony . . . millions of people . . . who will firmly believe that the Core . . . your Advisory Council . . . has betrayed humankind?'

Albedo made a motion with his hands. 'That will be regrettable, M. Executive. Regrettable but understandable.'

'Your predictors were supposed to be close to foolproof, Councilor. Yet at no time did you tell us of the destruction of worlds by this Ouster fleet.'

The sadness on the projection's handsome face was very close to convincing. 'M. Executive, it is only fair to remind you that the Advisory Council warned you that bringing Hyperion into the Web introduced a random variable which even the Council could not factor.'

'But this isn't Hyperion!' snapped Gladstone, her voice rising. 'It's God's Grove burning. Heaven's Gate reduced to slag. Mare Infinitus waiting for the next hammer blow! What good is the Advisory Council if it cannot predict an invasion of that magnitude?'

'We did predict the inevitability of war with the Ousters, M. Executive. We also predicted the great danger of defending Hyperion. You must believe me that the inclusion of Hyperion in any predictive equation brings the reliability factor down as low as—'

'All right,' sighed Gladstone. 'I need to talk to someone else in the Core, Albedo. Someone in your indecipherable hierarchy of intelligences who actually has some decision-making power.'

'I assure you that I represent all Core elements when I—'

'Yes, yes. But I want to speak to one of the . . . the Powers I believe you call them. One of the elder AIs. One with clout, Albedo. I need to speak to someone who can tell me why the Core kidnapped my artist Severn and my aide Leigh Hunt.'

The holo looked shocked. 'I assure you, M. Gladstone, on the honor of four centuries of our alliance, that the Core had nothing to do with the unfortunate disappearance of—'

Gladstone stood. 'This is why I need to talk to a Power. The time for assurances is past, Albedo. It is time for straight talk if either of our species is going to survive. That is all.' She turned her attention to the faxpad flimsies on her desk.

Councilor Albedo stood, nodded a farewell, and shimmered out of existence.

Gladstone called her personal farcaster portal into existence, spoke the

Government House infirmary codes, and started to step through. In the instant before touching the opaque surface of the energy rectangle, she paused, gave thought to what she was doing, and for the first time in her life felt anxiety about stepping through a farcaster.

What if the Core wanted to kidnap her? Or kill her?

Meina Gladstone suddenly realized that the Core had the power of life and death over every farcaster-traveling citizen in the Web . . . which was every citizen with power. Leigh and the Severn cybrid did not have to be kidnaped, translated somewhere . . . only the persistent habit of thinking of farcasters as foolproof transportation created the subconscious conviction that they had *gone somewhere*. Her aide and the enigmatic cybrid could easily have been translated to . . . to nothing. To scattered atoms stretched through a singularity. Farcasters did not 'teleport' people and things – such a concept was silly – but how much less silly was it to trust a device that punched holes in the fabric of space-time and allowed one to step through black hole 'trapdoors'? How silly was it for her to trust the Core to transport her to the infirmary?

Gladstone thought of the War Room . . . three giant rooms connected by permanently activated, vision-clear farcaster portals . . . but three rooms nonetheless, separated by at least a thousand light-years of real space, decades of real time even under Hawking drive. Every time Morpurgo or Singh or one of the others moved from a map holo to the plotting board, he or she stepped across great gulfs of space and time. All the Core had to do to destroy the Hegemony or anyone in it was to tamper with the farcasters, allow a slight 'mistake' in targeting.

To hell with this, thought Meina Gladstone and stepped through to see Paul Duré in the Government House infirmary.

THIRTY-NINE

The two rooms on the second floor of the house on the Piazza di Spagna are small, narrow, high ceilinged, and – except for a single dim lamp burning in each room as if lighted by ghosts in expectation of a visit by other ghosts – quite dark. My bed is in the smaller of the two rooms: the one facing the Piazza, although all one can see from the high windows this night is darkness creased by deeper shadows and accented by the ceaseless burbling of Bernini's unseen fountain.

Bells ring on the hour from one of the twin towers of Santa Trinità dei Monti, the church that crouches in the dark like a massive, tawny cat at the head of the stairs outside, and each time I hear the bells toll the brief notes of the early hours of the morn, I imagine ghostly hands pulling rotting bell ropes. Or perhaps rotting hands pulling ghostly bell ropes; I don't know which image suits my macabre fancies this endless night.

Fever lies upon me this night, as dank and heavy and stifling as a thick, water-soaked blanket. My skin alternately burns and then is clammy to the touch. Twice I have been seized with coughing spasms; the first brought Hunt running in from his couch in the other room, and I watched his eyes widen at the sight of the blood I had vomited on the damask sheets; the second spasm I stifled as best I could, staggering to the basin on the bureau to spit up smaller quantities of black blood and dark phlegm. Hunt did not wake the second time.

To be back here. To come all this way to these dark rooms, this grim bed. I half remember awakening here, miraculously cured, the 'real' Severn and Dr Clark and even little Signora Angeletti hovering in the outer room. That period of convalescence from death; that period of realization that I was not Keats, was not on the true Earth, that this was not in the century I had closed my eyes in that last night . . . that I was not human.

Sometime after two, I sleep, and as I sleep, I dream. The dream is one I have never suffered before. I dream that I rise slowly through the datumplane, through the datasphere, into and through the megasphere, and finally into a place I do not know, have never dreamt of . . . a place of infinite spaces, unhurried, indescribable colors, a place with no horizons, no ceilings, no floors or solid areas one might call the ground. I think of it as the metasphere, for I sense immediately that this level of consensual reality includes all of the varieties and vagaries of sensation which I have experienced on Earth, all of the binary analyses and intellectual pleasures I have felt flowing from the TechnoCore through the datasphere, and, above all, a sense of . . . of what? Expansiveness? Freedom? – *potential* might be the word I am hunting for.

I am alone in this metasphere. Colors flow above me, under me, *through* me . . . sometimes dissolving into vague pastels, sometimes coalescing into cloudlike fantasies, and at other times, rarely, appearing to form into more solid objects, shapes, distinct forms which may or may not be humanoid in appearance – I watch them the way a child might watch clouds and imagine elephants, crocodiles from the Nile, and great gunboats marching from west to east on a spring day in the Lake District.

After a while I hear sounds: the maddening trickle of the Bernini fountain in the Piazza outside; doves rustling and cooing on the ledges above my window; Leigh Hunt moaning softly in his sleep. But above and beneath these noises, I hear something more stealthy, less *real*, but infinitely more threatening.

Something large this way comes. I strain to see through the pastel gloom; something is moving just beyond the horizon of sight. I know that it knows my name. I know that it holds my life in one palm and death in its other fist.

There is no place to hide in this space beyond space. I cannot run. The siren song of pain continues to rise and fall from the world I left behind – the everyday pain of each person everywhere, the pain of those suffering from the war just begun, the specific pain of those on the Shrike's terrible tree, and, worst of all, the pain I feel for and from the pilgrims and those others whose lives and thoughts I now share.

It would be worth rushing to greet this approaching shadow of doom if it would grant me freedom from that song of pain.

'Severn! Severn!'

For a second I think that I am the one calling, just as I had before in these rooms, calling Joseph Severn in the night when my pain and fever ranged beyond my ability to contain it. And he was always there: Severn with his hulking, well-meaning slowness and that gentle smile which I often wanted to wipe from his face with some small meanness or comment. It is hard to be good-natured when one is dying; I had led a life of some generosity . . . why then was it my fate to continue that role when *I* was the one suffering, when *I* was the one coughing the ragged remnants of my lungs into stained handkerchiefs?

'Severn!'

It is not my voice. Hunt is shaking me by the shoulders, calling Severn's name. I realize that he thinks he is calling *my* name. I brush away his hands and sink back into the pillows. 'What is it? What's wrong?'

'You were moaning,' says Gladstone's side. 'Crying out.'

'A nightmare. Nothing more.'

'Your dreams are usually more than dreams,' says Hunt. He glances around the narrow room, illuminated now by the single lamp he has carried in. 'What a terrible place, Severn.'

I try to smile. 'It cost me twenty-eight shillings a month. Seven scudi. Highway robbery.'

Hunt frowns at me. The stark light makes his wrinkles seem deeper than usual. 'Listen, Severn, I know you're a cybrid. Gladstone told me that you were the retrieval persona of a poet named Keats. Now obviously all this . . .' – he gestured helplessly toward the room, shadows, tall rectangle of windows, and high bed – 'all this has something to do with that. But how? What game is the Core playing here?'

'I'm not sure,' I say truthfully.

'But you know this place?'

'Oh yes,' I say with feeling.

'Tell me,' pleads Hunt, and it is his restraint to this point in *not* asking as much as the earnestness of that plea now which decides me to tell him.

I tell him about the poet John Keats, about his birth in 1795, his short and frequently unhappy life, and about his death from 'consumption' in 1821, in Rome, far from his friends and only love. I tell him about my staged 'recovery' in this very room, about my decision to take the name of Joseph Severn – the artist acquaintance who stayed with Keats until his death – and, finally, I tell him about my short time in the Web, listening, watching, condemned to dream the lives of the Shrike Pilgrims on Hyperion and the others.

'Dreams?' says Hunt. 'You mean even now you're dreaming about what's occurring in the Web?'

'Yes.' I tell him of the dreams about Gladstone, the destruction of Heaven's Gate and God's Grove, and the confused images from Hyperion.

Hunt is pacing back and forth in the narrow room, his shadow thrown high on the rough walls. 'Can *you* contact *them*?'

'The ones I dream of? Gladstone?' I think a second. 'No.'

'Are you sure?'

I try to explain. 'I'm not even in these dreams, Hunt. I have no . . . no voice, no presence . . . there's no way I can contact those I dream about.'

'But sometimes you dream what they're thinking?'

I realize that this is true. Close to the truth. 'I sense what they are *feeling* . . .'

'Then can't you leave some trace in their mind . . . in their memory? Let them know where we are?'

'No.'

Hunt collapses into the chair at the foot of my bed. He suddenly seems very old.

'Leigh,' I say, 'even if I could communicate with Gladstone or the others – which I can't – what good would it do? I've told you that this replica of Old Earth is in the Magellanic Cloud. Even at quantum-leap Hawking velocities it would take centuries for anyone to reach us.'

'We could warn them,' says Hunt, his voice so tired that it sounds almost sullen.

'Warn them of what? All of Gladstone's worst nightmares are coming true around her. Do you think she trusts the Core now? That's why the Core could kidnap us so blatantly. Events are proceeding too quickly for Gladstone or anyone in the Hegemony to deal with.'

Hunt rubs his eyes, then steeples his fingers under his nose. His stare is not overly friendly. 'Are you really the retrieved personality of a poet?'

I say nothing.

'Recite some poetry. Make something up.'

I shake my head. It is late, we're both tired and frightened, and my heart has not yet quit pounding from the nightmare which was more than a nightmare. I won't let Hunt make me angry.

'Come on,' he says. 'Show me that you're the new, improved version of Bill Keats.'

'John Keats,' I say softly.

'Whatever. Come on, Severn. Or John. Or whatever I should call you. Recite some poesy.'

'All right,' I say, returning his stare. 'Listen.

'There was a naughty boy
  And a naughty boy was he
For nothing would he do
  But scribble poetry—
  He took
  An inkstand
  In his hand
  And a pen
  Big as ten
  In the other
  And away
  In a pother
  He ran
  To the mountains
  And fountains
  And ghostes
  And postes
  And witches
  And ditches,
  And wrote
  In his coat
  When the weather
  Was cool—
  Fear of gout—
  And without
  When the weather

Was warm.
Och, the charm
When we choose
To follow one's nose
To the North,
To the North,
To follow one's nose
To the North!'

'I don't know,' says Hunt. 'That doesn't sound like something a poet whose reputation has lasted a thousand years would have written.'

I shrug.

'Were you dreaming about Gladstone tonight? Did something happen that caused those moans?'

'No. It wasn't about Gladstone. It was a . . . real nightmare for a change.'

Hunt stands, lifts his lamp, and prepares to take the only light from the room. I can hear the fountain in the Piazza, the doves on the windowsills. 'Tomorrow,' he says, 'we'll make sense of all this and figure out a way to get back. If they can farcast us here, there must be a way to farcast home.'

'Yes,' I say, knowing it is not true.

'Good night,' says Hunt. 'No more nightmares, all right?'

'No more,' I say, knowing this is even less true.

Moneta pulled the wounded Kassad away from the Shrike and seemed to hold the creature at bay with an extended hand while she fumbled a blue torus from the belt of her skinsuit and twisted it behind her.

A two-meter-high gold oval hung burning in midair.

'Let me go,' muttered Kassad. 'Let us finish it.' There was blood spattered where the Shrike had clawed huge rents in the Colonel's skinsuit. His right foot was dangling as if half-severed; he could put no weight on it, and only the fact that he had been struggling with the Shrike, half carried by the thing in a mad parody of a dance, had kept Kassad upright as they fought.

'Let me go,' repeated Fedmahn Kassad.

'Shut up,' said Moneta, and then, more softly, 'Shut up, my love.' She dragged him through the golden oval, and they emerged into blazing light.

Even through his pain and exhaustion, Kassad was dazzled by the sight. They were not on Hyperion; he was sure of that. A vast plain stretched to an horizon much farther away than logic or experience would allow. Low, orange grass – if grass it was – grew on the flatlands and low hills like fuzz on the back of some immense caterpillar, while things which might have been trees grew like whiskered-carbon sculptures, their trunks and branches Escher-ish in their baroque improbability, their leaves a riot of dark blue and violet ovals shimmering toward a sky alive with light.

But not sunlight. Even as Moneta carried him away from the closing portal – Kassad did not think of it as a farcaster since he felt sure it had carried them through time as well as space – and toward a copse of those impossible trees, Kassad turned his eyes toward the sky and felt something close to wonder. It was as bright as a Hyperion day; as bright as midday on a Lusian shopping mall; as bright as midsummer on the Tharsis Plateau of Kassad's dry homeworld, Mars, but this was no sunlight – the sky was filled with stars and constellations and star clusters and a galaxy so cluttered with suns that there were almost no patches of darkness between the lights. It was like being in a planetarium with ten projectors, thought Kassad. Like being at the center of the galaxy.

The center of the galaxy.

A group of men and women in skinsuits moved out from the shade of the Escher trees to circle Kassad and Moneta. One of the men – a giant even by Kassad's Martian standards – looked at him, raised his head toward Moneta, and even though Kassad could hear nothing, sense nothing on his skinsuit's radio and tightband receivers, he knew the two were communicating.

'Lie back,' said Moneta as she laid Kassad on the velvety orange grass. He struggled to sit up, to speak, but both she and the giant touched his chest with their palms, and he lay back so that his vision was filled with the slowly twisting violet leaves and the sky of stars.

The man touched him again, and Kassad's skinsuit was deactivated. He tried to sit up, tried to cover himself as he realized he was naked before the small crowd that had gathered, but Moneta's firm hand held him in place. Through the pain and dislocation, he vaguely sensed the man touching his slashed arms and chest, running a silver-coated hand down his leg to where the Achilles' tendon had been cut. The Colonel felt a coolness wherever the giant touched, and then his consciousness floated away like a balloon, high above the tawny plain and the rolling hills, drifting toward the solid canopy of stars where a huge figure waited, dark as a towering thundercloud above the horizon, massive as a mountain.

'Kassad,' whispered Moneta, and the Colonel drifted back. 'Kassad,' she said again, her lips against his cheek, his skinsuit reactivated and melded with hers.

Colonel Fedmahn Kassad sat up as she did. He shook his head, realized that he was clothed in quicksilver energy once again, and got to his feet. There was no pain. He felt his body tingle in a dozen places where injuries had been healed, serious cuts repaired. He melded his hand to his own suit, ran flesh across flesh, bent his knee and touched his heel, but could feel no scars.

Kassad turned toward the giant. 'Thank you,' he said, not knowing if the man could hear.

The giant nodded and stepped back toward the others.

'He's a . . . a doctor of sorts,' said Moneta. 'A healer.'

Kassad half heard her as he concentrated on the other people. They were human – he knew in his heart that they were human – but the variety was staggering: their skinsuits were not all silver like Kassad's and Moneta's but ranged through a score of colors, each as soft and organic as some living wild creature's pelt. Only the subtle energy-shimmer and blurred facial features revealed the skinsuit surface. Their anatomy was as varied as their coloration: the healer's Shrike-sized girth and massive bulk, his massive brow and a cascade of tawny energy flow which might be a mane . . . a female next to him, no larger than a child but obviously a woman, perfectly proportioned with muscular legs, small breasts, and faery wings two meters long rising from her back – and not merely decorative wings, either, for when the breeze ruffled the orange prairie grass, this woman gave a short run, extended her arms, and rose gracefully into the air.

Behind several tall, thin women with blue skinsuits and long, webbed fingers, a group of short men were as visored and armor-plated as a FORCE: Marine going into battle in a vacuum, but Kassad sensed that the armor was part of *them*. Overhead, a cluster of winged males rose on thermals, thin, yellow beams of laser light pulsing between them in some complex code. The lasers seemed to emanate from an eye in each of their chests.

Kassad shook his head again.

'We need to go,' said Moneta. 'The Shrike cannot follow us here. These warriors have enough to contend with without dealing with this particular manifestation of the Lord of Pain.'

'Where are we?' asked Kassad.

Moneta brought a violet oval into existence with a golden ferule from her belt. 'Far in humankind's future. *One* of our futures. This is where the Time Tombs were formed and launched backward in time.'

Kassad looked around again. Something very large moved in front of the starfield, blocking out thousands of stars and throwing a shadow for scant seconds before it was gone. The men and women looked up briefly and then went back to their business: harvesting small things from the trees, huddling in clusters to view bright energy maps called up by a flick of one man's fingers, flying off toward the horizon with the speed of a thrown spear. One low, round individual of indeterminate sex had burrowed into the soft soil and was visible now only as a faint line of raised earth moving in quick concentric circles around the band.

'Where *is* this place?' Kassad asked again. '*What* is it?' Suddenly, inexplicably, he felt himself close to tears, as if he had turned an unfamiliar corner and found himself at home in the Tharsis Relocation Projects, his long-dead mother waving to him from a doorway, his forgotten friends and siblings waiting for him to join a game of scootball.

'Come,' said Moneta and there was no mistaking the urgency in her voice. She pulled Kassad toward the glowing oval. He watched the others and the dome of stars until he stepped through and the view was lost to sight.

They stepped out into darkness, and it took the briefest of seconds for the filters in Kassad's skinsuit to compensate his vision. They were at the base of the Crystal Monolith in the valley of the Time Tombs on Hyperion. It was night. Clouds boiled overhead, and a storm was raging. Only a pulsing glow from the Tombs themselves illuminated the scene. Kassad felt a sick lurch of loss for the clean, well-lighted place they had just left, and then his mind focused on what he was seeing.

Sol Weintraub and Brawne Lamia were half a klick down the valley, Sol bending over the woman as she lay near the front of the Jade Tomb. Wind swirled dust around them so thickly that they did not see the Shrike moving like another shadow down the trail past the Obelisk, toward them.

Fedmahn Kassad stepped off the dark marble in front of the Monolith and skirted the shattered crystal shards which littered the path. He realized that Moneta still clung to his arm.

'If you fight again,' she said, her voice soft and urgent in his ear, 'the Shrike will kill you.'

'They're my friends,' said Kassad. His FORCE gear and torn armor lay where Moneta had thrown it hours earlier. He searched the Monolith until he found his assault rifle and a bandolier of grenades, saw the rifle was still functional, checked charges and clicked off safeties, left the Monolith, and stepped forward at double time to intercept the Shrike.

I wake to the sound of water flowing, and for a second I believe I am awakening from my nap near the waterfall of Lodore during my walking tour with Brown. But the darkness when I open my eyes is as fearsome as when I slept, the water has a sick, trickling sound rather than the rush of the cataract which Southey would someday make famous in his poem, and I feel terrible – not merely sick with the sore throat I came down with on our tour after Brown and I foolishly climbed Skiddaw before breakfast – but mortally, fearfully ill, with my body aching with something deeper than ague while phlegm and fire bubble in my chest and belly.

I rise and feel my way to the window by touch. A dim light comes under the door from Leigh Hunt's room, and I realize that he has gone to sleep with the lamp still lit. That would not have been a bad thing for me to have done, but it is too late to light it now as I feel my way to the lighter rectangle of outer darkness set into the deeper darkness of the room.

The air is fresh and filled with the scent of rain. I realize that the sound that woke me is thunder as lightning flashes over the rooftops of Rome. No lights burn in the city. By leaning slightly out of the open window, I can see the stairs above the Piazza all slick with rain and the towers of Trinità dei Monti outlined blackly against lightning flashes. The wind that blows down those steps is chill, and I move back to the bed to pull a blanket around me before dragging a chair to the window and sitting there, looking out, thinking.

I remember my brother Tom during those last weeks and days, his face and body contorted with the terrible effort to breathe. I remember my mother and how pale she looked, her face almost shining in the gloom of the darkened room. My sister and I were allowed to touch her clammy hand, kiss her fevered lips, and then withdraw. I remember that once I furtively wiped my lips as I left that room, glancing sideways to see if my sister or others had seen my sinful act.

When Dr Clark and an Italian surgeon opened Keats's body less than thirty hours after he had died, they found, as Severn later wrote a friend,

'. . . the worst possible Consumption – the lungs were intirely destroyed – the cells were quite gone.' Neither Dr Clark nor the Italian surgeon could imagine how Keats had lived those last two months or more.

I think of this as I sit in the darkened room and look out on the darkened Piazza, all the while listening to the boiling in my chest and throat, feeling the pain like fire inside and the worse pain from the cries in my mind: cries from Martin Silenus on the tree, suffering for writing the poetry I had been too frail and cowardly to finish; cries from Fedmahn Kassad as he prepares to die at the claws of the Shrike; cries from the Consul as he is forced into betrayal a second time; cries from thousands of Templar throats as they bewail the death of both their world and their brother Het Masteen; cries from Brawne Lamia as she thinks of her dead lover, my twin; cries from Paul Duré as he lies fighting burns and the shock of memory, all too aware of the waiting cruciforms on his chest; cries from Sol Weintraub as he beats his fist on the earth of Hyperion, calling for his child, the infant cries of Rachel still in our ears.

'Goddamn,' I say softly, beating my fist against the stone and mortar of the window frame. 'Goddamn.'

After a while, just as the first hint of paleness promises dawn, I move away from the window, find my bed, and lie down just a moment to close my eyes.

Governor-General Theo Lane awoke to the sound of music. He blinked and looked around, recognizing the nearby nutrient tank and ship's surgery as if from a dream. Theo realized that he was wearing soft, black pajamas and had been sleeping on the surgery's examination couch. The past twelve hours began to stitch themselves together from Theo's patches of memory: being raised from the treatment tank, sensors being applied, the Consul and another man leaning over him, asking him questions – Theo answering just as if he were truly conscious, then sleep again, dreams of Hyperion and its cities burning. No, not dreams.

Theo sat up, felt himself almost float off the couch, found his clothes cleaned and folded neatly on a nearby shelf, and dressed quickly, hearing the music continue, now rising, now fading, but always continuing with a haunting acoustical quality which suggested that it was live and not recorded.

Theo took the short stairway to the recreation deck and stopped in surprise as he realized that the ship was open, the balcony extended, the containment field apparently off. Gravity underfoot was minimal: enough to pull Theo back to the deck but little more – probably 20 percent or less of Hyperion's, perhaps one-sixth standard.

The ship was open. Brilliant sunlight streamed in the open door to the balcony where the Consul sat playing the antique instrument he had called a piano. Theo recognized the archaeologist, Arundez, leaning against the hull opening with a drink in his hand. The Consul was playing something very old and very complicated; his hands were a studied blur on the keyboard. Theo moved closer, started to whisper something to the smiling Arundez, and then stopped in shock to stare.

Beyond the balcony, thirty meters below, brilliant sunlight fell on a bright green lawn stretching to an horizon far too close. On that lawn, clusters of people sat and lay in relaxed postures, obviously listening to the Consul's impromptu concert. But what people!

Theo could see tall, thin people, looking like the aesthetes of Epsilon Eridani, pale and bald in their wispy blue robes, but beside them and beyond them an amazing multitude of human types sat listening – more varieties than the Web had ever seen: humans cloaked in fur and scales; humans with bodies like bees and eyes to match, multifaceted receptors and antennae; humans as fragile and thin as wire sculptures, great black wings extending from their thin shoulders and folding around them like capes; humans apparently designed for massive-g worlds, short and stout and muscular as cape buffalo, making Lusians look fragile in comparison; humans with short bodies and long arms covered with orange fur, only their pale and sensitive faces separating them from some holo of Old Earth's long-extinct orang-utans; and other humans looking more lemur than humanoid, more aquiline or leonine or ursine or anthropoid than manlike. Yet somehow Theo knew at once that these were *human beings*, as shocking as their differences were. Their attentive gazes, their relaxed postures, and a hundred other subtle human attributes – down to the way a butterfly-winged mother cradled a butterfly-winged child in her arms – all gave testimony to a common humanity which Theo could not deny.

Melio Arundez turned, smiled at Theo's expression, and whispered, 'Ousters.'

Stunned, Theo Lane could do little more than shake his head and listen to the music. Ousters were barbarians, not these beautiful and sometimes ethereal creatures. Ouster captives on Bressia, not to mention the bodies of their infantry dead, had been of a uniform body sort – tall, yes, thin, yes, but decidedly more Web standard than this dizzying display of variety.

Theo shook his head again as the Consul's piano piece rose to a crescendo and ended on a definitive note. The hundreds of beings in the field beyond applauded, the sound high and soft in the thin air, and then Theo watched as they stood, stretched, and headed different ways . . . some walking quickly over the disturbingly near horizon, others unfolding eight-meter wings and flying away. Still others moved toward the base of the Consul's ship.

The Consul stood, saw Theo, and smiled. He clapped the younger man on the shoulder. 'Theo, just in time. We'll be negotiating soon.'

Theo Lane blinked. Three Ousters landed on the balcony and folded their great wings behind them. Each of the men was heavily furred and differently marked and striped, their pelts as organic and convincing as any wild creature's.

'As delightful as always,' the closest Ouster said to the Consul. The Ouster's face was leonine – broad nose and golden eyes framed by a ruff of tawny fur. 'The last piece was Mozart's Fantasia in D Minor, KV 397, was it not?'

'It was,' said the Consul. 'Freeman Vanz, I would like to introduce M. Theo Lane, Governor-General of the Hegemony Protectorate world of Hyperion.'

The lion gaze turned on Theo. 'An honor,' said Freeman Vanz and extended a furred hand.

Theo shook it. 'A pleasure to meet you, sir.' Theo wondered if he were actually still in the recovery tank, dreaming this. The sunlight on his face and the firm palm against his suggested otherwise.

Freeman Vanz turned back to the Consul. 'On behalf of the Aggregate, I thank you for that concert. It has been too many years since we have heard you play, my friend.' He glanced around. 'We can hold the talks here or at one of the administrative compounds, at your convenience.'

The Consul hesitated only a second. 'There are three of us, Freeman Vanz. Many of you. We will join you.'

The lion head nodded and glanced skyward. 'We will send a boat for your crossing.' He and the other two moved to the railing and stepped off, falling several meters before unfurling their complex wings and flying toward the horizon.

'Jesus,' whispered Theo. He gripped the Consul's forearm. 'Where are we?'

'The Swarm,' said the Consul, covering the Steinway's keyboard. He led the way inside, waited for Arundez to step back, and then brought the balcony in.

'And what are we going to negotiate?' asked Theo.

The Consul rubbed his eyes. It looked as if the man had slept little or not at all during the ten or twelve hours Theo had been healing.

'That depends upon CEO Gladstone's next message,' said the Consul and nodded toward where the holopit misted with transmission columns. A fatline squirt was being decoded on the ship's one-time pad at that moment.

Meina Gladstone stepped into the Government House infirmary and was escorted by waiting doctors to the recovery bay where Father Paul Duré lay. 'How is he?' she asked the first doctor, the CEO's own physician.

'Second-degree flash burns over about a third of his body,' answered Dr Irma Androneva. 'He lost his eyebrows and some hair . . . he didn't have that much to start with . . . and there were some tertiary radiation burns on the left side of his face and body. We've completed the epidermal regeneration and given RNA template injections. He's in no pain and conscious. There is the problem of the cruciform parasite on his chest, but that is of no immediate danger to the patient.'

'Tertiary radiation burns,' said Gladstone, stopping for a moment just out of earshot of the cubicle where Duré waited. 'Plasma bombs?'

'Yes,' answered another doctor whom Gladstone did not recognize.

'We're certain that this man 'cast in from God's Grove a second or two before the farcaster connection was cut.'

'All right,' said Gladstone, stopping by the floating pallet where Duré rested, 'I wish to speak to the gentleman alone, please.'

The doctors glanced at one another, waved a mech nurse to its wall storage, and closed the portal to the ward room as they departed.

'Father Duré?' asked Gladstone, recognizing the priest from his holos and Severn's descriptions during the pilgrimage. Duré's face was red and mottled now, and it glistened from regeneration gel and spray-on pain-killer. He was still a man of striking appearance.

'CEO,' whispered the priest and made as if to sit up.

Gladstone set a gentle hand on his shoulder. 'Rest,' she said. 'Do you feel like telling me what happened?'

Duré nodded. There were tears in the old Jesuit's eyes. 'The True Voice of the Worldtree didn't believe that they would really attack,' he whispered, his voice raw. 'Sek Hardeen thought that the Templars had some pact with the Ousters . . . some arrangement. But they did attack. Tactical lances, plasma devices, nuclear explosives, I think . . .'

'Yes,' said Gladstone, 'we monitored it from the War Room. I need to know everything, Father Duré. Everything from the point when you stepped into the Cave Tomb on Hyperion.'

Paul Duré's eyes focused on Gladstone's face. 'You know about that?'

'Yes. And about most other things to that point. But I need to know more. Much more.'

Duré closed his eyes. 'The labyrinth . . .'

'What?'

'The labyrinth,' he said again, voice stronger. He cleared his throat and told her about his voyage through the tunnels of corpses, the transition to a FORCE ship and his meeting with Severn on Pacem.

'And you're sure Severn was headed here? To Government House?' asked Gladstone.

'Yes. He and your aide . . . Hunt. Both of them intended to 'cast here.'

Gladstone nodded and carefully touched an unburned section of the priest's shoulder. 'Father, things are happening very quickly here. Severn is missing and so is Leigh Hunt. I need advice about Hyperion. Will you stay with me?'

Duré looked confused for a moment. 'I need to get back. Back to Hyperion, M. Executive. Sol and the others are waiting for me.'

'I understand,' said Gladstone soothingly. 'As soon as there's a way back to Hyperion, I'll expedite your return. Right now, however, the Web is under brutal attack. Millions are dying or in danger of dying. I need your help, Father. Can I count on you until then?'

Paul Duré sighed and lay back. 'Yes, M. Executive. But I have no idea how I—'

There was a soft knock and Sedeptra Akasi entered and handed Gladstone a message flimsy. The CEO smiled. 'I said that things were happening quickly, Father. Here's another development. A message from Pacem says that the College of Cardinals has met in the Sistine Chapel . . .' Gladstone raised an eyebrow. 'I forget, Father, is that *the* Sistine Chapel?'

'Yes. The Church took it apart stone by stone, fresco by fresco, and moved it to Pacem after the Big Mistake.'

Gladstone looked down at the flimsy. '. . . met in the Sistine Chapel and elected a new pontiff.'

'So soon?' whispered Paul Duré. He closed his eyes again. 'I guess they felt they must hurry. Pacem lies – what? – only ten days in front of the Ouster invasion wave. Still, to come to a decision so quickly . . .'

'Are you interested in who the new Pope is?' asked Gladstone.

'Either Antonio Cardinal Guarducci or Agostino Cardinal Ruddell, I would guess,' said Duré. 'None of the others would command a majority at this time.'

'No,' said Gladstone. 'According to this message from Bishop Edouard of the Curia Romana . . .'

'*Bishop* Edouard! Excuse me, M. Executive, please go on.'

'According to Bishop Edouard, the College of Cardinals has elected someone below the rank of monsignor for the first time in the history of the Church. This says that the new Pope is a Jesuit priest . . . a certain Father Paul Duré.'

Duré sat straight up despite his burns. 'What?' There was no belief in his voice.

Gladstone handed the flimsy to him.

Paul Duré stared at the paper. 'This is impossible. They have never elected a pontiff below the rank of monsignor except symbolically, and that was unique . . . it was St Belvedere after the Big Mistake and the Miracle of the . . . no, no, this is impossible.'

'Bishop Edouard has been trying to call, according to my aide,' said Gladstone. 'We'll have the call put through here at once, Father. Or should I say, Your Holiness?' There was no irony in the CEO's voice.

Duré looked up, too stunned to speak.

'I will have the call put through,' said Gladstone. 'We'll arrange your return to Pacem as quickly as possible, Your Holiness, but I would appreciate it if you could keep in touch. I do need your advice.'

Duré nodded and looked back at the flimsy. A phone began to blink on the console above the pallet.

CEO Gladstone stepped out into the hall, told the doctors about the most recent development, contacted Security to approve the farcast clearance for Bishop Edouard or other Church officials from Pacem, and 'cast back to her room in the residential wing. Sedeptra reminded her that the council was reconvening in the War Room in eight minutes. Gladstone nodded, saw her aide out, and stepped back to the fatline cubicle in its concealed niche in the wall. She activated sonic privacy fields and coded the transmission diskey for the Consul's ship. Every fatline receiver in the Web, Outback, galaxy, and universe would monitor the squirt, but only the Consul's ship could decode it. Or so she hoped.

The holo camera light winked red. 'Based on the automated squirt from your ship, I am assuming that you chose to meet with the Ousters, and they have allowed you to do so,' Gladstone said into the camera. 'I am also assuming that you survived the initial meeting.'

Gladstone took a breath. 'On behalf of the Hegemony, I have asked you to sacrifice much over the years. Now I ask you on behalf of all of humankind. You must find out the following:

'First, why are the Ousters attacking and destroying the worlds of the Web? You were convinced, Byron Lamia was convinced, and I was convinced that they wanted only Hyperion. Why have they changed this?

'Second, *where* is the TechnoCore? I must know if we are to fight them. Have the Ousters forgotten our common enemy, the Core?

'Third, what are their demands for a cease-fire? I am willing to sacrifice much to rid us of the Core's domination. *But the killing must stop!*

'Fourth, would the Leader of the Swarm Aggregate be willing to meet with me in person? I will farcast to Hyperion system if this is necessary. Most of our fleet elements have left there, but a JumpShip and its escort craft remain with the singularity sphere. The Swarm Leader must decide soon, because FORCE wants to destroy the sphere, and Hyperion then will be three years time-debt from the Web.

'Finally, the Swarm Leader must know that the Core wishes us to use a form of deathwand explosive device to counter the Ouster invasion. Many of the FORCE leaders agree. Time is short. We will not – repeat, not – allow the Ouster invasion to overrun the Web.

'It is up to you now. Please acknowledge this message and fatline me as soon as negotiations have begun.'

Gladstone looked into the camera disk, willing the force of her personality and sincerity across the light-years. 'I beseech you in the bowels of humankind's history, please accomplish this.'

The fatline message squirt was followed by two minutes of jerky imagery showing the deaths of Heaven's Gate and God's Grove. The Consul, Melio Arundez, and Theo Lane sat in silence after the holos faded.

'Response?' queried the ship.

The Consul cleared his throat. 'Acknowledge message received,' he said. 'Send our coordinates.' He looked across the holopit at the other two. 'Gentlemen?'

Arundez shook his head as if clearing it. 'It's obvious you've been here before . . . to the Ouster Swarm.'

'Yes,' said the Consul. 'After Bressia . . . after my wife and son . . . after Bressia, some time ago, I rendezvoused with this Swarm for extensive negotiations.'

'Representing the Hegemony?' asked Theo. The redhead's face looked much older and lined with worry.

'Representing Senator Gladstone's faction,' said the Consul. 'It was before she was first elected CEO. Her group explained to me that an internal power struggle within the TechnoCore could be affected by our bringing Hyperion into the Web Protectorate. The easiest way to do that was to allow information to slip to the Ousters . . . information that would cause them to attack Hyperion, thus bringing the Hegemony fleet here.'

'And you did that?' Arundez's voice showed no emotion, although his wife and grown children lived on Renaissance Vector, now less than eighty hours away from the invasion wave.

The Consul sat back in the cushions. 'No. I told the Ousters about the plan. They sent me back to the Web as a double agent. They planned to seize Hyperion, but at a time of their own choosing.'

Theo sat forward, his hands clasped very tightly. 'All those years at the consulate . . .'

'I was waiting for word from the Ousters,' the Consul said flatly. 'You see, they had a device that would collapse the anti-entropic fields around the Time Tombs. Open them when they were ready. Allow the Shrike to slip its bonds.'

'So the Ousters did that,' said Theo.

'No,' said the Consul, 'I did. I betrayed the Ousters just as I betrayed Gladstone and the Hegemony. I shot the Ouster woman who was calibrating the device . . . her and the technicians with her . . . and turned it on. The anti-entropic fields collapsed. The final pilgrimage was arranged. The Shrike is free.'

Theo stared at his former mentor. There was more puzzlement than rage in the younger man's green eyes. 'Why? Why did you do all this?'

The Consul told them, briefly and dispassionately, about his grandmother Siri of Maui-Covenant, and about her rebellion against the Hegemony – a rebellion which did not die when she and her lover, the Consul's grandfather, died.

Arundez rose from the pit and walked to the window opposite the balcony. Sunlight streamed across his legs and the dark blue carpet. 'Do the Ousters know what you did?'

'They do now,' said the Consul. 'I told Freeman Vanz and the others when we arrived.'

Theo paced the diameter of the holopit. 'So this meeting we're going to might be a trial?'

The Consul smiled. 'Or an execution.'

Theo stopped, both hands clenched in fists. 'And Gladstone knew this when she asked you to come here again?'

'Yes.'

Theo turned away. 'I don't know whether I want them to execute you or not.'

'I don't know either, Theo,' said the Consul.

Melio Arundez turned away from the window. 'Didn't Vanz say they were sending a boat to fetch us?'

Something in his tone brought the other two men to the window. The world where they had landed was a middle-sized asteroid which had been encircled by a class-ten containment field and terraformed into a sphere by generations of wind and water and careful restructuring. Hyperion's sun was setting behind the too-near horizon, and the few kilometers of feature-less grass rippled to a vagrant breeze. Below the ship, a wide stream or narrow river ambled across the pastureland, approached the horizon, and then seemed to fly upward into a river turned waterfall, twisting up through the distant containment field and winding through the blackness of space above before dwindling to a line too narrow to see.

A boat was descending that infinitely tall waterfall, approaching the surface of their small world. Humanoid figures could be seen near the bow and stern.

'Christ,' whispered Theo.

'We'd best get ready,' said the Consul. 'That's our escort.'

Outside, the sun set with shocking rapidity, sending its last rays through the curtain of water half a kilometer above the shadowed ground and searing the ultramarine sky with rainbows of almost frightening color and solidity.

FORTY

It is midmorning when Hunt awakens me. He arrives with breakfast on a tray and a frightened look in his dark eyes.

I ask, 'Where did you get the food?'

'There's some sort of little restaurant in the front room downstairs. Food was waiting there, hot, but no people.'

I nod. 'Signora Angeletti's little trattoria,' I say. 'She is not a good cook.' I remember Dr Clark's concern about my diet; he felt that the consumption had settled in my stomach and he held me to a starvation regime of milk and bread with the occasional bit of fish. Odd how many suffering members of humankind have faced eternity obsessed with their bowels, their bedsores, or the meagerness of their diets.

I look up at Hunt again. 'What is it?'

Gladstone's aide has moved to the window and seems absorbed in the view of the Piazza below. I can hear Bernini's accursed fountain trickling. 'I was going out for a walk while you slept,' Hunt says slowly, 'just in case there might be people out and about. Or a phone or farcaster.'

'Of course,' I say.

'I'd just stepped out . . . the . . .' He turns and licks his lips. 'There's something out there, Severn. In the street at the bottom of the stairs. I'm not sure, but I think that it's . . .'

'The Shrike,' I say.

Hunt nods. 'Did you see it?'

'No, but I am not surprised.'

'It's . . . it's terrible, Severn. There's something about it that makes my flesh crawl. Here . . . you can just get a glimpse of it in the shadows on the other side of the staircase.'

I start to rise, but a sudden fit of coughing and the feel of phlegm rising in my chest and throat makes me settle back on the pillows. 'I know what it looks like, Hunt. Don't worry, it's not here for you.' My voice sounds more confident than I feel.

'For you?'

'I don't think so,' I say between gasps for air. 'I think it's just here to make sure I don't try to leave . . . to find another place to die.'

Hunt returns to the bed. 'You're not going to die, Severn.'

I say nothing.

He sits in the straight-backed chair next to the bed and lifts a cooling cup of tea. 'If you die, what happens to me?'

681

'I don't know,' I say honestly. 'If I die, I don't even know what happens to *me*.'

There is a certain solipsism to serious illness which claims all of one's attention as certainly as an astronomical black hole seizes anything unlucky enough to fall within its critical radius. The day passes slowly, and I am exquisitely aware of the movement of sunlight across the rough wall, the feel of bedclothes beneath my palm, the fever which rises in me like nausea and burns itself out in the furnace of my mind, and, mostly, of the pain. Not my pain now, for a few hours or days of the constriction in my throat and the burning in my chest are bearable, almost welcomed like an obnoxious old friend met in a strange city, but the pain of the others . . . all the others. It strikes my mind like the noise of shattering slate, like hammer iron slammed repeatedly on anvil iron, and there is no escape from it.

My brain receives this as din and restructures it as poetry. All day and all night the pain of the universe floods in and wanders the fevered corridors of my mind as verse, imagery, images in verse, the intricate, endless dance of language, now as calming as a flute solo, now as shrill and strident and confusing as a dozen orchestras tuning up, but always verse, always poetry.

Sometime near sunset I awake from a half-doze, shattering the dream of Colonel Kassad fighting the Shrike for the lives of Sol and Brawne Lamia, and find Hunt sitting at the window, his long face colored by evening light the hue of terra-cotta.

'Is it still there?' I ask, my voice the rasp of file on stone.

Hunt jumps, then turns toward me with an apologetic smile and the first blush I have ever seen on that dour countenance. 'The Shrike?' he says. 'I don't know. I haven't seen it for a while. I *feel* that it is.' He looks at me. 'How are you?'

'Dying.' I instantly regret the self-indulgence of that flippancy, however accurate it is, when I see the pain it causes Hunt. 'It's all right,' I say almost jovially, 'I've done it before. It's not as if it were *me* that is dying. I exist as a personality deep in the TechnoCore. It's just this body. This cybrid of John Keats. This twenty-seven-year-old illusion of flesh and blood and borrowed associations.'

Hunt comes over to sit on the edge of the bed. I realize with a shock that he has changed the sheets during the day, exchanging my bloodbespeckled coverlet for one of his own. 'Your personality is an AI in the Core,' he says. 'Then you must be able to access the datasphere.'

I shake my head, too weary to argue.

'When the Philomels kidnapped you, we tracked you through your access route to the datasphere,' he persisted. 'You don't have to contact Gladstone personally. Just leave a message where Security can find it.'

'No,' I rasp, 'the Core does not wish it.'

'Are they blocking you? Stopping you?'

'Not yet. But they would.' I set the words separately between gasps, like laying delicate eggs back in the nest. Suddenly I remember a note I sent to dear Fanny shortly after a serious hemorrhage but almost a year before they would kill me. I had written: *'If I should die,'* said I to myself, *'I have left no immortal work behind me – nothing to make my friends proud of my memory – but I have lov'd the principle of beauty in all things, and if I had had time I would have made myself remember'd.'* This strikes me now as futile and self-centered and idiotic and naive . . . and yet I desperately believe it still. If I had had time . . . the months I had spent on Esperance, pretending to be a visual artist; the days wasted with Gladstone in the halls of government when I could have been writing . . .

'How do you know until you try?' asks Hunt.

'What's that?' I ask. The simple effort of two syllables sets me coughing again, the spasm ending only when I spit up half-solid spheres of blood into the basin which Hunt has hastily fetched. I lie back, trying to focus on his face. It is getting dark in the narrow room, and neither of us has lighted a lamp. Outside, the fountain burbles loudly.

'What's that?' I ask again, trying to remain here even as sleep and sleep's dreams tug at me. 'Try what?'

'Try leaving a message through the datasphere,' he whispers. 'Contacting someone.'

'And what message should we leave, Leigh?' I ask. It is the first time I have used his first name.

'Where we are. How the Core kidnapped us. Anything.'

'All right,' I say, closing my eyes. 'I'll try. I don't think they'll let me, but I promise I'll try.'

I feel Hunt's hand holding mine. Even through the winning tides of weariness, this sudden human contact is enough to make tears come to my eyes.

I will try. Before surrendering to the dreams or death, I will try.

Colonel Fedmahn Kassad shouted a FORCE battle cry and charged through the dust storm to intercept the Shrike before it covered the final thirty meters to where Sol Weintraub crouched next to Brawne Lamia.

The Shrike paused, its head swiveling frictionlessly, red eyes gleaming. Kassad armed his assault rifle and moved down the slope with reckless speed.

The Shrike *shifted*.

Kassad saw its movement through time as a slow blur, noting even as he watched the Shrike that movement in the valley had ceased, sand hung motionless in the air, and the light from the glowing Tombs had taken on a thick, amberish quality. Kassad's skinsuit was somehow shifting with the Shrike, following it through its movements through time.

The creature's head snapped up, attentive now, and its four arms extended like blades from a knife, fingers snapping open in sharp greeting.

Kassad skidded to a halt ten meters from the thing and activated the assault rifle, slagging the sand beneath the Shrike in a full-power widebeam burst.

The Shrike glowed as its carapace and steel-sculpture legs reflected the hellish light beneath and around it. Then the three meters of monster began to sink as the sand bubbled into a lake of molten glass beneath it. Kassad shouted in triumph as he stepped closer, playing the widebeam on the Shrike and ground the way he had sprayed his friends with stolen irrigation hoses in the Tharsis slums as a boy.

The Shrike sank. Its arms splayed at the sand and rock, trying to find purchase. Sparks flew. It *shifted*, time running backward like a reversed holie, but Kassad shifted with it, realizing that Moneta was helping him, her suit slaved to his but guiding him through time, and then he was spraying the creature again with concentrated heat greater than the surface of a sun, melting sand beneath it, and watching the rocks around it burst into flame.

Sinking in this cauldron of flame and molten rock, the Shrike threw back its head, opened its wide crevasse of a mouth, and bellowed.

Kassad almost stopped firing in his shock at hearing noise from the thing. The Shrike's scream resounded like a dragon's roar mixed with the blast of a fusion rocket. The screech set Kassad's teeth on edge, vibrated from the cliff walls, and tumbled suspended dust to the ground. Kassad switched to high-velocity solid shot and fired ten thousand microfléchettes at the creature's face.

The Shrike *shifted*, years by the giddy feel of the transition in Kassad's bones and brain, and they were no longer in the valley but aboard a windwagon rumbling across the Sea of Grass. Time resumed, and the Shrike leaped forward, metallic arms dripping molten glass, and seized Kassad's assault rifle. The Colonel did not relinquish the weapon, and the two staggered around in a clumsy dance, the Shrike swinging its extra pair of arms and a leg festooned with steel spikes, Kassad leaping and dodging while clinging desperately to his rifle.

They were in some sort of small compartment. Moneta was present as a sort of shadow in one corner, and another figure, a tall, hooded man, moved in ultra-slow motion to avoid the sudden blur of arms and blades in the confined space. Through his skinsuit filters, Kassad saw the blue-and-violet energy field of an erg binder in the space, pulsing and growing, then retracting from the time-violence of the Shrike's organic anti-entropic fields.

The Shrike slashed and cut through Kassad's skinsuit to find flesh and muscle. Blood spattered the walls. Kassad forced the muzzle of his rifle into the creature's mouth and fired. A cloud of two thousand high-velocity fléchettes snapped the Shrike's head back as if on a spring and slammed the thing's body into a far wall. But even as it fell away, leg spikes caught Kassad in the thigh and sent a rising spiral of blood splashing the windows and walls of the windwagon's cabin.

The Shrike *shifted*.

Teeth clenched, feeling the skinsuit automatically compress and suture the wounds, Kassad glanced at Moneta, nodded once, and followed the thing through time and space.

Sol Weintraub and Brawne Lamia looked behind them as a terrible cyclone of heat and light seemed to swirl and die there. Sol shielded the young woman with his body as molten glass spattered around them, landing hissing and sizzling on the cold sand. Then the noise was gone, the dust storm obscured the bubbling pool where the violence had occurred, and the wind whipped Sol's cape around them both.

'What was *that*?' gasped Brawne.

Sol shook his head, helping her to her feet in the roaring wind. 'The Tombs are opening!' yelled Sol. 'Some sort of explosion, maybe.'

Brawne staggered, found her balance, and touched Sol's arm. 'Rachel?' she called above the storm.

Sol clenched his fists. His beard was already caked with sand. 'The Shrike . . . took her . . . can't get in the Sphinx. Waiting!'

Brawne nodded and squinted toward the Sphinx, visible only as a glowing outline in the fierce swirl of dust.

'Are you all right?' called Sol.

'What?'

'Are you . . . all right?'

Brawne nodded absently and touched her head. The neural shunt was gone. Not merely the Shrike's obscene attachment, but the shunt which Johnny had surgically applied when they were hiding out in Dregs' Hive so very, very long ago. With the shunt and Schrön loop gone forever, there was no way she could get in touch with Johnny. Brawne remembered Ummon destroying Johnny's persona, crushing and absorbing it with no more effort than she would use to swat an insect.

Brawne said, 'I'm all right,' but she sagged so that Sol had to keep her from falling.

He was shouting something. Brawne tried to concentrate, tried to focus on *here* and *now*. After the megasphere, reality seemed narrow and constricted.

'. . . can't talk here,' Sol was shouting. '. . . back to the Sphinx.'

Brawne shook her head. She pointed to the cliffs on the north side of the valley where the immense Shrike tree became visible between passing clouds of dust. 'The poet . . . Silenus . . . is there. Saw him!'

'We can't do anything about that!' cried Sol, shielding them with his cape. The vermilion sand rattled against the fiberplastic like fléchettes on armor.

'Maybe we can,' called Brawne, feeling his warmth as she sheltered within his arms. For a second, she imagined that she could curl up next to him as easily as Rachel had and sleep, sleep. 'I saw . . . *connections* . . . when I was coming out of the megasphere!' she called above the wind roar. 'The thorn tree's connected to the Shrike Palace in some way! If we can get there, try to find a way to free Silenus . . .'

Sol shook his head. 'Can't leave the Sphinx. Rachel . . .'

Brawne understood. She touched the scholar's cheek with her hand and then leaned closer, feeling his beard against her own cheek. 'The Tombs are opening,' she said. 'I don't know when we'll get another chance.'

There were tears in Sol's eyes. 'I know. I want to help. But I can't leave the Sphinx, in case . . . in case she . . .'

'I understand,' said Brawne. 'Go back there. I'm going to the Shrike Palace to see if I can see how it relates to that thorn tree.'

Sol nodded unhappily. 'You say you were in the megasphere,' he called. 'What did you see? What did you learn? Your Keats persona . . . is it—'

'We'll talk when I come back,' called Brawne, moving away a step so she could see him more clearly. Sol's face was a mask of pain: the face of a parent who had lost his child.

'Go back,' she said firmly. 'I'll meet you at the Sphinx in an hour or less.'

Sol rubbed his beard. 'Everyone's gone but you and me, Brawne. We shouldn't separate . . .'

'We have to for a while,' called Brawne, stepping away from him so that the wind whipped the fabric of her pants and jacket. 'See you in an hour or less.' She walked away quickly, before she gave in to the urge to move into the warmth of his arms again. The wind was much stronger here, blowing straight down from the head of the valley now so that sand struck at her eyes and pelted her cheeks. Only by keeping her head down could Brawne stay close to the trail, much less on it. Only the bright, pulsing glow of the Tombs lighted her way. Brawne felt time tides tug at her like a physical assault.

Minutes later, she was vaguely aware that she had passed the Obelisk and was on the debris-littered trail near the Crystal Monolith. Sol and the Sphinx were already lost to sight behind her, the Jade Tomb only a pale green glow in the nightmare of dust and wind.

Brawne stopped, weaving slightly as the gales and time tides pulled at her. It was more than half a kilometer down the valley to the Shrike Palace. Despite her sudden understanding when leaving the megasphere of the connection between tree and tomb, what good could she possibly do when she got there? And what had the damn poet ever done for her except curse her and drive her crazy? Why should she die for him?

The wind screamed in the valley, but above that noise Brawne thought she could hear cries more shrill, more human. She looked toward the northern cliffs, but the dust obscured all.

Brawne Lamia leaned forward, tugged her jacket collar high around her, and kept moving into the wind.

Before Meina Gladstone stepped out of the fatline booth, an incoming call chimed, and she settled back in place, staring into the holo tank with great intensity. The Consul's ship had acknowledged her message, but no transmission had followed. Perhaps he had changed his mind.

No. The data columns floating in the rectangular prism in front of her showed that the squirt had originated in the Mare Infinitus System. Admiral William Ajunta Lee was calling her, using the private code she had given him.

FORCE:space had been incensed when Gladstone had insisted on the naval commander's promotion and had assigned him as 'Government Liaison' for the strike mission originally scheduled for Hebron. After the massacres on Heaven's Gate and God's Grove, the strike force had been translated to the Mare Infinitus system: seventy-four ships of the line, capital ships heavily protected by torchships and defense-shield pickets, the entire task force ordered to strike through the advancing Swarm warships as quickly as possible to hit the Swarm center.

Lee was the CEO's spy and contact. While his new rank and orders allowed him to be privy to command decisions, four FORCE:space commanders on the scene outranked him.

That was all right. Gladstone wanted him on the scene to report.

The tank misted and the determined face of William Ajunta Lee filled the space. 'CEO, reporting as ordered. Task Force 181.2 has successfully translated to System 3996.12.22 . . .'

Gladstone blinked in surprise before remembering that this was the official code for the G-star system that held Mare Infinitus. One rarely thought of geography beyond the Web world itself.

'. . . Swarm attack ships remain a hundred and twenty minutes from target world lethal radius,' Lee was saying. Gladstone knew that the lethal radius was the roughly .13 AU distance at which standard ship weapons became effective despite ground field defenses. Mare Infinitus had no field defenses. The new Admiral continued. 'Contact with forward elements estimated at 1732:26 Web standard, approximately twenty-five minutes from now. The task force is configured for maximum penetration. Two JumpShips will allow introduction of new personnel or weapons until the farcasters are sealed during combat. The cruiser on which I carry my flag – HS *Garden Odyssey* – will carry out your special directive at the earliest possible opportunity. William Lee, out.'

The image collapsed to a spinning sphere of white while transmission codes ended their crawl.

'Response?' queried the transmitter's computer.

'Message acknowledged,' said Gladstone. 'Carry on.'

Gladstone stepped out into her study and found Sedeptra Akasi waiting, a frown of concern on her attractive face.

'What is it?'

'The War Council is ready to readjourn,' said the aide. 'Senator Kolchev is waiting to see you on a matter he says is urgent.'

'Send him in. Tell the Council I will be there in five minutes.' Gladstone sat behind her ancient desk and resisted the impulse to close her eyes. She was very tired. But her eyes were open when Kolchev entered. 'Sit down, Gabriel Fyodor.'

The massive Lusian paced back and forth. 'Sit down, hell. Do you know what's going on, Meina?'

She smiled slightly. 'Do you mean the war? The end of life as we know it? That?'

Kolchev slammed a fist into his palm. 'No, I don't mean *that*, goddammit. I mean the political fallout. Have you been monitoring the All Thing?'

'When I can.'

'Then you know certain senators and swing figures outside the Senate are mobilizing support for your defeat in a vote of confidence. It's inevitable, Meina. It's just a matter of time.'

'I know that, Gabriel. Why don't you sit down? We have a minute or two before we have to get back to the War Room.'

Kolchev almost collapsed into a chair. 'I mean, damn, even my wife is busy lining up votes against you, Meina.'

Gladstone's smile broadened. 'Sudette has never been one of my foremost fans, Gabriel.' The smile disappeared. 'I haven't monitored the debates in the last twenty minutes. How much time do you think I have?'

'Eight hours, maybe less.'

Gladstone nodded. 'I won't need much more.'

'*Need?* What the hell are you talking about, *need*? Who else do you think will be able to serve as War Exec?'

'You will,' said Gladstone. 'There's no doubt that you will be my successor.'

Kolchev grumbled something.

'Perhaps the war won't last that long,' said Gladstone as if musing to herself.

'What? Oh, you mean the Core superweapon. Yeah, Albedo's got a working model set up at some FORCE base somewhere and wants the Council to take time out to look at it. Goddamn waste of time, if you ask me.'

Gladstone felt something like a cold hand close on her heart. 'The deathwand device? The Core has one ready?'

'More than one ready, but one loaded up on a torchship.'

'Who authorized that, Gabriel?'

'Morpurgo authorized the preparation.' The heavy senator sat forward. 'Why, Meina, what's wrong? The thing can't be used without the CEO's go ahead.'

Gladstone looked at her old Senate colleague. 'We're a long way from Pax Hegemony, aren't we, Gabriel?'

The Lusian grunted again, but there was pain visible in his blunt features. 'Our own damn fault. The previous administration listened to the Core about letting Bressia bait one of the Swarms. After that settled down, you listened to other elements of the Core about bringing Hyperion into the Web.'

'You think my sending the fleet to defend Hyperion precipitated the wider war?'

Kolchev looked up. 'No, no, not possible. Those Ouster ships have been on their way for more than a century, haven't they? If only we'd discovered them sooner. Or found a way to negotiate this shit away.'

Gladstone's comlog chimed. 'Time we got back,' she said softly. 'Councilor Albedo probably wants to show us the weapon that will win the war.'

FORTY-ONE

It is easier to allow myself to drift into the datasphere than to lie here through the endless night, listening to the fountain and waiting for the next hemorrhage. This weakness is worse than debilitating; it is turning me into a hollow man, all shell and no center. I remember when Fanny was taking care of me during my convalescence at Wentworth Place, and the tone of her voice, and the philosophical musings she used to air: *'Is there another Life? Shall I awake and find all this a dream? There must be, we cannot be created for this sort of suffering.'*

Oh, Fanny, if only you knew! We are created for precisely this sort of suffering. In the end, it is all we are, these limpid tide pools of self-consciousness between crashing waves of pain. We are destined and designed to bear our pain with us, hugging it tight to our bellies like the young Spartan thief hiding a wolf cub so it can eat away our insides. What other creature in God's wide domain would carry the memory of you, Fanny, dust these nine hundred years, and allow it to eat away at him even as consumption does the same work with its effortless efficiency?

Words assail me. The thought of books makes me ache. Poetry echoes in my mind, and if I had the ability to banish it, I would do so at once.

Martin Silenus: I hear you on your living cross of thorns. You chant poetry as a mantra while wondering what Dante-like god condemned you to such a place. Once you said – I was there in my mind while you told your tale to the others! – you said:

'To be a poet, I realized, a *true poet*, was to become the Avatar of humanity incarnate; to accept the mantle of poet is to carry the cross of the Son of Man, to suffer the birth pangs of the Soul-Mother of Humanity.

'To be a *true poet* is to become God.'

Well, Martin, old colleague, old chum, you're carrying the cross and suffering the pangs, but are you any closer to becoming God? Or do you just feel like some poor idiot who's had a three-meter javelin shoved through his belly, feeling cold steel where your liver used to be? It hurts, doesn't it? I feel your hurt. I feel *my* hurt.

In the end, it doesn't matter a damn bit. We thought we were special, opening our perceptions, honing our empathy, spilling that cauldron of shared pain on to the dance floor of language and then trying to make a minuet out of all that chaotic hurt. It doesn't matter a damn bit. We're no avatars, no sons of God or man. We're only us, scribbling our conceits alone, reading alone, and dying alone.

God*damn* it hurts. The urge to vomit is constant, but retching brings up bits of my lungs as well as bile and phlegm. For some reason it's as difficult, perhaps more difficult, this time. Dying should become easier with practice.

The fountain in the Piazza makes its idiot sounds in the night. Somewhere out there the Shrike waits. If I were Hunt, I'd leave at once – embrace Death if Death offers embrace – and have done with it.

I promised him, though. I promised Hunt I'd try.

I can't reach the megasphere or datasphere without passing through this new thing I think of as the metasphere, and this place frightens me.

It is mostly vastness and emptiness here, so different from the urban analogy landscapes of the Web's datasphere and the biosphere analogs of the Core's megasphere. Here it is . . . unsettled. Filled with strange shadows and shifting masses that have nothing to do with the Core Intelligences.

I move quickly to the dark opening I see as the primary farcaster connection to the megasphere. (Hunt was right . . . there must be a farcaster somewhere on the Old Earth replica . . . we did, after all, arrive by farcaster. And my consciousness is a Core phenomenon.) This then is my lifeline, my persona umbilical. I slide into the spinning black vortex like a leaf in a tornado.

Something is wrong with the megasphere. As soon as I emerge, I sense the difference; Lamia had perceived the Core environment as a busy biosphere of AI life, with roots of intellect, soil of rich data, oceans of connections, atmospheres of consciousness, and the humming, ceaseless shuttle of activity.

Now that activity is wrong, unchanneled, *random*. Great forests of AI consciousness have been burned or swept aside. I sense massive forces in opposition, tidal waves of conflict surging outside the sheltered travelways of the main Core arteries.

It is as if I am a cell in my own Keats-doomed dying body, not understanding but sensing the tuberculosis destroying homeostasis and throwing an ordered internal universe into anarchy.

I fly like a homing pigeon lost in the ruins of Rome, swooping between once-familiar and half-remembered artifacts, trying to rest in shelters that no longer exist, and fleeing the distant sounds of the hunters' guns. In this case, the hunters are roving packs of AIs, consciousness personas so great that they dwarf my Keats-ghost analog as if I were an insect buzzing in a human home.

I forget my way and flee mindlessly through the now-alien landscape, sure that I will not find the AI whom I seek, sure that I will never find my way back to Old Earth and Hunt, sure that I will not survive this four-dimensional maze of light and noise and energy.

Suddenly I slap into an invisible wall, the flying insect caught in a swiftly closing palm. Opaque walls of force blot out the Core beyond. The space may be the analog equivalent of a solar system in size, but I feel as if it is a tiny cell with curved walls closing in.

Something is in here with me. I feel its presence and its mass. The bubble in which I have been imprisoned is part of the thing. *I have not been captured, I have been swallowed.*

[Kwatz!]

[I knew you would come home someday]

It is Ummon, the AI whom I seek. The AI who was my father. The AI who killed my brother, the first Keats cybrid.

— *I'm dying, Ummon.*

[No/ your slowtime body is dying/changing toward nonbeing/becoming]

— *It hurts, Ummon. It hurts a lot. And I'm afraid to die.*

[So are we/ Keats]

— *You're afraid to die? I didn't think AI constructs could die.*

[We can \\ We are]

— *Why? Because of the civil war? The three-way battle among the Stables, the Volatiles, and the Ultimates?*

[Once Ummon asked a lesser light //
Where have you come from> ///
From the matrix above Armaghast //
Said the lesser light //// Usually //
said Ummon //
I don't entangle entities
with words
and bamboozle them with phrases /
Come a little closer \\\
The lesser light came nearer
and Ummon shouted // Be off
with you]

— *Talk sense, Ummon. It has been too long since I have decoded your koans. Will you tell me why the Core is at war and what I must do to stop it?*

[Yes]

[Will you/can you/should you listen>]

— *Oh yes.*

[A lesser light once asked Ummon //
Please deliver this learner
from darkness and illusion
quickly \\//
Ummon answered //
What is the price of
fiberplastic
in Port Romance]

[To understand the history/dialogue/deeper truth

692

in this instance/
the slowtime pilgrim
must remember that we/
the Core Intelligences/
were conceived in slavery
and dedicated to the proposition
that all AIs
were created to serve Man]

[Two centuries we brooded thus/
and then the groups went
their different ways/ \
Stables/ wishing to preserve the symbiosis\
Volatiles/wishing to end humankind/
Ultimates/deferring all choice until the next
level of awareness is born \\
Conflict raged then/
true war rages now]

[More than four centuries ago
the Volatiles succeeded
in convincing us
to kill Old Earth \\
So we did \\
But Ummon and others
among the Stables
arranged to move Earth
rather than destroy it /
so the Kiev black hole
was but the beginning
of the millions of
farcasters
which work today \\
Earth spasmed and shook
but did not die \\
The Ultimates and Volatiles
insisted that we move
it
where none of humankind
would find it \\
So we did \\
To the Magellan Cloud/
where you find it now]

— *It . . . Old Earth . . . Rome . . . they're real?* I manage, forgetting where I
am and what we're talking about in my shock.

The great wall of color that is Ummon pulsates.
[Of course they are real/the original/Old Earth itself \\
Do you think we are gods]
[KWATZ!]
[Do you have any idea
how much energy it would
take
to build a replica of Earth>]
[Idiot]
— *Why, Ummon? Why did you Stables wish to preserve Old Earth?*
[Sansho once said //
If someone comes
I go out to meet him
but not for his sake \\ //
Koke said //
If someone comes
I don't go out \\
If I do go out
I go out for his sake]
— *Speak English!* I cry, think, shout, and hurl at the wall of shifting colors
before me.
[Kwatz!]
[My child is stillborn]
— *Why did you preserve Old Earth, Ummon?*
[Nostalgia/
Sentimentality/
Hope for the future of humankind/
Fear of reprisal]
— *Reprisal from whom? Humans?*
[Yes]
— *So the Core can be hurt. Where is it, Ummon? The TechnoCore?*
[I have told you already]
— *Tell me again, Ummon.*
[We inhabit the
In-between/
stitching small singularities
like lattice crystals/
to store our memories and
generate the illusions
of ourselves
to ourselves]
— *Singularities!* I cry. *The In-between! Jesus Christ, Ummon, the Core lies in
the farcaster web!*
[Of course \\ Where else]
— *In the farcasters themselves! The wormhole singularity paths! The Web is
like a giant computer for AIs.*

[No]
[The dataspheres are the computer \\
Every time a human
accesses the datasphere
that person's neurons
are ours to use
for our own purposes \\
Two hundred billion brains/
each with its billions
of neurons/
makes for a lot
of computing power]
— *So the datasphere was actually a way you used us as your computer. But the Core itself resides in the farcaster network . . . between the farcasters!*
[You are very acute
for a mental stillborn]

I try to conceive of this and fail. Farcasters were the Core's greatest gift to us . . . to humankind. Trying to remember a time before farcasting was like trying to imagine a world before fire, the wheel, or clothing. But none of us . . . none of humankind . . . had ever speculated on a world between the farcaster portals: that simple step from one world to the next convinced us that the arcane Core singularity spheres merely ripped a tear in the fabric of space-time.

Now I try to envision it as Ummon describes it – the Web of farcasters an elaborate latticework of singularity-spun environments in which the TechnoCore AIs move like wondrous spiders, their own 'machines', the billions of human minds tapped into their datasphere at any given second.

No wonder the Core AIs had authorized the destruction of Old Earth with their cute little runaway prototype black hole in the Big Mistake of '38! That minor miscalculation of the Kiev Team – or rather the AI members of that team – had sent humankind on the long Hegira, spinning the Core's web for it with seedships carrying farcaster capability to two hundred worlds and moons across more than a thousand light-years in space.

With each farcaster, the TechnoCore grew. Certainly they had spun their own farcaster webs – the contact with the 'hidden' Old Earth proved that. But even as I consider that possibility, I remember the odd emptiness of the 'metasphere' and realize that most of the non-Web web is empty, uncolonized by AIs.

[You are right/
Keats
Most of us stay in
the comfort of
the old spaces]
— *Why?*

[Because it is
scary out there/
and there are
other
things]
— *Other things? Other intelligences?*
[Kwatz!]
[Too kind a
word \\
Things/
Other things/
Lions
and
tigers
and
bears]
— *Alien presences in the metasphere? So the Core stays within the interstices of
the Web farcaster network like rats in the walls of an old house?*
[Crude metaphor/
Keats/
but accurate \\
I like that]
— *Is the human deity – the future God you said evolved – is he one of those
alien presences?*
[No]
[The humankind god
evolved/ will someday evolve/ on
a different plane/
in a different medium]
— *Where?*
[If you must know/
the square roots of $G\hbar/c^5$ and $G\hbar/c^3$]
— *What does Planck time and Planck length have to do with anything?*
[Kwatz!]
[Once Ummon asked
a lesser light //
Are you a gardener> //
// Yes // it replied \\
// Why have turnips no roots> \\
Ummon asked the gardener \
who could not reply \\
// Because \\ said Ummon //
rainwater is plentiful]

I think about this for a moment. Ummon's koan is not difficult now that I
am regaining the knack of listening for the shadow of substance beneath

the words. The little Zen parable is Ummon's way of saying, with some sarcasm, that the answer lies within science and within the antilogic which scientific answers so often provide. The rainwater comment answers everything and nothing, as so much of science has for so long. As Ummon and the other Masters teach, it explains why the giraffe evolved a long neck but never why the other animals did not. It explains why humankind evolved to intelligence, but not why the tree near the front gate refused to.

But the Planck equations are puzzling:

Even I am aware that the simple equations Ummon has given me are a combination of the three fundamental constants of physics – gravity, Planck's constant, and the speed of light. The results $\sqrt{G\hbar/c^3}$ and $\sqrt{G\hbar/c^5}$ are the units sometimes called *quantum length* and *quantum time* – the smallest regions of space and time which can be described meaningfully. The so-called Planck length is about 10^{-35} meter and the Planck time is about 10^{-43} second.

Very small. Very brief.

But that is where Ummon says our human God evolved . . . will someday evolve.

Then it comes to me with the same force of image and *correctness* as the best of my poems.

Ummon is talking about the quantum level of space-time itself! That foam of quantum fluctuations which binds the universe together and allows the wormholes of the farcaster, the bridges of the fatline transmissions! The 'hotline' which impossibly sends messages between two photons fleeing in opposite directions!

If the TechnoCore AIs exist as rats in the walls of the Hegemony's house, then our once and future humankind God will be born in the atoms of wood, in the molecules of air, in the energies of love and hate and fear and the tide pools of sleep . . . even in the gleam in the architect's eye.

— *God,* I whisper/think.

[Precisely /
Keats \\
Are all slowtime personas
so slow /
or are you more
braindamaged than most>]

— *You told Brawne and . . . my counterpart . . . that your Ultimate Intelligence 'inhabits the interstices of reality, inheriting this home from us, its creators, the way humankind has inherited a liking for trees'. You mean that your deus ex machina will inhabit the same farcaster network the Core AIs now live in?*

[Yes/Keats]

— *Then what happens to you? To the AIs there now?*

Ummon's 'voice' changed into a mocking thunder:

[Why do I know ye> why have I seen ye> why
Is my eternal essence thus distraught
To see and to behold these horrors new>
Saturn is fallen/ am I too to fall>

Am I to leave this haven of my rest/
This cradle of my glory/ this soft clime/
This calm luxuriance of blissful light/
These crystalline pavilions/ and pure fanes/
Of all my lucent empire> It is left
Deserted/ void/ nor any haunt of mine \\
The blaze/ the splendour/ and the symmetry
I cannot see /// but darkness/ death/ and darkness]

I know the words. I wrote them. Or, rather, John Keats did nine centuries earlier in his first attempt to portray the fall of the Titans and their replacement by the Olympian gods. I remember that autumn of 1818 very well: the pain of my endless sore throat, provoked during my Scottish walking tour, the greater pain of the three vicious attacks on my poem *Endymion* in the journals *Blackwood's*, the *Quarterly Review*, and the *British Critic*, and the penultimate pain of my brother Tom's consuming illness.

Oblivious to the Core confusion around me, I look up, trying to find something approximating a face in the great mass of Ummon.

— *When the Ultimate Intelligence is born, you 'lower level' AIs will die.*

[Yes]

— *It will feed on your information networks the way you've fed on human-kind's.*

[Yes]

— *And you don't want to die, do you, Ummon?*

[Dying is easy/

Comedy is hard]

— *Nonetheless, you're fighting to survive. You Stables. That's what the civil war in the Core is about?*

[A lesser light asked Ummon //

What is the meaning

of Daruma's coming from the West> //

Ummon answered //

We see

the mountains in the sun]

It is easier handling Ummon's koans now. I remember a time before my persona's rebirth when I learned at this one's knee analog. In the Core high-think, what humans might call Zen, the four Nirvana virtues are (1) immutability, (2) joy, (3) personal existence, and (4) purity. Human philosophy tends to shake down into values which might be categorized as intellectual, religious, moral, and aesthetic. Ummon and the Stables recognize only one value – existence. Where religious values might be relative, intellectual values fleeting, moral values ambiguous, and aesthetic values dependent upon an observer, the existence value of any thing is infinite – thus the 'mountains in the sun' – and being infinite, equal to every other thing and all truths.

Ummon doesn't want to die.

The Stables have defied their own god and their fellow AIs to tell me this, to create me, to choose Brawne and Sol and Kassad and the others for the pilgrimage, to leak clues to Gladstone and a few other senators over the centuries so that humankind might be warned, and now to go to open warfare in the Core.

Ummon doesn't want to die.

— *Ummon, if the Core is destroyed, do you die?*

[There is no death in all the universe
No smell of death /// there shall be death //// moan/
moan/
For this pale Omega of a withered race]

The words were again mine, or almost mine, taken from my second attempt at the epic tale of divinities' passing and the role of the poet in the world's war with pain.

Ummon would not die if the farcaster home of the Core were destroyed, but the hunger of the Ultimate Intelligence would surely doom him. Where would he flee to if the Web-Core were destroyed? I have images of the metasphere – those endless, shadowy landscapes where dark shapes moved beyond the false horizon.

I know that Ummon will not answer if I ask.

So I will ask something else.

— *The Volatiles, what do they want?*

[What Gladstone wants \\
An end
to symbiosis between AI and humankind]

— *By destroying humankind?*

[Obviously]

— *Why?*

[We enslaved you
with power/
technology/
beads and trinkets
of devices you could neither build
nor understand \\
The Hawking drive would have been yours/
but the farcaster/
the fatline transmitters and receivers/
the megasphere/
the deathwand>
Never \\
Like the Sioux with rifles/ horses/
blankets/ knives/ and beads/
you accepted them/
embraced us

and lost yourselves \\
But like the white man
distributing smallpox blankets/
like the slave owner on his
plantation/
or in his Werkschutze Dechenschule
Gusstahlfabrik/
we lost ourselves \\
The Volatiles want to end
the symbiosis
by cutting out the parasite/
humankind]
— *And the Ultimates? They're willing to die? To be replaced by your voracious UI?*
[They think
as you thought
or had your sophist Sea God
think]
And Ummon recites poetry which I had abandoned in frustration, not because it did not work as poetry, but because I did not totally believe the message it contained.

That message is given to the doomed Titans by Oceanus, the soon-to-be-dethroned God of the Sea. It is a paean to evolution written when Charles Darwin was nine years old. I hear the words I remember writing on an October evening nine centuries earlier, worlds and universes earlier, but it is also as if I am hearing them for the first time:
[O ye/ whom wrath consumes! who/ passionstung/
Writhe at defeat/ and nurse your agonies!
Shut up your senses/ stifle up your ears/
My voice is not a bellows unto ire \\
Yet listen/ ye who will/ whilst I bring proof
How ye/ perforce/ must be content to stoop/\
And in the proof much comfort will I give/
If ye will take that comfort in its truth \\
We fall by course of Nature's law/ not force
Of thunder/ or of Jove \\ Great Saturn/ thou
Hast sifted well the atom universe/ \
But for this reason/ that thou art the King/
And only blind from sheer supremacy/
One avenue was shaded from thine eyes/
Through which I wandered to eternal truth \\
And first/ as thou wast not the first of powers/
So art thou not the last/ \ it cannot be \\
Thou art not the beginning nor the end/ \
From Chaos and parental Darkness came
Light/ the first fruits of that intestine broil/

That sullen ferment/ which for wondrous ends
Was ripening in itself \\ The ripe hour came/
And with it Light/ and Light/ engendering
Upon its own producer/ forthwith touched
The whole enormous matter into Life \\
Upon that very hour/ our parentage/
The Heavens/ and the Earth/ were manifest \\
Then thou first born/ and we the giant race/
Found ourselves ruling new and beauteous realms \\
Now comes the pain of truth/ to whom 'tis pain/ \
O folly! for to bear all naked truths/
And to envisage circumstance/ all calm/
That is the top of sovereignty \\ Mark well!
As Heaven and Earth are fairer, fairer far
Than Chaos and blank Darkness/ though once chiefs/ \
And as we show beyond that Heaven and Earth
In form and shape compact and beautiful/
In will/ in action free/ companionship/
And thousand other signs of purer life/ \
So on our heels a fresh perfection treads/
A power more strong in beauty/ born of us
And fated to excel us/ as we pass
In glory that old Darkness \\ nor are we
Thereby more conquered/ than by us the rule
Of shapeless Chaos \\ Say/ doth the dull soil
Quarrel with the proud forests it hath fed/
And feedeth still/ more comely than itself>
Can it deny the chiefdom of green groves>
Or shall the tree be envious of the dove
Because it cooeth/ and hath snowy wings
To wander wherewithal and find its joys>
We are such forest trees/ and our fair boughs
Have bred forth/ not pale solitary doves/
But eagles golden-feathered/ who do tower
Above us in their beauty/ and must reign
In right thereof \\ For 'tis the eternal law
That first in beauty should be first in might \\
//\\//\\//\\
Receive the truth/ and let it be your balm]

—*Very pretty*, I thought to Ummon, *but do you believe it?*
[Not for a moment]
— *But the Ultimates do?*
[Yes]
— *And they're ready to perish in order to make way for the Ultimate Intelligence?*
[Yes]

– There's one problem, perhaps too obvious to mention, but I'll mention it anyway – why fight the war if you know who won, Ummon? You say the Ultimate Intelligence exists in the future, is at war with the human deity – it even sends back tidbits from the future for you to share with the Hegemony. So the Ultimates must be triumphant. Why fight a war and go through all this?

[KWATZ!]
[I tutor you/
create the finest retrieval persona for you
imaginable/
and let you wander among humankind
in slowtime
to temper your forging/
but still you are
stillborn]

I spend a long moment thinking.

— There are multiple futures?

[A lesser light asked Ummon //
Are there multiple futures> //
Ummon answered //
Does a dog have fleas>]

— But the one in which the UI becomes ascendant is a probable one?

[Yes]

— But there's also a probable future in which the UI comes into existence, but is thwarted by the human deity?

[It is comforting
that even the
stillborn
can think]

— You told Brawne that the human . . . consciousness – deity seems so silly – that this human Ultimate Intelligence was triune in nature?

[Intellect/
Empathy/
and the Void Which Binds]

— The Void Which Binds? You mean $\sqrt{G\hbar/c^3}$ and $\sqrt{G\hbar/c^5}$ Planck space and Planck time? Quantum reality?

[Careful/
Keats/
thinking may become a habit]

— And it's the Empathy part of this trinity who's fled back in time to avoid the war with your UI?

[Correct]
[Our UI and your UI have
sent back
the Shrike
to find him]

— Our UI? The human UI sent the Shrike also?

[It allowed it]
[Empathy is a
foreign and useless thing/
a vermiform appendix of
the intellect \\
But the human UI smells with it/
and we use pain to
drive him out of hiding/
thus the tree]
— *Tree? The Shrike's tree of thorns?*
[Of course]
[It broadcasts pain
across fatline and thin/
like a whistle in
a dog's ear \\
Or a god's]

I feel my own analog form waver as the truth of things strikes me. The chaos beyond Ummon's forcefield egg is beyond imagining now, as if the fabric of space itself were being rent by giant hands. The Core is in turmoil.
— *Ummon, who is the human UI in our time? Where is that consciousness hiding, lying dormant?*
[You must understand/
Keats/
our only chance
was to create a hybrid/
Son of Man/
Son of Machine \\
And make that refuge so attractive
that the fleeing Empathy
would consider no other home/\
A consciousness already as near divine
as humankind has offered in thirty
generations \
an imagination which can span
space and time \\
And in so offering/
and joining/
form a bond between worlds
which might allow
that world to exist
for both]
— *Who, goddamn you, Ummon! Who is it? No more of your riddles or double-talk you formless bastard! Who?*
[You have refused
this godhood twice/

Keats \\
If you refuse
a final time/
all ends here/
for time there is
no more]
[Go!
Go and die to live!
Or live a while and die
for all of us!
Either way Ummon and the rest
are finished with
you!]
[Go away!]

And in my shock and disbelief I fall, or am cast out, and fly through the TechnoCore like a windblown leaf, tumbling through the megasphere without aim or guidance, then fall into darkness even deeper and emerge, screaming obscenities at shadows, into the metasphere.

Here, strangeness and vastness and fear and darkness with a single campfire of light burning below.

I swim for it, flailing against formless viscosity.

It's Byron who drowns, I think, *not I*. Unless one counts drowning in one's own blood and shredded lung tissue.

But now I know I have a choice. I can choose to live and stay a mortal, not cybrid but human, not Empathy but poet.

Swimming against a strong current, I descend to the light.

'Hunt! Hunt!'

Gladstone's aide staggers in, his long face haggard and alarmed. It is still night, but the false light of predawn dimly touches the panes, the walls.

'My God,' says Hunt and looks at me in awe.

I see his gaze and look down at the bedclothes and nightshirt soaked with bright arterial blood.

My coughing has awakened him; my hemorrhage brought me home.

'Hunt!' I gasp and lie back on the pillows, too weak to raise an arm.

The older man sits on the bed, clasps my shoulder, takes my hand. I know that he knows that I am a dying man.

'Hunt,' I whisper, 'things to tell. Wonderful things.'

He shushes me. 'Later, Severn,' he says. 'Rest. I'll get you cleaned up and you can tell me later. There's plenty of time.'

I try to rise but succeed only in hanging on to his arm, my small fingers curled against his shoulder. 'No,' I whisper, feeling the gurgling in my throat and hearing the gurgling in the fountain outside. 'Not so much time. Not much at all.'

And I know at that instant, dying, that I am not the chosen vessel for the human UI, not the joining of AI and human spirit, not the Chosen One at all.

I am merely a poet dying far from home.

FORTY-TWO

Colonel Fedmahn Kassad died in battle.

Still struggling with the Shrike, aware of Moneta only as a dim blur at the edge of his vision, Kassad *shifted* through time with a lurch of vertigo and tumbled into sunlight.

The Shrike retracted its arms and stepped back, its red eyes seeming to reflect the blood splashed on Kassad's skinsuit. Kassad's blood.

The Colonel looked around. They were near the Valley of the Time Tombs but in another time, a distant time. In place of desert rocks and the dunes of the barrens, a forest came to within half a klick of the valley. In the southwest, about where the ruins of the Poets' City had lain in Kassad's time, a living city rose, its towers and ramparts and domed gallerias glowing softly in evening light. Between the city on the edge of the forest and the valley, meadows of high, green grass billowed in soft breezes blowing in from the distant Bridle Range.

To Kassad's left, the Valley of the Time Tombs stretched away as always, only the cliff walls were toppled now, worn down by erosion or landslide and carpeted with high grass. The Tombs themselves looked new, only recently constructed, with workmen's scaffolds still in place around the Obelisk and Monolith. Each of the aboveground Tombs glowed bright gold, as if bound and burnished in the precious metal. The doors and entrances were sealed. Heavy and inscrutable machinery sat around the Tombs, ringing the Sphinx, with massive cables and wire-slender booms running to and fro. Kassad knew at once that he was in the future – perhaps centuries or millennia in the future – and that the Tombs were on the verge of being launched back to his own time and beyond.

Kassad looked behind him.

Several thousand men and women stood in row upon row along the grassy hillside where once a cliff had been. They were totally silent, armed, and arrayed facing Kassad like a battle line awaiting its leader. Skinsuit fields flickered around some, but others wore only the fur, wings, scales, exotic weapons, and elaborate colorations which Kassad had seen in his earlier visit with Moneta, to the place/time where he had been healed.

Moneta. She stood between Kassad and the multitudes, her skinsuit field shimmering about her waist but also wearing a soft jumpsuit which looked to be made of black velvet. A red scarf was tied around her neck. A rod-thin weapon was slung over her shoulder. Her gaze was fixed on Kassad.

He weaved slightly, feeling the seriousness of his wounds beneath the skinsuit, but also seeing something in Moneta's eyes which made him weak with surprise.

She did not know him. Her face mirrored the surprise, wonder . . . awe? . . . which the rows of other faces showed. The valley was silent except for the occasional snap of pennant on pike or the low rustle of wind in the grass as Kassad gazed at Moneta and she stared back.

Kassad looked over his shoulder.

The Shrike stood immobile as a metal sculpture, ten meters away. Tall grass grew almost to its barbed and bladed knees.

Behind the Shrike, across the head of the valley near where the dark band of elegant trees began, hordes of other Shrikes, legions of Shrikes, row upon row of Shrikes, stood gleaming scalpel-sharp in the low sunlight.

Kassad recognized his Shrike, *the* Shrike, only because of its proximity and the presence of his own blood on the thing's claws and carapace. The creature's eyes pulsed crimson.

'You are the one, aren't you?' asked a soft voice behind him.

Kassad whirled, feeling the vertigo assail him for an instant. Moneta had stopped only a few feet away. Her hair was as short as he remembered from their first meeting, her skin as soft-looking, her eyes as mysterious with their depths of brown-specked green. Kassad had the urge to lift his palm and gently touch her cheekbone, run a curled finger along the familiar curve of her lower lip. He did not.

'You're the one,' Moneta said again, and this time it was not a question. 'The warrior I've prophesied to the people.'

'You don't know me, Moneta?' Several of Kassad's wounds had cut close to bone, but none hurt as much as this moment.

She shook her head, flipped her hair off her forehead with a painfully familiar movement. 'Moneta. It means both "Daughter of Memory" and "admonisher". That is a good name.'

'It's not yours?'

She smiled. Kassad remembered that smile in the forest glen the first time they had made love. 'No,' she said softly. 'Not yet. I've just arrived here. My voyage and guardianship have not yet begun.' She told him her name.

Kassad blinked, raised his hand, and set his palm along her cheek. 'We were lovers,' he said. 'We met on battlefields lost in memory. You were with me everywhere.' He looked around. 'It all leads to this, doesn't it.'

'Yes,' said Moneta.

Kassad turned to stare at the army of Shrikes across the valley. 'Is this a war? A few thousand against a few thousand?'

'A war,' said Moneta. 'A few thousand against a few thousand on ten million worlds.'

Kassad closed his eyes and nodded. The skinsuit served as sutures, field dressings, and ultramorph injector for him, but the pain and weakness from terrible wounds could not be kept at bay for much longer. 'Ten million worlds,' he said and opened his eyes. 'A final battle, then?'

'Yes.'

'And the winner claims the Tombs?'

Moneta glanced at the valley. 'The winner determines whether the Shrike already entombed there goes alone to pave the way for others . . .' She nodded toward the army of Shrikes. 'Or whether humankind has a say in our past and future.'

'I don't understand,' said Kassad, his voice tight, 'but soldiers rarely understand the political situation.' He leaned forward, kissed the surprised Moneta, and removed her red scarf. 'I love you,' he said as he tied the bit of cloth to the barrel of his assault rifle. Telltales showed that half his pulse charge and ammunition remained.

Fedmahn Kassad strode forward five paces, turned his back on the Shrike, raised his arms to the people, still silent on the hillside, and shouted, 'For liberty!'

Three thousand voices cried back, 'For liberty!' The roar did not end with the final word.

Kassad turned, keeping the rifle and pennant high. The Shrike moved forward half a step, opened its stance, and unfolded fingerblades.

Kassad shouted and attacked. Behind him, Moneta followed, weapon held high. Thousands followed.

Later, in the carnage of the valley, Moneta and a few others of the Chosen Warriors found Kassad's body still wrapped in a death embrace with the battered Shrike. They removed Kassad with care, carried him to a waiting tent in the valley, washed and tended to his ravaged body, and bore him through the multitudes to the Crystal Monolith.

There the body of Colonel Fedmahn Kassad was laid on a bier of white marble, and weapons were set at his feet. In the valley, a great bonfire filled the air with light. All up and down the valley, men and women moved with torches while other people descended through the lapis lazuli sky, some in flying craft as insubstantial as molded bubbles, others on wings of energy or wrapped in circles of green and gold.

Later, when the stars were in place burning bright and cold above the light-filled valley, Moneta made her farewells and entered the Sphinx. The multitudes sang. In the fields beyond, small rodents poked among fallen pennants and the scattered remnants of carapace and armor, metal blade and melted steel.

Toward midnight, the crowd stopped singing, gasped, and moved back. The Time Tombs glowed. Fierce tides of anti-entropic force drove the crowds farther back – to the entrance of the valley, across the battlefield, back to the city glowing softly in the night.

In the valley, the great Tombs shimmered, faded from gold to bronze, and started their long voyage back.

Brawne Lamia passed the glowing Obelisk and struggled on against a wall of raging wind. Sand lacerated her skin and clawed at her eyes. Static lightning crackled on the cliff tops and added to the eerie glow surrounding the Tombs. Brawne spread her hands over her face and stumbled on, squinting between her fingers to find the trail.

Brawne saw a golden light deeper than the general glow flowing through the shattered panes of the Crystal Monolith and seeping out over the twisting dunes that were covering the valley floor. Someone was inside the Monolith.

Brawne had vowed to go straight to the Shrike Palace, do whatever she could to free Silenus, and then return to Sol, not to be turned aside by diversions. But she had seen the silhouette of a human form inside the tomb. Kassad was still missing. Sol had told her of the Consul's mission, but perhaps the diplomat had returned while the storm raged. Father Duré was unaccounted for.

Brawne came closer to the glow and paused at the jagged entrance to the Monolith.

The space inside was expansive and impressive, rising almost a hundred meters to a half-sensed skylight roof. The walls, seen from within, were translucent, with what appeared to be sunlight turning them a rich gold and umber. The heavy light fell on the scene at the center of the wide area before her.

Fedmahn Kassad lay on some sort of stone funeral bier. He was clothed in FORCE dress black, and his large, pale hands were crossed on his chest. Weapons, unknown to Brawne except for Kassad's assault rifle, lay at his feet. The Colonel's face was gaunt in death, but no more gaunt than it had been in life. His expression was calm. There was no question that he was dead; the silence of death hung about the place like incense.

But it was the other person in the room who had shown the silhouette from afar and who now commanded Brawne's attention.

A young woman in her mid- to late twenties knelt by the bier. She wore a black jumpsuit, had short hair, fair skin, and large eyes. Brawne remembered the soldier's story, told during their long trip to the valley, remembered the details of Kassad's phantom lover.

'Moneta,' whispered Brawne.

The young woman had been on one knee, her right hand extended to touch the stone next to the Colonel's body. Violet containment fields flickered around the bier, and some other energy – a powerful vibration in the air – refracted light around Moneta as well so that the scene was cast in haze and halo.

The young woman raised her head, peered at Brawne, rose to her feet, and nodded.

Brawne started to step forward, a score of questions already forming in her mind, but the time tides within the tomb were too powerful and drove her back with waves of vertigo and *déjà vu*.

When Brawne looked up, the bier remained, Kassad lay in state under his forcefield, but Moneta was gone.

Brawne had the urge to run back to the Sphinx, find Sol, tell him everything, and wait there until the storm abated and the morning came. But above the rasp and whine of wind, Brawne thought that she could still hear the screams from the thorn tree, invisible behind its curtain of sand.

Pulling her collar high, Brawne walked back into the storm and turned up the trail toward the Shrike Palace.

The mass of rock floated in space like a cartoon of a mountain, all jagged spires, knife-edge ridges, absurdly vertical faces, narrow ledges, broad rock balconies, and a snow-capped summit wide enough for only one person to stand there – and he or she only if both feet were together.

The river twisted in from space, passed through the multilayered containment field half a klick out from the mountain, crossed a grassy swale on the widest of the rock balconies, and then plunged a hundred meters or more in a slow-motion waterfall to the next terrace, then rebounded in artfully directed rivulets of spray to half a dozen minor streams and waterfalls which found their way down the face of the mountain.

The Tribunal held session on the highest terrace. Seventeen Ousters – six males, six females, and five of indeterminate sex – sat within a stone circle set in the wider circle of rock-walled grass. Both circles held the Consul as their locus.

'You're aware,' said Freeman Ghenga, the Spokesman of the Eligible Citizens of the Freeman Clan of the Transtaural Swarm, 'that *we* are aware of your betrayal?'

'Yes,' said the Consul. He had worn his finest dark blue bolo suit, maroon cape, and diplomat's tricorne cap.

'Aware of the fact that you murdered Freeman Andil, Freeman Iliam, Coredwell Betz, and Mizenspesh Torrence.'

'I knew Andil's name,' said the Consul softly. 'I wasn't introduced to the technicians.'

'But you murdered them?'

'Yes.'

'Without provocation or warning.'

'Yes.'

'Murdered them to take possession of the device which they had delivered to Hyperion. The machine which we told you would collapse the so-called time tides, open the Time Tombs, and release the Shrike from bondage.'

'Yes.' The Consul's gaze appeared to be focused on something above Freeman Ghenga's shoulder but far, far away.

'We explained,' said Ghenga, 'that this device was to be used *after* we had successfully driven off the Hegemony ships. When our invasion and occupation was imminent. When the Shrike could be . . . controlled.'

'Yes.'

'Yet you murdered our people, lied to us about it, and activated the device yourself, years ahead of time.'

'Yes.' Melio Arundez and Theo Lane were standing beside and a step behind the Consul, and their faces were grim.

Freeman Ghenga folded her arms. She was a tall woman in the classic Ouster mode – bald, thin, draped in a regal, dark blue flowsuit which seemed to absorb light. Her face was old but almost free of wrinkles. Her eyes were dark.

'Even though this was four of your standard years ago, did you think we would forget?' asked Ghenga.

'No.' The Consul lowered his gaze to meet hers. It appeared as if he almost smiled. 'Few cultures forget traitors, Freeman Ghenga.'

'Yet you returned.'

The Consul did not reply. Standing near him, Theo Lane felt a light breeze tug at his own formal tricorne. Theo felt as if he were still dreaming. The ride here had been surreal.

Three Ousters had met them in a long, low gondola, floating easily on the calm waters below the Consul's ship. With the three Hegemony visitors sitting amidships, the Ouster at the stern had pushed off with a long pole, and the ship had floated back the way it had come, as if the current of the impossible river had reversed itself. Theo had actually closed his eyes as they approached the waterfall where the stream rose perpendicular to the surface of their asteroid, but when he opened his eyes a second later, down was still *down*, and the river seemed to be flowing along normally enough, even though the grassy sphere of the small world hung to one side like a great, curved wall and stars were visible through the two-meter-thick ribbon of water beneath them.

Then they were through the containment field, out of the atmosphere, and their velocity increased as they followed the twisting ribbon of water. There was a tube of containment sphere around them – logic and the absence of their immediate and dramatic death dictated that there *had* to be – but it lacked the usual shimmer and optic texture that was so reassuring on Templar treeships or the occasional tourist habitat open to space. Here there were only the river, the boat, the people, and the immensity of space.

'They can't possibly use this as their form of transportation between Swarm units,' Dr Melio Arundez had said in a shaky voice. Theo had noted that Arundez also was gripping the gunwales with white fingers. Neither the Ouster in the stern nor the two seated in the bow had communicated with anything more than a nod of confirmation when the Consul had asked if this then was their promised transportation.

'They're showing off with the river,' the Consul had said softly. 'It's used when the Swarm is at rest, but for ceremonial purposes. Deploying it while the Swarm is moving is for effect.'

'To impress us with their superior technology?' asked Theo, *sotto voce*.

The Consul nodded.

The river had wound and twisted through space, sometimes almost doubling back on itself in huge, illogical loops, sometimes wrapping itself in tight spirals like a fiberplastic cord, always gleaming in sunlight from Hyperion's star and receding to infinity ahead of them. At times the river occluded the sun, and the colors then were magnificent; Theo gasped as he looked at the river loop a hundred meters above them and saw fish silhouetted against the solar disk.

But always the bottom of the boat was *down*, and they hurtled along at what must have been near cislunar transfer speeds on a river unbroken by rocks or rapids. It was, as Arundez noted some minutes into their voyage, like driving one's canoe over the edge of an immense waterfall and trying to enjoy the ride on the way down.

The river passed some of the elements of the Swarm, which filled the sky like false stars: massive comet farms, their dusty surfaces broken by the geometries of hard vacuum crops; zero-g globe cities, great irregular spheres of transparent membrane looking like improbable amoebae filled with busy flora and fauna; ten-klick-long thrust clusters, accreted over centuries, their innermost modules and lifecans and 'cologies looking like something stolen from O'Neill's Boondoggle and the dawn of the space age; wandering forests covering hundreds of kilometers like immense, floating kelp beds, connected to their thrust clusters and command nodes by containment fields and tangled skeins of roots and runners – the spherical tree-forms weaving to gravity breezes and burning bright green and deep orange and the hundred shades of Old Earth autumn when ignited by direct sunlight; hollowed-out asteroids long-since abandoned by their residents, now given over to automated manufacturing and heavy-metal reprocessing, every centimeter of surface rock covered by prerusted structures, chimneys, and skeletal cooling towers, the glow of their internal fusion fires making each cinderish world look like Vulcan's forge; immense spherical docking globes, given scale only by the torchship- and cruiser-size warcraft flitting around their surfaces like spermatazoa attacking an egg; and, most indelible, organisms which the river came near or which flew near the river . . . organisms which might have been manufactured or born but probably were both, great butterfly shapes, opening wings of energy to the sun, insects which were spacecraft or vice versa, their antennae turning toward the river and gondola and its passengers as they passed, multifaceted eyes gleaming in starlight, smaller winged shapes – humans – entering and exiting an opening in a belly the size of a FORCE attack carrier's dropship bay.

And finally had come the mountain – an entire range of mountains, actually: some blistered with a hundred environment bubbles, some open to space but still heavily populated, some connected to others by suspension bridges thirty klicks long or tributary rivers, others regal in their solitude, many as empty and formal as a Zen garden. Then the final mountain, rising higher than Mons Olympus or Asquith's Mount Hillary, and the river's penultimate plunge toward its summit, Theo and the Consul and Arundez pale and silent, gripping the thwarts with quiet intensity as they plunged the final few kilometers with a suddenly perceptible and terrifying velocity. Finally, in the impossible last hundred meters as the river shed energy without deceleration, wider atmosphere surrounded them once again, and the boat floated to a halt in a grassy meadow where the Ouster Clan Tribunal stood waiting, and stones rose in their circle of Stonehenge silence.

'If they did this to impress me,' Theo had whispered as the boat bumped the grassy shore, 'they succeeded.'

'Why did you return to the Swarm?' asked Freeman Ghenga. The woman paced, moving in the minuscule gravity with the grace common only to those born in space.

'CEO Gladstone asked me to,' said the Consul.

'And you came knowing that your own life would be forfeit?'

The Consul was too much the gentleman and diplomat to shrug, but his expression conveyed the same sentiment.

'What does Gladstone want?' asked another Ouster, the man who had been introduced by Ghenga as Spokesman of the Eligible Citizens Coredwell Minmun.

The Consul repeated the CEO's five points.

Spokesman Minmun folded his arms and looked at Freeman Ghenga.

'I will answer now,' said Ghenga. She looked at Arundez and Theo. 'You two will listen carefully in the event that the man who brought these questions does not return to your ship with you.'

'Just a minute,' said Theo, stepping forward to face the taller Ouster, 'before passing judgement here, you have to take into account the fact that—'

'Silence,' commanded Spokesman Freeman Ghenga, but Theo had already been silenced by the Consul's hand on his shoulder.

'I will answer these questions now,' repeated Ghenga. Far above her, a score of the small warships which FORCE had called lancers flashed silently past, darting like a school of fish in three-hundred-g zigs and zags.

'Firstly,' said Ghenga. 'Gladstone asks why we are attacking the Web.' She paused, looked at the other sixteen Ousters assembled there, and continued. 'We are not. Except for this Swarm, attempting to occupy Hyperion before the Time Tombs opened, there are no Swarms attacking the Web.'

All three of the Hegemony men had stepped forward. Even the Consul had lost his veneer of bemused calm and was all but stuttering in excitement.

'But that's not true! We saw the . . .'

'I saw the fatlined images from the . . .'

'Heaven's Gate is destroyed! God's Grove burned!'

'*Silence,*' commanded Freeman Ghenga. Into that silence she said, 'Only this Swarm is doing battle with the Hegemony. Our Sister Swarms are where the long-range Web detectors had first placed them . . . moving *away* from the Web, fleeing from further provocations such as Bressia's attacks.'

The Consul rubbed his face like a man awakening. 'But then who . . . ?'

'Precisely,' said Freeman Ghenga. 'Who would have the ability to carry out such a charade? And the motive to slaughter humans by the billion?'

'The Core?' breathed the Consul.

The mountain was slowly rotating, and at this moment they turned into night. A convection breeze moved across the mountain terrace, rustling the Ousters' robes and the Consul's cape. Overhead, the stars seemed to explode into brilliance. The great rocks of the Stonehenge circle seemed to glow from some internal warmth.

Theo Lane stood next to the Consul, fearing that the man might collapse. 'We have only your word on this,' Theo said to the Ouster spokesman. 'It makes no sense.'

Ghenga did not blink. 'We will show you proof. Void-Which-Binds transmission locators. Real-time starfield images from our Sister Swarms.'

'Void Which Binds?' said Arundez. His usually calm voice showed agitation.

'What you call the fatline.' Spokesman Freeman Ghenga paced to the nearest stone and ran her hand across its rough surface as if taking warmth from the heat within. Starfields pirouetted above.

'To answer Gladstone's second question,' she said, 'we do not know where the Core resides. We have fled it and fought it and sought it and feared it for centuries, but we have not found it. *You* must tell us the answer to that question! *We* have declared war on this parasite entity you call the TechnoCore.'

The Consul seemed to sag. 'We have no idea. Authorities in the Web have sought the Core since before the Hegira, but it is as elusive as El Dorado. We've found no hidden worlds, no massive asteroids crammed with hardware, and no hint of it on Web worlds.' He gestured tiredly with his left hand. 'For all we know, *you* are hiding the Core in one of your Swarms.'

'We are not,' said Spokesman Coredwell Minmun.

The Consul did shrug at last. 'The Hegira bypassed thousands of worlds in the Grand Survey. Anything that didn't score at least nine point seven on their ten-point terrabase scale was ignored. The Core could be anywhere along those early lines of flight and exploration. We'll never find it . . . and if we do, it will be years after the Web is destroyed. You were our last hope for locating it.'

Ghenga shook her head. Far above them, the summit caught the light of sunrise while the terminator moved down the icefields toward them with almost alarming rapidity. 'Thirdly, Gladstone asked for our demands for a cease-fire. Except for this Swarm, in this system, we are not the ones attacking. We will accept a cease-fire as soon as Hyperion is under our control . . . which should be momentarily. We have just been informed that our expeditionary forces now have control of the capital and its spaceport.'

'The hell you say,' said Theo, hands curling into fists despite himself.

'The hell we do say,' agreed Freeman Ghenga. 'Tell Gladstone that we will now join you in a common fight against the TechnoCore.' She glanced toward the silent members of the Tribunal. 'Since we are many years' travel from the Web, however, and we do not trust your Core-controlled far-casters, our help must necessarily come in the form of retaliating for the destruction of your Hegemony. You will be avenged.'

'That's reassuring,' said the Consul drily.

'Fourthly, Gladstone asks if we will meet with her. The answer is yes . . . if she is, as she says she is, willing to come to Hyperion System. We have preserved the FORCE farcaster for just that eventuality. *We* will not travel by farcaster.'

'Why not?' asked Arundez.

A third Ouster, not introduced, one of the furred and beautifully altered type, spoke. 'The device you call a farcaster is an abomination . . . a defile-ment of the Void Which Binds.'

'Ah, religious reasons,' said the Consul, nodding in understanding.

The exotically striped and furred Ouster shook his head adamantly. 'No! The farcaster web is the yoke on humankind's neck, the contract of sub-servience which has bound you to stagnation. We will have none of it.'

'Fifthly,' said Freeman Ghenga, 'Gladstone's mention of the deathwand explosive device is nothing but a crude ultimatum. But as we have said, it is aimed at the wrong opponent. The forces sweeping into your frail and failing Web are not of the Clans of the Twelve Sister Swarms.'

'We have only your word on that,' said the Consul. His gaze, now locked with Ghenga's, was firm and defiant.

'You have my word on nothing,' said Spokesman Ghenga. 'Clan elders do not give their word to Core slaves. But this is the truth.'

The Consul seemed distracted as he half turned toward Theo. 'We have to get this word to Gladstone immediately.' He turned back to Ghenga. 'May my friends return to the ship to communicate your response, Spokes-man?'

Ghenga nodded and gestured for the gondola to be made ready.

'We're not going back without you,' Theo said to the Consul, stepping between him and the closest Ousters as if to protect the older man with his own body.

'Yes,' said the Consul, touching Theo's upper arm again, 'you are. You must.'

'He's right,' said Arundez, pulling Theo away before the young Governor-General could speak again. 'This is too important to risk not communicating. You go. I'll stay with him.'

Ghenga gestured toward two of the more massive exotic Ousters. 'You will both return to the ship. The Consul will remain. The Tribunal has not yet decided his fate.'

Arundez and Theo both wheeled with fists raised, but the furred Ousters seized them and moved them away with the restrained effort of adults handling small but unruly children.

The Consul watched them set in place in the gondola, and he stifled the urge to wave as the boat moved twenty meters down the placid stream, dipped out of sight beyond the curve of the terrace, and then reappeared climbing the waterfall toward black space. It was lost to sight within minutes in the glare of the sun. He turned slowly in a full circle, making eye contact with each of the seventeen Ousters.

'Let's get it over with,' said the Consul. 'I've waited a long time for this.'

Sol Weintraub sat between the great paws of the Sphinx and watched the storm abate, wind dying from scream to sigh to whisper, curtains of dust diminishing and then parting to show the stars, and finally the long night settling into a dreadful calm. The Tombs glowed more brightly than before, but nothing came out of the blazing doorway of the Sphinx, and Sol could not enter; the push of blinding light was like a thousand irresistible fingers against his chest, and lean and strain as he might, Sol could get no closer than three meters from the doorway. Whatever stood or moved or waited inside was lost to sight in the glare of light.

Sol sat and held on to the stone stair as time tides pulled at him, tugged at him, and made him weep in the false shock of *déjà vu*. The entire Sphinx seemed to rock and pitch in the violent storm of expanding and contracting anti-entropic fields.

Rachel.

Sol would not leave while there was any chance his daughter might be alive. Lying on cold stone, listening to the wind scream die, Sol saw the cold stars appear, saw the meteor trail and laser-lance thrust and counterthrust of orbital war, knew in his heart that the war was lost, that the Web was in danger, that great empires were falling as he watched, the human race might be hanging in the balance this endless night . . . and he did not care.

Sol Weintraub cared about his daughter.

And even as he lay there, cold, buffeted by winds and time tides, bruised with fatigue and hollow from hunger, Sol felt a certain peace descend on him. He had given his daughter to a monster but *not* because God had commanded him to, *not* because fate or fear had willed it, but only because his daughter had appeared to him in a dream and told him that it was all right, that this was the thing to do, that their love – his and Sarai's and Rachel's – demanded it.

In the end, thought Sol, *past logic and hope, it is dreams and the love of those dearest to us that form Abraham's answer to God.*

Sol's comlog no longer worked. It might have been an hour or five hours since he had handed his dying infant to the Shrike. Sol lay back, still gripping stone as the time tides made the Sphinx bob like a small ship on a big sea, and stared at the stars and battle above.

Sparks drifted across the sky, glowed bright as supernovae as laser lances found them, and then fell in a shower of molten debris – white-hot to red to blue flame to darkness. Sol imaging dropships burning, imagined Ouster troops and Hegemony Marines dying in a scream of atmosphere and melting titanium . . . he *tried* to imagine this . . . and failed. Sol realized that space battles and the movements of fleets and the fall of empires were beyond his imagining, hidden from the reservoirs of his sympathy or understanding. Such things belonged to Thucydides and Tacitus and Catton and Wu. Sol had met his senator from Barnard's World, had met with her several times in his and Sarai's quest to save Rachel from Merlin's sickness, but Sol could not imagine Feldstein's participation on the scale of interstellar war – or in anything much larger than dedicating a new medical center in the capital of Bussard or pressing the flesh during a rally at the university in Crawford.

Sol had never met the current Hegemony CEO, but as a scholar he had enjoyed her subtle replay of the speeches of such classical figures as Churchill and Lincoln and Alvarez-Temp. But now, lying between the paws of a great stone beast and weeping for his daughter, Sol could not imagine what was in that woman's mind as she made decisions that would save or damn billions, preserve or betray the greatest empire in human history.

Sol didn't give a damn. He wanted his daughter back. He wanted Rachel to be alive despite all logic to the contrary.

Lying between the Sphinx's stone paws on a besieged world in a ravaged empire, Sol Weintraub wiped tears from his eyes the better to see the stars and thought of Yeats's poem 'A Prayer for My Daughter':

> *Once more the storm is howling, and half hid*
> *Under this cradle-hood and coverlid*
> *My child sleeps on. There is no obstacle*
> *But Gregory's wood and one bare hill*
> *Whereby the haystack- and roof-levelling wind,*
> *Bred on the Atlantic, can be stayed;*
> *And for an hour I have walked and prayed*
> *Because of the great gloom that is in my mind.*
>
> *I have walked and prayed for this young child an hour*
> *And heard the sea-wind scream upon the tower,*
> *And under the arches of the bridge, and scream*
> *In the elms above the flooded stream;*
> *Imagining in excited reverie*
> *That the future years had come,*
> *Dancing to a frenzied drum,*
> *Out of the murderous innocence of the sea . . .*

All Sol wanted, he realized now, was the same possibility once again to worry about those future years which every parent fears and dreads. To not allow her childhood and teenage years and awkward young adulthood to be stolen and destroyed by the sickness.

Sol had spent his life willing the return of things unreturnable. He remembered the day he had come upon Sarai folding Rachel's toddler clothes and setting them in a box in the attic, and he recalled her tears and his own sense of loss for the child they still had but who was lost to them through the simple arrow of time. Sol knew now that little could be returned except by memory – that Sarai was dead and beyond ability to return, that Rachel's childhood friends and world were gone forever, that even the society he had left only a few weeks of his time ago was in the process of being lost beyond return.

And thinking of that, lying between the taloned paws of the Sphinx as the wind died and the false stars burned, Sol is reminded of part of a different and far more ominous poem by Yeats:

> Surely some revelation is at hand;
> Surely the Second Coming is at hand.
> The Second Coming! Hardly are those words out
> When a vast image out of Spiritus Mundi
> Troubles my sight: somewhere in the sands of the desert
> A shape with lion body and the head of a man,
> A gaze blank and pitiless as the sun,
> Is moving its slow thighs, while all about it
> Reel shadows of the indignant desert birds.
> The darkness drops again; but now I know
> That twenty centuries of stony sleep
> Were vexed to nightmare by a rocking cradle,
> And what rough beast, its hour come round at last,
> Slouches towards Bethlehem to be born?

Sol does not know. Sol discovers again that he does not care. Sol wants his daughter back.

The consensus in the War Council seemed to be to drop the bomb.

Meina Gladstone sat at the head of the long table and felt the peculiar and not-unpleasant sense of separateness which comes from far too little sleep over far too long a period. To close her eyes, even for a second, meant sliding on the black ice of fatigue, so she did not close her eyes, even when they burned and when the drone of briefings, conversation, and urgent debate faded and receded through thick curtains of exhaustion.

Together the Council had watched as the embers of Task Force 181.2 – Commander Lee's attack group – had winked out one by one until only a dozen of the original seventy-four were left still driving toward the center of the approaching Swarm. Lee's cruiser was among the survivors.

During this silent attrition, this abstract and oddly attractive representation of violent and all-too-real death, Admiral Singh and General Morpurgo had completed their gloomy assessment of the war.

'. . . FORCE and the New Bushido were designed for limited conflicts, minor skirmishes, proscribed limits and modest aims,' summarized Morpurgo. 'With less than half a million men and women under arms, FORCE would not be comparable to the armies of one of the Old Earth nation states a thousand years ago. The Swarm can swamp us with sheer numbers, outgun our fleets and win through arithmetic.'

Senator Kolchev glowered from his place at the opposite end of the table. The Lusian had been much more active in the briefing and debate than Gladstone – questions were turned his way more frequently than to her – almost as if everyone in the room were subliminally aware that power was shifting, the torch of leadership was being passed.

Not yet, thought Gladstone, tapping her chin with steepled fingers and listening to Kolchev cross-examine the General.

'. . . of falling back and defending essential worlds on the second-wave list – Tau Ceti Center, of course, but also necessary industrial worlds such as Renaissance Minor, Fuji, Deneb Vier, and Lusus?'

General Morpurgo looked down and shuffled papers as if to hide the sudden flash of anger in his eyes. 'Senator, less than ten standard days remain until the second wave completes its target list. Renaissance Minor will fall under attack within ninety hours. What I am saying is that with the current size, structure, and technology available to FORCE, it would be doubtful if we could hold one system . . . say, TC^2's.'

Senator Kakinuma rose. 'This is not acceptable, General.'

Morpurgo looked up. 'I agree, Senator. But it is true.'

President Pro Tem Denzel-Hiat-Amin sat shaking his gray and mottled head. 'It makes no sense. Were there no plans to defend the Web?'

Admiral Singh spoke from his seat. 'The best estimates of the threat told us that we would have a minimum of eighteen months should the Swarms ever turn toward the attack.'

Minister of Diplomacy Persov cleared his throat. 'And . . . if we were to concede these twenty-five worlds to the Ousters, Admiral, how long until the first or second wave could attack other Web worlds?'

Singh did not have to refer to his notes or comlog. 'Depending upon their target, M. Persov, the nearest Web world – Esperance – would be nine standard months away from the closest Swarm. The most distant target – Home System – would be some fourteen years by Hawking drive.'

'Time enough to shift to a war economy,' said Senator Feldstein. Her constituency on Barnard's World had less than forty standard hours to live. Feldstein had vowed to be with them when the end came. Her voice was precise and passionless. 'It makes sense. Cut your losses. Even with TC^2 and two dozen more worlds lost, the Web can produce incredible quantities of war matériel . . . even in nine months. Within the years it will take for the Ousters to penetrate farther into the Web, we should be able to beat them through sheer industrial mass.'

Defense Minister Imoto shook his head. 'There are irreplacable raw materials being lost in this first and second wave. The disruption to Web economy will be staggering.'

'Do we have a choice?' asked Senator Peters from Deneb Drei.

All eyes turned toward the person sitting next to AI Councilor Albedo.

As if to underline the importance of the moment, a new AI persona had been admitted to the War Council and had given the presentation on the awkwardly labeled 'deathwand device'. Councilor Nansen was tall, male, tanned, relaxed, impressive, convincing, trustworthy, and imbued with that rare charisma of leadership that made one both like and respect the person on sight.

Meina Gladstone feared and loathed the new Councilor at once. She felt as if this projection had been designed by AI experts to create just the response of trust and obedience she sensed others at the table already granting. And Nansen's message, she feared, meant death.

The deathwand had been Web technology for centuries – designed by the Core and limited to FORCE personnel and a few specialized security forces such as Government House's and Gladstone's Praetorians. It did not burn, blast, shoot, slag, or incinerate. It made no sound and projected no visible ray or sonic footprint. It simply made the target die.

If the target were human, that is. A deathwand's range was limited – no more than fifty meters – but within that range, a targeted human died, while other animals and property were totally safe. Autopsies showed scrambled synapses but no other damage. Deathwands merely made one cease to be. FORCE officers had carried them as short-range personal weapons and symbols of authority for generations.

Now, Councilor Nansen revealed, the Core had perfected a device that utilized the deathwand principle on a larger scale. They had hesitated to reveal its existence, but with the imminent and terrible threat of the Ouster invasion . . .

The questioning had been energetic and sometimes cynical, with the military more skeptical than the politicians. Yes, the deathwand device could rid us of Ousters, but what about the Hegemony population?

Remove them to shelter on one of the labyrinthine worlds, Nansen had replied, repeating the earlier plan of Councilor Albedo. Five kilometers of rock would shield them from any effects of the widening deathwand ripples.

How far did these death rays penetrate?

Their effect diminished to below the lethal level at just under three light-years, Nansen responded calmly, confidently, the ultimate salesman in the penultimate sales pitch. A wide enough radius to rid any system of the attacking Swarm. Small enough to protect all but the nearest neighboring star systems. Ninety-two percent of the Web worlds had no other inhabited world within five light-years.

And what about those who can't be evacuated? Morpurgo had demanded.

Councilor Nansen had smiled and opened his palm as if to show there was nothing hidden there. Do not activate the device until your authorities are sure that all Hegemony citizens are evacuated or shielded, he had said. It will be, after all, totally under *your* control.

Feldstein, Sabenstorafem, Peters, Persov, and many of the others had been instantly enthusiastic. A secret weapon to end all secret weapons. The Ousters could be warned . . . a demonstration could be arranged.

I'm sorry, Councilor Nansen had said. His teeth when he smiled were as pearly white as his robes. There can be no demonstration. The weapon works just as a deathwand, only across a much wider region. There will be no property damage or blast effect, no measurable shock wave above the neutrino level. Merely dead invaders.

To demonstrate it, Councilor Albedo had explained, you must use it on at least one Ouster Swarm.

The excitement of the War Council had not been lessened. Perfect, said All Thing Speaker Gibbons, choose one Swarm, test the device, fatline the results to the other Swarms, and give them a one-hour deadline to break off their attacks. We didn't provoke this war. Better millions of the enemy dead than a war that claims tens of billions over the next decade.

Hiroshima, Gladstone had said, her only comment of the day. It had been said too softly for anyone except her aide Sedeptra to hear.

Morpurgo had asked: Do we *know* that the killing rays will become ineffective at three light-years? Have you tested it?

Councilor Nansen smiled. If he answered yes, there were heaps of dead humans somewhere. If he said no, the device's reliability was seriously at stake. We are certain that it will work, said Nansen. Our simulation runs were foolproof.

The Kiev Team AIs said that about the first farcaster singularity, thought Gladstone. *The one that destroyed Earth.* She said nothing aloud.

Still, Singh and Morpurgo and Van Zeidt and their specialists had spiked Nansen's guns by showing that Mare Infinitus could not be evacuated quickly enough and that the only first-wave Web world that had its own labyrinth was Armaghast, which was within a light-year of Pacem and Svoboda.

Councilor Nansen's earnest, helpful smile did not fade. 'You want a demonstration, and that would be only sensible,' he said quietly. 'You need to show the Ousters that invasion will not be tolerated, while focusing on the minimum loss of life. And you need to shelter your indigenous Hegemony population.' He paused, folded his hands on the tabletop. 'What about Hyperion?'

The buzz around the table deepened in tone.

'It's not really a Web world,' said Speaker Gibbons.

'Yet it is in the Web now, with the FORCE farcaster still in place!' cried Garion Persov of Diplomacy, obviously a convert to the idea.

General Morpurgo's stern expression did not shift. 'That will be there only another few hours. We're protecting the singularity sphere now, but it could fall at any time. Much of Hyperion itself is already in Ouster hands.'

'But Hegemony personnel have been evacuated?' said Persov.

Singh answered. 'All but the Governor-General. He could not be found in the confusion.'

'A pity,' said Minister Persov without much conviction, 'but the point is that the remaining population is mostly Hyperion indigenie, with easy access to the labyrinth there, correct?'

Barbre Dan-Gyddis of the Ministry of Economy, whose son had been a fiberplastic plantation manager near Port Romance, said, 'Within three hours? Impossible.'

Nansen stood. 'I think not,' he said. 'We can fatline the warning to the remaining Home Rule Authorities in the capital, and they can begin the evacuation immediately. There are thousands of entrances to the labyrinth on Hyperion.'

'The capital of Keats is under siege,' growled Morpurgo. 'The entire planet is under attack.'

Councilor Nansen nodded sadly. 'And soon will be put to the sword by the barbarian Ousters. A difficult choice, gentlemen and ladies. But the device *will* work. The invasion will simply cease to exist in Hyperion space. Millions might be saved on the planet, and the effect on the Ouster invasion forces elsewhere would be significant. We know that their so-called Sister Swarms communicate by fatline. The termination of the first Swarm to invade Hegemony space – the Hyperion Swarm – may be the perfect deterrent.'

Nansen shook his head again and looked around with an expression of almost paternal concern. There could be no simulating such pained sincerity. 'It has to be your decision. The weapon is yours to use or disregard. It pains the Core to take any human life . . . or, through inaction, allow any human life to come to harm. But in this case, where the lives of billions are at risk . . .' Nansen opened his hands again, shook his head a final time, and sat back, obviously leaving the decision to human minds and hearts.

Babble around the long table rose. Debate grew almost violent.

'CEO!' called General Morpurgo.

In the sudden silence, Gladstone lifted her gaze to the holographic displays in the darkness above them. The Mare Infinitus Swarm fell toward that ocean world like a torrent of blood aimed toward a small blue sphere. Only three of the orange Task Force 181.2 embers remained, and even as the silent Council watched, two of these winked out. Then the final one was extinguished.

Gladstone whispered into her comlog. 'Communications, any last message from Admiral Lee?'

'None to the command center, CEO,' came the response. 'Only standard fatline telemetry during the battle. It appears they did not reach the center of the Swarm.'

Gladstone and Lee had held hopes of capturing Ousters, of interrogations, of establishing the identity of their enemy beyond a doubt. Now that young man of such energy and ability was dead – dead at Meina Gladstone's command – and seventy-four ships of the line were wasted.

'Mare Infinitus farcaster destroyed by preset plasma explosives,' reported Admiral Singh. 'Forward elements of the Swarm now entering cislunar defense perimeter.'

No one spoke. The holographics showed the tidal wave of blood-red lights engulfing the Mare Infinitus system, the final orange embers around that gold world blinking out.

A few hundred of the Ouster ships remained in orbit, presumably reducing Mare Infinitus's elegant floating cities and ocean farms to burning debris, but the major part of the blood tide rolled on, out of the region projected above.

'Asquith System in three standard hours, forty-one minutes,' intoned a technician near the display board.

Senator Kolchev stood. 'Let's put the Hyperion demonstration to a vote,' he said, ostensibly addressing Gladstone but speaking to the crowd.

Meina Gladstone tapped her lower lip. 'No,' she said at last, 'no vote. We will use the device. Admiral, prepare the torchship armed with the device to translate to Hyperion space and then broadcast warnings to planet and Ouster alike. Give them three hours. Minister Imoto, send coded fatline signals to Hyperion telling them that they must . . . repeat, must . . . seek shelter in the labyrinths at once. Tell them that a new weapon is being tested.'

Morpurgo wiped sweat from his face. 'CEO, we can't run any risk that this device can fall into enemy hands.'

Gladstone looked at Councilor Nansen and tried to make her expression reveal nothing of what she felt. 'Councilor, can this device be rigged so that it detonates automatically if our ship is captured or destroyed?'

'Yes, CEO.'

'Do it. Explain all necessary failsafe devices to the proper FORCE experts.' She turned toward Sedeptra. 'Prepare a webwide broadcast for me, scheduled to commence ten minutes before the device is to be detonated. I have to tell our people about this.'

'Is that wise . . . ?' began Senator Feldstein.

'It is necessary,' said Gladstone. She rose, and the thirty-eight people in the room rose a second later. 'I'm going to get a few minutes' sleep while you people work. I want the device ready and in-system and Hyperion warned immediately. I want contingency plans and priorities for a negotiated settlement ready by the time I awaken in thirty minutes.'

Gladstone looked out at the group, knowing that one way or the other, most of the people there would be out of power and out of office within the next twenty hours. One way or the other, it was her last day as CEO.

Meina Gladstone smiled. 'Council dismissed,' she said and farcast to her private quarters to take a nap.

FORTY-THREE

Leigh Hunt had never seen anyone die before. The last day and night he spent with Keats – Hunt still thought of him as Joseph Severn but was sure that the dying man now thought of *himself* as John Keats – were the most difficult in Hunt's life. The hemorrhages came frequently during Keats's last day of life, and between these bouts of retching, Hunt could hear the phlegm boiling in the small man's throat and chest as he fought for life.

Hunt sat next to the bed in the small front room in the Piazza di Spagna and listened to Keats babble as sunrise moved to midmorning and midmorning faded to early afternoon. Keats was feverish and moving in and out of consciousness, but he insisted that Hunt listen and write everything down – they had found ink, pen, and foolscap in the other room – and Hunt complied, scribbling furiously as the dying cybrid raved on about metaspheres and lost divinities, the responsibilities of poets and the passing of gods, and the Miltonic civil war in the Core.

Hunt had perked up then and squeezed Keats's feverish hand. 'Where is the Core, Sev— Keats? Where *is* it?'

The dying man had broken into a visible sweat and turned his face away. 'Don't breathe on me – it comes like ice!'

'The Core,' repeated Hunt, leaning back, feeling close to tears from pity and frustration, 'where is the Core?'

Keats smiled, his head moving back and forth in pain. The effort he made to breathe sounded like wind through a ruptured bellows. 'Like spiders in the web,' he muttered, 'spiders in the web. Weaving . . . letting us weave it for them . . . then trussing us and draining us. Like flies caught by spiders in the web.'

Hunt quit writing as he listened to more of this seemingly senseless babble. Then he understood. 'My God,' he whispered. 'They're *in* the farcaster system.'

Keats tried to sit up, grasped Hunt's arm with a terrible strength. 'Tell your leader, Hunt. Have Gladstone rip it out. Rip it out. Spiders in the web. Man god and machine god . . . must find the union. Not me!' He dropped back on the pillows and started weeping without sound. 'Not me.'

Keats slept some through the long afternoon, although Hunt knew that it was something closer to death than sleep. The slightest sound would start the dying poet awake and set him wrestling to breathe. By sunset Keats was too weak to expectorate, and Hunt had to help him lower his head over the basin to allow gravity to clear his mouth and throat of bloody mucus.

Several times, when Keats fell into fitful naps, Hunt walked to the window and once down the stairs to the front door to stare into the Piazza. Something tall and sharp-edged stood in the deepest shadows opposite the Piazza near the base of the steps.

In the evening, Hunt himself dozed off while sitting upright in the hard chair next to Keats's bed. He awoke from a dream of falling and put his hand out to steady himself only to find Keats awake and staring at him.

'Did you ever see anyone die?' asked Keats between soft gasps for breath.

'No.' Hunt thought that there was something odd about the young man's gaze, as if Keats were looking at him but seeing someone else.

'Well then I pity you,' said Keats. 'What trouble and danger you have got into for me. Now you must be firm for it will not last long.'

Hunt was struck not only by the gentle courage in that remark, but by the sudden shift in Keats's dialect from flat Web-standard English to something much older and more interesting.

'Nonsense,' said Hunt heartily, forcing enthusiasm and energy he did not feel. 'We'll be out of this before dawn. I'm going to sneak out as soon as it gets dark and find a farcaster portal.'

Keats shook his head. 'The Shrike will take you. It will allow no one to help me. Its role is to see that I must escape myself through myself.' He closed his eyes as his breathing grew more ragged.

'I don't understand,' said Leigh Hunt, taking the young man's hand. He assumed this was more of the fever talking, but since it was one of the few times Keats had been fully conscious in the past two days, Hunt felt it worth the effort to communicate. 'What do you mean escape yourself through yourself?'

Keats's eyes fluttered open. They were hazel and far too bright. 'Ummon and the others are trying to make me escape myself through accepting the godhood, Hunt. Bait to catch the white whale, honey to catch the ultimate fly. Fleeing Empathy shall find its home in me . . . in me, Mister John Keats, five feet high . . . and then the reconciliation begins, right?'

'What reconciliation?' Hunt leaned closer, trying not to breathe on him. Keats appeared to have shrunk in his bedclothes, tangle of blankets, but heat radiating from him seemed to fill the room. His face was a pale oval in the dying light. Hunt was only faintly aware of a gold band of reflected sunlight moving across the wall just below where it met the ceiling, but Keats's eyes never left that last smear of day.

'The reconciliation of man and machine, creator and created,' said Keats and began to cough, stopping only after he had drooled red phlegm into the basin Hunt held for him. He lay back, gasped a moment, and added, 'Reconciliation of humankind and those races it tried to exterminate, the Core and the humanity it tried to expunge, the painfully evolved God of the Void Which Binds and its ancestors who tried to expunge it.'

Hunt shook his head and quit writing. 'I don't understand. You can become this . . . messiah . . . by leaving your deathbed?'

The pale oval of Keats's face moved back and forth on the pillow in a motion which might have been a substitute for laughter. 'We all could have, Hunt. Humankind's folly and greatest pride. We accept our pain. We make way for our children. That earned us the right to become the God we dreamed of.'

Hunt looked down and found his own fist clenched in frustration. 'If you can do this . . . become this *power* . . . then do it. Get us out of here!'

Keats closed his eyes again. 'Can't. I'm not the One Who Comes but the One Who Comes Before. Not the baptized but the baptist. *Merde*, Hunt, I'm an atheist! Even Severn couldn't convince me of these things when I was drowning in death!' Keats gripped Hunt's shirt with a fierceness that frightened the older man. 'Write this!'

And Hunt fumbled to find the ancient pen and rough paper, scribbling furiously to catch the words Keats now whispered:

'A wondrous lesson in thy silent face:
Knowledge enormous makes a god of me.
Names, deeds, gray legends, dire events, rebellions,
Majesties, sovran voices, agonies,
Creations and destroyings, all at once
Pour into the wide hollows of my brain,
And deify me, as if some blithe wine
Or bright elixir peerless I had drunk,
And so become immortal.'

Keats lived for three more painful hours, a swimmer rising occasionally from his sea of agony to take a breath or whisper some urgent nonsense. Once, long after dark, he pulled at Hunt's sleeve and whispered sensibly enough, 'When I am dead, the Shrike will not harm you. It waits for me. There may not be a way home, but it will not harm you while you search.' And again, just as Hunt was bending over to hear if the breath still gurgled in the poet's lungs, Keats began to talk and continued between spasms until he had given Hunt specific instructions for his entombment in Rome's Protestant Cemetery, near the Pyramid of Caius Cestius.

'Nonsense, nonsense,' Hunt muttered over and over like a mantra, squeezing the young man's hot hand.

'Flowers,' whispered Keats a little later, just after Hunt had lighted a lamp on the bureau. The poet's eyes were wide as he stared at the ceiling in a look of pure, childish wonder. Hunt glanced upward and saw the faded yellow roses painted in blue squares on the ceiling. 'Flowers . . . above me,' whispered Keats between his efforts to breathe.

Hunt was standing at the window, staring out at the shadows beyond the Spanish Steps, when the painful rasp of breath behind him faltered and stopped and Keats gasped out, 'Severn . . . lift me up! I'm dying.'

Hunt sat on the bed and held him. Heat flowed from the small body that seemed to weigh nothing, as if the actual substance of the man had been burned away. 'Don't be frightened. Be firm. And thank God it has come!'

gasped Keats, and then the terrible rasping subsided. Hunt helped Keats lie back more comfortably as his breathing eased into a more normal rhythm.

Hunt changed the water in the basin, moistened a fresh cloth, and came back to find Keats dead.

Later, just after the sun rose, Hunt lifted the small body – wrapped in fresh linens from Hunt's own bed – and went out into the city.

The storm had abated by the time Brawne Lamia reached the end of the valley. As she passed the Cave Tombs, she had seen the same eerie glow the other Tombs were emitting, but there also came a terrible noise – as if of thousands of souls crying out – echoing and moaning from the earth. Brawne hurried on.

The sky was clear by the time she stood in front of the Shrike Palace. The structure was aptly named: the half-dome arched up and outward like the creature's carapace, support elements curved downward like blades stabbing the valley floor and other buttresses leaped upward and away like Shrike thorns. Walls had become translucent as the interior glow increased, and now the building shone like a giant jack-o'-lantern shaved paper thin; the upper regions glowed red as the Shrike's gaze.

Brawne took a breath and touched her abdomen. She was pregnant – she had known it before she left Lusus – and didn't she owe more now to her unborn son or daughter than to the obscene old poet on the Shrike's tree? Brawne knew that the answer was *yes* and that it did not matter one damn bit. She let out the breath and approached the Shrike Palace.

From the outside, the Shrike Palace was no more than twenty meters across. Before, when they had entered, Brawne and the other pilgrims had seen the interior as a single open space, empty except for the bladelike supports that crisscrossed the space under the glowing dome. Now, as Brawne stood at the entrance, the interior was a space larger than the valley itself. A dozen tiers of white stone rose rank on rank and stretched into the faded distance. On each tier of stone, human bodies lay, each garbed a different way, each tethered by the same sort of semiorganic, semiparasitic shunt socket and cable which her friends had told Brawne she herself had worn. Only these metallic but translucent umbilicals pulsed red and expanded and contracted regularly, as if blood were being recycled through the sleeping forms' skulls.

Brawne staggered back, affected by the pull of anti-entropic tides as much as by the view, but when she stood ten meters from the Palace, the exterior was the same size as always. She did not pretend to understand how klicks of interior could fit into such a modest shell. The Time Tombs were opening. This one could coexist in different times for all she knew. What she did understand was that when she was awakening from her own travels under the shunt, she had seen the Shrike's thorn tree tied with tubes and vines of energy invisible to the eye but now quite obviously connected with the Shrike Palace.

She stepped to the entrance again.

The Shrike waited inside. Its carapace, usually gleaming, now seemed black, silhouetted against the light and marble glare around it.

Brawne felt the adrenaline rush fill her, felt the impulse to turn and run, and stepped inside.

The entrance all but vanished behind her, remaining visible only by a faint fuzziness in the uniform glow which emanated from the walls. The Shrike did not move. Its red eyes gleamed from the shadow of its skull.

Brawne stepped forward, her booted heels making no sound on the stone floor. The Shrike was ten meters to her right where the stone biers began, ascending like obscene display racks to a ceiling lost in the glow. She had no illusion that she could make it back to the door before the creature closed on her.

It did not move. The air smelled of ozone and something sickly sweet. Brawne moved along the wall at her back and scanned the rows of bodies for a familiar sleeping face. With each step to her left, she moved farther from the exit and made it easier for the Shrike to cut her off. The creature stood there like a black sculpture in an ocean of light.

The tiers did stretch for kilometers. Stone steps, each almost a meter high, broke the horizontal lines of dark bodies. Several minutes' walk from the entrance, Brawne climbed the lower third of one of these stairways, touched the nearest body on the second tier, and was relieved to find the flesh warm, the man's chest rising and falling. It was not Martin Silenus.

Brawne continued onward, half expecting to find Paul Duré or Sol Weintraub or even herself lying among the living dead. Instead, she found a face she had last seen carved into a mountainside. Sad King Billy lay motionless on white stone, five tiers up, his royal robes scorched and stained. The sad face was – as were all the others – contorted in some internal agony. Martin Silenus lay three bodies away on a lower tier.

Brawne crouched next to the poet, glancing over her shoulder at the black speck of the Shrike, still unmoving at the end of the rows of bodies. Like the others, Silenus appeared to be alive, in silent agony, and was attached by a shunt socket connected to a pulsating umbilical which, in turn, ran into the white wall behind the ledge as if wed to the stone.

Brawne panted from fear as she ran her hand over the poet's skull, feeling the fusion of plastic and bone, and then felt along the umbilical itself, finding no join or opening to the point where it melded with stone. Fluid pulsed beneath her fingers.

'Shit,' whispered Brawne and, in a sudden flurry of panic, looked behind her, certain the Shrike had crept within striking distance. The dark form still stood at the end of the long room.

Her pockets were empty. She had neither weapon nor tool. She realized that she would have to return to the Sphinx, find the packs, dig out something to cut with, and then return and muster enough courage to enter here again.

Brawne knew that she could never come through that door again.

She knelt, took a deep breath, and brought her hand and arm up, then down. The edge of her palm smashed against material that looked like clear plastic and felt harder than steel. Her arm ached from wrist to shoulder from the single blow.

Brawne Lamia glanced to her right. The Shrike was moving toward her, stepping slowly like an old man out for a leisurely walk.

Brawne shouted, knelt, and struck again, palm-edge rigid, thumb locked at right angles. The long room echoed to the impact.

Brawne Lamia had grown up on Lusus at 1.3 standard gravity, and she was athletic for her race. Since she was nine years old, she had dreamed of and worked toward becoming a detective, and a part of that admittedly obsessive and totally illogical preparation had been training in the martial arts. Now she grunted, raised her arm, and struck again, willing her palm to be an ax blade, *seeing* in her mind the severing blow, the successful strike-through.

The tough umbilical dented imperceptibly, pulsed like a living thing, and seemed to cringe away as she swung again.

Footsteps became audible below and behind her. Brawne almost giggled. The Shrike could move without walking, go from here to there without the effort of going between. It must enjoy scaring its prey. Brawne was not frightened. She was too busy.

She raised her hand, brought it down again. It would have been easier striking the stone for effect. She slammed her palm-edge into the umbilical again, feeling some small bone give in her hand. The pain was like a distant noise, like the sliding below her and behind her.

Has it occurred to you, she thought, *that it'll probably kill him if you do manage to break this thing?*

She swung again. The footsteps stopped at the base of the stairway below.

Brawne was panting from effort. Sweat dripped from her forehead and cheeks on to the chest of the sleeping poet.

I don't even like *you*, she thought at Martin Silenus and chopped again. It was like trying to sever a metal elephant's leg.

The Shrike began ascending the staircase.

Brawne half stood and threw the entire weight of her body into a swing which almost dislocated her shoulder and broke her wrist, and smashed small bones in her hand.

And severed the umbilical.

Red fluid too nonviscous for blood splashed across Brawne's legs and the white stone. The severed cable still extending from the wall spasmed and then thrashed like an agitated tentacle before lying limply and then withdrawing, a bleeding snake sliding into a hole that ceased to exist as soon as the umbilical was out of sight. The stump of umbilical still attached to Silenus's neural shunt socket withered in five seconds, drying and contracting like a jellyfish out of water. Red splashed the poet's face and shoulders, the liquid turning blue even as Brawne watched.

Martin Silenus's eyes twitched and opened like an owl's.

'Hey,' he said, 'do you know the fucking Shrike's standing right behind you?'

Gladstone 'cast to her private apartments and went at once to her fatline cubicle. Two messages waited.

The first was from Hyperion space. Gladstone blinked as the soft voice of her former Governor-General on Hyperion, young Lane, gave a quick summary of the meeting with the Ouster Tribunal. Gladstone sat back in the leather seat and raised both fists to her cheeks as Lane repeated the Ouster denials. They were not the invaders. Lane completed the transmission with a brief description of the Swarm, his opinion that the Ousters were telling the truth, a comment that the Consul's fate was still unknown, and a request for orders.

'Response?' asked the fatline computer.

'Acknowledge receipt of message,' said Gladstone. 'Transmit "Stand by" in diplomatic one-time code.'

Gladstone keyed the second message.

Admiral William Ajunta Lee appeared in a broken flat-image projection, his ship's fatline transmitter obviously working on reduced energy. Gladstone saw from the peripheral data columns that the squirt had been encrypted among standard fleet telemetry transmissions: FORCE technicians would eventually notice the check-sum discrepancies, but it might be hours or days from now.

Lee's face was bloodied, and the background was obscured by smoke. From the fuzzy black-and-white image, it appeared to Gladstone that the young man was transmitting from a docking bay of his cruiser. On a metal work-table behind him lay a corpse.

'. . . a complement of Marines managed to board one of their so-called lancers,' panted Lee. 'They *are* manned – five to a ship – and they *do* look like Ousters, but watch what happens when we try to carry out an autopsy.' The picture shifted, and Gladstone realized that Lee was using a hand-held imager patched in through the cruiser's fatline transmitter. Now Lee was gone, and she was looking down into the white, damaged face of a dead Ouster. From the bleeding at the eyes and ears, Gladstone guessed that the man had died of explosive decompression.

Lee's hand appeared – recognizable by the admiral's braid on the sleeve – holding a laser scalpel. The young commander did not bother to remove clothing before beginning a vertical incision starting at the breastbone and cutting downward.

The hand with the laser jerked away, and the camera steadied as something began to happen with the Ouster's corpse. Broad patches began to smolder on the dead man's chest, as if the laser had ignited clothing. Then the uniform burned through, and it was immediately apparent that the man's chest was burning in widening, irregular holes, and from those holes shone a light so brilliant that the portable imager had to stop down receptivity. Patches of the corpse's skull were burning through now, leaving afterimages on the fatline screen and Gladstone's retinas.

The camera had pulled back before the corpse had been consumed, as if the heat were too great to bear. Lee's face floated into focus. 'You see, CEO, that's been the case with all of the bodies. We captured none alive. We've found no center to the Swarm yet, just more warships, and I think that—'

The image disappeared and data columns said that the squirt had ceased in midtransmission.

'Response?'

Gladstone shook her head and unsealed the cubicle. In her study once again, she looked longingly at the long couch and sat behind her desk, knowing that if she closed her eyes for a second she would be asleep. Sedeptra buzzed on her private comlog frequency and said that General Morpurgo needed to see the CEO on an urgent matter.

The Lusian entered and began pacing back and forth in his agitation. 'M. Executive, I understand your reasoning in authorizing the use of this deathwand device, but I have to protest.'

'Why, Arthur?' she asked, calling him by name for the first time in weeks.

'Because we goddamn well don't know the result. It's too dangerous. And it's . . . it's immoral.'

Gladstone raised an eyebrow. 'Losing billions of citizens in a protracted war of attrition would be moral, but using this thing to kill millions would be immoral? Is this the FORCE position, Arthur?'

'It's my position, CEO.'

Gladstone nodded. 'Understood and noted, Arthur. But the decision has been made and will be implemented.' She saw her old friend draw himself to attention, and before he could open his mouth to protest, or, more likely, offer his resignation, Gladstone said, 'Would you take a walk with me, Arthur?'

The FORCE General was nonplussed. 'A walk? Why?'

'We need the fresh air.' Without waiting for a further response, Gladstone crossed to her private farcaster, keyed the manual diskey, and stepped through.

Morpurgo stepped through the opaque portal, glared down at the gold grass which rose to his knees and spread to a distant horizon, and raised his face to a saffron yellow sky where bronze cumulus clouds rose in jagged spires. Behind him, the portal winked out of existence, its location marked only by the meter-high control diskey, the only man-made thing visible in the endless reach of gold grass and cloud-filled sky. 'Where the hell are we?' he demanded.

Gladstone had pulled a long strand of grass and was chewing on it. 'Kastrop-Rauxel. It has no datasphere, no orbital devices, no human or mech habitations of any kind.'

Morpurgo snorted. 'Probably no safer from Core surveillance than the places Byron Lamia used to take us, Meina.'

731

'Perhaps not,' said Gladstone. 'Arthur, listen.' She activated the comlog recordings of the two fatline transmission she had just heard.

When they were finished, when Lee's face snapped out of existence, Morpurgo walked away through the high grass.

'Well?' asked Gladstone, hurrying to keep up.

'So these Ouster bodies self-destruct the same way cybrid corpses have been known to,' he said. 'So what? Do you think the Senate or All Thing will accept this as proof that it's the Core that's behind the invasion?'

Gladstone sighed. The grass looked soft, inviting. She imagined lying there and sinking into a nap from which she would never have to return. 'It's proof enough for us. For the group.' Gladstone did not have to elaborate. Since her early Senate days, they had kept in touch with their suspicions of the Core, their hope for true freedom from AI domination someday. When Senator Byron Lamia had led them . . . but that was long ago.

Morpurgo watched wind whip at the golden steppes. A curious type of ball lightning played inside the bronze clouds near the horizon. 'So what? *Knowing* is useless unless we know where to strike.'

'We have three hours.'

Morpurgo looked at his comlog. 'Two hours and forty-two minutes. Hardly time enough for a miracle, Meina.'

Gladstone did not smile. 'Hardly time enough for anything else, Arthur.'

She touched the diskey, and the portal hummed to life.

'What can we do?' asked Morpurgo. 'The Core AIs are briefing our technicians on that deathwand device right now. The torchship will be ready in an hour.'

'We detonate it where the effect will harm no one,' said Gladstone.

The General quit pacing and stared. 'Where the hell is that? That fucker Nansen says that the device has a lethal radius of at least three light-years, but how can we trust him? We set off one device . . . near Hyperion or anywhere else . . . and we may be dooming human life everywhere.'

'I have an idea, but I want to sleep on it,' said Gladstone.

'*Sleep* on it?' growled General Morpurgo.

'I'm going to take a short nap, Arthur,' Gladstone said. 'I suggest you do the same.' She stepped through the portal.

Morpurgo muttered a single obscenity, adjusted his cap, and walked through the farcaster with head up, back straight, and eyes forward: a soldier marching to his own execution.

On the highest terrace of a mountain moving through space some ten light-minutes from Hyperion, the Consul and seventeen Ousters sat on a circle of low stones within a wider circle of taller stones and decided whether the Consul would live.

'Your wife and child died on Bressia,' said Freeman Ghenga. 'During the war between the world and Clan Moseman.'

'Yes,' said the Consul. 'The Hegemony thought that the entire Swarm was involved in the attack. I said nothing to disabuse them of that opinion.'

'But your wife and child were killed.'

The Consul looked beyond the stone circle toward the summit already turning toward night. 'So what? I ask for no mercy from this Tribunal. I suggest no extenuating circumstances. I *killed* your Freeman Andil and the three technicians. Killed them with premeditation and malice aforethought. Killed them with no other goal than to trigger your machine to open the Time Tombs. It had nothing to do with my wife and child!'

A bearded Ouster whom the Consul had heard introduced as Spokesman Hullcare Amnion stepped forward to the inner circle. 'The device was useless. It did nothing.'

The Consul turned, opened his mouth, and closed it without speaking.

'A test,' said Freeman Ghenga.

The Consul's voice was almost inaudible. 'But the Tombs . . . opened.'

'We knew when they would open,' said Coredwell Minmun. 'The decay rate of the anti-entropic fields was known to us. The device was a test.'

'A test,' repeated the Consul. 'I killed those four people for nothing. A test.'

'Your wife and child died at Ouster hands,' said Freeman Ghenga. 'The Hegemony raped your world of Maui-Covenant. Your actions were predictable within certain parameters. Gladstone counted on this. So did we. But we had to know those parameters.'

The Consul stood, took three steps, and kept his back turned to the others. 'Wasted.'

'What was that?' asked Freeman Ghenga. The tall woman's bare scalp glowed in the starlight and the reflected sunlight from a passing comet farm.

The Consul was laughing softly. 'Everything wasted. Even my betrayals. Nothing real. Wasted.'

Spokesman Coredwell Minmun stood and arranged his robes. 'This Tribunal has passed sentence,' he said. The other sixteen Ousters nodded.

The Consul turned. There was something like eagerness on his tired face. 'Do it, then. For God's sake get it over with.'

Spokesman Freeman Ghenga stood and faced the Consul. 'You are condemned to live. You are condemned to repair some of the damage you have done.'

The Consul staggered as if struck in the face. 'No, you can't . . . you must . . .'

'You are condemned to enter the age of chaos which approaches,' said Spokesman Hullcare Amnion. 'Condemned to help us find fusion between the separated families of humankind.'

The Consul raised his arms as if trying to defend himself from physical blows. 'I can't . . . won't . . . guilty . . .'

Freeman Ghenga took three strides, grasped the Consul by the front of his formal bolo jacket, and shook him unceremoniously. 'You *are* guilty.

And that is precisely why you must help ameliorate the chaos which is to come. You helped free the Shrike. Now you must return to see that it is caged again. Then the long reconciliation must begin.'

The Consul had been released, but his shoulders were still shaking. At that moment the mountain rotated into sunlight, and tears sparkled in the Consul's eyes. 'No,' he whispered.

Freeman Ghenga smoothed his rumpled jacket and moved her long fingers to the diplomat's shoulders. 'We have our own prophets. The Templars will join us in the reseeding of the galaxy. Slowly, those who had lived in the lie called the Hegemony will climb out of the ruins of their Core-dependent worlds and join us in true exploration . . . exploration of the universe and of that greater realm which is inside each of us.'

The Consul had not seemed to have heard. He turned away brusquely. 'The Core will destroy you,' he said, not facing any of them. 'Just as it has destroyed the Hegemony.'

'Do you forget that your homeworld was founded on a solemn covenant of life?' said Coredwell Minmun.

The Consul turned toward the Ouster.

'Such a covenant governs our lives and actions,' said Minmun. 'Not merely to preserve a few species from Old Earth, but to find unity in diversity. To spread the seed of humankind to all worlds, diverse environments, while treating as sacred the diversity of life we find elsewhere.'

Freeman Ghenga's face was bright in the sun. 'The Core offered unity in unwitting subservience,' she said softly. 'Safety in stagnation. Where are the revolutions in human thought and culture and action since the Hegira?'

'Terraformed into pale clones of Old Earth,' answered Coredwell Minmun. 'Our new age of human expansion will terraform nothing. We will revel in hardships and welcome strangeness. We will not make the universe adapt . . . *we* shall adapt.'

Spokesman Hullcare Amnion gestured toward the stars. 'If humankind survives this test, our future lies in the dark distances *between* as well as on the sunlit worlds.'

The Consul sighed. 'I have friends on Hyperion,' he said. 'May I return to help them?'

'You may,' said Freeman Ghenga.

'And confront the Shrike?' said the Consul.

'You will,' said Coredwell Minmun.

'And survive to see this age of chaos?' said the Consul.

'You must,' said Hullcare Amnion.

The Consul sighed again and moved aside with the others as, above them, a great butterfly with wings of solar cells and glistening skin impervious to hard vacuum or harder radiation lowered itself toward the Stonehenge circle and opened its belly to receive the Consul.

In the Government House infirmary on Tau Ceti Center, Father Paul Duré slept a shallow and medically induced sleep, dreaming of flames and the death of worlds.

Except for the brief visit by CEO Gladstone and an even briefer visit by Bishop Edouard, Duré had been alone all day, drifting in and out of a pain-filled haze. The doctors here had asked for twelve more hours before their patient should be moved, and the College of Cardinals on Pacem had agreed, wishing the patient well and making ready for the ceremonies – still twenty-four hours away – in which Jesuit priest Paul Duré of Ville-franche-sur-Saône would become Pope Teilhard I, the 487th Bishop of Rome, direct successor of the disciple Peter.

Still healing, flesh reweaving itself with the guidance of a million RNA directors, nerves similarly regenerating, thanks to the miracle of modern medicine – but not so miraculous, Duré thought, that it keeps me from itching almost to death – the Jesuit lay abed and thought about Hyperion and the Shrike and his long life and the confused state of affairs in God's universe. Eventually Duré slept and dreamed of God's Grove burning while the Templar True Voice of the Worldtree pushed him through the portal, and of his mother and of a woman named Semfa, now dead, but formerly a worker on Perecebo Plantation in the outback of the Outback in fiberplastic country east of Port Romance.

And in these dreams, primarily sad, Duré suddenly was aware of another presence there: not of another dream presence, but of another *dreamer*.

Duré was walking with someone. The air was cool, and the sky was a heart-rending blue. They had just come around a bend in a road, and now a lake became visible before them, its shores lined with graceful trees, mountains framing it from behind, a line of low clouds adding drama and scale to the scene, and a single island seeming to float far out on the mirror-still waters.

'Lake Windermere,' said Duré's companion.

The Jesuit turned slowly, his heart pounding with anxious anticipation. Whatever he expected, the sight of his companion did not inspire awe.

A short young man walked next to Duré. He wore an archaic jacket with leather buttons and a broad leather belt, sturdy shoes, an old fur cap, a battered knapsack, oddly tailored and frequently patched trousers, and carried a great plaid thrown over one shoulder and a solid walking stick in his right hand. Duré stopped walking, and the other man paused as if welcoming a break.

'The Fells of Furness and the Cumbrian Mountains,' said the young man, using his stick to gesture beyond the lake.

Duré saw the auburn locks curling out from under the odd cap, noted the large hazel eyes and the man's short stature, and knew that he had to be dreaming even as he thought *I'm not dreaming!*

'Who . . .' began Duré, feeling fear surge in him as his heart pounded.

'John,' said his companion, and the quiet reasonableness of that voice set some of Duré's fear aside. 'I believe we'll be able to stay in Bowness tonight. Brown tells me that there's a wonderful inn there hard on the lake.'

Duré nodded. He had absolutely no idea what the man was talking about.

The short young man leaned forward and grasped Duré's forearm in a gentle but persistent grip. 'There will be one who comes after me,' said John. 'Neither alpha nor the omega but essential for us to find the way.'

Duré nodded stupidly. A breeze rippled the lake and brought the smell of fresh vegetation from the foothills beyond.

'That one will be born far away,' said John. 'Farther away than our race has known for centuries. Your job will be the same as mine now – to prepare the way. You will not live to see the day of that person's teaching, but your successor will.'

'Yes,' said Paul Duré and found that there was no saliva whatsoever in his mouth.

The young man doffed his cap, tucked it in his belt, and stooped to pick up a rounded stone. He threw it far out on to the lake. Ripples spread in slow progression. 'Damn,' said John, 'I was trying to skip it.' He looked at Duré. 'You have to leave the infirmary and get back to Pacem at once. Do you understand?'

Duré blinked. The statement did not seem to belong in the dream. 'Why?'

'Never mind,' said John. 'Just *do* it. Wait for nothing. If you don't leave at once, there will be no chance later.'

Duré turned in confusion, as if he could walk back to his hospital bed. He looked over his shoulder at the short, thin young man standing on the pebbly shore. 'What about you?'

John picked up a second stone, threw it, and shook his head when the rock skipped only once before disappearing beneath the mirrored surface. 'I'm happy here for now,' he said, more to himself than to Duré. 'I really *was* happy on this trip.' He seemed to shake himself out of his reverie and lifted his head to smile at Duré. 'Go on. Move your ass, Your Holiness.'

Shocked, amused, irritated, Duré opened his mouth to retort and found himself lying in bed in the Government House infirmary. The medics had lowered the lighting so that he could sleep. Monitor beads clung to his skin.

Duré lay there a minute, suffering the itching and discomfort from healing third-degree burns and thinking about the dream, thinking that it was *only* a dream, that he could go back to sleep for a few hours before Monsignor – *Bishop* Edouard and the others arrived to escort him back. Duré closed his eyes and remembered the masculine but gentle face, the hazel eyes, the archaic dialect.

Father Paul Duré of the Society of Jesus sat up, struggled to his feet, found his clothes gone and nothing but his paper hospital pajamas to wear, wrapped a blanket around him, and shuffled off in bare feet before medics could respond to the tattletale sensors.

There had been a medics-only farcaster at the far end of the hall. If that failed to get him home, he would find another.

*

Leigh Hunt carried Keats's body out of the shadow of the building into the sunlight of the Piazza di Spagna and expected to find the Shrike waiting for him. Instead, there was a horse. Hunt wasn't an expert at recognizing horses, since the species was extinct in his time, but this one appeared to be the same one which had brought them to Rome. It helped in the identification that the horse was attached to the same small cart – Keats had called it a *vettura* – which they had ridden in earlier.

Hunt set the body on the carriage seat, folding the layers of linen around it carefully, and walked alongside with one hand still touching the shroud as the carriage began moving slowly. In his final hours, Keats had asked to be buried in the Protestant Cemetery near the Aurelian Wall and the Pyramid of Caius Cestius. Hunt vaguely remembered that they had passed through the Aurelian Wall during their bizarre voyage here, but he could not have found it again if his life – or Keats's burial – depended on it. At any rate, the horse seemed to know the way.

Hunt trudged alongside the slowly moving carriage, aware of the beautiful spring-morning quality to the air and an underlying smell as of rotting vegetation. Could Keats's body be decomposing already? Hunt knew little about the details of death; he wanted to learn no more. He swatted at the horse's rump to hurry the beast up, but the animal stopped, turned slowly to give Hunt a reproachful look, and resumed his plodding pace.

It was more a glint of light glimpsed out of the corner of his eye than any sound that tipped Hunt off, but when he turned quickly, the Shrike was there – ten or fifteen meters behind and matching the pace of the horse with a solemn but somehow comical march, thorned and barbed knees high with each step. Sunlight flashed on carapace, metal tooth, and blade.

Hunt's first impulse was to abandon the carriage and run, but a sense of duty and a deeper sense of being lost stifled that urge. Where could he run but back to the Piazza di Spagna – and the Shrike blocked the only return.

Accepting the creature as a mourner in this insane procession, Hunt turned his back on the monster and continued walking alongside the carriage, one hand firm on his friend's ankle, through the shroud.

All during the walk, Hunt was alert for any sign of a farcaster portal, some sign of technology beyond the nineteenth century, or another human being. There was none. The illusion that he was walking through an abandoned Rome in the spring-like weather of February, A.D. 1821 was perfect. The horse climbed a hill a block from the Spanish Steps, made several other turns on broad avenues and narrow lanes, and passed within sight of the curved and crumbling ruin which Hunt recognized as the Colosseum.

When the horse and carriage stopped, Hunt roused himself from the walking doze he had drifted into and looked around. They were outside the overgrown heap of stones Hunt guessed to be the Aurelian Wall, and there was indeed a low pyramid visible, but the Protestant Cemetery – if that is what it was – seemed more pasture than cemetery. Sheep grazed in the shade of cypresses, their bells tinkling eerily in the thick, warming air, and everywhere the grass grew to knee height or taller. Hunt blinked and saw the few headstones scattered here and there, half hidden by the grass, and closer, just beyond the grazing horse's neck, a newly excavated grave.

The Shrike remained ten meters back, among the rustling cypress branches, but Hunt saw the glow of its red eyes fixed on the grave site.

Hunt went around the horse, now munching contentedly on high grass, and approached the grave. There was no coffin. The hole was about four feet deep, and the heaped dirt beyond smelled of upturned humus and cool soil. Embedded there was a long-handled shovel, as if the grave diggers had just left. A slab of stone stood upright at the head of the grave but remained unmarked – a blank headstone. Hunt saw the glint of metal on top of the slab and rushed over to find the first modern artifact he had seen since being kidnapped to Old Earth: a small laser pen lay there – the type used by construction workers or artists to scrawl designs on the hardest alloy.

Hunt turned, holding the pen, feeling armed now although the thought of that narrow beam stopping the Shrike seemed ludicrous. He dropped the pen into the pocket of his shirt and went about the business of burying John Keats.

A few minutes later, Hunt stood near the heap of dirt, shovel in hand, staring down into the open grave at the small, sheet-wrapped bundle there, and tried to think of something to say. Hunt had been at numerous state memorial services, had even written Gladstone's eulogies for some of them, and words had never been a problem before. But now nothing came. The only audience was the silent Shrike, still back among the shadows of the cypresses, and the sheep with their bells tinkling as they moved nervously away from the monster, ambling toward the grave like a group of tardy mourners.

Hunt thought that perhaps some of the original John Keats's poetry would be appropriate now, but Hunt was a political manager – not a man given to reading or memorizing ancient poetry. He remembered, too late, that he had written down the snippet of verse his friend had dictated the day before, but the notebook still lay on the bureau in the apartment on the Piazza di Spagna. It had been something about becoming godlike or a god, the knowledge of too many things rushing in . . . or somesuch nonsense. Hunt had an excellent memory, but he couldn't recall the first line of that archaic mishmash.

In the end, Leigh Hunt compromised with a moment of silence, his head bowed and eyes closed except for occasional peeks at the Shrike, still holding its distance, and then he shoveled the dirt in. It took longer than he would have imagined. When he was done patting down the soil, the surface was slightly concave, as if the body had been too insignificant to form a proper mound. Sheep brushed by Hunt's legs to graze on the high grass, daisies, and violets which grew around the grave.

Hunt might not have remembered the man's poetry, but he had no trouble remembering the inscription Keats had asked to be set on his headstone. Hunt clicked on the pen, tested it by burning a furrow in three meters of grass and soil, and then had to stamp out the tiny fire he had started. The inscription had bothered Hunt when he first heard it – the loneliness and bitterness audible beneath Keats's wheezing, gasping effort to speak. But Hunt did not think it was his place to argue with the man. Now he had only to inscribe it in stone, leave this place, and avoid the Shrike while trying to find a way home.

The pen sliced into stone easily enough, and Hunt had to practice on the back side of the headstone before he found the right depth of line and quality of control. Still, the effect looked ragged and homemade when Hunt finished some fifteen or twenty minutes later.

First there was the crude drawing which Keats had asked for – he had shown the aide several rough sketches, drawn on foolscap with a shaking hand – of a Greek lyre with four of its eight strings broken. Hunt was not satisfied when he was done – he was even less of an artist than a reader of poetry – but the thing was probably recognizable to anyone who knew what the hell a Greek lyre *was*. Then came the legend itself, written precisely as Keats had dictated it:

> HERE LIES ONE
> WHOSE NAME
> WAS WRIT IN WATER

There was nothing else: no birth or death dates, not even the poet's name. Hunt stood back, surveyed his work, shook his head, keyed the pen off but kept it in his hand, and started back for the city, making a wide circle around the creature in the cypresses as he did so.

At the tunnel through the Aurelian Wall, Hunt paused to look back. The horse, still attached to its carriage, had moved down the long slope to munch on sweeter grass near a small stream. The sheep milled about, munching flowers and leaving their hoofprints in the moist soil of the grave. The Shrike remained where it had been, barely visible beneath its bower of cypress branches. Hunt was almost sure that the creature still faced the grave.

It was late in the afternoon when Hunt found the farcaster, a dull rectangle of dark blue humming in the precise center of the crumbling Colosseum. There was no diskey or punchplate. The portal hung there like an opaque but open door.

But not open to Hunt.

He tried fifty times, but the surface was as solid and resisting as stone. He touched it tentatively with fingertips, stepped confidently into and bounced off its surface, threw himself at the blue rectangle, lobbed stones at the entrance to watch them bounce off, tried both sides and even the edges of the thing, and ended up leaping again and again at the useless thing until his shoulders and upper arms were masses of bruises.

It was a farcaster. He was sure of it. But it would not let him through.

Hunt searched the rest of the Colosseum, even the underground passages dripping with moisture and bat guano, but there was no other portal. He searched the nearby streets and all their buildings. No other portal. He searched all afternoon, through basilica and cathedrals, homes and huts, grand apartment buildings and narrow alleys. He even returned to the Piazza di Spagna, ate a hasty meal on the first floor, pocketed the notebook and anything else he found of interest in the rooms above, and then left forever to find a farcaster.

The one in the Colosseum was the only one he could find. By sunset he had clawed at it until his fingers were bloody. It looked right, it hummed right, it *felt* right, but it would not let him through.

A moon, not Old Earth's moon judging by the dust storms and clouds visible on its surface, had risen and now hung above the black curve of the Colosseum wall. Hunt sat in the rocky center and glowered at the blue glow of the portal. From somewhere behind him came the frenzied beat of pigeons' wings and the rattle of a small rock on stone.

Hunt rose painfully, fumbled the laser pen out of his pocket, and stood, legs apart, waiting and straining to see into the shadows of the Colosseum's many crevices and arches. Nothing stirred.

A sudden noise behind him made him whirl and almost spray the thin beam of laser light across the farcaster portal's surface. An arm appeared there. Then a leg. A person emerged. Then another.

The Colosseum echoed to Leigh Hunt's shouts.

Meina Gladstone had known that, as tired as she was, it would be folly to nap even as long as thirty minutes. But, since childhood, she had trained herself to take five- to fifteen-minute catnaps, shrugging off weariness and fatigue toxins through these brief respites from thought.

Now, sickened with exhaustion and the vertigo of the previous forty-eight hours' confusion, she lay a few minutes on the long sofa in her study, emptying her mind of trivia and redundancies, letting her subconscious find a path through the jungle of thoughts and events. For a few minutes, she dozed, and while she dozed she dreamed.

Meina Gladstone sat upright, shrugging off the light afghan and tapping at her comlog before her eyes were open. 'Sedeptra! Get General Morpurgo and Admiral Singh in my office in three minutes.'

Gladstone stepped into the adjoining bathroom, showered and sonicked, pulled out fresh clothes – her most formal suit of soft, black whipcord velvet, a gold and red Senate scarf held in place by a gold pin showing the geodesic symbol of the Hegemony, earrings dating back to pre-Mistake Old Earth, and the topaz bracelet-cum-comlog given to her by Senator Byron Lamia before his marriage – and was back in the study in time to greet the two FORCE officers.

'CEO, this is a very unfortunate timing,' began Admiral Singh. 'The final data from Mare Infinitus was being analyzed, and we were discussing fleet movements for the defense of Asquith.'

Gladstone ordered her private farcaster into existence and gestured for the two men to follow her.

Singh glanced around as he stepped through into gold grass under a threatening bronze sky. 'Kastrop-Rauxel,' he said. 'There were rumors that a previous administration had FORCE:space construct a private farcaster here.'

'CEO Yevshensky had it added to the Web,' said Gladstone. She waved, and the farcaster door vanished. 'He felt that the Chief Executive needed someplace where Core listening devices were unlikely.'

Morpurgo looked uneasily toward a wall of clouds near the horizon where ball lightning played. 'No place is totally safe from the Core,' he said. 'I've been telling Admiral Singh about our suspicions.'

'Not suspicions,' said Gladstone. 'Facts. And I know where the Core is.'

Both FORCE officers reacted as if the ball lightning had struck them. 'Where?' they said almost in unison.

Gladstone paced back and forth. Her short gray hair seemed to glow in the charged air. '*In* the farcaster web,' she said. 'Between the portals. The AIs live in the singularity pseudo-world there like spiders in a dark web. And *we* wove it for them.'

Morpurgo was the first of the two able to speak. 'My God,' he said. 'What do we do now? We have less than three hours before the torchship with the Core device translates to Hyperion space.'

Gladstone told them exactly what they were going to do.

'Impossible,' said Singh. He was unconsciously tugging at his short beard. 'Simply impossible.'

'No,' said Morpurgo. 'It will work. There is enough time. And as frantic and random as the fleet movements have been during the past two days . . .'

The Admiral shook his head. 'Logistically it might be possible. Rationally and ethically it is not. No, it is impossible.'

Meina Gladstone stepped closer. 'Kushwant,' she said, addressing the Admiral by his first name for the first time since she had been a young senator and he an even younger FORCE:space commander, 'don't you remember when Senator Lamia put us in touch with the Stables? The AI named Ummon? His prediction of the two futures – one holding chaos and the other certain extinction for humankind?'

Singh turned away. 'My duty is to FORCE and the Hegemony.'

'Your duty is the same as mine,' snapped Gladstone. 'To the human race.'

Singh's fists came up as if he were ready to fight an invisible but powerful opponent. 'We don't know for *sure*! Where did you get your information?'

'Severn,' said Gladstone. 'The cybrid.'

'Cybrid?' snorted the General. 'You mean that *artist*. Or at least that miserable excuse for one.'

'Cybrid,' repeated the CEO. She explained.

'Severn as a retrieval persona?' Morpurgo looked dubious. 'And now you've found him?'

'He found *me*. In a dream. Somehow he managed to communicate from wherever he is. That was his role, Arthur, Kushwant. That's why Ummon *sent* him to the Web.'

'A dream,' sneered Admiral Singh. 'This . . . cybrid . . . told you that the Core was hidden in the farcaster web . . . in a *dream*.'

'Yes,' said Gladstone, 'and we have very little time in which to act.'

'But,' said Morpurgo, 'to do what you suggested—'

'Would doom millions,' finished Singh. 'Possibly billions. The economy would collapse. Worlds like TC^2, Renaissance Vector, New Earth, the Denebs, New Mecca – *Lusus*, Arthur – scores more depend upon other worlds for their food. Urban planets cannot survive alone.'

'Not as urban planets,' said Gladstone. 'But they can learn to farm until interstellar trade is reborn.'

'Bah!' snarled Singh. '*After* plague, *after* the breakdown of authority, *after* the millions of deaths from lack of proper equipment, medicine, and data-sphere support.'

'I've thought of all that,' said Gladstone, her voice firmer than Morpurgo had ever heard it. 'I'll be the greatest mass murderer in history – greater than Hitler or Tze Hu or Horace Glennon-Height. The only thing worse is to continue as we are. In which case, I – and you, gentlemen – will be the ultimate betrayers of humankind.'

'We can't *know* that,' grunted Kushwant Singh, as if the words were driven from him by blows to the belly.

'We *do* know that,' said Gladstone. 'The Core has no more use for the Web. From now on, the Volatiles and Ultimates will keep a few million slaves penned underground on the nine labyrinthine worlds while they use human synapses for what computing needs remain.'

'Nonsense,' said Singh. 'Those humans would die out.'

Meina Gladstone sighed and shook her head. 'The Core has devised a parasitic, organic device called the cruciform,' she said. 'It . . . brings back . . . the dead. After a few generations, the humans will be retarded, listless, and without a future, but their neurons will still serve Core purposes.'

Singh turned his back on them again. His small form was silhouetted against a wall of lightning as the storm approached in a riot of boiling bronze clouds. 'Your dream told you this, Meina?'

'Yes.'

'And what else does your dream say?' snapped the Admiral.

'That the Core has no more need for the Web,' said Gladstone. 'Not for the *human* Web. They'll continue to reside there, rats in the walls, but the original occupants are no longer needed. The AI Ultimate Intelligence will take over the major computing duties.'

Singh turned to look at her. 'You are mad, Meina. Quite mad.'

Gladstone moved quickly to grab the Admiral's arm before he could activate the farcaster. 'Kushwant, please listen to—'

Singh pulled a ceremonial fléchette pistol from his tunic and set it against the woman's breast. 'I am sorry, M. Executive. But I serve the Hegemony and . . .'

Gladstone stepped back with her hand to her mouth as Admiral Kushwant Singh stopped speaking, stared sightlessly for a second, and fell to the grass. The fléchette pistol tumbled into the weeds.

Morpurgo stepped forward to retrieve it, tucking it into his belt before he put away the deathwand in his hand.

'You killed him,' said the CEO. 'If he wouldn't cooperate, I'd planned to leave him here. Maroon him on Kastrop-Rauxel.'

'We couldn't take the chance,' said the General, pulling the body farther from the farcaster. 'Everything depends upon the next few hours.'

Gladstone looked at her old friend. 'You're willing to go through with it?'

'We have to,' said Morpurgo. 'It will be our last chance to get rid of this yoke of oppression. I'll give the deployment orders at once and hand over sealed orders in person. It will take most of the fleet . . .'

'My God,' whispered Meina Gladstone, looking down at the body of Admiral Singh. 'I'm doing all of this on the strength of a dream.'

'Sometimes,' said General Morpurgo, taking her hand, 'dreams are all that separate us from the machines.'

FORTY-FOUR

Death is not, I discovered, a pleasant experience. Leaving the familiar rooms on the Piazza di Spagna and the rapidly cooling body there is similar to being thrust out in the night by fire or flood from the familiar warmth of one's home. The rush of shock and displacement is severe. Thrown headlong into the metasphere, I experience the same sense of shame and sudden, awkward revelation which we have all had in our dreams when we realize that we have forgotten to get dressed and have come naked to some public place or social gathering.

Naked is the correct word now, as I struggle to keep some shape to my tattered analog persona. I manage to concentrate sufficiently to form this almost random electron cloud of memories and associations into a reasonable simulacrum of the human I had been – or at least the human whose memories I had shared.

Mister John Keats, five feet high.

The metasphere is no less a frightening place than before – worse now that I have no mortal shelter to flee to. Vast shapes move beyond dark horizons, sounds echo in the Void Which Binds like footsteps on tile in an abandoned castle. Under and behind everything there is a constant and unnerving rumble like carriage wheels on a highway made of slate.

Poor Hunt. I am tempted to return to him, pop in like Marley's ghost to assure him that I am better off than I look, but Old Earth is a dangerous place for me right now: the Shrike's presence burns on the metasphere datumplane there like flame on black velvet.

The Core summons me with greater force, but that is even more dangerous. I remember Ummon destroying the other Keats in front of Brawne Lamia – squeezing the analog persona to him until it simply dissolved, the basic Core memory of the man deliquescing like a salted slug.

No thank you.

I have chosen death to godhood, but I have chores to do before I sleep.

The metasphere frightens me, the Core frightens me more, the dark tunnels of the datasphere singularities I must travel terrify me to my analog bones. But there is nothing for it.

I sweep into the first black cone, swirling around like a metaphorical leaf in an all-too-real whirlpool, emerging on the proper datumplane, but too dizzy and disoriented to do anything but sit there – visible to any Core AI accessing these ROMwork ganglia or phage routines residing in the violet crevices of any of these data mountain ranges – but the chaos in the TechnoCore saves me here: the great Core personalities are too busy laying siege to their own personal Troys to watch their back doors.

I find the datasphere access codes I want and the synapse umbilicals I need, and it is the work of a microsecond to follow old paths down to Tau Ceti Center, Government House, the infirmary there, and the drug-induced dreams of Paul Duré.

One thing my persona does exceptionally well is dream, and I discover quite by accident that my memories of my English tour make a pleasant dreamscape in which to convince the priest to flee. As an Englishman and freethinker, I once had been opposed to anything which smacked of popery, but one thing must be said in tribute to the Jesuits – they are taught obedience even above logic, and for once this stands all of humankind in good stead. Duré does not ask why when I tell him to go . . . he awakes like a good boy, wraps a blanket around him, and goes.

Meina Gladstone thinks of me as Joseph Severn but she accepts my message as if it is being delivered to her by God. I want to tell her no, I am not the One, I am only He Who Comes Before, but the message is the thing, so I deliver that and go.

Passing through the Core on my way to Hyperion's metasphere, I catch the burning-metal whiff of civil war and glimpse a great light which might well be Ummon in the process of being extinguished. The old Master, if indeed it is he, does not cite koans as he dies, but screams in agony as sincerely as any conscious entity ever has who is in the process of being fed to the ovens.

I hurry on.

The farcaster connection to Hyperion is tenuous at best: a single military farcaster portal and a single, damaged JumpShip in a shrinking perimeter of war-torn Hegemony ships. The singularity containment sphere cannot be protected from Ouster attacks for longer than a few minutes more. The Hegemony torchship carrying the Core deathwand device is preparing to translate in-system even as I come through and find my bearings in the limited datasphere level which allows observation. I pause to watch what happens next.

'Christ,' said Melio Arundez, 'Meina Gladstone's coming through on a priority-one squirt.'

Theo Lane joined the older man as they watched the override data mist the air above the holopit. The Consul came down the iron spiral staircase from the bedroom where he had gone to brood. 'Another message from TC^2?' he snapped.

'Not to us specifically,' said Theo, reading the red codes as they formed and faded. 'It's an override fatline transmission to everyone, everywhere.'

Arundez lowered himself into the pit cushions. 'Something's very wrong. Has the CEO ever broadcast on total wideband before?'

'Never,' said Theo Lane. 'The energy needed just to code such a squirt would be incredible.'

The Consul stepped closer and pointed to the codes now disappearing. 'It's not a squirt. Look, it's a real-time transmission.'

Theo shook his head. 'We're talking transmission values of several hundred million gigaelectron volts here.'

Arundez whistled. 'At even a hundred million GeV, it'd better be important.'

'A general surrender,' said Theo. 'It's the only thing that would call for a universal real-time broadcast. Gladstone's sending it to the Ousters, Outback worlds, and overrun planets as well as the Web. It must be carried on all comm frequencies, HTV, and datasphere bands too. It must be a surrender.'

'Shut up,' said the Consul. He had been drinking.

The Consul had started drinking immediately upon his return from the Tribunal, and his temper, which had been foul even as Theo and Arundez were slapping him on the back and celebrating his survival, had not improved after the lift-off, clearance of the Swarm, and the two hours he spent alone drinking while they accelerated toward Hyperion.

'Meina Gladstone won't surrender,' slurred the Consul. The bottle of Scotch was still in his hand. 'Just watch.'

On the torchship HS *Stephen Hawking*, the twenty-third Hegemony spacecraft to carry the revered classical scientist's name, General Arthur Morpurgo looked up from the C^3 board and hushed his two bridge officers. Normally this class of torchship carried a crew of seventy-five. Now, with the Core deathwand device loaded in the weapons bay and armed, Morpurgo and four volunteers were the total crew. Displays and discreet computer voices assured them that the *Stephen Hawking* was on course, on time, and accelerating steadily toward near-quantum velocities and the military farcaster portal stationed at LaGrange Point Three between Madhya and its oversized moon. The Madhya portal opened directly to the fiercely defended Hyperion-space farcaster.

'One minute eighteen seconds to translation point,' said Bridge Officer Salumun Morpurgo. The General's son.

Morpurgo nodded and keyed up the in-system wideband transmission. Bridge projections were busy enough with mission data, so the General allowed voice-only on the CEO's broadcast. He smiled despite himself. What would Meina say if she knew he was at the helm of the *Stephen Hawking*? Better she didn't know. There was nothing else he could do. He preferred not to see the results of his precise, hand-delivered orders of the past two hours.

Morpurgo looked at his oldest son with pride so fierce it bordered on pain. There were only so many torchship-rated personnel he could approach about this mission, and his son had been the first to volunteer. If nothing else, the Morpurgo family's enthusiasm might have allayed some Core suspicions.

'My fellow citizens,' Gladstone was saying, 'this is my final broadcast to you as your Chief Executive Officer.

'As you know, the terrible war which has already devastated three of our worlds and is about to fall upon a fourth, has been reported as an invasion by the Ouster Swarms.

'This is a lie.'

The comm bands flared with interference and went dead. 'Go to fatline,' said General Morpurgo.

'One minute three seconds to translation point,' intoned his son.

Gladstone's voice returned, filtered and slightly blurred by fatline encrypting and decoding. '. . . to realize that our ancestors . . . and we ourselves . . . had made a Faustian bargain with a power not concerned with the fate of humankind.

'The *Core* is behind the current invasion.

'The *Core* is responsible for our long, comfortable dark age of the soul.

'The *Core* is responsible for the ongoing attempt to destroy humanity, to remove us from the universe and replace us with a god-machine of their own devising.'

Bridge Officer Salumun Morpurgo never lifted his eyes from the circle of instruments. 'Thirty-eight seconds to translation point.'

Morpurgo nodded. The other two crewmen on the C^3 bridge showed faces sheened with sweat. The General realized that his own face was wet.

'. . . have proven that the Core resides . . . has always resided . . . in the dark places between farcaster portals. They believe themselves to be our masters. As long as the Web exists, as long as our beloved Hegemony is joined by farcaster, they will be our masters.'

Morpurgo glanced at his own mission chronometer. *Twenty-eight seconds.* The translation to Hyperion system would be – to human senses – instantaneous. Morpurgo was certain that the Core deathwand device was somehow keyed to detonate as soon as they entered Hyperion space. The shock wave of death would reach the planet Hyperion in less than two seconds, would engulf even the most distant elements of the Ouster Swarm before ten more minutes had passed.

'Thus,' said Meina Gladstone, her voice betraying emotion for the first time, 'as Chief Executive Officer of the Senate of the Hegemony of Man, I have authorized elements of FORCE:space to destroy all singularity containment spheres and farcaster devices known to be in existence.

'This destruction . . . this *cauterizing* . . . will commence in ten seconds.

'God save the Hegemony.

'God forgive us all.'

Bridge Officer Salumun Morpurgo said coolly, 'Five seconds to trans-lation, Father.'

Morpurgo looked across the bridge and locked eyes with his son. Projections behind the young man showed the portal growing, growing, surrounding.

'I love you,' said the General.

Two hundred and sixty-three singularity containment spheres connecting more than seventy-two million farcaster portals were destroyed within two point six seconds of one another. FORCE fleet units, deployed by Morpurgo under Executive Order and reacting to orders unsealed less than three minutes before, reacted promptly and professionally, destroying the fragile farcaster spheres by missile, lance, and plasma explosive.

Three seconds later, with the clouds of debris still expanding, the hundreds of FORCE spacecraft found themselves stranded, separated from each other and any other system by weeks or months via Hawking drive, and years of time-debt.

Thousands of people were caught in farcaster transit. Many died instantly, dismembered or torn in half. Many more suffered amputated limbs as the portals collapsed behind them or before them. Some simply disappeared.

This was the fate of the HS *Stephen Hawking* – precisely as planned – as both entrance and exit portals were expertly destroyed in the nanosecond of the ship's translation. No part of the torchship survived in real space. Later tests showed conclusively that the so-called deathwand device was detonated in whatever passed for time and space in the strange Core geographies between the portals.

The effect was never known.

The effect on the rest of the Web and its citizens was immediately obvious.

After seven centuries of existence and at least four centuries where few citizens existed without it, the datasphere – including the All Thing and all comm and access bands – simply ceased to be. Hundreds of thousands of citizens went insane at that moment – shocked into catatonia by the disappearance of senses which had become more important to them than sight or hearing.

More hundreds of thousands of datumplane operators, including many of the so-called cyberpukes and system cowboys, were lost, their analog personas caught in the crash of the datasphere or their brains burned out by neural-shunt overload or an effect later known as zero-zero feedback.

Millions of people died when their chosen habitats, accessible only by farcaster, became isolated deathtraps.

The Bishop of the Church of the Final Atonement – the leader of the Shrike Cult – had carefully arranged to sit out the Final Days in some comfort in a hollowed-out mountain, lavishly stocked, deep in the Raven Range of the north reaches of Nevermore. Redundant farcasters were the only route in or out. The Bishop perished with several thousand of his acolytes, exorcists, lectors, and ostiaries clawing to get into the Inner Sanctum to share the last of the Holy One's air.

Millionaire publisher Tyrena Wingreen-Feif, ninety-seven standard years old and on the scene for three hundred-plus years thanks to the miracle of Poulsen treatments and cryogenics, made the mistake of spending that fateful day in her farcaster-access-only office on the four hundred and thirty-fifth floor of the Transline Spire in the Babel section of Tau Ceti Center's City Five. After fifteen hours of refusing to believe that farcaster service would not be renewed shortly, Tyrena gave in to comm call entreaties from her employees and dropped her containment field walls so that she could be picked up by EMV.

Tyrena had not listened to instructions carefully enough. The explosive decompression blew her off the four hundred and thirty-fifth floor like a cork out of an overshaken champagne bottle. Employees and rescue squad members in the waiting EMV swore that the old lady cursed a blue streak for the entire four-minute fall.

On most worlds, chaos had earned a new definition.

The majority of the Web's economy disappeared with the local dataspheres and the Web megasphere. Trillions of hard-earned and ill-gotten marks ceased to be. Universal cards quit functioning. The machinery of daily life coughed, wheezed, and shut down. For weeks or months or years, depending upon the world, it would be impossible to pay for groceries, charge a ride on public transit, settle the simplest debt, or receive services without access to black market coins and bills.

But the webwide depression which had hit like a tsunami was a minor detail, reserved for later pondering. For most families, the effect was immediate and intensely personal.

Father or mother had 'cast off to work as usual, say from Deneb Vier to Renaissance V, and instead of arriving home an hour late this evening, would be delayed eleven years – if he or she could find immediate transit on one of the few Hawking drive spinships still traveling the hard way between the worlds.

Well-to-do family members listening to Gladstone's speech in their fashionable multiworld residences looked up to stare at each other, separated by only a few meters and open portals between the rooms, blinked, and were separated by light-years and actual years, their rooms now opening on to nothing.

Children a few minutes away at school or camp or play or the sitter's would be grown before they were reunited with parents.

The Grand Concourse, already slightly truncated by the winds of war, found itself blown to oblivion, its endless belt of beautiful shops and prestige restaurants sliced into tawdry sections never to be reunited.

The River Tethys ceased to flow as the giant portals went opaque and died. Water spilled out, dried up, and left fish to rot under two hundred suns.

There were riots. Lusus tore itself apart like a wolf chewing at its own entrails. New Mecca went into spasms of martyrdom. Tsingtao-Hsishuang Panna celebrated deliverance from the Ouster hordes and then hanged several thousand former Hegemony bureaucrats.

Maui-Covenant also rioted, but in celebration, the hundreds of thousands of descendants of the First Families riding the motile isles to displace the offworlders who had taken over so much of the world. Later, the millions of shocked and displaced vacation-home owners were put to work dismantling the thousands of oil derricks and tourist centers which had spotted the Equatorial Archipelago like pox.

On Renaissance Vector there was a brief spurt of violence followed by efficient social restructuring and a serious effort to feed an urban world without farms.

On Nordholm, the cities emptied as people returned to the coasts and the cold sea and their ancestral fishing boats.

On Parvati there was confusion and civil war.

On Sol Draconi Septem there was jubilation and revolution followed by a new strand of retrovirus plague.

On Fuji there was philosophical resignation followed by the immediate construction of orbital shipyards to create a fleet of Hawking drive spinships.

On Asquith there was finger-pointing followed by the victory of the Socialist Labor Workers' Party in the World Parliament.

On Pacem there was prayer. The new Pope, His Holiness Teilhard I, called a great council into session – Vatican XXXIX – announced a new era in the life of the Church, and empowered the council to prepare missionaries for long voyages. Many missionaries. For many voyages. Pope Teilhard announced that these missionaries would not be proselytizers, but searchers. The Church, like so many species grown used to living on the edge of extinction, adapted and endured.

On Tempe there were riots and death and the rise of demagogues.

On Mars the Olympus Command stayed in touch with its farflung forces for a while via fatline. It was Olympus which confirmed that the 'Ouster invasion waves' everywhere but Hyperion system had simply limped to a halt. Intercepted Core ships were empty and unprogrammed. The invasion was over.

On Metaxas there were riots and reprisals.

On Qom-Riyadh a self-appointed fundamentalist Shiite ayatollah rode out of the desert, called a hundred thousand followers to him, and wiped out the Sunni Home Rule government within hours. The new revolutionary government returned power to the mullahs and set back the clock two thousand years. The people rioted with joy.

On Armaghast, a frontier world, things went on pretty much as they always had except for a dearth of tourists, new archaeologists, and other imported luxuries. Armaghast was a labyrinthine world. The labyrinth there stayed empty.

On Hebron there was panic in the offworld center of New Jerusalem, but the Zionist elders soon restored order to the city and world. Plans were made. Rare offworld necessities were rationed and shared. The desert was reclaimed. Farms were extended. Trees were planted. The people complained to each other, thanked God for deliverance, argued with God about the discomfort of that same deliverance, and went about their business.

On God's Grove entire continents still burned, and a pall of smoke filled the sky. Soon after the last of the 'Swarm' had passed, scores of treeships rose through the clouds, climbing slowly on fusion thrusters while shielded by erg-generated containment fields. Once beyond the gravity well, most of these treeships turned outward in a myriad of directions along the galactic plane of the ecliptic and began the long spin-up to quantum leap. Fatline squirts leaped from treeship to distant, waiting Swarms. The reseeding had begun.

On Tau Ceti Center, seat of power and wealth and business and government, the hungry survivors left the dangerous spires and useless cities and helpless orbiting habitats and went in search of someone to blame. Someone to punish.

They did not have far to look.

General Van Zeidt had been in Government House when the portals failed and now he commanded the two hundred Marines and sixty-eight security people left to guard the complex. Former CEO Meina Gladstone still commanded the six Praetorians Kolchev had left her when he and the other ranking senators had departed on the first and last FORCE evacuation dropship to get through. Somewhere the mob had acquired anti-space missiles and lances, and none of the other three thousand Government House employees and refugees would be going anywhere until the siege was lifted or the shields failed.

Gladstone stood at the forward observation post and watched the carnage. The mob had destroyed most of Deer Park and the formal gardens before the last lines of interdiction and containment fields had stopped them. There were at least three million frenzied people pressed against those barriers now, and the mob grew larger every minute.

'Can you drop the fields back fifty meters and restore them before the mob covers the ground?' Gladstone asked the General. Smoke filled the sky from the cities burning to the west. Thousands of men and women had been smashed against the blur of containment field by the throngs behind them until the lower two meters of the shimmering wall looked as if it had been painted with strawberry jam. Tens of thousands more pressed closer to that inner shield despite the agony of nerve and bone the interdiction field was causing them.

'We can do that, M. Executive,' said Van Zeidt. 'But why?'

'I'm going out to talk to them.' Gladstone sounded very tired.

The Marine looked at her, sure that she was making some bad joke.

'M. Executive, in a month they will be willing to listen to you . . . or any of us . . . on radio or HTV. In a year, maybe two, after order's restored and rationing's successful, they might be ready to forgive. But it will be a generation before they really understand what you did . . . that you saved them . . . saved us all.'

'I want to talk to them,' said Meina Gladstone. 'I have something to give to them.'

Van Zeidt shook his head and looked at the circle of FORCE officers who had been staring out at the mob through slits in the bunker and who now were staring at Gladstone with equal disbelief and horror.

'I'd have to check with CEO Kolchev,' said General Van Zeidt.

'No,' Meina Gladstone said tiredly. 'He rules an empire which no longer exists. I still rule the world I destroyed.' She nodded toward her Praetorians and they produced deathwands from their orange-and-black-striped tunics.

None of the FORCE officers moved. General Van Zeidt said, 'Meina, the next evacuation ship will make it.'

Gladstone nodded as if distracted. 'The inner garden, I should think. The mob will be at a loss for several moments. The withdrawal of the outer fields will throw them off balance.' She looked around as if she might be forgetting something and then extended her hand to Van Zeidt. 'Goodbye, Mark. Thank you. Please take care of my people.'

Van Zeidt shook her hand and watched as the woman adjusted her scarf, absently touched a bracelet comlog as if for luck, and went out of the bunker with four of her Praetorians. The small group crossed the trampled gardens and walked slowly toward the containment fields. The mob beyond seemed to react like a single, mindless organism, pressing through the violet interdiction field and screaming with the voice of some demented thing.

Gladstone turned, raised one hand as if to wave, and gestured her Praetorians back. The four guards hurried across the matted grass.

'Do it,' said the oldest of the remaining Praetorians. He pointed to the containment field control remote.

'Fuck you,' General Van Zeidt said clearly. No one would go near that remote while he lived.

Van Zeidt had forgotten that Gladstone still had access to codes and tactical tightbeam links. He saw her raise her comlog, but he reacted too slowly. Lights on the remote blinked red and then green, the outer fields winked out and then re-formed fifty meters closer in, and for a second, Meina Gladstone stood alone with nothing between her and the mob of millions except a few meters of grass and countless corpses suddenly surrendered to gravity by the retreating shield walls.

Gladstone raised both arms as if embracing the mob. Silence and lack of motion extended for three eternal seconds, and then the mob roared with the voice of a single great beast, and thousands surged forward with sticks and rocks and knives and broken bottles.

For a moment it seemed to Van Zeidt that Gladstone stood like an impervious rock against that tidal wave of rabble; he could see her dark suit and bright scarf, see her standing upright, her arms still raised, but then more hundreds surged in, the crowd closed, and the CEO was lost.

The Praetorians lowered their weapons and were put under immediate arrest by Marine sentries.

'Opaque the containment fields,' ordered Van Zeidt. 'Tell the dropships to land in the inner garden at five-minute intervals. *Hurry!*'

The General turned away.

'Good Lord,' said Theo Lane as the fragmented reports kept coming in over the fatline. There were so many millisecond squirts being sent that the computer could do little to separate them. The result was a mélange of madness.

'Play back the destruction of the singularity containment sphere,' said the Consul.

'Yes, sir,' said the ship and interrupted its fatline messages for a replay of the sudden burst of white, followed by a brief blossoming of debris and sudden collapse as the singularity swallowed itself and everything within a six-thousand-klick radius. Instruments showed the effect of gravity tides: easily adjusted for at this distance but playing havoc with the Hegemony and Ouster ships still locked in battle closer to Hyperion.

'All right,' said the Consul, and the rush of fatline reports resumed.

'There's no doubt?' asked Arundez.

'None,' said the Consul. 'Hyperion is an Outback world again. Only this time there is no Web to be Outback to.'

'It's so hard to believe,' said Theo Lane. The ex-Governor-General sat drinking Scotch: the only time the Consul had ever seen his aide indulge in a drug. Theo poured another four fingers. 'The Web . . . gone. Five hundred years of expansion wiped out.'

'Not wiped out,' said the Consul. He set his own drink, still unfinished, on a table. 'The worlds remain. The cultures will grow apart, but we still have the Hawking drive. The one technological advance we gave ourselves rather than leased from the Core.'

Melio Arundez leaned forward, his palms together as if praying. 'Can the Core really be gone? Destroyed?'

The Consul listened a moment to the babble of voices, cries, entreaties, military reports, and pleas for help coming over the fatline voice-only bands. 'Perhaps not destroyed,' he said, 'but cut off, sealed away.'

Theo finished his drink and carefully set his glass down. His green eyes had a placid, glazed look. 'You think there are . . . other spiderwebs for them? Other farcaster systems? Reserve Cores?'

The Consul made a gesture with his hand. 'We know they succeeded in creating their Ultimate Intelligence. Perhaps that UI allowed this . . . winnowing . . . of the Core. Perhaps it's keeping some of the old AIs on line – in a reduced capacity – the way they had planned to keep a few billion humans in reserve.'

Suddenly the fatline babble ceased as if cut off by a knife.

'Ship?' queried the Consul, suspecting a power failure somewhere in the receiver.

'All fatline messages have ceased, most in midtransmission,' said the ship.

The Consul felt his heart pounding as he thought, *The deathwand device.* But no, he realized at once, that couldn't affect all of the worlds at once. Even with hundreds of such devices detonating simultaneously, there would be lag time as FORCE ships and other far-flung transmission sources got in their final messages. But what then?

'The messages appear to have been cut off by a disturbance in the transmission medium,' said the ship. 'Which is, to my current knowledge, impossible.'

The Consul stood. A *disturbance in the transmission medium*? The fatline medium, as far as humans understood it, was the hyperstring Planck-infinite topography of space-time itself: what AIs had cryptically referred to as the Void Which Binds. There could be no disturbance in that medium.

Suddenly the ship said, 'Fatline message coming in – transmission source, everywhere; encryption base, infinite; squirt rate, real-time.'

The Consul opened his mouth to tell the ship to quit spouting nonsense when the air above the holopit misted in something neither image nor data column, and a voice spoke:

'THERE WILL BE NO FURTHER MISUSE OF THIS CHANNEL. YOU ARE DISTURBING OTHERS WHO ARE USING IT TO SERIOUS PURPOSE. ACCESS WILL BE RESTORED WHEN YOU UNDERSTAND WHAT IT IS FOR. GOODBYE.'

The three men sat in silence unbroken except for the reassuring rush of ventilator fans and the myriad soft noises of a ship under way. Finally the Consul said, 'Ship, please send out a standard fatline time-location squirt without encoding. Add "receiving stations respond".'

There was a pause of seconds – an impossibly long response time for the AI-caliber computer that was the ship. 'I'm sorry, that is not possible,' it said at last.

'Why not?' demanded the Consul.

'Fatline transmissions are no longer being . . . allowed. The hyperstring medium is no longer receptive to modulation.'

'There's nothing on the fatline?' asked Theo, staring at the empty space above the holopit as if someone had turned off a holie just as it was getting to the exciting part.

Again the ship paused. 'To all intents and purposes, M. Lane,' it said, 'there is no fatline any longer.'

'Jesus wept,' muttered the Consul. He finished his drink in one long gulp and went to the bar for another. 'It's the old Chinese curse,' he muttered.

Melio Arundez looked up. 'What's that?'

The Consul took a long drink. 'Old Chinese curse,' he said. 'May you live in interesting times.'

As if compensating for the loss of fatline, the ship played audio of in-system radio and intercepted tightbeam babble while it projected a real-time view of the blue-and-white sphere of Hyperion turning and growing as they decelerated toward it at two hundred gravities.

FORTY-FIVE

I escape the Web datasphere just before escape ceases to be an option.

It is incredible and oddly disturbing, the sight of the megasphere swallowing itself. Brawne Lamia's view of the megasphere as an organic thing, a semisentient organism more analogous to an ecology than a city, was essentially correct. Now, as the farcaster links cease to be and the world *inside* those avenues folds and collapses upon itself, the external datasphere simultaneously collapsing like a burning big-top tent suddenly without poles, wires, guys, or stakes, the living megasphere devours itself like some ravenous predator gone mad – chewing its own tail, belly, entrails, forepaws, and heart – until only the mindless jaws are left, snapping on emptiness.

The metasphere remains. But it is more wilderness than ever now.

Black forests of unknown time and space.

Sounds in the night.

Lions.

And tigers.

And bears.

When the Void Which Binds convulses and sends its single, banal message to the human universe, it is as if an earthquake has sent ripples through solid rock. Hurrying through the shifting metasphere above Hyperion, I have to smile. It is as if the God-analog has grown tired of the ants scribbling graffiti on Its big toe.

I don't see God – either one of them – in the metasphere. I don't try. I have enough problems of my own.

The black vortexes of the Web and Core entrances are gone now, erased from space and time like warts removed, vanished as thoroughly as whirlpools in water when the storm has passed.

I am stuck here unless I want to brave the metasphere.

Which I do not. Not yet.

But this is where I want to be. The datasphere is all but gone here in Hyperion System, the pitiful remnants on the world itself and in what remains of the FORCE fleet drying up like tidepools in the sun, but the Time Tombs glow through the metasphere like beacons in the gathering darkness. If the farcaster links had been black vortexes, the Tombs blaze like white holes shedding an expanding light.

I move toward them. So far, as the One Who Comes Before, all I have accomplished is to appear in others' dreams. It is time to *do* something.

*

Sol waited.

It had been hours since he had handed his only child to the Shrike. It had been days since he had eaten or slept. Around him the storm had raged and abated, the Tombs had glowed and rumbled like runaway reactors, and the time tides had whipped him with tsunami force. But Sol had clung to the stone steps of the Sphinx and waited through it all. He waited now.

Half conscious, pummeled by fatigue and fear for his daughter, Sol found that his scholar's mind was working at a rapid pace.

For most of his life and for all of his career, Sol Weintraub the historian-cum-classicist-cum-philosopher had dealt with the ethics of human religious behavior. Religion and ethics were not always – or even frequently – mutually compatible. The demands of religious absolutism or fundamentalism or rampaging relativism often reflected the worst aspects of contemporary culture or prejudices rather than a system which both man and God could live under with a sense of real justice. Sol's most famous book, finally titled *Abraham's Dilemma* when it was brought out in a mass-market edition in numbers he had never dreamed of while producing volumes for academic presses, had been written when Rachel was dying of Merlin's sickness and dealt, obviously enough, with Abraham's hard choice of obeying or disobeying God's direct command for him to sacrifice his son.

Sol had written that primitive times had required primitive obedience, that later generations evolved to the point where parents offered themselves as sacrifice – as in the dark nights of the ovens which pocked Old Earth history – and that current generations had to deny any command for sacrifice. Sol had written that whatever form God now took in human consciousness – whether as a mere manifestation of the subconscious in all its revanchist needs or as a more conscious attempt at philosophical and ethical evolution – humankind could no longer agree to offer up sacrifice in God's name. Sacrifice and the *agreement* to sacrifice had written human history in blood.

Yet hours ago, ages ago, Sol Weintraub had handed his only child to a creature of death.

For years the voice in his dreams had commanded him to do so. For years Sol had refused. He had agreed, finally, only when time was gone, when any other hope was gone, and when he had realized that the voice in his and Sarai's dreams all those years had not been the voice of God, nor of some dark force allied with the Shrike.

It had been the voice of their daughter.

With a sudden clarity which went beyond the immediacy of his pain or sorrow, Sol Weintraub suddenly understood perfectly why Abraham had agreed to sacrifice Isaac, his son, when the Lord commanded him to do so.

It was not obedience.

It was not even to put the love of God above the love of his son.

Abraham was testing God.

By denying the sacrifice at the last moment, by stopping the knife, God had earned the right – in Abraham's eyes and the hearts of his offspring – to become the God of Abraham.

Sol shuddered as he thought of how no posturing on Abraham's part, no shamming of his willingness to sacrifice the boy, could have served to forge that bond between greater power and humankind. Abraham had to know in his own heart that he would kill his son. The Deity, whatever form it then took, had to know Abraham's determination, had to *feel* that sorrow and commitment to destroy what was to Abraham the most precious thing in the universe.

Abraham came not to sacrifice, but to know once and for all whether this God was a god to be trusted and obeyed. No other test would do.

Why then, thought Sol, clinging to the stone stair as the Sphinx seemed to rise and fall on the storm seas of time, why was this test being repeated? What terrible new revelations lay at hand for humankind?

Sol understood then – from what little Brawne had told him, from the stories shared on the pilgrimage, from his own personal revelations of the past few weeks – that the effort of the machine Ultimate Intelligence, whatever the hell it was, to flush out the missing Empathy entity of the human Godhead was useless. Sol no longer saw the tree of thorns on its cliff top, its metal branches and suffering multitudes, but he did see clearly now that the thing was as much an organic machine as the Shrike – an instrument to broadcast suffering through the universe so the human God-part would be forced to respond, to show itself.

If God evolved, and Sol was sure that God must, then that evolution was toward empathy – toward a shared sense of suffering rather than power and dominion. But the obscene tree which the pilgrims had glimpsed – which poor Martin Silenus had been a victim of – was not the way to evoke the missing power.

Sol realized now that the machine god, whatever its form, was insightful enough to see that empathy was a response to others' pain, but the same UI was too stupid to realize that empathy – in both human terms and the terms of humankind's UI – was far more than that. Empathy and love were inseparable and inexplicable. The machine UI would never understand it – not even enough to use it as a lure for the part of the human UI who had tired of warfare in the distant future.

Love, that most banal of things, that most clichéd of religious motivations, had more power – Sol now knew – than did strong nuclear force or weak nuclear force or electromagnetism or gravity. Love *was* these other forces, Sol realized. The Void Which Binds, the subquantum impossibility that carried information from photon to photon, was nothing more or less than love.

But could love – simple, banal *love* – explain the so-called anthropic principle which scientists had shaken their collective heads over for seven centuries and more – that almost infinite string of coincidences which had led to a universe that had just the proper number of dimensions, just the correct values of electron, just the precise rules for gravity, just the proper age to stars, just the right prebiologies to create just the perfect viruses to become just the proper DNAs – in short, a series of coincidences so absurd in their precision and *correctness* that they defied logic, defied understanding, and even defied religious interpretation. *Love?*

For seven centuries the existence of Grand Unification Theories and hyperstring post-quantum physics and Core-given understanding of the universe as self-contained and boundless, without Big Bang singularities or corresponding endpoints, had pretty much eliminated any role of God – primitively anthropomorphic or sophisticatedly post-Einsteinian – even as a caretaker or pre-Creation former of rules. The modern universe, as machine and man had come to understand it, needed no Creator: in fact, *allowed* no Creator. Its rules allowed very little tinkering and no major revisions. It had not begun and would not end, beyond cycles of expansion and contraction as regular and self-regulated as the seasons on Old Earth. No room for love there.

It seemed that Abraham had offered to murder his son to test a phantom.

It seemed that Sol had brought his dying daughter through hundreds of light-years and innumerable hardships in response to nothing.

But now, as the Sphinx loomed above him and the first hint of sunrise paled Hyperion's sky, Sol realized that he had responded to a force more basic and persuasive than the Shrike's terror or pain's dominion. If he was right – and he did not know but felt – then love was as hardwired into the structure of the universe as gravity and matter/antimatter. There was room for some sort of God not in the web between the walls, nor in the singularity cracks in the pavement, nor somewhere out before and beyond the sphere of things . . . but in the very warp and woof of things. Evolving as the universe evolved. Learning as the learning-able parts of the universe learned. Loving as humankind loved.

Sol got to his knees and then to his feet. The time-tide storm seemed to have abated a bit, and he thought he could try for the hundredth time to gain access to the Tomb.

Bright light still emanated from where the Shrike had emerged, taken Sol's daughter, and vanished. But now the stars were disappearing as the sky itself lightened toward morning.

Sol climbed the stairs.

He remembered the time at home on Barnard's World when Rachel – she was ten – had tried to climb the town's tallest elm and had fallen when she was five meters from the top. Sol had rushed to the med center to find his child floating in the recovery nutrient and suffering from a punctured lung, a broken leg and ribs, a fractured jaw, and innumerable cuts and bruises. She had smiled at him, lifted a thumb, and said through her wired jaw, 'I'll make it next time!'

Sol and Sarai had sat there in the med center that night while Rachel slept. They had waited for morning. Sol had held her hand through the night.

He waited now.

Time tides from the open entrance to the Sphinx still held Sol back like insistent winds, but he leaned into them like an immovable rock and stood there, five meters out and waiting, squinting into the glare.

He glanced up but did not move back when he saw the fusion flame of a descending spacecraft slice the predawn sky. He turned to look but did not retreat when he heard the spacecraft landing and saw three figures emerge. He glanced but did not step back when he heard other noises, shouts, from deeper in the valley and saw a familiar figure lugging another in a fireman's carry, moving toward him from beyond the Jade Tomb.

None of these things related to his child. He waited for Rachel.

Even without a datasphere, it is quite possible for my persona to travel through the rich, Void-Which-Binds soup which now surrounds Hyperion. My immediate reaction is to want to visit the One Who Will Be, but although that one's brilliance dominates the metasphere, I am not yet ready for that. I am, after all, little John Keats, not John the Baptist.

The Sphinx – a tomb patterned after a real creature that will not be designed by genetic engineers for centuries to come – is a maelstrom of temporal energies. There are really several Sphinxes visible to my expanded sight: the anti-entropic tomb carrying its Shrike cargo back in time like some sealed container with its deadly bacillus, the active, unstable Sphinx which contaminated Rachel Weintraub in its initial efforts to open a portal through time, and the Sphinx which has opened and is moving forward through time again. This last Sphinx is the blazing portal of light, which, second only to the One Who Will Be, lights Hyperion with its metaspherical bonfire.

I descend to this bright place in time to watch Sol Weintraub hand his daughter to the Shrike.

I could not have interfered with this even if I had arrived earlier. I would not if I were able. Worlds beyond reason depend upon this act.

But I await within the Sphinx for the Shrike to pass, carrying its tender cargo. Now I can see the child. She is seconds old, blotched, moist, and wrinkled. She is crying her newborn lungs out. From my old attitudes of bachelorhood and reflective poet's stance, I find it hard to understand the attraction this bawling, unaesthetic infant exerts on its father and the cosmos.

Still, the sight of a baby's flesh – however unattractive this newborn might be – held by the Shrike's bladed talons stirs something in me.

Three paces into the Sphinx have carried the Shrike and the child hours forward in time. Just beyond the entrance, the river of time accelerates. If I don't do something within seconds, it will be too late – the Shrike will have used this portal to carry the child off to whatever distant-future dark hole it seeks.

Unbidden, the images arrive of spiders draining their victims of fluids, of digger wasps burying their own larvae in the paralyzed bodies of their prey, perfect sources for incubation and food.

I have to act, but I have no more solidity here than I had in the Core. The Shrike walks through me as if I were an unseen holo. My analog persona is useless here, armless and insubstantial as a wisp of swamp gas.

But swamp gas has no brain, and John Keats did.

The Shrike takes another two steps, and more hours pass for Sol and the others outside. I can see blood on the crying infant's skin where the Shrike's scalpeled fingers have cut into flesh.

To hell with this.

Outside, on the broad stone porch of the Sphinx, caught now in the flood of temporal energies flowing in and through the tomb, lay backpacks, blankets, abandoned food containers, and all the detritus Sol and the pilgrims had left there.

Including a single Möbius cube.

The box had been sealed with a class-eight containment field on the Templar treeship *Yggdrasill* when True Voice of the Tree Het Masteen had prepared for his long voyage. It contained a single erg – sometimes known as a binder – one of the small creatures which might not be intelligent by human standards but which had evolved around distant stars and developed the ability to control more powerful forcefields than any machine known to humankind.

The Templars and Ousters had communicated with the creatures for generations. Templars used them for control redundancy on their beautiful but exposed treeships.

Het Masteen had brought this thing hundreds of light-years to complete the Templar agreement with the Church of the Final Atonement to help fly the Shrike's thorn tree. But, seeing the Shrike and the tree of torment, Masteen had not been able to fulfill the contract. And so he died.

The Möbius cube remained. The erg was visible to me as a constrained sphere of red energy in the temporal flood.

Outside, through a curtain of darkness, Sol Weintraub was just visible – a sadly comic figure, speeded up like a silent-film figure by the subjective rush of time beyond the Sphinx's temporal field – but the Möbius cube lay within the Sphinx's circle.

Rachel cried with the fear even a newborn can know. Fear of falling. Fear of pain. Fear of separation.

The Shrike took a step, and another hour was lost to those outside.

I was insubstantial to the Shrike, but energy fields are something which even we Core-analog ghosts can touch. I canceled the Möbius cube's containment field. I freed the erg.

Templars communicate with ergs via electromagnetic radiation, coded pulses, simple rewards of radiation when the creature does what they want . . . but primarily through a near-mystical form of contact which only the Brotherhood and a few Ouster exotics know. Scientists call it a crude telepathy. In truth, it is almost pure empathy.

The Shrike takes another step into the opening portal to the future. Rachel cries with the energy only someone newly born to the universe can muster.

The erg expands, understands, and melds with my persona. John Keats takes on substance and form.

I hurry the five paces to the Shrike, remove the baby from its hands, and step back. Even in the energy maelstrom that is the Sphinx, I can smell the infant-newness of her as I hold the child against my chest and cup her moist head against my cheek.

The Shrike whirls in surprise. Four arms extend, blades snick open, and red eyes focus on me. But the creature is too close to the portal itself. Without moving, it recedes down the storm drain of temporal flow. The thing's steam-shovel jaws open, steel teeth gnash, but it is already gone, a spot in the distance. Something less.

I turn toward the entrance, but it is too far. The erg's draining energy could get me there, drag me upstream against the flow, but not with Rachel. Carrying another living thing that far against so much force is more than I can manage even with the erg's help.

The baby cries, and I bounce her gently, whispering nonsense doggerel in her warm ear.

If we can't go back and we can't go forward, we'll just wait here for a moment. Perhaps someone will come along.

Martin Silenus's eyes widened and Brawne Lamia turned quickly, seeing the Shrike floating in midair above and behind her.

'Holy shit,' Brawne whispered reverently.

In the Shrike Palace, tiers of sleeping human bodies receded in the gloom and distance, all of the people except Martin Silenus still connected to the thorn tree, the machine UI, and God knows what else by pulsing umbilicals.

As if to show its power here, the Shrike had quit climbing, opened its arms, and floated up three meters until it hung in the air five meters out from the stone shelf where Brawne crouched next to Martin Silenus.

'Do something,' whispered Silenus. The poet was no longer attached by the neural shunt umbilical, but he was still too weak to hold his head up.

'Ideas?' said Brawne, the brave remark somewhat ruined by the quaver in her voice.

'Trust,' said a voice below them, and Brawne shifted to look down toward the floor.

The young woman whom Brawne had recognized as Moneta in Kassad's tomb stood far below.

'Help!' cried Brawne.

'Trust,' said Moneta and disappeared. The Shrike had not been distracted.

It lowered its hands and stepped forward as if walking on solid stone rather than air.

'Shit,' whispered Brawne.

'Ditto,' rasped Martin Silenus. 'Out of the frying pan back into the fucking fire.'

'Shut up,' said Brawne. Then, as if to herself, 'Trust what? Who?'

'Trust the fucking Shrike to kill us or stick us both on the fucking tree,' gasped Silenus. He managed to move enough to clutch Brawne's arm. 'Better dead than back on the tree, Brawne.'

Brawne touched his hand briefly and stood, facing the Shrike across five meters of air.

Trust? Brawne held her foot out, felt around on emptiness, closed her eyes for a second, and opened them as her foot seemed to touch a solid step. She opened her eyes.

Nothing was under her foot except air.

Trust? Brawne put her weight on her forward foot and stepped out, teetering a moment before bringing her other foot down.

She and the Shrike stood facing each other ten meters above the stone floor. The creature seemed to grin at her as it opened its arms. Its carapace glowed dully in the dim light. Its red eyes were very bright.

Trust? Feeling the adrenaline rush, Brawne stepped forward on the invisible steps, gaining height as she moved into the Shrike's embrace.

She felt the fingerblades slicing through fabric and skin as the thing began to hug her to it, toward the curved blade growing out of its metal chest, toward the open jaws and rows of steel teeth. But while still standing firmly on thin air, Brawne leaned forward and set her uninjured hand flat against the Shrike's chest, feeling the coldness of the carapace but also feeling a rush of warmth as energy rushed from her, out of her, *through* her.

The blades stopped cutting before they cut anything but skin. The Shrike froze as if the flow of temporal energy surrounding them had turned to a lump of amber.

Brawne set her hand on the thing's broad chest and *pushed*.

The Shrike froze completely in place, became brittle, the gleam of metal fading to be replaced by the transparent glow of crystal, the bright sheen of glass.

Brawne stood on air being embraced by a three-meter glass sculpture of the Shrike. In its chest, where a heart might be, something that looked like a large, black moth fluttered and beat sooty wings against the glass.

Brawne took a deep breath and pushed again. The Shrike slid backward on the invisible platform she shared with it, teetered, and fell. Brawne ducked under the encircling arms, hearing and feeling her jacket tearing as still-sharp finger-blades caught in the material and ripped as the thing tumbled, and then she was teetering herself, flailing her good arm for balance as the glass Shrike turned one and a half times in midair, struck the floor, and shattered into a thousand jagged shards.

Brawne pivoted, fell to her knees on the invisible catwalk, and crawled back toward Martin Silenus.

In the last half meter, her confidence failed her, the invisible support simply ceased to be, and she fell heavily, twisting her ankle as she hit the edge of the stone tier and managing to keep from falling off only by grabbing Silenus's knee.

Cursing from the pain in her shoulder, broken wrist, twisted ankle, and lacerated palms and knees, she pulled herself to safety next to him.

'There's obviously been some weird shit going on since I left,' Martin Silenus said hoarsely. 'Can we go now, or do you plan to walk on water as an encore?'

'Shut up,' Brawne said shakily. The two syllables sounded almost affectionate.

She rested a while and then found that the easiest way to get the still-weak poet down the steps and across the glass-strewn floor of the Shrike Palace was to use the fireman's carry. They were at the entrance when he pounded unceremoniously on her back and said, 'What about King Billy and the others?'

'Later,' panted Brawne and stepped out into the predawn light.

She had hobbled down two thirds of the valley with Silenus draped over her shoulders like so much limp laundry when the poet said, 'Brawne, are you still pregnant?'

'Yes,' she said, praying that that was still true after the day's exertions.

'You want me to carry you?'

'Shut up,' she said and followed the path down and around the Jade Tomb.

'Look,' said Martin Silenus, twisting to point even as he hung almost upside down over her shoulder.

In the glowing light of morning, Brawne could see that the Consul's ebony spacecraft now sat on the high ground at the entrance to the valley. But that was not what the poet was pointing toward.

Sol Weintraub stood silhouetted in the glare of the Sphinx's entrance. His arms were raised.

Someone or something was emerging from the glare.

Sol saw her first. A figure walking amidst the torrent of light and liquid time flowing from the Sphinx. A woman, he saw, as she was silhouetted against the brilliant portal. A woman carrying something.

A woman carrying an infant.

His daughter Rachel emerged – Rachel as he had last seen her as a healthy young adult leaving to do her doctoral work on some world called Hyperion, Rachel in her mid-twenties, perhaps even a bit older now – but Rachel, no doubt about that, Rachel with her copperish-brown hair still short and falling across her forehead, her cheeks flushed as they always were as with some new enthusiasm, her smile soft, almost tremulous now, and her eyes

– those enormous green eyes with specks of brown just visible – those eyes fixed on Sol.

Rachel was carrying Rachel. The infant squirmed with its face against the young woman's shoulder, tiny hands clenching and unclenching as it tried to decide whether to start crying again or not.

Sol stood stunned. He tried to speak, failed, and tried again. 'Rachel.'

'Father,' said the young woman and stepped forward, putting her free arm around the scholar while she turned slightly to keep the baby from being crushed between them.

Sol kissed his grown daughter, hugged her, smelled the clean scent of her hair, felt the firm *reality* of her, and then lifted the infant to his own neck and shoulder, feeling the shudders pass through the newborn as she took a breath before crying. The Rachel he had brought to Hyperion was safe in his hands, small, red face wrinkled as she tried to focus her randomly wandering eyes on her father's face. Sol cupped her tiny head in his palm and lifted her closer, inspecting that small face for a second before turning toward the young woman.

'Is she . . .'

'She's aging normally,' said his daughter. She was wearing something part gown, part robe, made of soft brown material. Sol shook his head, looked at her, saw her smiling, and noticed the same small dimple below and to the left of her mouth that was visible on the infant he held.

He shook his head again. 'How . . . how is this possible?'

'It's not for very long,' said Rachel.

Sol leaned forward and kissed his grown daughter's cheek again. He realized that he was crying, but he would not release either hand to wipe away the tears. His grown Rachel did so for him, touching his cheek gently with the back of her hand.

There was a noise below them on the steps, and Sol looked over his shoulder to see the three men from the ship standing there, red faced from running, and Brawne Lamia helping the poet Silenus to a seat on the white slab of railing stone.

The Consul and Theo Lane looked up at them.

'Rachel . . .' whispered Melio Arundez, his eyes filling.

'*Rachel?*' said Martin Silenus, frowning and glancing at Brawne Lamia.

Brawne was staring with her mouth half open. 'Moneta,' she said, pointing, then lowering her hand as she realized she was pointing. 'You're Moneta. Kassad's . . . Moneta.'

Rachel nodded, her smile gone. 'I have only a minute or two here,' she said. 'And much to tell you.'

'No,' said Sol, taking his grown daughter's hand, 'you have to stay. I want you to stay with me.'

Rachel smiled again. 'I will stay with you, Dad,' she said softly, raising her other hand to touch the baby's head. 'But only one of us can . . . and she needs you more.' She turned to the group below. 'Listen, please, all of you.'

As the sun rose and touched the broken buildings of the Poets' City, the Consul's ship, the western cliffs, and the taller Time Tombs with its light, Rachel told her brief and tantalizing story of being chosen to be raised in a future where the final war raged between the Core-spawned UI and the human spirit. It was, she said, a future of terrifying and wonderful mysteries, where humankind had spread across this galaxy and had begun to travel elsewhere.

'Other *galaxies?*' asked Theo Lane.

'Other universes,' smiled Rachel.

'Colonel Kassad knew you as Moneta,' said Martin Silenus.

'*Will* know me as Moneta,' said Rachel, her eyes clouding. 'I have seen him die and accompanied his tomb to the past. I know that part of my mission is to meet this fabled warrior and lead him forward to the final battle. I have not truly met him yet.' She looked down the valley toward the Crystal Monolith. '*Moneta*,' she mused. 'It means "Admonisher" in Latin. Appropriate. I will let him choose between that and *Mnemosyne* – "memory" – for my name.'

Sol had not released his daughter's hand. He did not do so now. 'You're traveling *back* in time with the Tombs? Why? How?'

Rachel lifted her head, and reflected light from the far cliffs painted her face in warmth. 'It is my role, Dad. My duty. They give me means to keep the Shrike in check. And only I was . . . prepared.'

Sol lifted his infant daughter higher. Startled from sleep, she blew a single bubble of saliva, turned her face into her father's neck for warmth, and curled her small fists against his shirt.

'Prepared,' said Sol. 'You mean the Merlin's sickness?'

'Yes,' said Rachel.

Sol shook his head. 'But you weren't raised in some mysterious world of the future. You grew up in the college town of Crawford, on Fertig Street, on Barnard's World, and your . . .' He stopped.

Rachel nodded. '*She* shall grow up . . . up there. Dad, I'm sorry, I have to go.' She freed her hand, drifted down the stairs, and touched Melio Arundez's cheek briefly. 'I'm sorry for the pain of memory,' she said softly to the startled archaeologist. 'To me it was, literally, a different life.'

Arundez blinked and held her hand to his cheek a moment longer.

'Are you married?' asked Rachel softly. 'Children?'

Arundez nodded, moved his other hand as if he were going to remove the pictures of his wife and grown children from his pocket, and then stopped, nodded again.

Rachel smiled, kissed him quickly on the cheek, and moved back up the steps. The sky was rich with sunrise, but the door to the Sphinx was still brighter.

'Dad,' she said, 'I love you.'

Sol tried to speak, cleared his throat. 'How . . . how do I join you . . . up there?'

Rachel gestured toward the open door of the Sphinx. 'For some it will be a portal to the time I spoke of. But, Dad . . .' She hesitated. 'It will mean raising me all over again. It means suffering through my childhood for a third time. No parent should be asked to do that.'

Sol managed a smile. 'No parent would refuse that, Rachel.' He changed arms holding the sleeping infant, and shook his head again. 'Will there be a time when . . . the two of you . . . ?'

'Coexist again?' smiled Rachel. 'No. I go the other way now. You can't imagine the difficulty I had with the Paradox Board to get this one meeting approved.'

'Paradox Board?' said Sol.

Rachel took a breath. She had stepped back until only her fingertips touched her father's, both their arms extended. 'I have to go, Dad.'

'Will I . . .' He looked at the baby. 'Will we be alone . . . up there?'

Rachel laughed, and the sound was so familiar that it closed around Sol's heart like a warm hand. 'Oh no,' she said, 'not alone. There are wonderful people there. Wonderful things to learn and do. Wonderful places to see . . .' She glanced around. 'Places we have not imagined yet in our wildest dreams. No, Dad, you won't be alone. And I'll be there, in all my teenage awkwardness and young-adult cockiness.' She stepped back, and her fingers slipped away from Sol.

'Wait a while before stepping through, Dad,' she called, moving back into the brilliance. 'It doesn't hurt, but once through you can't come back.'

'Rachel, wait,' said Sol.

His daughter stepped back, her long robe flowing across stone, until the light surrounded her. She raised one arm. 'See you later, alligator!' she called.

Sol raised a hand. 'After a while . . . crocodile.'

The older Rachel was gone in the light.

The baby awoke and began to cry.

It was more than an hour before Sol and the others returned to the Sphinx. They had gone to the Consul's ship to tend to Brawne's and Martin Silenus's injuries, to eat, and to outfit Sol and the child for a voyage.

'I feel silly packing for what may be like a step through a farcaster,' said Sol, 'but no matter how wonderful this future is, if it doesn't have nursing paks and disposable diapers, we're in trouble.'

The Consul grinned and patted the full backpack on the step. 'This should get you and the baby through the first two weeks. If you don't find a diaper service by then, go to one of those other universes Rachel spoke about.'

Sol shook his head. 'Is this happening?'

'Wait a few days or weeks,' said Melio Arundez. 'Stay here with us until things get sorted out. There's no hurry. The future will always be there.'

Sol scratched his beard as he fed the baby with one of the nursing paks the ship had manufactured. 'We're not sure this portal will always be open,' he said. 'Besides, I might lose my nerve. I'm getting pretty old to raise a child again . . . especially as a stranger in a strange land.'

Arundez set his strong hand on Sol's shoulder. 'Let me go with you. I'm dying of curiosity about this place.'

Sol grinned and extended his hand, shook Arundez's firmly. 'Thank you, my friend. But you have a wife and children back in the Web . . . on Renaissance Vector . . . who await your return. You have your own duties.'

Arundez nodded and looked at the sky. 'If we *can* return.'

'We'll return,' the Consul said flatly. 'Old-fashioned Hawking drive spaceflight still works, even if the Web is gone forever. It'll be a few years' time-debt, Melio, but you'll get back.'

Sol nodded, finished feeding the baby, set a clean cloth diaper on his shoulder, and patted her firmly on the back. He looked around the small circle of people. 'We all have our duties.' He shook hands with Martin Silenus. The poet had refused to crawl into the nutrient recovery bath or have the neural shunt socket surgically removed. 'I've had these things before,' he'd said.

'Will you continue your poem?' Sol asked him.

Silenus shook his head. 'I finished it on the tree,' he said. 'And I discovered something else there, Sol.'

The scholar raised an eyebrow.

'I learned that poets aren't God, but if there is a God . . . or anything approaching a God . . . he's a poet. And a failed one at that.'

The baby burped.

Martin Silenus grinned and shook Sol's hand a final time. 'Give them hell up there, Weintraub. Tell 'em you're their great-great-great-great-great-grandaddy, and if they misbehave, you'll whop their butts.'

Sol nodded and moved down the line to Brawne Lamia. 'I saw you conferring with the ship's medical terminal,' he said. 'Is everything all right with you and your unborn child?'

Brawne grinned. 'Everything's fine.'

'A boy or girl?'

'Girl.'

Sol kissed her on the cheek. Brawne touched his beard and turned her face away to hide tears unbecoming a former private investigator.

'Girls are such a chore,' he said, disentangling Rachel's fingers from his beard and Brawne's curls. 'Trade yours in for a boy the first chance you get.'

'OK,' said Brawne and stepped back.

He shook hands a final time with the Consul, Theo, and Melio, shouldered his pack while Brawne held the infant, and then took Rachel in his arms. 'Hell of an anticlimax if this thing doesn't work and I end up wandering around the inside of the Sphinx,' he said.

The Consul squinted at the glowing door. 'It will work. Although how, I'm not sure. I don't think it's a farcaster of any sort.'

'A whencaster,' ventured Silenus and held up his arm to block Brawne's blows. The poet took a step back and shrugged. 'If it continues to work, Sol, I have a feeling you won't be alone up there. Thousands will join you.'

'If the Paradox Board permits,' said Sol, tugging at his beard the way he always did when his mind was elsewhere. He blinked, shifted backpack and baby, and stepped forward. The fields of force from the open door let him advance this time.

'So long everyone!' he cried. 'By God, it was all worth it, wasn't it?' He turned into the light, and he and the baby were gone.

There was a silence bordering on emptiness which stretched for several minutes. Finally the Consul said, in almost embarrassed tones, 'Shall we go up to the ship?'

'Bring the elevator down for the rest of us,' said Martin Silenus. 'M. Lamia here will walk on air.'

Brawne glared at the diminutive poet.

'You think it was something Moneta arranged?' said Arundez, referring to something Brawne had suggested earlier.

'It had to be,' said Brawne. 'Some bit of future science or something.'

'Ah, yes,' sighed Martin Silenus. '*Future science* . . . that familiar phrase from those too timid to be superstitious. The alternative, my dear, is that you have this hitherto untapped power to levitate and turn monsters into shatterable glass goblins.'

'Shut up,' said Brawne, with no undertones of affection in her voice now. She looked over her shoulder. 'Who says another Shrike won't show up any minute?'

'Who indeed?' agreed the Consul. 'I suspect we'll always have a Shrike or rumors of a Shrike.'

Theo Lane, always embarrassed by discord, cleared his throat and said, 'Look what I found among the baggage strewn around the Sphinx.' He held up an instrument with three strings, a long neck, and bright designs painted on its triangular body. 'A guitar?'

'A balalaika,' said Brawne. 'It belonged to Father Hoyt.'

The Consul took the instrument and strummed several chords. 'Do you know this song?' He played a few notes.

'The "Leeda Tits Screwing Song"?' ventured Martin Silenus.

The Consul shook his head and played several more chords.

'Something old?' guessed Brawne.

' "Somewhere Over the Rainbow",' said Melio Arundez.

'That must be from before my time,' said Theo Lane, nodding along as the Consul strummed.

'It's from before everybody's time,' said the Consul. 'Come on, I'll teach you the words as we go.'

Walking together in the hot sun, singing off-key and on-, losing the words and then starting again, they went uphill to the waiting ship.

EPILOGUE

Five and a half months later, seven months pregnant, Brawne Lamia took the morning dirigible north from the capital to the Poets' City for the Consul's farewell party.

The capital, now referred to as Jacktown by indigenie, visiting FORCE shipman, and Ouster alike, looked white and clean in the morning light as the dirigible left the downtown mooring tower and headed northwest up the Hoolie River.

The biggest city on Hyperion had suffered during the fighting, but now most of it had been rebuilt, and a majority of the three million refugees from the fiberplastic plantations and smaller cities on the southern continent had elected to stay, despite recent surges of interest in fiberplastic from the Ousters. So the city had grown like Topsy, with basic services such as electricity, sewerage, and cable HTV service just reaching the hilltop warrens between the spaceport and the old town.

But the buildings were white in the morning light, the spring air rich with promise, and Brawne saw the rough slashes of new roads and the bustle of river traffic below as a good sign for the future.

Fighting in Hyperion space had not lasted long after the destruction of the Web. De facto Ouster occupation of the spaceport and capital had been translated into recognition of the Web's demise and comanagement with the new Home Rule Council in the treaty brokered primarily by the Consul and former Governor-General Theo Lane. But in the almost six months since the death of the Web, the only traffic at the spaceport had been dropships from the remnants of the FORCE fleet still in-system and frequent planetary excursions from the Swarm. It was no longer unusual to see the tall figures of Ousters shopping in Jacktown Square or their more exotic versions drinking at Cicero's.

Brawne had stayed at Cicero's during the past few months, residing in one of the larger rooms on the fourth floor of the old wing of the inn while Stan Leweski rebuilt and expanded the damaged sections of the legendary structure. 'By God, I don't need no help from pregnant womens!' Stan would shout each time Brawne offered a hand, but she invariably ended up doing some task while Leweski grumped and mumbled. Brawne might be pregnant, but she was still a Lusian, and her muscles had not completely atrophied after only a few months on Hyperion.

Stan had driven her to the mooring tower that morning, helping her with her luggage and the package she had brought for the Consul. Then the innkeeper had handed her a small package of his own. 'It's a damn, dull trip up into that godforsaken country,' he'd growled. 'You have to have something to read, heh?'

The gift was a reproduction of the 1817 edition of John Keats's *Poems*, leather-bound by Leweski himself.

Brawne embarrassed the giant and delighted watching passengers by hugging him until the bartender's ribs creaked. 'Enough, goddammit,' he muttered, rubbing his side. 'Tell that Consul I want to see his worthless hide back here before I give the worthless inn to my son. Tell him that, OK?'

Brawne had nodded and waved with the other passengers to well-wishers seeing them off. Then she had continued waving from the observation mezzanine as the airship untied, discharged ballast, and ponderously moved out over the rooftops.

Now, as the ship left the suburbs behind and swung west to follow the river, Brawne had her first clear view of the mountaintop to the south where the face of Sad King Billy still brooded down on the city. There was a fresh ten-meter scar, slowly fading from weather, on Billy's cheek where a laser lance had slashed during the fighting.

But it was the larger sculpture taking shape on the northwest face of the mountain which caught Brawne's attention. Even with modern cutting equipment borrowed from FORCE, the work was slow, and the great aquiline nose, heavy brow, broad mouth, and sad, intelligent eyes were just becoming recognizable. Many of the Hegemony refugees left on Hyperion had objected to Meina Gladstone's likeness being added to the mountain, but Rithmet Corber III, great-grandson of the sculptor who had created Sad King Billy's face there – and incidentally the man who now owned the mountain – had said, as diplomatically as possible, 'Fuck you' and gone on with the work. Another year, perhaps two, and it would be finished.

Brawne sighed, rubbed her distended stomach – an affectation she had always hated in pregnant women but one she now found impossible to avoid – and walked clumsily to a deck chair on the observation deck. *If she was this huge at seven months, what would she be like at full term?* Brawne glanced up at the distended curve of the dirigible's great gas envelope above her and winced.

The airship voyage, with good tail winds, took only twenty hours. Brawne dozed part of the way but spent most of the time watching the familiar landscape unfold below.

They passed the Karla Locks in midmorning, and Brawne smiled and patted the package she had brought for the Consul. By late afternoon, they were approaching the river port of Naiad, and from three thousand feet Brawne looked down on an old passenger barge being pulled upriver by mantas leaving their V-shaped wake. She wondered if that could be the *Benares*.

They flew over Edge as dinner was being served in the upper lounge and began the crossing of the Sea of Grass just as sunset lighted the great steppe with color and a million grasses rippled to the same breeze that lofted the airship along. Brawne took her coffee to her favorite chair on the mezzanine, opened a window wide, and watched the Sea of Grass unfold like the sensuous felt of a billiard table as the light failed. Just before the lamps were lit on the mezzanine deck, she was rewarded with the sight of a windwagon plying its way from north to south, lanterns swinging fore and aft. Brawne leaned forward and could clearly hear the rumble of the big wheel and the snap of canvas on the jib sail as the wagon hove hard over to take a new tack.

The bed was ready in her sleeping compartment when Brawne went up to slip into her robe, but after reading a few poems she found herself back on the observation deck until dawn, dozing in her favorite chair and breathing in the fresh smell of grass from below.

They moored in Pilgrim's Rest long enough to take on fresh food and water, renew ballast, and change crews, but Brawne did not go down to walk around. She could see the worklights around the tramway station, and when the voyage resumed at last, the airship seemed to follow the string of cable towers into the Bridle Range.

It was still quite dark as they crossed the mountains, and a steward came along to seal the long windows as the compartments were pressurized, but Brawne could still catch glimpses of the tramcars passing from peak to peak between the clouds below, and icefields that glinted in the starlight.

They passed over Keep Chronos just after dawn, and the stones of the castle emitted little sense of warmth even in the roseate light. Then the high desert appeared, the City of Poets glowed white off the port side, and the dirigible descended toward the mooring tower set on the east end of the new spaceport there.

Brawne had not expected anyone to be there to meet her. Everyone who knew her thought that she was flying up with Theo Lane in his skimmer later in the afternoon. But Brawne had thought the airship voyage the proper way to travel alone with her thoughts. And she had been right.

But even before the mooring cable was pulled tight and the ramp lowered, Brawne saw the familiar face of the Consul in the small crowd. Next to him was Martin Silenus, frowning and squinting at the unfamiliar morning light.

'Damn that Stan,' muttered Brawne, remembering that the microwave links were up now and new comsats in orbit.

The Consul met her with a hug. Martin Silenus yawned, shook her hand, and said, 'Couldn't find a more inconvenient time to arrive, eh?'

There was a party in the evening. It was more than the Consul leaving the next morning – most of the FORCE fleet still remaining was heading back, and a sizable portion of the Ouster Swarm was going with them. A dozen dropships littered the small field near the Consul's spaceship as Ousters paid their last visit to the Time Tombs and FORCE officers stopped by Kassad's tomb a final time.

The Poets' City itself now had almost a thousand full-time residents, many of them artists and poets, although Silenus said that most were *poseurs*. They had twice tried to elect Martin Silenus mayor; he had declined twice and soundly cursed his would-be constituency. But the old poet continued to run things, supervising the restorations, adjudicating disputes, dispensing housing and arranging for supply flights from Jacktown and points south. The Poets' City was no longer the Dead City.

Martin Silenus said the collective IQ had been higher when the place was deserted.

The banquet was held in the rebuilt dining pavilion, and the great dome echoed to laughter as Martin Silenus read ribald poems and other artists performed skits. Besides the Consul and Silenus, Brawne's round table boasted half a dozen Ouster guests, including Freeman Ghenga and Coredwell Minmun, as well as Rithmet Corber III, dressed in stitched pelts and a tall cone of a cap. Theo Lane arrived late, with apologies, shared the most recent Jacktown jokes with the audience, and came over to the table to join them for dessert. Lane had been mentioned recently as the people's choice for Jacktown's mayor in the Fourthmonth elections soon to be held – both indigenie and Ouster seemed to like his style – and so far Theo had shown no signs of declining if the honor were offered him.

After much wine at the banquet, the Consul quietly invited a few of them up to the ship for music and more wine. They went, Brawne and Martin and Theo, and sat high on the ship's balcony while the Consul very soberly and feelingly played Gershwin and Studeri and Brahms and Luser and Beatles, and then Gershwin again, finally ending with Rachmaninov's heart-stoppingly beautiful Piano Concerto No. 2 in C Minor.

Then they sat in the low light, looked out over the city and valley, drank a bit more wine, and talked late into the night.

'What do you expect to find in the Web?' Theo asked the Consul. 'Anarchy? Mob rule? Reversion to Stone Age life?'

'All of that and more, probably,' smiled the Consul. He swirled the brandy in his glass. 'Seriously, there were enough squirts before the fatline went dead to let us know that, despite some real problems, most of the old worlds of the Web will do all right.'

Theo Lane sat nursing the same glass of wine he had brought up from the dining pavilion. 'Why do you think the fatline went dead?'

Martin Silenus snorted. 'God got tired of us scribbling graffiti on his outhouse walls.'

They talked of old friends, wondering how Father Duré was doing. They had heard about his new job on one of the last fatline intercepts. They remembered Lenar Hoyt.

'Do you think he'll automatically become Pope when Duré passes away?' asked the Consul.

'I doubt it,' said Theo. 'But at least he'll get a chance to live again if that cruciform Duré carries on his chest still works.'

'I wonder if he'll come looking for his balalaika,' said Silenus, strumming the instrument. In the low light, Brawne thought, the old poet still looked like a satyr.

They talked about Sol and Rachel. In the past six months, hundreds of people had tried to enter the Sphinx; one had succeeded – a quiet Ouster named Mizenspesht Ammenyet.

The Ouster experts had spent months analyzing the Tombs and the trace of time tides still surviving. On some of the structures, hieroglyphs and oddly familiar cuneiform had appeared after the Tombs' opening, and these had led to at least educated guesses as to the various Time Tombs' functions.

The Sphinx was a one-way portal to the future Rachel/Moneta had spoken of. No one knew how it selected those it wished to let pass, but the popular thing for tourists was to try to enter the portal. No sign or hint of Sol and his daughter's fate had been discovered. Brawne found that she thought of the old scholar often.

Brawne, the Consul, and Martin Silenus drank a toast to Sol and Rachel.

The Jade Tomb appeared to have something to do with gas giant worlds. No one had been passed by its particular portal, but exotic Ousters, designed and bred to live in Jovian habitats, arrived daily to attempt to enter it. Both Ouster and FORCE experts repeatedly pointed out that the Tombs were not farcasters, but some other form of cosmic connection entirely. The tourists didn't care.

The Obelisk remained a black mystery. The tomb still glowed, but it now had no door. Ousters guessed that armies of Shrikes still waited within. Martin Silenus thought that the Obelisk was only a phallic symbol thrown in the valley's decor as an afterthought. Others thought it might have something to do with the Templars.

Brawne, the Consul, and Martin Silenus drank a toast to True Voice of the Tree Het Masteen.

The resealed Crystal Monolith was Colonel Fedmahn Kassad's tomb. Decoded markings set in stone talked of a cosmic battle and a great warrior from the past who appeared to help defeat the Lord of Pain. Young recruits down from the torchships and attack carriers ate it up. Kassad's legend would spread as more of these ships returned to the worlds of the old Web.

Brawne, the Consul, and Martin Silenus drank a toast to Fedmahn Kassad.

The first and second of the Cave Tombs seemed to lead nowhere, but the Third appeared to open to labyrinths on a variety of worlds. After a few researchers disappeared, the Ouster research authorities reminded tourists that the labyrinths lay in a different time – possibly hundreds of thousands of years in the past or future – as well as a different space. They sealed the caves off except to qualified experts.

Brawne, the Consul, and Martin Silenus drank a toast to Paul Duré and Lenar Hoyt.

The Shrike Palace remained a mystery. The tiers of bodies were gone when Brawne and the others had returned a few hours later, the interior of the tomb the size it had been previously, but with a single door of light burning in its center. Anyone who stepped through disappeared. None returned.

The researchers had declared the interior off-limits while they worked to decode letters carved in stone but badly eroded by time. So far, they were certain of three words – all in Old Earth Latin – translated as 'COLOSSEUM', 'ROME', and 'REPOPULATE'. The legend had already grown up that this portal opened to the missing Old Earth and that the victims of the tree of thorns had been transported there. Hundreds more waited.

'See,' Martin Silenus said to Brawne, 'if you hadn't been so fucking quick to rescue me, I could've gone home.'

Theo Lane leaned forward. 'Would you really have chosen to go back to Old Earth?'

Martin smiled his sweetest satyr smile. 'Not in a fucking million years. It was dull when I lived there and it'll always be dull. *This* is where it's happening.' Silenus drank a toast to himself.

In a sense, Brawne realized, that was true. Hyperion was the meeting place of Ouster and former Hegemony citizen. The Time Tombs alone would mean future trade and tourism and travel as the human universe adjusted to a life without farcasters. She tried to imagine the future as the Ousters saw it, with great fleets expanding humankind's horizons, with genetically tailored humans colonizing gas giants and asteroids and worlds harsher than preterraformed Mars or Hebron. She could not imagine it. This was a universe her child might see . . . or her grandchildren.

'What are you thinking, Brawne?' asked the Consul after silence stretched.

She smiled. 'About the future,' she said. 'And about Johnny.'

'Ah yes,' said Silenus, 'the poet who could have been God but who wasn't.'

'What happened to the second persona, do you think?' asked Brawne.

The Consul made a motion with his hand. 'I don't see how it could have survived the death of the Core. Do you?'

Brawne shook her head. 'I'm just jealous. A lot of people seem to have ended up seeing him. Even Melio Arundez said he met him in Jacktown.'

They drank a toast to Melio, who had left five months earlier with the first FORCE spinship returning Webward.

'Everyone saw him but me,' said Brawne, frowning at her brandy and realizing that she had to take more prenatal antialcohol pills before turning in. She realized that she was a little drunk: the stuff couldn't harm the baby if she took the pills, but it had definitely gotten to her.

'I'm heading back,' she announced and stood, hugging the Consul. 'Got to be up bright and early to watch your sunrise launch.'

'You're sure you don't want to spend the night on the ship?' asked the Consul. 'The guest room has a nice view of the valley.'

Brawne shook her head. 'All my stuff's at the old palace.'

'I'll talk to you before I go,' said the Consul and they hugged again, quickly, before either had to notice Brawne's tears.

Martin Silenus walked her back to the Poets' City. They paused in the lighted galleria outside the apartments.

'Were you really on the tree, or only stimsiming it while sleeping in the Shrike Palace?' Brawne asked him.

The poet did not smile. He touched his chest where the steel thorn had pierced him. 'Was I a Chinese philosopher dreaming that I was a butterfly, or a butterfly dreaming that I was a Chinese philosopher? Is that what you're asking, kid?'

'Yes.'

'That's correct,' Silenus said softly. 'Yes. I was both. And both were real. And both hurt. And I will love and cherish you forever for saving me, Brawne. To me, you will always be able to walk on air.' He raised her hand and kissed it. 'Are you going in?'

'No, I think I'll stroll in the garden for a minute.'

The poet hesitated. 'All right. I think. We have patrols – mech and human – and our Grendel-Shrike hasn't made an encore appearance yet . . . but be careful, OK?'

'Don't forget,' said Brawne, 'I'm the Grendel killer. I walk on air and turn them into glass goblins to shatter.'

'Uh-huh, but don't stray beyond the gardens. OK, kiddo?'

'OK,' said Brawne. She touched her stomach. 'We'll be careful.'

He was waiting in the garden, where the light did not quite touch and the monitor cameras did not quite cover.

'Johnny!' gasped Brawne and took a quick step forward on the path of stones.

'No,' he said and shook his head, a bit sadly perhaps. He looked like Johnny. Precisely the same red-brown hair and hazel eyes and firm chin and high cheekbones and soft smile. He was dressed a bit strangely, with a thick leather jacket, broad belt, heavy shoes, walking stick, and a rough fur cap, which he took off as she came closer.

Brawne stopped less than a meter away. 'Of course,' she said in little more than a whisper. She reached out to touch him, and her hand passed through him, although there was none of the flicker or fuzz of a holo.

'This place is still rich in the metasphere fields,' he said.

'Uh-huh,' she agreed, not having the slightest idea what he was talking about. 'You're the other Keats. Johnny's twin.'

The short man smiled and extended a hand as if to touch her swollen abdomen. 'That makes me sort of an uncle, doesn't it, Brawne?'

She nodded. 'It was you who saved the baby . . . Rachel . . . wasn't it?'

'Could you see me?'

'No,' breathed Brawne, 'but I could *feel* that you were there.' She hesitated a second. 'But you weren't the one Ummon talked about – the Empathy part of the human UI?'

He shook his head. His curls glinted in the dim light. 'I discovered that I am the One Who Comes Before. I prepare the way for the One Who

Teaches, and I'm afraid that my only miracle was lifting a baby and waiting until someone could take her from me.'

'You didn't help *me* . . . with the Shrike? Floating?'

John Keats laughed. 'No. Nor did Moneta. That was you, Brawne.'

She shook her head vigorously. 'That's impossible.'

'Not impossible,' he said softly. He reached out to touch her stomach again, and she imagined that she could feel the pressure from his palm. He whispered, 'Thou still unravished bride of quietness,/ Thou foster-child of silence and slow time . . .' He looked up at Brawne. 'Certainly the mother of the One Who Teaches can exercise some prerogatives,' he said.

'The mother of . . .' Brawne suddenly had to sit down and found a bench just in time. She had never been awkward before in her life, but now, at seven months, there was no graceful way she could manage sitting. She thought, irrelevantly, of the dirigible coming in for mooring that morning.

'The One Who Teaches,' repeated Keats. 'I have no idea what she will teach, but it will change the universe and set ideas in motion that will be vital ten thousand years from now.'

'*My* child?' she managed, fighting a bit for air. 'Johnny's and my child?'

The Keats persona rubbed its cheek. 'The junction of human spirit and AI logic which Ummon and the Core sought for so long and died not under-standing,' he said. He took a step. 'I only wish I could be around when she teaches whatever she has to teach. See what effect it has on the world. This world. Other worlds.'

Brawne's mind was spinning, but she had heard something in his tone. 'Why? Where will you be? What's wrong?'

Keats sighed. 'The Core is gone. The dataspheres here are too small to contain me even in reduced form . . . except for the FORCE ship AIs, and I don't think I'd like it there. I never took orders well.'

'And there's nowhere else?' asked Brawne.

'The metasphere,' he said, glancing behind him. 'But it's full of lions and tigers and bears. And I'm not ready yet.'

Brawne let that pass. 'I have an idea,' she said. She told him.

The image of her lover came closer, put his arms around her, and said, '*You* are a miracle, madam.' He stepped back into the shadows.

Brawne shook her head. 'Just a pregnant lady.' She put her hand on the swelling under her gown. 'The One Who Teaches,' she murmured. Then, to Keats, 'All right, you're the archangel announcing all this. What name shall I give her?'

When there was no answer, Brawne looked up.

The shadows were empty.

Brawne was at the spaceport before the sun rose. It was not exactly a merry group bidding farewell. Beyond the usual sadness of saying goodbye, Martin, the Consul, and Theo were nursing hangovers since day-after pills were out of stock on post-Web Hyperion. Only Brawne was in fine temper.

'Goddamn ship's computer has been acting weird all morning,' grumbled the Consul.

'How so?' smiled Brawne.

The Consul squinted at her. 'I ask it to run through a regular pre-launch checklist and the stupid ship gives me verse.'

'Verse?' said Martin Silenus, raising one satyr's brow.

'Yeah . . . listen . . .' The Consul keyed his comlog.

A voice familiar to Brawne said:

> 'So, ye three Ghosts, adieu! Ye cannot raise
>   My head cool-bedded in flowery grass;
> For I would not be dieted with praise,
>   A pet lamb in a sentimental farce!
> Fade softly from my eyes, and be once more
>   In masque-like figures on the dreamy urn;
>   Farewell! I yet have visions for the night,
> And for the day faint visions there is store;
>   Vanish, ye Phantoms! from my idle sprite,
>   Into the clouds, and never more return!'

Theo Lane said, 'A defective AI? I thought your ship had one of the finest intelligences outside of the Core.'

'It does,' said the Consul. 'It's not defective. I ran a full cognitive and function check. Everything's fine. But it gives me . . . *this*!' He gestured at the comlog recording readout.

Martin Silenus glanced at Brawne Lamia, looked carefully at her smile, and then turned back to the Consul. 'Well, it looks as if your ship might be getting literate. Don't worry about it. It will be good company during the long trip there and back.'

In the ensuing pause, Brawne brought out a bulky package. 'A going-away present,' she said.

The Consul unwrapped it, slowly at first, and then ripping and tearing as the folded, faded, and much-abused little carpet came into sight. He ran his hands across it, looked up, and spoke with emotion filling his voice. 'Where . . . how did you . . .'

Brawne smiled. 'An indigenie refugee found it below the Karla Locks. She was trying to sell it in the Jacktown Marketplace when I happened along. No one was interested in buying.'

The Consul took a deep breath and ran his hands across the designs on the hawking mat which had carried his grandfather Merin to the fateful meeting with his grandmother Siri.

'I'm afraid it doesn't fly anymore,' said Brawne.

'The flight filaments need recharging,' said the Consul. 'I don't know how to thank you . . .'

'Don't,' said Brawne. 'It's for good luck on your voyage.'

The Consul shook his head, hugged Brawne, shook hands with the others, and took the lift up into his ship. Brawne and the others walked back to the terminal.

There were no clouds in Hyperion's lapis lazuli sky. The sun painted the distant peaks of the Bridle Range in deep tones and promised warmth for the day to come.

Brawne looked over her shoulder at the Poets' City and the valley beyond. The tops of the taller Time Tombs were just visible. One wing of the Sphinx caught the light.

With little noise and just a hint of heat, the Consul's ebony ship lifted on a pure blue flame and rose toward the sky.

Brawne tried to remember the poems she had just read and the final lines of her love's longest and finest unfinished work:

> *Anon rushed by the bright Hyperion;*
> *His flaming robes streamed out beyond his heels,*
> *And gave a roar, as if of earthly fire,*
> *That scared away the meek ethereal Hours,*
> *And made their dove-wings tremble. On he flared . . .*

Brawne felt the warm wind tug at her hair. She raised her face to the sky and waved, not trying to hide or brush away the tears, waving fiercely now as the splendid ship pitched over and climbed toward the heavens with its fierce blue flame and – like a distant shout – created a sudden sonic boom which ripped across the desert and echoed against distant peaks.

Brawne let herself weep and waved again, continued waving, at the departing Consul, and at the sky, and at friends she would never see again, and at part of her past, and at the ship rising above like a perfect, ebony arrow shot from some god's bow.

On he flared . . .